A
MEMORY
OF
LIGHT

Book Fourteen of The Wheel of Time®

For twenty years The Wheel of Time has enthralled more than forty million readers in over thirty-two languages. *A Memory of Light* brings this majestic fantasy creation to its richly satisfying conclusion. Working from notes and partials left by Robert Jordan when he died in 2007, and consulting with Jordan's widow, who edited all of Jordan's books, established fantasy writer Brandon Sanderson has recreated the vision Jordan left behind.

The Wheel of Time turns, and ages come and pass.
What was, what will be, and what is,
may yet fall under the Shadow.

Let the Dragon ride again on the winds of time.

A MEMORY OF LIGHT

Book Fourteen of The Wheel of Time®

ROBERT JORDAN

AND

BRANDON SANDERSON

www.orbitbooks.net

ORBIT

First published in Great Britain in 2013 by Orbit
This paperback edition published in 2013 by Orbit

Maps by Ellisa Mitchell
Interior illustrations by Matthew C. Nielsen and Ellisa Mitchell

A CIP catalogue record for this book
is available from the British Library.

ISBN 978-1-84149-871-3

Printed and bound in Great Britain by
Clays Ltd, St Ives plc

Papers used by Orbit are from well-managed forests
and other responsible sources.

MIX
Paper from
responsible sources
FSC
www.fsc.org   FSC® C104740

Orbit
An imprint of
Little, Brown Book Group
100 Victoria Embankment
London EC4Y 0DY

An Hachette UK Company
www.hachette.co.uk

www.orbitbooks.net

For Harriet,
the light of Mr. Jordan's life,
and for Emily,
the light of mine.

CONTENTS

And the Shadow fell upon the Land, and the World was riven stone from stone. The oceans fled, and the mountains were swallowed up, and the nations were scattered to the eight corners of the World. The moon was as blood, and the sun was as ashes. The seas boiled, and the living envied the dead. All was shattered, and all but memory lost, and one memory above all others, of him who brought the Shadow and the Breaking of the World. And him they named Dragon.

—from *Aleth nin Taerin alta Camora,*
The Breaking of the World.
Author unknown, the Fourth Age.

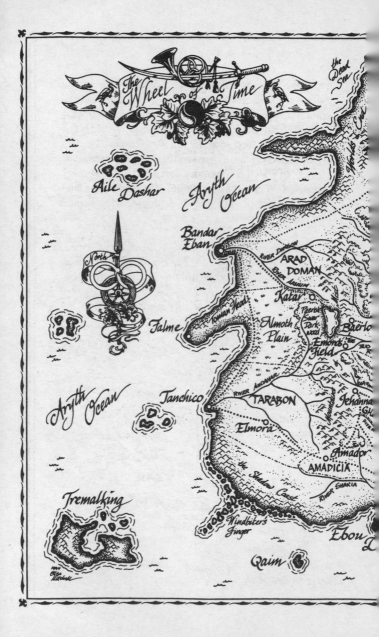

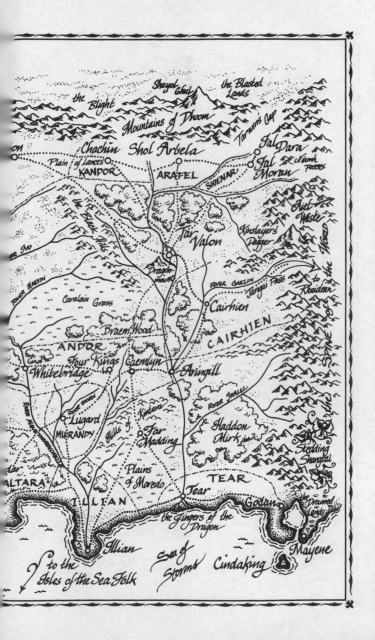

A
MEMORY
OF
LIGHT

PROLOGUE

By Grace and Banners Fallen

Bayrd pressed the coin between his thumb and forefinger. It was thoroughly unnerving to feel the metal *squish*.

He removed his thumb. The hard copper now clearly bore its print, reflecting the uncertain torchlight. He felt chilled, as if he'd spent an entire night in a cellar.

His stomach growled. Again.

The north wind picked up, making torches sputter. Bayrd sat with his back to a large rock near the center of the war camp. Hungry men muttered as they warmed their hands around firepits; the rations had spoiled long ago. Other soldiers nearby began laying all of their metal—swords, armor clasps, mail—on the ground, like linen to be dried. Perhaps they hoped that when the sun rose, it would change the material back to normal.

Bayrd rolled the once-coin into a ball between his fingers. *Light preserve us*, he thought. *Light . . .* He dropped the ball to the grass, then reached over and picked up the stones he'd been working with.

"I want to know what happened here, Karam," Lord Jarid snapped. Jarid and his advisors stood nearby in front of a table draped with maps. "I want to know how they drew so close, and I want that bloody Darkfriend Aes Sedai queen's head!" Jarid pounded his fist down on the table. Once, his eyes hadn't displayed such a crazed fervor. The pressure of it all—the lost rations, the strange things in the nights—was changing him.

Behind Jarid, the command tent lay in a heap. Jarid's hair—grown long during their exile—blew free, face bathed in ragged torchlight. Bits of dead grass still clung to his coat from when he'd crawled out of the tent.

Baffled servants picked at the iron tent spikes, which—like all metal in the camp—had become soft to the touch. The tent's mounting rings had stretched and snapped like warm wax.

The night smelled wrong. Of staleness, of rooms that hadn't been entered in years. The air of a forest clearing should not smell like ancient dust. Bayrd's stomach growled again. Light, but he would've liked to have something to eat. He set his attention on his work, slapping one of his stones down against the other.

He held the stones as his old pappil had taught him as a boy. The feeling of stone striking stone helped push away the hunger and coldness. At least something was still solid in this world.

Lord Jarid glanced at him, scowling. Bayrd was one of ten men Jarid had insisted guard him this night. "I *will* have Elayne's head, Karam," Jarid said, turning back to his captains. "This unnatural night is the work of her witches."

"Her head?" Eri's skeptical voice came from the side. "And how, precisely, is someone going to bring you her head?"

Lord Jarid turned, as did the others around the torchlit table. Eri stared at the sky; on his shoulder, he wore the mark of the golden boar charging before a red spear. It was the mark of Lord Jarid's personal guard, but Eri's voice bore little respect. "What's he going to use to cut that head free, Jarid? His teeth?"

The camp stilled at the horribly insubordinate line. Bayrd stopped his stones, hesitating. Yes, there had been talk about how unhinged Lord Jarid had become. But this?

Jarid sputtered, face growing red with rage. "You dare use such a tone with me? One of my own *guards*?"

Eri continued inspecting the cloud-filled sky.

"You're docked two months' pay," Jarid snapped, but his voice trembled. "Stripped of rank and put on latrine duty until further notice. If you speak back to me again, I'll cut out your tongue."

Bayrd shivered in the cold wind. Eri was the best they had in what was left of their rebel army. The other guards shuffled, looking down.

Eri looked toward the lord and smiled. He didn't say a word, but somehow, he didn't have to. Cut out his tongue? Every scrap of metal in the camp had gone soft as lard. Jarid's own knife lay on the table, twisted and warped—it had stretched thin as he pulled it from his sheath. Jarid's coat flapped, open; it had had silver buttons.

"Jarid ..." Karam said. A young lord of a minor house loyal to Sarand, he had a lean face and large lips. "Do you really think ... really think this was the work of Aes Sedai? All of the metal in the camp?"

"Of course," Jarid barked. "What else would it be? Don't tell me you believe those campfire tales. The Last Battle? *Phaw*." He looked back at the table. Unrolled there, with pebbles weighting the corners, was a map of Andor.

Bayrd turned back to his stones. *Snap, snap, snap.* Slate and granite. It had taken work to find suitable sections of each, but Pappil had taught Bayrd to recognize all kinds of stone. The old man had felt betrayed when Bayrd's father had gone off and become a butcher in the city, instead of keeping to the family trade.

Soft, smooth slate. Bumpy, ridged granite. Yes, some things in the world were still solid. Some few things. These days, you couldn't rely on much. Once immovable lords were now soft as ... well, soft as metal. The sky churned with blackness, and brave men—men Bayrd had long looked up to—trembled and whimpered in the night.

"I'm worried, Jarid," Davies said. An older man, Lord Davies was as close as anyone was to being Jarid's confidant. "We haven't seen anyone in days. Not farmer, not queen's soldier. Something is happening. Something wrong."

"She cleared the people out," Jarid snarled. "She's preparing to pounce."

"I think she's ignoring us, Jarid," Karam said, looking at the sky. Clouds still churned there. It seemed like months since Bayrd had seen a clear sky. "Why would she bother? Our men are starving. The food continues to spoil. The signs—"

"She's trying to squeeze us," Jarid said, eyes wide with fervor. "This is the work of the Aes Sedai."

Stillness came suddenly to the camp. Silence, save for Bayrd's stones. He'd never felt right as a butcher, but he'd found a home in his lord's guard. Cutting up cows or cutting up men, the two were strikingly similar. It bothered him how easily he'd shifted from one to the other.

Snap, snap, snap.

Eri turned. Jarid eyed the guard suspiciously, as if ready to scream out harsher punishment.

He wasn't always this bad, was he? Bayrd thought. *He wanted the throne for his wife, but what lord wouldn't?* It was hard to look past the name. Bayrd's family had followed the Sarand family with reverence for generations.

Eri strode away from the command post.

"Where do you think you're going?" Jarid howled.

Eri reached to his shoulder and ripped free the badge of the Sarand house guard. He tossed it aside and left the torchlight, heading into the night toward the winds from the north.

Most men in the camp hadn't gone to sleep. They sat around firepits, wanting to be near warmth and light. A few with clay pots tried boiling cuts of grass, leaves, or strips of leather as something, anything, to eat.

They stood up to watch Eri go.

"Deserter," Jarid spat. "After all we've been through, now he leaves. Just because things are difficult."

"The men are *starving*, Jarid," Davies repeated.

"I'm aware. Thank you so much for telling me about the problems with every *bloody breath you have.*" Jarid wiped his brow with his trembling palm, then slammed it on his map. "We'll have to strike one of the cities; there's no running from her, not now that she knows where we are. Whitebridge. We'll take it and resupply. Her Aes Sedai must be weakened after the stunt they pulled tonight, otherwise she'd have attacked."

Bayrd squinted into the darkness. Other men were standing, lifting quarterstaffs or cudgels. Some went without weapons. They gathered sleeping rolls, hoisted packs of clothing to their shoulders. Then they began to trail out of the camp, their passage silent, like the movement of ghosts. No rattling of chain mail or buckles on armor. The metal was all gone. As if the soul had been stripped from it.

"Elayne doesn't dare move against us in strength," Jarid said, perhaps convincing himself. "There must be strife in Caemlyn.

All of those mercenaries you reported, Shiv. Riots, maybe. Elenia will be working against Elayne, of course. Whitebridge. Yes, Whitebridge will be perfect.

"We hold it, you see, and cut the nation in half. We recruit there, press the men in western Andor to our banner. Go to ... what's the place called? The Two Rivers. We should find able hands there." Jarid sniffed. "I hear they haven't seen a lord for decades. Give me four months, and I'll have an army to be reckoned with. Enough that she won't dare strike at us with her witches ... "

Bayrd held his stone up to the torchlight. The trick to creating a good spearhead was to start outward and work your way in. He'd drawn the proper shape with chalk on the slate, then had worked toward the center to finish the shape. From there, you turned from hitting to tapping, shaving off smaller bits.

He'd finished one side earlier; this second half was almost done. He could almost hear his pappil whispering to him. *We're of the stone, Bayrd. No matter what your father says. Deep down, we're of the stone.*

More soldiers left the camp. Strange, how few of them spoke. Jarid finally noticed. He stood up straight and grabbed one of the torches, holding it high. "What are they doing? Hunting? We've seen no game in weeks. Setting snares, perhaps?"

Nobody replied.

"Maybe they've seen something," Jarid muttered. "Or maybe they think they have. I'll stand no more talk of spirits or other foolery; the witches are creating apparitions to unnerve us. That's ... that's what it has to be."

Rustling came from nearby. Karam was digging in his fallen tent. He came up with a small bundle.

"Karam?" Jarid said.

Karam glanced at Lord Jarid, then lowered his eyes and began to tie a coin pouch at his waist. He stopped and laughed, then emptied it. The gold coins inside had melted into a single lump, like pigs' ears in a jar. Karam pocketed this lump. He fished in the pouch and brought out a ring. The blood-red gemstone at the center was still good. "Probably won't be enough to buy an apple, these days," he muttered.

"I *demand* to know what you are doing," Jarid snarled. "Is this your doing?" He waved toward the departing soldiers. "You're staging a mutiny, is that it?"

"This isn't my doing," Karam said, looking ashamed. "And it's not really yours, either. I'm . . . I'm sorry."

Karam walked away from the torchlight. Bayrd found himself surprised. Lord Karam and Lord Jarid had been friends from childhood.

Lord Davies went next, running after Karam. Was he going to try to hold the younger man back? No, he fell into step beside Karam. They vanished into the darkness.

"I'll have you hunted down for this!" Jarid yelled after them, voice shrill. Frantic. "I will be consort to the Queen! No man will give you, or any member of your Houses, shelter or succor for ten generations!"

Bayrd looked back at the stone in his hand. Only one step left, the smoothing. A good spearhead needed some smoothing to be dangerous. He brought out another piece of granite he'd picked up for the purpose and carefully began scraping it along the side of the slate.

Seems I remember this better than I'd expected, he thought as Lord Jarid continued to rant.

There was something powerful about crafting the spearhead. The simple act seemed to push back the gloom. There had been a *shadow* on Bayrd, and the rest of the camp, lately. As if . . . as if he couldn't stand in the light no matter how he tried. He woke each morning feeling as if someone he'd loved had died the day before.

It could crush you, that despair. But the act of creating something—anything—fought back. That was one way to challenge . . . *him*. The one none of them spoke of. The one that they all knew was behind it, no matter what Lord Jarid said.

Bayrd stood up. He'd want to do more smoothing later, but the spearhead actually looked good. He raised his wooden spear haft—the metal blade had fallen free when evil had struck the camp—and lashed the new spearhead in place, just as his pappil had taught him all those years ago.

The other guards were looking at him. "We'll need more of those," Morear said. "If you're willing."

Bayrd nodded. "On our way out, we can stop by the hillside where I found the slate."

Jarid finally stopped yelling, his eyes wide in the torchlight. "No. You are my personal guard. You will not defy me!"

Jarid jumped for Bayrd, murder in his eyes, but Morear and Rosse caught the lord from behind. Rosse looked aghast at his own mutinous act. He didn't let go, though.

Bayrd fished a few things out from beside his bedroll. After that, he nodded to the others, and they joined him—eight men of Lord Jarid's personal guard, dragging the sputtering lord himself through the remnants of camp. They passed smoldering fires and fallen tents, abandoned by men who were trailing out into the darkness in greater numbers now, heading north. Into the wind.

At the edge of camp, Bayrd selected a nice, stout tree. He waved to the others, and they took the rope he'd fetched and tied Lord Jarid to the tree. The man sputtered until Morear gagged him with a handkerchief.

Bayrd stepped in close. He tucked a waterskin into the crook of Jarid's arm. "Don't struggle too much or you'll drop that, my Lord. You should be able to push the gag off—it doesn't look too tight—and angle the waterskin up to drink. Here, I'll take out the cork."

Jarid stared thunder at Bayrd.

"It's not about you, my Lord," Bayrd said. "You always treated my family well. But, here, we can't have you following along and making life difficult. There's just something that we need to do, and you're stopping everyone from doing it. Maybe someone should have said something earlier. Well, that's done. Sometimes, you let the meat hang too long, and the entire haunch has to go."

He nodded to the others, who ran off to gather bedrolls. He pointed Rosse toward the slate outcropping nearby and told him what to look for in good spearhead stone.

Bayrd turned back to the struggling Lord Jarid. "This isn't witches, my Lord. This isn't Elayne . . . I suppose I should call her the Queen. Funny, thinking of a pretty young thing like that as queen. I'd rather have bounced her on my knee at an inn than bow to her, but Andor will need a ruler to follow to the Last Battle, and it isn't your wife. I'm sorry."

Jarid sagged in his bonds, the anger seeming to bleed from him. He was weeping now. Odd thing to see, that.

"I'll tell people we pass—if we pass any—where you are,"

Bayrd promised, "and that you probably have some jewels on you. They might come for you. They might." He hesitated. "You shouldn't have stood in the way. Everyone seems to know what is coming but you. The Dragon is reborn, old bonds are broken, old oaths done away with ... and I'll be *hanged* before I let Andor march to the Last Battle without me."

Bayrd left, walking into the night, raising his new spear onto his shoulder. *I have an oath older than the one to your family, anyway. An oath the Dragon himself couldn't undo.* It was an oath to the land. The stones were in his blood, and his blood in the stones of this Andor.

Bayrd gathered the others and they left for the north. Behind them in the night, their lord whimpered, alone, as the ghosts began to move through camp.

Talmanes tugged on Selfar's reins, making the horse dance and shake his head. The roan seemed eager. Perhaps Selfar sensed his master's anxious mood.

The night air was thick with smoke. Smoke and screams. Talmanes marched the Band alongside a road clogged with refugees smudged with soot. They moved like flotsam in a muddy river.

The men of the Band eyed the refugees with worry. "Steady!" Talmanes shouted to them. "We can't sprint all the way to Caemlyn. Steady!" He marched the men as quickly as he dared, nearly at a jog. Their armor clanked. Elayne had taken half of the Band with her to the Field of Merrilor, including Estean and most of the cavalry. Perhaps she had anticipated needing to withdraw quickly.

Well, Talmanes wouldn't have much use for cavalry in the streets, which were no doubt as clogged as this roadway. Selfar snorted and shook his head. They were close now; the city walls just ahead—black in the night—held in an angry light. It was as if the city were a firepit.

By grace and banners fallen, Talmanes thought with a shiver. Enormous clouds of smoke billowed over the city. This was bad. Far worse than when the Aiel had come for Cairhien.

Talmanes finally gave Selfar his head. The roan galloped along the side of the road for a time; then Talmanes reluctantly forced his way across, ignoring pleas for help. Time he'd spent with Mat made him wish there were more he could offer these people. It was downright strange, the effect Matrim Cauthon had on a person. Talmanes looked at common folk in a very different light now. Perhaps it was because he still didn't rightly know whether to think of Mat as a lord or not.

On the other side of the road, he surveyed the burning city, waiting for his men to catch up. He could have mounted all of them—though they weren't trained cavalry, every man in the Band had a horse for long-distance travel. Tonight, he didn't dare. With Trollocs and Myrddraal lurking in the streets, Talmanes needed his men in immediate fighting shape. Crossbowmen marched with loaded weapons at the flanks of deep columns of pikemen. He would not leave his soldiers open to a Trolloc charge, no matter how urgent their mission.

But if they lost those dragons . . .

Light illumine us, Talmanes thought. The city seemed to be boiling, with all that smoke churning above. Yet some parts of the Inner City—rising high on the hill and visible over the walls—were not yet aflame. The Palace wasn't on fire yet. Could the soldiers there be holding?

No word had come from the Queen, and from what Talmanes could see, no help had arrived for the city. The Queen must still be unaware, and that was bad.

Very, *very* bad.

Ahead, Talmanes spotted Sandip with some of the Band's scouts. The slender man was trying to extricate himself from a group of refugees.

"Please, good master," one young woman was crying. "My child, my daughter, in the heights of the northern march . . . "

"I must reach my shop!" a stout man bellowed. "My glass-wares—"

"My good people," Talmanes said, forcing his horse among them, "I should think that if you want us to help, you might wish to back away and allow us to reach the bloody city."

The refugees reluctantly pulled back, and Sandip nodded to Talmanes in thanks. Tan-skinned and dark-haired, Sandip was one of the Band's commanders and an accomplished hedge-doctor. The affable man wore a grim expression today, however.

"Sandip," Talmanes said, pointing, "there."

In the near distance, a large group of fighting men clustered, looking at the city.

"Mercenaries," Sandip said with a grunt. "We've passed several batches of them. Not a one seemed inclined to lift a finger."

"We shall see about that," Talmanes said. People still flooded out through the city gates, coughing, clutching meager possessions, leading crying children. That flow would not soon slacken. Caemlyn was as full as an inn on market day; the ones lucky enough to be escaping would be only a small fraction compared to those still inside.

"Talmanes," Sandip said quietly, "that city's going to become a death trap soon. There aren't enough ways out. If we let the Band become pinned inside . . ."

"I know. But—"

At the gates a wave of feeling surged through the refugees. It was almost a physical thing, a shudder. The screams grew more intense. Talmanes spun; hulking figures moved in the shadows inside the gate.

"Light!" Sandip said. "What is it?"

"Trollocs," Talmanes said, turning Selfar. "Light! They're going to try to seize the gate, stop the refugees." There were five gates out of the city; if the Trollocs held all of them . . .

This was already a slaughter. If the Trollocs could stop the frightened people from fleeing, it would grow far worse.

"Hurry the ranks!" Talmanes yelled. "All men to the city gates!" He spurred Selfar into a gallop.

The building would have been called an inn elsewhere, though Isam had never seen anyone inside except for the dull-eyed women who tended the few drab rooms and prepared tasteless meals. Visits here were never for comfort. He sat on a hard stool at a pine table so worn with age, it had likely grayed long before Isam's birth. He refrained from touching the surface overly much, lest he come away with more splinters than an Aiel had spears.

Isam's dented tin cup was filled with a dark liquid, though he wasn't drinking. He sat beside the wall, near enough the inn's single window to watch the dirt street outside, dimly lit in the evening by a few rusty lanterns hung outside buildings. Isam took care not to let his profile show through the smeared glass. He never looked directly out. It was always best not to attract attention in the Town.

That was the only name the place had, if it could be said to have a name at all. The sprawling ramshackle buildings had been put up and replaced countless times over two thousand years. It actually resembled a good-sized town, if you squinted. Most of the buildings had been constructed by prisoners, often with little or no knowledge of the craft. They'd been supervised by men equally ignorant. A fair number of the houses seemed held up by those to either side of them.

Sweat dribbled down the side of Isam's face, as he covertly watched that street. Which one would come for him?

In the distance, he could barely make out the profile of a mountain splitting the night sky. Metal rasped against metal somewhere out in the Town like steel heartbeats. Figures moved on the street. Men, heavily cloaked and hooded, with faces hidden up to the eyes behind blood-red veils.

Isam was careful not to let his eyes linger on them.

Thunder rumbled. The slopes of that mountain were filled with odd lightning bolts that struck upward toward the ever-present gray clouds. Few humans knew of this Town not so far from the valley of Thakan'dar, with Shayol Ghul itself looming above. Few knew *rumors* of its existence. Isam would not have minded being among the ignorant.

Another of the men passed. Red veils. They kept them up always. Well, almost always. If you saw one lower his veil, it was time to kill him. Because if you didn't, he'd kill you. Most of the red-veiled men seemed to have no reason to be out, beyond scowling at each other and perhaps kicking at the numerous stray dogs—slat-ribbed and feral—whenever one crossed their path. The few women who had left shelter scuttled along the edges of the street, eyes lowered. There were no children to be seen, and likely few to be found. The Town was no place for children. Isam knew. He had grown from infancy here.

One of the men passing on the street looked up at Isam's window and stopped. Isam went very still. The *Samma N'Sei*, the Eye Blinders, had always been touchy and full of pride. No, touchy was too mild a term. They required no more than whim to take a knife to one of the Talentless. Usually it was one of the servants who paid. Usually.

The red-veiled man continued to regard him. Isam stilled his nerves and did not make a show of staring back. His summons here had been urgent, and one did not ignore such things if one wished to live. But still ... if the man took one step toward the building, Isam would slip into *Tel'aran'rhiod*, secure in the knowledge that not even one of the Chosen could follow him from here.

Abruptly the *Samma N'Sei* turned from the window. In a flash he was moving away from the building, striding quickly. Isam felt some of his tension melt away, though it would never truly leave him, not in this place. This place was not home, despite his childhood here. This place was death.

Motion. Isam glanced toward the end of the street. Another tall man, in a black coat and cloak, was walking toward him, his face exposed. Incredibly, the street was emptying as *Samma N'Sei* darted off down other streets and alleys.

So it was Moridin. Isam had not been there to witness the Chosen's first visit to the Town, but he had heard. The *Samma N'Sei* had thought Moridin one of the Talentless until he demonstrated differently. The constraints that held them did not hold him.

The numbers of dead *Samma N'Sei* varied with the telling, but the claim never dipped below a dozen. By the evidence of his eyes, Isam could believe it.

When Moridin reached the inn, the street was empty save for the dogs. And Moridin walked right on past. Isam watched as closely as he dared. Moridin seemed uninterested in him or the inn, which was where Isam had been instructed to wait. Perhaps the Chosen had other business, and Isam would be an afterthought.

After Moridin passed, Isam finally took a sip of his dark drink. The locals just called it "fire." It lived up to its name. It was supposedly related to some drink from the Waste. Like everything else in the Town, it was a corrupt version of the original.

How long was Moridin going to make him wait? Isam didn't like being here. It reminded him too much of his childhood. A servant passed—a woman with a dress so frayed that it was practically rags—and dropped a plate onto the table. The two didn't exchange a word.

Isam looked at his meal. Vegetables—peppers and onions, mostly—sliced thin and boiled. He picked at one and took a taste, then sighed and pushed the meal aside. The vegetables were as bland as unseasoned millet porridge. There wasn't any meat. That was actually good; he didn't like to eat meat unless he'd seen it killed and slaughtered himself. That was a remnant of his childhood. If you hadn't seen it slaughtered yourself, you couldn't know. Not for certain. Up here, if you found meat, it *could* have been something that had been caught in the south, or maybe an animal that had been raised up here, a cow or a goat.

Or it could be something else. People lost games up here and couldn't pay, then disappeared. And often, the *Samma N'Sei* who didn't breed true washed out of their training. Bodies vanished. Corpses rarely lasted long enough for burial.

Burn this place, Isam thought, stomach unsettled. *Burn it with—*

Someone entered the inn. He couldn't watch both approaches to the door from this direction, unfortunately. She was a pretty woman, dressed in black trimmed with red. Isam didn't recognize her slim figure and delicate face. He was increasingly certain he could recognize all of the Chosen; he'd seen them often enough in the dream. They didn't know that, of course. They thought themselves masters of the place, and some of them *were* very skilled.

He was equally skilled, and also exceptionally good at not being seen.

Whoever this was, she was in disguise, then. Why bother hiding herself here? Either way, she had to be the one who had summoned him. No woman walked the Town with such an imperious expression, such self-assurance, as if she expected the rocks themselves to obey if told to jump. Isam went quietly down on one knee.

That motion woke the ache inside his stomach from where he'd been wounded. He still hadn't recovered from the fight with the wolf. He felt a stirring inside of him; Luc hated Aybara. Unusual. Luc tended to be the more accommodating one, Isam the hard one. Well, that was how he saw himself.

Either way, on this particular wolf, they agreed. On one hand,

Isam was thrilled; as a hunter, he'd rarely been presented with such a challenge as Aybara. However, his hatred was deeper. He *would* kill Aybara.

Isam covered a grimace at the pain and bowed his head. The woman left him kneeling and took a seat at his table. She tapped a finger on the side of the tin cup for a few moments, staring at its contents, and did not speak.

Isam remained still. Many of those fools who named themselves Darkfriends would squirm and writhe when another asserted power over them. Indeed, he admitted with reluctance, Luc would probably squirm just as much.

Isam was a hunter. That was all he cared to be. When you were secure with what you were, there was no cause to resent being shown your place.

Burn it, but the side of his belly *did* ache.

"I want him dead," the woman said. Her voice was soft, yet intense.

Isam said nothing.

"I want him gutted like an animal, his bowels spilled onto the ground, his blood a milkpan for ravens, his bones left to bleach, then gray, then *crack* in the heat of the sun. I want him *dead*, hunter."

"Al'Thor."

"Yes. You have failed in the past." Her voice was ice. He felt a chill. This one was hard. Hard as Moridin.

In his years of service, he had learned contempt for most of the Chosen. They bickered like children, for all their power and supposed wisdom. This woman made him pause, and he wondered if he actually *had* spied on all of them. She seemed different.

"Well?" she asked. "Do you speak for your failures?"

"Each time one of the others has tasked me with this hunt," he said, "another has come to pull me away and set me on some other task."

In truth, he'd rather have continued his hunt for the wolf. He would not disobey orders, not direct ones from the Chosen. Other than Aybara, one hunt was much the same to him as another. He would kill this Dragon, if he had to.

"Such won't happen this time," the Chosen said, still staring at his cup. She hadn't looked at him, and she did not give him leave to stand, so he remained kneeling. "All others have renounced claim on you. Unless the Great Lord tells you otherwise—unless he *summons you himself*—you are to keep to this task. Kill al'Thor."

Motion outside the window caused Isam to glance to the side. The Chosen didn't look as a group of black-hooded figures passed. The winds didn't cause the cloaks of these figures to stir.

They were accompanied by carriages; an unusual sight in the Town. The carriages moved slowly, but still rocked and thumped on the uneven street. Isam didn't need to see into the carriages' curtained windows to know that thirteen women rode inside, matching the number of Myrddraal. None of the *Samma N'Sei* returned to the street. They tended to avoid processions like this. For obvious reasons, they had ... strong feelings about such things.

The carriages passed. So. Another had been caught. Isam would have assumed that the practice had ended, once the taint was cleansed.

Before he turned back to look at the floor, he caught sight of something more incongruous. A small, dirty face watching from the shadows of an alleyway across the street. Wide eyes but a furtive posture. Moridin's passing, and the coming of the thirteens, had driven the *Samma N'Sei* off the street. Where they were not, the urchins could go in some safety. Maybe.

Isam wanted to scream at the child to go. Tell it to run, to risk crossing the Blight. To die in the stomach of a Worm was better than to live in this Town, and suffer what it did to you. Go! Flee! *Die!*

The moment passed quickly, the urchin retreating to the shadows. Isam could remember being that child. He'd learned so many things then. How to find food that you could mostly trust, and wouldn't vomit back up once you found out what was in it. How to fight with knives. How to avoid being seen or noticed.

And how to kill a man, of course. Everyone who survived long enough in the Town learned that particular lesson.

The Chosen was still looking at his cup. It was her reflection she was looking at, Isam realized. What did she see there?

"I will need help," Isam finally said. "The Dragon Reborn has guards, and he is rarely in the dream."

"Help has been arranged," she said softly. "But you are to *find* him, hunter. None of this playing as you did before, trying to draw him to you. Lews Therin will sense such a trap. Besides, he will not deviate from his cause now. Time is short."

She spoke of the disastrous operation in the Two Rivers. Luc had been in charge then. What knew Isam of real towns, real people? Almost, he felt a longing for those things, though he suspected that was really Luc's emotion. Isam was just a hunter. People held little interest for him beyond the best places for an arrow to enter so as to hit the heart.

That Two Rivers operation, though ... it stank like a carcass left to rot. He still didn't know. Had the point really been to lure al'Thor, or had it been to keep Isam away from important events? He knew his abilities fascinated the Chosen; he could do something that they could not. Oh, they could imitate the way he stepped into the dream, but they needed channeling, gateways, time.

He was tired of being a pawn in their games. Just let him hunt; stop changing the prey with each passing week.

One did not say such things to the Chosen. He kept his objections to himself.

Shadows darkened the doorway to the inn, and the serving woman disappeared into the back. That left the place completely empty save for Isam and the Chosen.

"You may stand," she said.

Isam did, hastily, as two men stepped into the room. Tall, muscular and red-veiled. They wore brown clothing like Aiel, but didn't carry spears or bows. These creatures killed with weapons far deadlier.

Though he kept his face impassive, Isam felt a surge of emotion. A childhood of pain, hunger and death. A lifetime of avoiding the gaze of men like these. He fought hard to keep himself from trembling as they strode to the table, moving with the grace of natural predators.

The men dropped their veils and bared their teeth. *Burn me.* Their teeth were filed.

These had been Turned. You could see it in their eyes—eyes that weren't quite right, weren't quite *human*.

Isam nearly fled right then, stepping into the dream. He couldn't kill both of these men. He'd have been reduced to ash before he managed to take down one of them. He'd seen *Samma N'Sei* kill; they often did it just to explore new ways of using their powers.

They didn't attack. Did they know this woman was Chosen? Why, then, lower their veils? *Samma N'Sei* never lowered their veils except to kill—and only for the kills they were most eagerly anticipating.

"They will accompany you," the Chosen said. "You shall have a handful of the Talentless as well to help deal with al'Thor's guards." She turned to him and, for the first time, she met his eyes. She seemed . . . revolted. As if she were disgusted to need his aid.

"They will accompany you," she had said. Not *"They will serve you."*

Bloody son of a dog. This was going to be a hateful job.

Talmanes threw himself to the side, narrowly avoiding the Trolloc's axe. The ground trembled as the axe broke cobblestones; he ducked and rammed his blade through the creature's thigh. The thing had a bull's snout, and it threw back its head to bellow.

"Burn me, but you have horrid breath," Talmanes growled, whipping his sword free and stepping back. The thing went down on one leg, and Talmanes hacked off its weapon hand.

Panting, Talmanes danced back as his two companions struck the Trolloc through the back with spears. You always wanted to fight Trollocs in a group. Well, you always wanted to fight *anyone* with a team on your side, but it was more important with Trollocs, considering their size and strength.

Corpses lay like heaps of trash in the night. Talmanes had been forced to fire the city gate's guardhouses to give light; the half-dozen or so guards who had remained were now recruits in the Band, for the time being.

Like a black tide, the Trollocs began to retreat from the gate. They'd overextended themselves in pushing for it. Or, rather, *being* pushed for it. There had been a Halfman with this crew. Talmanes lowered his hand to the wound in his side. It was wet.

The guardhouse fires were burning low. He'd have to order a few of the shops set on fire. That risked letting the blaze spread, but the city was already lost. No sense in holding back now. "Brynt!" he yelled. "Set that stable aflame!"

Sandip came up as Brynt went running past with a torch. "They'll be back. Soon, probably."

Talmanes nodded. Now that the fighting was done, townspeople began to flood out of alleys and recesses, timidly making for the gate and—presumably—safety.

"We *can't* stay here and hold this gate," Sandip said. "The dragons . . ."

"I know. How many men did we lose?"

"I don't have a count yet. A hundred, at least."

Light, Mat's going to have my hide when he hears about that. Mat hated losing troops. There was a softness to the man equal to his genius—an odd, but inspiring, combination. "Send some scouts to watch the city roadways nearby for approaching Shadowspawn. Heap some of these Trolloc carcasses to make barriers; they'll work as well as anything else. You, soldier!"

One of the wearied soldiers walking past froze. He wore the Queen's colors. "My Lord?"

"We need to let people know this gate out of the city is safe. Is there a horn call that Andoran peasants would recognize? Something that would bring them here?"

"'Peasants,'" the man said thoughtfully. He didn't seem to like the word. They didn't use it often, here in Andor. "Yes, the Queen's March."

"Sandip?"

"I'll set the sounders to it, Talmanes," Sandip said.

"Good." Talmanes knelt to clean his sword on a fallen Trolloc's shirt, his side aching. The wound wasn't bad. Not by normal terms. Just a nick, really.

The shirt was so grimy he almost hesitated to wipe his weapon, but Trolloc blood was bad for a blade, so he swabbed down the sword. He stood up, ignoring the pain in his side, then walked toward the gate, where he'd tied Selfar. He hadn't dared trust the horse against Shadowspawn. He was a good gelding, but not Borderland-trained.

None of the men questioned him as he climbed into the saddle and turned Selfar westward, out of the city gate, toward those mercenaries he'd seen watching earlier. Talmanes wasn't surprised to find that they'd moved closer to the city. Fighting drew warriors like fire drawing cold travelers on a winter night.

They hadn't joined in the battle. As Talmanes rode up, he was greeted by a small group of the sell-swords: six men with thick arms, and—likely—thick wits. They recognized him and the Band. Mat was downright famous these days, and so was the Band, by association. They undoubtedly also noticed the Trolloc bloodstains on Talmanes' clothing and the bandage at his side.

That wound had really begun to burn fiercely now. Talmanes reined in Selfar, then patiently patted at his saddlebags. *I stowed some tabac here somewhere . . .*

"Well?" one of the mercenaries asked. The leader was easy to pick out; he had the finest armor. A man often became leader of a band like this by staying alive.

Talmanes fished his second-best pipe out of his saddlebag. Where was that tabac? He never took the best pipe into battle. His father had called that bad luck.

Ah, he thought, pulling out the tabac pouch. He placed some in the bowl, then removed a lighting twig and leaned over to stick it into a torch held by a wary mercenary.

"We aren't going to fight unless paid," the leader said. He was a stout man, surprisingly clean, though he could have done with a beard trim.

Talmanes lit his pipe, puffing smoke out. Behind him, the horns started blowing. The Queen's March turned out to be a catchy tune. The horns were accompanied by shouts, and Talmanes looked back. Trollocs on the main thoroughfare, a larger batch this time.

Crossbowmen fell into ranks and began loosing at an order Talmanes couldn't hear.

"We're not—" the head man began again.

"Do you know what this is?" Talmanes asked softly around his pipe. "This is the beginning of the end. This is the fall of nations and the unification of humankind. This is the *Last Battle*, you bloody fool."

The men shuffled uncomfortably.

"Do you . . . do you speak for the Queen?" the leader said, trying to salvage something. "I just want to see my men taken care of."

"If you fight," Talmanes said, "I'll promise you a great reward."

The man waited.

"I promise you that you'll continue to draw breath," Talmanes said, taking another puff.

"Is that a threat, Cairhienin?"

Talmanes blew out smoke, then leaned down from his saddle, putting his face closer to the leader. "I killed a Myrddraal tonight, Andoran," he said softly. "It nicked me with a Thakan'dar blade, and the wound has gone black. That means I have a few hours at best before the blade's poison burns me from the inside out and I die in the most agonizing way a man can. Therefore, friend, I suggest that you trust me when I tell you that I really have nothing to lose."

The man blinked.

"You have two choices," Talmanes said, turning his horse and speaking loudly to the troop. "You can fight like the rest of us and help this world see new days, and maybe you'll earn some coin in the end. I can't promise that. Your other option is to sit here, watch people be slaughtered and tell yourselves that you don't work for free. If you're lucky, and the rest of us salvage this world without you, you'll draw breath long enough to be strung up by your cowardly necks."

Silence. Horns blew from the darkness behind.

The chief sell-sword looked toward his companions. They nodded in agreement.

"Go help hold that gate," Talmanes said. "I'll recruit the other mercenary bands to help."

Leilwin surveyed the multitude of camps dotting the place known as the Field of Merrilor. In the darkness, with the moon not due to rise for some time, she could almost imagine that the cook fires were shipborne lanterns in a busy port at night.

That was probably a sight she would never see again. Leilwin Shipless was not a captain; she would never be one again. To wish otherwise was to defy the very nature of who she had become.

Bayle put a hand on her shoulder. Thick fingers, rough from many days of work. She reached up and rested her hand on his. It had been simple to slip through one of those gateways being made at Tar Valon. Bayle knew his way around the city, though he had grumbled about being there. "This place do set the hairs on my arms to points," he'd said, and, "I did wish to never walk these streets again. I did wish it."

He'd come with her anyway. A good man, Bayle Domon. As good as she'd found in these unfamiliar lands, despite moments of unsavory trading in his past. That was behind him. If he didn't understand the right way of things, he did try.

"This do be a sight," he said, scanning the quiet sea of lights. "What want you to do now?"

"We find Nynaeve al'Meara or Elayne Trakand."

Bayle scratched at his bearded chin; he wore it after the Illianer style, with the upper lip shaved. The hair on his head was of varying lengths; he'd stopped shaving a portion of his head, now that she had freed him. She'd done that so they could marry, of course.

It was well; the shaven head would have drawn attention here. He'd done quite well as *so'jhin* once certain ... issues had been resolved. In the end, however, she had to admit that Bayle Domon was not meant to be *so'jhin*. He was too rough-cut, and no tide would ever soften those sharp edges. That was how she wanted him, though she'd never say so out loud.

"It do be late, Leilwin," he said. "Perhaps we should wait until morning."

No. There was a quiet to the camps, true, but it was not the quiet of slumber. It was the quiet of ships waiting for the right winds.

She knew little of what was happening here—she hadn't dared open her mouth in Tar Valon to ask questions, lest her accent reveal her as Seanchan. A gathering of this size did not occur without dedicated planning. She was surprised at the immensity of it; she'd heard of the meeting here, one that most of the Aes Sedai had come to attend. This exceeded anything she'd anticipated.

She started across the field, and Bayle followed, both of them joining the group of Tar Valon servants they had been allowed to accompany, thanks to Bayle's bribe. His methods did not please her, but she had been able to think of no other way. She tried not to think too much about his original contacts in Tar Valon. Well, if she was never to be on a ship again, then Bayle would find no more opportunities for smuggling. That was a small comfort.

You're a ship's captain. That's all you know, all you want. And now,

Shipless. She shivered, and clenched her hands into fists to keep
from wrapping her arms around herself. To spend the rest of her
days on these unchanging lands, never able to move at a pace
brisker than what a horse could provide, never to smell the deep-
sea air, never to point her prow toward a horizon, hoist anchor, set
sail and simply ...

She shook herself. Find Nynaeve and Elayne. She might be
Shipless, but she would not let herself slip into the depths and
drown. She set her course and started walking. Bayle hunched
down slightly, suspicious, and tried to watch all around them at
once. He also glanced at her a few times, lips drawn to a line. She
knew what that meant, by now.

"What is it?" she asked.

"Leilwin, what do we be doing here?"

"I've told you. We need to find—"

"Yes, but why? What do you think you will do? They do be
Aes Sedai."

"They showed me respect before."

"And so you do think they'll take us in?"

"Perhaps." She eyed him. "Speak it, Bayle. You have something
on your mind."

He sighed. "Why do we need be taken in, Leilwin? We could
find ourselves a ship somewhere, in Arad Doman. Where there do
be no Aes Sedai *or* Seanchan."

"I wouldn't run the kind of ship you prefer."

He regarded her flatly. "I do know how to run an honest business, Leilwin. It would no be—"

She raised a hand, quieting him, then rested it on his shoulder.
They stopped on the pathway. "I know, my love. I know. I'm
speaking words to distract, to set us spinning in a current that
goes nowhere."

"Why?"

That single word scratched at her like a splinter under a fingernail. Why? Why *had* she come all this way, traveling with
Matrim Cauthon, putting herself dangerously near the Daughter
of the Nine Moons? "My people live with a grave misconception
of the world, Bayle. In doing so, they create injustice."

"They did reject you, Leilwin," he said softly. "You do no
longer be one of them."

"I will *always* be one of them. My name was revoked, but not my blood."

"I do be sorry for the insult."

She nodded curtly. "I am still loyal to the Empress, may she live forever. But the *damane* ... they are the very *foundation* for her rule. They are the means by which she creates order, by which she holds the Empire together. And the *damane* are a lie."

Sul'dam could channel. The talent could be learned. Now, months after she had discovered the truth, her mind could not encompass all of the implications. Another might have been more interested in the political advantage; another might have returned to Seanchan and used this to gain power. Almost, Leilwin wished she had done that. Almost.

But the pleas of the *sul'dam* ... growing to know those Aes Sedai, who were nothing like what she'd been taught ...

Something had to be done. And yet, in doing it, did she risk causing the entire Empire to collapse? Her movements must be considered very, very carefully, like the last rounds of a game of *shal*.

The two continued to follow the line of servants in the dark; one Aes Sedai or another often sent servants for something they'd left in the White Tower, so traveling back and forth was common—a good thing for Leilwin. They passed the perimeter of the Aes Sedai camp without being challenged.

She was surprised at the ease of it until she spotted several men alongside the path. They were very easy to miss; something about them blended into the surroundings, particularly in the darkness. She noticed them only when one moved, breaking off from the others to fall into step a short distance behind her and Bayle.

In seconds, it was obvious that he'd picked the two of them out. Perhaps it was the way they walked, the way they held themselves. They'd been careful to dress plainly, though Bayle's beard would mark him as Illianer.

Leilwin stopped—laying a hand on Bayle's arm—and turned to confront the one following them. A Warder, she assumed from descriptions.

The Warder stalked up to them. They were still near the perimeter of the camp, the tents organized in rings. She had noticed with discomfort that some of the tents glowed with a light too steady to come from candle or lamp.

"Ho," Bayle said, raising a friendly hand to the Warder. "We do be seeking an Aes Sedai named Nynaeve al'Meara. If she is not here, perhaps one named Elayne Trakand?"

"Neither makes their camp here," the Warder said. He was a long-armed man, and he moved with grace. His features, framed by long, dark hair, looked ... unfinished. Chiseled from rock by a sculptor who had lost interest in the project partway through.

"Ah," Bayle said. "That do be our mistake, then. Could you point us to where they do be making camp? It do be a matter of some urgency, you see." He spoke smoothly, easily. Bayle could be quite charming, when necessary. Much more so than Leilwin could.

"That depends," the Warder said. "Your companion, she wishes to find these Aes Sedai, too?"

"She do—" Bayle began, but the Warder held up a hand.

"I would hear it from her," he said, inspecting Leilwin.

"It do be what I wish," Leilwin said. "My aged grandmother! These women, they did promise us payment, and I *do* mean to have it. Aes Sedai do not lie. Everyone do know this fact. If you will not take us to them, then provide someone who will!"

The Warder hesitated, eyes widening at the barrage of words. Then, blessedly, he nodded. "This way." He led them away from the center of the camp, but he no longer seemed suspicious.

Leilwin let out a quiet breath and fell into step with Bayle behind the Warder. Bayle looked at her proudly, grinning so widely he'd certainly have given the two of them away if the Warder had looked back. She couldn't help a hint of a smile herself.

The Illianer accent had not come naturally to her, but both had agreed that her Seanchan tongue was dangerous, particularly when traveling among Aes Sedai. Bayle claimed that no true Illianer would accept her as one of them, but she was clearly good enough to fool an outsider.

She felt relieved when they moved away from the Aes Sedai camp into the dark. Having two friends—they were friends, despite their troubles with one another—who were Aes Sedai did not mean she wanted to be inside a camp full of them. The Warder led them to an open area near the middle of the Field of Merrilor. There was a very large camp here, with a great number of small tents.

"Aiel," Bayle said softly to her. "There do be tens of thousands of them."

Interesting. Fearsome stories were told of Aiel, legends that could not all possibly be true. Still, the tales—if exaggerated—suggested that these were the finest warriors this side of the ocean. She would have welcomed sparring with one or two of them, had the situation been different. She rested a hand on the side of her pack; she'd stowed her cudgel in a long pocket on the side, easily within reach.

They certainly were a *tall* folk, these Aiel. She passed some of them lounging by campfires, seemingly relaxed. Those eyes, however, watched more keenly than the Warders' had. A dangerous people, ready for killing while relaxing beside fires. She could not make out the banners that flapped above this camp in the night sky.

"Which king or queen do rule this camp, Warder?" she called.

The man turned to her, his features lost in the night shadow. "Your king, Illianer."

At her side, Bayle stiffened.

My . . .

The Dragon Reborn. She was proud that she didn't miss a step as they walked, but it was a near thing. A man who could channel. That was worse, far worse, than the Aes Sedai.

The Warder led them to a tent near the center of the camp. "You are fortunate; her light is on." There were no guards at the tent entrance, so he called in and received permission to enter. He pulled back the flap with one arm and nodded to them, yet his other hand was on his sword, and he stood in fighting posture.

She hated putting that sword to her back, but she entered as ordered. The tent was lit by one of those unnatural globes of light, and a familiar woman in a green dress sat at a writing desk, working on a letter. Nynaeve al'Meara was what, back in Seanchan, one would call a *telarti*—a woman with fire in her soul. Leilwin had come to understand that Aes Sedai were supposed to be calm as placid waters. Well, this woman might be that on occasion—but she was the kind of placid water found one bend away from a furious waterfall.

Nynaeve continued to write as they entered. She no longer

wore braids; her hair was loose around the top of her shoulders. It was a sight as strange as a ship with no mast.

"I'll be with you in a moment, Sleete," Nynaeve said. "Honestly, the way you lot have been hovering over me lately makes me think of a mother bird who has lost an egg. Don't your Aes Sedai have work for you to do?"

"Lan is important to many of us, Nynaeve Sedai," the Warder—Sleete—said in a calm, gravelly voice.

"Oh, and he's not important to me? Honestly, I wonder if we should send you out to chop wood or something. If one more Warder comes to see if I need—"

She glanced up, finally seeing Leilwin. Nynaeve's face immediately grew impassive. Cold. Burningly cold. Leilwin found herself sweating. This woman held her life in her hands. Why couldn't it have been Elayne that Sleete had brought them to? Perhaps they shouldn't have mentioned Nynaeve.

"These two demanded to see you," Sleete said. His sword was out of its sheath. Leilwin hadn't seen that. Domon muttered softly to himself. "They claim that you promised to pay them money, and they have come for it. They did not identify themselves in the Tower, however, and found a way to slip through one of the gateways. The man is from Illian. The woman, somewhere else. She's disguising her accent."

Well, perhaps she wasn't as good with the accent as she'd assumed. Leilwin glanced at his sword. If she rolled to the side, he'd probably miss a strike, assuming he went for the chest or neck. She could pull the cudgel and—

She was facing an Aes Sedai. She'd never stand up from that roll. She'd be caught in a weave of the One Power, or worse.

"I know them, Sleete," Nynaeve said, voice cool. "You did well in bringing them to me. Thank you."

His sword was sheathed at once, and Leilwin felt cool air on her neck as he slipped out of the tent, quiet as a whisper.

"If you've come to beg forgiveness," Nynaeve said, "you've come to the wrong person. I've half a mind to give you over to the Warders to question. Maybe they can bleed something useful about your people from that treacherous mind of yours."

"It is good to see you again too, Nynaeve," Leilwin said coolly.

"So what happened?" Nynaeve demanded.

What happened? What was the woman talking about?

"I did try," Bayle suddenly said, regretfully. "I did fight them, but I was taken easily. They could have fired my ship, sunk us all, killed my men."

"Better that you and all aboard should have died, Illianer," Nynaeve said. "The *ter'angreal* ended up in the hands of one of the Forsaken; Semirhage was hiding among the Seanchan, pretending to be some kind of judge. A Truthspeaker? Is that the word?"

"Yes," Leilwin said softly. She understood now. "I regret breaking my oath, but—"

"You *regret* it, Egeanin?" Nynaeve said, standing, knocking her chair back. "'Regret' is not a word I would use for endangering the world itself, bringing us to the brink of darkness and all but shoving us over the edge! She had copies of that device made, woman. One ended up around the neck of the Dragon Reborn. The *Dragon Reborn himself*, controlled by one of the Forsaken!"

Nynaeve flung her hands into the air. "Light! We were *heartbeats* from the end, because of you. The end of everything. No more Pattern, no more world, nothing. Millions of lives could have winked out because of your carelessness."

"I . . ." Leilwin's failures seemed monumental, suddenly. Her life, lost. Her very name, lost. Her ship, stripped from her by the Daughter of the Nine Moons herself. All were immaterial in light of this.

"I did fight," Bayle said more firmly. "I did fight with what I could give."

"I should have joined you, it appears," Leilwin said.

"I did try to explain that," Bayle said grimly. "Many times now, burn me, but I did."

"Bah," Nynaeve said, raising a hand to her forehead. "What are you doing here, Egeanin? I had hoped you were dead. If you had died trying to keep your oath, then I could not have blamed you."

I handed it to Suroth myself, Leilwin thought. *A price paid for my life, the only way out.*

"Well?" Nynaeve glared at her. "Out with it, Egeanin."

"I no longer bear that name." Leilwin went down on her knees. "I have had all stripped from me, including my honor, it now appears. I give myself to you as payment."

Nynaeve snorted. "We don't keep people as if they were animals, unlike you Seanchan."

Leilwin continued kneeling. Bayle rested a hand on her shoulder, but did not try to pull her to her feet. He understood well enough now why she had to do as she had. He was quite nearly civilized.

"On your feet," Nynaeve snapped. "Light, Egeanin. I remember you being so strong you could chew rocks and spit out sand."

"It is my strength that compels me," she said, lowering her eyes. Did Nynaeve not understand how difficult this was? It would be easier to slit her own throat, only she had not the honor left to demand such an easy end.

"Stand!"

Leilwin did as told.

Nynaeve grabbed her cloak off the bed and threw it on. "Come. We'll take you to the Amyrlin. Maybe she'll know what to do with you."

Nynaeve barged out into the night, and Leilwin followed. Her decision had been made. There was only one path that made sense, one way to preserve a shred of honor, and perhaps to help her people survive the lies they had been telling themselves for so long.

Leilwin Shipless now belonged to the White Tower. Whatever they said, whatever they tried to do with her, that fact would not change. They owned her. She would be a *da'covale* to this Amyrlin, and would ride this storm like a ship whose sail had been shredded by the wind.

Perhaps, with what remained of her honor, she could earn this woman's trust.

"It's part of an old Borderlander relief for the pain," Melten said, removing the bandage at Talmanes' side. "The blisterleaf slows the taint left by the cursed metal."

Melten was a lean, mop-haired man. He dressed like an Andoran woodsman, with a simple shirt and cloak, but spoke like a Borderlander. In his pouch he carried a set of colored balls that he'd sometimes juggle for the other members of the Band. In another life, he must have been a gleeman.

He was an unlikely man to be in the Band, but they all were, in one way or another.

"I don't know how it dampens the poison," Melten said. "But it does. It's no natural poison, mind you. You can't suck it free."

Talmanes pressed his hand to the side. The burning pain felt like thorny vines crawling in under his skin, creeping forward and tearing at his flesh with every movement. He could *feel* the poison moving through his body. Light, but it hurt.

Nearby, the men of the Band fought through Caemlyn up toward the Palace. They'd come in through the southern gate, leaving the mercenary bands—under Sandip's command—holding the western gate.

If there was human resistance anywhere in the city, it would be at the Palace. Unfortunately, fists of Trollocs roved the area between Talmanes' position and the Palace. They kept running across the monsters and getting drawn into fights.

Talmanes couldn't find out if, indeed, there was resistance above without getting there. That meant leading his men up toward the Palace, fighting all the way, and leaving himself open to being cut off from behind if one of those roving groups worked around behind him. There was nothing for it, though. He needed to find out what—if anything—remained of the Palace defenses. From there, he could strike further into the city and try to get the dragons.

The air smelled of smoke and blood; during a brief pause in the fighting, they'd piled dead Trollocs against the right side of the street to make room for passage.

There were refugees in this quarter of the city, too, though not a flood of them. A stream, maybe, seeping in from the darkness as Talmanes and the Band seized sections of the thoroughfare leading up toward the Palace. These refugees never demanded that the Band protect their goods or rescue their homes; they sobbed with joy at finding human resistance. Madwin was in charge of sending them toward freedom along the corridor of safety the Band had carved free.

Talmanes started up toward the Palace, atop the hill but only barely visible in the night. Though most of the city burned, the Palace was not aflame; its white walls hung in the smoky night like phantoms. No fire. That *had* to indicate resistance, didn't it?

Wouldn't the Trollocs have attacked it as one of their first actions in the city?

He'd sent scouts along the street up ahead as he gave his men—and himself—a short breather.

Melten finished tying Talmanes' poultice tight.

"Thank you, Melten," Talmanes said, nodding to the man. "I can feel the poultice working already. You said this is part of the cure for the pain. What is the other part?"

Melten unhooked a metal flask from his belt and handed it over. "Shienaran brandy, full strength."

"It's not a good idea to drink in combat, man."

"Take it," Melten said softly. "Keep the flask and drink it deep, my Lord. Or come the next bell, you won't be standing."

Talmanes hesitated, then took the flask and took a long swallow. It burned like the wound. He coughed, then tucked the brandy away. "I believe you mistook your bottles, Melten. That was something you found in a tanning vat."

Melten snorted. "And it's said you have no sense of humor, Lord Talmanes."

"I haven't one," Talmanes said. "Stay close with that sword of yours."

Melten nodded, eyes solemn. "Dreadbane," he whispered.

"What's that?"

"Borderlander title. You slew a Fade. Dreadbane."

"It had about seventeen bolts in it at the time."

"Doesn't matter." Melten clasped him on the shoulder. "Dreadbane. When you can't take the pain any longer, make two fists and raise them toward me. I will see the deed done."

Talmanes stood up, unable to suppress a groan. They both understood. The several Borderlanders in the Band agreed; wounds made by a Thakan'dar blade were unpredictable. Some festered quickly, others made men sick. When one went black like Talmanes', though . . . that was the worst. Nothing short of finding an Aes Sedai in the next few hours could save him.

"See," Talmanes muttered, "it is a good thing I have no sense of humor, otherwise I should think the Pattern was playing a joke on me. Dennel! You have a map handy?" Light, but he missed Vanin.

"My Lord," Dennel said, hurrying across the dark street carrying a torch and a hastily drawn map. He was one of the Band's dragon captains. "I think I've found a faster way through the streets to where Aludra had the dragons stored."

"We're fighting to the Palace first," Talmanes said.

"My Lord." Dennel's words came more softly from his wide lips. He was picking at his uniform, as if it didn't fit right. "If the Shadow reaches those dragons . . ."

"I'm well aware of the dangers, Dennel, thank you. How fast could you move the things, assuming we reach them? I'm worried about extending ourselves too far, and this city is going up faster than oil-soaked love letters to a High Lord's mistress. I want to get the weapons and leave the city as quickly as possible."

"I can level an enemy bulwark in a shot or two, my Lord, but the dragons do *not* move quickly. They are attached to carts, so that will help, but they aren't going to be any faster than . . . say, a line of supply wagons. And they would take time to set up properly and fire."

"Then we continue to the Palace," Talmanes said.

"But—"

"At the Palace," he said sternly, "we might find women who can channel us a gateway straight to Aludra's warehouse. Besides, if we find the Palace Guard still fighting, we know we have a friend at our backs. We *will* retrieve those dragons, but we'll do it smartly."

He noticed Ladwin and Mar hurrying down from above. "There are Trollocs up there!" Mar said, hastening up to Talmanes. "A hundred strong at least, hunkered down in the street."

"Form ranks, men!" Talmanes shouted. "We push for the Palace!"

The sweat tent fell completely still.

Aviendha had anticipated incredulity, perhaps, at her tale. Questions, certainly. Not this painful silence.

Though she had not expected it, she did understand it. She had felt it herself after seeing her vision of the Aiel slowly losing *ji'e'toh* in the future. She had witnessed the death, dishonor and ruination of her people. At least now she had someone with whom to share that burden.

The heated stones in the kettle hissed softly. Someone should pour more water, but none of the room's six occupants moved to tend it. The other five were all Wise Ones, naked—as was Aviendha—after the manner of sweat tents. Sorilea, Amys, Bair, Melaine and Kymer of the Tomanelle Aiel. All stared straight ahead, each alone for the moment with her thoughts.

One by one, they straightened their backs and sat up, as if accepting a new burden. That comforted Aviendha; not that she'd expected the news to break them. It was still good to see them set their faces toward the danger instead of away from it.

"Sightblinder is too close to the world now," said Melaine. "The Pattern has been twisted somehow. In the dream we still see many things that may or may not happen, but there are too many possibilities; we cannot tell one from another. The fate of our people is unclear to the dreamwalkers, as is the fate of the *Car'a'carn* once he spits in Sightblinder's eye on the Last Day. We do not know the truth of what Aviendha saw."

"We must test this," Sorilea said, eyes like stone. "We must know. Is each woman now shown this vision instead of the other, or was the experience unique?"

"Elenar of the Daryne," Amys said. "Her training is nearly complete; she will be the next to visit Rhuidean. We could ask Hayde and Shanni to encourage her."

Aviendha suppressed a shudder. She understood too well how "encouraging" the Wise Ones could be.

"That would be well," Bair said, leaning forward. "Perhaps this is what happens whenever someone goes through the glass columns a second time? Maybe that is why it is forbidden."

None of them looked at Aviendha, but she could feel them considering her. What she had done *was* forbidden. Speaking of what happened in Rhuidean was also taboo.

There would be no reprimand. Rhuidean had not killed her; this was what the Wheel had spun. Bair continued to stare into the distance. Sweat trickled down the sides of Aviendha's face and her breasts.

I do not miss taking baths, she told herself. She was no soft wetlander. Still, a sweat tent wasn't truly necessary on this side of the mountains. There was no bitter cold at night, so the heat of the tent felt stifling, not comforting. And if water *was* plentiful enough for bathing . . .

No. She set her jaw. "May I speak?"

"Don't be foolish, girl," Melaine said. The woman was round in the belly, nearly to term. "You're one of us now. No need to ask permission."

Girl? It would take time for them to see her truly as one of them, but they did make an effort. Nobody ordered her to make tea or to throw water on the kettle. With no apprentice around and no *gai'shain* handy, they took turns doing these tasks.

"I am less concerned with whether the vision repeats," Aviendha said, "than with what I was shown. Will it happen? Can we stop it?"

"Rhuidean shows two types of vision," Kymer said. She was a younger woman, perhaps less than a decade Aviendha's senior, with deep red hair and a long, tanned face. "The first visit is what could be, the second, to the columns, what has happened."

"This third vision could be either," Amys said. "The columns always show the past accurately; why would they not show the future with equal accuracy?"

Aviendha's heart lurched.

"But why," Bair said softly, "would the columns show a despair that cannot change? No. I refuse to believe it. Rhuidean has always shown us what we needed to see. To help us, not destroy us. This vision must have a purpose as well. To encourage us toward greater honor?"

"It's unimportant," Sorilea said curtly.

"But—" Aviendha began.

"It's unimportant," Sorilea repeated. "If this vision were unchangeable, if our destiny is to . . . fall . . . as you have spoken, would any of us stop fighting to change it?"

The room grew still. Aviendha shook her head.

"We must treat it as if it can be changed," Sorilea said. "Best not to dwell on your question, Aviendha. We must decide what course to take."

Aviendha found herself nodding. "I . . . Yes, yes, you are correct, Wise One."

"But what do we do?" Kymer asked. "What do we change? For now, the Last Battle *must* be won."

"Almost," Amys said, "I wish for the vision to be unchangeable, for at least it proves we win this fight."

"It proves nothing," Sorilea said. "Sightblinder's victory would break the Pattern, and so no vision of the future can be sure or trusted. Even with prophecies of what might happen in Ages to come, if Sightblinder wins this battle, all will become nothing."

"This vision I saw has to do with whatever Rand is planning," Aviendha said.

They turned to her.

"Tomorrow," she said. "From what you've told me, he's preparing for an important revelation."

"The *Car'a'carn* has a . . . fondness for dramatic presentations," Bair said, her tone itself fond. "He's like a crockobur who has toiled all night making a nest so that he can sing of it in the morning to all who will listen."

Aviendha had been surprised to discover the gathering at Merrilor; she had found it only by using her bond to Rand al'Thor to determine where he was. Arriving here to find so many together, the wetlander forces collected, she wondered if this was part of what she'd seen. Was this gathering the start of what would become her vision?

"I feel as if I know more than I should." She spoke almost to herself.

"You have had a deep glimpse of what the future may hold," Kymer said. "It will change you, Aviendha."

"Tomorrow is key," Aviendha said. "His plan."

"From what you said," Kymer replied, "it sounds as if he intends to ignore the Aiel, his own people. Why would he give boons to everyone else, but not to those who are most deserving? Does he seek to insult us?"

"I don't think that is the reason," Aviendha said. "I think he intends to make demands of those who attend, not grant them gifts."

"He did mention a price," Bair said. "A price he intends to make the others pay. No one has been able to pry the secret of this price from him."

"He went through a gateway to Tear earlier this evening and returned with something," Melaine said. "The Maidens report it—he keeps his oath to bring them with him, now. When we have inquired after his price, he has said that it is something that the Aiel need not worry about."

Aviendha scowled. "He is making men pay him in order to do what we all know he must? Perhaps he has been spending too much time with that minder the Sea Folk sent him."

"No, this is well," Amys said. "These people demand much of the *Car'a'carn*. He has a right to demand something of them in return. They are soft; perhaps he intends to make them hard."

"And so he leaves us out," Bair said softly, "because he knows that we are already hard."

The tent fell silent. Amys, looking troubled, ladled some water onto the kettle's heated stones. It hissed as the steam rose.

"That is it," Sorilea said. "He does not intend to insult us. He intends to do us honor, in his own eyes." She shook her head. "He should know better."

"Often," Kymer agreed, "the *Car'a'carn* gives insult by accident, as if he were a child. We are strong, so his demand—whatever it is—matters not. If it is a price the others can pay, so can we."

"He would not make these mistakes if he had been trained properly in our ways," Sorilea murmured.

Aviendha met their eyes evenly. No, she had not trained him as well as he could have been trained—but they knew that Rand al'Thor was obstinate. Besides, she was their equal now. Although she had trouble feeling that way while facing Sorilea's tight-lipped disapproval.

Perhaps it was spending so much time with wetlanders like Elayne, but suddenly, she did see things as Rand must. To give the Aiel an exemption from his price—if, indeed, that was what he intended—was an act of honor. If he *had* made a demand of them with the others, these very Wise Ones might have taken offense at being lumped with the wetlanders.

What was he planning? She saw hints of it in the visions, but increasingly, she was certain that the next day would start the Aiel on the road to their doom.

She *must* see that did not happen. This was her first task as a Wise One, and would likely be the most important she was ever given. She *would not* fail.

"Her task was not just to teach him," Amys said. "What I wouldn't give to know that he was safely under the watchful eyes of a good woman." She looked at Aviendha, face laden with meaning.

"He will be mine," Aviendha said, firmly. *But not for you, Amys, or for our people.* She was shocked at the strength of that sentiment within her. She was Aiel. Her people meant everything to her.

But this choice was not their choice. This choice was hers.

"Be warned, Aviendha," Bair said, laying a hand on her wrist. "He has changed since you left. He has grown strong."

Aviendha frowned. "In what way?"

"He has embraced death," Amys said, sounding proud. "He may still carry a sword and wear the clothing of a wetlander, but he is ours now, finally and truly."

"I must see this," Aviendha said, standing. "I will discover what I can regarding his plans."

"There is not much time remaining," Kymer warned.

"One night remains," Aviendha said. "It will be enough."

The others nodded, and Aviendha started to dress. Unexpectedly, the others joined her, dressing as well. It appeared that they considered her news important enough that they would be going to share it with the other Wise Ones, rather than continuing to sit in conference.

Aviendha was the first to step out into the night; the cool air, away from the sweltering heat of the sweat tent, felt good on her skin. She took a deep breath. Her mind was heavy with fatigue, but sleep would need to wait.

The tent flaps rustled behind the other Wise Ones, Melaine and Amys speaking softly to one another as they hastened into the night. Kymer walked purposefully toward the Tomanelle section of the camp. Perhaps she would speak with her sister-father, Han, the Tomanelle chief.

Aviendha started to move off herself, but a bony hand took her arm. She glanced over her shoulder to see Bair standing behind her, dressed again in blouse and skirt.

"Wise One," Aviendha said by reflex.

"Wise One," Bair replied with a smile.

"Is there something . . ."

"I would go to Rhuidean," Bair said, glancing at the sky. "Would you kindly make a gateway for me?"

"You're going through the glass columns."

"One of us needs to. Despite what Amys said, Elenar is not ready, particularly not to see . . . something of this nature. That girl spends half of her days squawking like a buzzard over the last scrap of a rotting carcass."

"But—"

"Oh, don't you start, too. You're one of us now, Aviendha, but I'm still old enough to have tended your *greatmother* when she was a child." Bair shook her head; her white hair almost seemed to glow in the filtered moonlight. "I am the best one to go," she continued. "Channelers must be preserved for the battle to come. I would not have some child walk into those columns now. I will do it. Now, that gateway? Will you grant my request, or do I need to bully Amys into doing so?"

Aviendha would have liked to see anyone bully Amys into anything. Maybe Sorilea could do it. She said nothing, however, and created the proper weave to open a gateway.

The thought of another seeing what she'd seen made her stomach twist. What would it mean if Bair returned with the exact same vision? Would that indicate the future was more likely?

"It was that terrible, was it?" Bair asked softly.

"Horrible. It would have made spears weep and stones crumble, Bair. I would rather have danced with Sightblinder himself."

"Then it is much better that I go than another. It should be the strongest of us who does this."

Aviendha stopped herself from raising an eyebrow. Bair was as tough as good leather, but the other Wise Ones weren't exactly flower petals. "Bair," Aviendha said, a thought occurring to her. "Have you ever met a woman named Nakomi?"

"Nakomi." Bair tried the word in her mouth. "An ancient name. I have never known anyone who uses it. Why?"

"I met an Aiel woman while traveling to Rhuidean," Aviendha said. "She claimed not to be a Wise One, but she had a way about her . . ." She shook her head. "The question was merely idle curiosity."

"Well, we shall know some of the truth of these visions," Bair said, stepping toward the gateway.

"What if they *are* true, Bair?" Aviendha found herself asking. "What if there isn't anything we can do?"

Bair turned. "You saw your children, you said?"

Aviendha nodded. She hadn't spoken in detail of that segment of the vision. It had seemed more personal to her.

"Change one of their names," Bair said. "Never speak of the name that child was called in the vision, not even to us. Then you shall know. If one thing is different, then others may be different as well. *Will* be different. This is not our fate, Aviendha. It is a path we will avoid. Together."

Aviendha found herself nodding. Yes. A simple change, a small change, but full of meaning. "Thank you, Bair."

The aging Wise One nodded to her, then stepped through the gateway, running in the night toward the city ahead.

Talmanes threw his shoulder against a hulking, boar-faced Trolloc in crude chain armor. The beast smelled horrid, like smoke, wet fur and unwashed flesh. It grunted at the force of Talmanes' assault; the things always seemed surprised when he attacked them.

Talmanes pulled back, ripping his sword out of the beast's side as it collapsed. He then lunged forward and rammed his sword into its throat, heedless of its ragged fingernails scratching at his legs. Life faded from the beady, too-human eyes.

Men fought, called, grunted, killed. The street ran up a steep incline toward the Palace. Trolloc hordes had entrenched here, holding position and keeping the Band from reaching the top.

Talmanes sagged against the side of a building—the one next to it was on fire, lighting the street with violent colors and bathing him in heat. Those fires seemed chilly compared to the flaring, horrible pain of his wound. The flare ran down his leg to his foot and was beginning to work its way across his shoulder.

Blood and bloody ashes, he thought. *What I'd give for another few hours with my pipe and book, alone and peaceful.* The people who spoke of glorious death in battle were complete flaming fools. There was nothing glorious about dying in this mess of fire and blood. Give him a quiet death any day.

Talmanes pushed himself back up to his feet, drops of sweat falling from his face. Below, Trollocs amassed themselves behind his rear position. They had closed the road behind Talmanes' force, but Talmanes was able to proceed, cutting through the Trollocs ahead.

Retreat would be difficult to pull off. As well as this roadway being full of Trollocs, fighting in the city meant that Trollocs could wind through the streets in small groups and attack his flanks, as they advanced and later when they retreated.

"Throw everything you've got at them, men!" he bellowed, hurling himself up the street and into the Trollocs blocking the way up. The Palace was quite close now. He caught a goat-faced Trolloc's sword on his shield right before it would have taken off Dennel's head. Talmanes tried to shove the beast's weapon back, but *Light*, Trollocs were strong. Talmanes barely kept this one from throwing him to the ground as Dennel recovered and attacked its thighs, bringing it down.

Melten fell in beside Talmanes. The Borderlander was true to his word to stay close, in case Talmanes needed a sword to end his life. The two led the push up the hill. The Trollocs began to give, then rallied, a snarling, roaring heap of dark fur, eyes and weapons in the firelight.

There were so many of them

"Steady!" Talmanes yelled. "For Lord Mat and the Band of the Red Hand!"

If Mat were here, he would probably curse a lot, complain as much, then proceed to save them all with some battlefield miracle. Talmanes couldn't reproduce Mat's blend of insanity and inspiration, but his yell did seem to encourage the men. The ranks tightened. Gavid arrayed his two dozen crossbowmen—the last Talmanes had with him—atop a building that hadn't burned away. They started driving flight after flight of bolts into the Trollocs.

That might have broken human enemies, but not Trollocs. The bolts dropped a few, but not as many as Talmanes would have hoped.

There's another Fade back there, Talmanes thought. *Pushing them forward. Light, I can't fight another. I shouldn't have fought the one I did!*

He shouldn't be on his feet. Melten's flask of brandy was gone, long since drained to deaden what it could. His mind was already as fuzzy as he dared allow. He fell in with Dennel and Londraed at the front, fighting, concentrating. Letting Trolloc blood out onto the cobbles to stream down the hillside.

The Band gave a good fight of it, but they were outnumbered and exhausted. Down below, another Trolloc fist joined the ones on the street behind him.

That was it. He would have to either hit that force behind—turning his back on the one in front—or break his men into smaller units and send them retreating through side streets to regroup at the gate below.

Talmanes prepared to give the orders.

"Forward the White Lion!" voices yelled. "For Andor and the Queen!"

Talmanes spun as men in white and red broke through the Trolloc lines atop the hill. A second force of Andoran pikemen poured out of a side alleyway, coming in behind the Trolloc horde that had just surrounded him. The Trollocs broke before the oncoming pikemen, and in moments the entire mass—like a pus-filled blister—burst, Trollocs scattering in all directions.

Talmanes stumbled back. Momentarily he had to prop himself up with his sword as Madwin took command of the counterstrike and his men killed many of the fleeing Trollocs.

A group of officers in bloodied Queen's Guard uniforms rushed down the hillside; they didn't look any better than the Band. Guybon led them. "Mercenary," he said to Talmanes, "I thank you for showing up."

Talmanes frowned. "You act as if we saved you. From my perspective, it happened the other way around."

Guybon grimaced in the firelight. "You gave us some respite; those Trollocs were attacking the Palace gates. I apologize for taking so long to reach you—we didn't realize, at first, what had drawn them in this direction."

"Light. The Palace still stands?"

"Yes," Guybon said. "We're full of refugees, though."

"What of channelers?" Talmanes asked, hopeful. "Why haven't the Andoran armies returned with the Queen?"

"Darkfriends." Guybon frowned. "Her Majesty took most of the Kinswomen with her, the strongest ones at least. She left four with enough power to make a gateway together, but—the attack—an assassin killed two of them before the other two could stop him. Alone, the two aren't strong enough to send for help. They're using their strength to Heal."

"Blood and bloody ashes," Talmanes said, though he felt a stab of hope as he said it. Perhaps these women could not make a gateway, but they *might* be able to Heal his wound. "You should lead the refugees out of the city, Guybon. My men hold the southern gate."

"Excellent," Guybon said, straightening. "But you will have to lead the refugees. I must defend the Palace."

Talmanes raised an eyebrow at him; he didn't take orders from Guybon. The Band had its own command structure, and reported only to the Queen. Mat had made that clear when accepting the contract.

Unfortunately, Guybon didn't take orders from Talmanes, either. Talmanes took a deep breath, but then wavered, dizzy. Melten grabbed his arm to keep him from toppling over.

Light, but it hurt. Couldn't his side just do the decent thing and grow numb? Blood and bloody ashes. He needed to get to those Kinswomen.

Talmanes said hopefully, "Those two women who can Heal?"

"I have sent for them already," Guybon said. "As soon as we saw this force here."

Well, that was something.

"I do mean to stay here," Guybon warned. "I won't abandon this post."

"Why? The city is lost, man!"

"The Queen ordered us to send regular reports through gateways," Guybon said. "Eventually, she's going to wonder why we haven't sent a messenger. She will send a channeler to see why we haven't reported, and that messenger will arrive at the Palace's Traveling ground. It—"

"My Lord!" a voice called. "My Lord Talmanes!"

Guybon cut off, and Talmanes turned to find Filger—one of the scouts—scrambling up the bloodied cobbles of the hillside toward him. Filger was a lean man with thinning hair and a couple of days' worth of scruff, and the sight of him filled Talmanes with dread. Filger was one of those they'd left guarding the city gate below.

"My Lord," Filger said, panting, "the Trollocs have taken the city walls. They're packing the ramparts, loosing arrows or spears at anyone who draws too close. Lieutenant Sandip sent me to bring you word."

"Blood and ashes! What of the gate?"

"We're holding," Filger said. "For now."

"Guybon," Talmanes said, turning back. "Show some mercy,

man; someone needs to defend that gate. Please, take the refugees out and reinforce my men. That gate will be our only method of retreat from the city."

"But the Queen's messenger—"

"The Queen will figure out what bloody happened once she thinks to look here. Look about you! Trying to defend the Palace is madness. You don't have a city any longer, but a pyre."

Guybon's face was conflicted, his lips a tight line.

"You know I'm right," Talmanes said, his face twisted in pain. "The best thing you can do is reinforce my men at the southern gate to hold it open for as many refugees as can reach it."

"Perhaps," Guybon said. "But to let the Palace burn?"

"You can make it worth something," Talmanes said. "What if you left some soldiers to fight at the Palace? Have them hold off the Trollocs as long as they can. That will draw the Trollocs away from the people escaping out this way. When they can hold no longer, your soldiers can escape the Palace grounds on the far side, and make their way around to the southern gate."

"A good plan," Guybon said, grudgingly. "I will do as you suggest, but what of you?"

"I have to get to the dragons," Talmanes said. "We can't let them fall to the Shadow. They're in a warehouse near the edge of the Inner City. The Queen wanted them kept out of sight, away from the mercenary bands outside. I have to find them. If possible, retrieve them. If not, destroy them."

"Very well," Guybon said, turning away, looking frustrated as he accepted the inevitable. "My men will do as you suggest; half will lead the refugees out, then help your soldiers hold the southern gate. The other half will hold the Palace a little longer, then withdraw. But *I'm* coming with you."

"Do we really need so many lamps in here?" the Aes Sedai demanded from her stool at the back of the room. It might as well have been a throne. "Think of the oil you're wasting."

"We need the lamps." Androl grunted. Night rain pelted the window, but he ignored it, trying to focus on the leather he was sewing. It would be a saddle. At the moment, he was working on the girth that would go around the horse's belly.

He poked holes into the leather in a double row, letting the work calm him. The stitching chisel he used made diamond-shaped holes—he could use the mallet on them for speed, if he wanted, but right now he liked the feel of pressing the holes without it.

He picked up his stitch-mark wheel, measuring off the locations for the next stitches, then worked another of the holes. You had to line the flat sides of the diamonds toward one another for holes like this, so that when the leather pulled, it didn't pull on the flats. The neat stiches would help keep the saddle in good shape over the years. The rows needed to be close enough together to reinforce one another, but not so close that there was danger of them ripping into one another. Staggering the holes helped.

Little things. You just had to make sure the little things were done right, and—

His fingers slipped, and he punched a hole with the diamond pointing the wrong way. Two of the holes ripped into one another at the motion.

He nearly tossed the entire thing across the room in frustration. That was the fifth time tonight!

Light, he thought, pressing his hands on the table. *What's happened to my self-control?*

He could answer that question with ease, unfortunately. *The Black Tower is what happened.* He felt like a multilegged *nachi* trapped in a dried-up tidal pool, waiting desperately for the water to return while watching a group of children work their way down the beach with buckets, gathering up anything that looked tasty . . .

He breathed in and out, then picked up the leather. This would be the shoddiest piece he'd done in years, but he *would* finish it. Leaving something unfinished was nearly as bad as messing up the details.

"Curious," said the Aes Sedai—her name was Pevara, of the Red Ajah. He could feel her eyes on his back.

A *Red*. Well, common destinations made for unusual shipmates, as the old Tairen saying went. Perhaps he should use the Saldaean proverb instead. *If his sword is at your enemy's throat, don't waste time remembering when it was at yours.*

"So," Pevara said, "you were telling me about your life prior to coming to the Black Tower?"

"I don't believe that I was," Androl said, beginning to sew. "Why? What did you want to know?"

"I'm simply curious. Were you one of those who came here on his own, to be tested, or were you one of those they found while out hunting?"

He pulled a thread tight. "I came on my own, as I believe Evin told you yesterday, when you asked him about me."

"Hmmm," she said. "I'm being monitored, I see."

He looked toward her, lowering the leather. "Is that something they teach you?"

"What?" Pevara asked innocently.

"To twist a conversation about. There you sit, all but accusing me of spying on you—when you were the one interrogating my friends about me."

"I want to know what my resources are."

"You want to know why a man would *choose* to come to the Black Tower. To learn to channel the One Power."

She didn't answer. He could see her deciding upon a response that would not run afoul of the Three Oaths. Speaking with an Aes Sedai was like trying to follow a green snake as it slipped through damp grass.

"Yes," she said.

He blinked in surprise.

"Yes, I want to know," she continued. "We are allies, whether either of us desires it or not. I want to know what kind of person I've slipped into bed with." She eyed him. "Figuratively speaking, of course."

He took a deep breath, *forcing* himself to become calm. He hated talking with Aes Sedai, with them twisting everything about. That, mixed with the tension of the night and the inability to get this saddle right . . .

He would be calm, Light burn him!

"We should practice making a circle," Pevara said. "It will be an advantage to us—albeit a small one—against Taim's men, should they come for us."

Androl put his dislike of the woman from his mind—he had other things to worry about—and forced himself to think objectively. "A circle?"

"Do you not know what one is?"

"Afraid not."

She pursed her lips. "Sometimes I forget how ignorant all of you are . . ." She paused, as if realizing she'd said too much.

"All men are ignorant, Aes Sedai," Androl said. "The topics of our ignorance may change, but the nature of the world is that no man may know everything."

That didn't seem to be the answer she'd been expecting, either. Those hard eyes studied him. She didn't like men who could channel—most people didn't—but with her it was more. She had spent her life hunting down men like Androl.

"A circle," Pevara said, "is created when women and men join their strength in the One Power together. It must be done in a specific way."

"The M'Hael will know about it, then."

"Men require women to form a circle," Pevara said. "In fact, a circle must contain more women than men except in very limited cases. One woman and man can link, as can one woman and two men, as can two women and two men. So the largest we could create is a circle of three, with me and two of you. Still, it *could* be of use to us."

"I'll find you two of the others to practice with," Androl said. "Among those I trust, I'd say that Nalaam is the strongest. Emarin is very powerful too, and I don't think he's yet reached the height of his strength. Same for Jonneth."

"They are the strongest?" Pevara asked. "Not yourself?"

"No," he said, returning to his work. That rain picked up again outside, and chill air slipped under the door. One of the room's lamps was burning low nearby, letting shadows into the room. He watched the darkness uncomfortably.

"I find that hard to believe, Master Androl," she said. "They all look to you."

"Believe what you wish, Aes Sedai. I'm weakest among them. Perhaps the weakest man in the Black Tower."

This quieted her, and Androl rose to refill that dwindling lamp. As he sat back down, a rap on the door announced the entrance of Emarin and Canler. Although both were wet from the rain, they were nearly as opposite as men could be. One was tall, refined and careful, the other crotchety and prone to gossip. They had found common ground, somewhere, and seemed to enjoy one another's company.

"Well?" Androl asked.

"It *might* work," Emarin said, taking off his rain-soaked coat and hanging it on a hook beside the door. He wore clothing underneath embroidered after the Tairen style. "It would need to be a powerful rainstorm. The guards watch carefully."

"I feel like the prize bull at a fair," Canler grumbled, stomping some of the mud off his boots after hanging up his coat. "Everywhere we go, Taim's favored watch us from the corners of their eyes. Blood and ashes, Androl. They *know*. They know we're going to try running."

"Did you find any weak points?" Pevara asked, leaning forward. "Someplace where the walls are less guarded?"

"It appears to depend upon the guards chosen, Pevara Sedai," Emarin said, nodding to her.

"Hmm ... I suppose that it would. Have I mentioned how intriguing I find it that the one of you who treats me with the most respect is a Tairen?"

"Being polite to a person is not a sign of respect for them, Pevara Sedai," Emarin said. "It is merely a sign of a good upbringing and a balanced nature."

Androl smiled. Emarin was an absolute *wonder* with insults. Half the time, the person didn't figure out that he'd been mocked until they'd parted ways.

Pevara's mouth pursed. "Well, then. We watch the rotation of guards. When the next storm arrives, we will use it as cover and escape over the wall near the guards we think are less observant."

The two men turned to Androl, who caught himself watching the corner of the room where the shadow fell from a table. Was it growing larger? Reaching toward him ...

"I don't like leaving men behind," he said, forcing himself to look away from the corner. "There are dozens upon dozens of men and boys here who aren't yet under Taim's control. We can't possibly lead all of them out without drawing attention. If we leave them, we risk ... "

He couldn't say it. They didn't know what was happening, not really. People were *changing*. Once-trustworthy allies became enemies overnight. They looked like the same people, yet different at the same time. Different behind the eyes. Androl shivered.

"The women sent by the rebel Aes Sedai are still outside the gates," Pevara said. They had been camped out there for a time, claiming the Dragon Reborn had promised them Warders. Taim had yet to let any of them in. "If we can reach them, we can storm the Tower and rescue those left behind."

"Will it really be that easy?" Emarin asked. "Taim will have an entire village of hostages. A lot of the men brought their families."

Canler nodded. His family was one of those. He wouldn't willingly leave them.

"Beyond that," Androl said softly, turning on his stool to face Pevara, "do you honestly think the Aes Sedai can win here?"

"Many of them have decades—some centuries—of experience."

"How much of that was spent fighting?"

Pevara did not answer.

"There are hundreds of men who can channel in here, Aes Sedai," Androl continued. "Each one has been trained—at length—to be a *weapon*. We don't learn about politics or history. We don't study how to influence nations. We learn to kill. Every man and boy here is pushed to the edges of his capacity, forced to stretch and grow. Gain more power. Destroy. And a lot of them are insane. Can your Aes Sedai fight that? Particularly when many of the men we trust—the very men we're trying to save—will likely fight alongside Taim's men if they see the Aes Sedai trying to invade?"

"Your arguments are not without merit," Pevara said.

Just like a queen, he thought, unwillingly impressed at her poise.

"But surely we need to send information out," Pevara continued. "An all-out assault may be unwise, but sitting here until we are all taken, one at a time . . ."

"I do believe it would be wise to send someone," Emarin said. "We need to warn the Lord Dragon."

"The Lord Dragon," Canler said with a snort, taking a seat by the wall. "He's abandoned us, Emarin. We're nothing to him. It—"

"The Dragon Reborn carries the world on his shoulders, Canler," Androl said softly, catching Canler up short. "I don't know why he's left us here, but I'd prefer to assume it's because he thinks we can handle ourselves." Androl fingered the straps of leather, then stood up. "This is our time of proving, the test of the

Black Tower. If we have to run to the Aes Sedai to protect us from our own, we subject ourselves to their authority. If we have to run to the Lord Dragon, then we will be nothing once he is gone."

"There can be no reconciliation with Taim, now," Emarin said. "We all know what he is doing."

Androl didn't look at Pevara. She had explained what she suspected was happening, and she—despite years of training at keeping her emotions in check—had not been able to quiet the fear in her voice as she spoke of it. Thirteen Myrddraal and thirteen channelers, together in a horrifying rite, could turn any channeler to the Shadow. Against his will. "What he does is pure, undiluted evil," Pevara said. "This is no longer a division between the men who follow one leader and those who follow another. This is the Dark One's work, Androl. The Black Tower has fallen under the Shadow. You must accept that."

"The Black Tower is a dream," he said, meeting her eyes. "A shelter for men who can channel, a place of our own, where men need not fear, or run, or be hated. I will not surrender that to Taim. I *will not*."

The room fell silent save for the sounds of rain on the windows. Emarin began to nod, and Canler stood up, taking Androl by the arm.

"You're right," Canler said. "Burn me if you ain't right, Androl. But what can we *do*? We're weak, outnumbered."

"Emarin," Androl said, "did you ever hear about the Knoks Rebellion?"

"Indeed. It caused quite a stir, even outside of Murandy."

"Bloody Murandians," Canler spat. "They'll steal your coat off your back and beat you bloody if you don't offer your shoes, too."

Emarin raised an eyebrow.

"Knoks was well outside Lugard, Canler," Androl said. "I think you'd find the people there not dissimilar to Andorans. The rebellion happened about . . . oh, ten years back, now."

"A group of farmers overthrew their lord," Emarin said. "He deserved it, by all accounts—Desartin was a horrid person, particularly to those beneath him. He had a force of soldiers, one of the largest outside of Lugard, and was looking as if he'd set up his own little kingdom. There wasn't a thing the King could do about it."

"And Desartin was overthrown?" Canler asked.

"By simple men and women who had had too much of his brutality," Androl said. "In the end, many of the mercenaries who had been his cronies stood with us. Though he'd seemed so strong, his rotten core led to his downfall. It seems bad here, but most of Taim's men are not loyal to him. Men like him don't inspire loyalty. They collect cronies, others who hope to share in the power or wealth. We *can* and *will* find a way to overthrow him."

The others nodded, though Pevara simply watched him with pursed lips. Androl couldn't help feeling a bit of the fool; he didn't think the others should be looking to him, instead of someone distinguished like Emarin or someone powerful like Nalaam.

From the corner of his eye, he saw the shadows underneath the table lengthen, reaching for him. He set his jaw. They wouldn't dare take him with so many people around, would they? If the shadows were going to consume him, they'd wait until he was alone, trying to sleep.

Nights terrified him.

They're coming when I don't hold to saidin *now,* he thought. *Burn me, the Source was cleansed! I'm not supposed to be losing more of my wits!*

He gripped the seat of his stool until the terror retreated, the darkness withdrawing. Canler—looking uncharacteristically cheerful—said he was going to fetch them something to drink. He wandered toward the kitchen, but nobody was to go about alone, so he hesitated.

"I suppose I could use a drink as well," Pevara said with a sigh, joining him.

Androl sat down to continue his work. As he did, Emarin pulled over a stool, settling down beside him. He did so nonchalantly, as if merely looking for a good place to relax and wanting a view out the window.

Emarin, however, wasn't the type to do things without several motivations. "You fought in the Knoks Rebellion," Emarin said softly.

"Did I say that?" Androl resumed his work on the leather.

"You said that when the mercenaries switched sides, they fought with you. You used the word 'us' to refer to the rebels."

Androl hesitated. *Burn me. I* really *need to watch myself.* If Emarin had noticed, Pevara would have as well.

"I was just passing through," Androl said, "and was caught up in something unanticipated."

"You have a strange and varied past, my friend," Emarin said. "The more I learn of it, the more curious I become."

"I wouldn't say that I'm the only one with an interesting past," Androl said softly. "Lord Algarin of House Pendaloan."

Emarin pulled back, eyes widening. "How did you know?"

"Fanshir had a book of Tairen noble lines," Androl said, mentioning one of the Asha'man soldiers who had been a scholar before coming to the Tower. "It included a curious notation. A house troubled by a history of men with an unmentionable problem, the most recent one having shamed the house not a few dozen years ago."

"I see. Well, I suppose that it is not too much of a surprise that I am a nobleman."

"One who has experience with Aes Sedai," Androl continued, "and who treats them with respect, despite—or because of—what they did for his family. A *Tairen* nobleman who does this, mind you. One who does not mind serving beneath what you would term farmboys, and who sympathizes with citizen rebels. If I might say, my friend, that is *not* a prevalent attitude among your countrymen. I wouldn't hesitate to guess you've had an interesting past of your own."

Emarin smiled. "Point conceded. You would be wonderful at the Game of Houses, Androl."

"I wouldn't say that," Androl said with a grimace. "Last time I tried my hand at it, I almost . . . " He stopped.

"What?"

"I'd rather not say," Androl said, face flushing. He was *not* going to explain that period of his life. *Light, people will think I'm as much a tale-spinner as Nalaam if I continue on like this.*

Emarin turned to watch the rain hitting the window. "The Knoks Rebellion succeeded for only a short time, if I remember correctly. Within two years the noble line had reestablished itself and the dissenters were driven out or executed."

"Yes," Androl said softly.

"So we do a better job of it here," Emarin said. "I'm your man, Androl. We all are."

"No," Androl said. "We are the *Black Tower's* men. I'll lead you, if I must, but this isn't about me, or about you, or any of us individually. I am only in charge until Logain returns."

If he ever returns, Androl thought. *Gateways into the Black Tower don't work any longer. Is he trying to return, but finding himself locked out?*

"Very well," Emarin said. "What do we do?"

Thunder crashed outside. "Let me think," Androl said, picking up his piece of leather and his tools. "Give me one hour."

"I'm sorry," Jesamyn said softly, kneeling beside Talmanes. "There is nothing I can do. This wound is too far along for my skill."

Talmanes nodded, replacing the bandage. The skin all along his side had turned black as if from terrible frostbite.

The Kinswoman frowned at him. She was a youthful-looking woman with golden hair, though with channelers, ages could be very deceptive. "I'm amazed you can still walk."

"I'm not certain it could be defined as walking," Talmanes said, limping back toward the soldiers. He could still gimp along on his own, mostly, but the dizzy moments came more frequently now.

Guybon was arguing with Dennel, who kept pointing at his map and gesturing. There was such a haze of smoke in the air that many of the men had tied kerchiefs to their faces. They looked like a band of bloody Aiel.

". . . even the Trollocs are pulling out of that quarter," Guybon insisted. "There's too much fire."

"The Trollocs are pulling back to the walls all through the city," Dennel replied. "They're going to let the city burn all night. The only sector not burning is the one where the Waygate is. They knocked down all of the buildings there to create a firewall."

"They used the One Power," Jesamyn said from behind Talmanes. "I felt it. Black sisters. I would not suggest going in that direction."

Jesamyn was the only Kinswoman remaining; the other had fallen. Jesamyn wasn't powerful enough to create a gateway, but neither was she useless. Talmanes had watched her burn six Trollocs that had broken through his line.

He'd spent that skirmish sitting back, overcome by the pain. Fortunately, Jesamyn had given him some herbs to chew. They made his head feel fuzzier, but made the pain manageable. It felt as if his body were in a vise, being smashed slowly, but at least he could stay on his feet.

"We take the quickest route," Talmanes said. "The quarter that isn't burning is too close to the dragons; I won't risk the Shadowspawn discovering Aludra and her weapons." *Assuming they haven't already.*

Guybon glared at him, but this was the Band's operation. Guybon was welcome, but he wasn't part of their command structure.

Talmanes' force continued through the dark city, wary of ambushes. Though they knew the approximate location of the warehouse, getting there was problematic. Many large streets were blocked by wreckage, fire or the enemy. His force had to crawl through alleyways and lanes so twisted that even Guybon and the others from Caemlyn had difficulty following their intended direction.

Their path skirted portions of the city that burned with a heat so strong, it was probably melting cobblestones. Talmanes stared at these flames until his eyes felt dry, then led his men in further detours.

Inch by inch, they approached Aludra's warehouse. Twice they encountered Trollocs prowling for refugees to kill. They finished these off, the remaining crossbowmen felling over half of each group before they had time to respond.

Talmanes stood to watch, but did not trust himself to fight any longer. That wound had left him too weak. Light, why had he left his horse behind? Fool move, that. Well, the Trollocs would have chased it off anyway.

My thoughts are starting to go in circles. He pointed with his sword down a crossing alley. The scouts scurried on ahead and looked in both directions before giving the all clear. *I can barely think. Not much longer now before the darkness takes me.*

He would see the dragons protected first. He had to.

Talmanes stumbled out of the alley onto a familiar street. They were close. On one side of the street, structures burned. The statues there looked like poor souls trapped in the flames. The fires raged around them, and their white marble was slowly being overcome with black.

The other side of the street was silent, nothing there burning. Shadows thrown by the statues danced and played, like revelers watching their enemies burn. The air smelled oppressively of smoke. Those shadows—and the burning statues—seemed to move, to Talmanes' fuzzy mind. Dancing creatures of shadow. Dying beauties, consumed by a sickness upon the skin, darkening it, feasting upon it, killing the soul . . .

"We're close now!" Talmanes said. He pushed himself forward into a shambling run. He couldn't afford to slow them down. *If that fire reaches the warehouse . . .*

They arrived at a burned-out patch of ground; the fire had been here, and gone, apparently. A large wooden warehouse had stood here once, but it had fallen in. Now the timbers only smoldered, and were heaped with rubble and half-burned Trolloc corpses.

The men gathered around him, silent. The only sound was that of crackling flames. Cold sweat dripped down Talmanes' face.

"We were too late," Melten whispered. "They took them, didn't they? The dragons would have made explosions if they'd burned. The Shadowspawn arrived, took the dragons and burned the place down."

Around Talmanes, exhausted members of the Band sank down to their knees. *I'm sorry, Mat,* Talmanes thought. *We tried. We—*

A sudden sound like thunder cracked through the city. It shook Talmanes to his bones, and the men looked up.

"Light," Guybon said. "The Shadowspawn are using the dragons?"

"Maybe not," Talmanes said. Strength surged through him, and he broke into a run again. His men filled in around him.

Each footfall sent a jolt of agony up his side. He passed down the street with the statues, flames to his right, cold stillness to his left.

BOOM.

Those explosions didn't sound loud enough to be dragons. Dared he hope for an Aes Sedai? Jesamyn seemed to have perked up at the sounds, and was running in her skirts alongside the men. The group barreled around a corner two streets from the warehouse and came up on the back ranks of a snarling force of Shadowspawn.

Talmanes bellowed with a startling ferocity and raised his sword in two hands. The fire of his wound had spread through his entire body; even his fingers burned with it. He felt as if he'd become one of those statues, consigned to burn with the city.

He beheaded a Trolloc before it knew he was there, then threw himself at the next creature in line. It drew back with an almost liquid grace, turning a face on him that had no eyes, a cloak that did not stir in the wind. Pale lips drew back in a snarl.

Talmanes found himself laughing. *Why not?* And men said he didn't have a sense of humor. Talmanes moved into Apple Blossoms in the Wind, striking forward wildly with a strength and fury to match the fire that was killing him.

The Myrddraal obviously had him at a disadvantage. At his best, Talmanes would have needed help fighting one. The thing moved like a shadow, flowing from one form to the next, its terrible blade darting toward Talmanes. It obviously felt it only needed to nick him.

It scored a hit on his cheek, the tip of its sword catching on his skin there and slicing a neat ribbon through the flesh. Talmanes laughed and struck at the weapon with his sword, causing the Fade's mouth to open wide in surprise. That wasn't how men were supposed to react. They were supposed to stumble at the burning flare of pain, cry out as they knew their life had ended.

"I've already had one of your flaming swords in me, you son of a goat," Talmanes screamed, attacking time and time again. Blacksmith Strikes the Blade. Such an inelegant form. It fit his mood perfectly.

The Myrddraal stumbled. Talmanes swept back in a smooth motion, bringing his sword to the side and slicing the thing's pale white arm free at the elbow. The limb twisted in the air, the Fade's blade dropping from spasming fingers. Talmanes spun for momentum and brought his sword across with two hands, severing the Fade's head from its neck.

Dark blood sprayed free and the thing fell, its remaining hand clawing at the bloodied stump as it collapsed. Talmanes stood over it, his sword suddenly feeling too heavy to hold. It slipped from his fingers, clanging to the paving stones. He tipped and lost his balance, falling face-first, but a hand caught him from behind.

"Light!" Melten exclaimed, looking at the body. "*Another* one?"

"I've found the secret to defeating them," Talmanes whispered. "You just have to be dead already." He chuckled to himself, though Melten just looked at him, seeming baffled.

Around them, dozens of Trollocs collapsed to the ground, writhing. They'd been linked to the Fade. The Band gathered around Talmanes, some bearing wounds; a few were down for good. They were exhausted and worn down; this batch of Trollocs could have ended them.

Melten retrieved Talmanes' sword and swabbed it clean, but Talmanes found he was having trouble standing, so he sheathed it and had a man fetch a Trolloc spear for him to lean on.

"Ho, the back of the street!" a distant voice called. "Whoever you are, thank you!"

Talmanes limped forward, Filger and Mar scouting on ahead without needing orders. The street here was dark and cluttered with Trollocs that had fallen moments ago, so it was a moment before Talmanes could climb over the corpses and see who had called to him.

Someone had built a barricade at the end of the street. People stood atop it, including one who held aloft a torch. She had hair in braids, and wore a plain brown dress with a white apron. It was Aludra.

"Cauthon's soldiers," Aludra said, sounding unimpressed. "Your time, you certainly did take it coming for me." In one hand, she held a stubby leather cylinder larger than a man's fist, with a short length of dark fuse attached. Talmanes knew they exploded after she lit and threw them. The Band had used them before, hurling them from slings. They weren't as devastating as dragons, but still powerful.

"Aludra," Talmanes called, "you have the dragons? Please, tell me you saved them."

She sniffed, waving for some people to pull apart a side of the barricade to admit his men. She appeared to have several hundred—maybe several thousand—townspeople back there, filling the street. As they opened the way for him, he saw a beautiful sight. Surrounded by townspeople, a hundred dragons rested there.

The bronze tubes had been fitted to wooden dragon carts to

comprise a single unit, pulled by two horses. They were really quite maneuverable, all things considered. Those carts could be anchored in the ground to manage recoil, Talmanes knew, and the dragons fired once the horses were detached. There were more than enough people here to do the work horses should have been available to do.

"You think I would *leave* them?" Aludra asked. "This lot, they do not have the training to fire them. But they can pull a cart as well as anyone else."

"We have to get them out," Talmanes said.

"This, it is a new revelation to you?" Aludra asked. "As if I haven't been trying to do that very thing. Your face, what is wrong with it?"

"I once ate a rather sharp cheese, and it has never quite sat right with me."

Aludra cocked her head at him. *Maybe if I smiled more when I made jokes*, he thought idly, leaning against the side of the barricade. *Then they'd understand what I meant.* That, of course, raised the question: Did he want people to understand? It was often more amusing the other way. Besides, smiling was so *garish*. Where was the subtlety? And . . .

And he was *really* having trouble focusing. He blinked at Aludra, whose face had grown concerned in the torchlight.

"What about my face?" Talmanes raised a hand to his cheek. Blood. The Myrddraal. Right. "Just a cut."

"And the veins?"

"Veins?" he asked, then noticed his hand. Tendrils of blackness, like ivy growing beneath the skin, had wound down his wrist and across the back of his hand toward the fingers. They seemed to be growing darker as he watched. "Oh, that. I'm dying, unfortunately. Terribly tragic. You wouldn't happen to have any brandy, would you?"

"I—"

"My Lord!" a voice called.

Talmanes blinked, then forced himself to turn about, leaning on the spear. "Yes, Filger?"

"More Trollocs, my Lord. Lots of them! They're filling in behind us."

"Lovely. Set the table. I hope we have enough dinnerware. I

knew we should have sent the maid for that five thousand seven hundred and thirty-first set."

"Are you . . . feeling all right?" Aludra asked.

"Blood and bloody ashes, woman, do I *look* like I'm feeling well? Guybon! Retreat is cut off. How far from the east gates are we?"

"East gates?" Guybon called. "Maybe a half-hour march. We need to head further down the hill."

"Onward we go, then," Talmanes said. "Take the scouts and go on point. Dennel, make sure those local folk are organized to haul those dragons! Be ready to set up the weapons."

"Talmanes," Aludra said, stepping in. "Dragons' eggs and powder, we have few of them left. We will need the supplies from Baerlon. Today, if you set up the dragons . . . A few shots for each dragon, this is all I can give you."

Dennel nodded. "Dragons aren't meant to make up frontline units all by themselves, my Lord. They need support to keep the enemy from coming too close and destroying the weapons. We can man those dragons, but we won't last long without infantry."

"That's why we're running," Talmanes said. He turned, took a step, and was so woozy he almost fell. "And I believe . . . I believe I'll need a horse . . ."

Moghedien stepped onto a platform of stone floating in the middle of an open sea. Glassy and blue, the water rippled in the occasional breeze, but there were no waves. Neither was there land in sight.

Moridin stood at the side of the platform, hands clasped behind his back. In front of him, the sea burned. The fire gave off no smoke, but it was hot, and the water near it hissed and boiled. Stone flooring in the middle of an endless sea. Water that burned. Moridin always *had* enjoyed creating impossibilities within his dreamshards.

"Sit," Moridin said to her, not turning.

She obeyed, choosing one of the four chairs suddenly arranged near the center of the platform. The sky was deep blue, cloudless, and the sun hung at about three-quarters of the way to its zenith. How long had it been since she'd seen the sun in *Tel'aran'rhiod*?

Lately, that omnipresent black storm had blanketed the sky. But, then, this wasn't completely *Tel'aran'rhiod*. Nor was it Moridin's dream, but a ... melding of the two. Like a temporary lean-to built off the side of the dream world. A bubble of merged realities.

Moghedien wore a gown of black and gold, lacework on the sleeves faintly reminiscent of a spider's web. Only faintly. One did well not to overuse a theme.

As she sat, Moghedien tried to exude control and self-confidence. Once, both had come easily for her. Today, trying to capture either was like trying to snatch dandelion seeds from the air, only to have them dance away from her hand. Moghedien gritted her teeth, angry at herself. She was one of the *Chosen*. She had made kings weep, armies tremble. Her name had been used by generations of mothers to frighten their children. And now ...

She felt at her neck, found the pendant hanging there. It was still safe. She knew it was, but touching it brought her calmness.

"Do not grow too comfortable wearing that," Moridin said. A wind blew across him, rippling the pristine ocean surface. On that wind she heard faint screams. "You are not completely forgiven, Moghedien. This is a probation. Perhaps when you fail next, I will give the mindtrap to Demandred."

She sniffed. "He would toss it aside in boredom. Demandred wants only one thing. Al'Thor. Anyone who does not lead him toward his goal is unimportant to him."

"You underestimate him," Moridin said softly. "The Great Lord is pleased with Demandred. Very pleased. You, however ... "

Moghedien sank down in her chair, feeling her tortures anew. Pain such as few in this world had ever known. Pain beyond what a body should be able to endure. She held to the *cour'souvra* and embraced *saidar*. That brought some relief.

Before, channeling in the same room as the *cour'souvra* had been agonizing. Now that she, rather than Moridin, wore the pendant, it was not so. *Not just a pendant*, she thought, clutching it. *My soul itself*. Darkness within! She had never thought that she, of all people, would find herself subject to one of these. Was she not the spider, careful in all that she did?

She reached her other hand up, clasping it over the one that held the pendant. What if it fell, what if someone took it? She wouldn't lose it. She *couldn't* lose it.

This is what I have become? She felt sick. *I have to recover. Somehow.* She forced herself to let go of the mindtrap.

The Last Battle was upon them; already, Trollocs poured into the southern lands. It was a new War of the Shadow, but only she and the other Chosen knew the deeper secrets of the One Power. The ones she hadn't been forced to give up to those horrible women . . .

No, don't think about that. The pain, the suffering, the *failure*.

In this war, they faced no Hundred Companions, no Aes Sedai with centuries of skill and practice. She would prove herself, and past errors would be forgotten.

Moridin continued to stare at those impossible flames. The only sounds were that of the fire and of the water that boiled near it. He would eventually explain his purpose in summoning her, wouldn't he? He had been acting increasingly strange, lately. Perhaps his madness was returning. Once, the man named Moridin—or Ishamael, or Elan Morin Tedronai—would have delighted in holding a *cour'souvra* for one of his rivals. He would have invented punishments, thrilled in her agony.

There had been some of that at the start; then . . . he had lost interest. He spent more and more time alone, staring into flames, brooding. The punishments he had administered to her and Cyndane had seemed almost routine.

She found him more dangerous this way.

A gateway split the air just to the side of the platform. "Do we really need to do this every other day, Moridin?" Demandred asked, stepping through and into the World of Dreams. Handsome and tall, he had jet hair and a prominent nose. He gave Moghedien a glance, noting the mindtrap on her neck before continuing. "I have important things to do, and you interrupt them."

"There are people you need to meet, Demandred," Moridin said softly. "Unless the Great Lord has named you Nae'blis without informing me, you *will* do as you are told. Your playthings can wait."

Demandred's expression darkened, but he did not object further. He let the gateway close, then moved to the side, looking down into the sea. He frowned. What was in the waters? She hadn't looked. She felt foolish for not having done so. What had happened to her caution?

Demandred walked to one of the chairs near her, but did not sit. He stood, contemplating Moridin from behind. What *had* Demandred been doing? During her period bound to the mindtrap, she had done Moridin's bidding, but had never found an answer to Demandred.

She shivered again, thinking of those months under Moridin's control. *I will have vengeance.*

"You've let Moghedien free," Demandred said. "What of this . . . Cyndane?"

"She is not your concern," Moridin said.

Moghedien had not failed to notice that Moridin still wore Cyndane's mindtrap. Cyndane. It meant "last chance" in the Old Tongue, but the woman's true nature was one secret that Moghedien *had* discovered. Moridin himself had rescued Lanfear from *Sindhol*, freeing her from the creatures that feasted upon her ability to channel.

In order to rescue her, and of course to punish her, Moridin had slain her. That had allowed the Great Lord to recapture her soul and place it in a new body. Brutal, but very effective. Precisely the kind of solution the Great Lord preferred.

Moridin was focused on his flames, and Demandred on him, so Moghedien used the chance to slip out of her seat and walk to the edge of the floating stone platform. The water below was completely clear. Through it she could see people very distinctly. They floated with their legs chained to something deep below, arms bound behind them. They swayed like kelp.

There were thousands of them. Each of them looked up at the sky with wide, horrified eyes. They were locked in a perpetual state of drowning. Not dead, not allowed to die, but constantly gasping for air and finding only water. As she watched, something dark reached up from below and pulled one of them down into the depths. Blood rose like a blooming flower; it caused the others to struggle all the more urgently.

Moghedien smiled. It did her good to see someone other than herself suffering. These might simply be figments, but it was possible that they were ones who had failed the Great Lord.

Another gateway opened at the side of the platform, and an unfamiliar woman stepped through. The creature had alarmingly unpleasant features, with a hooked yet bulbous nose and pale eyes that were off center with one another. She wore a dress that tried to be fine, of yellow silk, but it only served to highlight the woman's ugliness.

Moghedien sneered and returned to her seat. Why was Moridin admitting a stranger to one of their meetings? This woman could channel; she must be one of those useless women who called themselves Aes Sedai in this Age.

Granted, Moghedien thought, sitting, *she* is *powerful*. How had Moghedien missed noticing one with this talent among the Aes Sedai? Her sources had picked out that wretched lightskirt Nynaeve almost immediately, yet they'd missed this hag?

"This is who you wish us to meet?" Demandred said, lips turning down.

"No," Moridin said absently. "You've met Hessalam before."

Hessalam? It meant ... "without forgiveness" in the Old Tongue. The woman met Moghedien's eyes proudly, and there was something familiar about her stance.

"I have things to be about, Moridin," the newcomer said. "This had better be—"

Moghedien gasped. The tone in that voice ...

"Do not take that tone with me," Moridin cut in, speaking softly, not turning. "Do not take it with any of us. Currently, even Moghedien is favored more than you."

"*Graendal?*" Moghedien asked, horrified.

"Do not use that name!" Moridin said, spinning on her, the burning water flaring up. "It has been stripped from her."

Graendal—Hessalam—sat down without looking again at Moghedien. Yes, the way the woman carried herself was right. It *was* her.

Moghedien almost chortled with glee. Graendal had always used her looks as a bludgeon. Well, now they were a bludgeon of a different type. How perfect! The woman must be positively *writhing* inside. What had she done to earn such a punishment? Graendal's stature—her authority, the myths told about her—were all linked to her beauty. What now? Would she have to start searching for the most horrid people alive to keep as pets, the only ones who could compete with her ugliness?

This time, Moghedien did laugh. A quiet laugh, but Graendal

heard. The woman shot her a glare that could have set a section of the ocean aflame all on its own.

Moghedien returned a calm gaze, feeling more confident now. She resisted the urge to stroke the *cour'souvra*. *Bring what you will, Graendal,* she thought. *We are on level footing now. We shall see who ends this race ahead.*

A stronger wind blew past, and ripples started to rise around them, though the platform itself remained secure. Moridin let his fire die out, and nearby, waves rose. Moghedien could make out bodies, little more than dark shadows, inside those waves. Some were dead. Others struggled for the surface, their chains removed, but as they neared the open air, something always towed them back down again.

"We are few, now," Moridin said. "We four, and the one who is punished most, are all that remain. By definition, that makes us the strongest."

Some of us are, Moghedien thought. *One of us was slain by al'Thor, Moridin, and required the Great Lord's hand to return him.* Why had Moridin never been punished for his failure? Well, it was best not to look too long for fairness in the Great Lord's hand.

"Still, we are too few." Moridin waved a hand, and a stone doorway appeared on the side of the platform. Not a gateway, just a door. This was Moridin's dreamshard; he could control it. The door opened, and a man strode through it and out onto the platform.

Dark-haired, the man had the features of a Saldaean—a nose that was faintly hooked, eyes that tilted. He was handsome and tall, and Moghedien recognized him. "The leader of those fledgling male Aes Sedai? I know this man, Mazri—"

"That name has been discarded," Moridin said. "Just as each of us, upon being Chosen, discarded what we were and the names men called us. From this moment on, this man shall be known only as M'Hael. One of the Chosen."

"Chosen?" Hessalam seemed to choke on the word. "This *child*? He—" She cut off.

It was not their place to debate if one was Chosen. They could argue among themselves, even plot, if they did so with care. But questioning the Great Lord . . . that was not allowed. Ever.

Hessalam said no more. Moridin would not dare call this man

Chosen if the Great Lord had not decided it. There was no argument to be made. Still, Moghedien shivered. Taim ... M'Hael ... was said to be strong, perhaps as strong as the rest of them, but elevating one from this Age, with all of their ignorance ... It galled her to consider that this M'Hael would be regarded as her equal.

"I see the challenge in your eyes," Moridin said, looking at the three of them, "though only one of you was foolish enough to start voicing it. M'Hael has earned his reward. Too many of our number threw themselves into contests with al'Thor when he was presumed to be weak. M'Hael instead earned Lews Therin's trust, then took charge of the training of his weapons. *He* has been raising a new generation of Dreadlords to the Shadow's cause. What do the three of you have to show for your work since being released?"

"You will know the fruits I have harvested, Moridin," Demandred said, voice low. "You will know them in bushels and droves. Just remember my requirement: I face al'Thor on the field of battle. His blood is mine, and no one else's." He met each of their eyes in turn, then finally those of M'Hael. There seemed to be a familiarity to them. The two had met before.

You will have competition with that one, Demandred, Moghedien thought. *He wants al'Thor nearly as much as you do.*

Demandred had been changing lately. Once, he wouldn't have cared who killed Lews Therin—so long as the man died. What made Demandred insist on doing the deed himself?

"Moghedien," Moridin said. "Demandred has plans for the war to come. You are to assist him."

"*Assist* him?" she said. "I—"

"Do you forget yourself so quickly, Moghedien?" Moridin's voice was silky. "You will do as you are told. Demandred wants you watching over one of the armies that now lacks proper monitoring. Speak a single word of complaint, and you will realize that the pain you have known up to now is but a shadow of true agony."

Her hand went to the *cour'souvra* at her neck. Looking into his eyes, she felt her authority evaporate. *I hate you,* she thought. *I hate you more for doing this to me in front of the others.*

"The last days are upon us," Moridin said, turning his back on them. "In these hours, you will earn your final rewards. If you have grudges, put them behind you. If you have plots, bring them to completion. Make your final plays, for this . . . this is the end."

Talmanes lay on his back, staring up at a dark sky. The clouds above seemed to be reflecting light from below, the light of a dying city. That was wrong. Light came from above, didn't it?

He'd fallen from the horse not long after starting for the city gate. He could remember that, most of the time. Pain made it hard to think. People yelled at one another.

I should have . . . I should have taunted Mat more, he thought, a hint of a smile cracking his lips. *Stupid time to be thinking of such things. I have to . . . have to find the dragons. Or did we find them already . . . ?*

"I'm telling you, the bloody things don't work like that!" Dennel's voice. "They're not bloody Aes Sedai on wheels. We can't make a wall of fire. We can send these balls of metal hurtling through the Trollocs."

"They explode." Guybon's voice. "We could use the extras like I say."

Talmanes' eyes drifted closed.

"The balls explode, yes," Dennel said. "But we have to launch them first. Setting them all in a row and letting the Trollocs run over them won't do much."

A hand shook Talmanes' shoulder. "Lord Talmanes," Melten said. "There is no dishonor in letting it end now. I know the pain is great. May the last embrace of the mother shelter you."

A sword being drawn. Talmanes steeled himself.

Then he found that he really, *really* didn't want to die.

He forced his eyes open and held up a hand to Melten, who stood over him. Jesamyn hovered nearby with arms folded, looking worried.

"Help me to my feet," Talmanes said.

Melten hesitated, then did so.

"You shouldn't be standing," Jesamyn said.

"Better than being beheaded in honor," Talmanes grumbled, gritting his teeth against the pain. Light, was that his hand? It was so dark, it looked as if it had been charred in a fire. "What . . . what is going on?"

"We're cornered, my Lord," Melten said grimly, eyes solemn. He thought them all as good as dead. "Dennel and Guybon are arguing over placement of the dragons for a last stand. Aludra is measuring the charges."

Talmanes, finally standing, sagged against Melten. Before him, two thousand people clustered in the large city square. They huddled like men in the wilderness seeking one another's warmth on a cold night. Dennel and Guybon had set up the dragons in a half-circle bowed outward, pointing toward the center of the city, refugees behind. The Band was now committed to manning the dragons; three pairs of hands were needed to operate each weapon. Almost all of the Band had had at least some training.

The buildings nearby had caught fire, but the light was doing strange things. Why didn't it reach the streets? Those were all too dark. As if they'd been painted. Like . . .

He blinked, clearing the tears of pain from his eyes, realization dawning. Trollocs filled the streets like ink flowing toward the half-circle of dragons that were pointed at them.

Something held the Trollocs back for the moment. *They're waiting until they are all together for a rush*, Talmanes thought.

Calls and snarls came from behind. Talmanes pivoted, then clutched Melten's arm as the world lurched. He waited for it to steady. The pain . . . the pain was actually dulling. Like glowing flames running out of fresh coal. It had feasted upon him, but there wasn't much left of him for it to eat.

As things steadied, Talmanes saw what was creating the snarls. The square they were in adjoined the city wall, but the townspeople and soldiers had kept their distance from the wall, for it was coated with Trollocs, like a thick grime. They raised weapons in the air and roared down at the people.

"They throw down spears at anyone who comes too close," Melten said. "We'd been hoping to reach the wall, then follow it along to the gate, but we can't—not with those things up there raining death upon us. All other routes are cut off."

Aludra approached Guybon and Dennel. "Charges, I can set under the dragons," she said to them; softly, but not as softly as she should have. "These charges, they will destroy the weapons. They may hurt the people in an unpleasant way."

"Do it," Guybon said very softly. "What the Trollocs would do is worse, and we cannot allow the dragons to fall into the Shadow's hands. That's why they're waiting. Their leaders are hoping that a sudden rush will give them time to overwhelm us and seize the weapons."

"They're moving!" a soldier called from beside the dragons. "Light, they're coming!"

That dark slime of Shadowspawn bubbled down the streets. Teeth, nails, claws, too-human eyes. The Trollocs came from all sides, eager for the kill. Talmanes struggled to draw breath.

On the walls, the calls grew excited. *We're surrounded*, Talmanes thought. *Pressed back against the wall, caught in a net. We . . .*

Pressed back against the wall.

"Dennel!" Talmanes shouted over the din. The captain of dragons turned from his line, where men waited with burning punks for the call to launch the one volley they'd have.

Talmanes took a deep breath that made his lungs burn. "You told me that you could level an enemy bulwark in only a few shots."

"Of course," Dennel called. "But we're not trying to enter . . ." He trailed off.

Light, Talmanes thought. *We're all so exhausted. We should have seen this.* "You in the middle, Ryden's dragon squad, about-face!" Talmanes screamed. "The rest of you, stay in position and fire at the oncoming Trollocs! Move, move, *move!*"

The dragoners sprang into motion, Ryden and his men hastily turning their weapons about, wheels creaking. The other dragons began to fire a pattern of shot that sprayed through the streets entering the square. The booms were deafening, causing refugees to scream and cover their ears. It sounded like the end of the world. Hundreds, thousands of Trollocs went down in pools of blood as dragons' eggs exploded in their midst. The square filled with white smoke that poured from the mouths of the dragons.

The refugees behind, already terrified by what they had just witnessed, shrieked as Ryden's dragons turned on them, and most of them fell to the ground in fright, clearing a path. A path that exposed the Trolloc-infested city wall. Ryden's line of dragons bowed inward like a cup, the reverse formation of those firing into the Trollocs behind, so that the tubes were pointed at the same section of city wall.

"Give me one of those bloody punks!" Talmanes shouted, holding out a hand. One of the dragoners obeyed, passing him a flaming brand with a glowing red tip. He pushed away from Melten, determined to stand on his own for the moment.

Guybon stepped up. The man's voice sounded soft to Talmanes' strained ears. "Those walls have stood for hundreds of years. My poor city. My poor, poor city."

"It's not your city any longer," Talmanes said, raising his flaming brand high in the air, defiant before a wall thick with Trollocs, a burning city to his back. "It's theirs."

Talmanes swiped the brand down in the air, leaving a trail of red. His signal ignited a roar of dragonfire that echoed throughout the square.

Trollocs—pieces of them, at least—blew into the air. The wall under them exploded like a stack of children's blocks kicked at a full run. As Talmanes wavered, his vision blackening, he saw the wall crumble outward. When he toppled, slipping into unconsciousness, the ground seemed to tremble from the force of his fall.

CHAPTER 1

Eastward the Wind Blew

The Wheel of Time turns, and Ages come and pass, leaving memories that become legend. Legend fades to myth, and even myth is long forgotten when the Age that gave it birth comes again. In one Age, called the Third Age by some, an Age yet to come, an Age long past, a wind rose in the Mountains of Mist. The wind was not the beginning. There are neither beginnings nor endings to the turning of the Wheel of Time. But it was *a* beginning.

Eastward the wind blew, descending from lofty mountains and coursing over desolate hills. It passed into the place known as the Westwood, an area that had once flourished with pine and leather-leaf. Here, the wind found little more than tangled underbrush, thick save around an occasional towering oak. Those looked stricken by disease, bark peeling free, branches drooping. Elsewhere needles had fallen from pines, draping the ground in a brown blanket. None of the skeletal branches of the Westwood put forth buds.

North and eastward the wind blew, across underbrush that crunched and cracked as it shook. It was night, and scrawny foxes picked over the rotting ground, searching in vain for prey or carrion. No spring birds had come to call, and—most telling—the howls of wolves had gone silent across the land.

The wind blew out of the forest and across Taren Ferry. What was left of it. The town had been a fine one, by local standards. Dark buildings, tall above their redstone foundations, a cobbled street, built at the mouth of the land known as the Two Rivers.

The smoke had long since stopped rising from burned buildings, but there was little left of the town to rebuild. Feral dogs hunted through the rubble for meat. They looked up as the wind passed, their eyes hungry.

The wind crossed the river eastward. Here, clusters of refugees carrying torches walked the long road from Baerlon to Whitebridge despite the late hour. They were sorry groups, with heads bowed, shoulders huddled. Some bore the coppery skin of Domani, their worn clothing displaying the hardships of crossing the mountains with little in the way of supplies. Others came from farther off. Taraboners with haunted eyes above dirty veils. Farmers and their wives from northern Ghealdan. All had heard rumors that in Andor, there was food. In Andor, there was hope.

So far, they had yet to find either.

Eastward the wind blew, along the river that wove between farms without crops. Grasslands without grass. Orchards without fruit.

Abandoned villages. Trees like bones with the flesh picked free. Ravens often clustered in their branches; starveling rabbits and sometimes larger game picked through the dead grass underneath. Above it all, the omnipresent clouds pressed down upon the land. Sometimes, that cloud cover made it impossible to tell if it was day or night.

As the wind approached the grand city of Caemlyn, it turned northward, away from the burning city—orange, red and violent, spewing black smoke toward the hungry clouds above. War had come to Andor in the still of night. The approaching refugees would soon discover that they'd been marching toward danger. It was not surprising. Danger was in all directions. The only way to avoid walking toward it would be to stand still.

As the wind blew northward, it passed people sitting beside roads, alone or in small groups, staring with the eyes of the hopeless. Some lay as they hungered, looking up at those rumbling, boiling clouds. Other people trudged onward, though toward what, they knew not. The Last Battle, to the north, whatever that meant. The Last Battle was not hope. The Last Battle was death. But it was a place to *be*, a place to *go*.

In the evening dimness, the wind reached a large gathering far to the north of Caemlyn. This wide field broke the forest-patched landscape, but it was overgrown with tents like fungi on a decaying log. Tens of thousands of soldiers waited beside campfires that were quickly denuding the area of timber.

The wind blew among them, whipping smoke from fires into the faces of soldiers. The people here didn't display the same sense of hopelessness as the refugees, but there was a dread to them. They could see the sickened land. They could feel the clouds above. They knew.

The world was dying. The soldiers stared at the flames, watching the wood be consumed. Ember by ember, what had once been alive turned to dust.

A company of men inspected armor that had begun to rust despite being well oiled. A group of white-robed Aiel collected water—former warriors who refused to take up weapons again, despite their *toh* having been served. A cluster of frightened servants, sure that tomorrow would bring war between the White Tower and the Dragon Reborn, organized stores inside tents shaken by the wind.

Men and women whispered the truth into the night. *The end has come. The end has come. All will fall. The end has come.*

Laughter broke the air.

Warm light spilled from a large tent at the center of the camp, bursting around the tent flap and from beneath the sides.

Inside that tent, Rand al'Thor—the Dragon Reborn—laughed, head thrown back.

"So what did she do?" Rand asked when his laughter subsided. He poured himself a cup of red wine, then one for Perrin, who blushed at the question.

He's become harder, Rand thought, *but somehow he hasn't lost that innocence of his. Not completely.* To Rand, that seemed a marvelous thing. A wonder, like a pearl discovered in a trout. Perrin was strong, but his strength hadn't broken him.

"Well," Perrin said, "you know how Marin is. She somehow manages to look at even *Cenn* as if he were a child in need of mothering. Finding Faile and me lying there on the floor like two fool youths . . . well, I think she was torn between laughing at us and sending us into the kitchen to scrub dishes. Separately, to keep us out of trouble."

Rand smiled, trying to picture it. Perrin—burly, solid Perrin—so weak he could barely walk. It was an incongruous image. Rand wanted to assume his friend was exaggerating, but Perrin didn't have a dishonest hair on his head. Strange, how much about a man could change while his core remained exactly the same.

"Anyway," Perrin said after taking a drink of wine, "Faile picked me up off the floor and set me on my horse, and the two of us pranced about looking important. I didn't do much. The fighting was accomplished by the others—I'd have had trouble lifting a cup to my lips." He stopped, his golden eyes growing distant. "You should be proud of them, Rand. Without Dannil, your father and Mat's father, without all of them, I wouldn't have managed half what I did. No, not a tenth."

"I believe it." Rand regarded his wine. Lews Therin had loved wine. A part of Rand—that distant part, the memories of a man he had been—was displeased by the vintage. Few wines in the current world could match the favored vintages of the Age of Legends. Not the ones he had sampled, at least.

He took a small drink, then set the wine aside. Min still slumbered in another part of the tent, sectioned off with a curtain. Events in Rand's dreams had awakened him. He had been glad for Perrin's arrival to take his mind off what he had seen.

Mierin . . . No. He would not let that woman distract him. That was probably the point of what he had seen.

"Walk with me," Rand said. "I need to check on some things for tomorrow."

They went out into the night. Several Maidens fell into step behind them as Rand walked toward Sebban Balwer, whose services Perrin had loaned to Rand. Which was fine with Balwer, who was prone to gravitate toward those holding the greatest power.

"Rand?" Perrin asked, walking beside him with a hand on *Mah'alleinir*. "I've told you about all of this before, the siege of the Two Rivers, the fighting . . . Why ask after it again?"

"I asked about the events before, Perrin. I asked after what happened, but I did not ask after the people it happened to." He looked at Perrin, making a globe of light for them to see by as they walked in the night. "I need to remember the *people*. Not doing so is a mistake I have made too often in the past."

The stirring wind carried the scent of campfires from Perrin's nearby camp and the sounds of smiths working on weapons. Rand had heard the stories: Power-wrought weapons discovered again. Perrin's men were working overtime, running his two Asha'man ragged, to make as many as possible.

Rand had lent him as many more Asha'man as he could spare, if only because—as soon as they'd heard—he'd had dozens of Maidens presenting themselves and demanding Power-wrought spearheads. *It only makes sense, Rand al'Thor*, Beralna had explained. *His smiths can make four spearheads for every sword.* She'd grimaced saying the word "sword," as if it tasted like seawater.

Rand had never tasted seawater. Lews Therin had. Knowing facts like that had greatly discomforted him once. Now he had learned to accept that part of him.

"Can you believe what has happened to us?" Perrin asked. "Light, sometimes I wonder when the man who owns all these fancy clothes is going to walk in on me and start yelling, then send me out to muck the stables for being too bigheaded for my collar."

"The Wheel weaves as the Wheel wills, Perrin. We've become what we needed to become."

Perrin nodded as they walked on the path between tents, lit by the glow of the light above Rand's hand.

"How does it . . . feel?" Perrin asked. "Those memories you've gained?"

"Have you ever had a dream that, upon waking, you remembered in stark clarity? Not one that faded quickly, but one that stayed with you through the day?"

"Yes," Perrin said, sounding oddly reserved. "Yes, I can say that I have."

"It's like that," Rand said. "I can remember being Lews Therin, can remember doing what he did, as one remembers actions in a dream. It *was* me doing them, but I don't necessarily like them— or think I'd take those actions if I were in my waking mind. That doesn't change the fact that, in the dream, they seemed like the right actions."

Perrin nodded.

"He's me," Rand said. "And I'm him. But at the same time, I'm not."

"Well, you still seem like yourself," Perrin said, though Rand caught a slight hesitation on the word "seem." Had Perrin been about to say "smell" instead? "You haven't changed *that* much."

Rand doubted he could explain it to Perrin without sounding mad. The person he became when he wore the mantle of the Dragon Reborn ... that wasn't simply an act, wasn't simply a mask.

It was who he was. He had not changed, he had not transformed. He had merely *accepted*.

That didn't mean he had all of the answers. Despite four hundred years of memories nestled in his brain, he still worried about what he had to do. Lews Therin hadn't known how to seal the Bore. His attempt had led to disaster. The taint, the Breaking, all for an imperfect prison with seals that were now brittle.

One answer kept coming to Rand. A dangerous answer. One that Lews Therin hadn't considered.

What if the answer *wasn't* to seal the Dark One away again? What if the answer, the final answer, was something else? Something more permanent.

Yes, Rand thought to himself for the hundredth time. *But is it possible?*

They arrived at the tent where the clerks worked, the Maidens fanning out behind them, Rand and Perrin entering. The clerks were up late, of course, and they didn't look surprised to see Rand enter.

"My Lord Dragon," Balwer said, bowing stiffly from where he stood beside a table of maps and stacks of paper. The dried-up little man sorted his papers nervously, one knobby elbow protruding from a hole in his oversized brown coat.

"Report," Rand said.

"Roedran will come," Balwer said, his voice thin and precise. "The Queen of Andor has sent for him, promising him gateways made by those Kinswomen of hers. Our eyes in his court say he is angry that he needs her help to attend, but is insistent that he needs to be at this meeting—if only so he doesn't look left out."

"Excellent," Rand said. "Elayne knows nothing of your spies?"

"My Lord!" Balwer said, sounding indignant.

"Have you determined who is spying for her among our clerks?" Rand asked.

Balwer sputtered. "Nobody—"

"She'll have someone, Balwer," Rand said with a smile. "She all but taught me how to do this, after all. No matter. After tomorrow, my intentions will be manifest for all. Secrets won't be needed."

None save the ones I keep closest to my own heart.

"That means everyone will be here for the meeting, right?" Perrin asked. "Every major ruler? Tear and Illian?"

"The Amyrlin persuaded them to attend," Balwer said. "I have copies of their exchanges here, if you wish to see them, my Lords."

"I would," Rand said. "Send them to my tent. I will look them over tonight."

The shaking of the ground came suddenly. Clerks grabbed stacks of papers, holding them down and crying out as furniture crashed to the ground around them. Outside, men shouted, barely audible over the sound of trees breaking, metal clanging. The land groaned, a distant rumble.

Rand felt it like a painful muscle spasm.

Thunder shook the sky, distant, like a promise of things to come. The shaking subsided. The clerks remained holding their stacks of paper, as if afraid to let go and risk them toppling.

It's really here, Rand thought. *I'm not ready—we're not ready—but it's here anyway.*

He had spent many months fearing this day. Ever since Trollocs had come in the night, ever since Lan and Moiraine had dragged him from the Two Rivers, he had feared what was to come.

The Last Battle. The end. He found himself unafraid now that it had come. Worried, but not afraid.

I'm coming for you, Rand thought.

"Tell the people," Rand said to his clerks. "Post warnings. Earthquakes will continue. Storms. Real ones, terrible ones. There will be a Breaking, and we cannot avoid it. The Dark One will try to grind this world to dust."

The clerks nodded, shooting concerned glances at one another by lamplight. Perrin looked contemplative, but nodded faintly, as if to himself.

"Any other news?" Rand asked.

"The Queen of Andor may be up to something tonight, my Lord," Balwer said.

"'Something' is not a very descriptive word, Balwer," Rand said.

Balwer grimaced. "I'm sorry, my Lord. I don't have more for you yet; I only just received this note. Queen Elayne was awakened by some of her advisors a short time ago. I don't have anyone close enough to know why."

Rand frowned, resting his hand on Laman's sword at his waist.

"It could just be plans for tomorrow," Perrin said.

"True," Rand said. "Let me know if you discover anything, Balwer. Thank you. You do well here."

The man stood taller. In these last days—days so dark—every man looked for something useful to do. Balwer was the best at what he did, and was confident in his own abilities. Still, it did no harm to be reminded of the fact by one who employed him, particularly if his employer was none other than the Dragon Reborn.

Rand left the tent, Perrin following.

"You're worried about it," Perrin said. "Whatever it was that awoke Elayne."

"They would not awaken her without good cause," Rand said softly. "Considering her state."

Pregnant. Pregnant with *his* children. Light! He had only just learned of it. Why hadn't she been the one to tell him?

The answer was simple. Elayne could feel Rand's emotions as he felt hers. She would have been able to feel how he had been, recently. Before Dragonmount. Back when . . .

Well, she wouldn't have wanted to confront him with a pregnancy when he'd been in such a state. Beyond that, he hadn't exactly made himself easy to find.

Still, it was a shock.

I'm going to be a father, he thought, not for the first time. Yes, Lews Therin had had children, and Rand could remember them and his love for them. It wasn't the same.

He, Rand al'Thor, would be a father. Assuming he won the Last Battle.

"They wouldn't have awakened Elayne without good reason," he continued, returning to task. "I'm worried, not because of what might have happened, but because of the potential distraction. Tomorrow will be an important day. If the Shadow has any inkling of tomorrow's importance, it will try whatever it can to keep us from meeting, from unifying."

Perrin scratched at his beard. "I have people close to Elayne. People who keep watch on things for me."

Rand raised his hand. "Let's go talk to them. I have a great deal to do tonight, but ... Yes, I can't let this slip."

The two turned toward Perrin's camp nearby, picking up their pace, Rand's bodyguards following like shadows with veils and spears.

The night felt too quiet. Egwene, in her tent, worked on a letter to Rand. She was not certain if she would send it. Sending it was not important. Writing it was about organizing her thoughts, determining what she wished to say to him.

Gawyn pushed his way into the tent again, hand on his sword, Warder cloak rustling.

"Are you going to stay in this time?" Egwene asked, dipping her pen, "or are you going to go right back out?"

"I don't like this night, Egwene." He looked over his shoulder. "Something feels wrong about it."

"The world holds its breath, Gawyn, waiting upon the events of the morrow. Did you send to Elayne, as I requested?"

"Yes. She won't be awake. It's too late for her."

"We shall see."

It wasn't long before a messenger arrived from Elayne's camp, bearing a small folded letter. Egwene read it, then smiled. "Come," she said to Gawyn, rising and gathering a few things. She waved a hand, and a gateway split the air.

"We're Traveling there?" Gawyn asked. "It's only a short walk."

"A short walk would require the Amyrlin to call upon the Queen of Andor," Egwene said as Gawyn stepped through the gateway first and checked the other side. "Sometimes, I don't want to take an action that starts people asking questions."

Siuan would have killed for this ability, Egwene thought as she stepped through the gateway. How many more plots could that woman have spun if she'd been able to visit others as quickly, quietly and easily as this?

On the other side, Elayne stood beside a warm brazier. The Queen wore a pale green dress, her belly swollen from the babes within. She hastened over to Egwene and kissed her ring. Birgitte stood to one side of the tent flaps, arms folded, wearing her short red jacket and wide, sky-blue trousers, her golden braid down over her shoulder.

Gawyn cocked an eyebrow at his sister. "I'm surprised you are awake."

"I'm waiting for a report," Elayne said, gesturing for Egwene to join her in a pair of cushioned chairs beside the brazier.

"Something important?" Egwene asked.

Elayne frowned. "Jesamyn forgot to check in again from Caemlyn. I left the woman *strict* orders to send to me every two hours, and yet she dallies. Light, it's probably nothing. Still, I asked Serinia to go to the Traveling grounds to check on things for me. I hope you don't mind."

"You need rest," Gawyn said, folding his arms.

"Thank you very much for the advice," Elayne said, "which I will ignore, as I ignored Birgitte when she said the same thing. Mother, what is it you wished to discuss?"

Egwene handed over the letter she had been working on.

"To Rand?" Elayne asked.

"You have a different perspective on him than I. Tell me what you think of this letter. I might not send it to him. I haven't decided yet."

"The tone is . . . forceful," Elayne noted.

"He doesn't seem to respond to anything else."

After a moment of reading Elayne lowered the letter. "Perhaps we should simply let him do as he wishes."

"Break the seals?" Egwene asked. "Release the Dark One?"

"Why not?"

"Light, Elayne!"

"It has to happen, doesn't it?" Elayne asked. "I mean, the Dark One's going to escape. He's practically free already."

Egwene rubbed her temples. "There is a difference between touching the world and being free. During the War of Power, the Dark One was never truly released into the world. The Bore let him touch it, but that was resealed before he could escape. If the Dark One had entered the world, the Wheel itself would have been broken. Here, I brought this to show you."

Egwene retrieved a stack of notes from her satchel. The sheets had been hastily gathered by the librarians of the Thirteenth Depository. "I'm not saying that we shouldn't break the seals," Egwene said. "I'm saying that we can't afford to risk one of Rand's crackbrained schemes with this."

Elayne smiled fondly. Light, but she was smitten. *I can rely on her, can't I?* It was hard to tell with Elayne these days. The woman's ploy with the Kinswomen . . .

"We have unfortunately found nothing pertinent in your library *ter'angreal.*" The statue of the smiling bearded man had nearly caused a riot in the Tower; every sister had wanted to read the thousands of books that it held. "All of the books seem to have been written before the Bore was opened. They will keep searching, but these notes contain everything we could gather on the seals, the prison and the Dark One. If we break the seals at the wrong time, I fear it would mean an end to all things. Here, read this." She handed a page to Elayne.

"*The Karaethon Cycle?*" Elayne asked, curious. "'And light shall fail, and dawn shall not come, and still the captive rails.' The captive is the Dark One?"

"I think so," Egwene said. "The Prophecies are never clear. Rand intends to enter the Last Battle and break the seals immediately, but that is a dreadful idea. We have an extended war ahead of us. Freeing the Dark One now will strengthen the forces of the Shadow and weaken us.

"If it is to be done—and I still don't know that it has to be— we should wait until the last possible moment. At the very least, we need to discuss it. Rand has been right about many things, but he has been *wrong,* too. This is not a decision he should be allowed to make alone."

Elayne shuffled through the sheets of paper, then stopped on one of them. "'His blood shall give us the Light . . .'" She rubbed the page with her thumb, as if lost in thought. "'Wait upon the Light.' Who added this note?"

"That is Doniella Alievin's copy of the Termendal translation of *The Karaethon Cycle,*" Egwene said. "Doniella made her own notes, and they have been the subject of nearly as much discussion among scholars as the Prophecies themselves. She was a Dreamer, you know. The only Amyrlin that we know of to have been one. Before me, anyway."

"Yes," Elayne said.

"The sisters who gathered these for me came to the same conclusion that I have," Egwene said. "There may be a time to break the seals, but that time is not at the start of the Last Battle, whatever Rand thinks. We must wait for the right moment, and as the Watcher of the Seals, it is my duty to choose that moment. I won't risk the world on one of Rand's overly dramatic stratagems."

"He has a fair bit of gleeman in him," Elayne said, again fondly. "Your argument is a good one, Egwene. Make it to him. He will listen to you. He does have a good mind, and can be persuaded."

"We shall see. For now, I—"

Egwene suddenly sensed a spike of alarm from Gawyn. She glanced over to see him turning. Hoofbeats outside. His ears weren't any better than Egwene's, but it was his job to listen for things like this.

Egwene embraced the True Source, causing Elayne to do likewise. Birgitte already had the tent flaps open, hand on her sword.

A frazzled messenger leaped from horseback outside, eyes wide. She scrambled into the tent, Birgitte and Gawyn falling in beside her immediately, watching in case she came too close.

She didn't. "Caemlyn is under attack, Your Majesty," the woman said, gasping for breath.

"What!" Elayne leaped to her feet. "How? Did Jarid Sarand finally—"

"Trollocs," the messenger said. "It started near dusk."

"Impossible!" Elayne said, grabbing the messenger by the arm and hauling her out of the tent. Egwene followed hastily. "It's been over six hours since dusk," Elayne said to the messenger. "Why haven't we heard anything until now? What happened to the Kinswomen?"

"I was not told, my Queen," the messenger said. "Captain Guybon sent me to fetch you at speed. He just arrived through the gateway."

The Traveling ground was not far from Elayne's tent. A crowd had gathered, but men and women made way for the Amyrlin and Queen. In moments the two of them reached the front.

A group of men in bloodied clothing trudged through the open gateway, pulling carts laden with Elayne's new weapons, the dragons. Many of the men seemed near collapse. They smelled of smoke, and their skin was blackened by soot. Not a few of them slumped unconscious as Elayne's soldiers grabbed the carts, which were obviously meant for horses to pull, to help them.

Other gateways opened nearby as Serinia Sedai and some of the stronger of the Kinswomen—Egwene wouldn't think of them as *Elayne's* Kinswomen—created them. Refugees poured through like the waters of a suddenly unstopped river.

"Go," Egwene said to Gawyn, weaving her own gateway—one to the Traveling grounds in the White Tower camp nearby. "Send for as many Aes Sedai as we can rouse. Tell Bryne to ready his soldiers, tell them to do as Elayne orders and send them through gateways to the outskirts of Caemlyn. We will show solidarity with Andor."

Gawyn nodded, ducking through the gateway. Egwene let it vanish, then joined Elayne near the gathering of wounded, confused soldiers. Sumeko, of the Kinswomen, had taken charge of seeing that Healing was given to those in immediate danger.

The air was thick with the smell of smoke. As Egwene hurried to Elayne, she caught sight of something through one of the gateways. Caemlyn afire.

Light! She stood stunned for a moment, then hurried on. Elayne was speaking with Guybon, commander of the Queen's Guard. The handsome man seemed barely able to remain on his feet, his clothing and arms alarmingly bloodied.

"Darkfriends killed two of the women you left to send messages, Your Majesty," he was saying in a tired voice. "Another fell in the fighting. But we retrieved the dragons. Once we . . . we escaped . . ." He seemed pained by something. "Once we escaped through the hole in the city wall, we found that several mercenary bands were making their way around the city toward the gate that Lord Talmanes had left defended. By coincidence they were near enough to aid in our escape."

"You did well," Elayne said.

"But the city—"

"You did *well*," Elayne repeated, voice firm. "You retrieved the dragons and rescued all of these people? I will see you rewarded for this, Captain."

"Give your reward to the men of the Band, Your Majesty. It was their work. And please, if you can do anything for Lord Talmanes ..." He gestured to the fallen man whom several members of the Band had just carried through the gateway.

Elayne knelt beside him, and Egwene joined her. At first, Egwene assumed that Talmanes was dead, with his skin blackened. Then he drew a ragged breath.

"Light," Elayne said, Delving his prostrate form. "I've never seen anything like this."

"Thakan'dar blades," Guybon said.

"This is beyond either of us," Egwene said to Elayne, standing. "I ..." She trailed off, hearing something over the groans of soldiers and carts creaking.

"Egwene?" Elayne asked softly.

"Do what you can for him," Egwene said, standing and rushing away. She pushed through the confused crowd, following the voice. Was that ... yes, *there*. She found an open gateway at the edge of the Traveling grounds, Aes Sedai in a variety of clothing hurrying through to see to the wounded. Gawyn had done his work well.

Nynaeve was asking, quite loudly, who was in charge of this mess. Egwene approached her from the side and grabbed her by the shoulder, surprising her.

"Mother?" Nynaeve asked. "What is this about Caemlyn burning? I—"

She cut off as she saw the wounded. She stiffened, then tried to go to them.

"There is one you need to see first," Egwene said, leading her to where Talmanes lay.

Nynaeve drew in a sharp breath, then went to her knees and pushed Elayne gently aside. Nynaeve Delved Talmanes, then froze, eyes wide.

"Nynaeve?" Egwene said. "Can you—"

An *explosion* of weaves burst from Nynaeve like the sudden light of a sun coming out from behind clouds. Nynaeve wove the

Five Powers together in a column of radiance, then sent it driving into Talmanes' body.

Egwene left her to her work. Perhaps it would be enough, though he looked far gone. The Light willing, the man would live. She had been impressed with him in the past. He seemed precisely the type of man that the Band—and Mat—needed.

Elayne was near the dragons and was questioning a woman with her hair in braids. That must be Aludra, who had created the dragons. Egwene walked up to the weapons, resting her fingers on one of the long bronze tubes. She had been given reports on them, of course. Some men said they were like Aes Sedai, cast in metal and fueled by the powders from fireworks.

More and more refugees poured though the gateway, many of them townspeople. "Light," Egwene said to herself. "There are too many of them. We can't house all of Caemlyn here at Merrilor."

Elayne finished her conversation, leaving Aludra to inspect the wagons. It appeared that the woman wasn't willing to rest for the night and see to them in the morning. Elayne walked toward the gateways.

"The soldiers say the area outside the city is secure," Elayne said, passing Egwene. "I'm going through to have a look."

"Elayne . . ." Birgitte said, coming up behind her.

"We're going! Come on."

Egwene left the Queen to it, stepping back to supervise the work. Romanda had taken charge of the Aes Sedai and was organizing the injured, separating them into groups depending on the urgency of their wounds.

As Egwene surveyed the chaotic mix, she noticed a pair of people standing nearby. A woman and man, Illianers by the looks of them. "What do you two want?"

The woman knelt before her. The fair-skinned, dark-haired woman had a firmness to her features, despite her tall, slender build. "I am Leilwin," she said in an unmistakable accent. "I was accompanying Nynaeve Sedai when the call for Healing was raised. We followed her here."

"You're Seanchan," Egwene said, startled.

"I have come to serve you, Amyrlin Seat."

Seanchan. Egwene still held the One Power. Light, not *every*

Seanchan she met was dangerous to her; still, she would not take chances. As some members of the Tower Guard came through one of the gateways, Egwene pointed to the Seanchan pair. "Take these somewhere safe and keep watch on them. I'll deal with them later."

The soldiers nodded. The man went reluctantly, the woman more easily. She couldn't channel, so she wasn't a freed *damane*. That didn't mean she wasn't a *sul'dam*, though.

Egwene returned to Nynaeve, who still knelt beside Talmanes. The sickness had retreated from the man's skin, leaving it pale. "Take him somewhere to rest," Nynaeve said tiredly to several watching members of the Band. "I've done what I can."

She looked up at Egwene as the men carried him away. "Light," Nynaeve whispered, "that took a lot out of me. Even with my *angreal*. I'm impressed that Moiraine managed it with Tam, all that time ago . . . " There seemed to be a note of pride in Nynaeve's voice.

She had wanted to heal Tam, but could not—though, of course, Nynaeve had not known what she had been doing at the time. She had come a long, long way since then.

"Is it true, Mother?" Nynaeve asked, rising. "About Caemlyn?"
Egwene nodded.

"This is going to be a long night," Nynaeve said, looking at the wounded still pouring through the gateways.

"And a longer tomorrow," Egwene said. "Here, let us link. I'll lend you my strength."

Nynaeve looked shocked. "Mother?"

"You are better at Healing than I." Egwene smiled. "I may be Amyrlin, Nynaeve, but I am still Aes Sedai. Servant of all. My strength will be of use to you."

Nynaeve nodded and they linked. The two of them joined the group of Aes Sedai that Romanda had set Healing the refugees with the worst wounds.

"Faile has been organizing my network of eyes-and-ears," Perrin said to Rand as the two of them hurried toward Perrin's camp. "She might be there with them tonight. I'll warn you, I'm not certain she likes you."

She would be a fool to like me, Rand thought. *She probably knows what I'm going to require of you before this is over.*

"Well," Perrin said, "I guess that she does like that I know you. She's cousin to a queen, after all. I think she still worries you'll go mad and hurt me."

"The madness has already come," Rand said, "and I have it in my grip. As for hurting you, she's probably right. I don't think I can avoid hurting those around me. It was a hard lesson to learn."

"You implied that you're mad," Perrin said, hand resting on his hammer again as he walked. He wore it at his side, large though it was; he'd obviously needed to construct a special sheath for it. An amazing piece of work. Rand kept intending to ask whether it was one of the Power-wrought weapons his Asha'man had been making—"But Rand, you're not. You don't seem at all crazy to me."

Rand smiled, and a thought fluttered at the edge of his mind. "I *am* mad, Perrin. My madness is these memories, these impulses. Lews Therin tried to take over. I was two people, fighting over control of myself. And one of them was completely insane."

"Light," Perrin whispered, "that sounds horrible."

"It wasn't pleasant. But … here's the thing, Perrin. I'm increasingly certain that I needed these memories. Lews Therin was a good man. *I* was a good man, but things went wrong—I grew too arrogant, I assumed I could do everything myself. I needed to remember that; without the madness … without these memories, I might have gone charging in alone again."

"So you are going to work with the others?" Perrin asked, looking up toward where Egwene and the other members of the White Tower were camped. "This looks an *awful* lot like armies gathering to fight one another."

"I'll make Egwene see sense," Rand said. "I'm right, Perrin. We need to break the seals. I don't know why she denies this."

"She's the Amyrlin now." Perrin rubbed his chin. "She's Watcher of the Seals, Rand. It's up to her to make sure they're cared for."

"It is. Which is why I will persuade her that my intentions for them are correct."

"Are you *sure* about breaking them, Rand?" Perrin asked. "Absolutely sure?"

"Tell me, Perrin. If a metal tool or weapon shatters, can you stick it back together and make it work properly?"

"Well, you *can*," Perrin said. "It's better not to. The grain of the steel ... well, you're almost always better off reforging it. Melting it down, starting from scratch."

"It is the same here. The seals are broken, like a sword. We can't just patch the pieces. It won't work. We need to remove the shards and make something new to go in their place. Something better."

"Rand," Perrin said, "that's the most reasonable thing anyone has said on this topic. Have you explained it that way to Egwene?"

"She's not a blacksmith, my friend." Rand smiled.

"She's smart, Rand. Smarter than either of us. She'll understand if you explain it the right way."

"We shall see," Rand said. "Tomorrow."

Perrin stopped walking, his face lit by the glow of Rand's Power-summoned orb. His camp, beside Rand's, contained a force as large as any on the field. Rand still found it incredible that Perrin had gathered so many, including—of all things—the Whitecloaks. Rand's eyes-and-ears indicated that everyone in Perrin's camp seemed loyal to him. Even the Wise Ones and Aes Sedai with him were more inclined to do what Perrin said than not.

Sure as the wind and the sky, Perrin had become a king. A different kind of king than Rand—a king of his people, who lived among them. Rand couldn't take that same path. Perrin could be a man. Rand had to be something more, for a little time yet. He had to be a symbol, a force that everyone could rely upon.

That was terribly tiring. Not all of it was physical fatigue, but instead something deeper. Being what people needed was wearing on him, grinding as surely as a river cut at a mountain. In the end, the river would always win.

"I'll support you in this, Rand," Perrin said. "But I want you to promise me that you won't let it come to blows. I won't fight Elayne. Going up against the Aes Sedai would be worse. We can't afford to squabble."

"There won't be fighting."

"Promise me." Perrin's face grew so hard, one could have broken rocks against it. "Promise me, Rand."

"I promise it, my friend. I'll bring us to the Last Battle united."

"That'll do, then." Perrin walked into his camp, nodding to the sentries. Two Rivers men, both of them—Reed Soalen and Kert Wagoner. They saluted Perrin, then eyed Rand and bowed somewhat awkwardly.

Reed and Kert. He'd known them both—Light, he'd looked up to them, as a child—but Rand had grown accustomed to people he'd known treating him as a stranger. He felt the mantle of the Dragon Reborn harden upon him.

"My Lord Dragon," Kert said. "Are we ... I mean ..." He gulped and looked at the sky, and the clouds that seemed to be—despite Rand's presence—creeping in on them. "Things look bad, don't they?"

"The storms are often bad, Kert," Rand said. "But the Two Rivers survives them. Such it will do again."

"But ..." Kert said again. "It looks bad. Light burn me, but it does."

"It will be as the Wheel wills," Rand said, glancing northward. "Peace, Kert, Reed," Rand said softly. "The Prophecies have nearly all been fulfilled. This day was seen, and our tests are known. We do not walk into them unaware."

He hadn't promised them they would win or that they would survive, but both men stood up straighter and nodded, smiling. People liked to know that there was a plan. The knowledge that someone was in control might be the strongest comfort that Rand could offer them.

"That's enough bothering the Lord Dragon with your questions," Perrin said. "Make sure you guard this post well—no dozing, Kert, and no dicing."

Both men saluted again as Perrin and Rand passed into the camp. There was more cheer here than there was in other camps on the Field. The campfires seemed faintly brighter, the laughter faintly louder. It was as if the Two Rivers folk had managed, somehow, to bring *home* with them.

"You lead them well," Rand said softly, moving quickly beside Perrin, who nodded toward those out at night.

"They shouldn't need me to tell them what to do, and that's that." However, when a messenger came running into camp,

Perrin was immediately in charge. He called the spindly youth by name and, seeing the boy's flushed face and trembling legs—he was frightened of Rand—Perrin pulled him aside and spoke softly, but firmly, with him.

Perrin sent the boy off to find Lady Faile, then stepped over. "I need to talk to Rand again."

"You're talking to—"

"I need the real Rand, not the man who's learned to talk like an Aes Sedai."

Rand sighed. "It really *is* me, Perrin," he protested. "I'm more me than I've been for ages."

"Yes, well, I don't like talking to you when your emotions are all masked."

A group of Two Rivers men passed and saluted. He felt a sudden spike of cold solitude at seeing those men and knowing he could never be one of them again. It was hardest with the Two Rivers men. But he did let himself be more ... relaxed, for Perrin's sake.

"So, what was it?" he asked. "What did the messenger say?"

"You were right to be worried," Perrin said. "Rand, Caemlyn has fallen. It's overrun with Trollocs."

Rand felt his face grow hard.

"You're not surprised," Perrin said. "You're worried, but not surprised."

"No, I'm not," Rand admitted. "I thought it would be the south where they struck—I've heard word of Trolloc sightings there, and I'm half-certain that Demandred is involved. He has never been comfortable without an army. But Caemlyn ... yes, it's a clever strike. I told you they would try to distract us. If they can undercut Andor and draw her away, my alliance grows much shakier."

Perrin glanced at where Elayne's camp was set up right beside that of Egwene. "But wouldn't it be good for you if Elayne ran off? She's on the other side of this confrontation."

"There is no other side, Perrin. There is *one* side, with a disagreement on how that side should proceed. If Elayne isn't here to be part of the meeting, it will undermine everything I'm trying to accomplish. She's probably the most powerful of all the rulers."

Rand could feel her, of course, through the bond. Her spike of alarm let him know that she'd received this information. Should he go to her? Perhaps he could send Min. She had gotten up, and was moving away from the tent where he'd left her. And—

He blinked. Aviendha. She was here, at Merrilor. She hadn't been here moments ago, had she? Perrin glanced at him, and he didn't bother to wipe the shock from his face.

"We can't let Elayne leave," Rand said.

"Not even to protect her homeland?" Perrin asked, incredulous.

"If the Trollocs have already taken Caemlyn, then it's too late for Elayne to do anything meaningful. Elayne's forces will focus on evacuation. She doesn't need to be there for that, but she *does* need to be here. Tomorrow morning."

How could he make certain she stayed? Elayne reacted poorly to being told what to do—all women did—but if he implied . . .

"Rand," Perrin said, "what if we sent in the Asha'man? All of them? We could make a fight of it at Caemlyn."

"No," Rand said, though the word hurt. "Perrin, if the city really is overrun—I'll send men through gateways to be certain—then it's lost. Taking back those walls would take far too much effort, at least right now. We *cannot* let this coalition break apart before I have a chance to forge it together. Unity will preserve us. If each of us goes running off to put out fires in our homelands, then we will lose. That's what this attack is about."

"I suppose that's possible . . . " Perrin said, fingering his hammer.

"The attack might unnerve Elayne, make her more eager to act," Rand said, considering a dozen different lines of action. "Perhaps this will make her more vulnerable to agreeing with my plan. This could be a good thing."

Perrin frowned.

How quickly I've learned to use others. He had learned to laugh again. He had learned to accept his fate, and to charge toward it smiling. He had learned to be at peace with who he had been, what he had done.

That understanding would not stop him from using the tools given him. He needed them, needed them all. The difference now was that he would see the people they were, not just the tools he would use. So he told himself.

"I still think we should do something to help Andor," Perrin said, scratching his beard. "How did they sneak in, do you think?"

"By Waygate," Rand said absently.

Perrin grunted. "Well, you said that Trollocs can't Travel through gateways; could they have learned how to fix that?"

"Pray to the Light they haven't," Rand said. "The only Shadowspawn they managed to make that could go through gateways were *gholam*, and Aginor wasn't foolish enough to make more than a few of *those*. No, I'd bet against Mat himself that this was the Caemlyn Waygate. I thought she had that thing guarded!"

"If it *was* the Waygate, we can do something," Perrin said. "We can't have Trollocs rampaging in Andor; if they leave Caemlyn, they'll be at our backs, and that will be a disaster. But if they're coming in at a single point, we might be able to disrupt their invasion with an attack on that point."

Rand grinned.

"What's so funny?"

"At least *I* have an excuse for knowing and understanding things no youth from the Two Rivers should."

Perrin snorted. "Go jump in the Winespring Water. You really think this is Demandred?"

"It's exactly the sort of thing he'd try. Separate your foes, then crush them one at a time. It's one of the oldest strategies in warfare."

Demandred himself had discovered it in the old writings. They'd known nothing of war when the Bore had first opened. Oh, they'd *thought* they understood it, but it had been the understanding of the scholar looking back on something ancient, dusty.

Of all those to turn to the Shadow, Demandred's betrayal seemed the most tragic. The man could have been a hero. *Should* have been a hero.

I'm to blame for that, too, Rand thought. *If I'd offered a hand instead of a smirk, if I'd congratulated instead of competed. If I'd been the man then that I am now . . .*

Never mind that. He had to send to Elayne. The proper course was to send help for evacuating the city, Asha'man and loyal Aes Sedai to make gateways and free as many people as possible—and to make certain that for now, the Trollocs remained in Caemlyn.

"Well, I guess those memories of yours are good for something, then," Perrin said.

"Do you want to know the thing that twists my brain in knots, Perrin?" Rand said softly. "The thing that gives me shivers, like the cold breath of the Shadow itself? The taint is what made me mad *and* what gave me memories from my past life. They came as Lews Therin whispering to me. But that very insanity is the thing giving me the clues I need to win. Don't you see? If I win this, it will be the *taint itself* that led to the Dark One's fall."

Perrin whistled softly.

Redemption, Rand thought. *When I tried this last time, my madness destroyed us.*

This time, it will save us.

"Go to your wife, Perrin," Rand said, glancing at the sky. "This is the last night of anything resembling peace you shall know before the end. I'll investigate and see how bad things are in Andor." He looked back at his friend. "I will not forget my promise. *Unity* must come before all else. I lost last time precisely because I threw unity aside."

Perrin nodded, then rested a hand on Rand's shoulder. "The Light illumine you."

"And you, my friend."

CHAPTER
2

The Choice of an Ajah

Pevara did her very best to pretend that she was not terrified. If these Asha'man had known her, they'd have realized that sitting still and quiet was not her natural state. She retreated to basic Aes Sedai training: *appearing* in control when she felt anything but.

She forced herself to rise. Canler and Emarin had withdrawn to visit the Two Rivers lads and make sure they were going about in pairs. That left only her and Androl again. He quietly tinkered with his leather straps as the rain continued outside. He used two needles at once to stitch, crossing the holes on either side. The man had the concentration of a master craftsman.

Pevara strolled over, causing him to look up sharply when she drew close. She smothered a smile. She might not look it, but she could move silently, when necessary.

She stared out of the windows. The rain had grown worse, splashing curtains of water against the glass. "After so many weeks of *looking* as if it would storm at any moment, it finally comes."

"Those clouds had to break open eventually," Androl said.

"The rain doesn't feel natural," she said, hands clasped behind her. She could feel the coldness through the glass. "It doesn't ebb and flow. Just the same steady torrent. A great deal of lightning, but very little thunder."

"You think it's one of those?" Androl asked. He didn't need to say what "those" meant. Earlier in the week, common people in the Tower—none of the Asha'man—had begun bursting into flame. Just . . . flame, inexplicably. They'd lost some forty people. Many still blamed a rogue Asha'man, though the men had sworn nobody had been channeling nearby.

She shook her head, watching a group of people trudge past on the muddy street outside. She had been one of those, at first, who had called the deaths the work of an Asha'man gone mad. Now she accepted these events, and other oddities, as something far worse.

The world was unraveling.

She needed to be strong. Pevara herself had devised the plan of bringing women here to bond these men, though Tarna had suggested it. She couldn't let them discover how disturbing she found it to be trapped in here, facing down enemies who could force a person to the Shadow. Her only allies men who, only months ago, she would have pursued with diligence and gentled without remorse.

She sat down on the stool Emarin had used earlier. "I would like to discuss this 'plan' you are developing."

"I'm not sure I've actually developed one yet, Aes Sedai."

"I might be able to offer some suggestions."

"I wouldn't say no to hearing them," Androl said, though he narrowed his eyes.

"What's wrong?" she asked.

"Those people outside. I don't recognize them. And . . ."

She looked back out the window. The only light came from buildings, shining an occasional red-orange glow into the drenched night. The passersby still moved very slowly down the street, in and out of the light of windows.

"Their clothing isn't wet," Androl whispered.

With a chill, Pevara realized he was right. The man at the front walked with a wide-brimmed, drooping hat on his head, but it didn't break the rain or stream water. His rustic clothing was untouched by the downpour. And the dress of the woman beside him wasn't blowing at all in the wind. Now Pevara saw that one of the younger men was holding his hand behind him, as if pulling the reins of a pack animal—but there was no animal there.

Pevara and Androl watched in silence until the figures passed too far into the night to be seen. Visions of the dead were growing increasingly common.

"You said you had a suggestion?" Androl's voice trembled.

"I . . . Yes." Pevara tore her eyes away from the window. "So far, Taim's focus has been on the Aes Sedai. My sisters have all been taken. I am the last."

"You're offering yourself as bait."

"They *will* come for me," she said. "It is only a matter of time."

Androl fingered the leather strap and looked pleased with it. "We should sneak you out."

"Is that so?" she said, eyebrow raised. "I have been elevated to the position of maiden in need of rescue, have I? Very valiant of you."

He blushed. "Sarcasm? From an Aes Sedai? I wouldn't have thought I'd hear that."

Pevara laughed. "Oh my, Androl. You really don't know *anything* about us, do you?"

"Honestly? No. I've avoided your kind for most of my life."

"Well, considering your . . . innate tendencies, perhaps that was wise."

"I couldn't channel before."

"But you suspected. You came here to learn."

"I was curious," he said. "It's something I hadn't tried before."

Interesting, Pevara thought. *Is that what drives you then, leatherworker? What has set you drifting on the winds, from place to place?*

"I suspect," she said, "you have never tried jumping off a cliff before. The fact that you haven't done something shouldn't *always* be a reason to try it."

"Actually, I have jumped off a cliff. Several of them."

She raised an eyebrow at him.

"The Sea Folk do it," he explained. "Off into the ocean. The braver you are, the higher the cliff you choose. And you have changed the topic of the conversation again, Pevara Sedai. You are quite skilled at that."

"Thank you."

"The reason," he said, holding up a finger, "that I suggested we sneak you out is because this isn't your battle. You shouldn't have to fall here."

"It isn't because you want to hurry an Aes Sedai away, out of meddling in your business?"

"I came to you for help," Androl said. "I don't want to be rid of you; I'll happily use you. However, if you fall here, you do so in a fight that is not your own. That isn't fair."

"Let me explain something to you, Asha'man," Pevara said, leaning in. "This *is* my fight. If the Shadow takes this tower, it will mean terrible things for the Last Battle. I have accepted responsibility for you and yours; I will not turn away from it so easily."

"You've 'accepted responsibility' for us? What does that mean?"

Ah, perhaps I shouldn't have shared that. Still, if they were going to be allies, perhaps he needed to know.

"The Black Tower needs guidance," she explained.

"So that's the point of bonding us?" Androl asked. "So we can be . . . corralled, like stallions to be broken?"

"Don't be a fool. Surely you admit the value of the White Tower's experience."

"I'm not sure I'd say that," Androl said. "With experience comes a determination to be set in your ways, to avoid new experiences. You Aes Sedai all assume that the way things have been done is the only way to do them. Well, the Black Tower will not be subject to you. We can look after ourselves."

"And you've done a *wonderful* job of that so far, haven't you?"

"That was unfair," he said softly.

"Perhaps it was," she admitted. "I'm sorry."

"Your motivations don't surprise me," he said. "What you were doing here was obvious to the weakest of soldiers. The question I've had is this: Why, of all women, did the White Tower send *Red* sisters to bond us?"

"Who better? Our entire lives have been dedicated to dealing with men who can channel."

"Your Ajah is doomed."

"Is that so?"

"You exist to hunt down men who can channel," he said. "To

gentle them. See them ... disposed of. Well, the Source is cleansed—"

"So you all say."

"It *is* cleansed, Pevara. All things come and pass, and the Wheel turns. It was once pure, so it must someday be pure again. It has happened."

And the way you look at shadows, Androl? Is that a sign of purity? The way that Nalaam mutters in unknown languages? Do you think we don't notice such things?

"You have two choices, as an Ajah," Androl continued. "You can either continue to hunt us—ignoring the proof that we offer, that the Source is cleansed—or you can give up on being Red Ajah."

"Nonsense. Of all Ajahs, the Reds should be your greatest ally."

"You exist to destroy us!"

"We exist to make certain that men who can channel do not accidentally hurt themselves or those around them. Would you not agree that is a purpose of the Black Tower as well?"

"I suppose that might be part of it. The only purpose I have been told was that we are to be a weapon for the Dragon Reborn, but keeping good men from hurting themselves without proper training is important as well."

"Then we can unite on that idea, can we not?"

"I would like to believe that, Pevara, but I've seen the way you and yours look at us. You see us as ... as some stain that needs to be cleansed, or poison to be bottled."

Pevara shook her head. "If what you say is true, and the Source is cleansed, then changes *will* come, Androl. The Red Ajah and the Asha'man will grow together in common purpose, over time. I'm willing to work with you now, here."

"Contain us."

"Guide you. Please. Trust me."

He studied her by the light of the room's many lamps. He did have a sincere face. She could see why the others followed him, though he was weakest among them. He had a strange mixture of passion and humility. If only he hadn't been one of ... well ... what he was.

"I wish I could believe you," Androl said, looking away. "You're different from the others, I'll admit. Not like a Red at all."

"I think you'll find we're more varied than you suppose," Pevara said. "There isn't one single motive that makes a woman choose the Red."

"Other than hatred of men."

"If we hated you, would we have come here looking to bond you?" That was a sidestep, in truth. Though Pevara herself did not hate men, many Reds did—at the very least, many regarded men with suspicion. She hoped to change that.

"Aes Sedai motivations are odd sometimes," Androl said. "Everyone knows that. Anyway, different though you are from many of your sisters, I've seen that look in your eyes." He shook his head. "I won't believe you're here to help us. No more than I believed that the Aes Sedai who hunted down male channelers really thought they were helping the men. No more than I believe a headsman thinks he's doing a criminal a favor by killing him. Just because a thing needs to be done doesn't make the one doing it a friend, Pevara Sedai. I'm sorry."

He turned back to his leather, working by the close light of a lantern on the table.

Pevara found her annoyance rising. She'd almost had him. She *liked* men; she had often thought Warders would be useful. Couldn't the fool recognize a hand extended across the chasm when he saw it?

Calm yourself, Pevara, she thought. *You won't get anywhere if anger rules you.* She needed this man on her side.

"That will be a saddle, won't it?" she said.

"Yes."

"You're staggering the stitches."

"It's my own method," he said. "Helps prevent rips from spreading. I think it looks nice, too."

"Good linen thread, I assume? Waxed? And do you use a single lacing chisel for those holes, or a double? I didn't get a good look."

He glanced at her, wary. "You know leatherworking?"

"From my uncle," she said. "He taught me a few things. Let me work in the shop, when I was little."

"Maybe I've met him."

She fell still. For all Androl's comments that she was good at steering a conversation, she had blundered this one directly into places she didn't like to go.

"Well?" he asked. "Where does he live?"

"Back in Kandor."

"You're *Kandori*?" he asked, surprised.

"Of course I am. Don't I look it?"

"I just thought I could pick out any accent," he said, pulling a pair of stitches tight. "I've been there. Maybe I do know your uncle."

"He's dead," she said. "Murdered by Darkfriends."

Androl fell silent. "I'm sorry."

"It's been over a hundred years now. I miss my family, but they'd be dead by now even if the Darkfriends hadn't killed them. Everyone I knew back home is dead."

"My sorrow is deeper, then. Truly."

"It is long past," Pevara said. "I can remember them with fondness without having the pain intrude. But what of your family? Siblings? Nieces, nephews?"

"A smattering of each group," Androl said.

"Do you ever see them?"

He eyed her. "You're trying to engage me in friendly conversation to prove that you don't feel awkward around me. But I've seen how you Aes Sedai look at people like me."

"I—"

"Say you don't find us repulsive."

"I hardly think what you do should be—"

"Straight answer, Pevara."

"Very well, fine. Men who can channel *do* discomfort me. You make me itch all over, and it has only grown worse the longer I've been here, surrounded by you."

Androl nodded in satisfaction at having pulled it from her.

"However," Pevara continued, "I feel this way because it has been ingrained in me over decades of life. What you do is terribly unnatural, but you yourself do *not* disgust me. You are just a man trying to do your best, and I hardly think that is worthy of disgust. Either way, I am willing to look beyond my inhibitions in the name of common good."

"That's better than I could have expected, I suppose." He looked back toward the rain-splattered windows. "The taint is cleansed. This isn't unnatural any longer. I wish ... I wish I could just *show* you, woman." He looked toward her sharply. "How does one form one of those circles you mentioned?"

"Well," Pevara said, "I've never actually done it with a male channeler, of course. I did some reading before coming down here, but much of what we have is hearsay. So much has been lost. To start with, you must put yourself on the edge of embracing the Source, then open yourself to me. That is how we establish the link."

"All right," he said. "You're not holding the Source, however."

It was downright unfair, that a man could tell when a woman was holding the One Power and when she wasn't. Pevara embraced the Source, flooding herself with the sweet nectar that was *saidar*.

She reached out to link with Androl as she would with a woman. That was how one was supposed to begin, according to the records. But it was not the same. *Saidin* was a torrent, and what she had read was true; she could do nothing with the flows.

"It's working; my power is flowing into you."

"Yes," Pevara said. "But when a man and woman link, the man must be in control. You must take the lead."

"How?" Androl asked.

"I don't know. I'll try to pass it. You *must* control the flows."

He eyed her, and she prepared herself to pass control to him. Instead, he somehow *seized* it. She was caught in the tempestuous link, yanked—as if by her hair—right in.

The force of it nearly made her teeth rattle, and it felt as if her skin was being pulled off. Pevara closed her eyes, breathed deeply, and did not let herself fight back. She had wanted to try this; it could be useful. But she couldn't help a moment of sheer panic.

She was linked with a *male channeler*, one of the most feared things the land had ever known. Now he had control of her, completely. Her Power flowed through her, washing over him, and Androl gasped.

"So much . . . " he said. "Light, you're strong."

She allowed herself a smile. The link brought with it a storm of awareness. She could feel Androl's emotions. He was as fearful as she was. He was also *solid*. She'd imagined that being linked to him would be terrible, because of his madness, but she sensed none of it.

But *saidin* . . . that liquid fire that he wrestled with, like a serpent that was trying to consume him. She pulled back. Was it tainted? She wasn't certain she could tell. *Saidin* was so different, so alien. Reports from the early days fragmented, spoke of the taint like an oil slick upon a river. Well, she could see a river— more a stream, really. It appeared that Androl had been honest with her, and wasn't very powerful. She could not sense any taint—but then again, she did not know what to look for.

"I wonder . . ." Androl said. "I wonder if I can make a gateway with this power."

"Gateways don't work in the Black Tower anymore."

"I know," he said. "But I keep feeling that they're just beyond my fingertips."

Pevara opened her eyes, looking at him. She could feel his honesty within the circle, but creating a gateway required a *lot* of the One Power, at least for a woman. Androl would have to be orders of magnitude too weak for that weave. Could it require a different level of strength for a man?

He reached out a hand, using her Power somehow, mixed with his own. She could feel him pulling the One Power through her. Pevara tried to maintain her composure, but she did not like him having control. She could do nothing!

"Androl," she said. "Release me."

"It's wonderful . . ." he whispered, eyes unfocused as he stood up. "Is this what it feels like, to be one of the others? Those with strength in the Power?"

He drew more of her power and used it. Objects in the room began to rise into the air.

"Androl!" Panic. It was the panic she'd felt after hearing that her parents were dead. She hadn't known this sense of horror in over a hundred years, not since taking the test for her shawl.

He had control of her channeling. Absolute control. She began to gasp, trying to reach for him. She could not use *saidar* without him releasing it back to her—but he could use it against her. Images of him using her own strength to tie her in Air ran through her mind. She could not end the link. Only he could.

He noticed, suddenly, and his eyes widened. The circle vanished like a wink of the eye, and her power was her own again. Without thinking, she lashed out. This would not happen again. *She* would have the control. The weaves sprang from her before she knew what she was doing.

Androl fell to his knees, hand sweeping across his table as he threw his head back, brushing tools and scraps of leather to the floor. He gasped. "What have you done?"

"Taim said we could pick any of you," Pevara muttered as she realized what she *had* done. She'd bonded him. The reverse, after a fashion, of what he'd done to her. She tried to calm her thundering heart. An awareness of him blossomed in the back of her mind, like what they'd known in the circle, but somehow more personal. Intimate.

"Taim is a monster!" Androl growled. "You know that. You take his word on what you can do, and you do it without my permission?"

"I ... I ..."

Androl clenched his jaw, and Pevara immediately felt *something*. Something alien, something strange. It felt like looking at herself. Feeling her emotions circled back on her endlessly.

Her *self* melded with *his* for a seeming eternity. She knew what it was like to be him, think his thoughts. She saw his life in the blink of an eye, was absorbed by his memories. She gasped and fell to her knees in front of him.

It faded. Not completely, but it faded. It felt like swimming a hundred leagues through boiling water, and only now emerging, having forgotten what it was like to have normal sensations.

"Light ..." she whispered. "What was that?"

He lay on his back. When had he fallen? He blinked, looking up at the ceiling. "I saw one of the others do it. Some of the Asha'man bond their wives."

"You *bonded* me?" she said, horrified.

He groaned, rolling over. "You did it to me first."

She realized, with horror, that she could still feel his emotions. His self. She could even understand some of what he was thinking. Not the actual thoughts, but some impressions of them.

He was confused, worried and ... curious. He was curious about the new experience. *Foolish man!*

She'd hoped that the two bonds would have somehow canceled one another out. They did not. "We have to stop this," she said. "I'll release you. I vow it. Just ... just release me."

"I don't know how," he said, standing up and breathing in deeply. "I'm sorry."

He was telling the truth. "That circle was a bad idea," she said. He offered a hand to help her to her feet. She stood on her own without accepting it.

"I believe it was *your* bad idea before it was mine."

"So it was," she admitted. "It isn't my first one, but it might be one of my worst." She sat down. "We need to think through this. Find a way to—"

The door to his shop slammed open.

Androl spun, and Pevara embraced the Source. Androl had grabbed his stitching groover in one hand like a weapon. He'd also seized the One Power. She could sense that molten force within him—weak because of his lack of talent, like a single small jet of magma, but still burning and hot. She could feel his awe. So it was the same for him as it was for her. Holding the One Power felt like opening your eyes for the first time, the world coming to life.

Fortunately, neither weapon nor the One Power was needed. Young Evin stood in the doorway, raindrops dribbling down the sides of his face. He shut the door and hurried to Androl's workbench.

"Androl, it—" He froze, seeing Pevara.

"Evin," Androl said. "You're alone."

"I left Nalaam to watch," he said, breathing in and out. "It was important, Androl."

"We are *never* to be alone, Evin," Androl said. "Never. Always in pairs. No matter the emergency."

"I know, I know," Evin said. "I'm sorry. It's just—the news, Androl." He glanced at Pevara.

"Speak," Androl said.

"Welyn and his Aes Sedai are back," Ewan said.

Pevara could feel Androl's sudden tension. "Is he . . . one of us, still?"

Evin shook his head, sick. "He's one of them. Probably Jenare Sedai is, too. I don't know her well enough to tell for sure. Welyn, though . . . his eyes aren't his own any longer, and he now serves Taim."

Androl groaned. Welyn had been with Logain. Androl and the others had been holding to the hope that although Mezar had been taken, Logain and Welyn were still free.

"Logain?" Androl whispered.

"He isn't here," Evin said, "but Androl, Welyn says Logain will come back soon—and that he's met with Taim, and they have reconciled their differences. Welyn is promising that Logain will come tomorrow to prove it. Androl . . . that's it. We have to admit it now. They have him."

Pevara could feel Androl's agreement, and his horror. It mirrored her own.

Aviendha moved through the darkened camps silently.

So many groups. There had to be at least a hundred thousand people gathered here at the Field of Merrilor. All waiting. Like a breath taken in and held before a great leap.

The Aiel saw her, but she did not approach them. The wetlanders didn't notice her, save for a Warder who spotted her as she skirted the Aes Sedai camp. That camp was a place of motion and activity. Something had happened, though she caught only fragments. A Trolloc attack somewhere?

She listened enough to determine that the attack was in Andor, in the city of Caemlyn. There was worry the Trollocs would leave the city and rampage across the land.

She needed to know more; would the spears be danced tonight? Perhaps Elayne would share news with her. Aviendha moved silently out of the Aes Sedai camp. Stepping softly in these wet lands, with their lush plants, presented different challenges than the Three-fold Land did. There, the dry ground was often dusty, which could muffle footsteps. Here, a dry twig could inexplicably be buried beneath wet grass.

She tried not to think about how dead that grass seemed. Once, she'd have considered those browns lush. Now, she knew these wetland plants should *not* look so wan and . . . and hollow.

Hollow plants. What was she thinking? She shook her head and crept through the shadows out of the Aes Sedai camp. She briefly contemplated sneaking back to surprise that Warder— he'd been hiding in a moss-worn cleft in the rubble of an old, fallen building and watching the Aes Sedai perimeter—but discarded the idea. She wanted to get to Elayne and ask her for details on the attack.

Aviendha approached another busy camp, ducked beneath the leafless branches of a tree—she didn't know what type, but its limbs spread wide and high—and slipped inside the guard perimeter. A pair of wetlanders in white and red stood on "watch" near a fire. They didn't come close to spotting her, though they did jump up and level polearms toward a thicket a good thirty feet away when an animal rustled in it.

Aviendha shook her head and passed them.

Forward. She needed to keep moving forward. What to do about Rand al'Thor? What were his plans for tomorrow? These were other questions she wanted to ask Elayne.

The Aiel needed a purpose once Rand al'Thor finished with them. That was clear from the visions. She had to find a way to give this to them. Perhaps they should return to the Three-fold Land. But . . . no. No. It tore her heart, but she had to admit that if the Aiel did so, they would be going to their graves. Their death, as a people, might not be immediate, but it would come. The changing world, with new devices and new ways of fighting, would overtake the Aiel, and the Seanchan would never leave them alone. Not with women who could channel. Not with armies full of spears that could, at any time, invade.

A patrol approached. Aviendha drew some fallen brown under-growth over herself for camouflage, then lay down flat beside a dead shrub and remained perfectly still. The guards walked two handspans from her.

We could attack the Seanchan now, she thought. *In my vision, the Aiel waited nearly a generation to attack—and that let the Seanchan strengthen their position.*

The Aiel already spoke of the Seanchan and the confrontation that must inevitably come. The Seanchan would force it, everyone whispered. Except, in her vision, years had passed with the Seanchan failing to attack. Why? What could possibly have held them back?

Aviendha rose and crept across to the pathway the guards had taken. She took out her knife and rammed it down into the ground. She left it there, right beside a lantern on a pole, clearly visible even to wetlander eyes. Then she slipped back into the night, hiding near the back of the large tent that was her goal.

She crouched low and practiced her silent breathing, using the rhythm to calm herself. There were hushed, anxious voices inside the tent. Aviendha did her best not to pay attention to what they were saying. It wouldn't be proper to eavesdrop.

As the patrol passed again, she stood up. When they cried out, having found her dagger, she slipped around to the front of the tent. There, avoiding the attention of guards distracted by the commotion, she lifted the flap and stepped inside the tent behind them.

Some people sat at a table on the far side of the very large tent, huddled around a lamp. They were so busy with their conversation that they did not see her, so she settled down near some cushions to wait.

It was very hard not to listen in, now that she was so close.

"... *must* send our forces back!" one man barked. "The fall of the capital is a symbol, Your Majesty. A *symbol*! We cannot let Caemlyn go or the entire nation will collapse into chaos."

"You underestimate the strength of the Andoran people," said Elayne. She looked very much in control, very strong, her red-gold hair practically glowing in the lamplight. Several of her battle commanders stood behind her, lending authority and a sense of stability to the meeting. Aviendha was pleased to see the fire in her first-sister's eyes.

"I have been to Caemlyn, Lord Lir," Elayne continued. "And I have left a small force of soldiers there to watch and give warning if the Trollocs leave the city. Our spies will use gateways to sneak through the city and find where the remaining Trollocs are herding captives, and then we can mount rescue operations if the Trollocs continue to hold the city."

"But the city itself!" Lord Lir said.

"Caemlyn is lost, Lir," Lady Dyelin snapped. "We'd be fools to try to mount any kind of assault now."

Elayne nodded. "I have held conference with the other High Seats, and they agree with my assessment. For now, the refugees who escaped are safe—I sent them on along toward Whitebridge with guards. If there are people alive within, we will try to rescue them with gateways, but I will *not* commit my forces to an all-out attack on Caemlyn's walls."

"But—"

"Taking the city again would be fruitless," Elayne said, voice hard. "I know full well the damage that can be done to an army assaulting those walls! Andor will not collapse because of the loss of one city, no matter how important a city." Her face was a mask, her voice as cold as good steel.

"The Trollocs will eventually leave the city," Elayne continued. "They gain nothing by holding it—they will starve themselves out, if nothing else. Once they leave, we can fight them—and on far fairer ground. If you wish, Lord Lir, you may visit the city yourself and see that what I say is true. The soldiers there could use the inspiration of a High Seat."

Lir frowned, but nodded. "I think I will."

"Then go knowing my plan. We will begin sending in scouts before the night is through, trying to find pens of civilians to save, and *Aviendha, what in the name of a bloody goat's left stone are you doing!*"

Aviendha looked up from trimming her fingernails with her second knife. *Bloody goat's left stone?* That was a new one. Elayne always knew the most interesting curses.

The three High Seats at the table jumped up, scrambling, throwing down chairs and reaching for swords. Elayne sat in her place, eyes and mouth wide.

"It is a bad habit," Aviendha admitted, slipping her knife back into her boot. "My nails were growing long, but I should not have done it in your tent, Elayne. I am sorry. I hope I did not offend."

"I'm not talking about your flaming nails, Aviendha," Elayne said. "How ... when did you arrive? Why didn't the guards announce you?"

"They didn't see me," Aviendha said. "I didn't wish to make a fuss, and wetlanders can be touchy. I thought they might turn me away, now that you are Queen." She smiled as she said the last part. Elayne had much honor; the way of becoming a leader among the wetlanders was different from proper ways—things could be so backward over here—but Elayne had handled herself well and obtained her throne. Aviendha couldn't have been more proud of a spear-sister who had taken a clan chief *gai'shain*.

"They didn't ... " Elayne said. Suddenly, she was smiling. "You crept through the *entire camp*, to my tent at the center, and then slipped inside and sat down not five feet from me. And nobody saw."

"I didn't wish to make a fuss."

"You have a strange way of not making a fuss."

Elayne's companions did not react with such calm. One of the three, young Lord Perival, gazed around him with worried eyes, as if searching for other intruders.

"My Queen," Lir said. "We must punish this breach in security! I will find the men who were lax in their duty and see that they—"

"Peace," Elayne said. "I will speak to my guards and suggest they keep their eyes a little more open. Still, guarding the front of a tent is a silly precaution—and always has been—as someone can just cut their way into the back."

"And ruin a good tent?" Aviendha said, lips turning down. "Only if we had blood feud, Elayne."

"Lord Lir, you may go inspect the city—from a good distance—if you wish," Elayne said, standing. "If any of the rest of you wish to accompany him, you may. Dyelin, I will see you in the morning."

"Very well," the lords said in turn, then walked from the tent. Both kept distrustful eyes on Aviendha as they left. Dyelin just shook her head before following them, and Elayne sent her battle commanders out to coordinate scouting of the city. That left Elayne and Aviendha alone in the tent.

"Light, Aviendha," Elayne said, embracing her, "if the people who want me dead had half of your skill . . . "

"Did I do something wrong?" Aviendha said.

"Other than sneaking into my tent like an assassin?"

"But you are my first-sister . . . " Aviendha said. "Should I have asked? But we are not under a roof. Or . . . among wetlanders, is a tent considered a roof, as in a hold? I'm sorry, Elayne. Do I have *toh*? You are such an unpredictable people, it's hard to know what will offend you and what will not."

Elayne just laughed. "Aviendha, you're a gem. A complete and total *gem*. Light, but it's good to see your face. I needed a friendly one tonight."

"Caemlyn has fallen?" Aviendha asked.

"Near enough," Elayne said, face growing colder. "It was that bloody Waygate. I thought it was safe—I had that thing all but bricked up, with fifty guards at the door and the *Avendesora* leaves taken and both put on the outside."

"Someone inside Caemlyn let them in, then."

"Darkfriends," Elayne said. "A dozen members of the Guard—we were lucky enough that one man survived their betrayal and found his way out. Light, I don't know why I should be surprised. If they're in the White Tower, they're in Andor. But these were men who had rejected Gaebril, and who seemed loyal. They waited all this time only to betray us now."

Aviendha grimaced, but took one of the chairs to join Elayne at the table, rather than staying on the floor. Her first-sister preferred sitting that way. Her stomach had swelled with the children she bore.

"I sent Birgitte with the soldiers to the city to see what can be done," Elayne said. "But we've done what we can for the night, the city watched, the refugees seen to. Light, I wish I could do more. The worst thing about being Queen is not the things you must do, but the things that you cannot."

"We will bring the battle to them soon enough," Aviendha said.

"We will," Elayne said, eyes smoldering. "I will bring them fire and fury, repayment in kind for the flames they brought to my people."

"I heard you speak to those men of not attacking the city."

"No," Elayne said. "I will not give them the satisfaction of holding my own walls against me. I have given Birgitte an order—the Trollocs will eventually abandon Caemlyn, of this we are sure. Birgitte will find a way to hasten that, so we can fight them outside of the city."

"Do not let the enemy choose your battleground," Aviendha said with a nod. "A good strategy. And . . . Rand's meeting?"

"I will attend," Elayne said. "I must, so it will be done. He had better not give us theatrics and stalling. My people die, my city burns, the world is two steps from the edge of a cliff. I will stay through the afternoon only; after that, I go back to Andor." She hesitated. "Will you come with me?"

"Elayne . . ." Aviendha said. "I cannot leave my people. I am a Wise One now."

"You went to Rhuidean?" Elayne asked.

"Yes," Aviendha said. Though it pained her to keep secrets, she said nothing of her visions there.

"Excellent. I—" Elayne began, but was cut off.

"My Queen?" the tent guard called from outside. "Messenger for you."

"Let them in."

The guard opened the flaps for a young Guardswoman with a messenger's ribbon on her coat. She performed an ornate bow, one hand removing her hat as the other held out a letter.

Elayne took the letter but didn't open it. The messenger retreated.

"Perhaps we can still fight together, Aviendha," Elayne said. "If I have my way, I will have Aiel at my side as I reclaim Andor. The Trollocs in Caemlyn present a serious threat to all of us; even if I draw their main force out, the Shadow can continue to pour Shadowspawn through that Waygate.

"I'm thinking that while my armies fight the main body of Trollocs outside of Caemlyn—I will have to make the city inhospitable to the Shadowspawn somehow—I will send a smaller force through a gateway to seize the Waygate. If I could gain the aid of Aiel for that . . . "

As she spoke, she embraced the Source—Aviendha could see the glow—and absently sliced the letter open, breaking the seal with a ribbon of Air.

Aviendha raised an eyebrow.

"Sorry," Elayne said, "I've reached the point in my pregnancy where I can channel again reliably, and I keep finding excuses . . . "

"Do not endanger the babes," Aviendha said.

"I'm not going to endanger them," Elayne said. "You're as bad as Birgitte. At least no one has any goat's milk here. Min says . . . " She trailed off, eyes flickering back and forth as she read the letter. Elayne's expression darkened, and Aviendha prepared herself for a shock.

"Oh, that man . . . " Elayne said.

"Rand?"

"I think I may strangle him one of these days."

Aviendha set her jaw. "If he's offended—"

Elayne turned the letter around. "He *insists* that I return to Caemlyn to see to my people. He gives a dozen reasons why, going so far as to 'release me from my obligation' to meet with him tomorrow."

"He should not be insisting on anything with you."

"Particularly not so forcefully," Elayne said. "Light, this is clever. He's obviously trying to bully me into *staying*. There's a touch of *Daes Dae'mar* in this."

Aviendha hesitated. "You seem proud. Yet I gather this letter is only one step away from being insulting!"

"I am proud," Elayne said. "And angry at him. But proud because he knew to make me angry like that. Light! We'll make a king out of you yet, Rand. Why does he want me at the meeting so badly? Does he think I'll support his side just because of my affection for him?"

"You don't know what his plan is, then?"

"No. It obviously involves all of the rulers. But I will attend, even though I'm likely to do so without having had any sleep tonight. I am meeting with Birgitte and my other commanders in an hour to go over plans for drawing out, then destroying, the Trollocs." A fire still burned behind those eyes of hers. Elayne was a warrior, as true a one as Aviendha had ever known.

"I must go to him," Aviendha said.

"Tonight?"

"Tonight. The Last Battle will soon begin."

"As far as I'm concerned, it started the moment those bloody Trollocs set foot in Caemlyn," Elayne said. "May the Light favor us. It is here."

"Then the day of dying will come," Aviendha said. "Many of us will soon wake from this dream. There may not be another night for Rand and myself. I came to you, in part, to ask you about this."

"You have my blessing," Elayne said softly. "You are my first-sister. Have you spent time with Min?"

"Not enough, and under other circumstances I would remedy that lack immediately. There is no time."

Elayne nodded.

"I do think she feels better about me," Aviendha said. "She did me a great honor in helping me understand the last step to becoming a Wise One. It may be appropriate to bend some of the customs. We have done well, under the circumstances. I would speak to her together with you, if there is time."

Elayne nodded. "I can spare a moment or two between meetings. I'll send for her."

CHAPTER
3

A Dangerous Place

"Lord Logain and Taim have indeed patched up their differences," Welyn said, sitting inside the common room of The Great Gathering. He wore bells in his dark braids, and he smiled widely. He always had smiled too much. "Both were worried about the division we've been suffering and agree it isn't good for morale. We need to be focused on the Last Battle. This isn't a time for squabbling."

Androl stood just inside the door, Pevara beside him. It was surprising, how quickly this building—a former warehouse—had been transformed into a tavern. Lind had done her work well. There were a respectable bar and stools, and though the tables and chairs spread through the room didn't match yet, the place could seat dozens. She also had a library with a considerable number of books, although she was very particular about who she allowed to use it. On the second floor, she planned private dining chambers and sleeping rooms for visitors to the Black Tower. Assuming Taim started letting visitors in again.

The room was quite packed, and the crowd included a large number of newer recruits, men who didn't yet fall on either side of the growing dispute—either with Taim and his men, or with those loyal to Logain.

Androl listened to Welyn, feeling chilled. Welyn's Aes Sedai, Jenare, sat beside him, hand resting fondly on his arm. Androl didn't know her well, but he *did* know Welyn. And this thing with Welyn's face and voice was *not* the same man.

"We met with the Lord Dragon," Welyn continued. "Surveying the Borderlands, preparing for humankind's assault against the Shadow. He has rallied the armies of all nations to his banner. There are none who do not support him, other than the Seanchan, of course—but they have been driven back.

"This is the time, and we will soon be called upon to strike. We need to focus one last time on our skills. The Sword and Dragon will be awarded liberally in the next two weeks. Work hard, and we will be the weapons that break the Dark One's hold upon this land."

"You say Logain is coming," a voice demanded. "Why isn't he back yet?"

Androl turned. Jonneth Dowtry stood near Welyn's table. With his arms folded, glowering at Welyn, Jonneth was an intimidating sight. The Two Rivers man often had a friendly way about him, and it was easy to forget that he stood a head taller than you and had arms like those of a bear. He wore his black Asha'man coat, though it had no pins on the high collar—despite the fact that he was as strong in the One Power as any Dedicated.

"Why isn't he here?" Jonneth demanded. "You said that you returned with him, that he and Taim have spoken. Well, where is he?"

Don't push, lad, Androl thought. *Let him think we believe his lies!*

"He took the M'Hael to visit the Lord Dragon," Welyn said. "Both should be back on the morrow, the day after at the latest."

"Why did Taim need Logain to show him the way?" Jonneth said stubbornly. "He could have gone on his own."

"That boy is a fool," Pevara hissed.

"He's honest," Androl replied quietly, "and he wants honest answers." These Two Rivers lads were a good lot—straightforward and loyal. They weren't particularly practiced in subterfuge, however.

Pevara fell silent, but Androl could *feel* her as she considered channeling and hushing Jonneth with some bindings of Air. They weren't serious thoughts, just idle fancies, but Androl could sense them. Light! What had they done to one another?

She's in my head, he thought. *There's an Aes Sedai, inside my head.*

Pevara froze, then glanced at him.

Androl sought the void, that old soldier's trick to help him seek clarity before a battle. *Saidin* was there, too, of course. He didn't reach for it.

"What did you do?" Pevara whispered. "I can feel you there, but sensing your thoughts is harder."

Well, that was something at least.

"Jonneth," Lind called across the common room, interrupting the lad's next question to Welyn. "Didn't you hear the man saying how much traveling he's been doing? He's exhausted. Let him drink his ale and rest a spell before you pry stories out of him."

Jonneth glanced at her, looking hurt. Welyn smiled deeply as the lad withdrew, pushing his way out of the common room. Welyn continued talking about how well the Lord Dragon was doing, and about how much each of them would be needed.

Androl released the void, feeling more relaxed. He looked around the room, trying to judge who in here he could rely upon. He liked many of these men, and many weren't completely for Taim, yet he still couldn't trust them. Taim had complete control of the Tower now, and private lessons with him and his chosen were coveted by the newcomers. Only the Two Rivers lads could be counted on to give any sort of support to Androl's cause—and most of them other than Jonneth were too unpracticed to be of use.

Evin had joined Nalaam on the other side of the room, and Androl nodded his head to him, sending him out to follow Jonneth into the storm. Nobody was to be alone. That done, Androl listened to Welyn's boasting, and noticed Lind picking her way through the crowd toward him.

Lind Taglien was a short, dark-haired woman; her dress was covered in lovely embroidery. She had always seemed to him a model of what the Black Tower *could* be. Civilized. Educated. Important.

Men made way for her; they knew not to spill their drinks or start fights in her inn. Lind's anger was not something a wise man ever wanted to know. It was a good thing she ran the place so tightly. In a city full of male channelers, a simple tavern brawl could potentially go very, very wrong.

"Does this bother you as much as it does me?" Lind asked softly as she stepped up beside him. "Wasn't he the one who, just a few weeks back, was talking about how Taim should be tried and executed for some of the things he'd done?"

Androl didn't reply. What could he say? That he suspected that the man they'd known as Welyn was dead? That the entire Black Tower would soon be nothing but these monsters with the wrong eyes, the false smiles, the dead souls?

"I don't believe him about Logain," Lind said. "Something's going on here, Androl. I'm going to have Frask follow him tonight, see where he—"

"No," Androl said. "No. Don't." Frask was her husband, a man who had been hired to help Henre Haslin teach swordsmanship in the Black Tower. Taim thought that swordfighting was useless for Asha'man, but the Lord Dragon had insisted that the men be taught.

She eyed him. "You're not saying you believe—"

"I'm saying that we're in great danger right now, Lind, and I don't want Frask making it worse. Do me a favor. Take note of what else Welyn says tonight. Maybe some of it will be useful for me to know."

"All right," she said, sounding skeptical.

Androl nodded toward Nalaam and Canler, who rose and headed over. Rain beat against the rooftop and the porch outside. Welyn kept right on talking, and the men were listening. Yes, it was incredible that he'd swapped sides so quickly, and that would make some suspicious. But many people respected him, and the way he was *off* just slightly wasn't noticeable unless you knew him.

"Lind," Androl said as she started to walk away.

She glanced back at him.

"You . . . lock this place up tightly tonight. Then maybe you and Frask should find your way into the cellar with some supplies, all right? You have a sturdy cellar door?"

"Yes," she said. "For all the good it will do." It wouldn't matter how thick a door was if someone with the One Power came looking.

Nalaam and Canler reached them, and Androl turned to go, only to run directly into a man standing in the doorway behind him, someone he hadn't heard approach. Rain dripped from his Asha'man coat, with the Sword and the Dragon on the high collar. Atal Mishraile had been one of Taim's from the start. He didn't have the hollow eyes; his evil was all his own. Tall, with long golden hair, he had a smile that never seemed to reach his eyes.

Pevara jumped when she saw him, and Nalaam cursed, seizing the One Power.

"Now, now," a voice said. "No need for strife." Mezar stepped in from the rain beside Mishraile. The short Domani man had graying hair and an air of wisdom to him, despite his transformation.

Androl met Mezar's eyes, and it was like looking into a deep cavern. A place where light had never shone.

"Hello, Androl," Mezar said, putting a hand on Mishraile's shoulder, as if the two had been friends for a long time. "Why is it that Goodwoman Lind would need to fear, and shut herself in her cellar? Surely the Black Tower is as safe a place as there is?"

"I don't trust a dark night full of storms," Androl said.

"Perhaps that is wise," Mezar replied. "Yet you go out into it. Why not stay where it is warm? Nalaam, I should like to hear one of your stories. Perhaps you could tell me of the time your father and you visited Shara?"

"It's not that good a story," Nalaam said. "I don't know if I remember it that well."

Mezar laughed, and Androl heard Welyn stand up behind him. "Ah, there you are! I was telling them you'd talk about defenses in Arafel."

"Come listen," Mezar said. "This will be important for the Last Battle."

"Maybe I will return," Androl said, voice cool. "Once my other work is done."

The two stared at one another. To the side, Nalaam still held the One Power. He was as strong as Mezar, but would never be able to face both him and Mishraile—particularly not in a room crammed with people who would probably take the side of the two full Asha'man.

"Don't waste your time with the pageboy, Welyn," Coteren said from behind. Mishraile stepped aside to make room for this third newcomer. The bulky, beady-eyed man pressed a hand against Androl's chest and shoved him aside as he passed. "Oh, wait. You can't play pageboy anymore, can you?"

Androl entered the void and seized the Source.

Shadows immediately started moving in the room. Lengthening. There weren't enough lights! Why didn't they light more lamps? The darkness invited those shadows in, and he could *see* them. These were real, each one a tendril of blackness, reaching for him. To pull him into them, to destroy him.

Oh, Light. I'm mad. I'm mad . . .

The void shattered, and the shadows—thankfully—retreated. He found himself shaking, pulling back against the wall, panting. Pevara watched him with an expressionless face, but he could feel her concern.

"Oh, by the way," Coteren said. He was one of Taim's most influential toadies. "Have you heard?"

"Heard what?" Androl managed to force out.

"You've been demoted, pageboy," Coteren said, pointing toward the sword pin. "Taim's orders. As of today. Back to soldier you go, Androl."

"Oh, yes," Welyn called from the center of the room. "I'm sorry I forgot to mention it. It *has* been cleared with the Lord Dragon, I'm afraid. You never should have been promoted, Androl. Sorry."

Androl reached to his neck, to the pin there. It shouldn't matter to him; what did it really mean?

But it *did* matter. He'd spent his entire life searching. He'd apprenticed to a dozen different professions. He'd fought in revolts, sailed two seas. All the while searching, searching for something he hadn't been able to define.

He'd found it when he'd come to the Black Tower.

He pushed through the fear. Shadows be *burned*! He seized *saidin* again, the Power flooding him. He straightened up, going eye-to-eye with Coteren.

The larger man smiled and seized the One Power as well. Mezar joined him, and in the middle of the room, Welyn stood. Nalaam was whispering to himself in worry, eyes darting back and forth. Canler seized *saidin* and looked resigned.

Everything Androl could hold—all of the One Power he could muster—flooded into him. It was minuscule compared to the others. He was the weakest man in the room; the newest of recruits could manage more than he could.

"Are you going to make a go of it, then?" Coteren asked softly. "I asked them to leave you, because I knew you'd try it eventually. I wanted the satisfaction, pageboy. Come on. Strike. Let's see it."

Androl reached out, trying to do the one thing he could do, form a gateway. To him, this was something beyond weaves. It was just him and the Power, something intimate, something *instinctive*.

Trying to make a gateway now felt like trying to scramble up a hundred-foot glass wall with only his fingernails to give him purchase. He leaped, scrambled, *tried*. Nothing happened. He felt so close: if he could just push a little harder, he could ...

The shadows lengthened. The panic rose in him again. Teeth gritted, Androl reached to his collar and ripped the pin free. He dropped it on the floorboards before Coteren with a clink. Nobody in the room spoke.

Then, burying his shame under a mountain of determination, he released the One Power and pushed past Mezar into the night. Nalaam, Canler and Pevara followed with anxious steps.

The rain washed over Androl. He felt the loss of that pin as he might have felt the loss of a hand.

"Androl ..." Nalaam said. "I'm sorry."

Thunder rumbled. They splashed through muddy puddles on the unpaved street. "It doesn't matter," Androl said.

"Maybe we should have fought," Nalaam said. "Some of the lads in there would have supported us; they're not all in his pocket. Once, Father and I, we fought down six Darkhounds—Light upon my grave, we did. If we survived that, we can deal with a few Asha'man dogs."

"We'd have been slaughtered," Androl said.

"But—"

"We'd have been *slaughtered*!" Androl said. "We don't let them pick the battlefield, Nalaam."

"But there will be a battle?" Canler asked, catching up to Androl on the other side.

"They have Logain," Androl said. "They wouldn't make the

promises they're making unless they did. Everything dies—our rebellion, our chances at a unified Black Tower—if we lose him."

"So . . ."

"So we're going to rescue him," Androl said, continuing forward. "Tonight."

Rand worked by the soft, steady light of a *saidin* globe. Before Dragonmount, he'd begun avoiding this kind of common use of the One Power. Seizing it had made him sick, and using it had revolted him more and more.

That had changed. *Saidin* was part of him, and he needed to fear it no longer, now that the taint was gone. More importantly, he had to stop thinking of it—and of himself—as merely a weapon.

He would work by globes of light whenever he could. He intended to go to Flinn to learn Healing. He had little skill in it, but a little skill could save the life of someone wounded. All too often, Rand had used this wonder—this gift—only to destroy or kill. Was it any wonder that people looked upon him with fear? What would Tam say?

I guess I could ask him, Rand thought idly as he made a notation to himself on a piece of paper. It was still hard to get used to the idea of Tam being there, just one camp over. Rand had dined with him earlier. It had been awkward, but no more so than expected for a king inviting his father from a rural village to "dine." They had laughed about it, which had made him feel much better.

Rand had let Tam return to Perrin's camp rather than seeing him given honors and wealth. Tam didn't want to be hailed as the Dragon Reborn's father. He wanted to be what he'd always been—Tam al'Thor, a solid, dependable man by anyone's measure, but not a lord.

Rand went back to the document in front of him. Clerks in Tear had advised him on the proper language, but he had done the actual writing; he hadn't trusted any other hand—or any other eyes—with this document.

Was he being too careful? What his enemies could not anticipate, they could not work against. He had grown too distrustful after Semirhage had nearly captured him. He recognized this.

However, he'd been holding secrets close to him for so long, it was difficult to let them out.

He started at the top of the document, rereading. Once, Tam had sent Rand to examine a fence for weak spots. Rand had done so, but when he'd returned, Tam had sent him on the same duty again.

It hadn't been until the third pass that Rand had found the loose post that needed replacing. He still didn't know if Tam had known about the post, or if his father had just been being his careful self.

This document was far more important than a fence. Rand would look it over a dozen more times this night, searching for problems he had not foreseen.

Unfortunately, it was hard to concentrate. The women were up to something. He could feel them through the balls of emotion in the back of his mind. There were four of those—Alanna was still there, somewhere to the north. The other three had been near to one another all night; now they'd made their way almost to his tent. What *were* they up to? It—

Wait. One of them had split off from the others. She was nearly here. Aviendha?

Rand stood up, walking to the front of his tent and throwing back the flaps.

She froze in place just outside, as if she'd been intending to sneak into his tent. She raised her chin, meeting his eyes.

Suddenly, shouts rose in the night. For the first time, he noticed that his guards were not in attendance. However, the Maidens made camp near his tent, and they appeared to be shouting at him. Not with joy, as he'd expected. Insults. Terrible ones. Several were screaming about what they'd do to certain parts of his body when they caught him.

"What is this?" he murmured.

"They don't mean it," Aviendha said. "It is a symbol to them of you taking me away from their ranks—but I have already left their ranks to join the Wise Ones. It is a . . . thing of the Maidens. It is actually a sign of respect. If they did not like you, they would not act this way."

Aiel. "Wait," he said. "How have I taken you from them?"

Aviendha looked him in the eyes, but color rose in her cheeks. Aviendha? Blushing? That was unexpected.

"You should understand already," she said. "If you'd paid attention to what I told you about us . . . "

"Unfortunately, you had a complete woolhead of a student."

"It is fortunate for him that I have decided to extend my training." She took a step closer. "There are many things I still need to teach." Her blush deepened.

Light. She was beautiful. But so was Elayne . . . and so was Min . . . and . . .

He was a fool. A Light-blinded fool.

"Aviendha," he said. "I love you, I truly do. But that's a problem, burn it! I love all *three* of you. I don't think I could accept this and choose—"

Suddenly, she was laughing. "You *are* a fool, aren't you, Rand al'Thor?"

"Often. But what—"

"We are first-sisters, Rand al'Thor, Elayne and I. When we get to know her better, Min will join us. We three will share in all things."

First-sisters? He should have suspected, following that odd bonding. He raised a hand to his head. *We* will *share you,* they had said to him.

Leaving four bonded women to their pains was bad enough, but three bonded women who loved him? Light, he did not want to bring them pain!

"They say you have changed," Aviendha said. "So many have spoken of it in the short time since my return that almost, I grow weary of hearing about you. Well, your face may be calm, but your emotions are not. Is this so terrible a thing to consider, being with the three of us?"

"I want it, Aviendha. I should hide myself because I do. But the pain . . . "

"You have embraced it, have you not?"

"It is not my pain I fear. It is yours."

"Are we so weak, then, that we cannot bear what you can?"

That look in her eyes was unnerving.

"Of course not," Rand said. "But how can I hope for pain in those I love?"

"The pain is ours to accept," she said, raising her chin. "Rand al'Thor, your decision is simple, though you strive to make it difficult. Choose yes or no. Be warned; it is all three of us, or none of us. We will not let you come between us."

He hesitated, then—feeling a complete lecher—he kissed her. Behind him, Maidens he hadn't realized were watching began to yell louder insults, though he could now hear an incongruous joy to them. He pulled back from the kiss, then reached out, cupping the side of Aviendha's face with his hand. "You're bloody fools. All three of you."

"Then it is well. We are your equals. You should know that I am a Wise One now."

"Then perhaps we are not equals," Rand said, "for I've only just begun to understand how little wisdom I possess."

Aviendha sniffed. "Enough talk. You will bed me now."

"Light!" he said. "A little forward, aren't you? Is that the Aiel way of doing things?"

"No," she said, blushing again. "I just . . . I am not very skilled with this."

"You three decided this, didn't you? Which of you came to me?"

She hesitated, then nodded.

"I'm never going to get to choose, am I?"

She shook her head.

He laughed and pulled her close. She was stiff, initially, but then melted against him. "So, do I go fight them first?" He nodded toward the Maidens.

"That is only for the wedding, if we decide you are worth marriage, fool man. And it would be our families, not members of our society. You really did ignore your lessons, didn't you?"

He looked down at her. "Well, I'm glad there's no fighting to do. I'm not sure how much time we have, and I was hoping to get some sleep tonight. Still . . ." He trailed off at the look in her eyes. "I'm . . . not getting any sleep, am I?"

She shook her head.

"Ah, well. At least I don't have to worry about you freezing to death this time."

"Yes. But it may happen that I die of boredom, Rand al'Thor, if you do not stop rambling."

She took him by the arm and gently, but firmly, pulled him

back into his tent—the calls of the Maidens growing louder, more insulting and more exuberant all at the same time.

"I suspect the reason is some kind of *ter'angreal*," Pevara said. She crouched with Androl in the back room of one of the Black Tower's general storehouses, and she did not find the position terribly comfortable. The room smelled of dust, grain and wood. Most buildings in the Black Tower were new, and this was no exception, the cedar boards still fresh.

"You know of a *ter'angreal* that could prevent gateways?" Androl asked.

"Not specifically, no," Pevara replied, shifting to a better position. "But it is generally accepted that what we know of *ter'angreal* comprises only the smallest portion of what was once known. There must be thousands of different types of *ter'angreal*, and if Taim is a Darkfriend, he has access to the Forsaken—who could likely explain to him the use and construction of things we can only dream about."

"So we need to find this *ter'angreal*," Androl said. "Block it, or at least figure out how it functions."

"And escape?" Pevara asked. "Haven't you already determined that leaving would be a poor choice?"

"Well . . . yes," Androl admitted.

She concentrated, and could catch glimmers of what he was thinking. She'd heard that the Warder bond allowed an empathic connection. This seemed deeper. He was . . . yes, he *really* wished he could make gateways. He felt disarmed without them.

"It's my Talent," he said begrudgingly. He knew she'd sift out the reason eventually. "I can make gateways. At least, I could."

"Really? With your level of strength in the One Power?"

"Or lack of it?" he asked. She could sense a little of what he was thinking. Though he accepted his weakness, he worried that it made him unfit to lead. A curious mix of self-confidence and self-consciousness.

"Yes," he continued. "Traveling requires great strength in the One Power, but I can make large gateways. Before this all went wrong, the largest I ever made was a gateway thirty feet across."

Pevara blinked. "Surely you're exaggerating."

"I'd show you, if I could." He seemed completely honest. Either he was telling the truth, or his belief was due to his madness. She remained quiet, uncertain how to approach that.

"It's all right," he said. "I know that there are . . . things wrong with me. With most of us. You can ask the others about my gateways. There's a reason Coteren calls me pageboy. It's because the only thing I'm good at is delivering people from one place to another."

"That's a remarkable Talent, Androl. I'm certain the Tower would *love* to study it. I wonder how many people were born with it, but never knew, because the weaves for Traveling were unknown?"

"I'm not going to the White Tower, Pevara," he said, putting an emphasis on the *White*.

She changed the topic. "You long for Traveling, yet you don't want to leave the Black Tower. So what does this *ter'angreal* matter?"

"Gateways would be . . . useful," Androl said.

He thought something, but she couldn't catch hold of it. A quick flash of images and impressions.

"But if we're not going anywhere . . . " she protested.

"You'd be surprised," he said, raising his head to peer out over the windowsill at the alleyway. It was drizzling outside; the rain had finally let up. The sky was still dark, though. Dawn wouldn't come for a few hours yet. "I've been . . . experimenting. Trying a few things I don't think anyone else has ever tried."

"I doubt they are things that haven't *ever* been tried," she said. "The Forsaken had access to the knowledge of Ages."

"You really think one might be involved here?"

"Why not?" she asked. "If you were preparing for the Last Battle and wanted to make certain your enemies couldn't resist you, would you let a crop of channelers train together, teach one another and become strong?"

"Yes," he said softly. "I would, and then I'd steal them."

Pevara closed her mouth. That was probably right. Talking of the Forsaken troubled Androl; she could feel his thoughts, clearer than before.

This bond was unnatural. She needed to be rid of it. After that, she wouldn't mind having him properly bonded to her.

"I will *not* take responsibility for this situation, Pevara," Androl said, again looking out. "You bonded me first."

"After you betrayed the trust I gave you by offering a circle."

"I didn't hurt you. What did you *expect* to happen? Wasn't the purpose of a circle to allow us to join our powers?"

"This argument is pointless."

"You only say that because you're losing." He said it calmly, and he felt calm as well. She was coming to realize that Androl was a difficult man to rile.

"I say it because it's true," she said. "Do you disagree?"

She felt his amusement. He saw how she took control of the conversation. And . . . beside his amusement, he actually seemed impressed. He was thinking that he needed to learn to do what she did.

The inner door to the room creaked open, and Leish peered in. She was a white-haired woman, round and pleasant, an odd match for the surly Asha'man Canler, to whom she was married. She nodded to Pevara, indicating that half an hour had passed, then shut the door. Canler had reportedly bonded the woman, making her some kind of . . . what? Female Warder?

Everything was backward with these men. Pevara supposed she could see the reason for bonding one's spouse, if only so that each could have the comfort of knowing where the other was, but it felt wrong to use the bond in such a mundane way. This was a thing for Aes Sedai and Warders, not wives and husbands.

Androl regarded her, obviously trying to figure out what she was thinking—though these thoughts were complex enough to give him trouble. Such an odd man, this Androl Genhald. How did he so fully mix determination and diffidence, like two threads woven together? He did what needed to be done, all the while worrying that he shouldn't be the one doing it.

"I don't understand myself either," he said.

He was also *infuriating*. How had he grown so good at understanding what she was thinking? She still had to fish to figure out his thoughts.

"Can you think that again?" he asked. "I didn't catch it."

"Idiot," Pevara muttered.

Androl smiled, then peeked over the windowsill again.

"It's not time," Pevara said.

"You're sure?"

"Yes," she said. "And if you keep peeking, you might scare him off when he actually comes."

Androl reluctantly crouched down again.

"Now," Pevara said. "When he comes, you have to let me take the lead."

"We should link."

"No." She would *not* put herself in his hands again. Not after what had happened last time. She shivered, and Androl glanced at her.

"There are very good reasons," she said, "for not linking. I don't mean to insult you, Androl, but your ability isn't great enough to make the trade worthwhile. Better that there be two of us. You must accept this. On a battlefield, which would you rather have? One soldier? Or two—with one being only slightly less skilled— that you can send on different tasks and duties?"

He thought about it, then sighed. "All right, fine. You talk sense, this time."

"I always talk sense," she said, rising. "It's time. Be ready."

The two of them moved to either side of the doorway that led out into the alley. It stood open a crack by intention, the sturdy lock on the outside left hanging as if someone had forgotten to close it.

They waited silently, and Pevara began to worry that her calculations had been off. Androl would have a good laugh about that, and—

The door pushed open the rest of the way. Dobser poked his head in, lured by Evin's offhanded comment that he'd nicked a bottle of wine from the back room after finding that Leish had forgotten to lock the door. According to Androl, Dobser was a known drunkard, and Taim had beaten him senseless more than once for getting into the wine.

She could feel Androl's reaction to the man. Sadness. Deep, crushing sadness. Dobser had the darkness behind his eyes.

Pevara struck quickly, tying Dobser in Air and slamming a shield into place between the unsuspecting man and the Source. Androl hefted a cudgel, but it wasn't needed. Dobser grew wide-eyed as he was hoisted into the air; Pevara put her hands behind her back, regarding him critically.

"Are you certain about this?" Androl asked softly.

"Too late now, regardless," Pevara replied, tying off the weaves of Air. "The accounts *seem* to agree. The more dedicated a person was to the Light before being taken, the more dedicated they'll be to the Shadow after falling. And so . . ."

And so this man, who had always been rather lukewarm, *should* be easier to break, bribe or convert than others. That was important, as Taim's lackeys would likely realize what had happened as soon as—

"Dobser?" a voice asked. Two figures darkened the doorway. "Do you have the wine? No need to watch the front; the woman isn't—"

Welyn and another of Taim's favored, Leems, stood in the doorway.

Pevara reacted immediately, throwing weaves at the two men while forming a thread of Spirit. They rebuffed her attempts at shielding them—it was tough to get a shield between the Source and a person holding the One Power—but her gags snapped into place, stopping their yells.

She felt Air wrapping around her, a shield trying to come between her and the Source. She lashed out with Spirit, slicing down the weaves by guessing where they would be.

Leems stumbled back, looking surprised as his weaves vanished. Pevara threw herself forward, weaving another shield and smashing it between him and the Source as she slammed her body into him, throwing him back against the wall. The distraction worked, and her shield cut him off from the One Power.

She flung a second shield at Welyn, but he hit her with his own threads of Air. They hurled her backward across the room. She wove Air as she crashed into the wall, grunting. Her vision swam, but she kept hold of that single thread of Air and by instinct, sweeping it forward, grabbed Welyn's foot as he tried to run out of the building.

She felt the ground tremble from someone falling. He'd tripped, hadn't he? Dizzy, she couldn't see straight.

She sat up, aching all over, but clung to the threads of Air she'd woven as gags. Let those go, and Taim's men would be able to scream. If they did that, she died. They all died. Or worse.

She blinked the tears of pain from her eyes to find Androl

standing over the two Asha'man, cudgel in his hand. He'd knocked them both out, it appeared, not trusting in shields he couldn't see. Good thing, too, as her second shield hadn't gotten into place. She set it now.

Dobser still hung where she'd put him, his eyes wider now. Androl looked at Pevara. "Light!" he said. "Pevara, that was incredible. You brought down two Asha'man, practically by yourself!"

She smiled in satisfaction and woozily took Androl's hand, letting him help her to her feet. "What did you think the Red Ajah does with its time, Androl? Sit around and complain about men? We train to fight other channelers."

She felt Androl's respect as he busied himself, pulling Welyn into the building and shutting the door, then checking at the windows to make certain they hadn't been seen. He drew the shades quickly, then channeled to make a light.

Pevara took a breath, then raised a hand and steadied herself against the wall.

Androl looked up sharply. "We need to take you to one of the others for Healing."

"I'll be fine," she said. "Just took a thump to the head and it has the room shaking. It will wear off."

"Let me see," Androl said, walking over—his light hovering beside him. Pevara allowed him to putter about for a moment, checking her eyes, feeling her head for lumps. He moved his light closer to her eyes. "Does it hurt to look at this?"

"Yes," she admitted, glancing away.

"Nausea?"

"Slight."

He grunted, then took a handkerchief out of his pocket and poured some water on it from his flask. He adopted a look of concentration, and his light winked out. The handkerchief crackled softly, and when he handed it to her, it was frozen. "Hold this to the wound," he said. "Tell me if you start to feel drowsy. It could grow worse if you fall asleep."

"Are you worried for me?" she asked, amused, doing as he said.

"Just . . . what was it you told me earlier? Keeping watch over our assets?"

"I'm sure," she said, pressing the iced bandanna to her head. "So you know field medicine as well?"

"I apprenticed with a town's Wise Woman once," he said absently as he knelt to bind the fallen men. Pevara was glad to release the weaves of Air on them, though she did keep the shields up.

"A Wise Woman took on a *male* apprentice?"

"Not at first," Androl said. "It's . . . a long story."

"Excellent; a long story will keep me from falling asleep until the others come for us." Emarin and the others had been instructed to go and be seen, establishing an alibi for the group, in case Dobser's disappearance was noted.

Androl eyed her, replacing his light. Then he shrugged, continuing his work. "It started when I lost a friend to the fevers during a silverpike run out of Mayene. When I came back to the mainland, I started thinking that we could have saved Sayer if any of us had known what to do. So I went looking for someone who could teach me . . ."

CHAPTER 4

Advantages to a Bond

"And that was the end of it," Pevara said, sitting against the wall.

Androl could feel her emotions. They sat in the storeroom where they'd fought Taim's men, waiting for Emarin—who claimed he could make Dobser talk. Androl himself had little skill in interrogation. The scent of grain had changed to a rancid stench. It spoiled suddenly, sometimes.

Pevara had grown quiet, both outside and in, as she'd spoken of the murder of her family by longtime friends.

"I still hate them," she said. "I can think about my family without pain, but the Darkfriends ... I *hate* them. At least I have some vengeance, as the Dark One certainly didn't defend them. They spent all their lives following him, hoping for a place in his new world, only to have the Last Battle come long after their deaths. I suppose the ones living now won't be any better off. Once we win the Last Battle, he will have their souls. I hope their punishment is lengthy."

"You're so certain we will win?" Androl asked.

"Of course we will win. It's not a question, Androl. We can't afford to make it one."

He nodded. "You're right. Continue."

"There's no more to say. Odd, to tell the story after all these years. For a long while, I couldn't speak of it."

The room fell silent. Dobser hung in his bonds, facing the wall, his ears plugged by Pevara's weaves. The other two were still unconscious. Androl had hit them hard, and he intended to see that they didn't awaken anytime soon.

Pevara had shielded them, but she couldn't possibly maintain three shields at once if the men tried to break free. Aes Sedai usually used more than one sister to hold one man. Three would be impossible for any single channeler, strong or not. She could tie off those shields, but Taim had set the Asha'man at practicing how to escape a tied-off shield.

Yes, best to make certain the other two didn't wake. Useful though it would be just to cut their throats, he didn't have the stomach for it. Instead he sent a tiny thread of Spirit and Air to touch each of their eyelids. He had to use a single weave, and a weak one, but he managed to touch all of their eyes. If the lids cracked a tiny bit, he'd know. That would have to be enough.

Pevara was still thinking about her family. She had been telling the truth; she did hate the Darkfriends. All of them. It was a measured hate, not out of control, but it was still strong after all of these years.

He would not have suspected that in this woman who seemed so often to smile. He could sense that she hurt. And, oddly, that she felt . . . lonely.

"My father killed himself," Androl said, without really intending to.

She looked at him.

"My mother pretended it was an accident for years," Androl continued. "He did it out in the woods, leaped from a cliff. He'd sat down with her the night before and explained what he was going to do."

"She didn't try to stop him?" Pevara asked, aghast.

"No," Androl said. "Only a few years before she found the mother's last embrace, I was able to pry some answers out of her. She was frightened of him. That was shocking to me; he'd always been so gentle. What had changed, in those last few years, to make her fear him?" Androl turned to Pevara. "She said that he saw things in the shadows. That he'd started to go mad."

"Ah . . ."

"You asked me why I came to the Black Tower. You wanted to know why I *asked* to be tested. Well this thing that I am, it answers a question for me. It tells me who my father was, and why he did what he felt he needed to do.

"I can see the signs now. Our business did too well. Father could find quarries of stone and veins of metal when nobody else could. Men hired him to find valuable deposits for them. He was the best. Uncannily good. I could . . . see it in him at the end, Pevara. I was only ten, but I remember. The fear in his eyes. I *know* that fear now." He hesitated. "My father jumped off that cliff to save his family's lives."

"I'm sorry," Pevara said.

"Knowing what I am, what *he* was, helps."

It had started raining again, fat drops hitting the window like pebbles. The door into the shop opened, and Emarin, finally, peered in. He saw Dobser, hanging there, and looked relieved. Then he saw the other two and started. "What have you two done?"

"What needed to be done," Androl said, standing. "What took you so long?"

"I nearly started another confrontation with Coteren," Emarin said, still staring at the two captive Asha'man. "I think our time is short, Androl. We didn't let them goad us, but Coteren seemed annoyed—more so than normal. I don't think they're going to tolerate us much longer."

"Well, these captives put us on a countdown anyway," Pevara said, moving Dobser over to make room for Emarin. "You really think you can make this man talk? I've tried interrogating Darkfriends before. They can be tough to crack."

"Ah," Emarin said, "but this is *not* a Darkfriend. This is Dobser."

"I don't think it's really him," Androl said, studying the man floating in his bonds. "I can't accept that someone can be *made* to serve the Dark One."

He could sense Pevara's disagreement; she really did think that was how it happened. Anyone who could channel could be Turned, she'd explained. The old texts spoke of it.

The idea made Androl want to sick up. Forcing someone to be evil? That shouldn't be possible. Fate moved people about, put them in terrible positions, cost them their lives, sometimes their sanity. But the choice to serve the Dark One or the Light ... surely that one choice could not be taken from a person.

The shadow he saw behind Dobser's eyes was enough proof for Androl. The man he'd known was gone, killed, and something else—something evil—had been put into his body. A new soul. It had to be that.

"Whatever he is," Pevara said, "I'm still skeptical that you can force him to speak."

"The best persuasions," Emarin said, hands clasped behind his back, "are those that aren't forced. Pevara Sedai, if you would be so kind as to remove the weaves blocking his ears so that he can start to hear—but only remove them in the most minor way, as if the weave has been tied off and is failing. I want him to overhear what I'm about to say."

She complied. At least, Androl assumed she did. Being double-bonded didn't mean they could see one another's weaves. He could feel her anxiety, however. She was thinking of Darkfriends she'd interrogated, and was wishing for ... something. A tool she'd used against them?

"I do think we can hide at my estates," Emarin said in a haughty voice.

Androl blinked. The man held himself taller, more proudly, more ... authoritatively. His voice became powerful, dismissive. Just like that, he had become a nobleman.

"No one will think to look for us there," Emarin continued. "I will accept you as my associates, and the lesser among us—young Evin, for instance—can enter my employ as servants. If we play our hand correctly, we can build up a rival Black Tower."

"I ... don't know how wise that would be," Androl said, playing along.

"Silence," Emarin said. "I will ask your opinion when it is required. Aes Sedai, the *only* way we will rival the White and Black Towers is if we create a place where male and female channelers work together. A ... Gray Tower, if you will."

"It is an interesting proposal."

"It is the only thing that makes sense," Emarin said, then turned to their captive. "He cannot hear what we say?"

"No," Pevara said.

"Release him, then. I would speak to him."

Pevara hesitantly did as instructed. Dobser dropped to the floor, barely catching himself. He stumbled for a moment, unsteady on his feet, then immediately glanced toward the exit.

Emarin reached behind his back, pulled something from his belt and tossed it to the floor. A small sack. It clinked as it hit. "Master Dobser," Emarin said.

"What's this?" Dobser asked, tentatively crouching down, taking the sack. He peeked into it, and his eyes widened noticeably.

"Payment," Emarin said.

Dobser narrowed his eyes. "To do what?"

"You mistake me, Master Dobser," Emarin said. "I'm not asking you to do anything, I'm paying you in apology. I sent Androl here to request your aid, and he seems to have ... overstepped the bounds of his instructions. I merely wished to speak with you. I did not intend to see you wrapped up in Air and tormented."

Dobser glanced about himself, suspicious. "Where'd you find money like this, Emarin? What makes you think you can start giving orders? You're just a soldier ... " He looked at the pouch's contents again.

"I see that we understand each other," Emarin said, smiling. "You'll maintain my front for me, then?"

"I ... " Dobser frowned. He looked at Welyn and Leems, lying unconscious on the floor.

"Yes," Emarin said. "That *is* going to be a problem, isn't it? You don't suppose we could just give Androl to Taim and blame him for this?"

"Androl?" Dobser said, snorting. "The pageboy? Taking down two Asha'man? Nobody would believe it. Nobody."

"A valid point, Master Dobser," Emarin said.

"Just give 'em the Aes Sedai," Dobser said, jerking a finger toward her.

"Alas, I have need of her. A mess, this is. A pure mess."

"Well," Dobser said, "maybe I could talk to the M'Hael for you. You know, straighten it out."

"That would be much appreciated," Emarin said, taking a chair from beside the wall and setting it down, then placing another before it. He sat, waving for Dobser to sit down. "Androl, make yourself useful. Find something for Master Dobser and me to drink. Tea. You like sugar?"

"No," Dobser said. "Actually, I heard there was wine round here somewhere . . ."

"Wine, Androl," Emarin said, snapping his fingers.

Well, Androl thought, *best to play the part.* He bowed, shooting Dobser a calculated glare, then fetched some cups and wine from the storeroom. When he returned, Dobser and Emarin were chatting amicably.

"I understand," Emarin said. "I have had *such* trouble finding proper help inside the Black Tower. You see, the need to preserve my identity is *imperative*."

"I can see that, m'Lord," Dobser said. "Why, if anyone else knew a High Lord of Tear was among our ranks, there'd be no end to the boot licking. That I can tell you! And the M'Hael, well, he wouldn't like someone with so much authority being here. No, not at all!"

"You see why I had to maintain my distance," Emarin explained, holding out a hand and accepting a cup of wine as Androl poured it.

A High Lord of Tear? Androl thought, amused. Dobser seemed to be drinking it in as he did strong liquor.

"And we all thought you were fawning over Logain because you was stupid!" Dobser said.

"Alas, the lot I've been given. Taim would see through me in a moment if I were to spend too much time around him. So I was forced to go with Logain. He and that Dragon fellow, both are obviously farmers and wouldn't recognize a highborn man."

"I'll say, m'Lord," Dobser said, "I was suspicious."

"As I thought," Emarin said, taking a sip of the wine. "To prove it's not poisoned," he explained, before passing the cup to Dobser.

"'S all right, m'Lord," Dobser said. "I trust you." He gulped down the wine. "If you can't trust a High Lord himself, who can you trust, right?"

"Quite right," Emarin said.

"I can tell you this," Dobser said, holding out his cup and wagging it for Androl to refill, "you'll need to find a better way of

keeping away from Taim. Following Logain won't work anymore."

Emarin took a long, contemplative sip from his cup of wine.
"Taim has him. I see. I did guess it would be so. Welyn and the
others showing up tells the tale."

"Yeah," Dobser said, letting Androl refill his cup again.
"Logain is a strong one, though. Takes a lot of work to Turn a
man like him. Willpower, you know? It will be a day or two to
Turn him. Anyway, you might as well come out to Taim, explain
what you're up to. He'll understand, and he keeps saying men are
more useful to him if he doesn't have to Turn them. Don't know
why. No choice but to Turn Logain, though. Awful process."
Dobser shivered.

"I'll go and speak with him then, Master Dobser. Would you
vouch for me, by chance? I'll ... see you paid for the effort."

"Sure, sure," Dobser said. "Why not?" He downed his wine,
then lurched to his feet. "He'll be checking on Logain. Always
does, this time of night."

"And that would be where?" Emarin said.

"The hidden rooms," Dobser said. "In the foundations we're
building. You know the eastern section, where the collapse made
all of that extra digging? That was no collapse, just an excuse for
covering up extra work being done. And ... " Dobser hesitated.

"And that's enough," Pevara said, tying the man up in air again
and stopping his ears. She folded her arms, looking at Emarin.
"I'm impressed."

Emarin spread his hands apart in a gesture of humility. "I have
always had a talent for making men feel at ease. In truth, I didn't
suggest picking Dobser because I thought he'd be easy to bribe.
I picked him because of his ... well, understated powers of cog-
nitive expression."

"Turning someone to the Shadow doesn't make him any less
stupid," Androl said. "But if you could do this, why did we have
to jump him in the first place?"

"It's a matter of controlling the situation, Androl," Emarin
said. "A man like Dobser mustn't be confronted in his element,
surrounded by friends with more wits than he. We had to scare
him, make him writhe, then offer him a way to wiggle out."
Emarin hesitated, glancing at Dobser. "Besides, I don't think we

wanted to risk him going to Taim, which he very well might have done if I'd approached him in private without the threat of violence."

"And now?" Pevara asked.

"Now," Androl said, "we douse these three with something that will keep them sleeping until Bel Tine. We gather Nalaam, Canler, Evin and Jonneth. We wait for Taim to finish his inspection of Logain; we break in, rescue him and seize the Tower back from the Shadow."

They stood in silence for a moment, the room lit only by the single, flickering lamp. Rain sprayed the window.

"Well," Pevara said, "so long as it's not a *difficult* task you're proposing, Androl . . ."

Rand opened his eyes to the dream, somewhat surprised to find that he had fallen asleep. Aviendha had finally let him doze. In truth, she was probably letting herself doze as well. She'd seemed as tired as he had. More, perhaps.

He climbed to his feet in the meadow of dead grass. He had been able to sense her concern not only through the bond but in the way she had held him. Aviendha was a fighter, a warrior, but even a warrior needed something to hold on to once in a while. Light knew that he did.

He looked about. This didn't feel like *Tel'aran'rhiod*, not completely. The dead field extended into the distance on all sides, presumably into infinity. This wasn't the true World of Dreams; it was a dreamshard, a world created by a powerful Dreamer or dreamwalker.

Rand began walking, feet crunching on dead leaves, though there were no trees. He could probably have sent himself back to his own dreams; though he had never been as good as many of the Forsaken at walking dreams, he could manage that much. Curiosity drove him forward.

I shouldn't be here, he thought. *I set wards.* How had he come to this place and who had created it? He had a suspicion. There was one person who had often made use of dreamshards.

Rand felt a presence nearby. He continued walking, not turning, but knew that someone was now walking beside him.

"Elan," Rand said.

"Lews Therin." Elan still wore his newest body, the tall, handsome man who wore red and black. "It dies, and the dust soon will rule. The dust . . . then nothing."

"How did you pass my wards?"

"I don't know," Moridin said. "I knew that if I created this place, you would join me in it. You can't keep away from me. The Pattern won't allow it. We are drawn together, you and I. Time after time after time. Two ships moored on the same beach, beating against one another with each new tide."

"Poetic," Rand said. "You've finally let Mierin off her leash, I've seen."

Moridin stopped, and Rand paused, looking at him. The man's rage seemed to come off him in waves of heat.

"She came to you?" Moridin demanded.

Rand said nothing.

"Do not *pretend* that you knew she still lived. You didn't know, you couldn't have known."

Rand kept still. His emotions regarding Lanfear—or whatever she called herself now—were complicated. Lews Therin had despised her, but Rand had known her primarily as Selene, and had been fond of her—until, at least, she tried to kill Egwene and Aviendha.

Thinking of her made him think of Moiraine, made him *hope* for things he shouldn't hope for.

If Lanfear still lives . . . might Moiraine as well?

He faced Moridin with calm confidence. "Loosing her is pointless, now," Rand said. "She no longer holds any power over me."

"Yes," Moridin said. "I believe you. She does not, but I do think she still harbors something of a . . . grievance with the woman you chose. What is her name again? The one who calls herself Aiel but carries weapons?"

Rand did not rise to the attempt to rile him.

"Mierin hates you now, anyway," Moridin continued. "I think she blames you for what happened to her. You should call her Cyndane. She has been forbidden to use the name she took upon herself."

"Cyndane . . ." Rand said, trying out the word. "'Last Chance'? Your master has gained humor, I see."

"It was not meant to be humorous," Moridin said.

"No, I suppose that it was not." Rand looked at the endless landscape of dead grass and leaves. "It is hard to think that I was so afraid of you during those early days. Did you invade my dreams then, or bring me into one of these dreamshards? I was never able to figure it out."

Moridin said nothing.

"I remember one time . . . " Rand said. "Sitting up by the fire, surrounded by nightmares that felt like *Tel'aran'rhiod*. You would not have been able to pull someone fully into the World of Dreams, yet I'm no dreamwalker, able to enter on my own."

Moridin, like many of the Forsaken, had usually entered *Tel'aran'rhiod* in the flesh, which was dangerous. Some said that entering in the flesh was an evil thing, that it lost you a part of your humanity. It also made you more powerful.

Moridin gave no clue as to what had happened on that night. Rand remembered those days faintly, traveling toward Tear. He remembered visions in the night, visions of his friends or family that would try to kill him. Moridin . . . Ishamael . . . had been pulling him against his will into dreams intersecting *Tel'aran'rhiod*.

"You were mad, during those days," Rand said softly, looking into Moridin's eyes. He could almost see the fires burning there. "You're still mad, aren't you? You just have it contained. No one could serve him without being at least a little mad."

Moridin stepped forward. "Taunt as you wish, Lews Therin. The ending dawns. All will be given to the great suffocation of the Shadow, to be stretched, ripped, *strangled*."

Rand took a step forward as well, right up to Moridin. They were the same height. "You hate yourself," Rand whispered. "I can *feel* it in you, Elan. Once you served him for power; now you do it because his victory—and an end to all things—is the only release you'll ever know. You'd rather not exist than continue to be you. You must know that he will not release you. Not ever. Not you."

Moridin sneered. "He'll let me kill you before this ends, Lews Therin. You, and the golden-haired one, and the Aiel woman, and the little dark-haired—"

"You act as if this is a contest between you and me, Elan," Rand interrupted.

Moridin laughed, throwing his head back. "Of course it is! Haven't you seen that *yet*? By the blood falls, Lews Therin! It is about us two. Just as in Ages past, over and over, we fight one another. You and I."

"No," Rand said. "Not this time. I'm done with you. I have a greater battle to fight."

"Don't try to—"

Sunlight exploded through the clouds above. There was often no sunlight in the World of Dreams, but now it bathed the area around Rand.

Moridin stumbled back. He looked up at the light, then gazed at Rand and narrowed his eyes. "Don't think ... don't think I will believe your simple tricks, Lews Therin. Weiramon was shaken by what you did to him, but it's not such a difficult thing, holding *saidin* and listening for people's heartbeats to speed up."

Rand exerted his will. The crackling dead leaves began to transform at his feet, turning green again, and shoots of grass broke through the leaves. The green spread from him like spilled paint, and clouds above boiled away.

Moridin's eyes opened wider. He stumbled, staring at the sky as the clouds retreated ... Rand could feel his shock. This was *Moridin's* dreamshard.

However, to draw another in, he had had to place it close to *Tel'aran'rhiod*. Those rules applied. There was something else, too, something about the connection between the two of them ...

Rand strode forward, lifting his arms out to the sides. Grass sprouted in waves, red blossoms burst from the ground like a blush upon the land. The storm stilled, the dark clouds burned away by light.

"Tell your master!" Rand commanded. "Tell him this fight is not like the others. Tell him I've tired of minions, that I'm finished with his petty movement of pawns. Tell him that *I'm coming for HIM*!"

"This is wrong," Moridin said, visibly shaken. "This isn't ..." He looked at Rand for a moment, standing beneath the blazing sun, then vanished.

Rand let out a deep breath. The grass died around him, the clouds sprang back, the sunlight faded. Though Moridin was gone, holding on to that transformation of the landscape had been difficult. Rand sagged, panting, recovering from the exertion.

Here, willing something to be true could make it so. If only things were that simple in the real world.

He closed his eyes and sent himself away, to sleep for the short time before he had to rise. Rise, and save the world. If he could.

Pevara crouched beside Androl in the rainy night. Her cloak was soaked completely through. She knew a couple of weaves that would have been useful for that, but she didn't dare channel. She and the others would be facing Turned Aes Sedai and women of the Black Ajah. They could sense it if she channeled.

"They're definitely guarding the area," Androl whispered. Ahead of them, the ground broke away into a large sequence of mazelike brickworks and trenches. These were the foundation rooms of what would eventually become the Black Tower proper. If Dobser was right, other rooms had been created within the foundation—hidden chambers, already complete, that would continue to be secret as the Tower itself was constructed.

A pair of Taim's Asha'man stood chatting nearby. Though they tried to appear nonchalant, the effect was spoiled by the weather. Who would *choose* to stand outside on a night like this one? Despite a warm brazier lighting them and a weave of Air to send the rain streaming away, their presence was suspicious.

Guards. Pevara tried sending the thought to Androl directly.

It worked. She could feel his surprise as the thought intruded onto his own.

Something returned, fuzzy. *We should take advantage.*

Yes, she sent back. The next thought was too complex, though, so she whispered it. "How have you never before noticed that he left the foundation guarded at night? If there really are secret rooms, then the work on them would be done at night as well."

"Taim set a curfew," Androl whispered. "He lets us ignore it only when convenient to him—such as for Welyn's return tonight. Besides, this area is dangerous, with those pits and trenches. It would be a good enough reason to set guards, except . . ."

"Except," Pevara said, "Taim isn't exactly the type to care if a child or two break their necks poking around."

Androl nodded.

Pevara and Androl waited in the rain, counting their breaths, until three ribbons of fire flew from the night and struck the guards directly in their heads. The two Asha'man dropped like sacks of grain. Nalaam, Emarin and Jonneth had done their work perfectly. Quick channeling; with luck, it either wouldn't be noticed or would be thought the work of Taim's men on guard.

Light, Pevara thought. *Androl and the others really are weapons.* She hadn't stopped to consider that Emarin and the others would lead with lethal attacks. It was completely outside her experience as an Aes Sedai. Aes Sedai didn't even kill false Dragons if they could help it.

"Gentling kills," Androl said, eyes forward. "Albeit slowly."

Light. Yes, there might be advantages to their bond—but it was also blasted inconvenient. She would have to practice shielding her thoughts.

Emarin and the others came in from the darkness, joining Pevara and Androl at the brazier. Canler remained behind, with the other Two Rivers lads, ready to lead them from the Black Tower in an escape attempt if something went wrong tonight. It made sense to leave him, despite his protests. He had a family.

They dragged the corpses into the shadows, but left the brazier burning. Someone looking for the guards would see that the light was still there, but the night was so misty and rainy one would have to draw close to realize that its attendants had vanished.

Though he often complained that he didn't know why the others followed him, Androl immediately took charge of this group, sending Nalaam and Jonneth to watch at the edge of the foundation. Jonneth carried his bow, unstrung in the wet night. They were hoping the rain would let up, and that he'd be able to use it when they couldn't risk channeling.

Androl, Pevara and Emarin slid down one of the muddy slopes into the foundation pits that had been dug. Mud splashed over her as she landed, but she was already soaked, and the rain washed away the grime.

The foundation was made of stones built up to form walls between rooms and hallways; down here, this became a labyrinth, with a steady stream of rain falling from above. In the morning, the Asha'man soldiers would be set to drying out the foundation.

How do we find the entrance? Pevara sent.

Androl knelt, a very small globe of light hovering above his hand. Drops of rain passed through the light, looking like tiny meteorites for a moment as they flashed and vanished. He rested fingers in the pooling water on the ground.

He looked up, then pointed. "It runs this way," he whispered. "It's going somewhere. That is where we'll find Taim."

Emarin grunted appreciatively. Androl raised a hand, summoning Jonneth and Nalaam down into the foundation with them, then led the way, stepping softly.

You. Quietly. Move. Well, she sent.

Trained as scout, he sent back. *In woods. Mountains of Mist.*

How many jobs had he done in his life? She had worried about him. A life such as he had led could indicate a dissatisfaction with the world, an impatience. The way he spoke of the Black Tower, though ... the passion with which he was willing to fight ... that said something different. This wasn't just about a loyalty to Logain. Yes, Androl and the others respected Logain, but to them, he represented something far greater. A place where men like them were accepted.

A life like Androl's *could* indicate a man who would not commit or be satisfied, but it could also indicate something else: a man who searched. A man who knew that the life he wanted existed out there. He just had to find it.

"They teach you to analyze people like that in the White Tower?" Androl whispered to her as he stopped beside a doorway and moved his globe of light in, then waved the others to follow.

No, she sent back, trying to practice this method of communicating, to make her thoughts smoother. *Is something a woman picks up after her first century of life.*

He sent back tense amusement. They passed into a series of unfinished rooms, none of them roofed, before reaching a section of unworked earth. Some barrels here held pitch, but they had been shifted to the side and the boards they normally sat upon had been pulled away. A pit opened in the ground here. The water trailed over the lip of the pit and down into darkness. Androl knelt and listened, then nodded to the others before slipping down into it. His splash came a second later.

Pevara followed him, dropping only a few feet. The water was

cold on her feet, but she was already soaked. Androl hunched,
leading the way under an earthen overhang, then stood up on the
other side. His little globe of light revealed a tunnel. A trench
had been dug here to hold the rainwater. Pevara judged they'd
been standing directly above this when they'd taken down the
guards.

Dobser right, she sent as the others splashed down behind. *Taim
building secret tunnels and chambers.*

They crossed the trench and continued on. A short distance
down the tunnel, they reached an intersection where the earthen
walls were shored up, like the shafts of a mine. The five of them
gathered there, looking in one direction, then another. Two paths.

"That way slopes upward," Emarin whispered, pointing left.
"Perhaps to another entrance into these tunnels?"

"We should probably move deeper," Nalaam said. "Don't you
think?"

"Yes," Androl said, licking his finger and testing the air. "The
wind is blowing right. We'll go that way first. Be careful. There
will be other guards."

The group slipped further down into the tunnels. How long
had Taim been working on this complex? It didn't seem terribly
extensive—they didn't pass other branchings—but still, it was
impressive.

Suddenly Androl stopped, and the others pulled to a halt. A
grumbling voice echoed up the tunnel, too soft for them to make
out the words, accompanied by a flickering light on the walls.
Pevara embraced the Source and prepared weaves. If she channeled, would someone in the foundation notice? Androl was
obviously hesitant as well; channeling above, to kill the guards,
had been suspicious enough. If Taim's men down here sensed the
One Power being used . . .

The figure was approaching, the light illuminating him.

A creak came from beside her, as Jonneth drew his restrung
Two Rivers bow. There was barely room in the tunnel for it. He
loosed with a snap, the air whistling. The grumbling cut off, and
the light fell.

The group scrambled forward to find Coteren down on the
ground, eyes staring up glassily, the arrow through his chest. His
lantern burned fitfully on the ground beside him. Jonneth

retrieved his arrow, then wiped it on the dead man's clothing. *"That's* why I still carry a bow, you bloody son of a goat."

"Here," Emarin said, pointing at a thick door. "Coteren was guarding it."

"Prepare yourselves," Androl whispered, then shoved open the thick wooden door. Beyond, they found a line of crude cells built into the earthen wall—each one little more than a roofed cubbyhole burrowed into the earth with a door set in the opening. Pevara peeked in one, which was empty. The cubby didn't have enough room for a man to stand up inside, and the room was unlit. Being locked in those cells would mean being trapped in blackness, squeezed into a space like a grave.

"Light!" Nalaam said. "Androl! He's in here. It's Logain!"

The others hurried to join him, and Androl picked the door's lock with a surprisingly adept hand. They pulled open the cell door, and Logain rolled out with a groan. He looked horrible, covered in grime. Once, that curling dark hair and strong face might have made him handsome. He looked as weak as a beggar.

He coughed, then rose to his knees with Nalaam's help. Androl knelt immediately, but not in reverence. He looked Logain in the eyes as Emarin gave the Asha'man leader his flask for a drink.

Well? Pevara asked.

It's him, Androl thought, a wave of relief coming through the bond. *It's still him.*

They'd have let him go if they'd Turned him, Pevara sent back, growing increasingly comfortable with this method of communicating.

Maybe. Unless this is a trap. "My Lord Logain."

"Androl." Logain's voice was raspy. "Jonneth. Nalaam. And an Aes Sedai?" He inspected Pevara. For a man who had apparently suffered days, perhaps weeks, of incarceration, he looked remarkably lucid. "I remember you. What Ajah are you, woman?"

"Does it matter?" she replied.

"Greatly," Logain said, trying to stand. He was too weak, and Nalaam had to support him. "How did you find me?"

"That is a story for once we are safe, my Lord," Androl said. He peeked out the doorway. "Let's move. We still have a difficult night ahead of us. I—"

Androl froze, then slammed the door.

"What is it?" Pevara asked.

"Channeling," Jonneth said. "Powerful."

Yells, muffled by the door and the dirt walls, sounded outside in the hallway.

"Someone found the guards," Emarin said. "My Lord Logain, can you fight?"

Logain tried to stand on his own, then sagged again. His face grew determined, but Pevara felt Androl's disappointment. Logain had been given forkroot; either that, or he was simply too tired to channel. Not surprising. Pevara had seen women in better shape than this who were too worn out to embrace the Source.

"Back!" Androl shouted, stepping to the side of the door— against the earthen wall. The door exploded in a weave of fire and destruction.

Pevara didn't wait for the debris to settle; she wove Fire and released a column of destruction down the corridor beyond. She knew she was facing Darkfriends, or worse. The Three Oaths did not hinder her here.

She heard shouts, but something deflected the fire. Immediately, a shield tried to slam between her and the Source. She fought it off, barely, and ducked to the side, breathing deeply.

"Whoever it is, they're strong," Pevara said.

A voice called orders distantly, echoing in the tunnels.

Jonneth knelt down beside her, bow out. "Light, that's Taim's voice!"

"We cannot stand here," Logain said. "Androl. A gateway."

"I'm trying," Androl said. "Light, I'm trying!"

"Bah," Nalaam set Logain down beside the wall. "I've been in tighter spots before!" He joined the others at the doorway, flinging weaves down the corridor. Blasts shook the side walls, and dirt rained down from the roof above.

Pevara jumped in front of the doorway, releasing a weave, then knelt down beside Androl. He stared ahead, not seeing, face a mask of concentration. She could feel determination and frustration pulsing through the bond. She took his hand.

"You can do it," she whispered.

The doorway erupted, and Jonneth fell back, arm burned. The ground trembled; the walls started to break apart.

Sweat dripped down the sides of Androl's face. He gritted his teeth, his face going red, eyes opening wide. Smoke poured through the doorway, making Emarin cough as Nalaam Healed Jonneth.

Androl yelled, and he neared the top of that wall in his mind. He was almost there! He could—

A weave *thumped* against the room, a ripple in the earth, and the strained roof finally gave out. Earth poured down atop them, and all went black.

CHAPTER

5

To Require a Boon

Rand al'Thor awoke and drew in a deep breath. He slipped from the blankets in his tent, leaving Aviendha slumbering there, and threw on a robe. The air smelled wet.

He was reminded, in passing, of mornings during his youth, rising before dawn to milk the cow, which would need milking twice a day. Eyes closed, he remembered the sounds of Tam—already up—cutting new fence posts in the barn. Remembering the chilly air, stomping his feet into his boots, washing his face with water left to warm beside the stove.

On any morning, a farmer could open his door and look out on a world that was still new. Crisp frost. The first, tentative calls of birds. Sunlight breaking the horizon, like the morning yawn of the world.

Rand stepped up to the flaps of his tent and drew them back, nodding to Katerin, a short, golden-haired Maiden who was on guard. He looked out on a world that was far from new. This world was old and tired, like a peddler who had been to the Spine of the World and back on foot. Tents crowded the Field of Merrilor, cook fires trailing pillars of smoke toward the still-dark morning sky.

Everywhere, men worked. Soldiers oiled armor. Smiths sharpened spearheads. Women prepared feathers for fletching arrows. Breakfasts were served from meal wagons to men who should have slept better than they had. Everyone knew these were their last moments before the storm arrived.

Rand closed his eyes. He could *feel* it, the land itself, like a faint Warder bond. Beneath his feet, grubs crawled through the soil. The roots of the grasses continued to spread, ever so slowly, seeking nutrients. The skeletal trees were not dead, for water seeped through them. They slumbered. Bluebirds clustered in a nearby tree. They did not call out with the arrival of dawn. They huddled together, as if for warmth.

The land still lived. It lived like a man clinging to the edge of a cliff by his fingertips.

Rand opened his eyes. "Have my clerks returned from Tear?"

"Yes, Rand al'Thor," said Katerin.

"Send word to the other rulers," Rand said. "I will meet with them in one hour at the center of the field where I commanded no tents be placed."

Katerin went off to relay his command, leaving three other Maidens nearby to guard. Rand let the tent flaps close in front of him and turned around, then jumped as he found Aviendha—as bare as the day she'd been born—standing in the tent.

"It is very difficult to sneak up on you, Rand al'Thor," she announced with a smile. "The bond gives you too much of an advantage. I have to move very slowly, like a lizard at midnight, so that your sense of where I am does not change too quickly."

"Light, Aviendha! Why do you need to sneak up on me in the first place?"

"For this," she said, then jumped forward, snatching his head and kissing him, her body pressed against his.

He relaxed, letting the kiss linger. "Unsurprisingly," he mumbled around her lips, "this is much more fun now that I don't have to worry about freezing my bits off while doing it."

Aviendha pulled back. "You should not speak of that event, Rand al'Thor."

"But—"

"My *toh* is paid, and I am now first-sister to Elayne. Do not remind me of a shame that is forgotten."

Shame? Why would she be ashamed of that when just now . . .
He shook his head. He could hear the land breathing, could sense
a beetle on a leaf half a league away, but sometimes he could not
fathom Aiel. Or maybe it was just women.

In this case, it was probably both.

Aviendha hesitated beside the tent's barrel of fresh water. "I
suppose that we will not have time for a bath."

"Oh, you like baths now?"

"I have accepted them as a part of life," she said. "If I am going
to live in the wetlands, then I will adopt some wetlander customs.
When they are not foolish." Her tone indicated that most of them
were.

"What's wrong?" Rand asked, stepping up to her.

"Wrong?"

"Something bothers you, Aviendha. I can see it in you, feel it
in you."

She looked him over with a critical eye. Light, but she was
beautiful. "You were much easier to manage before you received
the ancient wisdom of your former self, Rand al'Thor."

"I was?" he asked, smiling. "You didn't act that way at the
time."

"That was when I was as a new child, inexperienced in Rand
al'Thor's boundless capacity to be frustrating." She dipped her
hands into the water and washed her face. "It is well; if I had
known some of what was to come with you, I might have put on
the white and never removed it."

He smiled, then channeled, weaving Water and drawing the
liquid from the barrel in a stream. Aviendha stepped back, watching with curiosity.

"You no longer seem bothered by the idea of a man channeling," he noted as he fanned the water out into the air and heated
it with a thread of Fire.

"There is no longer a reason to be bothered. If I were to be
uncomfortable with you channeling, I would be behaving like a
man refusing to forget a woman's shame after her *toh* has been
met." She eyed him.

"I can't imagine anyone being that crass," he said, tossing aside
his robe and stepping up to her. "Here. This is a relic from that
'ancient wisdom' you apparently find so frustrating."

He brought the water in, warmed perfectly, and shattered it into a thick misting spray that wove about them in a rush. Aviendha gasped, clutching his arm. She might be growing more comfortable with wetlander ways, but water still made her both uncomfortable and reverent.

Rand snatched some soap with Air and shaved it into part of the mix of water, sending a spinning whirl of bubbles around them, swirling up their bodies and pulling their hair into the air, twisting Aviendha's about like a column before dropping it back lightly to her shoulders.

He used another wave of warm water to remove the soap, then pulled most of the wetness away, leaving them damp but not soaked. He dumped the water back into the barrel and, with a hint of reluctance, released *saidin*.

Aviendha was panting. "That ... That was completely crackbrained and irresponsible."

"Thank you," he said, fetching a towel and tossing it to her. "You would consider most of what we did during the Age of Legends to be crackbrained and irresponsible. That was a different time, Aviendha. There were many more channelers, and we were trained from a young age. We didn't need to know things like warfare, or how to kill. We had eliminated pain, hunger, suffering, war. Instead, we used the One Power for things that might seem common."

"You'd only assumed that you'd eliminated war," Aviendha said with a sniff. "You were wrong. Your ignorance left you weak."

"It did. I can't decide if I would have changed things, though. There were many good years. Good decades, good centuries. We believed we were living in paradise. Perhaps that was our downfall. We wanted our lives to be perfect, so we ignored imperfections. Problems were magnified through inattention, and war might have become inevitable if the Bore hadn't ever been made." He toweled himself dry.

"Rand," Aviendha said, stepping up to him. "Today, I will require a boon." She laid her hand on his arm. The skin of her hand was rough, callused from her days as a Maiden. Aviendha would never be a milk-softened lady like those from the courts of Cairhien and Tear. Rand liked that just fine. Hers were hands that had known work.

"What boon?" he asked. "I'm not certain I could deny you anything today, Aviendha."

"I'm not yet certain what it will be."

"I don't understand."

"You needn't understand," she said. "And you needn't promise me you will agree. I felt I needed to give you warning, as one does not ambush a lover. My boon will require you to change your plans, perhaps in a drastic way, and it will be important."

"All right . . ."

She nodded, as mystifying as ever, and began gathering up her clothing to dress for the day.

Egwene strode around a frozen pillar of glass in her dream. It almost looked like a column of light. What did it mean? She could not interpret it.

The vision changed, and she found a sphere. The world, she knew somehow. Cracking. Frantic, she tied it with cords, striving to hold it together. She could keep it from breaking, but it took so much effort . . .

She faded from the dream and started awake. She embraced the Source immediately and wove a light. Where was she?

She was wearing a nightgown and lying in bed back in the White Tower. Not her own rooms, which were still in disrepair following the assassins' attack. Her study had a small sleeping chamber, and she'd bedded down in that.

Her head pounded. She could vaguely remember growing bleary-eyed the night before, listening in her tent at the Field of Merrilor to reports of Caemlyn's fall. At some point during the late hours of the night, Gawyn had insisted that Nynaeve make a gateway back to the White Tower so Egwene could sleep in a bed, rather than on a pallet on the ground.

She grumbled to herself, rising. He'd probably been right, though she could remember feeling *distinctly* annoyed at his tone. Nobody had corrected him on it, not even Nynaeve. She rubbed at her temples. The headache wasn't as bad as those she'd had when Halima had been "caring" for her, but it did hurt mightily. Undoubtedly, her body was expressing displeasure at the lack of sleep she'd given it in recent weeks.

A short time later—dressed, washed and feeling a *little* better—she left her rooms to find Gawyn sitting at Silviana's desk, looking over a report, ignoring a novice who was lingering near the doorway.

"She'd hang you out the window by your toes if she saw you doing that," Egwene said dryly.

Gawyn jumped. "It's not a report from her stack," he protested. "It's the latest news from my sister about Caemlyn. It came by gateway for you just a few minutes ago."

"And you're reading it?"

He blushed. "Burn me, Egwene. It's my *home*. It wasn't sealed. I thought . . ."

"It's all right, Gawyn," she said with a sigh. "Let's see what it says."

"There's not much," he said with a grimace, handing it to her. At a nod from him the novice scurried away. A short time later, the girl came back with a tray of wizened bellfruit, bread and a pitcher of milk.

Egwene sat down at her desk in the study to eat, feeling guilty as the novice left. The bulk of the Tower's Aes Sedai and soldiers camped in tents on the Field of Merrilor while she dined on fruit, no matter how old, and slept in a comfortable bed?

Still, Gawyn's arguments had made sense. If everyone thought she was in her tent on the Field, then potential killers would strike there. After her near-death at the hands of the Seanchan assassins, she was willing to accept a few extra precautions. Particularly those that helped her get a good night's sleep.

"That Seanchan woman," Egwene said, staring into her cup. "The one with the Illianer. Did you speak with her?"

He nodded. "I have some Tower guards watching the pair. Nynaeve vouched for them, in a way."

"In a way?"

"She called the woman several variations of wool-headed, but said she probably wouldn't do you any *intentional* harm."

"Wonderful." Well, Egwene could make use of a Seanchan who was willing to talk. Light. What if she had to fight them and the Trollocs at the same time?

"You didn't take your own advice," she said, noting Gawyn's red eyes as he sat down in the chair in front of her desk.

"Someone had to watch the door," he said. "Calling for guards would have let everyone know that you were not at the Field."

She took a bite of her bread—what *had* it been made of?—and looked over the report. He was right, but she didn't like the idea of him going without sleep on a day like this. The Warder bond would only help him so far.

"So the city is truly gone," she said. "Walls breached, palace seized. The Trollocs didn't burn all of the city, I see. Much of it, but not all."

"Yes," Gawyn said. "But it is obvious that Caemlyn is lost." She felt his tension through the bond.

"I'm sorry."

"Many people escaped, but it's hard to say what the city population was before the attack, with so many refugees. Hundreds of thousands are likely dead."

Egwene breathed out. A large army's worth of people, wiped out in one night. That was probably only the start of the brutality to come. How many had died in Kandor so far? They could only guess.

Caemlyn had held much of the Andoran army's food supply. She felt sick, thinking of so many people—hundreds of thousands of them—stumbling across the landscape away from the burning city. Yet that thought was less terrifying than the risk of starvation to Elayne's troops.

She drew up a note to Silviana, requiring her to send all sisters strong enough to provide Healing for the refugees, and gateways to carry them to Whitebridge. Perhaps she could deliver supplies there, though the White Tower was strained as it was.

"Did you see the note at the bottom?" Gawyn asked.

She had not. She frowned, then scanned a sentence added at the bottom in Silviana's hand. Rand al'Thor had demanded that everyone meet with him by . . .

She looked up at the room's old, freestanding wooden clock. The meeting was in a half-hour. She groaned, then began shoveling the rest of her breakfast into her mouth. It wasn't dignified, but Light *burn* her if she was going to meet with Rand on an empty stomach.

"I'm going to throttle that boy," she said, wiping her face. "Come on, let's move."

"We could always be last," Gawyn said, rising. "Show him he doesn't order us about."

"And allow him the chance to meet with everyone else while I'm not there to counter what he has to say? I don't like it, but Rand holds the reins right now. Everyone's too curious to see what he's going to do."

She made a gateway back to her tent, into the corner that she'd set aside for Traveling. She and Gawyn stepped through and left the tent, into the clamor of the Field of Merrilor. People shouted outside; with a distant thunder of hooves, troops cantered and galloped as they took positions for the meeting. Did Rand realize what he'd done here? Putting soldiers together like this, leaving them edgy and uncertain, was like tossing a handful of fireworks into a stewpot and setting it onto the stove. Eventually, things were going to start exploding.

Egwene needed to manage the chaos. She strode out of her tent, Gawyn a step behind and to her left, and smoothed her face. The world needed an Amyrlin.

Silviana waited outside, dressed formally with stole and staff, as if she were going to a meeting of the Hall of the Tower.

"See to this, once the meeting starts," Egwene said, handing her the note.

"Yes, Mother," the woman said, then fell into step just behind Egwene and to her right. Egwene didn't need to look to know that Silviana and Gawyn were pointedly ignoring each other.

At the west side of her camp, Egwene found a cluster of Aes Sedai arguing with one another. She passed through them and pulled silence in her wake. A groom brought her horse Sifter, a testy dapple gelding, and as she mounted, she looked at the Aes Sedai. "Sitters only."

That produced a sea of calm, orderly complaints, each made with an Aes Sedai sense of authority. Each woman thought she had a right to be at the meeting. Egwene stared at them, and the women slowly came into line. They were Aes Sedai; they knew that squabbling was beneath them.

The Sitters gathered, and Egwene looked out over the Field of Merrilor as she waited. It was a large triangular area of Shienaran grassland, bounded on two sides by converging rivers—the Mora and the Erinin—and on the other by woods. The grass was broken by Dashar Knob, a rocky outcrop about a hundred feet high, with cliff walls, and on the Arafellin side of the Mora by Polov Heights, a flat-topped hill about forty feet high, with gradual slopes on three sides and a steeper slope on the river side. Southwest of Polov Heights lay an area of bogs, and nearby, the River Mora's shallows, known as Hawal Ford, a convenient crossing place between Arafel and Shienar.

There was an Ogier *stedding* nearby, opposite some old stone ruins to the north. Egwene had paid her respects soon after arriving, but Rand had not invited the Ogier to his meeting.

Armies were converging. Borderlander flags came in from the west, where Rand had made his camp. Perrin's own flag flew among those. Odd, that Perrin should have a flag.

From the south, Elayne's procession wound its way toward the meeting place, smack in the middle of the Field. The Queen rode at the front. Her palace had burned, but she kept her eyes forward. Between Perrin and Elayne, the Tairens and Illianers—Light, who had let those armies camp so near one another?—marched in separate columns, both bringing almost their entire forces.

Best to be quick. Her presence would calm the rulers, perhaps prevent problems. They wouldn't like being near so many Aiel. Each clan but the Shaido was represented. She *still* didn't know if they'd support Rand or her. Some of the Wise Ones seemed to have listened to Egwene's pleas, but she had received no commitments.

"Look there," Saerin said, pulling up beside Egwene. "Did you invite the Sea Folk?"

Egwene shook her head. "No. I thought there was little chance they'd side against Rand." In truth, after her meeting with the Windfinders in *Tel'aran'rhiod*, she hadn't wanted to swim in negotiations with them again. She was afraid she'd wake up and find that she'd traded away not only her firstborn, but the White Tower itself.

They put up quite a show, appearing through gateways near Rand's camp, wearing their colorful clothing, Wavemistresses and Swordmasters as proud as monarchs.

Light, Egwene thought. *I wonder how long it's been since a meeting of this scale occurred.* Nearly every nation was represented, and then some, considering the Sea Folk and the Aiel. Only Murandy, Arad Doman and the Seanchan-held lands were missing.

The last of the Sitters finally mounted and pulled up beside her. Eager to move forward, but not daring to show it, Egwene started a slow ride toward the meeting place. Bryne's soldiers fell in and formed an escort of tromping boots and pikes held high. Their white tabards were emblazoned with the Flame of Tar Valon, but they did not outshine the Aes Sedai. The way they marched accented the women at their center. Other armies relied on the strength of arms. The White Tower had something better.

Each army converged on the meeting place, the center of the field, where Rand had ordered no tents erected. So many armies together on ground perfect for a charge. This had better not go wrong.

Elayne set precedent by leaving the vast bulk of her force halfway there, continuing on with a smaller guard of about a hundred men. Egwene did the same. Other leaders began to trickle forward, their retinues coming to rest in a large ring around the central field.

Sunlight shone down upon Egwene as she approached the center. She couldn't help but notice the large, perfectly broken circle of clouds above the field. Rand did affect things in strange ways. He needed no announcement to say that he was in attendance, no banner. The clouds pulled back and sunlight shone down when he was near.

It did not seem that he'd arrived at the center yet, however. She met up with Elayne. "Elayne, I'm sorry," she said, not for the first time.

The golden-haired woman kept her eyes forward. "The city is lost, but the city is not the nation. We must have this meeting, but do so quickly, so that I can return to Andor. Where is Rand?"

"Taking his time," Egwene said. "He's always been like that."

"I have spoken to Aviendha," Elayne said, her bay horse shifting and snorting. "She spent last night with him, but he wouldn't tell her what he intends this day."

"He has mentioned demands," Egwene said, watching the rulers gather with their retinues. Darlin Sisnera, King of Tear, was first. He would support her, for all the fact that he owed Rand his crown. The Seanchan threat still bothered him deeply. The middle-aged man with a dark, pointed beard was not particularly handsome, but self-composed and sure of himself. He bowed from horseback to Egwene, and she held out her ring.

He hesitated, then dismounted and came forward, bowing his head and kissing the ring. "The Light illumine you, Mother."

"I am glad to see you here, Darlin."

"So long as your promise holds. Gateways to my homeland should the moment require it."

"It will be done."

He bowed again, eyeing a man riding up toward Egwene from the other side. Gregorin, Steward of Illian, was Darlin's equal in many ways—-but not all. Rand had named Darlin Steward of Tear, but the High Lords had asked for him to be crowned king. Gregorin remained merely a Steward. The tall man had lost weight recently, his round face—with its customary Illianer beard—starting to look sunken. He didn't wait for Egwene to prod him; he swung from his horse and seized her hand, executing a flourishing bow and a kiss to the ring.

"I'm pleased the two of you could put aside differences to join me in this endeavor," Egwene said, drawing their attention away from glares at one another.

"The Lord Dragon's intentions are . . . troubling," Darlin said. "He chose me to lead Tear because I opposed him when I felt it necessary. I believe he will listen to reason if I present it to him."

Gregorin snorted. "The Lord Dragon do be perfectly reasonable. We do need to offer a good argument, and I do think he will listen."

"My Keeper has some words for each of you," Egwene said. "Please listen to what she has to say. Your cooperation will be remembered."

Silviana rode forward and drew Gregorin aside to speak to him. There wasn't much of importance to say, but Egwene had feared these two would end up chipping at one another. Silviana's instruction was to keep them apart.

Darlin regarded her with a discerning gaze. He seemed to understand what she was doing, but didn't complain as he mounted his horse.

"You seem troubled, King Darlin," she said.

"Some old rivalries run deeper than the ocean's depths, Mother. I can almost wonder if this meeting was the work of the Dark

One, hoping that we would end up destroying one another and doing his work for him."

"I understand," Egwene said. "Perhaps it would be best if you advised your men—again, if you've already done so—that there are to be *no* 'accidents' this day."

"A wise suggestion." He bowed, pulling back.

They were both with her, as was Elayne. Ghealdan would stand for Rand, if what Elayne said about Queen Alliandre was true. Ghealdan wasn't so powerful that Alliandre worried her—the Borderlanders were another matter. Rand seemed to have won them over.

Each of their flags flew over their respective armies, and each ruler was in attendance save Queen Ethenielle, who was in Kandor trying to organize the refugees fleeing her homeland. She had left a sizable contingent for this meeting—including Antol, her eldest son—as if to state that what happened here was as important to Kandor's survival as fighting on the border.

Kandor. The first casualty of the Last Battle. The entire country was said to be aflame. Would Andor be next? The Two Rivers? *Steady,* Egwene thought.

It felt awful to have to consider who was "for" whom, but it was her duty to do so. Rand could not direct the Last Battle personally, as he would undoubtedly wish to do. His mission would be to fight the Dark One; he would have neither the presence of mind nor the time to act as a commanding general as well. She intended to come from this meeting with the White Tower acknowledged as leading the collected forces against the Shadow, and she would *not* give up responsibility for the seals.

How much could she trust this man Rand had become? He wasn't the Rand she'd grown up with. He was more akin to the Rand she'd come to know out in the Aiel Waste, only more confident. And, perhaps, more cunning. He had grown quite proficient at the Game of Houses.

None of these changes in him were terrible things, assuming he could still be reasoned with.

Is that the flag of Arad Doman? she thought, surprised. It wasn't just the flag, it was the *King's* flag, indicating he was riding with those forces that had just arrived on the field. Had Rodel Ituralde finally ascended to the throne, or had Rand picked someone else?

The Domani king's flag flew next to that of Davram Bashere, uncle to the Queen of Saldaea.

"Light." Gawyn nudged his horse up beside hers. "That flag . . ."

"I see it," Egwene said. "I'll have to pin down Siuan: have her sources mentioned who took the throne? I was afraid the Domani would ride into battle without a leader."

"The Domani? I was talking about *that*."

She followed his eyes. A new force was approaching, moving with apparent haste, under the banner of the red bull. "Murandy," Egwene said. "Curious. Roedran has finally decided to join the rest of the world."

The newly arrived Murandians made more show than they probably deserved. Their apparel, at least, was pretty: yellow and red tunics over mail; brass helmets with wide brims. The wide red belts bore the symbol of the charging bull. They kept their distance from the Andorans, wrapping around behind the Aiel forces and coming in from the northwest.

Egwene looked toward Rand's camp. Still no sign of the Dragon himself.

"Come," she said, nudging Sifter into motion toward the Murandian force. Gawyn fell in beside her, and Chubain brought a force of twenty soldiers as a guard.

Roedran was a corpulent man swathed in red and gold; she could practically hear the man's horse groaning with each step. His thinning hair was more white than black, and he watched her with an unexpectedly keen expression. The King of Murandy was little more than ruler of one city, Lugard, but her reports indicated that this man wasn't doing a bad job of expanding his rule. Given a few years, he might actually have a full kingdom to call his own.

Roedran held up a meaty hand, stopping his procession. She reined in her horse and waited for him to approach her, as would be customary. He didn't.

Gawyn muttered a curse. Egwene let a smile tug at the edges of her lips. Warders could be useful, if only to express what she should not. Finally, she nudged her horse forward.

"So." Roedran looked her over. "You're the new Amyrlin. An Andoran."

"The Amyrlin has no nationality," Egwene said coolly. "I am curious to find you here, Roedran. When did the Dragon extend an invitation to you?"

"He didn't." Roedran waved for a cupbearer to bring him some wine. "I thought it was high time Murandy stopped being left out of events."

"And through whose gateways did you arrive? Surely you didn't cross Andor to reach here."

Roedran hesitated.

"You came from the south," Egwene said, studying him. "Andor. Elayne sent for you?"

"She did not *send* for me," Roedran snapped. "The bloody Queen promised me if I supported her cause, she'd release a proclamation of intention, promising not to invade Murandy." He hesitated. "Besides, I've been curious to see this false Dragon. Everybody in the world seems to have taken leave of their senses regarding him."

"You *do* know what this meeting is about, don't you?" Egwene said.

He waved a hand. "Talking this man out of his conquering ways, or something like that."

"Good enough." Egwene leaned forward. "I hear your rule is consolidating nicely, and that Lugard may actually have some real authority in Murandy for once."

"Yes," Roedran said, sitting up a bit straighter. "That is true."

Egwene leaned forward further. "You're welcome," she said softly, then smiled. She turned Sifter and led her retinue away.

"Egwene," Gawyn said softly, trotting his horse beside hers, "did you really just do that?"

"Does he look troubled?"

Gawyn glanced over his shoulder. "Very."

"Excellent."

Gawyn continued riding for a moment, then broke into a deep grin. "That was positively evil."

"He's as boorishly rude as reports have made him out to be," Egwene said. "He can suffer a few nights spent wondering how the White Tower has been pulling strings in his realm. If I'm feeling particularly vengeful, I'll set up some good secrets for him to unearth. Now, where *is* that sheepherder? He has the audacity to demand that we . . ."

She trailed off as she saw him coming. Rand strode across the browning grass of the field, wearing red and gold. A tremendous bundle hovered in the air beside him, held up by weaves she could not see.

The grass greened at his feet.

It wasn't a large change. Where he trod, the turf recovered, spreading from him like a soft wave of light through opening shutters. Men stepped back; horses stamped their hooves. Within minutes, the entire ring of troops stood on grass that lived again.

How long had it been since she'd seen a simple field of green? Egwene breathed out. Some of the gloom to the day had been lightened. "I'd give good coin to know how he does that," she murmured under her breath.

"A weave?" Gawyn asked. "I've seen Aes Sedai make flowers bloom in winter."

"I know of no weave that would be so extensive," Egwene said. "It feels so *natural*. Go see if you can find out how he's doing it. Maybe one of the Aes Sedai with Asha'man Warders will let the truth out."

Gawyn nodded, slipping away.

Rand continued his walk, trailed by that large floating bundle, Asha'man in black and an honor guard of Aiel. The Aiel spurned regular ranks, sweeping the land like a swarm, fanning out. Even soldiers who followed Rand shied back from the Aiel. For many of the older soldiers, a wave of browns and tans like that meant death.

Rand walked calmly, purposefully. The cloth bundle he carried with Air began to unravel in front of him. Large swaths of canvas rippled in the wind before Rand, braiding with one another, leaving long trails behind themselves. Wooden poles and metal stakes fell from inside them, and Rand caught those in unseen threads of Air, spinning them.

He never broke stride. He didn't look at the maelstrom of cloth, wood and iron, as canvas rippled in front of him like fish from the depths. Small clods of soil erupted from the ground. Some soldiers jumped.

He's grown into quite the showman, Egwene thought as the poles spun and came down in the holes. Sweeping bands of cloth wrapped around them, tying themselves. In seconds, a massive pavilion settled into place, the Dragon banner flapping from one end, the banner with the ancient symbol of the Aes Sedai on the other.

Rand didn't break stride as he reached the pavilion, cloth sides parting for him. "You may each bring five," he announced as he stepped inside.

"Silviana," Egwene said, "Saerin, Romanda, Lelaine. Gawyn will be our fifth when he returns."

Sitters behind suffered the decision in silence. They couldn't complain about her taking her Warder for protection or her Keeper for support. The other three she'd chosen were widely considered among the most influential in the Tower, and together the four she brought included two Aes Sedai each from Salidar and the White Tower loyalists.

The other rulers allowed Egwene to enter before them. All understood that this confrontation was, at its core, between Rand and Egwene. Or, rather, the Dragon and the Amyrlin Seat.

There were no chairs inside the pavilion, though Rand hung *saidin* globes of light at the corners, and one of the Asha'man deposited a small table at the center. She did a quick count. Thirteen glowing globes.

Rand stood facing her, arms behind his back, hand clasping his other forearm as had become his habit. Min stood at his side, one hand on his arm.

"Mother," he said, nodding his head.

So he would pretend respect, would he? Egwene nodded back. "Lord Dragon."

The other rulers and their small retinues filed in, many doing so with timidity until Elayne swept in, the sorrow on her face lightening as Rand smiled warmly at her. The wool-headed woman was still impressed with Rand, pleased with how he'd managed to bully everyone into coming here. Elayne considered it a matter of pride when he did well.

And you don't feel a small measure of pride? Egwene asked herself. *Rand al'Thor, once simple village boy and your near-betrothed, now the most powerful man in the world? You don't feel proud of what he's done?*

Perhaps a little.

The Borderlanders entered, led by King Easar of Shienar, and there was nothing timid about them. The Domani were led by an older man that Egwene did not know.

"Alsalam," Silviana whispered, sounding surprised. "He has returned."

Egwene frowned. Why hadn't any of her informants told her he had shown up? Light. Did Rand know that the White Tower had tried to take him into custody? Egwene herself had discovered that fact only a few days before, buried in a pile of Elaida's papers.

Cadsuane entered, and Rand nodded to her, as if giving permission. She didn't bring five, but neither did he seem to require her to be counted among Egwene's five. That struck her as a bothersome precedent. Perrin stepped in with his wife, and they stayed to the side. Perrin folded his tree-trunk arms, wearing his new hammer at his belt. He was far easier to read than Rand was. He was worried, but he trusted Rand. Nynaeve did, too, burn her. She took her position near Perrin and Faile.

The Aiel clan chiefs and Wise Ones entered in a large mass—Rand's "Bring only five" probably meant that each clan chief could bring five. Some Wise Ones, including Sorilea and Amys, made their way to Egwene's side of the tent.

Light bless them, Egwene thought, releasing a held breath. Rand's eyes flickered toward the women, and Egwene caught a tightening of his lips. He was surprised that all the Aiel didn't back him, each and every one.

King Roedran of Murandy was one of the last to enter the tent, and Egwene noticed something curious as he did. Several of Rand's Asha'man—Narishma, Flinn, Naeff—moved in behind Roedran. Others, near Rand, looked as alert as cats who had seen a wolf wander by.

Rand stepped over to the shorter, wider man and looked down into his eyes. Roedran stuttered for a moment, then started wiping his brow with a handkerchief. Rand continued to stare at him.

"What is it?" Roedran demanded. "You're the Dragon Reborn, so they say. I do not know that *I'd* have let you—"

"Stop," Rand said, raising a finger.

Roedran quieted immediately.

"Light burn me," Rand said. "You're not him, are you?"

"Who?" Roedran asked.

Rand turned away from him, waving his hand to make Narishma and the others stand down. They did so reluctantly. "I thought for certain . . . " Rand said, shaking his head. "Where *are* you?"

"Who?" Roedran asked loudly, almost squeaking.

Rand ignored him. The flaps to the pavilion had finally stilled, everyone inside. "So," Rand said. "We are all here. Thank you for coming."

"It's not like we did have much of a bloody choice," Gregorin grumbled. He'd brought a handful of Illianer nobility with him as his five, all members of the Council of Nine. "We did be caught between you and the White Tower itself. Light burn us."

"You know by now," Rand continued, "that Kandor has fallen and Caemlyn has been taken by the Shadow. The last remnants of Malkier are under assault at Tarwin's Gap. The end is upon us."

"Then why are we standing here, Rand al'Thor?" demanded King Paitar of Arafel. The aging man had only a thin ribbon of gray hair remaining on his head, but he was still broad-shouldered and intimidating. "Let us put an end to this posturing and be to it, man! There is fighting to be done."

"I promise you fighting, Paitar," Rand said softly. "All that you can stomach, and then some. Three thousand years ago, I met the Dark One's forces in battle. We had the wonders of the Age of Legends, Aes Sedai who could do things that would make your mind reel, *ter'angreal* that could enable people to fly and make them immune to blows. We still *barely won*. Have you considered that? We face the Shadow in much the same state as it was then, with Forsaken who have not aged. But we are not the same people, not by far."

The tent fell silent. Flaps blew in the breeze.

"What are you saying, Rand al'Thor?" Egwene said, folding her arms. "That we are doomed?"

"I'm saying we need to plan," Rand said, "and present a unified attack. That we did poorly last time, and it nearly cost us the war. We each thought we knew the best way to go." He met Egwene's eyes. "In those days, every man and woman considered themselves to be the leader on the field. An army of generals. *That* is why we nearly lost. *That* is what left us with the taint, the Breaking, the madness. I was as guilty of it as anyone. Perhaps the most guilty.

"I will not have that happen again. I will not save this world only to have it broken a second time! I will not die for the nations of humanity, only to have them turn upon one another the moment the last Trolloc falls. You're planning it. Light burn me, I *know* that you are!"

It would have been easy to miss the glances that Gregorin and Darlin shot at one another, or the covetous way Roedran watched Elayne. Which nations would be broken by this conflict, and which would step in—out of altruism—to help its neighbors? How quickly would altruism become greed, the chance to hold another throne?

Many of the rulers here were decent people. It took more than a decent person to hold that much power and not look afield. Even Elayne had gobbled up another country when the opportunity presented itself. She would do so again. It was the nature of rulers, the nature of nations. In Elayne's case, it even seemed appropriate, as Cairhien would be better off beneath her rule than it had been.

How many would assume the same? That they, of course, could rule better—or restore order—in another land?

"Nobody wants war," Egwene said, drawing the crowd's attention. "However, I think what you are trying to do here is beyond your calling, Rand al'Thor. You cannot change human nature and you cannot bend the world to your whims. Let people live their lives and choose their own paths."

"I *will not*, Egwene," Rand said. There was a fire in his eyes, like the one she'd seen when he first sought to bring the Aiel to his cause. Yes, that emotion seemed very like Rand—frustration that people didn't see the world as clearly as he thought he did.

"I don't see what else you can do," Egwene said. "Would you appoint an emperor, someone to rule over us all? Would you become a true tyrant, Rand al'Thor?"

He didn't snap back a retort. He held out his hand to the side, and one of his Asha'man slipped a rolled paper into it. Rand took it and placed it on the table. He used the Power to unroll it and to keep it flat.

The oversized document was filled with tight, cramped letters. "I call it the Dragon's Peace," Rand said softly. "And it is one of the three things which I will require of you. Your payment, to me, in exchange for my life."

"Let me see that." Elayne reached for it, and Rand obviously let it go, because she was able to snatch it off the table before any of the other surprised rulers.

"It locks the borders of your nations to their current positions," Rand said, arms behind his back again. "It forbids country from attacking country, and it requires the opening of a great school in each capital—fully funded and with doors open to those who wish to learn."

"It does more than that," Elayne said, one finger to the document as she read. "Attack another land, or enter into a minor armed border dispute, and the other nations of the world have an obligation to defend the country attacked. Light! Tariff restrictions to prevent the strangling of economies, barriers on marriage between rulers of nations unless the two lines of rule are clearly divided, provisions for stripping the land from a lord who starts a conflict . . . Rand, you *really* expect us to sign this?"

"Yes."

The outrage from the rulers was immediate, though Egwene stood calmly, and shot a few glances at the other Aes Sedai. They seemed troubled. As well they should be—and this was only part of Rand's "price."

The rulers muttered, each wanting a chance at the document, but not wanting to shoulder in and look over Elayne's shoulder. Fortunately, Rand had thought ahead, and smaller versions of the document were distributed.

"But there are very good reasons for conflict, sometimes!" Darlin said, looking over his document. "Such as creating a buffer between you and an aggressive neighbor."

"Or what if some people from our country do be living across the border?" Gregorin added. "Do we not have the mandate to step in and protect them, if they do be oppressed? Or what if someone like the Seanchan do claim land that is ours? Forbidding war do seem ridiculous!"

"I agree," Darlin said. "Lord Dragon, we should have the *mandate* to defend land that is rightfully ours!"

"I," Egwene said, cutting through the arguments, "am more interested to hear his other two requirements."

"You know one of them," Rand said.

"The seals," Egwene said.

"Signing this document would mean nothing to the White Tower," Rand said, apparently ignoring the comment. "I can't very well forbid all of you to influence the others; that would be foolishness."

"It's *already* foolishness," Elayne said.

Elayne was not feeling so proud of him any longer, Egwene thought.

"And as long as there are political games to be played," Rand continued to Egwene, "the Aes Sedai will master them. In fact, this document benefits you. The White Tower always *has* believed war to be, as they say, shortsighted. Instead, I demand something else of you. The seals."

"I am their Watcher."

"In name only. They were only just discovered, and I possess them. It is out of respect for your traditional title that I approached you about them first."

"Approached me? You didn't make a request," she said. "You didn't make a *demand*. You came, told me what you were going to do and walked away."

"I have the seals," he repeated. "And I will break them. I won't allow anything, not even you, to come between me and protecting this world."

All around them arguments over the document continued, rulers muttering with their confidants and neighbors. Egwene stepped forward, facing Rand across the small table, the two of them ignored for the moment. "You won't break them if I stop you, Rand."

"Why would you want to stop me, Egwene? Give me a single reason why it would be a bad idea."

"A single reason other than that it will let the Dark One loose on the world?"

"He was not loose during the War of Power," Rand said. "He could touch the world, but the Bore being opened will not loose him. Not immediately."

"And what was the cost of letting him touch the world? What are they now? Horrors, terrors, destruction. You know what is happening to the land. The dead walking, the strange twisting of the Pattern. This is what happens with the seals only weakened!"

What happens if we actually break them? The Light only knows."

"It is a risk that must be taken."

"I don't agree. Rand, you don't know what releasing his seals will do—you don't know if it might let him escape. You don't know how close he was to getting out when the Bore was last secured. Shattering those seals could destroy the world itself! What if our only hope lies in the fact that he's hindered this time, not completely free?"

"It won't work, Egwene."

"You don't know that. How can you?"

He hesitated. "Many things in life are uncertain."

"So you *don't* know," she said. "Well, I have been looking, reading, listening. Have you read the works of those who have studied this, thought about it?"

"Aes Sedai speculation."

"The only information we have, Rand! Open the Dark One's prison and all could be lost. We have to be more careful. This is what the Amyrlin Seat is for, this is part of why the White Tower was founded in the first place!"

He actually hesitated. Light, he was *thinking*. Could she be getting through to him?

"I don't like it, Egwene," Rand said softly. "If I go up against him and the seals are not broken, my only choice will be to create another imperfect solution. A patch, even worse than the one last time—because with the old, weakened seals there, I'll just be spreading new plaster over deep cracks. Who knows how long the seals would last this time? In a few centuries, we could have this same fight all over again."

"Is that so bad?" Egwene said. "At least it's sure. You sealed the Bore last time. You know how to do it."

"We could end up with the taint again."

"We're ready for it, this time. No, it wouldn't be ideal. But Rand . . . do we really want to risk this? Risk the fate of every living being? Why not take the simple path, the known path? Mend the seals again. Shore up the prison."

"No, Egwene." Rand backed away. "Light! Is this what it's about? You want *saidin* to be tainted again. You Aes Sedai . . . you're threatened by the idea of men who can channel, undermining your authority!"

"Rand al'Thor, don't you *dare* be that level of a fool."

He met her eyes. The rulers seemed to be paying little attention to this conversation, despite the fact that the world depended on it. They pored over Rand's document, muttering in outrage. Perhaps that was what he had intended, to distract them with the document, then pounce for the real fight.

Slowly, the rage melted from his face, and he raised his hand to the side of his head. "Light, Egwene. You can still do it, like the sister I never had—tie my mind in knots and have me raving at you and loving you at the same time."

"At least I'm consistent," she said. They were now speaking very softly, leaning across the table toward one another. To the side, Perrin and Nynaeve were probably close enough to hear, and Min had joined them. Gawyn had returned, but he kept his distance. Cadsuane rounded the room, looking in the other direction—too pointedly. She was listening in.

"I am not making this argument in some fool hope to restore the taint," Egwene said. "You know I'm better than that. This is about protecting humankind. I can't believe you are willing to risk everything on a slender chance."

"A slender chance?" Rand said. "We're talking about entering darkness instead of founding another Age of Legends. We could have peace, an end to suffering. Or we could have another Breaking. Light, Egwene. I don't know for certain if I *could* mend the seals, or make new ones, in the same way. The Dark One has to be ready for that plan."

"And you have another one?"

"I've been telling it to you. I break the seals to get rid of the old, imperfect plug, and try again in a new way."

"The world itself is the cost of failure, Rand." She thought a moment. "There's more here. What aren't you telling me?"

Rand looked hesitant, and for a moment, he seemed the child she'd once caught sneaking bites of Mistress Cauthon's pies with Mat. "I'm going to kill him, Egwene."

"Who? Moridin?"

"The Dark One."

She drew back in shock. "I'm sorry. What did you—"

"I'm going to *kill* him," Rand said passionately, leaning in. "I'm going to end the Dark One. We will never have true peace so long as he is there, lurking. I'll rip open the prison, I'll enter it and I'll face him. I'll build a new prison if I have to, but first, I'm going to try to end all of this. Protect the Pattern, the Wheel, for good."

"Light, Rand, you're *insane*!"

"Yes. That is part of the price I have paid. Fortunately. Only a man with shaken wits would be daring enough to try this."

"I'll fight you, Rand," she whispered. "I won't let you pull all of us into this. Listen to reason. The White Tower should be guiding you here."

"I've known the White Tower's guidance, Egwene," he replied. "In a box, beaten each day."

The two locked eyes across the table. Nearby, other arguments continued.

"I don't mind signing this," Tenobia said. "It looks fine to me."

"Bah!" Gregorin snarled. "You Borderlanders never care anything for southern politics. You'll sign it? Well, good for you. I, however, won't chain my country to the wall."

"Curious," Easar said. The calm man shook his head, pure white topknot bobbing. "As I understand, it's not your country, Gregorin. Unless you're assuming that the Lord Dragon will die, and that Mattin Stepaneos will not demand his throne back. He may be willing for the Lord Dragon to wear the Laurel Crown, but not you, I'm sure."

"Isn't all of this meaningless?" Alliandre asked. "The *Seanchan* are our worry now, aren't they? Peace can never exist so long as they are there."

"Yes," Gregorin said. "The Seanchan and those cursed Whitecloaks."

"We will sign it," Galad said. Somehow the Lord Captain Commander of the Children of the Light had ended up holding the official copy of the document. Egwene didn't look at him. It was hard not to stare. She loved Gawyn, and not Galad, but . . . well . . . it was hard not to stare.

"Mayene will sign it as well," Berelain said. "I find the Lord Dragon's will to be perfectly just."

"Of course *you'd* sign it." Darlin sniffed. "My Lord Dragon, this document seems designed to protect the interests of some nations more than others."

"I want to hear what his third requirement is," Roedran said. "I don't care anything for talk of the seals; that is Aes Sedai business. He claimed there were three requirements, and we have heard only two."

Rand raised an eyebrow. "The third and final price—the last thing you will pay me in exchange for my life on the slopes of Shayol Ghul—is this: I command your armies for the Last Battle. Utterly and completely. You do as I say, go where I say, fight where I say."

This caused a larger eruption of arguments. It was obviously the least outrageous of the three demands, though it *was* impossible for reasons Egwene had already determined.

The rulers treated it as an attack on their sovereignty. Gregorin glowered at Rand through the din, only maintaining the most threadbare respect. Amusing, since he had the least authority of them all. Darlin shook his head, and Elayne's face was *livid*.

Those on Rand's side argued back, primarily the Borderlanders. *They're desperate*, Egwene thought. *They're being overrun.* They probably thought that if command were given to the Dragon, he would immediately march to the defense of the Borderlands. Darlin and Gregorin would never agree to that. Not with the Seanchan breathing down their necks.

Light, what a mess.

Egwene listened to the arguments, hoping they would set Rand on edge. Once, they might have. Now, he stood and watched, arms folded behind his back. His face became serene, though she was increasingly certain that was a mask. She'd seen flashes of his temper inside. Rand certainly was more in control of himself now, but he was by no means emotionless.

Egwene actually found herself smiling. For all of his complaints about Aes Sedai, for all of his insistence that he wouldn't be controlled by them, he was acting more and more like one of them himself. She prepared to speak and take control, but something in the tent changed. A ... feeling to the air. Her eyes seemed drawn to Rand. Sounds came from outside, sounds she couldn't place. A faint cracking sound? What was he doing?

The arguments trailed off. One by one the rulers turned toward him. The sunlight outside dimmed, and she was glad for those spheres of light he had made.

"I need you," Rand said softly to them. "The land itself needs you. You argue; I knew that you would, but we no longer have time for arguments. Know this. You cannot talk me out of my designs. You cannot make me obey you. No force of arms, nor weave of the One Power, can *make* me face the Dark One for you. I must do it of my own choice."

"You would really toss the world for this, Lord Dragon?" Berelain asked.

Egwene smiled. The lightskirt suddenly didn't seem so certain of the side she had chosen.

"I won't have to," Rand said. "You'll sign it. To fail to do so means death."

"So it's extortion," Darlin snapped.

"No," Rand said, smiling toward the Sea Folk, who had said little as they stood near Perrin. They had simply read the document and nodded among themselves, as if impressed. "No, Darlin. It's not extortion . . . it's an arrangement. I have something you want, something you need. Me. My blood. I will die. We've all known this from the start; the Prophecies demand it. As you wish this of me, I will sell it to you in exchange for a legacy of peace to balance out the legacy of destruction I gave the world last time."

He scanned the meeting, looking at each ruler in turn. Egwene felt his determination almost like a physical thing. Perhaps it was his *ta'veren* nature, or perhaps it was just the weight of the moment. A pressure rose inside the pavilion, making it difficult to breathe.

He's going do it, she thought. *They'll complain, but they'll bend.*

"No," Egwene said loudly, her voice breaking the air. "No, Rand al'Thor, we will not be bullied into signing your document, into giving you sole control of this battle. And you're an utter fool if you think I believe you'd let the world—your father, your friends, all those you love, all of humanity—be slaughtered by Trollocs if we defy you."

He met her eyes, and suddenly she wasn't certain. Light, he wouldn't *really* refuse, would he? Would he really sacrifice the world?

"You dare call the Lord Dragon foolish?" demanded Narishma.

"The Amyrlin is *not* to be spoken to that way," Silviana said, stepping up beside Egwene.

The arguments began again, this time louder. Rand kept Egwene's eyes, and she saw the flush of anger rise in his face. The shouting rose, tension mounting. Unrest. Anger. Old hatreds, flaring anew, fueled by terror.

Rand rested his hand on the sword he wore these days—the one with the dragons on the scabbard—his other arm folded behind his back.

"I *will* have my price, Egwene," he growled.

"Require if you wish, Rand. You are *not* the Creator. If you go to the Last Battle with this foolishness, we're all dead anyway. If I fight you, then there is a chance I can change your mind."

"Ever the White Tower has been a spear at my throat," Rand snapped. "Ever, Egwene. And now you really have become one of them."

She met his stare. Inside, however, she was beginning to lose certainty. What if these negotiations did break down? Would she really drive her soldiers to fight Rand's?

She felt as if she had tripped over a rock at the top of a cliff and was tipping toward the fall. There had to be a way to stop this, to salvage it!

Rand started to turn away. If he left the pavilion, that would be the end of it.

"Rand!" she said.

He froze. "I will not budge, Egwene."

"Don't do this," she said. "Don't throw it all away."

"It cannot be helped."

"Yes it can! All you have to do is stop being such a Light-burned, wool-headed, stubborn fool for once!"

Egwene drew herself back. How could she have spoken to him as if they were back in Emond's Field, at their beginning?

Rand stared at her for a moment. "Well, you could certainly stop being a spoiled, self-certain, unmitigated *brat* for once, Egwene." He threw up his arms. "Blood and ashes! This was a waste of time."

He was very nearly right. Egwene didn't notice someone new entering the tent. Rand did, however, and he spun as the flaps parted and let in light. He frowned at the interloper.

His frown died as soon as he saw the person who entered. Moiraine.

CHAPTER
6

A Knack

The pavilion grew quiet again. Perrin hated a racket, and the people's scents weren't any better. Frustration, anger, fear. Terror.

Much of it was directed at the woman standing just inside the entrance to the pavilion.

Mat, you blessed fool, Perrin thought, breaking into a grin. *You did it. You actually did it.*

For the first time in a while, thinking of Mat made the colors swirl in his vision. He saw Mat on a horse, riding along a dusty road, tinkering with something he held. Perrin dismissed the image. Where had Mat gotten to now? Why hadn't he come back with Moiraine?

It didn't matter. Moiraine was back. Light, Moiraine! Perrin started toward her to give her an embrace, but Faile caught him by the sleeve. He followed her eyes.

Rand. His face had grown pale. He stumbled away from the table, as if all else had been forgotten, and pushed his way to Moiraine. He hesitantly reached out and touched her face. "By my mother's grave," Rand whispered, then fell to his knees before her. "How?"

Moiraine smiled, resting a hand on his shoulder. "The

Wheel weaves as the Wheel wills, Rand. Have you forgotten that?"

"I . . ."

"Not as you will, Dragon Reborn," she said gently. "Not as any of us will. Perhaps one day it will weave itself out of existence. I do not believe that day is today, nor a day soon."

"Who is this woman?" Roedran said. "And what is she blathering about? I—" He cut off as something unseen flicked him on the side of the head, causing him to jump. Perrin glanced at Rand, then noticed the smile on Egwene's lips. He caught the scent of her satisfaction despite all of the people in the pavilion.

Nynaeve and Min, standing nearby, smelled utterly shocked. The Light willing, Nynaeve would stay that way for a little while. Shouting at Moiraine wouldn't help right now.

"You haven't answered my question," Rand said.

"But I have," Moiraine replied fondly. "It just was not the answer you wanted."

Rand knelt, then threw his head back and laughed. "Light, Moiraine! You haven't changed, have you?"

"We all change day by day," she replied, then smiled. "Me more than some, lately. Stand up. It is I who should be kneeling before you, Lord Dragon. We all should."

Rand rose and stepped back to allow Moiraine farther into the pavilion. Perrin caught another scent, and smiled as Thom Merrilin slipped into the tent behind her. The old gleeman winked at Perrin.

"Moiraine," Egwene said, stepping forward. "The White Tower welcomes you back with open arms. Your service has not been forgotten."

"Hmmm," Moiraine said. "Yes, I should think that having discovered a future Amyrlin would reflect well upon me. That is a relief, as I believe I was on a path to stilling, if not execution, before."

"Things have changed."

"Obviously." Moiraine nodded. "Mother." She passed Perrin, and gave him a squeeze on the arm, eyes twinkling.

One by one, the Borderlander rulers took swords in hands and bowed or curtsied toward her. Each one seemed to know her personally. Many of the others in the tent still looked baffled, though

Darlin obviously knew who she was. He was more . . . thoughtful than confused.

Moiraine hesitated beside Nynaeve. Perrin couldn't catch Nynaeve's scent right then. That seemed ominous to him. *Oh, Light. Here it comes . . .*

Nynaeve enfolded Moiraine in a powerful embrace.

Moiraine stood for a moment, smelling distinctly shocked, hands out to the sides. Finally, she returned the embrace in a somewhat maternal way, patting Nynaeve on the back.

Nynaeve released her, pulling back, then wiped a tear from her eye. "Don't you *dare* tell Lan about this," she growled.

"I would not dream of it," Moiraine said, moving on to stand in the center of the pavilion.

"Insufferable woman," Nynaeve grumbled as she wiped a tear from the other eye.

"Moiraine," Egwene said. "You've come at just the right time."

"I have a knack for that."

"Well," Egwene continued as Rand stepped back up to the table, "Rand . . . the Dragon Reborn . . . has decided to hold this land for ransom to his demands, refusing to do his duty unless we agree to his whims."

Moiraine pursed her lips, taking up the contract for the Dragon's Peace as Galad set it on the table for her. She scanned it.

"Who *is* this woman?" Roedran said. "And why do we— Would you stop that!" He raised a hand as if he'd been smacked by a thread of Air, then glared at Egwene—however, this time one of the nearby Asha'man was the one who smelled satisfied.

"Nice shot, Grady," Perrin whispered.

"Thank you, Lord Perrin."

Grady would know her only by legend, of course, but tales of Moiraine had spread among those who followed Rand.

"Well?" Egwene said.

"'And it shall come to pass that what men made shall be shattered,'" Moiraine whispered. "'The Shadow shall lie across the Pattern of the Age, and the Dark One shall once more lay his hand upon the world of man. Women shall weep and men quail as the nations of the earth are rent like rotting cloth. Neither shall anything stand nor abide.'"

The people shuffled their feet. Perrin looked questioningly at Rand.

"'Yet one shall be born to face the Shadow,'" Moiraine said more loudly. "'Born once more as he was born before and shall be born again, time without end! The Dragon shall be Reborn, and there shall be wailing and gnashing of teeth at his rebirth. In sackcloth and ashes shall he clothe the people, and he shall break the world again by his coming, tearing apart all ties that bind!

"'Like the unfettered dawn shall he blind us, and burn us, yet shall the Dragon Reborn confront the Shadow at the Last Battle, and his blood shall give us the Light. Let tears flow, O ye people of the world. Weep for your salvation!'"

"Aes Sedai," Darlin said, "pardon, but that is very ominous."

"At least it shall be a salvation," Moiraine said. "Tell me, Your Majesty. That prophecy commands you to shed tears. Are you to weep because your salvation comes with such pain and worry? Or, instead, are you to weep *for* your salvation? For the man who will suffer for you? The only one we know for certain will not walk away from this fight?"

She turned to Rand.

"These demands are unfair," Gregorin said. "He requires us to keep our borders as they are!"

"'He shall slay his people with the sword of peace,'" Moiraine said, "'and destroy them with the leaf.'"

It's The Karaethon Cycle. *I've heard these words before.*

"The seals, Moiraine," Egwene said. "He's planning to break them. He defies the authority of the Amyrlin Seat."

Moiraine did not look surprised. Perrin suspected she'd been listening outside before entering. It was very like her.

"Oh, Egwene," Moiraine said. "Have you forgotten? 'The unstained tower breaks and bends knee to the forgotten sign ...'"

Egwene blushed.

"'There can be no health in us, nor any good thing grow,'" Moiraine quoted, "'for the land is one with the Dragon Reborn, and he one with the land. Soul of fire, heart of stone.'"

She looked to Gregorin. "'In pride he conquers, forcing the proud to yield.'"

To the Borderlanders. "'He calls upon the mountains to kneel ...'"

To the Sea Folk. "'. . . and the seas to give way.'"

To Perrin, then Berelain. "'. . . and the very skies to bow.'"

To Darlin. "'Pray that the heart of stone remembers tears . . .'"

Then, finally, to Elayne. "'. . . and the soul of fire, love.' You cannot fight this. None of you can. I am sorry. You think he came to this on his own?" She held up the document. "The Pattern is balance. It is not good nor evil, not wisdom nor foolishness. To the Pattern, these things matter not, yet it *will* find balance. The last Age ended with a Breaking, and so the next one will begin with peace—even if it must be shoved down your throats like medicine given to a screaming babe."

"If I may speak?" An Aes Sedai wearing a brown shawl stepped forward.

"You may," Rand said.

"This is a wise document, Lord Dragon," the Brown said. She was a stout woman, more direct of tone than Perrin expected from a Brown. "But I see an enormous flaw to it, one that was raised earlier. So long as the Seanchan are exempt from it, it will be meaningless. There will be no peace so long as they conquer."

"That's an issue," Elayne said, arms folded. "But not the only one. Rand, I see what you're trying to do, and I love you for it. That does not remove the fact that this document is fundamentally untenable. For a peace treaty to work, both sides must continue to wish for peace because of the benefits presented.

"This grants no way to settle disputes. They *will* arise, they always do. Any document like this must give a way to settle such things; you must set up a way to punish an infraction save for the other countries to enter all-out war. Without that change, little grievances will mount and build pressure over years until they explode.

"As this is, it all but requires the nations to fall upon the first that breaks the peace. It doesn't stop them from setting up a puppet regime in the fallen kingdom, or even in another kingdom. Over time, I fear this treaty will be viewed as null; what good is it if it protects only on paper? The end result of this will be war. Massive, overpowering war. You will have peace for a time, particularly while those who revere you live. But for every year of peace you gain, you will earn one of greater destruction once the thing falls apart."

Rand rested his fingers on the document. "I will make peace with the Seanchan. We will add a provision. If their ruler does not sign, then the document is voided. Will you all agree to it then?"

"That fixes the lesser problem," Elayne said softly, "but not the larger one, Rand."

"There is yet a greater issue here," a new voice said.

Perrin turned, surprised. Aviendha? She and the other Aiel had not participated in the arguments. They'd only watched. Perrin had almost forgotten they were there.

"You, too?" Rand said. "Come to walk on the shards of my dreams, Aviendha?"

"Don't be a child, Rand al'Thor," the woman said, striding up to place her finger on the document. "You have *toh*."

"I left you out of it," Rand protested. "I trust you, and all of the Aiel."

"The Aiel aren't in it?" Easar said. "Light, how did we miss that!"

"It is an insult," Aviendha said.

Perrin frowned. She smelled very serious. From any other Aiel, he'd expect that sharp scent to be followed by a pulled-up veil and a raised spear.

"Aviendha," Rand said, smiling. "The others are about to hang me for putting them in it, and you are angry for being left out?"

"I demand my boon of you," she said. "This is it. Place the Aiel in your document, your 'Dragon's Peace.' We will leave you otherwise."

"You don't speak for all of them, Aviendha," Rand said. "You can't—"

All of the tent's Wise Ones stepped up behind Aviendha, as if in rhythm together. Rand blinked.

"Aviendha carries our honor," Sorilea said.

"Do not be foolish, Rand al'Thor," Melaine added.

"This is a thing of the women," Sarinde added. "We will not be satisfied until we are treated equally with the wetlanders."

"Is this thing too difficult for us?" Amys asked. "Do you insult us by implying we are weaker than the others?"

"You're all insane!" Rand said. "Do you realize that this would *forbid* you from fighting one another?"

"Not from fighting," Aviendha said. "From fighting without cause."

"War is your purpose," Rand said.

"If you believe that, Rand al'Thor," she said, voice cold, "I have trained you poorly indeed."

"She speaks wisdom," Rhuarc said, stepping up to the front of the crowd. "Our purpose was to prepare for your need of us at this Last Battle—our purpose was to be strong enough to be preserved. We will need another purpose. I have buried blood feuds for you, Rand al'Thor. I would not take them up again. I have friends now that I would rather not kill."

"Madness," Rand said, shaking his head. "All right, I'll put you in."

Aviendha seemed satisfied, but something bothered Perrin. He didn't understand the Aiel—Light, he didn't understand Gaul, who had been with him for so long. Still, he'd noticed that the Aiel liked to be doing something. Even when they lounged, they were alert. When other men gamed or diced, the Aiel were often quietly doing something of use.

"Rand," Perrin said, stepping up, taking him by the arm. "A moment, please?"

Rand hesitated, then nodded to him and waved his hand. "We're sealed off; they can't hear us now. What is this about?"

"Well, I just noticed something. The Aiel are like tools."

"All right . . ."

"And tools that aren't used grow rusty," Perrin said.

"Which is why they raid one another," Rand said, rubbing his temple. "To keep up their skills. That is why I exempted them. Light, Perrin! I think this is going to be a disaster. If we include them in this document . . ."

"I don't think you have a choice, now," Perrin said. "The others will never sign it if the Aiel are left out."

"I don't know if they'll sign it anyway," Rand said. He looked longingly at the sheet on the table. "It was such a beautiful dream, Perrin. A dream of good for humanity. I thought I had them. Right up until Egwene called my bluff, I thought I had them."

It was a good thing others couldn't smell Rand's emotions, or everyone there would have known that he'd never refuse to go against the Dark One. Rand showed not a hint of it on his face, but inside, Perrin knew he had been as nervous as a boy at his first shearing.

"Rand, don't you see?" Perrin said. "The solution."

Rand frowned at him.

"The *Aiel*," Perrin said. "The tool that needs to be used. A treaty that needs to be enforced . . ."

Rand hesitated, then grinned widely. "You're a genius, Perrin."

"So long as it's about blacksmithing, I suppose I know a thing or two."

"But this . . . this isn't about blacksmithing, Perrin . . ."

"Of course it is," Perrin said. How could Rand not see that?

Rand turned, no doubt ending his weave. He strode up to the document, then held it up toward one of his clerks in the back of the pavilion. "I want two provisions added. First, this document is void if not signed by either the Seanchan Daughter of the Nine Moons or the Empress. Second . . . the Aiel—all but the Shaido— are to be written into the document as enforcers of the peace and mediators of disputes between nations. Any nation may call upon them if they feel abused, and the Aiel—not enemy armies—will provide redress. They can hunt criminals across national borders. They are to be *subject* to the laws of the nations in which they reside at the time, but they are not *subjects* of that nation."

He turned to Elayne. "There is your enforcement, Elayne, the way to keep your small pressures from building."

"The Aiel?" she asked skeptically.

"Will you agree to this, Rhuarc?" Rand asked. "Bael, Jheran, the rest of you? You claim to be left without purpose, and Perrin sees you as a tool that needs to be worked. Will you take this charge? To prevent war, to punish those who do wrong, to work with the rulers of nations to see justice served?"

"Justice as we see it, Rand al'Thor," Rhuarc said, "or as they see it?"

"It will have to be according to the conscience of the Aiel," Rand said. "If they call for you, they will have to know that they'll receive your justice. This will not work if the Aiel simply become pawns. Your autonomy will be what makes this effective."

Gregorin and Darlin began to complain, but Rand silenced

them with a look. Perrin nodded to himself, arms folded. Their complaints were weaker now than they had been before. He smelled ... thoughtfulness from many of them.

They see this as an opportunity, he realized. *They view the Aiel as savages, and think they'll be easy to manipulate once Rand is gone.* Perrin grinned, imagining their defeat should they attempt that course.

"This is very sudden," Rhuarc said.

"Welcome to the dinner party," Elayne added, still staring daggers at Rand. "Try the soup." Oddly, she smelled *proud*. Strange woman.

"I warn you, Rhuarc," Rand said. "You will need to change your ways. The Aiel will have to act together on these matters; the chiefs and Wise Ones will need to hold council to make decisions together. One clan cannot fight a battle while other clans disagree and fight for the other side."

"We will speak of it," Rhuarc said, nodding to the other Aiel chiefs. "This will mean an end to the Aiel."

"A beginning as well," Rand said.

The Aiel clan chiefs and the Wise Ones gathered separately to one side, and spoke in soft voices. Aviendha lingered, with Rand staring away, troubled. Perrin heard him whisper something, so soft Perrin's ears barely made it out.

"... your dream now ... when you wake from this life, we will be no more ..."

Rand's clerks, smelling frantic, came forward to begin working on the document's additions. The woman Cadsuane watched all events with a stern expression.

She smelled extremely proud.

"Add a provision," Rand said. "The Aiel can call upon other nations to aid them in their enforcement if they decide that their own numbers will not be enough. Give formal methods by which nations can petition the Aiel for redress or for permission to attack a foe."

The clerks nodded, working harder.

"You act as if this were settled," Egwene said, eyes on Rand.

"Oh, it is far from that," Moiraine said. "Rand, I have some words for you."

"Are they words I will like?" he asked.

"I suspect not. Tell me, why do you need to command the armies yourself? You will be traveling to Shayol Ghul where you will no doubt be unable to contact anyone."

"Somebody needs to be in command, Moiraine."

"On this point, I believe all would agree."

Rand folded his arms behind his back, smelling troubled. "I have taken responsibility for this people, Moiraine. I want to see that they're cared for, that the brutalities of this battle are minimized."

"I fear that is a poor reason to lead a battle," Moiraine said softly. "You do not fight to preserve your troops; you fight to win. This leader need not be you, Rand. It should not be you."

"I won't have this battle turn into a tangle, Moiraine," he said. "If you could see the mistakes we made last time, the confusion that can result when everyone thinks *they* are in control. Battle is turmoil, but we still need an ultimate commander to make decisions, to hold everything together."

"What of the White Tower?" Romanda asked, stepping—half shoving—her way up beside Egwene. "We have the resources for efficient travel between battlefronts, we are coolheaded in times that would crush others, and we are trusted by all nations."

That last bit prompted a raised eyebrow from Darlin.

"The White Tower *does* seem the optimal choice, Lord Dragon," Tenobia added.

"No," Rand said. "The Amyrlin is many things, but a leader of war . . . I do not think it a wise choice."

Egwene, oddly, said nothing. Perrin studied her. He'd have thought that she'd jump at the chance to lead the war herself.

"It should be one of us," Darlin said. "Chosen from those who would go to battle here."

"I suppose," Rand said. "So long as you all know who is in command, I will cede this point. You must meet my other demands, however."

"You still insist that you must break the seals?" Egwene said.

"Do not worry, Egwene," Moiraine said, smiling. "He is not going to break the seals."

Rand's face darkened.

Egwene smiled.

"You are going to break them," Moiraine said to Egwene.

"What? Of course I'm not!"

"You are the Watcher of the Seals, Mother," Moiraine said. "Did you not hear what I said earlier? 'It shall come to pass that what men made shall be *shattered*, and the Shadow shall lie across the Pattern of the Age, and the Dark One shall once more lay his hand upon the world of man . . .' It must happen."

Egwene seemed troubled.

"You have seen this, have you not?" Moiraine whispered. "What have you dreamed, Mother?"

Egwene didn't respond at first.

"What did you see?" Moiraine pressed, stepping closer to her.

"His feet crunching," Egwene said, staring Moiraine in the eyes. "As he strode forward, Rand's feet stepped on the shards of the Dark One's prison. I saw him, in another dream, hacking away at it to open it. But I never actually saw him *opening* it, Moiraine."

"The shards were there, Mother," Moiraine said. "The seals had been broken."

"Dreams are subject to interpretation."

"You know the truth of this one. It does need to be done, and the seals are yours. You will break them, when the time is right. Rand, Lord Dragon Reborn, it is time to give them to her."

"I don't like this, Moiraine," he said.

"Then not much has changed, has it?" she asked lightly. "I believe you have often resisted doing what you are supposed to. Particularly when *I* am the one to point it out to you."

He paused for a moment, then laughed, reaching into the pocket of his coat. He slipped out three discs of *cuendillar*, each split by a sinuous line down the center. He set them on the table.

"How will she know the time?" he asked.

"She will," Moiraine said.

Egwene smelled skeptical, and Perrin didn't blame her. Moiraine always had believed in following the weave of the Pattern and bowing to the Wheel's turnings. Perrin didn't see it that way. He figured you made your own path, and trusted in your own arms to do what needed to be done. The Pattern wasn't a thing to depend on.

Egwene was Aes Sedai. It seemed that she felt she should see it as Moiraine did. Either that, or she was willing to agree and just take those seals into her hands. "I'll break them, when I feel it must be done," she said, taking the seals.

"You'll sign, then." Rand took the document as the clerks protested the hastiness with which they'd had to work. It now had several additions on the back. One of the clerks cried out, reaching for the sand, but Rand did something with the One Power, drying the ink instantly as he placed the document before Egwene.

"I will," she said, holding out a hand for a pen. She read the provisions carefully, the other sisters looking over her shoulders. They nodded one at a time.

Egwene put pen to paper.

"And now the rest," Rand said, turning to measure reactions.

"Light, he's grown clever," Faile whispered beside Perrin. "Do you realize what he did?"

"What?" Perrin said, scratching his beard.

"He brought with him all he knew would support him," Faile whispered. "The Borderlanders, who would sign practically anything to garner help for their homelands. Arad Doman, which he helped most recently. The Aiel ... well, all right, who knows what the Aiel will do at a given time? But the idea stands.

"Then he let Egwene gather the others. It's genius, Perrin. That way, with her bringing this coalition against him, all he *really* had to do was convince her. Once he swayed her to his side, the others would look foolish to stand apart."

Indeed, as the rulers began to sign—Berelain going first and most eagerly—those who had supported Egwene started to fidget. Darlin stepped up and took the pen. He hesitated for a moment, then signed.

Gregorin followed. Then the Borderlanders, each in turn, followed by the King of Arad Doman. Even Roedran, who still seemed to find this entire thing a fiasco, signed. Perrin found that curious.

"He blusters a lot," Perrin said to Faile, "but he knows this is good for his kingdom."

"Yes," she said. "He's been acting a buffoon partially to throw everyone off, make them dismiss him. The document outlines current borders of nations to remain as they are," Faile said. "That's a huge boon to someone trying to stabilize his rule. But ..."

"But?"

"The Seanchan?" Faile said softly. "If Rand persuades them, does that allow them to keep the countries they have now? The women who are *damane*? Are they allowed to slap one of those collars on any woman who passes their border?"

The tent stilled; perhaps Faile had spoken more loudly than she'd intended. Perrin sometimes had trouble remembering what ordinary people could and couldn't hear.

"I will deal with the Seanchan," Rand said. He stood over the table, watching as each ruler looked over the document, spoke with the counselors they'd brought, then signed.

"How?" Darlin asked. "They do *not* wish to make peace with you, Lord Dragon. I do think they'll make this document meaningless."

"Once we are done here," Rand said softly, "I will go to them. They will sign."

"And if they do not?" Gregorin demanded.

Rand rested his hand on the table, fingers spread. "I may have to destroy them. Or at least their ability to make war in the near future."

The pavilion grew still.

"Could you *do* that?" Darlin asked.

"I'm not certain," Rand admitted. "If I can, it may leave me weakened in a time when I need all of my strength. Light, it may be my only choice. A terrible choice, when I left them last time . . . We *cannot* have them striking at our backs while we fight the Shadow." He shook his head, and Min stepped up to take his arm. "I will find a way to deal with them. Somehow, I'll find a way."

The signing progressed. Some did it with great flourish, others in more casual fashion. Rand had Perrin, Gawyn, Faile and Gareth Bryne sign as well. He seemed to want anyone here who might rise to a position of leadership to have their names on the document.

Finally, only Elayne remained. Rand held out the quill to her.

"This is a difficult thing you ask of me, Rand," Elayne said, arms folded, golden hair gleaming in the light of his globes. Why *had* the sky gone dim outside? Rand didn't seem worried, but Perrin feared that the clouds had consumed the sky. A dangerous sign, if they now held sway where Rand had once kept them back.

"I know it is difficult," Rand said. "Perhaps if I gave you something in return . . . "

"What?"

"The war," Rand said. He turned to the rulers. "You wanted one of you to lead the Last Battle. Will you accept Andor, and its queen, in this role?"

"Too young," Darlin said. "Too new. No offense, Your Majesty."

Alsalam snorted. "You're one to talk, Darlin. Half the monarchs present have held their thrones for a year or less!"

"What of the Borderlanders?" Alliandre asked. "They've fought against the Blight all of their lives."

"We are overrun," Paitar said. He shook his head. "One of us cannot coordinate this. Andor is as good a choice as any."

"Andor is suffering an invasion of its own," Darlin noted.

"You all are, or soon will be," Rand said. "Elayne Trakand is a leader to her core; she taught me much of what I know about leadership. She has learned tactics from a great captain, and I'm certain she will rely upon all the great captains for advice. Someone *must* lead. Will you all accept her in this position?"

The others reluctantly nodded agreement. Rand turned to Elayne.

"All right, Rand," she said. "I'll do this, and I will sign, but you had *better* find a way to deal with the Seanchan. I want to see their ruler's name on this document. None of us will be safe until it's there."

"What of the women held by the Seanchan?" Rhuarc asked. "I will admit, Rand al'Thor, our intention was to declare a blood feud with these invaders the moment more pressing battles were won."

"If their ruler signs it," Rand said, "I will ask about trading for goods to retrieve those channelers they have stolen. I will try to persuade them to release the lands they hold and return to their own country."

"What if they refuse?" Egwene asked, shaking her head. "Will you let them sign it without giving on those points? Thousands are enslaved, Rand."

"We cannot defeat them," Aviendha said, speaking softly.

Perrin eyed her. She smelled frustrated, but determined. "If we go to war with them, we will fall."

"Aviendha is right," Amys said. "The Aiel will *not* fight the Seanchan."

Rhuarc, startled, looked back and forth between the two.

"They have done horrible things," Rand said, "but so far, the lands they have taken have benefited from strong leadership. If forced to it, I am content to allow them the lands they have, so long as they do not spread further. As for the women . . . what is done is done. Let us worry about the world itself first, then do what we can for those held captive."

Elayne held the document for a moment, perhaps for the drama of it, then bent down and added her name to the bottom with a flourish.

"It is done," Moiraine said as Rand picked up the document. "You *will* have peace this time, Lord Dragon."

"We must survive first," he said, holding the document with reverence. "I will leave you to make your battle preparations. I need to complete some tasks, Seanchan included, before I travel to Shayol Ghul. I do have a request for you, however. There is a dear friend who needs us . . . "

Angry lightning blistered the clouded sky. Despite the shade, sweat lined Lan's neck, matting his hair underneath his helmet. He'd not worn one in years; much of his time with Moiraine had required them to be nondescript, and helmets were anything but.

"How . . . how bad is it?" Andere grimaced, holding his side, and leaning back against a rock.

Lan looked to the battle. The Shadowspawn were amassing again. The monsters almost seemed to blend and shift together, one enormous dark force of howling, *miasmic* hatred as thick as the air—which seemed to hold in the heat and the humidity, like a merchant hoarding fine rugs.

"It's bad," Lan said.

"Knew it would be," Andere said, breathing in and out quickly, blood seeping between his fingers. "Nazar?"

"Gone," Lan said. The white-haired man had gone down in the

same set-to that had nearly taken Andere. Lan's rescue had not been quick enough. "I saw him gut a Trolloc as it killed him."

"May the last embrace of the mother—" Andere spasmed in pain. "May the—"

"May the last embrace of the mother welcome you home," Lan said softly.

"Don't look at me that way, Lan," Andere said. "We all knew what this was going to be when we . . . when we joined you."

"That is why I tried to stop you."

Andere scowled. "I—"

"Peace, Andere," Lan said, rising. "What I wished was selfish. I came to die for Malkier. I have no right to deny that privilege to others."

"Lord Mandragoran!" Prince Kaisel rode up, his once-fine armor bloodstained and dented. The Kandori prince still looked too young for this battle, but he'd proven himself to be as cool-headed as any grizzled veteran. "They're forming up again."

Lan walked across the rocky ground to where a groom held Mandarb. The black stallion bore cuts on his flanks from Trolloc weapons. Thank the Light, they were superficial. Lan rested a hand on the horse's neck as Mandarb snorted. Nearby, his standard-bearer, a bald man named Jophil, raised the flag of Malkier, the Golden Crane. This was his fifth standard-bearer since yesterday.

Lan's forces had seized the Gap with their initial charge, shoving the Shadowspawn back before they were able to emerge into the valley. That was more than Lan had expected. The Gap was a long, narrow piece of rocky ground nestled between craggy rises and peaks.

Holding this position required nothing clever. You stood, you died and you killed—as long as you could.

Lan commanded a cavalry. It wasn't ideal for this kind of work—cavalries did best where they could spread out and had room to charge—but the passage through Tarwin's Gap was narrow enough that only a small number of Trollocs could come through at once. That gave Lan a chance. At least it was more difficult for the Trollocs to take advantage of their superior numbers. They would have to pay a butcher's bill for every yard they gained.

Trolloc carcasses had formed an almost furlike blanket leading through the canyon. Each time the creatures tried to push through the gorge, Lan's men had resisted them with lances and polearms, swords and arrows, eventually slaughtering thousands and leaving them heaped for their fellows to climb over. But each clash similarly reduced Lan's numbers.

Each assault forced his men to withdraw a little farther, toward the mouth of the Gap. They were less than a hundred feet from it now.

Lan felt the fatigue pressing deep into his bones.

"Our forces?" Lan asked Prince Kaisel.

"Maybe six thousand still able to ride, Dai Shan."

Less than half of what they'd started with a day before. "Tell them to mount up."

Kaisel looked shocked. "We're going to retreat?"

Lan turned to the lad.

Kaisel paled. Lan had been told that his gaze could unnerve any man; Moiraine had liked to joke that he could outstare rocks and had the patience of an oak. Well, he didn't feel as sure of himself as people thought, but this boy should have known better than to ask if they were retreating.

"Of course," Lan said, "and then we're going to attack."

"*Attack?*" Kaisel said. "We are on the defensive!"

"They'll sweep us out," Lan said, pulling himself into Mandarb's saddle. "We're exhausted, worn out and nearly broken. If we stand here and let them come at us again, we'll fall without a whimper."

Lan knew an ending when he saw one.

"Pass these orders," Lan said to Prince Kaisel. "We will slowly pull out of the pass. You have the rest of the troops assemble on the plain, mounted and ready to attack the Shadowspawn as they come out of the Gap. A charge will do great damage; they won't know what hit them."

"Won't we be surrounded and overrun if we leave the pass?" Kaisel asked.

"This is the best we can do with the resources we have."

"And then?"

"And then they eventually break through, slice our force into pieces and overrun us."

Kaisel sat for a moment, then nodded. Again, Lan was impressed. He'd assumed this boy had come with him to find the glory of battle, to fight at the side of Dai Shan and sweep their enemies away. But no. Kaisel was a Borderlander to the core. He hadn't come for glory. He'd come because he'd had to. *Good lad.*

"Give the order now. The men will be glad to get back on their horses again." Too many of them had been forced to fight on foot because of the lack of maneuverability in the narrow confines.

Kaisel gave the orders, and those orders burned through Lan's men like an autumn fire. Lan saw Andere being helped into his saddle by Bulen.

"Andere?" Lan said, heeling Mandarb toward him. "You are in no condition to ride. Go join the wounded at the back camp."

"So I lie back there and let the Trollocs butcher me after finishing you lot?" Andere leaned forward in the saddle, teetering slightly, and Bulen looked up with concern. Andere waved him off and forced himself upright. "We've already moved the mountain, Lan. Let's budge this feather and be through with it."

Lan could offer no argument. He called the retreat to the men ahead of him in the pass. His remaining men bunched around him, slowly backing out toward the plain.

The Trollocs hooted and yelled in excitement. They knew that once they were free of the walls that restricted their movement, they would win this fight easily.

Lan and his small force left the narrow confines of the Gap, those on foot running toward their horses tethered near the mouth of the canyon.

The Trollocs—for once—needed no push from the Myrddraal to charge. Their footfalls were a low rumble on the stony ground.

Several hundred yards out of the Gap, Lan slowed Mandarb and turned. Andere brought his horse up beside Lan's with difficulty, and they were joined by the other riders, who formed long lines of cavalry. Bulen cantered up to the other side of Lan.

The storm of Shadowspawn neared the mouth of the Gap, a charging force of thousands of Trollocs that would soon burst out into the open—and try to consume them.

Lan's forces were silently lined up around him. Many were old men, the last remnants of their fallen kingdom. This force that had managed to plug the narrow gap now seemed tiny on the much larger plain.

"Bulen," Lan said.

"Yes, Lord Mandragoran?"

"You claim to have failed me, years ago."

"Yes, my Lord. It—"

"Any failing on your part is forgotten," Lan said, eyes forward. "I am proud to have given you your *hadori*."

Kaisel rode up, nodding to Lan. "We are ready, Dai Shan."

"This is for the best," Andere said, grimacing, still holding to his wound, barely able to remain in the saddle.

"It is what must be," Lan said. Not an argument. Not exactly.

"No," Andere said. "It is more than that, Lan. Malkier is like a tree that lost its roots to whiteworms, the branches withering slowly. I'd rather be burned away in a flash."

"I'd rather charge," Bulen said, voice growing firm. "I'd rather charge now than let them overrun us. Let us die on the attack, with swords pointed home."

Lan nodded, turning and raising his sword high above his head. He gave no speeches. He had given those already. The men knew what this was. One more charge, while they still had some strength, would mean something. Fewer Shadowspawn to flood into civilized lands. Fewer Trollocs to kill those who could not fight back.

The enemy seemed endless. A slavering, rampaging horde without battle line or discipline. Anger, destruction incarnate. Thousands upon thousands of them. They came forward like floodwaters suddenly released, surging out of the canyon.

Lan's little force was but a pebble before them.

The men silently raised their swords to him, a final salute.

"Now!" Lan yelled. *Now as they begin to spread out. It will do the most damage.* Lan kicked Mandarb forward, leading the way.

Andere galloped beside Lan, clinging to his pommel with both hands. He didn't try to raise a weapon; he'd have fallen from his saddle if he had.

Nynaeve was too far away for Lan to feel much of her through the bond, but sometimes very powerful emotions could stand out despite the distance. He tried to project confidence in case it reached her. Pride in his men. Love for her. He wished deeply for those to be the last things she remembered of him.

My arm will be the sword . . .

Hooves clattered on the ground. The Trollocs ahead hooted in delight, realizing that their prey had transformed a retreat into a charge of men rushing right into their grasp.

My breast itself a shield . . .

Lan could hear a voice, his father's voice, speaking these words. That was foolish, of course. Lan had been a baby when Malkier had fallen.

To defend the Seven Towers . . .

He had never seen the Seven Towers stand against the Blight. He'd only heard stories.

To hold back the darkness . . .

The horses' hooves were becoming a thunder. So loud, louder than he'd have thought possible. He held himself straight, sword out.

I will stand when all others fall.

The oncoming Trollocs leveled spears as the distance between the two opposing forces narrowed.

Al Chalidholara Malkier. For my sweet land Malkier.

It was the oath a Malkieri soldier took during their first posting to the Border. Lan had never spoken it.

He did so now in his heart.

"*Al Chalidholara Malkier!*" Lan screamed. "Lances, set!" Light, but those hoofbeats were loud! Could six thousand make so much noise? He turned to look at those behind him.

At least ten thousand rode there.

What?

He pressed Mandarb forward through his surprise.

"Forward the Golden Crane!"

Voices, shouts, screams of power and joy.

The air ahead to the left *split* with a sudden vertical slash. A gateway three dozen paces wide—as large as Lan had ever seen—opened as if into the sun itself. From the other side, the brightness spilled out, *exploded* out. Charging men in full armor burst from the gateway, falling into place at Lan's flank. They flew the flag of Arafel.

More gateways. Three, then four, then a dozen. Each broke the field in coordination, charging horsemen bursting forth with lances leveled, flying the flags of Saldaea, Shienar, Kandor. In seconds, his charge of six thousand had become a hundred thousand.

Trollocs in the front lines screamed, and some of them stopped running. Some held steady, spears angled to impale oncoming horses. Bunching up behind them—not being able to see clearly what was happening in front—other enraged hordes pushed eagerly forward, waving large swords with scythelike blades and double-bitted battle-axes.

Those Trollocs at the front, holding spears, exploded.

From somewhere behind Lan, Asha'man began to send weaves to rip the earth, completely destroying the front ranks of Trollocs. As the carcasses collapsed to the ground, the middle ranks found themselves completely exposed, facing a storm of hooves, swords and lances.

Lan hit, swinging, crashing Mandarb through the snarling Trollocs. Andere was laughing.

"Back, you fool!" Lan yelled to him as he lashed out at the nearby Trollocs. "Direct the Asha'man to our wounded; have them protect the camp!"

"I want to see you smile, Lan!" Andere shouted, clinging to his horse's saddle. "Show more emotion than a stone, for once! Surely this deserves it!"

Lan looked at the battle he'd never thought to win, seeing a last stand instead become a promising fight, and couldn't help himself. He didn't just smile, he laughed.

Andere obeyed his order, riding off to seek Healing and organize the back lines.

"Jophil," Lan called. "Raise my banner high! Malkier lives on this day!"

CHAPTER
7

Into the Thick of It

Elayne stepped out of the pavilion after the meeting—and entered a grove of a dozen or so trees. And not just any trees: they were towering, healthy, huge-limbed, beautiful trees, hundreds of feet tall with massive trunks. The way she froze and gaped would have been embarrassing if everyone else hadn't been doing the same. She looked to the side, where Egwene stood, mouth open, as she stared up into the huge trees. The sun still shone above, but the green leaves shaded the area, explaining why the light had dimmed inside the tent.

"These trees," Perrin said, stepping forward and resting his hand on the thick, ribbed bark. "I've seen Great Trees like this before. Inside a *stedding*."

Elayne embraced the Source. The glow of *saidar* was there, a warmth alongside that of the sun. She breathed in the Power, and was amused to notice that most of the women who could channel had done as she had the moment a *stedding* was mentioned.

"Well, whatever Rand is now," Egwene said, folding her arms, "he can't just make *stedding* appear." She seemed to find the thought comforting.

"Where did he go?" Elayne asked.

"He strolled out there," Perrin said, waving toward the trees. "And vanished."

People were walking among the massive trunks: soldiers from the various camps, staring upward. She heard a Shienaran talking to Lord Agelmar close by. "We watched them grow, my Lord. They burst from the ground; it took less than five minutes for them to become so tall. I swear it, my Lord, or may I never draw blade again."

"All right," Elayne said, releasing the Source. "Let's begin. Nations are burning. Maps! We need maps!"

The other rulers turned toward her. In the meeting, with Rand standing there, few of them had objected to her being chosen to lead them. That was how it could be around him; a person was swept up in the tides of Rand's will. Things seemed so logical when he spoke of them.

Many now looked displeased to have her put above them. Best to give them no time to dwell on it. "Where is Master Norry?" she said to Dyelin. "Could he have—"

"I have maps, Your Majesty," Gareth Bryne said as he left the pavilion, Siuan at his side.

He seemed grayer than she remembered him; he wore a stiff white coat and trousers, the breast marked with the Flame of Tar Valon. He bowed in respect, but did not step too close. His uniform made his allegiance plain, as did Siuan's protective hand on his arm.

Elayne remembered him standing with that same quiet expression behind her mother. Never presuming, always protecting the Queen. That queen had put him out to pasture. That event hadn't been Elayne's fault, but she could read the breached trust in Bryne's face.

Elayne could not change what had come and gone. She could look only to the future. "If you have maps of this area and the potential battlefields presented to us, Lord Bryne, we would love to see them. I would like maps for the area between here and Caemlyn, a detailed map of Kandor and your best maps of the other Borderland areas." To the rulers, she continued, "Gather your commanders and advisors! We must meet immediately with the other great captains to discuss our next course of action."

It didn't take long, though the confusion was pervasive as two dozen different factions set to work. Servants pulled open the sides of the pavilion, and Elayne ordered Sumeko to gather Kinswomen and guards to fetch tables and some chairs through a gateway from her camp. Elayne also sent for specific reports of what was happening at the Gap, where Rand had asked the bulk of the Borderlander armies to go and rescue Lan. The rulers and great captains had remained behind for the planning.

Shortly, Elayne and Egwene stood surveying Bryne's detailed maps, which had been spread out across four tables. The rulers stood back and allowed the commanders to deliberate.

"This is good work, Bryne," Lord Agelmar said. The Shienaran was one of the four remaining great captains. Bryne was another. The final two great captains—Davram Bashere and Rodel Ituralde—stood side by side at the end of another table, making corrections to a map of the western Borderlands. Ituralde had bags under his eyes, and his hands sometimes shook. From what Elayne had heard, he had suffered quite an ordeal in Maradon, having been rescued only very recently. She was surprised he was here, actually.

"All right," Elayne said to the assembly. "We must fight. But how? Where?"

"Large forces of Shadowspawn have invaded three locations," Bryne said. "Caemlyn, Kandor and Tarwin's Gap. The Gap should not be abandoned, assuming our armies are enough to help Lord Mandragoran stabilize there. The likely result of our push there today will be the Shadowspawn pulling back into the pass. Keeping the enemy plugged up there is an unsuitable task for the Malkieri heavy cavalry alone. Perhaps we would best send him some pike companies? If he continues to plug that breach, we can devote the majority of our forces to combat in Andor and Kandor."

Agelmar nodded. "Yes. That should be viable if we give Dai Shan the proper support. But we cannot risk letting Shienar become overrun as Kandor was. If they push out of the Gap ... "

"We are prepared for an extended battle," Lord Easar said. "Kandor's resistance and Lan's fight at the Gap have given us the time we need. Our people are pulling into our fortresses. We can hold, even if we lose the Gap."

"Brave words, Your Majesty," Gareth Bryne said, "but it would be best if we did not have to test the Shienarans in that way. Let us plan to hold the Gap with whatever force it takes to do so."

"And Caemlyn?" Elayne asked.

Ituralde nodded. "An enemy force that deep behind our lines, with a Waygate to use for reinforcements . . . that is trouble."

"Early reports from this morning," Elayne said, "indicate they're staying put for the time being. They burned large quarters of the city, but left other sections alone—and now that they have the city, the Trollocs have been set to work smothering the flames."

"They will have to leave eventually," Bryne said. "But it will be better if we can flush them out sooner, rather than later."

"Why not consider a siege?" Agelmar asked. "I think the bulk of our armies should go to Kandor. I would not let the Throne of Clouds and the Three Halls of Trade fall as did the Seven Towers."

"Kandor already has fallen," Prince Antol said softly.

The great captains looked at the eldest son of the Kandori queen. A tall man, he had a silent way about him. Now he spoke boldly. "My mother fights for our country," he said, "but it is a fight of vengeance and redemption. Kandor burns, and it rips my heart to know it, but we cannot stop that. Give Andor your greatest attention; it is too tactically important to ignore, and I would not see another land fall as mine has."

The others nodded. "Wise advice, Highness," Bashere said. "Thank you."

"Also, do not forget Shayol Ghul," Rhuarc said from the periphery, where he stood alongside Perrin, some Aes Sedai and several other Aiel chiefs. The great captains turned toward Rhuarc, as if having forgotten he was there.

"The *Car'a'carn* soon will assault Shayol Ghul," Rhuarc said. "He will need spears at his back when he does so."

"He will have them," Elayne said. "Though that means four battlefronts. Shayol Ghul, Tarwin's Gap, Kandor and Caemlyn."

"Let us focus on Caemlyn first," Ituralde said. "I don't like the idea of a siege there. We *need* to flush the Trollocs out. If we simply besiege them, it gives them more time to reinforce their numbers through that Waygate. We have to take them out now, on our terms."

Agelmar nodded with a grunt, looking at the map of Caemlyn

an aide had put on the table. "Can we stanch that flow? Retake the Waygate?"

"I've tried," Elayne said. "This morning, we sent three separate forces through a gateway into the basement with the Waygate, but the Shadow is prepared and entrenched. None of the forces returned. I don't know if we *can* take the Waygate back, or even destroy it."

"What if we tried from the other side?" Agelmar asked.

"The other side?" Elayne asked. "You mean from *inside* the Ways?"

Agelmar nodded.

"Nobody travels the Ways," Ituralde said, aghast.

"The Trollocs do," Agelmar said.

"I've been through them," Perrin said, approaching the table. "And I'm sorry, my Lords, but I don't think that taking the Waygate from the other side would work. From what I understand, we couldn't destroy it—even with the One Power. And we couldn't hold it inside, not with the Black Wind in there. Our best choice is to somehow get those Trollocs out of Caemlyn and then hold this side of the Waygate. If it is properly guarded, the Shadow would never be able to use it against us."

"Very well," Elayne said. "We will consider other options. Though, it occurs to me that we should send to the Black Tower for their Asha'man also. How many are there?"

Perrin cleared his throat. "I think you might want to be careful about that place, Your Majesty. Something's going on there."

Elayne frowned. "'Something'?"

"I don't know," Perrin said. "I spoke to Rand about it, and he was worried, and said he was going to investigate. Anyway ... just be careful."

"I'm always careful," Elayne said absently. "So how do we get those Trollocs out of Caemlyn?"

"Perhaps we can hide a large assault force in Braem Wood; it's here, almost fifty leagues north of Caemlyn." Bryne pointed at the map. "If a smaller company of soldiers were to go up to the city gates and get the Trollocs to chase them back to the Wood as bait in the trap ... I always worried that an invading army would use the Wood for cover as a base for attacking the city. I never thought I'd be considering the same option myself."

"Interesting," Agelmar said, studying a map of the terrain around Caemlyn. "That seems like a solid prospect."

"But what of Kandor?" Bashere asked. "The Prince is right that the country is beyond rescue, but we cannot simply let the Trollocs pour out into other lands."

Ituralde scratched at his chin. "This entire matter is going to be difficult. Three Trolloc armies, with us forced to divide our attention between them. Yes, more and more, I realize that the right move is to focus on one of them and set delaying forces against the other two."

"The Shadow's army at Caemlyn is likely the smallest," Agelmar said, "as the size of the Waygate has restricted their entry into the city."

"Yes," Bashere agreed. "Our chance for a quick victory on one of the battlefronts is best at Caemlyn. We should strike hard there with the largest of our assault forces. If we can win in Andor, it will reduce the number of fronts we have to fight on—and that will be extremely advantageous."

"Yes," Elayne said. "We reinforce Lan, but tell him that his job will be to hold there as long as he can. We place a second force at the border of Kandor, with the purpose of delaying there as well—perhaps a slow withdrawal, as conditions dictate. While those two fronts are held, we can focus our true attention—and our largest army—at breaking the Trollocs in Caemlyn."

"Good," Agelmar said. "I like it. But what force do we place in Kandor? What army can slow the Trollocs, but won't require a large commitment of troops?"

"The White Tower?" Elayne asked. "If we send the Aes Sedai to Kandor, they can slow the Trollocs' advance across the border. That will let the rest of us concentrate on Caemlyn."

"Yes," Bryne said. "I like it."

"And what of the fourth battlefront?" Ituralde asked. "Shayol Ghul? Does anyone know what the Lord Dragon plans there?"

Nobody spoke.

"The Aiel will see to his needs," Amys said from beside the clan chiefs. "You needn't worry about us. Make your battle plans, and we will make ours."

"No," Elayne said.

"Elayne?" Aviendha said. "We—"

"This is precisely what Rand wished to avoid," Elayne said forcefully. "The Aiel will work with the rest of us. The battle at Shayol Ghul could be the most important of all. I won't have one group presuming to keep to themselves and fight alone. You'll accept our help."

And, she added to herself, *our direction*. The Aiel were excellent warriors, but there were some things they just wouldn't admit. The usefulness of cavalry, for one.

The Aiel obviously did *not* like the prospect of wetlander command. They bristled, eyes narrowing.

"The Aiel are excellent irregulars," Bryne said, looking to them. "I faced you on the Blood Snow, and I know how deadly you can be. However, if the Lord Dragon attacks Shayol Ghul, we will likely need to seize the valley and then hold it for as long as it takes him to battle with the Dark One. I don't know how long that will take, but it could take hours. Days. Tell me, have you ever had to entrench and fight a protracted, defensive war?"

"We will do what needs to be done," Rhuarc said.

"Rhuarc," Elayne said. "You yourselves insisted on signing the Dragon's Peace. You yourselves insisted that you be part of our coalition. I expect you to live up to your word. You *will* do as you are told."

Bryne's and Ituralde's questions had set them off, but being told directly what to do made them back down. Rhuarc nodded. "Of course," he said. "I have *toh*."

"Meet it by listening," Elayne said, "and offering your opinion. If we're going to fight on four different fronts at once, we'll need a lot of coordination." She looked at the gathered generals. "It occurs to me. We have four battlefronts, and four great captains . . ."

Bashere nodded. "No coincidence, that."

"Well, it might be one."

"There are no coincidences, Highness," Bashere said. "If I've learned one thing traveling with the Lord Dragon, that is it. Four of us, four battlefronts. We each take one, with Queen Elayne coordinating among us and overseeing the war effort as a whole."

"I will go to the Malkieri," Agelmar said. "Most of the Borderlanders fight there now."

"What of Kandor?" Elayne said.

"If the Aes Sedai are to fight there," Bryne said, "so will I. My place is with the White Tower."

He doesn't want to fight in Andor, Elayne thought. *He doesn't want to fight alongside me. He wishes the break to be clean.* "Who comes to Andor with me, then?"

"I'll go," Bashere said.

"And I to Shayol Ghul, then," Ituralde said, nodding. "To fight alongside Aiel. A day I never thought I'd see, in truth."

"Good," Elayne said, pulling over a chair. "Then let's dig into the thick of it and get to details. We need a central location for me to work from, and Caemlyn is lost. For now, I will use Merrilor. It is central, and has plenty of room to move troops and supplies around in. Perrin, do you think you could take charge of the logistics of this camp? Set up a Traveling ground, and organize the channelers to help with communications and supply operations?"

Perrin nodded.

"The rest of you," she said, "let's get to dividing the forces in detail and fleshing out the plans. We need a firm idea of how we are going to push those Trollocs out of Caemlyn so we can fight them on even ground."

Hours later, Elayne stepped from the pavilion, her mind spinning with details of tactics, supply needs and troop placements. When she blinked, she could see maps in her mind's eye, covered with Gareth Bryne's cramped notations.

The others from the meeting began trailing away to their separate camps to begin executing their battle plans. The dimming sky had required lanterns to be set up around the pavilion. She vaguely remembered both lunch and dinner being brought to the meeting. She'd eaten, hadn't she? There had simply been so much to *do*.

She nodded to those rulers who passed her, giving farewells. Most of the initial planning details had been worked out. On the morrow, Elayne would take her troops to Andor and begin the first leg of the counterattack against the Shadow.

The ground here was now soft and springy with deep green grass. Rand's influence lingered, though he had departed. As

Elayne inspected those towering trees, Gareth Bryne stepped up beside her.

She turned, surprised he hadn't left the pavilion already. The only ones still here now were the servants and Elayne's guards. "Lord Bryne?" she asked.

"I just wanted to say that I'm proud," Bryne told her softly. "You did well in there."

"I had hardly anything to add."

"You added leadership," Bryne said. "You aren't a general, Elayne, and nobody expects you to be one. But when Tenobia complained about Saldaea being left exposed, you were the one who diverted her back to what matters. Tensions are high, but you kept us together, smoothed over bad feelings, prevented us from snapping at one another. Good work, Your Majesty. *Very* good work."

She grinned. Light, but it was hard not to positively beam at his words. He wasn't her father, but in many ways, he was as close to one as she had. "Thank you. And Bryne, the crown apologizes for—"

"Not a word of that," he said. "The Wheel weaves as it wills. I don't blame Andor for what happened to me." He hesitated. "I'm still going to fight together with the White Tower, Elayne."

"I understand."

He bowed to her and strode off toward Egwene's section of camp.

Birgitte stepped up to Elayne. "Back to our camp, then?" the woman asked.

"I . . ." Elayne hesitated, hearing something. A faint sound, yet somehow deep and powerful. She frowned, walking toward it, holding up a hand to still Birgitte as she started to ask what was happening.

The two of them rounded the pavilion, crossing green grass and blossoming morning's breath, walking toward the sound, which grew stronger and stronger. A song. A beautiful song, unlike any she had ever heard, that made her tremble with its striking sonority.

It washed over her, enveloped her, vibrated *through* her. A joyful song, a song of awe and wonder, though she could not understand the words. She approached a group of towering creatures, like trees themselves, standing with their hands on the gnarled trunks of the trees Rand had grown, their eyes closed.

Three dozen Ogier of various ages, from those with eyebrows as white as new snow to those as young as Loial. He stood there with them, a smile raising the sides of his mouth as he sang.

Perrin, arms folded, stood nearby with his wife. "Your talk of going to the Asha'man had me thinking—if we need allies, what about the Ogier? I was going to see if I could find Loial, but before I could set out, I found them already here among these trees."

Elayne nodded, listening to the Ogier song reach its climax, then fade, the Ogier bowing their heads. For a moment, all was peaceful.

Finally, an ancient Ogier opened his eyes and turned toward Elayne. His white beard reached low on his chest, below the white mustaches that drooped on either side of his mouth. He stepped forward, other ancients both male and female joining him. With them came Loial.

"You are the Queen," the ancient Ogier said, bowing to her. "The one who leads this journey. I am Haman, son of Dal son of Morel. We have come to lend our axes to your fight."

"I am pleased," Elayne said, nodding to him. "Three dozen Ogier will add strength to our battle."

"Three dozen, young one?" Haman laughed a rumbling laugh. "The Great Stump did not meet, did not debate this long time, to send you three *dozen* of our numbers. The Ogier will fight alongside humans. All of us. Every one of us who can hold an axe or long knife."

"Wonderful!" Elayne said. "I will put you to good use."

An older Ogier woman shook her head. "So hasty. So quick. Know this, young one. There were some who would have abandoned you, and the world, to the Shadow."

Elayne blinked in shock. "You would have actually done it? Just . . . left us alone? To fight?"

"Some argued for it," Haman said.

"I myself took that position," the woman said. "I made the argument, though I did not truly believe it was right."

"What?" Loial asked, stumbling forward. This seemed news to him. "You didn't?"

The woman looked to him. "Trees will not grow if the Dark One claims this world."

Loial looked surprised. "But why did you—"

"An argument must have opposition if it is to prove itself, my son," she said. "One who argues truly learns the depth of his commitment through adversity. Did you not learn that trees grow roots most strongly when winds blow through them?" She shook her head, though she did seem fond. "That is not to say you should have left the *stedding* when you did. Not alone. Fortunately, that has been taken care of."

"Taken care of?" Perrin asked.

Loial blushed. "Well, you see, Perrin, I am married now."

"You didn't mention this earlier!"

"Everything has come so quickly. I am married to Erith, though, you see. She's just over there. Did you hear her singing? Isn't her song beautiful? Being married is not so bad, Perrin. Why didn't you tell me it was not so bad? I think I am rather fond of it."

"I am pleased for you, Loial," Elayne cut in. Ogier could talk quite long on tangents if one was not careful. "And thankful, to all of you, for joining us."

"It is worth the price, perhaps," Haman said, "just to see these trees. In all my life, men have only *cut* Great Trees. To see someone growing them instead . . . We made the correct decision. Yes, yes, we did. The others will need to see this . . . "

Loial waved to Perrin, apparently wanting to catch up. "Allow me to borrow him for a moment, Loial," Elayne said, steering Perrin toward the center of the grove.

Faile and Birgitte joined her, and Loial waited behind. He seemed distracted by the mighty trees.

"I have a duty I want to assign you," Elayne said softly to Perrin. "Losing Caemlyn threatens to send our armies into a supply crisis. Despite complaints of food prices, we had been keeping everyone fed, as well as accumulating stores for the battle ahead. Those stores are now gone."

"What of Cairhien?" Perrin asked.

"It still has some food," Elayne said. "As do the White Tower and Tear. Baerlon has good supplies of metals and powder—I need to find what we can draw from the other nations, and discover their food situation. It will be a massive task to coordinate stores and rations for all the armies. I'd like one person in charge of it all."

"You were thinking of me?" Perrin said.

"Yes."

"I'm sorry," Perrin said. "Elayne, Rand needs me."

"Rand needs us all."

"He needs me more," Perrin said. "Min saw it, he said. Without me at the Last Battle, he'll die. Besides, I have a few fights to finish."

"I'll do it," Faile said.

Elayne turned toward her, frowning.

"It is my duty to manage the affairs of my husband's army," Faile said. "You are his liege lady, Your Majesty, so your needs are his needs. If Andor is to command the Last Battle, then the Two Rivers will see it fed. Give me access to gateways large enough for wagons to drive through, give me troops to protect my movements, and give me access to the quartermaster records of anyone I want. I will see it done."

It was logical and rational, but not what Elayne needed. How far did she trust this woman? Faile had proven herself deft at politics. That was useful, but did she really consider herself part of Andor? Elayne studied the woman.

"There is nobody better you can trust with this task, Elayne," Perrin said. "Faile *will* see it done."

"Perrin," Elayne said. "There is a different matter involved in this. May we speak privately for a moment?"

"I'll just tell her what it is when we're done, Your Majesty," Perrin said. "I don't keep secrets from my wife."

Faile smiled.

Elayne eyed the two of them, then sighed softly. "Egwene came to me during our battle preparations. There is a certain . . . item of importance to the Last Battle that she needs to be delivered."

"The Horn of Valere," Perrin said. "You still have it, I hope."

"We do. In the Tower, hidden. We moved it from the strongroom none too quickly. Last night, that room was broken into. I know only because of certain wards we set. The Shadow knows we have the Horn, Perrin, and the Dark One's minions are looking for it. They can't use it; it's tied to Mat until he dies. But if the

Shadow's minions can capture it, he can keep Mat from using it. Or, worse—kill him, then blow it themselves."

"You want to mask moving it," Faile said, "using the supply runs to hide where you're taking it."

"We'd *rather* just give it to Mat straight out," Elayne said. "But he can be . . . difficult, sometimes. I had hoped he would be here at this meeting."

"He's in Ebou Dar," Perrin said. "Doing something with the Seanchan."

"He told you?" Elayne asked.

"Not exactly," Perrin said, looking uncomfortable. "We . . . have some kind of connection. I sometimes see where he is and what he's doing."

"That man," Elayne said, "is *never* where he needs to be."

"And yet," Perrin said, "he always arrives there eventually."

"The Seanchan are the enemy," Elayne said. "Mat doesn't seem to understand that, considering what he's done. Light, I hope that man isn't putting himself in trouble somehow . . ."

"I will do this," Faile said. "I'll care for the Horn of Valere. I'll see it gets to Mat, guard it."

"No offense to either of you," Elayne said, "but I am hesitant to trust this to someone I don't know well. That is why I came to you, Perrin."

"That's going to be a problem, Elayne," Perrin said. "If they really are watching for the Horn, then they'll *expect* you and Egwene to give it to someone you know well. Choose Faile. There is nobody I trust more than her, but she won't be suspected, as she has no direct relationship with the White Tower."

Elayne nodded slowly. "Very well. I'll send word to you on how it will be delivered. For now, begin running supplies to establish precedent. Too many people know about the Horn. After we give it to you, I will send five suspect envoys from the White Tower and seed the right rumors. We hope that the Shadow will assume the Horn is being carried by one of those envoys. I want it to be where nobody expects, at least until we can put it into Matrim's hands."

"Four battlefronts, Lord Mandragoran," Bulen repeated. "That's what the messengers are saying. Caemlyn, Shayol Ghul, Kandor, and here. They want to try to bottle up the Trollocs here and in Kandor while trying hard to defeat those in Andor first."

Lan grunted, guiding Mandarb around the reeking heap of dead Trollocs. The carcasses served as a bulwark now that his five Asha'man had pushed them up into mounds like dark, bloody hills before the Blight, where the Shadowspawn gathered.

The stench was horrible, of course. Many of the guards he passed in his rounds had thrown sprigleaf onto their fires to cover up the smell.

Evening approached, bringing its most dangerous hours. Fortunately, those black clouds above made nights so dark that Trollocs had trouble seeing anything. Dusk, however, was a time of strength to them—a time when the eyes of humans were hampered but the eyes of Shadowspawn were not.

The power of the united Borderlander attack had pushed the Trollocs back toward the mouth of the Gap. Lan was getting reinforced by the hour with pikemen and other foot to help him hold position. All in all, it looked far better here now than it had just a day before.

Still grim, though. If what Bulen said was right, his army would be stationed here as a stalling force. That meant fewer troops for him than he would have liked. He could not fault the tactics presented, however.

Lan passed into the area where the Shienaran lancers cared for their horses. A figure emerged from them and rode up beside Lan. King Easar was a compact man with a white topknot, recently arrived from the Field of Merrilor following a long day making battle plans. Lan began a horseback bow, but stopped as King Easar bowed to *him*.

"Your Majesty?" Lan asked.

"Agelmar has brought his plans for this battlefront, Dai Shan," King Easar said, falling in beside him. "He would like to go over them with us. It is important that you are there; we fight beneath the banner of Malkier. We all agreed to it."

"Tenobia?" Lan asked, genuinely surprised.

"In her case, a little encouragement was required. She came around. I also have word that Queen Ethenielle will leave Kandor and come here. The Borderlands fight together in this battle, and we do it with you at our head."

They rode on in the fading light, row upon row of lancers saluting Easar. The Shienarans were the finest heavy cavalry in the world, and they had fought—and died—upon these rocks countless times, defending the lush lands to the south.

"I will come," Lan agreed. "The weight of what you have given me feels like three mountains."

"I know," Easar said. "But we shall follow you, Dai Shan. Until the sky is rent asunder, until the rocks split underfoot, and until the Wheel itself stops turning. Or, Light send its blessing, until every sword is favored with peace."

"What of Kandor? If the Queen comes here, who will lead that battle?"

"The White Tower rides to fight the Shadowspawn there," Easar said. "You raised the Golden Crane. We were sworn to come to your aid, so we have." He hesitated, and then his voice grew grim. "Kandor is beyond recovery now, Dai Shan. The Queen admits it. The White Tower's job is not to recover it, but to stop the Shadowspawn from taking more territory."

They turned and rode through the ranks of lancers. The men were required to spend dusk within a few paces of their mounts, and they made themselves busy, caring for armor, weapons and horses. Each man wore a longsword, sometimes two, strapped to his back, and all had maces and daggers at their belts. The Shienarans did not rely solely upon their lances; an enemy who thought to pin them without room to charge soon discovered that they could be very dangerous in close quarters.

Most of the men wore yellow surcoats over their plate-and-mail, bearing the black hawk. They gave their salutes with stiff backs and serious faces. Indeed, the Shienarans were a serious people. Living in the Borderlands did that.

Lan hesitated, then spoke in a loud voice. "Why do we mourn?"

The soldiers nearby turned toward him.

"Is this not what we have trained for?" Lan shouted. "Is this not our purpose, our very *lives*? This war is not a thing to mourn. Other men may have been lax, but we have not been. We are prepared, and so this is a time of glory.

"Let there be laughter! Let there be joy! Let us cheer the fallen and drink to our forefathers, who taught us well. If you die on the morrow, awaiting your rebirth, be proud. The Last Battle is upon us, and *we are ready*!"

Lan wasn't sure, exactly, what had made him say it. His words inspired a round of "Dai Shan! Dai Shan! Forward the Golden Crane!" He saw that some of the men were writing the speech down, to pass among the other men.

"You do have the soul of a leader, Dai Shan," Easar said as they rode on.

"It is not that," Lan said, eyes forward. "I cannot stand self-pity. Too many of the men looked as if they were preparing their own shrouds."

"A drum with no head," Easar said softly, flicking his horse's reins. "A pump with no grip. A song with no voice. Still it is mine. Still it is mine."

Lan turned, frowning, but the King gave no explanation for the poem. If his people were a serious people, their king was more so. Easar had wounds deep within that he chose not to share. Lan did not fault him in this; Lan himself had done the same.

Tonight, however, he caught Easar smiling as he considered whatever it was that had brought the poem to his lips.

"Was that Anasai of Ryddingwood?" Lan asked.

Easar looked surprised. "You have read Anasai's work?"

"She was a favorite of Moiraine Sedai. It sounded as though it might be hers."

"Each of her poems was written as an elegy," Easar said. "This was for her father. She left instructions; it can be read, but should not be spoken out loud, except when it was right to do so. She did not explain when it would be right to do so."

They reached the war tents and dismounted. No sooner had they done so, however, than the horns of alarm began to sound. Both men reacted, and Lan unconsciously touched the sword on his hip.

"Let us go to Lord Agelmar," Lan shouted as men began to yell and equipment to rattle. "If you fight beneath my banner, then I will accept the role of leader gladly."

"No hesitation at all?" Easar said.

"What am I?" Lan asked, swinging into the saddle. "Some sheepherder from a forgotten village? I will do my duty. If men are foolish enough to put me in charge of them, I'll send them about theirs as well."

Easar nodded, then saluted, the corners of his mouth rising in another smile. Lan returned the salute, then galloped Mandarb through the center of the camp. The men at the outskirts were lighting bonfires; Asha'man had created gateways to one of the many dying forests in the south for soldiers to gather wood. If Lan had his way, those five channelers would never waste their strength killing Trollocs. They were far too useful otherwise.

Narishma saluted Lan as he passed. Lan could not be certain that the great captains had chosen Borderlander Asha'man for him on purpose, but it seemed not to be a coincidence. He had at least one from each Borderlander nation—even one born to Malkieri parents.

We fight together.

CHAPTER
8

That Smoldering City

Atop Moonshadow, her deep brown mare from the royal stables, Elayne Trakand rode through a gateway of her own making.

Those stables were now in the hands of Trollocs, and Moonshadow's stablemates had undoubtedly found their way into cookpots by now. Elayne did not think too hard about what else—*who* else—might have ended up in those same pots. She set her face in determination. Her troops would not see their queen look uncertain.

She had chosen to come to a hill about a thousand paces to the northwest of Caemlyn, well out of bow range but close enough to see the city. Several mercenary bands had made their camp in these hills during the weeks following the Succession War. Those had all either joined the armies of Light or had disbanded, becoming roving thieves and brigands.

The foreguard had already secured the area, and Captain Guybon saluted as members of the Queen's Guard—both male and female—surrounded Elayne's horse. The air still smelled of smoke, and seeing Caemlyn smoldering like Dragonmount itself tossed a handful of bitter powder into the stew of emotions churning inside of her.

The once-proud city was dead, a pyre that pitched a hundred different columns of smoke toward the storm clouds above. The smoke reminded her of the spring burnings, when farmers would occasionally fire their fields to help clear them for planting. She hadn't ruled Caemlyn for a hundred days, and already it was lost.

If dragons can do that to a city, she thought, surveying the hole that Talmanes had made in the nearest wall, *the world will need to change. Everything we know about warfare will change.*

"How many, would you say?" she asked the man who rode up beside her. Talmanes was only one day of rest away from the ordeal that should have cost him his life. He probably should have remained at Merrilor; he certainly wouldn't be doing any front-line fighting in the near future.

"It is impossible to count their numbers, hidden as they are in the city, Your Majesty," he said, bowing respectfully. "Tens of thousands, but probably not hundreds of thousands."

The fellow was nervous around her, and he manifested it in a very Cairhienin way—by speaking with flowery respect. He was said to be one of Mat's most trusted officers; she would have assumed that, by now, Mat would have corrupted the fellow far more. He didn't curse once. Pity.

Other gateways opened nearby onto the yellow grass, and her forces came through, filling the fields and topping the hills. She had taken charge of a large army of warriors, which included many of the *siswai'aman*, to bolster her Queen's Guard and the Andoran regulars under the command of Birgitte and Captain Guybon. A second contingent of Aiel—Maidens, Wise Ones and the remaining warriors—had been chosen to travel north to Shayol Ghul with Rand.

Only a handful of Wise Ones had come with Elayne, the ones who followed Perrin. Elayne would have liked more channelers than that. Still, she did have the Band and their dragons, which should make up for the fact that her only other channelers were the Kinswomen, many of whom were on the weaker side of strength in the Power.

Perrin and his force had come with her. That included Mayene's Winged Guards, the Ghealdanin cavalry, the Whitecloaks—she still wasn't sure what she thought of *that*—and a company of Two Rivers archers with Tam. Filling out her army was the group who called themselves the Wolf Guard, mostly refugees turned soldiers, some of whom had received combat training. And, of course, she had Captain Bashere and his Legion of the Dragon.

She had approved Bashere's plan for the battle at Caemlyn. *We will need to draw the fighting into the woods*, he had explained. *The archers will be deadly, loosing at the Trollocs upon their approach. If these lads can move as well as I am told they can in the forest, they'll be just as dangerous once they've pulled back.*

The Aiel, too, would be deadly in a forest, where the Trollocs wouldn't be able to use their masses to overrun their opponents. Bashere himself rode nearby. Apparently, Rand had specifically told him to watch over her. As if she didn't have Birgitte jumping every time she moved.

Rand had better stay safe so I can tell him what I think of him, she thought as Bashere approached in quiet conversation with Birgitte. Bashere was a bowlegged man with a thick mustache. He didn't talk to Elayne the way a man should a queen ... but then, the Queen of Saldaea was his niece, so perhaps he was just very comfortable around royalty.

He is first in line for the throne, Elayne reminded herself. Working with him would offer opportunities to further secure her ties to Saldaea. She still liked the idea of seeing one of her children on that throne. She lowered a hand to her stomach. The babes kicked and elbowed frequently now. Nobody had told her it would feel so much like ... well, indigestion. Unfortunately, Melfane had, against all expectation, found some goat's milk.

"What word?" Elayne asked as Birgitte and Bashere arrived, Talmanes moving his horse aside to make room.

"Scout reports of the city are in," Bashere said.

"Bashere was right," Birgitte said. "The Trollocs have been reined in, and the burning has mostly died out. A good half of the city still stands. Much of that smoke you see is from cook fires, not buildings."

"Trollocs are stupid," Bashere said, "but Halfmen are *not*. The Trollocs would have gleefully ransacked the city and lit fires all across it, but that would have threatened to let the fires get away from them. Either way, the truth is we don't know what the Shadow is planning here, but they at least have the option of trying to hold the city for a time, should they desire."

"Will they try that?" Elayne asked.

"I can't say, honestly," Bashere replied. "We don't know their goals. Was this attack on Caemlyn intended to sow chaos and bring fear to our armies, or is it intended to take a stronghold and hold it long-term as a base from which to harry our forces? Back during the Trolloc Wars, the Fades did hold cities for that purpose."

Elayne nodded.

"Pardon, Your Majesty?" a voice said. She turned to see one of the Two Rivers men stepping up. One of their leaders, Tam's second-in-command. *Dannil*, she thought, *that's his name.*

"Your Majesty," Dannil repeated. He fumbled a little, but actually spoke with some polish. "Lord Goldeneyes has his men set up in the forest."

"Lord Talmanes, do you have your dragons in position?"

"Almost," Talmanes said. "Pardon, Your Majesty, but I'm not certain the bows will be needed once those weapons fire. Are you certain you don't want to lead with the dragons?"

"We need to goad the Trollocs into battle," Elayne said. "The placement I outlined will work best. Bashere, what of my plan for the city itself?"

"I think everything is almost ready, but I'll want to check," Bashere said, knuckling his mustache in thought. "Those women of yours made gateways well enough, and Mayene gave us the oil. You're sure you want to go through with something so drastic?"

"Yes."

Bashere waited for more of a response, perhaps an explanation. When she didn't give one, he moved off, issuing the last orders. Elayne turned Moonshadow to ride down the ranks of soldiers here at the front lines, where they'd set up near the forests. There wasn't much she could do now, in these last moments as her commanders gave orders, but she *could* be seen riding with confidence. Where she passed, the men raised their pikes higher, lifted their chins.

Elayne kept her own eyes on that smoldering city. She would not look away, and she would not let anger control her. She would use the anger.

Bashere returned to her a short time later. "It's done. The basements of many buildings that are still standing have been filled with oil. Talmanes and the others are in place. Once your Warder returns with word that the Kinswomen are prepared to open another round of gateways, we can proceed."

Elayne nodded, and then removed her hand from her belly as Bashere glanced at it. She hadn't realized she'd been holding it again. "What do you think of me going to battle while pregnant? Is it a mistake?"

He shook his head. "No. It proves just how desperate our situation is. It will make the soldiers think. Make them more serious. Besides . . ."

"What?"

Bashere shrugged. "Perhaps it will remind them that not *everything* in this world is dying."

Elayne turned back, looking at the distant city. Farmers burned their fields in the spring to prepare them for new life. Maybe that was what Andor was suffering now.

"Tell me," Bashere said. "Are you going to tell the men that you're carrying the Lord Dragon's child?"

Children, Elayne corrected in her head. "You presume to know something that may or may not be true, Lord Bashere."

"I have a wife, and a daughter. I recognize the look in your eyes when you see the Lord Dragon. No woman with child touches her hand to her womb so reverently when looking on a man who is not the father."

Elayne drew her lips into a line.

"Why do you hide it?" Bashere asked. "I've heard what some of the men think. They talk of some other man, a Darkfriend named Mellar, once Captain of your Guardswomen. I can see that the rumors are false, but others are not so wise. You could kill those rumors if you wished."

"Rand's children will be targets," she said.

"Ah . . ." he replied. He knuckled his mustache for a moment.

"If you disagree with the reasoning, Bashere, speak your mind. I will not suffer a toady."

"I'm no toady, woman," he said with a huff. "But regardless, I hardly doubt your child could be a greater target than he or she already is. You're high commander of the armies of the Light! I think your men deserve to know what exactly they're fighting for."

"It is not your business to know," Elayne said, "nor is it theirs."

Bashere raised an eyebrow at her. "The heir to the realm," he said flatly, "is not the business of its subjects?"

"I believe you are overstepping your bounds, *General*."

"Perhaps I am," he said. "Maybe spending so much time with the Lord Dragon has warped the way I do things. That man ... you could never tell what he was thinking. Half of the time, he wanted to hear my mind, as raw as I could lay it out. The other half of the time, it seemed like he'd break me in two just for commenting that the sky looked a little dark." Bashere shook his head. "Just give it some thought, Your Majesty. You remind me of my daughter. She might have done something similar, and this is the advice I'd give her. Your men will fight more bravely if they know that you carry the Dragon Reborn's heir."

Men, Elayne thought. *The young ones try to impress me with every stunt that comes into their fool heads. The old ones assume every young woman is in need of a lecture.*

She turned her eyes toward the city again as Birgitte rode up and gave her a nod. The basements were filled with oil and pitch.

"Burn it," Elayne said loudly.

Birgitte waved a hand. The Kinswomen opened their round of gateways, and men hurled lit torches through into the basements of Caemlyn. It didn't take long for the smoke rising above the city to grow darker, more ominous.

"They won't soon put *that* out," Birgitte said softly. "Not with the dry weather we've been having. The entire city will go up like a haystack."

The army gathered to stare at the city, particularly the members of the Queen's Guard and the Andoran military. A few of them saluted, as one might salute the pyre of a fallen hero.

Elayne ground her teeth, then said, "Birgitte, make it known among the Guards. The children I carry were fathered by the Dragon Reborn."

Bashere's smile deepened. *Insufferable man!* Birgitte was smiling as she went to spread the word. She was insufferable, too.

The men of Andor seemed to stand taller, prouder, as they watched their capital burn. Trollocs started pouring from the gates, driven by the fires. Elayne made sure the Trollocs saw her army, then announced, "Northward!" She turned Moonshadow.

"Caemlyn is dead. We take to the forests; let the Shadowspawn follow!"

Androl awoke with dirt in his mouth. He groaned, trying to roll over, but found himself bound in some way. He spat, licked his lips and blinked crusty eyes.

He lay with Jonneth and Emarin against an earthen wall, tied by ropes. He remembered . . . Light! The roof had fallen in.

Pevara? he sent. Incredible how natural that method of communication was beginning to feel.

He was rewarded with a groggy sensation from her. The bond let him know that she was nearby, probably tied up as well. The One Power was also lost to him; he clawed at it, but ran up against a shield. His bonds were tied to some kind of hook in the ground behind him, hindering his movement.

Androl shoved panic down with some effort. He couldn't see Nalaam. Was he here? The group of them lay tied in a large chamber, and the air smelled of damp earth. They were still underground in a part of Taim's secret complex.

If the roof fell in, Androl thought, *the cells were probably destroyed.* That explained why he and the others were tied up, but not locked away.

Someone was sobbing.

He strained around and found Evin tied nearby. The younger man wept, shaking.

"It's all right, Evin," Androl whispered. "We'll find a way out of this."

Evin glanced at him, shocked. The youth was tied in a different way, in a seated position, hands behind his back. "Androl? Androl, I'm *sorry*."

Androl felt a twisting emotion. "For what, Evin?"

"They came right after the rest of you left. They wanted Emarin, I think. To Turn him. When he wasn't there, they began asking questions, demands. They broke me, Androl. I broke so easily. I'm sorry . . . "

So Taim hadn't discovered the fallen guards. "It's not your fault, Evin."

Footsteps sounded on the ground nearby. Androl feigned

unconsciousness, but someone kicked him. "I saw you talking, pageboy," Mishraile said, leaning down his golden-haired head. "I'm going to enjoy killing you for what you did to Coteren."

Androl opened his eyes and saw Logain sagging in the grip of Mezar and Welyn. They dragged him near and dropped him roughly to the ground. Logain stirred and groaned as they tied him up. They stood, and one spat on Androl before moving over to Emarin.

"No," Taim said from somewhere near. "The youth is next. The Great Lord demands results. Logain is taking too long."

Evin's sobs grew louder as Mezar and Welyn moved over to seize him under the arms.

"No!" Androl said, twisting. "No! Taim, burn you! Leave him alone! Take me!"

Taim stood nearby, hands clasped behind his back, in a sharp black uniform that resembled those of the Asha'man, but trimmed with silver. He wore no pins at his neck. He turned toward Androl, then sneered. "Take you? I am to present to the Great Lord a man who couldn't channel enough to break a pebble? I should have culled you long ago."

Taim followed the other two, who were dragging away the frantic Evin. Androl screamed at them, yelling until he was hoarse. They took Evin somewhere on the other side of the chamber—it was very large—and Androl could not see them because of the angle at which he was tied. Androl dropped his head back against the floor, closing his eyes. That didn't prevent him from hearing poor Evin's screams of terror.

"Androl?" Pevara whispered.

"Quiet." Mishraile's voice was followed by a thump and a grunt from Pevara.

I am really starting to hate that one, Pevara sent to him.

Androl didn't reply.

They took the effort to dig us out of the collapsed room, Pevara continued. *I remember some of it, before they shielded me and knocked me unconscious. It seems to have been less than a day since then. I guess Taim hasn't yet hit his quota of Dreadlords Turned to the Shadow.*

She sent it, almost, with levity.

Behind them, Evin's screams stopped.

Oh, Light! Pevara sent. *Was that Evin?* All wryness vanished from her tone. *What's happening?*

They're Turning him, Androl sent back. *Strength of will has something to do with resisting. That is why Logain hasn't been Turned yet.*

Pevara's concern was a warmth through the bond. Were all Aes Sedai like her? He'd assumed they had no emotions, but Pevara felt the full range—although she accompanied it with an almost inhuman control over how those emotions affected her. Another result of decades of practice?

How do we escape? she sent.

I'm trying to untie my bonds. My fingers are stiff.

I can see the knot. It's a hefty one, but I might be able to guide you.

He nodded, and they began, Pevara describing the turns of the knot as Androl tried to twist his fingers around them. He failed to get enough purchase on the bonds; he tried pulling his hands free and wiggling them out, but the ropes were too tight.

By the time he accepted defeat, his fingers were numb from the lack of circulation. *It's not going to work,* he sent.

I've been trying to push out of this shield, Pevara replied. *It's possible, and I think our shields might be tied off. Tied-off shields fail.*

Androl sent back agreement, though he couldn't keep from feeling frustrated. How long could Evin hold out?

The silence taunted him. Why couldn't he hear any sounds? Then he sensed something. Channeling. Could that be thirteen men? Light. If there were thirteen Myrddraal as well, the situation was dire. What would they do *if* they escaped? They couldn't fight so many.

Which cliff did you choose? Pevara sent him.

What?

You said that when you were among the Sea Folk, they jumped off cliffs to prove their bravery. The higher the cliff, the braver the jumper. Which cliff did you choose?

The highest, he admitted.

Why?

I figured that once you've decided to jump off a cliff, you might as well pick the highest one. Why accept the risk, if not for the greatest prize?

Pevara sent back approval. *We will escape, Androl. Somehow.*

He nodded, mostly for himself, and set back at his knot.

A few moments later, Taim's cronies returned. Evin squatted

down beside Androl. Behind his eyes lurked something different, something awful. He smiled. "Well, that was certainly not as bad as I had assumed it would be, Androl."

"Oh, Evin . . ."

"Don't worry about me," Evin said, resting a hand on Androl's shoulder. "I feel great. No more fear, no more worry. We shouldn't have been fighting all of this time. We are the Black Tower. We need to work together."

You are not my friend, Androl thought. *You might have his face, but Evin . . . Oh, Light. Evin is dead.*

"Where is Nalaam?" Androl asked.

"Died in the cave-in, I'm afraid." Evin shook his head. He leaned in. "They're planning to kill you, Androl, but I think I can convince them that you're worth Turning instead. You'll thank me, eventually."

The terrible thing inside of Evin's eyes smiled, patted Androl on the shoulder, then rose and began chatting with Mezar and Welyn.

Behind them, Androl could barely see thirteen shadows trailing over to grab Emarin and drag him away to be Turned next. Fades, with cloaks that did not move.

Androl thought how lucky Nalaam was to be crushed in the collapse.

CHAPTER
9

To Die Well

Lan split the head of the Myrddraal in half down to the neck. He danced Mandarb back, letting the Fade thrash as it died, its convulsions twisting the pieces of its skull from the neck. Putrid black blood poured onto the rock, which had already been bloodied a dozen times.

"Lord Mandragoran!"

Lan wheeled toward the call. One of his men pointed back toward their camp, where a spout of bright red light was shooting into the air.

Noon already? Lan thought, raising his sword and signaling for his Malkieri to retreat. The Kandori and Arafellin troops were swinging in, light cavalry with bows, sending wave after wave of arrows into the mass of Trollocs.

The stench was tremendous. Lan and his men rode away from the front lines, passing two Asha'man and an Aes Sedai— Coladara, who had insisted on staying on as King Paitar's advisor—channeling to set the Trolloc corpses aflame. That would make it more difficult for the next wave of Shadowspawn.

Lan's armies had continued their brutal work, holding the Trollocs at the Gap like pitch holding back the spray of water in a leaking boat. The army fought in short rotations, an hour at a time. Bonfires and Asha'man lit the way at night, never giving the Shadowspawn the opportunity to advance.

After two days of grueling battle, Lan knew that this tactic would eventually favor the Trollocs. Humans were killing them by the wagonload, but the Shadow had been building its forces for years. Each night, the Trollocs fed upon the dead; they didn't have to worry about mess supplies.

Lan kept his shoulders from sagging as he rode away from the front lines, making way for the next group of his troops, but he wanted to collapse and sleep for days. Despite the greater numbers given him by the Dragon Reborn, every man was required to take several shifts on the front lines each day. Lan always joined a few extra.

Finding sleep was not easy for his troops while also caring for their equipment, gathering wood for the bonfires and bringing supplies through gateways. As he surveyed those leaving the front lines with him, Lan sought for what he could do to strengthen them. Nearby, faithful Bulen was sagging. Lan would need to make sure the man slept more, or—

Bulen slid from the saddle.

Lan cursed, stopping Mandarb, and leaped down. He dashed to Bulen's side and found the man staring blankly into the sky. Bulen had a massive wound in his side, the mail there ripped like a sail that had seen too much wind. Bulen had covered the wound by putting his coat on over his armor. Lan hadn't seen him hit, nor had he seen the man covering up the wound.

Fool! Lan thought, feeling at Bulen's neck.

No pulse. He was gone.

Fool! Lan thought again, bowing his head. *You wouldn't leave my side, would you? That's why you hid it. You were afraid I'd die out there while you came back for Healing.*

Either that, or you didn't want to demand strength from the channelers. You knew they were pushed to their limits.

With teeth clenched, Lan picked up Bulen's corpse and slung it over his shoulder. He hefted the body onto Bulen's horse and tied it across the saddle. Andere and Prince Kaisel—the Kandori youth and his squad of a hundred usually rode with Lan—sat nearby, watching solemnly. Conscious of their eyes, Lan put his hand on the corpse's shoulder.

"You did well, my friend," he said. "Your praises will be sung for generations. May you shelter in the palm of the Creator's hand, and may the last embrace of the mother welcome you home." He turned to the others. "I will not mourn! Mourning is for those who regret, and I do *not* regret what we do here! Bulen could not have died a better death. I do not cry for him, I *cheer*!"

He swung up into Mandarb's saddle, holding the reins of Bulen's horse, and sat tall. He would not let them see his fatigue. Or his sorrow. "Did any of you see Bakh fall?" he asked those riding near him. "He had a crossbow tied to the back of his horse. He always carried that thing with him. I swore that if it ever went off by accident, I'd have the Asha'man hang him by his toes from the top of a cliff.

"He died yesterday when his sword caught in a Trolloc's armor. He left it and reached for his spare, but two more Trollocs pulled his horse out from underneath him. I thought he was dead then, and was trying to reach him, only to see him come up with that Light-burned crossbow of his and shoot a Trolloc right in the eye from two feet away. The bolt went clear through its head. The second Trolloc gutted him, but not before he put his boot knife in its neck." Lan nodded. "I remember you, Bakh. You died well."

They rode for a few moments, and then Prince Kaisel added, "Ragon. He died well, too. Charged his horse straight at a group of thirty Trollocs that were coming in at us from the side. Probably saved a dozen men with that move, buying us time. He kicked one in the face as they pulled him down."

"Yes, Ragon was a right insane man," Andere said. "I'm one of the men he saved." He smiled. "He did die well. Light, but he did. Of course, the *craziest* thing I've seen these last few days is what Kragil did when fighting that Fade. Did any of you see it . . ."

By the time they reached the camp, the men were laughing and toasting the fallen with words. Lan split off from them, and took Bulen to the Asha'man. Narishma was holding open a gateway for a supply cart. He nodded to Lan. "Lord Mandragoran?"

"I need to put him someplace cold," Lan said, dismounting. "When this is done, and Malkier is reclaimed, we will want a proper resting place for the noble fallen. Until then, I will not have him burned or left to rot. He was the first Malkieri to return to Malkier's king."

Narishma nodded, Arafellin bells tinkling on the ends of his braids. He ushered a cart through the gateway, then held up a hand for the others to stop. He closed that gateway, then opened one to the top of a mountain.

Icy air blew through. Lan took Bulen off his horse. Narishma moved to help, but Lan waved him away, grunting as he heaved the corpse up onto his shoulder. He stepped through into the snows, the biting wind sharp on his cheeks, as if someone had taken a knife to them.

He laid Bulen down, then knelt and gently took the *hadori* from Bulen's head. Lan would carry it into battle—so that Bulen could continue to fight—then return it to the body when the battle was through. An old Malkieri tradition. "You did well, Bulen," Lan said softly. "Thank you for not giving up on me."

He stood up, boots crunching the snow, and strode out through the gateway, *hadori* in hand. Narishma let the gateway close, and Lan asked for the location of the mountain—in case Narishma died in the fighting—so he could locate Bulen again.

They wouldn't be able to preserve all of the Malkieri corpses this way, but one was better than none. Lan wrapped the leather *hadori* about the hilt of his sword, just below the crossguard, and tied it tight. He handed Mandarb off to a groom, holding up a finger to the horse and meeting his dark, liquid eyes. "No more biting grooms," he growled at the stallion.

After that, Lan went looking for Lord Agelmar. He found the commander speaking with Tenobia outside the Saldaean section of camp. Men stood with bows nearby in lines of two hundred, watching the skies. There had already been a number of Draghkar attacks. As Lan stepped up, the ground started to shake and rumble.

The soldiers didn't cry out. They were growing used to this. The land groaned.

The bare rock ground near Lan split. He jumped back in alarm as the shaking continued, watching tiny rents appear in the rock—hairline cracks. There was something profoundly *wrong* about the cracks. They were too dark, too deep. Though the area was still shaking, he stepped up, looking at the tiny cracks, trying to make them out in detail through the rumbling earthquake.

They seemed to be cracks into nothingness. They drew the

light in, sucked it away. It was as if he was looking at fractures in the nature of reality itself.

The quakes subsided. The darkness within the cracks lingered for a few breaths, then faded away, the hairline fractures becoming just ordinary breaks in stone. Wary, Lan knelt down, inspecting them closely. Had he seen what he'd thought? What did it mean?

Chilled, he rose to his feet and continued on his way. *It is not men alone who grow tired*, he thought. *The mother is weakening.*

He hastened through the Saldaean camp. Of those fighting at the Gap the Saldaeans had the most well-kept camp, run by the stern hands of the officers' wives. Lan had left most of the Malkieri noncombatants in Fal Dara, and the other forces had come with few others except the warriors.

That wasn't the Saldaean way. Though they normally didn't go into the Blight, the women otherwise marched with their husbands. Each one could fight with knives, and would hold their camp to the death if the need arose. They had been extremely useful here in gathering and distributing supplies and tending the wounded.

Tenobia was arguing tactics with Agelmar again. Lan listened as the Shienaran great captain nodded to her demands. She didn't have a bad grasp of things, but she was too bold. She wanted them to push into the Blight, and take the fight to the Trolloc spawning grounds.

Eventually, she noticed Lan. "Lord Mandragoran," she said, eyeing him. She was a pretty enough woman, with fire in her eyes and long black hair. "Your latest sortie was a success?"

"More Trollocs are dead," Lan said.

"We fight a glorious battle," she said with pride.

"I lost a good friend."

Tenobia paused, then looked at his eyes, perhaps searching for emotion in them. Lan didn't give any. Bulen had died well. "The men who fight have glory," Lan said to her, "but the battle itself is not glory. It simply is. Lord Agelmar, a word."

Tenobia stepped aside and Lan drew Agelmar away. The aged general gave Lan a grateful look. Tenobia watched for a moment, then stalked off with two guards following hastily at her heels.

She'll be off into battle herself at some point if we don't watch her, Lan thought. *Her head is full of songs and stories.*

Hadn't he just encouraged his men to tell those same stories? No. There was a difference, he could *feel* a difference. Teaching the men to accept that they might die and to revere the honor of the fallen . . . that was different from singing songs about how wonderful it was to fight on the front lines.

Unfortunately, it took actual fighting to teach the difference. The Light send Tenobia wouldn't do anything too rash. Lan had seen many a young man with that look in his eyes. The solution then was to work them to exhaustion for a few weeks, drilling them to the point that they thought only of their bed, not of the "glories" they would someday find. He doubted that would be appropriate for the Queen herself.

"She has been growing more rash ever since Kalyan married Ethenielle," Lord Agelmar said quietly, joining Lan as they walked the back lines, nodding to passing soldiers. "I think that he was able to dampen her a featherweight or two, but now— without him *or* Bashere watching her . . ." He sighed. "Well, regardless. What is it you wished of me, Dai Shan?"

"We fight well here," Lan said. "But I'm worried about how tired the men are. Will we be able to keep holding back the Trollocs?"

"You are right; the enemy will force its way through eventually," Agelmar said.

"What do we do, then?" Lan asked.

"We will fight here," Agelmar said. "And then, once we cannot hold, we will retreat to buy time."

Lan stiffened. "Retreat?"

Agelmar nodded. "We are here to slow the Trollocs down. We will accomplish that by holding here for a time, then slowly pulling back across Shienar."

"I did not come to Tarwin's Gap to retreat, Agelmar."

"Dai Shan, I'm led to believe you came here to die."

That was nothing but the truth. "I will not abandon Malkier to the Shadow a second time, Agelmar. I came to the Gap—the Malkieri followed me here—to show the Dark One that we had not been beaten. To leave after we've actually been able to gain a footing . . ."

"Dai Shan," Lord Agelmar said in a softer voice as they walked, "I respect your decision to fight. We all do; your march here alone inspired thousands. That may not have been your purpose, but it is the purpose the Wheel wove for you. The determination of a man set upon justice is a thing not lightly ignored. However, there is a time to put yourself aside and see the greater importance."

Lan stopped, eyeing the aged general. "Take care, Lord Agelmar. It almost sounds as if you are calling me selfish."

"I am, Lan," Agelmar said. "And you are."

Lan did not flinch.

"You came to throw your life away for Malkier. That, in itself, is noble. However, with the Last Battle upon us, it's also stupid. We need you. Men will die because of your stubbornness."

"I did not ask for them to follow me. Light! I did all that I could to stop them."

"Duty is heavier than a mountain, Dai Shan."

That time, Lan did flinch. How long had it been since someone had been able to do that to him with mere words? He remembered teaching that same concept to a youth out of the Two Rivers. A sheepherder, innocent of the world, fearful of the fate laid out before him by the Pattern.

"Some men," Agelmar said, "are destined to die, and they fear it. Others are destined to live, and to lead, and they find it a burden. If you wished to keep fighting here until the last man fell, you could do it, and they'd die singing the glory of the fight. Or, you could do what we both need to do. Retreat when we're forced to it, adapt, continue delaying and stalling the Shadow as long as we can. Until the other armies can send us aid.

"We have an exceptionally mobile force. Each army sent you their finest cavalry. I've seen nine thousand Saldaean light horse perform complex maneuvers with precision. We can hurt the Shadow here, but their numbers are proving too great. Greater than I thought they would be. We will hurt more of them as we withdraw. We will find ways to punish them with every step we take backward. Yes, Lan. You made me commanding general of the field. That is my advice to you. It won't be today, or perhaps for another week, but we *will* need to fall back."

Lan walked on in silence. Before he could formulate a reply, he saw a blue light exploding in the air. The emergency signal from the Gap. The units that had just rotated onto the field needed help.

I will consider it, Lan thought. Pushing aside his fatigue, he dashed for the horselines where the groom would have delivered Mandarb.

He didn't need to ride on this sortie. He had just gotten off one. He decided to go anyway, and caught himself yelling for Bulen to prepare a horse, and felt a fool. Light, but Lan had grown accustomed to the man's help.

Agelmar is right, Lan thought as the grooms fell over themselves, saddling Mandarb. The stallion was skittish, sensing his mood. *They will follow me. Like Bulen did. Leading them to death in the name of a fallen kingdom ... leading myself to the same death ... how is that any different from Tenobia's attitude?*

Before long, he was galloping back toward the defensive lines to find the Trollocs almost breaking through. He joined the rally, and this night, they held. Eventually, they would fail to do so. What then?

Then ... then he would abandon Malkier again, and do what had to be done.

Egwene's force had gathered at the southern portion of the Field of Merrilor. They had been slated to Travel to Kandor once Elayne's force had been dispatched to Caemlyn. Rand's armies had not yet entered Thakan'dar, but had instead moved to staging areas on the northern part of the Field, where supplies could be assembled more easily. He claimed the time wasn't quite right for his assault; the Light send he was making progress with the Seanchan.

Moving so many people was a tremendous headache. Aes Sedai created gateways in a huge line, like the doorways along one side of a grand feast hall. Soldiers bunched up, waiting their turn to pass through. Many of the strongest channelers were not involved in this task; they would be channeling in combat soon enough, and creating gateways would only consume needed strength before the important work had begun.

The soldiers made way for the Amyrlin, of course. With the foreguard in place and a camp established on the other side, it was time for her to cross. She had spent the morning meeting with the Hall as they went over the supply reports and terrain assessments. She was glad she had allowed the Hall to take a larger role in the war; there was a great deal of wisdom to the Sitters, many of whom had lived well over a century.

"I don't like being forced to wait this long," Gawyn said, riding beside her.

She eyed him.

"I trust General Bryne's battlefield assessment, as does the Hall," Egwene said as they rode past the Illianer Companions, each man's brilliant breastplate worked with the Nine Bees of Illian on the front. They saluted her, faces hidden behind their conical helmets, barred at the front.

She wasn't certain she liked having them in her army—they would be more loyal to Rand than to her—but Bryne had insisted on it. He said that her force, though enormous, lacked an elite group like the Companions.

"I still say we should have left sooner," Gawyn said as the two of them passed through the gateway to the border of Kandor.

"It has only been a few days."

"A few days while Kandor burns." She could sense his frustration. She could also feel that he loved her, fiercely. He was her husband, now. The marriage had been performed by Silviana in a simple ceremony the night before. It still felt odd to know that Egwene had authorized her own wedding. When you were the highest authority, what else could you do?

As they moved into the camp on the Kandori border, Bryne rode by, giving terse orders to scouting patrols. When he reached Egwene, he climbed out of the saddle and bowed low, kissing her ring. He then remounted and continued. He was very respectful, considering that he'd essentially been bullied into leading this army. Of course, he'd made his demands and they had been met, so perhaps he'd bullied them as well. Leading the White Tower's armies had been an opportunity for him; no man liked being put out to pasture. The great captain shouldn't have found himself there in the first place.

Egwene noted Siuan riding at Bryne's side and smiled in satisfaction. *He is bound tightly to us now.*

Egwene surveyed the hills on the southeastern border of Kandor. Though they lacked greenery—like most places in the world now—their peaceful serenity gave no hint that the country beyond them burned. The capital, Chachin, was now little more than rubble. Before withdrawing to join the fight with the other Borderlanders, Queen Ethenielle had turned over rescue operations to Egwene and the Hall. They had done what they could, sending scouts through gateways along major roadways looking for refugees, then bringing them away to safety—if anywhere could be called safe now.

The main Trolloc army had left the burning cities and was now moving southeast toward the hills and the river that made up Kandor's border with Arafel.

Silviana rode up beside Egwene, opposite Gawyn. She spared him only a glare—those two really would have to stop snapping at one another; it was growing tiresome—before kissing Egwene's ring. "Mother."

"Silviana."

"We have received an update from Elayne Sedai."

Egwene allowed herself a smile. Both of them, independently, had taken to calling Elayne by her White Tower title as opposed to her civil title. "And?"

"She suggests that we set up a location where the wounded can be sent for Healing."

"We'd talked about having the Yellows move from battlefield to battlefield," Egwene said.

"Elayne Sedai is worried about exposing the Yellows to attack," Silviana said. "She wants a stationary hospital."

"That *would* be more efficient, Mother," Gawyn said, rubbing his chin. "Finding the wounded after a battle is a brutal affair. I don't know what I'd think of sending sisters to comb through the dead. This war could stretch weeks, even months, if the great captains are right. Eventually, the Shadow is going to start picking off Aes Sedai on the field."

"Elayne Sedai was quite . . . insistent," Silviana said. Her face was a mask, her tone steady, yet she also managed to convey severe displeasure. Silviana was proficient at that.

I helped put Elayne in charge, Egwene reminded herself. *Refusing her would set a bad precedent.* As would obeying her. Perhaps they could remain friends through it.

"Elayne Sedai shows wisdom," Egwene said. "Tell Romanda that it must be done this way. Have the entire Yellow Ajah gather for Healing, but not at the White Tower."

"Mother?" Silviana asked.

"The Seanchan," Egwene said. She had to smother the serpent deep inside of her that writhed whenever she thought of them. "I will not risk the Yellows being attacked while alone and exhausted from Healing. The White Tower is exposed, and is a focus for the enemy—if not the Seanchan, then the Shadow."

"A valid point." Silviana sounded reluctant. "But where else? Caemlyn has fallen, and the Borderlands are too exposed. Tear?"

"Hardly," Egwene said. That was Rand's territory, and it seemed too obvious. "Send back to Elayne with a suggestion. Perhaps the First of Mayene will be willing to provide a suitable building, a very large one." Egwene tapped the side of her saddle. "Send the Accepted and the novices with the Yellows. I don't want those women on the battlefield, but their strength can be put to use in Healing."

Linked to a Yellow, the weakest of novices could lend a trickle of strength and save lives. Many would be disappointed; they imagined slaying Trollocs. Well, this would be a way for them to fight without getting underfoot, untrained in combat as they were.

Egwene glanced over her shoulder. Movement through the gateways would not be finished any time soon. "Silviana, relay my words to Elayne Sedai," Egwene said. "Gawyn, I have something I want to do."

They found Chubain supervising the setup of a command camp in a valley west of the river that formed the boundary between Kandor and Arafel. They'd press forward into this hilly country to meet the oncoming Trollocs, deploying harrying forces in the adjoining valleys, with archers atop the hills alongside defensive units. The plan would be to strike hard at Trollocs as they tried to take the hills, doing as much damage as possible. The harrying units could swipe at enemy flanks while the defenders held the hills as long as they could.

The odds were good that they would eventually be pushed out of those hills and across the border into Arafel, but on the wide plains of Arafel their cavalries could be used to better advantage. Egwene's force, like Lan's, was meant to delay and slow the Trollocs until Elayne could defeat those in the south. Ideally they would hold until reinforcements could arrive.

Chubain saluted and led them to a tent that had already been erected nearby. Egwene dismounted and started to enter, but Gawyn laid a hand on her arm. She sighed, nodded and let him enter first.

Inside, on the floor with legs folded, sat the Seanchan woman that Nynaeve had called Egeanin, although the woman insisted on being called Leilwin. Three members of the Tower Guard watched over her and her Illianer husband.

Leilwin looked up as Egwene entered, then immediately rose to her knees and performed a graceful bow, forehead touching the tent floor. Her husband did as she did, though his motions seemed more reluctant. Perhaps he was merely a worse actor than she was.

"Out," Egwene said to the three guards.

They did not argue, though their withdrawal was slow. As if she couldn't handle herself with her Warder against two people who could not channel. Men.

Gawyn took up position at the side of the tent, leaving her to address the two prisoners.

"Nynaeve tells me you are marginally trustworthy," Egwene said to Leilwin. "Oh, sit up. Nobody bows that low in the White Tower, not even the lowest of servants."

Leilwin sat up, but kept her eyes lowered. "I have failed greatly in the duty assigned me, and in so doing have endangered the Pattern itself."

"Yes," Egwene said. "The bracelets. I'm aware. Would you like a chance to repay that debt?"

The woman bowed herself, forehead to the ground again. Egwene sighed, but before she could order the woman to rise, Leilwin spoke. "By the Light and my hope for salvation and rebirth," Leilwin said, "I vow to serve you and protect you, Amyrlin, ruler of the White Tower. By the Crystal Throne and the blood of the Empress, I bind myself to you, to do as commanded in all things, and to put your life before my own. Under the Light, may it be so." She kissed the floor.

Egwene looked at her, stunned. Only a Darkfriend would betray an oath such as that one. Of course, every Seanchan was close to being a Darkfriend.

"You think I'm not well protected?" Egwene asked. "You think that I need another servant?"

"I think only of repaying my debt," Leilwin said.

In her tone, Egwene sensed a stiffness, a bitterness. That rang of authenticity. This woman did not like humbling herself in this manner.

Egwene folded her arms, troubled. "What can you tell me of the Seanchan military, its arms and strength, and of the plans of the Empress?"

"I know some things, Amyrlin," Leilwin said. "But I was a ship's captain. What I do know is of the Seanchan navy, and that will be of little use to you."

Of course, Egwene thought. She glanced at Gawyn, who shrugged.

"Please," Leilwin said softly. "Allow me to prove myself to you somehow. I have little left to me. My name itself is no longer my own."

"First," Egwene said, "you will talk of the Seanchan. I don't care if you think it's irrelevant. Anything you tell me might be helpful." Or, it might reveal Leilwin as a liar, which would be equally useful. "Gawyn, fetch me a chair. I'm going to listen to what she says. After that, we'll see . . . "

Rand rifled through the pile of maps, notes and reports. He stood with his arm folded behind his back, a single lamp burning on the desk. Sheathed in glass, the flame danced as breezes eddied through the tent where he stood alone.

Was the flame alive? It ate, it moved on its own. You could smother it, so in a way, it breathed. What was it to be alive?

Could an idea live?

A world without the Dark One. A world without evil.

Rand turned back to the maps. What he saw impressed him. Elayne was preparing well. He had not attended the meetings planning each battle. His attention was directed toward the north. Toward Shayol Ghul. His destiny. His grave.

He hated the way these battle maps, with notes for formations and groups, reduced men's lives to scribbles on a page. Numbers and statistics. Oh, he admitted that the clarity—the distance—was essential for a battlefield commander. He hated it nonetheless.

Here before him was a flame that lived, yet here were also men who were dead. Now that he could not lead the war himself, he hoped to stay away from maps such as this one. He knew seeing these preparations would make him grieve for the soldiers he could not save.

A sudden chill ran across him, the hairs on his arms standing on end—a distinct shiver halfway between excitement and terror. A woman was channeling.

Rand raised his head and found Elayne frozen in the tent doorway. "Light!" she said. "Rand! What are you doing here? Are you trying to kill me with fright?"

He turned, settling his fingers on the battle maps, taking her in. Now *here* was life. Flushed cheeks, golden hair with a hint of honey and rose, eyes that burned like a bonfire. Her dress of crimson showed the swell of the children she bore. Light, she was beautiful.

"Rand al'Thor?" Elayne asked. "Are you going to talk to me, or do you wish to ogle me further?"

"If I can't ogle you, whom can I ogle?" Rand asked.

"Don't grin at me like that, farmboy," she said. "Sneaking into my tent? Really. What would people say?"

"They'd say that I wanted to see you. Besides, I didn't sneak in. The guards let me in."

She folded her arms. "They didn't tell me."

"I asked them not to."

"Then, for all intents and purposes, you *were* sneaking." Elayne brushed by him. She smelled wonderful. "Honestly, as if Aviendha weren't enough . . ."

"I didn't want the regular soldiers to see me," Rand said. "I worried it would disturb your camp. I asked the guards not to mention that I was here." He stepped up to her, resting his hand on her shoulder. "I had to see you again, before . . ."

"You saw me at Merrilor."

"Elayne . . ."

"I'm sorry," she said, turning back to him. "I *am* happy to see you, and I *am* glad you came. I'm just trying to get into my head how you fit into all of this. How *we* fit into all of this."

"I don't know," Rand said. "I've never figured it out. I'm sorry."

She sighed, sitting down in the chair beside her desk. "I suppose it is good to find there are some things you can't fix with a wave of your hand."

"There is much I can't fix, Elayne." He glanced at the desk, and the maps. "So much."

Don't think about that.

He knelt before her, getting a cocked eyebrow until he placed his hand on her belly—hesitantly, at first. "I didn't know," he said. "Not until just recently, the night before the meeting. Twins, it is said?"

"Yes."

"So Tam will be a grandfather," Rand said. "And I will be . . ."

How was a man supposed to react to this news? Was it supposed to shake him, upend him? Rand had been given his share of surprises in life. It seemed he could no longer take two steps without the world changing on him.

But this . . . this wasn't a surprise. He found that deep down, he'd hoped that someday he would be a father. It had happened. That gave him warmth. One thing was going right in the world, even if so many had gone wrong.

Children. *His* children. He closed his eyes, breathing in, enjoying the thought.

He would never know them. He would leave them fatherless before they were even born. But, then, Janduin had left Rand fatherless—and he had turned out all right. Just a few rough edges, here and there.

"What will you name them?" Rand asked.

"If there is a boy, I've been thinking of naming him Rand."

Rand let himself go still as he felt her womb. Was that motion? A kick?

"No," Rand said softly. "Please do not name either child after me, Elayne. Let them live their own lives. My shadow will be long enough as it is."

"Very well."

He looked up to meet her eyes, and he found her smiling with fondness. She rested a smooth hand on his cheek. "You will be a fine father."

"Elayne—"

"Not a word of it," she said, raising a finger. "No talk of death, of duty."

"We cannot ignore what will happen."

"We needn't dwell on it either," she said. "I taught you so

much about being a monarch, Rand. I seem to have forgotten one lesson. It is all right to plan for the worst possibilities, but you must not bask in them. You must not fixate on them. A queen must have hope before all else."

"I do hope," Rand said. "I hope for the world, for you, for everyone who must fight. That does not change the fact that I have accepted my own death."

"Enough," she said. "No more talk of this. Tonight, I will have a quiet dinner with the man I love."

Rand sighed, but rose, seating himself in the chair beside hers as she called to the guards at the tent flap for their meal.

"Can we at least discuss tactics?" Rand asked. "I am truly impressed by what you've done here. I don't think I could have done a better job."

"The great captains did most of it."

"I saw your annotations," Rand said. "Bashere and the others are wonderful generals, geniuses even, but they think only of their specific battles. Someone needs to coordinate them, and you are doing that marvelously. You have a head for this."

"No, I don't," Elayne said. "What I *do* have is a lifetime spent as the Daughter-Heir of Andor, being trained for wars that might come. Thank General Bryne and my mother for what you see in me. Did you find anything in my notes that you would change?"

"There is more than a hundred and fifty miles between Caemlyn and Braem Wood, where you plan to ambush the Shadow," Rand noted. "That's risky. What if your forces get over-run before they reach the Wood?"

"Everything depends on them beating the Trollocs to the Wood. Our harrying forces will be using the strongest, fastest mounts available. It will be a grueling race, there's no question, and the horses will be near death by the time they reach the Wood. But we are hoping that the Trollocs will be the worse for wear by then as well, which should make our job easier."

They talked tactics, and evening became night. Servants arrived with dinner, broth and wild boar. Rand had wished to keep his presence in the camp quiet, but there was nothing for that now that the servants knew.

He settled himself to dine, and let himself flow into the conversation with Elayne. Which battlefield was in the most danger?

Which of the great captains should she champion when they dis-
agreed, which they often did? How would this all work with
Rand's army, which still waited for the right time to attack Shayol
Ghul?

The conversation reminded him of their time in Tear, stealing
hidden kisses in the Stone between sessions of political training.
Rand had fallen in love with her during those days. Real love.
Not the admiration of a boy falling off a wall, looking at a
princess—back then, he hadn't understood love any more than a
farmboy swinging a sword understood war.

Their love was born of the things they shared. With Elayne, he
could speak of politics and the burden of rule. She understood.
She truly did, better than anyone he knew. She knew what it was
to make decisions that changed the lives of thousands. She understood what it was to be owned by the people of a nation. Rand
found it remarkable that, though they had often been apart, their
connection held. In fact, it felt even stronger. Now that Elayne
was queen, now that they shared the children growing within her.

"You wince," Elayne said.

Rand looked up from his broth. Elayne's dinner was half-
finished—he had been making her speak a great deal. She seemed
through anyway, and held a warm cup of tea.

"I what?" Rand asked.

"You wince. When I mentioned the contingents fighting for
Andor, you flinched, just a little."

It was not surprising she had noticed—Elayne had been the
one to teach him to watch for minor tells in the expressions of
those with whom he spoke.

"All of these people fight under my name," Rand said. "So
many people I do not even know will die for me."

"That has ever been the burden of a ruler at war."

"I should be able to protect them," Rand said.

"If you think you can protect everyone, Rand al'Thor, you are
far less wise than you pretend."

He looked at her, meeting her eyes. "I don't believe I can, but
their deaths weigh on me. I feel as if I should be able to do more,
now that I remember. He tried to break me, and he failed."

"Is that what happened that day atop Dragonmount?"

He hadn't spoken of it to anyone. He pulled his seat closer to hers. "Up there, I realized that I had been thinking too much on strength. I wanted to be *hard*, so hard. In driving myself so, I risked losing the ability to care. That was wrong. For me to win, I *must* care. That, unfortunately, means I must allow myself pain at their deaths."

"And you remember Lews Therin now?" she whispered. "Everything he knew? That is not just an air you put on?"

"I am him. I always was. I remember it now."

Elayne breathed out, eyes widening. "What an *advantage*."

Of all the people he had told that to, only she had responded in such a way. What a wonderful woman.

"I have all of this knowledge, yet it doesn't tell me what to do." He stood up, pacing. "I should be able to *fix* it, Elayne. No more should need to die for me. This is my fight. Why must everyone else go through such suffering?"

"You deny us the right to fight?" she said, sitting up straight.

"No, of course not," Rand said. "I could deny you nothing. I just wish that somehow . . . somehow I could make this all stop. Shouldn't my sacrifice be enough?"

She stood, taking his arm. He turned to her.

Then she kissed him.

"I love you," she said. "You *are* a king. But if you would try to deny the good people of Andor the right to defend themselves, the right to stand in the Last Battle . . . " Her eyes flared, her cheeks flushed. Light! His comments had truly made her angry.

He never quite knew what she was going to say or do, and that excited him. Like the excitement of watching nightflowers, knowing that what was to come would be beautiful, but never knowing the exact form that beauty would take.

"I said I wouldn't deny you the right to fight," Rand said.

"It's about more than just me, Rand. It's about everyone. Can you understand *that*?"

"I suppose that I can."

"Good." Elayne settled back down and took a sip of her tea, then grimaced.

"It's gone bad?" Rand asked.

"Yes, but I'm used to it. Still, it's almost worse than drinking nothing at all, with how spoiled everything is."

Rand walked to her and took the cup from her fingers. He held

it for a moment, but did not channel. "I brought you something.
I forgot to mention it."

"Tea?"

"No, this is just an aside." He handed the cup back to her and
she took a sip.

Her eyes widened. "It's *wonderful*. How do you do it?"

"I don't," Rand said, sitting. "The Pattern does."

"But—"

"I am *ta'veren*," Rand said. "Things happen around me, unpredictable things. For the longest time, there was a balance. In one
town, someone would discover a great treasure unexpectedly
under the stairs. In the next I visited, people would discover that
their coins were fakes, passed to them by a clever counterfeiter.

"People died in terrible ways; others were saved by a miracle of
chance. Deaths and births. Marriages and divisions. I once saw a
feather drift down from the sky and fall point-first into the mud
so it stuck there. The next ten that fell did the same thing. It was
all random. Two sides to a flipping coin."

"This tea is not random."

"Yes, it is," Rand said. "But, you see, I get only one side of the
coin these days. Someone else is doing the bad. The Dark One
injects horrors into the world, causing death, evil, madness. But
the Pattern . . . the Pattern is balance. So it works, through me, to
provide the other side. The harder the Dark One works, the more
powerful the effect around me becomes."

"The growing grass," Elayne said. "The splitting clouds. The
food unspoiled . . . "

"Yes." Well, some other tricks helped on occasion, but he
didn't mention them. He fished in his pocket for a small pouch.

"If what you say is true," Elayne replied, "then there can never
be good in the world."

"Of course there can."

"Will the Pattern not balance it out?"

He hesitated. That line of reasoning cut too close to the way he
had begun thinking before Dragonmount—that he had no
options, that his life was planned for him. "So long as we care,"
Rand said, "there can be good. The Pattern is not about emotions—it is not even about good or evil. The Dark One is a force
from outside of it, influencing it by force."

And Rand would end that. If he could.

"Here," Rand said. "The gift I mentioned." He pushed the pouch toward her.

She looked at him, curious. She untied the strings, and took from it a small statue of a woman. She stood upright, with a shawl about her shoulders, though she did not look like an Aes Sedai. She had a mature face, aged and wise, with a wise look about her and a smile on her face.

"An *angreal*?" Elayne asked.

"No, a Seed."

"A . . . seed?"

"You have the Talent of creating *ter'angreal*," Rand said. "Creating *angreal* requires a different process. It begins with one of these, an object created to draw your Power and instill it into something else. It takes time, and will weaken you for several months, so you should not attempt it while we are at war. But when I found it, forgotten, I thought of you. I had wondered what I could give you."

"Oh, Rand, I have something for you as well." She hurried over to an ivory jewelry chest that rested on a camp table and took a small object from it. It was a dagger with a short, dull blade and a handle made of deerhorn wrapped in gold wire.

Rand glanced at the dagger quizzically. "No offense, but that looks like a poor weapon, Elayne."

"It's a *ter'angreal*, something that may be of use when you go to Shayol Ghul. With it, the Shadow cannot see you." She reached up to touch his face.

He placed his hand on hers.

They stayed together long into the night.

CHAPTER 10

The Use of Dragons

Perrin rode Stayer, light cavalry from Elayne's forces following behind him: Whitecloaks, Mayeners, Ghealdanin, joined by some of the Band of the Red Hand. Only a fraction of their armies. That was the point.

They swept along diagonally toward the Trollocs camped outside of Caemlyn. The city still smoldered; Elayne's plan with the oil had driven the creatures out, for the most part, but some still held the walls above.

"Archers," Arganda yelled, "loose!" His voice would be lost to most in the roar of the charge, the snorting of horses, the gallop of hooves. Enough would hear to start shooting, and the rest knew what to do anyway.

Perrin leaned low, hoping his hammer would not be needed on this sortie. They charged past the Trollocs, sweeping in front of them, launching arrows; then they turned away from the city.

Perrin glanced over his shoulder as he rode, and he was rewarded with the sight of Trollocs falling. The Band followed after Perrin's cavalry, getting close enough to launch arrows.

Trolloc arrows followed—thick and black, almost like spears, loosed from enormous bows. Some of Perrin's riders fell, but his attack had been swift.

The Trollocs didn't break from their position outside the city walls. The riders slowed, Arganda coming up beside Perrin, watching over his shoulder.

"They still aren't charging," Arganda said.

"Then we'll hit them again and again," Perrin said. "Until they break."

"Our attacks are continuing, Your Majesty," the messenger said, riding through a gateway made by a pair of Kinswomen to where Elayne had her camp in the Wood. "Lord Goldeneyes sends word; they'll continue through the day, if need be."

She nodded, and the messenger rode back the way he had come. Braem Wood slumbered, trees bare, as if in winter. "It takes too much work to relay information back and forth to me," Elayne said with dissatisfaction. "I wish we could have made those *ter'angreal* work; Aviendha said that one let you see over distance, and another talk that way. But wish and want trip the feet, as Lini says. Still, if I could see the fighting with my own eyes—"

Birgitte said nothing. Eyes forward, the golden-haired Warder gave no sign at all that she'd heard the comment.

"After all," Elayne said, "I *can* defend myself, as I have proven on a number of occasions."

No response. The two horses walked softly beside one another, hooves on soft earth. The camp around them had been designed to be broken down and moved on the run. The soldiers' "tents" were canvas tarps set over ropes pulled tight between trees. The only travel furniture was that of her own pavilion and the battle pavilion. The Kinswomen had one group ready with gateways to move Elayne and her commanders further into the woods.

Most of her forces waited at the ready, like a taut bow with the arrow nocked. She would *not* engage the Trollocs on their terms, however. By report, some of their fists still topped the city walls, and attacking directly would be a disaster, with them raining death on her from above.

She would draw them out. If that required patience, so be it. "I've decided," Elayne continued to Birgitte. "I'll just hop through a gateway to take a look at the Trolloc army myself. From a safe distance. I could—"

Birgitte reached beneath her shirt and removed the foxhead medallion she wore, one of the three imperfect copies Elayne had made. Mat had the original and a copy. Mellar had escaped with the other copy.

"You try anything like that," Birgitte said, eyes still forward, "and I'll *throw* you over my bloody shoulder like a drunken man with a barmaid on a rowdy night and carry you back to camp. Light help me, I'll *do* it, Elayne."

Elayne frowned. "Remind me why, exactly, I gave you one of those medallions?"

"I'm not sure," Birgitte said. "It showed remarkable foresight and an actual sense of self-preservation. Completely unlike you."

"I hardly think that is fair, Birgitte."

"I know! It *is* extremely unfair for me to have to deal with you. I wasn't certain you'd noticed. Are all young Aes Sedai as reckless as you are, or did I just end up with the pick of this particular litter?"

"Stop whining," Elayne muttered, maintaining a smile and a nod for the men who saluted as she passed. "I'm beginning to wish I had a Tower-trained Warder. Then, at least, I wouldn't hear so much sauce."

Birgitte laughed. "I don't think you understand Warders half as well as you think you do, Elayne."

Elayne let the matter die as they passed the Traveling ground, where Sumeko and the other Kinswomen were shuttling messengers back and forth from the battlefields. For now, Elayne's agreement with them held.

In her dress pocket, Elayne carried Egwene's—the Amyrlin Seat's—official reply regarding the Kin and what Elayne had done. Elayne could almost sense heat radiating from the letter, but it was hidden behind official language and an agreement that now wasn't the time to worry about such things.

Elayne would have to do more work there. Egwene would eventually see the logic of letting the Kinswomen work in Andor, beneath Elayne's supervision. Just beyond the Traveling ground she noticed a tired-looking Shienaran accepting a waterskin from one of the Two Rivers men. The top-knotted man had an eyepatch and familiar features.

"Uno?" Elayne asked with shock, pulling Moonshadow to a halt.

He started, nearly spilling water over himself as he drank. "Elayne?" he asked, wiping his brow with his sleeve. "I'd heard that you're the flaming—the Queen now. I guess that's what should have happened, with you being the bloody Daughter-Heir. Sorry. The Daughter-Heir. Not bloody at all." The Shienaran man grimaced.

"You can swear all you want, Uno," Elayne said dryly. "Nynaeve isn't around. What are you doing here?"

"The Amyrlin," he said. "She flaming wanted a messenger, and I was bloody chosen. Already gave Egwene's bloody report to your commanders, for all the bloody good it will do. We've set up our flaming battle positions and started scouting out Kandor, and the place is a bloody mess. You want details?"

Elayne smiled. "I'll hear the report from my commanders, Uno," she said. "Have a rest, and go have a flaming bath, you son of a shepherd's boil."

Uno blew a mouthful of water out at the comment. Elayne smiled. She'd heard that last curse from a soldier just the day before, and still didn't know why it was considered to be so vile. It had the proper effect.

"I . . . No flaming bath for me," Uno said. "Er, Your Majesty. I've had my five minutes of rest. The Trollocs could attack soon up in bloody Kandor, and I won't have the others fighting without me." He saluted her, hand across chest, and bowed before hurrying back toward the Traveling ground.

"Pity," Birgitte said, "he was a good drinking companion. I'd have liked him to stay a little while." Through the bond, Elayne felt a different reaction from her, as she watched Uno's backside.

Elayne blushed. "There's no time for that right now. *Either* of those things."

"Just looking," Birgitte said innocently. "I suppose we should go listen to the reports from the other battlefields."

"We should," Elayne said firmly.

Birgitte didn't voice her annoyance, but Elayne could feel it. Birgitte hated battle planning, something Elayne found odd in a woman who had fought in thousands of battles, a hero who had saved countless lives during some of the great moments in history.

They came to the battle pavilion, one of the few full-sized tents the army carried. Inside, she found Bashere conferring with several of the commanders: Abell Cauthon, Gallenne and Trom, second-in-command of the Whitecloaks. Galad himself, like Perrin, was with the harrying forces at Caemlyn. Elayne found Trom surprisingly agreeable—much more so than Galad himself.

"Well?" she asked.

"Your Majesty," Trom said, bowing. He didn't like the fact that she was Aes Sedai, but he hid it well. The others in the room saluted, though Bashere gave merely a friendly wave, then pointed at their battle maps.

"Reports from all fronts are in," Bashere said. "Refugees from Kandor are flocking to the Amyrlin and her soldiers, and that includes a fair number of fighting men. House soldiers or merchant guards, for the most part. Lord Ituralde's forces still await the Lord Dragon before moving on Shayol Ghul." Bashere knuckled his mustache. "Once they move into that valley, there won't be any retreat available."

"And the Borderlander army?" Elayne asked.

"Holding," Bashere said, pointing to another map, showing Shienar. Elayne wondered, idly, if Uno wished he were fighting with the rest of his people at the Gap. "Last messenger said they feared being overwhelmed, and were considering a controlled retreat."

Elayne frowned. "Are things so bad there? They were supposed to hold until I could finish the Trollocs in Andor and join them. That was the plan."

"It was," Bashere agreed.

"You're going to tell me that a plan, in warfare, lasts only until the first sword is drawn," Elayne said. "Or maybe until the first arrow falls?"

"First lance is raised," Bashere said under his breath.

"I realize that," Elayne said, stabbing a finger at the map. "But I also know that Lord Agelmar is a good enough general to hold a pack of Trollocs, especially with the Borderlander armies there to back him up."

"They are holding for now," Bashere said. "But they're still being mightily pressed." He held up a hand to her objection. "I know you're worried about a retreat, but I counsel that you shouldn't try to overrule Agelmar. He deserves his reputation as a great captain, and he's there, while we are far away. He will know what to do."

She took a deep breath. "Yes. You are right. Do see if Egwene can send him any troops. Meanwhile, *we* need to win our battle here quickly." Fighting on four fronts was going to drain resources quickly.

Elayne had not only familiar terrain to fight on, but also the best odds. If the other armies could hold steady while she obliterated the Trollocs in Andor, she could join Lan and Agelmar and turn the Gap from a stalemate into a victory. From there, she could reinforce Egwene and reclaim Kandor.

Elayne's army was the linchpin of the entire operation. If she didn't win in Andor, the other armies would have no eventual reinforcement. Lan and Ituralde would waste away, losing wars of attrition. Egwene might have a chance, depending on what the Shadow hurled her direction. Elayne didn't want to find out.

"We need the Trollocs to charge us," she said. "Now."

Bashere nodded.

"Step up the harrying," Elayne said. "Hit them with constant waves of arrows. Make it clear that if they don't charge, we're going to wear them down to nothing."

"And if they just retreat back into the city?" Trom asked. "The fires are dying down."

"Then, like it or not, we'll bring those dragons in to start leveling Caemlyn. We cannot wait any longer."

Androl struggled to stay awake. The drink they had given him . . . it made him drowsy. What was the purpose of that?

Something to do with channeling, Androl thought in a daze. The One Power was lost to him, though there was no shield. What kind of drink could do that to a man?

Poor Emarin lay weeping in his bonds. They had not managed to Turn him yet, but as the hours wore on, he seemed closer and closer to breaking. Androl stretched, twisting his head. He could barely make out the thirteen men Taim had been using for the process. They slumped as they sat around a table in the dim room. They were exhausted.

Androl remembered . . . Taim yelling the day before. He railed against the men, claiming their work went too slowly. They had expended much strength on the first men and women they'd Turned, and now they were apparently having a more difficult time.

Pevara slept. The tea had knocked her out. They'd given it to Androl after her, but almost as an afterthought. They seemed to forget about him much of the time. Taim had actually been angry when he'd found his minions had given the tea to Pevara. He'd wanted to Turn her next, apparently, and the process required the victim to be able to channel.

"Release me!"

Androl twisted at the new voice. Abors and Mishraile pulled someone in through the door, a short woman with coppery skin. Toveine, one of the Aes Sedai that Logain had bonded.

Nearby, Logain—eyes closed, looking as if he'd been beaten by a mob of angry men—stirred.

"What are you doing!" Toveine demanded. "Light! I—" She cut off as Abors gagged her. The thick-browed man was one of those who had gone to Taim willingly, during the days before Turning had begun.

Androl tried, thoughts still cloudy, to pull his hands free from the bonds. The ropes were bound more tightly. That was right. Evin had noticed the bonds and retied them.

He felt so helpless. Useless. He hated that feeling. If there was one thing Androl had dedicated his life to, it was to never being useless. Always knowing something about the situation.

"Turn her next," Taim's voice said.

Androl twisted, craning his neck. Taim sat at the table. He liked to be there for the Turnings, but he wasn't watching Toveine. He fondled something in his hands. Some kind of disc . . .

He stood up suddenly, tucking the object into a pouch at his waist. "The others complain about exhaustion from so much Turning. Well, if they Turn this one, she can join their ranks and lend her strength. Mishraile, you come with me. It's time."

Mishraile and several others joined Taim; they'd been standing where Androl couldn't see them.

Taim stalked toward the door. "I want that woman Turned by the time I get back," he said.

Lan galloped across the rocky ground, riding toward the Gap for what seemed like the hundredth time, though he had been fighting here less than a week.

Prince Kaisel and King Easar fell in beside him, riding hard. "What is it, Dai Shan?" Kaisel yelled. "Another attack? I did not see the emergency signal!"

Lan leaned down grimly in the dusk, bonfires made of carcasses and wood blazing to either side of him as he led the charge of several hundred Malkieri. Burning carcasses was difficult, but not only did they need the light; they wanted to deny the Trollocs some meals.

Lan heard something ahead, something that horrified him. Something he had been dreading.

Explosions.

The distant eruptions sounded like boulders crashing against one another. Each one made the air shake.

"Light!" Queen Ethenielle of Kandor joined them, galloping on her white gelding. She yelled to him. "Is that what I think it is?"

Lan nodded. Enemy channelers.

Ethenielle called back to her retinue, yelling something he did not catch. She was a plump woman, somewhat matronly for a Borderlander. Her retinue included Lord Baldhere—her Swordbearer—and the grizzled Kalyan Ramsin, her new husband.

They approached the Gap, where warriors fought to keep the beasts contained. A group of Kandori riders near the bonfires at the front were suddenly thrown into the air.

"Lord Mandragoran!" A figure in a black coat waved to them. Narishma hurried up, his Aes Sedai accompanying him. Lan always had one channeler at the front lines, but had given them orders not to fight. He needed them fresh for emergencies.

Like this one.

"Channeling?" Lan asked, slowing Mandarb.

"Dreadlords, Dai Shan," Narishma said, panting. "Maybe as many as two dozen."

"Twenty or more channelers," Agelmar said. "They'll cut through us like a sword through a spring lamb."

Lan looked across the bitter landscape, once his homeland. A homeland he'd never known.

He would have to abandon Malkier. Admitting it felt like a knife twisting inside him, but he would do it. "You have your retreat, Lord Agelmar," Lan said. "Narishma, can you channelers do anything?"

"We can try to cut their weaves from the air if we ride up close enough," Narishma said. "But that will be hard, perhaps impossible, with them using just ribbons of Fire and Earth. Besides, with so many on their side ... well, they'll target us. I fear we would be cut down—"

A nearby blast rocked the earth, and Mandarb reared, nearly throwing Lan to the ground. Lan fought the horse, nearly blind from the flash of light.

"Dai Shan!" Narishma's voice.

Lan blinked tears from his eyes.

"Go to Queen Elayne!" Lan bellowed. "Bring back channelers to cover our retreat. We'll be cut to ribbons without them. Go, man!"

Agelmar was yelling the retreat, bringing forward archers to target the channelers and drive them beneath cover. Lan unsheathed his sword, galloping to bring the horsemen back.

Light protect us, Lan thought, yelling himself ragged and salvaging what he could of his cavalry. The Gap was lost.

Elayne waited nervously just inside Braem Wood.

It was an old forest, the type that seemed to have a soul of its own. The ancient trees were its gnarled fingers, reaching out of the earth to feel the wind.

It was difficult not to feel tiny in a wood like Braem. Though many of the trees were bare, Elayne could feel a thousand eyes watching her from the depths of the forest. She found herself thinking of the stories told to her as a child, stories of the Wood being full of brigands—some goodly, others with hearts as twisted as those of Darkfriends.

In fact ... Elayne thought, remembering one of the stories. She turned to Birgitte. "Didn't you once lead a band of thieves out of this forest?"

Birgitte grimaced. "I was hoping you hadn't heard that one."

"You robbed the Queen of Aldeshar!" Elayne said.

"I was very polite about it," Birgitte said. "She *wasn't* a good queen. Many claimed she wasn't the rightful one."

"It's the principle!"

"That's exactly why I did it." Birgitte frowned. "At least ... I think it was ... "

Elayne didn't push the topic any farther. Birgitte always grew anxious when reminded that her memories of past lives were fading. At times, she had no recollection of her past lives at all; at other times, certain incidents would come flooding back to her, only to disappear the next moment.

Elayne led the rear guard, which would—in theory—do the bulk of the damage to the enemy.

Dry leaves crunched as a winded messenger arrived from the Traveling ground. "I've come from Caemlyn, Your Majesty," the woman said with a bobbing bow from her mount. "Lord Aybara has successfully engaged the Trollocs. They are on their way."

"Light, they took the bait," Elayne said. "Now we make our preparations. Go get some rest; you'll be needing all your strength soon enough."

The messenger nodded, galloping away. Elayne relayed the latest news to Talmanes, the Aiel and Tam al'Thor.

As Elayne heard something in the forest she raised a hand, stopping a Guardswoman's report. Moonshadow danced forward, anxious, past the men who crouched in the underbrush around Elayne. No one spoke. The soldiers barely seemed to be drawing breath.

Elayne embraced the Source. Power flooded her, and with it the sweetness of a world expanded. The dying wood seemed more colorful within the embrace of *saidar*. Yes. There was something climbing over the hills in the near distance. Her soldiers, thousands of them, whipping at horses past the point of exhaustion, were fast approaching the Wood. Elayne raised her spyglass to make out the twisting mass of Trollocs chasing behind like black waves flooding onto an already shadowed land.

"Finally!" Elayne exclaimed. "Archers, to the front!"

The Two Rivers men scrambled out of the woods before her, forming up just inside the tree line. They were one of the smallest forces in her army, but if reports on their prowess weren't exaggerations, they'd be as useful as an ordinary force of archers three times their size.

A few of the younger men began nocking arrows to bows.

"Hold!" Elayne yelled. "Those are *our* men coming toward you."

Tam and his leaders repeated the order. The men lowered their bows nervously.

"Your Majesty," Tam said, stepping up to her horse. "The lads can hit them at this range."

"Our soldiers are still too close," Elayne said. "We need to wait for them to break to the sides."

"Pardon, my Lady," Tam said. "But no Two Rivers man would miss a shot like this. Those riders are safe, and the Trollocs have bows of their own."

He was right on that last count. Some of the Trollocs were pausing in their pursuit long enough to draw their massive black-wood bows. Perrin's men were riding with their backs exposed, and more than a few had dark-fletched arrows protruding from their limbs or their horses.

"Loose," Elayne said. "Archers, loose!" Birgitte relayed the orders as she rode down the line. Tam barked orders to those nearby.

Elayne lowered the spyglass as a breeze blew through the forest, crackling dried leaves, rattling skeletal branches. The Two Rivers men drew. Light! Could they *really* shoot that far and still be accurate? The Trollocs were hundreds of paces away.

Arrows flew high, like hawks breaking from their roosts. She'd heard Rand brag about his bow, and she'd seen a Two Rivers long-bow used on occasion. But this . . . so many arrows climbing into the air with incredible precision . . .

The arrows arced and dropped, not a one falling too short. They rained onto the Trolloc ranks, especially on the Trolloc archers. A few straggling Trolloc arrows returned, but the Two Rivers men had handily broken up their lines.

"That's some fine archery," Birgitte said, riding back up. "Fine indeed . . ."

The Two Rivers men loosed more volleys in quick succession as Perrin's riders entered the forest.

"Crossbowmen!" Elayne ordered, drawing her sword and raising it high. "Forward the Legion of the Dragon!"

The Two Rivers men fell back into the trees and the crossbowmen came out. She had two full banners of them from the Legion of the Dragon, and Bashere had drilled them well. They formed three ranks, one standing at a time to loose while the others reloaded while kneeling. The death they sent at the Trollocs hit like a crashing wave, driving a tremble through the advancing army, thousands falling dead.

Elayne leveled her sword at the Trollocs. The Two Rivers men had climbed the branches of the first line of trees and were loosing arrows from them. The men weren't nearly as accurate from the precarious perches, but they didn't need to be. The Trollocs faced death from the front and from above, and the creatures began to stumble over their dead.

Come on . . . Elayne thought.

The Trollocs advanced, forcing their way toward the archers. A large contingent of Trollocs broke off from the advance and headed to the east. The roadway that bordered Braem Wood was that way, and it would make sense for the Trollocs to seize it, then push along it to surround Elayne's forces. Or so the Fades would think.

"Fall back into the Wood!" Elayne said, waving the sword. "Hurry!"

The crossbowmen each loosed one more bolt, then melted into the forest, pushing through the underbrush. The Two Rivers men dropped to the ground, then moved carefully through the trees. Elayne turned and rode in at a cautious trot. A short distance into the forest, she reached a banner of Alliandre's Ghealdanin standing in ranks with pikes and halberds.

"Be sure to fall back as soon as they hit," Elayne yelled to them. "We want to draw them deeper!" Deeper into the forest, where the *siswai'aman* awaited their arrival.

The soldiers nodded. Elayne passed Alliandre herself, sitting her horse with a small guard surrounding her. The dark-haired queen did a horseback curtsy to Elayne. Her men had wanted their queen to join Berelain at Mayene's hospital, but Alliandre had refused. Perhaps seeing Elayne lead her troops directly had spurred the woman's decision.

Elayne left them behind as the first Trollocs hit the Wood, grunting and yelling. They'd have a difficult time fighting in the forest. The humans could use the forest cover far more effectively, ambushing the huge Trollocs barreling through the woods, skewering and hamstringing them from behind. Mobile forces of bowmen and crossbowmen could shoot from cover—if they did it right, the Trollocs wouldn't even know which direction the arrows were coming from.

As Elayne led her Queen's Guard toward the roadway, she heard distant explosions and screams from Trollocs. The slingmen were tossing Aludra's explosive roarsticks at the Trollocs through the trees. Flashes of light reflected off dim tree trunks.

Elayne reached the roadway just in time to see the Trollocs, led by several Myrddraal in deep black cloaks, come pouring onto it. They could quickly flank Elayne's force—but the Band of the Red Hand had already set up the dragons on the road. Talmanes stood with hands clasped behind his back atop a pile of boxes, overlooking his force. The banner of the Red Hand flapped behind him, a bloody palm stamped on a field of red-fringed white, with Aludra yelling out measurements, aiming instructions and the occasional curse at dragoners making mistakes or moving too slowly.

Arrayed in front of Talmanes were the dragons, nearly a hundred of them, strung across the broad roadway in four ranks, spilling out into the fields around the roadway here. Elayne was too far away to hear him give the order to fire. That was perhaps a good thing, for the thunder that followed shook her as if Dragonmount itself had decided to erupt. Moonshadow bucked, neighing, and Elayne had to fight to keep the animal from tossing her on her backside. In the end, she plugged the horse's ears with a weave of Air as the dragoners rolled their weapons to the side and let the second rank open fire.

Elayne plugged her own ears as she calmed Moonshadow. Birgitte continued fighting her own terrified mount, eventually leaping free, but Elayne paid little attention. She peered through the smoke that choked the roadway. The third line of dragons was rolling up to fire.

Despite having her ears plugged, she could *feel* the blast jolt the ground, shake the trees. The fourth round followed, rattling her to the bones. Elayne breathed in and out, stilling her heart, waiting for the smoke to clear.

First, she made out Talmanes, standing tall. The first line of dragons had rolled back into place, reloaded. The other three ranks were hastily doing their own reloads, slipping powder and the large metal spheres into place.

A strong breeze from the west cleared the smoke enough for her to see ... Elayne gasped softly.

Thousands of Trollocs lay in smoldering pieces, many blown off the road completely. Arms, legs, strands of coarse hair, *pieces* lay scattered amid holes in the ground fully two paces wide. Where there had once been many thousands of Trollocs, only blood, broken bones and smoke remained. Many of the trees had been shattered into splintered trunks. Of the Myrddraal that had been at the front, there was no sign at all.

The dragoners lowered their flame-sticks, not firing their reloaded rounds. A few surviving Trollocs near the back scrambled away into the forest.

Elayne looked at Birgitte and grinned. The Warder looked on, solemn, while several Guardswomen ran to chase down her horse.

"Well?" Elayne asked, unstopping her ears.

"I think ..." Birgitte said. "Those things are messy. And imprecise. And bloody *effective*."

"Yes," Elayne said proudly.

Birgitte shook her head. Her horse was returned to her, and she remounted. "I used to think that a man and his bow were the most dangerous combination this land would ever know, Elayne. Now—as if it weren't bad enough that men channel openly and the Seanchan use channelers in combat—we have those things. I don't like the way this is going. If any boy with a tube of metal can destroy an entire army ..."

"Don't you see?" Elayne said. "There won't be war any more. We win this, and there *will* be peace, as Rand intends. Nobody but Trollocs would go into battle, knowing they face weapons like these!"

"Perhaps," Birgitte said. She shook her head. "Maybe I have less faith in the wisdom of people than you do."

Elayne sniffed, raising her sword to Talmanes, who drew his and raised it back. The first step in destroying this Trolloc army had been taken.

CHAPTER
11

Just Another Sell-sword

"I realize there have been ... disagreements between us in the past," Adelorna Bastine said, riding beside Egwene as they passed through camp. Adelorna was a slim, regal woman; her tilted eyes and dark hair bespoke her Saldaean heritage. "I would not have you consider us enemies."

"I have not," Egwene said carefully, "and do not." She did not ask what Adelorna meant by using the word "us." She was Green, and Egwene had suspected for a time that she was the Captain-General, the name the Greens gave to the head of their Ajah.

"That is well," Adelorna said. "Some within the Ajah have acted in foolishness. They have been ... informed of their mistakes. You will find no further resistance from those who should have loved you best, Mother. Whatever has passed, let it be buried."

"Let it be buried," Egwene agreed, amused. *Now*, she thought. *After all of this, the Greens try to claim me?*

Well, she would use them. She had been worried that her relationship with them was beyond repair. Choosing Silviana as her Keeper had made many determine to treat her as an enemy. Egwene had heard whispers that many thought she would have chosen the Red as her Ajah, despite the fact that she not only had a Warder, but had married him.

"If I may ask," Egwene said. "Is there a particular incident which has brought about this . . . bridge across our difficulties?"

"Some are willfully ignorant of what you did during the Seanchan invasion, Mother," Adelorna said. "You proved to have the spirit of a warrior. Of a general. This is something the Green Ajah must not ignore. Indeed, we must embrace it as an example. So it has been decided, and so those who lead the Ajah have spoken." Adelorna met Egwene's eyes, then bowed her head.

The implication was obvious. Adelorna *was* the head of the Green Ajah. To speak it outright would not be appropriate, but to give Egwene this knowledge was to give a measure of trust and respect.

If you had truly been raised from us, the action said, *you would have known who led us. You would have known our secrets. I give them to you.* There was also gratitude to the motion. Egwene had saved Adelorna's life during the Seanchan assault of the White Tower.

The Amyrlin was of no Ajah—and Egwene actually expressed this virtue more than any before her, for she never *had* belonged to an Ajah. Still, this gesture was moving. She rested her hand on Adelorna's arm in thanks, then gave her leave to depart.

Gawyn, Silviana and Leilwin rode off to the side, where Egwene had sent them after Adelorna asked for a private word. That Seanchan . . . Egwene vacillated between keeping her close to watch her, and sending her far, far away.

Leilwin's information about the Seanchan *had* been useful. So far as she could determine, Leilwin had told her the exact truth. For now, Egwene kept her close—if only because she frequently thought of more questions about the Seanchan. Leilwin acted more like a bodyguard than a prisoner. As if Egwene would trust her safety to one of the Seanchan. She shook her head, riding among the gathered tents and campfires of the army. Most were empty, as Bryne had the men forming battle lines. He expected the Trolloc approach within the hour.

Egwene found Bryne calmly organizing his maps and papers in a tent near the center of the camp. Yukiri was there, arms folded. Egwene dismounted and went in.

Bryne looked up sharply. "Mother!" he exclaimed, causing her to freeze.

She looked down. There was a hole in the floor of the tent, and she had nearly stepped into it.

It was a *gateway*. The other side appeared to open into the air itself, looking down on the Trolloc army, which was crossing the hills. The recent week had involved many skirmishes, with Egwene's archers and riders slaughtering Trollocs who marched, in force, toward the hills and the border into Arafel.

Egwene peered through this gateway in the floor. It was high up, well outside of bow range, but looking down through it at the Trollocs made her dizzy.

"I'm not sure if this is brilliant," she said to Bryne, "or incredibly foolhardy."

Bryne smiled, turning back to his maps. "Winning wars is about information, Mother. If I can see exactly what they are doing—where they are trying to envelop us and how they are bringing in reserves—I can prepare. This is better than a battle tower. I should have thought of it ages ago."

"The Shadow has Dreadlords who can channel, General," Egwene said. "Peeking through this gateway could get you burned to a crisp. That's not to mention Draghkar. If a flock of them tried to fly through this—"

"Draghkar are Shadowspawn," Bryne said. "I've been told that they'd die passing through the gateway."

"I guess that's true," Egwene said, "but you'd have a flock of dead Draghkar in here. Regardless, channelers can still attack through it."

"I will take that chance. The advantage offered is incredible."

"I'd still rather you use scouts to look through the gateway," Egwene said, "not your own eyes. You are a resource. One of our most valuable. Risks are unavoidable, but please take care to minimize them."

"Yes, Mother," he said.

She inspected the weaves, then eyed Yukiri.

"I volunteered, Mother," Yukiri said before Egwene could ask how a Sitter ended up doing simple gateway duty. "He sent to us, asking if forming a gateway like this—horizontal, instead of vertical—was possible. I thought it an interesting puzzle."

She was not surprised he had sent to the Grays. There was a growing sentiment among them that, just as the Yellows specialized in Healing weaves and the Greens specialized in Battle weaves, the Grays should take particular interest in weaves for

Traveling. They seemed to consider travel part of their calling as mediators and ambassadors.

"Can you show me our own lines?" Egwene asked.

"Certainly, Mother," Yukiri said, closing the gateway. She opened another, letting Egwene look down on the battle lines of her army as they formed up in defensive positions on the hills.

This *was* more efficient than maps. No map could completely convey the lay of a land, the way that troops moved. Egwene felt as if she were looking at an exact replica of the landscape in miniature.

Vertigo hit her suddenly. She was standing at the edge of a drop of hundreds of feet. Her mind reeled, and she stepped back, taking a deep breath.

"You need to put a rope up around this thing," Egwene said. "Someone could step right off." *Or pitch headfirst while staring down ...*

Bryne grunted. "I sent Siuan for something like that." He hesitated. "She didn't much like being sent, though, so she might come back with something completely useless."

"I keep wondering," Yukiri said. "Shouldn't there be a way to create a gateway like this, but make it so it can only let light through? Like a window. You could stand on it and look down, without fearing that you could slip through. With the right weaves, you might be able to make it invisible from the other side ..."

Stand on *it? Light. You'd have to be mad.*

"Lord Bryne," Egwene said, "your battle lines seem very solid."

"Thank you, Mother."

"They are also lacking."

Bryne raised his head. Other men might have risen to the challenge, but he did not. Perhaps it was all of that practice in dealing with Morgase. "How so?"

"You form up the troops as usual," Egwene said. "Archers at the front and on the hills to slow the enemy advance, heavy cavalry to charge and hit, then withdraw. Pikes to hold the line, light cavalry to protect our flanks and keep us from being surrounded."

"The soundest battle strategies are often those that are time-tested," Bryne said. "We may have a large force, with all of those Dragonsworn, but we're still outnumbered. We can't be more aggressive than I've been here."

"Yes, you can be," Egwene said calmly. She met his eyes. "This is unlike any battle you've ever fought, and your army is not like any you've ever led, General. You have a major advantage that you are not taking into account."

"You mean the Aes Sedai?"

Bloody right I do, she thought. Light, she'd been spending too much time around Elayne.

"I did account for you, Mother," Bryne said. "I had planned for the Aes Sedai to be a reserve force to aid companies in disengaging so we can rotate in fresh troops."

"Pardon, Lord Bryne," Egwene said. "Your plans are wise, and certainly some of the Aes Sedai should be used that way. However, the White Tower did not prepare and train for thousands of years to sit out the Last Battle as a *reserve* force."

Bryne nodded, slipping a new set of documents out from underneath his pile. "I did consider other more . . . dynamic possibilities, but I did not want to overstep my authority." He handed her the documents.

Egwene scanned them, raising an eyebrow. Then she smiled.

Mat had not remembered so many Tinkers around Ebou Dar. Brilliantly colored wagons grew like vibrant mushrooms on an otherwise dun field. There were enough of them to make a bloody city. A city of Tinkers? That would be like . . . like a city of Aiel. It was just wrong.

Mat trotted Pips along the roadway. Of course, there *was* an Aiel city. Maybe there would be a Tinker city someday, too. They would buy up all of the colored dye, and everyone else in the world would have to wear brown. There would be no fighting in the city, so it would be downright boring, but there also would not be a single bloody pot with a hole in the bottom for thirty leagues!

Mat smiled, patting Pips. He had covered over his *ashandarei* as best he could to make it look like a walking pole strapped to the side of the horse. His hat lay inside the pack he had hung from the saddlebags, along with all of his nice coats. He had ripped the lace off the one he wore. It was a shame, but he did not want to be recognized.

He wore a crude bandage wrapped around the side of his head, covering his missing eye. As he approached the Dal Eira gate, he fell into line behind the others awaiting permission to enter. He should look just like another wounded sell-sword riding into the city, seeking refuge or perhaps work.

He made certain to slump in the saddle. Keep your head down: good advice on the battlefield *and* when entering a city where people knew you. He could not be Matrim Cauthon here. Matrim Cauthon had left the queen of this city tied up to be murdered. Many would suspect him of the murder. Light, he would have suspected *himself*. Beslan would hate him now, and there was no telling how Tuon would feel about him, now that they had had some time apart.

Yes, best to keep his head down and stay quiet. He would feel the place out. If, that was, he ever reached the front of this bloody line. Who ever heard of a line to enter a city?

Eventually, he reached the gate. The bored soldier there had a face like an old shovel—it was half-covered in dirt and would be better off locked in a shed somewhere. He looked Mat up and down.

"You have sworn the oaths, traveler?" the guard asked in a lazy Seanchan drawl. On the other side of the gate, a different soldier waved over the next person in line.

"Yes, I have indeed," Mat said. "The oaths to the great Seanchan Empire, and the Empress herself, may she live forever. I'm just a poor, traveling sell-sword, once attendant to House Haak, a noble family in Murandy. I lost my eye to some bandits in the Tween Forest two years back while protecting a young child I discovered in the woods. I raised her as my own, but—"

The soldier waved him on. The fellow did not look as if he had been listening. Mat considered staying put out of principle. Why would the soldiers force people to wait in such a long line and give them time to think of a cover story, only to not hear it out? That could offend a man. Not Matrim Cauthon, who was always lighthearted and never offended. But someone else, surely.

He rode on, containing his annoyance. Now, he just needed to make his way to the right tavern. Pity Setalle's place was not an option any longer. That had—

Mat stiffened in the saddle, though Pips continued his leisurely pace forward. Mat had just taken a moment to look at the other guard at the gate. It was *Petra*, the strongman from Valan Luca's menagerie!

Mat looked the other way and slumped again in his saddle, then shot another glance over his shoulder. That was Petra, all right. There was no mistaking those log arms and that tree-stump neck. Petra was not a tall man, but he was so wide, an entire army could have taken shade in his shadow. What was he doing back in Ebou Dar? Why was he wearing a Seanchan uniform? Mat almost went over to talk to him, as they had always been amiable, but that Seanchan uniform made him reconsider.

Well, at least his luck was with him. If he had been sent to Petra instead of the guard he had ended up talking to, he would have been recognized for sure. Mat breathed out, then climbed down to lead Pips. The city was crowded, and he did not want the horse pushing someone over. Besides, Pips was laden down enough to look like a packhorse—if the looker knew nothing of horses—and walking might make Mat less memorable.

Perhaps he should have started his search for a tavern in the Rahad. Rumors were always easy to find in the Rahad, as was a game of dice. It was also the easiest place to find a knife in your gut, and that was saying something in Ebou Dar. In the Rahad people were as likely to take out their knives and begin killing as they were to say hello in the morning.

He did not go into the Rahad. The place looked different, now. There were soldiers camped outside it. Generations of successive rulers in Ebou Dar had allowed the Rahad to fester unchecked, but the Seanchan were not so inclined.

Mat wished them luck. The Rahad had fought off every invasion so far. Light. Rand should have just hidden there, instead of going up to fight the Last Battle. The Trollocs and Darkfriends would have come for him, and the Rahad would have left them all unconscious in an alley, their pockets turned inside out and their shoes sold for soup money. Mat caught a glimpse of Rand shaving, but he squashed the image.

Mat shouldered his way over a crowded canal bridge, keeping a close eye on his saddlebags, but so far, not a single cutpurse had tried for them. With a Seanchan patrol on every other corner, he could see why. As he passed a man yelling out the day's news, with hints that he had good gossip for a little coin, Mat found himself smiling. He was surprised at how familiar, even comfortable, this city felt. He had liked it here. Though he could vaguely remember grumbling about wanting to be away—probably just after the wall fell on him, as Matrim Cauthon was not often one for grumbling—he now realized that his time in Ebou Dar had been among the best of his life. Plenty of cards and dice in the city.

Tylin. Bloody ashes, but that had been a fun game. She had had the better of him time and again. Light send him plenty of women who could do that, though not in rapid succession, and always when he knew how to find the back door. Tuon was one. Come to think of it, he would probably never need another. She was enough of a handful for any man. Mat smiled, patting Pips on the neck. The horse blew down Mat's neck in return.

Strangely, this place felt more like home to him than the Two Rivers did. Yes, the Ebou Dari were prickly, but all peoples had their quirks. In fact, as Mat thought about it, he had never met a people who were not prickly about one thing or another. The Borderlanders were baffling, and so were the Aiel—that went without saying. The Cairhienin and their strange games, the Tairens and their ridiculous hierarchies, the Seanchan and their . . . Seanchan-ness.

That was the truth of it. Everyone outside the Two Rivers, and to a lesser extent Andor, was *bloody* insane. A man just had to be ready for that.

He strolled along, careful to be polite, lest he find a knife in his gut. The air smelled of a hundred sweetmeats, the chattering crowd a low roar in his ears. The Ebou Dari still wore their colorful outfits—maybe that was why the Tinkers had come here, drawn to the bright colors like soldiers drawn to dinner—anyway, the Ebou Dari women wore dresses with tight-laced tops that showed plenty of bosom, not that Mat looked. Their skirts had colorful petticoats underneath and they pinned up the side or front to show them off. That never had made sense to him. Why put the colorful parts underneath? And if you did, why take such pains to cover them over, then go around with the outside pinned up?

The men wore long vests that were equally colorful, perhaps to hide the bloodstains when they were stabbed. No point in throwing away a good vest just because the fellow wearing it was murdered for inquiring after the weather. Though ... as Mat walked along, he found fewer duels than he had expected. They never had been as common in this part of the city as in the Rahad, but some days, he had hardly been able to take two steps without passing a pair of men with knives out. This day, he saw not a single one.

Some of the Ebou Dari—you could often tell them by their olive skin—were parading around in Seanchan dress. Everyone was very polite. As polite as a six-year-old boy who had just heard that you had a fresh apple pie back in the kitchen.

The city was the same, but different. The feel was off a shade or two. And it was not just that there were no Sea Folk ships in the harbor any longer. It was the Seanchan, obviously. They'd made rules since he'd left. What kind?

Mat took Pips to a stable that seemed reputable enough. A quick glance at their stock told him that; they were caring well for the animals, and many were very fine. It was best to trust a stable with fine horses, though it cost you a little more.

He left Pips, took his bundle, and used the still-wrapped *ashandarei* as a walking staff. Choosing the right tavern was as tough as choosing a good wine. You wanted one that was old, but not broken down. Clean, but not too clean—a spotless tavern was one that never saw any real use. Mat could not stand the types of places where people sat around quietly and drank tea, coming there primarily to be seen.

No, a good tavern was worn and used, like good boots. It was also sturdy, again like good boots. So long as the ale did not *taste* like good boots, you would have a winner. The best places for information were over in the Rahad, but his clothing was too nice to visit, and he did not want to run into whatever the Seanchan were doing there.

He stuck his head into an inn named The Winter Blossom, and immediately turned around and stalked away. Deathwatch Guards in uniform. He did not want to take any slight chance of running into Furyk Karede. The next inn was too well lit, and the next too dark. After about an hour of hunting—and not a duel to be seen—he began to despair of ever finding the right place. Then he heard dice tumbling in a cup.

At first, he jumped, thinking that it was those blasted dice in his head. Fortunately, it was just ordinary dice. Blessed, wonderful dice. The sound was gone in a moment, carried on the wind through the throng of people in the streets. Hand on his coin purse, pack over his shoulder, he pushed through the crowd, muttering a few apologies. In a nearby alleyway, he saw a sign hanging from a wall.

He stepped up to it, reading the words "The Yearly Brawl" in copper on its face. It had a picture of clapping people, and the sounds of dice mixed with the smells of wine and ale. Mat stepped inside. A round-faced Seanchan stood just inside the door, leaning casually against the wall, a sword on his belt. He gave Mat a distrustful stare. Well, Mat had never met a shoulderthumper who did not give that look to every man who entered. Mat reached up to tip his hat to the man, but of course he was not wearing it. Bloody ashes. He felt naked without it, sometimes.

"Jame!" a woman called from beside the bar. "You aren't glaring at customers again, are you?"

"Only the ones that deserve it, Kathana," the man called back with a Seanchan slur. "I'm sure this one does."

"I'm just a humble traveler," Mat said, "looking for some dicing and some wine. Nothing more. Certainly not trouble."

"And that's why you're carrying a polearm?" Jame asked. "Wrapped up like that?"

"Oh, stop it," the woman, Kathana, said. She had crossed the common room and took Mat by the sleeve of his coat, dragging him toward the bar. She was a short thing, dark-haired and fair-skinned. She was not that much older than he was, but she had an unmistakable motherly air. "Don't mind him. Just don't make trouble, and he won't be forced to stab you, kill you, or anything in between."

She plunked Mat down on a bar stool and started busying herself behind the bar. The common room was dim, but in a friendly way. People diced at one side, the good kind of dicing. The kind that had people laughing or clapping their friends on the back at a good-natured loss. No haunted eyes of men gambling their last coin, here.

"You need food," Kathana declared. "You have the look of a man who hasn't eaten anything hearty in a week. How'd you lose that eye?"

"I was a lord's guard in Murandy," Mat said. "Lost it in an ambush."

"That's a great lie," Kathana said, slapping a plate down in front of him, full of slices of pork and gravy. "Better than most. You said it really straight, too. I almost believe you. Jame, you want food?"

"I have to guard the door!" he called back.

"Light, man. You expect someone to walk off with it? Get over here."

Jame grumbled but made his way over to the bar beside Mat, settling down on a stool. Kathana put a mug of ale down, and he took it up to his lips, staring straight ahead. "I'm watching you," he muttered to Mat.

Mat was not certain this was the right inn for him, but he also was not certain he would be able to escape with his head unless he ate the woman's food as instructed. He took a taste; it was pretty good. She had moved over and was wagging a finger while lecturing a man at one of the tables. She seemed the type who would lecture a tree for growing in the wrong spot.

This woman, Mat thought, *must never be allowed to enter the same room as Nynaeve. At least not when I'm within shouting distance.*

Kathana came bustling back. She wore a marriage knife at her neck, though Mat did not stare for more than a few seconds on account of him being a married man. She had her skirt pinned up on the side after the fashion of Ebou Dari commoners. As she came back to the bar and readied a plate of food for Jame, Mat noticed him watching her fondly, and made a guess. "You two been married long?" Mat asked.

Jame eyed him. "No," he finally said. "Haven't been on this side of the ocean for long."

"I suppose that would make sense," Mat said, taking a drink of the ale she set before him. It was not bad, considering how awful most things tasted these days. This was only a little awful.

Kathana walked over to the dicing men and demanded they eat more food, as they were looking pale. It was a wonder this Jame fellow did not weigh as much as two horses. She did talk some, though, so perhaps he could wiggle the information he needed out of her.

"There don't seem to be as many duels as there used to be," Mat said to her as she passed.

"That's because of a Seanchan rule," Kathana said, "from the new Empress, may she live forever. She didn't forbid duels entirely, and a bloody good thing she didn't. The Ebou Dari won't riot at something as unimportant as being conquered, but take away our duels ... *then* you'll see something. Anyway, duels now have to be witnessed by an official of the government. You can't duel without answering a hundred different questions and paying a fee. It's drained the whole life out of it all."

"It has saved lives," Jame said. "Men can still die by each other's knives if they are determined. They simply have to give themselves time to cool down and think."

"Duels aren't about thinking," Kathana said. "But I suppose it *does* mean that I don't have to worry about your pretty face being cut up on the street."

Jame snorted, resting his hand on his sword. The hilt, Mat noticed for the first time, was marked with herons—though he could not see if the blade was or not. Before Mat could ask another question, Kathana marched away and began squawking at some men who had spilled ale on their table. She did not seem the type to stand in one place for very long.

"How's the weather, to the north?" Jame asked, eyes still straight ahead.

"Dreary," Mat replied, honestly. "As everywhere."

"Men say it's the Last Battle," Jame said.

"It is."

Jame grunted. "If it is, it would be a bad time for interfering with politics, wouldn't you think?"

"Bloody right it would be," Mat said. "People need to stop playing games and have a look at the sky."

Jame eyed him. "That's the truth. You should listen to what you are saying."

Light, Mat thought. *He must think I'm a spy of some sort.* "It's not my choice," Mat said. "Sometimes, people will only listen to what they want to hear." He took another bite of his meat, which tasted as good as could be expected. Eating a meal these days was like going to a dance where there were only ugly girls. This, however, was among the better of the bad that he had had the misfortune of eating, lately.

"A wise man might just learn the truth," Jame said.

"You have to find the truth first," Mat said. "It's harder than most men think."

From behind, Kathana snorted, bustling past. "The 'truth' is something men debate in bars when they're too drunk to remember their names. That means it's not in good company. I wouldn't put too much stock in it, traveler."

"The name's Mandevwin," Mat said.

"I'm sure it is," Kathana said. She looked him over then. "Has anyone ever told you that you should wear a hat? It would fit the missing eye quite well."

"Is that so," Mat said dryly. "You give fashion advice as well as force-feeding men?"

She swatted him on the back of the head with her cleaning rag. "Eat your food."

"Look, friend," Jame said, turning toward him. "I know what you are and why you are here. The fake eye bandage is not fooling me. You have throwing knives tucked into your sleeves and six more on your belt that I can count. I've never met a man with one eye who could throw worth a dried bean. She's not as easy a target as you foreigners think. You'll never make it into the palace, let alone through her bodyguards. Go find some honest work instead."

Mat gaped at the man. He thought Mat was an *assassin*? Mat reached up and took off the bandage, exposing the hole where his eye had been.

Jame started at that.

"There are assassins," Mat said calmly, "after Tuon?"

"Don't use her name like that," Kathana said, beginning to snap her cleaning rag at him again.

Mat reached up beside his head without looking, catching the tip of the rag. He held Jame's eyes with his single one, not flinching.

"There are assassins," Mat repeated calmly, "after Tuon?"

Jame nodded. "Mostly foreigners who don't know the right way of things. Several have moved through the inn. Only one admitted the reason he was here. I saw that his blood fed the dusty earth of the dueling grounds."

"Then I count you a friend," Mat said, standing. He reached into his bundle and took out his hat and put it upon his head.

"Who is behind it? Who has brought them in, put the bounty on her head?"

Nearby, Kathana inspected his hat and nodded in satisfaction. Then she hesitated and squinted at his face.

"This isn't what you think," Jame said. "He isn't hiring the best assassins. They're foreigners, so they aren't meant to succeed."

"I don't care how bloody likely their chances are," Mat said. "Who is hiring them?"

"He's too important for you to—"

"*Who?*" Mat said softly.

"General Lunal Galgan," Jame said. "Head of the Seanchan armies. I can't make you out, friend. Are you an assassin, or are you here hunting assassins?"

"I'm no bloody assassin," Mat said, pulling the brim of his hat down and picking up his bundle. "I never kill a man unless he demands it—demands it with screams and thunder so loudly, I figure it would be impolite not to agree to the request. If I stab you, friend, you'll know that it is coming, and you will know why. I promise you that."

"Jame," Kathana hissed. "It's *him*."

"What now?" Jame asked as Mat brushed past, raising his covered *ashandarei* to his shoulder.

"The one the guards have been looking for!" Kathana said. She looked to Mat. "Light! Every soldier in Ebou Dar has been told to watch for your face. How did you make it through the city gates?"

"By luck," Mat said, then stepped out into the alleyway.

"What are you waiting for?" Moiraine asked.

Rand turned toward her. They stood in Lan's command tent in Shienar. He could smell the smoke of burning fields, set aflame by Lan and Lord Agelmar's troops as they withdrew from the Gap.

They were burning the lands they would rather defend. A desperate tactic, but a good one. It was the sort of all-in tactic that Lews Therin and his people in the Age of Legends had been hesitant to try, at least at first. It had cost them dearly then.

The Borderlanders showed no such timidity.

"Why are we here?" Moiraine pressed, stepping up to him. His

Maidens guarded the tent from the inside; better to not let the enemy know Rand was here. "You should be at Shayol Ghul right now. That is your destiny, Rand al'Thor. Not these lesser fights."

"My friends die here."

"I thought you were beyond such weaknesses."

"Compassion is not a weakness."

"Is it not?" she said. "And if, in sparing your enemy because of compassion, you allow them to kill you? What then, Rand al'Thor?"

He had no answer.

"You cannot risk yourself," Moiraine said. "And regardless of whether or not you agree that compassion itself can be a weakness, acting foolishly because of it certainly is."

He had often thought about the moment when he had lost Moiraine. He had agonized over her death, and he still reveled in her return. At times, however, he had forgotten how ... insistent she could be.

"I will move against the Dark One when the time is right," Rand said, "but not before. He must think I am with the armies, that I am waiting to seize more ground before striking at him. We must coax his commanders to commit their forces southward, lest we be overwhelmed at Shayol Ghul once I enter."

"It will not matter," Moiraine said. "You will face him, and that will be the time of determination. All spins on that moment, Dragon Reborn. All threads in the Pattern are woven around your meeting, and the turning of the Wheel pulls you toward it. Do not deny that you feel it."

"I feel it."

"Then go."

"Not yet."

She took a deep breath. "Stubborn as ever."

"And a good thing," Rand said. "Stubbornness is what brought me this far." Rand hesitated, then fished in his pocket. He came out with something bright and silvery—a Tar Valon mark. "Here," he said, holding it out to her. "I've been saving this."

She pursed her lips. "It cannot be ... "

"The same one? No. That is long lost, I fear. I've been carrying this one around as a token, almost without realizing what I'd been doing."

She took the coin, turning it over in her fingers. She was still inspecting it when the Maidens looked with alertness toward the tent flap. A second later, Lan lifted the flap and strode in, flanked by two Malkieri men. The three could have been brothers, with those grim expressions and hard faces.

Rand stepped up, resting his hand on Lan's shoulder. The man did not look tired—a stone could not look tired—but he did look *worn*. Rand understood that feeling.

Lan nodded to him, then looked at Moiraine. "Have you two been arguing?"

Moiraine tucked the mark away, face becoming impassive. Rand didn't know what to make of the interaction between the two of them since Moiraine's return. They were civil, but there was a distance between them that he had not expected.

"You should listen to Moiraine," Lan said, turning back to Rand. "She has prepared for these days longer than you have been alive. Let her guide you."

"She wants me to leave this battlefield," Rand said, "and strike immediately for Shayol Ghul instead of trying to fight those channelers for you so you can retake the Gap."

Lan hesitated. "Then perhaps you should do as she—"

"No," Rand said. "Your position here is dire, old friend. I can do something, and so I will. If we can't stop those Dreadlords, they'll have you retreating all the way back to Tar Valon."

"I have heard what you did at Maradon," Lan said. "I will not turn away a miracle here if one is determined to find us."

"Maradon was a mistake," Moiraine said tersely. "You cannot afford to expose yourself, Rand."

"I cannot afford not to, either. I won't just sit back and let people die! Not when I can protect them."

"The Borderlanders do not need to be sheltered," Lan said.

"No," Rand replied, "but I've never known one who would refuse a sword when one was offered in a time of need."

Lan met his eyes, then nodded. "Do what you can."

Rand nodded to the two Maidens, who nodded back.

"Sheepherder," Lan said.

Rand raised an eyebrow.

Lan saluted him, arm across his chest, bowing his head.

Rand nodded back. "There is something for you on the floor over there, Dai Shan."

Lan frowned, then walked to a pile of blankets. There were no tables in this tent. Lan knelt, then raised a bright, silvery crown—thin, yet strong. "The crown of Malkier," he whispered. "This was lost!"

"My smiths did what they could with old drawings," Rand said. "The other is for Nynaeve; I think it will suit her. You have ever been a king, my friend. Elayne taught me to rule, but you . . . you taught me how to stand. Thank you." He turned to Moiraine. "Keep a space clear for my return."

Rand seized the One Power and opened a gateway. He left Lan kneeling, holding the crown, and followed his Maidens out onto a black field. Burned stalks crunched beneath his boots and smoke wreathed the air.

The Maidens immediately sought shelter in a small depression in the field, huddling against the blackened earth, prepared to weather the storm.

Because one was *certainly* brewing. Trollocs milled in a large mass before Rand, prodding at the soil and at the remains of farmhouses. The River Mora rushed nearby; this was the first cultivated land south of Tarwin's Gap. Lan's forces had burned it before preparing to retreat downriver ahead of the Trolloc advance.

There were tens of thousands of the beasts here. Perhaps more. Rand raised his arms, forming a fist, drawing in a deep breath. In the pouch at his belt, he carried a familiar object. The small fat man with the sword, the *angreal* he had recently found at Dumai's Wells. He had returned there for one last look and found it buried in the mud. It had been useful at Maradon. Nobody knew he had it. That was important.

But there was more to what he would do here than tricks. Trollocs shouted as the winds whipped up around Rand. This was not the result of channeling, not yet.

It was Rand. Being here. Confronting *him*.

Seas grew choppy when different streams of water crashed into one another. Winds grew powerful when hot air and cool mixed. And where Light confronted Shadow . . . storms grew. Rand shouted, letting his nature stir the tempest. The Dark One pressed upon the land, seeking to smother it. The Pattern needed equalization. It needed balance.

It needed the Dragon.

The winds grew more powerful, lightning breaking the air, black dust and burned stalks flipping up, twisting about in the maelstrom. Rand finally channeled as Myrddraal forced the Trollocs to attack him; the beasts charged against the wind, and Rand directed the lightning.

It was so much easier to *direct* than *control*. With a storm already in place, he didn't need to force the lightning—he needed only to cajole it.

Strikes destroyed the front groups of Trollocs, a hundred bolts of lightning in succession. The pungent scent of burned flesh soon swirled in the storm, joining the charred stalks of grain. Rand roared as the Trollocs kept coming. Deathgates sprang up around him, gateways that zipped across the ground like water striders, sweeping Trollocs into death. Shadowspawn could not survive Traveling.

The stormwinds rose around Rand as he struck down those Trollocs who tried to reach him. The Dark One thought to rule here? He would see that this land already had a king! He would see that the fight would not—

A shield tried to sever Rand from the Source. He laughed, spinning, trying to pinpoint the shield's origin. "Taim!" he yelled, though the storm captured his voice and overwhelmed it. "I had hoped you would come!"

This was the fight that Lews Therin had constantly demanded of him, a fight Rand hadn't dared begin. Not until now, not until he had control. He summoned his strength, but then another shield struck at him, and another.

Rand drew in more of the One Power, tapping nearly all that he could through the fat man *angreal*. Shields continued to snap at him like biting flies. None were strong enough to sever him from the Source, but there were *dozens* of them.

Rand calmed himself. He sought peace, the peace of destruction. He was life, but he was also death. He was the manifestation of the land itself.

He struck, destroying an unseen Dreadlord hiding in the rubble of a burned building nearby. He summoned fire and directed it at a second, burning him to nothingness.

He could not see the weaves of the women out there—he could only feel their shields.

Too weak. Each shield was too weak, and yet their attacks had him worried. They had come quickly, at least three dozen Dreadlords, each trying to cut him off from the Source. This was dangerous—that they had anticipated him. That was why they had hit Lan so hard with channelers. To draw Rand out.

Rand fought off the attacks, but none of them were in danger of truly shielding him. A single person could not cut off someone holding as much *saidin* as he was. They should have ...

He saw it right before it happened. The other attacks were cover, feints. One that was coming would be created by a circle of men and women. A man would be leading.

There! A shield slammed against him, but Rand had had just enough time to prepare. He channeled Spirit in the tempest, weaving by instinct from Lews Therin's memories, and rebuffed the shield. He shoved it away, but could not destroy it.

Light! That had to be a full circle. Rand grunted as the shield slipped closer to him; it made a vibrant pattern in the sky, motionless despite the tempest. Rand resisted it with his own surge of Spirit and Air, holding it back as if it were a knife hanging above his throat.

He lost control of the tempest.

Lightning crashed around him. The other channelers wove to enhance the storm—they didn't try to control it, for they didn't need to. It being out of control served them, as at any moment, it could strike Rand.

He roared again, louder this time, more determined. *I will beat you, Taim! I will finally do what I should have months ago!*

But he did not let the anger, the wildness, force him into conflict. He couldn't afford to. He had learned better than that.

This was not the place. He could not fight here. If he did, he would lose.

Rand pushed with a surge of strength, throwing back Taim's shield, then used the moment of respite to weave a gateway. His Maidens went through immediately, and Rand, ducking his head against the wind, reluctantly followed.

He leaped into Lan's tent, where Moiraine had done as he requested and kept space open for him. He closed his gateway, and the winds stilled, the noise dampened.

Rand formed a fist, panting, sweat running down the sides of his face. Here, back with Lan's army, the tempest was distant, although Rand could hear it rumbling, and faint winds stirred the tent.

Rand had to fight to keep from sinking to his knees. He sucked in large breaths. With difficulty, he slowed his racing heart and brought calmness to his face. He wanted to *fight*, not run! He could have beaten Taim!

And in so doing, would have weakened himself so far that the Dark One would have taken him with ease. He forced his fist to open and wrestled control of his emotions.

He looked up at Moiraine's calm, knowing face.

"It was a trap?" she asked.

"Not so much a trap," Rand said, "as a battlefield well-prepared with sentinels. They know what I did at Maradon. They must have teams of Dreadlords waiting to Travel to wherever I'm spotted and attack me."

"You have seen the error in this line of attack?" she asked.

"Error . . . no. Inevitability, yes."

He couldn't fight this war personally. Not this time.

He would have to find another way to protect his people.

CHAPTER
12

A Shard of a Moment

Birgitte dashed through the forest, accompanied by a group of thirty Aiel, all with bows out. They made sound—they couldn't help but make sound—but the Aiel made less than they should. They would leap up onto fallen logs and run deftly along them or would find stones to step upon. They would writhe out of the way of hanging branches, ducking, twisting, moving.

"Here," she said in a hushed tone, rounding the side of a broken hill. Fortunately, the cave was still there, overgrown with vines, a small creek running past it. The Aiel ducked in, the water removing any scent of their passage.

Two of the men continued down the game trail, now moving much more loudly, scraping against every branch they passed. Birgitte joined the ones hiding in the cavern. It was dark inside and smelled of mold and earth.

Had she hidden in this cave, centuries ago when she'd lived in these woods as a bandit? She didn't know. She rarely remembered any of her past lives, sometimes only fleeting memories of the in-between years during her life in the World of Dreams before being brought into this world unnaturally by Moghedien.

She considered that with sickness. It was all right to be reborn, fresh and new. But to have her memories—her very sense of self—ripped away? If she lost her memories of her time in the World of Dreams, would she forget Gaidal completely? Would she forget herself?

She clenched her teeth. *It's the Last Battle, fool woman*, she thought. *Who cares about that?*

But she did. A question had begun to haunt her. What if, in being cast out of the World of Dreams, Birgitte had been broken from the Horn? She didn't know if it was possible. She no longer remembered enough to tell.

But if she had, she'd lose Gaidal forever.

Outside, leaves crunched, twigs cracking. The clatter was so loud, she would have sworn that a thousand soldiers were marching past—though she knew the fist of Trollocs was only fifty strong. Still, fifty had her band outnumbered. She didn't worry. Though she complained to Elayne that she didn't know much about warfare, this hiding in a forest with a team of well-trained companions . . . this she'd done before. Dozens of times. Perhaps hundreds, though her memories were so fuzzy, she couldn't say for certain.

When the Trollocs were nearly all the way past, she and her Aiel burst from cover. The brutes had started down the false trail made by the two Aielmen earlier, and Birgitte attacked them from behind, downing a number of Trollocs with arrows before the rest were able to react.

Trollocs did not die easily. They could often take two or three arrows before slowing. Well, that only happened when you missed the eyes or the throat. She never did. Monster after monster dropped to her bow. The Trollocs had begun downslope of the cave, which meant every one she or the Aiel killed was another corpse the others had to try to climb over to reach her.

Fifty became thirty in mere seconds. As that thirty rushed upward, half of the Aiel pulled out spears and engaged them while Birgitte and the others took a few steps downslope and flanked the Trollocs.

Twenty became ten, who tried to flee. Despite the wooded landscape, they were easy to pick off—though it meant hitting them in the legs or back of the neck, taking them down so that spears could finish them off.

Ten of the Aiel saw to the Trollocs, sticking a spear in each one to make certain it was dead. Others gathered arrows. Birgitte pointed to Nichil and Ludin, two of the Aiel, and they joined her to scout the area.

Her steps felt familiar, these woods felt familiar. Not just because of past lives she could no longer remember. During her centuries spent living in the World of Dreams, she and Gaidal had spent many a year in these forests. She remembered his caress upon her cheek. Her neck.

I can't lose this, she thought, fighting down panic. *Light, I can't. Please . . .* She didn't know what was happening to her. She could remember something, a faint discussion about . . . about what? She had lost it. People couldn't be unbound from the Horn, could they? Hawkwing might know. She'd have to ask him. Unless she had already?

Burn me!

Movement in the forest stopped her cold. She crouched down next to a rock, bow out in front of her. Underbrush crackled close at hand. Nichil and Ludin had vanished at the first sound. Light, but they were good. It took her a moment to pick them out hiding nearby.

She raised a finger, pointed at herself, then pointed before her. She would scout; they would cover her.

Birgitte moved silently. She'd show these Aiel that they weren't the only ones who knew how to avoid detection. Besides, these were *her* woods. She wouldn't be shown up by a bunch of desert folk.

She moved stealthily, avoiding thickets of withered thorn bushes. Were there more of those around of late? They seemed to be one of the only plants that hadn't died off completely. The ground smelled stale in a way that no forest should, though that was overpowered by the stench of death and rot. She passed another group of fallen Trollocs. The blood on them was dry. They were several days dead.

Elayne ordered her forces to bring back their dead. Thousands upon thousands of Trollocs moved through these woods like crawling beetles. Elayne wanted them to find only their own dead, hoping it would give them reason to fear.

Birgitte moved toward the sounds. She saw large shadows approaching in the dim light. Trollocs, sniffing at the air.

The creatures continued to press through the woods. They were forced to avoid the roads where an ambush of dragons could prove deadly. Elayne's plan called for teams like the one Birgitte led to hack away at the Trollocs, leading groups of them off into the woods, whittling down their numbers.

This group was far too big for her team to take, unfortunately. Birgitte withdrew, waving for the Aiel to follow, and slipped quietly back toward camp.

That night, following his failure with Lan's army, Rand fled to his dreams.

He sought out his valley of peace, appearing amid a grove of wild cherry trees in full bloom, their perfume lacing the air. With those beautiful pink-throated white blossoms, the trees almost looked aflame.

Rand wore simple Two Rivers clothing. After months in a king's garments of brilliant colors and soft textures, the loose wool trousers and linen felt very comfortable. He placed sturdy boots on his feet, like those he'd worn growing up. They fit him in a way that no new boot, no matter how well made, ever could.

He wasn't allowed old boots any longer. If his boots showed a hint of wear, one servant or another made them vanish.

Rand stood up in the dream hills and made himself a walking staff. He then began to walk upward through the mountains. This wasn't a real place, not any longer. He'd crafted it from memory and desire, somehow mixing both familiarity and a sense of exploration. It smelled fresh, of overturned leaves and sap. Animals moved in the underbrush. A hawk cried somewhere distant.

Lews Therin had known how to create dreamshards like this. Though he had not been a Dreamer, most Aes Sedai of that era had made use of *Tel'aran'rhiod* in one way or another. One thing they learned was how to slice out a dream for themselves, a haven within their own mind, more controlled than regular dreams. They learned how to enter a fragment like this while meditating, somehow giving the body rest as real as sleep.

Lews Therin had known these things, and more. How to reach into someone's mind if they entered his dreamshard. How to tell if someone else had invaded his dreams. How to expose his dreams to others. Lews Therin had liked to *know* things, like a traveler who wanted to have one of everything useful in his rucksack.

Lews Therin had rarely used these tools. He'd left them stored on a back shelf in his mind, gathering dust. Would things have gone differently if he'd taken time, each night, to wander a peaceful valley such as this? Rand didn't know. And, truth be told, this valley was no longer safe. He passed a deep cavern to his left. He had not put it there. Another attempt by Moridin to draw him? Rand passed it by without looking.

The forest didn't seem as alive as it had moments ago. Rand kept walking, trying to enforce his will upon the land. He had not practiced that enough, however—so as he walked, the forest grayed, looking washed out.

The cavern came again. Rand stopped at its mouth. Cold, humid air blew out over him, chilling his skin, smelling of fungus. Rand cast aside his walking staff, then strode into the cavern. As he passed into darkness, he wove a globe of white-blue light and hung it beside his head. The glow reflected from the wet stone, shining on smooth knobs and clefts.

Panting echoed from deep within the cavern. It was followed by gasps. And . . . splashes. Rand walked forward, though by now he had guessed what this was. He had begun to wonder if she would try again.

He came to a small chamber, perhaps ten paces wide, at the end of the tunnel, where the stone sank down into a clear pool of water, perfectly circular. The blue depths seemed to extend downward forever.

A woman in a white dress struggled to stay afloat in the center of it. The fabric of her dress rippled in the water, forming a circle. Her face and hair were wet. As Rand watched, she gasped and sank, flailing in the crystalline water.

She came up a moment later, gasping.

"Hello, Mierin," Rand said softly. His hand formed into a fist. He would *not* jump into that water to rescue her. This was a dreamshard. That pool could actually be water, but more likely it represented something else.

His arrival seemed to buoy her, and her vigorous thrashings

became more effective. "Lews Therin," she said, wiping her face with one hand, panting.

Light! Where was his peace? He felt like a child again, a boy who thought Baerlon the grandest city ever built. Yes, her face was different, but faces were no longer of much matter to him. She was still the same person.

Of all the Forsaken, only Lanfear had chosen her new name. She had always wanted one of those.

He remembered. He *remembered*. Walking into grand parties with her on his arm. Her laughter over the music. Their nights alone. He had not wanted to remember making love to another woman, particularly not to one of the Forsaken, but he could not pick and choose what was in his mind.

Those memories mixed with his own, when he had desired her as the Lady Selene. A foolish, youthful lust. He no longer felt these things, but the memories of them remained.

"You can free me, Lews Therin," Lanfear said. "He has claimed me. Must I beg? He has claimed me!"

"You pledged yourself to the Shadow, Mierin," Rand said. "This is your reward. You expect pity from me?"

A dark something reached up and wrapped around her legs, yanking her down into the abyss again. Despite his words, Rand found himself stepping forward, as if to leap into the pool.

He held himself back. He finally felt like a whole person again, after a long fight. That gave him strength, but in his peace was a weakness—the weakness he had always feared. The weakness that Moiraine had rightfully spotted in him. The weakness of compassion.

He needed it. Like a helmet needed a hole through which to see. Both could be exploited. He admitted to himself that it was true.

Lanfear surfaced, sputtering, looking helpless. "Must I beg?" she said again.

"I don't think you are capable of it."

She lowered her eyes. ". . . Please?" she whispered.

Rand's insides twisted. He had fought through darkness himself in seeking the Light. He had given himself a second chance; should he not give one to another?

Light! He wavered, remembering what it had felt like in that moment seizing the True Power. That agony and that thrill, that power and that horror. Lanfear had given herself to the Dark One. But in a way, Rand had as well.

He looked into her eyes, searching them, *knowing* them. Finally, Rand shook his head. "You've grown better at this kind of deception, Mierin. But not good enough."

Her expression darkened. In a moment, the pool was gone, replaced by a stone floor. Lanfear sat there, cross-legged, in her silver-white dress. Wearing her new face, but still the same.

"So you *are* back," she said, sounding not entirely pleased. "Well, I am no longer forced to deal with a simple farmboy. That is some small blessing."

Rand snorted, entering the chamber. She *was* still imprisoned—he could sense a darkening around her, like a dome of shadow, and he stayed outside of it. The pool, however—the act of drowning—had been mere theatrics. She was prideful, but was not above maintaining a weak front when the situation required it. If he'd been able to embrace Lews Therin's memories earlier, Rand would never have been fooled so easily by her in the Waste.

"Then I shall address you not as a damsel in need of a hero," Lanfear said, eyeing him as he walked around her prison, "but as an equal, seeking asylum."

"An equal?" Rand said, laughing. "Since when have you ever considered *anyone* your equal, Mierin?"

"You care nothing for my captivity?"

"It pains me," Rand said, "but no more than it pained me when you swore yourself to the Shadow. Did you know I was there, when you revealed it? You did not see me, as I did not want to be seen, but I was watching. Light, Mierin, you swore to *kill* me."

"Did I mean it?" she asked, turning to look him in the eyes.

Had she? . . . No, she had not meant it. Not then. Lanfear did not kill people that she thought would be useful, and she had always considered him useful.

"We shared something special, once," she said. "You were my—"

"I was an ornament to you!" Rand snapped. He breathed deeply, trying to calm himself. Light, but it was hard around her. "The past is done. I care nothing for it, and would gladly give you a second chance at the Light. Unfortunately, I *know* you. You're just doing it again. Playing us all, including the Dark One himself. You care nothing for the Light. You care only for power, Mierin. You honestly want me to believe that you've changed?"

"You do not know me so well as you think that you do," she said, watching him as he rounded the perimeter of her prison. "You never did."

"Then prove it to me," Rand said, stopping. "Show me your mind, Mierin. Open it to me completely. Give me control over you here, in this place of mastered dreams. If your intentions are pure, I will free you."

"What you ask is forbidden."

Rand laughed. "When has *that* ever stopped you?"

She seemed to consider it; she must actually have been worried about her imprisonment. Once, she would have laughed at a suggestion such as this. Since this was, ostensibly, a place where he had complete control, if she gave him leave, he could strip her down, delve within her mind.

"I . . . " Lanfear said.

He stepped forward, right to the lip of the prison. That tremble in her voice . . . that felt real. The first genuine emotion from her.

Light, he thought, searching her eyes. *Is she actually going to do it?*

"I cannot," she said. "I cannot." She said it the second time more softly.

Rand exhaled. He found his hand shaking. So close. So close to the Light, like a feral cat in the night, stalking back and forth before the fire-lit barn! He found himself angry, angrier than before. Always, she did this! Flirting with what was right, but always choosing her own path.

"I am done with you, Mierin," Rand said, turning away and walking from the chamber. "Forever."

"You mistake me!" she called out. "You have *always* mistaken me! Would *you* show yourself to someone in that way? I cannot do it. I have been slapped too many times by those I should have trusted. Betrayed by those who should have loved me."

"You blame this on me?" Rand asked, spinning on his heel.

She did not look away. She sat, imperious, as if her prison were a throne.

"You really remember it that way, don't you?" Rand said. "You think I betrayed you for her?"

"You said that you loved me."

"I never said that. *Never.* I could not. I did not know what love was. Centuries of life, and I never discovered it until I met her." He hesitated, then continued, speaking so softly his voice did not echo in the small cavern. "You have never really felt it, have you? But of course. Who could you love? Your heart is claimed already, by the power you so strongly desire. There is no room left."

Rand let go.

He let go as Lews Therin never had been able to. Even after discovering Ilyena, even after realizing how Lanfear had used him, he had held on to hatred and scorn. *You expect me to pity you?* Rand had asked her.

He now felt just that. Pity for a woman who had never known love, a woman who would not let herself know it. Pity for a woman who could not choose a side other than her own.

"I . . ." she said softly.

Rand raised his hand, and then he opened himself to her. His intentions, his mind, his self appeared as a swirl of color, emotions and power around him.

Her eyes opened wide as the swirl played before her, like pictures on a wall. He could hold nothing back. She saw his motives, his desires, his wishes for mankind. She saw his intentions. To go to Shayol Ghul, to kill the Dark One. To leave a better world than he had the last time.

He did not fear revealing these things. He had touched the True Power, and so the Dark One knew his heart. There were no surprises here, at least nothing that *should* have been a surprise.

Lanfear was surprised anyway. Her jaw dropped as she saw the truth—the truth that, down deep, it was not Lews Therin who made up Rand's core. It was the sheepherder, raised by Tam. His lives played out in moments, his memories and feelings exposed.

Last, he showed her his love for Ilyena—like a glowing crystal, set upon a shelf and admired. Then his love for Min, Aviendha, Elayne. Like a burning bonfire, warming, comforting, passionate.

There was no love for Lanfear in what he exposed. Not a sliver. He had squelched Lews Therin's loathing of her as well. And so, to him, she really was nothing.

She gasped.

The glow around Rand faded. "I'm sorry," he said. "I really did mean it. I am finished with you, Mierin. Keep your head down during the storm to come. If I win this fight, you will no longer have reason to fear for your soul. There will be no one left to torment you."

He turned from her again, and walked from the cave, leaving her silent.

Evening in the Braem Wood was accompanied by the scent of fires smoldering in their pits and the sounds of men groaning softly as they settled into uneasy sleep, swords ready at hand. An unnatural chill to the summer air.

Perrin walked through the camp, among the men under his command. The fighting had been hard in these woods. His people were hurting the Trollocs, but Light, there always seemed to be more Shadowspawn to replace those that fell.

After seeing that his people were properly fed, that the watch had been set and the men knew what to do if awakened in the night by an assault of Shadowspawn, he went seeking the Aiel. The Wise Ones in particular. Nearly all of them had gathered to go with Rand when he marched on Shayol Ghul—for now, they waited his order—but a few had remained with Perrin, including Edarra.

She and the other Wise Ones did not march at his command. And yet, like Gaul, they stayed with him when their fellows went elsewhere. Perrin had not asked them why. He didn't really care why. Having them with him was useful, and he was grateful.

The Aiel let him pass their perimeter. He found Edarra sitting beside a fire, well rimmed with stones to prevent the chance of a stray spark escaping. These woods, dry as they were, could go up easier than a barn full of last harvest's hay.

She glanced at Perrin as he settled down near her. The Aiel looked young but smelled of patience, inquisitiveness and control. Wisdom. She did not ask why Perrin had come to her. She waited for him to speak.

"Are you a dreamwalker?" Perrin asked.

She studied him in the night; he had the distinct impression this was not a question a man—or an outsider—was supposed to ask.

He was surprised, then, when she answered.

"No."

"Do you know much of it?" Perrin asked.

"Some."

"I need to know of a way to enter the World of Dreams physically. Not just in my dreams, but in my real body. Have you heard of such a thing?"

She inhaled sharply. "Do not think of that, Perrin Aybara. It is evil."

Perrin frowned. Strength in the wolf dream—in *Tel'aran'rhiod*—was a delicate thing. The more strongly Perrin put himself into the dream—the more solidly *there* he was—the easier he found it to change things there, manipulate that world.

That came at a risk, however. Going into the dream too strongly, he risked cutting himself off from his sleeping body in the real world.

That apparently didn't bother Slayer. Slayer was strong there, so *very* strong; the man was in the dream physically. Perrin was increasingly sure of it.

Our contest will not end, Perrin thought, *until you are the prey, Slayer. Hunter of wolves. I will end you.*

"In many ways," Edarra muttered, looking at him, "you are still a child, for all the honor you have found." Perrin had grown accustomed to—though not fond of—women who looked not a year or two older than he addressing him so. "None of the dreamwalkers will teach you this thing. It is evil."

"Why is it evil?" Perrin said.

"To enter into the world of dreams in the flesh costs you part of what makes you human. What's more, if you die while in that place—and you are in the flesh—it can make you die forever. No more rebirth, Perrin Aybara. Your thread in the Pattern could end forever, you yourself destroyed. This is not a thing you should contemplate."

"The servants of the Shadow do this, Edarra," Perrin said. "They take these risks to dominate. We need to take the same risks in order to stop them."

Edarra hissed softly, shaking her head. "Do not cut off your foot for fear that a snake will bite it, Perrin Aybara. Do not make a terrible mistake because you fear something that seems worse. This is all I will say on the topic."

She stood and left him sitting by the fire.

CHAPTER
13

What Must Be Done

The army split before Egwene as she rode forward toward the hills in southeastern Kandor where they would shortly engage the advancing enemy. She led over a hundred Aes Sedai, many of them from the Green Ajah. Bryne's tactical revisions had been quick and efficient. He had something better than archers for breaking a charge, something more destructive than heavy cavalry for causing sheer damage.

It was time to use it.

Two other smaller forces of Aes Sedai made their way to the flanks of the army. These hills might once have been lush and green. Now they were yellow and brown, as if burned by sunlight. She tried to see the advantages. At least they would have sure footing, and though the sky broke with periodic lightning, rain seemed unlikely.

The approaching Trollocs seemed to extend forever in either direction. Though Egwene's army was enormous, it suddenly felt tiny. Fortunately, Egwene had a single advantage: The Trolloc army was driven by a need to continue moving forward. Trolloc armies fell apart if they were not constantly advancing. They'd start bickering. They'd run out of food.

Egwene's army was a barrier in their way. And bait. The

Shadowspawn couldn't afford to leave such a force as theirs at large, and so Egwene would draw them along a course she determined.

Her Aes Sedai reached the battlefront. Bryne had split his army into large, highly mobile strike units to hit the Trollocs wherever and whenever they showed vulnerability.

The offensive structure of Bryne's forces seemed to confuse the Trollocs. At least, that was how Egwene read the shuffling in their ranks, the churning movement, the increase of noise. Trollocs rarely had to worry about being on the defensive. Trollocs attacked, humans defended. Humans worried. Humans were food.

Egwene reached the top of a low hill, looking out at the plain in Kandor where the Trollocs amassed, her Aes Sedai arraying in a long line to either side of her. Behind them, the men of the army seemed uncertain. They knew Egwene and the others were Aes Sedai, and no man was comfortable around Aes Sedai.

Egwene reached to her side, and slipped something long, white and slender from the leather case tied to her belt. A fluted rod, Vora's *sa'angreal*. It felt comfortable in her hand, familiar. Though she had only used this *sa'angreal* once, she felt as if it had claimed her and she it. During the fight against the Seanchan, this had been her weapon. For the first time, she understood why a soldier might feel a bond with his sword.

The glow of the Power winked on around the women in the line, like a row of lanterns being lit. Egwene embraced the Source and felt the One Power flow into her like a waterfall, filling her and opening her eyes. The world became sweeter, the scents of oil from armor and of beaten grass growing stronger.

Within the embrace of *saidar* she could see the signs of color that the Shadow wanted them to ignore. The grass wasn't all dead; there were tiny hints of green, slivers where the grass clung to life. There were voles beneath it; she could now easily make out the ripples in the earth. They ate at the dying roots and clung to life.

Smiling widely, she pulled the One Power through the fluted rod. Within that torrent she was atop a sea of strength and energy, riding a lone vessel and embracing the wind. The Trollocs finally surged into motion. They roared, a huge rush of weapons, teeth, stink and eyes that were too human. Perhaps the Myrddraal had seen Aes Sedai up front, and thought to attack and destroy the human channelers.

The other women waited for Egwene's sign. They were not in a circle—a circle was best for one focused, precise stream of the One Power. That wasn't the goal today. The goal today was simply to destroy.

Once the Trollocs were halfway to the hills, Egwene began her offensive. She had always been unusually strong in Earth, so she led with the most simple and destructive of weaves. She sent threads of Earth into the ground beneath the Trollocs in a long line, then heaved it up. With the aid of Vora's *sa'angreal*, it felt as easy as tossing a handful of pebbles into the air.

At this sign, the entire line of women formed weaves. The air rippled with glowing threads. Pure streams of fire, of earth to heave, of gusts of wind to blow the Trollocs into one another and make them trip and tumble.

The Trollocs that Egwene had thrown into the air toppled back to the ground, many of them missing legs or feet. Bones broke and Trollocs screamed in agony as their fellows fell upon them. Egwene let the second rank stumble across the fallen, then struck again. This time, she didn't focus on the earth, but on *metal*.

Metal in armor, in weapons and on wrists. She shattered axes and swords, mail and the occasional breastplate. This released fragments of metal with deadly speed. The air grew red with spraying blood. The next ranks tried to stop to avoid the shrapnel, but the Trollocs behind them had too much momentum. They shoved their fellows forward into the zone of death and trampled them.

Egwene also killed the next wave with exploding metal. It was harder than casting up the earth, but it also didn't give as much sign to the back ranks, so she was able to continue killing without them realizing what they were doing by shoving their fellows forward.

Then Egwene returned to rupturing the earth. There was something energizing about using raw power, sending weaves in their most basic forms. In that moment—maiming, destroying, bringing death upon the enemy—she felt as if she were one with the land itself. That she was doing the work it had longed for someone to do for so long. The Blight, and the Shadowspawn it grew, were a disease. An infection. Egwene—afire with the One Power, a blazing beacon of death and judgment—was the cauterizing flame that would bring healing to the land.

The Trollocs tried hard to push through the Aes Sedai weaves, but that only put more and more of them into the White Tower's reach. The Greens lived up to their Ajah's reputation—releasing wave after wave of destruction at the Trollocs—but the other Ajahs did well, also.

The ground trembled, and the air clogged with the howls of the dying. Bodies ripped. Flesh burned. Not a few of the soldiers in the front lines emptied their stomachs at the sight. And still, the Aes Sedai pounded the Trolloc lines. Specific sisters sought out Myrddraal, as they had been ordered. Egwene struck one herself, ripping its eyeless head from its neck with a weave of Fire and Air. Each Fade they killed dropped fists of Trollocs linked to them.

Egwene doubled her attack. She hit a rank with a wave of exploding earth, then slammed a wave of air into the bodies as they fell, pushing them back so they dropped onto the ranks behind. She ripped holes in the earth and made the stones in the ground explode. She butchered Trollocs for what seemed like hours. Finally, the Shadowspawn broke, the Trollocs pulling back despite the whips of the Myrddraal. Egwene took a deep breath—she was starting to feel limp—and struck down more Fades. Finally, they too broke and fled back away from the hills.

Egwene sagged in her saddle, lowering her *sa'angreal*. She wasn't sure exactly how much time had passed. The soldiers nearby stared, wide eyed. Their blood had not been required this day.

"That was *impressive*," Gawyn said, pulling his horse up beside hers. "It was as if they were assaulting city walls, trying to run ladders to a siege . . . only without the walls or the ladders."

"They'll return," Egwene said tiredly. "We killed just a small percentage of them."

On the morrow, or the day after at the latest, they would try again. New tactics, perhaps—they might spread out waves of attackers to make it more difficult for the Aes Sedai to kill large batches of them at once.

"We surprised them," Egwene said. "They will come stronger next time. For now, for this night, we've held."

"You didn't just hold, Egwene," Gawyn said with a smile. "You sent them running. I don't know that I've ever seen an army so thoroughly trounced."

The rest of the army seemed to agree with Gawyn's assessment, for they began to cheer, raising weapons. Egwene forced back her fatigue and tucked away the fluted rod. Nearby, other Aes Sedai lowered small statues, bracelets, brooches, rings and rods. They had emptied the White Tower's storehouse of every *angreal* and *sa'angreal*—the few of those they had—and distributed them among the sisters on the battlefront. At the end of each day, they would be collected and delivered to the women providing Healing.

The Aes Sedai turned and rode back through the cheering army. The time for sorrows would, unfortunately, come. The Aes Sedai could not fight each battle. For now, however, Egwene was content to let the soldiers enjoy their victory, for it was the very best kind. The kind that left no holes in their ranks.

"The Lord Dragon and his scouts have begun to reconnoiter Shayol Ghul." Bashere pointed to one of the shaded maps. "Our resistance in Kandor and Shienar is forcing the Shadow to commit more and more troops to those fights. Soon, the Blasted Lands will be mostly empty, save for a skeleton force of defenders. He will be able to strike more easily then."

Elayne nodded. She could feel Rand somewhere in the back of her mind. He was worried about something, though he was too distant for her to feel more than that. He occasionally visited her, at her camp in the Braem Wood, but for now he was on one of the other battlefronts.

Bashere continued. "The Amyrlin should be able to hold in Kandor, considering the number of channelers she has. I'm not worried about her."

"But you are about the Borderlanders," Elayne said.

"Yes. They've been pushed out of Tarwin's Gap."

"I wish they had been able to hold where they were, but they've been overwhelmed. There is nothing to be done for it save siphon to them what aid we can."

Bashere nodded. "Perhaps Lord Mandragoran could reverse his retreat if he had more Aes Sedai or Asha'man."

Of which there were none to spare. She had sent him some Aes Sedai from Egwene's army to help him with his initial retreat, and that had helped. But if Rand himself couldn't fight off the Dreadlords there . . .

"Lord Agelmar will know what to do," Elayne said. "The Light willing, he'll be able to pull the Trollocs away from more populated areas."

Bashere grunted. "A retreat like this—almost a rout—usually affords no chance for directing the course of battle." Bashere pointed toward the map of Shienar.

Elayne studied it. The path of the Trollocs would *not* avoid inhabited land. Fal Dara, Mos Shirare, Fal Moran . . . And with Dreadlords, city walls would be useless.

"Send word to Lan and the lords of Shienar," she said quietly. "Order Fal Dara and Ankor Dail burned, along with Fal Moran and villages like Medo. They're already burning what farmland they can—emptying the cities as well. Evacuate the civilians to Tar Valon."

"I'm sorry," Bashere said softly.

"It is what must be done, isn't it?"

"Yes," Bashere said.

Light, what a mess. *Well, what did you expect? Neatness and simplicity?*

Footsteps on the leaves announced Talmanes approaching with one of his commanders. The Cairhienin looked tired. Everyone did. A week of battle was only the beginning, but the thrill of the fight was dying. Now came the real work of the war. Days fighting or waiting to fight, nights spent sleeping with sword in hand.

Elayne's current location in the Wood—she'd begun the morning a thousand paces further south, but their constant retreat through the forest kept her moving—was ideal. Three small streams with easy access, room for plenty of troops to camp, trees atop the hill that worked as well as watchtowers. A pity they'd have to leave this site behind in the morning.

"The Trollocs control the entire southern section of the forest," Bashere said, knuckling his mustaches. "They are avoiding the clearings. That means our cavalry won't be able to operate effectively."

"The dragons are practically useless in here, Your Majesty,"

Talmanes said, entering the tent. "Now that the Trollocs are keeping off the roadways, we have trouble doing any damage. It's nearly impossible to maneuver the dragon carts in the forest, and when we do get a shot, we kill more trees than we do Shadowspawn."

"What of that ... whatever it was that Aludra was talking about?"

"Her dragon teeth?" Talmanes said. "It's better—the dragon shoots out a bunch of bits of metal, rather than one ball. It has a big spread to it, and works reasonably well inside the forest, but I maintain that the dragons are doing less damage than it is worth risking them to achieve."

"I think that the forest has done us the good it can," Bashere said, moving some Trolloc tokens on their maps. "We have whittled down their numbers, but they're getting smart, keeping to the thick woods and trying to surround us."

"Suggestions?"

"Pull back," Bashere said. "Head out to the east of here."

"Make for the Erinin? There's no bridge this far north," Talmanes said.

Bashere nodded. "So you know what I'm going to ask. You have a company of men who can build bridges. Send them with some of your dragons for protection and have them build raft bridges directly east of us. The rest of us won't be far behind. The open terrain there will give our cavalry and the dragons the chance to do more damage. We can rely on the Erinin to slow the Trollocs, especially once we torch the bridges. A few dragons placed there should slow their progress. We'll continue east to the Alguenya, and repeat the process. Then we'll be on the road to Cairhien. We'll head north and when we find a suitable place to make a stand—I think I know just the spot—we'll turn and face the Shadow with Cairhien at our backs."

"Surely you don't think we'll need to go all that way," Elayne said.

Bashere stared at the map, squinting, as if seeing through the parchment itself to the land it depicted. "We're stirring this battle," he said softly, "but we don't control it. We're riding it, as a man might ride a stampeding horse. I can't say where the gallop will stop. I'll divert it, I'll send it through patches of thorns. But I can't stop it, not so long as the Trollocs keep coming."

Elayne frowned. She couldn't afford an endless retreat; she needed to defeat these Shadowspawn as soon and as thoroughly as possible so she could join the remainder of her forces to Lan's and Egwene's armies to beat back the invasions from the north.

That was the only way they'd win. Otherwise, it wouldn't matter what Rand was able to do against the Dark One.

Light, what a *mess*.

"Do it."

Perrin rested his hammer on his shoulder, listening as the sweating young messenger relayed Elayne's orders. A gentle breeze blew through the branches of the forest behind. The Ogier fought in there. He'd worried they would refuse to endanger the trees, but their fighting . . . Light, Perrin had never seen savagery to rival it.

"These tactics aren't bad," Tam said reading the orders. "The Queen has a good head for warfare."

Perrin waved away the messenger boy. He passed Galad and several of his Whitecloak commanders, conferring nearby. "She listens well to those who know their tactics," Perrin said, "and she doesn't interfere."

"That's what I meant, lad," Tam said with a smile. "Being in charge isn't always about telling people what to do. Sometimes, it's about knowing when to step out of the way of people who know what they're doing."

"Wise words, Tam," Perrin said, turning northward. "I suggest you adopt them, as you have command now."

Perrin could see Rand. The colors swam. Rand, speaking with Moiraine on a bleak rocky ridge he did not recognize. They were almost ready for the invasion of Shayol Ghul. Perrin felt a tug from Rand, growing stronger. Soon, Rand would need him.

"Perrin?" Tam asked. "What's this nonsense about command?"

"You have our forces, Tam," Perrin said. "The men are working together now; let Arganda, Gallenne and Galad assist you." Nearby, Grady held open a gateway through which the wounded from the most recent skirmish were being sent for Healing. Berelain ran the hospital on the other side, which the Yellow Ajah had placed in Mayene. The air coming from the other side was warm.

"I don't know if they'll listen to me, Perrin," Tam said. "I'm just a common farmer."

"They listened to you well enough before."

"That was when we were traveling the wilderness," Tam said. "You were always nearby. They answered to me on your authority." He rubbed his chin. "I have a feeling, from the way you keep looking north, that you don't intend to be here much longer."

"Rand needs me," Perrin said softly. "Burn me, Tam, I hate it—but I can't fight along with you here in Andor. Someone needs to watch Rand's back, and it . . . well, it's going to be me. I know it, somehow."

Tam nodded. "We'll just go to Arganda or Gallenne, and tell them they're in charge of our men. Queen Elayne is giving most of the orders anyway, and—"

"Men!" Perrin yelled, looking toward the assembled soldiers. Arganda was consulting with Gallenne. They turned to Perrin, as did the nearby members of the Wolf Guard, along with Galad and his Whitecloaks. Young Bornhald regarded Perrin through dark eyes. That one grew more and more unpredictable lately. The Light send Galad had been able to keep him from the brandy.

"You all accept my authority, as granted by the crown of Andor?" Perrin asked.

"Of course, Lord Goldeneyes," Arganda called. "I thought that was established."

"I'm hereby making Tam al'Thor a lord," Perrin called. "I am making him steward over the Two Rivers in the name of his son, the Dragon Reborn. He carries all of my authority, which is the Dragon's own authority. If I do not survive this battle, Tam succeeds me."

The camp grew still, then the men nodded, several saluting Tam. Tam groaned so softly, Perrin doubted anyone else could hear.

"Is it too late to turn you over to the Women's Circle for a good talking-to?" Tam asked. "Maybe a sound swat on the behind and a week spent carrying water for Widow al'Thone?"

"Sorry, Tam," Perrin said. "Neald, try making a gateway to the Black Tower."

The young Asha'man adopted a look of concentration. "It still doesn't work, Lord Goldeneyes."

Perrin shook his head. He'd heard the reports from Lan's battlefront, that members of the Black Tower were fighting for the Shadow. Something had happened there, something terrible. "All right, back to Merrilor, then," Perrin said.

Neald nodded, concentrating.

As he worked, Perrin turned to the men. "I hate to leave you, but I have these hooks in me, pulling me north. I *have* to go to Rand, and there's just no arguing with it. I'll try to come back. If I can't . . . well, I want you all to know that I'm proud of you. All of you. You're welcome in my home when this is over. We'll open a cask or two of Master al'Vere's best brandy. We'll remember those who fell, and we'll tell our children how we stood when the clouds turned black and the world started to die. We'll tell them we stood shoulder to shoulder, and there was just no space for the Shadow to squeeze through."

He raised *Mah'alleinir* toward them, and he bore their cheering. Not because he deserved it, but because they certainly did.

Neald opened the gateway. Perrin started toward it, then hesitated as his name was called. He frowned, looking at Dain Bornhald as the man hurried over.

Perrin rested his hand on his hammer, wary. This man had saved his life against the Trollocs, and against a fellow Whitecloak, but Perrin saw the dislike the man had for him. He might not blame Perrin for the death of his father, but that didn't mean he liked—or even accepted—Perrin.

"A word, Aybara," Bornhald said, looking toward Gaul standing nearby. "In private."

Perrin waved Gaul away, and the Aiel reluctantly retreated. He stepped with Bornhald away from the open gateway. "What is this about? If it's because of your father—"

"Light, just be quiet," Bornhald said, glancing away. "I don't want to say this. I hate saying this. But you need to know. Light burn me, you need to know."

"Know what?"

"Aybara," Bornhald said, taking a deep breath. "It wasn't Trollocs who killed your family."

A shock went through Perrin's body.

"I'm sorry," Bornhald said, looking away. "It was Ordeith. Your father insulted him. He tore apart the family, and we blamed the

Trollocs. I didn't kill them, but I didn't say anything. So much blood . . ."

"What?" Perrin grabbed the Whitecloak by the shoulder. "But they said . . . I mean . . ." Light, he'd *dealt* with this already!

The look in Bornhald's eyes when his met Perrin's dredged it all up again. The pain, the horror, the loss, the fury. Bornhald reached up and took Perrin's wrist, then yanked it free of his shoulder.

"This is an awful time to tell you this, I know," Bornhald said. "But I couldn't keep it in. I just . . . We may fall. Light, it might all fall. I had to speak, say it."

He pulled away, moving back toward the other Whitecloaks with eyes downcast. Perrin stood alone, his entire world shaking.

Then he pulled it back together. He *had* dealt with this; he had mourned his family. It was over, through.

He could and would go on. Light, the old hurts returned, but he shoved them down and turned his eyes toward the gateway. Toward Rand, and his duty.

He had work to do. But Ordeith . . . Padan Fain . . . This only added to that man's terrible crimes. Perrin would see that he paid, one way or another.

He approached the gateway to Travel to find Rand, where he was joined by Gaul.

"I'm going to a place you cannot, my friend," Perrin said softly, his pain subsiding. "I'm sorry."

"You'll go to the dream within a dream," Gaul said, then yawned. "Turns out I'm tired."

"But—"

"I'm coming, Perrin Aybara. Kill me if you wish me to remain behind." Perrin didn't dare push him on it. He nodded.

Perrin glanced behind him, raising his hammer once more. As he did so, he caught a glimpse through the other gateway, the one to Mayene that Grady still held open. Inside, two white-robed forms watched Gaul. He raised a spear to them. How must it feel, for a pair of warriors to wait out this, the Last Battle? Perhaps Rand should have tried to have the *gai'shain* released from their vows for a few weeks.

Well, that would probably have turned every single Aiel against him. Light protect the wetlander who dared tamper with *ji'e'toh*.

Perrin ducked through the gateway, stepping onto the ground of Merrilor. From there, he and Gaul packed as if for a long trip—foodstuffs and water aplenty, as much as they dared carry.

It took Perrin the better part of a half hour to convince Rand's Asha'man to tell him where their leader had gone. Finally, a grudging Naeff opened a gateway for Perrin. He left Merrilor, and stepped out into what seemed to be the Blight. Only the rocks were cold.

The air smelled of death, of desolation. The fetor took Perrin aback, and it was minutes before he could sort out normal scents from the stench. Rand stood just ahead, at the edge of a ridge, arms folded behind his back. A group of his advisors, commanders and guards stood behind, including Moiraine, Aviendha and Cadsuane. At this moment, though, Rand stood alone at the end of the ridge.

Distant, in front of them, rose the peak of Shayol Ghul. Perrin felt a shiver. It was distant, but Perrin could not mistake the intense determination in Rand's expression as he regarded the peak.

"Light," Perrin said. "Is it time?"

"No," Rand said softly. "This is a test, to see if he senses me."

"Perrin?" Nynaeve asked from the hillside behind. She had been speaking with Moiraine and for once, she didn't smell a twinge hateful. Something had happened between those two women.

"I only need him for a moment," Perrin said, walking up to join Rand at the end of the outcropping of rock. There were some Aiel back there, and Perrin didn't want them—particularly any Wise Ones—to hear what he was going to ask Rand.

"You have this moment and many, Perrin," Rand said. "I owe you dearly. What is it you want?"

"Well . . ." Perrin looked over his shoulder. Would Moiraine or Nynaeve know enough to try to stop him? Probably. Women were always trying to keep a man from doing what he must, as if worried he'd break his neck. Never mind that it was the Last Battle.

"Perrin?" Rand asked.

"Rand, I need to enter the wolf dream."

"*Tel'aran'rhiod?*" Rand said. "Perrin, I don't know what you do there; you've told me little. I figured that you would know how to—"

"I know how to enter it one way," Perrin said, whispering so that the Wise Ones and the others behind couldn't hear. "The easy way. I need something else. You know things, you remember things. Is there anything in that ancient brain of yours that remembers how to enter into the World of Dreams in the flesh?"

Rand grew solemn. "It's a dangerous thing you ask."

"As dangerous as going to do what you're about to do?"

"Perhaps." Rand frowned. "If I'd known back when I . . . Well, let's just say that some would call your request very, very evil."

"It's not evil, Rand," Perrin said. "I know something evil when I smell it. This isn't evil, it's just incredibly stupid."

Rand smiled. "And still you ask?"

"The good options are gone, Rand. Better to do something desperate than to do nothing at all."

Rand didn't reply.

"Look," Perrin said. "We've spoken of the Black Tower. I know you're worried about it."

"I will need to go there," Rand said, expression darkening. "And yet, it's obviously a trap."

"I think I know part of what is to blame," Perrin said. "There's someone I need to face, and I can't beat him without being able to face him on equal terms. There, in the dream."

Rand nodded slowly. "The Wheel weaves as the Wheel wills. We will have to leave the Blasted Lands; you cannot enter the dream from . . ."

He trailed off, then did something, crafting a weave. A gateway opened beside him. Something about it was different from ordinary ones.

"I see," Rand said. "The worlds are drawing together, compressing. What was once separate is no longer so. This gateway will take you into the dream. Take care, Perrin. If you die in that place while in the flesh, it can have . . . ramifications. What you face could be worse than death itself, particularly now. At this time."

"I know," Perrin said. "I will need a way out. Can you have one of your Asha'man make one of these gateways once a day, at dawn? Say, at the Traveling grounds of Merrilor?"

"Dangerous," Rand whispered. "But I will do it."

Perrin nodded in thanks.

"The Light willing, we will see one another again," Rand said. He held out his hand to Perrin. "Watch out for Mat. I'm honestly not sure what he's going to do, but I have a feeling it will be highly dangerous for all involved."

"Not like us," Perrin said, clasping Rand's forearm. "You and I, we're *much* better at keeping to the safe paths."

Rand smiled. "May the Light shelter you, Perrin Aybara."

"And you, Rand al'Thor." Perrin hesitated, and realized what was happening. They were saying goodbye. He took Rand in an embrace.

"You take care of him, you two," Perrin said, looking toward Nynaeve and Moiraine as he pulled back from the embrace. "You hear me?"

"Oh, *now* you want me to watch after Rand?" Nynaeve said, hands on hips. "I don't believe I ever stopped, Perrin Aybara. Don't think I didn't hear you two whispering over there. You're doing something foolish, aren't you?"

"Always," Perrin said, raising a hand in farewell to Thom. "Gaul, you certain you want to do this?"

"I am," the Aielman said, loosening his spears and looking through Rand's gateway.

Without another word, the two hefted their heavy packs and stepped into the World of Dreams.

CHAPTER
14

Doses of Forkroot

"L ight ..." Perrin whispered to Gaul, looking across the landscape. "It's dying."

The boiling, thrashing, churning black sky of the wolf dream was nothing new, but the storm that the sky had been fore-shadowing for months had finally arrived. Wind blew in enormous gusts, moving this way, then that, in unnatural patterns. Perrin closed his cloak, then strengthened it with a thought, imagining the ties holding it to be fixed strongly in place.

A little bubble of calmness extended out from him, deflecting the worst of the winds. It was easier than he anticipated, as if he'd reached for a heavy piece of oak and found it as light as pine.

The landscape seemed less real than it usually did. The raging winds actually *smoothed* out hills, like erosion at high speed. In other places, the land swelled up, forming ripples of rock and new hillsides. Chunks of earth sprayed into the air, shattering. The land itself was coming apart.

He grabbed Gaul's shoulder and *shifted* the two of them away from the place. It was too close to Rand, Perrin suspected. Indeed, as they appeared on the familiar plain to the south—the place where he'd hunted with Hopper—they found the storm less powerful.

They stowed their heavy packs, laden with food and water, in a thicket of bushes. Perrin didn't know if they could survive on food or water found in the dream, but he didn't want to have to find out. They should have enough here for a week or so, and as long as they had a gateway waiting for them, he felt comfortable—or, at least, satisfied—with the risks he was taking here.

The landscape here wasn't coming apart in the same way as it had been near Shayol Ghul. However, if he watched a section long enough, he could catch bits of . . . well, everything being pulled up in the winds. Stalks of dead grain, fragments of tree trunks, gobs of mud and slivers of rock—all were slowly being pulled toward those gluttonous black clouds. After the way of the wolf dream, when he looked back, things that had been broken apart would often be whole again. He understood. This place was being consumed, slowly, as was the waking world. Here, it was simply easier to see.

The winds whipped at them, but weren't so strong that he had to keep them at bay. They felt like the winds at the beginning of a storm, right before the rain and lightning. The heralds of oncoming destruction.

Gaul had pulled the *shoufa* over his face, and looked about suspiciously. His clothing had changed in shade to match the grasses.

"You have to be very careful here, Gaul," Perrin said. "Your idle thoughts can become reality."

Gaul nodded, then hesitantly unveiled his face. "I will listen and do as instructed."

It was encouraging that Gaul's clothing didn't change too much as they walked through the field. "Just try to keep your mind clear," Perrin said. "Free of thought. Act by instinct and follow my lead."

"I will hunt like the *gara*," Gaul said, nodding. "My spear is yours, Perrin Aybara."

Perrin walked through the field, worried that Gaul would accidentally send himself somewhere by thinking of it. The man barely suffered any effects of the wolf dream, however. His clothing would change a little if he was startled, his veil snapping into place without him reaching for it, but that seemed to be the extent of it.

"All right," Perrin said. "I'm going to take us to the Black Tower. We hunt a dangerous prey, a man named Slayer. You remember Lord Luc?"

"The *lopinginny*?" Gaul said.

Perrin frowned.

"It is a type of bird," Gaul said. "From the Three-fold Land. I did not see this man often, but he seemed to be the type who talked big, but was inwardly a coward."

"Well, that was a front," Perrin said. "And either way, he is a very different person in the dream—here, he is a predator named Slayer who hunts wolves and men. He's powerful. If he decides to kill you, he can appear behind you in an eyeblink and imagine you captured by vines and unable to move. You'll be trapped as he slits your throat."

Gaul laughed.

"That's funny?" Perrin asked.

"You act as if it is something new," Gaul explained. "Yet in the first dream, wherever I go, I am surrounded by women and men who could tie me in air with a thought and kill me at any time. I am accustomed to being powerless around some, Perrin Aybara. It is the way of the world in all things."

"Still," Perrin said sternly, "if we find Slayer—he's a square-faced fellow, with eyes that don't seem totally alive, and he dresses in dark leather—I want you to stay away from him. Let me fight him."

"But—"

"You said you'd obey, Gaul," Perrin said. "This is *important*. He took Hopper; I won't have him taking you as well. You don't fight Slayer."

"Very well," Gaul said. "I give my oath on it. I will not dance the spears with this man unless you order it."

Perrin sighed, imagining Gaul standing with his spears put away, letting Slayer kill him because of this oath. Light, but Aiel could be prickly. "You can fight him if he attacks you," Perrin said, "but only as a means of escape. Don't hunt him, and if I'm fighting him, stay out of the way. Understand?"

Gaul nodded. Perrin put a hand on the Aiel's shoulder, then *shifted* them in the direction of the Black Tower. Perrin had never been there before, so he had to guess and try to find it. The first *shift* was off, taking them to a section of Andor where grass-covered hills seemed to dance in the churning winds. Perrin would have preferred to just leap from hilltop to hilltop, but he didn't think Gaul was ready for that. He used *shifting* instead.

After four or five tries, Perrin took them to a place where he spotted a translucent, faintly purple dome rising in the distance.

"What is it?" Gaul asked.

"Our goal," Perrin said. "That is the thing keeping Grady and Neald from creating gateways to the Black Tower."

"Just as we were afflicted in Ghealdan."

"Yes." Seeing that dome brought back memories, vivid ones, of wolves dying. Perrin suppressed them. Memories like that could lead to idle thoughts, here. He allowed himself a burning anger deep within, like the warmth of his hammer, but that was all.

"Let's go," Perrin said, *shifting* them down in front of the dome. It looked like glass. "Pull me free if I collapse," he said to Gaul, then stepped into the barrier.

It felt as if he'd hit something incredibly cold. It sucked away his strength. He stumbled, but kept his mind on his goal. Slayer. Killer of wolves. Hopper's murderer.

Perrin straightened as his strength returned. This was easier than it had been last time; being in the wolf dream in the flesh *did* make him stronger. He didn't have to worry about pulling himself into the dream too strongly, and leaving his body to die in the real world.

He moved slowly through the barrier, as if through water, and stepped out onto the other side. Behind, Gaul reached out with a curious expression on his face, then tapped the dome wall with his index finger.

Gaul immediately dropped to the ground, going limp like a doll. His spears and arrows tumbled away from his body, and he lay perfectly still, his chest not rising. Perrin reached through—his arm slow—and seized Gaul by the leg to pull him through.

Once on the other side, Gaul gasped, then rolled over, groaning. He sat up, holding his head. Perrin quietly fetched the man's arrows and spears for him.

"This is going to be a good experience for building our *ji*," Gaul said. He stood up and rubbed his arm where he'd hit the ground. "The Wise Ones call coming to this place as we do evil?

It seems to me they would enjoy bringing men here to teach them."

Perrin eyed Gaul. He hadn't realized that the man had heard him speaking to Edarra of the wolf dream. "What did I do to deserve your loyalty, Gaul?" Perrin said, mostly to himself.

Gaul laughed. "It is not anything you did."

"What do you mean? I cut you down from that cage. That's why you follow me."

"That's why I began following you," Gaul said. "It is not why I remained. Come, is there not a danger that we hunt?"

Perrin nodded, and Gaul veiled his face. Together, they walked beneath the dome, approaching the structure within. It was a goodly distance from the edge of one of these domes to the center, but Perrin didn't want to jump and be surprised, so they continued on foot, crossing a landscape of open grasslands patched with groves of trees.

They walked for about an hour before they spotted the walls. Tall and imposing, they looked like those around a large city. Perrin and Gaul walked up to them, Gaul scouting with great care, as if he expected to be fired upon at any moment. However, in the wolf dream, these walls wouldn't be guarded. If Slayer were in here, he would lurk at the heart of the dome, at the center. And he'd probably have laid a trap.

Perrin rested his hand on Gaul's shoulder and brought them to the top of the wall in an instant. Gaul prowled to one side, crouching low and peeking into one of the covered guard posts.

Perrin went to the inner edge of the wall, looking in. The Black Tower wasn't as imposing as the outside implied: a distant village of huts and small houses, and beyond that a large building project.

"They're arrogant, wouldn't you say?" a feminine voice asked.

Perrin jumped, spinning, summoning his hammer to his hands and readying a brick wall around himself for protection. A short young woman with silver hair stood next to him, standing straight as if to try to appear taller than she was. She wore white clothing, tied at the waist with a silver belt. He didn't recognize the face, but he did know her scent.

"Moonhunter," Perrin said, almost a growl. "Lanfear."

"I'm not allowed to use that name any longer," she said, tapping one finger on the wall. "He's so strict with names."

Perrin backed away, glancing from side to side. Was she working with Slayer? Gaul appeared out of the guard post and froze, seeing her. Perrin held out a hand to stop him. Could he jump to Gaul and be away before she attacked?

"Moonhunter?" Lanfear asked. "Is that what the wolves call me? That's not right, not at all. I don't *hunt* the moon. The moon is mine already." She leaned down, resting her arms on the chest-high battlement.

"What do you want?" Perrin demanded.

"Vengeance," she whispered. Then she looked at him. "The same as you, Perrin."

"I'm to believe *you* want Slayer dead too?"

"Slayer? That orphan errand boy of Moridin's? He doesn't interest me. My vengeance will be against another."

"Who?"

"The one who caused my imprisonment," she said softly, passionately. Suddenly, she looked toward the skies. Her eyes widened in alarm, and she vanished.

Perrin passed his hammer from one hand to the other as Gaul crept forward, trying to watch all directions at once. "What was that?" he whispered. "Aes Sedai?"

"Worse," Perrin said with a grimace. "Do the Aiel have a name for Lanfear?"

Gaul drew in a sharp breath.

"I don't know what she wants," Perrin said. "She's never made any sense to me. With any luck, we merely crossed paths, and she will go on with what she was about."

He didn't believe that, not after what the wolves had told him earlier. Moonhunter wanted him. *Light, as if I didn't have enough trouble.*

He *shifted* them down to the bottom of the wall, and they continued.

Toveine knelt beside Logain. Androl was forced to watch as she caressed his chin, his wearied eyes open and watching her with horror.

"It's all right," she said sweetly. "You can stop resisting. Relax, Logain. Give in."

She had been Turned easily. Apparently, linked with thirteen Halfmen, it was easier for male channelers to Turn female channelers, and vice versa. That was why they were having so much trouble with Logain.

"Take him," Toveine said, pointing at Logain. "Let's see this done, once and for all. He deserves the peace of the Great Lord's bounty."

Taim's minions dragged Logain away. Androl watched with despair. Taim obviously considered Logain a prize. Turn him, and the rest of the Black Tower would go easily. Many of the boys up above would come willingly to their fate if Logain ordered them to it.

How can he keep fighting? Androl thought. Stately Emarin had been reduced to a whimpering wreck after only two sessions, though he hadn't yet been Turned. Logain had suffered nearly a dozen, and still he resisted.

That would change, for Taim now had women. Soon after Toveine's Turning, others had arrived, sisters of the Black Ajah led by a horridly ugly woman who spoke with authority. The other Reds who had come with Pevara had joined them.

Drowsy concern flowed through Pevara's bond to Androl. She was awake, but full of that drink that stopped her from channeling. Androl's own mind felt relatively clear. How long had it been since they'd forced him to drink the dregs out of the cup they'd first given to Emarin?

Logain ... will not last much longer. Pevara's sending was laced with fatigue and growing resignation. *What are ...* She cut off, thoughts growing muddled. *Burn me! What are we going to do?*

Logain screamed in pain. He hadn't done that before. It seemed a very bad sign. By the doorway, Evin stood and watched. He looked over his shoulder suddenly, jumping at something.

Light, Androl thought. *Could it be ... his madness, caused by the taint? Is it still there?*

Androl noticed for the first time that he was shielded, which they never did to captives unless letting their dose of forkroot wane so they could be Turned.

That sent a spike of panic through him. Were they coming for him next?

Androl? Pevara sent. *I have an idea.*

What?

Androl started coughing through his gag. Evin jumped, then

came over, bringing out his water flask and pouring water on the gag. Abors—one of Taim's flunkies—lounged against the wall. He was holding the shield. He glanced at Androl, but something at the other side of the room drew his attention.

Androl coughed worse, so Evin untied the gag and rolled him to the side, letting him spit out the water.

"Quiet now," Evin said, glancing back at Abors, who was too far away to hear. "Don't make them angry at you, Androl."

The Turning of a man to the Shadow was not perfect. While it changed their allegiance, it did not change everything about them. The thing in Evin's head had his memories, his personality, and—the Light send—his failings.

"Have you convinced them?" Androl whispered. "Not to kill me?"

"I have!" Evin said, leaning low, eyes frenzied. "They keep saying you're useless, since you can't channel very well, but none of them like making gateways to shuffle people about. I told them you'd do it for them. You will, won't you?"

"Of course," Androl said. "It's better than dying."

Evin nodded. "They stopped your dose of forkroot. They'll take you next, after Logain. M'Hael was finally sent new women from the Great Lord, women who aren't tired from channeling all the time. Them and Toveine and the Reds mean it should go quickly now. M'Hael should have Logain by the end of the day."

"I'll serve them," Androl said. "I'll swear to the Great Lord."

"That's good, Androl," Evin said. "But we can't let you go until you've been Turned. M'Hael won't accept just an oath. It will be all right. I told them that you'd Turn easily. You will, won't you? Not resisting?"

"I won't resist."

"Thank the Great Lord," Evin said, relaxing.

Oh, Evin. You never were terribly bright.

"Evin," Androl said softly, "you need to watch out for Abors. You know that, right?"

"I'm one of them now, Androl," Evin said. "I don't have to worry about them."

"That's good," Androl whispered. "What I heard him say about you must have been nothing."

Evin fidgeted. That look in his eyes . . . it was fright. The taint had been cleansed. Jonneth, Emarin and the other new Asha'man would never have to suffer the madness.

It manifested differently in different Asha'man, and at different rates. However, the fear was the most common. It came in waves; it had been consuming Evin when the cleansing happened. Androl had seen Asha'man need to be put down as the taint overwhelmed them. He knew that look in Evin's eyes well. Though the lad had been Turned, he still carried the madness with him. He would do so forever.

"What did he say?" Evin said.

"He didn't like it that you had been Turned," Androl said. "He thinks you'll take his place."

"Oh."

"Evin . . . he might be planning to kill you. Take care."

Evin stood up. "Thank you, Androl."

He walked away, leaving Androl ungagged.

That . . . can't possibly work, Pevara sent drowsily.

She hadn't lived among them long enough. She hadn't seen what the madness could do, and didn't know to recognize it in the eyes of the Asha'man. Normally, when one of them became like this, they would take him and confine him until he rode it out. If that didn't work, Taim added something to their wine, and they didn't wake up.

If they weren't stopped, they would descend to destruction. They would kill those closest to them, lashing out first at people they should have loved.

Androl knew that madness. He knew it was inside of him, too. *That is a mistake, Taim*, he thought. *You use our own friends against us, but we know them better than you do.*

Evin struck at Abors. It came in a burst of the One Power. A second later, Androl's shield dropped.

Androl embraced the Source. He was not very strong, but he had enough Power to burn away a few ropes. He rolled free of his bindings, hands bloodied, and took stock of the room. He hadn't been able to see it before, not entirely.

The room was bigger than he'd assumed, the size of a small throne room. A wide circular dais dominated the far end, topped by a double ring of Myrddraal and women. He shivered as he saw the Fades. Light, but that eyeless gaze was awful.

Taim's exhausted men stood by the far wall, the Asha'man who had failed to Turn Logain. He sat on the dais, slouching and tied to a chair in the center of the double ring. Like a throne. Logain's head rolled to the side, his eyes closed. He appeared to be whispering something.

Taim had spun, furious, toward Evin, who fought with Mishraile beside Abors' smoking corpse. Evin and Mishraile each held the One Power, wrestling on the floor, a knife in Evin's hands.

Androl scrambled toward Emarin, then nearly fell on his face as his legs gave out. Light! He was weak, but he did manage to burn away Emarin's bonds, then Pevara's. She shook her head, trying to clear it. Emarin nodded in gratitude.

"Can you weave?" Androl whispered. Taim's attention was on Evin's fight.

Emarin shook his head. "The drink they gave us . . ."

Androl clung to the One Power. Shadows began to lengthen around him.

No! he thought. *No, not now!*

A gateway. He needed a gateway! Androl sucked in the One Power, forming the weave for Traveling. And yet, as before, he hit some kind of barrier—like a wall, preventing him from opening the gateway. Frustrated, he tried to make one to a closer destination. Perhaps distance mattered. Could he make a gateway to Canler's store above them?

He struggled against that wall, fighting with everything he had. He strained, inching closer; he could almost do it . . . He felt as if something was happening.

"Please," he whispered. "Please, open. We need to get out of here . . ."

Evin fell to Taim's weave.

"What was that?" Taim bellowed.

"I don't know," Mishraile said. "Evin attacked us! He had been talking to the pageboy, and—"

Both spun toward Androl. Androl stopped trying to make the gateway, instead flinging a weave of Fire in desperation toward Taim.

Taim smiled. By the time Androl's tongue of fire reached him, it vanished into a weave of Air and Water that dissipated it.

"You *are* a persistent one," Taim said, slamming Androl against the wall with a weave of Air.

Androl gasped in pain. Emarin stumbled dizzily to his feet, but a second weave of Air knocked him down. Dazed, Androl felt himself hoisted up and pulled across the room.

The ugly woman wearing black stepped out of the circle of Aes Sedai and walked up beside Taim. "So, M'Hael," she said. "You are not nearly as in control of this place as you indicated."

"I have inferior tools," Taim said. "I should have been given more women earlier!"

"You ran your Asha'man to exhaustion," the woman replied. "You squandered their strength. I will take charge here."

Taim stood on the dais, beside Logain's slumped form, the women and the Fades. He seemed to consider this woman, perhaps one of the Forsaken, a greater threat than anyone else in the room.

"You think that will work, do you?" Taim asked.

"When the Nae'blis hears of how you are bungling—"

"The Nae'blis? I care not for Moridin. I have already provided a gift to the Great Lord himself. Beware, I am in his favor. I hold the keys in my hands, Hessalam."

"You mean . . . you actually did it? You stole them?"

Taim smiled. He turned back to Androl, who hung in the air, struggling without success. He wasn't shielded. He flung another weave at Taim, but the man blocked it indifferently.

Androl wasn't even worth shielding. Taim dropped him from the weaves of Air. Androl hit the ground hard. He grunted.

"How long have you trained here, Androl?" Taim asked. "You shame me. That is the *best* you can do when trying to kill?"

Androl struggled to his knees. He felt pain and worry from Pevara behind, her mind clouded with forkroot. In front of him, Logain sat on his throne, locked in place, surrounded by the enemy. The man's eyes were closed; he was barely conscious.

"We are done here," Taim said. "Mishraile, kill these captives. We will take those above and carry them to Shayol Ghul. The Great Lord has promised me more resources for my work there."

Taim's lackeys approached. Androl looked up from his knees. The darkness grew all around, shapes moving in the shadows. The darkness . . . it terrified him. He had to let go of *saidin*, he *had* to. And yet, he could not.

He had to begin weaving.

Taim glanced at him, then smiled and wove balefire.

Shadows, all around!

Androl clung to the Power.

The dead, they come for me!

He wove by instinct, the best weave he knew. A gateway. He hit that wall, that blasted wall.

So tired. Shadows . . . Shadows will take me.

A white-hot bar of light sprang from Taim's fingers, pointed right at Androl. Androl shouted, straining, thrusting his hands forward and snapping his weave into place. He hit that wall and *heaved*.

A gateway the width of a coin opened in front of him. He caught the stream of balefire in it.

Taim frowned, and the room grew still, stunned Asha'man pausing their weaves. At that moment, the door to the room exploded inward.

Canler, holding the One Power, roared in. He was followed by the twenty or so Two Rivers boys who had come to train in the Black Tower.

Taim yelled, embracing the Source. "We are attacked!"

The dome seemed to be centered on the building project he'd noted. That was bad; with those foundations and pits, Slayer would have plenty of places to hide and ambush him.

Once they reached the village, Perrin pointed to a particularly large building. Two stories, built like an inn, with a solid wooden roof. "I'm going to take you up there," Perrin whispered. "Ready your bow. Yell if you spot anyone trying to sneak up on me, all right?"

Gaul nodded. Perrin *shifted* them up onto the top of the building, and Gaul took position by the chimney. His clothing blended to match the color of the clay bricks, and he stayed low, bow out. It wouldn't have the range of a longbow, but from here, he'd be deadly.

Perrin dropped to the ground, floating softly the last inch or so in order to keep from making noise. He crouched and *shifted* to

the side of a building just ahead. He *shifted* again, to the edge of
the last building in the row before the excavation, then looked
over his shoulder. Gaul, hidden quite well up above, raised his
fingers. He had tracked Perrin.

From here, Perrin crept forward on his belly, not wanting to
shift to a place he couldn't see directly. He reached the lip of the
first cavernous foundation hole and looked down on a dirt floor.
The wind still blew, and dust swirled down below, obscuring any
tracks that might have been left.

Perrin rose to a crouch and began to make his way around the
perimeter of the large foundation. Where would the exact center
of the dome be? He couldn't tell; it was too large. He kept his
eyes open.

His attention was so focused on the foundation holes that he
nearly walked right into the guards. A quiet chuckle from one of
them alerted him, and he *shifted* immediately, jumping to the
other side of the foundation and dropping to his knees, Two
Rivers longbow appearing in his hands. He scanned the area he'd
left, now distant.

Fool, he thought, finally spotting them. The two men lounged
in a shack built beside the foundations. The shack was the type of
structure you'd expect workers to take meals in. Perrin looked
about anxiously, but Slayer did not rise out of hiding to attack
him, and the two guards failed to spot him.

He couldn't make out many details, so he cautiously *shifted*
back to near where he'd been. He dropped down into the foundation and created an earthen ledge on its side to stand on while
peering over the lip of the hole into the shack.

Yes, there were two of them. Men in black coats. Asha'man. He
thought he recognized them from the aftermath of Dumai's
Wells, where they had rescued Rand. They were loyal to him,
weren't they? Had Rand sent help for Perrin?

Light burn that man, Perrin thought. *Couldn't he just be up front
with everyone for once?*

Of course, even Asha'man could be Darkfriends. Perrin
debated climbing out of the pit and confronting them.

"Broken tools," Lanfear said idly.

Perrin jumped, cursing to find her standing on the ledge beside
him, peeking up at the two men.

"They've been Turned," she said. "I've always found that to be a wasteful business. You lose something in the transformation— they will never serve as well as if they'd come willingly. Oh, they'll be loyal, but the light is gone. The self-motivation, the spark of ingenuity that makes people into people."

"Be quiet," Perrin said. "Turned? What do you mean? Is that . . ."

"Thirteen Myrddraal and thirteen Dreadlords." Lanfear sneered. "Such crudeness. Such a waste."

"I don't understand."

Lanfear sighed, speaking as if she were explaining to a child. "Those who can channel can be Turned to the Shadow by force in the right circumstances. M'Hael has been having trouble here making the process work as easily as he should. He needs women if he's going to Turn men easily."

Light, Perrin thought. Did Rand know this could happen to people? Were they planning to do the same thing to him?

"I'd be careful around those two," Lanfear said. "They're powerful."

"Then you should be speaking more softly," Perrin whispered.

"Bah. It's easy to bend sound in this place. I could shout for all I'm worth, and they wouldn't hear. They're drinking, you see? They brought the wine through with them. They're here in the flesh, of course. I doubt their leader warned them of the dangers of that."

Perrin looked up at the guards. The two men sipped at their wine, chuckling to one another. As Perrin watched, the first slumped to the side, then the other did as well. They slipped out of their seats and hit the ground.

"What did you do?"

"Forkroot in the wine," Lanfear said.

"Why are you helping me?" Perrin demanded.

"I'm fond of you, Perrin."

"You're one of the Forsaken!"

"I was," Lanfear said. "That . . . privilege has been removed from me. The Dark One discovered I was planning to help Lews Therin win. Now, I—" She froze, looking toward the sky again. What did she see in those clouds? Something that made her grow pale. She vanished a moment later.

Perrin tried to decide what to do. He couldn't trust her, of course. However, she was *good* with the wolf dream. She managed to appear next to him without making any sound at all. That was tougher than it seemed; she had to still the air as it was moved out of the way when she arrived. She had to land just precisely so that she didn't make noise, and had to mute her clothing's rustle.

With a start, Perrin realized that this time she'd also been masking her scent. He'd only been able to smell her—her scent was that of soft night lily—after she'd begun speaking to him.

Uncertainly, he crawled out of the pit and approached the shack. Both men were asleep. What happened to men who slept in the dream? Normally, this would have sent them back to the waking world—but they were here in the flesh.

He shivered, thinking of what had been done to them. "Turned"? Was that the word she'd used? Light. It seemed unfair. *Not that the Pattern is ever fair*, Perrin acknowledged, quickly searching through the hut.

He found the dreamspike driven into the ground under the table. The silvery piece of metal looked like a long tent spike, carved with designs down its length. It was similar to the other one he'd seen, but not exactly the same. He pulled it free, then waited, hand on his hammer, expecting Slayer to come for him.

"He's not here," Lanfear said.

"Light!" Perrin jumped, hammer raised. He turned. "Why do you keep appearing like that, woman?"

"He searches for me," she said, glancing skyward. "I'm not supposed to be able to do this, and he's grown suspicious. If he finds me, he'll know for certain, and I will be destroyed, captured and burned for an eternity."

"You expect me to feel sorry for you, one of the Forsaken?" Perrin snapped.

"I chose my master," she said, studying him. "This is my price—unless I can find a way free of it."

"What?"

"I think you have the best chance," she said. "I need you to win, Perrin, and I need to be at your side when you do."

He snorted. "You haven't learned any new tricks, have you? Take your offers elsewhere. I'm not interested." He turned the dreamspike over in his fingers. He had never been able to figure out how the other one worked.

"You have to twist it at the top." Lanfear held out a hand.

Perrin eyed her.

"You don't think I could have taken it on my own if I'd wanted?" she asked, amused. "Who was it who put M'Hael's little pets down for you?"

He hesitated, then handed it over. She ran her thumb from tip to midlength, and something clicked inside it. She reached up and twisted the head about. Outside, the faint wall of violet shrank and vanished.

She handed it back. "Twist it again to set up the field—the longer you twist, the larger it will grow—then slide your finger in the reverse of what I did to lock it. Be careful. Wherever you set it will have ramifications in the waking world as well as this world, and it will stop even your allies from moving in or out. You can get through with a key, but I do not know it for this spike."

"Thank you," Perrin said grudgingly. At his feet, one of the slumbering men grunted, then rolled to his side. "Is there . . . Is there really no way to resist being Turned? Nothing they can do?"

"A person can resist for a short time," she said. "A short time only. The strongest will fail eventually. If you are a man facing women, they will beat you quickly."

"It shouldn't be possible," Perrin said, kneeling. "Nobody should be able to *force* a man to turn to the Shadow. When all else is taken from us, this choice should remain."

"Oh, they have the choice," Lanfear said, idly nudging one with her foot. "They could have chosen to be gentled. That would have removed the weakness from them, and they could never have been Turned."

"That's not much of a choice."

"This is the weave of the Pattern, Perrin Aybara. Not all options will be good ones. Sometimes you have to make the best of a bad lot and ride the storm."

He looked at her sharply. "And you imply that's what you did? You joined the Shadow because it was the 'best' option? I don't buy it for a moment. You joined for power. Everyone knows it."

"Think what you will, wolf pup," she said, eyes growing hard.

"I've suffered for my decisions. I've borne pain, agony, *excruciating* sorrow because of what I've done in my life. My suffering goes beyond what you could conceive."

"And of all of the Forsaken," Perrin said, "you chose your place and accepted it most readily."

She sniffed. "You think you can believe stories three thousand years old?"

"Better to trust them than the words of one such as yourself."

"As you wish," she said, then looked down again at the sleeping men. "If it helps you to understand, wolf pup, you should know that many think men like these are killed when the Turning happens. And then something else invades the body. Some think that, at least." She vanished.

Perrin sighed, then tucked the dreamspike away and *shifted* back to the rooftop. As soon as he appeared, Gaul spun about, drawing an arrow. "Is it you, Perrin Aybara?"

"It's me."

"I wonder if I should ask for proof," Gaul said, arrow still drawn. "It seems to me that in this place, one could easily change one's appearance."

Perrin smiled. "Appearance isn't all. I know that you have two *gai'shain*, one you want, one you do not. Neither seems content to act as proper *gai'shain*. If we live through this, one might marry you."

"One might," Gaul agreed, lowering his bow. "It's looking like I'll have to take both or neither. Perhaps it is punishment for making them put away their spears, though it is not my choice that makes them do so, but their own." He shook his head. "The dome is gone."

Perrin held up the dreamspike. "It is."

"What is our next task?"

"To wait," Perrin said, settling down on the rooftop, "and see if removing the dome draws Slayer's attention."

"What if it does not?"

"Then we go to the next likely place to find him," Perrin said, rubbing his chin. "And that is wherever there are wolves to kill."

"We heard you!" Canler yelled to Androl amid the firefight. "Burn me if it isn't true! We were in my shop above and we heard you speak, begging! We decided we had to attack. Now or never."

Weaves exploded through the room. Earth erupted, and Fire shot from Taim's people at the dais toward the Two Rivers men. Fades slunk across the room with cloaks that did not move, unsheathing swords.

Androl scrambled away from Canler, head low, making for Pevara, Jonneth and Emarin at the side of the room. Canler had heard him? The gateway he'd made, just before Taim heaved him in air. It must have opened, so small he hadn't been able to see it.

He could make gateways again. But only very small ones. What good was that? *Enough to stop Taim's balefire*, he thought, reaching Pevara and the others. None of the three were in a state to fight. He wove a gateway, hitting the wall, pushing to—

Something changed.

The wall vanished.

Androl sat, stunned for a moment. Blasts and explosions in the room assaulted his ears. Canler and the others fought well, but the Two Rivers lads faced fully trained Aes Sedai and maybe one of the Forsaken. They were dropping one by one.

The wall was gone.

Androl stood up slowly, then walked back toward the center of the room. Taim and his people fought on the dais; the weaves coming from Canler and his lads were flagging.

Androl looked to Taim and felt a powerful, overwhelming surge of anger. The Black Tower belonged to the Asha'man, not this man.

It was time for the Asha'man to reclaim it.

Androl roared, raising his hands beside him, and wove a gateway. The power rushed through him. As always, his gateways snapped into place faster than any others, growing larger than a man of his strength should be able to make.

He built this one the size of a large wagon. He opened it facing Taim's channelers, snapping it in place right as they released their next round of deadly weaves.

The gateway only covered the distance of a few paces, and opened behind them.

Weaves crafted by Taim's women and men hit the open gateway—which hung before Androl like a haze in the air—then exploded out behind them.

Weaves killed their own masters, burning away Aes Sedai, killing Asha'man and the few remaining Myrddraal. Straining at the exertion, Androl bellowed louder and opened small gateways on Logain's bonds, snapping them. He opened another one directly in the floor beneath Logain's chair, dropping it from the room to a place far away from the Black Tower—one that was, the Light send, safe.

The woman called Hessalam fled. As she darted through a gateway of her own, Taim followed with a couple of others. The rest were not so wise—for a moment later, Androl opened a gateway as wide as the floor, dropping the other women and Asha'man through it to plummet hundreds of feet.

CHAPTER
15

Your Neck in a Cord

The Tarasin Palace of Ebou Dar was *far* from the most difficult place that Mat had broken into. He told himself that over and over again as he dangled outside a balcony three stories above the gardens.

He clung to a marble ledge with one hand while holding his hat on his head with the other, his *ashandarei* strapped to his back. He'd stowed his bundle in the gardens below. The night air was cool against the sweat running down the sides of his face.

Above, a pair of Deathwatch Guards clanked as they moved on the balcony. Blood and bloody ashes. Did those fellows never take off their armor? They looked like beetles. He could barely make them out. The balcony was surrounded by an ironwork screen to keep people from looking in at the occupants from below, but Mat was close enough to see the guards moving inside through it.

Light, they were spending a long time in there. Mat's arm started to ache. The two men murmured to one another. Perhaps they were going to sit down and have some tea. Pull out a book, start reading into the night. Tuon really needed to dismiss these two. Why were they having a leisurely conversation on a balcony? There could be assassins out here!

Eventually, thank the Light, the two moved

count to ten before swinging up, but only lasted to seven. He pushed open one of the unlatched screens, and scrambled over the balcony railing.

Mat exhaled softly, arms aching. This palace—those two guards notwithstanding—was nowhere near as impregnable as the Stone had been, and Mat had gotten in there. He had another advantage here, of course: He had lived in this palace, free to come and go. For the most part. He scratched at his neck, and the scarf he wore there. For a moment it felt like a ribbon that felt like a chain.

Mat's father had an adage: Always know which way you are going to ride. There never was a man as honest as Abell Cauthon, and everyone knew it, but some folk—like those up in Taren Ferry—could not be trusted farther than they could spit. In trading horses, Abell had always said, you needed to be ready to ride, and you always had to know which way you were going to go.

In his two months living in this palace, Mat had learned every way out—every crack and passage, every loose window. Which balcony screens were easy to open, which were usually locked tight. If you could sneak out, you could sneak in. He rested a moment on the balcony, but did not enter the room it was attached to. He was on the third floor, where guests stayed. He might have been able to sneak in this way, but the guts of a building were always better guarded than the skin. Best to go up the outside.

Doing so involved a lot of *not* looking down. Fortunately, the side of the building was not difficult to scale. Stonework and wood with plenty of handholds. He remembered chastising Tylin about that once.

Sweat crept down Mat's brow like ants down a hill as he crawled out onto the screen, pulled himself upward and started toward the fourth level. The *ashandarei* occasionally banged his legs from behind. He could smell the sea on the breeze. Things always smelled better when one was up high. Perhaps that was because heads smelled better than feet did.

Stupid thought, that, Mat told himself. Anything to keep from thinking about the height. He pulled himself up onto a piece of stonework, slipping with one foot below and lurching. He breathed in and out, panting, then continued on.

There. Above, he could see Tylin's balcony. Her quarters had several, of course; he went for the one at her bedroom, not the one attached to her sitting room. That one was on the Mol Hara Square, and climbing there, he would be as obvious as a fly in a white pudding.

He looked up again at the arabesque-covered iron balcony. He had always wondered if he could climb to it. He had certainly considered climbing *out* of it.

Well, he would not be a fool and try this sort of thing again, that was for certain. Just this once, and grudgingly. Matrim Cauthon knew to look out for his own neck. He had not survived this long by taking fool chances, luck or no luck. If Tuon wanted to live in a city where the head of her armies was trying to have her assassinated, that was her choice.

He nodded to himself. He would climb up, explain to her in very rational tones that she needed to leave the city and that this General Galgan was betraying her. Then he could saunter on his way and find himself some games of dice. That was why he had come to the city, after all. If Rand was up north, where all the Trollocs were, then Mat wanted to be as far from the man as possible. He felt bad for Rand, but any sane person would see that Mat's choice was the only one. The swirl of colors started to form, but Mat suppressed it.

Rational. He would be very rational.

Sweating, cursing, his hands aching, Mat pulled himself up to the balcony on the fourth floor. One of the screen latches was loose here, as it had been when he lived in the palace. Quick work with a small wire hook was all he needed to get in. He entered the enclosed balcony, took off the *ashandarei*, then lay down on his back, panting as if he had just run all the way from Andor to Tear.

After a few minutes of that, he hauled himself to his feet, then looked out the unlatched screen down four stories. Mat felt pretty good about that climb.

He picked up the *ashandarei* and went to the balcony doors. Tuon would undoubtedly have moved in here, to Tylin's rooms. They were the finest in the palace. Mat cracked the doors open. He would just peek and—

Something shot from the shadows before him and slammed into the door just above his head.

Mat dropped, rolling, pulling out a knife with one hand and holding the *ashandarei* with the other. The door creaked open from the force of the crossbow bolt lodged in its wood.

Selucia looked out a moment later. She had the right side of her head shaven clean, the other side covered in cloth. Her skin was the color of cream, but any man who thought her soft would soon learn otherwise. Selucia could teach sandpaper a thing or two about being tough.

She leveled a small crossbow at him, and Mat found himself smiling. "I knew it!" he exclaimed. "You're a bodyguard. You always were."

Selucia scowled. "What are you doing here, you fool?"

"Oh, just going for a stroll," Mat said, picking himself up and sheathing his knife. "The night air is said to be good for a fellow. The sea breeze. That sort of thing."

"Did you *climb* up here?" Selucia asked, glancing over the side of the balcony, as if looking for a rope or ladder.

"What? You don't climb up normally? It's very good for the arms. Improves grip."

She gave him a suffering look, and Mat found himself grinning. If Selucia was on the lookout for assassins, then Tuon was probably all right. He nodded toward the crossbow, which was still leveled toward him. "Are you going to . . . "

She paused, then sighed and lowered it.

"Many thanks," Mat said. "You could put a man's eye out with that thing, and normally I wouldn't mind, but I'm running short on eyes these days."

"What did you do?" Selucia asked dryly. "Go dicing with a bear?"

"Selucia!" Mat said, walking past her to enter the rooms. "That was quite near to a joke. I should think that, with a little effort, we might be able to grow you a sense of humor. That would be so unexpected, we could put you in a menagerie and charge money to see you. 'Come see the marvelous laughing *so'jhin*. Two coppers only, tonight . . . '"

"You bet the eye on something, didn't you?"

Mat stumbled, pushing open the door. He chuckled. Light! That was strangely close to the truth. "Very cute."

It's a bet I won, he thought, *no matter how it may seem.* Matrim

Cauthon was the only man to have diced with the fate of the world itself in the prize pouch. Of course, next time, they could find some fool hero to take his place. Like Rand or Perrin. Those two were so full of heroism, it was practically dripping out their mouths and down their chins. He suppressed the images that tried to form. Light! He had to stop thinking of those two.

"Where is she?" Mat asked, looking about the bedchamber. The sheets of the bed were disturbed—he earnestly did not imagine pink ribbons tied to that headboard—but Tuon was nowhere to be seen.

"Out," Selucia said.

"*Out?* It's the middle of the night!"

"Yes. A time when only assassins would visit. You are lucky that my aim was off, Matrim Cauthon."

"Never you bloody mind that," Mat said. "You're her bodyguard."

"I don't know what you mean," Selucia said, making the little crossbow vanish into her robes. "I am *so'jhin* to the Empress, may she live forever. I am her Voice and her Truthspeaker."

"Lovely," Mat said, glancing at the bed. "You're decoying for her, aren't you? Lying in her bed? With a crossbow ready, should assassins try to sneak in?"

Selucia said nothing.

"Well, where is she?" Mat demanded. "Bloody ashes, woman! This is serious. General Galgan himself has hired men to kill her!"

"That?" Selucia asked. "You're worried about *that?*"

"Bloody right, I am."

"Galgan is nothing to worry about," Selucia said. "He's too good a soldier to jeopardize our current stabilization efforts. Krisa is the one you should be worried about. She has brought in three assassins from Seanchan." Selucia glanced at the balcony doorway. Mat noticed for the first time a stain on the floor that might have been blood. "I have caught two so far. Pity. I assumed you were the third." She eyed him, as if considering that he might—against all logic—somehow be that assassin.

"You're bloody insane," Mat said, tugging on his hat and fetching his *ashandarei*. "I'm going to Tuon."

"That is no longer her name, may she live forever. She is known as Fortuona; you should not address her by either name, but instead as 'Highest One' or 'Greatest One.'"

"I'll call her what I bloody well please," Mat said. "Where is she?"

Selucia studied him.

"I'm *not* an assassin," he said.

"I don't believe that you are. I am trying to decide if she would like me to tell you her location."

"I'm her husband, am I not?"

"Hush," Selucia said. "You just tried to convince me you weren't an assassin, now you bring up that? Fool man. She is in the palace gardens."

"It's the—"

"—middle of the night," Selucia said. "Yes, I know. She does not always . . . listen to logic." He caught a hint of exasperation in her tone. "She has an entire squad of the Deathwatch Guard with her."

"I don't care if she has the Creator himself with her," Mat snapped, walking back toward the balcony. "I'm going to go sit her down and explain some things to her."

Selucia followed and leaned against the doorway, raising a skeptical gaze to him.

"Well, maybe I won't sit her down, really," Mat said, looking through the open screen at the gardens below. "But I will explain to her—logically—why she can't just go wandering in the night like this. At least, I'll mention it to her. Blood and bloody ashes. We really are high up, aren't we?"

"Normal people use stairs."

"Every soldier in the city is looking for me," Mat said. "I think Galgan is trying to make me vanish."

Selucia pursed her lips.

"You didn't know about this?" Mat asked.

She hesitated, then shook her head. "It's not impossible that Galgan would be on the watch for you. The Prince of the Ravens would be competition, under normal circumstances. He is general of our armies, but that is a task often assigned to the Prince of the Ravens."

Prince of the Ravens. "Don't bloody remind me," Mat said. "I thought that was my title when I was married to the Daughter of the Nine Moons. It hasn't changed at her elevation?"

"No," Selucia said. "Not yet."

Mat nodded, then sighed as he looked at the climb ahead of him. He lifted one leg up onto the railing.

"There is another way," Selucia said. "Come before you break your fool neck. I do not know yet what she wants with you, but I doubt it involves you falling to your death."

Mat gratefully hopped off the balcony railing, following Selucia into the room. She opened a wardrobe, and then opened the back into a dark passageway enclosed in the wood and stone of the palace.

"Blood and bloody ashes," Mat said, sticking his head in. "This was here all along?"

"Yes."

"This might be how it got in," Mat murmured. "You need to board this thing up, Selucia."

"I've done better. When the Empress sleeps—may she live forever—she sleeps in the attic. She never slumbers in this room. We have not forgotten how easily Tylin was taken."

"That's good," Mat said. He shuddered. "I found the thing that did that. He won't be ripping out any more throats. Tylin and Nalesean can have a little dance together about that. Farewell, Selucia. Thank you."

"For the passageway?" she asked. "Or for failing to kill you with the crossbow?"

"For not bloody calling me Highness like Musenge and the others," Mat muttered, entering the passage. He found a lantern hung on the wall, and lit it with his flint and tinder.

Behind him, Selucia laughed. "If that bothers you, Cauthon, you have a very irritating life ahead of you. There is only one way to stop being the Prince of the Ravens, and that is to find your neck in a cord." She closed the door to the wardrobe.

What a pleasant woman she is, Mat thought. He almost preferred the days when she would not talk to him. Shaking his head, he started down the passage, realizing she had never told him exactly where it led.

Rand strode through Elayne's camp at the eastern edge of Braem Wood, accompanied by a pair of Maidens. The camp was dark, evening upon them, but few slept. They were making preparations to break camp and move the army east toward Cairhien the next morning.

Only two guards for Rand tonight. He felt almost *exposed* with two guards, though once he had thought any number of guards at all to be excessive. The inevitable turning of the Wheel had changed his perception as surely as it changed the seasons.

He walked a lantern-lit pathway that had obviously once been a game trail. This camp hadn't been here long enough to have pathways otherwise. Soft noises broke the night's calm: supplies being loaded on to carts, sword blades being ground on whetstones, meals being distributed to hungry soldiers.

The men did not call to one another. Not only was it night, but the Shadow's forces were near in the forest, and Trollocs had good ears. Best to be in the habit of speaking softly, not shouting from one side of the camp to another. The lanterns had shields to give only a soft light, and cook fires were kept to a minimum.

Rand left the trail, carrying his long bundle, passing through rustling high grass in the clearing on his way to Tam's tent. This would be a quick trip. He nodded to those soldiers who saluted as he passed on the path. They were shocked to see him, but not surprised that he walked the camp. Elayne had made her armies aware of his earlier visit.

I lead these armies, she had said as they parted last time, *but you are their heart. You gathered them, Rand. They fight for you. Please let them see you when you come.*

And so he did. He wished he could protect them better, but he would simply have to carry that burden. The secret, it turned out, had not been to harden himself to the point of breaking. It had not been to become numb. It had been to walk in pain, like the pain of the wounds at his side, and accept that pain as part of him.

Two men from Emond's Field guarded Tam's tent. Rand nodded to them as they straightened up, saluting. Ban al'Seen and Dav al'Thone—once, he would never have thought to see them salute. They did it well, too.

"You have a solemn task, men," Rand said to them. "As important as any on this battlefield."

"Defending Andor, my Lord?" Dav asked, confused.

"No," Rand said. "Watching over my father. Take care you do it well." He pushed into the tent, leaving the Maidens outside.

Tam stood over a travel table, inspecting maps. Rand smiled. It was the same look Tam had worn when inspecting a sheep that had gotten caught in the thicket.

"You seem to think I'll need watching," Tam said.

Responding to that comment, Rand decided, would be like walking up to an archer's nest and daring anyone inside to hit him. Instead, he set his bundle down on the table. Tam regarded the long, cloth-wrapped bundle, then tugged at its covering. The cloth came off, revealing a majestic sword with a black-lacquered sheath painted with entwined dragons of red and gold.

Tam looked up with a question in his eyes.

"You gave me your sword," Rand said. "And I wasn't able to return it. This is a replacement."

Tam slid the sword from its sheath, and his eyes widened. "This is too fine a gift, son."

"Nothing is too fine for you," Rand whispered. "Nothing."

Tam shook his head, slipping the blade back into the sheath. "It will just end up in a trunk, forgotten like the last one. I should never have brought that thing home. You put too much care into that blade." He moved to hand the sword back.

Rand put his hand over Tam's. "Please. A blademaster deserves a fitting weapon. Take it—that will ease my conscience. Light knows, any burden I can lighten now will help in the days to come."

Tam grimaced. "That's a dirty trick, Rand."

"I know. I've been spending my time with all kinds of unsavory types lately. Kings, clerks, lords and ladies."

Tam reluctantly took the sword back.

"Think of it as a thank-you," Rand said, "from all the world to you. If you had not taught me of the flame and the void all those years ago ... Light, Tam. I wouldn't be here right now. I'd be dead, I'm sure of that." Rand looked down at the sword. "To think. If you hadn't wanted me to be a good archer, I'd have never learned the thing that kept me sane through the rough times."

Tam sniffed. "The flame and the void aren't about archery."

"Yes, I know. They are a swordsman's technique."

"They're not about swords either," Tam said, strapping the sword onto his belt.

"But—"

"The flame and the void are about center," Tam said. "And about peace. I would teach it to each and every person in this land, soldier or not, if I could." His expression softened. "But, Light, what am I doing? Lecturing you? Tell me, where did you get this weapon?"

"I found it."

"It's as fine a blade as I've ever seen." Tam pulled it out again, looking at the folds of the metal. "It's ancient. And used. Well-used. Cared for, certainly, but this didn't just sit in some warlord's trophy case. Men have swung this blade. Killed with it."

"It belonged . . . to a kindred soul."

Tam looked at him, searching his eyes. "Well, I suppose I should try it out, then. Come on."

"In the night?"

"It's early evening still," Tam said. "This is a good time. The practice grounds won't be clogged."

Rand raised an eyebrow, but stepped aside as Tam rounded the table and left the tent. Rand followed, the Maidens falling in behind them, and trailed his father to the nearby practice grounds, where a few Warders sparred, lit by glowing lanterns on poles.

Near the rack of wooden practice weapons, Tam took the new sword out and moved into a few forms. Though his hair was gray, his face creased around the eyes, Tam al'Thor moved like a ribbon of silk in the wind. Rand had never seen his father fight, not even spar. In truth, a piece of him had had trouble imagining gentle Tam al'Thor killing anything other than a grouse for the firepit.

Now he saw. Lit by flickering lantern light, Tam al'Thor slipped into the sword forms like a comfortable pair of boots. Oddly, Rand found himself jealous. Not of his father specifically, but of any who could know the peace of sword practice. Rand held up his hand, then the stump of the other. Many of the forms required two hands. To fight as Tam did was not the same as fighting with shortsword and shield, as many men in the infantry did. This was something else. Rand might still be able to fight, but he could never do *this*. No more than a man missing one foot could dance.

Tam completed Hare Finds Its Hole, sliding the weapon into its sheath in one smooth motion. Orange lantern light reflected off of the blade as it slipped into its cover. "Beautiful," Tam said. "Light, the weight, the construction . . . Is it Power-forged?"

"I don't know," Rand said.

He'd never had a chance to fight with it.

Tam took a cup of water from a serving boy. A few newer recruits ran through pike formations in the distance, working late into the night. Every moment of training was precious, particularly for those who were not often on the front lines.

New recruits, Rand thought, watching them. *These, too, are my burden. Every man who fights.*

He would find a way to defeat the Dark One. If he did not, these men fought in vain.

"You're worried, son," Tam said, handing the cup back to the serving boy.

Rand calmed himself, finding peace, turning to Tam. He remembered, from his old memories, something from a book. *The key to leadership is in the rippling waves.* You could not find stillness on a body of water if there was turmoil underneath. Likewise, you could not find peace and focus in a group unless the leader himself had peace within.

Tam eyed him, but did not challenge Rand on the sudden mask of control that he had adopted. Instead, Tam reached to the side and took one of the balanced wooden practice swords from the rack. He tossed it to Rand, who caught it, standing with his other arm folded behind his back.

"Father," Rand said warningly as his father picked up another sparring sword. "This is not a good idea."

"I've heard you became quite the swordsman," Tam said, taking a few swipes with the practice sword to test its balance. "I'd like to see what you can do. Call it a father's pride."

Rand sighed, holding up his other arm, displaying the stump. People's eyes tended to slide off it, as if they were seeing a Gray Man. They didn't like the idea that their Dragon Reborn was flawed.

He never let them know how tired he felt, inside. His body was worn, like a millstone that had worked for generations. He was still tough enough to do his job, and he *would*, but Light, he felt tired sometimes. Carrying the hopes of millions was heavier than lifting any mountain.

Tam didn't pay any heed to the stump. He took out a hand-kerchief and wrapped it around one of his hands, then tied it tight using his teeth. "I won't be able to grip a thing with my off hand," he said, swinging the sword again. "It will be a fair fight. Come on, son."

Tam's voice carried authority—the authority of a father. It was the same tone he had once used to get Rand out of bed to go muck the milking shed.

Rand couldn't disobey that voice, not Tam's. It was just built into him. He sighed, stepping forward. "I don't need the sword to fight any longer. I have the One Power."

"That would be important," Tam said, "if sparring right now had anything to do with fighting."

Rand frowned. What—

Tam came at him.

Rand parried with a halfhearted swing. Tam moved into Feathers in the Wind, spinning his sword and delivering a second blow. Rand stepped back, parrying again. Something stirred inside of him, an eagerness. As Tam attacked a second time, Rand lifted the sword and—by instinct—brought his hands together.

Only, he didn't have his other hand to grip the bottom of the sword. That left his grip weak, and when Tam hit again, it nearly twisted the sword out of Rand's grip.

Rand set his teeth, stepping back. What would Lan say, if he'd seen this shoddy performance by one of his students? *What would he say?* He'd say, *"Rand, don't get into swordfights. You can't win them. Not any longer."*

Tam's next attack feinted right, then came around and hit Rand on the thigh with a solid thump. Rand danced backward, smarting. Tam had actually *hit* him, and hard. The man certainly wasn't holding back.

How long had it been since Rand had sparred with someone who was actually willing to hurt him? Too many treated him like glass. Lan had never done that.

Rand threw himself into the fight, trying Boar Rushes Down the Mountain. He beat at Tam for a few moments, but then a slap from Tam's weapon almost twisted the sword from Rand's hand again. The long swords, designed for swordmasters, were difficult to stabilize correctly without a second hand.

Rand growled, again trying to fall into a two-handed stance, again failing. He'd learned, by now, to deal with what he had lost—in normal life, at least. He hadn't spent time sparring since the physical loss, although he'd intended to.

He felt like a chair that was missing one of its legs. He could balance, with effort, but not very well. He fought, he tried form after form, but he barely held on against Tam's attacks.

He couldn't do it. Not well, so why was he bothering? In this activity, he was defective. Sparring made no sense. He turned, sweat streaming from his brow, and threw his coat aside. He tried again, stepping carefully on the trampled grass, but again Tam got the better of him, nearly knocking his feet out from under him.

This is pointless! Why fight one-handed? Why not find another way? Why . . .

Tam was doing it.

Rand continued to fight, defensive, but he directed his attention to Tam. His father must have practiced fighting one-handed; Rand could read it in his movements, the way he didn't try—by instinct—to keep grabbing the hilt with his bound hand. Upon consideration, Rand probably should have practiced sparring one-handed. Many wounds could hurt the hand, and some forms focused on arm attacks. Lan had told him to practice reversing his grips. Perhaps fighting with one hand would have come next.

"Let go, son," Tam said.

"Let go of what?"

"Everything." Tam came rushing in, throwing shadows in the lantern light, and Rand sought the void. All emotion went into the flame, leaving him empty and whole at once.

The next attack nearly cracked his head. Rand cursed, coming into Heron in the Reeds as Lan had taught him, sword up to block the next blow. Again, that missing hand of his tried to grip the hilt. One could not unlearn years of training in an evening!

Let go.

Wind blew through across the field, carrying with it the scents of a dying land. Moss, mold, rot.

Moss lived. Mold was a living thing. For a tree to rot, life had to progress.

A man with one hand was still a man, and if that hand held a sword, he was still dangerous.

Tam fell into Hawk Spots the Hare, a very aggressive form. He charged Rand, swinging. Rand saw the next few moments before they happened. He saw himself raising his sword in the proper form to block—a form that required him to expose his sword to bad balance, now that he had no second hand. He saw Tam slicing down on the sword to twist it in Rand's grip. He saw the next attack coming back and taking Rand at the neck.

Tam would freeze before hitting. Rand would lose the spar.

Let go.

Rand shifted his grip on the sword. He didn't think about why; he did what felt right. When Tam came near, Rand flung his left arm up to stabilize his hand while pivoting his sword to the side. Tam connected, weapon sliding off Rand's sword, but not unhanding it.

Tam's backswing came as expected, but hit Rand's elbow, the elbow of the useless arm. Not so useless after all. It blocked the sword effectively, though the *crack* of it hitting sent a shiver of pain down Rand's arm.

Tam froze, eyes widening—first in surprise that he'd been blocked, then in apparent worry over connecting with a solid blow on Rand's arm. He had probably fractured the bone.

"Rand," Tam said, "I . . ."

Rand stepped back, folded his wounded arm behind his back, and lifted his sword. He breathed in the deep scents of a world wounded, but not dead.

He attacked. Kingfisher Strikes in the Nettles. Rand didn't choose it; it happened. Perhaps it was his posture, sword out, other arm folded behind his back. That led him easily into the offensive form.

Tam blocked, wary, stepping to the side in the brown grass. Rand swung to the side, flowing into his next form. He stopped trying to turn off his instincts, and his body adapted to the challenge. Safe within the void, he didn't need to wonder how.

The contest continued in earnest, now. Swords clacking with sharp blows, Rand keeping his hand behind his back and *feeling* what his next strike should be. He did not fight as well as he once had. He could not; some forms were impossible for him, and he could not strike with as much force as he once could.

He did match Tam. To an extent. Any swordsman could tell

who was the better as they fought. Or, at least, they could tell who had the advantage. Tam had it here. Rand was younger and stronger, but Tam was just so *solid*. He *had* practiced fighting with one hand. Rand was certain of it.

He did not care. This focus . . . he had missed this focus. With so much to worry about, so much to carry, he had not been able to dedicate himself to something as simple as a duel. He found it now, and poured himself into it.

For a time, he wasn't the Dragon Reborn. He wasn't even a son with his father. He was a student with his master.

In this, he remembered that no matter how good he had become, no matter how much he now remembered, there was still much he could learn.

They continued to spar. Rand did not count who had won which exchange; he just fought and enjoyed the peace of it. Eventually, he found himself exhausted in the good way—not in the worn-down way he had begun to feel lately. It was the exhaustion of good work done.

Sweating, Rand raised his practice sword to Tam, indicating that he was through. Tam stepped back, raising his own sword. The older man wore a grin.

Nearby, standing near the lanterns, a handful of Warders began clapping. Not a large audience—only six men—but Rand had not noticed them. The Maidens lifted their spears in salute.

"It has been quite a weight, hasn't it?" Tam asked.

"What weight?" Rand replied.

"That lost hand you've been carrying."

Rand looked down at his stump. "Yes. I believe it has been at that."

Tylin's secret passage led to the gardens, opening up in a very narrow hole not far from where Mat had begun his climb. He crawled out, brushing the dust off of his shoulders and knees, then craned his neck back and looked up to the balcony far above. He had ascended to the building's heights, then crawled out through its bowels. Maybe there was a lesson in that somewhere. Maybe it was that Matrim Cauthon should look for secret passages before deciding to scale a bloody four-story building.

He stepped softly into the gardens. The plants were not doing well. These ferns should have far more fronds, and the trees were as bare as a Maiden in the sweat tent. Not surprising. The entire land wilted faster than a boy at Bel Tine with no dancing partners. Mat was pretty sure Rand was to blame. Rand or the Dark One. Mat could trace every bloody problem in his life to one or the other. Those flaming colors . . .

Moss still lived. Mat had not ever heard of moss being used in a garden, but he could have sworn that here it had been made to grow on rocks in patterns. Perhaps, when everything died off, the gardeners used what they could find.

It took him some searching, poking through dried shrubs and past dead flower beds, to find Tuon. He had expected to find her sitting peacefully in thought, but he should have known better.

Mat crouched beside a fern, unseen by the dozen or so Deathwatch Guards who stood in a ring around Tuon as she went through a series of fighting stances. She was lit by a pair of lanterns that gave off a strange, steady blue glow. Something burned within them, but it was not a regular flame.

The light shone on her soft, smooth skin, which was the shade of good earth. She wore a pale *a'solma*, a gown that was split at the sides, showing blue leggings underneath. Tuon had a slight frame; he had once made the mistake of assuming that meant she was frail. Not so.

She had shaved her head again properly, now that she was no longer hiding. Baldness looked good on her, strange though it was. She moved in the blue glow, running through a sequence of hand combat forms, her eyes closed. She seemed to be sparring with her own shadow.

Mat preferred a good knife—or, better, his *ashandarei*—to fighting with his hands. The more space he had between himself and a fellow trying to kill him, the better. Tuon did not seem to need either. Watching her, he realized how fortunate he had been the night he had taken her. Unarmed, she was deadly.

She slowed, waving her hands in front of her in a gentle pattern, then thrusting them quickly to the side. She breathed in and brought her arms to the other side, her entire body twisting.

Did he love her?

The question made Mat uncomfortable. It had been scratching

at the edges of his mind for weeks now, like a rat trying to have at the grain. It was not the sort of question Matrim Cauthon was supposed to have to ask. Matrim Cauthon worried only about the girl on his knee and the next toss of the dice. Questions about matters like love were best left to Ogier who had time to sit and watch trees grow.

He had married her. That was an accident, was it not? The bloody foxes had told him he would. She had married him back. He still did not know why. Something to do with those omens she talked about? Their courtship had been more of a game than a romance. Mat liked games, and he always played to win. Tuon's hand had been the prize. Now that he had it, what did he do with it?

She continued her forms, moving like a reed in the wind. A tilt this way, then a wave of motion that way. The Aiel called fighting a dance. What would they think of this? Tuon moved as gracefully as any Aiel. If battle were a dance, most of it was done to the music of a rowdy barroom. This was done to the swaying melody of a master singer.

Something moved over Tuon's shoulder. Mat tensed, peering into that darkness. Ah, it was just a gardener. An ordinary-looking fellow with a cap on his head and freckled cheeks. Barely worth noticing. Mat put him out of his mind and leaned forward to take a better look at Tuon. He smiled at her beauty.

Why would a gardener be out at this time? he thought. *Must be a strange type of fellow.*

Mat glanced at the man again, but had trouble picking him out. The gardener stepped between two members of the Deathwatch Guard. They did not seem to care. Mat should not either. They must trust the man . . .

Mat reached into his sleeve and freed a knife. He raised it without letting himself think about why. In doing so, his hand brushed one of the branches ever so softly.

Tuon's eyes snapped open, and despite the dim light, she focused directly on Mat. She saw the knife in his hand, ready to throw.

Then she looked over her shoulder.

Mat threw, the knife reflecting blue light as it spun. It passed less than a finger's width from Tuon's chin, hitting the gardener in the shoulder as he raised a knife of his own. The man gasped, stumbling back. Mat would have preferred to take him in the throat, but he had not wanted to risk hitting Tuon.

Rather than doing the sensible thing and moving away, Tuon leaped for the man, hands shooting toward his throat. That made Mat smile. Unfortunately, the man had just enough time—and she was just enough off-balance—that he managed to push backward and scramble between the baffled Deathwatch Guards. Mat's second dagger hit the ground behind the assassin's heel as he vanished into the night.

A second later, three men—each weighing roughly the same as a small building—crashed down on top of Mat, slamming his face against the dry ground. One stepped on his wrist, and another ripped his *ashandarei* away from him.

"Stop!" Tuon barked. "Release him! Go after the other one, you fools!"

"Other one, Majesty?" one of the guards asked. "There was no other one."

"Then to whom does that blood belong?" Tuon asked, pointing at the dark stain on the ground that the assassin had left behind. "The Prince of the Ravens saw what you did not. Search the area!"

The Deathwatch Guards slowly climbed off Mat. He let out a groan. What did they feed these men? Bricks? He did not like being called "Highness," but a little respect would have been nice here. If it had prevented him from being sat upon, that was.

He climbed to his feet, then held out his hand to a sheepish Deathwatch Guard. The fellow's face had more scars than skin. He handed Mat the *ashandarei*, then went off to help search the garden.

Tuon folded her arms, obviously unshaken. "You have chosen to delay your return to me, Matrim."

"Delay my . . . I came to bloody warn you, not 'return to' you. I'm my own man."

"You may pretend whatever you wish," Tuon said, looking over her shoulder as the Deathwatch Guards beat at the shrubbery. "But you must not stay away. You are important to the Empire, and I have use for you."

"Sounds delightful," Mat grumbled.

"What was it?" Tuon asked softly. "I did not see the man until you drew attention. These guards are the best of the Empire. I have seen Daruo there catch an arrow in flight with his bare hand, and Barrin once stopped a man from breathing on me because he suspected an assassin whose mouth was filled with poisons. He was right."

"It's called a Gray Man," Mat said, shivering. "There's something freakishly ordinary about them—they're hard to notice, hard to fixate upon."

"Gray Man," Tuon said idly. "More myths come to life. Like your Trollocs."

"Trollocs are real, Tuon. Bloody—"

"Of course Trollocs are real," she said. "Why wouldn't I believe that they are?" She looked at him defiantly, as if daring him to mention the times she had called them myths. "This Gray Man appears to be real as well. There is no other explanation for why my guards let him pass."

"I trust the Deathwatch Guards well enough," Mat said, rubbing his shoulder where one of them had placed his knee. "But I don't know, Tuon. General Galgan is trying to have you killed; he could be working with the enemy."

"He's not serious about having me killed," Tuon said indifferently.

"Are you bloody insane?" Mat asked.

"Are you bloody stupid?" she asked. "He hired assassins from this land only, not true killers."

"That Gray Man is from this land," Mat pointed out.

That quieted her. "With whom did you gamble away that eye?"

Light! Was everyone going to ask him about it that way? "I went through a rough patch," he said. "I made it through alive, which is all that matters."

"Hmm. And did you save her? The one you went to rescue?"

"How did you know about that?"

She did not reply. "I have decided not to be jealous. You are fortunate. The missing eye suits you. Before, you were too pretty."

Too pretty? Light. What did that mean?

"Good to see you, by the way," Mat said. He waited a few moments. "Usually, when a fellow says something like that, it's customary to tell them that you're happy to see them as well."

"I am the Empress now," Tuon said. "I do not wait upon others,

and do not find it 'good' that someone has returned. Their return
is expected, as they serve me."

"You know how to make a fellow feel loved. Well, I know how
you feel about me."

"And how is that?"

"You looked over your shoulder."

She shook her head. "I had forgotten that you are supremely
good at saying that which has no meaning, Matrim."

"When you saw me," Mat explained, "with a dagger in hand—
as if to throw at you—you didn't call for your guards. You didn't
fear I was here to kill you. You looked over your shoulder to see
what I was aiming at. That's the most loving gesture I think a
man could receive from a woman. Unless you'd like to sit on my
knee for a little while . . . "

She did not reply. Light, but she seemed cold. Was it all going
to be different, now that she was the Empress? He could not have
lost her already, could he?

Furyk Karede, the captain of the Deathwatch Guard, soon
arrived with Musenge walking behind him. Karede looked like he
had just found his house on fire. The other Deathwatch Guards
saluted him and seemed to wither before him.

"Empress, my eyes are lowered," Karede said, going down on
his belly before her. "I will join those who failed you in spilling
our lives before you as soon as a new squad has arrived to see to
your protection."

"Your lives are mine," Tuon said, "and you do not end them
unless I give you leave. This assassin was not of natural birth, but
a creation of the Shadow. Your eyes are not lowered: The Prince of
the Ravens will teach you how to spot this kind of creature, so
you will not be so surprised again."

Mat was fairly certain that Gray Men *were* of natural birth, but
then, so were Trollocs and Fades. It did not seem appropriate to
point this out to Tuon. Besides, something else in her orders drew
his attention.

"I'm going to do what, now?" Mat asked.

"Teach them," Tuon said softly. "You are Prince of the Ravens.
This will be part of your duties."

"We need to talk about that," Mat said. "Everyone calling me
'Highness' is not going to do, Tuon. It just won't."

She did not reply. She waited as the search proceeded, and made no move to retreat to the palace.

Finally, Karede approached again. "Highest One, there is no sign of the thing in the gardens, but one of my men has found blood on the wall. I suspect the assassin fled into the city."

"He is unlikely to try again tonight," Tuon said, "while we are alerted. Do not spread news of this to the common soldiers or guards. Inform my Voice that our ruse has stopped being effective, and that we will need to consider a new one."

"Yes, Empress," Karede said, bowing low again.

"For now," Tuon said, "clear out and secure the perimeter. I will be spending time with my consort, who has requested that I 'make him feel loved.'"

"That's not exactly—" Mat said as the members of the Deathwatch Guard faded into the darkness.

Tuon studied Mat for a moment, then began to disrobe.

"Light!" Mat said. "You *meant* it?"

"I'm not going to sit on your knee," Tuon said, pulling one arm out of her robe, exposing her breasts, "though I may allow you to sit on mine. Tonight, you have saved my life. That will earn you special privilege. It—"

She cut off as Mat grabbed her and kissed her. She was tense with surprise. *In the bloody garden*, he thought. *With soldiers standing all about, well within earshot.* Well, if she expected Matrim Cauthon to be shy, she had a surprise coming.

He released her lips from the kiss. Her body was pressed against his, and he was pleased to find her breathless.

"I won't be your toy," Mat said sternly. "I won't have it, Tuon. If you intend it to be that way, I will leave. Mark me. Sometimes, I do play the fool. With Tylin, I did for sure. I won't have that with you."

She reached up and touched his face, surprisingly tender. "I would not have said the words I did if I had found in you only a toy. A man missing an eye is no toy anyway. You have known battle; everyone who sees you now will know that. They will not mistake you for a fool, and I have no use for a toy. I shall have a prince instead."

"And do you love me?" he asked, forcing the words out.

"An empress does not love," she said. "I am sorry. I am with

you because the omens state it so, and so with you I will bring the
Seanchan an heir."

Mat had a sinking feeling.

"However," Tuon said. "Perhaps I can admit that it is ... good
to see you."

Well, Mat thought, *guess I can take that. For now.*

He kissed her again.

CHAPTER
16

A Silence Like Screaming

L oial, son of Arent son of Halan, had secretly always wanted to be hasty.

Humans fascinated him, of *that* he made no secret. He was sure most of his friends knew, though he could not be certain. It amazed him what humans didn't hear. Loial could speak to them all day, then find that they had heard only part. Did they think that someone would speak without intending for others to listen?

Loial listened when they spoke. Every word out of their mouths revealed more about them. Humans were like the lightning. A flash, an explosion, power and *energy*. Then gone. What would it be like?

Hastiness. There were things to learn from hastiness. He was starting to wonder if he had learned that particular lesson too well.

Loial strode through a forest of too-silent trees, Erith at his side, other Ogier surrounding them. All held axes on shoulders or carried long knives as they marched toward the battlefront. Erith's ears twitched; she was not a Treesinger, but she could sense that the trees did not feel right.

It was horrible, horrible indeed. He could not explain the sense of a healthy stand of trees any more than he could explain the sensation of wind on his skin. There was a rightness, like the scent of morning rain, to healthy trees. It was not a sound, but it felt like a melody. When he sang to them, he found himself swimming in that rightness.

These trees had no such rightness. If he drew close to them, he felt he could hear something. A silence like screaming. It was not a sound, but a feeling.

Fighting raged ahead of them in the forest. Queen Elayne's forces carefully withdrew eastward, out of the trees. They were nearly to the edge of Braem Wood now; once out, they would march for the bridges, cross them and burn them behind. Then the soldiers would launch volleys of destruction at the Trollocs trying to cross the river after them on their own bridges. Bashere hoped to reduce the enemy's numbers considerably at the Erinin before they continued east.

Loial was certain this would all make fascinating information for his book, once he wrote it. If he was able to write it. He laid his ears flat as the Ogier began their war song. He lent his voice to theirs, glad for the terrible song—the call to blood, to death— as it filled the silence left by the trees.

He started running with the others, Erith at his side. Loial drew out in front, axe raised above his head. Thoughts left him as he found himself angry, *furious*, at the Trollocs. They didn't just kill trees. They took the peace from the trees.

The call to blood, to death.

Bellowing his song, Loial laid into the Trollocs with his axe, Erith and the other Ogier joining him and stopping the brunt of this Trolloc flanking force. He had not intended to lead the Ogier charge. He did anyway.

He hacked at the shoulder of a ram-faced Trolloc, shearing its arm free. The thing yelled and fell to its knees, and Erith kicked it in the face, throwing it back into the legs of a Trolloc behind.

Loial did not stop his song, the call to blood, to death. Let them hear! Let them *hear*! Swing after swing. Chopping dead wood, that was all this was. Dead, rotting, horrible wood. He and Erith fell into place with Elder Haman, who—with ears laid back—looked utterly fierce. Placid Elder Haman. He felt the rage too.

A beleaguered line of Whitecloaks—whom the Ogier had relieved—stumbled back, making way for the Ogier.

He sang and fought and roared and killed, hacking at Trollocs with an axe meant for cutting wood, and never flesh. Working with wood was a reverent business. This ... this was killing weeds. Poisonous weeds. Strangling weeds.

He continued to chop the Trollocs, losing himself in the call to blood, to death. The Trollocs began to fear. He saw terror in their beady eyes, and he loved it. They were used to fighting men, who were smaller than themselves.

Well, let the Trollocs fight someone their own size. They snarled as the Ogier line forced them back. Loial landed blow after blow, shearing through arms, hacking through torsos. He shoved his way between two bear Trollocs, laying about him with his axe, yelling in fury—fury now for what the Trollocs had done to the Ogier. They should be enjoying the peace of the *stedding*. They should be able to build, sing, and grow.

They could not. Because of these ... these *weeds*, they could not! The Ogier were forced to kill. The Trollocs made builders into destroyers. They forced Ogier and humans to be like themselves. The call to blood, to death.

Well, the Shadow would see just how dangerous the Ogier could be. They *would* fight, and they *would* kill. And they would do it better than any human, Trolloc or Myrddraal could imagine.

By the fear Loial saw in the Trollocs—by their terrified eyes—they were beginning to understand.

"Light!" Galad exclaimed, falling back from the thick of the fight. "*Light!*"

The Ogier attack was terrible and glorious. The creatures fought with ears drawn back, eyes wide, broad faces flat as anvils. They seemed to transform, all placidity gone. They cut through ranks of Trollocs, hacking the beasts to the ground. The second row of Ogier, made up mostly of females, sliced up Trollocs with long knives, bringing down any who made it through the first line.

Galad had thought Trollocs fearsome with their twisted mix of human and animal features, but the Ogier disturbed him more.

Trollocs were simply horrible ... but Ogier were gentle, soft-spoken, kindly. Seeing them enraged, bellowing their terrible song and attacking with axes nearly as long as men were tall ... Light!

Galad waved the Children back, then ducked as a Trolloc slammed into a tree nearby. Some of the Ogier were seizing wounded Trollocs by their arms and hurling them out of the way. Many of the other Ogier were blood-soaked to their waists, hacking and chopping like butchers preparing meat. Now and then, one of them fell, but unarmored though they were, their skin seemed tough.

"Light!" Trom said, moving up to Galad. "Have you ever seen anything like that?"

Galad shook his head. It was the most honest answer he could think of.

"If we had an army of those ... " Trom said.

"They're Darkfriends," Golever said, joining them. "Shadowspawn for certain."

"Ogier are no more Shadowspawn than I am," Galad said dryly. "Look, they're *slaughtering* the Trollocs."

"Any moment now, they'll all turn on us," Golever said. "Watch ... " He trailed off, listening to the Ogier chant their war song. One large group of Trollocs broke, fleeing back around cursing Myrddraal. The Ogier didn't let them go. Enraged, the giant Builders chased after the Trollocs, long-handled axes chopping their legs, dropping them in sprays of blood and cries of agony.

"Well?" Trom asked.

"Maybe ... " Golever said. "Maybe it's a scheme of some kind. To gain our trust."

"Don't be a fool, Golever," Trom said.

"I'm not—"

Galad held up a hand. "Gather our wounded. Let's head toward the bridge."

Rand let the swirling colors fade from his vision. "It is nearly time for me to go," he said.

"To battle?" Moiraine asked.

"No, to Mat. He is in Ebou Dar."

He had returned from Elayne's camp to Merrilor. The conversation with Tam still bounced around in his head. *Let go.* It wasn't nearly so easy. And yet, something had lifted from him in speaking with his father. *Let go.* There seemed a depth to Tam's words, one far beyond the obvious.

Rand shook his head. He couldn't afford to waste time on such thoughts. The Last Battle ... it had to claim his attention.

I have been able to draw close without drawing attention, he thought, fingering the deerhorn-hilted dagger at his belt. *It seems to be true. The Dark One can't sense me when I carry this.*

Before he could move against the Dark One, he had to do something about the Seanchan. If what Thom said was true, Mat might be the key. The Seanchan *had* to join the Dragon's Peace. If they did not ...

"That is an expression I remember," a soft voice said. "Consternation. You do it so well, Rand al'Thor."

He turned toward Moiraine. Beyond her, on the table in his tent, maps that Aviendha had sent by messenger showed positions where his army could gather in the Blight.

Moiraine stepped up beside Rand. "Did you know that I used to spend hours in thought, trying to discover what that mind of yours was conjuring? It is a wonder I did not pull every hair from my head in frustration."

"I was a fool for not trusting you," Rand said.

She laughed. A soft laugh, the laugh of an Aes Sedai who was in control. "You trusted me enough. That was what made it all the more frustrating that you would not share."

Rand breathed in deeply. The air here at Merrilor was sweeter than in other places. He had coaxed the land here back to life. Grass grew. Flowers budded. "Tree stumps and men," he said to Moiraine. "The Two Rivers has both, and one is about as likely to budge as the other."

"Perhaps that is too harsh," Moiraine said. "It was not merely stubbornness that drove you; it was a will to prove to yourself, and to everyone else, that you could do this on your own." She touched his arm. "But you cannot do this on your own, can you?"

Rand shook his head. He reached up to *Callandor*, strapped on his back, touching it. The sword's final secret lay bare to him now.

It was a trap, and a clever one, for this weapon was a *sa'angreal* not for just the One Power, but for the True Power as well.

He had thrown away the access key, but on his back he carried something so very tempting. The True Power, the Dark One's essence, was the sweetest thing he had ever touched. With *Callandor*, he could draw it forth in strength such as no man had ever before felt. Because *Callandor* lacked the safety measures of most other *angreal* and *sa'angreal*, there was no telling how much of the Powers it could draw.

"There it is again," Moiraine murmured. "What are you planning, Rand al'Thor, Dragon Reborn? Can you finally let go enough to tell me?"

He eyed her. "Did you set this entire conversation up to pull that secret from me?"

"You think very highly of my conversational abilities."

"An answer that says nothing," Rand said.

"Yes," Moiraine said. "But might I point out that you did it first in deflecting my question?"

Rand thought back a few steps in the conversation, and realized he'd done just that. "I'm going to kill the Dark One," Rand said. "I'm not just going to seal up the Dark One, I'm going to end him."

"I thought you had grown up while I was away," Moiraine said.

"Only Perrin grew up," Rand said. "Mat and I have simply learned to pretend to be grown up." He hesitated. "Mat did not learn it so well."

"The Dark One is beyond killing," Moiraine said.

"I think I can do it," Rand said. "I remember what Lews Therin did, and there was a moment . . . a brief moment . . . It can happen, Moiraine. I'm more confident that I can do *that* than I am that I could seal the Dark One away." That was true, though he had no real confidence that he could manage either.

Questions. So many questions. Shouldn't he have some answers by now?

"The Dark One is part of the Wheel," Moiraine said.

"No. The Dark One is outside the Pattern," Rand countered. "Not part of the Wheel at all."

"Of course the Dark One is part of the Wheel, Rand," Moiraine said. "*We* are the threads that make up the Pattern's substance, and the Dark One affects us. You cannot kill him. That is a fool's task."

"I have been a fool before," Rand said. "And I shall be one again. At times, Moiraine, my entire life—all that I've done—feels like a fool's task. What is one more impossible challenge? I've met all the others. Perhaps I can accomplish this one too."

She tightened her grip on his arm. "You have grown so much, but you are still just a youth, are you not?"

Rand immediately seized control of his emotions, and did not lash back at her. The surest way to be thought of as a youth was to act like one. He stood straight-backed, and spoke softly. "I have lived for four centuries," he said. "Perhaps I am still a youth, in that all of us are, compared to the timeless age of the Wheel itself. That said, I am one of the oldest people in existence."

Moiraine smiled. "Very nice. Does that work on the others?"

He hesitated. Then, oddly, he found himself grinning. "It worked pretty well on Cadsuane."

Moiraine sniffed. "That one . . . Well, knowing her, I doubt you fooled her as well as you assume. You may have the memories of a man four centuries old, Rand al'Thor, but that does not make you ancient. Otherwise, Matrim Cauthon would be the patriarch of us all."

"Mat? Why Mat?"

"It is nothing," Moiraine said. "Something I am not supposed to know. You are still a wide-eyed sheepherder at heart. I would not have it any other way. Lews Therin, for all of his wisdom and power, could not do what you must. Now, if you would be kind, fetch me some tea."

"Yes, Moiraine Sedai," he said, immediately starting toward the teapot over the fire. He froze, then looked back at her.

She glanced at him slyly. "Merely seeing if that still worked."

"I *never* fetched you tea," Rand protested, walking back to her. "As I remember, I spent our last few weeks together ordering *you* around."

"So you did," Moiraine said. "Think about what I said regarding the Dark One. But now I ask you a different question. What will you do *now*? Why go to Ebou Dar?"

"The Seanchan," Rand said. "I must try to bring them to our side, as I promised."

"If I remember," Moiraine said, "you did not promise that you would try, you promised that you would make it happen."

"Promises to 'try' don't achieve much in political negotiations," Rand said, "no matter how sincere." He held up his hand before him, arm outstretched, fingers up, and looked out of his open tent flaps. As if he were preparing to grab the lands to the south. Scoop them up, claim them as his, protect them.

The Dragon on his arm shone, gold and crimson. "Once the Dragon, for remembrance lost." He held up his other arm, ending at the stump near the wrist. "Twice the Dragon . . . for the price he must pay."

"What will you do if the Seanchan leader refuses again?" Moiraine asked.

He hadn't told her that the Empress had refused him the first time. Moiraine didn't need to be told things. She simply discovered them.

"I don't know," Rand said softly. "If they don't fight, Moiraine, we will lose. If they don't join the Dragon's Peace, then we have nothing."

"You spent too much time on that pact," Moiraine said. "It distracted you from your goal. The Dragon does not bring peace, but destruction. You cannot change that with a piece of paper."

"We shall see," Rand said. "Thank you for your advice. Now, and always. I don't believe I have said that enough. I owe you a debt, Moiraine."

"Well," she said. "I *am* still in need of a cup of tea."

Rand looked at her, incredulous. Then he laughed and walked away to bring her some.

Moiraine held her warm cup of tea, which Rand had fetched for her before leaving. He had become ruler of so much since they had parted, and he was as humble now as when she had first found him in the Two Rivers. Maybe more so.

Humble toward me, perhaps, she thought. *He believes he can slay the Dark One. That is not the sign of a humble man.* Rand al'Thor, such an odd mixture of self-effacement and pride. Did he finally have the balance right? Despite what she had said, his action toward her today proved he was no youth, but a man.

A man could still make mistakes. Often, they were of a more dangerous sort.

"The Wheel weaves as the Wheel wills," she murmured to herself, sipping the tea. Prepared by Rand's hand, and not someone else's, it was as flavorful and vibrant as it had been during better days. Not touched in the least bit by the Dark One's shadow.

Yes, the Wheel wove as it willed. Sometimes, she wished that weaving were easier to understand.

"Everyone knows what to do?" Lan asked, turning in Mandarb's saddle.

Andere nodded. He'd carried the word himself to the rulers, and from them it had gone to their generals and commanders. Only at the last moments had it been passed to the soldiers themselves.

There would be Darkfriends among them. There always were. It was impossible to exterminate rats from a city, no matter how many cats you brought in. The Light willing, this news would come too late for those rats to give warning to the Shadow.

"We ride," Lan said, setting heels into Mandarb's ribs. Andere raised his banner high, the flag of Malkier, and galloped at his side. He was joined by his ranks of Malkieri. Many of those had only a little Malkieri blood in them, and were truly Borderlanders of other nations. They still chose to ride beneath his banner, and had taken up the *hadori*.

Thousands upon thousands of horsemen rode with him, hooves shaking the soft earth. It had been a long, hard retreat for their army. The Trollocs had superior numbers and presented a serious threat of surrounding Lan's men. Lan's mounted army was highly mobile, but there was only so much speed you could force upon soldiers, and Trollocs could march quickly. Faster than people could, particularly with those Fades whipping them. Fortunately, the fires in the countryside were slowing the Shadow's army. Without that, Lan's men might not have been able to escape.

Lan crouched in the saddle as the explosions from the Dreadlords began. To his left, the Asha'man Deepe rode, tied to his saddle because of his missing leg. As a ball of fire crackled through the air and arced down toward Lan, Deepe adopted a look of concentration and thrust his hands forward. The fire exploded in the air above them.

Burning embers fell like crimson rain, trailing smoke. One hit Mandarb's neck, and Lan brushed it aside with a gauntleted hand. The horse didn't seem to notice.

The ground here was of deep clay. The terrain consisted of rolling hills, covered with sere grass, rocky outcrops and groves of defoliated trees. The retreat followed the banks of the Mora; the river would prevent the Trollocs flanking them from the west.

Smoke bled from two distinct points on the horizon. Fal Dara and Fal Moran. The two grandest cities in Shienar, torched by their own people, along with the lands of their farms and orchards, everything that could provide even a handful of sustenance to the invading Trollocs.

Holding the cities had not been an option. That meant they had to be destroyed.

It was time to start hitting back. Lan led a charge at the center of the mass, and the Trollocs set spears against the oncoming rush of Malkieri and Shienaran heavy cavalry. Lan brought his lance down, setting it in position along Mandarb's neck. He leaned forward in his stirrups, holding tightly with his knees, and hoped that the channelers—Lan now had fourteen, after a small reinforcement from Egwene—could do their part.

The ground ripped up before the Trollocs. The front line of Trollocs broke.

Lan chose his target, a massive boar Trolloc that was yelling at its companions as they shied away from the explosions. Lan took the creature in the neck; the lance pierced it, and Mandarb threw the Trolloc to the side while trampling one of the cowering beasts nearby. The roar of the cavalry became a crash as the riders hit hard, letting momentum and weight carry them into the thick of the Trollocs.

Once they slowed, Lan tossed the lance to Andere, who caught it deftly. Lan's guards moved in and he slipped his sword from its sheath. Woodsman Tops the Sapling. Apple Blossom on the Wind. The Trollocs made for easy targets when he was in the saddle—the Trollocs' height presented their necks, shoulders and faces at just the right level.

It was quick, brutal work. Deepe watched for attacks from the enemy Dreadlords, countering them. Andere moved up to Lan's side.

Lan's banner was a lodestone for the Shadowspawn. They began to roar and rage, and he heard two Trolloc words spoken over and over in their language. *Murdru Kar. Murdru Kar. Murdru Kar.* He laid about himself with his sword, spilling their blood, coldly, within the void.

They had taken Malkier from him twice now. They would never be able to taste his sense of defeat, his sense of loss, at leaving his homeland again, this time by choice. But by the Light, he *could* bring them close to it. His sword through their chests would do that best.

The battle descended into chaos, as so many did. The Trollocs fell into frenzy; his army had spent the last four days not engaging the beasts at all. They had only retreated, finally having gained some control over their withdrawal, enough to avoid clashes, at least, which their fires had made possible.

Four days without a conflict, now this all-out attack. That was the first piece of the plan.

"Dai Shan!" someone called. Prince Kaisel. He pointed to where the Trollocs had managed to divide Lan's guard. His banner was tipping.

Andere. The man's horse fell, pulled down as Lan urged Mandarb between two Trollocs. Prince Kaisel and a handful of other soldiers joined him.

Lan couldn't continue on horseback, lest he accidentally trample his friend. He threw himself from the saddle, hit the ground and crouched beneath a Trolloc swing. Kaisel took that beast's leg off at the knee.

Lan dashed past the falling Trolloc. He saw his banner and a body beside it. Alive or dead, Lan did not know, but there *was* a Myrddraal raising a dark blade.

Lan arrived in a rush of wind and spinning steel. He blocked the Thakan'dar blade with a swing of his own, trampling his own banner as he fought. Within the void, there was no time for thought. There was only instinct and action. There was—

There was a second Myrddraal, rising up from behind Andere's fallen horse. So, a trap. Take down the banner, draw Lan's attention.

The two Fades attacked, one from each side. The void did not shake. A sword could not feel fear, and for that moment, Lan *was* the sword. The Heron Spreads Its Wings. Slashing all around him, blocking their blades with his own, back and forth. The

Myrddraal were like water, flowing, but Lan was the wind itself. He spun between their blades, knocking back the attack to the right, then the one to the left.

The Fades began cursing in fury. The one to his left rushed Lan, a sneer on its pale lips. Lan stepped to the side, then parried the creature's thrust and lopped its arm off at the elbow. He continued in a fluid stroke, his swing continuing to where he knew the other Fade would be attacking, and took its hand off at the wrist.

Both Thakan'dar blades clanged to the ground. The Fades froze, stupefied for a second. Lan cut the head of one from its neck, then twisted and drove his sword through the neck of the other. Black Pebbles on Snow. He stepped back and swiped his sword to the side to spray some of the deadly blood free of the blade. Both Fades fell, thrashing, flailing at one another, mindless, dark blood staining the ground.

A good hundred and fifty Trollocs nearby fell writhing to the ground. They'd been linked to the Fades. Lan stepped over to haul Andere out of the mud. The man looked dazed, blinking, and his arm hung at a strange angle. Lan tossed Andere over his shoulder, and kicked his banner by its staff up into his free hand.

He ran back toward Mandarb—the area around him now clear of Trollocs—and handed the banner to one of Prince Kaisel's men. "See that cleaned, then raise it." He slung Andere across the front of his saddle, mounted, and wiped his sword on his saddle blanket. The man didn't look mortally wounded.

He faintly heard Prince Kaisel behind. "By my fathers!" the man said. "I'd heard he was good, but . . . but *Light*!"

"This will do," Lan said, surveying the battlefield, releasing the void. "Send the signal, Deepe."

The Asha'man complied, sending a red streak of light into the air. Lan turned Mandarb and pointed his sword back toward the camp. His forces rallied around him. Their attack had always been meant to be a hit and retreat. They hadn't maintained a solid battle line. That was difficult with a cavalry charge.

His troops pulled back, and the Saldaeans and Arafellin arrived, riding in quick waves to break up the Trolloc lines and protect the retreat. Mandarb was wet with sweat; carrying two armored men was a difficult order for the horse, following a charge. Lan slowed the pace, now that they were out of direct harm.

"Deepe," Lan asked as they reached the back lines. "How is Andere?"

"He has a few broken ribs, a broken arm, and a head injury," Deepe said. "I'd be surprised if he could count to ten on his own right now, but I've seen worse. I'll Heal the head wound; the rest can wait."

Lan nodded, reining in. One of his guards—a surly man named Benish who wore a Taraboner veil, though he wore a *hadori* above it—helped take Andere off Mandarb; they held him up beside Deepe's horse. The one-legged Asha'man leaned down from the arrangement of straps that supported him in the saddle, placing his hand on Andere's head and concentrating.

The dazed look left Andere's eyes, and awareness took over. Then he started swearing.

He'll be fine, Lan thought, looking at the battlefield. The Shadowspawn were now falling back. It was near dusk.

Prince Kaisel cantered up beside Lan. "That Saldaean flag bears the red stripe of the Queen," he said. "She's riding with them again, Lan."

"She is their queen. She can do as she wishes."

"You should talk to her," Kaisel said, shaking his head. "It's not right, Lan. Other women from the Saldaean army are starting to ride with them as well."

"I've seen Saldaean women spar," Lan said, still watching the battlefield. "If I were to place a bet on a contest between one of them and a man from any army in the South, I'd bet on the Saldaean any day."

"But . . ."

"This war is everything or nothing. If I could round up each woman in the Borderlands and put a sword in her hands, I would. For now, I'll settle for not doing something stupid—like forbidding some trained and passionate soldiers from fighting. If you, however, decide not to exercise that prudence, you are free to tell them what you think. I promise to give you a good burial once they let me take your head down off the pole."

"I . . . Yes, Lord Mandragoran," Kaisel said.

Lan took out his spyglass and surveyed the field.

"Lord Mandragoran?" Kaisel said. "Do you really think this plan will work?"

"There are too many Trollocs," Lan said. "The leaders of the Dark One's armies have been breeding them for years, growing them like weeds. Trollocs eat a lot; each one requires more food than a man to keep it going.

"By now, they must have eaten the Blight out of anything that could sustain them. The Shadow expended every bit of food they could to create this army, counting on the Trollocs being able to eat the corpses of the fallen."

Sure enough, now that the battle had broken off, the Trollocs swarmed the field in their gruesome scavenging. They preferred human meat, but would eat their own fallen. Lan had spent four days running before their army, not giving them any bodies to feast upon.

They'd managed it only because of the burning of Fal Dara and Fal Moran and other cities in western Shienar. Scouring those cities for food had slowed the Trollocs, allowing Lan's army to get its feet underneath it and organize its retreat.

The Shienarans had left nothing edible in any of the nearby cities. Four days without food. The Trollocs didn't use supply lines; they ate what they came across. They'd be starving. Ravenous. Lan studied them with his spyglass. Many did not wait for the cookpots. They were far more animal than they were human.

They're far more Shadow than they are either one, Lan thought, lowering his spyglass. His plan was morbid, but the Light send it would be effective. His men would fight, and there would be casualties. Those casualties would become the bait for the real battle.

"Now," Lan whispered.

Lord Agelmar saw it, too. The horns blew, and a yellow streak of light rose into the air. Lan turned Mandarb, the horse snorting at the command. He was tired, but so was Lan. Both could stand another battle. They had to.

"*Tai'shar Malkier!*" Lan roared, lowering his sword and leading his force back onto the field. All five Borderlander armies converged on the fractured Shadowspawn horde. The Trollocs had broken lines completely to fight over the corpses.

As Lan thundered toward them, he heard the Myrddraal yelling, trying to force the Trollocs back into order. It was far too late. Many of the famished beasts didn't look up until the armies were nearly upon them.

When Lan's forces hit this time, the effect was very different from before. Earlier, their attack had been slowed by the Trollocs' close ranks, and they had managed to penetrate only a dozen paces before being forced to take up swords and axes. This time, the Trollocs were spread out. Lan signaled the Shienarans to hit first; their line was so tight, one would have been hard-pressed to find an opening of more than two paces between the horses.

That left no room for the Trollocs to run or dodge. The riders trampled them in a thunder of hooves and clanking barding, skewering Trollocs on their lances, firing horsebows, laying about themselves with two-handed swords. There seemed to be a special viciousness to the Shienarans as they attacked, wearing their open-fronted helmets and armor made up of flat plates.

Lan brought his Malkieri cavalry in behind, riding cross-field behind the Shienarans to kill any Trollocs that survived the initial onslaught. Once they'd passed, the Shienarans broke to the right to gather for another pass, but the Arafellin slammed in behind them, slaying more Shadowspawn that were attempting to form up. After them came a wave of Saldaeans crossing as the Malkieri had, then the Kandori sweeping from the other direction.

Sweating—sword-arm tired—Lan prepared again. Only then did he realize that Prince Kaisel himself was carrying the banner of Malkier. The lad was young, but his heart was right. Though he was somewhat stupid about women.

Light, but we all are, in one way or another, Lan thought. Nynaeve's distant emotions in the bond comforted him. He could not sense much over the distance, but she seemed determined.

As Lan began his second sweep, the ground started exploding beneath his men. The Dreadlords had finally realized what was happening and had made their way back to the front lines. Lan directed Mandarb around a crater that erupted in the ground just before him, soil spraying across his chest. The Dreadlords' appearance was his signal to stop the sweeps; he wanted to ride in, hit hard, and ride out. To fight the Dreadlords, he'd have to commit all of his channelers, which was something he didn't want to do.

"Blood and bloody ashes!" Deepe swore as Lan rounded another explosion. "Lord Mandragoran!"

Lan looked back. Deepe was slowing his horse.

"Keep moving, man," Lan said, reining in Mandarb. He signaled for his forces to keep riding, though Prince Kaisel and Lan's battlefield guard stopped with him.

"Oh, *Light*," Deepe said, concentrating.

Lan surveyed the scene. Around them, Trollocs lay dead or dying, howling or simply whimpering. To his left, the mass of Shadowspawn was belatedly forming up. They'd have a unified line soon, and if Lan and the others didn't move, they'd find themselves alone on the field.

Deepe had his eyes on a figure standing atop what appeared to be a large siege engine; it had a flat bed, and was perhaps twenty feet tall. A group of Trollocs were heaving it forward, and it rolled on large wooden wheels.

Yes, there was a figure up there. There were several of them. Balls of fire began to fall toward the Borderlanders as they rode away, and lighting flashed from the sky. Lan suddenly felt like a target on an archery practice field.

"Deepe!"

"It's the M'Hael!" Deepe explained.

Taim had not been with the enemy army for the last week or so—but now the man had returned, it seemed. It was impossible to tell for sure because of the distance, but the way the man flung weaves in rapid succession, he seemed angry about something.

"Let's ride!" Lan yelled.

"I could take him," Deepe said. "I could—"

Lan saw a flash of light, and suddenly Mandarb reared. Lan cursed, trying to blink the afterimage from his eyes. There was something wrong with his ears, too.

Mandarb bucked and curvetted, quivering. It took a lot to shake the stallion, but a lightning bolt that close would unnerve any horse. A second flash of lightning threw Lan to the ground. He tumbled, grunting, but something—deep within—knew what to do. When he came to himself, he was already on his feet, dizzy, sword in hand. He groaned, staggering.

Hands grabbed him, hauling him up into a saddle. Prince Kaisel, face bloodied from fighting, held the reins. Lan's guard made sure he was steady on his mount as they rode away.

He caught sight of Deepe's corpse, mangled and lying in pieces, as they fled.

CHAPTER
17

Older, More Weathered

" . . . Was not fruitful, Majesty," the voice said through Mat's doze.

Something was pricking Mat's face. This mattress was the absolute worst he had ever slept on. He was going to thrash the innkeeper until he got his money back.

"The assassin is very difficult to follow," that annoying voice continued. "People he passes do not remember him. If the Prince of the Ravens has information on how the creature may be tracked, I would very much like to hear it."

Why would the innkeeper let these people into Mat's room? He drifted toward consciousness, leaving behind a lovely dream involving Tuon and no cares in the world. He opened a bleary eye, looking up at a cloudy sky. Not an inn's ceiling at all.

Bloody ashes, Mat thought, groaning. They had fallen asleep in the gardens. He sat up, finding himself totally bare except for the scarf around his neck. His and Tuon's clothing was spread out beneath them. His face had been in a patch of weeds.

Tuon sat beside him, ignoring the fact that she was completely naked, speaking with a member of the Deathwatch Guard. Musenge was on one knee, head bowed, face toward the ground. But still!

"Light!" Mat said, reaching for his clothing. Tuon was sitting on his shirt, and gave him an annoyed look as he tried to yank it free.

"Honored One," the guard said to Mat, face still down. "Greetings upon your waking."

"Tuon, why are you just sitting there?" Mat demanded, finally retrieving his shirt from under that luscious rump.

"As my consort," Tuon said sternly, "you may call me Fortuona or Majesty. I would hate to have you executed before you give me a child, as I am growing fond of you. Regarding this guard, he is of the Deathwatch. They are needed to watch me at all times. I have often had them with me when bathing. This is their duty, and his face is averted."

Mat hurriedly began dressing.

She started to dress, though not quickly enough for his taste. He did not think much of a guard ogling his wife. The place where they had slept was rimmed by small blue fir trees—an oddity here in the South, perhaps cultivated because they were exotic. Though the needles were browning, they offered some measure of privacy. Beyond the firs was a ring of other trees—peaches, Mat thought, but it was hard to tell without the leaves.

He could barely hear the city waking up outside the garden, and the air smelled faintly of the fir needles. The air was warm enough that sleeping outside had not been uncomfortable, though he was glad to be back in his clothing.

A Deathwatch Guard officer approached just as Tuon finished dressing. He crunched dried fir needles, bowing low before her. "Empress, we may have caught another assassin. It is not the creature from last night, as he bears no wounds, but he was trying to sneak into the palace. We thought you might wish to see him before we begin our interrogation."

"Bring him forward," Tuon said, straightening her gown. "And send for General Karede."

The officer withdrew, passing Selucia, who stood near the pathway that led to the clearing. She walked in to stand beside Tuon. Mat put his hat on his head and went up to her other side, setting the *ashandarei* butt down in the dead grass.

Mat felt sorry for this poor fool caught sneaking into the palace. Maybe the man was an assassin, but he could just be a beggar or other fool looking for excitement. Or he could be . . .

. . . the Dragon Reborn.

Mat groaned. Yes, that was Rand they led along the path. Rand looked older, more weathered, than the last time Mat had seen him in person. Of course, he had seen the man recently in those blasted visions. Although Mat had trained himself to stop thinking of Rand to avoid those colors, he still slipped on occasion.

Anyway, seeing Rand in person was different. It had been . . . Light, how long *had* it been? *The last time I saw him with my own eyes was when he sent me to Salidar after Elayne.* That felt like an eternity ago. It had been before he had come to Ebou Dar, before he had seen the *gholam* for the first time. Before Tylin, before Tuon.

Mat frowned as Rand was led up to Tuon, his arms bound behind his back. She spoke with Selucia, wiggling her fingers in their handtalk. Rand did not seem the least bit worried; his face was calm. He wore a nice coat of red and black, a white shirt underneath, black trousers. No gold or jewelry, no weapon at all.

"Tuon," Mat began. "That's—"

Tuon turned from Selucia to see Rand. *"Damane!"* Tuon said, cutting Mat off. "Bring my *damane*! Run, Musicar! *RUN!*"

The Deathwatch Guard stumbled backward, then ran, yelling for the *damane* and for Banner-General Karede.

Rand watched the man go, nonchalant though he was bound. *You know,* Mat thought idly, *he kind of does look like a king.* Of course, Rand was mad, most likely. That would explain why he had strolled up to Tuon like this.

Either that, or Rand was just planning on killing her. Bonds did not matter one bit to a man who could channel. *Blood and ashes,* Mat thought. *How did I end up in this situation?* He had done whatever he could to avoid Rand!

Rand met Tuon's stare. Mat took a big breath, then jumped in front of her. "Rand. Rand, here now. Let's be calm."

"Hello, Mat," Rand said, voice pleasant. Light, he *was* mad! "Thank you for leading me to her."

"Leading you . . ."

"What is this?" Tuon demanded.

Mat spun. "I . . . Really, it's just . . . "

Her stare could have drilled holes in steel. "You did this," she said to Mat. "You came, you lured me to be affectionate, then you brought him in. Is this true?"

"Don't blame him," Rand said. "The two of us needed to meet again. You know it is true."

Mat stumbled out between them, raising one hand either direction. "Here now! Both of you, stop. You hear me!"

Something seized Mat, hauling him into the air. "Stop that, Rand!" he said.

"It isn't me," Rand said, adopting a look of concentration. "Ah. I am shielded."

As Mat hung in the air he felt at his chest. The medallion. *Where was his medallion?*

Mat stared at Tuon. She looked ashamed for a brief moment, reaching into the pocket of her gown. She brought out something silver in her hand, perhaps intending to use the medallion as protection against Rand.

Brilliant, Mat thought, groaning. She had taken it off him while he slept, and he had not noticed. *Bloody brilliant.*

The weaves of Air set him down beside Rand; Karede had returned with a *sul'dam* and *damane*. All three were flushed, as if having run quickly. The *damane* had been doing the channeling.

Tuon looked over Rand and Mat, then began gesturing with handtalk at Selucia with sharp motions.

"Thanks a bundle for this," Mat muttered to Rand. "You're such a bloody good friend."

"It's good to see you too," Rand said, a hint of a smile on his lips.

"Here we go," Mat said with a sigh. "You've pulled me into trouble again. You always do this."

"I do?"

"Yes. In Rhuidean and the Waste, in the Stone of Tear . . . back in the Two Rivers. You do realize that I went south, instead of coming to your little party with Egwene in Merrilor, to *escape*?"

"You think you could stay away from me?" Rand asked, smiling. "You really think *it* would let you?"

"I could bloody try. No offense, Rand, but you're going to go mad and all. I figured I'd give you one less friend nearby to kill. You know, save you some trouble. What did you do to your hand, by the way?"

"What did you do to your eye?"

"A little accident with a corkscrew and thirteen angry innkeepers. The hand?"

"Lost it capturing one of the Forsaken."

"Capturing?" Mat said. "You're growing soft."

Rand snorted. "Tell me you've done better."

"I killed a *gholam*," Mat said.

"I freed Illian from Sammael."

"I married the Empress of the Seanchan."

"Mat," Rand said, "are you *really* trying to get into a bragging contest with the Dragon Reborn?" He paused for a moment. "Besides, I cleansed *saidin*. I win."

"Ah, that's not really worth much," Mat said.

"Not worth much? It's the single most important event to happen since the Breaking."

"Bah. You and your Asha'man are already crazy," Mat said, "so what does it matter?" He glanced to the side. "You look nice, by the way. You've been taking better care of yourself lately."

"So you *do* care," Rand said.

"Of course I do," Mat grumbled, looking back at Tuon. "I mean, you have to keep yourself alive, right? Go have your little duel with the Dark One and keep us all safe? It's good to know you're looking up to it."

"That's nice to hear," Rand said, smiling. "No wisecracks about my nice coat?"

"What? Wisecracks? You aren't still sore because I teased you a little a couple of years ago?"

"Teased?" Rand said. "You spent weeks refusing to talk to me."

"Here now," Mat said. "It wasn't all that bad. I remember that part easily."

Rand shook his head, as if bemused. Bloody ungrateful was what he was. Mat had gone off to fetch Elayne, as Rand had asked, and this was the thanks he was given. Sure, Mat had been a little sidetracked after that. He had still done it, had he not?

"All right," Mat said very softly, tugging at the bonds of Air holding him. "I'll get us out of this, Rand. I'm married to her. Let me do the talking, and—"

"Daughter of Artur Hawkwing," Rand said to Tuon. "Time spins toward the end of all things. The Last Battle has begun, and the threads are being woven. Soon, my final trial will begin."

Tuon stepped forward, Selucia waving a few last finger-talk

words toward her. "You will be taken to Seanchan, Dragon Reborn," Tuon said. Her voice was collected, firm.

Mat smiled. Light, but she made a good Empress. *There was no need to filch my medallion, though,* he thought. They were going to have words about that. Assuming he survived this. She would not *really* execute him, would she?

Again, he tried the invisible bonds tying him.

"Is that so?" Rand asked.

"You have delivered yourself to me," Tuon said. "It is an omen." She seemed almost regretful. "You did not truly think that I would allow you to stroll away, did you? I must take you in chains as a ruler who resisted me—as I have done to the others I found here. You pay the price of your ancestors' forgetfulness. You should have remembered your oaths."

"I see," Rand said.

You know, Mat thought, *he does a fair job of sounding like a king, too.* Light, what kind of people had Mat surrounded himself with? What had happened to the fair barmaids and carousing soldiers?

"Tell me something, Empress," Rand said. "What would you all have done if you'd returned to these shores and found Artur Hawkwing's armies still ruling? What if we hadn't forgotten our oaths, what if we had stayed true? What then?"

"We would have welcomed you as brothers," Tuon said.

"Oh?" Rand said. "And you would have bowed to the throne here? Hawkwing's throne? If his empire still stood, it would have been ruled over by his heir. Would you have tried to dominate them? Would you instead have accepted their rule over you?"

"That is not the case," Tuon said, but she seemed to find his words intriguing.

"No, it is not," Rand said.

"By your argument, you must submit to us." She smiled.

"I did not make that argument," Rand said, "but let us do so. How do you claim the right to these lands?"

"By being the only legitimate heir of Artur Hawkwing."

"And why should that matter?"

"This is his empire. He is the only one to have unified it, he is the only leader to have ruled it in glory and greatness."

"And there you are wrong," Rand said, voice growing soft. "You accept me as the Dragon Reborn?"

"You must be," Tuon said slowly, as if wary of a trap.

"Then you accept me for who I am," Rand said, voice growing loud, crisp. Like a battle horn. "*I* am Lews Therin Telamon, the Dragon. *I* ruled these lands, unified, during the Age of Legends. *I* was leader of all the armies of the Light, *I* wore the Ring of Tamyrlin. *I* stood first among the Servants, highest of the Aes Sedai, and I could summon the Nine Rods of Dominion."

Rand stepped forward. "*I* held the loyalty and fealty of all seventeen Generals of Dawn's Gate. Fortuona Athaem Devi Paendrag, my authority supersedes your own!"

"Artur Hawkwing—"

"My authority supersedes that of Hawkwing! If you claim rule by the name of he who conquered, then you must bow before my prior claim. I conquered before Hawkwing, though I needed no sword to do so. You are here on *my* land, Empress, at my sufferance!"

Thunder broke in the distance. Mat found himself shaking. Light, it was just Rand. Just Rand . . . was it not?

Tuon backed away, eyes wide, her lips parted. Her face was full of horror, as if she had just seen her own parents executed.

Green grass spread around Rand's feet. The guards nearby jumped back, hands to swords, as a swath of life extended from Rand. The brown and yellow blades colored, as if paint had been poured on them, then came upright—stretching as if after long slumber.

The greenness filled the entire garden clearing. "He's still shielded!" the *sul'dam* cried. "Honored One, he is *still shielded*!"

Mat shivered, and then noticed something. Very soft, so easy to miss.

"Are you singing?" Mat whispered to Rand.

Yes . . . it was unmistakable. Rand *was* singing, under his breath, very softly. Mat tapped his foot. "I swear I've heard that tune somewhere, once . . . Is it 'Two Maids at the Water's Edge'?"

"You're not helping," Rand whispered. "Quiet."

Rand continued his song. The green spread to the trees, the firs strengthening their limbs. The other trees began to shoot out leaves—they were indeed peach trees—growing at great speed, life flooding into them.

The guards looked about themselves, spinning, trying to watch all of the trees at once. Selucia had cringed. Tuon remained upright, her eyes focused on Rand. Nearby, the frightened *sul'dam* and *damane* must have stopped concentrating, for the bonds holding Mat vanished.

"Do you deny my right?" Rand demanded. "Do you deny that my claim to this land precedes your own by thousands of years?"

"I . . ." Tuon took a deep breath and stared at him defiantly. "You broke the land, abandoned it. I can deny your right."

Behind her, blossoms *exploded* onto the trees like fireworks, white and deep pink. The bursts of color surrounded them. Petals sprayed outward with their growth, breaking from the trees, catching in the wind and swirling through the clearing.

"I allowed you to live," Rand said to Tuon, "when I could have destroyed you in an instant. This is because you have made life better for those under your rule, though you are not without guilt for the way you have treated some. Your rule is as flimsy as paper. You hold this land together only through the strength of steel and *damane*, but your homeland burns.

"I have not come here to destroy you. I come to you now to offer you peace, Empress. I have come without armies, I have come without force. I have come because I believe that you need me, as I need you." Rand stepped forward and, remarkably, went down on one knee, bowing his head, his hand extended. "I extend my hand to you in alliance. The Last Battle is upon us. Join me, and fight."

The clearing fell still. The wind stopped blowing, the thunder stopped rumbling. Peach blossoms wafted to the now-green grass. Rand remained where he was, hand extended. Tuon stared at that hand as if at a viper.

Mat hurried forward. "Nice trick," he said under his breath to Rand. "Very nice trick." He approached Tuon, taking her by the shoulders and turning her to the side. Nearby, Selucia looked stunned. Karede was not in much better shape. They would not be any help.

"Hey, look," Mat said to her softly. "He's a good fellow. He's rough at the corners sometimes, but you can trust his word. If he's offering you a treaty, he'll make good on it."

"That was a very impressive display," Tuon said softly. She was trembling faintly. "What *is* he?"

"Burn me if I know," Mat said. "Listen, Tuon. I grew up with Rand. I vouch for him."

"There is a darkness in that man, Matrim. I saw it when last he and I last met."

"Look at me, Tuon. Look at me."

She looked up, meeting his gaze.

"You can trust Rand al'Thor with the world itself," Mat said. "And if you can't trust him, trust me. He's our only choice. We don't have time to take him back to Seanchan.

"I've been in the city long enough to have a little peek at your forces. If you're going to fight the Last Battle *and* recapture your homeland, you're going to need a stable base here in Altara. Take his offer. He just claimed this land. Well, make him secure your borders as they are and announce it to the others. They might listen. Take a little pressure off you. Unless, that is, you want to fight the Trollocs, the nations of this land, *and* the rebels in Seanchan at the same time."

Tuon blinked. "Our forces."

"What?"

"You called them my forces," she said. "They are *our* forces. You are one of us now, Matrim."

"Well, I guess I am at that. Listen, Tuon. You have to do this. Please."

She turned, looking at Rand, kneeling in the middle of a pattern of peach blossoms that seemed to have circled out from him. Not a one had fallen on him.

"What is your offer?" Tuon asked.

"Peace," Rand said, standing, hand still out. "Peace for a hundred years. Longer, if I can make it so. I have persuaded the other rulers to sign a treaty and work together to fight the armies of the Shadow."

"I would have my borders secured," Tuon said.

"Altara and Amadicia shall be yours."

"Tarabon and Almoth Plain as well," Tuon said. "I hold them now. I will not be forced from them by your treaty. You wish peace? You will give me this."

"Tarabon and half of Almoth Plain," Rand said. "The half you already control."

"I would have all of the women this side of the Aryth Ocean who can channel as *damane*," Tuon said.

"Do not strain your luck, Empress," Rand said dryly. "I . . . I will allow you to do what you will in Seanchan, but I *will* require you to relinquish any *damane* you have taken while in this land."

"Then we have no agreement," Tuon said.

Mat held his breath.

Rand hesitated, hand lowering. "The fate of the world itself could hang on this, Fortuona. Please."

"If it is that important," she said firmly, "you can agree to my demand. Our property is our own. You wish a treaty? Then you will get it with this clause: We keep the *damane* we already have. In exchange, I will allow you to leave in freedom."

Rand grimaced. "You're as bad as one of the Sea Folk."

"I should hope I'm worse," Tuon said, no emotion in her voice. "The world is your charge, Dragon, not mine. I care for my empire. I will greatly need those *damane*. Choose now. As I believe you said, your time is short."

Rand's expression darkened; then he thrust his hand outward. "Let it be done. Light be merciful, let it be done. I will carry this weight too. You may keep the *damane* you already have, but you shall not take any from among my allies while we fight the Last Battle. Taking any afterward who are not in your own land will be seen as breaking the treaty and attacking the other nations."

Tuon stepped forward, then took Rand's hand in her own. Mat let out his breath.

"I have documents for you to review and sign," Rand said.

"Selucia will take them," Tuon said. "Matrim, with me. We must prepare the Empire for war." Tuon walked away down the path, her step controlled, though Mat suspected that she wanted to be away from Rand as quickly as possible. He understood the sentiment.

He followed, but stopped beside Rand. "Seems you have a bit of the Dark One's luck yourself," he muttered to Rand. "I can't believe that worked."

"Honestly?" Rand said softly. "I can't either. Thank you for the good word."

"Sure," Mat said. "By the way, *I* saved Moiraine. Chew on that as you try to decide which of the two of us is winning."

Mat followed Tuon, and behind him rose the laughter of the Dragon Reborn.

CHAPTER
18

To Feel Wasted

Gawyn stood on a field near the area where the Aes Sedai had first fought the Trollocs. They'd come off the hills, and had moved deeper onto the Kandor plain. They continued to stem the Trolloc advances, and they even managed to push back the enemy's main forces a few hundred paces. All in all, this battle was going better than could have been expected.

They'd fought here for a week on this open, unnamed Kandori field. This place had been churned and torn as if in preparation for planting. There were so many bodies here—almost all Shadowspawn—that even Trolloc appetites couldn't consume them all.

Gawyn carried a sword in one hand, shield in the other, stationed in front of Egwene's horse. His job was to bring down the Trollocs that came through the Aes Sedai attacks. He preferred to fight two-handed, but against Trollocs, he needed that shield. Some of the others thought him a fool for using the sword. They preferred pikes or halberds, anything to keep the Trollocs at a distance.

You couldn't really *duel* with a pike, though; as a pikeman, you were like a brick in a larger wall. You weren't so much a soldier as a barrier. A halberd was better—at least it had a blade that required some skill to use—but nothing gave the same feel as a sword. When Gawyn fought with the sword, he controlled the fight.

A Trolloc came for him, snorting, face bearing the melded features of a ram and a man. This one was more human than most, including a sickeningly human mouth with bloodied teeth. The thing brandished a mace that bore the Flame of Tar Valon on its haft, stolen from a fallen member of the Tower Guard. Though it was a two-handed weapon, the creature wielded it easily in one.

Gawyn dodged to the side, then brought his shield up and to the right under the expected blow. The shield shook with repeated impacts. One, two, three. Standard Trolloc berserking— hit hard, hit fast and assume that the opponent would break.

Many did. They would trip, or their arms would go numb from the pounding. That was the value of pikewalls or halberd lines. Bryne used both, and a newly improvised half-spear, half-halberd line. Gawyn had read of its like in history books. Bryne's army used them for hamstringing Trollocs. The pike lines would keep them back, and then the halberds would reach through and slice their legs.

Gawyn ducked to the side, and the Trolloc wasn't ready for his burst of speed. The thing turned, too slow, as Gawyn separated its hand from its wrist, using Whirlwind on the Mountain. As it screamed, Gawyn spun about, ramming his sword into the stomach of another Trolloc that had plowed through the Aes Sedai defense.

He whipped his sword out of that body and sheathed it in the first Trolloc's neck. The dead beast slid off his blade. That was four that Gawyn had killed today. He carefully wiped his sword on the bloody cloth he wore tied at his waist.

He checked on Egwene. Mounted, she used the One Power to rip apart Trollocs in droves. The Aes Sedai used a rotation, with only a small portion of them on the field at a time. Using so few Aes Sedai at a time required the soldiers to take the brunt of the fighting, but the Aes Sedai always came to the battle rested. Their job was to blast apart the groups of Trollocs, shattering lines and letting the soldiers work on the scattered remnants.

With the Aes Sedai keeping the Trollocs from solid battle formations, the fight—though grueling—was proceeding well.

They hadn't had to fall back since leaving the hills behind, and had effectively stalled the Trolloc advance for a week here.

Silviana sat atop a roan gelding beside Egwene, and did her best to keep the Trollocs from coming too close. The ground was ripped and furrowed just in front of them, Silviana's attacks having torn it asunder, leaving trenchlike depressions all over the field. Despite that, the occasional Trolloc would crawl through the mire and come for Gawyn.

Gawyn saw movement in the nearest trench and strode forward. A wolf-featured Trolloc crouched inside. It snarled at him, scrambling up.

Water Flows Downhill.

The Trolloc fell back into the trench, and Gawyn wiped his blade on the bloody rag. Five. Not bad for one of his two-hour shifts. Often the Aes Sedai were able to repel the Trollocs, and he just ended up standing beside Egwene. Of course, today she was accompanied by Silviana—they always came to the battlefront in pairs—and Gawyn was half-convinced the Keeper let a few through now and then just to keep him working.

A sudden series of explosions nearby drove him backward, and he glanced over his shoulder. Their relief had arrived. Gawyn raised his sword to Sleete as the man took up position with Piava Sedai's Warder to guard the area.

Gawyn joined Egwene and Silviana as they left the battlefield. He could feel Egwene's growing exhaustion. She was pushing herself too hard, insisting on joining too many shifts.

They made their way across the trampled grass, passing a group of Illianer Companions charging into the fray. Gawyn didn't have a good enough view of the battle as a whole to know where specifically they were needed. He watched them go with a hint of envy.

He knew Egwene needed him. Now more than ever. Fades slipped into camp at night, bringing Thakan'dar-forged blades to take the lives of Aes Sedai. Gawyn kept watch personally when Egwene slept, relying on her to wash his fatigue away when it overwhelmed him. He slept when she was in conference with the Hall of the Tower.

He insisted that she sleep in a different tent each night. Once in a while, he convinced her to Travel to Mayene and the beds in the palace. She hadn't done that in a few days. His arguments that she should check on the Yellows, and inspect the Healing work, were growing thin. Rosil Sedai had things in hand there.

Gawyn and the two women continued on into the camp. Some soldiers bowed, the ones who were not currently on duty, while others hastened toward the battlefield. Gawyn eyed some of these. Too young, too new.

Others were Dragonsworn, and who knew what to make of them? There were Aiel among the Dragonsworn, which made sense to him, since all Aiel seemed basically Dragonsworn to him. But there were also Aes Sedai among the Dragonsworn ranks. He didn't think much of their choice.

Gawyn shook his head and continued on. Their camp was enormous, though it contained virtually no camp followers. Food was brought in daily through gateways in wagons—some pulled by those unreliable metal machines from Cairhien. When those wagons left, they carried away clothing for washing, weapons to be repaired and boots to be mended.

It made for a very efficient camp; one not heavily populated, however, as almost everyone spent long hours on the battlefield fighting. Everyone but Gawyn.

He knew he was needed, and that what he did was important, but he couldn't help feeling wasted. He was one of the finest swordsmen in the army, and he stood on the battlefield for a few hours a day, killing only the occasional Trolloc stupid enough to charge two Aes Sedai. What Gawyn did was more like putting them out of their misery than fighting them.

Egwene nodded farewell to Silviana, then turned her horse toward the command tent.

"Egwene . . ." Gawyn said.

"I only want to check on things," she said calmly. "Elayne was supposed to have sent new orders."

"You need sleep."

"It seems that all I do these days is sleep."

"When you fight on the battlefield, you are easily worth a thousand soldiers," Gawyn said. "If sleeping twenty-two hours a day were required to keep you in good enough shape to protect the men for two, I'd suggest you do it. Fortunately, that isn't required—and neither is it required that you run yourself as hard as you do."

He could feel her annoyance through the bond, but she snuffed it out. "You are right, of course." She eyed him. "And you needn't feel surprised to hear me admit it."

"I wasn't surprised," Gawyn said.

"I can feel your emotions, Gawyn."

"That was from something else entirely," he said. "I remembered something Sleete said a few days back, a joke I didn't understand until now." He looked at her innocently.

That, finally, earned a smile. A hint of one, but that was enough. She didn't smile much these days. Few of them did.

"In addition," he said, taking her reins and helping her dismount as they reached the command tent, "I'd never given much thought to the fact that a Warder can, of course, ignore the Three Oaths. I wonder how often sisters have found that convenient?"

"I hope not too often," Egwene said. A very diplomatic answer. Inside the command tent, they found Gareth Bryne looking down through his now customary gateway; it was being maintained by a mousy Gray whom Gawyn didn't know. Bryne stepped to his map-littered desk, where Siuan was attempting to bring order. He made a few notes on a map, nodding to himself, then looked to see who had entered.

"Mother," Bryne said, and took her hand to kiss her ring.

"The battle seems to be going well," Egwene said, nodding to Siuan. "We have held here well. You have plans to push forward, it seems?"

"We can't loiter here forever, Mother," Bryne said. "Queen Elayne has asked me to consider an advance farther into Kandor, and I think she is wise to do so. I worry that the Trollocs will pull back into the hills and brace themselves. You notice how they've been pulling more of the bodies off the field each night?"

"Yes."

Gawyn could sense her displeasure; she wished the Aes Sedai had the strength to burn the Trolloc carcasses with the One Power each day.

"They're gathering food," Bryne said. "They might decide to move eastward and try to get around us. We need to keep them engaged here, which might mean pushing into those hills. It would be costly, normally, but now . . . " He shook his head, walking over and looking down through his gateway onto the front lines. "Your Aes Sedai dominate this battlefield, Mother. I've never seen anything like it."

"There is a reason," she replied, "that the Shadow did everything in its power to bring down the White Tower. It knew. The White Tower has the ability to rule this war."

"We'll need to watch for Dreadlords," Siuan said, shuffling through papers. Scouting reports, Gawyn suspected. He knew little of Siuan Sanche, despite having spared her life, but Egwene commonly spoke of the woman's greed for information.

"Yes," Egwene said. "They will come."

"The Black Tower," Bryne said, frowning. "Do you trust the word from Lord Mandragoran?"

"With my life," Egwene said.

"Asha'man fighting for the enemy. Why wouldn't the Dragon Reborn have done something? Light, if all of the remaining Asha'man side with the Shadow . . ."

Egwene shook her head. "Bryne, I want you to saddle up riders and send them to the area outside the Black Tower where gateways can still be made. Send them, riding hard, to the sisters still camped outside the Black Tower."

"You want them to attack?" Gawyn asked, perking up.

"No. They are to retreat back as far as it takes to make gateways, and then they are to join us here. We can't afford any further delays. I want them here."

She tapped the table with one finger. "Taim and his Dreadlords *will* come. They have stayed away from this battlefield, instead focusing on Lord Mandragoran. That lets them dominate their battlefield as we have this one. I will choose more sisters to send to the Borderlander army. We will have to confront them eventually."

Gawyn said nothing, but drew his lips tight. Fewer sisters here meant more work for Egwene and the others.

"And now," Egwene said, "I need to . . ." She trailed off, seeing Gawyn's expression. "I suppose I need to sleep. If I am needed, send to . . . Light, I don't know where I'm sleeping today. Gawyn?"

"I have you in Maerin Sedai's tent. She's on duty in the rotation after this, so that should give you some hours of uninterrupted sleep."

"Unless I'm needed," Egwene reminded him. She walked toward the tent flaps.

"Of course," Gawyn said, following her out, but shaking his head toward Bryne and Siuan. Bryne smiled back, nodding. On a battlefield, there was little that would absolutely require the Amyrlin's attention. The Hall of the Tower had been given direct oversight of their armies.

Outside, Egwene sighed, closing her eyes. He put his arm around her, and let her slump against him. The moment lasted but a few seconds before she pulled back, standing up straight and putting on the face of the Amyrlin. *So young*, he thought, *to have so much required of her.*

Of course, she wasn't much younger than al'Thor himself. Gawyn was pleased, and a little surprised, that thinking of the man did not provoke any anger. Al'Thor would fight his fight. Really, what the man did was none of Gawyn's business.

Gawyn led Egwene to the Green Ajah section of camp, the several Warders at the perimeter greeting them with nods of respect. Maerin Sedai had a large tent. Most of the Aes Sedai had been allowed to bring what housing and furniture they wished, so long as they could make their own gateway for it and use their own Warders to carry it. If the army had to move quickly, such things would be abandoned. Many Aes Sedai had chosen to bring very little, but others . . . well, they were not accustomed to austerity. Maerin was one of those. Few had brought as much as she.

Leilwin and Bayle Domon waited outside the tent. They had been the ones to inform Maerin Sedai that her tent was being borrowed, and that she wasn't to tell anyone that Egwene was the one using it. The secret could be discovered if anyone asked around— they hadn't hidden themselves while walking here—but at the same time, someone asking where the Amyrlin was sleeping would draw attention. It was the best protection Gawyn could arrange, since Egwene was unwilling to Travel each day to sleep.

Egwene's emotions immediately turned sour when she saw Leilwin.

"You did say you wanted to keep her close," Gawyn said softly.

"I don't like her knowing where I sleep. If their assassins *do* come looking for me in camp, she might be the one to lead them to me."

Gawyn fought down the instinct to argue. Egwene was a cunning, insightful woman—but she had a blind spot regarding anything Seanchan. He, on the other hand, found himself trusting Leilwin. She seemed to be the type who dealt straight with people.

"I'll keep an eye on her," he said.

Egwene composed herself with a breath, then walked to the tent and passed Leilwin without saying a word. Gawyn didn't follow her inside.

"The Amyrlin seems intent on not letting me provide service," Leilwin said to Gawyn in that telltale Seanchan drawl.

"She doesn't trust you," Gawyn said frankly.

"Is one's oath worth so little on this side of the ocean?" Leilwin said. "I swore an oath to her that none would break, not even a Muyami!"

"A Darkfriend will break any oath."

The woman eyed him coolly. "I begin to think she assumes all Seanchan to be Darkfriends."

Gawyn shrugged. "You beat her and imprisoned her, making her into an animal to be led by a collar."

"*I* did not," Leilwin said. "If one baker made you foul bread, would you assume all of them seek to poison you? Bah. Do not argue. There is no point. If I cannot serve her, then I will serve you. Have you eaten today, Warder?"

Gawyn hesitated. When *had* he last had something to eat? This morning ... no, he'd been too eager for the fight. His stomach grumbled loudly.

"I know you will not leave her," Leilwin said, "particularly under the watch of a *Seanchan*. Come, Bayle. Let us fetch this fool some food so that he does not faint if assassins do come." She stalked off, her large Illianer husband following. The fellow shot a glare over his shoulder that could have cured leather.

Gawyn sighed and settled down on the ground. From his pocket, he pulled three black rings; he selected one, then shoved the others back into his pocket.

Talk of assassins always made him think of the rings, which he'd taken off the Seanchan who *had* come to kill Egwene. The rings were *ter'angreal*. They were the means by which those Bloodknives had moved quickly and blended into shadows.

He held up the ring toward the light. It didn't look like any *ter'angreal* he had seen, but an object of the Power could look like anything. The rings were of some heavy black stone he did not recognize. The outside was carved like thorns, though the inside surface—the side that touched the skin—was smooth.

He turned the ring over in his fingers. He knew that he should go to Egwene with it. He also knew how the White Tower treated *ter'angreal*. They locked the objects away, afraid to experiment with them. But this was the Last Battle. If there was ever a time to take risks . . .

You decided to stand in Egwene's shadow, Gawyn, he thought. *You decided you would protect her, do what she needed of you.* She was winning this war, she and the Aes Sedai. Would he let himself grow as jealous of her as he had been of al'Thor?

"Is that what I believe it to be?"

Gawyn snapped his head up, fist closing around the ring. Leilwin and Bayle Domon had been to the mess tent and returned with a bowl for him. From the smell of it, the meal was barley stew again. The cooks used so much pepper it was almost sickening. Gawyn suspected they did so because the black flakes hid the bits of weevil.

I can't act like I'm doing something suspicious, he thought immediately. *I can't let her go to Egwene.*

"This?" he asked, holding up the ring. "It's one of the rings we recovered from the Seanchan assassins who tried to kill Egwene. We assume it's a *ter'angreal* of some sort, though it's not one the White Tower has ever heard of."

Leilwin hissed softly. "Those are to be bestowed only by the Empress, may she—" She cut herself off and took a deep breath. "Only one appointed as a Bloodknife, one who has given their life to the Empress, is allowed to wear such a ring. For you to put one on would be very, very wrong."

"Fortunately," Gawyn said, "I'm not wearing it."

"The rings are dangerous," Leilwin said. "I do not know much of them, but they are said to kill those who use them. Do not let your blood touch the ring, or you will activate it, and that could be deadly, Warder." She handed him the bowl of stew, then strode away.

Domon didn't follow her. The Illianer scratched at his short beard. "She do not always be the most accommodating of women, my wife," he said to Gawyn. "But she do be strong and wise. You would do well to listen to her."

Gawyn pocketed the ring. "Egwene would never allow me to wear it in the first place." That was true. If she knew about it. "Tell your wife that I appreciate the warning. I should warn you that the subject of the assassins is still a very sore subject for the Amyrlin. I'd suggest avoiding the topic of the Bloodknives, or their *ter'angreal*."

Domon nodded and then went after Leilwin. Gawyn felt only a small prick of shame at the deception. He hadn't said anything untrue. He just didn't want Egwene asking any awkward questions.

That ring, and its brothers, represented something. They weren't the way of the Warder. Standing beside Egwene, watching for danger to her ... that was the way of the Warder. He would make a difference on the battlefield by serving her, not by riding out like some hero.

He told himself that time and time again as he ate his stew. By the time he was done, he was nearly certain he believed it.

He still didn't tell Egwene about the rings.

Rand remembered the first time he'd seen a Trolloc. Not when they had attacked his farm in the Two Rivers. The *true* first time he'd seen them. During the last Age.

There will come a time when they no longer exist, he thought, weaving Fire and Air, creating an explosive wall of flames that roared to life in the middle of a pack of Trollocs. Nearby, men of Perrin's Wolf Guard raised weapons in thanks. Rand nodded back. He wore the face of Jur Grady in this fight, for now.

Once Trollocs had not scourged the land. They could return to that state. If Rand killed the Dark One, would it happen immediately?

The flames of his fire wall brought sweat on his forehead. He drew carefully on the fat-man *angreal*—he couldn't afford to seem *too* powerful—and struck down another group of Trollocs here on the battlefield just west of the River Alguenya. Elayne's forces had crossed the Erinin and the countryside to the east, and were waiting for their bridges across the Alguenya to be constructed. These were almost completed, but meanwhile a vanguard of Trollocs had caught up with them, and Elayne's army had formed up in defensive positions to hold them off until they could cross the river.

Rand was happy to help. The real Jur Grady rested back in his camp in Kandor, worn out from Healing. A convenient face that Rand could wear and not draw the attention of the Forsaken.

The Trolloc screams were satisfying as they burned. He had loved that sound, near the end of the War of Power. It had always made him feel as if he were *doing* something.

He hadn't known what Trollocs were the first time he'd seen them. Oh, he'd known of Aginor's experiments. Lews Therin had named him a madman on more than one occasion. He hadn't understood; so many of them hadn't. Aginor had loved his projects far too much. Lews Therin had made the mistake of assuming that Aginor, like Semirhage, enjoyed the torture for its own sake.

And then the Shadowspawn had come.

The monsters continued burning, limbs twitching.

Still, Rand worried that these *things* might be humans reborn. Aginor had used people to create the Trollocs and Myrddraal. Was this the fate of some? To be reborn as twisted creations such as this? The idea sickened him.

He checked the sky. The clouds had begun to withdraw, as they did near him. He could force them to not do so, but ... no. Men needed the Light, and he could not fight here too long, lest it become obvious that one of the Asha'man was too strong for the face he wore.

Rand let the light come.

All across the battlefield near the river, people glanced toward the sky as sunlight fell on them, the dark clouds pulling back.

No more hiding, Rand thought, removing his Mask of Mirrors and raising his hand in a fist above his head. He wove Air, Fire and Water, creating a column of light extending from himself high into the sky. Soldiers across the battlefield cheered.

He would not bring down the traps the Dark One had waiting for him. He moved through a gateway back to Merrilor. He never stayed long at a battlefront, but he always revealed himself before he left. He let the clouds break above, proving he had been there, then withdrew.

Min waited for him at the Merrilor Traveling ground. He looked behind himself as his gateway closed, leaving the people to fight without him. Min placed a hand on his arm. His Maiden guards waited here; they reluctantly allowed him to fight alone as they knew that their presence would give him away.

"You look sad," Min said softly.

A hot breeze blew from somewhere north. Nearby soldiers saluted him. Most of what he had here were Domani, Tairens and Aiel. The assault force, led by Rodel Ituralde and King Darlin, that would try to hold the valley of Thakan'dar while Rand wrestled with the Dark One.

The time had almost arrived for that. The Shadow had seen him fighting on all fronts. He had joined Lan's fighting, Egwene's fighting and Elayne's in turn. By now the Shadow had committed most of its armies to the fighting in the south. The time for Rand to strike Shayol Ghul was at hand.

He looked to Min. "Moiraine calls me a fool for these attacks. She says that even a small risk to me is not worth what I accomplish."

"Moiraine is probably right," Min said. "She often is. But I prefer you as the person who would do this. *That* is the person who can defeat the Dark One: the man who cannot sit and plan while others die."

Rand put his arm around her waist. Light, what would he have done without her? *I'd have fallen*, he thought. *During the dark months . . . I'd have fallen for certain.*

Over Min's shoulder, Rand saw a gray-haired woman approaching. And behind her, a smaller figure in blue stopped and pointedly turned the other way. Cadsuane and Moiraine gave one another wide berth in the camp. He thought he caught a hint of a glare in Moiraine's eyes when she saw that Cadsuane had spotted Rand first.

Cadsuane came up to him, then walked around him, looking him up and down. She nodded to herself several times.

"Trying to decide if I'm up to the task?" Rand said to Cadsuane, keeping emotions—in this case, annoyance—from his voice.

"I never wondered," Cadsuane said. "Even before I found you

were reborn, I never wondered if I would be able to make you into the man you needed to be. Wondering, in that manner at least, is for fools. Are you a fool, Rand al'Thor?"

"An impossible question," Min replied. "If he says that he is, then a fool he becomes. If he says that he is not, then he implies he does not seek further wisdom."

"Phaw. You've been reading too much, child." Cadsuane seemed fond as she said it. She turned to Rand. "I hope you give her something nice."

"What do you mean?" Rand asked.

"You've been giving things to people," Cadsuane said, "in preparation for death. It's common for the elderly or for men riding into a battle they don't think they can win. A sword for your father, a *ter'angreal* for the Queen of Andor, a crown for Lan Mandragoran, jewelry for the Aiel girl, and for this one." She nodded at Min.

Rand stiffened. He'd known what he was doing, on some level, but to hear it explained was disconcerting.

Min's expression darkened. Her grip on him tightened.

"Walk with me," Cadsuane said. "Just you and me, Lord Dragon." She glanced at him. "If you will."

Min looked to Rand, but he patted her on the shoulder and nodded. "I'll meet you at the tent."

She sighed, but retreated. Cadsuane had already started on the path. Rand had to jog a few steps to catch up. She probably enjoyed seeing that.

"Moiraine Sedai grows restless with your delays," Cadsuane said.

"And what are your thoughts?"

"I think she has a portion of wisdom to her. However, I do not find your plan to be complete idiocy. You must not delay much longer, however."

He purposely did not say when he would give the order to attack Shayol Ghul. He wanted everyone guessing. If nobody around him knew when he would strike, then chances were good the Dark One wouldn't know either.

"Regardless," Cadsuane said, "I am not here to speak about your delays. I feel that Moiraine Sedai has your . . . education in that matter well in hand. Something else worries me far more."

"And that is?"

"That you expect to die. That you are giving so much away. That you do not even seek to live."

Rand took a deep breath. Behind, a group of Maidens trailed him. He passed the Windfinders in their small camp, huddled and speaking over the Bowl of Winds. They looked toward him and Cadsuane with placid faces.

"Leave me go to my fate, Cadsuane," Rand said. "I have embraced death. I will take it when it comes."

"I am pleased at that," she said, "and do not think—for a moment—that I would not trade your life for the world."

"You've made that obvious from the start," Rand said. "So why worry now? This fight will claim me. So it must be."

"You must not assume that you will die," Cadsuane said. "Even if it is nearly inevitable, you must not take it as *completely* inevitable."

"Elayne said much the same thing."

"Then she has spoken wisdom at least once in her life. A better average than I had assumed of that one."

Rand refused to rise to that comment, and Cadsuane let slip a smile. She was pleased at how he controlled himself now. That was why she tested him.

Would the tests never end?

No, he thought. *Not until the final one. The one that matters most.*

Cadsuane stopped in the path, causing him to stop as well. "Do you have a gift for me as well?"

"I am giving them to those I care about."

That actually made her smile more deeply. "Our interactions have not always been smooth, Rand al'Thor."

"That would be one way to say it."

"However," she continued, eyeing him, "I will have you know that I am pleased. You have turned out well."

"So I have your permission to save the world?"

"Yes." She looked upward, where the dark clouds boiled. They began to split at his presence, as he did not try to mask it or keep them back.

"Yes," Cadsuane repeated, "you have my permission. So long as you do it soon. That darkness grows."

As if in concert with her words, the ground rumbled. It did

that more and more lately. The camp shook, and men stumbled, wary.

"There will be Forsaken," Rand said. "Once I enter. Someone will need to face them. I intend to ask Aviendha to lead the resistance against them. She could use your aid."

Cadsuane nodded. "I will do my part."

"Bring Alivia," Rand said. "She is strong, but I worry about putting her with others. She does not understand limits in the way that she should."

Cadsuane nodded again, and from the look in her eyes, he wondered if she'd already planned to do just that. "And the Black Tower?"

Rand set his jaw. The Black Tower was a trap. He *knew* it was a trap. Taim wanted to lure Rand into a place where he couldn't escape through a gateway.

"I sent Perrin to help."

"And your determination to go yourself?"

I have to help them. Somehow. I let Taim gather them. I can't just leave them to him . . .

"You still aren't certain," Cadsuane said, dissatisfied. "You'd risk yourself, you'd risk us all, stepping into a trap."

"I . . ."

"They're free." Cadsuane turned to walk away. "Taim and his men have been cast out of the Black Tower."

"What?" Rand demanded, taking her by the arm.

"Your men there freed themselves," Cadsuane said. "Though, from what I've been told, they took a beating doing it. Few know it. Queen Elayne might not be able to use them in battle for some time. I don't know the details."

"They freed themselves?" Rand said.

"Yes."

They did it. Or Perrin did.

Rand exulted, but a wave of guilt slammed against him. How many had been lost? Could he have saved them, if he'd gone? He'd known for days now of their predicament, and yet he'd left them, obeying Moiraine's insistent counsel that this was a trap he could not afford to spring.

And now they'd escaped it.

"I wish that I'd been able to draw an answer out of you,"

Cadsuane said, "about what you intended to do there." She sighed, then shook her head. "You have cracks in you, Rand al'Thor, but you'll have to do."

She left him.

"Deepe was a good man," Antail said. "He survived the fall of Maradon. He was on the wall when it blew, but he lived and kept fighting. The Dreadlords came for him eventually, sending an explosion to finish the job. Deepe spent the last moments throwing weaves at them. He died well."

The Malkieri soldiers raised cups toward Antail, saluting the fallen. Lan raised his own cup, though he stood just outside the ring of men around the fire. He wished Deepe had followed orders. He shook his head, downing his wine. Though it was night, Lan's men were on rotation to be awake in case of an attack.

Lan turned his cup between two fingers, thinking of Deepe again. He found he couldn't drum up anger at the man. Deepe had wanted to kill one of the Shadow's most dangerous channelers. Lan couldn't say he would turn down a similar opportunity, if it were given him.

The men continued their toasts to the fallen. It had become a tradition every evening, and had spread among all of the Borderlander camps. Lan found it encouraging that the men here were starting to treat Antail and Narishma as fellows. The Asha'man were aloof, but Deepe's death had forged a link between the Asha'man and the ordinary soldiers. Now they'd all paid the butcher's bill. The men had seen Antail grieving, and had invited him to make a toast.

Lan stepped away from the fire and walked through the camp, stopping by the horselines to check on Mandarb. The stallion was holding up well, though he bore a large wound on his left flank where his coat would never grow back; it seemed to be healing well. The grooms still spoke in hushed tones about how the wounded horse had appeared out of the night following the fight where Deepe had died. Many riders had been killed or unhorsed in the fighting that day. Very few horses had escaped the Trollocs and made their way back to camp.

Lan patted Mandarb's neck. "We'll rest soon, my friend," he said softly. "I promise."

Mandarb snorted in the darkness, and nearby, several of the other horses nickered.

"We'll make a home," Lan said. "The Shadow defeated, Nynaeve and I will reclaim Malkier. We'll make the fields bloom again, cleanse the lakes. Green pastures. No more Trollocs to fight. Children to ride on your back, old friend. You can spend your days in peace, eating apples and having your pick of mares."

It had been a very long time since Lan had thought of the future with anything resembling hope. Strange to find it now, in this place, in this war. He was a hard man. At times, he felt he had more in common with the rocks and the sand than he did with the men who laughed together beside the fire.

That was what he'd made of himself. It was the person he'd needed to be, a person who could someday journey toward Malkier and uphold the honor of his family. Rand al'Thor had begun to crack that shell, and then Nynaeve's love had ripped it apart completely.

I wonder if Rand ever knew, Lan thought, taking out the currycomb and working on Mandarb's coat. Lan knew what it was like to be chosen, from childhood, to die. He knew what it was like to be pointed toward the Blight and told he would sacrifice his life there. Light, but he did. Rand al'Thor would probably never know how similar the two of them were.

Lan brushed Mandarb for a time, though he was bone tired. Perhaps he should have slept. Nynaeve would have told him to sleep. He played out the conversation in his head, allowing himself a smile. She'd have won, explaining that a general needed sleep and that there were plenty of grooms to care for the horses.

But Nynaeve wasn't there. He kept brushing.

Someone approached the horselines. Lan heard the footsteps long before the person arrived, of course. Lord Baldhere retrieved a brush from the groom station, nodding to one of the guards there, and walked toward his own horse. Only then did he notice Lan.

"Lord Mandragoran?" he said.

"Lord Baldhere," Lan said, nodding toward the Kandori. Queen Ethenielle's Swordbearer was slender, with streaks of white in his otherwise black hair. Though Baldhere was not one of the great captains, he was a fine commander, and had served Kandor well since his king's death. Many had assumed that the Queen would marry Baldhere. That, of course, was foolish; Ethenielle looked at him as she would a brother. Besides, anyone who paid attention would know that Baldhere clearly preferred men to women.

"I am sorry to disturb you, Dai Shan," Baldhere said. "I had not realized that anyone else would be here." He moved to withdraw.

"I was nearly done," Lan said. "Do not let me stop you."

"The grooms do well enough," Baldhere said. "I wasn't here to check on their work. I have found, at times, that doing something simple and familiar helps me think."

"You're not the only one to have noticed that," Lan said, continuing to brush Mandarb.

Baldhere chuckled, then fell silent for a moment. Finally, he spoke. "Dai Shan," he said, "are you worried about Lord Agelmar?"

"In what regard?"

"I worry that he's pushing himself too hard," Baldhere said. "Some of the choices he is making ... they confuse me. It's not that his battle decisions are *bad*. They simply strike me as too aggressive."

"It is war. I don't know that one can be too aggressive in defeating one's enemy."

Baldhere fell quiet for a time. "Of course. But did you notice the loss of Lord Yokata's two cavalry squadrons?"

"That was unfortunate, but mistakes do happen."

"This isn't one that Lord Agelmar should have made. He's been in situations like this before, Dai Shan. He should have seen."

It had happened during a recent raid against the Trollocs. The Asha'man had been setting fire to Fal Eisen and the surrounding countryside. At Agelmar's orders, Yokata had taken his cavalry in a swing around a large hill to attack the right flank of the Trolloc army advancing on the Asha'man. Using a classic pincer movement, Agelmar was to send in more cavalry against the enemy's left flank, and the Asha'man would turn to meet the Trollocs head-on.

But the Shadow's leaders had seen through the maneuver. Before Agelmar and the Asha'man could act, a large contingent of

Trollocs had come over the hill to hit Yokata's own right flank, while the remainder hit Yokata head-on, enveloping his cavalry.

The cavalry had been killed to the last man. Immediately after, the Trollocs went after the Asha'man, who had barely been able to save themselves.

"He is tired, Dai Shan," Baldhere said. "I *know* Agelmar. He would never have made a mistake like that if he were awake and alert."

"Baldhere, anyone could have made a mistake like that."

"Lord Agelmar is one of the great captains. He should see the battle differently than ordinary men do."

"Are you certain you aren't expecting too much of him?" Lan asked. "Agelmar is just a man. We all are, at the end of the day."

"I . . . Perhaps you are right," Baldhere said, hand on his sword, as if worried. He wasn't carrying the Queen's weapon, of course— he did that only when she was acting in her station. "I guess it comes down to an instinct, Lan. An itch. Agelmar seems tired a lot, and I worry it's affecting his ability to plan. Please, just watch him."

"I'll watch," Lan said.

"Thank you," Baldhere said. He seemed less troubled now than when he'd approached.

Lan gave Mandarb a final pat, left Baldhere to tend his horse and walked through camp to the command tent. He went in; the tent was lit and well guarded, though the soldiers on guard weren't allowed clear views of the battle maps.

Lan moved around the hung cloths that obscured the entry and nodded to the two Shienaran commanders, subordinates to Agelmar, who attended this inner sanctum. One was studying the maps spread out on the floor. Agelmar himself wasn't there. A leader needed to sleep sometime.

Lan squatted, looking at the map. After tomorrow's retreat, it appeared that they would reach a place called Blood Springs, named for the way the rocks beneath the water made the river seem to run red. At Blood Springs, they would have a slight advantage of height because of the adjacent hills, and Agelmar wanted to stage an offensive against the Trollocs with bowmen and cavalry lines working together. And, of course, there would be more burning of the land.

Lan knelt on one knee, looking over Agelmar's notes about which army would fight where and how he'd divide the attacks. It was ambitious, but nothing looked particularly troublesome to Lan.

As he was studying, the tent flaps rustled, and Agelmar himself entered, speaking softly with Lady Ells of Saldaea. He stopped when he saw Lan, excusing himself quietly from his conversation. He approached Lan.

Agelmar did not slump with exhaustion, but Lan had learned to read beyond a man's posture for signs of tiredness. Redness to the eyes. Breath that smelled faintly of flatwort, an herb chewed to keep the mind alert when one had been up too long. Agelmar was tired—but so was everyone else in camp.

"Do you approve of what you see, Dai Shan?" Agelmar asked, kneeling.

"It is very aggressive for a retreat."

"Can we afford any other action?" Agelmar asked. "We leave a swath of burned land behind us, destroying Shienar almost as surely as if the Shadow had taken her. I will bring Trolloc blood to quench those ashes."

Lan nodded.

"Baldhere came to you?" Agelmar asked.

Lan looked up sharply.

Agelmar smiled wanly. "I assume it was regarding the loss of Yokata and his men?"

"Yes."

"It was a mistake, to be certain," Agelmar said. "I wondered if anyone would confront me on it; Baldhere is one to believe I should never have made such an error."

"He thinks you're pushing yourself too hard."

"He is clever in tactics," Agelmar said, "but he does not know so much as he thinks. His head is full of the stories of great captains. I am not without flaw, Dai Shan. This will not be my only error. I will see them, as I saw this one, and learn from them."

"Still, perhaps we should see that you get more sleep."

"I am perfectly hale, Lord Mandragoran. I know my limits; I have spent my entire life learning them. This battle will push me to my utmost, and I must let it."

"But—"

"Relieve me or let me be," Agelmar said, cutting in. "I will listen to advice—I am not a fool—but I will not be second-guessed."

"Very well," Lan said, rising. "I trust your wisdom."

Agelmar nodded, lowering his eyes to his maps. He was still working on his plans when Lan finally left to turn in.

CHAPTER
19

The Choice of a Patch

E layne found Bashere pacing on the east bank of the river.
Riverbanks were among the few places that still felt
alive to her. So much was lifeless these days, trees that did
not put forth leaves, grass that did not grow, animals that huddled in their dens and refused to move.

The rivers kept flowing. There was a sense of life to that,
though the plants were dreary.

The Alguenya was one of those deceptively mighty rivers that
looked placid from a distance, but could pull a woman under its
surface until she drowned. She remembered Bryne making a
lesson of that to Gawyn once during a hunting trip they'd taken
along it. He'd been speaking to her, too. Maybe to her primarily,
though he'd always been careful not to overstep himself with the
Daughter-Heir.

Be careful of currents, he'd said. *River currents are one of the most
dangerous things under the Light, but only because men underestimate
them. The surface looks still because nothing is fighting it. Nothing wants
to. The fish go along with it and men stay out of it, all except the fools
who think to prove themselves.*

Elayne stepped down the rocky bank, toward Bashere. Her
guards stayed behind—Birgitte wasn't with them just now. She

was seeing to the archer companies miles downriver, where they were busy pounding the Trollocs building rafts to get them across the river. Birgitte's archers and Talmanes' dragons were doing an outstanding job of reducing the Trolloc numbers there, but it was still only a matter of time before their vast army would pour across the Alguenya.

Elayne had pulled her forces out of Andor a week before, and she and Bashere had been pleased with their progress. Until they had discovered the trap.

"Amazing, isn't it?" she asked, stepping up beside Bashere, who stood at the river's bank.

Bashere glanced at her, then nodded. "We don't have anything like it, back home."

"What of the Arinelle?"

"It doesn't grow this big until it's outside of Saldaea," he said absently. "This is almost like an ocean, settled right here, dividing bank from bank. It makes me smile, thinking of how the Aiel must have regarded it after first crossing the Spine."

The two of them were silent for a time.

"How bad is it?" Elayne finally asked.

"Bad," Bashere said. "I should have realized, burn me. I should have seen."

"You can't plan for everything, Bashere."

"Pardon," he said, "but that is *exactly* what I'm supposed to be doing."

Their march eastward from Braem Wood had gone according to plan. Burning the bridges across the Erinin and the Alguenya, they had taken out large numbers of Trollocs trying to cross after them. Elayne was now on the road that went upriver to the city of Cairhien. Bashere had planned to set up their final confrontation with the Trollocs in hills along the road that lay twenty leagues south of Cairhien.

The Shadow had out-thought them. Scouts had spotted a second army of Trollocs just to the north of their current position, marching east, heading toward the city of Cairhien itself. Elayne had stripped that city of defenders to fill out her army. Now it was filled only with refugees—and was as crowded as Caemlyn had been.

"How did they do it?" she asked. "Those Trollocs couldn't have come down from Tarwin's Gap."

"There hasn't been enough time for that," Bashere agreed.

"Another Waygate?" she asked.

"Perhaps," Bashere said. "Perhaps not."

"How, then?" she asked. "Where did that army come from?" That army of Trollocs was almost close enough to knock on the city gates. Light!

"I made the mistake of thinking like a human," Bashere said. "I accounted for Trolloc marching speed, but not for how the Myrddraal might push them. A foolish mistake. The army in the woods must have split in two, with half taking a northeastern route through the woods toward Cairhien. It's the only thing I can think of."

"We've been moving as quickly as we can," Elayne said. "How could they have overtaken us?" Her army had gateways. She couldn't move everyone through them, as she didn't have enough channelers to hold gateways for long periods. However, she *could* move the supply carts, the wounded, and the camp followers through. That let them march at the speed of trained soldiers.

"We've moved as quickly as we could *safely*," Bashere said. "A human commander would never have pushed his forces into such a terrible march. The terrain they went through had to have been awful—the rivers they had to cross, the forests, the wetlands, Light! They must have lost thousands of Trollocs to fatigue during such a march. The Fades risked it, and now they have us in a pincer. The city could be destroyed as well."

Elayne fell silent. "I *won't* let that happen," she finally said. "Not again. Not if we can prevent it."

"Do we have a choice?"

"Yes," Elayne said. "Bashere, you're one of the greatest military minds the land has known. You have resources that no man has ever had before. The dragons, the Kinswomen, Ogier willing to fight in battle . . . You can make this work. I know you can."

"You show surprising faith in me for someone you have known a very short time."

"Rand trusts you," Elayne said. "Even during the dark times, Bashere—when he would look at every second person around him with darkness in his eyes—he trusted you."

Bashere seemed troubled. "There is a way."

"What is it?"

"We march and hit the Trollocs near Cairhien as quickly as we can. They're tired; they have to be. If we could beat them quickly, before the horde to the south reaches us, we may have a chance. It will be difficult. The northern force probably wants to seize the city, then use it against us as the southern Trollocs arrive."

"Could we open gateways into the city and hold it?"

"I doubt it," Bashere said. "Not with channelers as tired as these. Beyond that, we need to *destroy* the northern Trollocs, not just hold against them. If we give them time to rest, they will recover from their march, be joined by the Trollocs from the south, then use Dreadlords to rip open Cairhien like an overripe apple. No, Elayne. We have to attack and *crush* that northern army while it is weak; only then could we possibly hold against the southern one. If we fail, the two will smash us between them."

"It is the risk we must take," Elayne said. "Make your plans, Bashere. We'll make them work."

Egwene stepped into *Tel'aran'rhiod*.

The World of Dreams had always been dangerous, unpredictable. Lately, it was even more so. The grand city of Tear reflected strangely in the dream, the buildings weathered as if by a hundred years of storms. The city walls were now little more than ten feet high, their tops rounded and smooth, blown by the wind. Buildings inside had worn away, leaving foundations and lumps of weathered stone.

Chilled by the sight, Egwene turned toward the Stone. It, at least, stood as it had. Tall, strong, unchanged by the weathering of the winds. That comforted her.

She sent herself into its heart. The Wise Ones waited for her. That, too, was comforting. Even in this time of change and tempest, they were solid like the Stone itself. Amys, Bair and Melaine waited for her. She overheard part of their conversation before they noticed her.

"I saw it just as she did," Bair was saying. "Though it was my own descendants who lent me their eyes. I think we will all see it now, if we return the third time. It should be required."

"Three visits?" Melaine said. "That brings change indeed. We still do not know if the second visit will show this, or the previous vision."

Conscious of her eavesdropping, Egwene cleared her throat. They turned toward her, immediately falling silent.

"I did not mean to intrude," Egwene said, walking among the columns and joining them.

"It is nothing," Bair said. "We should have guarded our tongues. We were the ones to invite you here to meet us, after all."

"It is good to see you, Egwene al'Vere," Melaine said, smiling with affection. The woman looked so far along in her pregnancy, she must be close to delivering. "From reports, your army gains much *ji*."

"We do well," Egwene said, settling herself on the floor with them. "You shall have your own chance, Melaine."

"The *Car'a'carn* delays," Amys said, frowning. "The spears grow impatient. We should be moving against Sightblinder."

"He likes to prepare and plan," Egwene said. She hesitated. "I cannot remain with you long. I have a meeting with him later today."

"About what?" Bair asked, leaning forward, curious.

"I don't know," Egwene said. "I found a letter from him on the floor of my tent. He said he wanted to see me, but not as Dragon and Amyrlin. As old friends."

"Tell him that he must not dally," Bair said. "But here, there is something we need to speak of with you."

"What is it?" Egwene asked, curious.

"Have you seen anything like this?" Melaine said, concentrating. On the floor between them, the rock split with cracks. She was imposing her will upon the World of Dreams, creating something specific for Egwene to see.

At first, she was confused. Cracks in the rock? Of course she had seen cracks in rock before. And with the earthquakes striking the land so often recently, they were probably becoming even more common.

There *was* something distinctive about these. Egwene leaned forward, and found that the cracks seemed to empty into *nothing*. A deep blackness. Unnaturally so.

"What is it?" Egwene asked.

"Our people report seeing these," Amys said softly. "Those

fighting in Andor and those in the Blasted Lands with Rand al'Thor. They appear like fractures in the pattern itself. They remain dark like that for a few moments, then fade, leaving behind ordinary cracks."

"It is a very dangerous sign," Bair said. "We sent one of ours to ask at the Borderlands, where Lan Mandragoran fights. It appears that the cracks are most common there."

"They appear more frequently when the Dreadlords fight," Amys said. "When they use the weave known as balefire."

Egwene stared at that darkness, shivering. "Balefire weakens the Pattern. During the War of Power, even the Forsaken grew to fear using it, lest they unravel the world itself."

"We must spread the word to all of our allies," Amys said. "We *must* not use this weave."

"It is forbidden of Aes Sedai already," Egwene said. "But I will make it known that nobody is to consider breaking that rule."

"That is wise," Melaine said. "For a people with so many rules for themselves, I have found that the Aes Sedai are very proficient at ignoring guidelines if their situation allows it."

"We trust our women," Egwene said. "The Oaths hold them; otherwise, their own wisdom must guide them. If Moiraine had not been willing to bend this rule, Perrin would be dead—as would Mat, had Rand ignored the rule. But I *will* speak to the women."

Balefire bothered her. Not that it existed or did what it did. It was uniquely dangerous. And yet, what was it Perrin had said to her in the dream? *It's only another weave . . .*

It seemed unfair that the Shadow should have access to such a weapon as this, one that unraveled the Pattern as it was used. How would they fight it, how could they counter it?

"This is not the only reason we sent to you, Egwene al'Vere," Melaine said. "You have seen the changes to the World of Dreams?"

Egwene nodded. "The storm grows worse here."

"We will not be visiting here often in the future," Amys said. "We have made the decision. And, despite our complaints about him, the *Car'a'carn* does prepare his armies to move. It will not be long before we march with him to the Shadow's own hold."

Egwene nodded slowly. "So this is it."

"I am proud of you, girl," Amys said. Amys, tough-as-rocks

Amys, looked teary-eyed. They rose, and Egwene embraced them one at a time.

"Light shelter you, Amys, Melaine, Bair," Egwene said. "Give my love to the others."

"It will be done, Egwene al'Vere," Bair said. "May you find water and shade, now and always."

One by one, they faded from Tear. Egwene took a deep breath, looking upward. The building groaned, like a ship in a tempest. The rock itself seemed to shift around her.

She had loved this place—not the Stone, but *Tel'aran'rhiod*. It had taught her so much. But she knew, as she prepared to leave, that it was like a river in dangerous flood. Familiar and loved it might be, but she could not risk herself here. Not while the White Tower needed her.

"And farewell to you, old friend," she said to the air. "Until I dream again."

She let herself wake.

Gawyn waited beside the bed, as usual. They were back in the Tower, Egwene fully dressed, in the chamber near her study. It was not yet evening, but the request from the Wise One was not something she had wished to ignore.

"He's here," Gawyn said quietly, glancing at the door to her study.

"Then let us meet him," Egwene said. She prepared herself, rising, smoothing her skirt. She nodded to Gawyn, and they stepped out and went to meet the Dragon Reborn.

Rand smiled when he saw her. He waited inside with two Maidens she did not know.

"What is this about?" Egwene asked tiredly. "Convincing me to break the seals?"

"You've grown cynical," Rand noted.

"The last two times we met," Egwene said, "you pointedly tried to infuriate me. Am I not to expect it again?"

"I am not trying to infuriate you," Rand said. "Look, here." He pulled something from his pocket. A hair ribbon. He held it out to her. "You always looked forward so to being able to braid your hair."

"So now you imply I'm a child?" Egwene asked, exasperated. Gawyn rested a hand on her shoulder, comforting.

"What? No!" Rand sighed. "Light, Egwene. I want to make

amends. You're like a sister to me; I never had siblings. Or, at least, the one I have doesn't know me. I only have you. Please. I'm not trying to rile you."

For a moment, he seemed just as he had long ago. An innocent boy, earnest. Egwene let her frustration melt away. "Rand, I'm busy. *We* are busy. There isn't time for things like this. Your armies are impatient."

"Their time will soon come," Rand said, growing harder. "Before this is through, they will wonder why they were so eager, and will look with longing at these restful days waiting." He still held the ribbon in his hand, forming a fist. "I just ... I didn't want to go to my fight with our last meeting having been an argument, even if it was an important one."

"Oh, Rand," Egwene said. She stepped forward, taking the ribbon. She embraced him. Light, but he'd been difficult to deal with lately—but she'd thought the same thing about her parents on occasion. "I support you. It doesn't mean I'm going to do as you say with the seals, but I *do* support you."

Egwene released Rand. She would *not* be teary-eyed. Even if it did seem like a last parting for them.

"Wait," Gawyn said. "Sibling? You have a sibling?"

"I am the son of Tigraine," Rand said, shrugging, "born after she went to the Waste and became a Maiden."

Gawyn looked stunned, though Egwene had figured this out ages ago. "You are Galad's *brother?*" Gawyn asked.

"Half-brother," Rand said. "Not that it would probably mean much to a Whitecloak. We had the same mother. His father, like yours, was Taringail, but mine was an Aiel."

"I think Galad would surprise you," Gawyn said softly. "But Elayne ... "

"Not to tell you your own family history, but Elayne is not related to me." Rand turned to Egwene. "May I see them? The seals. Before I go to Shayol Ghul, I would look upon them one last time. I promise not to do anything with them."

Reluctantly, she fished them from the pouch at her waist where she often kept them. Gawyn, still looking stunned, walked to the window and pushed it open, letting light into the room. The White Tower felt still ... silent. Its armies were gone, its masters at war.

She unwrapped the first seal and handed it to Rand. She would not give him all of them at once. Just in case. She did trust his word; it was Rand after all, but . . . just in case.

Rand held up the seal, staring at it, as if seeking wisdom in that sinuous line. "I crafted these," he whispered. "I made them to never break. But I knew, as I did it, that they would eventually fail. Everything eventually fails when he touches it . . ."

Egwene hefted another of the seals, holding it gingerly. It would not do to break the thing by accident. She kept them wrapped and the pouch stuffed with cloth; she worried about breaking them while carrying them, but Moiraine had indicated that Egwene would break them.

She felt that was foolish, but the words she had read, the things Moiraine had said . . . Well, if the moment did come to break them, Egwene would need to have them at hand. And so she carried them—carried with her the potential death of the world itself.

Rand suddenly went as white as a sheet. "Egwene," he said. "This does not fool me."

"What doesn't?"

He looked at her. "This is a fake. Please, it is all right. Tell me the truth. You made a copy and gave it to me."

"I did nothing of the sort," she said.

"Oh . . . Oh, *Light*." Rand raised the seal again. "It's a fake."

"What!" Egwene snatched it from his hand, feeling it. She sensed nothing wrong. "How can you be sure?"

"I made them," Rand said. "I know my handiwork. That is *not* one of the seals. It is . . . Light, someone took them."

"I've had these with me each moment since you gave them to me!" Egwene said.

"Then it happened before," Rand whispered. "I didn't look them over carefully after I fetched them. He knew, somehow, where I'd put them." Taking the other one from her, he shook his head. "It's not real either." He took the third. "Nor this one."

He looked at her. "He has them, Egwene. He's stolen them back, somehow. The Dark One holds the keys to his own prison."

For much of Mat's life, he had wished that people would not look at him so much. They gave him frowns at the trouble he had ostensibly caused—trouble that really was not his fault—and glances of disapproval when he walked about completely inno-cent, trying his best to be pleasant. Every boy filched a pie now and then. No harm in it. It was practically expected.

Normal life had been harder for Mat than for other boys. For no good reason, everyone watched him extra carefully. Perrin could have stolen pies all day, and people would have just smiled at him and maybe mussed his hair. Mat they came at with the broom.

When he entered a place to dice, he drew looks. People watched him as they would watch a cheater—though he never was—or with envy in their eyes. Yes, he had always figured that *not* being watched would be a grand situation. A cause for real celebration.

Now he had it, and it made him sick.

"You can look at me," Mat protested. "Really. Burn you, it's all right!"

"My eyes would be lowered," the serving woman said as she piled fabric on the low table against the wall.

"Your eyes are *already* lowered! They're staring at the bloody floor, aren't they? I want you to raise them."

The Seanchan continued her work. She was of fair skin with freckles under her eyes, not too bad to look at, though he was more in favor of darker shades these days. He still would not have minded if this girl showed him a smile. How could he talk to a woman if he could not try to make her smile?

A few other servants entered, eyes downcast, carrying other folds of fabric. Mat stood in what were apparently "his" chambers in the palace. They were more numerous than he would ever need. Perhaps Talmanes and some of the Band could move in with him and keep the place from feeling so empty.

Mat sauntered over to the window. Below, in the Mol Hara, an army organized. It was going to take longer than he wanted. Galgan—Mat had only met the man briefly, and he did not trust the fellow, no matter what Tuon said about his assassins not being intended to succeed—was gathering the Seanchan forces from the borders, but too slowly. He worried about losing Almoth Plain with the withdrawal.

Well, he had better listen to reason. Mat had little reason to like the man already, but if he delayed in this . . .

"Honored One?" the serving girl asked.

Mat turned, raising an eyebrow. Several *da'covale* had entered with the last of the fabric, and Mat found himself blushing. They hardly wore any clothing at all, and what they did wear was transparent. He could look, though, could he not? They would not wear clothing like that if a man was not supposed to look. What would Tuon think?

She doesn't own me, Mat thought, determined. *I will* not *be husbandly*.

The freckled servant—she was *so'jhin*, half of her head shaved—gestured toward a person who had entered behind the *da'covale*, a middle-aged woman with her dark hair in a bun, none of her head shaved. She was squat, shaped kind of like a bell, with a grandmotherly air.

The newcomer inspected him. Finally someone who would look at him! If only her face did not have the expression of one studying horses at the market.

"Black for his new station," the woman said, clapping her hands once. "Green for his heritage. A deep forest, in moderation. Someone bring me a variety of eyepatches, and someone else burn that hat."

"What?" Mat exclaimed. Servants swarmed around him, picking at his clothing. "Wait, now. What is this?"

"Your new regalia, Honored One," the woman said. "I am Nata, and I will be your personal tailor."

"You aren't burning my hat," Mat said. "Try, and we'll bloody well see if you can fly from four stories up. Do you understand me?"

The woman hesitated. "Yes, Honored One. Do not burn his clothing. Keep it safe, should it be needed." She seemed doubtful it ever would be.

Mat opened his mouth to complain further, and then one of the *da'covale* opened a box. Jewelry shone inside it. Rubies, emeralds, firedrops. Mat's breath caught in his throat. There was a *fortune* in there!

He was so stunned that he almost did not notice that the servants were undressing him. They pulled at his shirt, and Mat let them. Although he held on to his scarf, he was not bashful. That blush on his cheeks had nothing to do with his trousers being taken off. He was just surprised at the jewelry.

Then one of the young *da'covale* reached for Mat's smallclothes.

"You'd be real funny without any fingers," Mat growled.

The *da'covale* looked up—his eyes widening, face paling. He immediately looked down again, bowing, backing away. Mat was not bashful, but the smallclothes were far enough.

Nata clicked her tongue. Her servants began draping Mat in fine cloth, black and deep green—so dark it was nearly black itself. "We shall tailor you outfits for military expression, court attendance, private functions, and civic appearances. It—"

"No," Mat said. "Military only."

"But—"

"We're at the bloody Last Battle, woman," Mat said. "If we survive this, you can make me a bloody feastday cap. Until then, we're at war, and I don't need anything else."

She nodded.

Mat reluctantly stood with arms out to the sides, letting them drape him in the fabric, taking measurements. If he had to put up with this business of being called "Honored One" and "Highness," then he could at least make certain he was dressed in a reasonable way.

In truth, he *had* been growing tired of the same old clothing. There did not seem to be much lace used by the Seanchan tailor, which was a shame, but Mat did not want to correct her in doing her job. He could not complain about every little thing. Nobody liked a complainer, least of all Mat.

As they dealt with the measurements, a servant approached with a small, velvet-lined case displaying a variety of eyepatches. He hesitated, considering; some were marked with gemstones, others painted with designs.

"That one," he said, pointing at the least ornamented patch. Simple black with only two small rubies, cut thin and long, set at the right and left edges of the patch opposite one another. They fitted it on him as the other servants finished measuring.

That done, the tailor had her servants dress him in a costume she had brought. Apparently, he was not going to be allowed back to his old clothing while he waited for his new outfits to be tailored.

The clothing started off simple enough. A silk robe of fine weave. Mat would have preferred trousers, but the robe was comfortable. However, they overlaid it with a larger, stiffer robe. It was also silk, of dark green, every inch of it embroidered with scrollwork patterns. The sleeves were large enough to trot a horse through, and they felt heavy and bulky.

"I thought I said to give me warrior's clothing!" he said.

"This is a ceremonial warrior's uniform for a member of the Imperial family, Highness," Nata said. "Many will see you as an outsider, and though nobody would question your loyalty, it would be well for our soldiers to see you as Prince of the Ravens first and an outlander second. Would you agree?"

"I suppose," Mat said.

The servants continued, buckling on an ornate girdle and placing forearm bands of the same design on his arms inside the large sleeves. That was all right, Mat supposed, as the girdle pulled in the waist of the clothing and kept it from feeling quite so bulky.

Unfortunately, the next piece of clothing was the most ridiculous of all. The stiff, pale piece of cloth fitted onto his shoulders. It draped down his front and back like a tabard, the sides open, but they flared out to the sides a good foot each, making him seem inhumanly wide. They were like shoulder plates from heavy armor, only made of cloth.

"Here now," Mat said. "This isn't a kind of trick you play on a fellow, just because he's new, is it?"

"Trick, Honored One?" Nata asked.

"You can't really . . ." Mat trailed off as someone passed outside his door. Another commander. The man was wearing a costume not unlike Mat's, though not as ornate, and with shoulders not quite as wide. Not Imperial family armor, but ceremonial armor for one of the Blood. Still, it was almost as lavish.

The man stopped and bowed to Mat, then continued on his way.

"Burn me," Mat said.

Nata clapped and the servants began draping Mat in gemstones. They chose mostly rubies, which made Mat uncomfortable. That had to be a coincidence, did it not? He did not know what he thought of being covered in all of these gemstones. Perhaps he could sell them. Actually, if he could put these on a gambling table, he could probably end up owning all of Ebou Dar . . .

Tuon already owns it, he realized. *And I married her.* It sank in that he was rich. *Really* rich.

He sat there, letting them lacquer his fingernails, as he considered what this all meant. Oh, he had not needed to worry about money for some time, as he could always gamble for more. This was different. If he already had everything, what point was there to gambling? This did not sound like much fun. People were not supposed to give you things like this. You were supposed to find a way to come to them yourself, by wits, luck or skill.

"Burn me," Mat said, lowering his arms to his side as the lacquering finished. "I'm a *bloody* nobleman." He sighed, plucking his hat from the hands of a startled servant—who was walking past with his old clothing—and set it on his head.

"Honored One," Nata said. "Please forgive my forwardness, but it is my place to advise on fashion, if you please. That hat looks . . . particularly out of place with that uniform."

"Who cares?" Mat said, marching out of the room. He almost had to go out the door sideways! "If I'm going to look ridiculous, I might as well do it with style. Someone point me toward where our flaming generals are meeting. I need to figure out how many troops we have."

CHAPTER
20

Into Thakan'dar

Later in the day after her meeting with Rand, Egwene thrust Vora's *sa'angreal* out in front of her and wove Fire. Threads came together, tiny glowing ribbons forming a complex weave in the air before her. She could almost feel their heat shining upon her, turning her skin a violent orange.

She finished the weave, and a fiery ball as large as a boulder arced in the air, crackling and roaring. It fell upon the distant hilltop like a meteor. The blast flung bow-wielding Trollocs aside, scattering their carcasses.

Romanda opened a gateway beside Egwene. Romanda was among the Yellows who had insisted on staying at the battlefront to provide emergency Healing. She and her small crew had been invaluable in saving lives.

Today, however, there would be no opportunity for Healing. The Trollocs had pulled back into the hills, as Bryne had indicated they would. After a day and a half of rest, many of the Aes Sedai were recovered. Not to full strength—not after over a week of grueling combat—but enough.

Gawyn jumped through the gateway right after it opened, his sword out. Egwene followed, along with Romanda, Lelaine, Leane, Silviana, Raemassa and a handful of Warders and soldiers.

They stepped out onto the very hilltop Egwene had just cleared. The charred earth was still warm under her feet, blackened; the scent of burned flesh hung in the air.

This hill was in the very middle of the Trolloc army. All around, Shadowspawn scrambled for safety this way and that. Romanda held the gateway and Silviana began weaving Air to create a dome of wind against arrows. The rest of them began to send weaves outward.

The Trollocs reacted slowly—they'd been waiting here, in these hills, ready to surge down into the valleys as Egwene's army entered. Normally, this would have been a disaster. The Trollocs could rain projectiles down on Egwene's troops, and her cavalry would have been at a disadvantage trying to get up those hills. The hilltops would have given the Trollocs and Fades a better perspective to spot weak points in Egwene's forces, and attack accordingly.

Egwene and her commanders had been disinclined to give the enemy that advantage. The beasts scattered as the battle reversed on them, Aes Sedai seizing the hilltops. Some of the beasts tried to charge up and retake them, but others scrambled away for their lives. Egwene's heavy cavalry came next, thundering through the valleys. What had once been a very efficient position for the Trollocs became a killing field; with the Trolloc archers removed by Aes Sedai, the heavy cavalry could kill practically unmolested.

That opened the way for the foot, who marched in formation to sweep the Trollocs back, smashing them against hillsides so that the Aes Sedai could kill them in groups. Unfortunately, the Trollocs had grown more accustomed to facing the One Power. Either that, or the Myrddraal had grown more thorough at encouraging them.

Soon, more coordinated groups of Trollocs charged the hilltops, while others managed to form resistance to the foot assault. *Bryne is right*, Egwene thought, leveling a contingent of Trollocs that had almost clawed their way to her. *The Fades are linked to the Trollocs again.* The Shadowspawn had been hesitant to use that tactic recently, as killing the Fade would drop all linked Trollocs. However, she suspected that it was the only way they could make the Trollocs climb toward almost-certain death on these hills.

If she could find the Myrddraal linked to the Trollocs nearby, she could stop them all with one well-placed weave of Fire. Unfortunately, the Fades were crafty, and had begun hiding among the Trollocs.

"They're closing in," Lelaine said, panting.

"Fall back," Egwene said.

They ducked through Romanda's gateway, followed by their Warders. Romanda came last, leaping through as a group of Trollocs claimed their hilltop. One of the beasts, a shaggy-furred bearlike monstrosity, stumbled through the gateway after her.

The thing dropped dead immediately, a faint wisp of smoke rising from its carcass. Its fellows hooted and growled on the other side. Egwene glanced at the other women, then shrugged and released flame straight through the gateway. A few fell dead, twitching, while the others scrambled away, howling, dropping their weapons.

"That is effective," Leane noted, folding her arms and raising an immaculate eyebrow at the gateway. It was the middle of the Last Battle, and the woman *still* took time each morning to do her face.

Their gateway had taken them back to camp, which was now mostly empty. With the reserves formed up and ready to move when required, the only soldiers who remained in the camp were a force of five hundred guarding Bryne's command tent.

She still carried the pouch with the false seals at her side. Rand's words had shaken her hard. How would they get the seals back? If the minions of the Shadow broke them at the wrong time, it would be a catastrophe.

Had they broken them already? Would the world know? Egwene felt a dread she could not abandon. And yet, the war continued, and she had no recourse but to keep fighting. They would think of a way to recover the seals, if they could. Rand swore to try. She wasn't certain what he could do.

"They're fighting so hard," Gawyn said.

Egwene turned to find him standing a short distance away, inspecting the battlefield with his looking glass. She felt a longing from him. Without some men to lead as he had the Younglings, she knew, he felt useless in these battles.

"The Trollocs are driven by Myrddraal," Egwene said, "linked to give the Fades greater control over them."

"Yes, but *why* resist so strongly?" Gawyn said, still looking through the glass. "They don't care about this land. It's obvious that these hills are lost to them, and yet they fight savagely. Trollocs are base—they fight and win or they scatter and retreat. They don't hold land. They're trying to do so here. It's like ... like the Fades think that even after a rout like this one, they're in a good position."

"Who knows why Fades do what they do?" Lelaine remarked, arms folded, looking through the still-open gateway.

Egwene turned, looking through it, too. The hilltop was now empty, strangely isolated amid the battle. Her soldiers had crashed up against the Trollocs in the small valley between the hills, and the fighting was brutal down there. She heard grunts, yells, clangs. Bloodied pikes were raised in the air as a group of men were forced back, and halberdiers moved in to try to slow the Trollocs.

The Shadowspawn were taking terrible casualties. It *was* an oddity; Bryne had expected them to retreat.

"Something's wrong," Egwene said, the hairs of her arms standing on end. Her worry about the seals vanished, for now. Her army was in danger. "Gather the Aes Sedai and have the army pull back."

The other women looked at her as if she were mad. Gawyn took off at a dash toward the command tent to give her orders. He didn't question.

"Mother," Romanda said, letting her gateway die. "What is—"

Something split the air on the other side of Egwene's war camp, opposite the battlefield. A line of light, longer than any gateway Egwene had seen. It was nearly as wide as her *camp itself*.

The line of light turned upon itself, opening a view that was *not* of southern Kandor. Instead, it was a place of ferns and drooping trees—though they were brown, like everything else, they were still alien and unfamiliar.

An enormous army stood silently upon this unfamiliar landscape. Thousands of banners flew above it, emblazoned with symbols Egwene didn't recognize. The foot soldiers wore knee-length garments that appeared to be some kind of padded armor, reinforced with chain in a large-squared pattern. Others wore metal shirts that seemed sewn from coins tied together.

Many carried hand axes, though of a very strange design. They had long, thin handles that bulged like bulbs at the end and the axe heads were narrow and thin, almost like picks. The hafts of all of their weapons—from polearms to swords—had a flowing, organic design. Smooth and not of a uniform width, made of some dark red wood that had been painted with colorful dots down the sides.

Egwene took in all of this in moments, her mind searching for any kind of origin for this strange force. She found nothing to latch on to until she sensed the channeling. The glow of *saidar* surrounded *hundreds* of women, all of them riding, wearing strange dresses made entirely of stiff black silk. The dresses were not tied at the waists, but instead pulled relatively tight around the shoulders, and flared wide toward the bottoms. Long, rectangular tassels of a multitude of colors hung from ties at the front, just below the neck. The faces of the women were all tattooed.

"Release the Power," Egwene said, letting go of *saidar*. "Don't let them sense you!" She dashed to the side, Lelaine following, the glow winking out from around her.

Romanda ignored Egwene, letting out a curse. She began weaving a gateway to escape.

A dozen different weaves of fire suddenly thrashed the area where Romanda stood. The woman didn't have a chance to scream. Egwene and the other women scrambled through the camp as weaves of the One Power destroyed tents, consumed supplies and set the entire place aflame.

Egwene reached the command tent just as Gawyn stumbled out. She grabbed him and pulled him to the ground as a ball of fire passed just overhead, then crashed into a collection of tents nearby.

"Light!" Gawyn said. "What is it?"

"Sharans." Lelaine, breathless, huddled down beside them.

"Are you certain?" Egwene whispered.

Lelaine nodded. "Accounts from the Cairhienin before the Aiel War are plentiful, if not very informative. They weren't allowed to see much, but what they did see looked a lot like that army."

"Army?" Gawyn said, stretching to the side and looking between the tents toward the force marching through the unnaturally wide gateway. "Blood and bloody ashes!" he swore, ducking back. "There are thousands of them!"

"Far too many to fight," Egwene agreed, mind working furiously. "Not pinned between them and the Trollocs as we are. We have to fall back."

"I just passed the order to Bryne to disengage the troops," Gawyn said. "But ... Egwene. Where are we going to go? Trollocs in front, that army behind! Light. We'll be crushed between them!"

Bryne would react quickly. He'd send a messenger through a gateway to the line captains. *Oh no* ...

Egwene grabbed Gawyn and pulled him away from the command tent just as she felt channeling within. Lelaine cried out, ducking in the other direction.

The Sharan women reacted immediately to the channeling. The ground ripped up underneath the tent, destroying it in a burst of overwhelming power. Tattered shreds of cloth flew into the air amid stones and clods of earth.

Egwene fell backward, and Gawyn pulled her toward a toppled cart that had been hit, one wheel shattered, its burden of firewood tumbling out. Gawyn pulled Egwene to the sheltered place just under the edge of the cart, beside the tumble of wood. They huddled there, though the wood flickered with flames and the ground before them was afire. The heat was distressing, but not unbearable.

Egwene huddled against the ground, blinking through eyes that burned with smoke, searching for signs of Lelaine. Or ... Light! Siuan and Bryne had been inside that tent, along with Yukiri and many of their command staff.

Egwene and Gawyn hid as flames rained on the camp, tearing up the earth. The Sharans struck at any sign of movement; several serving women who ran by were instantly immolated.

"Be ready to run," Gawyn said, "once the fire stops falling."

The flames *did* wane, but just as they did, riders in Sharan armor charged through the camp. They hooted and yelled, leveling bows at anyone they saw, dropping dozens with arrows to the back. After that, the Sharan troops moved through the camp in tight formations. Egwene waited tensely, trying to think of how to slip away.

She saw no opportunity. Gawyn pulled Egwene back farther, rubbed soot on her cheeks and motioned for her to stay low, then

draped his Warder cloak over them both. With the smoke from
the wood burning nearby, perhaps they wouldn't be seen.

Her heart thumped urgently in her chest. Gawyn pressed
something to her face, a kerchief he had soaked with his waterskin. He held another one to his face and breathed through it. She
took the one he was holding to her, but barely breathed. Those
soldiers were so *close*.

One of the soldiers turned toward the cart, peering at the
woodpile, but when he glanced through the smoke toward them
he didn't seem to see anything. Egwene silently contemplated the
Warder cloak. Its color-shifting nature made them nearly invisible, if they were careful not to move.

Why don't I have one of these cloaks? she thought with annoyance.
Why should they only be for Warders?

The soldiers were busy flushing out servants. Those who ran,
they killed with arrows from bows that stretched extremely far.
Servants who moved more slowly, they rounded up and forced to
the ground.

Egwene longed to embrace the Source, to do something. To
bring down fire and lightning upon these invaders. She still had
Vora's *sa'angreal*. She could—

She quashed that line of thinking. She was surrounded by the
enemy, and the swift reaction of the channelers indicated that they
were watching for Aes Sedai. If she wove for a single moment, she'd
be killed before she could escape. She huddled beside Gawyn, under
his cloak, hoping none of the Sharan channelers walked close
enough to sense her ability. She could use a weave to hide that ability, but would have to channel first to use it. Dare she try that?

They hid for a good hour or more. If the cloud cover hadn't
been so complete, casting the land into perpetual twilight, they'd
certainly have been spotted, cloak or no cloak. She almost cried
out at one point when a few of the Sharan soldiers tossed some
buckets of water onto the woodpile, stifling the fire and soaking
both of them.

She couldn't make out anything of her own army, though she
feared the worst. The Sharan channelers and a large portion of
their army moved through the camp quickly, toward the battlefield. With Bryne and the Amyrlin gone, and with a surprise force
coming in from behind . . .

Egwene felt sick. How many were dying, dead? Gawyn caught her arm as he felt her stir, then shook his head, mouthing a few words. *Wait until night.*

They're dying! she mouthed.

You can't help.

It was true. She let him hold her, letting his familiar scent calm her. But how could she simply *wait* as soldiers and Aes Sedai who depended on her were slaughtered? Light, a huge portion of the White Tower was out there! If this army fell, and those women with it . . .

I am the Amyrlin Seat, she told herself firmly. *I will be strong. I will survive. So long as I live, the White Tower stands.*

She still let Gawyn hold her.

Aviendha crawled across the rock like a winter lizard seeking warmth. Her fingertips, though callused, were beginning to burn from the bitter cold. Shayol Ghul was cold, with air that smelled as if it came from a tomb.

Rhuarc crawled to her left, a Stone Dog named Shaen to her right. Both wore the red headband of the *siswai'aman*. She didn't know what to make of Rhuarc, a clan chief, donning that headband. He had never spoken of it; it was as if the headband did not exist. So it was with all of the *siswai'aman*. Amys crawled on Shaen's right. For once, no one had objected to Wise Ones joining the advance scouts. In a place such as this, at a time such as this, the eyes of one who could channel might see what ordinary eyes would not.

Aviendha pulled herself forward, making no noise, despite the necklaces she wore. No plants sprouted on these rocks, not even mold or lichen. They were deep within the Blasted Lands, now. Almost as deep as one could go.

Rhuarc reached the ridge first, and she saw him tense. Aviendha arrived next, peering over the side of the rock, keeping low so as not to be seen. Her breath stopped dead in her throat.

She'd heard stories of this place. Of the massive forge near the base of the slope, a single black stream running past it. That water had been poisoned to the point that it would kill any who touched it. Hearths dotted the valley like open wounds, reddening the fog around them. As a young Maiden, she'd listened with wide eyes as an ancient roofmistress told of the creatures who worked the Shadow's forges, creatures that were not dead and not alive. Silent and horrible, the brutish things moved with steps that held no life—like the ticking hands of a clock.

The forgers paid little heed to the cages full of humans whose blood would be spilled to temper newly forged blades. The captives might as well have been chunks of iron. Though Aviendha was too far to hear the humans' whimpers, she felt them. Her fingers grew taut upon the rocks.

Shayol Ghul itself dominated the valley, its black slopes rising like a serrated knife into the sky. The sides were rent with cuts, like the skin of a man who had been whipped a hundred times, each score leaving a gash that spat steam. Perhaps that steam created the fog that lay over the valley. The fog churned and surged, as if the valley were a cup holding liquid.

"Such a terrible place," Amys whispered.

Aviendha had never heard such dread in the woman's voice. That chilled Aviendha nearly as much as the bitter wind that ruffled their clothing. Distant *ping*s broke the air, the workers forging. A black column of smoke rose from the nearest forge, and did not dissipate. It rose like an umbilical cord to the clouds above, which rained down lightning with dreadful frequency.

Yes, Aviendha had heard stories of this place. Those stories had failed to convey the full truth. One could not *describe* this place. One had to experience it.

A scraping from behind, and in a few moments, Rodel Ituralde crawled up next to Rhuarc. He moved quietly, for a wetlander.

"You were so impatient that you could not await our report?" Rhuarc asked softly.

"No report can convey what a man's own eyes can," Ituralde said. "I didn't promise I'd stay behind. I told you to go ahead. And you did." He raised his looking glass, shading the front with his hand, though that probably wasn't necessary with those clouds.

Rhuarc frowned. He and the other Aiel who had come north had agreed to follow a wetlander general, but it did not sit well with them. Nor should it. They would do this thing without growing comfortable. Comfort was the great killer of men.

Let it be enough, Aviendha thought, turning back to look at the valley. *Enough for my people. Enough for Rand and the task he must accomplish.*

Seeing the end of her people had nauseated and horrified her, but also awakened her. If the end of the Aiel was the sacrifice required for Rand to win, she would make it. She would scream and curse the Creator's own name, but she would pay that price. Any warrior would. Better that one people should end than the world fall completely under Shadow.

The Light willing, it would not come to that. The Light willing, her actions with the Dragon's Peace would serve to protect and shelter the Aiel. She would not let the possibility of failure stop her. They would fight. Waking from the dream was always a possibility when the spears were danced.

"Interesting," Ituralde said softly, still looking through his glass. "Your thoughts, Aiel?"

"We need to create a distraction," Rhuarc said. "We can come down the slope just to the east of the forge and set those captives free and break the place apart. This stops the Myrddraal from receiving new weapons and will keep the Dark One's eyes on us and not the *Car'a'carn*."

"How long will it take the Dragon?" Ituralde asked. "What do you think, Aiel? How much time do we give him to save the world?"

"He will fight," Amys said. "Enter the mountain, duel with Sightblinder. It will take as long as a fight needs to take. A few hours, perhaps? I have not seen a duel last much longer than that, even between two men of great skill."

"Let us assume," Ituralde said with a smile, "that there is going to be more to it than a duel."

"I am not a fool, Rodel Ituralde," Amys said coolly. "I doubt that the *Car'a'carn*'s fight will be one of spears and shields. However, when he cleansed the Source, did that not happen in the space of a single day? Perhaps this will be similar."

"Perhaps," Ituralde said. "Perhaps not." He lowered the glass and looked to the Aiel. "Which possibility would you rather plan for?"

"The worst one," Aviendha said.

"So we plan to hold out as long as the Dragon needs," Ituralde said. "Days, weeks, months . . . years? As long as it takes."

Rhuarc nodded slowly. "What do you suggest?"

"The pass into the valley is narrow," Ituralde said. "Scout reports put most of the Shadowspawn left in the Blight out beyond the pass there. Even they spend as little time as they can in this forsaken place. If we can close off the pass and seize this valley—destroy those forgeworkers and the few Fades down there—we could hold this place for ages. You Aiel are good at slash-and-run tactics. Burn me, but I know *that* from personal experience. You lot attack that forge, and we'll set about closing up the pass."

Rhuarc nodded. "It is a good plan."

The four of them walked down the ridge to where Rand waited, dressed in red and gold, arms behind his back, accompanied by a force of twenty Maidens and six Asha'man, plus Nynaeve and Moiraine. He seemed very troubled by something—she could feel his anxiety—though he should have been pleased. He had convinced the Seanchan to fight. What was it that, in his meeting with Egwene al'Vere, had disturbed him so?

Rand turned and looked upward, toward the peak of Shayol Ghul. Staring at it, his emotions changed. He seemed a man looking at a fountain in the Three-fold Land, savoring the idea of cool water. Aviendha could feel his anticipation. There was also fear in him, of course. No warrior ever rid himself completely of the fear. He controlled it, overwhelmed it with the thirst to be on with the fight, to test himself.

Men or women could not know themselves, not truly, until they were strained to their absolute limit. Until they danced the spears with death, felt their blood seeping out to stain the ground, and drove the weapon home into the beating heart of an enemy. Rand al'Thor wanted this, and she understood him because of it. Strange to realize, after all of this time, just how alike they were.

She stepped up to him, and he moved so that he stood just beside her, his shoulder touching hers. He did not drape an arm around her, and she did not take his hand. He did not own her, and she did not own him. The act of his movement so that they faced the same direction meant far more to her than any other gesture could.

"Shade of my heart," he said softly, watching his Asha'man open a gateway, "what did you see?"

"A tomb," she replied.

"Mine?"

"No. That of your enemy. The place where he was buried once, and the place he will slumber again."

Something hardened inside Rand. She could feel it, his resolve.

"You mean to kill him," Aviendha whispered. "Sightblinder himself."

"Yes."

She waited.

"Others tell me I am a fool for thinking this," Rand said. His guards moved through the gateway to return to Merrilor.

"No warrior should enter a battle without intending to see that battle finished," Aviendha said. She hesitated after saying it, something else occurring to her.

"What is it?" Rand asked.

"Well, the *greatest* victory would be to take your enemy *gai'shain*."

"I doubt he would submit to that," Rand said.

"Don't make jest," she said, elbowing him in the side, earning a grunt. "This must be considered, Rand al'Thor. Which is the better way of *ji'e'toh*? Is imprisoning the Dark One like taking him *gai'shain*? If so, that would be the proper path."

"I'm not certain I care what is 'proper' this time, Aviendha."

"A warrior must *always* consider *ji'e'toh*," she said sternly. "Have I taught you nothing? Do not speak like that, or you will shame me again before the other Wise Ones."

"I had hoped that—considering how our relationship has progressed—we would be through with the lectures, Aviendha."

"You thought that growing closer to me would *end* the lectures?" she asked, baffled. "Rand al'Thor, I have been among wetlander wives, and I've seen that they—"

He shook his head, leading the way through the gateway, Aviendha following. He seemed amused, and that was good. Some of his anxiety had faded. But truly, this was not a jest. Wetlanders did not have good senses of humor. Sometimes, they did not understand at all when to laugh.

On the other side of the gateway, they entered a camp made up of many groups. Rand had command of the Maidens and the *siswai'aman*, along with most of the Wise Ones.

Just outside of the Aiel camp were the Aes Sedai. Rand had

command of some three dozen—all of the Aes Sedai who had sworn to him personally, and most who were bonded to his Asha'man. That meant another two dozen Asha'man, of various ranks.

He also had Rodel Ituralde and his force, composed primarily of Domani. Their king, with his wispy beard and the beauty mark on his cheek, rode with them as well, but left the command to the great captain. The monarch gestured, and Ituralde walked over to give a report. Alsalam seemed uncomfortable around Rand, and did not go on any excursions when the Dragon did. Aviendha liked that arrangement. She wasn't certain she trusted this Alsalam.

Outside the Aiel tents camped another large military force, the Tairen army, including the elite force known as the Defenders of the Stone, led by a man named Rodrivar Tihera. Their king was with them as well, and was generally considered the highest authority in their gathered armies, aside from Rand.

The Tairens would form a key part of Rodel Ituralde's plans. As much as it galled Aviendha to admit it, Ituralde was right. The Aiel were not a defensive force, and though they could hold a pass if needed, they would be better used for offensive maneuvers.

The Tairens would be perfect for holding ground. They had well-trained companies of pikemen, and a full banner of cross-bowmen with a new kind of crossbow crank, knowledge of which the smiths had only just received. They had spent the last week converting the equipment to the new style.

There was one other group in Rand's force, and it was the most baffling to Aviendha. Dragonsworn in large numbers. They camped together, and flew a flag that placed the image of the dragon over the ancient symbol of the Aes Sedai. The group was made up of common men, soldiers, lords, ladies and some Aes Sedai and Warders. They came from all nations, including the Aiel, and shared only one common bond: They had put aside all loyalties, broken all bonds, to fight in the Last Battle. Aviendha had heard discomforting rumors that many of the Aiel among them were *gai'shain* who had put aside the white, claiming they would take it up again when the Last Battle was won.

Rand's coming was said to remove all bonds from men. Oaths shattered when he drew near, and any loyalty or alliance was secondary to the need to serve him in this last fight for humankind. Part of her wanted to name that wetlander foolishness, but perhaps she used that term too easily. A Wise One had to see with better eyes than that.

Now that they were on the other side of the gateway, Aviendha finally allowed herself to release *saidar*. The world dulled around her, the added sense of life and wonder evaporating. Every time she released the One Power, she felt slightly hollow, the joy and thrill now passed, over.

Ituralde and Rhuarc went to join King Darlin, speaking together about their battle plans. Aviendha joined Rand as he walked toward his tent.

"The dagger worked," Rand said. He reached down and fingered the black sheath that held the dull dagger. "Artham. I had heard them spoken of, back in the Age of Legends, but nobody created one. I wonder who finally managed it . . . "

"Are you certain it worked?" Aviendha said. "He could have been watching you, but not exposed his hand."

"No, I would have felt the attention," Rand said. "It *did* work. With this, he won't sense me until I step right up to the Bore. Once he does know I'm there, he will have trouble envisioning me, striking at me directly. Aviendha, that you should find this and identify it when you did, that Elayne should give it to me . . . The Pattern weaves us all where we need to be."

Rand smiled, then added, "Elayne sounded sad when she gave me the dagger. I think a part of her wanted to keep it because it would let her curse by the Dark One's name without drawing his attention."

"Is this really a time for levity?" Aviendha asked, scowling at him.

"If ever there was a need for laughter, this is it," Rand said, though the laughter seemed to have left his voice. That anxiety of his returned as they reached his tent.

"What is troubling you?" Aviendha asked him.

"They have the seals," Rand said.

"What!"

"Only Egwene knows, but it is true. They were stolen, perhaps from my hiding place, perhaps after I delivered them to Egwene."

"Then they are broken."

"No," Rand said. "I would feel that. I think they must be waiting. Perhaps they know that in breaking the seals, they clear the
way for me to reforge his prison. They'll break them at just the
wrong moment, to let the Dark One touch the world, perhaps to
give him the strength to overwhelm me as I face him . . ."

"We will find a way to stop this," Aviendha said, voice firm.

He looked to her and smiled. "Always the warrior."

"Of course." What else would she be?

"I have another concern. The Forsaken will try to strike at me
when I enter to face him. The Dark One cannot see me, does not
know where I am, and so is committing some of his forces to each
of the different battlefronts. The Shadow pushes hard at Lan,
trying to destroy him—the Dark One presses Elayne almost as
badly in Cairhien. Only Egwene seems to be having some success.

"He searches for me at each of these battlefields, committing
his creatures in large numbers. When we attack Shayol Ghul, we
should be able to hold the valley against armies. The Forsaken,
however, will come through gateways. Holding a pass will not
stop them, or the Dreadlords, male or female. My confrontation
with the Dark One will draw them as the cleansing did—only a
thousand times more urgently. They will come, with fire and
thunder, and they will kill."

"So will we."

"I'm counting on it," Rand said. "But I cannot afford to take
you into the cavern with me, Aviendha."

She felt a sinking feeling, though she attacked it, stabbed it,
left it to die. "I suspected. Do not think to send me away to safety,
Rand al'Thor. You would—"

"I wouldn't dare," he said. "I'd fear for my life if I were to try—
there isn't any place that is safe, now. I cannot take you into the
cavern because you will be needed out in the valley, watching for
the Forsaken and the seals. I *need* you, Aviendha. I need all three
of you to watch, to be my hands—my heart—during this fight. I
am going to send Min to Egwene. Something is going to happen
there, I'm certain. Elayne will fight in the south, and you . . . I
need you in the valley of Thakan'dar, watching my back.

"I will leave orders for the Aes Sedai and Asha'man, Aviendha.
Ituralde leads our troops, but *you* command our channelers at
Shayol Ghul. You must keep the enemy from entering the cavern

after me. You are my spear in this battle. If they reach me while I am in the cavern, I will be helpless. What I must do will take all of me—all of my concentration, every scrap of power I have. I'll be like a babe lying in the wilderness, defenseless against the beasts."

"And how is this different from how you usually are, Rand al'Thor?" she asked.

He laughed. It felt good to be able to both see and feel that smile. "I thought you said this wasn't a time for levity."

"Someone must keep you humble," Aviendha said. "It would not do for you to think yourself something grand, simply because you save the world."

He laughed again, leading her up to the tent where Min was. Nynaeve and Moiraine waited there, too, one with annoyance on her face, the other serenity. Nynaeve looked very odd with her hair not long enough to braid. Today, she'd pulled it up and pinned it back.

Moiraine sat quietly on a large stone, *Callandor*—the Sword That Is Not a Sword—lying across her lap, one hand resting protectively on its hilt. Thom sat beside her, whittling a stick and whistling softly to himself.

"You should have taken me, Rand," Nynaeve said, folding her arms.

"You had work to do," Rand said. "You have tried as I instructed?"

"Time and time again," Nynaeve said. "There's no way around the flaw, Rand. You *cannot* use *Callandor*. It will be too dangerous."

Rand came up to Moiraine, reaching out his hand, and she lifted *Callandor* for him to take. He raised it up before him, looking through its crystalline substance. It started to glow softly. "Min, I have a task for you," he whispered. "Egwene is progressing well, and I feel her battlefront will be key. I wish you to go and watch her and the Seanchan Empress, whom I have asked to join that battlefront once their forces are ready."

"You would have the Seanchan join *Egwene's* battlefront?" Moiraine asked, aghast. "Is that wise?"

"I cannot tell wisdom from brashness these days," Rand said. "But I would feel better if someone were keeping an eye on those two factions. Min, will you do it?"

"I was hoping . . ." Min looked away.

Hoping he'd take her into the cavern, Aviendha thought. But of course he could not.

"I'm sorry, Min," Rand said. "But I need you."

"I will do it."

"Rand," Nynaeve said. "You are taking *Callandor* when you attack him? Its weakness . . . so long as you are channeling into that . . . *thing*, anyone can seize control of you. They can use you, and can draw the One Power through *Callandor* into you until it burns you out—leaving you powerless, and leaving them with the strength to level mountains, destroy cities."

"I will take it," Rand said.

"But it's a trap!" Nynaeve said.

"Yes," Rand said, sounding tired. "A trap I must stride into and allow to spring shut upon me." He laughed, suddenly, throwing his head back. "As always! Why should I be surprised? Spread the word, Nynaeve. Tell Ituralde, Rhuarc, King Darlin. Tomorrow, we invade Shayol Ghul and claim it as our own! If we must put our head into the lion's mouth, let us make certain that he chokes upon our flesh!"

CHAPTER
21

Not a Mistake to Ignore

Siuan rolled her shoulder. She grimaced at the sharp pain. "Yukiri," she grumbled, "that weave of yours still needs work."

The tiny Gray cursed softly, standing up from beside a soldier who had lost his hand. She hadn't Healed him, instead leaving him to more mundane healers with bandages. To spend energy Healing this man would be a waste, as he would never fight again. They needed to save their strength for soldiers who could rejoin the battle.

It was brutal reasoning. Well, these were brutal times. Siuan and Yukiri moved on to the next soldier in the line of wounded. The man with the missing hand would survive without Healing. Probably. They had the Yellows in Mayene, but their energy was consumed in Healing Aes Sedai who had survived the escape and soldiers who could still fight.

All through the makeshift camp, set up on Arafellin soil east of the river's ford, soldiers wept and groaned. So many wounded, and Siuan and Yukiri were among the few Aes Sedai left with any strength to Heal. Most of the others had drained themselves making gateways to bring their army out from between the two attacking forces.

The Sharans had attacked aggressively, but securing the White Tower's camp had occupied them for a while, giving time for the army to flee. Pieces of it, at least.

Yukiri Delved the next man, then nodded. Siuan knelt down and began a Healing weave. She'd never been very good at this, and even with an *angreal*, it took a lot out of her. She brought the soldier back from the edge of death, Healing the wound in his side. He gasped, much of the energy for the Healing coming from his own body.

Siuan wavered, then fell to her knees in exhaustion. Light, she was as unsteady as a noblewoman on her first day on the deck of a ship!

Yukiri looked her over, then reached out for the *angreal*, a small stone flower. "Go rest, Siuan."

Siuan clenched her teeth, but handed over the *angreal*. The One Power slipped from her, and she let out a deep sigh, half-relieved and half-saddened at losing the beauty of *saidar*.

Yukiri moved to the next soldier. Siuan lay back where she was, her body complaining of its numerous bruises and aches. The events of the battle were a blur to her. She remembered young Gawyn Trakand bursting into the command tent, yelling that Egwene wanted the army to retreat.

Bryne had moved quickly, dropping a written order through the gateway in the floor. That was his newest method of passing commands—an arrow shaft with a note and a long ribbon tied to it, dropped through a gateway high above. There were no heads on the shafts, just a small stone to weight them.

Bryne had been restless before Gawyn appeared. He hadn't liked the way the battle had been playing out. The way the Trollocs moved had warned him that the Shadow had been planning something. Siuan was certain he'd already prepared the orders.

Then there had been the explosions in camp. And Yukiri yelling for them to jump *through* the hole in the floor. Light, she'd assumed the woman was mad! Mad enough to save all of their lives, apparently.

Burn me if I'm going to lie here like a piece of yesterday's catch on the deck, Siuan thought, staring up at the sky. She hauled herself to her feet and started stalking through the new camp.

Yukiri claimed her weave wasn't all *that* obscure, though Siuan had never heard of it. A massive cushion of Air, meant to cradle someone who had fallen a great distance. Crafting it had drawn the attention of the Sharans—*Sharans*, of all things!—but they'd escaped. She, Bryne, Yukiri and a few aides. Burn her, they'd gotten out, though that fall still made her wince to remember. And Yukiri kept saying she thought the weave might be the secret behind discovering how to fly! Fool woman. There was a good reason the Creator hadn't given people wings.

She found Bryne at the edge of the new camp, sitting exhausted on a stump. Two battle maps spread out by stones lay on the ground in front of him. The maps were wrinkled; he'd grabbed them as the tent started to explode around him.

Fool man, she thought. *Risking his life for a couple of pieces of paper.*

". . . from reports," said General Haerm, the new commander of the Illianer Companions. "I'm sorry, my Lord. The scouts don't dare sneak too close to the old camp."

"No sign of the Amyrlin?" Siuan asked.

Bryne and Haerm both shook their heads.

"Keep looking, young man." Siuan wagged a finger at Haerm. He raised an eyebrow at her use of the word "young." Burn this youthful face she'd been given. "I mean it. The Amyrlin is alive. You *find* her, you hear me?"

"I . . . Yes, Aes Sedai." He showed some measure of respect, but not enough. These Illianers didn't know how to treat Aes Sedai.

Bryne waved the man off, and for once, it didn't look as if anyone was waiting to meet with him. Everyone was probably too exhausted. Their "camp" looked more like a collection of refugees from a terrible fire than it did an army. Most of the men had rolled themselves in cloaks and gone to sleep. Soldiers were better than sailors at sleeping whenever, and wherever, they could.

She couldn't blame them. She'd been exhausted *before* the Sharans arrived. Now she was tired as death itself. She sat down on the ground beside Bryne's stump.

"Arm still hurting you?" Bryne asked, reaching down to rub her shoulder.

"You can feel that it is," Siuan grumbled.

"Merely trying to be pleasant, Siuan."

"Don't think I have forgotten that you're to blame for this bruise."

"Me?" Bryne said, sounding amused.

"You pushed me through the hole."

"You didn't seem ready to move."

"I was just about to jump. I was almost there."

"I'm certain," Bryne said.

"It's your fault," Siuan insisted. "I tumbled. I hadn't intended to tumble. And Yukiri's weave . . . horrible thing."

"It worked," Bryne said. "I doubt many people can claim to have fallen three hundred paces and survived."

"She was too eager," Siuan said. "She was probably longing to make us jump, you know. All that talk about Traveling and weaves of movement . . ." She trailed off, partly because she was annoyed at herself. This day had gone poorly enough without her griping at Bryne. "How many did we lose?" Not a much better topic, but she needed to know. "Do we have reports yet?"

"Nearly one in two of the soldiers," Bryne said softly.

Worse than she'd suspected. "And the Aes Sedai?"

"We have somewhere around two hundred and fifty left," Bryne said. "Though a number of those are in shock at having lost Warders."

That was more of a disaster. A hundred and twenty Aes Sedai dead in a matter of hours? The White Tower would require a very long time to recover from that.

"I'm sorry, Siuan," Bryne said.

"Bah," Siuan said, "most of them treated me like fish guts anyway. They resented me as Amyrlin, laughed when I was cast down, and then made a servant of me when I returned."

Bryne nodded, still rubbing her shoulder. He could feel that she was hurt, despite her words. There were good women among the dead. Many good sisters.

"She's out there," Siuan said stubbornly. "Egwene will surprise us, Bryne. You watch."

"If I'm watching, it won't be much of a surprise, will it?"

Siuan grunted. "Fool man."

"You're right," he said solemnly. "On both counts. I think Egwene *will* surprise us. I'm also a fool."

"Bryne . . ."

"I *am*, Siuan. How could I miss that they were stalling? They wanted to occupy us until this other force could gather. The

Trollocs pulled back into those hills. A defensive move. Trollocs aren't defensive. I assumed they were trying to set up an ambush only, and that was why they were pulling back corpses and preparing to wait. If I'd attacked them earlier, this could have been avoided. I was too careful."

"A man who thinks all day about the catch he missed because of stormy weather ends up wasting time when the sky is clear."

"A clever proverb, Siuan," he said. "But there's a saying among generals, written by Fogh the Tireless. 'If you do not learn from your losses, you will be ruled by them.' I can't see how I let this happen. I've trained better than this, prepared better than this! It's *not* just a mistake I can ignore, Siuan. The Pattern itself is at stake."

He rubbed his forehead. In the dim light of the setting sun, he looked older, his face wrinkled, his hands frail. It was as if this battle had stolen decades from him. He sighed, hunching forward.

Siuan found herself at a loss for words.

They sat in silence.

Lyrelle waited outside the gates to the so-called Black Tower. It took every ounce of her training not to let her frustration show.

This entire expedition had been a disaster from the start. First, the Black Tower had refused them entry until the Reds had done their business, and that had been followed by the trouble with gateways. *That* had been followed by three bubbles of evil, two attempts by Darkfriends to murder the lot of them and the warning from the Amyrlin that the Black Tower had joined the Shadow to fight.

Lyrelle had sent most of her women to fight alongside Lan Mandragoran at the Amyrlin's insistence. She'd remained behind with a few sisters to watch the Black Tower. And now ... now this. What to make of it?

"I can assure you," the young Asha'man said, "the danger has passed. We drove off the M'Hael and the others who turned to the Shadow. The rest of us walk in the Light."

Lyrelle turned to her companions. A representative from each Ajah, along with backup—sent for desperately this morning when the Asha'man had first approached her—in the form of thirty other sisters. They accepted Lyrelle's leadership here, if only reluctantly.

"We will discuss it," she said, dismissing the young Asha'man with a nod.

"What do we do?" Myrelle asked. The Green had been with Lyrelle from the start, one of the few that she'd not sent away, partially because she wanted the woman's Warders near. "If some of their members are fighting for the Shadow . . ."

"Gateways can be made again," Seaine said. "Something has changed about this place in the days since we felt that channeling inside."

"I don't trust it," Myrelle said.

"We must know for certain," Seaine said. "We cannot leave the Black Tower unattended during the Last Battle itself. We *must* see these men taken care of, one way or another." The Black Tower men claimed that only a few of their number had joined the Shadow, and that the channeling had been the result of an attack by the Black Ajah.

It galled her to hear them use those words. Black Ajah. For centuries, the White Tower had denied the existence of Darkfriends among Aes Sedai. The truth had, unfortunately, been revealed. That didn't mean Lyrelle wanted to hear men tossing around the term so casually. Particularly men like these.

"If they'd wanted to attack us," Lyrelle said speculatively, "they'd have done it when we couldn't escape with gateways. For now, I will assume they have cleansed the . . . problems among their ranks. As was required of the White Tower itself."

"So we go in?" Myrelle asked.

"Yes. We bond the men we were promised, and from them draw out the truth, if it is obscured." It troubled Lyrelle that the Dragon Reborn had refused them the highest-ranking among the Asha'man, but Lyrelle had devised a plan when she first came here. It should still work. She would first ask for a display of channeling among the men, and would bond the one she felt was strongest. She would then have that one tell her which among the trainees were the most talented so her sisters could bond those.

From there . . . well, she hoped that would contain the majority of these men. Light, what a mess. Men who could *channel*, walking about unashamed! She did not accept this fable of the taint having been cleansed. Of course these ... men ... would claim such a thing.

"Sometimes," Lyrelle muttered, "I wish I could go back and slap myself for accepting this commission."

Myrelle laughed. She never *did* take events as seriously as she should. Lyrelle felt annoyed at having missed the chances to be had at the White Tower during her long absence. Reunification, fighting the Seanchan ... These were the times when leadership could be proven, and a woman could gain a reputation for strength.

Opportunities appeared during times of upheaval. Opportunities now lost to her. Light, but she hated that thought.

"We will enter," she called up to the walls framing the gate before her. Then, more softly, she continued to her women: "Hold the One Power and be careful. We do not know what could happen here." Her women would be a match for a larger number of untrained Asha'man, if it came to that. It shouldn't, logically. Of course, the men *were* likely mad. So perhaps assuming logic from them was imprudent.

The large gates opened to allow her people in. It said something about these Black Tower men that they chose to finish the walls around their grounds before actually building their tower.

She kneed her horse forward, and Myrelle and the others followed in a clopping of hooves. Lyrelle embraced the Source and used the new weave, which would tell her if a man channeled nearby. It was not the young man from a short time ago who met them at the gates, however.

"What is this?" Lyrelle asked as she was joined by Pevara Tazanovni. Lyrelle knew the Red Sitter, though not well.

"I've been asked to accompany you," Pevara said cheerfully. "Logain thought that a familiar face might make you more comfortable."

Lyrelle held in a sneer. Aes Sedai should not be cheerful. Aes Sedai should be calm, collected, and—if anything else—stern. A man should look at an Aes Sedai and immediately wonder what he had done wrong and how he could fix it.

Pevara fell in beside her as they rode onto the grounds of the Black Tower. "Logain, who is in charge now, sends his regards,"

Pevara continued. "He was gravely wounded in the attacks and has not yet fully recovered."

"Will he be well?"

"Oh, certainly. He should be up and about in another day or two. He will be needed to lead the Asha'man as they join the Last Battle, I suspect."

Pity, Lyrelle thought. The Black Tower would have been more easily controlled without a false Dragon at their head. Better that he had died.

"I am certain his aid will be useful," Lyrelle said. "His leadership, however . . . Well, we shall see. Tell me, Pevara. I have been told that bonding a man who can channel is different from bonding a normal man. Have you been through the process?"

"Yes," Pevara said.

"Is it true, then?" Lyrelle asked. "Ordinary men can be compelled with the bond to obey, but not these Asha'man?"

Pevara smiled, seeming wistful. "Ah, what would that be like? No, the bond cannot force Asha'man. You will have to use more inventive means."

That was not good. "How obedient are they?" Aledrin asked from the other side.

"It depends on the man, I suspect," Pevara said.

"If they cannot be forced," Lyrelle said, "will they obey their Aes Sedai in battle?"

"Probably," Pevara said, though there was something ambiguous about the way she said it. "I must tell you something, all of you. The mission I was sent on, and the one you also pursue, is a fool's errand."

"Is that so?" Lyrelle asked evenly. She was hardly going to trust a Red after what they had done to Siuan. "Why is that?"

"I was once where you are," Pevara said. "Ready to bond all of the Asha'man in an attempt to control them. But would you ride into another city and select fifty men there, at a whim, and bond them as Warders? Bonding the Asha'man just to bond them is foolish. It will not control them. I do think some Asha'man will make excellent Warders, but—like many men—others will not. I suggest that you abandon your plan to bond exactly forty-seven and take those who are most willing. You will gain better Warders."

"Interesting advice," Lyrelle said. "But, as you mentioned, the

Asha'man will be needed at the battlefront. There is not time. We will take the forty-seven most powerful."

Pevara sighed, but said nothing further as they passed several men in black coats with two pins on the high collars. Lyrelle felt her skin crawling, as if insects burrowed beneath it. Men who could channel.

Lelaine felt that the Black Tower was vital to the White Tower's plans. Well, Lyrelle did not belong to Lelaine. She was her own person, and a Sitter in her own right. If she could find a way to bring the Black Tower under her direct authority, then perhaps she could finally wiggle out from under Lelaine's thumb.

For that prize, bonding Asha'man was worthwhile. Light, but she wasn't going to enjoy it. They needed all of these men controlled, somehow. The Dragon would be growing mad, unreliable by this point, tainted by the Dark One's touch on *saidin*. Could he be manipulated into letting the rest of the men be bonded?

Not having control through the bond . . . that will be dangerous. She imagined going into battle with ranks of two or three dozen Asha'man, bonded and forced to her will. How could she make it happen?

They reached a line of men in black coats waiting at the edge of the village. Lyrelle and the others approached them, and Lyrelle did a quick count. Forty-seven men, including the one standing at the front. What trick were they trying to pull?

The one at the front came forward. He was a sturdy man in his middle years, and he looked as if he'd recently suffered some kind of ordeal. He had bags under his eyes and wan skin. His step was firm, however, and his gaze steady as he met Lyrelle's eyes, then bowed to her.

"Welcome, Aes Sedai," he said.

"And you are?"

"Androl Genhald," he said. "I've been put in charge of your forty-seven until they have been bonded."

"*My* forty-seven? I see that you have forgotten the terms already. We are to be given any soldier or Dedicated we wish, and they cannot refuse us."

"Yes, indeed," Androl said. "That is true. Unfortunately, all of the men in the Black Tower other than these are either full

Asha'man, or have been called away on urgent business. The others would, of course, follow the Dragon's commands if they were here. We made certain to keep forty-seven for you. Actually, forty-six. I've already been bonded by Pevara Sedai, you see."

"We will wait until the others return," Lyrelle said coldly.

"Alas," Androl said, "I do not think they will return any time soon. If you intend to join the Last Battle, you will have to make your selections quickly."

Lyrelle narrowed her eyes at him, then looked at Pevara, who shrugged.

"This is a trick," Lyrelle said to Androl. "And a childish one."

"I thought it clever myself," Androl returned, voice cool. "Worthy of an Aes Sedai, one might say. You were promised that any member of the Black Tower, save full Asha'man, would respond to your request. They will. Any of them to whom you can *make* the request."

"Undoubtedly, you chose for me the weakest among your numbers."

"Actually," Androl said, "we took those who volunteered. They are good men, every one of them. They are the ones who wanted to be Warders."

"The Dragon Reborn will hear of this."

"From what I've heard," Androl said, "he's heading to Shayol Ghul any time now. Are you going to join him there just to make your complaint?"

Lyrelle drew her lips into a line.

"Here's the thing, Aes Sedai," Androl said. "The Dragon Reborn sent a message to us, just earlier today. He instructed us to learn one last lesson: that we're not to think of ourselves as weapons, but as men. Well, men have a choice in their fate, and weapons do not. Here are your *men*, Aes Sedai. Respect them."

Androl bowed again and walked away. Pevara hesitated, then turned her horse, following him. Lyrelle saw something in the woman's face as she looked at the man.

So that is it, Lyrelle thought. *No better than a Green, that one is. I would have expected more of one her age.*

Lyrelle was tempted to refuse this manipulation, to go to the Amyrlin and protest what had happened. Only . . . news from the

Amyrlin's battlefront was jumbled. Something about an unexpected army appearing; details were not available.

Certainly the Amyrlin would not be happy to hear complaints at this point. And certainly, Lyrelle admitted to herself, she also wanted to be done with the Black Tower.

"Each of you pick two," Lyrelle said to her companions. "A few of us will take only one. Faolain and Theodrin, you are among those. Be quick about it, all of you. I want away from this place as soon as possible."

Pevara caught up to Androl as he slipped into one of the huts.

"Light," she said. "I'd forgotten how *cold* some of us can be."

"Oh, I don't know," Androl replied. "I've heard that some of you aren't quite so bad."

"Be careful of them, Androl," she said, looking back out. "Many will see you as only a threat or a tool to be used."

"We won you over," Androl said, walking into a room where Canler, Jonneth and Emarin waited with cups of warm tea. All three were beginning to recover from the fighting, Jonneth most quickly. Emarin bore the worst scars, most of them emotional. He, like Logain, had been subjected to the Turning process. Pevara noticed him staring blankly, sometimes, face etched by fear as if remembering something horrible.

"You three shouldn't be here," Pevara said, hands on hips, facing Emarin and the other two. "I know Logain promised you advancement, but you still wear only the sword on your collars. If any of those women saw you, they could take you as Warders."

"They won't see us," Jonneth said with a laugh. "Androl would have us through a gateway before we had time to curse!"

"So what do we do now?" Canler asked.

"Whatever Logain wishes of us," Androl said.

Logain had . . . changed since the ordeal. Androl whispered to her that he was darker now. He spoke less. He did still seem determined to get to the Last Battle, but for now, he gathered the men in and pored over things they'd found in Taim's rooms. Pevara worried that the Turning had broken him inside.

"He thinks there might be something in those battle maps he found in Taim's chambers," Emarin said.

"We'll go where Logain decides we can be of most use," Androl replied. A straightforward answer, but one that didn't actually say much.

"And what of the Lord Dragon?" Pevara asked carefully.

She felt Androl's uncertainty. The Asha'man Naeff had come to them, bearing news and instructions—and with them, some implications. The Dragon Reborn had known all was not well at the Black Tower.

"He left us alone on purpose," Androl said.

"He would have come if he could have!" Jonneth said. "I promise you."

"He left us to escape on our own," Emarin said, "or to fall on our own. He has become a harsh man. Perhaps callous."

"It doesn't matter," Androl said. "The Black Tower has learned to survive without him. Light! It always survived without him. He barely had anything to do with us. It was Logain who gave us hope. It is Logain who will have my allegiance."

The others nodded. Pevara felt something important happening here. *They couldn't have leaned upon him forever anyway*, she thought. *The Dragon Reborn will die at the Last Battle.* By intention or not, he had given them the chance to become their own men.

"I will take his last order to heart, however," Androl said. "I will not be merely a weapon. The taint is cleansed. We fight not to die, but to live. We have a *reason* to live. Spread the word among the other men, and let us take oaths to uphold Logain as our leader. And then, to the Last Battle. Not as minions of the Dragon Reborn, not as pawns of the Amyrlin Seat, but as the Black Tower. Our own men."

"Our own men," the other three whispered, nodding.

CHAPTER
22

The Wyld

Egwene was shocked awake as Gawyn clamped his hand over her mouth. She tensed, memories returning like the light of a sunrise. They were still hiding beneath the broken cart; the air still smelled of burned wood. The land nearby was dark as coal. Night had fallen.

She looked to Gawyn and nodded. Had she really drifted off? She wouldn't have thought it possible, under the circumstances.

"I'm going to try to slip away," Gawyn whispered, "and make a distraction."

"I'll go with you."

"I can go more quietly."

"Obviously you've never tried to sneak up on someone from the Two Rivers, Gawyn Trakand," she said. "I'd bet you a hundred Tar Valon marks that I'm the quieter of us two."

"Yes," Gawyn whispered, "but if you draw within a dozen steps of one of their channelers, you'll be spotted, no matter how quiet. They've been patrolling through camp, particularly at the perimeters."

She frowned. How did he know that? "You went out scouting."

"A little," he whispered. "I wasn't seen. They're scavenging through the tents, taking captive anyone they find. We won't be able to hide here much longer."

He should not have gone out without asking her. "We—"

Gawyn stiffened, and Egwene cut off, listening. Feet, shuffling. The two of them pulled back, watching as ten or twelve captives were led into an open space near where the command tent had stood. Sharans placed torches on poles around the ragged prisoners. A few of these were soldiers, beaten to the point where they could barely walk. There were cooks and laborers as well. They had been lashed, their trousers frayed. All of their shirts had been removed.

On their backs, someone had tattooed a symbol that Egwene did not recognize. At least, she thought they were tattoos. The symbols might have been burned into them.

As the captives were gathered, someone yelled nearby. In a few minutes, a dark-skinned Sharan guard walked up, dragging a young messenger boy he'd apparently found hiding in camp. He ripped off the boy's shirt and shoved him, crying, to the ground. The Sharans, oddly, wore clothing that had a large diamond shape cut out of the back. Egwene could see that the guard bore a mark on his own back, a tattoo she could barely make out against his dark skin. His clothing was very formal, with a large, stiff robe that came almost to his knees. It didn't have sleeves, but underneath he wore a shirt, with a diamond cut-out, that had long sleeves.

Another Sharan came out of the darkness, and this man was almost completely naked. He wore ripped trousers, but no shirt. Instead of a tattoo on his back, he had tattoos all across his shoulders. They crept up his neck, like twisted vines, before reaching up to cup his jaw and cheeks. They looked like a hundred twisted hands, long fingers with claws holding his head from below.

This man went over to the kneeling messenger boy. The other guards shuffled; they weren't comfortable with this fellow, whoever he was. He held out a hand, sneering.

The boy's back burned, suddenly, with a tattoo mark like that of the other captives. Smoke rose, and the boy cried out in pain. Gawyn exhaled softly in shock. That man with the tattoos running up onto his face . . . that man could channel.

Several of the guards muttered. She could *almost* understand the words, but they had a thick accent. The channeler snapped like a feral dog. The guards stepped back, and the channeler prowled off, disappearing into the shadows.

Light! Egwene thought.

Rustling in the darkness resolved into two women in wide silk dresses. One had lighter skin, and as Egwene searched, she found that some of the soldiers did, too. Not all Sharans were dark as the fellows she'd seen so far.

The women's faces were very beautiful. Delicate. Egwene shrank back. From what she had seen earlier, these two would probably be channelers. If they stepped too close to Egwene, they might sense her.

The two women inspected the captives. By the light of their lanterns, Egwene made out tattoos on their faces as well, though theirs were not as disturbing as those upon the men. These were like leaves, tattooed from the back of the neck forward, going under the ears and spreading like blossoms on the cheeks. The two women whispered to one another, and again Egwene felt as if she could almost understand them. If she could weave a thread to listen—

Idiot, she thought. Channeling would get her killed here.

Others gathered around the captives. Egwene held her breath. A hundred, two hundred, more people approached. They did not talk much; they seemed a quiet, solemn people, these Sharans. Most of those who came had open backs to their garments, revealing their tattoos. Were those symbols of status?

She had assumed that the more important one was, the more intricate the tattoos. However, officers—she had to assume that was what they were, with their feathered helmets and fine silken coats and golden armor made as if of coins that had been sewn together through the holes at their centers—they had only small openings, revealing tiny tattoos at the base of shoulders.

They've removed pieces of armor to display the tattoos, she thought. Surely they did not do battle with the skin exposed. This was something done during more formal times.

The last people who joined the crowd—ushered to the front— were the strangest of all. Two men and a woman atop small donkeys, all three wearing beautiful silk skirts, their animals draped with gold and silver chains. Plumes of vibrant colors fanned out from intricate headdresses upon these three. They were nude from the waist up, including the woman, save for the jewelry and necklaces that covered much of their chests. Their backs were exposed, their heads shaven just on the back to show their necks. There were no tattoos.

So . . . lords of some sort? Except all three had hollow, haunted expressions. They slumped forward, eyes down, faces wan. Their arms seemed thin, almost skeletal. So frail. What had been done to these people?

It made no sense to her. The Sharans were undoubtedly a people as baffling as the Aiel, probably more so. *But why come now?* Egwene thought. *Why, after centuries upon centuries of isolation, have they finally decided to invade?*

There were no coincidences, not of this magnitude. These had come to ambush Egwene's people, and had worked with the Trollocs. She let herself seize upon that. Whatever she learned here would be of vital importance. She could not help her army right now—Light send that some of its members, at least, had managed to flee—so she should learn what she could.

Gawyn prodded her softly. She looked to him, and felt his worry for her.

Now? he mouthed, gesturing behind them. Perhaps, with everyone's attention drawn by . . . whatever was happening, the two of them could sneak away. They started to back up, shuffling quietly.

One of the Sharan channelers called out. Egwene froze. She'd been spotted!

No. No. Egwene breathed deeply, trying to calm her heart, which seemed to be trying to beat its way out through her chest. The woman was speaking to the others. Egwene thought she'd heard the words "It is done" through the thick accent.

The group of people knelt down. The bejeweled trio bowed their heads further. And then, near the captives, the air *bent*.

Egwene couldn't describe it any other way. It warped and . . . and seemed to rip apart, twisting like it did above the road on a hot day. Something formed from this disruption: a tall man in glistening armor.

He wore no helmet and had dark hair and light skin. His nose was slightly hooked, and he was very handsome, particularly in that armor. It looked to be constructed all of *coins*, silvery and overlapping. The coins were polished to such a shine, they reflected the faces around him like a mirror.

"You have done well," the man announced to those bowing before him. "You may stand." His voice bore hints of the Sharan accent, but it was not nearly as thick.

The man placed his hand on the pommel of the sword at his waist as the others rose. From the darkness behind, a group of the channelers crawled forward. They bobbed for this newcomer in a kind of bow. He removed one of his gauntlets, reached out with an offhanded gesture and scratched the head of one of the men, as a lord might favor a hound.

"So these are the new *inacal*," the man said speculatively. "Do any of you know who I am?"

The captives cringed before him. Though the Sharans had risen, the captives were smart enough to remain on the ground. None of them spoke.

"I suspected not," the man said. "Though one can never tell if one's fame has spread unexpectedly. Tell me, if you know who I am. Speak it, and I will let you free."

No replies.

"Well, you will listen and remember," the man said. "I am Bao, the Wyld. I am your savior. I have crawled through the depths of sorrow and have risen up to accept my glory. I have come seeking what was taken from me. Remember that."

The captives cowered further, obviously uncertain what to do. Gawyn tugged on Egwene's sleeve, motioning backward, but she did not move. There was something about that man . . .

He looked up suddenly. He focused on the women channelers, then gazed about, peering into the darkness. "Do any of you *inacal* know the Dragon?" he asked, though he sounded distracted. "Speak up. Tell me."

"I did see him," said one of the captive soldiers. "Several times."

"Did you speak with him?" Bao asked, strolling away from the captives.

"No, great Lord," the soldier said. "The Aes Sedai, they did speak with him. Not I."

"Yes. I worried you would be of no use," Bao said. "Servants, we are being watched. You have not searched this camp as well as you claimed. I sense a woman nearby who can channel."

Egwene felt a spike of alarm. Gawyn pulled on her arm, meaning to go, but if they ran, they'd be captured for certain. Light! She—

The crowd turned at a sudden noise near one of the fallen tents. Bao raised a hand, and Egwene heard a furious yell in the darkness. Moments later, Leane floated through the crowd of Sharans, tied in Air, her eyes wide. Bao brought her up close to him, holding her wrapped in weaves that Egwene could not see.

Her heart continued to pound. Leane was alive. How had she remained hidden? Light! What could Egwene do?

"Ah," Bao said. "One of these . . . Aes Sedai. You, you have spoken with the Dragon?"

Leane didn't respond. To her credit, she kept her face blank.

"Impressive," Bao said, reaching up fingers and touching her chin. He held up another hand, and the collected captives suddenly started to writhe and scream. They burst into flames, yelling in agony. Egwene had to forcibly stop herself from reaching for the True Source as she watched. She was crying by the time it ended, though she did not remember starting.

The Sharans shuffled.

"Do not be displeased," Bao said to them. "I know you went to great trouble to take some alive for me, but they would have made poor *inacal*. They are not raised to it, and during this war, we do not have time to train them. Killing them now is a mercy compared to what they would have had to endure. Besides, this one, this . . . Aes Sedai will serve our purpose."

Leane's mask had cracked, and despite the distance, Egwene could see her hatred.

Bao still had her chin cupped in his hand. "You are a beautiful thing," he said. "Unfortunately, beauty is meaningless. You are to deliver a message for me, Aes Sedai, to Lews Therin. The one who calls himself the Dragon Reborn. Tell him that I have come to slay him, and in so doing, I will claim this world. I will take what originally should have been mine. Tell him that. Tell him you have seen me, and describe me to him. He will know me.

"Just as the people here awaited him with prophecy, just as they showered him with glory, the people of *my* land awaited me.

I have fulfilled their prophecies. He is false, and I am true. Tell him I will finally have satisfaction. He is to come to me, so that we may face one another. If he does not, I will slaughter and destroy. I will seize his people. I will enslave his children, I will take his women for my own. One by one, I will break, destroy, or dominate everything he has loved. The only way for him to avoid this is for him to come and face me.

"Tell him this, little Aes Sedai. Tell him that an old friend awaits. I am Bao, the Wyld. He Who Is Owned Only by the Land. The dragonslayer. He knew me once by a name I have scorned, the name Barid Bel."

Barid Bel? Egwene thought, memories from her lessons in the White Tower returning to her. *Barid Bel Medar . . . Demandred.*

The storm in the wolf dream was a changeable thing. Perrin spent hours prowling the Borderlands, visiting packs of wolves as he ran down dry riverbeds and across broken hills.

Gaul had learned quickly. He wouldn't stand for a moment against Slayer, of course, but at least he had learned to keep his clothing from changing—though his veil did still snap up to cover his face when he was startled.

The two of them bounded through Kandor, leaving blurs in the air as they moved from hilltop to hilltop. The storm was sometimes strong, sometimes weak. At the moment, Kandor was hauntingly still. The grassy highland landscape was strewn with all kinds of debris. Tents, roofing tiles, the sail of a large ship, even a blacksmith's anvil, deposited point-first into a muddy hillside.

The dangerously powerful storm could arise anywhere in the wolf dream and rip apart cities or forests. He'd found Tairen hats blown all the way to Shienar.

Perrin came to rest on a hilltop, Gaul streaking into place beside him. How long had they been searching for Slayer? A few hours, it seemed on one hand. On the other . . . how much ground had they crossed? They had returned to their food stores now three times to eat. Did that mean a day had passed?

"Gaul," Perrin said. "How long have we been at this?"

"I cannot say, Perrin Aybara," Gaul replied. He checked for the sun, though there was none. "A long while. Will we need to stop and sleep?"

That was a good question. Perrin's stomach suddenly growled, and he made them a meal of dried meat and a hunk of bread. He gave some to Gaul. Would summoned bread sustain them in the wolf dream, or would it merely vanish once they consumed it?

The latter. The food vanished even as Perrin ate it. They would need to rely upon their supplies, perhaps getting more from Rand's Asha'man during the daily opening of that portal. For now, he *shifted* back to their packs and dug out some dried meat, then rejoined Gaul in the north.

As they settled down on the hillside to eat again, he found himself dwelling on the dreamspike. He carried it with him, turned to its slumbering position, as Lanfear had taught him. It made no dome now, but he could make one when he wished.

Lanfear had all but given it to him. What did that mean? Why did she taunt him?

He ripped at a hunk of dried meat. Was Faile safe? If the Shadow discovered what she was doing ... Well, he wished he could at least check on her.

He took a long drink from his waterskin, then searched outward for the wolves. There were hundreds of them up here, in the Borderlands. Perhaps thousands. He gave those nearby a greeting, sending his scent mixed with his image. The dozen replies that came were not words, but his mind understood them as such.

Young Bull! This from a wolf named White Eyes. *The Last Hunt is here. Will you lead us?*

Many asked this, lately, and Perrin couldn't figure out how to interpret it. *Why do you need me to lead you?*

It will be by your call, White Eyes replied. *By your howl.*

I don't understand what you mean, Perrin sent. *Can you not hunt on your own?*

Not this prey, Young Bull.

Perrin shook his head. A response like others he'd received. *White Eyes,* he sent. *Have you seen Slayer? The killer of wolves? Has he stalked you here?*

Perrin sent it out broadly, and some of the other wolves replied. They knew of Slayer. His image and scent had been passed among many wolves, much as had Perrin's own. None had seen him recently, but time was an odd thing to wolves; Perrin wasn't certain how recent their "recently" really was.

Perrin took a bite of dried meat, and caught himself growling softly. He stifled that. He had come to a peace with the wolf inside of him, but that didn't mean he intended to let it start tracking mud into the house.

Young Bull, another wolf sent. Turn Bow, an aged female pack leader. *Moonhunter walks the dreams again. She seeks you.*

Thank you, he sent back. *I know this. I will avoid her.*

Avoid the moon? Turn Bow sent back. *A difficult thing, Young Bull. Difficult.*

She had the right of that.

I saw Heartseeker just now, sent Steps, a black-furred youth. *She wears a new scent, but it is her.*

Other wolves sent agreement. Heartseeker was in the wolf dream. Some had seen her to the east, but others said that she had been seen to the south.

But what of Slayer? Where was the man, if not hunting wolves? Perrin caught himself growling again.

Heartseeker. That must be one of the Forsaken, though he didn't recognize the images they sent of her. She was ancient, and so were the memories of wolves, but often the things they remembered were fragments of fragments that their ancestors had seen.

"Any news?" Gaul said.

"Another one of the Forsaken is here," Perrin said with a grunt. "Doing something to the east."

"Does it involve us?"

"The Forsaken always involve us," Perrin said, standing. He reached down, touched Gaul on the shoulder and *shifted* them in the direction Steps had indicated. The position wasn't exact, but once Perrin arrived, he found some wolves who had seen Heartseeker on their way to the Borderlands the day before. They sent Perrin eager greetings, asking if he was going to lead them.

He rebuffed their questions, pinpointing where Heartseeker had been spotted. It was Merrilor.

Perrin *shifted* there. A strange mist hung over the landscape here. Tall trees, the ones Rand had grown, reflected here, and their lofty tops poked out of the mist above.

Tents dotted the landscape, like the tops of mushrooms. Aiel tents were plentiful, and between them cook fires glowed in the mist. This camp had been here long enough to manifest in the wolf dream, though tent flaps changed places and bedrolls vanished, flickering in the insubstantial way of this place.

Perrin led Gaul between the neat rows of tents and horseless horse pickets. They both froze as they heard a sound. Someone muttering. Perrin used the trick he'd seen Lanfear use, creating a pocket of . . . something around himself that was invisible, but which stopped sound. It was strange, but he did it by creating a barrier with no air in it. Why would that make the sound stop?

He and Gaul crept forward to the canvas of a tent. That of the man Rodel Ituralde, one of the great captains, judging by the banner. Inside, a woman in trousers picked through documents on a table. They kept vanishing in her fingers.

Perrin didn't recognize her, though she was painfully homely. That certainly wasn't what he'd have expected from one of the Forsaken; not that large forehead, bulbous nose, uneven eyes or thinning hair. He didn't recognize her curses, though he grasped the meaning from her tone.

Gaul looked at him, and Perrin reached for his hammer, but hesitated. Attacking Slayer was one thing, but one of the Forsaken? He was confident of his ability to resist weaves here in the wolf dream. But still . . .

The woman cursed again as the paper she was reading vanished. Then she looked up.

Perrin's reaction was immediate. He created a paper-thin wall between her and him, her side painted with an exact replica of the landscape behind him, his side transparent. She looked right at him, but didn't see him, and turned away.

Beside him, Gaul let out a very soft breath of relief. *How did I do that?* Perrin thought. It wasn't something he had practiced; it had merely seemed *right*.

Heartseeker—this had to be she—waved her fingers, and the tent split in half above her, the canvas flaps hanging down. She rose through the air, moving toward the black tempest above.

Perrin whispered to Gaul, "Wait here and watch for danger."

Gaul nodded. Perrin cautiously followed Heartseeker, lifting himself into the air with a thought. He tried to form another wall between himself and her, but it was too difficult to keep the right image displayed while moving. Instead, he kept his distance and put a blank brownish-green wall between him and the Forsaken, hoping that if she happened to glance down, she'd pass over the small oddity.

She began to move more quickly, and Perrin forced himself to keep up. He glanced down, and was rewarded with the stomach-churning sight of Merrilor's landscape dwindling below. Then it grew dark and vanished into blackness.

They didn't pass through the clouds. As the ground faded away, so did the clouds, and they entered someplace black. Pinpricks of light appeared all around Perrin. The woman above stopped and hung in the air for a few moments before streaking away to the right.

Perrin followed again, coloring himself—his skin, his clothing, everything—black to hide. The woman approached one of the pinpricks of light until it expanded and dominated the sky in front of her.

Heartseeker reached her hands forward and pressed them against the light. She was muttering to herself. Feeling he *needed* to hear what she was saying, Perrin dared move closer, though he suspected that the pounding of his heart was so loud it would give him away.

". . . take it from me?" she said. "You think I care? Give me a face of broken stone. What do I care? That's not *me*. I will have your place, Moridin. It *will be mine*. This face will just make them underestimate me. Burn you."

Perrin frowned. He couldn't make much sense of what she was saying.

"Go ahead and throw your armies at them, you fools," she continued to herself. "I'll have the greater victory. An insect can have a thousand legs, but only one head. Destroy the head, and the day is yours. All you're doing is cutting off the legs, stupid fool. Stupid, arrogant, *insufferable* fool. I'll have what is due me, I'll . . ."

She hesitated, then pivoted. Perrin, spooked, immediately sent himself back to the ground. It worked, thankfully—he hadn't known if it would, up in that place of lights. Gaul jumped, and Perrin took a deep breath. "Let's——"

A ball of blazing fire crashed into the ground beside him.

Perrin cursed and rolled, cooling himself with a gust of wind, imagining his hammer up into his hand.

Heartseeker dropped to the ground in a wave of energy, power rippling around her. "Who are you?" she demanded. "Where are you? I—"

She focused suddenly on Perrin, seeing him completely for the first time, the blackness having faded from his clothing. "You!" she screeched. "You are to blame for this!"

She raised her hands; her eyes almost seemed to *glow* with hatred. Perrin could smell the emotion in spite of the blowing wind. She released a white-hot bar of light, but Perrin bent it around himself.

The woman started. They always did that. Didn't they realize that nothing was real here except what you thought to be real? Perrin vanished, appearing behind her, raising his hammer. Then he hesitated. A woman?

She spun about, screaming and ripping the earth beneath him. He jumped up into the sky, and the air around him tried to seize him—but he did what he'd done before, creating a wall of nothingness. There was no air to grab him. Holding his breath, he vanished and appeared back on the ground, summoning banks of earth in front of him to block the balls of fire that hurtled his way.

"I want you dead!" the woman screamed. "You *should* be dead. My plans were perfect!"

Perrin vanished, leaving behind a statue of himself. He appeared beside the tent, where Gaul watched carefully, spear raised. Perrin put a wall between them and the woman, coloring it to hide them, and made a barrier to block the sound.

"She can't hear us now," Perrin said.

"You are strong here," Gaul said thoughtfully. "Very strong. Do the Wise Ones know of this?"

"I'm still a pup compared to them," Perrin said.

"Perhaps," Gaul said. "I have not seen them, and they do not speak of this place to men." He shook his head. "Much honor, Perrin Aybara. You have much honor."

"I should have just struck her down," Perrin said as Heartseeker destroyed the statue of him, then stepped up to it, looking confused. She turned about, searching frantically.

"Yes," Gaul agreed. "A warrior who will not strike a Maiden is a warrior who refuses her honor. Of course, the greater honor for you . . ."

Would be to take her captive. Could he do it? Perrin took a breath, then sent himself behind her, imagining vines reaching around her to hold her in place. The woman howled curses at him, slicing the vines with unseen blades. She reached her hand toward Perrin, and he *shifted* to the side.

His feet crunched on bits of frost on the ground that he hadn't noticed, and she immediately spun on him and released another weave of balefire. *Clever*, Perrin thought, barely managing to bend the light away. It struck the hillside behind, drilling a hole straight through it.

Heartseeker continued the weave, snarling, hideous face distorted. The weave bent back toward Perrin, and he gritted his teeth, keeping it at bay. She *was* strong. She pushed hard, but finally, she released it, panting. "How . . . how can you possibly . . ."

Perrin filled her mouth with forkroot. It was difficult to do; changing anything directly about a person was always harder. However, this was much easier than trying to transform her into an animal or the like. She raised a hand to her mouth, eyes adopting a look of panic. She began to spit and hack, then desperately opened a gateway beside her.

Perrin growled, imagining ropes reaching for her, but she destroyed them with a weave of Fire—she must have gotten the forkroot out. She hurled herself through the gateway, and he *shifted* himself to be right in front of it, preparing to leap through. He froze when he saw her entering the middle of an enormous army of Trollocs and Fades at night. Many faced the gateway, eager.

Perrin stepped back as Heartseeker raised a hand to her mouth, looking aghast and coughing out more forkroot. The gateway closed.

"You should have killed her," Lanfear said.

Perrin turned to find the woman standing nearby, her arms folded. Her hair had changed from silver to dark brown. In fact, her face had changed, too, becoming slightly more like it had been before, when he'd first seen her nearly two years ago.

Perrin said nothing, returning his hammer to its straps.

"This is a weakness, Perrin," Lanfear said. "I found it charming in Lews Therin at one point, but that doesn't make it any less a weakness. You need to overcome it."

"I will," he snapped. "What was she doing, up there with the balls of light?"

"Invading dreams," Lanfear said. "She was here in the flesh. That affords one certain advantages, particularly when playing with dreams. That hussy. She thinks she knows this place, but it has always been mine. It would have been best if you'd killed her."

"That was Graendal, wasn't it?" Perrin asked. "Or was it Moghedien?"

"Graendal," Lanfear said. "Though, again, we are not to use that name for her. She's been renamed Hessalam."

"Hessalam," Perrin said, trying the word out in his mouth. "I don't know it."

"It means 'without forgiveness.'"

"And what is your new name, the one we're supposed to call you, now?"

That actually pulled a blush out of her. "Never mind," she said. "You are skilled here in *Tel'aran'rhiod*. Much better than Lews Therin ever was. I always thought I would rule at his side, that only a man who could channel would be worthy of me. But the power you display here . . . I think I may accept it as a substitute."

Perrin grunted. Gaul had moved across the small clearing between the camp tents, spear raised, *shoufa* covering his face. Perrin waved him off. Not only was Lanfear likely to be *much* better with the wolf dream than Gaul, but she hadn't done anything specifically threatening yet.

"If you've been watching me," Perrin said, "you'll know that I'm married, quite happily."

"So I have seen."

"Then stop looking at me like a flank of beef hung up for display in the market," Perrin growled. "What was Graendal doing here? What does she want?"

"I'm not certain," Lanfear said lightly. "She always has three or four plots going at the same time. Don't underestimate her, Perrin. She's not as skilled here as some others, but she *is* dangerous. She's a fighter, unlike Moghedien, who will run from you whenever she can."

"I'll keep that in mind," Perrin said, walking up to the place where she'd vanished by gateway. He prodded at the earth where the gateway had cut the ground.

"You could do that, you know," Lanfear said.

He spun on her. "What?"

"Go back and forth into the waking world," she said. "Without requiring the help of one like Lews Therin."

Perrin didn't like the way she sneered when she said his name. She tried to cover it up, but he smelled hatred on her whenever she mentioned him.

"I can't channel," Perrin said. "I suppose I could imagine being able to . . ."

"It wouldn't work," she said. "There are limits to what one can accomplish here, regardless of how strong the mind. The ability to channel is not a thing of the body, but a thing of the soul. There *are* still ways for one such as you to move back and forth between worlds in the flesh. The one you call Slayer does it."

"He's not a wolfbrother."

"No," she said. "But he is something similar. I'm honestly not certain another has had his skills before. The Dark One did . . . something to this Slayer when capturing his soul, or his souls. I suspect Semirhage might have been able to tell us more. It's a pity she's dead."

Lanfear didn't smell of pity at all. She glanced at the sky, but was calm, not worried.

"You don't seem as worried about being spotted as you once were," Perrin noted.

"My former master is . . . occupied. This last week watching you, I've rarely felt his eyes on me."

"Week?" Perrin asked, shocked. "But—"

"Time passes oddly here," she said, "and the barriers of time itself are fraying. The closer you are to the Bore, the more time will distort. For those who approach Shayol Ghul in the real world, it will be just as bad. For every day that passes to them, three or four might pass to those more distant."

A week? Light! How much had happened on the outside? Who lived, and who had died, while Perrin hunted? He should wait at the Traveling ground for his portal to open. But, judging by the darkness he'd seen through Graendal's gateway, it was night. Perrin's escape portal could be hours away.

"You could make a gateway for me," Perrin said. "A pathway out, then back in. Will you?"

Lanfear considered it, strolling past one of the flickering tents and letting her fingers trail on the canvas as it vanished. "No," she finally said.

"But—"

"You must learn to do this thing for yourself if we are to be together."

"We're *not* going to be together," he said flatly.

"You need this power of and for yourself," she said, ignoring what he had said. "You are weak so long as you are trapped only in one of the worlds; being able to come here when you want will give you great power."

"I don't care about power, Lanfear," he said, watching her as she continued to stroll. She *was* pretty. Not as pretty as Faile, of course. Beautiful nonetheless.

"Don't you?" She faced him. "Have you never thought of what you could do with more strength, more power, more authority?"

"That won't tempt me to—"

"Save lives?" she said. "Prevent children from starving? Stop the weak from being bullied, end wickedness, reward honor? Power to encourage men to be straightforward and honest with one another?"

He shook his head.

"You could do so much good, Perrin Aybara," she said, walking up to him, then touching the side of his face, running her fingers down his beard.

"Tell me how to do what Slayer does," Perrin said, pushing her hand away. "How does he move between worlds?"

"I cannot explain it to you," she said, turning away, "as it is a skill I have never had to learn. I use other methods. Perhaps you can beat it out of him. I would be quick, assuming you wish to stop Graendal."

"Stop her?" Perrin said.

"Didn't you realize?" Lanfear turned back to him. "The dream she was invading was not one of the people from this camp— space and distance matter not to dreams. That dream you saw her invading . . . it belongs to Davram Bashere. Father of your wife."

With that, Lanfear vanished.

CHAPTER
23

At the Edge of Time

Gawyn tugged urgently on Egwene's shoulder. Why wouldn't she move? Whoever that man was in the armor made of silver discs, he could sense female channelers. He'd picked Leane out of the darkness; he could do the same for Egwene. Light, he probably would, as soon as he took a moment to notice.

I'm going to haul her up onto my shoulder, if she doesn't move, he thought. *Light help me, I'll do it, no matter how much noise it makes. We're going to be caught anyway, if we—*

The one who called himself Bao moved off, towing Leane—still wrapped in Air—with him. The others followed in a mass, leaving the awful, charred remnants of the other captives behind.

"Egwene?" Gawyn whispered.

She looked at him, a cold strength in her eyes, and nodded. Light! How could she be so calm when he had to clench his teeth for fear they would start rattling together?

They wriggled out from under the cart backward, moving on their stomachs until they emerged. Egwene glanced in the direction of the Sharans. Her cold sense of control radiated into his mind from the bond. Hearing that man's name had done that to her, given her a sudden spike of shock followed by grim determination.

What was that name? Barid something? Gawyn thought he'd heard it before.

He wanted Egwene *out* of this death trap. He put the Warder cloak around her shoulders. "The best way out is directly east," he whispered. "Around the mess tent—what's left of it—then on to the camp perimeter. They have a guard post set up next to what was our Traveling ground. We'll go around that to the north side."

She nodded.

"I'll scout ahead, you follow," Gawyn said. "If I see anything, I'll toss a stone back toward you. Listen for it hitting, all right? Count to twenty, then follow me at a slow pace."

"But—"

"You can't go first, lest we run across some of those channelers. I need to take the lead."

"At least wear the cloak," she hissed.

"I'll be fine," he whispered, then slipped away before she could argue further. He did feel her spike of annoyance, and suspected he'd get an earful once they were out of this. Well, if they lived long enough for that to happen, he'd accept the reprimand happily.

Once he was a short distance from her, he slipped on one of the rings of the Bloodknives. He had activated it with his blood, as Leilwin had said was needed.

She'd also said it might kill him.

You're a fool, Gawyn Trakand, he thought as a tingling sensation ran across his body. Though he'd used the *ter'angreal* only once before, he knew that his figure had been blurred and darkened. If people glanced in his direction, their eyes would slide away from him. It worked particularly well in shadows. For once, he was pleased that those clouds blocked out any moonlight or starlight.

He moved on, stepping carefully. Earlier in the night, when he'd first tested the ring as Egwene slept, he'd been able to pass within a few steps of sentries holding lanterns. One had looked right at Gawyn, but hadn't seen him. In this much darkness, he might as well have been invisible.

The *ter'angreal* allowed him to move more quickly as well. The change was slight, but noticeable. He itched to try out the ability in a duel. How many of these Sharans could he take on his own while wearing one of these rings? A dozen? Two?

That would last right up until one of those channelers cooked you,

Gawyn told himself. He collected a few pebbles off the ground to toss back toward Egwene if he spotted one of the female channelers.

He looped around the mess tent, following the path he'd scouted earlier. It was important to keep reminding himself to be careful; earlier, the *ter'angreal*'s power had made him too bold. It was a heady thing, knowing how easily he could move.

He had told himself he wouldn't use the rings, but that had been during battle—when he'd been tempted to try to make a name for himself. This was different. This was protecting Egwene. He could allow an exception for this.

The moment she hit the count of twenty, Egwene moved into the darkness. She wasn't as good at sneaking as Nynaeve and Perrin were, but she was from the Two Rivers. Every child in Emond's Field learned how to move in the woods without startling game.

She turned her attention to the path before her, testing with her toes—she'd removed her shoes—to avoid dried leaves or weeds. Moving this way was second nature to her; that left her mind free, unfortunately.

One of the Forsaken led the Sharans. She could only guess from his words that their entire nation followed him. This was as bad as the Seanchan. Worse. The Seanchan captured and used Aes Sedai, but they didn't slaughter the common people with such recklessness.

Egwene *had* to survive to escape. She needed to bring this information to the White Tower. The Aes Sedai would have to face Demandred. Light send that enough of their number had escaped the battle earlier to do so.

Why had Demandred sent for Rand? Everyone knew where to find the Dragon Reborn.

Egwene reached the mess tent, then crept around it. Guards chatted in the near distance. That Sharan accent was oddly monotone, as if the people had no emotions at all. It was as if . . . the music was gone from their speech. Music that Egwene hadn't realized was normally there.

The ones speaking were men, so she probably didn't need to worry that they would sense her ability to channel. Still,

Demandred had done it with Leane; perhaps he had a *ter'angreal* for the purpose. Such things existed.

She gave the men a wide berth anyway and continued on into the darkness of what had once been her camp. She moved past fallen tents, the scent of smoldering fires still lingering in the air, and crossed a path that she had taken most evenings while collecting troop reports. It was disturbing, how quickly one could go from being in a position of power to slinking through camp like a rat. Being suddenly unable to channel changed so many things.

My authority is not drawn from my power to channel, she told herself. *My strength is in control, understanding, and care. I will escape this camp, and I will continue the fight.*

She repeated those words, fighting off a creeping sense of powerlessness—the feeling of despair at so many dead, the tingling between her shoulder blades, as if someone were watching her in the darkness. Light, poor Leane.

Something hit the bare earth near her. It was followed by two more pebbles dropping to the ground. Gawyn apparently didn't trust in just one. She moved quickly to the remnants of a nearby tent, half-burned, the other half of the canvas hanging from the poles.

She crouched down. At that moment she realized a half-burned body was lying on the ground mere inches from her. He was Shienaran, she saw in a flash of lightning from the rumbling clouds above, though he wore the symbol of the White Tower on his shirt. He lay with one eye up toward the sky, silent, the other side of his head burned down to the skull.

A light appeared from the direction she'd been heading. She waited, tense, as two Sharan guards approached, bearing a lantern. They didn't speak. As they turned to walk southward along their route, she could see that their armor had symbols etched across the back that mimicked the tattoos she'd seen on men earlier. These marks were quite extravagant, and so—by her best guess—the men were actually of low rank.

The system disturbed her. You could always add to a person's tattoo, but she knew of no way to remove one. Having the tattoos grow more intricate the lower one was in society implied something: people could fall from grace, but they could not rise once fallen—or born—to a lowly position.

She sensed the channeler behind her mere moments before a shield slammed between Egwene and the Source.

Egwene reacted immediately. She didn't give terror time to gain purchase; she grabbed her belt knife and spun toward the woman she could sense approaching from behind. Egwene lunged, but a weave of Air snatched her arm and held it tightly; another one filled her mouth, gagging her.

Egwene thrashed, but other weaves grabbed her and hauled her into the air. The knife dropped from her twitching fingers.

A globe of light appeared nearby, a soft blue aura, much dimmer than that of a lantern. It had been created by a woman with dark skin and very refined features. Delicate. A small nose, a slender frame. She stood up from her crouch, and Egwene found her to be quite tall, nearly as tall as a man.

"You are a dangerous little rabbit," the woman said, her thick, toneless accent making her difficult to understand. She emphasized words in the wrong places, and pronounced many sounds in a just-off way. She had the tattoos on her face, like delicate branches, reaching from the back of her neck forward onto her cheeks. She also wore one of those dresses shaped like a cow's bell, black, with strands of white tied a handspan below the neck.

The woman touched her arm, where Egwene's knife had nearly taken her. "Yes," the woman said, "very dangerous. Few of the Ayyad would reach for a dagger so quickly, rather than for the Source. You have been trained well."

Egwene struggled in her bonds. It was no use. They were tight. Her heart began racing, but she was better than that. Panic would not save her. She forced herself to be calm.

No, she thought. *No, panic won't save me . . . but it* may *alert Gawyn.* She could sense that he was worried, out there somewhere in the darkness. With effort, she allowed her terror to rise. She let go of all of her careful Aes Sedai training. It was not nearly as easy as she had expected.

"You move quietly, little rabbit," the Sharan woman said, inspecting Egwene. "I would never have been able to follow you if I hadn't already known you were moving in this direction." She walked around Egwene, looking curious. "You watched the Wyld's little show all the way through, did you? Brave. Or stupid."

Egwene shut her eyes and focused on her terror. Her sheer panic. She had to bring Gawyn to her. She reached within, and opened the tight little nugget of emotion she'd packed there. Her fear at being captured again by the Seanchan.

She could feel it. The *a'dam* on her neck. The name. Tuli. A name for a pet.

Egwene had been younger then, but no more powerless than she was now. It would happen again. She would be nothing. She would have her very self stripped away. She would rather be dead. Oh, *Light*! Why couldn't she have died?

She'd sworn she'd never be captured like this again. She began to breathe quickly, now unable to control her terror.

"Now, now," the Sharan said. She seemed amused, though her tone was so flat, Egwene couldn't completely tell. "It won't be that bad now, will it? I have to decide. Which will gain me more? Turning you over to him, or keeping you for myself? Hmmm . . ."

Strong channeling came suddenly from the far side of the camp, where Demandred had gone. The Sharan glanced that way, but didn't seem alarmed.

Egwene could feel Gawyn approaching. He was very worried. Her message had served its purpose, but he wasn't coming quickly enough, and he was farther away than she'd expected. What was wrong? Now that she'd let her worry out of its hidden place, it overwhelmed her, beating against her, a series of blows.

"Your man . . ." the Sharan said. "You have one of them. What are they called, again? Odd, that you should rely on the protection of a *man*, but you never reach your potential in this land, I am told. He will be taken. I've sent for him."

As Egwene had feared. Light! She'd led Gawyn to this. She'd led the army to disaster. Egwene squeezed her eyes shut. She'd led the White Tower to its destruction.

Her parents would be slaughtered. The Two Rivers would burn.

She should have been stronger.

She should have been smarter.

No.

She had not been broken by the Seanchan. She would not be broken by this. Egwene opened her eyes and met the gaze of the

Sharan in the soft blue light. Egwene wrestled her emotions to stillness, and felt the Aes Sedai calm envelop her.

"You ... are an odd one," the Sharan whispered, still held by Egwene's eyes. So transfixed was she that the woman didn't notice when the shadow moved up behind her. A shadow that could not have been Gawyn, for he was still distant.

Something smashed into the woman's head from behind. She crumpled, slumping to the ground. The globe winked out instantly, and Egwene was free. She dropped to a crouch, fingers finding her knife.

A figure moved up to her. Egwene raised her knife and prepared herself to embrace the Source. She would draw attention if she had to. She would *not* be taken again.

But who was this?

"Hush," the figure said.

Egwene recognized the voice. "*Leilwin?*"

"Others noticed this woman channeling," Leilwin said. "They will come to see what she was doing. We must move!"

"You saved me," Egwene whispered. "You *rescued* me."

"I take my oaths seriously," Leilwin said. Then, so softly that Egwene could barely hear it, she added, "Maybe too seriously. Such horrible omens this night ... "

They moved quickly through the camp for a few moments, until Egwene sensed Gawyn approaching. She couldn't make him out in the darkness. Finally, she whispered softly, "Gawyn?"

Suddenly, he was there, right next to her. "Egwene? Who did you find?"

Leilwin stiffened, then hissed softly through her teeth. Something seemed to have upset her greatly. Perhaps she was angry at having someone sneak up on her. If that was the case, Egwene shared the emotion. She'd been taking pride in her abilities, and then she'd been blindsided not only by a channeler, but now by Gawyn! Why should a boy raised in the city be able to move so well without her spotting him?

"I didn't find anyone," Egwene whispered. "Leilwin found me ... and she pulled me out of a fire."

"Leilwin?" Gawyn said, peering through the darkness. Egwene could feel his surprise, and his suspicion.

"We must keep moving," Leilwin said.

"I will not argue with that," Gawyn replied. "We're almost out. We'll want to go a little to the north, though. I left some bodies just to the right."

"Bodies?" Leilwin asked.

"Half a dozen or so Sharans jumped me," Gawyn said.

Half a dozen? Egwene thought. He made it sound as if it were nothing.

This was not the place for discussion. She joined the other two, heading out of the camp, Leilwin leading them in a specific direction. Each noise or shout from the camp made Egwene wince, worried that one of the bodies had been found. In fact, she nearly jumped all the way to the storm clouds above when someone spoke from the darkness.

"Do that be you?"

"It is us, Bayle," Leilwin said softly.

"My aged grandmother!" Bayle Domon exclaimed softly, joining them. "You *found* her? Woman, you do amaze me again." He hesitated. "I do wish you'd have let me come with you."

"My husband," Leilwin whispered, "you are as brave and stout a man as any woman could wish on her crew. But you move with all of the stillness of a bear charging through a river."

He grunted, but joined them as they left the edge of the camp, quietly and carefully. About ten minutes away, Egwene finally trusted herself to embrace the Source. Glorying in it, she made a gateway for them and Skimmed to the White Tower.

Aviendha ran with the rest of the Aiel through gateways. They surged, like floodwaters, into the valley of Thakan'dar. Two waves, rushing down from opposite sides of the valley.

Aviendha did not carry a spear; that was not her place. Instead, she *was* a spear.

She was joined by two men in black coats, five Wise Ones, the woman Alivia and ten of Rand's sworn Aes Sedai with Warders. None of them save Alivia had responded well to having Aviendha placed above them. The Asha'man did not like having to answer to any woman, the Wise Ones didn't like being ordered by Rand at all, and the Aes Sedai still thought of Aiel channelers as inferior. They all obeyed the order anyway.

Rand had whispered to her in a quiet moment to watch them all for Darkfriends. Fear did not make him speak those words, but his sense of realism. Shadows could creep anywhere.

There were Trollocs here in the valley and some Myrddraal, but they had not anticipated this attack. The Aiel took advantage of their disarray and commenced a slaughter. Aviendha led her group of channelers toward the forge, that massive gray-roofed building. The Shadow-forgers turned from their inexorable movement, showing just a hint of confusion.

Aviendha wove Fire at one, removing its head from its shoulders. The body turned to stone, then started to crumble.

That seemed a signal to the other channelers, and Shadow-forgers through the valley began to explode. They were said to be terrible warriors when provoked, with skin that turned aside swords. That might just be rumor, as few Aiel had ever actually danced the spears with a Shadow-forger.

Aviendha didn't particularly want to discover the truth. She let her team end the first group of Shadow-forgers, and tried not to think too hard about the death and destruction these things had caused during their unnatural lives.

The Shadowspawn tried to mount a defense, some of the Myrddraal screaming and whipping at their Trollocs to charge and break the Aiel attack that came at them across a broad front. It would have been easier to stop a river with a handful of twigs. The Aiel didn't slow, and those Shadowspawn who tried to resist were slain in their tracks, often falling to multiple spears or arrows.

Most of the Trollocs broke and ran, fleeing before the thunder of Aiel yells. Aviendha and her channelers reached the forges and the nearby pens of dirty, lifeless-eyed captives who had been awaiting death.

"Quickly!" Aviendha said to the Warders who accompanied her. The men broke open pens as Aviendha and the others attacked the last of the Shadow-forgers. As they died—falling to stone and dust—they dropped half-finished Thakan'dar blades to the rocks.

Aviendha looked upward to the right. A long serpentine path led up toward the cavern maw in the side of the mountain that loomed above. The hole there was *dark*. It seemed a trap that tempted light to enter, then never released it.

Aviendha wove Fire and Spirit, then released the weave into the air. A moment later, a gateway opened at the head of the path up to Shayol Ghul. Four figures stepped through. A woman in blue, small of stature but not of will. An aging man, white-haired and shrouded in a multihued cloak. A woman in yellow, her dark hair cut short, adorned with an assortment of gemstones set in gold.

And a tall man, hair the color of living coals. He wore his coat of red and gold, but under it a simple Two Rivers shirt. What he had become and what he had been, wrapped together in one. He carried two swords, like a Shienaran. One looked as if it were glass; he wore it upon his back. The other was the sword of the Treekiller, King Laman, tied at his waist. He carried that because of her. Fool man.

Aviendha raised her hand to him, and he raised his in return. That would be their only farewell if he failed in his task or she died during hers. With a last look, she turned away from him and toward her duty.

Two of her Aes Sedai had linked and created a gateway so that the Warders could usher the captives to safety. Many needed to be prodded into motion. They stumbled forward, eyes nearly as dead as those of the Shadow-forgers.

"Check inside the forge, too," Aviendha said, motioning to a few of the Warders. They charged in, Aes Sedai following. Weaves of the One Power shook the building as they found more Shadow-forgers, and the two Asha'man quickly went in as well.

Aviendha scanned the valley. The battle had become uglier; there were more Shadowspawn at the corridor leading out of the valley. These had been given more time to prepare and form up. Ituralde led his forces in behind the Aiel, securing the sections of the valley already taken.

Patience, Aviendha thought to herself. Her job would not be to join that battle ahead, but to guard Rand's back as he ascended and entered the Pit of Doom.

She worried about one thing. Couldn't the Forsaken just Travel directly into the cavern itself? Rand didn't seem worried about that, but he was also very distracted by what he had to do. Perhaps she should join him and . . .

She frowned, looking up. What was that shadow?

High above, the sun shone in a turbulent sky. Some storm clouds, in patches, some deep black, others brilliant white. It wasn't a cloud that had suddenly obscured the sun, however, but something solid and black sliding into place.

Aviendha felt a chill and found herself trembling as the light slipped away. Darkness, true darkness, fell.

Soldiers across the field looked up in awe, and even fear. The light went out. The end of the world had come.

Channeling came suddenly from the other end of the wide valley. Aviendha spun, shaking off her awe. The ground nearby was littered with torn garments, dropped weapons and corpses. All of the fighting was at the mouth of the valley, distant from her, where the Aiel were trying to push the Shadowspawn back into the pass.

Though Aviendha couldn't see much through the darkness, she could tell soldiers were staring at the sky. Even the Trollocs looked awestruck. But then the solid blackness began to move in the sky, revealing first the edge of the sun, and then the sun itself. Light! The end was not upon them.

The battle at the mouth of the valley resumed, but it was obviously difficult. Making the Trollocs retreat through such narrow confines was like trying to shove a horse through a small crack in a wall. Impossible, unless you started doing some carving.

"There!" Aviendha said, pointing toward the side of the valley, behind the Aiel lines. "I sense channeling by a woman."

"Light, but she's powerful," Nesune breathed.

"Circle!" Aviendha yelled. "Now!"

The others linked, feeding Aviendha control of the circle. Power filled her, unimaginable power. It was as if she drew in a breath, but just kept being able to take in more air, filling, expanding, crackling with energy. She was a thunderstorm, a vast sea of the One Power.

She thrust her hands forward, letting loose a raw weave, only half-formed. This was almost too much power for her to shape. Air and Fire spurted from her hands, a column of it as wide as a man with arms outstretched. The fire flared as a thick, hot near-liquid. Not balefire—she was smarter than that—but dangerous nonetheless. The air contained the fire in a concentrated mass of destruction.

The column streaked across the battlefield, melting the stone beneath and starting corpses aflame. A huge swath of fog vanished with a hiss, and the ground shook as the column plowed into the side of the valley wall where the enemy channeler—Aviendha could only assume it was one of the Forsaken, from her strength—had been attacking the back ranks of Aiel.

Aviendha released the weave, her skin slick with sweat. A smoldering black column of smoke rose from the valley wall. Molten rock trickled down the slope. She grew still, waiting, alert. The One Power inside of her actually started to *strain*, as if trying to escape her. Was that because some of the energy she used came from men? Never before had the One Power seemed to want to destroy her.

She had only a brief warning: a frantic moment of channeling from the other side of the valley, followed by an enormous rush of wind.

Aviendha sliced that wind down the center with an invisible weave the size of a great forest tree. She followed it with another blast of fire, this time more controlled. No, she didn't dare use balefire. Rand had warned her. That could widen the Bore, break the framework of reality in a place where that membrane was already thin.

Her enemy didn't have the same restriction. The woman's next attack came as a white-hot bar, narrowly missing Aviendha— drilling through the air a finger's width from her head—before hitting the wall of the forge behind. The balefire sliced a wide swath of stone and brick from the wall, and the building collapsed with a crash.

Good riddance, Aviendha thought, throwing herself to the ground. "Spread out!" she ordered the others. "Don't give her good targets!" She channeled, stirring up air to create a tempest of dust and debris in front of them. Then she used a weave to mask the fact that she was holding to the One Power and hide her from her enemy. She scuttled in a low crouch behind some nearby cover: a heap of slag and broken bits of iron, waiting to be smelted.

Balefire struck again, hitting the stony ground where she'd been before. It punctured stone as easily as a spear went through a melon. Aviendha's companions had all taken cover, and they continued to feed her their strength. Such *power*. It was distracting.

She judged the source of the attacks. "Be ready to follow," she said to the others, then made a gateway to the point where the weave had begun. "Come through after me, but take cover immediately!"

She leaped through, skirts swishing, the One Power held like thunder somehow contained. She landed on a slope overlooking the battlefield. Below, Maidens and men fought Trollocs; it looked as if the Aiel were holding back a vast black flood.

Aviendha didn't spare time for more than a quick glance. She dug into the ground with a primal weave of Earth and ripped up a horse-sized chunk of rock, popping it into the air. The beam that came for her a second later struck the chunk of rock.

Balefire was a dangerous spear to wield. Sometimes it cut, but if it hit a distinct object—a person, for example—it caused the entire thing to flash and vanish. The balefire burned Aviendha's chunk from existence in a flash, dropping motes of glowing dust that soon vanished. Behind her, the men and women in her circle dashed through her gateway and took cover.

Aviendha barely had time to notice that nearby, cracks had appeared in the rock. Cracks that seemed to look down into darkness. As the bar of light faded in Aviendha's vision, she released a burning column of fire. This time, she met flesh, burning away a coppery-skinned, slender woman in a red dress. Two other women nearby cursed, scrambling away. Aviendha launched a second attack at the others.

One of the two—the strongest—made a weave with such skill and speed that Aviendha barely caught sight of it. The weave went up in front of her column of fire, and the result was an explosion of blistering steam. Aviendha's fire was extinguished, and she gasped, temporarily blinded.

Battle instincts took over. Obscured by the cloud of steam, she dropped to her knees, then rolled to the side while grabbing a handful of rocks and tossing them away from her to create a distraction.

It worked. As she blinked tears from her eyes, a white-hot bar struck toward the sound of the rocks. Those dark cracks spread further.

Aviendha blew the steam away with a weave of Air while still blinking tears. She could see well enough to distinguish two black shapes crouching nearby on the rocks. One turned toward her, gasped—seeing the attack weaves that Aviendha was making—then *vanished*.

There was no gateway. The person just seemed to fold up on herself, and Aviendha sensed no channeling. She did feel something else, a faint ... *something*. A tremble to the air that wasn't entirely physical.

"No!" the second woman said. Just a blur to Aviendha's tear-streaked eyes. "Don't—"

Aviendha's vision cleared just enough to make out the woman's features—a long face and dark hair—as her weave struck the woman. The woman's limbs ripped from her body. A smoldering arm spun in the air, creating a swirl of black smoke before hitting nearby.

Aviendha coughed, then released the circle. "Healing!" she said, struggling to her feet.

Bera Harkin reached her first, and a Healing weave set Aviendha trembling. She panted, and her reddened skin—her singed eyes—were repaired. She nodded in thanks to Bera, whom she could now see clearly.

Ahead of her, Sarene—an Aes Sedai with a teardrop face and numerous dark braids—stepped up to the corpses Aviendha had made, her Warder Vitalien close by her side. She shook her head. "Duhara and Falion. Dreadlords now."

"There's a difference between Dreadlords and Black Ajah?" Amys asked.

"Of course," Sarene said with a calm tone.

Nearby, the others still held the One Power, expecting another attack. Aviendha didn't think there would be one. She had heard that gasp of surprise, sensed the panic in the way the final woman—the strongest of the three—had fled. Perhaps she hadn't anticipated facing such powerful resistance so quickly.

Sarene kicked at an arm that had been Falion's. "Better to have taken them alive for questioning. I am certain we could have learned the identity of that third woman. Did anyone recognize her?"

Members of the group shook their heads. "She was not anyone on the list of Black Ajah who escaped," Sarene said, taking the arm of her Warder. "She has a distinctive face—so bulbous, and lacking any qualities of charm. I am certain I would remember her."

"She was powerful," Aviendha said. "Very powerful." Aviendha would have guessed her as one of the Forsaken. But that certainly hadn't been Moghedien, and it didn't match the description of Graendal.

"We'll split into three circles," Aviendha said. "Bera will lead one of them, Amys and I the others. Yes, we *can* make circles larger than thirteen now, but it seems a waste. I don't need that much power to kill. One of our groups will attack the Trollocs below. The other two will avoid channeling, and hide nearby watching. That way, we can goad the enemy channeler into assuming we're still in one large circle, and the other two can strike at her from the sides when she comes to attack."

Amys smiled. She recognized this as a basic Maiden raiding tactic. She didn't seem particularly put out to be following Aviendha's orders, now that annoyance at Rand's presumption had faded. In fact, if anything, she and the other four Wise Ones looked proud.

As Aviendha's team obeyed, she sensed more channeling on the battlefield. Cadsuane and those who followed her liked to consider themselves outside Rand's orders. They fought while another group of Aes Sedai and Asha'man held open gateways to usher through the Domani and Tairen armies.

Too many people channeling all about. It was going to grow difficult to pinpoint an attack by one of the Forsaken.

"We need to set up Traveling grounds," Aviendha said. "And keep strict control over who is going to channel and where. That way, we'll be able to tell in an instant when we sense channeling if something is wrong." She raised her hand to her head. "This is going to be very difficult to organize."

Nearby, Amys' smile widened. *You are in command now, Aviendha*, that smile seemed to say. *And leadership's headaches are yours to endure.*

Rand al'Thor, the Dragon Reborn, turned away from Aviendha and left her and Ituralde to their battle. He had a different one to join.

At last, the time had come.

He approached the base of the mountain of Shayol Ghul. Above, a black hole burrowed into the mountain face, the only way to reach the Pit of Doom. Moiraine joined him, pulling close her rippling shawl, its blue fringe catching in the wind. "Remember. This is not the Bore, this is not the Dark One's prison. This is merely the place where his touch is strongest upon the world. He has control here."

"He touches the entire world now, to one extent or another," Rand said.

"And so his touch here will be stronger."

Rand nodded, setting his hand upon the dagger he wore at his belt. "No channeling until we strike at the Dark One directly. If possible, I would avoid a fight like the one we had at the cleansing. What comes will require all of my strength."

Nynaeve nodded. She wore her *angreal* and *ter'angreal* jewelry over a gown of yellow, one far more beautiful than she would ever have allowed herself during their days in the Two Rivers. She looked strange to him without her braid, her hair now barely to her shoulders. She seemed somehow older. That shouldn't be. The braid was a symbol of age and maturity in the Two Rivers. Why should Nynaeve look older without it?

Thom stepped up beside Rand, squinting up at the hole in the rock. "I suspect I'm not going in with you."

Moiraine looked at him, pursing her lips.

"Someone will need to guard the entry into the cave, my wife," Thom said. "That ledge up there right beside the opening has an excellent view of the battlefield. I can watch the battle below, maybe compose a good ballad or two."

Rand smiled at the spark of humor in Thom's eyes. They stood at the edge of time itself, and still Thom Merrilin found a smile.

Above them, dark clouds spun, the peak of Shayol Ghul their axis. Darkness assaulted the sun until it was nearly gone, entirely covered, in total oblivion.

Rand's forces stopped, staring in terror at the sky, and even the Trollocs paused, growling and hooting. But as the sun slowly emerged from its captivity, the fierce battle resumed in the valley below. It announced his intentions, but the dagger would shield him from the Dark One's eyes. The Light willing, the Shadow's leaders would focus on the battle and assume Rand would wait for its outcome before striking.

"Now?" Nynaeve asked, looking up the narrow, stony pathway to the cavern.

Rand nodded and led the way forward. A wind rose, whipping at the four as they climbed the pathway. He had chosen his clothing deliberately. His red coat, embroidered with long-thorned briars on the sleeves and golden herons on the collar, was a twin to one of those Moiraine had arranged for him to receive in Fal Dara. The white shirt, laced across the front, was of Two Rivers make. *Callandor* on his back, the sword of Laman at his hip. It had been a long time since he'd chosen to wear that, but it felt appropriate.

The winds buffeted him, threatening to throw him from the heights. He pushed forward anyway, climbing the steep hill, gritting his teeth against the pain in his side. Time seemed to have less meaning here, and he felt as if he'd been walking for days when he reached the flat area before the cavern. He turned, resting one hand against the rock of the open maw, and looked out over the valley.

His forces in the valley seemed so fragile, so insignificant. Would they be able to hold it long enough?

"Rand . . ." Nynaeve said, taking his arm. "Perhaps you should rest."

He looked down, following her eyes to his side. His wound, the old wound, had broken open again. He felt blood inside his boot. It had run down his side, down his leg, and when he moved his foot, he left a bloody footprint behind.

Blood on the rocks . . .

Nynaeve raised a hand to her mouth.

"It has to happen, Nynaeve," Rand said. "You cannot stop it. The prophecy does not say anything about me living through this. I've always found that odd, haven't you? Why would it speak of the blood, but not what comes after?" He shook his head, then unsheathed *Callandor* from his back. "Moiraine, Nynaeve, will you lend me your strength and join me in a circle?"

"Do you wish one of us to lead," Moiraine said hesitantly, "so you can use that safely?"

"I'm not planning to be safe," Rand said. "A circle, please."

The two women exchanged a look. So long as he led the circle, another could strike and seize control of him. Neither liked the request, obviously. He wasn't certain if he should be pleased that the two of them had started to get along—perhaps, instead, he should worry about them teaming up against him.

That seemed like a thought from simpler days. Easier days. He smiled wryly, but knew that the smile did not reach his eyes. Moiraine and Nynaeve fed him their strength, and he accepted it. Thom kissed Moiraine, and then the three of them turned to regard the opening before them. It led back down, toward the base of the mountain, and the fiery pit that was the closest thing this world knew to the Dark One's dwelling.

Shadows from a returned sun dimmed the cavern mouth around him. Wind tugged at him, his foot warm with his own blood. *I will not walk out of this pit alive*, he thought.

He no longer cared. Survival was not his goal. It had not been for some time.

He did want to do this right. He *had* to do this right. Was it the right time? Had he planned well enough?

IT IS TIME. LET THE TASK BE UNDERTAKEN.

The voice spoke with the inevitability of an earthquake, the words vibrating through him. More than sound in the air, far more, the words spoke as if from one soul to another. Moiraine gasped, eyes opening wide.

Rand was not surprised. He had heard this voice once before, and he realized that he had been expecting it. Hoping for it, at least.

"Thank you," Rand whispered, then stepped forward into the Dark One's realm, leaving footprints of blood behind.

CHAPTER
24

To Ignore the Omens

Fortuona, Empress of the Seanchan Empire, studied her husband as he gave orders to their forces. They were arrayed outside the palace in Ebou Dar, and she herself sat upon an elaborate mobile throne, outfitted with poles at the bottom so she could be carried by a dozen soldiers.

The throne lent her grandeur, but also gave an illusion of immobility. An assassin would assume that she could not move quickly while wearing her formal silks, her gown draping down in front and tumbling toward the ground. They would be surprised, then, that she could break free of the outer garments at the flick of a wrist.

"He has changed, Greatest One," Beslan said to her. "And yet he hasn't. I don't know what to make of him any longer."

"He is what the Wheel has sent us," Fortuona replied. "Have you considered what you will do?"

Beslan kept eyes forward. He was impetuous, often governed by his emotions, but no more so than the other Altarans. They were a passionate people, and were making a fine addition to the Empire now that they were properly tamed.

"I will do as has been suggested," Beslan said, face flushed.

"Wise," Fortuona said.

"May the throne stand forever," Beslan said. "And may your breath continue as long, Greatest One." He bowed, withdrawing to do as he should. Fortuona could march to war, but these were Beslan's lands to govern. He so wanted to be part of the battle, but now he understood that he was needed here.

Selucia watched him go, nodding in approval. *That one is becoming a strong asset as he learns proper restraint*, she signed.

Fortuona said nothing. Selucia's motions carried an implication, one that Fortuona would have missed save for their long association. Beslan *was* learning. Other men, however ...

Mat started cursing up a storm nearby, gathered with the Seanchan commanders. She could not hear exactly what had set him off. What had she done, in yoking herself to him?

I have followed the omens, she thought.

She caught him glancing toward her before he returned to his raving. He *would* have to be taught restraint, but teaching him ... it would be difficult. Far more difficult than teaching Beslan had been. At least Selucia did not speak her condemnations out loud. The woman was now Fortuona's Truthspeaker, though Fortuona could sense that Selucia was finding the position grating. She would prefer to remain only Fortuona's Voice. Perhaps the omens would show Fortuona someone else fitting as a Truthspeaker.

Are we really going to do as he says? Selucia signed.

This world is chaos, Fortuona signed back. Not a straight answer. She did not want to give straight answers at the moment. Selucia would puzzle out the meaning.

The Seanchan commonly said "may she live forever" in regard to the Empress. To some, it was a platitude or a mere ritual of allegiance. Fortuona had always seen much more to it. That phrase encapsulated the strength of the Empire. An Empress had to be crafty, strong, and skilled if she was to survive. Only the fittest deserved to sit on the Crystal Throne. If one of her siblings, or a member of the High Blood like Galgan, managed to kill her, then her death served the Empire—for she had obviously been too weak to lead it.

May she live forever. May she be strong enough to live forever. May she be strong enough to lead us to victory. She *would* bring order to this world. That was her goal.

Matrim stalked past on the army's gathering grounds, passing ten paces before Fortuona's throne. He wore an Imperial high general's uniform, although not well. He kept snagging the paltron-cloths on things. A high general's regalia was meant to give the bearer authority, to enhance his grace as cloth rippled in response to his careful movements. On Matrim, it was like wrapping a racehorse in silk and expecting him to run. He had a kind of grace, but it was not the grace of court.

Lesser commanders trailed after him. Matrim baffled the Blood. That was good, as it kept them off balance. But he also represented disorder, with his random ways and constant stabs at authority. Fortuona represented order, and she had married *chaos himself*. What had she been thinking?

"But what of the Sea Folk, Highness?" General Yulan said, stopping beside Matrim in front of Fortuona.

"Stop worrying about the bloody Sea Folk," Matrim snapped. "If you say the words 'Sea Folk' one more time, I'll hang you by your toenails from one of those *raken* you fly about on and send you off to Shara."

Yulan seemed perplexed. "Highness, I . . ."

He trailed off as Mat yelled, "Savara, we're leading with pikes, not cavalry, you goat-loving idiot! I don't *care* if the cavalry thinks it can do a better job. Cavalry always thinks that! What are you, a bloody Tairen High Lady? Well, I'll name you an honorary one if you keep this up!"

Matrim stormed off toward Savara, who sat her horse with arms folded, displeasure on her dark face. Yulan, left behind, looked completely bewildered. "How does one hang a person by their toenails?" Yulan asked, softly enough that Fortuona barely heard. "I do not think that is possible. The nails would break off." He walked away, shaking his head.

To the side, Selucia signed, *Beware. Galgan approaches.*

Fortuona steeled herself as Captain-General Galgan rode up. He wore black armor rather than a uniform like Mat's, and he wore it well. Commanding, almost towering, he was her greatest rival and her strongest resource. Any man in his position would be a rival, of course. That was the way of things—the proper way of things.

Matrim would never be a rival. She still did not know how to think of that. A piece of her—small, but not without strength—

thought she should have him put away for that very reason. Was not the Prince of the Ravens a check upon the Empress, to keep her strong by providing a constant threat? *Sa'rabat shaiqen nai batain pyast.* A woman was most resourceful with a knife at her throat. A proverb uttered by Varuota, her great-great-great-grandmother.

She would hate to put Matrim away. She couldn't until she had a child by him, anyway—it would be ignoring the omens to do otherwise.

Such a strange man he was. Each time she thought she could anticipate him, she was proved wrong.

"Greatest One," Galgan said, "we are nearly ready."

"The Prince of the Ravens is dissatisfied with the delays," she said. "He fears we are joining the battle too late."

"If the Prince of the Ravens has any *real* understanding of armies and battlefields," Galgan said, his tone indicating that he didn't believe such a thing was possible, "he will realize that moving a force of this size requires no small effort."

Up until Matrim's arrival, Galgan had been the highest-ranking member of the Blood in these lands other than Fortuona herself. He would dislike being superseded suddenly. As of yet, Galgan had command of their armies—and Fortuona intended to let him continue to lead. Earlier today, Galgan had asked Mat how he would gather their forces, and Mat had taken it as a suggestion to do just that. The Prince of the Ravens strode about giving orders, but he did *not* command. Not fully; Galgan could stop him with a word.

He did not. Obviously, he wished to see how Mat handled command. Galgan watched Mat, eyes narrowed. He did not fully know how the Prince of the Ravens fit into the command structure. Fortuona had yet to make a decision on that.

Nearby, a burst of wind carried away some dust. It revealed the small skull of a rodent, peeking from the earth. Another omen. Her life had been cluttered with them lately.

This was an omen of danger, of course. It was as if she strolled through deep grasses, passing between stalking *lopar* and among holes dug to catch the unwary. The Dragon Reborn had knelt before the Crystal Throne, and the omen of peach blossoms—the most powerful omen she knew—had accompanied him.

Troops marched past, officers shouting orders in time to the steps. The *raken* calls seemed timed to the beats of the falling feet. This was what she would be leaving for an unknown war in lands she barely knew. Her lands here would be virtually undefended, a foreigner of newly minted loyalty in command.

Great change. Her decisions could end her rule and, indeed, the Empire itself. Matrim did not understand that.

Summon my consort, Fortuona signed, tapping the armrest of her throne.

Selucia Voiced the order to a messenger. After a short time, Mat rode up on his horse. He had refused the gift of a new one, with good reason. He had a better eye for horseflesh than the Imperial stablemaster herself. Still. Pips. What a silly name.

Fortuona stood up. Immediately, those nearby bowed. Galgan dismounted and went down on his knees. Everyone else prostrated themselves to the ground. The Empress standing to proclaim meant an act of the Crystal Throne.

"Blood and ashes," Matrim said. "More bowing? Have you folks nothing better to do? I could think of a few dozen things, if you can't."

To the side, she saw Galgan smile. He thought he knew what she was going to do. He was wrong.

"I name you Knotai, for you are a bringer of destruction to the Empire's enemies. Let your new name only be spoken from now into eternity, Knotai. I proclaim that Knotai, Prince of the Ravens, is to be given the rank of Rodholder in our armies. Let it be published as my will."

Rodholder. It meant that should Galgan fall, Mat would have command. Galgan was no longer smiling. He would have to keep watch over his shoulder lest Mat overcome him and take control.

Fortuona sat down.

"Knotai?" Knotai said.

She glared at him. *Keep your tongue, for once*, she thought at him. *Please.*

"I kind of like it," Knotai said, turning his horse and trotting away.

Galgan regained his saddle. "He will need to learn to kneel," the general muttered, then kicked his horse forward.

It was an ever-so-small offense, deliberate and calculating.

Galgan had not addressed the words to Fortuona directly, instead acting as if they were just a comment to himself. He sidestepped calling her Greatest One.

It was enough to make Selucia growl softly and wiggle her fingers in a question.

No, Fortuona signed, *we need him.*

Once again, Knotai did not seem to realize what she had done, and the risk inherent in it. Galgan would have to consult with him on their battle plans; the Rodholder could not be left out of meetings, as he had to be ready to take control at any moment. Galgan would have to listen to his advice and incorporate it.

She bet upon her prince in this, hoping that he could manifest again the unexpected genius in battle that had so impressed Furyk Karede.

This is bold, Selucia said. *But what if he fails?*

We will not fail, Fortuona replied, *for this is the Last Battle.*

The Pattern had placed Knotai before her, had shoved her into his arms. The Dragon Reborn had seen and spoken truth about her—for all the illusion of order, her rule was like a heavy rock balanced on its smallest point. She was stretched thin, reigning over lands unaccustomed to discipline. She needed to take great risks to bring order to chaos.

She hoped that Selucia would see it that way and not publicly denounce her. Fortuona really would need to find a new Voice or appoint someone else as Truthspeaker. Having one person fill both roles was drawing criticism in court. It—

Knotai suddenly came riding back, holding to his hat. "Tuon!"

Why is it so hard for him to understand names? Selucia asked with a wiggle of her fingers. Fortuona could almost read the sigh in those motions.

"Knotai?" Fortuona asked. "You may approach."

"Bloody good," Knotai said, "since I'm already here. Tuon, we need to move *now*. The scouts just came back. Egwene's army is in trouble."

Yulan rode up just behind Knotai, then dismounted and bowed himself full to the ground.

"Rise," Fortuona said. "Is this true?"

"The army of the *marath'damane* has suffered a grave defeat," Yulan said. "The returning Fists of Heaven describe it in detail.

This Amyrlin's armies are scattered, in turmoil, and retreating at speed."

Galgan had stopped nearby to receive a messenger, no doubt being given a similar report. The general looked at her.

"We should move in to support Egwene's retreat," Knotai said. "I don't know what a Rodholder is, but from how everyone's reacting, I think it means I have control of the armies."

"No," Fortuona said. "You are third. Behind me. Behind Galgan."

"Then you can order a move right now," Knotai said. "We need to go! Egwene is getting stomped."

"How many *marath'damane* are there?" Fortuona asked.

"We have been watching this army," Yulan said. "There are hundreds. The entirety of the White Tower that remains. They are exhausted, being driven forth by a new force, one we do not recognize."

"Tuon . . ." Mat warned.

Great change. So this was the meaning of the Dragon's omen. Fortuona could swoop in and all of those *damane* would be hers. Hundreds upon hundreds. With that force, she could crush the resistance to her rule back in Seanchan.

It was the Last Battle. The world hung upon her decisions. Was it truly better to support these *marath'damane* in their desperate fight here, or should she use the chance to retreat to Seanchan, secure her rule there, then defeat the Trollocs and the Shadow with the might of the Empire?

"You gave your word," Knotai said softly.

"I signed a treaty," she said. "Any treaty can be broken, particularly by the Empress."

"Some empresses might be able to do that," Knotai said. "But not you. Right? Light, Tuon. You gave him your *word*."

Order in one hand—something known, something she could measure—chaos in the other. Chaos in the form of a one-eyed man who knew Artur Hawkwing's face.

Had she not just told Selucia she would bet upon him?

"The Empress cannot be constrained by words on a paper," Fortuona said. "However . . . in this case, the reason I signed the treaty remains, and is real. We will protect this world in its darkest days, and we will destroy the Shadow at its root. General

Galgan, you shall move our forces to protect these *marath'damane*, as we will require their aid in fighting the Shadow."

Knotai relaxed. "Good. Yulan, Galgan, let's get planning! And send for that woman, Tylee. She seems like the only bloody general around here with her head on her shoulders. And . . . "

He went on talking, riding off, giving orders that he really should have allowed Galgan to give. Galgan studied her from horseback, his face unreadable. He'd consider this a grave mistake, but she . . . she had the omens on her side.

Those dreadful black clouds had been Lan's companion for far too long. He had grown weary indeed of seeing them each day, expanding toward infinity in all directions, rumbling with thunder like growls from the stomach of a hungry beast.

"The clouds seem lower today," Andere said, from his horse beside Mandarb. "The lightning is touching down. It doesn't do that every day."

Lan nodded. Andere was right; it did look bad. That didn't change a thing. Agelmar had chosen the place for their battle alongside the river roaring on their western flank, using it to protect that side. Nearby hills provided archer positions, and it was atop one of these that Lan and Andere waited.

Ahead, the Trollocs gathered for an assault. They would come soon. Closer by, Agelmar had placed heavy cavalry in the valleys for flanking attacks once the Trollocs charged, light cavalry behind the hills to help the heavy cavalry withdraw when the time came. Agelmar kept grumbling about not having any pikes, though it was the lack of foot that had facilitated their successful retreat.

For all the good it has done, Lan thought gloomily as he studied the near-endless sea of Trollocs. His men had picked their battles carefully, killing tens of thousands while losing only thousands, leaving Shienar burned and unable to sustain the Trolloc advance. None of it seemed to have mattered.

They were losing this fight. Yes, they had delayed the Trollocs, but not well enough—and not long enough. They would soon be trapped and destroyed, with no aid coming from Elayne's army, which was pressed just as badly.

The sky darkened. Lan looked up sharply. Those clouds were still there, but they grew much more ominous. The land was cast into deep shadow.

"Blast it," Andere said, looking up. "Has the Dark One somehow swallowed the sun? We'll have to carry lanterns to fight, even though it's the middle of the day."

Lan placed his hand to his breastplate; beneath the armor, Nynaeve's letter rested next to his heart. *Light! May her fight go better than my own.* Earlier today, she and Rand had entered the Pit of Doom itself.

Across the battlefield, the tired channelers, pulling their eyes from the terrifyingly dark sky, sent up lights. It wasn't much to see by, but it would have to do. But then the darkness receded, and daylight returned, clouded as had become usual.

"Gather the High Guard of Malkier," Lan said. That was what his protectors were calling themselves. It was an old Malkieri term for the King's battlefield guard. Lan wasn't certain what to make of the fact that Prince Kaisel, who was from Kandor, considered himself one.

Many of Lan's Malkieri had very little true Malkier blood—they came to him as an honor more than anything else. The Prince was another matter. Lan had asked him and his companions if they should be swearing to a foreign king, no matter how friendly.

The only reply he'd received was, "Malkier represents the Borderlands in this war, Dai Shan."

Lightning flashed nearby; the clap of thunder beat against Lan like a physical thing. Mandarb barely stirred. The animal was growing accustomed to such strikes. The High Guard gathered, and Andere took up Lan's banner, affixing it in the socket on his saddle so that he could carry it, but still swing a sword.

Their orders arrived from Agelmar. Lan and his men would be in the very thick of the attack. Once the Trollocs charged, the heavy cavalry would hit the flanks to break up their momentum. Lan and his men would hit the creatures face-on.

As Lan preferred it. Agelmar knew better than to try to coddle him. Lan and his troops would hold the center ground before the hills, forcing the Trollocs to fight in such a way that the archers could lob volley after volley into their back ranks. Harrying forces would be held mostly in reserve, to prevent the enemy sweeping around their right flank; the river was on their left, a natural deterrent to the Trollocs. A good plan, if any plan could be considered a good one in the face of such overwhelming odds. Still, Agelmar was not making mistakes that Lan could see. He complained of troubled dreams lately, but considering the war they fought, Lan would have been more worried if the man *hadn't* dreamed of death and battle.

The Trollocs started to move.

"Forward!" Lan called as the trumpets sounded in the air, accompanied by thunder from above.

A short distance from the walls of Cairhien, Elayne rode Moonshadow along the front lines; the army had formed up according to Bashere's battle plans, but she was worried.

They had done it. A fast march upriver along the road to arrive at Cairhien in front of the Trolloc army. Elayne had positioned their force on the far northern side of Cairhien to face the Trolloc army coming in from that direction. She had also left some of the dragons and a company of bowmen downriver to deter the Trollocs trying to cross the river there; they would withdraw quickly northward when it became impossible to prevent the enemy from crossing.

Beat the army ahead; then face the one behind. It was their only chance. The Kinswomen were exhausted; Elayne had required many gateways to move her men. Their fatigue meant Elayne would have no channelers in this fight. The women would be hard-pressed to make small gateways to Mayene to deliver the wounded for Healing.

Elayne's army was slightly larger than that of the Shadowspawn, but her men were exhausted. Amid the anxiety of a coming battle, some slumped in their lines, pikes tipping forward. Those who stood firm had reddened eyes nonetheless. They still had Aludra's dragons. That would have to be enough.

Elayne hadn't slept the night before. She'd spent the time searching for inspiring words, seeking something she could say this day that would have meaning. What did you say when all was coming to an end?

She halted Moonshadow at the front of the line of Andoran soldiers. Her words would be relayed, using weaves, to the entire army. Elayne was surprised to see that some of the Aiel were drawing close to listen. She wouldn't have thought they'd care about the words of a wetlander queen.

She opened her mouth to speak, and the sun went out.

Elayne froze, looking upward with shock. The clouds had parted above them—they often did when she was near, one way the bond with Rand manifested—and so she'd been expecting an open sky and light for this battle.

The sun still shone up there, but occluded. Something solid and dark rolled in front of it.

All across her army, men looked up, raising fingers as they were swallowed by darkness. Light! It was hard to keep from trembling.

She heard cries through the army. Lamentations, worries, cries of despair. Elayne gathered her confidence and kicked her horse forward.

"This is the place," she announced, enhancing her voice with the One Power to project across the field, "where I promise you we will win. This is where I tell you that days will continue, that the land will recover. This is the time when I promise you that the light will return, that hope will survive, that we will continue to live."

She paused. Behind the army, people lined the top of Cairhien's city walls: children, women, and the elderly who were armed with kitchen knives and pots to throw down, should the Trollocs destroy the army and come for the city. There had barely been time to contact them; a skeleton force of soldiers guarded the city. Now, their distant figures huddled down as darkness ate the sky.

Those walls offered a false safety; they meant little when the enemy had Dreadlords. She needed to defeat the Trolloc army quickly, not hide and allow them to be reinforced by the larger force to the south.

"I am supposed to reassure you," Elayne shouted to the men. "But I cannot! I will *not* tell you that the land will survive, that the Light will prevail. Doing so would remove responsibility.

"This is our duty! Our blood that will be spilled this day. We have come here to fight. If we do not, then the land will die! The Light will fall to the Shadow. This is not a day for empty promises. Our blood! Our blood is the fire within us. Today, our blood must drive us to defeat the Shadow."

She turned her horse. The men had looked away from the darkness above, toward her. She wove a light, high in the sky above her, drawing their attention.

"Our blood is our passion," she shouted. "Too much of what I hear from my armies is about resistance. We cannot merely resist! We must show them our anger, our fury, at what they have done. We must not resist. Today, we must *destroy*.

"Our blood is our land. This place is ours, and we claim it! For our fathers and mothers, for our children.

"Our blood is our life. We have come to give it. Across the world, other armies are pushed back. We will not retreat. Our task is to spend our blood, to die *advancing*. We will not remain still, no!

"If we are to have the Light again, we must *make* it ours! We must reclaim it and cast out the Shadow! He seeks to make you despair, to win this battle before it begins. We will not give him that satisfaction! We will destroy this army before us, then destroy the one behind. And from there, we bring our blood—our life, our fire, our passion—to the others who fight. From there it spreads to victory and the Light!"

She honestly didn't know what kind of response to expect from a battlefield speech. She'd read all of the great ones, particularly those given by queens of Andor. When younger, she'd imagined the soldiers clapping and shouting—the response given to a gleeman at a rowdy tavern.

Instead, the men raised weapons to her. Drawn swords, pikes lifted, then thumped back against the ground. The Aiel did give some whoops, but the Andorans looked at her with solemn eyes. She had not inspired them to excitement, but to determination. That seemed the more honest emotion. They ignored the darkness in the sky and turned eyes on the goal.

Birgitte walked up beside her horse. "That was quite good, Elayne. When did you change it?"

Elayne blushed, thinking of the carefully prepared speech she'd memorized last night while repeating it half a dozen times to

Birgitte. It had been a work of beauty, with allusions to the sayings of queens through the ages.

She'd forgotten every word of it once that darkness had come. This one had spurted out instead.

"Come on," Elayne said, looking over her shoulder. The Trolloc army was arriving opposite hers. "I need to move into position."

"Into position?" Birgitte asked. "You mean that you need to go back to the command tent."

"I'm not going there," Elayne said, turning Moonshadow.

"Blood and bloody ashes, you aren't! I—"

"Birgitte," Elayne snapped. "I am in command, and you are my soldier. You *will* obey."

Birgitte recoiled as if slapped.

"Bashere has the command tent," Elayne said. "I'm one of the few channelers of any strength this army has, and I'll be drawn and quartered before I let myself sit out the fight. I'm easily worth a thousand soldiers on this battlefield."

"The babes—"

"Even if Min hadn't had that viewing, I'd still insist on fighting. You think the babes of these soldiers aren't at risk? Many of them line the walls of that city! If we fail here, they will be *slaughtered*. No, I will *not* keep myself out of danger, and no, I will *not* sit back and wait. If you think it's your duty as my Warder to stop me, then I will bloody sever this bond right here and now and send you to someone else! I'm not going to spend the Last Battle lounging on a chaise and drinking goat's milk!"

Birgitte fell silent, and Elayne could feel her shock through the bond. "Light," the woman finally said. "I won't stop you. But will you at least agree to back away for the initial arrow volleys? You can do more good helping the lines where they're weakened."

She allowed Birgitte and her guards to lead the way back to a hillside near Aludra's dragons. Talmanes, Aludra and their crews waited with more anxiety and eagerness than the regular troops. They were tired, too, but they'd also seen little use during the forest battles and the retreat. Today was their chance to shine.

Bashere's battle plan was as complex as any that Elayne had been a part of. The bulk of the army positioned itself almost a mile north of the city, beyond the Foregate ruins outside the city walls. The army's lines ran east from the Alguenya, across a

hillside that sloped down across an approach road to the Jangai
Gates on the flats, all the way to the ruins of the Illuminators'
chapter house.

Ranks of foot soldiers—mostly Andorans and Cairhienin, but
some Ghealdanin and Whitecloaks as well—bowed out like a
half-moon across the front of Elayne's forces. Six squadrons of
dragons rolled up atop the hill behind the foot.

The Trollocs would not reach the city without defeating this
army. Estean had the Band's cavalry on one flank while the
Mayener Winged Guards covered the other. The rest of the cavalry was held in reserve.

Elayne waited with patience, watching the Trolloc army prepare. Her biggest worry was that they'd just sit there, waiting for
their fellow Trollocs to arrive from the south and attack Elayne
simultaneously. Fortunately, that didn't happen—they had apparently been commanded to take the city, and they were planning
to do it.

Bashere's scout reports indicated that the second army was a
little over a day's march away, and could arrive late on the morrow
if they marched hard. Elayne had until then to defeat this northern force.

Come on, Elayne thought. *Move.*

The Trollocs finally began to surge forward. Bashere and Elayne
were counting on them to employ their usual tactic: Overwhelming
numbers and sheer force. Indeed, today, the Trollocs crashed forward in a large mass. Their goal would be to overwhelm the
defenders, shattering their lines.

Her troops stood firm, knowing what was coming next. The
dragons began to bellow, each like innumerable hammers falling
at exactly the same moment. Elayne was now a good hundred
paces from them, and still she had the urge to cover her ears.
Rolling clouds of white smoke began to fill the sky above the
dragons as they fired.

The first few shots fell short, but Aludra and her men used the
shots to adjust range. After that, the eggs fell among Trollocs,
ripping through their ranks, tossing them into the air. Thousands
of body parts fell to the crimson-splattered ground. For the first
time, Elayne was frightened of the weapons.

Light, Birgitte has been right all along, Elayne thought,

imagining what it would be like to charge a fortified position equipped with dragons. Normally, in war, at least a man could depend on one thing: that his skill would be placed against that of his foe. Sword against sword. Trollocs were bad enough. What would it be like for men to have to face this kind of power?

We'll make sure it doesn't happen, she told herself. Rand had been right to force that peace upon them.

The dragoners had trained well, and their reloading speeds were impressive. Each set off three volleys before the Trollocs hit the front lines. Elayne hadn't watched the exchange of arrows— she'd been too focused on the dragons—but she did see that some of her lines were struck with black-fletched arrows, and men were down and bleeding.

The Trollocs crashed into her front ranks of crossbowmen and pikemen, who were already fading back to make way for hal- berdiers. Nobody used swords and maces against Trollocs, at least not while on foot, if they could help it.

"Let's go," Elayne said, moving Moonshadow forward.

Birgitte followed; Elayne could sense the woman's reluctant resignation. They moved down off the hill through some reserve units and entered the battle.

Rodel Ituralde had almost forgotten what it was like to have ad- equate resources at his command.

It had been some time since he had commanded legions of men and full banners of archers. For once, his men weren't half-starved, and Healers, fletchers and good smiths stood ready to repair his troops and equipment nightly. What a wonder it was to be able to ask for something—no matter how unusual—and have it located and brought to him, often within the hour!

He was still going to lose. He faced a numberless host of foes, Dreadlords by the dozen and even some of the Forsaken. He'd brought his force into this dead-end valley, seizing the jewel of the Dark One's lands—his very footstool, the black mountain. And now the sun itself had gone out, though the Aes Sedai said that would pass.

Ituralde puffed on his pipe as he rode his horse along the ridge that edged the valley to the north. Yes, he was going to lose. But with these resources, he'd do it with *style*.

He followed along the ridge, reaching a point above the pass into Thakan'dar. The valley, deep in the heart of the Blasted Lands, ran east to west, with Shayol Ghul at the western side and the pass on the east. One could reach this vantage only after hours of very hard climbing—or one quick step through a gateway. Handy, that. It was perfect for surveying his defenses.

The pass into Shayol Ghul was like a large slot canyon, the top completely inaccessible from the eastern side except by gateway. With a gateway, he could reach the top and look down into the canyon, which was perhaps wide enough to march fifty men down shoulder-to-shoulder. A perfect bottleneck. And he could position archers up top here, to fire down on those coming through the pass.

The sun finally burned out from behind the blackness above, like a drop of molten steel. So the Aes Sedai had been right. Still, those swirling black thunderheads spun back, as if to consume all the sky.

Since Shayol Ghul lay in the Blasted Lands, the air was chill enough that Ituralde wore a woolen winter cloak and his breath was white in front of him. Fog hung over the valley, thinner than it had been when the forges worked.

He left the canyon mouth and moved back to a group of people that had come with him. Windfinders and other high-ranking Sea Folk stood in long coats that they had—hawkishly, of course—traded for before coming north. Colorful clothing peeked out beneath. It, and the many ornaments on their faces, seemed a strange contrast to the dull brown coats.

Ituralde was Domani. He'd had more than a share of dealings with the Sea Folk; if they proved half as tenacious in battle as they were in negotiations, he was happy indeed to have them with him. They had insisted on coming up here to the ridge so they could survey the valley below and the pass into it.

The woman at their front was the Mistress of the Ships herself, Zaida din Parede Blackwing. A short woman, she had dark skin, and gray strands wove through her short black hair. "The Windfinders send word to you, Rodel Ituralde," she said. "The attack has begun."

"The attack?"

"The Bringer of Gales," Zaida said, looking toward the sky, where the dark clouds rumbled and churned. "The Father of Storms. He would destroy you with the force of his ire."

"Your people can handle it, right?"

"The Windfinders already confront him with the power of the Bowl of the Winds," Zaida said. "If it were not so, he would have destroyed us all with tempests already."

She still watched the sky, as did many of her companions. There were only about a hundred Sea Folk with him, not counting the Windfinders. Most of the rest worked with the supply teams, relaying arrows, food and other equipment to the four battlefronts. They seemed particularly interested in the steamwagons, though Ituralde couldn't fathom why. The devices couldn't match a good team of horses. "Confronting the Dark One himself, gust for gust," Zaida said. "We will sing of this day." She looked back to Ituralde. "You must protect the Coramoor," she said sternly, as if scolding him.

"I'll do my part," Ituralde said, continuing on his way. "Just do yours."

"This bargain was sealed long ago, Rodel Ituralde," she called after him.

He nodded, continuing back along the ridge. Men stationed at watchposts saluted as he passed. Well, the ones that weren't Aiel. He had a lot of the Aiel up here, where they could use their bows. He'd put the bulk of his Tairens down below, where those pikes and polearms would be of maximum use. They would hold the path into Shayol Ghul.

A distant Aiel horn blew; a signal from one of the scouts. The Trollocs had entered the pass. It was time.

He galloped back along the ridge toward the valley, trailed by other commanders and King Alsalam. When they reached the point where he had set up his primary watchpost, a vantage from which he could see miles back into the pass, Ituralde took out his looking glass.

Shadows moved there. In moments, he could make out the Trolloc hordes charging forward, whipped to a frenzy. For a moment, he was back in Maradon, watching his men—good men—fall one by one. Overrun at the hill fortifications, pulled down in the streets of the city. The explosion on the wall.

Desperate act after desperate act. Killing as many as he could, like a screaming man clubbing wolves as they tore him to pieces, hoping to take at least one with him into the final darkness.

His hand, holding the looking glass, quivered. He forced himself back to the present and his current defenses. It felt as if he'd been fighting losing battles his entire life. That took a toll. At night, he would hear Trollocs coming. Snorting, sniffing the air, hooves on the cobbles. Flashbacks from Maradon.

"Steady, old friend," King Alsalam said, riding up beside him. The King had a soothing voice. He'd always been able to calm others. Ituralde was certain the merchants of Arad Doman had chosen him for that reason. Tensions could run high when trade and war were concerned—the Domani looked at the two as much the same beast. But Alsalam . . . he could calm a frantic merchant who had just lost her entire fleet at sea.

Ituralde nodded. The defense of this valley. He had to keep his mind on the defense of this valley. He'd hold, not let the Trollocs boil out of the pass into Thakan'dar. Burn him, he'd hold for *months* if the Dragon Reborn needed it. Every other fight—every battle man had fought, and was fighting—would be meaningless if Ituralde lost here. It was time to pull out every trick he knew, every last-ditch strategy. Here, one moment of delay could earn Rand al'Thor the time he needed.

"Remind the men to remain steady below," Ituralde said, surveying through his glass. "Prepare the logs."

Attendants relayed the orders, which went through gateway to the squads involved. That terrible force of Trollocs continued onward, clutching enormous swords, twisted polearms, or catchpoles to pull down riders. They clamored through the pass, lightning streaking between clouds above.

First the logs, Ituralde thought.

As the Trollocs reached the middle of the pass, the Aiel on both sides untied piles of oiled tree trunks—there were so many dead trees in forests now that Ituralde had had no trouble fetching them through gateways—and lit them aflame.

Hundreds of burning logs rolled down the sides of the pass, crashing into the Trollocs. The oiled logs set flesh alight. The beasts yelled, howled and screeched depending on the orifice they'd been given. Ituralde raised his looking glass and watched them, feeling an intense satisfaction.

That was new. In the past, he'd never been satisfied to see his foes die. Oh, he'd been pleased when a plan worked. And, in truth, the point of fighting was to see the other fellow dead and your men alive—but there had been no *joy* in that. The longer you fought, the more you saw the enemy as being like yourself. The banners changed, but the rank and file were much the same. They wanted to win, but usually they were more interested in a good meal, a blanket to sleep on and boots without holes in them.

This was different. Ituralde wanted to see those beasts dead. He *lusted* after it. Without them, he'd never have been forced to suffer the nightmare at Maradon. Without them, his hand wouldn't shake when the horns of war sounded. They'd ruined him.

He'd ruin them in return.

The Trollocs pushed through the jumble of logs with great difficulty. Many of them had been set alight, and the Myrddraal had to whip them to keep them moving. Many seemed to want to eat the flesh of the fallen. The rank scent of it made them hungry. Cooked bodies. To them, it was like the aroma of fresh bread.

The Fades succeeded in driving them on, but the Trollocs soon reached the next of Ituralde's defenses. Figuring out what to do had been a trick. You couldn't plant spikes or dig ditches in that solid rock, not without running your channelers to exhaustion. He could have made piles of rock or earth, but Trollocs were big, and mounds that would slow men were less effective against them. Beyond that, moving so much earth and stone would have meant diverting workers from building real fortifications in the valley. He'd learned early that in a defensive war, you wanted the fortifications to grow progressively better. You lasted longer that way, as you kept the enemy from gaining momentum.

In the end, the solution had been simple. Brambles.

He'd remembered huge thickets of them, dry and dead, back in Arad Doman. Ituralde's father had been a farmer, and had always complained about the thorn thickets. Well, if there was one thing mankind was not lacking, it was dead plants. Another was manpower. Thousands had flocked to the Dragon's call, and many of these Dragonsworn had little battle experience.

He'd still set them fighting when that time came. For now, however, he'd sent them to cut down enormous thornbushes. They'd placed these across the pass, lashed together, in masses twenty feet thick and eight feet tall. The thorn bales had been relatively easy to place—far lighter than stones or dirt—yet amassed as they were, the Trollocs couldn't move them simply by pushing. The first ranks ran up against them and tried, but were rewarded with five-inch thorns biting into them. The creatures in the rear pressed forward, causing the front ranks to turn in anger and rise up against those behind.

This left the bulk of the Trolloc forces frozen in the pass, at his mercy.

He didn't have much mercy for Shadowspawn.

Ituralde gave the signal, and the Asha'man with him—Awlsten, one of those who had served under him at Maradon—shot a bright burst of red light into the sky. Along the sides above the pass, more Aiel came out and began to roll boulders and more burning logs down upon the trapped Shadowspawn. Arrows and stones followed—anything they could shoot, throw or drop onto those below.

Most of these attacks from Ituralde's men happened farther down the pass, in the middle of the bulk of Trollocs. That caused half to pull back and shy away, while the others pushed forward to get away—shoving their allies in front into the brambles.

Some Trollocs carried shields, and tried to protect themselves against the deadly hail. Wherever they formed together defensively and began to make a shield wall above themselves, Ituralde's channelers struck, tearing them apart.

He couldn't spare many channelers for the work—most were back in the valley, making gateways to move supplies and watching for enemy channelers. They'd already had a second run-in with Dreadlords. Aviendha and Cadsuane Sedai had those operations in hand.

Some of the Trollocs shot arrows at the defenders above, but casualties mounted as the Shadowspawn at the front tried to hack their way through the abatis of thorns. It was slow going.

Ituralde watched, cold inside and out, as the Myrddraal whipped the Trollocs into a stampede. That shoved the ones working on the thorns forward, impaling them, trampling them.

Blood became a stream running back down toward the eastern end of the pass, making the Trollocs slip. They pushed the front five or six lines, breaking the thorns on the bodies of the beasts there.

It still took them the better part of an hour to break through. They left thousands dead as they surged forward, then found a *second* abatis, thicker and higher than the first. Ituralde had placed seven at intervals in the pass. The second was the largest, and it had the desired effect. Seeing it made the Trollocs at the front pull up short. Then they turned and broke backward.

Mass confusion resulted. Trollocs behind cried and shouted, pressing forward. Those in front snarled and howled as they tried to cut through the brambles. Some stood dazed. All the while arrows and rocks and burning logs continued to fall.

"Beautiful," Alsalam whispered.

Ituralde found that his arm was no longer quivering. He lowered his looking glass. "Let's go."

"The battle is not through!" the King protested.

"It is," Ituralde said, turning away. "For now."

True to his word, the entire Trolloc army broke behind him—he could hear it happening—and fled eastward down the pass, away from the valley.

One day held, Ituralde thought. They would be back on the morrow, and then they would be ready. More shields, better weapons at the front for cutting thorns.

They'd still bleed. Bleed dearly.

He'd make certain of it.

CHAPTER 25

Quick Fragments

Siuan let out a long, relieved breath as the Amyrlin—with eyes as if on fire—strode through the gateway and into their camp with Doesine, Saerin and several other Sitters.

Bryne came through the gateway after them, hurrying up to Siuan. "What was decided?" she asked.

"We stand, for now," Bryne said. "Elayne's orders, and the Amyrlin agrees with them."

"We're outnumbered," Siuan said.

"And so is everyone else," he said, looking westward.

The Sharans had spent the last few days gathering their forces, setting up a mile or two away from Egwene's army, which was stationed with its back to the wide river that formed the border between Kandor and Arafel.

The Shadow hadn't committed to an all-out attack yet, instead sending an occasional raiding group through gateways as they waited for the slower Trolloc army to catch up. The Trollocs were here now, unfortunately. Egwene's force could have retreated again through gateways, but Siuan admitted to herself that would accomplish little. They had to face this force eventually.

Bryne had selected this place at the southeastern tip of Kandor because the terrain gave them an advantage, albeit a small one.

The river that ran north-south on the eastern border of Kandor was deep, but a ford lay less than a quarter-mile away from the hills that ran east to west along the southern border of Kandor. The Shadow's army would be making for the ford to enter Arafel. By stationing his forces at the ford and on the hills overlooking it, Bryne could engage the invading army from two directions. If pressed, he could withdraw across the ford to the Arafellin side, the water barrier putting the Trollocs at a disadvantage against them. It was a small benefit, but in battle, sometimes the small things made all the difference.

On the plains west of the river, the Shadow formed up the Sharan and Trolloc armies. Both moved across the field toward the beleaguered Aes Sedai and troops under Bryne's command.

Nearby, Egwene surveyed the camp. Light, it was a relief to know that the Amyrlin had survived. Siuan had predicted it, but still ... Light. It was good to see Egwene's face.

If, indeed, it was her face. This was the first time that the Amyrlin had returned to camp following her ordeal, but she had spent several quiet meetings with the Sitters in secret locations. Siuan had not yet had a chance to speak with Egwene in quiet.

"Egwene al'Vere," Siuan called after the Amyrlin. "Tell me where we first met!"

The others looked at Siuan, frowning at her temerity. Egwene, however, seemed to understand. "Fal Dara," she said. "You bound me with Air on our trip down the river from there, as part of a lesson in the Power I have never forgotten."

Siuan breathed a second, deeper sigh of relief. Nobody had been in that lesson on the ship but Egwene and Nynaeve. But Siuan had unfortunately told Sheriam, Mistress of Novices and Black Ajah, about it. Well, she still believed that this was in fact Egwene. Imitating a woman's features was easy, but prying out her memories was another story.

Siuan made certain to look into the woman's eyes. There had been talk, of what had happened at the Black Tower. Myrelle had spoken of it, of events shared by her new Warders. Something dark.

They said you could tell. Siuan would see the change in Egwene if it had happened to her, wouldn't she?

If we can't tell, Siuan thought, *then we're already doomed.* She would have to trust the Amyrlin as she had so many times before.

"Gather the Aes Sedai," Egwene said. "Commander Bryne, you have your orders. We hold at this river unless the losses become so absolutely unbearable that ... " She trailed off. "How long have *those* been there?"

Siuan looked up at the *raken* scouts passing overhead. "All morning. You have his letter."

"Bloody man," Egwene said. The Dragon Reborn's message, delivered by Min Farshaw, had been brief.

The Seanchan fight the Shadow.

He'd sent Min to them, for reasons the woman wouldn't quite state. Bryne had given her tasks immediately: She was working for the supply masters as a clerk.

"Do you trust the Dragon Reborn's word regarding the Seanchan, Mother?" Saerin asked.

"I don't know," Egwene said. "Form up our battle lines anyway, but keep an eye on those things up there, in case they attack."

As Rand entered the cavern, something changed in the air. The Dark One only now sensed his arrival, and was surprised by it. The dagger had done its job.

Rand led the way, Nynaeve at his left, Moiraine at his right. The cavern led downward, and climbing down it lost them all of the elevation they'd gained. The passage was familiar to him, from another's memory, from another Age.

It was as if the cavern were swallowing them, forcing them down toward the fires below. The cavern's ceiling, jagged with fanglike stalactites, seemed to lower as they walked. Inching down with each step. It didn't move, and the cavern didn't gradually narrow. It just *changed*, tall one moment, shorter the next.

The cavern was a set of jaws, slowly tightening on its prey. Rand's head brushed the tip of a stalactite, and Nynaeve crouched down, looking upward and cursing softly.

"No," Rand said, stopping. "I will not come to you on my knees, Shai'tan."

The cavern rumbled. The cavern's dark reaches seemed to press inward, pushing against Rand. He stood motionless. It was as if he were a stuck gear, and the rest of the machine strained to keep turning the hands on the clock. He held firm.

The rocks trembled, then retreated. Rand stepped forward, and released a breath as the pressure lessened. This thing he had begun could not be stopped now. Slowing strained both him and the Dark One; his adversary was caught up in this inevitability as much as he was. The Dark One didn't exist within the Pattern, but the Pattern still affected him.

Behind Rand, where he had stopped, lay a small pool of blood. *I will need to be quick about this*, he thought. *I can't bleed to death until the battle is finished.*

The ground trembled again.

"That's right," Rand whispered. "I'm coming for you. I am not a sheep being led to the slaughter, Shai'tan. Today, I am the hunter."

The trembling of the ground seemed almost like laughter. Horrible laughter. Rand ignored Moiraine's worried look as she walked beside him.

Down they went. An odd sensation came to mind. One of the women was in trouble. Was it Elayne? Aviendha? He could not tell. The warping of this place affected the bond. He was moving through time differently than they, and he lost his sense of where they were. He could only feel that one was in pain.

Rand growled, walking faster. If the Dark One had hurt them . . . Shouldn't it be growing lighter in here? They had to rely on the glow of *Callandor* as he pulled *saidin* through it. "Where are the fires?" Rand asked, voice echoing. "The molten stone at the bottom of the path?"

"The fires have been consumed, Lews Therin," a voice said from the shadows ahead.

Rand stopped, then stepped forward, *Callandor* thrust out to illuminate a figure on one knee at the edge of the light, head bowed, sword held before him, tip resting against the ground.

Beyond the figure was . . . nothing. A blackness.

"Rand," Moiraine said, hand on his arm. "The Dark One wells up against his bonds. Do not touch that blackness."

The figure stood and turned, Moridin's now-familiar face reflecting *Callandor*'s glow. Beside him on the ground lay a husk. Rand could explain it no other way. It was like the shell some insects leave behind when they grow, only it was in the shape of a man. A man with no eyes. One of the Myrddraal?

Moridin looked to the husk, following Rand's gaze. "A vessel my master needed no longer," Moridin said. *Saa* floated in the whites of his eyes, bouncing, shaking, moving with crazed vigor. "It gave birth to what is behind me."

"There is nothing behind you."

Moridin raised his sword before his face in a salute. "Exactly." Those eyes were nearly completely black.

Rand waved for Moiraine and Nynaeve to stay a few steps back as he approached. "You demand a duel? Here? Now? Elan, you know what I do is inevitable. Slowing me has no purpose."

"No purpose, Lews Therin?" Moridin laughed. "If I weaken you even slightly, will my master's task not be that much easier? No, I think I shall *indeed* stand in your way. And if I win, what then? Your victory is not assured. It never has been."

I win again, Lews Therin . . .

"You could step aside," Rand said, raising *Callandor*, the glow of its light shifting off Moridin's black steel sword. "If my victory is not assured, neither is your fall. Let me pass. For once, make the choice you know you should."

Moridin laughed. "Now? *Now* you beg me to return to the Light? I have been promised oblivion. Finally, nothing, a destruction of my entire being. An *end*. You will not steal that from me, Lews Therin! By my grave, you will not!"

Moridin came forward swinging.

Lan executed Cherry Petal Kisses the Pond—not an easy task from horseback, as it was not a form designed for the saddle. His sword slashed into the neck of a Trolloc, just an inch into the creature's skin. That was enough to make fetid blood blossom in a spray. The bull-faced creature dropped its catchpole, reaching up to hold its neck, and let out a gurgling half-scream, half-groan.

Lan danced Mandarb backward as a second Trolloc came for his side. He cut its arm off as he spun. The Trolloc stumbled from the blow, and Andere ran it through from behind.

Andere moved his horse up beside Mandarb; over the din of battle, Lan could hear his friend panting. How long had they been fighting here at the battle's front? Lan's arms felt like lead on his shoulders.

It hadn't been this bad during the Blood Snow.

"Lan!" Andere shouted. "They keep coming!"

Lan nodded, then moved Mandarb back again as a pair of Trollocs shoved their way through corpses to attack. These two had catchpoles as well. That wasn't uncommon for Trollocs; they realized that men on foot were far less dangerous to them than men on horseback. Still, it made Lan wonder if they were trying to capture him.

He and Andere let the Trollocs come through and attack, as two members of the High Guard rode in from the side to distract their attention. The Trollocs came for Lan, and he lurched forward, swinging and cutting in half the shaft of each of their catchpoles.

The beasts didn't stop, reaching brutish fingers to try to pull him down. Lan could smell their putrid breath as he rammed his sword into the throat of one. How slowly his muscles moved! Andere had better be in position.

Andere's horse came in with a sudden gallop, slamming its armored flank into the second Trolloc, knocking it to the side. It stumbled, and the two mounted guardsmen butchered it with long-handled axes.

Those men were both bloodied, as was Andere. As was Lan himself. He only vaguely remembered taking that thigh wound. He was growing *so* tired. He wasn't in any condition to fight.

"We pull back," he announced reluctantly. "Let someone else take the point for now." Lan and his men were leading the heavy cavalry at the tip of the fight, pressing against the Trollocs in a triangular formation to shear through and pushing them to the sides for the flanking attacks to crush.

The others nodded, and he could sense their relief as he pulled himself and his fifty-something High Guards back. They retreated, and a group of Shienarans moved in to fill the point. Lan cleaned his sword, then sheathed it. Lightning rumbled above. Yes, those clouds *did* seem lower today. Like a hand, slowly pressing down upon the men as they died.

Lightning bolts cracked the air nearby, one after another. Lan turned Mandarb sharply. There had been a lot of lightning today, but those had been too close together. He smelled smoke on the air.

"Dreadlords?" Andere asked.

Lan nodded, eyes searching for the attackers. All he could see was the lines of men fighting, the swarming mass of Trollocs driving forward in waves. He needed higher ground.

Lan gestured at one of the hills, and heeled Mandarb toward it. Members of the rear guard watched him pass, giving a raised hand and a "Dai Shan." Their armor was stained with blood. The reserves had been rotated to the front, then back again, during the day.

Mandarb plodded up the hill. Lan patted the horse, then dismounted and trudged beside the stallion. At the top, he stopped to survey the battle. Borderlander armies made spikelike indentations of silver and color in the Trolloc sea.

So *many*. The Dreadlords had come out on their large platform again, the mechanism pulled by dozens of Trollocs as it rolled across the field. They needed height to see where to direct their attacks. Lan set his jaw, watching a series of lightning bolts strike the Kandori, hurling bodies into the air and opening a gap in their lines.

Lan's own channelers struck back, hurling lightning and fire at the advancing Trollocs to keep them from pouring through the hole in the Borderlander line. That would work for only so long. He had far fewer Aes Sedai and Asha'man than the Shadow had Dreadlords.

"Light," said Prince Kaisel, riding up next to him. "Dai Shan, if they rip enough holes in our lines . . ."

"Reserves are coming. There," Andere said, pointing. He was still mounted, and Lan had to step forward to look around him to see what he was indicating. A group of Shienaran riders were making for the lines upon which the lightning bolts were falling.

"There too," Kaisel said, pointing to the east. A group of Arafellin were making for the same place. The two forces became entangled as they both rushed to close the gap at the same time.

Lightning began to strike down from the sky, raining on the Dreadlords' platform. Good. Narishma and Merise had been told to watch for the Dreadlords and try to kill them. Perhaps it would distract the enemy. Lan focused on something else.

Why had two groups of reserves been sent to plug that same hole? Either unit would have been large enough for the job; with so many, they had interfered with one another. A mistake?

He climbed into Mandarb's saddle, reluctant to make the horse work again so soon. He would check on this error.

Within the wolf dream, Perrin and Gaul stopped on a ridge over-looking a valley with a mountain at the end of it. Above the mountain, the black clouds spun in a terrible vortex that didn't quite touch the mountain's tip.

The winds ravaged the valley, and Perrin was forced to create a pocket of stillness around himself and Gaul, deflecting debris. Down below, they caught quick fragments of an enormous battle. Aiel, Trollocs and men in armor appeared in the wolf dream for moments as if out of twisting smoke and dust, swung weapons, disintegrated in midblow. Thousands of them.

Many wolves were here in the dream, all around. They waited for . . . for something. Something they could not explain to Perrin. They had a name for Rand, Shadowkiller. Perhaps they were here to witness what he would do.

"Perrin?" Gaul asked.

"He's here, finally," Perrin said softly. "He has entered the Pit of Doom."

Rand was going to need Perrin at some point during this fight. Unfortunately, Perrin couldn't just stand here; there was work to be done. Gaul and he had, with help from the wolves, found Graendal near Cairhien. She had spoken to some people in their dreams. Darkfriends among the armies, perhaps?

She was peeking at Bashere's dreams before that, Perrin thought. *Or so Lanfear claimed.* He didn't trust her for a moment.

Anyway, he'd found Graendal earlier today, and had been plan-ning to strike, when suddenly she had vanished. He knew how to track someone in the wolf dream when they *shifted*, and he had followed her here, to Thakan'dar.

Her scent vanished sharply in the middle of the valley below. She'd Traveled back into the real world. Perrin wasn't certain how much time had passed in the wolf dream; he and Gaul still had food, but it felt as if it had been days and days. Lanfear said that the closer Perrin came to Rand, the more time would distort. He could probably test that statement, at least.

He is here, Young Bull! The sending came, sudden and urgent, from a wolf named Sunrise, here in the valley. *Slayer comes among us! Hurry!*

Perrin growled, grabbed Gaul by the shoulder without a word and *shifted* them. They appeared on the rocky path leading to a gaping hole in the rock above, the passage down to the Pit of Doom itself.

A wolf lay nearby, arrow in its side, smelling of death. Others howled in the near distance. The horrible wind whipped at him; Perrin lowered his head and charged into it, Gaul at his side. *Inside, Young Bull*, a wolf sent. *Inside the mouth of darkness.*

Not daring to think about what he was doing, Perrin burst into a long, narrow chamber filled with jagged rocks projecting from the floor and ceiling. Ahead, something bright sent pulsing waves through the space. Perrin raised a hand against the light, vaguely catching sight of shapes at the end of the chamber.

Two men, locked in battle.

Two women, as if frozen.

And just a few feet from Perrin, Slayer, drawing his bow to his cheek.

Perrin roared, hammer in his hand, and *shifted* himself between Slayer and Rand. He slapped the arrow from the air with his hammer a split second after it was loosed. Slayer's eyes widened, and he vanished.

Perrin *shifted* to Gaul, grabbing the man by the arm, then *shifted* back to where Slayer had been and caught the scent of his location. "Be wary," Perrin said, then *shifted* them after the man.

They dropped into the middle of a group of people. They were *Aiel*, but instead of wearing normal *shoufa*, they had strange red veils.

The *shift* hadn't taken Perrin and Gaul far; this was a village of some sort, close enough for the peak of Shayol Ghul to be visible in the distance.

The red-veils attacked. Perrin wasn't particularly surprised to find Aiel on the side of the Shadow. There were Darkfriends among all peoples. But why identify themselves with the color of their veils?

Perrin swung his hammer in a wide circle, keeping a group of them at bay, then *shifted* behind them, crushing the head of one from behind. Gaul became a blur of spears and brown clothing, dodging around red-veils, stabbing, then vanishing—and then appearing and stabbing again. Yes, he'd learned quickly, more quickly than these red-veils apparently had, for they failed to keep up with him. Perrin smashed another one in the kneecap, then searched for Slayer.

There. He stood on a hillock above, watching. Perrin glanced at Gaul, who, between jumps, gave him a quick nod. There were eight red-veils left, but—

The earth underneath Gaul's feet began to heave, exploding upward as Gaul jumped. Perrin managed to protect his friend, creating a steel plate beneath him to deflect the blast, but it was a close thing. Gaul landed shakily, and Perrin was forced to *shift* to him and attack the red-veil coming at him from behind.

"Take care," Perrin yelled at Gaul. "At least one of these fellows can channel!"

Light. As if Aiel fighting for the Shadow weren't enough. Channeling Aiel. Channeling Aiel *men*. Light!

As Perrin swung at another, Slayer arrived, a sword in one hand and a long hunting knife in the other—the type a man would use to skin his prey.

Growling, Perrin threw himself into the fight, and the two began a strange dance. One attacking the other, who vanished to appear nearby before attacking also. They spun about like that, one *shifting*, then the other, each trying for an edge. Perrin just missed crushing Slayer with a blow, then nearly caught steel in his gut.

Gaul was proving very useful—Perrin would have had a horrible time trying to stand alone against both Slayer and the red-veils. Unfortunately, Gaul could do little but distract his foes, and was having a very difficult time managing that.

As a column of fire from one of the red-veils nearly took him, Perrin made his decision. He *shifted* over to Gaul—and almost took a spear through the shoulder. Perrin turned the spear to cloth, and it bent on his skin.

Gaul started, seeing Perrin, then opened his mouth. Perrin didn't give him a chance to speak. He grabbed his friend by the arm, then *shifted* them away. They vanished just as flames welled up around them.

They reappeared before the entrance to the Pit of Doom.

Perrin's cloak was smoldering. Gaul was bleeding from the thigh. When had that happened?

Are you there? Perrin sent out, urgent.

Dozens upon dozens of wolves replied. *We are here, Young Bull. Do you lead us, Young Bull? The Last Hunt!*

Watch for Moonhunter, Young Bull. She stalks you like a lion in the high grass.

I need you, Perrin sent to the wolves. *Slayer is here. Will you fight him, and the men with him, for me?*

It is the Last Hunt, one sent back as many others agreed to help him. They appeared on the slopes of Shayol Ghul. Perrin could smell their wariness; they did not like this place. It was not a place wolves came, not in the waking world, nor in the dream.

Slayer came for him. Either he realized Perrin would be guarding this place, or he intended to finish his attack on Rand. Either way, Perrin caught sight of him standing on the ridge up above, looking down into the valley—a dark figure with a bow and a black cloak whipping in the tempest's winds. Beneath him, that battle still raged in dust and shadow. Thousands upon thousands of people dying, killing, struggling in the real world, only phantoms reaching this place.

Perrin gripped his hammer. "Come try me," he whispered. "You'll find me a different foe this time."

Slayer raised his bow, then loosed. The arrow split, becoming four, then sixteen, then a hail of shafts shooting toward Perrin.

Perrin growled, then attacked the column of air that Slayer had created to stop the wind. It dissolved, and the raging gale caught the arrows, spinning them about.

Slayer appeared in front of Perrin, brandishing knife and sword. Perrin leaped at him as the red-veils appeared nearby. The wolves and Gaul dealt with them. This time, Perrin could focus on his enemy. He swung with a roar, slapping Slayer's weapon away, then aiming for his head.

Slayer danced back and created stone arms that burst from the ground—throwing chips and shards of rock—to seize Perrin. Perrin concentrated, and they burst, tumbling back to the ground. He caught the sharp scent of Slayer's surprise.

"You're here in the flesh," Slayer hissed.

Perrin jumped for him, *shifting* in midleap to reach the man more quickly. Slayer blocked with a shield that appeared on his arm. *Mah'alleinir* left a large dent in the front as it was deflected.

Slayer vanished and appeared five strides back, on the rim of the pathway leading up to the cavern. "I'm so very glad you came hunting me, wolf pup. I was forbidden from seeking you, but now you are here. I skinned the sire; now the pup."

Perrin launched himself at Slayer in a blurring leap, like those he used to bound from hilltop to hilltop. He crashed into the man, throwing them both off of the ledge in front of the opening to the Pit of Doom, sending them tumbling dozens of feet toward the ground.

Perrin's hammer was at his belt—he didn't remember putting it there—but he didn't want to hit this man with the hammer. He wanted to feel Slayer as he slammed a fist into the man's face. The punch connected as they fell, but Slayer's face was suddenly hard as stone.

In that moment, the fight became not one of flesh against flesh, but will against will. As they fell together, Perrin imagined Slayer's skin becoming soft, giving beneath his punch, the bones brittle and cracking. Slayer, in response, imagined his skin as stone.

The result was that Slayer's cheek became hard as rock, but Perrin cracked it anyway. They hit the ground, and rolled apart. When Slayer stood, his right cheek looked like that of a statue hit with a hammer, small cracks moving out over the skin.

Blood began to trickle through those cracks, and Slayer opened his eyes in shock. He raised a hand to his cheek, feeling the blood. The skin became flesh again, and stitches appeared, as if sewn by a master surgeon. One could not heal oneself in the wolf dream.

Slayer sneered at Perrin, then lunged. The two of them danced back and forth, surrounded by churning dust that formed the faces and bodies of people struggling for their lives in another place, another world. Perrin crashed through a pair of them, dust streaming from *Mah'alleinir* as he swung. Slayer skidded back, creating a wind to blow him out of the way, then struck forward too quickly.

Perrin became a wolf without a thought, Slayer's sword passing over his head. Young Bull leaped into Slayer, slamming him backward through an impression of two Aiel fighting one another. Those exploded into sand and dust. Others formed to the sides, then blew away.

The howling tempest was a roar in Young Bull's ears, and the dust ground into his skin and eyes. He rolled across Slayer, then lunged for his throat. *How sweet it will be to taste this two-legs' blood in my mouth.* Slayer *shifted* away.

Young Bull became Perrin, with hammer at the ready, crouching on the plain of fragmentary fighting, changing people. *Careful,* he thought to himself. *You are a wolf, but more a man.* With a start, he realized that some of those impressions weren't completely human. He saw a couple that were distinctly snake-like in appearance, though they faded quickly.

Does this place reflect other worlds? he wondered, not certain what else to make of the phantoms.

Slayer came at him again, teeth clenched. Perrin's hammer grew hot in his fingers, and his leg throbbed where he'd been hit and then Healed during his last fight with Slayer. He roared, letting Slayer's sword close—letting it graze him on the cheek—as he crashed his own weapon into the man's side.

Slayer vanished.

Perrin followed through with the swing, and, for a moment, assumed he'd beaten the man. But no, his hammer had barely connected before Slayer disappeared. The man had been ready, waiting to *shift.* Perrin felt blood moving through the hair of his beard toward his chin; that graze had cut a gash on his cheek much in the same place as he'd landed that blow on Slayer's face.

He sniffed at the air, turning about, trying to catch the scent of Slayer's location. Where had he gone? There was nothing.

Slayer hadn't *shifted* to another place in the wolf dream. He knew that Perrin could follow him. Instead, he must have jumped back into the waking world. Perrin howled, realizing he'd lost his prey. The wolf railed against this, a failed hunt, and it was a struggle for Perrin to bring himself back under control.

It was a scent that brought him back to it. Burning fur. It was accompanied by howls of pain.

Perrin *shifted* himself back to the top of the pathway. Wolves lay burned and dying amid the corpses of red-veils. Two of the men were still up, back to back, and incongruously, they'd lowered their veils. They had teeth filed to points, and were smiling, almost with madness, as they channeled. Burning wolf after wolf to char. Gaul had been forced to take shelter beside a rock, his clothing smoldering. He smelled of pain.

The two smiling channelers didn't seem to care that their companions were bleeding to death on the ground around them. Perrin walked toward them. One raised a hand and released a jet of fire. Perrin turned it to smoke, then parted that by walking directly into it, the gray-black smoke eddying against him, then streaming off.

The other Aiel man also channeled, trying to rip the earth up beneath Perrin. Perrin knew that earth would not break, that it would resist the weaves. So it did. Perrin could not see the weaves, but he knew that the earth—suddenly far more solid—refused to budge as ordered.

The first Aiel reached for his spear with a growl, but Perrin grabbed him by the neck.

He wanted so badly to crush this man's throat. He had lost Slayer *again*, and wolves were dead because of these two. He held himself back. Slayer . . . Slayer deserved worse than death for what he had done. He didn't know about these men, and he wasn't certain if killing them here would kill them forever, without rebirth.

It seemed to him that everyone, including creatures like these, should have another chance. The red-veil in his hand struggled, trying with weaves of Air to envelop Perrin.

"You are an idiot," Perrin said softly. Then he looked to the other one. "You too."

Both blinked, then looked at him with eyes that grew slack. One started drooling. Perrin shook his head. Slayer hadn't trained them at all. Even Gaul, after only a . . . how long had it been? Anyway, even Gaul knew not to be caught like that, in the grip of someone who could change the very capacity of one's mind.

Perrin had to keep thinking of them as idiots to maintain the transformation. He knelt, seeking among the wolves for the wounded he could help. He imagined bindings on the wounds of those who were hurt. They would heal quickly in this place. Wolves seemed to be able to do that. They had lost eight of their members, for whom Perrin howled. The others joined him, but there was no regret to their sendings. They had fought. That was what they had come to do.

After that, Perrin saw to the fallen red-veils. All were dead. Gaul limped up beside him, holding a burned arm. The wound was bad, but not immediately life-threatening.

"We need to take you out of here," Perrin said to him, "and get you some Healing. I'm not certain what time it is, but I think we should go to Merrilor and wait for the gateway out."

Gaul gave him a toothy grin. "I killed two of those myself, Perrin Aybara. One could channel. I think myself great with honor, then you slide in and take two *captive*." He shook his head. "Bain would laugh herself all the way back to the Three-fold Land if she saw this."

Perrin turned to his two captives. Killing them here seemed heartlessly cruel, but to release them meant fighting them again—perhaps losing more wolves, more friends.

"I do not suspect these keep to *ji'e'toh*," Gaul said. "Would you take a man who could channel as *gai'shain* anyway?" He shuddered visibly.

"Just kill them and be done with it," Lanfear said.

Perrin eyed her. He didn't jump as she spoke—he had grown somewhat accustomed to the way she popped in and out. He did find it annoying, however.

"If I kill them here, will that kill them forever?"

"No," she said. "It doesn't work that way for men."

Did he trust her? On this point, for some reason, he found that he did. Why would she lie? Still, killing unarmed men . . . they were barely more than babies here to him.

No, he thought, considering the dead wolves, *not babies. Far more dangerous than that.*

"Those two have been Turned," she said, folding her arms, nodding to the two channelers. "Many are born to their life these days, but those two have the filed teeth. They were taken and Turned."

Gaul muttered something. It sounded like an oath, but it also sounded reverent. It was in the Old Tongue, and Perrin didn't catch its meaning. After that, however, Gaul raised a spear. He smelled regretful. "You spat in his eye, and so he uses you, my brothers. Horrible . . ."

Turned, Perrin thought. Like those men at the Black Tower. He frowned, walking up and taking the head of one of the men in his hands. Could he *will* the man back to the Light? If he could be forced to be evil, could he be restored?

Perrin hit something vast as he pushed against the minds of these men. His will bounced free, like a twig used to try beating down an iron gate. Perrin stumbled back.

He looked at Gaul, and shook his head. "I can do nothing for them."

"I will do it," Gaul said. "They are brothers."

Perrin nodded, reluctant, as Gaul slit the throats of the two men. It was better this way. Still, it ripped Perrin up inside to see it. He hated what fighting did to people, what it did to him. The Perrin of months ago could never have stood and watched this. Light . . . if Gaul hadn't done it, he would have himself. He knew it.

"You can be such a child," Lanfear said, arms still folded beneath her breasts as she watched him. She sighed, then took him by the arm. A wave of icy Healing washed through him. The wound on his cheek closed.

Perrin took a deep breath, then nodded toward Gaul.

"I am not your errand woman, wolf pup," she said.

"You want to convince me that you're not a foe?" he asked. "That's a good place to start."

She sighed, then waved impatiently for Gaul to approach. He did so, limping, and she Healed him.

A distant rumbling shook the cavern behind them. She looked at it, and narrowed her eyes. "I cannot stay here," she said. Then she was gone.

"I do not know what to make of that one," Gaul said, rubbing his arm where the clothing was burned, but the skin healed. "I believe she is gaming with us, Perrin Aybara. I do not know which game."

Perrin grunted in agreement.

"This Slayer . . . he will return."

"I'm thinking of a way to do something about that," Perrin said, reaching to his waist where he'd tied the dreamspike to his belt with straps. He freed it. "Watch here," he told Gaul, then entered the cavern.

Perrin walked past those stones like teeth. It was hard to escape the feeling that he was crawling into the mouth of a Darkhound. The light at the bottom of the descent was blinding, but Perrin created a bubble around himself that was shaded, like glass that was only translucent. He could make out Rand and someone else striking at one another with swords at the lip of a deep pit.

No. It wasn't a pit. Perrin gaped. The entire *world* seemed to end here, the cavern opening into a vast nothingness. An eternal expanse, like the blackness of the Ways, only this one seemed to be *pulling* him into it. Him, and everything else. He'd grown accustomed to the storm raging outside, so he hadn't noticed the wind in the tunnel. Now that he paid attention, he could feel it streaming through the cavern into that hole.

Looking into that gap, he knew that he'd never understood blackness before, not really. *This* was blackness. *This* was nothingness. The absolute end of all. Other darkness was frightening because of what it might hide. This darkness was different; if this engulfed you, you would cease completely.

Perrin stumbled back, though the wind blowing down the tunnel wasn't strong. Just . . . steady, like a stream running into nowhere. Perrin gripped the dreamspike, then forced himself to turn away from Rand. Someone knelt on the floor nearby, her head bowed, braced as if against some great force coming from the nothingness. Moiraine? Yes, and that was Nynaeve kneeling to her right.

The veil between worlds was very thin here. If he could see Nynaeve and Moiraine, perhaps they could see or hear him.

He stepped up to Nynaeve. "Nynaeve? Can you hear me?"

She blinked, turning her head. Yes, she could hear him! But she could not see him, it seemed. She searched about, confused as she clung to the stone teeth of the floor as if for life itself.

"Nynaeve!" Perrin yelled.

"Perrin?" she whispered, looking about. "Where are you?"

"I'm going to do something, Nynaeve," he said. "I will make it impossible to create gateways into this place. If you want to Travel to or from this area, you'll need to create your gateway out in front of the cavern. All right?"

She nodded, still looking about for him. Apparently, though the real world reflected in the wolf dream, it didn't work the other way around. Perrin rammed the dreamspike into the ground, then activated it as Lanfear had shown him, creating the bubble of purple just around the cavern itself. He hurried back into the tunnel, emerging through a wall of purple glass to rejoin Gaul and the wolves.

"Light," Gaul said. "I was about to go search for you. Why did it take so long?"

"So long?" Perrin asked.

"You were gone at least two hours."

Perrin shook his head. "It's the Bore playing with our sense of time. Well, at least with that dreamspike in place, Slayer will have trouble reaching Rand."

After having Slayer use the dreamspike against him, it was satisfying to turn the *ter'angreal* against the man. Perrin had made the protective bubble just large enough to fit inside the cavern and shelter Rand, the Bore and those with him. The placement meant all of the borders of the dome save the one here at the front were inside rock.

Slayer would not be able to jump into the middle of the cavern and strike; he would have to enter through the front. Either that, or find a way to burrow through the rock, which Perrin supposed was possible here in the wolf dream. However, it would slow him, and that was what Rand needed.

"I need you to protect this place," Perrin sent to the gathered wolves, many of whom were still licking their wounds. "Shadowkiller fights inside, hunting the most dangerous prey this world has known. We must not let Slayer reach him."

We will guard this place, Young Bull, one sent. *Others gather. He will not pass us.*

"Can you do this?" Perrin sent an image of wolves spaced through the Borderlands, relaying messages quickly between themselves. There were thousands upon thousands of them roaming the area.

Perrin was proud of his sending. He didn't send it as words, or as images, but as a concept mixed with scents, with a hint of instinct. With the wolves positioned as he sent, they could send to him through the network almost instantly if Slayer returned.

We can do it, the wolves sent.

Perrin nodded, then waved to Gaul.

"We are not staying?" he asked.

"There is too much happening," Perrin said. "Time moves too slowly here. I don't want the war to pass us by."

Besides, there was still the matter of whatever Graendal was doing.

CHAPTER
26

Considerations

"I don't like fighting beside those Seanchan," Gawyn said softly, coming up beside Egwene.

She didn't like it either, and she knew he would be able to sense that from her. What could she say? She couldn't turn the Seanchan away. The Shadow had brought the Sharans to fight under its banner. Egwene, therefore, would have to use what she had. Anything she had.

Her neck itched as she crossed the field to the meeting place about a mile or so east of the ford in Arafel. Bryne had already arrayed most of her forces at the ford. Aes Sedai could be seen atop the hills just south of the ford, and large squadrons of archers and pikemen were positioned below them on the slopes. The troops were feeling fresher. The days Egwene's force had spent retreating had relieved some of the pressure of warfare, despite attempts by the enemy to make them commit to combat.

Egwene's chances depended on the Seanchan joining the battle and engaging the Sharan channelers. Her stomach twisted. She had once heard that in Caemlyn, unscrupulous men would throw starving dogs into a pit together and bet on which one would survive the ensuing fight. This felt the same to her. The Seanchan *damane* were not free women; they could not choose to fight. From what she'd seen of the Sharan male channelers, they were little more than animals themselves.

Egwene should be fighting the Seanchan with every breath, not allying with them. Her instincts rebelled as she approached the gathering of Seanchan. The Seanchan leader demanded this audience with Egwene. The Light send it would be quick.

Egwene had received reports on this Fortuona, so she knew what to expect. The diminutive Seanchan Empress stood atop a small platform, watching the battle preparations. She wore a glittering dress whose train extended a ridiculous distance behind her, carried by eight *da'covale*, those servants in the horribly immodest clothing. Various members of the Blood stood in groups, waiting with careful poses. Deathwatch Guards, hulking in their near-black armor, stood like boulders around the Empress.

Egwene approached, guarded by her own soldiers and much of the Hall of the Tower. Fortuona had first tried to insist that Egwene come to visit her in her camp. Egwene had, of course, refused. It had taken hours to reach an agreement. Both would come to this location in Arafel, and both would stand rather than sit so that neither could give the impression of being above the other. Still, Egwene was irritated to find the woman waiting. She'd wanted to time this meeting so they both arrived at the same moment.

Fortuona turned from the battle preparations and looked at Egwene. It appeared that many of Siuan's reports were false. True, Fortuona did look something like a child, with that slight build and delicate features. Those similarities were minor. No child had ever had eyes so discerning, so calculating. Egwene revised her expectations. She'd imagined Fortuona as a spoiled adolescent, the product of a coddled lifetime.

"I have considered," Fortuona said, "whether it would be appropriate to speak to you in person, with my own voice."

Nearby, several of the Seanchan Blood—with their painted fingernails and partially shaved heads—gasped. Egwene ignored them. They stood near several pairs of *sul'dam* and *damane*. If she let those pairs draw her attention, her temper might get the better of her.

"I have considered myself," Egwene said, "whether it would be appropriate to speak to one such as yourself, who has committed such terrible atrocities."

"I have decided that I will speak to you," Fortuona continued, ignoring Egwene's remark. "I think that, for the time, it would be better if I see you not as *marath'damane*, but as a queen among the people of this land."

"No," Egwene said. "You will see me for what I am, woman. I demand it."

Fortuona pursed her lips. "Very well," she finally said. "I have spoken to *damane* before; training them has been a hobby of mine. To see you as such does not violate protocol, as the Empress may speak with her pet hounds."

"Then I will speak with you directly as well," Egwene said, keeping her face impassive. "For the Amyrlin judges many trials. She must be able to speak to murderers and rapists in order to pass sentence upon them. I think you would be at home in their company, though I suspect they would find you nauseating."

"I can see that this will be an uneasy alliance."

"You expected otherwise?" Egwene asked. "You hold my sisters captive. What you have done to them is worse than murder. You have tortured them, broken their wills. I wish to the Light you had simply killed them instead."

"I would not expect you to understand what needs to be done," Fortuona said, looking back toward the battlefield. "You are *marath'damane*. It is . . . natural for you to seek your own good, as you see it."

"Natural indeed," Egwene said softly. "This is why I insist that you see me as I am, for I represent the ultimate proof that your society and empire are built upon falsehoods. Here I stand, a woman you insist should be collared for the common good. And yet I display none of the wild or dangerous tendencies that you claim I should have. So long as I am free from your collars, I prove to every man and woman who draws breath that you are a liar."

The other Seanchan murmured. Fortuona herself maintained a cool face.

"You would be much happier with us," Fortuona said.

"Oh, would I?" Egwene said.

"Yes. You speak of hating the collar, but if you were to wear it and see, you would find it a more peaceful life. We do not torture our *damane*. We care for them, and allow them to live lives of privilege."

"You don't know, do you?" Egwene asked.

"I am the Empress," Fortuona said. "My domination extends across seas, and the realms of my protection encompass all that humankind knows and thinks. If there are things I do not know, they are known by those in my Empire, for I *am* the Empire."

"Delightful," Egwene said. "And does your Empire realize that I *wore* one of your collars? That I was once trained by your *sul'-dam*?"

Fortuona stiffened, then rewarded Egwene with a look of shock, although she covered it immediately.

"I was in Falme," Egwene said. "A *damane*, trained by Renna. Yes, I wore your collar, woman. I found no peace there. I found pain, humiliation, and terror."

"Why did I not know of this?" Fortuona asked loudly, turning. "Why did you not tell me?"

Egwene glanced at the collected Seanchan nobility. Fortuona seemed to be addressing one man in particular, a man in rich black and golden clothing, trimmed with white lace. He had an eyepatch over one eye, black to match, and the fingernails on both hands were lacquered to a dark—

"*Mat?*" Egwene sputtered.

He gave a kind of half-wave, looking embarrassed.

Oh, Light, she thought. *What has he thrown himself into?* She galloped through plans in her mind. Mat was imitating a Seanchan nobleman. They must not know who he really was. Could she trade something to save him?

"Approach," Fortuona said.

"This man is not—" Egwene began, but Fortuona spoke over her.

"Knotai," she said, "did you know that this woman was an escaped *damane*? You knew her as a child, I believe."

"You know who he is?" Egwene asked.

"Of course I do," Fortuona said. "He is named Knotai, but once was called Matrim Cauthon. Do not think he will serve you, *marath'damane*, though you did grow up together. He is the Prince of the Ravens now, a position he earned by his marriage to me. He serves the Seanchan, the Crystal Throne, and the Empress."

"May she live forever," Mat noted. "Hello, Egwene. Glad to hear you escaped those Sharans. How's the White Tower? Still . . . white, I guess?"

Egwene looked from Mat to the Seanchan Empress, then back at him again. Finally, unable to do anything else, she burst out laughing. "You married Matrim Cauthon?"

"The omens predicted it," Fortuona said.

"You let yourself draw too close to a *ta'veren*," Egwene said, "and so the Pattern bound you to him!"

"Foolish superstitions," Fortuona said.

Egwene glanced at Mat.

"Being *ta'veren* never did get me much," Mat said sourly. "I suppose I should be grateful the Pattern didn't haul me by my boots over to Shayol Ghul. Small blessing, that."

"You didn't answer my question, Knotai," Fortuona said. "Did you know this woman was an escaped *damane*? If so, why didn't you speak of it to me?"

"I didn't think too much about it," Mat said. "She wasn't one for very long, Tuon."

"We will speak of this on another occasion," Fortuona said softly. "It will not be pleasant." She turned back to Egwene. "To converse with a former *damane* is not the same as speaking to one recently captured, or one who has always been free. News of this event will spread. You have caused me . . . inconvenience."

Egwene regarded the woman, baffled. Light! These people were completely insane. "What was your purpose insisting upon this meeting? The Dragon Reborn says you will help our fight. Help us, then."

"I needed to meet you," Fortuona said. "You are my opposite. I have agreed to join this peace the Dragon offered, but there are conditions."

Oh, Light, Rand, Egwene thought. *What did you promise them?* She braced herself.

"Along with agreeing to fight," Fortuona said, "I will acknowledge the sovereign borders of nations as they are currently mapped. We will force the obedience of no *marath'damane* save those who violate our borders."

"And those borders are?" Egwene asked.

"As currently outlined, as I—"

"Be more specific," Egwene said. "Tell me with your own voice, woman. What borders?"

Fortuona drew her lips to a line. Obviously, she was not accustomed to being interrupted. "We control Altara, Amadicia, Tarabon, and Almoth Plain."

"Tremalking," Egwene said. "You'll release Tremalking and the other Sea Folk islands?"

"I did not list those because they are not of your land, but the sea. They are not your concern. Besides, they were not part of the agreement with the Dragon Reborn. He did not mention it."

"He has a lot on his mind. Tremalking will be part of the agreement with me."

"I wasn't aware we were making such an agreement," Fortuona said calmly. "You require our assistance. We could leave in a moment, should I order it. How would you fare against that army without our aid, which you so recently begged me to lend?"

Begged? Egwene thought. "Do you realize what happens if we lose the Last Battle? The Dark One breaks the Wheel, slays the Great Serpent, and all things will end. That's if we're lucky. If we aren't lucky, the Dark One will remake the world according to his own twisted vision. All people will be bound to him in an eternity of suffering, subjugation, and torment."

"I am aware of this," Fortuona said. "You act as if this particular fight—here, on this battlefield—is decisive."

"If my army were to be destroyed," Egwene said, "our entire effort would be jeopardized. Everything could indeed hinge on what happens here."

"I disagree," Fortuona said. "Your armies are not vital. They are populated by the children of oathbreakers. You fight the Shadow, and for that I grant you honor. If you were to lose, I would return to Seanchan and raise up the full might of the Ever Victorious Army and bring *it* to bear against this . . . horror. We would still win the Last Battle. It would be more difficult without you, and I would not waste useful lives or potential *damane*, but I am confident we could stand against the Shadow on our own."

She met Egwene's eyes.

So cold, Egwene thought. *She's bluffing. She must be.* Reports from Siuan's eyes-and-ears said that the Seanchan homeland was in chaos. A succession crisis.

Perhaps Fortuona really did believe that the Empire could stand against the Shadow on its own. If so, she was wrong.

"You *will* fight alongside us," Egwene said. "You made the treaty with Rand, gave him your oath, I assume."

"Tremalking is ours."

"Oh?" Egwene said. "And you have set up a leader there? One of the Sea Folk, to acknowledge your rule?"

Fortuona said nothing.

"You have the allegiance of most of the other lands you've conquered," Egwene said. "For better or worse, the Altarans and Amadicians follow you. The Taraboners seem to as well. But the Sea Folk . . . I have no reports whatsoever of a single one of their kind supporting you or living peacefully beneath your thumb."

"Borders—"

"The borders you just mentioned, as they exist on maps, show Tremalking as Sea Folk land. It is not yours. If our treaty holds current borders as they are, you would need a ruler in Tremalking to acknowledge you."

It seemed a tenuous argument to Egwene. The Seanchan were conquerors. What did they care if they had any kind of legitimacy? However, Fortuona seemed to consider Egwene's words. She frowned in thought.

"This . . . is a good argument," Fortuona finally said. "They have not accepted us. They are foolish to reject the peace we offer, but they have indeed done so. Very well, we will leave Tremalking, but I will add a condition to our agreement as you have."

"And your condition?"

"You will announce through your Tower and through your lands," Fortuona said. "Any *marath'damane* who wish to come to Ebou Dar and be properly collared must be allowed to do so."

"You think people would *want* to be collared?" She was insane. She had to be.

"Of course they would want to," Fortuona said. "In Seanchan, very occasionally one who can channel is missed in our searches. When they discover what they are, they come to us and demand to be collared, as is appropriate. You will not force anyone to stay away from us. You will let them come."

"I promise you, none will."

"Then you should have no trouble making the proclamation," Fortuona said. "We will send emissaries to educate your people on the benefits of *damane*—our teachers will come peacefully, for we will hold to the treaty. I believe you will be surprised. Some will see what is right."

"Do what you wish," Egwene said, amused. "Break no laws, and I suspect most will allow your . . . emissaries. I cannot speak for every ruler."

"What of the lands you control? Tar Valon? You will allow our emissaries?"

"If they break no laws," Egwene said, "I won't silence them. I'd allow in Whitecloaks, if they could say their piece without driving men to riot. But *Light*, woman. You can't actually believe . . . "

She trailed off, watching Fortuona. She did believe it. So far as Egwene could tell, she did.

At least she's sincere, Egwene thought. *Insane. Insane, but sincere.*

"And the *damane* you now hold?" Egwene said. "You'll let them go, if they wish to be released?"

"None who are properly trained would wish that."

"This must be equal on both sides," Egwene said. "What of a girl whom you discover to be able to channel? If she does not wish to be made *damane*, will you let her leave your lands and join ours?"

"That would be like letting an enraged *grolm* free in a city square."

"You said that people will see the truth," Egwene said. "If your way of life is strong, your ideals true, then people will see them for what they are. If they don't, you shouldn't force them. Let any who wish to be free go free, and I'll let your people speak in Tar Valon. Light! I'll give them room and free board, and I'll see the same done in every city!"

Fortuona eyed Egwene. "Many of our *sul'dam* have come to this war anticipating the chance to capture new *damane* from among those who serve the Shadow. These Sharans, perhaps. You would have us let them, or your sisters of the Shadow, free? To destroy, murder?"

"To be tried and executed, under the Light."

"Why not let them be put to use? Why waste their lives?"

"What you do is an abomination!" Egwene said, feeling exasperated. "Not even the Black Ajah deserves that."

"Resources should not be discarded so idly."

"Is that so?" Egwene said. "Do you realize that every one of your *sul'dam*, your precious trainers, is herself a *marath'damane*?"

Fortuona spun on her. "Do not spread such lies."

"Oh? Shall we test it, Fortuona? You said you trained them yourself. You are a *sul'dam*, I presume? Put the *a'dam* on your neck. I *dare* you. If I am wrong, it will do nothing to you. If I am right, you will be subject to its power, and will prove to be *marath'damane*."

Fortuona's eyes widened in anger. She had ignored Egwene's barbs calling her a criminal, but *this* accusation seemed to dig into her . . . so Egwene made certain to twist the knife a little deeper.

"Yes," Egwene said. "Let us do it and test the real strength of your commitment. If you prove to be able to channel, will you do as you claim others should? Will you stroll up to the collar and snap it around your own neck, Fortuona? Will you obey your own laws?"

"I have obeyed them," Fortuona said coldly. "You are very ignorant. Perhaps it is true, that *sul'dam* can learn to channel. But this is not the same thing as being a *marath'damane*—any more than a man who *can* become a murderer is to be considered one."

"We shall see," Egwene said, "once more of your people realize the lies they've been told."

"I will break you myself," Fortuona said softly. "Someday, your people will turn you over to me. You will forget yourself, and your arrogance will lead you to our borders. I will be waiting."

"I plan to live centuries," Egwene hissed. "I will watch your empire crumble, Fortuona. I will watch it with joy." She raised a finger to tap the woman on the chest, but Fortuona moved with blurring speed, her hand grabbing Egwene's by the wrist. For one so small, she certainly was quick.

Egwene embraced the Source by reflex. *Damane* nearby gasped, and the light of the One Power sprang up around them.

Mat pushed between Egwene and Fortuona and shoved them apart, holding one hand at each woman's chest. Egwene wove by instinct, intending to remove his hand with a thread of Air. It fell apart, of course.

Blood and ashes, that's inconvenient! She had forgotten he was there.

"Let's be civil, ladies," Mat said, eyeing one of them, then the other. "Don't make me throw the pair of you over my knee."

Egwene glared at him, and Mat met her eyes. He was trying to deflect her anger to him instead of Fortuona.

Egwene looked down at his hand, which was pressed against her chest uncomfortably close to her breasts. Fortuona was also looking at that hand.

Mat lowered both hands, but took his sweet time at it, as if completely unconcerned. "The people of this world need you two, and they need you levelheaded, you hear me? This is bigger than any of us. When you fight each other, the Dark One wins, and that is that. So stop behaving like children."

"We will have many words about this tonight, Knotai," Fortuona said.

"I love words," Mat said. "There are some deliciously pretty words out there. 'Smile.' That's always sounded like a pretty word to me. Don't you think? Or, perhaps, the words 'I promise not to kill Egwene right now for trying to touch me, the Empress, may I live forever, because we really bloody need her for the next couple of weeks or so.'" He eyed Fortuona pointedly.

"You really married him?" Egwene said to Fortuona. "Honestly?"

"It was . . . an unusual event," Fortuona replied. She shook herself, then glared at Egwene. "He is mine and I do not intend to release him."

"You don't seem the type to release anything, once you have your hands on it," Egwene said. "Matrim does not interest me at the moment; your army does. Will you fight, or won't you?"

"I will fight," Fortuona said. "But my army is not subject to you. Have your general send us suggestions. We will consider them. But I can see you are going to have a difficult time defending the ford against the invader without a larger number of your *marath'damane*. I will send you some of my *sul'dam* and *damane* to protect your army. That is all I will do for now." She started walking back toward her people. "Come, Knotai."

"I don't know how you fell into this," Egwene said under her breath to Mat. "I don't want to know. I'll do what I can to help free you, once we are done fighting."

"That's kind of you, Egwene," Mat said. "But I can handle this on my own." He rushed off after Fortuona.

That was what he always said. She'd find some way to help him. She shook her head, returning to where Gawyn waited for her. Leilwin had declined to come, though Egwene would have expected her to enjoy seeing some of those from her homeland.

"We'll need to keep them at arm's length," Gawyn said softly.

"Agreed," Egwene said.

"You'll still fight alongside the Seanchan, despite what they've done?"

"So long as they keep the Sharan channelers occupied, yes." Egwene looked toward the horizon—toward Rand, and the powerful struggle he must be embroiled in. "Our options are limited, Gawyn, and our allies dwindling. For now, whoever is willing to kill Trollocs is a friend. That is that."

The Andoran line buckled, and Trollocs ripped through, snarling beasts with stinking breath that clouded in the chill air. Elayne's halberdiers nearby scrambled as they fell over themselves to escape. The first few Trollocs ignored them, howling and leaping over them to make room for more to pour through the opening, like dark blood from a gash in the flesh.

Elayne tried to gather what little strength she had left. She felt as if *saidar* would slip from her at any moment, but the men fighting and dying wouldn't be any stronger than she at this point. They'd all been fighting for most of the day.

Somehow finding the strength to weave, she roasted the first few Trollocs with balls of fire, tripping up the flow through the wound in the human lines. Streaks of white, arrows from Birgitte's bow, followed. Trollocs gurgled, clawing at their necks where the arrows hit.

Elayne sent strike after strike from horseback, tired hands clinging to the saddle as she blinked eyes that seemed leaden. Dead Trollocs toppled, forming like a scab over the hole, blocking the others from ripping through. Reserve troops stumbled up, seizing ground and pushing the Trollocs back.

Elayne breathed out, wavering. Light! She felt as if she'd been forced to run around Caemlyn while pulling lead weights. She could barely sit upright, let alone hold the One Power. Her vision dimmed, then darkened further. Sound faded in her ears. Then . . . darkness.

Sound came back first. Distant yells, clangs. A very faint horn. The howls of the Trollocs. Occasional thundering from the dragons. *Those aren't firing as often*, she thought. Aludra had moved to a rhythm in her firing. Bashere would pull back one section of troops and let them rest. The Trollocs would pour through, and the dragons would bombard them for a short time. As the Trollocs tried to crawl up and destroy the dragons, cavalry would come in and smash them at the flanks.

It killed a lot of Trollocs. That was their job . . . kill Trollocs . . . *Too slow*, she thought. *Too slow* . . .

Elayne found herself on the ground, Birgitte's worried face hovering above her.

"Oh, Light?" Elayne mumbled. "Did I fall off?"

"We caught you in time," Birgitte muttered. "You slumped into our arms. Come on, we're pulling back."

"I . . . "

Birgitte raised an eyebrow at her, waiting for the argument.

It was hard to make one, lying on her back mere paces from the front lines. *Saidar* had fled her, and she probably couldn't take hold of it again if her life depended on it. "Yes," she said. "I should . . . should check on Bashere."

"Very wise," Birgitte said, waving for the guard to help Elayne back onto her horse. She hesitated, then. "You did well here, Elayne. They know how you fought. It was good for them to see."

They began a hurried trip through the back lines. Those were very shallow; most soldiers were committed to the fight. They needed to win before that second Trolloc army arrived, and that meant throwing everything they had at this force.

Still, Elayne was surprised at the depleted reserves, the small number that could be spared to rotate from the front and rest. How long had it been?

The clouds had enveloped the open sky that often accompanied her. That seemed a bad sign. "Curse those clouds," she muttered. "What time of day is it?"

"Maybe two hours from sunset," Birgitte said.

"Light! You should have made me return to camp hours ago, Birgitte!"

The woman glared at her, and Elayne vaguely remembered attempts to do just that. Well, no use arguing about it now. Elayne was recovering some of her strength, and forced herself to sit straight-backed on her horse as she was led to the small valley between hills near Cairhien where Bashere gave battle orders.

She rode right up to the command post, not trusting her legs to be able to support her walking, and remained in the saddle as she addressed Bashere. "Is it working?"

He looked up at her. "I assume I can't count on you any longer on the front?"

"Too weak to channel for now. I'm sorry."

"You lasted longer than you should have." He made a notation on his maps. "Good thing. I half think you were the only thing that kept the eastern flank from collapsing. I'll need to send more support that direction."

"Is it *working*?"

"Go have a look," Bashere said, nodding toward the hillside.

Elayne gritted her teeth, but nudged Moonshadow up to where she could find a vantage. She lifted her looking glass with fingers that shook *far* more than she would have liked.

The Trolloc force had hit their bowed line of defenders. The natural result of this had been the infantry falling back, the bowl inverting as the Trollocs pushed forward. This had let the Shadowspawn feel as if they were gaining the advantage, and had stopped them from realizing the truth.

As they pressed forward, the infantry line had wrapped up and surrounded the Trolloc sides. She'd missed the most important moment, when Bashere had ordered the Aiel to attack. Their quick sweep around to hit the Trollocs from behind had worked as hoped.

Elayne's forces had the Trollocs completely surrounded. An enormous circle of writhing Shadowspawn fought with her encircling force, pressing them together to constrict their movements and their ability to fight.

It was working. Light, it *was*. The Aiel beat against the back flanks of Trollocs, slaughtering them. The noose had been drawn.

Which of them was blowing those horns? Those were Trolloc horns.

Elayne searched through the Shadowspawn, but could not find

the ones sounding the horns. She did spot some dead Myrddraal near the Aiel ranks. One of Aludra's dragons—attached to its cart and pulled by a pair of horses—was with the Band's horsemen. They had been positioning the carts on different hilltops to fire down into the Trollocs.

"Elayne . . . " Birgitte said.

"Oh, sorry," Elayne said, lowering the looking glass and handing it to her Warder. "Have a look. It's going well."

"Elayne!"

With a start, she realized how worried the Warder was. Elayne spun, following the woman's gaze south, far beyond the city's walls. Those horns sounding . . . they'd been so soft, Elayne hadn't realized they were coming from behind.

"Oh, no . . . " Elayne said, hastily raising her looking glass.

There, like black filth on the horizon, approached the second Trolloc army.

"Didn't Bashere say they weren't supposed to be here until tomorrow?" Birgitte said. "At the earliest?"

"It doesn't matter," Elayne said. "One way or another, they're here. We need to get ready to turn those dragons the other way! Send the order to Talmanes, and find Lord Tam al'Thor! I want the Two Rivers men armed and ready. Light! The crossbowmen too. We have to slow that second army, any way possible."

Bashere, she thought. *I have to tell Bashere.*

She spun Moonshadow, moving so fast she became dizzy. She tried to embrace the Source, but it wouldn't come. She was so tired, she had trouble gripping the reins.

Somehow, she made it down the hill without falling off. Birgitte had left to convey her orders. Good woman. Elayne rode into camp to find an argument in progress.

"—won't listen to this!" Bashere yelled. "I will *not* stand by and be insulted in my own camp, man!"

The object of his scorn was none other than Tam al'Thor. The steady Two Rivers man glanced at Elayne, and his eyes opened wider, as if he was surprised to see her there.

"Your Majesty," Tam said. "I was told you were still out on the battlefield." He turned back to Bashere, who grew red-faced.

"I didn't want you going to her with—"

"Enough!" Elayne said, riding Moonshadow between them.

Why was *Tam* of all people arguing with Bashere? "Bashere, the second Trolloc army is almost upon us."

"Yes," Bashere said, breathing deeply. "I just had word. Light, this is a disaster, Elayne. We need to pull out through gateways."

"We exhausted the Kinswomen on our push up here, Bashere," Elayne said. "Most can barely channel enough now to warm a teacup, let alone make a gateway." *Light, and I couldn't warm the tea.* She forced her voice to remain firm. "That was part of the plan."

"I . . . That's right," Bashere said. He looked at the map. "Let me think. The city. We'll retreat into the city."

"And give the Shadowspawn time to rest, gather together, and assault us?" Elayne asked. "That's what they're probably *trying* to force us to do."

"I don't see any other choice," Bashere said. "The city is our only hope."

"The city?" Talmanes said, hurrying up, panting. "You can't be talking about pulling back into the city."

"Why not?" Elayne asked.

"Your Majesty, our infantry have just managed to surround a Trolloc army! They're going at it tooth and claw! We have no reserves left, and our cavalry is exhausted. We'd never manage to disengage from that contest without sustaining heavy losses. And then our survivors would be holed up in the city, trapped between two armies of the Shadow."

"Light," Elayne whispered. "It's like they planned it."

"I think they did," Tam said softly.

"Not this again," Bashere bellowed. He didn't seem like himself at all, though she knew that Saldaeans could have tempers. Bashere almost seemed like a different person. His wife had stepped up to his side, arms folded, and both confronted Tam.

"Have your say, Tam," Elayne said.

"I—" Bashere began, but Elayne held up a hand.

"He knew, Your Majesty," Tam said softly. "It's the only thing that makes sense. He hasn't been using the Aiel to scout."

"What?" Elayne said. "Of course he has. I read the scout reports."

"The reports are faked, or at least tampered with," Tam said. "I talked to Bael. He said that none of his Aiel had been sent on scouting duty the last few days of our march. He said he thought my men had been doing it, but they hadn't. I talked to Arganda, who thought Whitecloaks had been doing it, but Galad said that it was the Band."

"It wasn't us," Talmanes said, frowning. "None of my men have been used for scout details."

All eyes turned to Bashere.

"Who," Elayne asked, "has been watching our rear, Bashere?"

"I . . ." He looked up, anger flaring again. "I have the reports somewhere! I showed them to you, and you approved them!"

"It's all too perfect," Elayne said. She felt a sudden chill, right at the middle point of her back. It spread down through her body, a wave of icy wind blowing through her veins. They'd been trapped, perfectly. Channelers run to exhaustion, soldiers committed to a close-fought battle, a second army left to approach in secret a day ahead of where falsified reports said they would be . . .

Davram Bashere was a Darkfriend.

"Bashere is relieved of duty," she said.

"But—" he sputtered. His wife put her hand on his arm, looking at Elayne with fire in her eyes. Bashere leveled a finger at Tam. "I did send the Two Rivers men! Tam al'Thor must be the culprit. He's trying to distract you, Your Majesty!"

"Talmanes," Elayne said, feeling cold to the bone. "Have five Redarms put Lord Bashere and his wife under guard."

Bashere let out a string of curses. Elayne was surprised at how calm she felt. Her emotions were deadened. She watched him be dragged away.

There wasn't time for this. "Gather our commanders," Elayne said to the others. "Galad, Arganda . . . Finish off that Trolloc army above the city! Spread the word to the men. Throw everything we have into this battle! If we can't crush the Trollocs in the next hour, we die here!

"Talmanes, those dragons can't be much use against the Trollocs now that they're surrounded—you risk hitting our men. Have Aludra move all of the dragon carts up on the tallest hill to pound the new enemy coming up from the south. Tell the Ogier to make a cordon around the hill the dragons are on; we can't have them damaged. Tam, put your Two Rivers bowmen on the surrounding hills. And have the Legion of the Dragon form up the front lines, crossbowmen in the lead, heavy cavalry behind. Light willing, that will be enough to buy us time to finish off the surrounded Trollocs."

It would be close. Light! If that second army surrounded her men . . .

Elayne took a deep breath, then opened herself to *saidar*. The One Power flooded into her, though she could hold only a trickle. She could act as if she weren't exhausted, but her body knew the truth.

She would lead them anyway.

CHAPTER 27

Friendly Fire

Gareth Bryne strode through the camp he had set up on the Arafellin side, several hundred paces on the Kandor border east of the ford, ignoring soldiers who tried to salute him. Siuan hastened at one side, a messenger delivering reports at his other. They were trailed by a flurry of guards and attendants carrying maps, ink and paper.

The whole burning *place* shook with explosions of the Power. Crashing racket and calamity . . . it was like being in the middle of a rockslide.

He'd stopped being bothered by the scent of smoke. It was pervasive. At least some of the fires were put out; those Seanchan channelers had set up by the river and were drawing out streams of water.

Nearby, a rack of polearms tumbled to the ground in a clatter as a surge of the One Power hit in the camp nearby. He stumbled, and earth sprayed around him and Siuan, pebbles clattering against his helmet and breastplate.

"Keep talking, man," he snapped at Holcom, the messenger.

"Er, yes, my Lord." The spindly man had a face like a horse. "The Aes Sedai on the Red, Green, and Blue hilltops are all holding. The Gray have fallen back, and the White report that they're running out of strength."

"The other Aes Sedai will be tiring as well," Siuan said. "I'm not surprised that the Whites are the first to admit it. It won't be a point of shame to them, merely another fact."

Bryne grunted, ignoring another spray of earth as it fell over them. He had to keep moving. The Shadow had too many gateways now. They'd try to strike at his command centers. That was what he'd do, if he were them. The best counter to that strategy was to not *have* a command center, at least not one that was easy to find.

All things considered, the battle was going according to plan. It was a surprise, sometimes, when that happened; on a battlefield, you expected to have to rebuild your tactics from the ground up at every turn—but for once, everything had gone smoothly.

Aes Sedai were pounding the Sharans from the hilltops south of the ford, augmented by a steady stream of projectiles from archers stationed just below them on the slopes. Because of that, the Shadow's commander—Demandred himself—couldn't devote all his troops against the defenders at the river. Nor could he bring all his troops against the Aes Sedai—they would Travel away—so committing himself fully there would expose him with very little gain. Instead, he'd split his forces, sending the Trollocs off his right flank toward the hills—they would sustain heavy losses, but he'd keep the Aes Sedai pressed—and bringing his Sharans forward to engage the bulk of the White Tower troops at the river.

The Seanchan occupied most of the enemy channelers' attention. This did not prevent some Sharan channelers from lobbing fire at Bryne's camp across the river. There was no use worrying about being hit. He was as safe here as he would be anywhere, other than perhaps retreating all the way to the White Tower. He couldn't *stand* the idea of being safe in a room somewhere, miles from the battlefield.

Light, he thought. *That's how commanders will probably do it in the future. A secure command position accessed only by gateways.* But a general needed to feel the flow of the battlefield. He couldn't do that from miles away.

"How well are the pikemen on each of the hills doing?" he demanded.

"Very well, my Lord," said Holcom. "As well as can be expected after hours of holding off Trollocs." Bryne had placed defensive lines of pikemen halfway up each of the hills; any Trollocs that managed to get through the cordon could be picked off by archers above, without having to disturb the work of the Aes Sedai. "The pikes defending the Red Ajah on the middle hill will be needing reinforcement soon, though; they lost a fair number on the last assault."

"They'll have to hang on a bit longer. Those Reds are nasty enough to take care of any more Trollocs that break through the pike formations." He hoped. Another explosion flattened a tent nearby. "How about the archer squadrons up there?" Bryne kicked aside a fallen halberd.

"Some are getting low on arrows, my Lord."

Well, he couldn't do much about that. He glanced toward the ford, but it was a right mess of confusion. It rankled him to be this close to the fighting and not know how things were going for his troops.

"Does anyone have information about what's happening at the ford?" he bellowed, turning toward his aides. "I can't see a Light-blasted thing, just a churning of bodies and those balls of fire shooting back and forth, blinding us all!"

Holcom paled. "Those Seanchan women are channeling like they've got red-hot irons up . . . I mean, they're giving the Sharans a hard time, my Lord. Our left flank just took a lot of casualties, but they seem to be fighting back admirably now."

"Didn't I put Joni in command of the lancers there?"

"Captain Shagrin is dead, my Lord," said another messenger, stepping forward. He had a fresh cut on his scalp. "I've just come from there."

Burn me. Well, Joni had always wanted to fall in battle. Bryne kept his emotions in check. "Who commands now?"

"Uno Nomesta," the messenger said. "He pulled us together after Joni fell, but sends warning that they're being hard-pressed."

"Light, Nomesta's not even an officer!" Still, he'd been training heavy cavalry for years, and there probably wasn't a better man in the saddle than him. "All right, get back there and tell him I'm giving him some reinforcements."

Bryne turned back to Holcom. "Get over to Captain Denhold and have him send his cavalry reserve squadron across the ford to beef up our left flank. Let's see what those Illianers can do! We can't lose this river!"

The messenger rushed off. *I'll have to do something to take the pressure off those Aes Sedai soon.* He bellowed, "Annah, where are you?"

Two soldiers talking nearby were pushed aside as a heavyset young woman—a former merchant's guard and now foot soldier and messenger serving General Bryne—shoved through. "My Lord?"

"Annah, go beg that Imperial monster of a Seanchan leader if she'd be ever so kind as to lend us some of her bloody cavalry."

"Shall I phrase it exactly that way?" Annah asked, saluting, a smile on her lips.

"If you do, girl, I'll throw you off a cliff and let Yukiri Sedai test a few of her new falling weaves on you. Go!"

The messenger grinned, then dashed off toward the Traveling ground for passage.

Siuan eyed Bryne. "You're growing grouchy."

"You're a good influence on me," he snapped, glancing up as a shadow passed above. He reached for his sword, expecting to see another flight of Draghkar. Instead, it was only one of those Seanchan flying beasts. He relaxed.

A fireball knocked the creature from the sky. It spun, flapping burning wings. Bryne cursed, jumping back as the monstrous animal crashed into the path just ahead, where the messenger Annah was running. The animal's corpse rolled over her and crashed through one of the supply tents, which was filled with soldiers and quartermasters. The *raken*'s rider slapped the ground a fraction of a moment later.

Bryne recovered his wits and leaped forward, stooping beneath a fallen section of cloth and tent poles that covered the path. Two of his guards found a soldier half-pinned by the dead beast's wing and pulled him free, Siuan kneeling and removing her *angreal* from her pouch to perform Healing.

Bryne moved to where Annah had fallen. He found her crushed where the fallen beast had rolled. "Burn it!" He shoved aside thought for the dead to consider what to do next. "I need someone to go to the Seanchan!"

Of his entourage, only two guards and one clerk remained in

camp. He needed the Seanchan to give him some more cavalry; he was beginning to feel that a great deal depended on keeping those Aes Sedai on the hills safe. After all, the Amyrlin was up there with them.

"Looks like we're going ourselves," Bryne said, leaving Annah's corpse. "Siuan, are you strong enough to make a gateway with that *angreal*?"

She stood, masking her exhaustion, but he could see it. "I can, though it will be so small we'll have to crawl through. I don't know this area well enough. We'll have to move back to the center of camp."

"Burn me!" Bryne said, turning as a series of explosions sounded from the river. "We don't have time for this."

"I can go find us some more messengers," a guard said. The other was helping the soldier Siuan had Healed. The man stood on wobbly feet.

"I don't know if there are more messengers to be had," Bryne said. "Let's just—"

"I'll go."

Bryne saw Min Farshaw rising to her feet nearby and dusting herself off. He'd almost forgotten that he'd set her helping as a clerk for one of the supply regiments.

"It doesn't look like I'll be clerking here in the near future," Min said, inspecting the fallen supply tent. "I can run as well as any of your messengers. What do you want me to do?"

"Find the Seanchan Empress," Bryne said. "Her camp is a few miles north of here on the Arafellin side. Go to the Traveling ground; they'll know where to send you. Tell the Empress she needs to send me some cavalry. Our reserves are depleted."

"I'll do it," Min said.

She wasn't a soldier. Well, it seemed half of his army hadn't been soldiers until a few weeks back. "Go," he said, then smiled. "I'll count the day's work toward what you owe me."

She blushed. Did she think he'd let a woman forget her oath? It didn't matter to him whose company she kept. An oath was an oath.

Min ran through the army's back lines. The camp had more tents and carts—brought in from supply dumps in Tar Valon or Tear—

to replace the ones lost during the initial Sharan assault. Those proved to be obstacles to weave around as she sought out the Traveling ground.

The ground was a series of roped-off squares, numbered with painted planks shoved in the ground. A quartet of women in gray shawls spoke together in hushed voices as one of their number held open a gateway for a supply cart laden with arrows. The placid oxen didn't look up as a comet-like ball of fire hit the ground nearby, hurling glowing red stones into the air and across a pile of bedrolls, which began to smolder.

"I need to go to the Seanchan army," Min said to the Grays. "Lord Bryne's orders."

One of the Gray sisters, Ashmanaille, looked at her. She took in Min's breeches and curls, then frowned. "Elmindreda? Sweet thing, what are *you* doing here?"

"Sweet thing?" one of the others asked. "She's one of the clerks, isn't she?"

"I *need* to go to the Seanchan army," Min said, breathing deeply from her run. "Lord Bryne's orders."

This time, they seemed to hear her. One of the women sighed. "Square four?" she asked the others.

"Three, dear," Ashmanaille said. "A gateway could be opening to four from Illian any moment."

"Three," the first said, waving Min over. A small gateway split the air there. "All messengers crawl," she noted. "We have to conserve strength; gateways need to be made as small as reasonable."

This is reasonable? Min thought with annoyance, running to the small hole. She dropped to her hands and knees and crawled through.

She came out in a ring of grass that had been burned black to mark its location. A pair of Seanchan guards stood with tasseled spears nearby, their faces obscured by insectile helmets. Min started to walk forward, but one held up a hand.

"I'm a messenger from General Bryne," she said.

"New messengers wait here," one of the guards said.

"It's urgent!"

"New messengers wait here."

She received no further explanation, so she crossed her arms— stepping out of the black circle, in case another gateway opened—and waited. She could see the river from here, and a large military encampment stretched out along its banks. *The Seanchan could make a big difference to this battle*, Min thought. *There are so many of them.* She was far from the battle here, a few miles north of Bryne's camp, but still close enough to see the flashes of light as channelers traded deadly weaves.

She found herself fidgeting, so she forced herself to remain still. Explosions from channeling sounded like dull thumps. The sounds came after the flashes of light, like thunder trailing behind lightning. Why was that?

It doesn't really matter, Min thought. She needed cavalry for Bryne. At least she was doing something. She had spent the last week pitching in wherever she found that an extra hand was needed. It was surprising how much there was to do in a war camp other than fighting. It wasn't work that had required her, specifically, but it was better than sitting in Tear and worrying about Rand . . . or being angry at him for forbidding her to go to Shayol Ghul.

You'd have been a liability there, Min told herself. *You know it.* He couldn't worry about saving the world and protecting her from the Forsaken at the same time. Sometimes, it was hard not to feel insignificant in a world of channelers like Rand, Elayne and Aviendha.

She glanced at the guards. Only one had an image hovering above his head. A bloodied stone. He'd die by falling from someplace high. It seemed like decades since she'd seen anything *hopeful* around a person's head. Death, destruction, symbols of fear and darkness.

"And who is she?" a slurred Seanchan voice asked. A *sul'dam* had approached, one without a *damane*. The woman held an *a'dam* in her hand, tapping the silvery collar against her other palm.

"New messenger," the guard said. "She has not come through the gateways before."

Min took a deep breath. "I was sent by General Bryne—"

"He was supposed to clear all messengers with us," the *sul'dam* said. She was dark of skin, with curls that came down to her shoulders. "The Empress—may she live forever—must be protected. Our camp will be orderly. Every messenger cleared, no opportunities for assassins."

"I am no assassin," Min said flatly.

"And the knives in your sleeves?" the *sul'dam* asked.

Min started.

"The way your cuffs droop make it obvious, child," the *sul'dam* said, though she was no older than Min herself.

"A woman would be a fool to walk a battlefield without some kind of weapon," Min said. "Let me deliver my message to one of the generals. The other messenger was killed when one of your *raken* was hit and fell from the sky onto our camp."

The *sul'dam* raised an eyebrow. "I am Catrona," she said. "And you will do exactly as I say while in camp." She turned and waved for Min to follow.

Min hurried gratefully behind the woman as they crossed the ground. The Seanchan camp was very different from Bryne's. They had *raken* to fly their messages and reports, not to mention an empress to protect. They had set their camp away from the hostilities. It also looked far tidier than Bryne's camp, which had been nearly destroyed and rebuilt, and which included people from many different countries and military backgrounds. The Seanchan camp was homogeneous, full of trained soldiers.

At least that was the way Min decided to interpret its orderliness. Seanchan soldiers stood in ranks, silent, awaiting the call to battle. Sections of the camp had been marked with posts and ropes, everything clearly organized. Nobody bustled about. Men walked with quiet purpose or waited at parade rest. Speak what criticism one would about the Seanchan—and Min had a number of things she could add to *that* conversation—they certainly were organized.

The *sul'dam* led Min to a section of camp where several men stood at ledgers set on tall desks. Wearing robes and bearing the half-shaved head of upper servants, they quietly made notations. Immodestly dressed young women carrying lacquered trays threaded their way between the desks, placing on them thin white cups of steaming black liquid.

"Have we lost any *raken* in the last little while?" Catrona asked the men. "Was one hit by an enemy *marath'damane* while in flight, and could it have crashed into General Bryne's camp?"

"A report just came in of such a thing," a servant said, bowing. "I am surprised that you have heard of it."

Catrona's eyebrow inched a little higher as she inspected Min. "You hadn't expected the truth?" Min asked.

"No," the *sul'dam* said. She moved her hand, replacing a knife into its sheath at her side. "Follow."

Min let out a breath. Well, she had dealt with Aiel before; the Seanchan couldn't possibly be as prickly as they were. Catrona led the way along another path in the camp, and Min found herself growing anxious. How long had it been since Bryne had sent her? Was it too late?

Light, but the Seanchan liked things well guarded. There were two soldiers at every intersection of paths, standing with raised spears, watching through those awful helmets of theirs. Shouldn't all of these men be out fighting? Eventually, Catrona led her to an actual *building* they had constructed here. It wasn't a tent. It had walls that looked to be draped silk, stretched into wooden frames, a wooden floor and a ceiling covered with shingles. It probably broke down quickly to be transported, but it seemed frivolous.

The guards here were big fellows in armor of black and red. They had a wicked appearance. Catrona passed them as they saluted her. She and Min entered the building, and Catrona bowed. Not to the ground—the Empress wasn't in the room, it appeared—but still deep, since many members of the Blood were inside. Catrona glanced at Min. "Bow, you fool!"

"I think I'll be fine standing," Min said, folding her arms as she regarded the commanders inside. Standing at their forefront was a familiar figure. Mat wore silken Seanchan clothing—she had heard he was in this camp—but he topped it with his familiar hat. He had an eyepatch covering one eye. So that viewing had finally come to pass, had it?

Mat looked up at her and grinned. "Min!"

"I'm a total fool," she said. "I could have just said I knew you. They'd have brought me right here without all of the fuss."

"I don't know, Min," Mat said. "They rather like fuss around here. Don't you, Galgan?"

A wide-shouldered man with a thin crest of white hair on his otherwise shaven head eyed Mat, as if uncertain what to make of him.

"Mat," Min said, clearing her mind. "General Bryne needs cavalry."

Mat grunted. "I don't doubt it. He's been pushing his troops hard, even the Aes Sedai. Man ought to be given a medal for that. I've never seen one of those women budge so much as to take a step indoors when a man suggests, even if she's standing in the rain. First Legion, Galgan?"

"They will do," Galgan said, "so long as the Sharans don't manage to get across the ford."

"They won't," Mat said. "Bryne has set up a good defensive position that should punish the Shadow, with a little encouragement. *Laero lendhae an indemela.*"

"What was that?" Galgan asked, frowning.

Min missed it, too. Something about a flag? She had been studying the Old Tongue lately, but Mat spoke it so quickly.

"Hmm, what?" Mat said. "You've never heard it before? It's a saying of the Fallen Army of Kardia."

"Who?" Galgan sounded baffled.

"Never mind," Mat said. "Tylee, would you care to lead your legion on to the battlefield, assuming the good General approves?"

"I would be honored, Raven Prince," said a woman in a breastplate standing nearby, four plumes rising from the helmet she held under her arm. "I have wanted to watch the actions of this Gareth Bryne more directly."

Mat glanced to Galgan, who rubbed his chin, inspecting his maps. "Take your legion, Lieutenant-General Khirgan, as the Raven Prince suggests."

"And," Mat added, "we *need* to watch those Sharan archers. They're going to move north along the river for a better shot at Bryne's right flank."

"How can you be certain?"

"It's just obvious," Mat said, tapping at the map. "Send a *raken* to make sure, if you want."

Galgan hesitated, then gave the order. Min wasn't certain that she was needed any longer, so she started to walk away, but Mat caught her by the arm. "Hey. I could . . . uh . . . use you, Min."

"Use me?" she asked flatly.

"Make use of you," Mat said. "That's what I meant. I've had trouble with the words coming out of my mouth lately. Only the stupid ones seem to make it. Anyway, could you . . . uh . . . you know . . ."

"I don't see anything new around you," she said, "though I assume the eye on a balance scale finally makes sense to you."

"Yes," Mat said, wincing. "That one is bloody obvious. What about Galgan?"

"A dagger rammed through the heart of a raven."

"Bloody ashes . . ."

"I don't think it means you," she added. "I can't say why."

Galgan was speaking with some lesser nobles. At least, they had more hair than he did, which was the Seanchan mark of a lesser. Their tones were hushed, and Galgan would occasionally glance over at Mat.

"He doesn't know what to make of me," Mat said softly.

"How very uncommon. I can't think of anyone else who has reacted that way to you, Mat."

"Ha ha. You're sure that bloody dagger doesn't mean me? Ravens . . . well, ravens kind of mean me, right? Sometimes? I'm the flaming Prince of the bloody Ravens now."

"It's not you."

"He's trying to decide when to assassinate me," Mat said softly, gaze narrowing toward Galgan. "I've been put right beneath him in the army, and he worries I will supplant him. Tuon says he's a dedicated soldier, so he'll wait until after the Last Battle to strike."

"That's awful!"

"I know," Mat said. "He won't play cards with me first. I was hoping I could win him over. Lose on purpose a few times."

"I don't think you could manage that."

"Actually, I figured out how to lose bloody ages ago." He seemed to be completely serious. "Tuon says it would be a sign of disrespect if he didn't try to kill me. They're insane, Min. They're all *bloody* insane."

"I'm sure Egwene would help you escape if you ask, Mat."

"Well, I didn't say they weren't fun. Just insane." He straightened his hat. "But if any more of them bloody well try to—"

He cut off as the guards outside the door dropped to their knees, then completely prostrated themselves on the ground. Mat sighed. "'Say the name of Darkness, and his eye is upon you.' *Yalu kazath d'Zamon patra Daeseia asa darshi.*"

". . . What?" Min asked.

"You don't know that one either?" Mat said. "Doesn't anyone bloody read anymore?"

The Seanchan Empress stepped through the door. Min was surprised to see her wearing not a dress, but wide silvery trousers. Or ... well, maybe it *was* a dress. Min couldn't tell if those were skirts that had been divided for riding, or if it was a pair of trousers with very enveloping legs. Fortuona's top was of tight scarlet silk, and over it she wore an open-fronted blue robe with a very long train. It seemed the clothing of a warrior, a kind of uniform.

The people in the room fell to their knees, then bowed themselves down all the way to the floor, even General Galgan. Mat stayed standing.

Gritting her teeth, Min went down on one knee. The woman *was* the Empress, after all. Min wouldn't bow to Mat or the generals, but it was only proper to show respect to Fortuona.

"Who is this one, Knotai?" Fortuona asked, curious. "She thinks herself high."

"Oh, well," Mat said idly, "she's just the Dragon Reborn's woman."

Catrona, who at the side of the room had bowed herself to the ground, made a strangled sound. She looked up at Min with bulging eyes.

Light, Min thought. *She probably thinks she's offended me or something.*

"How curious," Fortuona said. "That would make her your equal, Knotai. Of course, you seem to have forgotten to bow again."

"My father would be mortified," Mat said. "He always *did* pride himself on my memory."

"You embarrass me in public again."

"Only as much as I embarrass myself." He smiled, then hesitated, as if thinking through those words a second time.

The Empress smiled as well, though she looked distinctly predatory. She moved into the room, and the people rose, so Min climbed to her feet. Mat immediately began to push her toward the door.

"Mat, wait," Min whispered.

"Just keep moving," he said. "Don't risk her deciding to snatch you up. She's not particularly good at letting things go, once she has them in hand." He actually sounded proud, saying that.

You're as crazy as they are, Min thought. "Mat, a bloody flower."

"What?" he said, still shoving her.

"A bloody flower around her head," Min said. "A death lily. Someone is going to try to kill her very soon."

Mat froze. Fortuona turned sharply.

Min didn't realize that two guards were moving until they had her pressed against the ground. They were the odd ones in the black armor—though now that she was close, Min could see it was actually a dark green.

Idiot, she thought as they pressed her face against the floor. *I should have let Mat pull me from the room first.* She hadn't made a mistake like that—speaking of one of her viewings loud enough for others to hear—in years. What was wrong with her?

"Stop!" Mat said. "Let her up!"

Mat might have been elevated to the Blood, but the guards obviously had no problem ignoring a direct order from him.

"How does she know this, Knotai?" Fortuona asked, stepping up to Mat. She sounded angry. Perhaps disappointed. "What is happening?"

"It's not what you assume, Tuon," Mat said.

No, don't—

"She sees things," Mat continued. "It's nothing to get all angry about. It's just a trick of the Pattern, Tuon. Min sees visions around people, like little pictures. She didn't mean anything by what she said." He laughed. It was forced.

The room grew very still. It was so quiet, Min could once again hear the explosions in the distance.

"Doomseer," Fortuona whispered.

The guards suddenly let her free, backing away. Min groaned, sitting up. The guards had moved to protect the Empress, but one who had touched her pulled his gauntlets off and tossed them to the ground. He wiped his hand against his breastplate, as if trying to clean his skin of something.

Fortuona didn't seem afraid. She stepped up to Min, lips parting, almost in awe. The young Empress reached out and touched Min's face. "What he says . . . it is true?"

"Yes," Min said, grudgingly.

"What do you see around me?" Fortuona said. "Speak it, Doomseer. I would know your omens, and judge you true or false!"

That sounded dangerous. "I see a bloody death lily, as I told Mat," Min said. "And three ships, sailing. An insect in the darkness. Red lights, spread across a field that should be lush and ripe. A man with the teeth of a wolf."

Fortuona drew in a sharp breath. She looked up at Mat. "This is a great gift you have brought me, Knotai. Enough to pay your penance. Enough for credit beyond. Such a grand gift."

"Well ... I ..."

"I don't belong to anyone," Min said. "Except maybe Rand, and him to me."

Fortuona ignored her, standing. "This woman is my new *Soe'feia*. Doomseer, Truthspeaker! Holy woman, she who may not be touched. We have been blessed. Let it be known. The Crystal Throne has not had a true reader of the omens for over three centuries!"

Min sat, stunned, until Mat pulled her to her feet. "Is that a good thing?" she whispered to him.

"I'll be bloody in the face if I know," Mat said back. "But you remember what I said about getting away from her? Well, you can probably forget about that now."

CHAPTER
28

Too Many Men

"Lord Agelmar sent us directly," the Arafellin said to Lan.
The man kept glancing toward the front line, where his
companions fought for their lives.

Thunder shook the battlefield here in Shienar. The scent of
burnt flesh was pungent in the air, alongside burnt hair. The
Dreadlords didn't care if their attacks killed Trollocs, so long as
they hit men as well.

"You're certain?" Lan asked from horseback.

"Of course, Dai Shan," the man said. He wore his braids long,
the bells painted red for some reason Lan did not understand.
Something to do with the Arafellin Houses and their approach to
the Last Battle. "If I lie, let me be whipped a hundred times and
left in the sun. I was surprised by the order, as I thought my men
were to guard the flanks. Not only did the messenger have the
proper passwords, but the man I sent to the command tent
returned to confirm."

"Thank you, Captain," Lan said, waving for him to go back to
his men. He glanced at Andere and Prince Kaisel, both of whom
sat nearby, looking confused. They had listened to Lan interrogate
the Kandori banner leader just before this, and that man had
made similar assertions.

Lord Agelmar had sent them both. Two reserve forces, sent separately, neither knowing the other was going to the same place. A cool breeze blew across the river to Lan's right as he turned and rode toward the back lines. The land's heat soon smothered that coolness. Those clouds above seemed so close, one could almost reach out and touch them.

"Lan?" Andere asked, as he and Kaisel trotted their horses up beside Mandarb. "What is this about?"

"Too many men sent to plug the same hole in our lines," Lan said softly.

"It is an easy mistake to make," Prince Kaisel said. "The worry that the Trollocs would punch through is a real one, now that the Dreadlords have joined the battle. The general sent two banners instead of one. Best to be safe. He probably did it intentionally."

No. It *had* been a mistake. A small one, but a mistake. The correct move would have been to pull the soldiers back and stabilize their battle lines. A single banner of cavalry then could ride in and cut off the Trollocs coming through. Two waves could have been coordinated, but without giving warning to the different captains, the risk was that they would trip one another up—which was what had happened.

Lan shook his head and scanned the battlefield. Queen Ethenielle's banner was not far away. He headed straight for it. The Queen waited with her honor guard, Lord Baldhere on one side, the Sword of Kirukan held with its hilt directly toward the Queen, though she had chosen not to ride into battle herself. Lan had half-wondered if she would follow Tenobia's lead on that point, but he shouldn't have. Ethenielle was a coolheaded woman. More importantly, she'd surrounded herself with coolheaded advisors.

Lord Ramsin—her new husband—spoke with a group of his commanders. A sly-looking fellow in the clothing of a scout brushed past Lan as he rode up, off to deliver orders. Lord Agelmar didn't usually give the squad-by-squad commands; his concern was the overall battle. He told his commanders what he wanted them to accomplish, but details of how they would carry out those objectives were left up to them.

A stout, round-faced woman sat beside the Queen, speaking calmly to her. She noticed Lan, and nodded. Lady Serailla was the

Queen's primary advisor. Lan and she had had . . . disagreements in the past. He respected her as much as he could someone he occasionally wanted to throttle and toss off a cliff.

"Dai Shan," the Queen said, nodding to him. Ramsin, standing a little ways off, gave a wave. Thunder rumbled. There was no rain, and Lan didn't expect any, despite the thick humidity. "You are wounded? Let me send for one of the Healers."

"They are needed elsewhere," Lan said tersely as her guards saluted him. Each man wore a green tabard over his breastplate, the Red Horse embroidered on it, and each lance trailed red and green streamers. The helmets had steel face-bars, as opposed to Lan's own open-fronted, wide Malkieri helmet. "Might I borrow Lord Baldhere, Your Majesty? I have a question for him."

"You need but make the request, Dai Shan," Queen Ethenielle said, though Lady Serailla narrowed her eyes at him. Obviously, she wondered what he needed of the Kandori queen's Swordbearer.

Baldhere moved up to Lan, shifting the Sword of Kirukan to his other arm, to keep the hilt still pointed at his queen. It was a formality, but Baldhere was a formal man. Andere and Prince Kaisel joined the two of them, and Lan did not make them fall back.

"Lord Agelmar committed a good fourth of our reserves to a small opening in our lines," Lan said softly enough that only Baldhere, Andere and Kaisel could hear. "I'm not certain all were needed."

"He just gave orders for our Saldaean light cavalry to pull away from the eastern flank," Baldhere said, "and hit the Trollocs' left flank deep behind their lines, a surprise hit-and-run attack. He says he wants the Dreadlords' attention spread out, and claims that making our defenses appear weaker than they are will tempt them into making a mistake."

"Your thoughts?" Lan asked.

"It's a good move," Baldhere said, "if you intend to force the battle to go long. Alone, it wouldn't worry me too much, not as long as the Saldaeans can get out with their necks intact. I hadn't heard about the reserves. That leaves us enormously exposed on the east."

"Let's assume," Lan said softly, carefully, "that one were in a position to sabotage the entire army. Let's assume that one wanted to do so, but do it with great subtlety, as to not be suspected. What would you do?"

"Put our back to the river," Baldhere said slowly. "Claim a position for the high ground, but leave us in danger of being surrounded. Commit us to a deadly fight, then expose an opening in our defenses and let us be split. Make each step seem rational."

"And your next step?" Lan said.

Baldhere considered, looking troubled. "You'd need to pull the archers off the hills to the east. The land is rough over there, and so Shadowspawn could come around our scouts—particularly with everyone's eyes up toward the front lines—and draw close.

"Archers would see them and raise the alarm, perhaps be able to hold the Trollocs back long enough for the other reserves to arrive. But if the archers were moved, and the eastern reserves committed, and the enemy could swing around our eastern flank and attack our back lines ... our whole army would be pinned back against the river. From there, it would be only a matter of time."

"Lord Mandragoran," Prince Kaisel said, nudging his horse forward. He looked about, as if ashamed. "I can't believe I'm hearing this. Surely you don't suspect Lord Agelmar of betraying us!"

"We can't afford to leave anyone above suspicion," Lan said grimly. "A caution I should have listened to with a keener ear. Perhaps it is nothing. Perhaps."

"We're going to have enough difficulty getting out of this position as it is," Andere said, frowning. "If we get pinned against the river ..."

"The plan originally was to use the reserve light cavalry to cover the retreat," Lan said. "The infantry could retreat first, crossing the river on foot, then we could bring the heavy cavalry through gateways. The river is not swift, and the horses of the light cavalry could ford it, while Trollocs wouldn't dare. Not until they were forced. It was a good enough plan."

Unless they got pressed too hard for the foot to disengage. Everything would fall apart then. And if they were surrounded, there was no way Lan would get his army out. They didn't have enough channelers to move the entire army. The only way out would be to leave the foot, abandoning half of his army to the slaughter. No, he'd die before he let that happen.

"Everything Lord Agelmar has been doing lately *is* a good enough plan," Baldhere said intensely. "Good enough to avoid suspicion, but not good enough to win. Lan ... something is wrong with him. I've known him for years. Please. I still believe that he's merely tired, but he *is* making mistakes. I'm right, I know I am."

Lan nodded. He left Lord Baldhere at his post and rode, with his guard, toward the back lines and the command tent.

The sense of dread that Lan felt was like a stone stuck in his throat. Those clouds seemed lower than before. They rumbled. The drums of the Dark One, come to claim the lives of men.

By the time Lan reached the command tent, he had a hundred good men at his back. As he drew near, Lan spotted a young Shienaran messenger—unarmored, topknot streaming behind him as he ran—making for his horse.

At Lan's wave, Andere dashed over and caught the man's reins, holding them tight. The messenger frowned. "Dai Shan?" he asked, saluting as Lan rode up.

"You are delivering orders for Lord Agelmar?" Lan asked, dismounting.

"Yes, my Lord."

"What orders?"

"The eastern Kandori archers," the messenger said. "Their hill is too far from the main part of the battlefield, and Lord Agelmar feels they would serve better coming forward and launching volleys at those Dreadlords."

The archers probably thought that the Saldaean light cavalry were still back there; the Saldaeans thought the archers would stay; the reserves thought that both would hold after they'd been deployed.

It could still be a coincidence. Agelmar was being worked too hard, or had some greater plan that was beyond the eyes of other generals. Never accuse a man of a killing offense unless you were ready to kill him yourself, right then, with your own sword.

"Belay that order," Lan said, cold. "Instead, send the Saldaean scouts out roving through those eastern hills. Tell them to watch for signs of a force of Shadowspawn sneaking in to strike at us. Warn the archers to prepare to shoot, then return here and bring me word. Be quick about it, but tell nobody but the scouts and archers themselves that you are doing it."

The man looked confused, but he saluted. Agelmar was commanding general of this army, but Lan—as Dai Shan—had final word on all orders, and the only authority greater than his in this battle was that of Elayne.

Lan nodded to a pair of men from the High Guard. Washim and Geral were Malkieri whom he'd grown to respect a great deal during their weeks fighting together.

Light, has it only been weeks? It feels like months . . .

He pushed the thought away as the two Malkieri followed the messenger to make certain he did as told. Lan would consider the ramifications of what was happening only after he knew all of the facts.

Only then.

Loial did not know much about warfare. One did not need to know much to realize that Elayne's side was losing.

He and the other Ogier fought, facing a horde of thousands upon thousands of Trollocs—the second army that had come up to crush from the south, skirting the city. Crossbowmen from the Legion of the Dragon flanked the Ogier, launching volleys of quarrels, having withdrawn from the front as the Trollocs hit their lines. The enemy had dispersed the Legion's heavy cavalry, exhausted as they had been. Companies of pikemen held desperately against the tide, and the Wolf Guard clung to a disintegrating line on the other hill.

He'd heard fragments of what was happening on other parts of the battlefield. Elayne's armies had crushed the northern force of Trollocs, finishing them off, and as the Ogier fought, guarding the dragons that fired from the hill above them, more and more soldiers came to join the new front. They came bloodied, exhausted and weak.

This new force of Trollocs would crush them.

The Ogier sang a song of mourning. It was the dirge they sang for forests that had to be leveled or for great trees that died in a storm. It was a song of loss, of regret, of inevitability. He joined in the final refrain.

> *"All rivers run dry,*
> *All songs must end,*

Every root will die,
Every branch must bend ... "

He downed a snarling Trolloc, but another one sank its teeth into his leg. He bellowed, breaking off his song as he grabbed the Trolloc by the neck. He had never considered himself strong, not by Ogier standards, but he lifted the Trolloc and flung it into its fellows behind.

Men—fragile men—were dead all around his feet. Their loss of life pained him. Each one had been given such a short time to live. Some, still alive, still fought. He knew they thought of themselves as bigger than they were, but here on the battlefield—with Ogier and Trollocs—they seemed like children running around underfoot.

No. He would not see them that way. The men and women fought with bravery and passion. Not children, but heroes. Still, seeing them broken made his ears lie back. He started singing again, louder, and this time it was not the song of mourning. It was a song he had not sung before, a song of growing, but not one of the tree songs that were so familiar to him.

He bellowed it loud and angry, laying about him with his axe. On all sides, grass turned green, cords and ribbons of life sprouted. The hafts of the Trolloc polearms began to grow leaves; many of the beasts snarled and dropped the weapons in shock.

Loial fought on. This song was not a song of victory. It was a song of life. Loial did not intend to die here on this hillside.

By the Light, he had a book to finish before he went!

Mat stood in the Seanchan command building, surrounded by skeptical generals. Min had only just returned, after being taken away and dressed in Seanchan finery. Tuon had gone as well, to see to some empressy duty.

Looking back at the maps, Mat felt like cursing again. Maps, maps and more maps. Pieces of paper. Most of them had been sketched by Tuon's clerks in the fading light of the previous evening. How could he know they were accurate? Mat had once seen a street artist drawing a pretty woman at night in Caemlyn, and the resulting picture could have been sold for gold as a dead-on representation of Cenn Buie in a dress.

More and more, he was thinking that battle maps were about as useful as a heavy coat in Tear. He needed to be able to *see* the battle, not how someone else thought the battle looked. The map was too simple.

"I'm going out to look at the battlefield," Mat declared.

"You're what?" Courtani asked. The Seanchan Banner-General was about as pretty as a bundle of sticks with armor bolted to it. Mat figured she must have eaten something very sour once and—upon finding the resulting grimace useful for frightening away birds—had decided to adopt it permanently.

"I'm going to go look at the battlefield," Mat said again. He set aside his hat, then reached up over his head and grabbed the back of his rich, bulky Seanchan robes. He pulled the clothing, awkward shoulder pieces and all, over his head with a rustle of silk and lace, then tossed it aside.

That left him clad in only his neck scarf, his medallion and the strange breeches the Seanchan had given him, black and somewhat stiff. Min raised an eyebrow at his bare chest, which made him blush. But what did it matter? She was with Rand, so that made her practically his sister. There *was* Courtani, too, but Mat was not convinced that she was female. He was not convinced she was human, either.

Mat dug under the table for a moment, and pulled out a bundle he had stashed there earlier, then straightened up. Min folded her arms. Her new clothing looked very nice on her, a dress nearly as rich as the ones worn by Tuon. Min's was a dark green shiny silk with black embroidery and wide, open sleeves that were at least long enough to stick your head into. They had done up her hair, too, sticking bits of metal into it, silver with inset firedrops. There were hundreds of them. If this whole Doomseer title did not work out for her, perhaps she could find work as a chandelier.

She was quite fetching in the outfit, actually. Odd. Mat had always considered Min on the boyish side, but now he found her appealing. Not that he looked.

The Seanchan in the room seemed stunned that Mat had suddenly stripped to the waist. He did not see why. They had servants that wore much less. Light, but they did.

"I'm tempted to do the same as you," Min muttered, grabbing the front of her dress.

Mat froze, then sputtered. He must have swallowed a fly or something. "Burn me," he said, throwing on the shirt he dug out of the bundle. "I'll give you a hundred Tar Valon marks if you do it, just so I can tell the story."

That earned him a glare, though he did not know why. She was the one talking about striding about like a bloody Aiel Maiden on her way to the sweat tent.

Min did not do it, and he was almost sad. Almost. He had to be careful around Min. He was certain that a smile in the wrong place would earn him a knifing not only from her, but from Tuon, and Mat was much happier with only one knife stuck in him at a time.

The foxhead medallion rested comfortably against his skin— thank the Light, Tuon had understood that he did need it—as he tossed on his coat, also retrieved from the bundle.

"How did you retain those?" Captain-General Galgan asked. "I was under the impression that your clothing had been burned, Raven Prince."

Galgan looked very silly with that one strip of white hair on his head, but Mat did not mention this. It was the Seanchan way. Folk could be funny, but he didn't doubt Galgan could handle himself in a battle, however he looked.

"These?" Mat said, gesturing to his coat and shirt. "I really have no idea. They were just down there. I'm completely baffled." He had been very pleased to learn that Seanchan guards—for all their stoic expressions and too-straight backs—responded to bribes like other people.

All but those Deathwatch Guards. Mat had learned not to try it with them; the glare they'd given him made him think that if he tried it again, he'd end up with his face in the mud. Perhaps it would be better not to even talk to a Deathwatch Guard again, as it was quite obvious that each and every one one of them had traded his sense of humor for an oversized chin.

In a pinch, though, he knew exactly who he would trust with Tuon's safety.

Mat strode out, grabbing his *ashandarei* from against the wall as he passed. Courtani and Min followed him out. It was too bad Tylee was so good at what she did. Mat would rather have kept her behind for company and sent the scarecrow instead. Maybe he should have. Some of the Trollocs might have mistaken her for one of them.

He had to wait as a groom ran for Pips, unfortunately, and that gave someone time to alert Tuon. He saw her approaching. Well, she had said she would return shortly anyway, so he had not really expected to avoid a confrontation.

Min shuffled, cursing softly at her skirts.

"Still trying to decide if you should run?" Mat asked Min under his breath as Tuon approached.

"Yes," Min said sourly.

"The beds are nice here, you know. And they know how to treat a fellow, so long as they don't end up beheading him. I still haven't figured out what keeps that from happening."

"Wonderful."

Mat turned to her. "You realize that if Rand were here, he'd probably ask you to stay."

Min glared at him.

"It's just the truth, Min. The bloody truth. I was there when Rand brought them to his side, and I can tell you, he was worried. The Seanchan and Aes Sedai don't get along too well, if you hadn't noticed."

"That's about as obvious as your pride is, Mat."

"Ouch. Here I'm trying to help. I tell you, Min. How much relief do you think it would bring Rand if he knew that someone he trusted had Tuon's ear, someone who could nudge her to play nicely with the Aes Sedai by giving the right 'omens' at the right time? Of course, you could be back at the camp hauling water and running messages. I'm sure that would be *just* as helpful as you would be keeping an eye on a foreign monarch and encouraging her to trust and respect the Dragon Reborn, building a bridge of friendship between her and the rest of the nations."

Min stood silently for a moment. "I hate you, bloody Mat Cauthon."

"That's the spirit," Mat said, raising a hand to greet Tuon. "Now, let's see which of my limbs she cuts off for throwing away her fancy clothing." Too bad about that. Nice embroidery on that robe. A man needed a little embroidery to keep him refined. Still, he was not *about* to wear that heap of cloth into battle. He would have better luck trying to fight while carrying Pips on his back.

The others did their usual bowing and scraping when Tuon walked up, though she had been gone only a few minutes. Mat gave her a nod. She took in his clothing with a long glance, up and down. Why was everyone so sour on a good shirt and jacket? He had not chosen the ratty one he had worn to visit Elayne. He had burned that.

"Greatest One," Courtani said. She was of the High Blood, and could address Tuon directly. "May you always draw breath. The Raven Prince has determined that he himself must visit the battlefield, as he has judged our messengers and generals to be lacking skill."

Mat hooked his thumbs into his belt, regarding Tuon, as a groom finally arrived with Pips. About bloody time. Had the boy stopped for lunch along the way, perhaps taken in a gleeman performance or two?

"Well, why are we waiting?" Tuon asked. "If the Prince of the Ravens wishes to see the battlefield, I would think that loyal servants of the Empire would have tripped over themselves in their haste to carry him there."

Courtani looked as if she had been slapped. Mat grinned at Tuon, and she favored him with a smile. Light, but he liked those smiles.

"So, you're coming along, then?" he asked Tuon.

"Of course. You see a reason why I should not?"

"Not a one," Mat said, groaning inside. "Not a single bloody one."

CHAPTER
29

The Loss of a Hill

"**F**ocus attention on the Fades!" Egwene said, releasing a burst of Air toward the Trollocs climbing up the hillside. The Trollocs had made a gaping hole in the ranks of pikemen defending the hill and were pouring through. Now accustomed to assaulting channelers, they squatted and braced themselves. That gave Egwene a good view of the fist and the Myrddraal hiding at the very center. It wore a brown coat over its usual clothing and held a Trolloc catchpole.

No wonder I had trouble spotting him, Egwene thought, destroying the creature with a weave of Fire. The Halfman writhed, shaking and screeching in the fire, its eyeless face turned toward the heavens. The fist of Trollocs dropped as well.

Egwene smiled in satisfaction, but her pleasure was short lived. Her archers were getting low on arrows, the pike ranks were tattered and some of the Aes Sedai were clearly fatigued. Another wave of Trollocs replaced those that Egwene had dropped. *Will we be able to stand another day of this?* she thought.

A banner of lancers suddenly broke from the left flank of Bryne's army fighting at the river. They flew the Flame of Tar Valon—that would be the unit of heavy cavalry that Bryne was proud of. He had cobbled them together under Captain Joni

Shagrin out of a mix of seasoned veterans from the cavalries of other countries and those soldiers from the Tower Guard who wanted to join this elite fighting force.

The lancers skirted the Sharans opposite them and rode furiously toward Egwene's hills, directly at the rear of the Trolloc army that was assaulting her position. Right behind them, a second cavalry unit followed in the dust of the first, this one displaying the dark green banner of Illian. It looked like the general was finally going to send her some relief.

But . . . Wait. Egwene frowned. From her vantage, she could see that the main army's left flank was completely unprotected now. *What is he doing? Some . . . some sort of trap for the Sharans?*

If there had been a trap planned, the jaws did not snap shut. Instead, a Sharan cavalry unit charged into Bryne's exposed left flank and began to inflict heavy casualties on the foot soldiers defending that position at the river. And then Egwene saw another movement on the field below that really horrified her— an even larger Sharan cavalry banner had broken off the enemy's right flank and was bearing down on the lancer unit that had come to help Egwene.

"Gawyn, get word to those lancers—it's a trap!"

But there was no time to do anything. Within moments, the Sharan cavalry had begun slaying the White Tower lancers from behind. At the same time, the back ranks of Trollocs had turned around to face the lancer charge. Egwene could see that these Trollocs all carried long polearms that ripped through the flesh of man and horse. The front ranks of lancers went down in a bloody heap, and the Trollocs waded between the bodies to pull down and thrust their weapons through the cavalrymen behind.

Egwene shouted, drawing what Power she could and trying to destroy that Trolloc force—and the other women joined her. It was a massacre on both sides. There were just too many Trollocs, and the lancers were unprotected. In minutes, it was over. Only a few cavalrymen had managed to survive, and Egwene saw them riding at full bore toward the river.

It shook her. At times, the armies seemed to move at the turgid pace of enormous ships at dock—and then, in an instant, everything would burst and entire banners would have perished.

She looked away from the corpses below. The Aes Sedai positions on the hilltops had been compromised. As the Trollocs returned their attention toward her force, Egwene gave orders for gateways. She had the pikemen withdraw uphill through the gateways as her archers continued to shoot projectiles into the Trollocs below. Then, Egwene and the remaining Aes Sedai rained destruction down on the Trollocs long enough to get the archers through the gateways.

Before disappearing through the last gateway on her hill, Egwene gave a final look at the battlefield. What had just happened? She shook her head as Gawyn stepped up to her side, faithful as always. He hadn't had an opportunity to draw his sword this battle. Neither had Leilwin; the two seemed to be having a little silent competition as to who could act as the better guard, remaining right by Egwene's side. She'd have found it annoying, but it was better than Gawyn's sullen regret in previous battle engagements.

He *was* looking pale, though. As if at the start of a sickness. Had he been getting enough sleep?

"I want to go to the camp and find General Bryne," Egwene said. "I want to know why this was allowed to happen. And then I will go to our troops defending the ford, and avenge our people who just lost their lives here."

They both gave her frowns.

"Egwene . . . " Gawyn said.

"I have strength yet," Egwene said. "I have been using the *sa'angreal* to keep from having to work too hard. The men fighting in that quarter need to see me, and I must do good where I can. I will take as many guards as you wish me to take."

Gawyn hesitated, glanced at Leilwin, then finally nodded.

Lan dismounted and handed the reins to Andere, then continued past the guards—who seemed shocked to see him and his numerous guards, many of them bloodied—toward the command tent. The tent was little more than an awning now, open on all sides, with soldiers moving in and out like ants in a hill. The air was hot here in Shienar today. He had not received reports recently from the other battlefronts, but had heard his would not be the only desperate stand today. Elayne fought at Cairhien; the Amyrlin on the border of Arafel.

Light send that they were having a better time of it than Lan. Inside the tent, Agelmar stood with maps on the ground all around him, pointing at them with a thin pole and moving bits of colored stone around as he gave orders. Runners would come and give updates on the progress of battle. The best battle plans lasted only until the first sword was drawn, but a good general could work battles like a potter working clay, taking the ebbs and flows of soldiers and molding them.

"Lord Mandragoran?" Agelmar asked, looking up. "Light, man! You look like the Blight itself. Have you seen the Aes Sedai for Healing?"

"I am well," Lan said. "How goes the battle?"

"I'm encouraged," Agelmar said. "If we can find some way to stall those Dreadlords for an hour or two, I think we actually have a fair shot of turning the Trollocs back."

"Surely not," Lan said. "There are so many."

"It's not about numbers," Agelmar said, waving Lan over, pointing at a map. "Lan, here is a thing that few men understand. Armies *can* and often *do* break when they have superior numbers, superior battlefield advantage, and a good chance of winning.

"When you spend time commanding, you start to think of an army as a single entity. A massive beast with thousands of limbs. That's a mistake. An army is made up of men—or, in this case, Trollocs—each one on the field, each one terrified. Being a soldier is about keeping your terror in check. The beast inside just wants to escape."

Lan crouched down, inspecting the battle maps. The situation was much as he'd seen it, only Agelmar still had the Saldaean light cavalry watching the eastern flank on the map. A mistake? Lan had confirmed for himself that they were no longer there. Shouldn't runners have brought Agelmar word that the map was wrong? Or was he somehow distracting them from noticing?

"I'll show you something today, Lan," Agelmar said softly. "I'll show you what the smallest man on the practice yard must learn if he is to survive. You can make the larger enemy break if you convince him that he is going to die. Hit him hard enough, and he will run, and won't return to let you hit again—even if you're secretly too weak to hit again."

"That's your plan, then?" Lan asked. "Today?"

"The Trollocs will break if we show them a display of force that frightens them," Agelmar said. "I know it can work. I'm hoping that we can bring down the leader of those Dreadlords. If the Trollocs assume they're losing, they will run. They are cowardly beasts."

Listening to Agelmar made it seem plausible. Perhaps Lan just wasn't seeing the entire picture. Perhaps the great captain's genius was beyond what others could fathom. Had he done right in countermanding the order to move the archers?

The messenger Lan had sent earlier came galloping back to the command center. One of Lan's High Guard was there, too, holding his own arm, a black-fletched arrow stuck in it. "An enormous force of Shadowspawn!" the messenger said. "Coming in from the east! Dai Shan, you were right!"

They knew to come in that way, Lan thought. *They couldn't have just noticed that we'd exposed ourselves, not with those hills blocking their view. It's come too quickly. The Shadow must have been told, or must have known what to expect.* He looked at Agelmar.

"Impossible!" Agelmar said. "What's this, now? Why didn't the scouts see it?"

"Lord Agelmar," one of his commanders said. "You sent the scouts in the east back to look at the river, remember? They were to inspect the crossing for us. You said the archers would . . . " The commander paled. "The archers!"

"The archers are still in their positions," Lan said, rising. "I want the front lines to begin withdrawing. Pull the Saldaeans out of the fighting, ready to strike to help the foot soldiers disengage. Pull the Asha'man back. We'll need gateways."

"Lord Mandragoran," Agelmar said. "This new development can be used. If we pull apart and then smash them between us, we can—"

"You are relieved of duty, Lord Agelmar," Lan said, not looking at the man. "And, unfortunately, I must request that you remain under supervision until I can sort through what has happened."

The command tent grew silent, every aide, messenger and officer turning toward Lan.

"Now, Lan," Agelmar said. "That *sounded* like you are having me arrested."

"I am," Lan said, motioning to the High Guard. They moved into the tent, taking positions to keep anyone from escaping. Some of Agelmar's men did reach for swords, but most looked confused, and only rested their hands on the hilts.

"This is an outrage!" Agelmar said. "Don't be a fool. This isn't the time—"

"What would you have me do, Agelmar?" Lan barked. "Let you run this army into the ground? Let the Shadow take us? Why are you doing this? *Why?*"

"You're overreacting, Lan," Agelmar said, keeping his calm with obvious difficulty, his eyes burning. "What's going through your head? Light!"

"Why did you pull the archers off of the eastern hills?"

"Because I needed them elsewhere!"

"And does that make *sense?*" Lan demanded. "Didn't you tell me that guarding that flank was vital?"

"I . . ."

"You drew away the scouts from that position too. Why?"

"They . . . It . . . " Agelmar raised a hand to his head, looking dazed. He looked down at the battle map, and his eyes widened.

"What's wrong with you, Agelmar?" Lan said.

"I don't know," the man said. He blinked, staring at the maps at his feet. His face adopted a look of horror, eyes wide, lips parting. "Oh, *Light!* What have I done?"

"Pass my orders!" Lan said urgently to his high guard. "Bring Lord Baldhere to the command tent. Queen Ethenielle and King Easar as well."

"Lan, you have to bring the . . . " Agelmar stopped. "Light! I can't say it. I start thinking about what to do, and the wrong thoughts come into my head! I'm still trying to sabotage us. I've doomed us." His eyes wide, he reached for his shortsword, sliding the blade free.

Lan caught the sword around the guard and the blade collar, stopping it just before Agelmar could ram it into his stomach and end his life. Blood seeped between Lan's fingers from where one brushed the sharp edge of the blade, just below the collar.

"Let me die with honor," Agelmar said. "I . . . I've destroyed us all. I've lost us this war, Lan."

"Not the war, just the battle," Lan said. "Something is wrong with you. A sickness, a fatigue or something of the Shadow. I suspect we'll find someone has been tampering with your mind."

"But—"

"You are a soldier!" Lan bellowed. "Act like one!"

Agelmar froze. He met Lan's eyes, then nodded once. Lan removed his fingers from the blade and Agelmar thrust it back in its sheath. The great captain sat down cross-legged in the traditional Shienaran meditation posture, eyes closed.

Lan strode away, calling orders. Prince Kaisel ran up to him, obviously afraid. "What's happening, Lord Mandragoran?"

"Compulsion, likely," Lan said. "We've been like rabbits in a snare, with the line being drawn slowly—but snugly—around our necks. Someone please tell me the Asha'man still have enough strength for gateways! And bring me news of the eastern flank! Those archers will need support. Commit the rest of the reserves to protecting them."

Prince Kaisel backed away as the orders continued, his eyes wide, his hand on his sword. He looked at Lord Agelmar, face pale. "We've really lost?" he asked Lan once the orders were out, messengers racing to deliver them.

"Yes," Lan said. "We have."

"Lan!" Agelmar said suddenly, opening his eyes.

Lan turned to him.

"Queen Tenobia," Agelmar said. "I've sent her into danger without understanding what I'd done. Whoever put these plans into my head wanted her dead!"

Lan swore softly, bolting out of camp and up the side of the nearest hill. The scouts there made room for him as he reached the top, pulling his looking glass from his belt. He didn't need it. He found the Queen's flag while scanning the battlefield.

She was surrounded. Whatever support she had thought she would receive had not been sent. Lan opened his mouth to call orders, but they died on his lips as the Trollocs swarmed over the small flag of white and silver where she'd been fighting. It fell, and in seconds, he couldn't pick out a living soldier in that section of the battlefield.

Coldness. He could do nothing for Tenobia. It was no longer about saving individuals.

He would be lucky to escape this day with any semblance of an army at all.

Mat rode with Tuon south toward the battlefield, along the banks of the river that was the western border of Arafel.

Of course, where Tuon went, so did Selucia. And now Min; Tuon wanted to keep her new Doomseer at her side at all times. Tuon kept asking for viewings, and Min kept reluctantly explaining what she saw.

Mat had tried to make her say she saw a hat floating around Mat's head. That would persuade Tuon to stop trying to get rid of his, would it not? It would have been better than Min explaining about the eye on a scale, and the dagger, and all of the other bloody things she had seen about Mat.

Where Tuon went, a hundred of the Deathwatch Guards *also* went. And Galgan and Courtani, who felt chastised for not acting quickly enough to help Mat. Furyk Karede was along, too, leading the Deathwatch Guard. Being around Karede was about as pleasant as finding another man's hand in your purse, but he was a good soldier, and Mat respected him. He would very much like to put Karede and Lan in a staring contest together. They could be at it for years.

"I need a better view," Mat said, scanning the battlefield when they came within range. "There."

He turned Pips and rode toward a rise close enough to where the opposing forces traded destruction at the river's edge. Tuon followed him without a word. When they all reached the rise, he noticed Selucia staring daggers at him.

"What's wrong?" Mat asked. "I'd have assumed you would be happy to have me back. It gives you someone else to scowl at."

"The Empress will follow where you go," she said.

"So she will," Mat said. "As I'll follow where she goes, I suppose. I hope that doesn't lead us in too many circles." He inspected the combat.

The river was not terribly wide—maybe fifty spans across— but it was swift-moving and deep on either side of the ford. The water made a nice barrier, and not just for Trollocs. The ford, though, made for an easy crossing—the water there was knee-deep and wide enough for at least twenty files of riders to cross at the same time.

In the distant middle of the Sharan army, a man sat upon a brilliant white horse. Mat could barely make him out with his glass; the man's glistening armor didn't seem like any Mat had seen, though the distance made it difficult to tell specifics. "I assume that's our Forsaken?" he asked, gesturing with the *ashandarei*.

"He seems to be yelling for the Dragon Reborn," Galgan said. Demandred's voice boomed across the battlefield right then, enhanced by the One Power. He was demanding that the Dragon come and face him in a duel.

Mat inspected the fellow through the glass. "Demandred, eh? Has he gone a bit dotty, or what?" Well, Mat knew which part of the battle to bloody stay away from. He had not signed up to fight Forsaken. In fact, so far as he remembered, he had not signed up at all. He had been bloody *press-ganged* every step of the way. Usually by force, and always by one fool woman or another.

Egwene could deal with Demandred, or maybe the Asha'man could. Rand said the Asha'man were not going crazy anymore, but that was a shallow promise. Any man who wanted to wield the One Power was *already* crazy, so far as Mat considered it. Adding more crazy to them would be like pouring tea into an already full cup.

At least Tuon's *damane* had those Sharan channelers occupied. Their firefight ripped up the ground on both riverbanks. It was impossible to get a clear picture of what was going on, though. There was just too much confusion.

Mat pointed his looking glass southward along the river once more, and frowned. There was a military camp set up just a few hundred paces opposite the ford, but it wasn't the haphazard arrangement of tents that caught his attention. At the eastern edge of the camp was a large body of troops and their horses, just standing there. He picked out a figure pacing in front of the assembly, who appeared to be in a foul mood. Mat might have been missing an eye, but it was no difficult task to recognize Tylee.

Mat lowered the looking glass. He rubbed his chin, adjusted his hat and set his *ashandarei* on his shoulder. "Give me five minutes on my own," he said, then kicked Pips into a gallop down the hill, hoping that Tuon would let him go alone. For once, she did, though as he reached the base of the rise, he could imagine her up there watching him with those curious eyes of hers. She seemed to find everything he did to be interesting.

Mat galloped alongside the river toward Tylee's location. Explosions rang out, painful to the ears, announcing that he had neared the heart of the battle.

Mat nudged Pips to the left and rode directly toward the pacing general. "Tylee, you Light-blinded fool! Why are you sitting around here instead of making yourself useful?"

"Highness," Tylee said, falling to her knees, "we were ordered to stay here until we were called."

"Who told you to do that? And get up."

"General Bryne, Highness," she said, rising. He could sense the annoyance in her tone, but she kept her face under control. "He said that we were only a reserve force, and that under no circumstances were we to move from here until he gave the order. He said many lives depended on it. But look, you can see for yourself," she said, gesturing toward the river, "the battle is not going well."

Mat had been too caught up with Tylee to see the state of affairs across the water, but now he gave the field a wide sweep with his eye.

While the *damane* still seemed to be holding their own against the Sharan channelers, the regular troops were clearly in a bind. The defenses on Bryne's left flank downriver had completely broken down, and the soldiers there were being mobbed by Sharans.

Where was the cavalry? It was supposed to be protecting the flanks. And, as Mat had predicted, Sharan archers had moved out into the field and were sending arrows into Bryne's cavalry on the right flank. It was all like a boil being squeezed, and Bryne's troops were the boil about to pop.

"This doesn't make any bloody sense," Mat said. "He's spinning this more and more into a disaster. Where is the general now, Tylee?"

"I cannot say, Highness, I have people out looking for him, but so far there is no word. But I have reports that our side has had a major setback just south of here. Two large cavalry units of

General Bryne's have been wiped out by the Sharans just below the hills on the border. It is said they had been sent there to relieve the *marath'damane* on the hilltops."

"Blood and bloody ashes." Mat considered this information. "All right, Tylee, we can't wait around any longer. Here's what we are going to do. Have Banner-General Makoti take the Second Banner right up the middle. He has to work his way around our troops fighting there and push back those Sharans. You take the Third Banner and swing around to the right flank; take out those archers and any other goat-kissers that cross your path. I'm going to take the First Banner over to the left flank and put a patch on those defenses. Get going, Tylee!"

"Yes, Highness. But surely you aren't going to get so close to the battle?"

"Yes I am. Now get going, Tylee!"

"Please, if I might make a humble suggestion, Highness? You are unprotected; let me at least give you some proper armor."

Mat thought for a moment, then agreed that her suggestion was a prudent one. *A person could get hurt out there, what with arrows flying and blades swinging.* Tylee called over one of her senior officers who seemed to be about the same size as Mat. She had the man remove his armor, which was extremely colorful, overlapping plates lacquered green, gold and red, outlined with silver. The officer looked bemused when Mat handed him his coat in trade, saying that he expected it to be returned at the end of the day in the same condition. Mat put on the armor, which covered his chest, the back of his arms and the front of his thighs, and it felt comfortable enough. When the officer held out his helmet, though, Mat ignored him, merely adjusting his wide-brimmed hat as he turned to Tylee.

"Highness, one more thing, the *marath'damane* . . . "

"I'll deal with those channelers personally," Mat said.

She gawked at him as if he were insane. Bloody ashes, he probably was.

"Highness!" Tylee said. "The Empress . . . " She stopped when she saw Mat's expression. "Let us at least send for some *damane* to protect you."

"I can take care of myself just fine, thank you very much. Those bloody women would just get in my way." He grinned. "Are you ready, Tylee? I would really like this over with before it's time for my bedtime mug of ale."

In response, Tylee turned and yelled, "Mount up!" Light, she had a strong set of lungs! With that, thousands of bottoms hit their saddles, producing a slapping sound that reverberated across the legion, and each soldier sat at attention, eyes straight ahead. He'd give the Seanchan one thing—they trained bloody good soldiers.

Tylee barked out a series of orders, turned back to Mat and said, "On your command, Highness."

Mat cried out, "*Los caba'drin!*" Words most of those assembled did not understand, and yet instinctively knew to mean "Horsemen forward!"

As Mat spurred Pips into the waters of the ford, the *ashandarei* raised above his head, he heard the ground rumble as the First Banner closed ranks around him. The blaring Seanchan horns behind were giving the call to charge, each horn pitched slightly differently from the next, producing a grating, dissonant sound meant to be heard at great distances. Ahead, soldiers of the White Tower glanced over their shoulders at the noise, and in the seconds it took Mat and the Seanchan to cross the passage, soldiers were flinging themselves out of the way to make room for the riders.

Just a short veer to the left and the Seanchan were suddenly in the thick of Sharan cavalry, which had been grinding through Egwene's foot soldiers. The speed of their approach enabled the Seanchan vanguard to smash hard into the Sharans, their well-trained steeds rearing up just before crashing down on the foe with their forelegs. Sharans and their mounts fell, many crushed as the Seanchan cavalry continued their relentless forward motion.

The Sharans appeared to know what they were about, but these were heavy cavalry, weighted down with burdensome armor and equipped with long lances; perfect for eliminating foot soldiers with their backs up against a wall, but disadvantaged against a highly mobile light cavalry in such tight quarters.

The First Banner were a crack unit that used a wide variety of weaponry, and they were trained to work in teams. Spears thrown by lead riders with deadly accuracy plunged into the visors of the Sharans, a surprising number of which went through the slits and into faces. Pushing through behind were riders wielding two-handed swords with curved blades, slicing their weapons across the vulnerable space that separated helmets from the top of body armor, or at other times slashing the vulnerable chests of armor-clad Sharan mounts, bringing their riders to the ground. Other Seanchan used hooked polearms to pull Sharans out of the saddle while their partners swung spiked maces at the enemy, denting their armor so much that movement was severely restricted. And when the Sharans were on the ground, trying with difficulty to rise, the spikers would descend on them, lightly armed Seanchan whose job it was to pull up visors of the fallen and thrust a narrow dagger into exposed eyes. The lances of the Sharans were useless under these conditions—in fact, they were a hindrance, and many Sharans died before they could drop their lances and draw swords.

Mat ordered one of his cavalry squadrons to ride along the water's edge until they reached the far left edge of battle, and then to swing around the Sharan cavalry. No longer overwhelmed by Sharan lances, the White Tower infantry on the left-center were able to use their pikes and halberds again, and with the addition of the efforts of the Seanchan Second and Third Banners, defenses were slowly reestablished at the ford. It was dirty, slippery work, as the ground within several hundred paces of the river got beaten down and became an expanse of churned-up mud. But the forces of Light stood their ground.

Mat found himself washed into the thick of the fray, and his *ashandarei* never stopped spinning. He quickly found, however, that his weapon was not very useful; a few of his swings met with vulnerable flesh, but most of the time his blade glanced off the armor of his opponents, and he was forced to duck and twist in the saddle repeatedly to avoid being struck by a Sharan blade.

Mat slowly worked his way forward through the brawl, and had nearly reached the back lines of Sharan cavalry when he realized that three of his companions were no longer in their saddles. Odd, they had just been there a minute ago. Two others stiffened up, scanning from side to side, and suddenly they both went up in flames, screaming in agony and throwing themselves to the ground before going limp. Mat looked to his right just in time to see a Seanchan flung back a hundred feet in the air by an unseen force.

When he turned back, his eye met the gaze of a most beautiful woman. She was oddly clad in a black silk dress that stood out from her body, adorned with white ribbons. She was a dark-skinned beauty, like Tuon, but there was nothing delicate about her bold, high cheekbones and wide sensuous mouth, lips that seemed to pout. Until they curved up into a smile, a smile that was not meant to comfort him.

As she stared at him, his medallion grew cold. Mat breathed out.

Luck seemed to be with him so far, but he did not want to press it too far, any more than you wanted to press your best race-horse. He would still have a healthy need of that luck in the days to come.

Mat dismounted and walked toward her as the woman gasped, trying another weave, her eyes wide with amazement. Mat flipped the *ashandarei* around and spun it, sweeping her feet from beneath her. He brought the haft just below the blade back down to his right, cracking her on the back of the head as she fell.

She landed facedown in the mud. Mat did not have time to pull her out, as he was suddenly confronted by dozens of Sharans. Ten of Mat's soldiers filled out around him, and he pressed forward. These Sharans only had swords. Mat fended them off with spinning blade and pole, and he and the Seanchan fought furiously.

The fight became a blur of sweeping weapons, his *ashandarei* spraying clods of mud into the air. Two of Mat's men grabbed the facedown woman before she could suffocate in the mire.

Mat pushed forward.

Men yelled, calling for reinforcements.

Steps taken cautiously, but inevitably forward.

The ground was turning red.

Sharan soldiers replaced the ones who were slain, and the bodies of the fallen sank deeper in the mud. Soldiers often were a grim folk, but each of these Sharans seemed personally intent on killing him—until the Sharans stopped coming. Mat looked around him; there were only four Seanchan remaining at his side.

Despite the chaos of the fight, Mat felt he saw more clearly than he had before. And the lull in fighting gave him a chance to act like a commander again.

"Bind that woman's hands behind her back," Mat said, panting, to the men around him, "and tie a cloth around her eyes so that she can't see anything." He wiped the sweat from his brow—Light, there was enough of it for a second river. "We are going to push our way back to the ford with our prisoner. I'll see if I can find a few more of those bloody *damane* to throw into this battle. The Sharans were wrong to leave only one of their channelers by herself on the battlefield. But let's get out of here before any more of them show up."

Mat shook his hand; he had cracked one of his nails, splitting the fine lacquer. He turned to a Seanchan officer, one of those who had fought alongside him. The man wore an expression of awe, as if he were staring at the Dragon bloody Reborn himself. Mat looked down at the ground, not liking the man's expression, but he supposed it wasn't any worse than looking at the blood-soaked muck littered with Sharan corpses. How many had Mat killed?

"Highness . . . " the officer said. "Great Lord, no man in the Empire's service would ever dare question the Empress, may she live forever. But if a man *had* wondered about some of her choices, he would do so no longer. Prince of the Ravens!" He raised his sword, prompting a cheer from those behind.

"Get yourselves some bloody polearms," Mat said. "Those swords are next to useless for foot soldiers in this battle." He chewed a bit off the offending fingernail, then spat it to the side. "You fellows did well. Anyone see my horse?"

Pips was nearby and so, taking his mount's reins, he headed back toward the ford. He even managed to stay out of more skirmishes, for the most part. That Seanchan captain reminded him a little too much of Talmanes, and Mat had enough people following him about. *I wonder if he plays dice*, Mat thought idly, stepping into the water. His boots were good, but all boots eventually leaked, and his feet squished inside his stockings as he walked across the ford with Pips. There was a commotion far to his right on the bank, what appeared to be a gathering of Aes Sedai channeling toward the battlefield. But Mat had no intention of sticking his nose into their business. He had larger issues on his mind.

Ahead Mat saw a man standing by a tree, dressed in voluminous pants and a familiar-looking coat. He approached the man and, after a brief conversation, exchanged garb with him. Feeling good about being back in his Two Rivers coat, Mat heaved himself into the saddle, legs still dripping water, and rode back toward where he had left Tuon. His men had brought that Sharan channeler—by his order, they'd gagged her and blindfolded her. Light, what would he do with her? She'd probably end up as a *damane*.

He left his soldiers and passed the guards, now set up at the base of the little rise, with barely a nod. The battlefield spread out in his mind, no longer little drawings on paper. He could see the field, hear the men fighting, smell the rancid breath of the enemy. It was real to him now.

"The Empress," Selucia said as he reached the top of the rise, "would like to know—with great specificity—exactly why you saw fit to put yourself into the skirmish in such an irresponsible way. Your life is no longer your own, Prince of the Ravens. You cannot toss it aside as you once might have."

"I had to know," Mat said, looking out. "I had to feel the pulse of the battle."

"The pulse?" Selucia said. Tuon was talking through her by wiggling her fingers like some bloody Maiden of the Spear. Not speaking to him directly. Bad sign.

"Every battle has a pulse, Tuon," Mat said, still staring into the middle distance. "Nynaeve ... she would sometimes feel a person's hand to check their heartbeat, and from there would know that something was wrong with their feet. It's the same thing. Step into the struggle, feel its motion. Know it ... "

A servant with his head half-shaven stepped up to Tuon, whispering to her and Selucia. He had come from the ford.

Mat kept looking out, remembering maps, but overlaying them with the real combat. Bryne failing to use Tylee in combat, exposing his defenses' left flank at the ford, sending his cavalry into a trap.

The battle opened to him, and he saw tactics, ten steps ahead of what was occurring. It was like reading the future, like what Min saw, only with flesh, blood, swords and battle drums.

Mat grunted. "Huh. Gareth Bryne is a Darkfriend."

"He *what*?" Min sputtered.

"This battle is one step away from being doomed," Mat said,

turning to Tuon. "I need absolute control of our armies right now. No more arguing with Galgan. Min, I need you to send to Egwene and warn her that Bryne is trying to lose this battle. Tuon, she'll need to go in person. I doubt Egwene will listen to anyone else."

Everyone looked at Mat with stunned expressions—everyone but Tuon, who gave him one of those soul-shaking stares of hers. The ones that had him feeling as if he were a mouse who had just been caught in an otherwise immaculately clean room. That made him sweat more than the battle had.

Come on, he thought. *There isn't time.* He could see it now, like a grand game of stones. Bryne's movements were complex and subtle, but the end result would be the destruction of Egwene's army.

Mat could stop it. But he had to act *now*.

"It is done," Tuon said.

The comment provoked almost as much surprise as Mat's announcement. Captain-General Galgan looked as if he would rather swallow his own boots than have Mat in command. Min found herself being led away by a group of servants and soldiers, and she gave a squawk of annoyance.

Tuon moved her horse nearer to Mat's. "I am told," she said softly, "that in the battle moments ago, you not only claimed a *marath'damane* for yourself, but also raised one of our officers to the low Blood."

"I *did*?" Mat asked, baffled. "I don't remember that."

"You dropped your nail at his feet."

"Oh. That ... All right, maybe I did that. Accidentally. And the *channeler* ... bloody ashes, Tuon. I didn't mean for her to ... I guess. Well, you can have her."

"No," Tuon said. "It is well for you to have taken one of your own. You cannot train her, of course, but there are many *sul'dam* who will be eager for the chance. It is very rare that a man captures a *damane* personally on the battlefield, very rare indeed. Though I know of your particular advantage, others do not. This will greatly increase your reputation."

Mat shrugged. What else could he do? Maybe, if the *damane* belonged to him, he could let her free or something.

"I will have the officer you raised transferred to be your

personal retainer," Tuon said. "He has a good record, perhaps too good. He had been assigned that duty at the ford because he was considered . . . potentially part of a faction who would have moved against us. He is now spouting your praises. I do not know what you did to change his opinion. You seem to have a particular skill at that."

"Let's just hope I have as much skill for retrieving a victory," Mat grumbled. "This is bad, Tuon."

"Nobody else thinks so." She said the words carefully, not arguing with him, really. Stating a fact.

"I'm right, anyway. I wish I wasn't, but I am. I bloody am."

"If you are not, I will lose influence."

"You'll be fine," Mat said, leading the way back toward the Seanchan camp a few miles north at a brisk pace. "I may lead you wrong now and then, but in the end, you can be sure that I'm always a safe bet."

CHAPTER
30

The Way of the Predator

Perrin and Gaul did another dismayed round of Egwene's camp—at least, the little of it that reflected in the wolf dream. Her army had been pushed far to the east, and the tents had not been placed long enough at the river to reflect strongly in the wolf dream.

The wolves had spotted Graendal here, but Perrin had not been able to catch her at whatever she was doing.

Three times now, Slayer had tried attacking the Bore, and the wolves had warned Perrin. Each time, Slayer had withdrawn before Perrin arrived. The man was testing them. It was the way of the predator, surveying the herd, searching for the weak.

At least Perrin's plan with the wolves had worked. Time progressed slowly in the Bore, and so Slayer—by necessity—was slowed down as he tried to reach Rand. That gave Perrin a chance to reach him in time.

"We need to warn the others about Graendal," Perrin said, stopping in the center of camp. "She must be communicating with Darkfriends in our camps."

"Perhaps we could go to those at the Bore? You managed to speak to Nynaeve Sedai."

"Maybe," Perrin said. "I don't know if it would be good to

distract Nynaeve again, considering what she is up to." Perrin turned about, looking at the bedrolls that flickered, then vanished in the wolf dream. He and Gaul had checked at Merrilor for a gateway, but none was there currently. If he wanted to go back to the waking world, he'd need to camp there and wait for hours. It seemed like such a waste.

If only he could figure out how to *shift* back to the real world himself. Lanfear implied that he might be able to learn the trick, but his only clue in how to do so lay in Slayer. Perrin tried remembering the moment when the man had *shifted* out. Had Perrin sensed anything? A hint to how Slayer did what he did?

He shook his head. He'd gone over and over that, and had come to no conclusions. With a sigh, he quested out for the wolves. *Any sign of Heartseeker?* he asked hopefully.

The wolves sent amusement. He had been asking them too frequently.

Have you seen any camps of two-legs, then? Perrin sent.

This earned a vague response. Wolves paid attention to men only to avoid them; in the wolf dream, that didn't matter much. Still, where men congregated, nightmares sometimes ran wild, so the wolves had learned to keep their distance.

He would have liked to know how the other battles were progressing. What of Elayne's army, Perrin's men, Lord and Lady Bashere? Perrin led Gaul away; they ran with quick strides, rather than jumping to a place immediately. Perrin wanted to think.

The longer he remained in the wolf dream in the flesh, the more he felt that he should know how to *shift* back. His body seemed to understand that this place was not natural for it. He hadn't slept here, despite . . . how long had it been? He could not say. They were almost at the end of their rations, though he felt as though he and Gaul had been here only a handful of hours. Part of that sensation was caused by frequent approaches to the Bore to check on the dreamspike, but it was generally so easy to lose track of time here.

There was also an ache of fatigue inside him, growing stronger. He didn't know if he could sleep in this place. His body wanted rest, but had forgotten how to find it. It reminded him a little of when Moiraine had dispelled their fatigue while fleeing the Two Rivers all that time ago. Two years now.

A very long two years.

Perrin and Gaul inspected Lan's camp next. It was even more ephemeral than Egwene's; using the wolf dream for surveillance here was pointless. Lan moved with lots of cavalry, retreating at speed. He and his men did not remain in one place long enough to reflect in the wolf dream except in the most fleeting of ways.

There were no signs of Graendal. "*Aan'allein* is retreating too," Gaul guessed, surveying the rocky ground that they thought was Lan's camp. There were no tents here, just the occasional fleeting appearance of sleeping rings marked by a pole at the center where horsemen would hobble their animals.

Gaul looked up, scanning the landscape to the west. "If they keep falling back from here, they will eventually reach the Field of Merrilor again. Perhaps that is the goal."

"Perhaps," Perrin said. "I want to visit Elayne's battlefront and—"

Young Bull, a wolf called to him. He found the "voice" of the sending to be familiar somehow. *She is here.*

Here? Perrin sent. *Heartseeker?*

Come.

Perrin grabbed Gaul by the arm and *shifted* them far to the north. Graendal was at Shayol Ghul? Was she trying to break in and kill Rand?

They arrived on a ledge overlooking the valley. He and Gaul went down immediately onto their stomachs, peering over the edge, inspecting the valley. An old, grizzled wolf appeared beside Perrin. He knew this wolf, he was certain of it—the scent was familiar, but he could not place a name to him, and the wolf did not send one.

"Where?" Perrin whispered. "Is she in the cavern?"

No, the grizzled wolf sent. *There.*

The wolf sent an image of tents clustered in the valley just below the entrance to the cavern. She had not been spotted in this valley since that first time Perrin had caught her here.

Ituralde's troops had been holding here for long enough that their tents were becoming more and more stable in the wolf dream. Perrin *shifted*, carefully, down below. Gaul and the wolf joined him as he prowled forward, relying on the wolf's Sending to lead him.

There, the wolf said, nodding toward a large tent at the center.

Perrin had seen Graendal here before, at this tent, the tent of Rodel Ituralde.

Perrin froze as the tent's flap rustled. Graendal stepped out. She looked as she had before, with a face like a slab of rock.

Perrin created a thin, painted wall to hide himself, but he needn't have bothered. Graendal immediately created a gateway and stepped into the waking world. It was night there, though time passed at such a strange rate this close to the Bore, that might not mean much for the rest of the world.

Perrin could see the same tent darkly on the other side of the gateway, two Domani guards out front. Graendal waved a hand, and both stood up straighter and saluted her.

The gateway began to close as Graendal slipped into the tent. Perrin hesitated, then *shifted* to stand just in front of the gateway. He had a moment to decide. Follow?

No. He had to keep watch on Slayer. However, being this close, he felt something . . . an awareness. Stepping through that gateway would be like . . .

Like waking up.

The gateway snapped shut. Perrin felt a stab of regret, but knew staying in the wolf dream had been right. Rand was all but defenseless against Slayer here; he would need Perrin's help.

"We need to send warning," Perrin said.

I suppose I could take the message for you, Young Bull, sent the unnamed wolf.

Perrin froze, then spun, pointing. "Elyas!"

I am Long Tooth here, Young Bull. Elyas sent amusement.

"I thought you said you didn't come here."

I said I avoided it. This place is strange and dangerous. I have enough strangeness and *danger in my life in the other world.* The wolf sat down on his haunches. *But someone needed to check on you, foolish pup.*

Perrin smiled. Elyas' thoughts were a strange mix of wolf and human. His way of sending was very wolflike, but the way he thought of himself was too individual, too *human*.

"How goes the fight?" Perrin asked eagerly. Gaul took up position nearby, watching, alert, in case Graendal or Slayer appeared. The field before them, the floor of the valley, was quiet for once. The winds had died down, the dust on the sandy ground stirring in small rifts and ripples. Like water.

I do not know of the other battlefields, Elyas sent, *and we wolves stay far from the two-legs. We fight, here and there, at the edges of the battle. Mostly, we have attacked the Twisted Ones and Neverborn from the other side of the canyon, where there are no two-legs except those strange Aiel.*

It is a grueling fight. Shadowkiller must do quick work. We have stood five days, but may not last many more.

Five days here in the north. Much longer had passed in the rest of the world since Rand entered to face the Dark One. Rand himself was so close to the Bore that it was likely only hours—maybe minutes—had passed for him. Perrin could feel how time moved differently when he drew near to where Rand fought.

"Ituralde," Perrin said, scratching at his beard. "He's one of the great captains."

Yes, Elyas sent, smelling of amusement. *Some call him "Little Wolf."*

"Bashere is with Elayne's army," Perrin said. "And Gareth Bryne is with Egwene. Agelmar is with the Borderlanders and Lan."

I do not know.

"He is. Four battlefronts. Four great captains. *That's* what she's doing."

"Graendal?" Gaul asked.

"Yes," Perrin said, anger gathering. "She's doing something to them, changing their minds, corrupting them. I overheard her saying . . . Yes. That's it, I'm certain. Instead of fighting our armies with armies of her own, she plans to bring down the great captains. Elyas, do you know how a man can *shift* in and out of the wolf dream in the flesh?"

Even if I knew this thing—which I do not—I would not teach it to you, Elyas said with a growl. *Has nobody told you it is a terrible, dangerous thing that you do?*

"Too many," Perrin said. "Light! We need to warn Bashere. I must—"

"Perrin Aybara!" Gaul said, pointing. "He is here!"

Perrin spun to see a dark blur streak upward toward the entrance to the Pit of Doom. Wolves whimpered and died. Others howled, beginning the hunt. This time, Slayer did not back away.

The way of the predator. Two or three quick lunges to determine weakness, then an all-out attack.

"Wake!" Perrin called to Elyas, running up the incline. "Warn Elayne, Egwene, anyone you can! And if you cannot, stop Ituralde somehow. The great captains are being corrupted. One of the Forsaken controls their minds, and their tactics cannot be trusted!"

I will do it, Young Bull, Elyas sent, fading.

"Go to Rand, Gaul!" Perrin roared. "Guard the way to him! Do not let any of those red-veils pass you!"

Perrin summoned his hammer to his hands, not waiting for a reply, then *shifted* to confront Slayer.

Rand clashed with Moridin, sword against sword, standing before the darkness that was the essence of the Dark One. The cold expanse was somehow both infinite and empty.

Rand held so much of the One Power that he nearly burst. He would need that strength in the fight to come. For now, he resisted Moridin sword against sword. He wielded *Callandor* as a physical weapon, fighting as if with a sword made of light itself, parrying Moridin's attacks.

Each step Rand took dripped blood to the ground. Nynaeve and Moiraine clung to stalagmites as if something were battering them, a wind that Rand could not sense. Nynaeve closed her eyes. Moiraine stared straight ahead as if determined not to look away, no matter the price.

Rand turned aside Moridin's latest attack, the blades throwing sparks. He had always been the better swordsman of the two, during the Age of Legends.

He had lost his hand, but thanks to Tam, that no longer mattered as it once might have. And he was also wounded. This place . . . this place changed things. Rocks on the ground seemed to move, and he often stumbled. The air grew alternately musty and dry, then humid and moldy. Time slipped around them like a stream. Rand felt as if he could see it. Each blow here took moments, yet hours passed outside.

He scored Moridin across the arm, drawing his blood to spray against the wall.

"My blood and yours," Rand said. "I have you to thank for this wound in my side, Elan. You thought you were the Dark One, didn't you? Has he punished you for that?"

"Yes," Moridin snarled. "He returned me to life." Moridin came swinging hard in a two-handed blow. Rand stepped backward, catching the blow on *Callandor*, but he misjudged the slope of the ground. Either that, or the slope changed on him. Rand stumbled, the blow forcing him down on one knee.

Blade against blade. Rand's leg slipped backward, and brushed the darkness behind, which waited like a pool of ink.

All went black.

The distant Ogier song was comforting to Elayne as she slumped in her saddle atop the hill just north of Cairhien.

The women around her weren't in any better shape than she was. Elayne had gathered all of the Kinswomen who could hold on to *saidar*—no matter how weak or tired—and formed two circles with them. She had twelve with her in her own circle, but their collective strength in the Power at the moment was barely more than that of a single Aes Sedai.

Elayne had stopped channeling in an attempt to let the women recover. Most of them slumped in their saddles or sat on the ground. In front of them extended a ragged battle line. Men fought desperately before the Cairhienin hills, trying to hold against the sea of Trollocs.

Their victory over the northern Trolloc army had been short-lived, as they now found themselves strung-out, exhausted and in serious danger of being surrounded by the southern one.

"We almost managed," Arganda said from beside her, shaking his head. "We almost made it."

He wore a plume in his helmet. It had belonged to Gallenne. Elayne hadn't been there when the Mayener commander had fallen.

That was the frustrating part. They *were* close. Despite Bashere's betrayal, despite the unexpected arrival of the southern force, they had almost pulled it off. If she'd had more time to position her men, if they'd been able to catch more than a moment's breather between defeating the northern army and then turning to meet this southern one . . .

But that was not the case. Nearby, the proud Ogier fought to protect the dragons, but the Ogier were slowly being overrun.

The ancient creatures had begun to collapse, like felled trees, pulled down by Trollocs. One by one, their songs broke off.

Arganda held a bloodied hand to his side, pale-faced, barely able to speak. She didn't have the strength to Heal him. "That Warder of yours is a *fiend* on the battlefield, Your Majesty. Her arrows fly like light itself. I'd swear . . . " Arganda shook his head. He might never hold a sword again, even if Healed.

He should have been sent with the other wounded . . . somewhere. There wasn't really anywhere to take them; the channelers were too exhausted to make gateways.

Her people were fracturing. The Aiel fought in clumps, the Whitecloaks nearly surrounded, the Wolf Guard in no better shape. The Legion of the Dragon heavy cavalry still rode, but Bashere's betrayal had shaken them.

Now and then, a dragon fired. Aludra had rolled them back up to the top of the highest hill, but they were out of ammunition, and the channelers didn't have strength to make gateways to Baerlon to fetch the new dragons' eggs. Aludra had fired bits of armor until her powder ran low. Now they had only enough for the occasional shot.

The Trollocs would push through her lines soon, fragmenting her army like ravenous lions. Elayne watched from one of the hilltops, guarded by ten of her Guardswomen. The rest had gone to fight. Trollocs broke through the Aiel to the east of her position, right near the dragoner hilltop position. The beasts charged up the hill, killing the few Ogier defenders on that side, roaring their victory as the dragoners pulled out sabers and grimly stood to defend.

Elayne wasn't ready to let the dragons go yet. She gathered strength through the circle; women groaned around her. She took up barely a dribble of the Power, far less than she'd hoped, and directed Fire at the lead Trollocs.

Her attack arced in the air toward the Shadowspawn. She felt she was trying to stop a storm by spitting at the wind. That lone ball of fire hit.

The earth exploded beneath it, ripping the hillside and hurling *dozens* of Trollocs back in the air.

Elayne started, causing Moonshadow to shuffle beneath her. Arganda cursed.

Someone rode up beside her on a large black horse, emerging as if from smoke. The man was of medium build and had dark curls of hair down to his shoulders. Logain looked thinner than she remembered from last time she'd seen him, his cheeks sunken, but his face was still handsome.

"Logain?" she said, shocked.

The Asha'man gestured sharply. Explosions sounded all across the battlefield. Elayne turned to see over a hundred men in black coats marching through a large gateway on top of her hill.

"Pull those Ogier back," Logain said. His ragged voice was raw. Those eyes of his seemed darker now than they once had been. "We will hold this position."

Elayne blinked, then nodded for Arganda to pass the command. *Logain shouldn't give orders to me*, she thought absently. For the moment, she let it pass.

Logain turned his horse and rode to the side of the hilltop, looking down at her army. Elayne followed, feeling numb. Trollocs fell as Asha'man called up strange attacks, gateways that seemed tied to the ground somehow. They stormed forward, killing the Shadowspawn.

Logain grunted. "You're in bad shape."

She forced her mind to work. The Asha'man were here. "Did Rand send you?"

"We sent ourselves," Logain said. "The Shadow has been planning this trap for a long time, according to notes in Taim's study. I only just managed to decipher them." He looked at her. "We came to you first. The Black Tower stands with the Lion of Andor."

"We need to get my people out of here," Elayne said, forcing her mind to think through the cloud of fatigue. Her army needed a queen. "Mother's milk in a cup! This is going to cost us." She'd probably lose half her force withdrawing. Better half than all of them. "I'll start bringing my men back in ranks. Can you make enough gateways to lead us to safety?"

"That wouldn't be a problem," Logain said absently, looking down the slope. His impassive face would have impressed any Warder. "But it will be a slaughter. There's no room for a good retreat, and your lines will grow weaker and weaker as you pull back. The last ranks will be overwhelmed and consumed."

"I don't see that we have any other choice," Elayne snapped, exhausted. Light! Here, help had come, and she was snapping. *Stop it.* She composed herself, sitting up straighter. "I mean to say that your arrival, while appreciated greatly, cannot turn a battle that is this far gone. A hundred Asha'man cannot stop a hundred thousand Trollocs on their own. If we could arrange our battle lines better, get at least a short rest for my men . . . but no. That is impossible. We must retreat—unless you can produce a miracle, Lord Logain."

He smiled, perhaps at her use of "lord" for him. "Androl!" he barked.

A middle-aged Asha'man hurried over, a plump Aes Sedai joining him. *Pevara?* Elayne thought, too exhausted to make sense of it. *A Red?*

"My Lord?" the man, Androl, asked.

"I need to slow that army of Trollocs long enough for the army to regroup and refield itself, Androl," Logain said. "How much will it cost us for a miracle?"

"Well, my Lord," Androl said, rubbing his chin. "That depends. How many of those women sitting back there can channel?"

It was a thing of legends.

Elayne had heard of the great works performed by large circles of men and women. Every woman in the White Tower was taught of these feats from the past, stories of different days, better days. Days when one half of the One Power had not been a thing to fear, when two halves of one whole had worked together to create incredible wonders.

She wasn't sure the days of legend had truly returned. Certainly, the Aes Sedai during those times hadn't been so worried, so desperate. But what they did now left Elayne in awe.

She joined in the circle, making the total fourteen women and twelve men. She barely had any strength to lend, but her trickle added to the increasingly large stream. More importantly, a circle had to have at least one more woman than it had men—and now that she had joined, Logain could come in last of all and add his considerable strength to the flow.

At the head of this circle was Androl, an odd choice. Now that she was part of the circle, she could feel his relative strength. He was extremely weak, weaker than many women who were turned away from the Tower, refused the shawl because of their lack of innate talent.

Elayne and the others had relocated to the far side of the battlefield. The rest of the Asha'man held back the attacking Trolloc horde as Androl prepared. Whatever he did, it would need to be swift. Elayne still had trouble believing anything could be done. Even with this much power, even with thirteen men and fourteen women working together.

"Light," Androl whispered, standing between her horse and Logain's. "Is this what it feels like to be one of you people? How do you handle so much of the One Power? How do you keep it from consuming you alive, burning you away?"

Pevara rested her hand on his shoulder in a gesture that was unmistakably tender. Elayne could barely rub two thoughts together amid her fatigue, but she still found herself shocked. She had not expected affection from a Red for a man who could channel.

"Move the soldiers back," Androl said softly.

Elayne gave the order, worried. The man beside her had never held this kind of power before. It could go to someone's head; she had seen it happen. Light send that he knew what he was doing.

The soldiers and others retreated, passing by Elayne's group. Several tired Ogier nodded to her in passing, their shoulders slumped, their arms scored with cuts. The Trollocs poured forward, but the Asha'man who weren't in the circle disrupted their attack with weaves of the One Power.

It wasn't enough. Though the Asha'man fought well, there were just *so* many Trollocs. The Asha'man could not stop this tide. What did Logain think could be done?

Androl smiled widely, and held his hands out in front of himself as if pressing against a wall. He closed his eyes. "Three thousand years ago the Lord Dragon created Dragonmount to hide his shame. His rage still burns hot. Today . . . I bring it to you, Your Majesty."

A beam of light split the air, easily a hundred feet tall. Moonshadow shied back and Elayne frowned. Why a column of light? What good would that . . . The beam of light began to twist in the air, rotating upon itself. Only then did Elayne recognize it for the start of a gateway. An enormous gateway, large enough to swallow buildings. She could have moved an entire wing of the Caemlyn palace through that thing!

The air shimmered in front of them, the way a gateway always looked from behind. She couldn't see where the gateway was leading. Did they have an army waiting on the other side?

She could see the expressions on the slavering Trolloc faces as they looked into the opening. Absolute horror. They broke away, running, and Elayne felt a sudden heat, almost overpowering.

Something exploded out of the gateway, as if pushed by an incredible force. A column of lava a hundred feet in diameter, blazing hot. The column broke apart as the lava crashed down, splashing to the battlefield, gushing forward in a river. The Asha'man outside the circle used weaves of Air to keep it from splashing back on the circle and to shepherd it in the right direction.

The river of fire washed through the foremost Trolloc ranks, consuming them, destroying hundreds in an eyeblink. The lava *was* under pressure on the other side; that was the only way she could explain the force with which it sprayed from the enormous gateway, turning Trollocs into cinders, burning a large swath through their army.

Androl held the gateway for long minutes as the Shadow's army pulled back. Asha'man to the sides used gusts of wind to blow the Shadowspawn back into the ever-widening river. By the time Androl finished, he had created a barrier of red-hot death between Elayne's army and the bulk of the Trollocs, whose backs were against the northern walls of Cairhien.

Androl took a breath, closed the gateway, then pivoted and made two others in quick succession, one pointing southeast, the other southwest.

A second and third column of lava spurted forth—smaller this time, as Androl was obviously weakened. These went tumbling over the land to the east and west of Cairhien, singeing away dead weeds and casting smoke into the air. Some of the Trolloc army had pulled back, but many others had perished, boxed in, with the walled city on one side and lava on others. It would be some time before the Fades could organize the survivors to resume their attacks on Elayne's forces.

Androl let the gateway close. He slumped, but Pevara caught him.

"One miracle, my Lord," Androl said, voice soft, as if strained. "Delivered as requested. That should hold them back for a few hours. Long enough?"

"Long enough," Elayne said. "We will be able to regroup, bring through supplies for the dragons, and fetch as many Aes Sedai from Mayene as we can get to Heal our men and wash away their fatigue. Then we can sort through who is strong enough to continue and reposition our ranks for a much more effective battle."

"You intend to keep fighting?" Androl asked, surprised.

"Yes," Elayne said. "I can barely stand, but yes. We cannot afford to leave that Trolloc horde here intact. You and your men give us an edge, Logain. We will use it, and everything we have, and we *will* destroy them."

CHAPTER
31

A Tempest of Water

Egwene looked across the river at the struggle raging between her forces and the Sharan army. She had arrived back at her camp on the Arafellin side of the ford. She was itching to join the battle against the Shadow again, but she also needed to talk with Bryne about what had happened at the hills. She had arrived to find the command tent empty.

The camp continued to fill with Aes Sedai and the surviving archers and pikemen who were coming through gateways from the hilltops to the south. The Aes Sedai were milling about and speaking to each other with some urgency. They all seemed worn out, but it was clear from their frequent glances toward the battle taking place across the river that they were as eager as Egwene was to rejoin the fight against the Shadow.

Egwene summoned the messenger who was standing in front of the command tent. "Get word to the sisters that they have less than an hour to rest. Those Trollocs we were fighting will be joining the battle at the river soon, now that we have left the hills."

She'd move the Aes Sedai downriver on this side, then attack them across the water as they moved across the fields to attack her soldiers. "Tell the archers they'll be marching with us as well," she added. "They may as well put their remaining arrows to good use, until we can get them another supply."

As the messenger rushed off, Egwene turned to Leilwin, who was standing with her husband, Bayle Domon, nearby. "Leilwin, those look like Seanchan cavalry troops across the river. Do you know anything about that?"

"Yes, Mother, they are Seanchan. That man standing over there—" She pointed to a man with shaved temples standing by a tree down toward the river; he wore voluminous trousers and, incongruously, a tattered brown coat which looked as if it might have come from the Two Rivers. "—he told me that a legion commanded by Lieutenant-General Khirgan had come from the Seanchan camp, and that they had been summoned by General Bryne."

"He also said that they do be accompanied by the Prince of Ravens," Domon interjected.

"Mat?"

"He did more than accompany them. He do be leading one of the cavalry banners, the ones giving the Sharans a hiding on our army's left flank. He got there just in time, our pikemen were getting the worst of it before he showed up."

"Egwene," Gawyn said, pointing.

To the south, a few hundred paces below the ford, a small number of soldiers were hauling themselves from the river. They had stripped to their smallclothes and carried swords tied to their backs. It was too far to be sure, but one of their leaders looked familiar.

"Is that Uno?" Egwene frowned, then waved for her horse. She mounted and galloped, with Gawyn and her guards, along the river to where the men lay gasping on the bank, and the sound of one man cursing filled the air.

"Uno!"

"It's about bloody flaming time someone came!" Uno stood as he saluted in respect. "Mother, we're in bad shape!"

"I saw." Egwene gritted her teeth. "I was in the hills when your force was attacked. We did what we could, but there were just too many of them. How did you get out?"

"How did we flaming get out, Mother? When the men started dropping all around us and we figured we was goners, we flaming rode out of there like a flaming lightning bolt had struck our flaming hindquarters! We got to the frog-kissing river on the run, stripped and jumped in, swimming for all we were bloody worth, Mother, with all due respect!" Uno's topknot danced as he continued to blaspheme, and Egwene could have sworn the eye painted on his eyepatch became a more intense red.

Uno took a deep breath and continued, a little more subdued. "I can't understand it, Mother. Some goat-headed messenger told us that the Aes Sedai on the hills were in trouble and we needed to go up the flaming backsides of the Trollocs attacking them. I said, who's going to mind the left flank at the river, and, for that bloody matter, our own bloody flank when we attack the Trollocs, and he said that General Bryne had that taken care of, reserve cavalry would move up into our position at the river, and the Illianers would watch out for our bloody flanks. Some protection they were, all right, one flaming squadron, like a flaming fly trying to fend off a flaming falcon! Oh, they were just waiting for us, like they knew we was coming. No, Mother, this can't be the fault of Gareth Bryne, we've been tricked by some sheep-gutted milk-drinking traitor! With all due respect, Mother!"

"I can't believe that, Uno. I just heard that General Bryne had brought in a legion of Seanchan cavalry. Maybe they were simply late getting here. We'll sort it all out when I find the general. Meanwhile, get your men back to camp so they can have a proper rest. Light knows you've earned it."

Uno nodded, and Egwene galloped back toward camp.

Using Vora's *sa'angreal*, Egwene wove Air and Water, spinning them together. A funnel of water surged up, drawn from the river beneath. Egwene blew her tornado of water into the Trollocs that were beginning their assault against her army's left flank on the Kandori side of the river. Her tempest of water surged across them. It wasn't strong enough to pull any of them into the air— she didn't have the energy for that—but it drove them back, hands to their faces.

Behind her and the other Aes Sedai positioned on the Arafellin side of the river, archers loosed volleys of arrows into the sky. Those didn't darken the sky the way she would have liked—there weren't so many—but they did take down more than a hundred Trollocs with each wave.

To the side, Pylar and a couple of other Browns—all adept with weaves of Earth—caused the ground to erupt under the charging Trollocs. Spread out next to her, Myrelle and a large contingent of Greens wove fireballs that they lobbed over the water into bunched-up groups of Trollocs, many of whom continued to run a considerable distance before they collapsed, engulfed in flames.

The Trollocs howled and roared, but continued their relentless progress against the defenders at the river's edge. At one point, several ranks of Seanchan cavalry moved out from the defensive lines and attacked the Trolloc onslaught head-on. It happened so quickly that many of the Trollocs were unable to raise their spears before contact was made; large swaths of the foe in the front ranks went down. The Seanchan swept to the side and returned to their lines at the river.

Egwene held to her channeling, forcing herself to work through sheer exhaustion. But the Trollocs didn't break; they grew enraged, attacking the humans with a frenzy. Egwene could hear their yells distinctly over the sounds of wind and water.

The Trollocs grew angry, did they? Well, they would not *know* anger until they had felt that of the Amyrlin Seat. Egwene pulled in more and more of the Power until she was at the very edges of her ability. She put heat into her tempest so that the scalding water burned Trolloc eyes, hands, hearts. She felt herself yelling, Vora's *sa'angreal* thrust before her like a spear.

What seemed like hours went by. Eventually, exhausted, she allowed Gawyn to talk her into pulling back for a time. Gawyn went to fetch her horse and as he was returning, Egwene looked across the river.

There was no doubt about it; her army's left flank had already been pushed another thirty paces. Even with the Aes Sedai aid, they were losing this battle.

It was long past time for her to find Gareth Bryne.

When Egwene and Gawyn got back to camp, she climbed from her horse and gave it to Leilwin, telling her to use it to help carry the wounded. There were plenty of those who had been dragged across the ford to safety, bloodied soldiers slumping against the arms of friends.

Unfortunately, she hadn't the strength for Healing, let alone a gateway to send wounded to Tar Valon or Mayene. Most of the Aes Sedai not busy at the riverbank didn't look as if they were doing any better.

"Egwene," Gawyn said softly. "Rider. Seanchan. Looks like a noblewoman."

One of the Blood? Egwene thought, standing and looking through camp toward where Gawyn pointed. At least he had the strength left to keep a lookout. Why any woman would voluntarily go without a Warder was beyond her.

The woman approaching wore fine Seanchan silks, and Egwene's stomach turned at the sight. That finery existed because of a foundation of enslaved channelers, forced into obedience to the Crystal Throne. The woman was certainly one of the Blood, as a contingent of Deathwatch Guards accompanied her. You had to be very important for . . .

"Light!" Gawyn exclaimed. "Is that *Min*?"

Egwene gaped. It *was*.

Min rode up, scowling. "Mother," she said to Egwene, bowing her head amid her stone-faced guards in dark armor.

"Min . . . are you well?" Egwene asked. *Careful, don't give out too much information.* Was Min a captive? Surely she couldn't have *joined* the Seanchan, could she?

"Oh, I'm well," Min said sourly. "I've been pampered, stuffed in this outfit, and offered all sorts of somewhat delicate foods. I might add that among the Seanchan, delicate does not necessarily mean tasty. You should see the things they *drink*, Egwene."

"I've seen them," Egwene said, unable to keep her tone from coldness.

"Oh. Yes. I suppose you have. Mother, we have a problem."

"What kind of problem?"

"Well, it depends on how much you trust Mat."

"I trust him to find trouble," Egwene said. "I trust him to find drinking and gambling, no matter where he goes."

"Do you trust him to lead an army?" Min asked.

Egwene hesitated. Did she?

Min leaned forward, sparing a glance for the Deathwatch Guards, who didn't seem *about* to let her draw any closer to Egwene. "Egwene," she said softly, "Mat thinks that Bryne is

leading your army to destruction. He says ... he says he thinks
Bryne is a Darkfriend."

Gawyn started laughing.

Egwene jumped. She would have expected anger from him,
outrage. "Gareth Bryne?" Gawyn asked. "A *Darkfriend*? I'd
believe my own *mother* to be a Darkfriend before him. Tell
Cauthon to stay out of his wife's royal brandy; he's obviously had
too much."

"I'm inclined to agree with Gawyn," Egwene said slowly. Still,
she could not ignore the irregularities in how the army was being
led.

She would sort through that. "Mat is always looking out for
people who don't need to be looked out for," she said. "He's just
trying to protect me. Tell him that we appreciate the ... warning."

"Mother," Min said. "He seemed certain. This isn't a joke. He
wants you to turn your armies over to him."

"My armies," Egwene said flatly.

"Yes."

"In the hands of Matrim Cauthon."

"Um ... yes. I should mention, the Empress has given him
command of all the Seanchan forces. He's now Marshal-General
Cauthon."

Ta'veren. Egwene shook her head. "Mat is a good tactician, but
handing him the White Tower's armies ... No, that is beyond
possibility. Besides, the armies are not mine to give him—the
Hall of the Tower has authority for them. Now, how can we persuade these gentlemen surrounding you that you'll be safe
accompanying me?"

As little as Egwene wanted to admit it, she needed the
Seanchan. She wouldn't risk their alliance to save Min, particularly since it didn't seem that she was in immediate danger. Of
course, if the Seanchan realized that Min had sworn their oaths
back in Falme, then fled ...

"Don't worry about me," Min said with a grimace. "I suppose
I'm better off with Fortuona. She ... knows about a certain talent
of mine, thanks to Mat, and it might let me help her. And you."

The statement was laden with meaning. The Deathwatch
Guards were too stoic to respond overtly to Min's use of the

Empress's name, but they did seem to stiffen, their faces hardening. *Take care, Min,* Egwene thought. *You're surrounded by autumn thornweeds.*

Min didn't seem to care. "Will you at least consider what Mat is saying?"

"That Gareth Bryne is a Darkfriend?" Egwene said. It really was laughable. "Go back and tell Mat to submit his battle suggestions to us, if he must. For now, I need to find my commanders to plan our next steps."

Gareth Bryne, where are you?

A flight of black arrows rose almost invisibly into the air, then fell like a breaking wave. They hit Ituralde's army at the mouth of the pass to the valley of Thakan'dar, some bouncing off shields, others finding flesh. One fell inches from where Ituralde stood atop a rocky outcropping.

Ituralde didn't flinch. He stood, straight-backed, hands clasped behind him. He did, however, mutter, "Letting things draw a little close, aren't we?"

Binde, the Asha'man who stood beside him in the night, grimaced. "Sorry, Lord Ituralde." He was supposed to keep the arrows away. He'd done well, so far. Sometimes, however, he got a distant look in his face and started muttering about "them" trying to "take his hands."

"Stay sharp," Ituralde said.

His head throbbed. More dreams earlier tonight, so real. He had seen Trollocs eating members of his family alive, and had been too weak to save them. He had struggled and wept as they ate Tamsin and his children, but at the same time had been lured by the scents of the boiling and burning flesh.

At the end of the dream, he had joined the monsters in their feast.

Put that from your mind, he thought. It was not easy to do so. The dreams had been so vivid. He had been glad to be awakened by a Trolloc attack.

He'd been ready for this. His men lit bonfires at the barricades. The Trollocs had finally pushed through his thorn fortifications, but their butcher's bill had been high. Now, Ituralde's men fought at the mouth of the pass, holding the tides back from entering the valley.

They had applied their time well during the days the Trollocs had pushed their way through arduous barriers to the mouth of the pass. The entrance to the valley was now fortified with a series of chest-high earthen bulwarks. Those would be excellent for crossbowmen to use as cover, if Ituralde's pike formations were ever pushed back too far.

For now, Ituralde had split his army into groups of around three thousand men each, then organized them into square formations of pikes, billhooks and crossbows. He used mounted crossbowmen as skirmishers in the front and on the flanks, and had formed up a vanguard—about six ranks deep—of pikemen. Big pikes, twenty feet long. He'd learned from Maradon that you wanted to keep your distance from the Trollocs.

Pikes worked wonderfully. Ituralde's pike squares could pivot and fight in all directions in case they were surrounded. Trollocs could be forced to fight in ranks, but these squares—properly applied—could break up their lines. Once the Trolloc ranks were shattered, the Aiel could kill with abandon.

Behind ranks of pikemen he positioned foot soldiers carrying billhooks and halberds. Sometimes Trollocs fought their way through the pikes, pushing the weapons aside or pulling them down with the weight of corpses. The billhookmen then moved up—slipping between the pikemen—and hamstrung the leading Trollocs. This gave the leading foot soldiers time to pull back and regroup while the next wave of soldiers—more foot, with pikes— moved up to engage the Trollocs.

It was working, so far. He had a dozen such squares of troops facing the Trollocs in the night. They fought defensively, doing whatever they could to break the surging tide. The Trollocs threw themselves at the pikemen, trying to crack them, but each square operated independently. Ituralde didn't worry about the Trollocs that made it through the gauntlet, because they would be handled by the Aiel.

Ituralde had to keep his hands clasped behind his back to conceal their shaking. Nothing had been the same after Maradon. He'd learned, but he'd paid dearly for that education.

Burn these headaches, he thought. *And burn those Trollocs.*

Three times, he had nearly given the order to send his armies in with a direct assault, abandoning the square formations. He could imagine them slaughtering, killing. No more delaying. He wanted *blood*.

Each time, he'd stopped himself. They weren't here for blood, they were here to hold. To give that man the time he needed in the cavern. That was what it was all about . . . wasn't it? Why did he have so much trouble remembering that lately?

Another wave of Trolloc arrows dropped onto Ituralde's men. The Fades had some of them stationed on the tops of the slopes above the pass, in places that Ituralde's own archers had once held. Getting them up there must have been quite an undertaking; the walls of the pass were very steep. How many would have dropped to their deaths making the attempt? Regardless, Trollocs weren't good shots with bows, but they didn't need to be, when firing at armies.

The halberdiers raised shields. They couldn't fight while holding those, but they kept them strapped to their backs for need. The falling arrows increased, plummeting through the lightly foggy night air. The storm rumbled overhead, but the Windfinders were at their task again, keeping it away. They claimed that at several moments, the army had been mere breaths away from an all-out storm of destruction. At one point, hail the size of a man's fist had fallen for about a minute before they'd wrested control of the weather again.

If that was what awaited them if the Windfinders weren't using their bowl, Ituralde was more than happy to leave them at their task. The Dark One wouldn't care how many Trollocs he destroyed while sending a blizzard, twister or hurricane to kill the humans they fought.

"They're gathering for another surge at the mouth of the pass!" someone yelled in the night air, followed by other calls confirming it. Ituralde peered through the mist, aided by light from the bonfires. The Trollocs were indeed regrouping.

"Withdraw the seventh and ninth infantry squads," Ituralde said. "They've been at it too long. Pull the fourth and fifth out of reserve and have them take flanking positions. Prepare for more arrows. And . . . " He trailed off, frowning. What *were* those Trollocs doing? They'd pulled back farther than he'd have expected, drawing into the darkness of the pass. They couldn't be retreating, could they?

A dark wave slid out of the mouth of the pass. Myrddraal. Hundreds upon *hundreds* of them. Black cloaks that did not move, in defiance of the breeze. Faces with no eyes, lips that sneered, black swords. The creatures moved like eels, sinuous and sleek.

They gave no time for orders, no time for response. They flowed into the squares of defenders, sliding between pikes, whipping deadly swords.

"Aiel!" Ituralde bellowed. "Bring in the Aiel! All of them, and channelers! Everyone except for those who guard at the Pit of Doom itself! Move, move!"

Messengers scrambled away. Ituralde watched in horror. An *army* of Myrddraal. Light, it was as bad as his nightmares!

The seventh infantry collapsed before the attack, square formation shattering. Ituralde opened his mouth to order the primary reserve—the one defending his position—to give support. He needed the cavalry to ride out and draw pressure off the infantry.

He didn't have much cavalry; he'd agreed that most of the horsemen would be needed on other fronts. But he did have some. They'd be essential here.

Except ...

He squeezed his eyes shut. Light, but he was exhausted. He had trouble thinking.

Pull back before the attack, a voice seemed to be saying to him. *Pull back to the Aiel, then make a stand there.*

"Pull back ... " he whispered. "Pull ... "

Something felt very, *very* wrong about doing that. Why was his mind insisting upon it?

Captain Tihera, Ituralde tried to whisper. *You have command.* It wouldn't come out. Something physical seemed to be holding his mouth shut.

He could hear men screaming. What was happening? Dozens of men could die fighting a single Myrddraal. At Maradon, he'd lost an entire company of archers—one hundred men—to two Fades who had slipped into the city at night. His defensive squads were built to deal with Trollocs, to hamstring them, to drop them.

The Fades would crack those pike squares open like eggs. Nobody was doing what needed to be done.

"My Lord Ituralde?" Captain Tihera said. "My Lord, what was it you said?"

If they retreated, the Trollocs would surround them. They needed to stand firm.

Ituralde's lips opened to give the order to retreat. "Pull the—"

Wolves.

Wolves appeared in the fog like shadows. They leaped at the Myrddraal, growling. Ituralde started, spinning, as a man in furs pulled himself up onto the top of the rocky outcrop.

Tihera stumbled back, calling for their guards. The newcomer in furs leaped for Ituralde and shoved him off the top of the rocks.

Ituralde did not fight back. Whoever this man was, Ituralde was grateful to him, feeling a moment of victory as he fell. He hadn't given the order to retreat.

He hit the ground not far below, and it knocked the wind out of him. The wolves took his arms in gentle mouths and pulled him off into the darkness as he slowly drifted into unconsciousness.

Egwene sat in the camp as the battle for the border of Kandor continued.

Her army held back the Trollocs.

The Seanchan fought alongside her troops just across the river.

Egwene herself held a small cup of tea.

Light, it was galling. She was the *Amyrlin*. But she was drained of energy.

She still hadn't found Gareth Bryne, but that wasn't unexpected. He moved about. Silviana was hunting him, and should have word soon.

Aes Sedai had been sent to take the wounded to Mayene. The sun drooped low in the sky, like an eyelid that refused to stay open. Egwene's hands shook as she held her cup. She could still hear the battle. It seemed that the Trollocs would fight into the night, grinding the human armies against the river.

Distant shouts rose like the calls of an angry crowd, but the explosions from the channelers had slowed.

She turned to Gawyn. He didn't seem tired at all, though he was strangely pale. Egwene sipped her tea and silently cursed him. It was unfair, but she wasn't concerned with fairness right now. She could grumble at her Warder. That was what they were for, wasn't it?

A breeze blew through camp. She was a few hundred paces east of the ford, but she smelled blood in the air. Nearby, a squad of archers drew their bows at their commander's call, launching a volley of arrows. A pair of black-winged Draghkar plummeted moments later, hitting the ground with dull thuds just beyond camp. More would come, as it grew dark and they had an easier time hiding against the sky.

Mat. She felt strangely sick thinking about him. He was such a blowhard. A carouser, leering at every pretty woman he met. Treating her like a painting and not a person. He ... he ...

He was Mat. Once, when Egwene had been around thirteen, he'd jumped into the river to save Kiem Lewin from drowning. Of course, she *hadn't* been drowning. She'd merely been dunked under the water by a friend, and Mat had come running, throwing himself into the water to help. The men of Emond's Field had made sport of him for months about that.

The next spring, Mat had pulled Jer al'Hune from the same river, saving the boy's life. People had stopped making fun of Mat for a while afterward.

That was how Mat was. He'd grumbled and muttered all winter about how people made sport of him, insisting that next time, he'd just let them drown. Then the moment he'd seen someone in danger, he'd gone splashing right back in. Egwene could remember gangly Mat stumbling from the river, little Jer clinging to him and gasping, a look of pure terror in his eyes.

Jer had gone down without making a sound. Egwene had never realized that could happen. People who started to drown didn't yell, or sputter, or call for help. They just slipped under the water, when everything seemed fine and peaceful. Unless Mat was watching.

He came for me in the Stone of Tear, she thought. Of course, he'd *also* tried to save her from the Aes Sedai, unwilling to believe she was Amyrlin.

So which was this? Was she drowning or not?

How much do you trust Matrim Cauthon? Min had asked. *Light. I do trust him. Fool that I am, I do.* Mat could be wrong. He often was wrong.

But when he was right, he saved lives.

Egwene forced herself to stand. She wavered, and Gawyn came to her side. She patted him on the arm, then stepped away from him. She would not let the army see its Amyrlin so weak that she had to lean against someone for support. "What reports do we have from the other battlefronts?"

"Not much, today," Gawyn said. He frowned. "In fact, it's been rather silent."

"Elayne was supposed to fight at Cairhien," Egwene said. "It was an important battle."

"She might be too occupied to send word."

"I want you to send a messenger by gateway. I need to know how that battle is going."

Gawyn nodded, hurrying off. After he was gone, Egwene walked at a steady pace until she found Silviana, who was talking with a pair of Blue sisters.

"Bryne?" Egwene asked.

"In the mess tent," Silviana said. "I only just had word. I sent a runner to tell him to stay put until you arrived."

"Come."

She walked over to the tent, the largest shelter in camp by far, and spotted him as she entered. Not eating, but standing beside the cook's travel table with his maps spread out. The table smelled of onions, which had probably been cut there time and time again. Yukiri had a gateway open in the floor to look down on the battlefield. She closed it as Egwene arrived. They didn't leave it open long, not with the Sharans watching for it and preparing weaves to send through it.

Egwene whispered very quietly to Silviana, "Gather the Hall of the Tower. Bring back any Sitters you can find. Get them all here, to this tent, as soon as you can."

Silviana nodded, her face betraying no hint of the confusion she likely felt. She hastened off and Egwene sat down in the tent.

Siuan wasn't there—she was likely helping with Healing again. That was good. Egwene wouldn't have wanted to attempt this with Siuan glaring at her. As it was, she worried about Gawyn. He loved Bryne like a father, and already his anxiety streamed through their bond.

She would have to approach this very delicately, and she didn't want to start until the Hall had arrived. She couldn't accuse Bryne, but she couldn't ignore Mat. He was a scoundrel and a fool, but she trusted him. Light help her, but she did. She'd trust him with her life. And things *had* been going oddly on the battlefield.

The Sitters gathered relatively quickly. They had charge of the war effort, and they met together each evening to get reports and tactical explanations from Bryne and his commanders. Bryne didn't seem to think it odd that they came to him now; he kept at his work.

Many of the women did give Egwene curious looks as they entered. She nodded to them, trying to convey the weight of the Amyrlin Seat.

Eventually, enough of them had arrived that Egwene decided she should begin. Time was wasting. She needed to dismiss Mat's accusations from her mind once and for all, or she needed to act on them.

"General Bryne," Egwene said. "Have you been well? We've had a difficult time finding you."

He looked up and blinked. His eyes were red. "Mother," he said. He nodded to the Sitters. "I feel tired, but probably no more than you. I've been all over the battlefield, tending to all kinds of details; you know how it is."

Gawyn hurried in. "Egwene," he said, his face pale. "Trouble."

"What?"

"I . . ." He took a deep breath. "General Bashere turned against Elayne. Light! He's a Darkfriend. The battle would have been lost had the Asha'man not arrived."

"What's this?" Bryne asked, looking up from his maps. "*Bashere*, a Darkfriend?"

"Yes."

"Impossible," Bryne said. "He was the Lord Dragon's companion for months. I don't know him well, but . . . a Darkfriend? It couldn't be."

"It *is* somewhat unreasonable to assume . . ." Saerin said.

"You can speak with the Queen yourself, if you wish," Gawyn said, standing tall. "I heard it from her own mouth."

The tent stilled. Sitters looked to one another with worried faces.

"General," Egwene said to Bryne, "how was it that you sent two cavalry units to protect us from the Trollocs on the hills south of here, sending them into a trap and leaving the main army's left flank exposed?"

"How was it, Mother?" Bryne asked. "It was obvious that you were about to be overrun, anyone could see that. Yes, I had them leave the left flank, but I moved the Illianer reserves into that position. When I saw that Sharan cavalry unit split off to attack Uno's right flank, I sent the Illianers out to intercept them; it was the right thing to do. I didn't know there would be so many Sharans!" His voice had raised to a shout, but he stopped, and his hands were trembling. "I made a mistake. I'm not perfect, Mother."

"This *was* more than a mistake," Faiselle said. "I have just returned from speaking with Uno and the other survivors of that cavalry massacre. Uno said he could smell a trap as soon as he and his men started riding toward the sisters, but that you had promised him help."

"I told you, I sent him reinforcements, I just didn't expect the Sharans would send such a large force. Besides, I had it all under control. I had ordered up a Seanchan cavalry legion to reinforce our troops; they were supposed to take care of those Sharans. I had them staged across the river. I just didn't expect them to be so late!"

"Yes," Egwene said, hardening her voice. "Those men—so many thousands of them—were crushed between the Trollocs and the Sharans, with no hope for escape. You lost them, and all for no good reason."

"I had to bring the Aes Sedai out!" Bryne said. "They're our most valuable resource. Pardon, *Mother*, but you have made that same point to me."

"The Aes Sedai could have waited," Saerin said. "I was there. Yes, we needed out—we were being pressed—but we held, and could have held longer.

"You left thousands of good men to die, General Bryne. And you know the worst part? It was unnecessary. You left all those Seanchan across the ford here, the ones who were going to save the day, waiting for your order to attack. But that order never came, did it, General? You abandoned them, just like you abandoned our cavalry."

"But I ordered them to attack; they finally went in, didn't they? I sent a messenger. I . . . I . . ."

"No. If it wasn't for Mat Cauthon, they would still be waiting on this side of the river, General!" Egwene turned away from him.

"Egwene," Gawyn said, taking her arm. "What are you saying? Just because—"

Bryne raised a hand to his head. Then he sagged, as if suddenly his limbs had lost their strength. "I don't know what's wrong with me," he whispered, sounding hollow. "I keep making mistakes, Mother. They are the kind a man can recover from, and I keep telling myself that. Then I make another mistake, and there is more scrambling to fix it."

"You're just tired," Gawyn said, voice pained, looking to him. "We all are."

"No," Bryne said softly. "No, it's *more* than that. I've been tired before. This is like . . . my instincts are suddenly wrong. I give the orders, then afterward, I see the holes, the problems. I . . ."

"Compulsion," Egwene said, feeling cold. "You've been Compelled. They're attacking our great captains."

Several women in the room embraced the Source.

"How would that be possible?" Gawyn protested. "Egwene, we have sisters watching the camp for signs of channeling!"

"I don't know how it happened," Egwene said. "Perhaps it was put in place months ago, before the battle began." She turned to the Sitters. "I move that the Hall relieve Gareth Bryne as commander of our armies. It is your decision, Sitters."

"Light," Yukiri said. "We . . . Light!"

"It must be done," Doesine said. "It is a clever move, a way to destroy our armies without us seeing the trap. We should have seen . . . The great captains should have been better protected."

"Light!" Faiselle said. "We need to send word to Lord Mandragoran and to Thakan'dar! This could involve them, too— an attempt to bring down all four battlefronts at once in a coordinated attack."

"I will see it done," Saerin said, moving toward the tent flaps. "For now, I agree with Mother. Bryne must be relieved."

One by one, the others nodded. It was not a formal vote in the Hall, but it would do. Beside the table, Gareth Bryne sat down. Poor man. He was no doubt shaken, worried.

Unexpectedly, he smiled.

"General?" Egwene asked.

"Thank you," Bryne said, looking relaxed.

"For what?"

"I feared I was losing my mind, Mother. I kept seeing what I'd done ... I left thousands of men to die ... but it wasn't me. It wasn't me."

"Egwene," Gawyn said. He covered his pain well. "The army. If Bryne has been *forced* to lead us toward danger, we need to change our command structure immediately."

"Bring in my commanders," Bryne said. "I will relinquish control to them."

"And if they have been corrupted as well?" Doesine asked.

"I agree," Egwene said. "This smells of one of the Forsaken, perhaps Moghedien. Lord Bryne, if you were to fall in this fight, she'd know that your commanders would be next to take charge. They might have the same faulty instincts that you do."

Doesine shook her head. "Who can we trust? Any bloody man or woman we put in command could have suffered Compulsion."

"We may have to lead ourselves," Faiselle said. "Getting to a man who cannot channel would be easier than a sister, who would sense channeling and notice a woman with the ability. We are more likely to be clean."

"But who among us has the knowledge of battlefield tactics?" Ferane asked. "I consider myself well-read enough to oversee plans, but to make them?"

"We will be better than someone who may have been corrupted," Faiselle said.

"No," Egwene said, pulling herself up on Gawyn's arm.

"Then what?" Gawyn asked.

Egwene clenched her teeth. Then what? She knew of only one man she could trust not to have been Compelled, at least not by Moghedien. A man who was immune to the effects of *saidar* and *saidin*. "We will have to put our armies under the command of Matrim Cauthon," she said. "May the Light watch over us."

CHAPTER
32

A Yellow Flower-Spider

The *damane* held open a hole in the floor for Mat. It looked down on the battlefield itself.

Mat rubbed his chin, still impressed, though he'd been using these holes for the last hour or so as he countered the trap that Bryne had laid for Egwene's armies. He had sent in additional banners of Seanchan cavalry to reinforce both flanks of his troops at the river, and additional *damane* to counter the Sharan channelers and stem the flood of Trollocs pressing against the defenders.

Of course, this still wasn't as good as being down on the battlefield himself. Maybe he should go out again and do a little more fighting. He glanced at Tuon, who sat on a throne—a massive, ten-foot-tall throne—at one side of the command building. Tuon narrowed her eyes at him, as if she could see right into his thoughts.

She's Aes Sedai, Mat told himself. *Oh, she can't channel—she hasn't let herself learn yet. She's bloody one of them anyway. And I married her.*

She *was* something incredible, though. He felt a thrill each time she gave orders; she did it so naturally. Elayne and Nynaeve could take lessons. Tuon did look very nice on that throne. Mat let his gaze linger on her, and that earned him a scowl, which was downright unfair. If a man couldn't leer at his wife, who *could* he leer at?

Mat turned back to the battlefield. "Nice trick," he said, stooping down to stick his hand through the hole. They were high up. If he fell, he'd have time to hum three verses of "She Has No Ankles That I Can See" before he hit. Maybe an extra round of the chorus.

"This one learned it," the *sul'dam* said, referring to her new *damane*, "from watching the weaves of the Aes Sedai." The *sul'dam*, Catrona, almost choked on the words "Aes Sedai." Mat couldn't blame her. Those could be tough words to speak.

He didn't look too hard at the *damane*, nor the tattoos of flowering branches on her cheeks, reaching from the back of her head like hands to cup her face. Mat was responsible for her being captured. It was better than her fighting for the Shadow, wasn't it?

Blood and bloody ashes, he thought to himself. *You are doing a fine job of persuading Tuon not to use* damane, *Matrim Cauthon. Capturing one yourself . . .*

It was unnerving how quickly the Sharan woman had taken to her captivity. The *sul'dam* had all remarked upon it. Barely a moment of struggle, then complete subservience. They expected a newly captured *damane* to take months to train properly, yet this one had been ready within hours. Catrona practically beamed, as if she were personally responsible for the Sharan woman's temperament.

That hole *was* remarkable. Mat stood right on the edge, looking down at the world, counting off the banners and squadrons as he marked them in his head. What would Classen Bayor have done with one of these, he wondered? Maybe the Battle of Kolesar would have turned out differently. He'd have never lost his cavalry in the marsh, that's for certain.

Mat's forces continued to hold back the Shadow at the eastern border of Kandor, but he was not pleased with the current situation. The nature of Bryne's trap had been subtle, as hard to see as a yellow flower-spider crouching on a petal. That's how Mat had known. It had taken true military genius to put the army into such a bad situation without it *looking* like the army was in a bad situation. That sort of thing didn't happen by accident.

Mat had lost more men than he wanted to count. His people

were pressed up against the river, and Demandred—despite continuing to rave about the Dragon Reborn—was continually testing Mat's defenses, trying to find a weak spot, sending out a heavy cavalry raid against one side, then an attack from Sharan archers and a Trolloc charge on the other. Consequently, Mat had to keep a close eye on Demandred's movements to be able to counter them in time.

Night was coming soon. Would the Shadow pull back? The Trollocs could fight into the darkness, but those Sharans probably couldn't. Mat gave another sequence of orders, and messengers galloped through gateways to deliver them. It seemed like only moments passed before his troops below responded. "So fast . . . " Mat said.

"This will change the world," General Galgan said. "Messengers can respond instantly; commanders can watch their battles and plan in the moment."

Mat grunted in agreement. "I'll bet it still takes all bloody evening to get dinner from the mess tent, though."

Galgan actually smiled. It was like seeing a boulder crack in half.

"Tell me, General," Tuon said. "What is your assessment of our consort's abilities?"

"I don't know where you found this one, Greatest One, but he is a diamond of great worth. I have watched him these last hours as he rescued the forces of the White Tower. For all of his . . . unconventional style, I have rarely seen a battle commander as gifted as he."

Tuon did not smile, but he could see from her eyes that she was pleased. They *were* nice eyes. And, actually, with Galgan not acting so gruff, perhaps this wouldn't be such a bad place to be after all.

"Thanks," Mat said under his breath to Galgan as they both leaned over to study the field below.

"I consider myself a man of truth, my Prince," Galgan said, rubbing his chin with a callused finger. "You will serve the Crystal Throne well. It would be a shame to see you assassinated too early. I will make certain that the first I send after you are newly trained, so that you may stop them with ease."

Mat felt his mouth drop open. The man said it with perfect

frankness, almost affection. As if he were planning to do Mat a *favor* by trying to kill him!

"The Trollocs here," he pointed at a group of them far below, "will pull back soon."

"I concur," Galgan said.

Mat rubbed his chin. "We'll have to see what Demandred does with them. I'm concerned that the Sharans may try to slip some of their *marath'damane* into our camp during the night. They show a remarkable dedication to their cause. Or a bloody foolish disregard for self-preservation."

Aes Sedai and *sul'dam* weren't particularly timid, but they *were* generally cautious. The Sharan channelers were anything but, particularly the men.

"Get me some *damane* to create lights for the river," Mat said. "And put the camp on lockdown, with a ring of *damane* spaced through camp to watch for channeling. Nobody channels, not even to light a bloody candle."

"The ... Aes Sedai ... may not like this," General Galgan said. He too hesitated upon using the words Aes Sedai. They had started using the term instead of *marath'damane* by Mat's order, one that he'd expected Tuon to rescind. She had not.

Figuring that woman out was going to be a real pleasure if they both survived this bloody mess.

Tylee entered the room. Tall and with a scarred face, the darkskinned woman walked with the confidence of a long-time soldier. She prostrated herself before Tuon, her clothing bloodied and her armor dented. Her legion had taken a beating today, and she probably felt like a rug did after a goodwife had been at it.

"I'm worried about our position here." Mat turned back and squatted down, looking through the hole. As he'd predicted, the Trollocs had begun to fall back.

"In what way?" General Galgan asked.

"We've run our channelers to the bone," Mat said. "And we're backed up against the river, a difficult position to defend longterm, especially against such a huge army. If they channel some gateways and move part of the Sharan army to this side of the river in the night, they could crush us."

"I see what you mean," Galgan said, shaking his head. "Given their strength, they will continue to wear us down, until we are so weak, they can throw a noose around us and tighten it."

Mat looked directly at Galgan. "I think it's time we abandon this position."

"I agree, that seems to be our only reasonable course of action," General Galgan said, nodding. "Why not choose a battlefield more to our advantage? Will your friends from the White Tower agree to a retreat?"

"Let's see," Mat said, straightening all the way up. "Someone send for Egwene and the Sitters."

"They will not come," Tuon said. "The Aes Sedai will not meet with us here. I doubt this Amyrlin will accept me into her camp, not with the protections I would require."

"Fine." Mat waved toward the gateway in the floor, which the *damane* was closing. "We'll use a gateway and talk through it like a door."

Tuon made no specific objection, so Mat sent the messengers. It took a little arranging, but Egwene seemed to like the idea well enough. Tuon entertained herself during the wait by having her throne moved to the other side of the room—Mat had no idea why. She then proceeded to begin annoying Min. "And this one?" Tuon asked as a lanky member of the Blood entered and bowed himself.

"He'll marry soon," Min said.

"You will give the omen first," Tuon said, "then interpretation, if you desire."

"I know exactly what this one means," Min protested. She had been set on a smaller throne beside that of Tuon. The girl was so decked in fine cloth and lace that she could have been mistaken for a mouse hiding in a bale of silk. "Sometimes, I know immediately, and—"

"You will give the omen first," Tuon said, her tone unchanged. "And you will refer to me as Greatest One. It is a high honor that you are given to speak with me directly. Do not let the Prince of the Ravens' attitude prove a model for your own."

Min quieted, though she didn't look cowed. She'd spent too long around Aes Sedai to let Tuon bully her. That gave Mat pause. He had an inkling of what Tuon might be capable of, if she grew displeased with Min. He loved her—Light, he was pretty sure he did. But he also let himself be a little afraid of her.

He'd have to keep watch so that Tuon didn't decide to "educate" Min.

"The omen for this man," Min said, controlling her tone with—it seemed—some difficulty, "is white lace trailing in a pond. I know that it will mean his marriage in the near future."

Tuon nodded. She wiggled her fingers at Selucia—the man they were discussing was of the low Blood, not of a high enough rank to speak directly to Tuon. His head was down so close to the ground as he bowed that it seemed that he had become fascinated with beetles and was trying to collect a specimen.

"Lord Gokhan of the Blood," Selucia Voiced, "is to be moved to the front lines. He is forbidden to marry until the end of this conflict. The omens have spoken that he will live long enough to find a wife, and so he will be protected."

Min grimaced, then opened her mouth, probably to object that it didn't work that way. Mat caught her eye and shook his head, and she backed down.

Tuon brought in the next, a young soldier, not of the Blood. The woman had fair skin and not a bad face, though Mat couldn't see much else beneath that armor. Men's armor and women's armor didn't actually look much different, which he found a shame. Mat had asked a Seanchan armorer if certain areas of the female breastplate shouldn't be emphasized, so to speak, and the armorer had looked at him like he was a half-wit. Light, these people had no sense of morality. A fellow needed to know if he was fighting a woman on the battlefield. It was only right.

As Min gave her omens, Mat settled back in his chair, putting his boots up on the map table and fishing in his pocket for his pipe. She *was* rather fine-looking, that soldier, though he could not see some of the important parts. She might make a good match for Talmanes. That fellow spent entirely too little time looking at women. He was shy around them, Talmanes was.

Mat ignored the looks of those nearby as he tipped his chair back onto two legs, set his heels on the table and packed his pipe. Seanchan could be so touchy.

He wasn't certain what he thought of so many Seanchan women being soldiers. A lot of them seemed like Birgitte, which wouldn't be so bad. Mat would rather spend an evening in the tavern with her than half the men he knew.

"You will be executed," Tuon Voiced through Selucia, speaking to the soldier.

Mat nearly fell off of his chair. He grabbed the table in front of him, the chair's front legs slamming down on the ground.

"*What?*" Min demanded. "No!"

"You saw the sign of the white boar," Tuon said.

"I don't know the meaning!"

"The boar is the symbol of one Handoin, one of my rivals in Seanchan," Tuon explained patiently. "The white boar is an omen of danger, perhaps betrayal. This woman works for him, or will in the future."

"You can't just *execute* her!"

Tuon blinked once, looking straight at Min. The room seemed to drop into shade, feeling colder. Mat shivered. He didn't like it when Tuon got like this. That stare of hers . . . it seemed like the stare of another person. A person without compassion. A statue had more life to it.

Nearby, Selucia wiggled her fingers at Tuon. Tuon glanced at them, then nodded.

"You are my Truthspeaker," she said to Min, almost reluctantly. "You may correct me in public. Do you see error in my decisions?"

"Yes, I do," Min said, not missing a beat. "You do not use my skills as you should."

"And how should I?" Tuon asked. The soldier who had been given a death sentence continued lying prostrate. She didn't object—she was not of a rank that could address the Empress. She was lowly enough that speaking to someone else in Tuon's presence would be a breach of honor.

"What someone *may* do is not grounds to kill them," Min said. "I intend no disrespect, but if you are going to kill people because of what I tell you, I will not speak."

"You can be made to speak."

"Try it," Min said softly. Mat started. Bloody ashes, she looked as cold as Tuon had a moment ago. "Let us see how the Pattern treats you, Empress, if you torture the bearer of omens."

Instead, Tuon smiled. "You take to this well. Explain to me what you desire, bringer of omens."

"I will tell you my viewings," Min said, "but from now on, the interpretations—whether my own, or those you read into the images—are to be kept quiet. Between the two of us would be best. You are allowed to watch someone because of what I've said, but not to punish them—not unless you catch them doing something. Set this woman free."

"Let it be so," Tuon said. "You are free," she Voiced through Selucia. "Walk in loyalty to the Crystal Throne. You will be watched."

The woman bowed lower, then retreated from the room, head down. Mat caught a trickle of sweat running down the side of her face. So she wasn't a statue.

He turned back to Tuon and Min. They were still staring at one another. No knives, but he felt as if someone had been stabbed. If only Min would learn a little respect. One of these days, he was going to have to haul her away from the Seanchan by her collar—a step in front of the headsman—he was certain of it.

A gateway suddenly split the air on the side of the room where Tuon had indicated it should go. Suddenly, it occurred to Mat why she had moved her throne. If that *damane* had been captured and forced to say where Tuon was sitting, an Aes Sedai could have opened a gateway where she sat, slicing her in two. It was so unlikely it was laughable—an Aes Sedai could sooner fly than kill someone who wasn't a Darkfriend—but Tuon took no chances.

The gateway opened to reveal the Hall of the Tower seated in a tent. Behind them, Egwene sat upon a large chair. The Amyrlin Seat itself, Mat realized. *Blood and ashes . . . she had them fetch it.*

Egwene looked exhausted, though she was doing a good job of hiding it. The others were no better. The Aes Sedai had been strained to their limits. If she were a soldier, he'd never send her into battle. Blood and bloody ashes—if he had a soldier with that cast to his skin and that look in his eyes, Mat would send the fellow to bed rest for a week.

"We are curious to know the purpose of this meeting," Saerin said calmly.

Silviana sat in a smaller chair by Egwene's side, and the other sisters were organized by Ajah. Some were missing, including one of the Yellows, by Mat's best guess.

Tuon nodded to Mat. He was to lead this meeting. He tipped

his hat to her, which earned him a half-raised eyebrow. Her dangerous look was gone, although she was still Empress.

"Aes Sedai," Mat said, standing up and tipping his hat to the Sitters. "The Crystal Throne appreciates you coming to your bloody senses and letting us direct the battle."

Silviana's eyes bulged as if someone had just stepped on her foot. From the corner of his eye, Mat caught a hint of a smile on Tuon's lips. Blood and bloody ashes, both women should know better than to encourage him so.

"You are as eloquent as ever, Mat," Egwene said dryly. "Do you still have your pet fox?"

"I do," Mat said. "He's snuggled up nice and warm."

"Take care of him," Egwene said. "I would not see you suffer Gareth Bryne's fate."

"So it was really Compulsion?" Mat asked. Egwene had sent him word.

"As near as we can tell," Saerin said. "Nynaeve Sedai can see the weaves on someone's mind, I'm told, but none of the rest of us can."

"We have our Healers looking at Bryne," said a stocky Domani Aes Sedai. "For now, we cannot trust any battle plans that he touched, at least not until we determine how long he's been under the Shadow's thumb."

Mat nodded. "That sounds good. Also, we need to withdraw our forces from the ford."

"Why?" Lelaine demanded. "We have stabilized here."

"Not well enough," Mat said. "I don't like this terrain, and we shouldn't have to fight where we don't want to."

"I hesitate to give an extra *inch* to the Shadow," Saerin said.

"A pace given up now could earn us two at the dawn," Mat replied.

General Galgan murmured in agreement, and Mat realized that he'd quoted Hawkwing.

Saerin frowned. The others seemed to be letting her lead the meeting. Egwene mostly stayed out of it, fingers laced before her, sitting at the back.

"I should probably tell you," Saerin said, "that our great captain was not the only one targeted. Davram Bashere and Lord Agelmar also tried to lead their respective armies to destruction.

Elayne Sedai did well in her battle, destroying a large force of Trollocs, but she was only able to do so because of the Black Tower's arrival. The Borderlanders were crushed, losing nearly two-thirds of their numbers."

Mat felt a chill. *Two-thirds?* Light! They were among the best troops the Light had. "Lan?"

"Lord Mandragoran lives," Saerin said.

Well, that was something. "And what of that army up in the Blight?"

"Lord Ituralde fell in battle," Saerin replied. "No one quite seems to know what happened to him."

"This was planned very well," Mat said, mind racing. "Blood and bloody ashes. They tried to crush all four battlefronts at once. I can't imagine the amount of coordination that would take . . ."

"As I noted," Egwene said softly, "we must be very careful. Keep that fox of yours near at all times."

"What does Elayne want to do?" Mat said. "Isn't she in charge?"

"Elayne Sedai is currently helping the Borderlanders," Saerin said. "She has instructed us that Shienar is all but lost, and is having the Asha'man bring Lord Mandragoran's army to a place of safety. Tomorrow, she plans to move her army through gateways and hold the Trollocs in the Blight."

Mat shook his head. "We need to make a unified stand." He hesitated. "Could we bring her through one of these gateways? At least contact her?"

There seemed to be no good objection. In a short time, another gateway opened in the tent with Egwene and the Sitters. Elayne strode through, thick with child, eyes practically on fire. Behind her, Mat caught a glimpse of soldiers with slumped postures, trudging across a dim evening field.

"Light," Elayne said, "Mat, what is it you want?"

"You've won your battle?" Mat asked.

"Barely, but yes. The Trollocs in Cairhien have been destroyed. The city is safe, as well."

Mat nodded. "I need to withdraw from our position here."

"Fine," Elayne said. "Perhaps we can meld your force with what's left of the Borderlanders."

"I want to do more than that, Elayne," Mat said, stepping forward. "This ploy the Shadow tried . . . it was clever, Elayne. *Bloody* clever. We're bloodied and almost broken. We don't have the luxury of fighting on multiple battlefronts anymore."

"What, then?"

"A last stand," Mat said softly. "All of us, together, at one place where the terrain favors us."

Elayne quieted, and someone brought her a chair to sit beside Egwene. She maintained the posture of a queen, but her disheveled hair and clothing burned in several places indicated what she'd been through. Mat could smell smoke coming from her battlefield, where the gateway was still open.

"That sounds desperate," Elayne finally said.

"We *are* desperate," Saerin said.

"We should ask our commanders . . . " Elayne trailed off. "If there are any we can trust not to be under Compulsion."

"There's only one," Mat said grimly, meeting her eyes. "And he's telling you we are finished if we continue as we have. The earlier plan was a good enough one, but after what we lost today . . . Elayne, we're dead unless we choose one place to stand, gather together, and fight."

One last toss of the dice.

Elayne sat for a time. "Where?" she finally asked.

"Tar Valon?" Gawyn asked.

"No," Mat said. "They'd just besiege it and move on. It can't be a city where we can get boxed in. We need a territory that will work in our favor, also a land that can't feed the Trollocs."

"Well, a place in the Borderlands should work for that," Elayne said with a grimace. "Lan's army burned almost every city or field they passed to deny the Shadow resources."

"Maps," Mat said, waving. "Someone get me maps. We need a location in southern Shienar or Arafel. Someplace close enough that the Shadow will see it as tempting, a place to fight us all at once . . . "

"Mat," Elayne asked. "Won't that be giving them what they want? A chance to wipe us out?"

"Yes," Mat said softly as the Aes Sedai sent over maps. These had markings on them, notations that appeared to be in General Bryne's hand, judging by what they said. "We have to be a tempting target. We have to draw them in, face them and either defeat them or be crushed."

A drawn-out fight would serve the Shadow. Once enough Trollocs reached southern lands, there would be no containing them. He had to win or lose quickly.

One last toss of the dice indeed.

Mat pointed at a location on the maps, a place that Bryne had annotated. It had a good water supply, a nice meeting of hills and rivers. "This place. Merrilor? You've been using it as a supply dump?"

Saerin chuckled softly. "And so we go back where we began, do we?"

"It does have some small fortifications," Elayne said. "The men built a palisade on one side, and we could expand it."

"It's what we need," Mat said, envisioning a battle there.

Merrilor would put them where the two major Trolloc armies could come in, try to crush the humans between them. That would be tempting. But the terrain would be wonderful for Mat to use . . .

Yes. It would be like the Battle of the Priya Narrows. If he put archers along those cliffs—no, dragons—and if he could give the Aes Sedai a few days of rest . . . Priya Narrows. He had counted on using a large river to trap the Hamarean army at the mouth of the Narrows. But as he sprung the trap, the blasted river dried up on him; the Hamareans had dammed it up on the other side of the Narrows. They had stepped right over the riverbed, and got clean away. *That's a lesson I won't forget.*

"This will do," Mat said, placing his hand on the map. "Elayne?"

"Let it be done," Elayne said. "I hope you know what you're doing, Mat."

As she spoke, the dice started tumbling inside his head.

Galad closed Trom's eyes. He'd searched the battlefield north of Cairhien for over an hour to find him. Trom had bled out, and only a few corners of his cloak were still white. Galad ripped the officer's knots off his shoulder—amazingly unsoiled—and stood up.

He felt weary to the bone. He started back across the battlefield, passing heaps of the dead. The crows and the ravens had come; they blanketed the landscape behind him. An undulating, quivering blackness that coated the ground like mold. From a distance, it seemed as if the ground had been burned, there were so many carrion birds.

Occasionally, Galad passed men like himself who sifted through the corpses for friends. There were surprisingly few looters—you had to watch for those on a battlefield. Elayne had caught a few trying to sneak out of Cairhien. She'd threatened to hang them.

She's grown harder, Galad thought, trudging back toward camp. His boots felt like lead on his feet. *That is good.* As a child, she had often made decisions with her heart. She was a queen now, and acted it. Now, if only he could right her moral compass. She wasn't a bad person, but Galad wished that she—like other monarchs—could see as clearly as he did.

He was beginning to accept that they didn't. He was beginning to accept that it was all right, so long as they tried their best. Whatever he had inside of him that allowed him to see the right of things was obviously a gift of the Light, and holding others to scorn because they had not been born with it was wrong. Just as it would be wrong to hold a man to scorn because he had been born with only one hand, and was therefore an inferior swordsman.

Many of the living he passed sat on the ground in the rare spots where there were no corpses and no blood. These men did not look like the victors of a battle, though the arrival of the Asha'man had saved this day. The trick with the lava had given Elayne's army the breather it needed to regroup and attack.

That battle had been swift, but brutal. Trollocs did not surrender, and they couldn't be allowed to break and flee. So Galad and the others had fought, bled and died long past when it was obvious they would be victorious.

The Trollocs were dead now. The remaining men sat and stared out at the blanket of corpses, as if numbed by the prospect of searching out the few living among the many thousands dead.

The setting sun and choking clouds made the light red, and gave faces a bloody cast.

Galad eventually reached the long hill that had marked the division between the two battlefields. He climbed it, slowly, forcing down thoughts of how good a bed would feel. Or a pallet on the floor. Or some flat rock in an out-of-the-way place, where he could roll up in his cloak.

The fresher air atop the hill shocked him. He'd been smelling blood and death for so long that now it was the clean air that smelled wrong. He shook his head, walking past tired Borderlanders who were trudging through gateways. The Asha'man had gone to hold off the Trollocs to the north so Lord Mandragoran's armies could escape.

From what Galad heard, the Borderlander armies were a fraction of what they had been. The betrayal of the great captains had been felt most deeply by Lord Mandragoran and his men. It sickened Galad, for this battle had not gone easily for him or anyone else with Elayne. It had been horrible—and as bad as it had been, the fight had gone more poorly for the Borderlanders.

Galad kept his stomach settled with difficulty as his view from atop the hill let him see just how many carrion birds had come to feast. The Dark One's minions fell, and the Dark One's minions glutted themselves.

Galad eventually found Elayne. Her passionate words, being spoken to Tam al'Thor and Arganda, took him by surprise.

"Mat is right," she said. "The Field of Merrilor is a good battlefield. Light! I wish we could give the people more time to rest. We'll have only a few days, a week at most, before the Trollocs reach Merrilor behind us." She shook her head. "We should have seen those Sharans coming. When the deck starts to look like it's stacked against the Dark One, of *course* he will just add a few new cards to the game."

Galad's pride demanded that he remain standing as he listened to Elayne talk to the other commanders. For once, however, his pride lost out, and he settled down on a stool and slumped forward.

"Galad," Elayne said, "you really should allow one of the Asha'man to wash away your fatigue. Your insistence upon treating them like outcasts is foolish."

Galad straightened up. "It has nothing to do with the Asha'man," he snapped. Too argumentative. He *was* tired. "This fatigue reminds me of what we lost today. It is an exhaustion my men must endure, and so I will, lest I forget just how tired they are and push them too far."

Elayne frowned at him. He had stopped worrying that his words offended her long ago. It seemed he couldn't claim that a day was pleasant or his tea warm without her taking offense somehow.

It would have been nice if Aybara hadn't run off. That man was a leader—one of the few that Galad had ever met—that one could actually talk to without worrying that he'd take offense. Perhaps the Two Rivers would be a good place for the Whitecloaks to settle.

Of course, there *was* something of a history of bad blood between them. He could work on that . . .

I called them Whitecloaks, he thought to himself a moment later. *Inside my head, that's how I thought of the Children just now.* It had been a long time since he'd done that by accident.

"Your Majesty," Arganda said. He stood beside Logain, the leader of the Asha'man, and Havien Nurelle, the new commander of the Winged Guard. Talmanes of the Band of the Red Hand trudged up with a few commanders from the Saldaeans and the Legion of the Dragon. Elder Haman of the Ogier sat on the ground a short distance away; he stared off, toward the sunset, seeming dazed.

"Your Majesty," Arganda continued, "I realize you consider this a great victory—"

"It *is* a great victory," Elayne said. "We must persuade the men to see it that way. Not eight hours ago, I assumed that our entire army would be slaughtered. We won."

"At a cost of half of our troops," Arganda said softly.

"I will count that a victory," Elayne insisted. "We were expecting complete destruction."

"The only victor today is the butcher," Nurelle said softly. He looked haunted.

"No," Tam al'Thor said, "she's right. The troops have to understand what their losses earned. We *must* treat this as a victory. It must be recorded that way in the histories, and the soldiers must be convinced to see it so."

"That is a lie," Galad found himself saying.

"It is not," al'Thor said. "We lost many friends today. Light, but we all did. Focusing on death, however, is what the Dark One wants us to do. I dare you to tell me I'm wrong. We must look and see Light, not Shadow, or we'll all be pulled under."

"By *winning* here," Elayne said, deliberately emphasizing the word, "we earn a reprieve. We can gather at Merrilor, entrench there, and make our last stand in our strength against the Shadow."

"Light," Talmanes whispered. "We're going to go through this again, aren't we?"

"Yes," Elayne said reluctantly.

Galad looked out over the fields of the dead, then shivered. "Merrilor will be worse. Light help us . . . it's going to get worse."

CHAPTER
33

The Prince's Tabac

Perrin chased Slayer through the skies.

He leaped from a churning, silver-black cloud, Slayer a blur before him in the charred sky. The air pulsed with the rhythm of lightning bolts and furious winds. Scent after scent assailed Perrin, with no logic behind them. Mud in Tear. A burning pie. Rotting garbage. A death-lily flower.

Slayer landed on the cloud ahead and *shifted*, turning around in an eyeblink, bow drawn. The arrow loosed so quickly the air cracked, but Perrin managed to slap it down with his hammer. He landed on the same thunderhead as Slayer, imagining footing beneath him, and the vapors of the storm cloud became solid.

Perrin charged forward through a churning dark gray fog, the top layer of the cloud, and attacked. They clashed, Slayer summoning a shield and sword. Perrin's hammer beat a rhythm against that shield, pounding alongside the booming of thunder. A crash with each blow.

Slayer spun away to flee, but Perrin managed to snatch the edge of his cloak. As Slayer attempted to *shift* away, Perrin imagined them staying put. He knew they would. It was not a possibility, it *was*.

They both fuzzed for a moment, then returned to the cloud.

Slayer growled, then swept his sword backward, shearing off the tip of his cloak and freeing himself. He turned to face Perrin, stalking to the side, sword held in wary hands. The cloud trembled beneath them, and a flash of phantom lightning lit the misty vapor at their feet.

"You become increasingly annoying, wolf pup," Slayer said.

"You've never fought a wolf that can fight you back," Perrin said. "You've killed them from afar. The slaughter was easy. Now you've tried to hunt a prey who has teeth, Slayer."

Slayer snorted. "You're like a boy with his father's sword. Dangerous, but completely unaware of why, or how to use your weapons."

"We'll see who—" Perrin began, but Slayer lunged, sword out. Perrin braced himself, imagining the sword growing dull, the air becoming thick to slow it, his skin turning hard enough to turn the weapon aside.

A second later, Perrin found himself tumbling through the air.

Fool! he thought. He'd focused so much on the attack that he hadn't been ready when Slayer changed their footing. Perrin passed through the rumbling cloud, breaking out into the sky below, wind tugging at his clothing. He prepared himself, waiting for the hail of arrows to follow him down out of the cloud. Slayer could be so predictable . . .

No arrows came. Perrin fell for a few moments, then cursed and twisted to see a storm of arrows shooting up from the ground below. He *shifted* seconds before they passed through where he'd been.

Perrin appeared in the air a hundred feet to the side, still falling. He didn't bother to slow himself; he hit the ground, increasing his body's strength to deal with the shock of the blow. The ground cracked. A ring of dust blew out from him.

The storm was far worse than it had been. The ground here— they were in the south, somewhere, with overgrown brush and tangled vines growing up the sides of the trees—was pocked and torn. Lightning lashed repeatedly, so frequent that he could hardly count to three without seeing a bolt.

There was no rain, but the landscape crumbled. Entire hills would suddenly disintegrate. The one just to Perrin's left dissolved like an enormous pile of dust, a trail of dirt and sand streaking out into the wind.

Perrin leaped through the debris-laden sky, hunting Slayer. Had the man *shifted* back up to Shayol Ghul? No. Two more arrows pierced the sky, heading for Perrin. Slayer was very good at making them ignore the wind.

Perrin slapped the arrows aside and hurled himself in Slayer's direction. He spotted the man on a peak of rock, ground crumbling to either side of him and whipping into the air.

Perrin came down with hammer swinging. Slayer *shifted* away, of course, and the hammer struck stone with a sound like thunder. Perrin growled. Slayer was too quick!

Perrin was fast, too. Sooner or later, one of them would slip. One slip would be enough.

He caught sight of Slayer bounding away, and followed. When Perrin jumped off the next hilltop, the stones shattered behind him, rising up into the wind. The Pattern was weakening. Beyond that, his will was much stronger now that he was here in the flesh. He no longer had to worry about entering the dream too strongly and losing himself. He had entered it as strongly as one could.

And so, when Perrin moved, the landscape shuddered around him. The next leap showed him sea ahead. They had traveled much farther to the south than Perrin had realized. Were they in Illian? Tear?

Slayer hit the beach, where water crashed against rocks; the sand—if there had been any—had been blown away. The land seemed to be returning to a primal state, grass ripped free, soil eroded, leaving only stone and crashing waves.

Perrin landed beside Slayer. For once, there was no *shifting*. Both men were intent on the fight, the swings of hammer and sword. Metal clanged against metal.

Perrin nearly landed a hit, his hammer brushing Slayer's clothing. He heard a curse, but the next moment, Slayer was rounding from his dodge with a large axe in hand. Perrin braced himself and took it on the side, hardening his skin.

The axe didn't draw blood, not with Perrin braced as he was, but it *did* carry a huge amount of force behind it. The blow tossed Perrin out over the sea.

Slayer appeared above him a second later, plunging down with that axe. Perrin caught it on his hammer as he fell, but the force of the blow flung him downward, toward the ocean.

He commanded the water to recede. It rushed away, churning and bubbling, as if pursued by a powerful wind. Perrin righted himself as he fell, landing and cracking the still-wet, rocky bottom of the bay. Seawater rose high to either side of him, a circular wall some thirty feet high.

Slayer crashed down nearby. The man was panting from the exertion of their fight. Good. Perrin's own fatigue manifested as a deep burning in his muscles.

"I'm glad you were there," Slayer said, raising his sword to his shoulder, his shield vanishing. "I had so hoped that, when I appeared to kill the Dragon, you would interfere."

"What are you, Luc?" Perrin asked, wary, *shifting* to the side, keeping opposite Slayer in the circle of stone with walls of sea. "What are you really?"

Slayer prowled to the side, talking—Perrin knew—to lull his prey. "I've seen him, you know," Slayer said softly. "The Dark One, the Great Lord as some would call him. Both terms are gross, almost insulting, understatements."

"Do you really think he'll reward you?" Perrin spat. "How can you not realize that once you've done what he wishes of you, he'll just discard you, as he has so many?"

Slayer laughed. "Did he discard the Forsaken, when they failed and were imprisoned with him in the Bore? He could have slaughtered them all and kept their souls in eternal torment. Did he?"

Perrin didn't reply.

"The Dark One does not discard useful tools," Slayer said. "Fail him, and he may exact punishment, but he never discards. He's like a goodwife, with her balls of tangled yarn and broken tea-kettles hidden away in the bottoms of baskets, waiting for the right moment to return them to usefulness. That is where you're wrong, Aybara. A mere human might kill a tool who succeeds, fearing that the tool will threaten him. That is not the Dark One's way. He *will* reward me."

Perrin opened his mouth to reply, and Slayer *shifted* right in front of him to attack, thinking him distracted. Perrin vanished and Slayer struck only air. The man spun about, sword splitting the air, but Perrin had *shifted* to the opposite side. Small sea creatures with many arms undulated near his feet, confused at the sudden lack of water. Something large and dark swam through the shadowy water behind Slayer.

"You never answered my question," Perrin said. "What *are* you?"

"I'm bold," Slayer said, striding forward. "And I'm tired of being afraid. In this life, there are predators and there are prey. Often, the predators themselves become food for someone else. The only way to survive is to move up the chain, become the hunter."

"That's why you kill wolves?"

Slayer smiled a dangerous smile, his face in shadows. With the storm clouds above and the high walls of water, it was dim here at the bottom—though the strange light of the wolf dream pierced this place, if in a muted way.

"Wolves and men are the finest hunters in this world," Slayer said softly. "Kill them, and you elevate yourself above them. Not all of us had the *privilege* of growing up in a comfortable home with a warm hearth and laughing siblings."

Perrin and Slayer rounded one another, shadows blending, lightning blasts above shimmering through the water.

"If you knew my life," Slayer said, "you'd howl. The hopelessness, the agony . . . I soon found my way. My power. In this place, I am a king."

He leaped across the space, his form a blur. Perrin prepared to swing, but Slayer didn't draw his sword. He crashed into Perrin, throwing them both into the wall of water. The sea churned and bubbled around them.

Darkness. Perrin created light, somehow making the rocks at his feet glow. Slayer had hold of his cloak with one hand and was swinging at him in the dark water, his sword trailing bubbles but moving as quickly as in the air. Perrin yelled, bubbles coming from his mouth. He tried to block, but his arms moved lethargically.

In that frozen moment, Perrin tried to imagine the water not impeding him, but his mind rejected that thought. It wasn't natural. It couldn't be.

In desperation, Slayer's sword nearly close enough to bite, Perrin froze the water solid around both of them. Doing so nearly crushed him, but it held Slayer still for a precarious moment while Perrin oriented himself. He made his cloak vanish so he wouldn't take Slayer with him, then *shifted* away.

Perrin landed on the rocky beach beside a steep hillside that was half broken away by the power of the sea. He fell on hands and knees, gasping. Water streamed from his beard. His mind felt . . . numb. He had trouble thinking the water away from him to dry himself.

What's happening? he thought, trembling. Around him, the storm raged, the bark ripping from tree trunks, their limbs already stripped away. He was just so . . . tired. Exhausted. How long had it been since he slept? Weeks had passed in the real world, but it couldn't actually have been weeks here, could it? It—

The sea boiled, churning. Perrin turned. He'd kept his hammer, somehow, and he raised it to face Slayer.

The waters continued to move, but nothing came from them. Suddenly, behind him, the hill split in half. Perrin felt something heavy hit him in the shoulder, like a punch. He fell to his knees, twisting to see the hillside broken in two, Slayer standing on the other side, nocking another arrow to his bow.

Perrin *shifted*, desperate, pain belatedly flaring up his side and across his body.

"All I'm saying is that battles are being fought," Mandevwin said, "and we are not there."

"Battles are always being fought *somewhere*," Vanin replied, leaning back against the wall outside a warehouse in Tar Valon. Faile listened to them with half an ear. "We've fought our share of them. All *I'm* saying is that I'm pleased to avoid this particular one."

"People are dying," Mandevwin said, disapproving. "This is not simply a battle, Vanin. It is Tarmon Gai'don itself!"

"Which means nobody is paying us," Vanin said.

Mandevwin sputtered, "Paying . . . to fight the Last Battle . . . You knave! This battle means life itself."

Faile smiled as she looked over the supply ledgers. The two Redarms idled by the doorway as servants wearing the Flame of Tar Valon loaded Faile's caravan. Behind them, the White Tower rose over the city.

At first, she had been annoyed by the banter, but the way Vanin poked at the other man reminded her of Gilber, one of her father's quartermasters back in Saldaea.

"Now, Mandevwin," Vanin said, "you hardly sound like a mercenary at all! What if Lord Mat heard you?"

"Lord Mat will fight," said Mandevwin.

"When he has to," Vanin said. "We *don't* have to. Look, these supplies are important, right? And someone has to guard them, right? Here we are."

"I just do not see why this job requires us. I should be helping Talmanes lead the Band, and you lot, you should be guarding Lord Mat . . ."

Faile could almost hear the end of that line, the one they were all thinking. *You should be guarding Lord Mat from those Seanchan.*

The soldiers had taken in stride Mat's disappearance, then his reappearance with the Seanchan. Apparently, they expected this kind of behavior from "Lord" Matrim Cauthon. Faile had a squad of fifty of the Band's best, including Captain Mandevwin, Lieutenant Sandip and several Redarms who came highly recommended by Talmanes. None of them knew their true purpose in guarding the Horn of Valere.

She would have brought ten times this number if she could. As it was, fifty was suspicious enough. Those fifty were the Band's very best, some pulled from command positions. They would have to do.

We're not going far, Faile thought, checking the next page of the ledgers. She had to look as if she were concerned about the supplies. *Why am I so worried?*

She needed only to carry the Horn to the Field of Merrilor, now that Cauthon had finally appeared. She'd already run three caravans from other locations using the same guards, so her current job wouldn't be suspicious in the least.

She'd chosen the Band very deliberately. In the eyes of most, they were just mercenaries, so the least important—and least trustworthy—troops in the army. However, for all of her complaints about Mat—she might not know him well, but the way Perrin spoke of him was enough—he did inspire loyalty in his men. The men who found their way to Cauthon were like him. They tried to hide from duty and preferred gambling and drinking to doing anything useful, but in a pinch they'd each fight like ten men.

At Merrilor, Cauthon would have good reason to check in on Mandevwin and his men. At that point, Faile could give him the Horn. Of course, she also had some members of *Cha Faile* with her as guards. She wanted some people she knew for certain she could trust.

Nearby, Laras—the stout mistress of the kitchens at Tar Valon—came out of the warehouse, wagging a finger at several of the serving girls. The woman walked to Faile, trailed by a lanky youth with a limp who was carrying a beat-up chest.

"Something for you, my Lady." Laras gestured to the trunk. "The Amyrlin herself added it to your shipment as an afterthought. Something about a friend of hers, from back home?"

"It's Matrim Cauthon's tabac," Faile said with a grimace. "When he found that the Amyrlin had a store of Two Rivers leaf left, he insisted upon purchasing it."

"Tabac, at a time like this." Laras shook her head, wiping her fingers on her apron. "I remember that boy. I've known a youth or two in my day like him, always skulking around the kitchens like a stray wanting scraps. Someone ought to find something useful for him to do."

"We're working on it," Faile said as Laras' servant placed the trunk in Faile's own wagon. She winced as he let it thump down, then dusted off his hands.

Laras nodded, walking back into her warehouse. Faile rested her fingers on the chest. Philosophers claimed the Pattern did not have a sense of humor. The Pattern, and the Wheel, simply *were*; they did not care, they did not take sides. However, Faile could not help thinking that somewhere, the Creator was grinning at her. She had left home with her head full of arrogant dreams, a child thinking herself on a grand quest to find the Horn.

Life had knocked those out from under her, leaving her to haul herself back up. She had grown up, had started paying mind to what was really important. And now ... now the Pattern, with almost casual indifference, dropped the Horn of Valere into her lap.

She removed her hand and pointedly refused to open the chest. She had the key, delivered to her separately, and she *would* check to see that the Horn was really in the chest. Not now. Not until she was alone and reasonably certain she was safe.

She climbed into the wagon and rested her feet on the chest.

"I still don't like it," Mandevwin was saying beside the warehouse.

"You don't like *anything*," Vanin said. "Look, the work we're doing is important. Soldiers have to eat."

"I suppose that is true," Mandevwin said.

"It is!" a new voice added. Harnan, another Redarm, joined them. Not one of the three, Faile noticed, jumped to help the servants load the caravan. "Eating is wonderful," Harnan said. "And if there is an expert on the subject, Vanin, it is certainly you."

Harnan was a sturdily built man with a wide face and a hawk tattooed on his cheek. Talmanes swore by the man, calling him a veteran survivor of both "the Six-Story Slaughter" and Hinderstap, whatever those were.

"Now, that wounds me, Harnan," Vanin said from behind. "That wounds me badly."

"I doubt it," Harnan said with a laugh. "To wound you badly, an attack would first have to penetrate through fat to reach the muscle. I'm not sure Trolloc swords are long enough for that!"

Mandevwin laughed, and the three of them moved off. Faile went over the last few pages of the ledger, then began to climb down, to call for Setalle Anan. The woman had been acting as her assistant for these caravan runs. As she was climbing down, however, Faile noticed that not all three members of the Band had moved off. Only two of them had. Portly Vanin still stood back there. She saw him, and paused.

Vanin immediately lumbered off toward some of the other soldiers. Had he been watching her?

"Faile! Faile! Aravine says she has finished checking over the manifests for you. We can go, Faile."

Olver scrambled eagerly into the wagon seat. He had insisted on joining the caravan, and the members of the Band had persuaded her to allow it. Even Setalle had suggested it would be wise to bring him. Apparently, they worried that Olver would find his way to the fighting somehow if he wasn't constantly under their watch. Faile had reluctantly set him to running errands.

"All right, then," Faile said, climbing back into the wagon. "I suppose we can be off."

The wagons lumbered into motion. She spent the entire trip out of the city trying not to look at the chest.

She tried to distract herself from thinking about it, but that only brought her mind to another pressing concern. Perrin. She had seen him only briefly during a supply run to Andor. He'd warned her he might have another duty, but had been reluctant to tell her about it.

Now he'd vanished. He'd made Tam steward in his place, had taken a gateway to Shayol Ghul and had vanished. She'd asked those who'd been there, but nobody had seen him since his conversation with Rand.

All would be well with him, wouldn't it? She was a soldier's daughter and a soldier's wife; she knew not to worry overly much. But a person could not help but worry a little. Perrin had been the one to suggest her as the keeper of the Horn.

She wondered, idly, if he had done it to keep her off the battlefield. She wouldn't mind terribly if he'd done so, though she would never tell him that. In fact, once this was all said and done, she would insinuate that she was offended and see how he reacted. He needed to know that she would not sit back and be coddled, even if her true name implied otherwise.

Faile pulled her wagon, which was first in the caravan, onto the Jualdhe Bridge out of Tar Valon. About halfway across, the bridge trembled. The horses stomped and tossed their heads as Faile slowed them and glanced over her shoulder. The sight of swaying buildings in Tar Valon proved to her that the trembling wasn't just the bridge, but an earthquake.

The other horses danced and whinnied, and the shaking rattled carts.

"We need to move off the bridge, Lady Faile!" Olver cried.

"The bridge is much too long for us to get to the other side before this ends," Faile said calmly. She had suffered earthquakes in Saldaea before. "We'd be more in danger of hurting ourselves in the scramble than we will be here. This bridge is Ogier work. We're probably safer here than we'd be on solid ground."

Indeed, the earthquake passed without so much as a stone being loosed from the bridge. Faile brought her horses under control and started ahead again. The Light willing, the damage to the city wasn't too bad. She didn't know if earthquakes were common here. With Dragonmount nearby, there would at least be occasional rumblings, wouldn't there?

Still, the earthquake worried her. People spoke of the land becoming unstable, the groanings of the earth coming to match the breaking of the sky by lightning and thunder. She had heard more than one account of the spiderweb cracks that appeared in rocks, pure black, as if they extended on into eternity itself.

Once the rest of the caravan left the city, Faile pulled her wagons up beside some mercenary bands waiting their turn at an Aes Sedai for Traveling. Faile could not afford to insist on preference; she had to avoid attention. So, nerve-racking though it was, she settled down to wait.

Her caravan was last in line for the day. Eventually, Aravine came up to Faile's wagon, and Olver scooted over to make room for her. She patted him on the head. A lot of women responded that way to Olver, and he *did* seem so innocent much of the time. Faile wasn't convinced; she narrowed her eyes at Olver as he snuggled up beside Aravine. Mat seemed to have had a strong influence on the child.

"I'm pleased with this shipment, my Lady," Aravine said. "With this canvas, we should have enough material to put tents over the heads of most men in the army. We *are* still going to need leather. We know that Queen Elayne marched her men hard, and we will be getting requests for new boots."

Faile nodded absently. A gateway ahead opened to Merrilor, and she could see the armies, still gathering. Over the last couple of days, they'd slowly limped back to lick their wounds. Three battlefronts, three disasters of varying degrees. Light. The arrival of the Sharans was devastating, as were the betrayals of the great captains, including Faile's own father. The armies of the Light had lost well over a third of their forces.

On the Field of Merrilor, commanders deliberated and their

soldiers repaired armor and weapons, awaiting what would come. A final stand.

". . . will also need some more meat," Aravine said. "We should suggest some quick hunting trips using gateways over the next few days to see what we can find."

Faile nodded. It was a comfort, having Aravine. Though Faile still reviewed reports and visited the quartermasters, Aravine's careful attention made the job much easier, like a good sergeant who had made certain his men were in shape before an inspection.

"Aravine," Faile said. "You haven't ever taken one of the gateways to check on your family in Amadicia."

"There is nothing for me there any longer, my Lady."

Aravine stubbornly refused to admit that she'd been a noble before being taken by the Shaido. Well, at least she didn't act as some of the former *gai'shain* did, docile and submissive. If Aravine was determined to leave her past behind her, then Faile would gladly give her the chance. It was the least she owed the woman.

As they talked, Olver climbed down to go chat with some of his "uncles" among the Redarms. Faile glanced to the side as Vanin rode past with two of the Band's other scouts. He spoke jovially to them.

You're misreading that look of his, Faile told herself. *There's nothing suspicious about the man; you're merely jumpy because of the Horn.*

Still, when Harnan came to ask if she needed anything—a member of the Band did that every half-hour—she asked him about Vanin.

"Vanin?" Harnan said from horseback. "Good fellow. He can chew your ear off griping at times, my Lady, but don't let that sour you. He's our best scout."

"I can't imagine how," she said. "I mean, he can't move quickly or quietly with that bulk, can he?"

"He'd surprise you, my Lady," Harnan said with a laugh. "I like to rib him, but he really is skilled."

"Has he ever presented any disciplinary problems?" Faile asked, trying to choose her words. "Fighting? Lifting things from other men's tents?"

"Vanin?" Harnan laughed. "He'll borrow your brandy if you let him, then return the flask mostly empty. And truth be told, he might have had a bit of thieving in his past, but I've never known him to fight. He's a good man. You don't need to worry about him."

Some thieving in his past? Harnan, though, looked like he didn't want to talk about it any further. "Thank you," she said, but she remained worried.

Harnan raised a hand to his head in a kind of salute, then rode off. It was three more hours before an Aes Sedai came to process them. Berisha strolled over, giving the caravan a critical inspection. She was hard of features and lean of figure. The other Aes Sedai working the Traveling ground had already returned to Tar Valon by this point, and the sun was dipping toward the horizon.

"Caravan of foodstuffs and canvas," Berisha said, examining Faile's ledger. "Bound for the Field of Merrilor. We've sent them seven caravans today so far. Why another? I suspect the Caemlyn refugees could use this as much."

"The Field of Merrilor is soon going to be a site of great battle," Faile said, keeping her temper with difficulty. Aes Sedai did not like to be snapped at. "I doubt we can oversupply it."

Berisha sniffed. "I say it's too much." The woman seemed chronically dissatisfied, as if annoyed at being left out of the fighting.

"The Amyrlin disagrees with you," Faile replied. "A gateway, please. The hour grows late." *And if you want to talk about a waste, why not consider how you made me march all the way out of the city and wait, instead of sending me straight from the White Tower grounds?*

The Hall of the Tower wanted a single Traveling ground for large troop or supply movements to keep better control over who entered and left Tar Valon. Faile could not blame them for the precaution, even if it was frustrating sometimes.

Bureaucracy was bureaucracy, and Berisha finally adopted a look of concentration in preparation for making a gateway. Before she could weave the gateway, however, the ground started to rumble.

Not again, Faile thought with a sigh. Well, there were commonly smaller quakes after an—

A series of sharp black crystal spikes split the ground nearby, jutting upward some ten or fifteen feet. One speared a Redarm's horse, splashing blood into the air as the spike went straight through both beast and man.

"Bubble of evil!" Harnan called from nearby.

Other crystalline spikes—some thin as a spear, others wide as a person—ripped up through the ground. Faile frantically tried to control her horses. They danced to the side, spinning her cart, nearly toppling it as she pulled on the reins.

Around her, madness ruled. The spikes punched up through the ground in groups, each sharp as a razor. One wagon splintered as crystals destroyed its left side. Foodstuffs spilled to the dead grass. Some horses went wild and other wagons overturned. The crystal spikes continued to rise, appearing all over the empty field. Shouts rose from the nearby village at the end of the bridge from Tar Valon.

"Gateway!" Faile screamed, still fighting her horses. "*Do it!*"

Berisha jumped back as spikes jutted out of the ground near her feet. She threw a pale-faced glance at them, and only then did Faile realize that something was *moving* inside the shadowy crystals. It seemed like smoke.

A crystal spike came up through Berisha's foot. She cried out, kneeling, just as a line of light split the air. Thank the Light, the woman held her weave, and—with what seemed glacial slowness—the line of light rotated and opened a hole large enough for a wagon.

"Through the gateway!" Faile shouted, but her voice was lost in the commotion. Crystals burst from the ground very near her left, tossing earth across her face. Her horses danced, then started to gallop. Rather than risking complete loss of control, Faile steered them toward the gateway. Right before they went through, however, she pulled them to a rearing halt.

"The gateway!" she shouted at the others. Again her voice was lost. Fortunately, the Redarms took up the call, riding down the disordered line, grabbing the reins of horses and steering wagons toward the gateway. Other men picked up those who had been tossed to the ground.

Harnan thundered past, carrying Olver. He was followed by Sandip with Setalle Anan clinging to him from behind. The frequency of the crystals increased. One jutted up near Faile, and with horror, she realized that the smoky movements inside had form. Figures of men and women, screaming, as if trapped inside.

She drew back, aghast. Nearby, the last working wagon rattled through the gateway. Soon the field would be nothing but crystals. Some straggling members of the Band helped the wounded onto horses, but two fell as the crystals started budding growths that shot out to the sides. It was time to go. Aravine passed by, grabbing Faile's reins to pull them to safety.

"Berisha!" Faile said. The Aes Sedai knelt beside the opening, sweat trickling down her pale face. Faile leaped from her wagon seat, grabbing the woman's shoulder as Aravine pulled the wagon through the gateway.

"Let's move!" Faile said to Berisha. "I'll carry you."

The woman teetered, then fell to the side, holding her stomach. Faile realized with a start that blood streamed around the woman's fingers. Berisha stared at the sky, mouth working, but no sounds came out.

"My Lady!" Mandevwin galloped up. "I don't care where it leads! We must get through!"

"What—"

She cut off as Mandevwin grabbed her by the waist and hauled her up, crystals exploding nearby. He galloped through the opening, holding her.

The gateway snapped shut a moment later.

Faile panted as Mandevwin let her down. She stared at where the gateway had been.

His words finally caught up with her. *I don't care where it leads . . .* He had seen something she, in her panic over getting everyone to safety, had not.

The gateway hadn't led to the Field of Merrilor.

"Where . . . " Faile whispered, joining the others, who stared at the horrid landscape. A sweltering heat, plants covered in spots of darkness, a scent of something awful in the air.

They were in the Blight.

Aviendha chewed on her rations, crunchy rolled oats that had been mixed with honey. They tasted good. Being near Rand meant that their food stores had stopped spoiling.

She reached for her water flask, then hesitated. She'd been drinking a lot of water lately. She rarely stopped to think about its value. Had she already forgotten the lessons she'd learned during her return to the Three-fold Land to visit Rhuidean?

Light, she thought, raising the flask to her lips. *Who cares? It's the Last Battle!*

She sat on the floor of a large Aiel tent in the valley of Thakan'dar. Melaine chewed on her own rations close by. The woman was near to term now with her twins, her belly bulging beneath her dress and shawl. Much as a Maiden was forbidden to fight while with child, Melaine was forbidden dangerous activity. She had voluntarily gone to work in Berelain's Healing station in Mayene—but she regularly checked on the progress of the battle. Many of the *gai'shain* had found their way through gateways to help as they could, though all they could do was carry water or soil for the earthen mounds Ituralde had ordered cast up to give the defenders some kind of protection.

A group of Maidens ate nearby, chatting with handtalk. Aviendha could have read it, but didn't. It would only make her wish she could join them. She'd become a Wise One and had forsaken her old life. That didn't mean she had purged herself of every bit of envy. Instead, she wiped out her wooden bowl and stowed it in her pack, stood up and slipped out of the tent.

Outside, the night air was cool. It was about an hour before dawn, and felt almost like the Three-fold Land at night. Aviendha looked up at the mountain that dominated the valley; despite the dark of early morning, she could see the pit leading inward.

It had been many days since Rand had entered. Ituralde had wandered back into camp the night before with a tale of being held by wolves and a man who claimed Perrin Aybara had sent him to kidnap the great captain. Ituralde had been taken into custody, and had not complained.

The Trollocs had not attacked the valley all day. The defenders still had them held in the pass. The Shadow seemed to be waiting for something. The Light send it was not another attack by Myrddraal. The last one had nearly ended the resistance. Aviendha had rallied the channelers once the Eyeless had emerged to kill the humans defending the mouth of the pass; they must have realized that exposing themselves in large numbers was unwise, and they fled back to the safety of the pass once the channeling began.

Either way, she felt grateful for this rare moment of rest and relative peace between attacks. She stared into that pit in the mountain, within which Rand fought. A strong pulse came from deep within it; channeling, in waves, powerful. Several days on the outside, but how long on the inside? A day? Hours? Minutes? Maidens who guarded the path up to the entrance claimed that after four hours of duty, they'd climb down the mountainside and find that eight hours had passed.

We have to hold, Aviendha thought. *We have to fight. Give him as much time as we can.*

At least she knew he still lived. She could sense that. And his pain.

She looked away.

As she did, she noticed something. A woman was channeling in the camp. It was faint, but Aviendha frowned. At this hour, with no fighting, the only channeling should have been happening on the Traveling ground, and this was in the wrong direction.

Muttering to herself, she started through the camp. It was probably one of the off-duty Windfinders again. They took turns rotating in and out of the group using the Bowl of the Winds, constantly, to keep the tempest at bay. That task was done atop the northern valley wall, well guarded by a large force of Sea Folk. They had to take gateways up there to change shifts.

When the Windfinders weren't on duty with the Bowl, they camped with the rest of the army. Aviendha had told them time and time again that, while in the valley, they were *not* allowed to channel for incidental reasons. One would think, after all the years they had spent never letting Aes Sedai see them use their powers, that they could be more self-controlled! If she caught another one of them using the One Power to warm her tea, she'd send her to Sorilea for an education. This was supposed to be a secure camp.

Aviendha froze in place. That channeling was *not* coming from the small ring of tents where the Windfinders made camp.

Had she sensed an incursion? A Dreadlord or Forsaken would probably assume that—in a camp this large filled with Aes Sedai, Windfinders and Wise Ones—no one would notice a tiny bit of channeling here or there. Aviendha immediately crouched beside a nearby tent, avoiding the light of a lantern on a pole. The channeling came again, very faint. She crept forward.

If this turns out to be someone heating water for a bath . . .

She moved between tents, across the hard earth. As she drew closer, she took off her boots and left them behind, then pulled her dagger from its sheath. She couldn't risk embracing the Source, lest she reveal herself to her prey.

The camp didn't truly sleep. Those warriors who were not on duty had trouble slumbering here. Fatigue among the spears, including the Maidens, was becoming a problem. They complained of terrible dreams.

Aviendha continued forward silently, slipping between tents, avoiding those that shone with light. This place disturbed all of them, so she was not surprised to hear of bad dreams. How could they sleep in peace so close to the Dark One's abode?

Logically, she knew that the Dark One was not nearby, not really. That wasn't what the Bore was. He didn't *live* in this place; he existed outside the Pattern, inside his prison. Still, bedding down here was like trying to sleep while a murderer stood beside your bed, holding a knife and contemplating the color of your hair.

There, she thought, slowing. The channeling stopped, but Aviendha was close. Draghkar attacks and the threat of Myrddraal slipping in at night had driven the camp leaders to spread the officers throughout the camp, in tents that bore no external sign of which belonged to a commander and which to a common foot soldier. Aviendha, however, knew this tent to belong to Darlin Sisnera.

Darlin had official command of this battlefield, now that Ituralde had fallen. He was not a general, but the Tairen army was the bulk of the defense, with the Defenders of the Stone their elite units. Their commander, Tihera, was good with tactics, and Darlin listened well to the man's suggestions. Tihera was not a great captain, but he was very clever. He, Darlin and Rhuarc had been devising their battle plans following Ituralde's fall . . .

In the darkness, Aviendha nearly missed the three figures crouched ahead of her, just outside Darlin's tent. They gestured to one another, silent, and she could see little about them—not even their clothing. She raised her knife, and then a bolt of lightning split the sky, giving her a better glimpse of one. The man was wearing a veil. Aiel.

They noticed the intruder too, she thought, stalking up to them and raising a hand to keep them from attacking. She whispered, "I felt channeling nearby, and I do not think it is from one of ours. What have you seen?"

The three men stared at her, as if stunned, though she couldn't make out much of their faces.

Then they attacked her.

Aviendha cursed, leaping backward as their spears came out and one threw a knife in her direction. Aiel Darkfriends? She felt a fool. She should have known better.

She reached out to embrace the Source. If a female Dreadlord was nearby, she'd feel what Aviendha did, but there was no help for it. She needed to survive these three.

However, as Aviendha reached for the One Power, something snapped into place between her and the Source. A shield, with weaves she could not see.

One of these men could channel. Aviendha's reaction was instinctive. She shoved down her panic, stopped scrambling to touch the Source and threw herself at the nearest of the men. She caught his spear-thrust with her off hand—ignoring the pain as the spearhead sliced against her ribs—and hauled him forward to ram her knife in his neck.

One of the other two cursed, and Aviendha suddenly found herself wrapped in weaves of Air, unable to speak or move. Blood soaked into her blouse and pooled against her wounded side. The man she'd struck gasped and thrashed on the ground as he died. The other two did not move to help him.

One of the Darkfriends stepped forward, lithe, almost invisible in the darkness. He pulled her face close to inspect her, then waved his hand to the other. A very soft light appeared beside them, giving them a better look at her—and her at them. They wore *red* veils, but this one had taken his down for the fight. Why? What was this? No Aiel she knew did that. Were these the Shaido? Had they joined the Shadow?

One of the men made a few gestures to the other. It was handtalk. Not Maiden handtalk, but something similar. The other man nodded.

Aviendha thrashed against her invisible bonds. She slammed her will against that shield, biting down on her gag of Air. The

Aiel on the right—the taller one, the one who probably held her shield—grunted. She felt as if her fingers were clawing at the edge of a nearly shut door, with light, warmth and power beyond. That door wouldn't budge an inch.

The tall Aiel narrowed his eyes at her. He let the light he'd summoned vanish, plunging them into darkness. Aviendha heard him take out a spear.

A foot fell on the ground nearby. The red-veils heard it and spun; Aviendha looked as best she could, but couldn't make out the newcomer.

The men stood perfectly still.

"What is this?" a woman's voice asked. Cadsuane. She approached, a lantern in her hand. Aviendha was jerked away as the man holding her weaves pulled her back into the shadows, and Cadsuane did not seem aware of her. Cadsuane saw only the other man, who stood closer to the pathway.

That Aiel man stepped from the shadows. He'd lowered his veil, too. "I thought I heard something near the tents here, Aes Sedai," he said. He had a strange accent, one that was slightly off. Only by a shade. A wetlander would never know the difference.

These aren't Aiel, Aviendha thought. *They're something different.* Her mind wrestled with the concept. Aiel who were not Aiel? Men who could channel?

The men we send, she realized with horror. Men discovered among the Aiel with the ability to channel were sent to try to kill the Dark One. Alone, they came to the Blight. Nobody knew what happened to them after that.

Aviendha began to struggle again, trying to make noise—any noise—to alert Cadsuane. The attempts were in vain. She hung tightly in the air, in the darkness, and Cadsuane wasn't looking in her direction.

"Well, did you find anything?" Cadsuane asked the man.

"No, Aes Sedai."

"I will speak to the guards," Cadsuane said, sounding dissatisfied. "We must be vigilant. If a Draghkar—or, worse, a Myrddraal—managed to sneak in, it could kill dozens before being discovered."

Cadsuane turned to go. Aviendha shook her head, tears of frustration in her eyes. So close!

The red-veil who had been with Cadsuane stepped back into the shadows, going up to Aviendha. In a flash of lightning, she caught a smile on his lips, mimicked by the one who still held her in the bonds.

The red-veil in front of her slid a dagger from his belt, then reached up for her. She watched that knife, helpless, as he raised it to her throat.

She sensed channeling.

The bonds holding her were gone instantly, and she dropped to the ground. Aviendha caught the man's knife hand as she fell, his eyes opening wide. Though she embraced the Source by raw, mad instinct, her hands were already moving. She twisted the man's wrist, snapping the bones where hand met arm. She caught the knife with her other hand, then slammed it into his eye as he started to scream in pain.

The scream cut off. The red-veil fell at her feet, and she looked with anxiety toward the one beside her—the one who had been holding her in weaves. He lay dead on the ground.

Gasping, she scrambled toward the path nearby, and found Cadsuane.

"It is a simple thing, to stop a man's heart," Cadsuane said, arms folded. She seemed dissatisfied. "So close to Healing, yet opposite in effect. Perhaps it is an evil thing, yet I've always failed to see how it would be worse than simply burning a man to ash with fire."

"How?" Aviendha asked. "How did you recognize what they were?"

"I am not a half-trained wilder," Cadsuane replied. "I would have liked to strike them down when I first arrived, but I had to be certain before I could act. When that one threatened you with the knife, I knew."

Aviendha breathed in and out, trying to still her heart.

"And, of course, there was the other one," Cadsuane said. "The one that channeled. How many male Aiel warriors can secretly channel? Was this an anomaly, or have your people been covering them up?"

"What? No! We don't. Or, we didn't." Aviendha wasn't certain what they would do now that the Source had been cleansed. Men, certainly, should stop being sent alone to die fighting the Dark One.

"You're certain?" Cadsuane asked, voice flat.

"Yes!"

"Pity. That could have been a large boon to us, now." Cadsuane shook her head. "I wouldn't have been surprised, after finding out about those Windfinders. So these were just run-of-the-mill Darkfriends, with one among them who had hidden his channeling ability? What were they about tonight?"

"These are anything but ordinary Darkfriends," Aviendha said softly, inspecting the corpses. Red veils. The man who had been able to channel wore his teeth filed to points, but the other two did not. What did it mean?

"We need to alert the camp," Aviendha continued. "It's possible that these three merely walked in, unchallenged. Many of the wetlander guards avoid challenging Aiel. They assume that all of us serve the *Car'a'carn*."

To many wetlanders, an Aiel was an Aiel. Fools. Though . . . to be honest, Aviendha had to admit that her own first instinct upon seeing Aiel had been to think them allies. When had that happened? Not two years back, if she'd caught unfamiliar *algai'd'siswai* prowling about, she'd have attacked.

Aviendha continued her inspection of the dead men—a knife on each man, spears and bows. Nothing else telling. However, her thoughts whispered to her that she was missing something.

"The female channeler," she said suddenly, looking up. "It was a *woman* using the One Power that drew me, Aes Sedai. Was that you?"

"I did not channel until I killed that man," Cadsuane said, frowning.

Aviendha dropped back into a battle stance, hugging the shadows. What would she find next? Wise Ones who served the Shadow? Cadsuane frowned, as Aviendha scouted the area further. She passed Darlin's tent, where soldiers outside huddled around lamps and cast shadows that danced on the canvas. She passed soldiers in tight groups walking along the pathways, not speaking. They carried torches, blinding their eyes to the night.

Aviendha had heard Tairen officers remark that it was nice, for once, to have no worry about their sentries dozing on duty. With the lightning, the Trolloc drums in the near distance, the occasional raids by Shadowspawn trying to slip into camp . . . soldiers knew to be wary. The frosted air smelled of smoke, with putrid scents blowing in from the Trolloc camps.

She eventually gave up the hunt and walked back the way she had come, finding Cadsuane speaking with a group of soldiers. Aviendha was about to approach when her eyes passed over a patch of darkness nearby, and her senses came alert. *That patch of darkness is channeling.*

Aviendha began weaving a shield immediately. The one in the darkness wove Fire and Air toward Cadsuane. Aviendha dropped her weave and instead lashed out with Spirit, slicing the enemy weave just as it was released.

Aviendha heard a curse, and a quick weave of fire blossomed in her direction. Aviendha ducked as it lashed overhead, hissing in the cold air. The wave of heat passed. Her enemy ducked out of the shadows—whatever weave she'd been using to hide had collapsed—revealing the woman Aviendha had fought before. The one with the face almost as ugly as a Trolloc's.

The woman dashed behind a group of tents just before the ground ripped up behind her—a weave that Aviendha hadn't made. A second later, the woman *folded* again, as she had before. Vanishing.

Aviendha stood warily. She turned toward Cadsuane, who walked up to her. "Thank you," the woman said, grudgingly. "For disrupting that weave."

"I suppose we are even, then," Aviendha said.

"Even? No, not by several hundred years, child. I will admit that I am thankful for your intervention." She frowned. "She vanished."

"She did that before."

"A method of Traveling we do not know," Cadsuane said, looking troubled. "I saw no flows for it. Perhaps a *ter'angreal*? It—"

A shot of red light rose from the front lines of the army. The Trollocs were attacking. At the same time, Aviendha felt channeling in different spots around the camp. One, two, three . . . She spun about, trying to locate each of the locations. She counted five.

"Channelers," Cadsuane said sharply. "Dozens of them."

"Dozens? I sense five."

"Most are men, fool child," Cadsuane said, waving a hand. "Go, gather the others!"

Aviendha dashed away, yelling the alarm. She would have words with Cadsuane later for ordering her about. Maybe. "Having words" with Cadsuane often left one feeling like a complete fool. Aviendha ran into the Aiel section of camp in time to see Amys and Sorilea pulling on their shawls, checking the sky. Flinn stumbled out of a nearby tent, blinking bleary eyes. "Men?" he said. "Channeling? Have more Asha'man arrived?"

"Unlikely," Aviendha said. "Amys, Sorilea, I need a circle."

They raised eyebrows at her. She might be one of them now, and she might have command by the *Car'a'carn's* authority, but reminding Sorilea of that would end with Aviendha buried to her neck in sand. "If you please," she added quickly.

"It is your say, Aviendha," Sorilea said. "I will go and speak with the others and send them to you, so you may have your circle. We will make two, I think, as you have suggested before. That would be for the best."

Stubborn as Cadsuane, that one is, Aviendha thought. The two of them could teach lessons on patience to trees. Still, Sorilea was not strong in the Power—in fact, she could barely channel—so it would be wise to use others as she suggested.

Sorilea began calling for the other Wise Ones and Aes Sedai. Aviendha suffered the delay with anxiety; already, she could hear screams and explosions in the valley. Streams of fire arced into the air, then dropped.

"Sorilea," Aviendha said softly to the elder Wise One as the women began to build the circles, "I was attacked in camp just now by three Aiel men. The battle we are about to fight, it will probably involve other Aiel who fight for the Shadow."

Sorilea turned sharply, meeting Aviendha's eyes. "Explain."

"I think they must be the men we sent to kill Sightblinder," Aviendha said.

Sorilea hissed softly. "If this is true, child, then this night will mark great *toh* for us all. *Toh* toward the *Car'a'carn*, *toh* toward the land itself."

"I know."

"Bring me word," Sorilea said. "I will organize a third circle; maybe make some of those off-duty Windfinders join in."

Aviendha nodded, then accepted control of the circle as it was handed to her. She had three Aes Sedai who had sworn to Rand and two Wise Ones. By her order, Flinn did not join the circle. She wanted him to be on the watch for signs of men channeling, ready to point the direction, and being in a circle might make that impossible for him to do.

They moved off like a squad of spear-sisters. They passed clusters of Tairen Defenders pulling on burnished breastplates over uniforms with wide striped sleeves. In one group, she found King Darlin bellowing orders.

"A moment," she said to the others, hastening to the Tairen.

" . . . them all!" Darlin said to his commanders. "*Don't* let the front lines weaken! We can't let those monsters spill into the valley!" It appeared that he'd been awakened from sleep by the attack, for he stood dressed only in trousers and a white undershirt. A disheveled serving man held out Darlin's coat, but the King, distracted by a messenger, turned away.

When Darlin saw Aviendha, he waved her forward urgently. The serving man heaved a sigh, lowering the coat.

"I'd given up on them attacking tonight," Darlin said, then glanced at the sky. "Or, well, this *morning*. The scout reports are so confused, I feel like I've been thrown into a coop full of crazed chickens and told to catch the one with a single black feather."

"Those reports," Aviendha said, "do they mention Aiel men, fighting for the Shadow? Possibly channeling?"

Darlin turned sharply. "It's true?"

"Yes."

"And the Trollocs are pushing with everything they have to force their way into the valley," Darlin said. "If those Aiel Dreadlords start attacking our troops, we won't stand a chance without you lot being there to hold them off."

"We're moving," Aviendha said. "Send for Amys and Cadsuane to make gateways. But I warn you. I caught a Dreadlord sneaking around near your tent . . ."

Darlin paled. "Like Ituralde . . . Light, they didn't touch me. I swear it. I . . . " He raised a hand to his head. "Who do we trust if we cannot trust our own minds?"

"We must make the dance of spears as simple as possible," Aviendha said. "Go to Rhuarc, gather your leaders. Plan how you will face the Shadow together, do not let one man control the battle—and set your plans in place; do not allow them to be changed."

"That could lead to disaster," Darlin said. "If we don't have flexibility . . . "

"What needs be changed?" Aviendha asked grimly. "We hold. With everything we have, we hold. We don't pull back. We don't try anything clever. We just *hold*."

Darlin nodded. "I'll send for gateways to put Maidens atop those slopes. They can take out those Trollocs shooting arrows down at our lads. Can you deal with the enemy channelers?"

"Yes."

Aviendha returned to her group, then started to draw on their power. The more of the One Power you held, the harder it was to cut you off from the True Source. She intended to hold so much that no man could separate her from it.

Helplessness. She *hated* feeling helpless. She let the anger at what had been done to her rage inside of her, and led her group toward the nearest source of male channeling that Flinn could identify.

CHAPTER
34

Drifting

R and stood in a place that was not.

A place outside of time, outside of the Pattern itself.

All around him spread a vast nothingness. Voracious and hungry, it longed to consume. He could actually *see* the Pattern. It looked like thousands upon thousands of twisting ribbons of light; they spun around him, above him, undulating and shimmering, twisting together. At least, that was how his mind chose to interpret it.

Everything that had ever been, everything that could be, everything that could have been ... it all lay right there, before him.

Rand could not comprehend it. The blackness around it sucked on him, *pulled* him toward it. He reached out to the Pattern and somehow anchored himself in it, lest he be consumed.

That changed his focus. It locked him, slightly, into a time. The pattern before him rippled, and Rand watched it being woven. It was not actually *the* Pattern, he knew, but his mind saw it that way. Familiar, as it had been described, the threads of lives weaving together.

Rand anchored himself in reality again and moved with it. Time had meaning again, and he could not see ahead or behind.

He still could see all places, like a man standing above a globe as it turned.

Rand faced the emptiness. "So," he said into it. "This is where it will really happen. Moridin would have had me believe that a simple sword fight would decide this all."

HE IS OF ME. BUT HIS EYES ARE SMALL.

"Yes," Rand said. "I have noticed the same."

SMALL TOOLS CAN BE EFFECTIVE. THE THINNEST OF KNIVES CAN STOP A HEART. HE HAS BROUGHT YOU HERE, ADVERSARY.

None of this had happened the last time, when Rand had worn the name of Lews Therin. He could only interpret that as a good sign.

Now the battle truly began. He looked into the nothingness and felt it welling up. Then, like a sudden storm, the Dark One brought all of his force against Rand.

Perrin fell back against a tree, gasping at the pain. Slayer's arrow had impaled his shoulder, the arrowhead coming out his back. He didn't dare pull it free, not with . . .

He wavered. Thoughts came lethargically. Where was he? He'd *shifted* away from Slayer as far as he could go, but . . . he didn't recognize this place. The trees were odd-shaped on top, too leafy, of a variety he'd never before seen. The storm blew here, but far more weakly.

Perrin slipped and hit the ground with a grunt. His shoulder flared with pain. He rolled over, staring up at the sky. He'd broken the arrow when falling.

It's . . . it's the wolf dream. I can just make the arrow vanish.

He tried to gather the strength to do so, but was too weak. He found himself floating, and he sent outward, seeking for wolves. He found the minds of some, and they started, sending back surprise.

A two-legs who can talk? What is this? What are you?

His nature seemed to frighten them, and they pushed him out of their minds. How could they not know what he was? Wolves had long, long memories. Surely . . . surely . . .

Faile, he thought. *So beautiful, so clever. I should go to her. I just need to ... need to close this Waygate ... and I can get back to the Two Rivers to her ...*

Perrin rolled over and crawled to his knees. Was that his blood on the ground? So much red. He blinked at it.

"Here you are," a voice said.

Lanfear. He looked up at her, his vision blurry.

"So he defeated you," she said, folding her arms. "Disappointing. I didn't want to have to choose that one. I find you much more appealing, wolf."

"Please," he croaked.

"I'm tempted, though I shouldn't be," she said. "You've proven yourself weak."

"I ... I can beat him." Suddenly, the shame of having failed in front of her crushed Perrin. When had he started worrying about what Lanfear thought of him? He couldn't quite point to it.

She tapped one finger on her arm.

"Please ... " Perrin said, raising a hand. "Please."

"No," she said, turning away. "I've learned the mistake of setting my heart on one who does not deserve it. Goodbye, wolf pup."

She vanished, leaving Perrin on hands and knees in this strange place.

Faile, a piece of his mind said. *Don't worry about Lanfear. You have to go to Faile.*

Yes ... Yes, he could go to her, couldn't he? Where was she? The Field of Merrilor. That was where he'd left her. It was where she would be. He *shifted* there, somehow gathering himself just enough to manage it. But of course she wasn't there. He was in the wolf dream.

The portal Rand would send. It would be here. He just had to get to it. He needed ... He needed ...

He collapsed to the ground and rolled to his back. He felt himself drifting into the nothingness. His vision blackened as he stared up at the churning sky. *At least ... at least I was there for Rand*, Perrin thought.

The wolves could hold Shayol Ghul on this side now, couldn't they? They could keep Rand safe ... They'd have to.

*

Faile poked a stick at their meager cook fire. Darkness had fallen, and the fire glowed with a faint red light. They hadn't dared make it larger. Deadly things prowled the Blight. Trollocs were the least of the dangers here.

The air here smelled pungent, and Faile expected to find a rotting corpse behind every black-speckled shrub. The ground cracked when she stepped, dry earth crushing beneath her boots, as if rain had not been seen in centuries. As she sat in the camp, she saw a group of sickly green lights—like glowing insects in a swarm—passing in the distance, over a stand of silhouetted trees. She knew enough of the Blight to hold her breath until they passed. She did not know what they were, and did not want to know.

She had led her group on a short hike to find this place for a camp. Along the way, one caravan worker had been killed by a twig, another by stepping in what looked like mud—but it had dissolved his leg. He'd gotten some of it on his face. He had thrashed and screamed as he died.

They'd had to forcibly gag him to keep the sounds from bringing other horrors.

The Blight. They couldn't survive up here. A simple walk had killed two of their members, and Faile had some hundred people to try to protect. Guards from the Band, some members of *Cha Faile* and the wagon drivers and workers from her supply caravan. Eight of the wagons still worked, and they'd brought those to this camp, for now. They would probably be too conspicuous to take farther.

She wasn't even certain they would survive this night. Light! Their only chance of rescue seemed to lie with the Aes Sedai. Would they notice what had happened and send help? It seemed a very faint hope, but she did not know about the One Power.

"All right," Faile said softly to those who sat with her— Mandevwin, Aravine, Harnan, Setalle and Arrela of *Cha Faile*. "Let's talk."

The others looked hollow. Probably, like Faile, they had been frightened with stories of the Blight since childhood. The quick deaths in their party soon after entering this land had reinforced that. They knew how dangerous this place was. They kept jumping at every sound in the night.

"I will explain what I can," Faile said, trying to divert them from the death all around. "During the bubble of evil, one of those crystals speared Berisha Sedai's foot right as she made the gateway."

"A wound?" Mandevwin asked from his place beside the fire. "Would that have been enough to make the gateway go awry? Truly, I know little of Aes Sedai business, nor have I wanted to. If one is distracted, is it possible to create an accidental opening to the wrong place?"

Setalle frowned, and the expression drew Faile's attention. Setalle was neither nobility nor an officer. There was something about the woman, however ... she projected authority and wisdom.

"You know something?" Faile asked her.

Setalle cleared her throat. "I know ... some little about channeling. It was once an area of curiosity to me. Sometimes, if a weave is done incorrectly, it simply does nothing. Other times, the result is disastrous. I have not heard of a weave doing something like this, working but in the wrong way."

"Well," Harnan said, watching that darkness and shivering visibly, "the alternative is to think that she *wanted* to send us to the Blight."

"Perhaps she was disoriented," Faile said. "The pressure of the moment made her send us to the wrong place. I've been turned about before in a moment of tension and found myself running in the wrong direction. It could be like that."

The others nodded, but again, Setalle looked concerned.

"What is it?" Faile prodded.

"Aes Sedai training is very extensive in relation to this type of situation," Setalle said. "No woman reaches the level of Aes Sedai without learning how to channel under extreme pressure. There are specific ... barriers a woman must clear in order to wear the ring."

So, Faile thought, *Setalle must have a relative who is Aes Sedai. Someone close, if they shared information so private. A sister, perhaps?*

"Then do we assume that this is some kind of trap?" Aravine sounded confused. "That Berisha was some kind of Darkfriend? Surely the Shadow has greater things to misdirect than a simple supply train."

Faile said nothing. The Horn was safe; the chest it was in now sat in her small tent nearby. They had circled the wagons, and had allowed only this one fire. The rest of the caravan slept, or tried to.

The still, too-silent air made Faile feel as if they were being watched by a thousand eyes. If the Shadow had planned a trap for her caravan, it meant the Shadow knew about the Horn. In that case, they were in very serious danger. More serious, even, than being in the Blight itself.

"No," Setalle said. "No, Aravine is right. This could not have been an intentional trap. If the bubble of evil hadn't come, we would never have burst through the opening without looking where it led. So far as we know, these bubbles are completely random."

Unless Berisha was simply taking advantage of the circumstances, Faile thought. Also, there was the woman's death. That wound in her stomach had not looked like one caused by the spikes. It had looked like a knife wound. As if someone had attacked Berisha once the Horn was through the gateway. To keep her from telling what she'd done?

Light, Faile thought. *I am growing suspicious.*

"So," Harnan said, "what do we do?"

"That depends," Faile said, looking toward Setalle. "Is there any way an Aes Sedai could tell where we'd been sent?"

Setalle hesitated, as if reluctant to reveal how much she knew. When she continued, however, she spoke with confidence. "Weaves leave behind a residue. So yes, an Aes Sedai could discover where we'd gone. The residue does not last long, however: a few days at most, for a powerful weave. And not all channelers can read residues—this is a rare talent."

The way she spoke, so commanding and authoritative ... the way she projected an immediate sense of being trustworthy. *It wasn't a relative, then*, Faile thought. *This woman trained in the White Tower.* Was she, perhaps, like Queen Morgase? Too weak in the One Power to become Aes Sedai?

"We will wait one day," Faile said. "If nobody has come for us by then, we will head south and try to escape the Blight as quickly as possible."

"I wonder how far north we are," Harnan said, rubbing his chin. "I don't fancy going over mountains to get back home."

"You'd rather remain in the Blight?" Mandevwin asked.

"Well, no," Harnan said. "But it could take *months* to walk back to safety. Months traveling through the Blight itself . . . "

Light, Faile thought. *Traveling months in a place where we're lucky to have lost only two in one day.* They'd never make it. Even without the wagons, the caravan would stand out in this landscape like a fresh wound on diseased skin. They'd be lucky to last another day or two.

She resisted the urge to glance back at the tent. What would happen if she didn't bring it to Mat in time?

"There is another option," Setalle said hesitantly.

Faile looked to her.

"That peak you see to the east of us," Setalle said, speaking with obvious reluctance. "That is Shayol Ghul."

Mandevwin whispered something quietly that Faile didn't catch, squeezing his eyes shut. The others looked sick. Faile, however, caught Setalle's implication.

"That is where the Dragon Reborn is making war against the Shadow," Faile said. "One of our armies will be there. With channelers who could get us out."

"Indeed," Setalle said. "And the area just around Shayol Ghul is known as the Blasted Lands, lands that the horrors of the Blight are said to avoid."

"Because it's so terrible!" Arrela said. "If they don't go there, it's because they fear the Dark One himself!"

"The Dark One and his armies might have their attention on the fighting," Faile said slowly, nodding her head. "We can't survive long in the Blight—we'll be dead before the week is out. But if the Blasted Lands are free of those horrors, and if we can reach our armies there . . . "

It seemed a far better hope—slim though it was—than trying to march for months in the most dangerous place in the world. She told the others she'd consider what to do and dismissed them.

Her advisors moved off to make their bedrolls, Mandevwin going to check the men on watch. Faile remained staring at the embers of the fire, feeling sick.

Someone did kill Berisha, she thought. *I'm certain of it.* The gateway's location really could have been an accident. Accidents happened, even to Aes Sedai, no matter what Setalle thought. But if there *was* a Darkfriend in the caravan, one who had ducked through the opening and seen that it went to the Blight, they could have easily decided to kill Berisha in order to leave the Horn and the caravan stranded.

"Setalle," Faile said as the woman passed, "a word."

Setalle sat down beside Faile, wearing a composed expression. "I know what you're going to ask."

"How long has it been," Faile asked, "since you were in the White Tower?"

"It has been decades now."

"Are you capable of making a gateway?"

Setalle laughed. "Child, I couldn't light a candle. I was burned out in an accident. I haven't held the One Power in over twenty-five years."

"I see," Faile said. "Thank you."

Setalle moved off, and Faile found herself wondering. How truthful was her story? Setalle had been very helpful in their days together, and Faile couldn't blame the woman for keeping secret her ties to the White Tower. In any other situation, Faile wouldn't have given the woman's story a moment of doubt.

However, there was no way out here to confirm what she said. If Setalle was Black Ajah in hiding, her story about being burned out could simply be that—a story. Perhaps she could still channel. Or perhaps she couldn't, but had been stilled as a punishment. Could this woman be an escaped prisoner of the most dangerous type, an agent who had waited decades for the right moment to strike?

Setalle had been the one to suggest they go to Shayol Ghul. Was she seeking to bring the Horn to her master?

Feeling cold, Faile entered her tent as several members of *Cha Faile* set up watch around it. Faile wrapped herself in her bedroll. She knew that she was being overly suspicious. But how else was she to be, considering the circumstances?

Light, she thought. *The Horn of Valere, lost in the Blight.* A nightmare.

Aviendha knelt on one knee beside the smoldering corpse, holding her *angreal*—the turtle brooch that Elayne had given her.

She breathed through her mouth as she gazed down on the man's face.

There were a surprising number of these red-veils. Whatever their origins, they were *not* Aiel. They did not follow *ji'e'toh*. During the night's fighting, she had seen two Maidens take a man captive. He had acted like *gai'shain*, but had then killed one from behind with a hidden knife.

"Well?" Sarene asked, breathless. While those at the Field of Merrilor rested and prepared for their challenge ahead, this battle at Shayol Ghul continued. The red-veil attack had lasted all through the night, the following day and now into the night again.

"I think I knew him," Aviendha said, disturbed. "He channeled for the first time when I was a child, making *algode* grow when it should not." She let the veil fall down on his face. "His name was Soro. He was kind to me. I watched him run across the dry ground at sunset after vowing to spit in Sightblinder's eye."

"I'm sorry," Sarene said, though her voice was uncolored by any sympathy. Aviendha was growing accustomed to that in the woman. It wasn't that Sarene didn't care; she just didn't let caring distract her. At least, not when her Warder was elsewhere. The Aes Sedai would have made a fine Maiden.

"Let's keep moving," Aviendha said, taking off with her pack of channelers. During the days and nights of fighting, Aviendha's team had shifted, melded and split as women needed rest. Aviendha herself had slept sometime during the day.

By common agreement, the one leading the circle avoided drawing on her own power—thus Aviendha was still at reasonable strength, despite so many hours of fighting. This allowed her to remain alert, on the hunt. The other women became wells of power to be drawn upon.

She had to be careful not to drain them too far. Tire a woman, and she could sleep for a few hours and be back up to fight again. Drain her completely, and she could be useless for days. At the moment, Aviendha had Flinn and three Aes Sedai with her. She had learned the weave to tell her when a man was channeling nearby—it was moving through the Aes Sedai and Wise Ones—but having a male channeler with her was far more useful.

Flinn pointed toward some flashes of fire on the side of the valley. They loped in that direction, passing corpses and places where the ground smoldered. With the growing light of dawn, Aviendha could see through the cold mist that Darlin's forces still held the mouth of the valley.

The Trollocs had pushed forward to the low earthen mounds that Ituralde had built. Killing had been done there on both sides. The Trollocs had taken far more losses—but then, they were also far more numerous. It seemed from her quick glance that they had overrun one of the earthen bulwarks, but Domani riders had come in from the reserves and were pushing them back.

Bands of Aiel roved and fought in the mouth of the valley itself. Some with red veils, some with black. *Too many*, Aviendha thought, as she slowed her team with a raised hand. She then continued forward on her own, quietly. She could draw a few hundred paces away from the women and still have access to their power.

She picked her way through the barren rocky fields of the valley. There were three dead bodies to her right, two with black veils. She tested them with a quick Delving; she would not be caught by the old trick of hiding among the corpses. She had used that one herself.

These three were truly dead, so she continued on in a crouch. In addition to the place where the Tairens and Domani held the Trollocs back, they had a second force guarding their camp and the pathway up to where Rand fought. In the space between, Aiel and red-veils roved in bands, each trying to best the other. Only, some of the red-veils could channel.

The ground thumped and shook nearby. A spray of soil fell through the air. Aviendha crouched down lower, but quickened her pace.

Ahead, over a dozen *siswai'aman* were rushing the position of two red-veils, both channelers. The red-veils cast up the earth beneath the attackers, sending bodies flying.

Aviendha understood why the Aiel kept going. These red-veils were an affront, a crime. The Seanchan, who would dare take Wise Ones captive, were not as disgusting as these. Somehow, the Shadow had taken the bravest of the Aiel and made them into these . . . these *things*.

Aviendha struck quickly, pulling strength through her *angreal* and her circle, weaving two lines of fire and hurling them at the red-veils. She began new weaves immediately, casting up the ground beneath the two channelers, and started a third set of weaves. She threw fire at the red-veils as they stumbled; one jumped away as the other was caught in her earthen blasts.

She struck the one who had fled with spears of flame. Then she hit both corpses with an extra burst of power, just to make certain. These men no longer held to *ji'e'toh*. They were no longer alive. They were weeds to be pulled.

She moved forward to check on the *siswai'aman*. Eight still lived, three of them wounded. Aviendha was not particularly good with Healing, but she was able to save the life of one man, keeping a wound in his throat from bleeding out. The other survivors gathered the wounded and moved back toward the camp.

Aviendha stood above the two corpses. She decided not to look at them closely. Seeing one man she had known was bad enough. These—

A shock went through her, and one of her wells of power vanished. Aviendha gasped. Another one winked out.

She immediately released the circle, then dashed back to where she had left the women. Flashes and explosions shook her. Aviendha clung to the One Power, her own strength now seeming pitifully small compared to what she'd been using.

She stumbled to a halt before the smoldering corpses of Kiruna and Faeldrin. The hideous woman she had seen before—the woman that Aviendha was increasingly certain was one of the Forsaken—stood there smiling at her. The horrid woman had her hand on Sarene's shoulder; the slender White stood with her head turned toward the Forsaken, staring at her with vapid, adoring eyes. Sarene's Warder lay dead at her feet.

Both vanished, twisting upon themselves, Traveling without use of a gateway. Aviendha fell to her knees beside the dead. Nearby, Damer Flinn groaned and tried to pull himself free of the cast-up earth. His left arm was completely gone, burned away at the shoulder.

Aviendha cursed and did what she could to Heal him, though he slipped into unconsciousness. She suddenly felt very tired and very, *very* alone.

CHAPTER
35

A Practiced Grin

Olver missed Wind. Bela—the stout, shaggy mare he now rode—wasn't bad, really. She was just slow. Olver knew this because he kept trying to nudge her forward, but she continued plodding along behind the other horses. Nothing he did could make her go any faster. Olver wanted to ride like a storm. Instead, he rode like a sturdy log in a placid river.

He wiped his brow. The Blight was pretty scary, and the others—most of them didn't have horses—walked as if each step was going to bring a thousand Trollocs down on them. The rest of the caravan spoke in hushed voices, and they looked at the hillsides with suspicion.

They passed a group of withered trees, with sap leaking from open sores in the bark. That sap looked too red. Almost like blood. Nearby, one of the caravan drivers stepped up to inspect it.

Vines snapped down from the limbs above—vines that looked brown and dead, yet moved like snakes. Before Olver could scream, the caravan driver was hanging, dead, from the upper branches of the tree.

The entire line of people froze in place, horrified. Above, the tree actually *pulled* the dead man into itself through a split in the bark. Ingesting him. Maybe that sap *was* blood.

Olver looked on, horrified.

"Steady," Lady Faile said, a slight tremor in her voice. "I've told you, don't draw close to plants! Don't touch anything."

They moved on, a solemn bunch. Sandip, riding nearby, muttered to himself. "That's the fifteenth one. Fifteen men, dead in a few days. Light! We're never going to survive this!"

If only it were Trollocs! Olver couldn't fight trees and insects. Who could? But Trollocs, those he'd be able to fight. Olver had his knife, and he'd learned a few things about using it from Harnan and Silvic. Olver wasn't that tall, but he figured that would make Trollocs underestimate him. He could lunge low and go for their vitals before they knew what was happening.

He told himself this to keep his hands from shaking as he kicked Bela, hoping to move up by Lady Faile. In the distance, he heard a screeching sound, like something dying in a horrible way. Olver shivered. He'd heard that same sound earlier in the day. Did it sound closer now?

Setalle gave him a worried glance as he neared the front. The others tried everything they could to keep him from danger. He steeled himself, ignoring that horrid screeching off in the distance. Everyone thought Olver was fragile, but he wasn't. They hadn't seen what he had, growing up. In truth, he didn't like thinking about those times. It seemed as if he'd lived three lives. One before his parents died, one when he'd been alone and now this one.

Anyway, he was used to fighting people bigger than he was. It was the Last Battle. They kept saying everyone would be needed. Well, why not him? When the Trollocs came, the first thing he'd do was climb down off this slow mount. He could *stroll* faster than this animal could gallop! Well, the Aiel didn't need horses. Olver hadn't gone to train with them yet, but he would. He had it planned out. He hated all Aiel, but mostly the Shaido, and he would need to learn their secrets if he was going to kill them.

He'd go among them and demand to be trained. They'd take him in, and would treat him poorly, but eventually they'd respect him and let him train with their warriors. There were stories about that. It was how things happened.

After he knew their secrets, he'd go to the Snakes and Foxes and receive answers on how to locate the Shaido who had murdered his father. From there, tracking and killing them would be a quest worthy of its own story.

I'll take Noal, he thought. *He's been everywhere. He can be my guide. He . . .*

Noal was dead.

Sweat crawled down the side of Olver's face as he stared at the rocky path ahead. They passed more of those terrible trees, and now everyone gave them a wide berth. Beside the path, though, one of the men pointed out a large patch of that killing mud. It looked brown and thick, and Olver spotted several bones peeking out.

This place was horrible!

He wished Noal were here. Noal had gone everywhere, seen everything. He'd know how to get them out of this place. But Noal was gone. Olver had only heard the news recently, filtered through things that the Lady Moiraine had shared about what happened at the Tower of Ghenjei.

Everyone's dying, Olver thought, eyes still forward. *Everyone . . .*

Mat had run off to the Seanchan, Talmanes to fight alongside Queen Elayne. One by one, everyone in this group was being eaten by trees, mud or monsters.

Why did they all leave Olver alone?

He rubbed at his bracelet. Noal had given it to him, shortly before leaving. Woven of rough fibers, it was of a type warriors wore in a faraway land, so Noal had told him. It was the mark of a man who had seen battle and lived.

Noal . . . dead. Would Mat die, too?

Olver felt hot, tired and very frightened. He nudged Bela forward, and fortunately she obeyed, trotting a little faster up the slope so Olver moved up the line. They'd abandoned the wagons, then left for some place called the Blasted Lands, which required them to climb some foothills. In the morning, they'd entered a pass between the mountains. Though he felt warm, the air *was* getting cooler as they climbed. He didn't mind that at all. It still smelled awful, though. Like rotting corpses.

Their group had started with fifty soldiers and almost half as many wagon drivers and workers. There were also a handful of others like Olver, Setalle and the half-dozen members of Lady Faile's bodyguard.

So far, they'd lost fifteen people to hazards of the Blight, including five killed by some horrible three-eyed things that had attacked the camp yesterday morning. He'd overheard Lady Faile saying that she considered them lucky to have lost only fifteen so far, that it could have been worse.

It didn't seem lucky to Olver. This place was awful and he wanted to be out of it. The Waste wouldn't be as bad as this, would it? *Cha Faile*'s men and women acted like Aiel. A little bit like Aiel. Maybe they'd done as Olver wanted to, and trained in the Waste. He'd have to ask them.

He rode on for another half-hour or so. Eventually, he coaxed Bela up to the front of the line. Lady Faile's brilliant black mare looked fast. Why couldn't Olver have been given a horse like that one?

Faile had Mat's chest tied to the back of her horse. At first, Olver had been pleased with that, as he figured Mat would want that tabac pretty badly. Mat always complained about not having good tabac. Then Olver had heard Faile explaining to someone else that the chest had simply been a convenient place to stow some of her things. Had she thrown away the tabac? Mat wouldn't like that.

Faile looked at him, and Olver grinned, giving it as much confidence as he could. It wouldn't do for her to see how scared he was.

Most women liked his grin. He'd been practicing it, though he didn't use Mat's grin as a model. Mat's always made him look guilty. You learned grins when you were forced to fend for yourself, and Olver needed one that made him seem innocent. And he *was* innocent. Mostly.

Faile did not smile back. Olver figured that she was pretty good to look at, despite that nose. She wasn't very soft, though. Bloody ashes, but she had a glare that could rust good iron.

Faile rode between Aravine and Vanin. Though they spoke softly, Olver could hear what they were saying. He made sure to stare in the other direction, so they'd think he wasn't eavesdropping. And he wasn't. He just wanted to be out of the trail dust of the other horses.

"Yes," Vanin was whispering. "It may not seem it, but we're close to the Blasted Lands. Burn my own mother, I can't believe we're going there. But do you feel the air? It's getting cooler. We haven't seen anything *really* nasty since those three-eyed things yesterday morning."

"We are close," Aravine agreed. "Soon, we will be near the Dark One, in a land where nothing grows, corrupted or not, where there is no life, not even the nastier things from the Blight."

"I suppose that should be a comfort."

"Not really," Vanin said, wiping his brow. "Because the Shadowspawn up here are more dangerous. If we survive, it will be because there's a bloody war going on. The Shadowspawn are all locked in battle. If we're lucky, the Blasted Lands, except right around Shayol Ghul, will be as empty as a man's purse after a deal with the bloody Sea Folk. Pardon my language, my Lady."

Olver squinted at the approaching mountain peak.

That's where the bloody Dark One lives, Olver thought. *And that's probably where Mat is, not Merrilor.* Mat talked about staying away from danger, but he always found his way to it anyway. Olver figured that Mat was just trying to be humble, but was bad at it. Why else would you say you don't want to be a hero, then always bloody end up charging right into danger?

"And this path?" Faile asked Vanin. "You said there might have been traffic here recently. Wouldn't that indicate that this place is far from as empty as you so colorfully described?"

Vanin grunted. "It does look used."

"So someone has been moving wagons through the area," Aravine said. "I don't know if that is a good sign or a bad one."

"I don't think there are *any* good signs up here," Vanin said. "Maybe we should just pick someplace nearby and hole up, waiting." He sighed, wiping his brow again, though Olver didn't see why. It was growing pretty cold—he could tell, even through the course of the day. And there seemed to be fewer plants, too. He was just fine with that.

He glanced over his shoulder at the stand of trees that had taken that poor man's life. There didn't seem to be any others like it nearby, particularly not ahead of them along the path.

"We can't afford to wait, Vanin," Faile said. "I intend to get back to Merrilor, one way or another. The Dragon Reborn will be fighting at Thakan'dar. That's where we need to go to get out of this forsaken place."

Vanin groaned, but Olver smiled. He *would* find his way to Mat, and show how dangerous he could be in battle. Then . . .

Well, then maybe Mat wouldn't leave him like the others had. That would be good, as Olver was going to need Mat's help tracking down those Shaido. After all he'd learned training with the Band, he was certain nobody would push him around. And nobody would take those he loved from him ever again.

"There are accounts in the archives that explain what we saw." Cadsuane picked up her cup of tea to warm her hands.

The Aiel girl, Aviendha, sat on the floor of the tent. *What I wouldn't give to have that one in the Tower*, Cadsuane thought. These Wise Ones . . . they had fight to them. Real bite, like the best of the women in the White Tower.

Cadsuane was increasingly convinced that the Shadow for years had been carrying out a complex plan to undermine the White Tower. It went deeper than Siuan Sanche's unfortunate unseating and Elaida's reign. It might be decades, centuries, before they understood the extent of the Shadow's planning. However, the sheer number of Black sisters—hundreds, not the few dozen Cadsuane had guessed—shouted of what had happened.

For now, Cadsuane had to work with what she had. That included these Wise Ones, poorly trained in using weaves but never lacking in grit. Useful. Like Sorilea, despite her weakness in the One Power, who sat farther back in the tent, watching.

"I have made some inquiries, child," Cadsuane said to Aviendha. "What this woman does is *indeed* Traveling. However, the only fragments of documents mentioning it date back to the War of Power."

Aviendha frowned. "I saw no weaves, Cadsuane Sedai."

Cadsuane masked a smile at the respectful tone. The al'Thor boy had put this girl in command—and, in truth, better her than some others. However, he *should* have chosen Cadsuane, and Aviendha likely knew it.

"That is because the woman was not weaving the One Power," Cadsuane replied.

"What else would it be?"

"Do you know why the Dark One was originally freed?"

Aviendha looked as if remembering something. "Ah ... yes. Then they are channeling the Dark One's power?"

"It is called the True Power," Cadsuane said. "The accounts say that Traveling by True Power works in the way you have seen this woman move. Few saw it happen. The Dark One was miserly with his essence during the War of Power, and only the most favored were granted access. I surmise from this fact that this is *most definitely* one of the Forsaken. From your description of what she did to poor Sarene, I would suspect it is Graendal."

"The stories never mentioned Graendal being so ugly," Sorilea said softly.

"If you were one of the Forsaken, easily recognized by description, would you not wish to change your appearance to remain unknown?"

"Perhaps," Sorilea said. "But then I would not use this ... True Power, as you name it. That would defeat the purpose of my disguise."

"From what Aviendha has told us," Cadsuane noted, "the woman did not have much of a choice. She had to escape quickly."

Cadsuane and Sorilea met eyes, and each nodded in agreement. They would hunt this Forsaken, the two of them.

I won't have you dying on me now, boy, Cadsuane thought, glancing over her shoulder toward where al'Thor, Nynaeve and Moiraine continued their work. Every channeler in the camp could feel that pulsing. *At least, not until you've done what you need to do.* Cadsuane had expected the Forsaken to be here. It was why she'd come to this battlefront.

Wind shook the tent, chilling Cadsuane down deep. This place was awful, even when the battle slowed. The dread that hung here was like that of a funeral for a child. It stifled laughter, killed smiles. The Dark One watched. Light, but it would be good to leave this place.

Aviendha drank her tea. The woman still looked haunted, although she had obviously lost allies in battle before.

"I left them to die," she whispered.

"Phaw," Cadsuane said to her. "You are not to blame for what one of the Forsaken did, child."

"You don't understand," Aviendha said. "We were in a circle, and they tried to break free—I felt them—but I didn't know what was happening. I held on to their Power, and so they couldn't fight her. I left them helpless."

"Well, from now on don't leave those in your circle behind," Cadsuane said briskly. "You could not have known what would happen."

"If you suspect this one is nearby, Aviendha," Sorilea said, "you will send word to Cadsuane, me or Amys. There is no shame in admitting that another is too strong to face alone. We will defeat this woman together and protect the *Car'a'carn*."

"Very well," Aviendha said. "But you will do the same for me. All of you."

She waited. Cadsuane reluctantly agreed, as did Sorilea.

Faile crouched in a dark tent. The air had grown even colder, now that they were close to Thakan'dar. She ran her thumb along the hilt of her knife, breathing in slowly and evenly, then releasing the breath in the same manner. She stared at the tent flaps, unblinking.

She'd placed the Horn's chest there with one corner sticking out into the night. She felt more alone here on the border of the Blasted Lands—surrounded by supposed allies—than she had in the Shaido camp.

Two nights ago, she'd been called out of her tent to inspect some odd tracks that had worried the men. They hadn't lost anyone since drawing so close to the Blasted Lands—that part of the plan was working—but tensions were still high. She'd been gone only a few minutes, but when she'd returned, the Horn's chest in her tent had been moved just slightly.

Someone had tried to open it. *Light*. Fortunately, they hadn't managed to break the lock, and the Horn had still been there when she'd looked.

The traitor could be anyone. One of the Redarms, a wagon driver, a member of *Cha Faile*. Faile had spent the past two nights being extra—even obviously—vigilant with the chest to frustrate the thief. Then, tonight, she'd complained of a headache and allowed Setalle to fix her some tea to help her sleep. She'd brought the tea back to her tent, had not taken a sip and now crouched, waiting.

The chest's corner would be obvious, poking out into the

night. Would they try again? As a precaution, she'd removed the Horn from the chest and taken it when she went out to answer the call of nature. She'd hidden it there in a cubby of rock and, upon returning, had put *Cha Faile* on patrol duty for the night, away from her tent. They had not liked leaving her unguarded, but Faile had made it clear that she was worried about tensions among the men.

That would be enough. Light, let it be enough.

Hours passed with Faile crouched in that same position, ready to leap up and call the alarm the moment someone tried to enter her tent. Surely they would try again tonight, when she was supposedly ill.

Nothing. Her muscles ached, but she didn't move. The thief could be out there, in the dark, waiting. Wondering if this was the right moment to strike, to grab the Horn and run off to his or her masters. It—

A scream shattered the night.

Faile wavered. A distraction?

That scream, she thought, judging the direction. *It came . . . from just west of here.*

Near where she'd hidden the Horn. Faile cursed, making a snap decision. The chest was empty. If she took the bait and it really was just a distraction, then she would not lose anything. If, on the other hand, the thief had anticipated her . . . She darted from the tent as others scrambled from bedrolls. Members of *Cha Faile* raced through the camp. The yell came again.

It was accompanied by a haunting screech, a type that had been following them in the distance.

She crashed through some thin, Blight-stained weeds. Running through them was a foolish move in a place where a twig could kill, but she was not thinking clearly.

She arrived first on the scene, reaching the area where she'd hidden the Horn. There stood not only Vanin, but Harnan as well. Vanin clutched the Horn of Valere in thick arms while Harnan fought against some kind of beast with dark fur, shouting and swinging his sword.

Vanin looked at Faile and grew as pale as a Whitecloak's shirt.

"Thief!" Faile shouted. "Stop him! He has stolen the Horn of Valere!"

Vanin cried out, tossing the Horn as if it had bitten him, then dashing away. Light, but he could move quickly for one of his bulk! He grabbed Harnan by the shoulder, pulling him to the side as the beast screamed that haunting wail.

Other roars came in the distance. Faile skidded to the ground, grabbing the Horn and clutching it close. These men were no common thieves. They had not only seen through her plan, but anticipated exactly where she'd hidden the Horn. She felt like a farmgirl who had just fallen for a townsman's three-cup scam.

Those who had come running with her stood stunned, either by the sight of the Horn or the monster. The creature screeched— it looked like some kind of bear with too many arms, though it was larger than any bear Faile had seen. She stumbled to her feet. There was no time to look for the thieves as the beast smashed its way into Faile's guards. It ripped the head off a member of *Cha Faile*, screeching.

Faile shouted, flinging a knife at the thing as Arrela hacked at one of its shoulders with her sword. Just then, a *second* beast came lumbering over the rocks next to Faile.

She cursed, leaping away, flinging a knife. She hit it—or, at least, the thing cried out in what sounded like anger and pain. As Mandevwin rode up on horseback, bearing a torch, the light revealed that the horrible things had faces like those of insects, with a multitude of fanglike teeth. Faile's knife protruded from one bulblike eye.

"Protect the lady!" Mandevwin yelled, throwing spears to nearby Redarms, who rammed them at the first monster, pushing it back from Arrela—who scrambled away, bleeding. The woman hadn't lost her sword, though.

Faile fell back as *Cha Faile* organized around her, then looked down at what she held. The Horn of Valere itself, pulled from the sack in which she'd hidden it. She could blow it . . .

No, she thought. *It is bound to Cauthon.* To her, it would be just an ordinary horn.

"Steady!" Mandevwin said, dancing his warhorse back as one of the beasts lunged at it. "Verdin, Laandon, we need more spears! Go! The things fight like boars. Draw them forward, impale them!"

The tactic worked on one of the monsters, but as Mandevwin

yelled, the other one charged at him and grabbed his horse by the neck. The beast brushed aside soldiers who tried to strike, and Mandevwin crashed to the ground, groaning.

Still clutching the Horn, Faile dashed past where a group of Redarms had managed to skewer the other beast. She grabbed a freshly lit torch and threw it at the other monster, lighting the fur on its back. The thing bellowed as fire raced up its spine, the fur burning like dry tinder. It dropped Mandevwin's dead horse, the head ripped nearly free, as it thrashed, yelling and howling.

"Grab the wounded!" Faile ordered. She took a member of the Band by the arm. "See to Mandevwin!"

The man looked down at the Horn she held, eyes wide, then shook himself and nodded, calling for two others to help him lift the man.

"My Lady?" Aravine asked, standing near the bushes behind. "What is happening?"

"Two Redarms tried to steal what I have been carrying," Faile said. "Now we're going to ride away into the night."

"But—"

"Listen!" Faile said, pointing into the darkness.

Distantly, a dozen different screeches sounded, responding to the cries of the dying beast.

"The screams will draw further horrors, as will the scent of spilled blood. We go. If we can get deeply enough into the Blasted Lands tonight, we might be safe. Rouse the camp and get the wounded onto horses. Prepare everyone else for a forced quick march. Quickly!"

Aravine nodded, scrambling off. Faile spared a glance in the direction Harnan and Vanin had gone. She longed to hunt them down, but tracking them in the night would require them to move slowly, and that would mean death this night. Besides, who knew what resources a pair of Darkfriends had access to?

They would flee. And Light, she hoped that she hadn't been deceived more than it seemed. If Vanin had somehow known to prepare a dummy Horn, a replica to drop and leave for Faile to "rescue" as he fled . . .

She'd never know. She'd reach the Last Battle with a fake Horn, and perhaps doom them all. That possibility haunted her as the caravan's members hastily moved into the darkness, hoping in Light and luck to escape the dangers of the night.

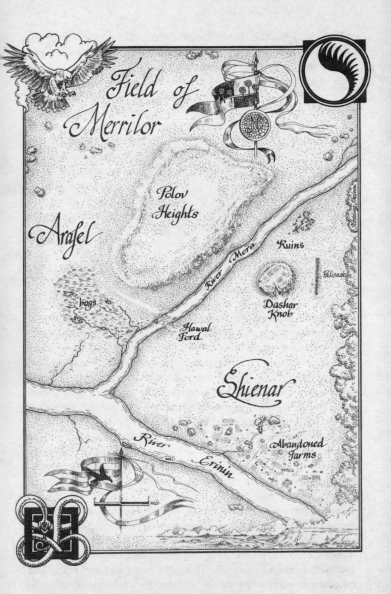

CHAPTER
36

Unchangeable Things

S omething was wrong with Rand.

Nynaeve clutched the stalagmite deep within the Pit of Doom, holding herself from being pulled by the winds into that nothingness in front of her. Moiraine had called it the Dark One's essence, but wouldn't that make it the True Power? Worse, if his essence was in the world, wouldn't that mean that he had broken free? Whatever it was, its nature was pure evil, and it filled Nynaeve with a terror like none she had ever felt before in her life.

It pulled with a powerful force, drawing all that was nearby into it. She feared that if she let go, she would be yanked in. Already, it had stolen her shawl, making it vanish. If that nothingness pulled her in, her life would end. Perhaps her soul as well.

Rand! Nynaeve thought. Could she do something to help him? He stood before Moridin, the two of them locked together, sword against sword. Frozen as if in a moment. Sweat trickled down Rand's face. He did not speak. He didn't so much as blink.

His foot had touched the darkness. At that moment, he had frozen, and so had Moridin. They were like statues. The air howled around them, but did not seem to affect them as it did

Nynaeve. They'd been standing like that, frozen, for a good fifteen minutes.

All in all, it had been less than an hour since the group of them had entered the pit to face the Dark One.

Nynaeve watched rocks slide across the ground, then be sucked into that blackness. Her clothing rippled and flapped as if in a strong wind, as did Moiraine's, who huddled nearby holding to her own tooth of stone. Mercifully, the stench of sulfur that had filled the cavern was drawn away here into the blackness.

She couldn't use the One Power. Rand drew every bit of it she could hold, though he didn't seem to be doing anything with it. Could she reach Moridin? He didn't seem to be able to move. What if she took a rock to his head? It would be better than waiting.

Nynaeve tested her weight against the pull of the nothingness ahead, relaxing her grip on the stalagmite. She immediately started to slip, and pulled herself back.

I am not spending the Last Battle clinging to a rock! she thought. *Not the same one the whole time, at the very least.* She had to risk moving. Going directly forward seemed too dangerous, but if she moved sideways . . . yes, there was another stalagmite nearby to her right. She managed to let go of her hold and half-slip, half-scuttle to the next stalagmite. From there, she picked out another one, carefully eased off her hold and grabbed it instead.

The process was very slow. *Rand, you wool-headed fool,* she thought. If he'd let her or Moiraine lead the circle, then maybe they could have done something while he was fighting!

She reached another stalagmite, then stopped as she saw something to her right. She almost screamed. A *woman* huddled there, hidden against the wall, sheltered from the wind by the rocks. She appeared to be crying.

Nynaeve glanced at Rand, who was still locked in stasis with Moridin, then approached the woman. The greater number of stalagmites here meant that Nynaeve could crawl more safely, the stones blocking the pull of the nothingness.

Nynaeve reached the woman. She was chained to the wall. "Alanna?" Nynaeve shouted over the wind. "Light, what are you doing here?"

The Aes Sedai blinked reddened eyes at Nynaeve. Her eyes

stared dully, as if she had no mind. As Nynaeve examined the woman, she noticed that the entire left side of Alanna's body was bloodied from a knife wound to the gut. Light! Nynaeve should have known that from the paleness of the woman's face.

Why stab her and leave her here? *She bonded Rand*, Nynaeve realized. *Oh, Light.* It was a trap. Moridin had left Alanna bleeding, then confronted Rand. When Alanna died, Rand—as her Warder—would be driven mad with rage, making him easy for Moridin to destroy.

Why hadn't he noticed? Nynaeve fished at her pouches for herbs, then stopped short. Could herbs do anything at this point? She needed to use the One Power to Heal such a wound. Nynaeve ripped the woman's clothing, making a bandage, then tried to draw *saidar* for Healing.

Rand had it, and he wouldn't let go. Frantic, she tried to batter him away, but Rand held tight. Tighter, as she tried to push against him. He *did* seem to be channeling it, somehow, but she couldn't see the weaves. She could feel something, but with the howling wind and the strange nature of the pit, it was like a tempest swirling around her. The Power was wrapped up in that somehow.

Blast it! She needed *saidar*! It wasn't Rand's fault. He could not give her any power while leading the circle.

Nynaeve pressed her hand against Alanna's wound, feeling helpless. Dare she call for Rand to release her from the circle? If she did, Moridin would undoubtedly turn on her and attack Alanna.

What to do? If this woman died, Rand would lose control. That, likely, would be the end of him . . . and of the Last Battle.

Mat hacked at the wood with his axe to sharpen it to a point. "See," he said, "it doesn't need to be fancy. Save your pretty carpentry to impress the mayor's daughter."

The watching men and women nodded with grim determination. They were farmers, villagers and craftsmen, like people he'd known back in the Two Rivers. Mat had thousands of them under his command. He'd never have suspected that there would be so many. The good people of the land had come to fight.

Mat figured they were insane, to a person. If he had been able to escape, he would be hiding in a basement somewhere. Burn him, but he would have tried.

Those dice rattled in his head, just as they'd been doing ever since Egwene gave him control of all of the armies of the Light. Being bloody *ta'veren* was not worth two beans.

He kept at it, shaping his stake for the palisade. One fellow watched particularly carefully, an old farmer with skin so leathery that Trolloc swords would likely just bounce off. He looked familiar to Mat for some reason.

Burn these memories, Mat thought. Undoubtedly, this fellow resembled someone from one of those old memories Mat had been given. Yes, that felt right. He could not *quite* remember. A . . . cart? A Fade?

"Come on, Renald," the fellow said to one of his companions— another farmer, Borderlander stock from the looks of him. "Let's go on down the line, and see if we can hurry the other lads up."

The two headed off as Mat finished his stake, then wiped his brow. He reached for another length of wood—he had better give these sheepherders another demonstration—when a *cadin'sor*-clad figure ran up along the mostly finished palisade wall.

Urien had bright red hair, kept short save for the tail in the back. He raised a hand to Mat as he passed. "They are agitated, Matrim Cauthon," Urien said, not stopping. "I believe they are coming in this direction."

"Thanks," Mat called. "I owe you."

The Aiel turned as he ran, jogging backward for a second and facing Mat. "Just win this battle! I have bet a skin of *oosquai* upon our success."

Mat snorted. The only thing more discomforting than a stoic Aiel was a grinning one. Bet? On the outcome of this battle? What kind of bet was that? If they lost, nobody would live long enough to collect . . .

Mat frowned. Actually, that was a pretty *good* bet to be making. "Who did you find to take that bet?" Mat called. "Urien?" But the man was already too far away to hear.

Mat grumbled, but handed his axe to one of the people nearby, a slender Tairen woman. "Keep them in line, Cynd."

"Yes, Lord Cauthon."

"I'm no bloody lord," Mat said by habit as he picked up his *ashandarei*. He walked off, then turned to look at the palisade being erected and caught sight of a handful of Deathwatch Guards walking along the rows of working people. Like wolves among the sheep. Mat hurried on.

His armies did not have much time left to prepare. Using gateways had put them ahead of the Trollocs, but they had not escaped. Light, there *was* no escape. Mat had been given his choice of battlefields, though, and this Merrilor place would work best.

Like picking the plot for your own grave, Mat thought. *Sure, I'd rather not have to choose in the first place.*

The palisade was rising in front of the woods east of the field. He did not have time to section off or surround the entire area with a palisade, and doing so would not make much sense anyway. With those Sharan channelers, the Shadow could rip through walls like a sword through silk. But some palisades, with catwalks on top, would give his archers height to target Trollocs.

Mat had two rivers to work with here. The River Mora flowed in a southwest direction, running between the Heights and Dashar Knob. Its southern bank was in Shienar, the northern bank in Arafel. It joined the River Erinin, which ran directly westward at the southern edge of the field.

Those rivers would serve better than any walls, particularly now that he had the resources to defend them correctly. Well, if you could call them resources. Half his soldiers were as new as spring grass and the other half had fought near to death the week before. The Borderlanders had lost two men out of three—Light, two out of *three*. A lesser army would have disbanded.

Counting everyone he had, Mat would be outnumbered four to one when those Trollocs arrived, at least according to the reports from the Fists of Heaven. It was going to be messy.

Mat pulled his hat down further, then scratched at the side of the new eyepatch that Tuon had given him. Red leather. He liked it.

"Here now," he said, passing some of the new Tower Guard recruits. They were sparring with quarterstaffs—spearheads were still being forged to go on the ends. The men looked more likely to hurt themselves than the enemy.

Mat handed his *ashandarei* to a man, then took a quarterstaff from another as the first hastily saluted. Most of these men were not old enough to need to shave more than once a month. If the boy whose staff he had taken was a day over fifteen, Mat would eat his boots. He would not even boil them first!

"You can't cringe every time the staff hits something!" Mat said. "Close your eyes on the battlefield, and you're dead. Didn't you lot pay any attention last time?"

Mat held up the staff, showing them where to grip it, then put them through the blocking practice his father had shown him back when he had been young enough to think fighting might actually be fun. He worked up a sweat, hitting at each of the new recruits in turn, forcing each to block.

"Burn me, but you *will* figure this out," Mat said loudly to all of them. "I wouldn't care so much, as you lot seem to have the wits of stumps, but if you get yourselves killed, your mothers will be expecting me to send them word. I won't do it, mind you. But I might feel a little guilty between games of dice, and I hate feeling guilty, so pay attention!"

"Lord Cauthon?" said the lad who had given him the staff.

"I'm not—" He stopped. "Well, yes, what is it?"

"Can't we just learn the sword?"

"Light!" Mat said. "What's your name?"

"Sigmont, sir."

"Well, Sigmont, how much time do you think we have? Maybe you could wander out, talk to the Dreadlords and the Shadowspawn and ask them to give me a few more months' time so I can train you all properly."

Sigmont blushed, and Mat handed back his staff. *City boys.* He sighed. "Look here, all I want is for you lot to be able to defend yourselves. I don't have time to make you great warriors, but I *can* teach you to work together, keep a formation, and not shy away when the Trollocs come. That will get you farther than any kind of fancy swordplay, trust me."

The youths nodded reluctantly.

"Get back to your practice," Mat said, wiping his brow and looking over his shoulder. Bloody ashes! The Deathwatch Guards were heading his way.

He grabbed his *ashandarei* and rushed off, then ducked around the side of a tent, only to stumble into a group of Aes Sedai approaching on the path.

"Mat?" Egwene asked from the middle of the group of women. "Are you well?"

"They're bloody chasing me," he said, glancing around the side of the tent.

"Who is chasing you?" Egwene said.

"Deathwatch Guards," Mat said. "I'm supposed to be back at Tuon's tent."

Egwene waved a few fingers, sending the other women off, except her two shadows—Gawyn and that Seanchan woman— who remained with her. "Mat," Egwene said in a suffering tone, "I'm glad you've finally decided to see reason and leave the Seanchan camp, but couldn't you have waited until *after* the battle was over to defect?"

"Sorry," he said, only half-listening. "But can we walk on toward the Aes Sedai quarter of camp? They won't follow me there." Maybe not. If all Deathwatch Guards were like Karede, maybe they would. Karede would dive after a man falling off a cliff in order to catch him.

Egwene started back, seeming displeased with Mat. How was it Aes Sedai could be so perfectly emotionless, yet still let a man know they disapproved of him? Come to think of it, an Aes Sedai would probably follow a man off a cliff, too, if only to explain to him—in detail—all the things he was doing incorrectly in the way he went about killing himself.

Mat wished so many of his thoughts lately did not involve feeling like he was the one jumping off the cliff.

"We'll have to find a way to explain to Fortuona why you ran," Egwene said as they approached the Aes Sedai quarter. Mat had placed it as far from the Seanchan as was reasonable. "The marriage is going to present a problem. I suggest that you—"

"Wait, Egwene," Mat said. "What are you talking about?"

"You are running from the Seanchan guards," Egwene said. "Weren't you listening . . . Of course you weren't. It is pleasant to know that, as the world crumbles, a few things are completely unchangeable. *Cuendillar* and Mat Cauthon."

"I'm running from them," Mat said, looking over his shoulder, "because Tuon wants me to sit in judgment. Any time a soldier is seeking the Empress's mercy for a crime, *I'm* the one who is supposed to bloody hear his case!"

"You," Egwene said, "passing judgment?"

"I know," Mat said. "Too much bloody work, if you ask me. I've been dodging guardsmen all day, trying to steal a little time for myself."

"A little honest work wouldn't kill you, Mat."

"Now, you know that's not true. Soldiering is honest work, and it gets men killed all the bloody time."

Gawyn Trakand was apparently practicing to be an Aes Sedai sometime, because he kept giving Mat glares that would have made Moiraine proud. Well, let him. Gawyn was a prince. He had been raised to do things like pass judgment. He probably sent a few men to the gallows each day at his lunch break, just to keep in practice.

But Mat . . . Mat was not going to order men to be executed, and that was that. They passed a group of Aiel sparring together. Was this group what Urien had been running to reach? Once they had passed—Mat trying to make the others walk faster so the Seanchan would not catch up—he drew closer to Egwene.

"Have you found it yet?" he asked softly.

"No," Egwene said, eyes forward.

No need to mention what *it* was. "How could you have lost the thing? After all the work we bloody went through to find it?"

"We? From the telling I hear, Rand, Loial and the Borderlanders had far more to do with finding it than you."

"I was there," Mat said. "I rode across the entire bloody continent, didn't I? Burn me, first Rand, then you. Is everybody going to chivvy me about those days? Gawyn, you want a turn?"

"Yes, please." He sounded eager.

"Shut up," Mat said. "It seems that nobody can remember straight but me. I hunted down that bloody Horn like a madman. And, I'll mention, it was me blowing the thing that let you all escape Falme."

"Is that how you remember it?" Egwene asked.

"Sure," Mat said. "I mean, I have some holes in there, but I've pieced it mostly together."

"And the dagger?"

"That trinket? Hardly worth anyone's time." He caught himself reaching to his side, to where he had once carried it. Egwene raised an eyebrow at him. "Anyway, that's not the point. We're going to need that bloody instrument, Egwene. We'll *need* it."

"We have people searching," she said. "We're not sure exactly what happened. There was a Traveling residue, but it's been a while and ... Light, Mat. We're trying. I promise it. It's not the only thing the Shadow has stolen from us recently ..."

He glanced at her, but she gave him no more. Flaming Aes Sedai. "Has anyone seen Perrin yet?" he asked. "I don't want to be the one to tell him his wife has gone missing."

"Nobody has seen him," Egwene said. "I assume he is at work helping Rand."

"Bah," Mat said. "Can you make a gateway for me up to the top of the Knob?"

"I thought you wanted to go to my camp."

"It's on the way," Mat said. Well, sort of, it was. "And those Deathwatch Guards won't expect it. Burn me, Egwene, but I think they've guessed where we were heading."

Egwene—after pausing for a moment—opened them a gateway to the Traveling ground atop the Knob. They stepped through onto it.

More than a hill, less than a mountain, Dashar Knob rose a good hundred feet into the air near the middle of the battlefield. The rock formation was unscalable, and gateways were the only way to reach the top. From here, Mat and his commanders would be able to watch the entire battle play out.

"I have never known anyone else," Egwene said to him, "who will work so hard to avoid hard work, Matrim Cauthon."

"You haven't spent enough time around soldiers." Mat waved at the men who saluted him as he walked out of the Traveling grounds.

He looked north toward the River Mora and across it into Arafel. Then northeast, toward the ruins of what had once been some kind of fort or watchtower. Eastward, toward the rising palisade and the forest. He continued to turn, southward to gaze at the River Erinin in the far distance, and the strange little grove of tall trees that Loial was so in awe of. They said Rand had grown those, during the meeting where the treaty had been signed. Mat looked southwest toward the only good ford on the Mora nearby, named Hawal Ford by the locals who had farmed this area; beyond the ford on the Arafel side was a large expanse of bogs.

Westward, across the Mora, lay Polov Heights—a forty-foot-tall plateau with a steep slope on the east and more gradual slopes on the other sides. Between the base of the southwestern slope and the bogs was a corridor roughly two hundred paces across, well worn by travelers who used the ford to cross between Arafel and Shienar. Mat could use these features to his advantage. He could use them all. Would that be enough? He could feel something pulling on him, tugging him northward. Rand would need him soon.

He turned, ready to bolt, as someone approached across the top of the Knob, but it was not the Deathwatch Guards. It was just leather-faced Jur Grady.

"I fetched those soldiers for you," Grady said, pointing. Mat could see a small force coming through a gateway to the Traveling grounds near the palisade. A hundred men of the Band, led by Delarn, flying a bloody red flag. The Redarms were accompanied by some five hundred people in worn clothing.

"What was the point of this?" Grady asked. "You sent those hundred to a village in the south to recruit, I assume?"

That, and more. *I saved your life, man*, Mat thought, trying to pick Delarn out of the group. *And then you volunteer for this. Bloody fool.* Delarn acted as if it were his fate.

"Take them upriver," Mat said. "The maps show there is only one good place to block the Mora, a narrow canyon a few leagues northeast of here."

"All right," Grady said. "There will be channelers involved."

"You will have to handle them," Mat said. "Mostly, though, I want you to let those six hundred men and women defend the river. Don't risk yourself too much. Let Delarn and his people do the work."

"Pardon," Grady said. "But that doesn't seem like a very large force. Most of them aren't trained soldiers."

"I know what I'm doing," Mat said. *I hope.*

Grady nodded reluctantly and moved off.

Egwene watched Mat with curious eyes.

"We can't fall back from this fight," Mat said softly. "We don't retreat. There isn't anywhere to go. We stand here, or we lose it all."

"There is *always* a retreat," Egwene said.

"No," Mat said. "Not anymore." He rested his *ashandarei* on his shoulder, his other hand out, palm forward. He scanned the landscape, memories appearing as if from light and dust before him. Rion at Hune Hill. Naath and the San d'ma Shadar. The Fall of Pipkin. Hundreds upon hundreds of battlefields, hundreds of victories. Thousands of deaths.

Mat watched figments of memories flash across the field. "Have you spoken to the supply masters? We're out of food, Egwene. We can't win a protracted war, fighting and falling back. The enemy will overwhelm us if we do that. Just like Eyal in the Marches of Maighande. We are at our strongest now, broken though we are. Fall back, and we resign ourselves to starvation as the Trollocs destroy us."

"Rand," Egwene said. "We just have to hold out until he is victorious."

"That's true in a fashion," Mat said, turning toward the Heights. In his mind's eye, he saw what could come, the possibilities. He imagined riders on the Heights, like shadows. He would lose if he tried to hold those Heights, but maybe ... "If Rand loses, it won't matter. The Wheel is bloody broken, and we all become nothing, if we're lucky. Well, we can't do anything more about it. But here's the thing. If he does what he's supposed to, we could still lose—we will lose, if we don't stop the Shadow's armies."

He blinked, seeing it, the entire battlefield spread before him. Fighting at the ford. Arrows from the palisade. "We can't just beat them, Egwene," Mat said. "We can't just stand and hold on. We have to destroy them, drive them away, then hunt them to the last Trolloc. We can't just survive ... we have to *win*."

"How are we going to do that?" Egwene asked. "Mat, you're not talking sense. Weren't you just saying yesterday how outnumbered we'll be?"

He looked toward the bog, imagining shadows trying to slog through it. Shadows of dust and memory. "I have to change it all," he said. He could not do what they would expect. He could not do what spies might have reported he was planning. "Blood and bloody ashes ... one last toss of the dice. Everything we have, piled into a heap ... "

A group of men in dark armor came through a gateway to the top of the Knob, panting deeply, as if they'd had to chase down a *damane* to get them up here. Their breastplates were lacquered a deep red, but this batch did not need a fearsome display to be frightening. They looked furious enough to scramble eggs with a stare.

"You," said the lead Deathwatch Guard, a man named Gelen, pointing at Mat, "are *needed* at the—"

Mat held up a hand to cut him off.

"I will not be denied again!" Gelen said. "I have orders from—"

Mat shot the man a glare, and he stopped short. Mat turned northward again. A cool, somehow *familiar* wind blew across him, rippling his long coat, brushing at his hat. He narrowed his eye. Rand was tugging on him.

The dice still tumbled in his head.

"They're here," Mat said.

"What did you say?" Egwene asked.

"They're here."

"The scouts—"

"The scouts are wrong," Mat said. He looked up, and noticed a pair of *raken* speeding back toward the camp. They had seen it. The Trollocs must have marched through the night.

Sharans will come first, Mat thought, *to give the Trollocs a breather. They'll have arrived through gateways.*

"Send runners," Mat said, pointing at the Deathwatch Guards, "get the men and women to their posts. And warn Elayne that I'm going to change the battle plan."

"What?" Egwene said.

"They're *here*!" Mat said, turning on the Guards. "Why aren't you bloody running! Go, *go*!" Above, the *raken* screeched. Gelen, to his credit, saluted, then ran—pounding in that massive armor—with his companions.

"This is it, Egwene," Mat said. "Take a deep breath, a last pull on the brandy, or burn your final pinch of tabac. Have a good look at the ground before you, as it's soon going to be covered in blood. In an hour, we'll be in the thick of it. The Light watch over us all."

Perrin drifted in darkness. He felt so *tired*.

Slayer still lives, a piece of himself thought. *Graendal is corrupting the great captains. The end is near. You can't slip away now! Hold on.*

Hold on to what? He tried to open his eyes, but was so exhausted. He should ... should have gotten out of the wolf dream sooner. His entire body felt numb, except ...

Except for his side. Moving fingers that felt like bricks, he touched the warmth. His hammer. It was blazing hot. That warmth seemed to move up his fingers, and Perrin took a deep breath.

He needed to wake up. He hovered at the edges of consciousness, as when he was close to sleep, but still partially aware. In that state, he felt as if he faced a forked pathway before him. One path led deeper into darkness. And one led ... He couldn't see, but he knew that it meant ... It meant waking up.

Warmth from the hammer radiated up his arm. His mind gathered sharpness. *Awaken.*

That was what Slayer had done. He had ... awakened ... somehow ...

Perrin's life was trickling away. Not much time left. Half within death's embrace, he gritted his teeth, drew in a deep breath and forced himself to *wake*.

The silence of the wolf dream shattered.

Perrin hit soft earth, and entered a place of shouts. Something about a battlefront, about preparing the lines ...

Nearby, someone cried out. And then someone else. And others.

"Perrin?" He knew that voice. "Perrin, lad!"

Master Luhhan? Perrin's eyelids felt so heavy. He couldn't open them. Arms grabbed him.

"Hang on. I have you, lad. I have you. *Hang on.*"

CHAPTER
37

The Last Battle

Dawn broke that morning on Polov Heights, but the sun did not shine on the Defenders of the Light. Out of the west and out of the north came the armies of Darkness, to win this one last battle and cast a Shadow across the earth; to usher in an Age where the wails of suffering would go unheard.

—from the notebook of Loial, son of Arent son of Halan, the Fourth Age

Lan held his sword aloft as he galloped Mandarb through camp.

Above, the morning clouds began to bleed red, reflecting enormous fireballs rising from the massive Sharan army that was approaching from the west. They arced in the sky gracefully, seeming slow because of the great distance.

Groups of riders broke out of the camp, joining Lan. The remaining Malkieri rode just behind him, but his force had swelled like a tide. Andere joined him at the front, the flag of Malkier—the Golden Crane—acting as a banner for all of the Borderlands.

They had been bloodied, but not beaten. Knock a man down, and you saw what he was made of. That man might run. If he didn't—if he stood back up with blood at the corner of his mouth and determination in his eyes—then you knew. That man was about to become truly dangerous.

The fireballs seemed to move more quickly as they dropped, crashing to the camp in bursts of red fury. Explosions shook the ground. Nearby screams rose to accompany the thunder of hoof-beats. Still men joined him. Mat Cauthon had spread word through all of the camps that more cavalry were needed to join Lan's advance and replace lost soldiers.

He had also disclosed the cost of doing so. The cavalry would be at the forefront of the fighting, breaking Trolloc and Sharan lines, and would find little rest. They'd carry the brunt of the casualties this day.

Still, men joined him. Borderlanders who should have been too old to ride. Merchants who had put aside the money pouch and taken up the sword. A surprising number of southerners, including many women, wearing breastplates and steel or leather caps, carrying spears. There weren't enough lances to go around.

"Half of those joining look like farmers more than soldiers!" Andere called to him over the hoofbeats.

"Have you ever seen a man or woman from the Two Rivers ride, Andere?" Lan yelled back.

"I can't say that I have."

"Watch and be surprised."

Lan's cavalry reached the River Mora, where a man with long, curling hair, wearing a black coat, stood with hands clasped behind his back. Logain now had forty Aes Sedai and Asha'man with him. He eyed Lan's force, then raised a hand toward the sky, crumpling an enormous falling fireball as if it were a piece of paper. The sky cracked like lightning, and the breaking fireball gushed sparks to every side, smoke churning in the air. Ashes drifted down, burning out, hitting the rushing river and scattering black and white on its surface.

Lan slowed Mandarb as he approached Hawal Ford, just south of the Heights. Logain thrust his other hand toward the river. The waters churned, then lurched up into the air as if flowing over an invisible ramp. They crashed down on the other side, a violent waterfall, while some of the water spilled over the banks of the river.

Lan nodded to Logain and continued on, guiding Mandarb under the waterfall and crossing the still-wet rocks of the ford. Sunlight filtered through the river waters above, sparkling down on Lan as he thundered through the tunnel, Andere and the Malkieri behind him. The waterfall roared down to his left, spraying a mist of water.

Lan shivered as he burst back out into the light, then charged through the corridor toward the Sharans. To his right rose the Heights, to his left the bogs, but there was a passage of solid, level ground here. Up on the Heights, archers, crossbowmen and dragoners prepared to release volleys at the oncoming foes.

Sharans at the front, a huge force of Trollocs gathering up behind, all directly west of the Heights. The thunder of dragon-fire shook the air from the top of the Heights, and soon the Sharans had explosions of their own to contend with.

Lan set his lance, took aim at a Sharan soldier charging toward Polov Heights, then braced himself.

Elayne whipped her head up, turning to the side. That terrible song, a croon, a hum, beautiful yet terrible at the same time. She heeled Moonshadow, drawn toward that soft sound. Where was it?

It rose from somewhere deeper in the Seanchan camp at the base of Dashar Knob. Chewing out Mat for not telling her his plan of war could wait. She needed to find the source of that sound, that wonderful sound, that . . .

"Elayne!" Birgitte said.

Elayne kicked her horse forward.

"Elayne! Draghkar!"

Draghkar. Elayne shook herself, then looked up to find the creatures falling like drops of water into the camp around them. Guardswomen lowered their swords, eyes opening wide as the crooning continued.

Elayne wove a thunderclap. It burst from her, splitting the air, washing across the Guardswomen and making them cry out and cover their ears. Pain stabbed Elayne's head and she cursed, closing her eyes at the shock. And then . . . then she heard nothing.

That was the point.

She forced her eyes open to see Draghkar all around, with their spindly bodies and inhuman eyes. They opened their lips to croon, but Elayne's deafened ears could not hear the song. She smiled, then wove whips of fire, striking the creatures down. She could not hear their screeches of pain, which was a pity.

Elayne's Guardswomen rallied, rising from knees, lowering hands from ears. She could tell from their dazed looks that they had been deafened. Birgitte soon had them striking at the surprised Draghkar. Three of the creatures tried to leap up and fly away, but Birgitte took each one with a white-fletched arrow, dropping the last so that it crashed into a nearby tent.

Elayne waved, getting Birgitte's attention. The first Draghkar sounds hadn't come from above, but from farther into camp. Elayne pointed, kicking Moonshadow into motion, leading her troops among the Seanchan. All about, men lay staring into the sky, mouths open. Many seemed to be breathing, but they stared with dead eyes. The Draghkar had consumed their souls, but left the bodies alive, like the crust cut off a rich man's bread.

Sloppy. This group of Draghkar—Light, there were well over a hundred of them—could have taken a man each, killed him, then retreated before their presence was discovered. The distant roars of the battle—the bleating horns, the booming dragons, the hissing fireballs, all of which Elayne now felt but could only barely make out with her broken ears—had covered the Draghkar attack. The creatures could have struck and fled, but they were greedy.

Her guards scattered, hacking at the surprised Draghkar—many of whom were holding soldiers. The beasts were not strong fighters if measured by strength of arm. Elayne waited, preparing weaves. Those Draghkar who tried to flee, she burned from the sky.

Once the last of them were dead—at least, the ones they could see—Elayne waved Birgitte to approach. The air smelled sharply of burned flesh. Elayne wrinkled her nose, and reached down from horseback to take Birgitte's head in her hands, Healing the woman's ears. The babes kicked as she did so. Did they react to times when she Healed someone, or was that her fancy? Elayne reached down to hold her stomach with one arm as Birgitte stepped back, looking about.

The Warder nocked an arrow, and Elayne felt her alarm. Birgitte loosed, and a Draghkar stumbled back from cover inside a nearby tent. A Seanchan stumbled out, eyes glassed over. The feeding had been interrupted halfway through; the poor fellow would never be right in the mind again.

Elayne turned her horse and saw some Seanchan troops charging into the area. Birgitte spoke to them, then turned to speak to Elayne. Elayne just shook her head, and Birgitte hesitated, then said something else to the Seanchan.

Elayne's guards grouped around her again, watching the Seanchan with distrust. Elayne understood the sentiment perfectly.

Birgitte waved her forward, and they continued on in the direction they had been going. As they did, a *damane* and *sul'dam* approached and—surprisingly—curtsied to Elayne. Perhaps this Fortuona had given them orders to respect foreign monarchs.

Elayne hesitated, but what was she going to do? She could return to her own camp for Healing, but that would take time, and it was urgent that she speak with Mat. What was the point of spending days drawing up war plans if he was going to throw them aside? She trusted him—Light, she had to—but she'd still rather know what he intended to do.

She sighed, then held out her foot to the *damane*. The woman frowned, then glanced to the *sul'dam*. Both seemed to take it as an insult. Elayne had certainly intended it as one.

The *sul'dam* nodded, and her *damane* reached to touch Elayne's leg just above her booted foot. Elayne's sturdy boots looked like something a soldier would wear, not a queen, but she didn't intend to ride into battle wearing slippers.

A small icy shock of Healing ran through her, and her hearing returned slowly. The low pitches returned first. Explosions. The distant boom of dragonfire, the rush of the river nearby. Several Seanchan talking. Midranges came next, then a flood of sound. Flaps rustling, screams of soldiers, calls of horns.

"Tell them to Heal the others," Elayne said to Birgitte.

Birgitte raised an eyebrow, probably wondering why Elayne wouldn't just give the order herself. Well, these Seanchan paid very close attention to which people could speak to one another. Elayne would not give them the honor of speaking to them directly.

Birgitte relayed the order, and the *sul'dam*'s lips drew to a line. She had had the sides of her hair shaved; she was highborn. Light willing, Elayne had managed to insult her again.

"I will do it," the woman said. "Though why any of you would want to be Healed by an animal is beyond me."

The Seanchan didn't believe in letting *damane* Heal. At least, that was what they kept claiming—that hadn't stopped them from reluctantly teaching the weaves to their captive women, now that they'd seen firsthand what an advantage it was in battle. From what Elayne had heard, the highborn rarely accepted that Healing, however.

"Let's go," Elayne said, riding forward. She waved for her soldiers to stay behind and be Healed.

Birgitte eyed her, but did not object. The two of them hurried on, Birgitte mounting her horse and riding with Elayne toward the Seanchan command building. One story, perhaps the size of a small farmhouse, it sat in a large, high-walled cleft at the southern base of Dashar Knob—they'd moved it from the top, as Mat worried it would be too exposed. The top would continue to be used for overseeing the battle at short intervals.

Elayne allowed Birgitte to help her dismount—Light, but she was starting to feel unwieldy. It was as if she were a ship in dry dock. She took a moment to properly compose herself. Smooth features, emotions in control. She picked at her hair, straightened her dress, then walked into the building.

"What," she bellowed as she stepped in, "in the name of a bloody, two-fingered Trolloc haystack-grunter do you think you are doing, Matrim Cauthon?"

Unsurprisingly, the curse made the man grin as he looked up from the map table. He wore his hat and coat over some very nice silken clothing that looked as if it had been tailored to match the hat's color, and to include tooled leather at the cuffs and collar so as to not be so out of place. It smelled of some kind of compromise. Why was his hat banded with pink ribbon, though?

"Hello, Elayne," Mat said. "I figured that I could look forward to seeing you soon." He waved to a chair, bearing the red and gold of Andor, at the side of the room. It was extra cushioned, with a cup of warm tea steaming on the stand beside it.

Burn you, Matrim Cauthon, she thought. *When did you grow so clever?*

The Seanchan Empress sat on her own throne at the head of the room, Min at her side, draped in enough green silk to supply a shop in Caemlyn for two weeks. Elayne did not miss the fact that Fortuona's throne was two fingers higher than Elayne's. Bloody insufferable woman. "Mat. There are Draghkar in your camp."

"Burn it," he said. "Where?"

"I should say there *were* Draghkar in your camp," Elayne said. "We dealt with them. You need to tell your archers to keep better watch."

"I've told them," Mat complained. "Bloody ashes. Somebody check on the archers, I—"

"Great Prince!" a Seanchan messenger said, skidding through the doorway. He went to his knees, then prostrated himself with a smooth motion, never stopping his narrative. "Archer bank is down! Hit by Sharan outriders—they masked their attack by smoke from fireballs."

"Blood and bloody ashes!" Mat said. "Send sixteen *damane* and *sul'dam* down there now! Send to the northern archery units and bring squads forty-two and fifty down. And tell the scouts I'll have them flogged if they let anything like this happen again."

"Great One," the scout said, saluting and scrambling to his feet, backing out of the room without looking up to avoid the risk of meeting Mat's gaze.

All in all, Elayne was impressed by how easily the scout mixed his obeisance and his report. She was also sickened. No ruler should demand such of her subjects. A nation's strength came from the strength of its people; break them, and you were breaking your own back.

"You knew I was coming," Elayne said after Mat gave a few more orders to his aides. "And you anticipated the anger your changing of plans would cause. Burn you, Matrim Cauthon, *why* did you feel the need to do this? I thought our battle plan was sound."

"It was," Mat said.

"Then why change it!"

"Elayne," Mat said, glancing at her. "Everyone put me in charge, against my will, because I can't have my mind changed by the Forsaken, right?"

"That was the general idea," Elayne said. "Though I'd guess it has less to do with that medallion of yours and more to do with you having too thick a head for Compulsion to penetrate."

"Bloody right," Mat said. "Anyway, if the Forsaken are using Compulsion on people in our camps, they probably have a few spies in our meetings."

"I suppose so."

"So they know our plan. Our great plan, that we spent so long preparing. They know it."

Elayne hesitated.

"Light!" Mat said, shaking his head. "The first and most important rule to winning a war is knowing what your enemy is going to do."

"I though the first rule was to know your terrain," Elayne said, folding her arms.

"That, too. Anyway, I realize that if the enemy knows what we're going to do, we have to change. Immediately. Bad battle plans are better than ones your enemy will anticipate."

"Why didn't you guess this would happen?" Elayne demanded.

He looked at her, expressionless. One side of his mouth twitched up, then he pulled his hat down, shading his eyepatch.

"Light," Elayne said. "You *knew*. You spent this whole week planning with us, and you knew the entire time you'd throw it out with the dishwater."

"That's giving me too much bloody credit," Mat said, looking back at his maps. "I think a part of me might have known all along, but I didn't figure it out until just before the Sharans got here."

"So what is the new plan?"

He didn't reply.

"You're going to keep it in your head," Elayne said, her legs feeling weak. "You're going to lead the battle, and none of us are going to know what in the Light you're planning, are we? Otherwise, someone might overhear, and the news would travel to the Shadow."

He nodded.

"Creator shelter us," she whispered.

Mat scowled. "You know, that's what Tuon said."

On the Heights, Uno held his ears as the nearby dragons belched fire at the Trollocs and Sharans west of them. The scent of something pungent burned in the air, and the blasts were so deafening, he couldn't hear his own bloody cursing.

Down below, Lan Mandragoran's riders were sweeping the sides of the assault force, keeping them contained so that the dragons could do more damage. The Sharans had Trollocs with them. They'd have channelers with them, too, lots of them. Farther upriver, another large army of Trollocs, the ones that had done so much damage to Dai Shan's forces, had come down from the northeast, and would soon reach the Field of Merrilor.

The dragons stilled momentarily, the dragoners stuffing the maws again with whatever it was that made them work. Uno wasn't going to step bloody close to them. Bad luck, those were. He was certain of it.

The leader of the dragoners was a wiry Cairhienin, and Uno had never had much use for those folk. They bloody scowled at him whenever he talked. This one sat haughtily upon his horse, and didn't flinch when the dragons fired again.

The Amyrlin Seat had thrown her lot in with these men, and with the Seanchan, too. Uno wasn't going to flaming complain. They needed every sword they could get, Cairhienin and bloody Seanchan included.

"You like our dragons, Captain?" the leader—Talmanes—called to Uno. Captain. Uno had bloody been promoted. He now led a force of newly recruited Tower pikemen and light cavalry.

He shouldn't have been in charge of bloody anything; he had been happy as a regular soldier. But he had both training and battle experience, things that were in slim supply these days, or so Queen Elayne had said. So now he was a flaming officer, and leading cavalry *and* foot soldiers no less! Well, he knew his way around a pike, if he had to use one, though he usually preferred to fight on horseback.

His men were ready to defend the rim of the Heights should the enemy make it up the slope. So far, the archers situated in front of the dragoners had prevented that, but soon enough, the archers would have to pull back, and then it would be bloody regular soldiers doing the bloody fighting. Below, the Sharans pulled aside to let the main Trolloc forces storm up onto the slope.

The pikemen would advance, resisting the Trolloc attack, and pikes would work well here, as the Trollocs would be pushing uphill. Add in some flaming cavalry on their flanks, and some bloody archers shooting through those gateways made high up in the air, and they could probably sit here for days. Maybe weeks. When they were pushed off by superior numbers, they'd let go inch by inch, clinging to every speck of ground.

Uno figured there was no way he was going to survive this flaming battle. He was surprised he'd made it this long. Really, flaming Masema should have had his head, or the Seanchan near Falme, or a Trolloc here and there. He had tried to keep himself lean so he'd taste flaming terrible when they stuffed him in one of those flaming cookpots.

The dragons fired again, blasting enormous holes in the hordes of advancing Trollocs. Uno clapped his hands to his ears. "Warn a man when you do that, you flaming bits hanging from a goat's—"

The next shot drowned him out.

The Trollocs below were blown into the air, the dragons pulverizing the ground beneath them. Those eggs *exploded* once they were shot from those cursed tubes. What kind of thing, other than the One Power, could make metal explode? Uno was certain he flaming didn't want to know.

Talmanes stepped up to the rim of the Heights, inspecting the damage. He was joined by a Taraboner woman, the one who had invented these weapons. She looked over and saw Uno, then tossed him something. A small bit of wax. The Taraboner woman tapped her ear, then began speaking with Talmanes, gesturing. He might have command of the troops, but the woman had charge of the devices. She told the men where to position the dragons to fight.

Uno grumbled, but pocketed the wax. A fist of Trollocs had pushed through the blast, about a hundred strong, and he didn't have time to bother with his ears. Uno grabbed a pike, leveling it and signaling for his men to do the same. They all wore the white of the Tower; Uno himself wore a white tabard.

He shouted orders, readying his pike by standing sideways near the top of the slope, the heel of its shaft raised. One hand gripped the shaft in front of him to guide and reinforce the thrust; the other hand, palm down, gripping it an arm's length from the heel, would drive home the thrust as the Trollocs came into range. Several ranks of pikemen behind Uno stood ready to advance following the initial impact.

"Steady with the pikes, you flaming sheepherders!" Uno bellowed. "Steady!"

The Trollocs scrambled up the hill, crashing into the line of pikes. The beasts in the vanguard tried to knock the pikes aside with sweeps of their weapons, but Uno's men stepped forward, skewering Trollocs, often two pikes per beast. Uno grunted, pulling his pike back into line to catch a Trolloc through the throat.

"First rank, back!" Uno yelled, pulling his pike backward to free it from the Trolloc he'd killed. His companions did the same, pulling their weapons free and leaving the corpses to roll down the slope.

The pikemen in the front rank fell back as those in the second rank came forward between them, ramming pikes into snarling Trollocs. Each rank rotated up front in succession until, minutes later, the entire group of Trollocs was dead. "Nice work," Uno said, raising his pike to the upright position, a trickle of rancid Trolloc blood winding down the shaft from the pike head. "Nice work."

He glanced toward the dragoners, who were feeding more eggs down those tubes. He hastily pulled the wax out of his pocket. Yes, they could hold this flaming position. They could hold it well. They just needed to—

A cry from above stopped him from putting the wax in. Something thumped to the ground beside Uno. A lead ball with streamers dropped from high up. "Flaming Seanchan goat!" Uno yelled, looking up and shaking his fist. "That nearly took me in the crown, you lover of rotting worms!"

The *raken* flew off, probably without its rider hearing a word of what Uno had shouted. Bloody Seanchan. He stooped down, removing the letter from the ball.

Retreat down the southwestern slope of the Heights.

"You're bloody *kicking* me," Uno muttered. "Kicking me in the head while I'm sleeping. Allin, you bloody fool, can you read this?"

Allin, a dark-haired Andorman, wore a half-beard, shaved at the sides. Uno had always thought those looked flaming ridiculous.

"Retreat?" Allin said. "Now?"

"They've flaming lost their minds," Uno said.

Nearby, Talmanes and the Taraboner woman were receiving a messenger—and she was relaying the same news, by the looks of the Taraboner woman's scowl. Retreat.

"Cauthon had better bloody know what he's doing," Uno said, shaking his head. He still didn't understand why anyone would put Cauthon in charge of anything. He remembered that boy, always snapping at people, eyes sunken in his head. Half-dead, half-spoiled. Uno shook his head.

But he'd do it. He'd sworn to the bloody White Tower. So he'd do it. "Pass the word," he said to Allin, stuffing the wax in his ears as Aludra, at the dragons, prepared a last volley before leaving. "We're pulling back from the bloody Heights, and—"

A clap of sound hit Uno physically, vibrating through him, bloody near stopping his heart. His head hit the ground before he realized he'd fallen.

He blinked dust from his eyes, groaning and rolling over as another flash, then another, struck the Heights where the dragons were. Lightning! His soldiers were down on their knees, eyes shut, hands over ears. Talmanes was already up, however, shouting orders that Uno could barely hear, waving for his men to pull back.

A dozen fireballs, enormous and incredibly fast, rose from the Sharan army behind the Trollocs. Uno cursed and threw himself in a depression for cover, rolling into place moments before the entire hill shook like an earthquake. Clods of earth fell upon him, almost burying him.

Everything was coming at them. *Everything.* Every bloody Sharan channeler in the army seemed to focus on the Heights at once. His people had Aes Sedai, placed to protect the dragons, but from the look of things they would be hard-pressed to fight back against *that*!

The attack lasted for what seemed an eternity. When it subsided, Uno crawled free. Some of the flaming dragons were in pieces, and Aludra was working with the dragoners to salvage those and protect the rest. Talmanes, holding a bloody hand to his head, was shouting. Uno pried the wax from one of his ears—that had probably saved his hearing—and scrambled toward Talmanes.

"Where are your bloody Aes Sedai?" Uno shouted. "They're bloody supposed to be stopping this!"

They had four dozen of them, ordered to cut weaves from the air or knock them aside to protect the dragons. They had claimed to be able to keep the Heights safe from anything but the coming of the Dark One. Now they were in shambles, the lightning strikes having fallen in their midst.

Trollocs were advancing up the hill again. Uno ordered Allin to form the pikewall and hold the creatures back, then ran toward the Aes Sedai with a few guards. He joined Warders, helping the women up, looking for their leader.

"Kwamesa Sedai?" Uno asked, finding the Aes Sedai in charge who was dusting herself off. The slender, dark-skinned Arafellin was muttering softly under her breath.

"What was *that*?" she demanded.

"Uh . . ." Uno said.

"That question wasn't intended for you," she said, scanning the sky. "Einar! Why didn't you spot those weaves?"

An Asha'man rushed over. "They came so quickly. They were upon us before I had time to give warning. And . . . Light! Whoever sent them was strong. Stronger than I've ever seen, stronger than—"

A line of light split the air behind them. It was enormous, as long as the keep of Fal Dara. It rotated upon itself, opening a vast gateway that split the ground at the center of the Heights. Standing on the other side was a man in brilliant armor made of silver, coinlike rings, his helmetless head bearing dark hair and a strong nose. He held before him a scepter of gold, the top shaped like an hourglass or a fine goblet.

Kwamesa reacted immediately, raising her hand and releasing a stream of fire. The man waved his hand, and the stream of fire deflected; then he pointed—almost indifferently—and something thin, hot and *white* connected him to Kwamesa. Her form glowed, and then she was gone, motes drifting toward the ground.

Uno jumped away, Einar joining him as he rolled behind the rubble of a broken dragon.

"I come for the Dragon Reborn!" the figure in silver announced. "You will send for him. Either that, or I will see that your screams bring him."

The ground beneath the dragons heaved into the air just a few feet from Uno. He threw his arm up in front of his face, bits of wood and soil flying across him.

"Light help us," Einar said. "I'm trying to stop him, but he's in a circle. A *full circle*. Seventy-two. I've never seen such power before! I—"

A bar of white-hot light cut through the broken dragon, vaporizing it and striking Einar. The man was gone in an instant, and Uno scrambled back, cursing. He ducked away as the wreckage of dragons crashed to the ground around him.

Uno yelled for his men to fall back, whipping them into motion, delaying only long enough to grab a wounded man under the arm and help him away. He no longer questioned the order to retreat from the Heights. It was the finest bloody order any man had ever given!

Logain Ablar released the One Power. He stood beside the Mora, below the Heights, and felt the attacks up above.

Releasing the One Power today was one of the most difficult things he'd ever done. More difficult than the decision to name himself Dragon, more difficult than keeping himself from strangling Taim during their early days together in the Black Tower.

The Power drained out of him, as if his veins had been opened and he was bleeding out across the ground. He took a deep breath. Holding that much of the One Power—that of thirty-nine people in a circle—had been intoxicating. Letting go reminded him of his gentling, when the Power had been stolen from him. When every breath had encouraged him to find a knife and slit his own throat.

He suspected this was his madness: the terror that releasing the One Power would cause him to lose it forever.

"Logain?" Androl asked.

Logain turned his head toward the shorter man and his companions. They were loyal. Logain didn't know why, but they were loyal. The whole lot of them. Fools. Faithful fools.

"Can you feel that?" Androl asked. The others—Canler, Emarin, Jonneth—were staring at the Heights. The Power being released there . . . it was amazing.

"Demandred," Emarin said. "It must be him."

Logain nodded slowly. *Such power . . .* Even one of the Forsaken could not be so strong. He must carry a *sa'angreal* of immense strength.

With such a tool, his thoughts whispered, *no man or woman could ever take the Power from you again.*

Taim had done it, during Logain's imprisonment. Held him captive, shielded, unable to touch the One Power. The attempts to Turn him had been painful, crushing. But being without *saidin* . . .

Strength, he thought, watching that powerful channeling. The lust to be so strong almost drowned out his hatred of Taim.

"For now, we will not engage him," Logain said. "Split yourselves into the prearranged teams." Those would be one woman and five or six men in each team. The woman and two men could form a circle, while the other two offered support. "We will hunt the traitors of the Black Tower."

Pevara, standing at Androl's side, raised an eyebrow. "You mean to go hunting Taim already? Didn't Cauthon want you here to help move men?"

"I've made it clear to Cauthon," Logain said. "I will not spend this battle delivering soldiers around the field. As for orders, we have a directive from the Dragon Reborn himself."

Rand al'Thor had called them his "last" orders for them, a note delivered with a small *angreal* of a man holding a sword. *The Shadow has stolen the seals of the Dark One's prison. Find them. If you can, please find them.*

During their captivity, Androl had heard what he thought was Taim bragging about the seals. It was their only lead. Logain scanned the distance. Their forces were retreating from the Heights. Logain could not see the array of dragons from where he stood, but the thick lines of smoke did not speak well for their safety.

He still gives orders, Logain thought. *Am I inclined to obey them any longer?*

For the chance at revenge on Taim? Yes, he would follow Rand al'Thor's orders. Once he wouldn't have questioned doing so nearly as much. That had been before his captivity and torture.

"Go," Logain said to his Asha'man. "You have read what the Lord Dragon wrote. We must recover the seals at all costs. Nothing is more important than this. We must hope that Taim indeed has them. Watch for signs of men channeling, hunt them, kill them."

It didn't matter if those men channeling were Sharans. The Asha'man would help this battle by removing enemy channelers anyway. They had discussed the tactic earlier. When they sensed channeling from men, they could use gateway jumps to pinpoint where they were, then try to surprise them and attack.

"If you see one of Taim's men," Logain said, "try to capture him so we can pry out of him where Taim has set up his base." He paused. "If we're lucky, the M'Hael himself will be here. Be wary that he might be carrying the seals; it would not do to destroy them in our attack. If you see him, return and bring me word of his location."

Logain's teams moved off. They left him with Gabrelle, Arel Malevin and Karldin Manfor. It was well that at least some of his more skilled men had been absent from the Tower during Taim's betrayal.

Gabrelle looked at Logain with level eyes. "What of Toveine?" she asked.

"We will kill her if we find her."

"It is that simple for you?"

"Yes."

"She—"

"Would you rather live, Gabrelle, if you were she? Live and serve *him*?"

She closed her mouth, lips drawn tight. She still feared him; he could sense that. Good.

Was this what you wished for, his mind whispered, *when you raised the banner of the Dragon? When you sought to save mankind? Did you do it to be feared? Hated?*

He ignored that voice. The only times he had accomplished

anything in life had come when he'd been feared. It was the only edge he'd had against Siuan and Leane. The primal Logain, that something deep inside that drove him to keep living, needed people to fear him.

"Can you sense her?" Gabrelle asked.

"I released the bond."

Her envy was sharp and immediate. It shocked him. He had thought that she was beginning to enjoy, or at least suffer, their place together.

But, of course, it was all an act so that she could try to manipulate him. That was the Aes Sedai way. Yes, he had felt lust from her before, perhaps even affection. He wasn't certain he could trust what he thought he'd felt from her. It seemed that for all he had tried to be strong and free, his strings had been pulled since he'd been a youngling.

Demandred's channeling radiated strength. Such *power*.

A loud boom sounded from the Heights. Logain laughed, throwing his head back. Bodies, like leaves, were thrown off the Heights and into the air.

"Link to me!" he commanded those who remained with him. "Join me in a circle, and let us hunt the M'Hael and his men as well. Light send that I can find him—my table deserves only the finest of meat, the head stag himself!"

And after that . . . Who knew? He had always wanted to test himself against one of the Forsaken. Logain seized the Source again, holding to the thrashings of *saidin* as if it were a serpent writhing and trying to bite him. He used his *angreal* to draw more, and then the Power from the others streamed into him. He laughed louder.

Gawyn felt so tired. This week of preparation would normally have rested him, but he felt today as if he'd hiked for tens of leagues.

There was no helping it. He forced his attention toward the gateway in the table in front of him, overlooking the battlefield. "You're certain they cannot see this?" he asked Yukiri.

"I'm certain," she replied. "It has been tested exhaustively."

She was becoming skilled with these viewing gateways. She

had created this one on top of a table brought through to their camp from Tar Valon. He was looking down at the battleground as he would a map.

"If you have truly made the other side invisible," Egwene said speculatively, "this might be useful indeed . . . "

"It would be easier to spot from up close," Yukiri admitted. "This one is so high in the sky that nobody below will be able to make it out."

Gawyn didn't like Egwene standing there, head and shoulders hanging out over the battlefield. He held his tongue; the gateway was as safe as they could make it. He couldn't protect her from everything.

"Light," Bryne said softly, "they're cutting us to pieces."

Gawyn glanced at him. The man rebuffed suggestions—even strong ones—that he return to his estates. He insisted that he was still capable of holding a sword; he just couldn't be allowed to lead. Besides, he argued, *any* of them could be under Compulsion. In a way, knowing that he was gave them an advantage. At least him they could watch.

And Siuan did, holding to his arm protectively. The only others in the tent were Silviana and Doesine.

The battle was not going well. Cauthon had lost the Heights already—the original plan had been to hold there as long as possible—and the dragons were in pieces. Demandred's attack with the One Power had come far more powerfully than any of them had anticipated. And the other large Trolloc army had arrived from the northeast and were pressing Cauthon's defenders upriver.

"What is he planning?" Egwene said, tapping the side of the table. Distant yells drifted through the opening. "If this keeps up, our armies are going to be surrounded."

"He's trying to bait the trap," Bryne said.

"What kind of trap?"

"It is a guess," Bryne said, "and Light knows, my own assessment cannot be trusted as it once was. It looks like Cauthon is planning to heap everything into one battle, no delaying, no trying to wear the Trollocs down. The way this is going, it will be decided in days. Maybe hours."

"That sounds exactly like something Mat would do," Egwene said, resigned.

"The strength of those weaves," Lelaine said, "that *power* . . . "

"Demandred is in a circle," Egwene said. "Eyewitnesses say a full circle. Something that hasn't been seen since the Age of Legends. And he has a *sa'angreal*. Some of the soldiers saw it—a scepter."

Gawyn watched the fighting far below, his hand on his sword. He could hear men scream as Demandred aimed wave after wave of fire at them.

The Forsaken's voice boomed, suddenly, reaching high into the air. "Where are you, Lews Therin! You were seen at each of the other battlefields in disguise. Are you here, too? Fight me!"

Gawyn's hand tightened on his sword. Soldiers flooded down the southwestern side of the Heights, to cross the ford. A few small groups held on the slopes, and dragoners there—tiny as insects to Gawyn—led the remaining dragons to safety, pulled by mules.

Demandred flung destruction at the fleeing troops. He was an army unto himself, hurling bodies into the air, exploding horses, burning and destroying. Around him, his Trollocs seized the high ground. Their brutish cheers floated through the gateway.

"We're going to have to deal with him, Mother," Silviana said. "Soon."

"He's trying to draw us out," Egwene said. "He has that *sa'angreal*. We could build a circle of seventy-two ourselves, but what then? Fall into his trap? Be slaughtered?"

"What choice have we, Mother?" Lelaine asked. "Light. He's killing thousands."

Killing thousands. And here they stood.

Gawyn stepped back.

Nobody seemed to notice his withdrawal other than Yukiri, who eagerly stepped up and took his place beside Egwene. Gawyn slipped out of the tent, and when the tent guards glanced at him, said he needed some fresh air. Egwene would approve. She sensed how tired he was lately; she'd mentioned it to him several times. His eyelids felt as if they had weights of iron pulling them down. Gawyn looked toward the blackened sky. He could hear the distant booms. How long would he just stand around and do nothing while men died?

You promised, he thought to himself. *You said you were willing to stand in her shadow.*

That didn't mean he had to stop doing important work, did it? He fished in his pouch and took out a ring of the Bloodknives. He put it on, and immediately his strength returned, his exhaustion fleeing.

He hesitated, then took out the other rings and slipped them on as well.

On the south bank of the River Mora, in front of the ruins northeast of Dashar Knob, Tam al'Thor summoned the void as Kimtin had taught him all of those years ago. Tam imagined the single flame, and poured his emotions into it. He grew calm, then the calmness left him, leaving nothing. Like a newly painted wall, beautiful and white, that had just been washed. Everything melted away.

Tam was the void. He drew his bow, the good black yew bending, arrow to his cheek. He took aim, but this was only a formality. When he was this strongly within the void, the arrow would do exactly as he commanded. He didn't *know* this, any more than the sun knew that it would rise or the branches knew that their leaves would fall. These were not things *known*; they were things that *were*.

He released, bowstring snapping, arrow drilling through the air. Another followed, then another. He had five in the air at once, each one aimed in anticipation of the shifting winds.

The first five Trollocs fell as they tried to make their way across one of several of the raft bridges they had managed to place on the river here. Trollocs hated water; even shallow water daunted them. Whatever Mat had done to protect the river upstream, it was working for now, and the river was still flowing. The Shadow would try to stop it. Was *trying* to stop it. Occasionally a Trolloc or mule carcass floated past from far upriver.

Tam continued to launch arrows, Abell and the other Two Rivers men joining him. Sometimes they aimed into the mass, not picking out an individual Trolloc—though that was rare. A regular soldier might shoot unsighted and assume his arrow would find flesh, but not a good Two Rivers archer. Arrows were cheap to soldiers, but not to woodsmen.

Trollocs fell in waves. Beside Tam and the Two Rivers men,

crossbowmen cranked their weapons and loosed wave after wave into the Shadowspawn. Fades behind whipped at the Trollocs, trying to urge them across the river—with little success.

Tam's arrow hit a Fade right where its eyes should have been. Nearby, a large man named Bayrd whistled in appreciation, leaning on his axe and watching the arrows fall. He was part of the group of soldiers set just behind the archers to move in and protect them, once the Trollocs were forced to cross.

Bayrd was one of the mercenary leaders who had drifted into the army, and though he was an Andoran, neither he nor the hundred or so men he led would speak of where they'd come from. "I need to get one of those bows," Bayrd said to his companions. "Burn me, do you *see* that?"

Nearby, Abell and Azi smiled, continuing to shoot. Tam did not smile. There was no humor within the void, though outside of the void, a thought did flutter. Tam knew why Abell and Azi had smiled. Having a Two Rivers bow did not make one into a Two Rivers archer.

"I think," Galad Damodred said from horseback nearby, "that you'd likely do more harm to yourself than to the enemy, should you try to use one of those. Al'Thor, how long?"

Tam released another arrow. "Five more," he said, reaching for the next arrow in his side quiver. He raised it, shot it, then continued. Two, three, four, five.

Five more Trollocs dead. In all, he'd loosed over thirty arrows. He'd missed once, but only because Abell had killed the Trolloc that Tam had aimed for.

"Archers, halt!" Tam yelled.

The Two Rivers men pulled back, Tam releasing the void, as a straggling group of Trollocs stumbled onto the riverbank. Tam still led Perrin's troops, to an extent. Whitecloaks, Ghealdanin and the Wolf Guard all looked to Tam for final say, but each had their own leaders as well. He personally commanded the archers.

Perrin, you'd better heal up strong. When Haral had found the boy lying in the grass on the outskirts of camp the day before, bloodied and near death . . . Light, that had given them all a fright.

Perrin was safely in Mayene, where he would likely spend the rest of the Last Battle. A man didn't quickly recover from the type of wound the lad had taken, even with Aes Sedai Healing. It would probably drive Perrin near mad to miss the fighting, but sometimes that happened. It was part of being a soldier.

Tam and the archers retreated back to the ruins to get a better vantage to watch the battle, and he organized his archers in case they were needed while runners brought them more arrows. Mat had positioned all of Perrin's troops alongside the Dragonsworn, led by Tinna, a statuesque woman. Tam had no idea where she'd come from or why she was in command—she had the bearing of a lady, the build of an Aiel and the coloring of a Saldaean. The others seemed to listen to her. Dragonsworn made little sense to Tam, so he stayed out of their way.

Tam's army had been told to hold. Mat had expected the Sharan and Trolloc attack from the west to be the strongest; therefore Tam was surprised to see Mat sending more reinforcements upriver from the ford. The Whitecloaks were a recent arrival, and their clothing rippled as they charged along the riverbank, cutting through the Trollocs stumbling off their unstable bridges.

Arrows started to fly from the Trollocs on the other bank toward Galad and his men. The clanks and pings of arrowheads on the Whitecloak armor and shields sounded like hail on a roof. Tam ordered Arganda to bring in their foot soldiers, including Bayrd and the mercenaries.

They didn't have enough pikes, so Arganda's men held halberds and spears. Men began to scream and die, Trollocs howling. Near Tam's rearward position, Alliandre came riding up, surrounded by well-armed foot soldiers. Tam raised the bow to her, and she nodded, then settled back to watch. She had wanted to be here for the battle. Tam couldn't blame her, nor could he blame her for ordering her soldiers to carry her off at the first sign that this battle was turning against them.

"Tam! Tam!" Dannil came riding up, and Tam waved for Abell to take command of the archers. He strode over to Dannil, meeting the lad in the shade of the ruins.

Inside those broken walls, Tam's reserves watched the battle with nervousness. Most of them were archers pulled from among the mercenaries and Dragonsworn. Many of that latter group had never been in battle before. Well, neither had most of the Two Rivers men until a few months back. They'd learn quickly.

Hitting a Trolloc with an arrow wasn't so different from hitting a deer.

Though, if you missed the deer, it didn't gut you with a sword a few seconds later.

"What is it, Dannil?" Tam asked. "Word from Mat?"

"He's sending you infantry banners from the Legion of the Dragon," Dannil said. "He says to hold the river here, no matter what."

"What is that boy up to?" Tam said, looking toward the Heights. The Legion of the Dragon had good infantry, well-trained crossbowmen who would be useful here. But what was happening on the Heights?

The flashes of light reflected off columns of thick black smoke, rising from the Heights toward the clouds above. The fighting was in earnest up there.

"I don't know, Tam," Dannil said. "Mat . . . he's changed. I hardly think I know him any longer. He was always a bit of a scoundrel, but now . . . Light, Tam. He's like someone from one of the stories."

Tam grunted. "We've all changed. Mat would probably say similar things about you."

Dannil laughed. "Oh, I doubt that, Tam. Though I do wonder, sometimes, what would have happened if I'd gone with the three of them. I mean, Moiraine Sedai was looking for boys the right age, and I guess I was just a little too old . . ."

He seemed wistful. Dannil could say, and think, what he wanted—but Tam doubted he would have liked to endure the things that had forced Mat, Perrin and Rand to become the people they now were. "Take command of this lot," Tam said, nodding to the reserve archers. "I'll see that Arganda and Galad know we're being reinforced."

Thick Trolloc arrows sprayed around Pevara as she desperately wove Air. Her gust blew away the arrows like stones swept off the board by a furious player. Sweating, she clung to *saidar* and wove a stronger shield of Air, moving it into the sky to defend against further volleys.

"It's safe!" she yelled. "Go!"

A group of soldiers dashed out from underneath an overhang on the steep riverside slope of the Heights. More thick black shafts fell from above. They hit her shield; it slowed them to the point that once they passed through, they dropped as idly as feathers.

The soldiers she'd helped dashed for the rallying point at Hawal Ford. Others decided to stand and fight as Trolloc bands poured down the slopes. Most of the Shadowspawn stayed atop the Heights to secure the position, and finish pushing humans off.

Where? Androl's furious thought came to her, a soft whisper inside her mind.

Here, she sent him. Not completely a thought, more an image, a sense of place.

A gateway split beside her, and he dashed through, Emarin on his heels. Both men carried swords, but Emarin spun and thrust his hand backward, a streak of fire shooting through the open gateway. Screaming sounded from the other side. Human screaming.

"You went all the way to the Sharan army?" Pevara demanded. "Logain wanted us to stay together!"

"So you care about what he wants, now?" Androl asked, grinning.

You're insufferable, she thought. Around them, arrows clattered to the ground. The Trollocs above hooted in anger.

"Nice weave," Androl said.

"Thank you." She glanced at the sword.

"I'm a Warder now." He shrugged. "Might as well look like one, eh?"

He could cut a Trolloc in half with a gateway at three hundred paces, and summon fire from inside Dragonmount itself, and he still wanted to carry a sword. It was, she decided, a male thing.

I heard that, Androl sent her. "Emarin, to me. Pevara Sedai, if you'd graciously agree to accompany us . . ."

She sniffed, but joined the other two as they moved along the southwestern base of the Heights, passing some wounded stumbling toward the rallying point. Androl glanced at them, then wove a gateway back to their camp. The flagging men cried out in surprise and thanks, and shambled through it to safety.

Androl had grown . . . more confident since they had left the

Black Tower. When they'd first met, he'd displayed hesitation about whatever he did. A kind of nervous humility. No more.

"Androl ..." Emarin said, pointing up the slope with his sword.

"I see them," Androl said. Above, Trollocs poured over the top of the Heights like pitch boiling over the side of a pot. Behind, Androl's gateway closed, that group of soldiers safe. Others cried out as they saw it close.

You can't save them all, Pevara thought sternly to Androl, sensing his spike of anguish. *Stay focused on the task at hand.*

The three of them moved through the soldiers, angling toward several channelers they could feel ahead. Jonneth, Canler and Theodrin were there, throwing fire at groups of Trollocs. Their position was being overrun.

"Jonneth, Canler, to me," Androl said, charging past them and opening a gateway in front of him. Pevara and Emarin ducked through after him, finding themselves on the top of the Heights, a few hundred paces away.

Jonneth and the others followed, joining them as the group dashed past a group of startled Trollocs.

"Channeling!" Pevara yelled. Light, but it was hard to run in these skirts. Androl did know that, didn't he?

Androl opened another gateway for them as a few bursts of flame came from the direction of some Sharans atop the Heights. Pevara ran through, beginning to pant. They appeared on the other side of the Sharans, who were firing at where Pevara had been moments before.

Pevara opened her senses, trying to spot—or feel—their quarry. The Sharans turned on them and pointed, but then cried out as Androl brought an avalanche of snow down on them from a gateway to the side. He had tried making those Deathgates that the other Asha'man used, but the weave was apparently just different enough that he had trouble. Instead, he stuck to what he was good at doing.

Groups of Tower Guards still fought atop the Heights, holding ground against orders. Pieces of the dragons, including the large bronze firing tubes, lay smoldering nearby amid burned corpses. Thousands upon thousands of Trollocs howled, most at the edges of the Heights, loosing arrows on those below. Their joyous roars set Pevara on edge, and she wove Earth and sent the flows toward the ground near a group of them. A large chunk of ground trembled, then split off, dumping two dozen Trollocs over the edge.

"We're drawing attention again!" Emarin said, setting ablaze a Myrddraal that had been slinking toward them. It thrashed in the flames, screeching in an inhuman voice, refusing to die. Sweating, Pevara lent her Fire to Emarin's, burning the creature until it was nothing more than bones.

"Well, that's not all bad!" Androl said. "If we draw enough attention, sooner or later, one of the Black Ajah or one of Taim's men will decide to confront us."

Jonneth cursed. "That's a little like jumping into an anthill and waiting to be bitten!"

"Actually, it's a *lot* like that," Androl said. "Keep watch. I'll deal with the Trollocs!"

That's quite a strong assertion, Pevara sent to him.

His answer was warm, like heat off a cooking plate. *It sounded heroic.*

I assume you could use some added strength?

Yes, please, he sent.

She initiated the link. He drew in her strength, taking control of their circle. As always, linking with him was an overwhelming experience. She felt her own emotions bounce back against him and to her again, and that made her blush. Did he sense how she was starting to regard him?

Foolish as a girl in knee-length skirts, she thought at herself—careful to shield her thoughts from him—*barely old enough to know the difference between boys and girls.* And in the middle of a war, too.

She found it hard to steel her emotions—as an Aes Sedai should—while linked with Androl. Their selves mixed, like swirling paints poured in the same bowl. She fought against it, determined to maintain her own identity. This was vital when linking, and she had been taught it time and time again.

Androl flung his hand forward at a group of Trollocs that had begun loosing arrows at him. The gateway went up, consuming the arrows. She glanced about, and found them falling on another group of Trollocs.

Gateways opened in the ground, dropping Trollocs through,

making them appear hundreds of feet in the air. A tiny gateway split the head off a Myrddraal at the neck, leaving it to thrash about, pumping inky blood on the soil. Androl's team stood near the western section of the Heights, where the dragons had once been positioned. There were Shadowspawn and Sharans on all sides.

Androl, channeling! She could feel it, rising above them on the Heights. Something powerful.

Taim! Androl's immediate flare of anger felt as if it would burn her away. In it was the loss of friends, and fury at betrayal by one who should have protected them.

Careful, she sent. *We don't know it's him.*

The one attacking them was in a circle with men and women, otherwise Pevara would not have been able to feel him. Of course, she could only see the weaves of *saidar*. A thick column of air struck at them, fully a pace wide, the heat of it enough to redden the rocky ground beneath.

Androl put a gateway up in time, barely, catching the column of fire and directing it back the way it had come. Twin streams burned Trolloc corpses and caused weeds and patches of grass to burst alight.

Pevara didn't see what happened next. Androl's gateway vanished, as if ripped from him, and an explosion of lightning struck right next to them. Pevara hit the ground in a heap, Androl slamming into her.

In that moment, she let go of herself.

She did it by accident because of the shock of impact. In most cases, the link would have slipped away, but Androl had a powerful grip. The dam holding back Pevara's self from his own broke, and they mixed. It was like stepping through a mirror, then looking back on herself.

She forcibly pulled herself out again, but with an awareness she couldn't describe. *We need to get out of here*, she thought, still linked with Androl. The others all seemed alive, but that would not last long if their enemy brought more lightning. Pevara began the complex weave for a gateway by instinct, though it wouldn't do anything. Androl was leading their circle, so only he—

The gateway snapped open. Pevara gaped. *She'd* done that, not him. This was among the most complex, most difficult and most power-intensive weaves she knew, but she'd done it as easily as waving her hand. While in a circle someone else was leading.

Theodrin stumbled through first. The lithe Domani woman tugged a stumbling Jonneth after her through the gateway. Emarin followed, limping, one arm hanging uselessly at his side.

Androl regarded the gateway, stunned. "I thought you aren't supposed to be able to channel if someone else is leading a circle you are in."

"You aren't," she said. "I did it by accident."

"Accident? But—"

"Through the gateway, you knothead," Pevara said, shoving him toward it. She followed, then collapsed on the other side.

"Damodred, I need you to stay where you are," Mat said. He did not look up, but he heard Galad's horse snort through the open gateway.

"One is led to question your sanity, Cauthon," Galad replied.

Mat finally looked up from his maps. He was not sure he would ever grow accustomed to these gateways. He stood in their command building, the one Tuon had erected in the cleft at the foot of Dashar Knob, and there was a gateway in his wall. Outside it Galad sat his horse wearing the gold and white of the Children of the Light. He was still positioned near the ruins, where a Trolloc army was trying to push its way across the Mora.

Galad Damodred was a man who could have used a few stiff drinks in him. He could have been a statue, with that pretty face and unchanging expression. No, statues had more life.

"You'll do as you're told," Mat said, looking back to his maps. "You are to hold the river up there and do as Tam tells you. I don't care if you think your place isn't important enough."

"Very well," Galad said, voice as cold as a corpse in the snow. He turned his horse away, and Mika the *damane* closed the gateway.

"It's a bloodbath out there, Mat," Elayne said. Light, her voice was colder than Galad's!

"You all put me in charge. Let me do my job."

"We made you commander of the armies," Elayne said. "You are *not* in charge."

Trust an Aes Sedai to argue over every little word. It ... He looked up, frowning. Min had just said something softly to Tuon. "What is it?" he asked.

"I saw his body alone, on a field," Min said, "as if dead."

"Matrim," Tuon said. "I am ... concerned."

"For once we agree," Elayne said from her throne on the other side of the room. "Mat, their general is outmatching you."

"It's not so bloody simple," Mat said, fingers on the maps. "It's never that bloody simple."

The man leading the Shadow *was* good. Very good. *It's Demandred*, Mat thought. *I'm fighting one of the bloody Forsaken.*

Together, Mat and Demandred were composing a grand painting. Each responded to the other's moves with subtle care. Mat was trying to use just a little *too* much red in one of his paints. He wanted to paint the wrong picture, but still a reasonable one.

It was hard. He had to be capable enough to keep Demandred back, but weak enough to invite aggression. A feint, ever so subtle. It was dangerous, possibly disastrous. He had to walk on a razor edge. There was no way to avoid cutting his feet. The question was not whether he would be bloodied, but whether he would reach the other side or not.

"Move in the Ogier," Mat said softly, fingers on the map. "I want them to reinforce the men at the ford." The Aiel fought there, guarding the way as the White Tower's men and the members of the Band of the Red Hand retreated off the Heights per his order.

The command was relayed to the Ogier. *Stay safe, Loial,* Mat thought, making a notation on the map where he had sent the Ogier. "Alert Lan, he's still on the western side of the Heights. I want him to swing around the back of the Heights, now that most of the Shadow's forces are on top, and back toward the Mora, behind the other Trolloc army trying to cross near the ruins. He's not to engage them; just stay out of sight and hold his position."

The messengers ran to do his bidding, and he made another notation. One of the *so'jhin* brought him some *kaf*, the cute one with the freckles. He was too absorbed by the battle to smile at her.

Sipping his *kaf*, Mat had the *damane* make him a gateway on the tabletop so he could see the battlefield itself. He leaned out over it, but kept one hand on the rim of the table. Only a bloody fool would let someone shove him through a hole two hundred feet over the ground.

He set down his *kaf* on a side table and took out his looking glass. The Trollocs were moving down the Heights toward the bogs. Yes, Demandred was good. The hulking beasts he had sent toward the bogs were slow but thick and powerful, like a rock-slide. Also, a group of mounted Sharans were about to ride down from the Heights. Light cavalry. They would hit Mat's troops holding Hawal Ford, and keep them from attacking the Trolloc left flank.

A battle was a swordfight on a grand scale. For every move, there was a counter—often three or four. You responded by moving a squad here, a squad there, trying to counter what your enemy did while putting pressure on him in places where he was thin. Back and forth, back and forth. Mat was outnumbered, but he could use that.

"Relay the following to Talmanes," Mat said, eye still to the looking glass. "'Remember when you bet me I couldn't throw a coin into a cup from across the entire inn?'"

"Yes, Great One," the Seanchan messenger said.

Mat had responded to the bet by saying he would try it once he was drunker—otherwise, there would have been no sport to it. Then Mat had pretended to get drunk, and provoked Talmanes to up the bet from silver to gold.

Talmanes had figured him out and insisted he really drink. *I still owe him a few marks for that, don't I?* Mat thought absently.

He pointed the looking glass to the northern part of the Heights. A group of Sharan heavy cavalry had gathered to move down the slope; he could make out their long, steel-tipped lances.

They were preparing to charge down the slope to intercept Lan's men as they swung around the northern side of the Heights. But the order hadn't even reached Lan yet.

It confirmed Mat's suspicions: Demandred not only had spies in the camp, he had one in or near the command tent. Someone who could send messages as soon as Mat gave orders. That probably meant a channeler, here, inside the tent and masking their ability.

Bloody ashes, Mat thought. *As if this weren't tough enough.*

The messenger returned from Talmanes. "Great One," he said, prostrating himself nose to the floor, "your man says that his forces are completely ruined. He wishes to follow your order, but says that the dragons will not be available for the rest of this day. It will take weeks to repair them. They are ... I'm sorry, Great One, but these were his exact words. They are worse off than a barmaid in Sabinel. I do not know what it means."

"Barmaids there work for tips," Mat said with a grunt, "but people in Sabinel don't tip."

That was, of course, a lie. Sabinel was a town where Mat had tried to make Talmanes help him win over a pair of barmaids. Talmanes had suggested that Mat feign a war wound to get sympathy.

Good man. The dragons could still fight, but they probably looked busted up something good. They had an advantage there; nobody knew how they worked except Mat and Aludra. Bloody ashes, and even he worried that each time one went off it would somehow blow up the wrong way.

Five or six dragons were completely functional; Mat had pulled them through a gateway to safety. Aludra had those set up south of the ford, aimed toward the Heights. Mat would use them, but leave the spy with the impression that the bulk of them had been destroyed. Talmanes could instead patch them up; then Mat could use them again.

But the moment I do, he thought, *Demandred will bring everything he has down on them.* It had to be just the right moment. Bloody ashes, lately his life had been completely *about* trying to find the right moments. He was running out of those kinds of moments. For now, he ordered Aludra to use the half-dozen functional dragons to pound Trollocs across the river who were coming down the southwestern slope of the Heights.

She was far enough away from the Heights, and she would keep moving, so Demandred would have a difficult time pinpointing her and bringing the dragons down. The smoke they made would obscure her position quickly.

"Mat," Elayne said from her throne on the side of the room. He noticed, with amusement, that in shifting it about for "comfort" she had somehow gotten Birgitte to wedge it up a few inches, so she now sat exactly level with Tuon. Maybe an inch higher. "Please. Can you at least explain *some* of what you're doing?"

Not without letting that spy hear, too, he thought, glancing about the room. Who was it? One of the three pairs of *damane* and *sul'dam*? Could a *damane* be a Darkfriend without her *sul'dam* knowing? What about the opposite? That noblewoman with the white streak in her hair looked suspicious.

Or was it one of the many generals? Galgan? Tylee? Banner-General Gerisch? She stood at the side of the room, glaring at him. Honestly. Women. She *did* have a nice backside, but Mat had only mentioned it to be friendly. He was a married man.

The fact was, there were so many people moving about, Mat figured he could have spread millet on the floor and had flour by the end of the day. Supposedly, they were all absolutely trustworthy and incapable of betraying the Empress, might she live forever. Which she would not, if spies kept slipping in.

"Mat?" Elayne said. "Someone else needs to know what you are planning. If you fall, we have to continue your plan."

Well, that was a good enough argument. He'd considered it himself. Assured that his current orders were being followed, he stepped over to Elayne. He glanced about the room, then smiled to the others innocently. They need not know he was suspicious of them.

"Why are you leering at everyone?" Elayne asked softly.

"I'm not bloody leering," Mat said. "Outside. I want to walk and take in some fresh air."

"Knotai?" Tuon asked, standing.

He did not look toward her—those eyes could drill through solid steel. Instead, he casually made his way out of the command building. Elayne and Birgitte followed a few moments later.

"What is this?" Elayne asked softly.

"There are many ears in there," Mat said.

"You suspect a spy inside of the command—"

"Wait," Mat said, taking her arm, pulling her away. He nodded agreeably to some Deathwatch Guards. They grunted in reply. For Deathwatch Guards, that was downright talkative.

"You can speak freely," Elayne said. "I just wove us a ward against eavesdropping."

"Thanks," Mat said. "I want you away from the command post. I'll tell you what I'm doing. If something goes wrong, you'll have to pick another general, all right?"

"Mat," Elayne said, "if you think there's a spy—"

"I know there's a spy," Mat said, "and so I'm going to use the fellow. It's going to work. Trust me."

"Yes, and you're so confident that you've already made a backup plan in case you fail."

He ignored that, nodding to Birgitte. She looked around them idly, watching for anyone who tried to draw too close.

"How good are you at cards, Elayne?" Mat asked.

"At . . . Mat, this isn't the time for gambling."

"It's the *exact* time for gambling. Elayne, do you see how badly we're outnumbered? Do you *feel* the ground when Demandred attacks? We're lucky he didn't decide to Travel directly to the command post here and attack us—I suspect he's afraid that Rand is hiding here somewhere, and he'll get ambushed. But blood and bloody ashes, he's *strong*. Without a gamble, we're dead. Finished. Buried."

She grew silent.

"Here's the thing about cards," Mat said, holding up a finger. "Cards aren't like dice. In dice, you want to win as many throws as possible. Lots of throws, lots of wins. It's random, see? But not cards. In cards, you need to make the other fellows start betting. Betting well. You do that by letting them win a little. Or a lot.

"That's not so hard here, since we're outnumbered and over-whelmed. The only way to win is to bet everything on the right hand. In cards, you can lose ninety-nine times but come out ahead if you win that right hand. So long as the enemy starts gambling recklessly. So long as you can ride the losses."

"And that's what you're doing?" Elayne asked. "You're faking that we're losing?"

"Bloody ashes, no," Mat said. "I can't fake that. He'd see through it. I *am* losing, but I'm also watching. Holding back for that last bet, the one that could win it all."

"So when do we move?"

"When the right cards come along," Mat said. He raised his hand, stilling her objection. "I'll know, Elayne. I just will *bloody* know. That's all I can say."

She folded her arms above her swollen belly. Light, it seemed bigger every day. "Fine. What are your plans for Andor's forces?"

"I already have Tam and his men committed along the river at the ruins," Mat said. "As for the rest of your armies, I'd like you to go help at the ford. Demandred is probably counting on those Trollocs north of here to cross the river and herd our defenders downriver on the Shienaran side while the rest of the Trollocs and the Sharans come off the Heights to push us back across the ford and upriver.

"They'll try to squeeze us tight, envelop us, and that will be that. Only, Demandred sent a force up the Mora to stop the river from flowing, and it's going to succeed very soon. We'll see if there's a way to make that work for us. But once the river's gone, we'll need a solid defense in place to stop the Trollocs when they try to surge over the riverbed. That's what your forces are for."

"We'll go," Elayne said.

"We?" Birgitte barked.

"I'm riding with my troops," Elayne said, walking toward the horselines. "It's increasingly obvious that I won't be able to do anything here, and Mat wants me away from the command position. I'll bloody go, then."

"Into *battle*?" Birgitte said.

"We're already in battle, Birgitte," Elayne said. "The Sharan channelers could have ten thousand men assaulting Dashar Knob, and this cleft, in minutes. Come. I promise I'll let you put so many Guards around me that I won't be able to sneeze without spraying a dozen of them."

Birgitte sighed, and Mat gave her a consoling look. She nodded farewell to him, then walked off with Elayne.

All right, Mat thought, turning back toward the command building. Elayne was doing what she had to, and Talmanes had caught his signal. Now the real challenge.

Could he coax Tuon into doing what he wanted?

Galad led the cavalry of the Children of the Light in a sweeping attack along the Mora, near the ruins. The Trollocs had constructed more raft bridges here, and bodies floated as thick as autumn leaves on a pond. The archers had done their work well.

Those Trollocs that finally crossed now had the Children to contend with. Galad leaned in low, lance held firmly, as he split the neck of a hulking, bear-faced Trolloc; he continued forward, lance tip streaming blood, the Trolloc falling to its knees behind him.

He guided his mount Sidama into the mass of Trollocs, knocking them down or causing them to leap out of the way. The power of a cavalry charge was in numbers, and those Galad forced aside could be trampled by the horses following him.

After his charge came a volley from Tam's men, who launched arrows into the main body of Trollocs as they stumbled onto the banks of the river. Those behind pushed over them, trampling the wounded.

Golever and several other Children joined Galad as their charge—which swept lengthwise across the front rank of Trollocs—ran out of enemies. He and his men reared and turned, lances up, galloping back to locate small groups of men separated and fighting alone.

The battlefield here was enormous. Galad spent the better part of an hour hunting out such groups, rescuing them and ordering them to the ruins so that Tam or one of his captains could form them into new banners. Slowly, as their numbers dwindled, original formations became mixed with one another. Mercenaries were not the only ones who now rode with the Children. Galad had Ghealdanin, Winged Guardsmen and a couple of Warders under his command. Kline and Alix. Both had lost their Aes Sedai. Galad didn't expect those two to last long, but they were fighting with terrible ferocity.

After sending another group of survivors back toward the ruins, Galad brought Sidama down to a slow walk, listening to the horse's labored breath. This field beside the river had become a bloody churn of bodies and mud. Cauthon had been right to leave the Children in position here. Perhaps Galad gave the man too little credit.

"How long have we been fighting, would you say?" Golever asked from beside him. The other Child's tabard had been ripped free, exposing his mail. A section of links along the right side had been crushed by a Trolloc blade. The mail had held, but the stain of blood there indicated that many of the links had been driven through Golever's quilted gambeson and into his side. The bleeding didn't look bad, so Galad said nothing.

"We've hit midday," Galad guessed, though he could not see

the sun for the clouds. He was reasonably certain they'd been fighting for four or five hours now.

"Think they'll stop for the night?" Golever asked.

"Doubtful," Galad said. "If this battle lasts that long."

Golever looked at him with concern. "You think—"

"I cannot follow what is happening. Cauthon sent so many troops up here, and he pulled everyone off the Heights, from what I can tell. I don't know why. And the water in the river . . . does it seem to be flowing in fits and spurts to you? The struggle upstream must be going poorly . . ." He shook his head. "Perhaps if I could see more of the battlefield, I could understand Cauthon's plan."

He was a soldier. A soldier need not understand the whole of the battle in order to follow his orders. However, Galad was usually able to at least piece together his side's strategy from commands given.

"Have you ever imagined a battle this large?" Golever asked, turning his head. Arganda's infantry was crashing into the Trollocs at the river. More and more of the Shadowspawn were getting across—with alarm, Galad realized that the river had stopped flowing completely.

The Shadowspawn had gotten a footing in the last hour. It was going to be a tough fight, but at least the numbers were more even now, with all the Trollocs they had killed earlier. Cauthon had known the river would stop flowing. That was why he'd sent so many troops up here, to stem this onslaught from the other side.

Light, Galad thought, *I'm watching the Game of Houses on the battlefield itself.* Yes, he had not given Cauthon nearly enough credit.

A lead ball with a red streamer suddenly fell from the sky about twenty paces ahead, hitting a dead Trolloc in the skull. Far overhead, the *raken* screeched and continued on its way. Galad heeled Sidama forward, and Golever climbed down to fetch the letter for him. Gateways were useful, but *raken* could see the battlefield in its expanse, search out banners for specific men and deliver orders.

Golever handed him the letter, and Galad pulled his list of ciphers from the leather envelope he carried in the top of his boot. The ciphers were simple—a list of numbers with words beside them. If orders didn't use the right word and the right number together, then they were suspect.

Damodred, the orders read, *bring yourself and a dozen of the best men from your twenty-second company and move along the river toward Hawal Ford. Stop when you can see Elayne's banner and hold there for more orders. P.S. If you see any Trollocs with quarterstaffs, I suggest you let Golever fight them instead, as I know you have trouble with those types. Mat.*

Galad sighed, showing the letter to Golever. The cipher authenticated it; the number twenty-two and the word "quarterstaff" were paired.

"What does he want of us?" Golever asked.

"I wish I knew," Galad said. He really did.

"I'll go gather some men," Golever said. "I assume you'll want Harnesh, Mallone, Brokel . . ." He continued through an entire list.

Galad nodded. "A good list. Well, I can't say I'm sad for this order. My sister has entered the field, it appears. I would keep watch on her." Beyond that, he wanted to look over another section of the battlefield. Perhaps that would help him understand what Cauthon was doing.

"As you order, Lord Captain Commander," Golever said.

The Dark One attacked.

It was an attempt to tear Rand apart, to destroy him bit by bit. The Dark One sought to claim the very elements that made up Rand's essence, then annihilate them.

Rand couldn't gasp, couldn't cry out. This attack wasn't at his body, for he had no true body in this place, just a memory of one.

Rand held himself together. With difficulty. In the face of this awesome attack, any notion of defeating the Dark One—of killing him—vanished. Rand couldn't defeat anything. He could barely hold on.

He could not have described the sensation if he'd tried. It was as if the Dark One was shredding him while at the same time trying to crush him entirely, coming at Rand from infinite directions, all at once, in a wave.

Rand fell to his knees. It was a projection of himself that did so, but it felt real to him.

An eternity passed.

Rand suffered it. The crushing pressure, the noise of destruction. He weathered it on his knees, fingers taut like claws, sweat streaming from his brow. He suffered it and looked up.

"That is all you have?" Rand growled.

I WILL WIN.

"You made me strong," Rand said, voice ragged. "Each time you or your minions tried to destroy me, your failure was like the blacksmith's hammer beating against metal. This attempt . . ." Rand took a deep breath. "This attempt of yours is nothing. I will not break."

YOU MISTAKE. THIS IS NOT AN ATTEMPT TO DESTROY YOU. THIS IS PREPARATION.

"For what?"

TO SHOW YOU TRUTH.

Fragments of the Pattern . . . threads . . . suddenly spun before Rand, splitting from the main body of light like hundreds of tiny flowing streams. He knew this was not actually the Pattern, no more than what he saw as himself was actually his body. In interpreting something so vast as the fabric of creation, his mind needed some kind of imagery. This was what his consciousness chose.

The threads spun, not unlike threads in a weave of the One Power, only there were thousands upon thousands of them, and the colors were more varied, more vibrant. Each was straight, like a string pulled taut. Or a beam of light.

They came together like the product of a loom, creating a vision around him. A ground of slimy soil, plants speckled with black, trees with limbs that drooped like arms bereft of strength.

It became a place. A *reality*. Rand pushed himself to his feet, and could feel the soil. He could smell smoke in the air. Could hear . . . moans of sorrow. Rand turned, and found that he was on a mostly barren slope above a dark city with black stone walls. Buildings huddled inside, squat and dull, like bunkers.

"What is this?" Rand whispered. Something about the place felt familiar. He looked up, but could not see the sun for the clouds that dominated the sky.

IT IS WHAT WILL BE.

Rand felt for the One Power, but drew back in revulsion. The taint had returned, but it was worse—far worse. Where it had once been a dark film on the molten light of *saidin*, it was now a sludge so thick that he could not pierce it. He would have to drink in the darkness, envelop himself in it, to seek out the One Power beneath—if, indeed, it was even still there. The mere thought made bile rise in his throat, and he had to fight to keep his stomach from emptying.

He was drawn toward that fortress nearby. Why did he feel he knew this place? He was in the Blight; the plants made that clear. If that wasn't enough, he could smell rot in the air. The heat was like that of a bog in the summer—sweltering, oppressive despite the clouds.

He walked down the shallow hillside, and caught sight of some figures working nearby. Men with axes, hacking at trees. There were maybe a dozen of them. As Rand approached, he glanced to the side, and saw the nothing that was the Dark One in the distance, consuming part of the landscape, like a pit on the horizon. A reminder that what Rand was seeing wasn't real?

He passed stumps of cut trees. Were the men gathering firewood? The *thock, thock* of axes—and the postures of the workers—had none of the steadfast strength Rand associated with woodsmen. The beats were lethargic, the men working with slumped shoulders.

That man on the left ... As Rand grew closer, he recognized him, despite the bent posture and wrinkled skin. Light. Tam had to be at least seventy, perhaps eighty. Why was he out working so hard?

It's a vision, Rand thought. *A nightmare. The Dark One's own creation. Not real.*

Yet, while standing within it, Rand found it difficult not to react as if this were indeed real. And it was, after a fashion. The Dark One used shadowed threads of the pattern—the *possibilities* that rippled from creation like waves from a dropped pebble in a pond—to create this.

"Father?" Rand asked.

Tam turned, but his eyes didn't focus on Rand.

Rand took Tam by the shoulder. "Father!"

Tam stood dully for a moment, then went back to his work, raising his axe. Nearby, Dannil and Jori hacked at a stump. They had aged as well, and were now men well into their middle years. Dannil seemed sick with something awful, his face pale, his skin having broken out in some kind of sores.

Jori's axe bit deep into the bitter earth, and a black flood seeped from the soil—insects that had been hiding at the base of the stump. The blade had pierced their lair.

The insects swarmed out and sped up the handle to cover Jori. He screamed, batting at them, but his open mouth let them climb inside. Rand had heard of such a thing, a deathswarm, one of the many dangers of the Blight. He raised a hand toward Jori, but the man slumped to the side, dead as quickly as a man could draw breath.

Tam yelled in horror and broke away, running. Rand spun as his father crashed into a thicket of brush nearby, trying to flee the deathswarm. Something jumped from a branch, quick as a snapping whip, and wrapped around Tam's neck, jerking him to a halt.

"No!" Rand said. It wasn't real. He still couldn't watch his father die. He seized the Source, punching through the sickly darkness of the taint. It seemed to suffocate him, and Rand spent an excruciating time trying to find *saidin*. When he did grasp it, only a trickle came through.

He wove anyway, roaring, sending a ribbon of flame to kill the vine that had grabbed his father. Tam dropped from its grip as the vines writhed, dying.

Tam didn't move. His eyes stared upward, dead.

"No!" Rand turned on the deathswarm. He destroyed it with a weave of Fire. Only seconds had passed, but all that remained of Jori was bones.

The insects popped as he burned them.

"A channeler," Dannil breathed, cowering nearby, eyes wide as he looked at Rand. Others of the woodsmen had fled into the wilderness. Rand heard several scream.

Rand could not stop himself from retching. The taint . . . it was so awful, so *putrid*. He could not hold to the Source any longer.

"Come," Dannil said, and grabbed Rand's arm. "Come, I need you!"

"Dannil," Rand croaked, standing up. "You don't recognize me?"

"Come," Dannil repeated, towing Rand toward the fortress.

"I'm Rand. Rand, Dannil. The Dragon Reborn."

No understanding shone in Dannil's eyes.

"What has he done to you?" Rand whispered.

THEY DO NOT KNOW YOU, ADVERSARY. I HAVE REMADE THEM. ALL THINGS ARE MINE. THEY WILL NOT KNOW THAT THEY LOST. THEY WILL KNOW NOTHING BUT ME.

"I deny you," Rand whispered. "I *deny* you."

DENYING THE SUN DOES NOT MAKE IT SET. DENYING ME DOES NOT PREVENT MY VICTORY.

"Come," Dannil said, towing Rand. "Please. You must save me!"

"End this," Rand said.

END IT? THERE ARE NO ENDINGS, ADVERSARY. IT IS. I HAVE CREATED IT.

"You imagine it."

"Please," Dannil said.

Rand allowed himself to be pulled along toward the dark fortress. "What were you doing out there, Dannil?" Rand demanded. "Why gather wood in the Blight itself? It isn't safe."

"It was our punishment," Dannil whispered. "Those who fail our master are sent out and told to bring back a tree they have cut down with their own hands. If the deathswarms or the twigs don't get you, the sound of cutting wood draws other things . . . "

Rand frowned as they stepped onto a road leading to the town and its dark fortress. Yes, this place *was* familiar. *The Quarry Road*, Rand thought with surprise. *And that ahead* . . . The fortress dominated what had once been the Green at the center of Emond's Field.

The Blight had consumed the Two Rivers.

The clouds overhead seemed to push down on Rand, and he heard Jori's screams in his head. He again saw Tam struggling as he was strangled.

It isn't real.

This was what would happen if Rand failed. So many people depended on him . . . so many. Some, he had already failed. He had to fight to keep from going over in his head the list of those who had died in his service. Even if he saved others, he had failed to protect these.

It was an attack of a different kind from the one that had tried to destroy his essence. Rand felt it, the Dark One forcing his tendrils into Rand, infecting his mind with worry, doubt, fear.

Dannil led him to the walls of the village where a pair of Myrddraal in unmoving cloaks guarded the gates. They slid forward. "You were sent to gather wood," one whispered with too-white lips.

"I . . . I brought this one!" Dannil said, stumbling away. "A gift for our master! He can channel. I found him for you!"

Rand growled, then plunged toward the One Power again, swimming in filth. He reached the trickle of *saidin*, seizing it.

It was immediately knocked from his grasp. A shield slid between him and the Source.

"It isn't real," he whispered as he turned to see who had channeled.

Nynaeve strode through the city gates, dressed in black. "A wilder?" she asked. "Undiscovered? How did he survive this long? You have done well, Dannil. I give you back your life. Do not fail again."

Dannil wept for joy, then scrambled past Nynaeve into the city.

"It isn't real," Rand said as Nynaeve tied him in weaves of Air, then dragged him into the Dark One's version of Emond's Field, the two Myrddraal rushing in ahead of her. It was a large city now. The houses had the feel of mice clustered together before a cat, each one of the same, uniform dullness. People scuttled through alleyways, eyes down.

People scattered before Nynaeve, sometimes calling her "mistress." Others named her Chosen. The two Myrddraal sped through the city, like shadows. When Rand and Nynaeve reached the fortress, a small group had gathered in the courtyard. Twelve people—Rand could sense that the four men in the group held *saidin*, though he only recognized Damer Flinn from among them. A couple of the women were girls he had known in the Two Rivers.

Thirteen of them. And thirteen Myrddraal, gathering beneath that clouded sky. For the first time since the start of the vision, Rand felt fear. Not this. Anything but this.

What if they Turned him? This wasn't real, but it was a version of reality. A mirror world, created by the Dark One. What would it do to Rand if they Turned him here? Had he been trapped that easily?

He began to struggle, panicked, against the bonds of Air. It was useless, of course.

"You *are* an interesting one," Nynaeve said, turning to him. She didn't look a day older than when he had left her in the cavern, but there were other differences. She wore her hair in a braid again, but her face was leaner, more ... harsh. And those eyes.

The eyes were all wrong.

"How did you survive out there?" she asked him. "How did you go undiscovered so long?"

"I come from a place where the Dark One does not rule."

Nynaeve laughed. "Ridiculous. A tale for children. The Great Lord has always ruled."

Rand could see it. His connection to the Pattern, the glimmering of half-truths and shadowed ways. This possibility ... it could happen. It was one path the world could take. The Dark One, here, had won the Last Battle and broken the Wheel of Time.

That had allowed him to remake it, to spin the pattern in a new way. Everyone alive had forgotten the past, and now knew only what the Dark One had inserted in their minds. Rand could read the truth, the history of this place, in the threads of the Pattern he had touched earlier.

Nynaeve, Egwene, Logain and Cadsuane were now members of the Forsaken, Turned to the Shadow against their will. Moiraine had been executed for being too weak.

Elayne, Min, Aviendha ... they had been given over to torture, endlessly, at Shayol Ghul.

The world was a living nightmare. Each member of the Forsaken ruled as a despot over their own little section of the world. An endless autumn played out as they threw armies, Dreadlords, and factions against one another. An eternal battle.

The Blight had extended to every ocean. Seanchan was no more, ruined and scorched until not even rats and crows could survive there. Anyone who could channel was discovered as a youth and Turned. The Dark One did not like the risk that some-one would bring hope back to the world.

And nobody ever would.

Rand screamed as the thirteen began to channel.

"This is your worst?" Rand yelled.

They pressed their wills against his own. He felt them, like nails being pounded into his skull, parting his flesh. He pushed back with everything he had, but the others started a thrumming pressure. Each thump, like the chop of an axe, came closer and closer to boring into him.

AND SO I WIN.

The failure hit Rand hard—the knowledge that what hap-pened here was his fault. Nynaeve, Egwene, Turned to the Shadow because of him. Those he loved, becoming playthings for the Shadow.

Rand should have protected them.

I WIN. AGAIN.

"You think I am the same youth that Ishamael tried so hard to frighten?" Rand shouted, fighting down his terror and shame.

THE FIGHT IS OVER.

"*IT HAS NOT YET BEGUN!*" Rand screamed.

The reality around him shattered again into ribbons of light. Nynaeve's face shredded, coming apart like lace with a loose thread. The ground disintegrated, and the fortress ceased to exist.

Rand dropped from bands of Air that had never been com-pletely there. The reality the Dark One had created, fragile, unwove into its component parts. Threads of light spiraled out, quivering like the strings of a harp.

They waited to be woven.

Rand drew breath, deeply, through his teeth and looked up at the darkness beyond the threads. "I will not sit passively and suffer it this time, Shai'tan. I will not be captive to your night-mares. I have become something greater than I once was."

Rand seized those threads spinning about him, taking them—hundreds upon hundreds of them. There was no Fire, Air, Earth, Water or Spirit here . . . these were somehow more base, somehow more varied. Each one was individual, unique. Instead of Five Powers, there were thousands.

Rand took them, gathered them and in his hand held the fabric of creation itself.

Then he channeled it, spinning it into a different possibility.

"Now," Rand said, breathing deeply, trying to banish the horror of what he had seen. "Now I will show *you* what is going to happen."

Bryne bowed. "The men are in position, Mother."

Egwene took a deep breath. Mat had sent the White Tower's forces across the dry riverbed below the ford and around the western side of the bogs; it was time for Egwene to join them. She hesitated for a moment, looking through the gateway to Mat's command post. Egwene met the eyes of the Seanchan woman across the table, where she sat imperiously on her throne.

I have not finished with you, Egwene thought.

"Let's go," she said, turning, waving for Yukiri to close the gateway to Mat's building. She fingered Vora's *sa'angreal*, held in one hand as she strode out of her tent.

She hesitated when she saw something there. Something slight, on the ground. Tiny spiderweb cracks in the rocks. She bent down.

"There are more and more of those around, Mother," Yukiri said, stooping down beside her. "We think that when Dreadlords channel, the cracks can spread. Particularly if balefire is used . . ."

Egwene felt them. Though they seemed like ordinary cracks to the touch, they looked down into pure nothing. Blackness, far too deep for simple cracks to have caused through shadows of the light.

She wove. All five powers, together, testing at the cracks. Yes . . .

She wasn't certain exactly what she did, but the fledgling weave covered the cracks like a bandage. The darkness faded, leaving behind only ordinary cracks—and a thin film of crystals.

"Interesting," Yukiri said. "What was that weave?"

"I don't know," Egwene said. "It felt right. Gawyn, have you . . ." She trailed off.

Gawyn.

Egwene stood up with a start. She vaguely remembered him

leaving her command tent for some air. How long ago had it been? She turned around slowly, sensing where he was. The bond let her tell his direction. She stopped when she was pointing toward him.

She was looking toward the riverbed, just up from the ford, where Mat had positioned Elayne's forces.

Oh, Light . . .

"What?" Silviana asked.

"Gawyn has gone to fight," Egwene said, keeping her voice calm with effort. That wool-headed idiot of a man! Could he not wait an hour or two until her armies were in position? She knew that he was eager to fight, but he should have at least asked!

Bryne groaned softly.

"Send someone to fetch him," Egwene said. Now her voice *was* cold, angry. She could not make it otherwise. "He has apparently joined the Andoran armies."

"I will do it," Bryne said, one hand on his sword, his other arm raised toward one of the grooms. "I cannot be trusted to lead armies. At least I can do this."

It made sense. "Take Yukiri with you," she said. "Once you've found my fool Warder, Travel to us west of the bogs."

Bryne bowed, then retreated. Siuan watched him, hesitant.

"You may go with him," Egwene said.

"Is that where you need me?" Siuan asked.

"Actually . . ." Egwene lowered her voice. "I want someone to join Mat and the Seanchan Empress and listen with ears accustomed to hearing what is not spoken."

Siuan nodded, approval—even pride—in her expression. Egwene was Amyrlin; she had no need of either emotion from Siuan, and yet it lifted a little of her grinding fatigue.

"You look amused," Egwene said.

"When Moiraine and I set out to find the boy," Siuan said, "I had no idea the Pattern would send you to us as well."

"Your replacement?" Egwene said.

"As a queen ages," Siuan said, "she begins to think about her legacy. Light, every goodwife probably starts to think the same things. Will she have an heir to hold what she has created? As a woman grows in wisdom, she realizes that what she alone can accomplish pales compared to what her legacy can achieve.

"Well, I suppose I can't claim you entirely as my own, and I wasn't exactly pleased to be succeeded. But it is . . . comforting to know I've had a hand in shaping what is to come. And if a woman were to wish for a legacy, she could not dream of greater than one such as you. Thank you. I'll watch this Seanchan woman for you, maybe help poor Min crawl out of the fangfish net she's found herself in."

Siuan moved away, calling for Yukiri to make her a gateway before going with Bryne. Egwene smiled, watching her give the general a kiss. Siuan. Kissing a man in the open.

Silviana channeled, and Egwene climbed into Daishar's saddle as a gateway opened for them. She embraced the Source, holding Vora's *sa'angreal* before her, and trotted through behind a group of Tower Guards. She was immediately assaulted by the scent of smoke.

High Captain Chubain waited for her on the other side. The dark-haired man had always struck her as being too young for his position, but she supposed not every commander had to be silvered like Bryne. After all, they were entrusting this battle to someone only a bit older than she, and she herself was the youngest Amyrlin ever.

Egwene turned toward the Heights and found that she could barely see them through fires that were burning along the slope and the eastern edge of the bogs.

"What happened?" she asked.

"Flaming arrows," Chubain said, "fired by our forces at the river. I thought Cauthon was mad at first, but I can see his reasoning now. He fired at the Trollocs to set the fields alight there on the Heights and at their base to give us cover. The undergrowth over there is dry and brittle as tinder. The fires drove the Trollocs and Sharan cavalry back up the slope for the time being. And I think Cauthon is counting on the smoke masking our movement around the bogs."

The Shadow would know someone was moving over here, but how many troops and in what configuration . . . they would have to rely on scouts, rather than their superior vantage atop the Heights.

"Our orders?" Chubain said.

"He didn't tell you?" Egwene asked.

He shook his head. "He just put us in position here."

"We continue on up the west side of the bog and come at the Sharans from behind," she said.

Chubain grunted. "This is fragmenting our forces a great deal. And now he assaults them on the Heights after relinquishing it to them?"

She didn't have an answer to that. Well, she had been the one—essentially—to put Mat in charge. She spared a glance across the bogs again, toward where she sensed Gawyn. He would be fighting at the . . .

Egwene hesitated. Her previous position had let her sense Gawyn in the direction of the river, but after moving through the gateway, she had a better sense of his position. He *wasn't* at the river with Elayne's armies.

Gawyn was on the Heights themselves, where the Shadow held the strongest.

Oh, Light! she thought. *Gawyn . . . What are you doing?*

Gawyn strode through smoke. Black tendrils of it curled around him, and the heat of smoldering grass warmed his boots, but the fire had mostly burned out here atop the Heights, leaving the ground dark with ash.

Bodies and some broken dragons lay blackened, like heaps of slag or coal. Gawyn knew that sometimes, to renew a field, farmers would burn the previous year's weeds. The world itself was alight now. As he slipped through the twisting black smoke—his kerchief wetted and tied across his face—he prayed for a renewal.

There were spiderweb cracks all over the ground. The Shadow was destroying this land.

Most of the Trollocs were gathering on the Heights overlooking Hawal Ford, though a handful busied themselves prodding at bodies on the slope. Perhaps they had been drawn by the scent of burning flesh. A Myrddraal emerged from the smoke and began scolding them in a language Gawyn did not understand. It lashed a whip at the Trollocs' backs.

Gawyn froze in place, but the Halfman did not notice him. It drove the stragglers toward where the rest of the Trollocs had gathered. Gawyn waited, breathing softly through his handkerchief, feeling the shadows of the Bloodknives wreathe him. The three rings had done things to him. He felt heady, and his limbs moved too quickly when he stepped. It had taken time to grow accustomed to the changes, to keep his balance each time he moved.

A wolf-featured Trolloc rose up from behind a nearby pile of rubble and sniffed the air, looking after the Fade. The Trolloc then crept out of hiding, a corpse thrown over its shoulder. It walked past Gawyn, passing not five feet away, where it paused and sniffed the air again. Then, hunching low, it continued. The body it carried over its shoulder trailed the cloak of a Warder. Poor Symon. He would never play another hand of cards. Gawyn growled softly, and before he could stop himself, leaped forward. He moved into Kissing the Adder, spinning and relieving the Trolloc's shoulders of its head.

The carcass crashed down to the ground. Gawyn stood with sword out, then cursed himself, crouching and moving back into the smoke. It would mask his scent, and the twisting blackness his blurred form. Fool, to risk exposing himself to kill one Trolloc. Symon's corpse would end up in a cookpot anyway. Gawyn couldn't kill the entire army. He was here for one man.

Gawyn crouched, waiting to see if his attack had been noticed. Perhaps they wouldn't have been able to see him—he wasn't certain how much the rings clouded him—but anyone watching would have seen the Trolloc fall.

No warning call. Gawyn rose and continued. Only then did he notice that his fingers were showing red among the black of the ash. He had burned them. The pain was distant. The rings. He had difficulty thinking straight, but that didn't—fortunately— stop his ability to fight. If anything, his instincts were stronger now.

Demandred. Where was Demandred? Gawyn sped back and forth across the top of the Heights. Cauthon had troops stationed at the river near the ford, but the smoke made it impossible to see who was involved. On the other side, the Borderlanders were engaged with a Sharan cavalry unit. Yet here, on top, it was peaceful, despite the presence of Shadowspawn and Sharans. Now Gawyn crept along the back lines of the Shadowspawn, keeping to the rougher patches of deadwood and weeds. Nobody seemed to notice him. There were shadows here, and shadows were protection. Down below, in the corridor between Heights and bog, the fires were going out. That seemed too quick for them to have burned themselves out. Channeling?

He had intended to find Demandred by seeking the origin of the man's attacks, but if he was just channeling to put out fires, then—

The Shadow's army charged, racing down the slope toward Hawal Ford. Though the Sharans remained behind, the bulk of the Trollocs moved. They obviously intended to push over the now-dry riverbed and engage Cauthon's army.

If Cauthon had intended to lure all of Demandred's forces off the Heights, he had failed. Many Sharans remained behind, infantry and cavalry units, watching impassively as the Trollocs thundered toward battle.

Explosions pounded along the slope, throwing Trollocs into the air like dirt from a beaten rug. Gawyn hesitated, crouching low. Dragons, the few working ones. Mat had set them up somewhere across the river; it was difficult to see an exact position because of the smoke. By the sound, there were only half a dozen or so, but the damage they caused was enormous, particularly considering the distance.

A burst of red light from nearby atop the Heights launched toward the smoke of the dragons. Gawyn smiled. *Thank you kindly.* He put his hand on his sword. Time to test just how well these rings worked.

He dashed, low and quick, out of cover. Most of the Trollocs were piling down the slope, loping toward the dry riverbed. Crossbow bolts and arrows assaulted them, and another round of dragon fire came from a slightly different location. Cauthon had the dragons moving, and Demandred had trouble pinpointing them.

Gawyn ran between howling Shadowspawn. The ground thumped like a beating heart from the impacts along the ground behind him. Smoke whipped around him, thick in his throat. His hands had been blackened, and he assumed his face had been as well. He hoped that would help keep him hidden.

Trollocs turned about, screeching or grunting, but none of them fixed upon him. They knew something had passed, but to them, he was merely a blur.

Egwene's anger poured through the bond. Gawyn smiled. He had not expected her to be pleased. As he ran, arrows slicing the earth around him, he found peace with his choice. Once, perhaps, he would have done this for the pride of the battle and the chance to pit himself against Demandred.

That was not his heart now. His heart was the need. Someone had to fight this creature, someone had to kill him or they would lose this battle. They could all see it. Risking Egwene or Logain would be too great a gamble.

Gawyn could be risked. No one would send him to do this— no one would dare—but it was necessary. He had a chance to change things, to really *matter*. He did it for Andor, for Egwene, for the world itself.

Ahead, Demandred bellowed his now familiar challenge. "Send me al'Thor, not these so-called dragons!" Another streak of fire flew from him.

Gawyn passed the charging Trollocs and came up behind a large group of Sharans with strange bows, almost as big as those of the Two Rivers. They surrounded a mounted man in inter-linking armor of coins, bound at holes in the centers, with a gorget and armguards. The faceplate on his fearsome helmet was open. That proud face was eerily familiar to Gawyn, handsome and imperious.

This will have to be quick, Gawyn thought. *And Light, I'd better not give him a chance to channel.*

The Sharan archers stood at the ready, but only two of them turned as Gawyn slipped between them. Gawyn pulled his knife from his belt sheath. He'd have to drag Demandred off his horse, then go for the face with his knife. It felt like a coward's attack, but it was the best way. Trip him, and Gawyn could—

Demandred spun, suddenly, and looked toward Gawyn. A second later, the man thrust his hand forward, and a beam of white-hot fire—thin as a twig—shot for Gawyn.

It missed, striking just beside Gawyn as he leaped away. Cracks opened all across the ground nearby. Deep, black cracks, that seemed to open into eternity itself.

Gawyn leaped forward, cutting at Demandred's saddle. So *fast*. These rings let him react while Demandred was still staring in confusion.

The saddle came off and Gawyn rammed his knife into the horse's side. The beast screamed and reared, throwing Demandred backward, saddle and all.

Gawyn leaped, bloodied knife out, as the horse bolted and the Sharan archers cried out. He loomed over Demandred, knife raised in two hands.

The Forsaken's body suddenly jolted, and the man was pushed to the side. Wind blew about the blackened ground, raising flakes of ash, as weaves of Air caught Demandred and spun him about, depositing him on his feet with a clink, sword unsheathed. The Forsaken crouched, and released another weave—Gawyn felt air spinning next to him, as if threads of it had tried to grab him. He was too quick, and Demandred obviously had trouble hitting him because of the rings.

Gawyn backed away and switched his knife to his off hand, unsheathing his sword in his right.

"So," Demandred said, "an assassin. And Lews Therin always spoke of the 'honor' of facing a man face-to-face."

"I wasn't sent by the Dragon Reborn."

"With Night's Shade surrounding you, a weave that none from this Age remember? Do you know that what Lews Therin has done to you will leak your life away? You are dead, little man."

"Then you can join me in the grave," Gawyn said.

Demandred stood up, taking his sword in two hands in an unfamiliar battle stance. He seemed able to track Gawyn somewhat despite the rings, but his responses were a hair slower than they should have been.

Apple Blossoms in the Wind, with three quick strikes, forced Demandred back. Several Sharans came forward with swords, but Demandred raised a gauntleted hand to warn them off. He did not smile at Gawyn—this man did not seem as if he ever smiled—but he performed something that was similar to Lightning of Three Prongs. Gawyn replied with The Boar Rushes Down the Mountain.

Demandred was good. With the edge granted by the rings, Gawyn narrowly escaped Demandred's riposte. The two danced through a small circle of open ground guarded by the watching Sharans. Distant booms threw iron spheres at the hillside, making the ground shake. There were only a few dragons still firing, but they seemed to be concentrating on this position.

Gawyn grunted, throwing himself into Storm Shakes the Branch, trying to push inside Demandred's guard. He would need to be close and ram his sword into the armpit or between the seams of the coin armor.

Demandred responded with skill and finesse. Gawyn was soon sweating beneath his mail. He felt faster than he'd ever been, his reactions like the darting movements of a hummingbird. Yet, try as he did, he could not land a hit.

"Who are you, little man?" Demandred growled, walking back with sword raised at his side. "You fight well."

"Gawyn Trakand."

"The little queen's brother," Demandred said. "You realize who I am."

"A murderer."

"And has your Dragon not murdered?" Demandred said. "Has your sister never killed to keep, dare I say *seize*, her throne?"

"That's different."

"So everyone always says." Demandred stepped forward. His sword forms were smooth, his back always straight but relaxed, and he used the broad, sweeping movements of a dancer. He had absolute mastery of his sword; Gawyn had not heard that Demandred was known for his swordsmanship, but this man was as good as any man Gawyn had ever faced. Better, truly.

Gawyn performed Cat Dances on the Wall, a beautiful, sweeping sword form that matched Demandred's. Then he ducked in with The Serpent's Tongue Dances, hoping his previous form would have lulled Demandred into letting a thrust slip past.

Something crashed into Gawyn, throwing him to the ground. He rolled, coming up in a crouch. His breathing grew labored. He did not feel pain because of the rings, but he had probably broken a rib.

A rock, Gawyn thought. *He channeled and brought a rock in to hit me.* He had trouble hitting Gawyn with weaves, because of the shadows, but something large could be tossed at the shadows and still hit him.

"You cheat," Gawyn said with a sneer.

"Cheat?" Demandred asked. "Are there rules, little swordsman? As I recall, you tried to stab *me* in the back while hiding in a shroud of darkness."

Gawyn breathed in and out, holding his side. A dragon's iron sphere thumped into the ground just a short distance away, then exploded. The blast ripped apart some Sharans, their bodies shielding Gawyn and Demandred from the brunt of the blast. The soil rained down, like a spray of surf on the deck of a ship. At least one of the dragons was still working.

"You name me a murderer," Demandred said, "and I am. I am also your savior, whether you wish it or not."

"You're mad."

"Hardly," Demandred walked around him, cutting the air with a few sweeps of his sword. "That man you follow, Lews Therin Telamon, *he* is mad. He thinks he can defeat the Great Lord. He cannot. That is simple fact."

"You'd have us join the Shadow instead?"

"Yes." Demandred's eyes were cold. "If I kill Lews Therin, in victory I will be given the right to remake the world as I wish. The Great Lord cares nothing for rule. The only way to protect this world is to destroy it, and then shelter its people. Is that not what your Dragon claims he can do?"

"Why do you keep calling him *my* Dragon?" Gawyn said, then spat blood to the side. The rings . . . they urged him forward. His limbs pulsed with strength, energy. *Fight! Kill!*

"You follow him," Demandred said.

"I do not!"

"Lies," Demandred said. "Or perhaps you are simply fooled. I know that Lews Therin leads this army. At first I was uncertain, but no longer. That weave about you is proof enough, but I have a greater one. No mortal general has such skill as this day has shown; I face a true master on the battlefield. Perhaps Lews Therin wears the Mask of Mirrors, or perhaps he leads by sending messages to this Cauthon through the One Power. It does not matter, I see the truth. I dice with Lews Therin this day.

"I was always the better general. I will prove it here. I would have you tell that to Lews Therin, but you will not live long enough, little swordsman. Prepare yourself." Demandred raised his sword.

Gawyn stood, dropping his knife, taking his sword in two hands. Demandred stalked toward him, using forms that were different from those Gawyn knew. They were still familiar enough for him to counter, but despite his greater speed, time and time again Demandred caught his sword and deflected it harmlessly to the side.

The man did not strike. He barely moved, feet set wide apart, sword in two hands, battering aside each and every attack Gawyn hurled at him. The Dove Takes Flight, The Falling Leaf, Leopard's Caress. Gawyn gritted his teeth, growling through them. The rings should have been enough. Why weren't the rings enough?

Gawyn stepped back, then ducked backward as another stone came hurtling toward him. It missed him by inches. *Thank the Light for these rings*, he thought.

"You fight with skill," Demandred said, "for one of this Age. But you still wield your sword, little man."

"What else would I do?"

"Become the sword yourself," Demandred said, as if baffled that Gawyn did not understand.

Gawyn growled and came in again, battering at Demandred. Gawyn was still faster. Demandred didn't attack; he was on the defensive, then, although he didn't retreat. He just stood there, turning aside each blow.

Demandred closed his eyes. Gawyn smiled, then thrust in Black Lance's Last Strike.

Demandred's sword became a blur.

Something struck Gawyn. He gasped, pulling to a stop. He wobbled and fell to his knees, looking down at a hole in his gut. Demandred had thrust straight through the mail, then pulled his sword free in a single fluid motion.

Why can't . . . why can't I feel anything?

"If you do survive this and see Lews Therin," Demandred said, "tell him I am very much looking forward to a match between the two of us, sword against sword. I have improved since we last met."

Demandred whipped his sword around, catching the back of the blade in the crook between his thumb and forefinger. He pulled the sword across, stripping the blood from the steel and splattering it to the ground.

He slid the weapon into his sheath. He shook his head, then released a ball of fire toward a still-firing dragon.

It fell silent. Demandred strode away along the edge of the

steep slope facing the river, his Sharan guard forming around him. Gawyn collapsed to the ground, stunned, spurting his life onto the burned grass. He tried to hold in the blood through trembling fingers.

Somehow Gawyn managed to push himself up to his knees. His heart cried out; he needed to return to Egwene. He began to crawl, blood mixing with the earth beneath him as it seeped from his wound. Through eyes clouded with cold perspiration, he spotted several cavalry mounts twenty paces ahead, poking at blackened tufts of grass at their feet and tethered to a picket-line. After minutes of struggle, an impossible interval of time that left him drained, he pulled himself up on to the back of the first horse he could reach and untether. Gawyn hunched over, dazed, grasping its mane in one hand. Summoning his remaining strength, he kicked his heel into the animal's rib cage.

"My Lady," Mandevwin said to Faile, "I have *known* those two men for years! They are not without a few spots in their past. No man comes to the Band without a few of those. But, Light provide, they are *not* Darkfriends!"

Faile ate her midday rations in silence, listening with as much patience as she could muster to Mandevwin's protests. She wished Perrin were here so she could have a good argument. She felt as if she would burst from pressure.

They were close to Thakan'dar, horribly close. The black sky rumbled with lightning, and they hadn't seen a living creature—dangerous or not—in days. Nor had they seen Vanin or Harnan again, though Faile set a double guard each night. The minions of the Dark One did not give up.

She now carried the Horn in a large bag tied to her waist. The others knew it, and moved between pride in their duty and horror at the import of it. At least she shared that with them now.

"My Lady," Mandevwin said, kneeling down. "Vanin is out there nearby somewhere. He is a very gifted scout, the best in the Band. We will not see him unless he wants us to, but I would swear that he is following us. Where else would he go? Perhaps if I call out to him, invite him in to tell his story, so we can resolve this."

"I will consider it, Mandevwin," Faile said.

He nodded. The one-eyed man was a good commander, but had the imagination of a brick. Uncomplicated men assumed others to have uncomplicated motivations, and he could not imagine someone like Vanin or Harnan helping the Band for so long—under orders, undoubtedly, to avoid suspicion—only to now do something so terrible.

At least now she knew that she hadn't been worried without cause. That look of pure terror in Vanin's eyes when he'd been caught was confirmation enough, if catching him with the Horn in his hands hadn't been. She had not expected *two* Darkfriends, and they had outsmarted her in their thievery. However, they had also underestimated the dangers of the Blight. She hated to think what would have happened if they hadn't drawn the attention of the bear-thing. Faile would have remained in her tent, anticipating the arrival of thieves who had already disappeared with one of the most powerful artifacts in the world.

The sky rumbled. Dark Shayol Ghul loomed ahead, rising out of the valley of Thakan'dar in a range of smaller mountains. The air had grown chill, almost wintery. Reaching that peak would be difficult—but one way or another, she was going to bring this Horn to the forces of the Light for the Last Battle. She rested her fingers on the sack at her side, feeling the metal within.

Nearby, Olver scampered across the lifeless gray rock of the Blasted Lands, wearing his knife at his belt like a sword. Perhaps she should not have brought him. Then again, boys his age in the Borderlands learned to run messages and carry supplies to besieged forts. They wouldn't go out with a war band or be given a post until they were at least twelve, but their training started much earlier.

"My Lady?"

Faile looked toward Selande and Arrela as they approached. Faile had put Selande in charge of the scouts, now that Vanin had revealed himself. The pale little woman looked less like an Aiel than many of the others in *Cha Faile*. But the attitude helped.

"Yes?"

"Movement, my Lady," Selande said softly.

"What?" Faile stood. "What kind?"

"Some kind of caravan."

"In the *Blasted Lands*?" Faile asked. "Show me."

It wasn't just a caravan. There was a *village* out there. Faile could make it out through the looking glass, though only as a smudge of darkness to indicate buildings. It was settled into the foothills near Thakan'dar. A village. Light!

Faile moved the looking glass down to where a caravan crept across the bleak landscape, heading toward a supply station set up a good distance outside the village.

"They're doing what we did," she whispered.

"What's that, my Lady?" Arrela lay on her stomach beside Faile. Mandevwin was on her other side, peering through his own looking glass.

"It's a central supply station," Faile explained, looking over the stacks of boxes and bundles of arrows. "Shadowspawn can't move through gateways, but their supplies can. They needn't have carried arrows and replacement weapons as part of the invasion. Instead, the supplies are being collected here, then sent to the battlefields when needed."

Indeed, down below, a ribbon of light announced a gateway opening. A large train of dirty-looking men trudged through it with packs on their backs, followed by dozens of others pulling small carts.

"Wherever those supplies are going," Faile said slowly, "there will be fighting nearby. Those carts carry arrows, but no food, as the Trollocs are dragging corpses away to feast on each night."

"So if we could slip through one of those gateways ..." Mandevwin said.

Arrela snorted, as if the conversation were a joke. She looked at Faile, and the smile slipped from her lips. "You're serious. Both of you."

"We are still a long hike from Thakan'dar," Faile said. "And that village blocks our way. It might be easier to sneak through one of those gateways than try to work our way into the valley."

"We'd end up behind the enemy lines!"

"We're already behind their lines," Faile said grimly, "so nothing would change there."

Arrela fell silent.

"That will be a problem," Mandevwin said softly, turning his looking glass. "Look at the fellows approaching the camp from the village."

Faile raised her looking glass again. "Aiel?" she whispered. "Light! The Shaido have joined with the forces of the Dark One?"

"Even the Shaido dogs would not do that," Arrela said, then spat to the side.

The newcomers *did* look different. They wore their veils up, as if for killing, but the veils were red. Either way, sneaking past Aiel would be nearly impossible. Likely, only the fact that her group was so distant had saved them from discovery. That, and the fact that no one would expect to find a group like Faile's here.

"Back," Faile said, inching back down the hillside. "We need to do some planning."

Perrin awoke, feeling as if he had been tossed into a lake during winter. He gasped.

"Lie down, you fool," Janina said, putting her hand on his arm. The flaxen-haired Wise One looked as exhausted as he felt.

He was in someplace soft. Too soft. A nice bed, clean sheets. Outside the windows, waves broke gently against a shore and gulls called. He also heard moans echoing from some place nearby.

"Where am I?" Perrin asked.

"At my palace," Berelain said. She stood near the doorway, and he hadn't noticed her before. The First wore her diadem, the hawk in flight, and had on a crimson dress with yellow trim. The room was lavish, with gold and bronze on the mirrors, windows and bedposts.

"I might add," Berelain said, "that this is a somewhat familiar situation for me, Lord Aybara. I took precautions this time, in case you were wondering."

Precautions? Perrin sniffed the air. Uno? He could smell the man. Indeed, Berelain nodded to the side, and Perrin turned to find Uno sitting in a chair nearby, his arm in a sling.

"Uno! What happened to you?" Perrin asked.

"Bloody Trollocs happened to me," Uno grumbled. "Waiting my turn for Healing."

"Those with life-threatening wounds are Healed first," Janina said. She was the most accomplished of the Wise Ones at Healing; she'd apparently decided to stay with the Aes Sedai and Berelain. "You, Perrin Aybara, were Healed to the point of survival. Only just to the point of survival. It wasn't until now that we could take care of the wounds that did not threaten your life."

"Wait!" Perrín said. He struggled to sit. Light, he was exhausted. "How long have I been here?"

"Ten hours," Berelain said.

"Ten hours! I have to go. The fighting . . ."

"The fighting will continue without you," Berelain said. "I'm sorry."

Perrin growled softly. So *tired*. "Moiraine knew a method of wiping away a man's fatigue. Do you know this, Janina?"

"I wouldn't do it for you if I did," Janina said. "You need sleep, Perrin Aybara. Your participation in the Last Battle is over."

Perrin gritted his teeth, then moved to stand.

"Step out of that bed," Janina said, turning her eyes toward him, "and I'll bundle you in Air and leave you hanging there for hours."

Perrin's first instinct was to *shift* away. He began forming the thought in his head, and felt foolish. He'd somehow returned to the real world. He couldn't *shift* here. He was as helpless as a babe.

He leaned back in his bed, frustrated.

"Be of good cheer, Perrin," Berelain said softly, walking up to the bed. "You should be dead. How did you reach that battlefield? If Haral Luhhan and his men hadn't spotted you lying there . . ."

Perrin shook his head. What he'd done defied explanation for one who did not know the wolf dream. "What is happening, Berelain? The war? Our armies?"

She pursed her lips.

"I can smell the truth on you," Perrin said. "Worry, anxiety." He sighed. "I saw that the battlefronts had moved. If the Two Rivers men are at the Field of Merrilor as well, all three of our armies have been pushed back to the same place. Everyone but those at Thakan'dar."

"We don't know how the Lord Dragon is doing," she said softly, gliding onto a stool beside his bed. Beside the wall, Janina took Uno by the arm. He shivered as the Healing coursed through him.

"Rand still fights," Perrin said.

"Too much time has passed," she said. There was something she wasn't telling him, something she was dancing around. He could smell it on her.

"Rand still fights," Perrin repeated. "If he had lost, we wouldn't be here." He leaned back, exhaustion deep in his bones. Light! He couldn't just lie here while men died, could he? "Time is different at the Bore. I visited it and saw firsthand. It has been many days out here, but I'll bet it has only been a day for Rand. Maybe less."

"That is well. I will pass what you say to the others."

"Berelain," Perrin said. "I need you to do something for me. I sent Elyas with a message to our armies, but I don't know if he delivered it. Graendal is interfering with the minds of our great captains. Will you find out for me if his message arrived?"

"It arrived," she said. "Almost too late, but it arrived. You did well. Sleep now, Perrin." She rose.

"Berelain?" he asked.

She turned back to him.

"Faile," he said. "What of Faile?"

Her anxiety sharpened. *No.*

"Her supply caravan was destroyed in a bubble of evil, Perrin," Berelain said softly. "I'm sorry."

"Was her body recovered?" he forced himself to ask.

"No."

"Then she still lives."

"It—"

"She *still lives*," Perrin insisted. He would have to assume that was true. If he didn't . . .

"There is, of course, hope," she said, then walked to Uno, who was flexing his Healed arm, and nodded for him to join her as she left the room. Janina was puttering around the washstand. Perrin could still hear moaning in the hallways outside, and the place smelled of healing herbs and of pain.

Light, he thought. Faile's caravan had carried the Horn. Did the Shadow now have it?

And Gaul. He *had* to return to Gaul. He'd left the man in the wolf dream, guarding Rand's back. If Perrin's exhaustion was any guide, Gaul couldn't hold much longer.

Perrin felt as if he could sleep for weeks. Janina returned to his bedside, then shook her head. "There is no good purpose in trying to force yourself to hold your eyes open, Perrin Aybara."

"I have too much to do, Janina. Please. I need to return to the battlefield and—"

"You will *stay here*, Perrin Aybara. You are of no use to anyone in your state, and will gain no *ji* by trying to prove otherwise. If the blacksmith who brought you here knew I'd let you stumble off and die on the battlefield, I believe he'd come try to hang me out the window by my heels." She hesitated. "And that one . . . I almost think he could manage it."

"Master Luhhan," Perrin said, recalling faintly those moments before he blacked out. "He was there. He found me?"

"He saved your life," Janina said. "That man threw you on his back and ran you to an Aes Sedai for a gateway. You were seconds from death when he arrived. Considering your size, just lifting you is some feat."

"I don't really need sleep," Perrin said, feeling his eyes droop. "I need . . . I need to get . . . "

"I'm sure you do," Janina said.

Perrin let his eyes shut. That would convince her that he was going to do as she said. Then, when she left, he could stand up.

"I'm sure you do," Janina repeated, her voice growing softer for some reason.

Sleep, he thought. *I'm falling asleep.* Again, he saw the three paths before himself. This time, one led to ordinary sleep, another to the wolf dream while sleeping, the path he usually took.

And between them, a third path. The wolf dream in the flesh.

He was sorely tempted, but in the moment, he chose not to take that path. He chose ordinary sleep, as—in a moment of understanding—he knew that his body would die without it.

Androl lay, gasping for breath, staring up at the sky somewhere far from the battlefield, following their flight from the top of the Heights.

That attack . . . it had been so powerful.

What was that? he sent to Pevara.

It wasn't Taim, she replied, standing up, dusting off her skirts. *I think it was Demandred.*

I purposefully brought us to a place far from where he was fighting.

Yes. How dare he move and interfere with the group of channelers attacking his forces?

Androl sat up, groaning. *You know, Pevara, you are unusually smart-lipped, for an Aes Sedai.*

He was surprised by her amusement. *You don't know Aes Sedai nearly as well as you assume.* She walked over to check on Emarin's wounds.

Androl took a deep breath, filled with the scents of autumn. Fallen leaves. Stagnant water. An autumn that had come too early. Their hillside looked down on a valley where, in defiance of the way the world was going, some farmers had tilled the earth in large squares.

Nothing had grown.

Nearby, Theodrin pulled herself up. "It's *madness* back there," she said, her face flushed.

Androl could feel Pevara's disapproval. The girl should not have been so free with her emotions; she hadn't learned proper Aes Sedai control yet.

She isn't a proper Aes Sedai, Pevara sent him, reading his thoughts. *Regardless of what the Amyrlin claims. She hasn't been through the testing yet.*

Theodrin seemed to know what Pevara thought, and the two kept their distance from one another. Pevara Healed Emarin, who took it stoically. Theodrin Healed a cut on Jonneth's arm. He seemed bemused at the motherly ministration.

She'll have him bonded before long, Pevara sent him. *Notice how she let one of the other women take her one of the fifty, then started following him about? We've barely been rid of her since the Black Tower.*

What if he bonds her back? Androl sent.

Then we'll see if what you and I have is unique or not. Pevara hesitated. *We are stumbling upon things that have never been known.*

He met her eyes. She was referring to whatever had happened during their linking this last time. She had opened a gateway, but had done it as he would have.

We're going to need to try that again, he sent her.

Shortly, she said, Delving Emarin to be certain her Healing had taken.

"I am quite all right, Pevara Sedai," he said, courteous as always. "And if I might note, you seem as if you could use some Healing of your own."

She looked down at the burned cloth on her arm. She was still timid about letting a man Heal her, but also annoyed at her own timidity.

"Thank you," she said, her voice level as she let him touch her arm and channel.

Androl unhooked the small tin cup from his belt, and absently lifted his hand, fingers downward. He pressed his fingers as if pinching something between them, and when he spread them, a small gateway opened in the middle. Water poured out, filling the cup.

Pevara sat down beside him, accepting the cup as he offered it. She drank, then sighed. "As cool as mountain springwater."

"That's what it is," Androl said.

"That reminds me, I've been meaning to ask you something. How do you do that?"

"Do this?" he said. "It's just a small gateway."

"That's not what I mean. Androl, you just got here. You couldn't possibly have had time to memorize this area well enough to open a gateway to some mountain spring hundreds of miles away."

Androl stared blankly at Pevara, as if he had just heard a surprising piece of news. "I don't know. Maybe it's something to do with my Talent."

"I see." Pevara was silent a moment. "By the way, what happened to your sword?"

Androl reached by reflex to his side. The sheath hung there, empty. He'd dropped his sword when the lightning had struck near them, and he hadn't had the presence of mind to grab it as they fled. He groaned. "Garfin would send me to grind barley at the quartermaster's for weeks straight if he heard of this."

"It's not that important," Pevara said. "You have better weapons."

"It's the principle," Androl said. "Carrying a sword reminds me. It's like ... well, seeing a net reminds me of fishing around

Mayene, and springwater reminds me of Jain. Small things, but small things matter. I need to be a soldier again. We have to find Taim, Pevara. The seals . . . "

"Well, we can't find him the way we've been trying. Do you agree?"

He sighed, but nodded.

"Excellent," she said. "I hate being a target."

"What do we do instead?"

"We approach this with careful study, not with swinging swords."

She probably had a point. "And . . . what we did? Pevara, you used my *Talent*."

"We shall see," she said, sipping from her cup. "Now, if only this were tea."

Androl raised his eyebrows. He took the cup back, opened a small gateway between two fingers and dropped a few dried tea leaves into the cup. He boiled it for a moment with a thread of Fire, then dropped in some honey through another gateway.

"Had some back in my workshop in the Black Tower," he said, handing the cup back. "It looks like nobody moved it."

She sipped the tea, then smiled warmly. "Androl, you are *wonderful*."

He smiled. Light! How long had it been since he'd felt this way about a woman? Love was supposed to be something for young fools, wasn't it?

Of course, the young fools never could see straight. They'd look for a pretty face, and stop there. Androl had been around long enough to know that a pretty face was nothing compared to the type of *solidity* a woman like Pevara displayed. Control, steadiness, determination. These were things that only proper seasoning could bring.

It was the same way with leather. New leather was fine, but really *good* leather was leather that had been used and worn, like a strap that had been cared for over the years. You never knew for certain if you could rely on a new strap. Once it had been your companion for a few seasons, you knew.

"I'm trying to read that thought," Pevara said. "Did you just . . . compare me to an old strap of leather?"

He blushed.

"I'll assume it's a leatherworker's thing." She sipped her tea.

"Well, you keep comparing me to . . . what is it? A bunch of little figurines?"

She smiled. "My family."

The ones killed by Darkfriends. "I'm sorry."

"It happened very, very long ago, Androl." He could sense that she was still angry about it, though.

"Light," he said. "I keep forgetting that you're older than most trees, Pevara."

"Hmmm . . ." she said. "First I'm a strap of leather, now I'm older than trees. I assume that, despite the several dozen jobs you've had in your life, none of your training involves how to speak with a lady?"

He shrugged. When younger, he might have been embarrassed to have his tongue tied in such knots, but he'd learned that there was just no way to avoid it. Trying to do so only made it worse. Oddly, the way he reacted pleased her. Women liked to see a man flummoxed, he supposed.

Her mirth died down, however, as she happened to glance at the sky. He was reminded, suddenly, of the empty fields below. The dead trees. The growling thunder. This was not a time for mirth, not a time for love. For some reason, though, he found himself clinging to both precisely because of that.

"We should be moving soon," he said. "What is your plan?"

"Taim will always be surrounded by minions. If we continue attacking as we have, we'll be cut to ribbons before we can get to him. We need to reach him stealthily."

"And how are we going to manage that?"

"That depends. How crazy can you be, if the situation warrants?"

The valley of Thakan'dar had become a place of smoke, mayhem and death.

Rhuarc stalked through it, Trask and Baelder at his sides. They were brothers of his from the Red Shields. He had never met these two before coming to this place, but they were brothers nonetheless, and their bond had been sealed by the spilled blood of Shadowspawn and traitors.

Lightning broke the air, striking nearby. As Rhuarc walked, his feet crunched on sand that had been turned to shards of glass by the lightning. He reached cover—some Trolloc corpses in a pile—and crouched down, Trask and Baelder joining him. The tempest had finally come, furious winds assaulting the valley, nearly enough to pull the veil from his face.

It was difficult to make out anything. The fog had blown away, but the sky had darkened, and the storm kicked up dust and smoke. Many people fought in prowling packs.

There were no more battle lines. Earlier in the day, a Myrddraal attack—and an all-out Trolloc assault afterward—had finally broken the Defenders' hold on the mouth of the valley. The Tairens and Dragonsworn had pulled back into the valley, toward Shayol Ghul, and now most of them fought near the base of the mountain.

Fortunately, the Trollocs that had piled through didn't have overwhelming numbers. The killing in the pass and the long siege had reduced the numbers of Trollocs at Thakan'dar. In all, the Trollocs remaining probably equaled the number of Defenders.

That still would be a problem—but in his opinion, the Honorless who wore red veils were a far greater threat. Those roved across the expanse of the valley, as did the Aiel. In this open killing field, obscured with fog and swirling dust to ruin visibility, Rhuarc hunted. Occasionally, he would run across Trollocs in groups, but most had been driven by the Fades to fight the regular forces, the Tairens and Domani.

Rhuarc waved to his brothers, and they moved through the tempest along one side of the valley. The Light send that the regular forces and the channelers could hold the path up to the mountain where the *Car'a'carn* fought Sightblinder.

Rand al'Thor would need to complete his battle soon, for Rhuarc suspected it would not be long before the Shadow won this valley.

He and his brothers passed a group of Aiel dancing the spears with the traitors who wore the red veils. While many of the red-veils could channel, it seemed that none in this group could. Rhuarc and his two leaped into the dance, spears thrusting.

These red-veils fought well. Trask woke from the dream during this fight, though he slew one of the red-veils as he fell. The skirmish ended when the remaining red-veils fled. Rhuarc killed one of them with the bow, and Baelder downed another. Shooting men in the back; it was a thing they would not have done if fighting true Aiel. These creatures were worse than Shadowspawn.

The three remaining Aiel they had helped nodded in thanks. They joined with him and Baelder, and together they moved back toward the Pit of Doom to check on the defenses there.

Thankfully, the army at this place still held. Many were of those Dragonsworn who had come to the battle last, and who were made up primarily of common men and women. Yes, there were some Aes Sedai among them, even some Aiel and a couple of Asha'man. However, most of them held old swords that hadn't seen use in years, or staffs that had probably once been farming tools.

They fought like cornered wolves against the Trollocs. Rhuarc shook his head. If the treekillers had fought so savagely, perhaps Laman would still have his throne.

A bolt of lightning came from the air, killing a number of the defenders. Rhuarc blinked the flash from his eyes, turned to the side, and scanned the surroundings through the blowing winds. *There.*

He motioned for his brothers to stay behind, then slipped forward in a crouch. He grabbed a handful of the gray, ashlike dust that covered the ground and rubbed it into his clothing and onto his face; the wind whipped some of it from his fingers.

He went prone on the ground, a dagger clenched in his jaw. His prey stood atop a small hill, watching the fight. One of the red-veils with his veil down, grinning. The creature's teeth were not filed to points. The ones with teeth filed to points could all channel; some without teeth like that could as well. Rhuarc did not know what that meant.

This fellow was a channeler, revealed as he summoned Fire like a spear and launched it toward fighting Tairens nearby. Rhuarc crept forward slowly, inching along the ground in a depression in the rocks.

He was forced to watch the red-veil killing Defender after Defender, but he did not speed up. He continued his excruciatingly slow crawl, listening to the fire sizzle as the red-veil stood with hands behind his back, weaves of the One Power striking around him.

The red-veil didn't see him. Though some of these men fought like Aiel, many did not. They were not quiet as they stalked, and did not seem to know the bow or the spear as well as they should. Men like the one in front of him ... Rhuarc doubted they had ever had to move quietly, sneak up on a foe, kill a deer in the wilderness. Why would they want to, when they could channel?

The man didn't notice as Rhuarc slid around a Trolloc corpse near the red-veil's feet, then reached out and sliced the man's hamstrings. He dropped with a cry, and before he could channel further, Rhuarc cut his throat, then slipped back into hiding between two corpses.

Two Trollocs came to see what the fuss was. Rhuarc killed the first, then dropped the second even as it turned, before they had a chance to see him. Then, once again, he melted into the landscape.

No more Shadowspawn came to investigate, so Rhuarc retreated back toward his men. As he moved—rising to a crouching run—he passed a small pack of wolves finishing off a pair of Trollocs. The wolves turned to him, muzzles bloodied and ears raised. They let him pass, moving silently out into the storm of wind to find other prey.

Wolves. They had come with the rainless tempest, and now fought alongside men. Rhuarc did not know much of how the overall battle was going. He could see that some of King Darlin's troops in the distance still held formation. The crossbowmen had set up next to the Dragonsworn. Last Rhuarc had seen, they'd nearly run out of bolts, and the strange steam-belching wagons that had been delivering supplies now lay in ruins. Aes Sedai and Asha'man continued to channel against the onslaught, but not with the energy he had seen from them earlier.

The Aiel did what they did best: kill. So long as those armies held the pathway to Rand al'Thor, perhaps that would be enough. Perhaps ...

Something hit him. He gasped, falling to his knees. He looked up, and someone beautiful stepped through the storm to inspect him. She had wonderful eyes, though the two were offset from one another. He'd never before realized how horribly balanced everyone else's eyes were. Thinking of it nauseated him. And all other women had too much hair on their heads. This creature, with thinning hair, was far more marvelous.

She neared, wonderful, amazing. Incredible. She touched his chin as he knelt on the ground, and her fingertips were as soft as clouds.

"Yes, you'll do," she said. "Come, my pet. Join the others."

She gestured toward a group following her. Several Wise Ones, a pair of Aes Sedai, a man with a spear. Rhuarc growled. Would this man try to take the affection of his beloved? He would *kill* the man for that. He would—

His mistress chuckled. "And Moridin thinks this face a punishment. Well, you don't care what face I wear, do you, my pet?" Her voice grew softer, and at the same time harsher. "When I'm through, nobody will. Moridin himself will praise my beauty, for he will see through eyes that I grant him. Just like you, pet. Just like you."

She patted Rhuarc. He joined her and the others and moved through the valley, leaving behind the men he had called brothers.

Rand stepped forward as a roadway formed itself from threads of light in front of him. His foot fell on a bright, clean paving stone and he passed from nothingness into majesty.

The road was wide enough to let six wagons pass one another at a time, but no vehicles clogged the roadway. Only people. Vibrant people, in colorful clothing, chatting, calling, eager. Sounds filled the emptiness—the sounds of life.

Rand turned, looking at the buildings as they grew around him. Tall houses lined the thoroughfare, ribbed with columns in front. Long and thin, they abutted one another, their faces toward the roadway. Beyond them lay domes and marvels, buildings that stretched toward the sky. It was like no city he had ever seen, though the workmanship was Ogier.

Partly Ogier work, that was. Nearby, workers repaired a stone facade that had broken during a storm. Thick-fingered Ogier laughed rumbling laughs as they worked alongside men. When the Ogier had come to the Two Rivers to repay Rand for his sacrifice, intending to build a monument here, the town's leaders had wisely requested help improving their city instead.

Over the years, the Ogier and Two Rivers people had worked closely together—to the extent that now, Two Rivers craftsmen were sought the world over. Rand walked up the roadway, moving among people from all nationalities. Domani trailing colorful, filmy clothing. Tairens—the division between commoner and noble vanishing more and more by the day—in baggy clothing and shirts marked by striped sleeves. Seanchan wearing exotic silks. Borderlanders with noble airs. Even some Sharans.

All had come to Emond's Field. The city now bore little resemblance to its name, and yet there were hints. More trees and open green spaces dotted the landscape than one would find in other great cities, like Caemlyn or Tear. In the Two Rivers, craftsmen were revered. And their marksmen were the best the world knew. An elite group of Two Rivers men, armed with the new firing sticks men were calling rifles, served with the Aiel in their peace-keeping campaigns in Shara. It was the only place war was known in the world. Oh, there were disputes here and there. The flare up between Murandy and Tear five years back had nearly given the land its first real war in the century since the Last Battle.

Rand smiled as he moved through the crowd, not jostling, but listening with pride to the joy in people's voices. The "flare-up" in Murandy had been dynamic by Fourth Age standards, but in truth it had been nothing. A single disgruntled nobleman had fired on an Aiel patrol. Three wounded, none dead, and this was the worst "fighting" in years, outside of the Sharan campaigns.

Above, sunlight broke through the thin cloud cover, bathing the roadway in light. Rand finally reached the city square, which had once been the Green in Emond's Field. What to think of the Quarry Road now that it was wide enough to march an army down? He walked around the massive fountain at the center of the square, a monument to those who had fallen in the Last Battle, crafted by the Ogier.

He saw familiar faces among the statuary in the center of the fountain, and turned away.

Not final yet, he thought. *This isn't real yet.* He'd built this reality out of threads of what could be, of mirrors of the world as it now played out. It wasn't set.

For the first time since entering this vision of his own design, his confidence shook. He knew the Last Battle wasn't a failure. But people were dying. Did he think to stop all death, all pain? *This should be my fight*, he thought. *They shouldn't have to die.* Wasn't his sacrifice enough?

So he'd asked time and time again.

The vision quivered, fine stones beneath his feet buzzing, buildings shaking and wavering. The people stopped in place, motionless, sound dying. Down a small side street, he saw a darkness appear like a pinprick that expanded, engulfing everything near it—sucking them in. It grew to the size of one of the houses, slowly expanding.

YOUR DREAM IS WEAK, ADVERSARY.

Rand asserted his will, and the quivering stopped. People who had frozen in place resumed walking, and the comfortable chatter sprang up again. Soft wind blew down the walkway, rustling banners on poles proclaiming celebration.

"I will see that it happens," Rand said to the darkness. "This is your failing. Happiness, growth, love . . . "

THESE PEOPLE ARE MINE NOW. I WILL TAKE THEM.

"You are darkness," Rand said loudly. "Darkness cannot push back Light. Darkness exists only when Light fails, when it flees. I will *not* fail. I will *not* flee. You cannot win so long as I bar your path, Shai'tan."

WE SHALL SEE.

Rand turned from the darkness and continued doggedly around the fountain. On the other side of the square, a large set of majestic white steps led up to a building four stories high and of incredible craftsmanship. Carved with reliefs, topped by a gleaming copper roof, the building was decked with banners. One hundred years. A hundred years of life, a hundred years of peace.

The woman who stood at the top of the steps had a familiarity to her features. Some Saldaean heritage, but also dark curls of hair that felt distinctly Two Rivers. Lady Adora, Perrin's granddaughter and mayor of Emond's Field. Rand walked up the steps as she gave her speech of commemoration. Nobody noticed him. He made it so that they didn't. He slipped like a Gray Man behind her as she proclaimed the day of celebration; then he entered the building.

It was not a government office, though it might seem so from the front. It was much more important.

A school.

To the right, grand hallways were hung with paintings and ornaments to rival those of any palace—but these depicted the great teachers and storytellers of the past, from Anla to Thom Merrilin. Rand strolled that hallway, looking in at rooms where any could come and gain knowledge, from the poorest farmer to the children of the Mayor. The building had to be large to accommodate all who wanted to learn.

YOUR PARADISE IS FLAWED, ADVERSARY.

Darkness hung in a mirror to Rand's right. It reflected not the hallway, but instead HIS presence.

YOU THINK YOU CAN ELIMINATE SUFFERING? EVEN IF YOU WIN, YOU WILL NOT. ON THOSE PERFECT STREETS, MEN ARE STILL MURDERED AT NIGHT. CHILDREN GO HUNGRY DESPITE THE EFFORTS OF YOUR MINIONS. THE WEALTHY EXPLOIT AND CORRUPT; THEY MERELY DO SO QUIETLY.

"It is better," Rand whispered. "It is good."

IT IS NOT ENOUGH, AND WILL NEVER BE ENOUGH. YOUR DREAM IS FLAWED. YOUR DREAM IS A LIE. I AM THE ONLY HONESTY YOUR WORLD HAS EVER KNOWN.

The Dark One attacked him.

It came like a storm. A burst of wind so terrible, it threatened to rip Rand's skin from his bones. He stood tall, eyes toward the nothing, crossing his arms behind his back. The attack ripped away the vision—the beautiful city, the laughing people, the monument to learning and peace. The Dark One consumed it, and once again, it became mere possibility.

Silviana held the One Power, felt it flooding her, lighting the world. When she held *saidar*, she felt as if she could see all. It was a glorious feeling, so long as she acknowledged that it *was* merely a feeling. It was not truth. The lure of *saidar*'s power had coaxed many a woman into foolhardy gestures. Certainly many Blues had made them, at one point or another.

Silviana sculpted fire from horseback, leveling Sharan soldiers. She had trained her gelding, Stinger, to never be skittish around channeling.

"Archers fall back!" Chubain yelled from just behind her. "Go, go! Heavy infantry companies, advance!" The armored foot soldiers marched past Silviana with axes and maces to confront the disoriented Sharans on the slopes. Pikes would have been better, but they didn't have nearly enough of those for everyone.

She wove one more burst of fire into the enemy, preparing the way, then turned her attention to the Sharan archers higher up on the slope.

Once Egwene's forces had rounded the bogs, they had split into two assault groups. The Aes Sedai had moved in with the White Tower infantry, attacking Sharans on the Heights from the west. By this time, the fires had been extinguished and most of the Trollocs had moved off the Heights to attack below.

The other half of Egwene's army, mainly cavalry, were sent into the corridor that skirted the bogs and led toward the ford; they attacked the vulnerable rear flanks of the Trollocs that had come down the slopes to hit Elayne's troops defending the area around the ford.

The first group's main job was to make its way up the western slope. Silviana began aiming a careful series of lightning blasts at the Sharans who were advancing to repel them.

"Once the infantry has forced its way up the slope a ways," Chubain said from beside Egwene, "we'll have the Aes Sedai start . . . Mother?" Chubain's voice had risen.

Silviana spun on horseback, looking with alarm at Egwene. The Amyrlin wasn't channeling. Her face had grown pale, and she was trembling. Was she being attacked by a weave? Not one Silviana could see.

Figures gathered at the top of the slope, pushing aside the Sharan infantry. They began to channel, and lightning fell on the White Tower army, each with a crack shattering the air and a flash of light bright enough to stun.

"Mother!" Silviana kneed her horse up beside Egwene's mount. Demandred must be attacking her. Touching the *sa'angreal* in Egwene's hands for an extra boost of power, Silviana wove a gateway. The Seanchan woman who rode behind Egwene grabbed the

Amyrlin's reins and yanked the horse to safety through the gateway. Silviana followed, yelling, "Stand against those Sharans! Warn the male channelers of Demandred's attack on the Amyrlin Seat!"

"No," Egwene said weakly, wavering in her saddle as the horses clopped into a large tent. Silviana would have liked to take her farther away, but she had not known the area well enough for a long jump. "No, it's not ... "

"What's wrong?" Silviana asked, pulling up beside her and letting the gateway vanish. "Mother?"

"It's Gawyn," she said, pale, trembling. "He's been hurt. Badly. He's dying, Silviana."

Oh, Light, Silviana thought. Warders! She had feared something like this from the moment she'd seen that fool boy.

"Where?" Silviana asked.

"On the Heights. I'm going to find him. I'll use gateways, Travel in his direction ... "

"Light, Mother," Silviana said. "Do you have any idea how dangerous that will be? Stay here and lead the White Tower. I will try to find him."

"You can't sense him."

"Pass his bond to me."

Egwene froze.

"You know it is the right thing to do," Silviana said. "If he dies, it could destroy you. Let me have his bond. It will let me find him, and it will protect you, should he die."

Egwene was aghast. How dare Silviana even suggest this? But, then, she was a Red—and they concerned themselves little with Warders. Silviana did not know what she was asking.

"No," Egwene said. "No, I won't even consider it. Besides, if he dies, that would only protect me by shifting the pain to you."

"I am not the Amyrlin."

"*No.* If he dies, I will survive it and keep fighting. Jumping to him by gateway would be foolish, as you say, and I will not let you do it either. He is on the Heights. We will force our way up there, as ordered, and that way we can reach him. It is the best choice."

Silviana hesitated, then nodded. That would do. Together, they returned to the western side of the Heights, but Silviana stewed.

Fool man! If he died, Egwene would have a very difficult time continuing to fight.

The Shadow didn't need to fell the Amyrlin herself to stop her. It just had to kill one idiot boy.

"What are those Sharans doing?" Elayne asked softly.

Birgitte steadied her horse, taking the looking glass from Elayne. She raised it, looking across the dry river toward the slope of the Heights where a large number of Sharan troops had gathered. She grunted. "They're probably waiting for the Trollocs to be filled with arrows."

"You don't sound very certain," Elayne said, retrieving the looking glass. She held the One Power, but wasn't using it for now. Her army had been fighting here at the river for two hours. The Trollocs had surged into the riverbed all up and down the Mora, but her troops were holding them off from stepping onto Shienaran soil. The bogs prevented the enemy from swinging around her left flank; her right flank was more vulnerable and would need to be watched. It would be much worse if all the Trollocs were pushing to cross the river, but Egwene's cavalry was hitting them from behind. That took some of the pressure off her army.

Men held the Trollocs back with pikes, and the small flow of water still trickling through the bed had turned completely red. Elayne sat resolute, watching and being seen by her troops. The finest of Andor bled and died, holding back the Trollocs with difficulty. The Sharan army appeared to be readying a charge off the Heights, but Elayne was unconvinced they would launch an attack just yet; the White Tower assault on the western side had to be a concern to them. Mat sending Egwene's army to attack from behind the Heights was a stroke of genius.

"I'm not very certain of what I said," Birgitte said softly. "Not at all. Not about much, any more."

Elayne frowned. She'd thought the conversation over. What was Birgitte saying? "What about your memories?"

"The first thing I remember now is waking up to you and Nynaeve," Birgitte said softly. "I can remember our conversations about being in the World of Dreams, but I cannot remember the place itself. It's all slipped away from me, like water between my fingers."

"Oh, Birgitte . . ."

The woman shrugged. "I can't miss what I don't remember." The pain in her voice belied the words.

"Gaidal?"

Birgitte shook her head. "Nothing. I feel that I'm supposed to know someone by that name, but I don't." She chuckled. "Like I said. I don't know what I've lost, so it's all right."

"Are you lying?"

"Bloody ashes, of *course* I am. It's like a hole inside of me, Elayne. A deep, gaping hole. Bleeding out my life and memories." She looked away.

"Birgitte . . . I'm sorry."

Birgitte turned her horse and moved off a way, obviously not wanting to discuss the matter further. Her pain radiated its spikes in the back of Elayne's mind.

What would it be like, to lose so much? Birgitte didn't have a childhood, parents. Her entire life, all she remembered, usually spanned less than a year. Elayne started to go after her, but her guards moved aside to let Galad approach, attired in the armor, tabard and cloak of the Lord Captain Commander of the Children of the Light.

Elayne tightened her lips. "Galad."

"Sister," Galad said. "I assume that it would be completely futile to inform you how inappropriate it is for a woman in your condition to be on the battlefield."

"If we lose this war, Galad, my children will be born into captivity to the Dark One, if they are born at all. I think fighting is worth the risk."

"So long as you refrain from holding the sword personally," Galad said, shading his eyes to inspect the battlefield. The words implied that he was giving her permission—*permission*—to lead her troops.

Streaks of light shot from the Heights, striking at the last dragons firing from the field just behind her troops. Such strength! Demandred had power that eclipsed Rand's. *If he turns that power against my troops . . .*

"Why would Cauthon bring me down here?" Galad said softly. "He wanted a dozen of my best men . . ."

"You're not asking me to guess the mind of Matrim Cauthon, are you?" Elayne asked. "I'm convinced that Mat only *acts* simple so that people will let him get away with more."

Galad shook his head. She could see a group of his men gathered nearby. They were pointing toward the Trollocs that were slowly making their way upriver on the Arafellin bank. Elayne realized her right flank was in jeopardy.

"Send for six companies of crossbowmen," Elayne said to Birgitte. "Guybon needs to reinforce our troops upriver."

Light. This is starting to look bad. The White Tower was out there on the west slope of the Heights, where the channeling was most furious. She couldn't see much of it, but she could feel it.

Smoke billowed over the top of the Heights, lit by splashing explosions of lightning. Like a beast of storm and hunger stirring amid the blackness, its eyes flashing as it woke.

Elayne was suddenly aware. Of the pervasive scent of smoke in the air, the cries of pain from men. Thunder from the sky, trembles in the earth. The cold air resting upon a land that would not grow, the breaking weapons, grinding of pikes against shields. The end. It really had come, and she stood upon its precipice.

A messenger galloped up, bearing an envelope. He gave the proper pass codes to Elayne's guard, dismounted and was allowed to step up to her and Galad. He addressed Galad, handing the letter to him. "From Lord Cauthon, sir. He said you'd be here."

Galad took the letter and, frowning, opened it. He slipped a sheet of paper from inside.

Elayne waited patiently—*patiently*—to a count of three, then moved her horse up beside Galad's mount and craned her neck to read. Honestly, one would think he'd take concern for the comfort of a pregnant woman.

The letter was written in Mat's hand. And, Elayne noticed with amusement, the handwriting was much neater and the spelling much better in this one than the one he'd sent her weeks ago. Apparently, the pressure of battle made Matrim Cauthon into a better clerk.

> *Galad,*
> *Not much time to be flowery. You're the only one I trust with this*
> *mission. You'll do what is right, even when nobody bloody wants*

you to. The Borderlanders might not have the stomach for this, but I'll bet I can trust a Whitecloak. Take this. Get a gateway from Elayne. Do what has to be done.

Mat

Galad frowned, then upended the envelope, dumping out something silvery. A medallion on a chain. A single Tar Valon mark slid out beside it.

Elayne breathed out, then touched the medallion and channeled. She could not. This was one of the copies she'd made, one of those she'd given Mat. Mellar had stolen another one. "It protects the wearer against channeling," Elayne said. "But why send it to you?"

Galad turned the sheet of paper over, apparently noticing something. Written on the back in a hastier scrawl was, *p.s. In case you don't know what "Do what needs to be done" means, it means that I want you to go bloody slaughter as many of those Sharan channelers as you can. I'll bet you a full Tar Valon mark—it's only been shaved on the sides a little—that you can't kill twenty. —MC*

"That's bloody devious," Elayne breathed out. "Blood and bloody ashes, it is."

"Hardly fitting language for a monarch," Galad said, folding the message and placing it in the pocket of his cloak. He hesitated, then put the medallion around his neck. "I wonder if he knows what he is doing by giving one of the Children an artifact that makes one immune to the touches of the Aes Sedai. The orders are good ones. I will see them carried out."

"You can do it, then?" Elayne asked. "Kill women?"

"Perhaps once I would have hesitated," Galad said, "but that would have been the wrong choice. Women are as fully capable of being evil as men. Why should one hesitate to kill one, but not the other? The Light does not judge one based on gender, but on the merit of the heart."

"Interesting."

"What is interesting?" Galad asked.

"You actually said something that doesn't make me want to strangle you. Perhaps there is hope for you someday, Galad Damodred."

He frowned. "This is neither the place nor the time for levity, Elayne. You should see to Gareth Bryne. He appears agitated."

She turned, surprised to find the aging general speaking with her guards. "General?" she called to him.

Bryne looked up, then bowed formally from horseback.

"Did my guard stop you?" Elayne asked, as he approached. Had word of Bryne's Compulsion spread?

"No, Your Majesty," he said. His horse was lathered. He had been riding hard. "I did not wish to bother you personally."

"Something is troubling you," Elayne said. "Out with it."

"Your brother, has he come this way?"

"Gawyn?" she asked, looking to Galad. "I haven't seen him."

"Nor I," Galad said.

"The Amyrlin was certain he'd be with your forces . . ." Bryne said, shaking his head. "He went to fight on the front lines. Perhaps he came in disguise."

Why would he . . . He was Gawyn. He would want to fight. Yet sneaking to the front lines in disguise didn't seem like him. He might gather some men loyal to him and lead a few charges. But sneak? Gawyn? It was difficult to imagine.

"I will spread word," Elayne said as Galad bowed to her, then withdrew on his mission. "Perhaps one of my commanders has seen him."

Ah . . . Mat thought, face so close to the maps that it was nearly level with them. Then he waved to the side, having Mika the *damane* open a gateway. Mat could have Traveled to the top of Dashar Knob to get an overview. However, the last time he had done so, enemy channelers had targeted him, shearing off part of the summit; and, despite being so high, Dashar Knob did not allow him to see everything happening below the western side of Polov Heights. He scrambled over, hands on the lip of the gateway in the table, inspecting the landscape below.

Elayne's line at the river was being pushed back. They had run archers to their right flank. Good. Blood and bloody ashes . . . those Trollocs had nearly the weight behind them of a cavalry push. He'd need to send word to Elayne to get her cavalry lined up behind the pikes.

Like when I fought Sana Ashraf at the falls of Pena, he thought.

Heavy cavalry, horseback archers, heavy cavalry, horseback archers. One after another. *Taer'ain dhai hochin dieb sene.*

Mat could not remember being this engaged by a battle. The fight against the Shaido had not been nearly so gripping, though Mat had not been leading that battle entirely. The fight against Elbar had not been this satisfying, either. Of course, that had been on a much smaller scale.

Demandred knew how to gamble. Mat could sense it through the movements of troops. Mat was playing against one of the best who had ever lived, and the stake this time was not wealth. They diced for the lives of men, and the final prize was the world itself. Blood and *bloody* ashes, but that excited him. He did feel guilty about that, but it was exciting.

"Lan is in position," Mat said, straightening up and returning to his maps, making some notations. "Tell him to strike."

The Trolloc army crossing the riverbed by the ruins needed to be crushed. He'd moved the Borderlanders around the Heights to attack their vulnerable rear flanks while Tam and his combined forces continued to pound them from the front. Tam had killed large numbers of them before and after the river had stopped. That Trolloc horde was close to being broken, and a coordinated action on two sides could do it.

Tam's men would be tired. Could they hold long enough for Lan to arrive and hit the Trollocs from behind? Light, Mat hoped they could. If they didn't . . .

Someone darkened the doorway of the command position, a tall man with dark, curling hair, wearing the coat of an Asha'man. He had the expression of a man who had just drawn a losing hand. Light. A *Trolloc* would have found that stare unnerving.

Min, who had been speaking with Tuon, choked off; Logain seemed to have a special glare for her. Mat straightened, dusting off his hands. "I hope you didn't do anything too nasty to the guards, Logain."

"The weaves of Air will untie on their own in a minute or two," the man said, voice harsh. "I didn't think they were likely to allow me in."

Mat glanced at Tuon. She had grown stiff as a well-starched apron. Seanchan did not trust *women* who could channel, let alone someone like Logain.

"Logain," Mat said. "I need you to fight alongside the White Tower army. Those Sharans are *pounding* them."

Logain had locked eyes with Tuon.

"Logain!" Mat said. "If you haven't noticed, we're fighting a bloody war here."

"It is not my war."

"This is *our* war," Mat snapped. "Every one of us."

"I stood forth to fight," Logain said. "And what was my reward? Ask the Red Ajah. They will tell you the reward of a man abused of the Pattern." He barked a laugh. "The Pattern demanded a Dragon! And so I came! Too soon. Just a little too soon."

"Listen here," Mat said, stepping up to Logain. "You're angry because you didn't get to be the Dragon?"

"Nothing so petty," Logain said. "I follow the Lord Dragon. Let *him* die. I wish no part of that feast. I and mine should be with him, not fighting here. This battle for the little lives of men is nothing compared to the battle happening at Shayol Ghul."

"And yet, you know we need you here," Mat said. "You would already be gone, otherwise."

Logain said nothing.

"Go to Egwene," Mat said. "Take everyone you have and *keep those Sharan channelers busy*."

"What of Demandred?" Logain asked softly. "He cries out for the Dragon. He has the power of a dozen men. None of us can face him."

"But you want to try, don't you?" Mat replied. "That's why you're really here, right now. You want me to send you against Demandred."

Logain hesitated, then nodded. "He cannot have the Dragon Reborn. He will have to take me instead. The Dragon's . . . replacement, if you will."

Blood and bloody ashes . . . they're all insane. Unfortunately, what else was Mat going to do against one of the Forsaken? Right now, his battle plan revolved around keeping Demandred occupied, forcing the man to respond. If Demandred had to act as general, he couldn't do as much damage channeling.

He would have to come up with something to deal with the Forsaken. He was working on that. He'd been working on it the whole bloody battle, and hadn't come up with anything.

Mat glanced back through his gateway. Elayne was being pressed too hard. He had to do something. Send in the Seanchan? He had them positioned at the southern end of the field on the banks of the Erinin. They would be a wildcard to Demandred, preventing him from committing all his troops in the battles being waged below the Heights. In addition, he had plans for them. Important ones.

Logain didn't have much of a shot against Demandred, in Mat's estimation. But he'd have to deal with the man somehow. If Logain wanted to try, then so be it.

"You may fight him," Mat said. "Do it now, or wait until he is weakened a little. Light, I hope we *can* weaken him. Anyway, I leave it to you. Pick your time and attack."

Logain smiled, then made a gateway right in the middle of the room and strode through, hand on his sword. He had enough pride to be the Dragon Reborn, that was for certain. Mat shook his head. What he would give to be done with all of these high heads. Mat might be one of them now, but that could be fixed. All he had to do was convince Tuon to forsake her throne and run off with him. That would not be easy, but bloody ashes, he was fighting the Last Battle. Compared to the challenge he now faced, Tuon seemed to be an easy knot to untie.

"Glory of men . . ." Min whispered. "It's still to come."

"Someone go check on those guards," Mat said, returning to his maps. "Tuon, we may want to move you. This place never has been secure, and Logain has just proven it."

"I can protect myself," she said haughtily.

Too haughty. He raised an eyebrow at her, and she nodded.

Really? Mat thought. *This is what you want to fight about?* He was not certain the spy would buy it. Too flimsy a reason.

His plan with Tuon was to take a cue from what Rand had once done with Perrin. If Mat could fake a split between himself and the Seanchan, and in so doing make Tuon pull her forces back, perhaps the Shadow would ignore her. Mat needed an edge of some sort.

Two guards came in. No, three. That one fellow was easy to miss. Mat shook his head at Tuon—they needed to find something more realistic to argue over—and glanced back at his maps.

Something itched at him about the little guard. *Looks more like a servant than a soldier*, Mat thought. He forced himself to look up, though he really should not let himself become distracted by common servants. Yes, there the fellow was, standing beside Mat's table. Not worth paying attention to, even if he was pulling a knife out.

A knife.

Mat stumbled back as the Gray Man attacked. Mat yelled, reaching for one of his own knives, just as Mika screamed. "Channeling! Nearby!"

Min threw herself at Fortuona as the wall of the command post went up in flame. Sharans in strange armor made of bands of metal, painted gold, ripped through the blazing opening. Channelers with tattooed faces accompanied them: the women in long, stiff black dresses, the men shirtless, trousers ragged. Min took this in just before she tipped Fortuona's throne over.

Fire burned through the air above Min, singeing her ornate silks and consuming the wall behind them. Fortuona scrambled out of Min's grip, lying low, and Min blinked in surprise. The woman had left her bulky costume behind—it was made to break away—and underneath wore sleek silken trousers and a tight shirt, both black.

Tuon came up with a knife in her hand, growling softly in an almost feral way. Nearby, Mat fell backward to the ground, a knife-wielding man on top of him. Where had that man come from? She didn't remember him entering.

Tuon ran for Mat as Sharan channelers began to pound the command post with fire. Min struggled to her feet in the awful clothing. She pulled a dagger out and huddled by the throne, putting her back to it as the ground heaved.

She couldn't reach Fortuona, so she forced herself out the back wall, which was made of the paperlike stuff the Seanchan called *tenmi*.

She coughed at the smoke, but now that she was outside, the air was clearer. None of the Sharans were here on this side of the building. They were all attacking from the other directions. She sprinted along the wall. Channelers were dangerous, but if she could put a knife in one, all of the One Power in the world wouldn't matter.

She peeked around the corner, and was surprised by a man crouching there, a feral look in his eyes. He had an angular face; his blood-red neck tattoos looked like claws, cupping his light-skinned head and chin.

He growled, and Min threw herself backward to the ground, ducking a ribbon of fire and throwing her knife.

The man caught it in the air. He prowled forward in a crouch, bestial, smiling at her.

Then he jerked, suddenly, and fell over, thrashing. A trickle of blood came from his lips.

"That," a woman said nearby, a sound of utter distaste in her tone, "is something I'm not supposed to know how to do, but stopping someone's heart with the One Power is quiet. It requires very little Power, surprisingly, which is pertinent to me."

"Siuan!" Min said. "You're not supposed to be here."

"Lucky for you I am," Siuan said with a snort, inspecting the body, staying low. "Bah. Nasty business that, but if you're going to eat a fish, you should be willing to gut it yourself. What's wrong, girl? You're safe now. No need to look so pale."

"You're not supposed to *be* here!" Min said. "I told you. Stay near Gareth Bryne!"

"I did stay near him, almost near as his own smallclothes, I'll have you know. We saved one another's lives because of it, so I guess the viewing was right. Are they ever wrong?"

"No, I've told you that," Min whispered. "Never. Siuan ... I saw an aura around Bryne that meant you had to stay together, or the two of you would die. It hangs above you, right now. Whatever you think you did, the viewing has not been accomplished yet. It's *still there*."

Siuan stood frozen for a moment. "Cauthon is in danger."

"But—"

"I don't care, girl!" Nearby, the ground trembled with the force of the One Power. The *damane* were fighting back. "If Cauthon falls, this battle is lost! I don't care if we both die from this. We *must* help. Move!"

Min nodded, then joined her as she moved around the side of the ragged building. The firefight outside was a raw mix of explosions, smoke and flames. Members of the Deathwatch Guard charged the Sharans, swords out, heedless of their companions being slaughtered around them. That, at least, was keeping the channelers busy.

The command post burned with such heat that Min had to shy back, raising an arm.

"Hold on," Siuan said, then used the One Power to draw a small column of water out of a nearby barrel, spraying them both. "I'll try to dampen the flames," she said, redirecting the small column of water to the command post. "All right. Let's go."

Min nodded, bursting through the flames, Siuan joining her. The *tenmi* walls inside had all started aflame, burning away quickly. Fire dripped from the ceiling.

"There," Min said, blinking away tears from the heat and the smoke. She pointed toward dark figures struggling near the center of the building and Mat's blazing map table. There seemed to be a group of three or four people fighting Mat. Light, they were all Gray Men—not just one of them! Tuon was down.

Min ran past the corpse of a *sul'dam* alongside several guards. Siuan used the One Power to haul one of the Gray Men away from Mat. Guards' corpses created shadows of firelight on the floor. One *damane* still lived, huddled in a corner, looking terrified, her leash on the floor. Her *sul'dam* lay a distance away, unmoving. Her grip had been knocked free, it appeared, and then she was killed as she tried to get back to her *damane*.

"Do something!" Min shouted at the girl, grabbing her by the arm.

The *damane* shook her head, crying.

"Burn you—" Min said.

The ceiling of the structure groaned. Min ran for Mat. One Gray Man was dead, but there were two others, wearing the uniforms of Seanchan guards. Min had trouble seeing the living ones; they were inhumanly average in every way. Utterly nondescript.

Mat bellowed, knifing one of the men, but he didn't have his spear. Min didn't know where it was. Mat pushed forward, reckless, taking a gash along his side. Why?

Tuon, Min realized, stumbling to a halt. One of the Gray Men knelt above her motionless form, raising a dagger, and—

Min threw.

Mat toppled to the ground a few feet from Tuon; the final Gray Man had him by the legs. Min's knife spun through the air, reflecting flames, and took the Gray Man over Tuon in the chest.

Min breathed out. Never in her life had she been so happy to see a knife fly true. Mat had cursed, turning about, booting his aggressor in the face. He followed that with a knife, then scrambled for Tuon, hauling her up onto his shoulder.

Min met him. "Siuan is here, too. She—"

Mat pointed. Siuan lay on the floor of the building. Her eyes stared sightlessly, and all the images were gone from above her.

Dead. Min froze, heart wrenching. Siuan! She moved toward the woman anyway, unable to believe she was dead, though her clothing burned from the explosion of fire that had taken her and about half of the wall nearby her.

"Out!" Mat said, coughing, cradling Tuon. He threw his shoulder against a wall that was only half-burned, breaking out into the air.

Min groaned, leaving Siuan's corpse, blinking away tears both from grief and from the smoke. She coughed as she followed Mat out into open air. The outside smelled so sweet, so *cold*. Behind them, the building groaned, then collapsed.

In moments, Min and Mat were surrounded by members of the Deathwatch Guard. Not a one tried to take Tuon—who was still breathing, if shallowly—away from Mat. From the look in his eye, Min doubted they'd have been able to do so.

Farewell, Siuan, Min thought, looking back as Guards ushered her away from the fighting below Dashar Knob. *May the Creator shelter your soul.*

She would send word to others to protect Bryne, but she knew—deep down—it would be futile. He would have gone into a vengeful rage the moment Siuan died, and discounting that, there was the viewing.

She was never wrong. Sometimes, Min hated her accuracy. But she was *never* wrong.

"Strike at their weaves," Egwene yelled. "I'll attack!"

She didn't wait to see if she was obeyed. She struck, holding as much power as she could, drawing it through Vora's *sa'angreal* and heaving three different bands of fire upslope at the entrenched Sharans.

Around her, Bryne's well-trained troops struggled to maintain battle lines as they fought Sharan soldiers, working their way up the western side of the Heights. The hillside was pocked with hundreds of furrows and holes, created by weaves from one side or the other.

Egwene fought forward desperately. She could feel Gawyn above, but she thought he was unconscious; his spark of life was so faint that she could barely sense his direction. Her only hope was to fight through the Sharans and reach him.

The ground rumbled as she vaporized a Sharan woman above; Saerin, Doesine and other sisters concentrated on deflecting the enemy weaves, while Egwene focused on sending attacks. She stepped forward. One step after another.

I'm coming, Gawyn, she thought, growing frantic. *I'm coming.*

"We come to report, Wyld."

Demandred ignored the messengers for the moment. He flew upon the wings of a falcon, inspecting the battle through the bird's eyes. Ravens were better, but each time he tried using one of those, one Borderlander or another shot it down. Of all the customs to remember through the Ages, why did it have to be that one?

No matter. A falcon would work, even if the bird did resist his control. He guided it about the battlefield, inspecting formations, deployments, advancements of troops. He did not have to rely upon the reports of others.

It should have been an almost insurmountable advantage. Lews Therin could not use such an animal; this was a gift only the True Power could grant. Demandred could channel only a thin trickle of the True Power—not enough for destructive weaves, but there were other ways to be dangerous. Unfortunately, Lews Therin had his own advantage. Gateways that looked down upon a battle-field? It was discomforting the things people of this time discovered, things that hadn't been known during the Age of Legends.

Demandred opened his eyes and broke his bond to the falcon.

His forces were advancing, but each step was a grueling ordeal. Tens of thousands of Trollocs had been slain. He had to be careful; their numbers were not limitless.

He was currently on the eastern side of the Heights, looking down at the river below and northeast of the place where Lews Therin's assassin had tried to kill him.

Here, Demandred was nearly opposite the hill that Moghedien said they called Dashar Knob. The rock formation rose high in the air; its base was a fine position for a command post, sheltered from attacks by the One Power.

It was so tempting to strike there himself, to Travel to it and lay waste. But was that what Lews Therin wanted? Demandred would fight the man. He *would*. However, Traveling into the enemy's stronghold and possibly a trap, surrounded as it was by those high rock walls ... Better to draw Lews Therin to him. Demandred dominated this battlefield. He could choose where their confrontation would occur.

The riverbed had been slowed to a muddy trickle below, and Demandred's Trollocs fought to seize the southern bank. The defenders held for now, but he would have them soon. Far upriver M'Hael had done his work well in diverting that water, though he had reported unusual resistance. Townspeople and a small unit of soldiers? An oddity that Demandred had not yet deciphered.

He had almost wished for failure from M'Hael. Though Demandred himself had been the one to recruit the man, he had not expected M'Hael to rise to the rank of Chosen so quickly.

Demandred turned to the side. Before him bowed three women in black with white ribbons. Next to them, Shendla.

Shendla. He had thought himself long past caring for a woman again—how could affection thrive beside the burning passion that was his hatred for Lews Therin? And yet, Shendla ... Devious, capable, powerful. Almost, it was enough to change his heart.

"What is your report?" he asked the three bowing women in black.

"The hunt was a failure," Galbrait said, her head low.

"He escaped?"

"Yes, Wyld. I have failed you." He heard the pain in the woman's voice. She was leader of the female Ayyad.

"You were not meant to kill him," Demandred said. "He is a foe beyond your skill. You have disrupted his command post?"

"Yes," Galbrait said. "We killed half a dozen of his channelers, set the building aflame and destroyed his maps."

"Did he channel? Did he reveal himself?"

She hesitated, then shook her head.

So he could not know for certain yet if this Cauthon was Lews Therin in disguise. Demandred suspected he was, but there were reports from Shayol Ghul that Lews Therin had been seen there, on the slopes of the mountain. He had proven devious in the Last Battle before, jumping between battlefields, showing himself here and there.

The more Demandred maneuvered against the enemy general, the more he believed that Lews Therin was here. It would be very like Lews Therin to send a decoy north while coming to fight this battle himself. Lews Therin had difficulty letting others fight for him. He always wanted to be doing everything himself, leading every battle—every charge, if he could.

Yes ... how else could Demandred explain the skill of the enemy general? Only a man with the experience of an ancient was so masterly at the dance of battlefields. At their core, many battle tactics were simple. Avoid being flanked, meet heavy force with pikes, infantry with a well-trained line, channelers with other channelers. And yet, the finesse of it ... the little details ... these took centuries to master. No man from this Age had lived long enough to learn the details with such care.

During the War of Power, the only thing that Demandred ever done better than his friend was as a battle general. It stung to admit that, but he would no longer hide from that truth. Lews Therin had been stronger in the One Power. Lews Therin had been better at capturing the hearts of men. Lews Therin had taken Ilyena.

But Demandred ... Demandred had been better at war. Lews Therin had never been able to correctly balance caution and boldness. The man would hold back and deliberate, worrying over his decisions, until boiling forward in a reckless military action.

If this Cauthon was Lews Therin, the man had grown better at that. The enemy general knew when to flip the coin and let fate rule, but did not let too much ride on each result. He would have made an excellent card player.

Demandred would still defeat him, of course. The battle would merely be more . . . interesting.

He rested his hand on his sword, considering his scan of the battlefield moments before. His Trollocs continued their attack at the riverbed, and Lews Therin had formed his pikemen, opposite them, into disciplined square formations, a defensive move. Behind Demandred, the shaking booms of channelers marked the greater war, that between his Sharan Ayyad and the Aes Sedai.

He held the advantage there. His Ayyad were far better at war than the Aes Sedai. When would Cauthon commit those *damane*? Moghedien had reported some dissension between them and the Aes Sedai. Could Demandred widen the fracture there somehow?

He gave orders, and the three Ayyad nearby retreated. Shendla remained, waiting his permission to leave. He had her scouting the area nearby and watching for more assassins.

"Are you worried?" he asked her. "You know now for which side we fight. So far as I know, you have not given yourself to the Shadow."

"I've given myself to you, Wyld."

"And for me you fight beside Trollocs? Halfmen? Creatures from nightmare?"

"You said some would call your actions evil," she said. "But I do not see them as such. Our path is clear. Once you are victorious, you will remake the world, and our people will be preserved." She took his hand, and something stirred within him. It was quickly smothered by his hatred.

"I would cast it all away," he said, looking into her eyes. "Everything for a chance at Lews Therin."

"You have promised to try," she said. "That will be enough. And if you destroy him, you will destroy one world and preserve another. I will follow you. *We* will follow you."

Her voice seemed to imply that perhaps, once Lews Therin was dead, Demandred would be able to become his own man again.

He was not certain. Rule only interested him insofar as he could use it against his ancient enemy. The Sharans, devoted and faithful, were just a tool. But within him, there was something that wished it was not so. That was new. Yes, it was.

The air nearby *warped*, bending. No weaves were visible—this was a ripping of the fabric of the Pattern, Traveling by the True Power. M'Hael had arrived.

Demandred turned, and Shendla released his arm, but did not leave his side. M'Hael had been given access to the Great Lord's essence. That did not make Demandred jealous. M'Hael was another tool. Still, it made him wonder. Was anyone denied the True Power, these days?

"You are going to lose the battle near the ruins, Demandred," M'Hael said with an arrogant smile. "Your Trollocs there will be crushed. You had the enemy vastly outnumbered, and yet they still will defeat you! I thought you were supposed to be our greatest general, yet you lose to this rabble? I'm disappointed."

Demandred raised his hand casually, two fingers up.

M'Hael jerked as two dozen nearby Sharan channelers slammed shields between him and the One Power. They wrapped him in the Air, jerking him backward. He fought back, the air-warping aura of the True Power surrounding him, but Demandred was faster. He wove a True Power shield, building it from burning threads of Spirit.

The threads trembled in the air, each one barbed with twisting strands of energy so small, the ends vanished into nothing. The True Power was so volatile, so dangerous. A shield crafted from it had a strange effect, drinking in the power of another trying to channel it.

Demandred's shield stole M'Hael's power, and used the man like a conduit. Demandred gathered the True Power and wove it into a crackling ball of *force* above his hand. Only M'Hael would be able to see it, and the man's proud eyes opened wide as Demandred drained him.

It was not unlike a circle. The pulling of energy made M'Hael tremble, sweat, as he was held up by the weaves of Demandred's Ayyad. This flow could burn M'Hael out, if unchecked—could flay his soul with the rushing of the True Power, like a river surging beyond its banks. The twisting mass of threads in Demandred's hands pulsed and crackled, warping the air, beginning to unravel the Pattern.

Tiny spiderweb cracks spread out on the ground from him. Cracks into nothingness.

He walked up to M'Hael. The man began to have a seizure, froth dripping from his lips.

"You will listen to me, M'Hael," Demandred said softly. "I am not as the other Chosen. I do not care one *whit* for your political games. I don't care which of you the Great Lord favors, which of you Moridin pats on the head. I care only for Lews Therin.

"This is my fight. You are mine. I brought you to the Shadow, and I can destroy you. If you interfere with what I do here, I will snuff you out like a candle. I realize you think yourself strong, with your stolen Dreadlords and untrained channelers. You are a child, an infant. Take your men, create what chaos you wish, but stay out of my way. And stay away from my prize. The enemy general is mine."

M'Hael's eyes, though his body betrayed him with trembles, were full of hatred, not fear. Yes, this one always had shown promise.

Demandred turned his hand and launched a stream of balefire with the gathered True Power. The white-hot line of liquid destruction burned through the armies at the river below, vaporizing each man or woman it touched. Their forms became points of light, then dust, hundreds of them vanishing. He left a long line of burned ground, like a furrow cut by an enormous cleaver.

"Release him," Demandred said, allowing the True Power shield to unravel.

M'Hael stumbled back, keeping his feet, sweat dripping from his face. He gasped, hand raised to his chest.

"Stay alive through this battle," Demandred said to him, turning away and beginning a weave to summon his falcon back. "If you do so, perhaps I will show you how to do as I just did. You may think you wish to kill me now, but know that the Great Lord watches. Beyond that, consider this. You may have a hundred pet Asha'man. I have over four hundred of my Ayyad. I am this world's savior."

When he looked back, M'Hael was gone, having Traveled away with the True Power. It was amazing that he could summon the strength, after what Demandred had just done. He hoped he wouldn't have to kill the man. He should prove useful.

I WILL WIN EVENTUALLY.

Rand stood before the blowing winds, stood strong, though his eyes watered as he stared into the darkness. How long had he been in this place? A thousand years? Ten thousand?

For the moment, he concerned himself only with defiance. He would not bend before this wind. He could not give in for a fraction of a heartbeat.

THE TIME HAS COME, FINALLY.

"Time is nothing to you," Rand said.

It was true, and it was not. Rand could see the threads swirling-around him, forming the Pattern. As it formed, he saw the battlefields below him. Those he loved fighting for their lives. These were not possibilities; this was the truth, what was actually happening.

The Dark One wrapped around the Pattern, unable to take it and destroy it, but able to touch it. Tendrils of darkness, spines, touched the world at points all along its length. The Dark One lay like shadow upon the Pattern.

When the Dark One touched the Pattern, time existed for him. And so, while time was nothing to the Dark One, he—or it, as the Dark One had no gender—could only work within its bounds. Like . . . like a sculptor who had marvelous visions and dreams but was still bound by the reality of the materials he worked with.

Rand stared at the Pattern, resisting the Dark One's attack. He did not move or breathe. Breath wasn't needed here.

People died below. Rand heard their screams. So many fell.

I WILL WIN EVENTUALLY, ADVERSARY. WATCH THEM SCREAM. WATCH THEM DIE.

THE DEAD ARE MINE.

"Lies," Rand said.

NO. I WILL SHOW YOU.

The Dark One spun possibility again, gathering up what could be, and thrust Rand into another vision.

Juilin Sandar was not a commander. He was a thief-catcher, not some nobleman. *Certainly* not a nobleman. He worked on his own.

Except, apparently, when he ended up on a battlefield, put in charge of a squad of men because he had successfully captured dangerous men as a thief-catcher. The Sharans pressed against his men, aiming for the Aes Sedai. They fought on the western side of the Heights, and his squad's job was to protect the Aes Sedai from Sharan infantry.

Aes Sedai. How had he ever gotten tangled up with Aes Sedai? Him, a good Tairen.

"Hold!" Juilin yelled to his men. "Hold!" He yelled it for his own benefit, too. His squad held to their spears and pikes, forcing the Sharan infantry backward up the slope. He wasn't sure why he was here, or why they were fighting in this sector. He just wanted to stay alive!

The Sharans shouted and cursed in an unfamiliar tongue. They had a lot of those channelers, but the outfit he faced was made up of regular troops who used a variety of hand weapons, mostly swords and shields. Corpses littered the ground, and that made it difficult for both sides as Juilin and his men followed orders, pushing against the Sharan troops while the Aes Sedai and enemy channelers traded weaves.

Juilin wielded a spear, a weapon he was only mildly familiar with. An armored Sharan squad forced its way between Myk and Charn's pikes. The officers wore breastplates, strangely wrapped in cloth of a variety of colors, while the common rank and file wore leather fitted with strips of metal. They all had their backs painted with strange patterns.

The leader of the Sharan troop wielded a wicked mace, smashing one pikeman, then the other. The man shouted at Juilin, curses he didn't understand.

Juilin feinted, and the Sharan raised his shield, so Juilin rammed his spear into the man's armor at the gap between breastplate and arm. Light, he didn't even flinch! He smashed his shield into Juilin, forcing him back.

The spear slipped from Juilin's sweaty fingers. He cursed, reaching for his sword breaker, a weapon he knew well. Myk and the others fought nearby, engaging the rest of this Sharan squad. Charn tried to help Juilin, but the crazed Sharan brought his mace down on Charn's head—splitting it in two like a cracked walnut.

"Die, you bloody monster!" Juilin cried, leaping forward and ramming his sword breaker into the man's neck just above the gorget. Other Sharans were moving quickly toward his position. Juilin fell back as the man in front of him collapsed and died. Just in time, as a Sharan to his left tried to take his head off with a broad swing of his sword. The tip of the sword went by his ear, and Juilin instinctively raised his own blade. His opponent's weapon broke in two, and he quickly dispatched the man with a backhand slice to the man's throat.

Juilin scrambled to pick up his spear. Fireballs fell nearby, attacks from the Aes Sedai behind and the Sharans on the Heights ahead. Soil coated Juilin's hair, and stuck in clumps to the blood on his arms.

"Hold!" Juilin shouted to his men. "Burn you, we need to hold!"

He attacked another Sharan who came at him. One of the pikemen raised his weapon in time to pin the man on the shoulder, and Juilin speared him through his leather-clad chest.

The air trembled. His ears rang faintly from all of the explosions. Juilin pulled back, yelling orders to his men.

He wasn't supposed to be here. He was supposed to be someplace warm, with Amathera, thinking about the next criminal he needed to catch.

He figured that every man on the field felt they should be someplace else. The only thing to do was keep on fighting.

You look good in black, Androl sent to Pevara as they moved through the enemy army on top of the Heights.

That, she replied back, *is something one should never, never say to an Aes Sedai. Ever.*

His only response was a sense of nervousness through the bond. Pevara understood. They—wearing inverted weaves of the Mask of Mirrors—walked among Darkfriends, Shadowspawn and Sharans. And it was working. Pevara wore a white dress and a black cloak over it—those weren't part of a weave—but anyone looking into her cloak's hood would see the face of Alviarin, a member of the Black Ajah. Theodrin wore the face of Rianna.

Androl and Emarin wore weaves that gave them the faces of Nensen and Kash, two of Taim's cronies. Jonneth looked very unlike himself, wearing the face of a nondescript Darkfriend, and he played the part well, skulking behind and carrying their gear. One would never have seen the good-natured Two Rivers man in that hawk-faced man with the greasy hair and nervous manner.

They moved at a brisk pace along the back lines of the Shadow's army on the Heights. Trollocs hauled bundles of arrows forward; others left the lines to feast on piles of corpses. Cookpots boiled here. That shocked Pevara. They were stopping to eat? Now?

Only some of them, Androl sent. *It's common for human armies too, though these moments don't make it into the ballads. The fighting has lasted all day, and soldiers need energy while fighting. Usually, you rotate in three batches. Your front lines, your reserves, and your off-duty—troops who will trudge away from the fight and eat as quickly as they can before grabbing a little sleep. Then back to the front lines.*

She'd once seen war differently. She'd imagined every man committed every moment of the day. A true battle, however, was not a sprint; it was an extended, soul-grinding trudge.

It was late afternoon already, approaching evening. To the east, below the Heights, battle lines extended far in both directions along the dry riverbed. Many thousands of men and Trollocs fought back and forth there. Large numbers of Trollocs fought there, but others were rotated back up the Heights to either eat or collapse into unconsciousness for a time.

She did not look too closely at the cookpots, though Jonneth fell to his knees and sicked up beside the path. He had noticed the body parts floating in the thick stew. As he emptied his stomach onto the ground, a passing group of Trollocs snorted and hooted in mockery.

Why are they pushing off the Heights to take the river? she sent to Androl. *It seems to be a better position up here.*

Maybe it is, Androl sent. *But the Shadow is the aggressor. If they stay in this position, it serves Cauthon's army. Demandred needs to keep pressing him. That means crossing the river.*

So Androl understood tactics, too. Interesting.

I've picked up a few things, he sent. *I won't be leading a battle any time soon.*

Just curious how many lives you've led, Androl.

An odd statement, coming from a woman who is old enough to be my grandmother's grandmother.

They continued along the eastern side of the Heights. Distant, on the far western side, the Aes Sedai were battling their way up to the top—but for now, the Heights were held by Demandred's forces. This area Pevara walked through was full of Trollocs. Some bowed in a lumbering way as Pevara and the others passed, others curled up on the stones to sleep, with no cushions or blankets. Each one kept its weapon at hand.

"This does not look promising," Emarin said softly from behind his mask. "I do not see Taim associating with Trollocs any more than he has to."

"Ahead," Androl said. "Look there."

The Trollocs were separated from a group of Sharans who could be seen up ahead, wearing unfamiliar uniforms. They wore armor that was wrapped in cloth, so none of the metal showed except on the very back, though the shape of the breastplates was still obvious. Pevara looked to the others.

"I could see Taim being part of that group," Emarin said. "It's likely to smell far less putrid than over here among the Trollocs, for one thing."

Pevara had been ignoring the stench—she had learned to do that years ago, snuffing out powerful scents in the same way she ignored heat and cold. As Emarin said it, however, a hint of what the others were smelling seeped through her defenses. She quickly regained control. It was *awful*.

"Will the Sharans let us pass?" Jonneth asked.

"We shall see," Pevara said, setting off toward the Sharans; their group fell in around her. The Sharan guards maintained an uneasy line against the Trollocs, watching them as they would enemies. This alliance, or whatever it was, did not sit terribly well with the Sharan soldiers. They didn't try to mask their looks of disgust, and many had tied cloths around their faces to mask the odors.

As Pevara passed their line, a nobleman—or such she assumed him to be, from his armor of brazen rings—moved to confront her. A well-practiced Aes Sedai look staved him off. *I am far too important for you to bother*, that look said. It worked beautifully, and they were in.

The Sharan reserve camp was orderly as men rotated in from

the west, where they fought the White Tower forces. The fierce channeling from that direction kept drawing Pevara's attention, like a bright light.

What do you think? Androl sent to her.

We're going to need to talk to someone. The battlefield is just too big for us to find Taim on our own.

He sent back his agreement. Not for the first time, Pevara found their bond distracting. She not only had to deal with her own nervousness, but Androl's as well. That crept from the back of her mind, and she had to constrain it forcefully, using breathing exercises she'd learned when first in the Tower.

She stopped in the center of the camp, looking about, trying to decide whom to approach. She could distinguish servants from nobles. Approaching the former would be less dangerous, but also less likely to yield results. Maybe—

"You!"

Pevara started, spinning around.

"You should not be here." The aged Sharan was completely bald, with a short gray beard. Twin sword hilts in the shape of serpents' heads peeked out over his shoulders; he wore the blades crossed at his back, and he carried a staff that had strange holes along its length. A flute of some sort?

"Come," the man said, his accent so thick, Pevara could barely make it out. "The Wyld will need to see you."

Who is the Wyld? Pevara sent Androl.

He shook his head, feeling as baffled as she did.

This could turn out very badly.

The old man stopped ahead of them with an annoyed expression. What would he do if they refused? Pevara was tempted to create a gateway for them to flee.

We follow, Androl thought, striding forward. *We're never going to find Taim in this unless we talk to someone.*

Pevara frowned as he walked after the man, the other Asha'man joining him. She hurriedly caught up. *I thought we had decided I was in charge,* she thought to him.

No, he replied, *I thought that we'd decided you would act like you were in charge.*

She sent back a calculated mix of cold displeasure and an implication that the conversation was not yet finished.

Androl sent back amusement. *Did you . . . just glare at me mentally? That's impressive.*

We're taking a risk, she sent back. *This man could lead us into anything.*

Yes, he replied.

Something smoldered inside of him, something only hinted at until now. *You want Taim that badly?*

. . . Yes. I do.

She nodded.

You understand? he sent.

I lost friends to him as well, Androl, she replied. *I watched them be taken right in front of me. We have to be careful, though. We can't take too many risks. Not yet.*

It's the end of the world, Pevara, Androl sent back. *If we can't take risks now, when will we?*

She followed without further argument, wondering at the determined focus she sensed in Androl. Taim had awoken something inside of him by taking his friends and Turning them to the Shadow.

As they followed the old Sharan, Pevara realized that she didn't understand what Androl was feeling, not completely. Aes Sedai friends of hers had been taken, but it wasn't the same as Androl losing Evin. Evin had trusted Androl, looked to Androl for protection. The Aes Sedai with Pevara had been acquaintances, friends, but it was different.

The old Sharan led them to a larger group of people, many of whom wore fine clothing. The highest noblemen and women among the Sharans didn't seem to fight, for not one of them carried a weapon. They made way for the older man, though several looked at his swords and sneered.

Jonneth and Emarin moved in around Pevara and Theodrin, one to each side, like bodyguards. They eyed the Sharans, hands on weapons, and she suspected that both were holding the One Power. Well, that would probably be expected of Dreadlords who were walking among allies they didn't fully trust. They didn't need to protect Pevara in such a way, but it was a nice gesture. She *had* always thought it would be useful to have a Warder. She had gone to the Black Tower with the intention of taking multiple Asha'man as Warders. Perhaps . . .

Androl immediately felt jealous. *What are you? Some Green with a flock of men fawning over her?*

She sent back amusement. *Why not?*

They're too young for you, he sent back. *Jonneth is, anyway. And Theodrin would fight you for him.*

I'm considering bonding them, she sent back, *not bedding them, Androl. Honestly. Besides, Emarin prefers men.*

Androl paused. *He does?*

Of course he does. Haven't you been paying attention?

Androl seemed baffled. Sometimes, men could be surprisingly dense, even observant ones like Androl.

Pevara embraced the One Power as they reached the center of the group. Would she have time to make a gateway if something went wrong? She did not know the area, but so long as she Traveled somewhere nearby, that wouldn't matter. She felt as if she was walking up to a noose and inspecting it, deciding how well it would fit her neck.

A tall man in armor made of silvery discs with holes in the middle stood at the center of the group, dispensing orders. As they watched, a cup moved toward him through the air. Androl stiffened. *He's channeling, Pevara.*

Demandred, then? It *must* be. Pevara let *saidar* flood her with its warm glow, letting it wash away emotions. The old man who had been leading them stepped forward and whispered something to Demandred. Despite the enhanced senses of *saidar*, Pevara could not hear what was said.

Demandred turned toward the group of them. "What is this? Has M'Hael so quickly forgotten his orders?"

Androl dropped to his knees, as did the others. Though it galled her, Pevara went down as well.

"Great One," Androl said, "we were merely—"

"No excuses!" Demandred yelled. "No games! M'Hael is to take all of his Dreadlords and destroy the White Tower forces. If I see *any* of you away from that fight, I will make you wish I'd given you to the Trollocs instead!"

Androl nodded eagerly, then began backing away. A whip of Air Pevara could not see—although she could feel his pain through the bond—cracked him in the face. The rest of them followed after him, scrambling away with heads low.

That was foolish and dangerous, Pevara thought at Androl.

And effective, he replied, eyes ahead, hand to his cheek, blood seeping between the fingers. *We know Taim is on the battlefield for sure, and we know where to find him. Let's move.*

Galad scrambled through a nightmare. He had known that the Last Battle might be the end of the world, but now ... now he *felt* it.

Channelers on both sides scourged one another, shaking Polov Heights. Lightning had struck so often that Galad could barely hear any longer, and his eyes watered from the pain of seeing blasts strike nearby.

He threw himself up against the hillside, digging his shoulder into the ground and ducking for cover as a series of explosions ripped up the earth in front of him. His team—twelve men in tattered white cloaks—dove for cover with him.

The White Tower's forces were strained under the attacks, but so were the Sharan forces. The power of so many channelers was incredible.

The main bulk of White Tower infantry and a large number of Sharan troops fought here on the western Heights. Galad stayed on the perimeter of that battle, looking for Sharan channelers alone or in small groups. In many places here, the battle lines on both sides had fractured. Not surprising; it was near impossible to maintain solid battle lines with all of that power being flung back and forth.

Bands of soldiers scrambled about, seeking cover in blown-out holes in the rock. Others protected groups of channelers. Nearby, women and men roamed about in small groups, destroying soldiers with fire and lightning.

These were what Galad hunted.

He raised his sword, pointing at a trio of Sharan women holding at the top of the Heights. He and his men were more than halfway up the slope.

Three. Three would be difficult. They turned their attention on a small band of men wearing the Flame of Tar Valon. Lightning struck the unfortunate soldiers.

Galad held up four fingers. Plan four. He leaped out of his

hollow and dashed toward the three women. His men waited a count of five, then followed behind.

The women saw him. If they'd remained turned away, Galad would have gained the advantage. One raised a hand and summoned Fire, hurling the weave at him. The flame struck him, and though he could feel its heat, the weave unraveled and dissipated—leaving him singed, but mostly unharmed.

The Sharan's eyes opened with shock. That look ... that look was becoming familiar to Galad now. It was the look of a soldier whose sword had broken in battle, the look of one who had seen something that should not be. What did you do when the One Power failed, the thing you relied upon to raise you above common folk?

You died. Galad's sword took the woman's head off as one of her companions tried to seize him with Air. He felt the metal grow cold at his chest, and sensed the rush of Air moving around him.

A poor choice, Galad thought, ramming his sword into the chest of a second woman. The third proved smarter, and she slammed him with a large rock. He barely raised his shield before the rock smashed into his arm, throwing him backward. The woman raised another stone right as Galad's team hit her. She fell to their swords.

Galad caught his breath, his head back, pain radiating from the impact of the rock. He groaned, sitting up. Nearby, his men hacked at the third Sharan woman's body. They didn't need to be so thorough, but some Children had strange ideas about what Aes Sedai could do. He'd caught Laird cutting off one of the Sharan women's heads to bury it separate from the body. Unless you did that, Laird claimed, they would return to life at the next full moon.

As the men butchered the other two corpses, Golever came over and offered Galad a hand. "Light burn me," Golever said, a wide grin splitting his bearded face, "if this isn't the finest work we've ever done, my Lord Captain Commander, I don't know what is!"

Galad stood up. "It is what must be done, Child Golever."

"I wish it had to be done more often! *This* is what the Children have awaited for centuries. You are the first to deliver it. The Light illumine you, Galad Damodred. The Light illumine you!"

"May the Light illumine a day when men need not kill at all," Galad said tiredly. "It is not fitting to take joy in death."

"Of course, my Lord Captain Commander." Golever continued grinning.

Galad looked across the bloody pandemonium of the western slope of the Heights. The Light send Cauthon could make some sense of this battle, for Galad certainly could not.

"Lord Captain Commander!" a frightened voice cried.

Galad spun about, hand on his sword. It was Alhanra, one of his scouts.

"What is it, Child Alhanra?" Galad asked as the spindly man ran up. No horses. They were on an incline, and the animals would not have reacted well to the lightning. Better to trust one's own feet.

"You need to see this, my Lord," Alhanra said, panting. "It's . . . It's your *brother*."

"Gawyn?" Impossible. *No*, he thought. *Not impossible. He would be with Egwene, fighting on their front.* Galad ran after Alhanra, Golever and the others falling in around him.

Gawyn's body lay ashen-faced in a gap between two rocks on the top of the Heights. Nearby a horse was munching on grass, a trail of blood streaming down its side. By the looks of it, not the horse's blood. Galad knelt down beside the younger man's corpse. Gawyn had not died easily. But what of Egwene?

"Peace, brother," Galad said, resting a hand on the body. "May the Light—"

"Galad . . ." Gawyn whispered, his eyes fluttering open.

"Gawyn?" Galad asked, shocked. Gawyn had a nasty gut wound. He wore some strange rings. There was blood everywhere. His hand, chest . . . his entire body . . .

How could the man still be alive?

The Warder bond, he realized. "We need to carry you to a Healer! One of the Aes Sedai." He reached into the hollow, scooping up Gawyn.

"Galad . . . I failed." Gawyn stared at the sky, eyes blank.

"You did well."

"No. I failed. I should have . . . I should have stayed with her. I killed Hammar. Did you know that? I killed him. Light. I should have picked a side . . ."

Galad cradled his brother and began running along the slope toward the Aes Sedai. He tried to shelter Gawyn amid the attacks of channelers. After only a few moments, an explosion of earth ripped up among the Children, flinging them aside, tumbling Galad to the ground. He dropped Gawyn as he collapsed to the earth beside him.

Gawyn trembled, eyes staring distantly.

Galad crawled over and tried to pick him up again, but Gawyn grabbed his arm, meeting his eyes. "I did love her, Galad. Tell her."

"If you are truly bonded, then she knows."

"This will hurt her," Gawyn said through pale lips. "And at the end of it, I failed. To kill him."

"Him?"

"Demandred," Gawyn whispered. "I tried to kill him, but I wasn't good enough. I've never . . . been quite good . . . enough . . ."

Galad found himself in a very cold place. He had seen men die, he had lost friends. This hurt more. Light, but it did. He had loved his brother, loved him deeply—and Gawyn, unlike Elayne, had returned the sentiment.

"I will bring you to safety, Gawyn," Galad said, picking him up, shocked to find tears in his eyes. "I will not be left without a brother."

Gawyn coughed. "You won't be. You have another brother, Galad. One you do not know. A son of . . . Tigraine . . . who went into the Waste . . . Son of a Maiden. Born on Dragonmount . . ."

Oh, Light.

"Don't hate him, Galad," Gawyn whispered. "I always hated him, but I stopped. I . . . stopped . . ."

Gawyn's eyes stopped moving.

Galad felt for a pulse, then sat back, looking down at his dead brother. The bandage Gawyn had made for himself at his side seeped blood onto the dry ground below, which hungrily soaked it up.

Golever moved up to him, helping Alhanra, whose blackened face and burned clothing smelled of smoke from the lightning strike. "Take the wounded to safety, Golever," Galad said, standing. He reached up and felt the medallion at his neck. "Take all of the men and go."

"And you, Lord Captain Commander?" Golever asked.

"I will do what needs to be done," Galad said, cold inside. Cold as winter steel. "I will bring Light to the Shadow. I will bring justice to the Forsaken."

Gawyn's thread of life vanished.

Egwene lurched to a stop on the battlefield. Something severed within her. It was as if a knife suddenly tore into her and scooped out the piece of Gawyn inside, leaving only emptiness.

She screamed, falling to her knees. No. No, it *couldn't* be. She could feel him, just ahead! She'd been running for him. She could . . . She could . . .

He was gone.

Egwene howled, opening herself to the One Power and drawing in as much as she could hold. She let it out as a wall of flames toward the Sharans who were all around now. They had once held the Heights, the Aes Sedai below, but it was madness now.

She assailed them with the Power, clutching Vora's *sa'angreal*. She would destroy them! Light! It hurt. It *hurt so badly*.

"Mother!" Silviana cried, seizing her arm. "You are out of control, Mother! You will kill our own people. Please!"

Egwene breathed in gasps. Nearby, a group of Whitecloaks stumbled by, carrying wounded down the hillside.

So *close*! Oh, Light. He was gone!

"Mother?" Silviana said. Egwene barely heard. She touched her face, and found tears there.

She had been bold before. She had claimed she could keep fighting through the loss. How naive that was. She let the fire of *saidar* die within her. With that gone, life went out of her. She slumped to the side, and felt hands carrying her away. Through a gateway, off the battlefield.

Tam used his last arrow to save a Whitecloak. It wasn't something he'd have ever imagined himself doing, but there he was. The wolfish Trolloc stumbled back with the arrow through its eye, refusing to go down until the young Whitecloak pulled himself from the mud and struck at its knees.

His men were now positioned on the catwalks of the palisade, shooting volleys of arrows at the Trollocs that had surged across the riverbed here. Their numbers were depleted, but there were still so many of them.

Until this point, the battle had been going well. Tam's combined forces spread out mightily along the river on the Shienaran side. Downriver the Legion of the Dragon, crossbow banners and heavy cavalry, stemmed the Trolloc advance. The same events were being played out here, farther upriver, with archers, foot soldiers and cavalry stopping the Trolloc incursion at the riverbed. Until the supplies began to dwindle and Tam was forced to withdraw his men to the relative safety of the palisade.

Tam looked to the side. Abell held up his bow, shrugging. He was out of arrows as well. All up and down the catwalk, the Two Rivers men held up their bows. No arrows.

"No more will be coming," Abell said softly. "The lad said that batch was the last."

The Whitecloak army fought desperately, mixed with members of Perrin's Wolf Guard, but they were being pushed back from the riverbed in droves. They fought on three sides, and another force of Trollocs had just swung around to box them in entirely. The banner of Ghealdan flew closer to the ruins. Arganda held that position along with Nurelle and the remnants of the Winged Guard.

If this were any other battle, Tam would have had his men save their arrows to cover a retreat. There would be no retreat this day, and the order to loose had been the right one; the lads had taken their time with each shot. They'd likely killed thousands of Trollocs during the hours of fighting.

But what was an archer without his bow? *Still a Two Rivers man*, Tam thought. *And still not willing to let this battle be lost.*

"Off the catwalks and form up with weapons," Tam called to the lads. "Leave the bows here. We will fetch them when more arrows come our way."

More arrows wouldn't come, but the Two Rivers men would be happier pretending that they might go back to their bows. They formed up into ranks as Tam had taught them, armed with spears, axes, swords, even some scythes. Everything and anything they'd had on hand, along with shields for those with axes or swords and good leather armor for them all. No pikes, unfortunately. After the heavy infantry had been outfitted, there hadn't been any of those left.

"Stay tight," Tam said to them. "Form into two wedges. We'll push into the Trollocs around the Whitecloaks." Best thing to do—at least, the best Tam could come up with—was to hit those Trollocs that had just come around the back of the Whitecloaks, fragment them and help the Whitecloaks break free.

The men nodded, though they probably had very little understanding of the tactics. It didn't matter. So long as they kept disciplined ranks as Tam had taught them.

They started forward, running, and Tam was reminded of another battlefield. Snow, cutting into his face, blown by terrible winds. In a way, that battlefield had begun this all. Now it ended here.

Tam placed himself at the point of the first wedge, then put Deoan—a man from Deven Ride who had served in the Andoran army—at the point of the other. Tam guided his men forward briskly, not letting them, or himself, dwell too much on what was about to happen.

As they approached the hulking Trollocs, with their swords, polearms and battle-axes, Tam sought the flame and the void. Nervousness vanished. All emotion evaporated. He unsheathed the sword Rand had given him, the one with the dragons painted on the sheath. It was as fine a weapon as Tam had ever seen. Those folds in the metal whispered of ancient origin. It seemed too good a weapon for Tam. He had felt that way about every sword he'd ever used.

"Remember, hold formation!" Tam yelled back at his men. "Don't let them break us apart. If someone falls, one man steps up and takes his place while another pulls the fallen man into the center of the wedge."

They nodded back at him, and then they hit the Trollocs in the back, where they had surrounded the Children of the Light at the river.

His formations hit, pounding forward. The huge Trollocs turned to fight.

Fortuona waved away the *so'jhin* who tried to replace her regal clothing. She smelled of smoke from the fire, and her arms had been burned and scored in several places. She would not accept *damane* Healing. Fortuona thought Healing to be a useful development—and some of her people were changing their attitudes toward it—but she was not certain the Empress should submit to it. Besides, her wounds were not dire.

The Deathwatch Guards kneeling before her would need some form of punishment. This was the second time they had allowed an assassin to reach her, and while she did not blame them for the failure, to deny them punishment would be to deny them their honor. It twisted her heart about, but she knew what she would have to do.

She gave the order herself. Selucia, as her Voice, should have done it—but Selucia's wounds were being tended. And Karede deserved this small honor of receiving his execution order from Fortuona herself.

"You will go to engage the enemy *marath'damane* directly," she ordered Karede. "Each of you who was on duty. Fight valiantly for the Empire there, and try to slay the enemy's *marath'damane*."

She could see Karede relax. It was a way to continue serving; he would probably have fallen on his own sword, if given the choice himself. This was a mercy.

She turned away from the man who had cared for her during her youth, the man who had defied what was expected of him. All for her. She would find her own penance for what she must do later. At this point, she would grant him the honor she could.

"Darbinda," she said, turning to the woman who insisted upon calling herself "Min" despite the honor of a new name that Fortuona had given her. It meant "Girl of Pictures" in the Old Tongue. "You have saved my life and possibly that of the Prince of the Ravens. I name you of the Blood, Doomseer. Let your name be venerated for generations to come."

Darbinda folded her arms. How like Knotai she was. Stubbornly humble, these mainlanders. They were actually proud—*proud*—of their lowborn heritage. Baffling.

Knotai himself sat on a nearby stump, receiving battle reports and snapping out orders. The Aes Sedai battle for the western Heights was descending into chaos. He met her eyes across the small gap between them, then nodded once.

If there was a spy—and Fortuona would be surprised if there

was not one—then now was the time to mislead them. Everyone who had survived the attack was gathered around. Fortuona had insisted on having them close, ostensibly for the purpose of rewarding those who had served her well and meting punishment to those who had not. Each and every guard, servant and noble could hear as she spoke.

"Knotai," she said, "we have yet to discuss what I should do about you. The Deathwatch Guard has charge of my safety, but *you* have charge of the defense of this camp. If you suspected that our command post was not safe, why did you not speak earlier?"

"Are you bloody suggesting that this is *my* fault?" Knotai stood up and stilled the scouts' reports with a gesture.

"I gave you command here," Fortuona said. "The ultimate responsibility for failure is yours then, is it not?"

Nearby, General Galgan frowned. He did not see it this way. Others looked toward Knotai with accusing eyes. Noble sycophants; they would blame him because he wasn't born of the Seanchan. Impressive, that Knotai had converted Galgan so quickly. Or was Galgan telegraphing his emotions purposefully? Was he the spy? He could have been manipulating Suroth, or simply have been a redundant plant if Suroth failed.

"I'm not taking responsibility for this, Tuon," Knotai said. "You are the one who bloody insisted on watching from the camp when you could have been somewhere safe."

"Perhaps I should have done just that," she replied coldly. "This entire battle has been a disaster. You lose ground each moment. You talk lightly and joke, refusing proper protocol; I do not think you approach this with the solemnity befitting your station."

Knotai laughed. It was a loud, genuine laugh. He was good at this. Fortuona thought she was the only one who saw the twin lines of smoke rising exactly behind him from the Heights. An appropriate omen for Knotai: a large gamble would yield large rewards. Or a great cost.

"I've had it with you," Knotai said, waving a hand at her. "You and your bloody Seanchan rules just keep getting in the way."

"Then I have had it with you as well," she said, raising her head. "We should never have joined this battle. We would be better preparing to defend our own lands to the southwest. I will not let you throw away the lives of my soldiers."

"Go, then," Knotai snarled. "What do I care?"

She spun about, stalking away. "Come," she said to the others. "Gather our *damane*. All but those Deathwatch Guards will Travel to our army's camp at the Erinin, then we will all return to Ebou Dar. We will fight the true Last Battle there once these fools have bloodied the Shadowspawn for us."

Her people followed. Had the ploy been convincing? The spy had seen her consign to death men who loved her; would that show that she was reckless? Reckless and self-important enough to pull her troops away from Knotai? It was plausible enough. In a way, she wanted to do as she said, and fight in the south instead.

To do that, of course, would be to ignore the breaking sky, the trembling land, and the Dragon Reborn's fight. These were not omens she could let pass her by.

The spy did not know that. It could not know her. The spy would see a young woman, foolish enough to want to fight on her own. So she hoped.

The Dark One spun a web of possibility around Rand.

Rand knew this struggle between them—the fight for what *could* be—was vital to the Last Battle. Rand could not weave the future. He was not the Wheel, nor anything like it. For everything that had happened to him, he was still merely a man.

Yet, in him was the hope of humankind. Humankind had a destiny, a choice for its future. The path they would take . . . this battle would decide it, his will clashing with that of the Dark One. As of yet, what *could* be might become what *would* be. Breaking now would be to let the Dark One choose that future.

BEHOLD, the Dark One said as the lines of light came together and Rand entered another world. A world that had not yet happened, but a world that very well might soon come to be.

Rand frowned, looking up at the sky. It was not red in this vision, the landscape not ruined. He stood in Caemlyn, much as he knew it. Oh, there were differences. Steamwagons rattled down the streets, mingling with the traffic of horse-drawn carriages and crowds walking.

The city had expanded beyond the new wall—he could see that

from the height of the central hill he stood upon. He could even make out the place where Talmanes had blown a hole in the wall. It had not been repaired. Instead, the city had spilled out through it. Buildings covered what had once been fields outside.

Rand frowned, turning and walking down the street. What game was the Dark One playing? Surely this normal, even prosperous, city would not be part of his plans for the world. The people were clean and did not look oppressed. He saw no sign of the depravity that had marked the previous world the Dark One had created for him.

Curious, he walked up to a stand where a woman sold fruit. The slender woman gave him an inviting smile, gesturing toward her wares. "Welcome, good sir. I am Renel, and my shop is a second home to all seeking the finest of fruits from around the world. I have fresh peaches from Tear!"

"Peaches!" Rand said, aghast. Everyone knew those were poisonous.

"Ha! Fear not, good sir! These have had the toxin removed. They are as safe as I am honest." The woman smiled, taking a bite of one to prove it. As she did, a grubby hand appeared from under the fruit stand—an urchin hid underneath, a young boy that Rand had not noticed earlier.

The little boy snatched a red fruit of a type Rand did not recognize, then dashed off. He was so thin that Rand could see his ribs pressing against the skin of his too-small form, and he ran on legs so slender that it was a wonder the boy could walk.

The woman continued smiling at Rand as she reached to her side, took out a small rod with a lever at the side for her finger. She pulled the lever, and the rod *cracked*.

The urchin died in a spray of blood. He fell, sprawling, to the ground. People moved around him in the flow of traffic, though somebody—a man with many guards—did scoop up the piece of fruit. He wiped the blood off of it and took a bite, continuing on his way. A few moments later, a steamwagon rolled over the corpse, pressing it into the muddy roadway.

Rand, aghast, looked back at the woman. She tucked away her weapon, a smile still on her face. "Were you looking for any type of fruit in particular?" she asked him.

"You just killed that child!"

The woman frowned in confusion. "Yes. Did it belong to you, good sir?"

"No, but . . . " Light! The woman didn't show a hint of remorse or concern. Rand turned, and nobody else seemed to care in the slightest about what had happened.

"Sir?" the woman asked. "I feel as if I should know you. That is fine clothing, if a little out of style. To which faction do you belong?"

"Faction?" Rand asked, looking back.

"And where are your guards?" the woman asked. "A man as rich as you has them, of course."

Rand met her eyes, then ran to the side as the woman reached for her weapon again. He ducked around a corner. The look in her eyes . . . utter lack of any kind of human sympathy or concern. She'd have killed him in a moment without a second thought. He knew it.

Others on the street saw him. They nudged companions, gesturing toward him. One man he passed called out, "Speak your faction!" Others gave chase.

Rand ducked around another corner. The One Power. Dared he use it? He didn't know what was going on in this world. As before, he had trouble separating himself from the vision. He knew that it wasn't completely real, but he couldn't help believing himself part of it.

He didn't risk the One Power, and trusted his own feet for now. He did not know Caemlyn terribly well, but he did remember this area. If he reached the end of this street and turned . . . yes, there! Ahead, he saw a familiar building, with a sign out front showing a man kneeling before a woman with red-gold hair. The Queen's Blessing.

Rand reached the front doors as those chasing him piled around the corner behind. They stopped as Rand scrambled up to the door, passing a brutish fellow standing to the side. A new door guard? Rand did not know him. Did Basel Gill still own the inn, or had it changed hands?

Rand burst into the large common room, heart thumping. Several men nursing pitchers of afternoon ale looked up at him. Rand was in luck; Basel Gill himself stood behind the counter, rubbing a cup with a cloth.

"Master Gill!" Rand said.

The stout man turned, frowning. "Do I know you?" He looked Rand up and down. "My Lord?"

"It's me, Rand!"

Gill cocked his head, then grinned. "Oh, you! I'd forgotten you. Your friend isn't with you, is he? The one with the dark look to his eyes?"

So people did not recognize Rand as the Dragon Reborn in this place. What had the Dark One done to them?

"I need to speak with you, Master Gill," Rand said, striding toward a private dining chamber.

"What is it, lad?" Gill asked, following after. "Are you in trouble of some sort? Again?"

Rand shut the door after Master Gill. "What Age are we in?"

"The Fourth Age, of course."

"So the Last Battle happened?"

"Yes, and we won!" Gill said. He looked at Rand closely, narrowing his eyes. "Are you all right, son? How could you not know ..."

"I spent my time in the woods these last years," Rand said. "Frightened of what was happening."

"Ah, then. You don't know about the factions?"

"No."

"Light, son! You're in some meaty trouble. Here, I'll get you a faction symbol. You'll need one in a hurry!" Gill pulled open the door and bustled out.

Rand folded his arms, noticing with displeasure that the fireplace in the room contained a *nothingness* beyond it. "What have you done to them?" Rand demanded.

I LET THEM THINK THEY WON.

"Why?"

MANY WHO FOLLOW ME DO NOT UNDERSTAND TYRANNY.

"What does that have to do with—" Rand cut off as Gill returned. He bore no "faction symbol," whatever that was. Instead, he'd gathered three thick-necked guards. He pointed in, toward Rand.

"Gill ..." Rand said, backing away and seizing the Source. "What are you doing?"

"Well, I figure that coat will sell for something," Gill said. He didn't sound the least bit apologetic.

"And so you'll rob me?"

"Well, yes." Gill seemed confused. "Why wouldn't I?"

The thugs stepped into the room, looking Rand over with careful eyes. They carried cudgels.

"Because of the law," Rand said.

"Why would there be laws against theft?" Gill asked, shaking his head. "What manner of person are you, to think such things? If a man cannot protect what he has, why should he have it? If a man cannot defend his life, what good is it to him?"

Gill waved the three men forward. Rand bound them in cords of Air.

"You took their consciences, didn't you?" he asked softly.

Gill's eyes widened at the use of the One Power. He tried to run. Rand grabbed him in cords of Air as well.

MEN WHO THINK THEY ARE OPPRESSED WILL SOMEDAY FIGHT. I WILL REMOVE FROM THEM NOT JUST THEIR WILL TO RESIST, BUT THE VERY SUSPICION THAT SOMETHING IS WRONG.

"So you leave them without compassion?" Rand demanded, looking into Gill's eyes. The man seemed terrified that Rand would kill him, as did the three thugs. No remorse. Not a bit of it.

COMPASSION IS NOT NEEDED.

Rand felt deathly cold. "This is different from the world you showed me before."

WHAT I SHOWED BEFORE IS WHAT MEN EXPECT. IT IS THE EVIL THEY THINK THEY FIGHT. BUT I WILL MAKE A WORLD WHERE THERE IS NOT GOOD OR EVIL.

THERE IS ONLY ME.

"Do your servants know?" Rand whispered. "The ones you name Chosen? They think they fight to become lords and rulers over a world of their own making. Instead you will give them this. The same world . . . except one without Light."

THERE IS ONLY ME.

No Light. No love of men. The horror of it sank deep within Rand, shaking him. This was one of the possibilities that the

Dark One could choose, if he won. It didn't mean he would, or that it had to happen, but ... oh Light, this was terrible. Far more terrible than a world of captives, far more terrible than a dark land with a broken landscape.

This was true horror. This was a full corruption of the world, it was taking everything beautiful from it, leaving behind only a husk. A pretty husk, but still a husk.

Rand would rather live a thousand years of torture, retaining the piece of himself that gave him the capacity for good, than live a moment in this world without Light.

He turned, enraged, upon the darkness. It consumed the far wall, growing larger. "You make a mistake, Shai'tan!" Rand yelled at that nothingness. "You think to make me despair? You think to shatter my will? This will not do it, I swear to you. This makes me sure to fight!"

Something rumbled inside of the Dark One. Rand yelled, pushing outward with his will, shattering the dark world of lies and men who would kill without empathy. It exploded into threads, and Rand was once again in the place outside of time, the Pattern rippling around him.

"You show me your true heart?" Rand demanded of the nothingness as he seized those threads. "I will show you mine, Shai'tan. There is an opposite to this Lightless world you would create.

"A world without Shadow."

Mat stalked away, calming his anger. Tuon had seemed really angry at him! Light. She *would* come back when he needed her to, would she not?

"Mat?" Min said, hurrying up beside him.

"Go with her," Mat said. "Keep an eye on her for me, Min."

"But—"

"She doesn't need much protecting," Mat said. "She's a strong one. Bloody ashes, but she is. She does need watching, though. She worries me, Min. Anyway, I have this bloody war to win. I can't do that and go with her. So would you go and watch her? Please?"

Min slowed, then gave him an unexpected hug. "Luck, Matrim Cauthon."

"Luck, Min Farshaw," Mat said. He let her go, then shouldered his *ashandarei*. The Seanchan had begun leaving Dashar Knob, pulling back to the Erinin before leaving the Field of Merrilor altogether. Demandred would let them go; he would be a fool not to. Blood and bloody ashes, what was Mat getting himself into? He had just sent away a good quarter of his troops.

They'll come back, he thought. If his gamble worked. If the dice fell as he needed them.

Only this battle was not a game of dice. There was too much subtlety to it for that. It was cards, if anything. Mat usually won at cards. Usually.

To his right, a group of men in dark Seanchan armor marched toward the battlefield. "Hey, Karede!" Mat yelled.

The large man gave Mat a dark look. Suddenly, Mat knew what an ingot of metal felt like when Perrin eyed it, hefting a hammer. Karede stalked up, and though he obviously was making an effort to keep his face calm, Mat could feel the thunder coming off him.

"Thank you," Karede said, voice stiff, "for helping protect the Empress, may she live forever."

"You think I should have kept her someplace secure," Mat said. "Not at the command post."

"It is not my place to question one of the Blood, Great One," Karede said.

"You're not questioning me," Mat said, "you're thinking of sticking something sharp in me. Entirely different."

Karede breathed out a long, deep breath. "Excuse me, Great One," he said, turning to leave. "I must take my men and die."

"I don't think so," Mat said. "You're coming with me."

Karede turned back toward him. "The Empress, may she live forever, ordered—"

"You to the front lines," Mat said, shading his eye as he scanned the riverbed, swarming with Trollocs . . . "Great. Where do you bloody think I'm going?"

"You ride to battle?" Karede asked.

"I was thinking more of a saunter," Mat said. He shook his head. "I need a feel for what Demandred is doing . . . I'm going out there, Karede, and putting you fellows between me and the Trollocs sounds delightful. Are you coming?"

Karede did not reply, though he did not continue walking away, either.

"Look, what are your choices?" Mat asked. "Ride out there and die for really no purpose? Or come try to keep me alive for your Empress? I'm *almost* certain that she's fond of me. Maybe. She's a hard one to read, Tuon is."

"You do not call her by that name," Karede said.

"I'll call her what I bloody well want."

"Not if we're to come with you," Karede said. "If I am to ride with you, Prince of the Ravens, I would not have my men hearing such from your lips. It would be a bad omen."

"Well, we wouldn't want any of those," Mat said. "Right, then, Karede. Let's dive back into this mess and see what we can do. In Fortuona's name."

Tam raised his sword as if to begin a duel, but found no honorable foes here. Only grunting, howling, ferocious Trollocs. Drawn away from the beleaguered Whitecloaks at this battle near the ruins.

The Trollocs turned on the Two Rivers men and attacked. Tam, holding the point of the wedge, fell into Reed in Wind. He refused to take a single step backward. He bent this way and that, but held firm as he broke the Trolloc line, slashing with his sword in quick movements.

The men of the Two Rivers pushed forward, a thorn to the Dark One's foot and a bramble to his hand. In the chaos that followed, they shouted and cursed, and fought to drive the Trollocs apart.

But soon their focus turned to holding their ground. The Trollocs surged around the men. The wedge formation, normally an offensive tactic, worked well here, too. Trollocs moved down the sides of the wedge, taking hits from the Two Rivers men with their axes, swords and spears.

Tam let the lads' training guide them. He would have preferred to be in the center of the wedge, calling out encouragement as Dannil now did—but he was one of the few who had any real battle training, and the wedge formation depended on having a point who could hold steady.

So hold steady he did. Calm within the void, he let the Trollocs break upon him. He moved from Shake Dew from the Branch, to Apple Blossoms in the Wind, to Stones Fall in the Pond—all forms that stabilized him in one position while fighting multiple opponents.

Despite practice over the last few months, Tam wasn't nearly as strong as he had been in his youth. Fortunately, a reed did not need strength. He was not as practiced as he once had been, but no reed practiced how to bend in the wind.

It simply *did*.

Years of maturing, years of age, had brought Tam an understanding of the void. He understood it now, better than he ever had. Years teaching Rand responsibility, years of living without Kari, years of listening to the wind blow and the leaves rustle . . .

Tam al'Thor became the void. He brought it to the Trollocs, showed it to them and sent them into its depths.

He danced around a goat-featured Trolloc, sweeping his sword to the side and slicing the beast's leg at the heel. It stumbled and Tam turned, letting the men behind take it. He flashed his sword up—the weapon trailing blood—and sprayed the dark droplets across the eyes of a charging Trolloc with nightmare features. It howled, blinded, and Tam flowed forward, arms out, and opened its stomach below the breastplate. It stumbled in front of a third Trolloc, who brought an axe down toward Tam, but hit its ally instead.

Each step was part of a dance, and Tam invited the Trollocs to join him. He had only fought like this once before, long ago, but memory was something that the void did not allow. He did not think of other times; he did not think of anything. If he knew that he'd done this once before, it was because of the resonance of his motions, an understanding that seemed to permeate his muscles themselves.

Tam stabbed the neck of a Trolloc with a face that was nearly human, with only a little too much hair on its cheeks. It fell backward and collapsed, and Tam suddenly found no more foes. He stopped, bringing his sword up, feeling a soft wind blow across him. The dark beasts were thundering away downriver in a rout, chased by horsemen flying Borderlander flags. Shortly they would hit a wall of troops, the Legion of the Dragon, and be crushed between them and the pursuing Borderlanders.

Tam cleaned his blade, leaving the void. The gravity of the situation hit him. Light! His men should be dead. If those Borderlanders hadn't arrived …

He placed his sword back into its lacquered sheath. The red and gold dragon caught sunlight, sparkling, though Tam wouldn't have thought there was anything to catch with that cloud cover above. He searched for the sun, and found it—behind the clouds—nearly at the horizon. It was almost night!

Fortunately, it looked like the Trollocs here at the battle by the ruins were finally breaking. Already weakened severely by the drawn-out river crossing, they now crumbled as Lan's men hit them from behind.

In a short time it was done. Tam had held.

Nearby, a black horse trotted up. Its rider, Lan Mandragoran—with standard-bearer and guards behind—looked over the Two Rivers men.

"I had long wondered," Lan said to Tam. "About the man who had given Rand that heron-marked blade. I wondered if he had truly earned it. Now I know." Lan raised his own sword in salute.

Tam turned back toward his men, an exhausted, bloodied group clutching weapons. The path of their wedge showed easily on the trampled plain; dozens of Trollocs lay behind where the wedge had cut into them. To the north, the men of the second wedge raised their weapons. They had been pushed back nearly to the forest, but they'd held there and some had survived. Tam couldn't help but see that dozens of good folk had died.

His exhausted men sat down right there on the battlefield, surrounded by corpses. Some weakly began tying their own bandages or seeing to the wounded they'd pulled into the interior of the wedge. To the south, Tam spotted a dismaying sight. Were those the Seanchan pulling out from their camp at Dashar Knob?

"Have we won, then?" Tam asked.

"Far from it," Lan said. "We've seized this part of the river, but it is the lesser fight. Demandred pressed his Trollocs hard here to keep us from drawing resources to the larger battle at the ford downriver." Lan turned his horse. "Gather your men, blademaster. This battle will not end with the setting sun. You will be needed again in the coming hours. *Tai'shar Manetheren.*"

· Lan thundered toward his Borderlanders.

"Tai'shar Malkier," Tam called after him, belatedly.

"So . . . we're not done yet?" Dannil asked.

"No, lad. We're not. But we'll take a break, get the men Healed and find some food." He saw gateways opening beside the field. Cauthon had been smart enough to send a means for Tam to take his wounded to Mayene. It—

People poured through the openings. Hundreds of them, thousands. Tam frowned. Nearby, the Whitecloaks were picking themselves up—they'd been hit hard by the Trolloc attacks, but Tam's arrival had kept them from being destroyed. Arganda's force was forming up at the ruins, and the Wolf Guard hoisted their flag high, bloodied, heaps of Trolloc corpses surrounding them.

Tam trudged across the field. Now his limbs felt like dead weights. He felt more exhausted than if he'd spent a month pulling stumps.

At the first of the gateways, he found Berelain herself, standing with a few Aes Sedai. The beautiful woman was terribly out of place here in this mud and death. Her gown of black and silver, the diadem in her hair . . . Light, she didn't belong here.

"Tam al'Thor," she said. "You command this force?"

"Near enough," Tam said. "Pardon, my Lady First, but who are all of these people?"

"The refugees from Caemlyn," Berelain said. "I sent some people to see if they needed Healing. They refused it, and insisted that I bring them to the battle."

Tam scratched at his head. To the battle? Any man—and many women—who could hold a sword had already been drawn into the army. The people he saw coming through the gateways were mostly children and the elderly, and some matrons who had remained back to care for the young.

"Pardon," Tam said, "but this is a *killing field*."

"So I tried to explain," Berelain said, a hint of exasperation in her voice. "They claim they can be of use. Better than waiting out the Last Battle huddled together on the road to Whitebridge, so they say."

Tam watched, frowning, as children scattered onto the field. His stomach lurched at them investigating the gruesome dead, and many did shy back at first. Others began picking through the fallen, looking for signs of those people who were still alive and could be Healed. A few aged soldiers who had been set to guard the refugees went among them, watching for Trollocs that weren't quite dead.

Women and children began to pick arrows out from among the fallen. That would be helpful. *Very* helpful. With surprise, Tam saw hundreds of Tinkers pour out of one gateway. They went searching for the wounded under the direction of several Yellow sisters.

Tam found himself nodding. It still worried him, allowing the children to see such sights. *Well*, he thought, *they'll see a worse sight if we fail here.* If they wanted to be of use, they should be allowed.

"Tell me, Tam al'Thor," Berelain asked, "is ... Galad Damodred well? I see his men here, but not his banner."

"He was called to other duties, my Lady First," Tam said. "Downriver. I haven't heard from him in hours, I'm afraid."

"Ah. Well, let's Heal and feed your men. Perhaps word of Lord Damodred will be forthcoming."

Elayne touched Gareth Bryne's cheek softly. She closed his eyes, one, then the other, before nodding to the soldiers who had found his body. They carried Bryne away, legs dangling over the edge of his shield, head hanging down on the other side.

"He just went riding off, screaming," Birgitte said. "Right into the enemy lines. There was no stopping him."

"Siuan is dead," Elayne said, feeling an almost overpowering sense of loss. Siuan ... Siuan had always been so strong. With effort, Elayne stilled her emotions. She had to keep her attention on the battle. "Is there word from the command post?"

"The camp at Dashar Knob has been abandoned," Birgitte said. "I don't know where Cauthon is. The Seanchan have forsaken us."

"Raise my banner high," Elayne said. "Until we hear from Mat, I'm taking command of this battlefield. Bring forward my advisors."

Birgitte moved to give the orders. Elayne's Guardswomen watched, shuffling nervously, as the Trollocs pushed against the Andorans at the river. They'd totally filled the corridor between Heights and bogs, and threatened to spill out on to Shienaran soil. Part of Egwene's army had hit the Trollocs from the other side of the corridor, which had taken some pressure off her own troops for a time; but more Trollocs had attacked from above, and it looked as if Egwene's men were getting the worst of it.

Elayne had had solid lessons in battlefield tactics, though little experience on the field, and she could see how badly things were going. Yes, she had received news that the Trollocs' position upriver had been destroyed by the arrival of Lan and the Borderlanders. But that brought scant relief with the situation here at the ford.

The sun began to slip beneath the horizon. The Trollocs made no sign of pulling back, and her soldiers reluctantly began to light bonfires and torches. Organizing her men into square formations made for better defense, but it meant giving up any hope of pushing forward. The Aiel fought here as well, as did the Cairhienin. But those pike squares were the core of their battle plan.

They're slowly surrounding us, she thought. If the Trollocs did so, they could squeeze until the Andorans popped. *Light, this is bad.*

The sun made a sudden blazing fire behind the horizon clouds. With night, the Trollocs gained another advantage. The air had grown cold in the advent of darkness. Her early assumptions that this battle would last days now seemed silly. The Shadow pushed with all of its might. Humankind did not have days remaining, but hours.

"Majesty," Captain Guybon said, riding up with her commanders. Their dented armor and bloodied tabards proved that nobody, not even the senior officers, could be spared from direct fighting.

"Advice," Elayne said, looking at him, Theodohr—commander of the cavalry—and Birgitte, who was Captain-General.

"Retreat?" Guybon asked.

"Do you really think we could disengage?" Birgitte replied.

Guybon hesitated, then shook his head.

"Right, then," Elayne said. "How do we win?"

"We hold," said Theodohr. "We hope the White Tower can win their fight against the Sharan channelers and come to our aid."

"I don't like just sitting here," Birgitte said. "It—"

A blazing beam of white-hot fire sliced through Elayne's

guards, vaporizing dozens of them. Guybon's horse vanished beneath him, though he narrowly missed being hit himself. Elayne's horse reared.

Swearing, she wrestled her mount under control. That had been balefire!

"Lews Therin!" A power-enhanced voice rang over the field. "I hunt a woman you love! Come to me, coward! *Fight!*"

The earth exploded near Elayne, heaving her standard-bearer into the air, the flag bursting into flames. This time Elayne *was* thrown from horseback, and she hit hard, grunting.

My babes! She groaned, rolling over as hands grabbed her. Birgitte. The woman hauled Elayne into the saddle behind her, helped by several Guardswomen.

"Can you channel?" Birgitte asked. "No. Never mind. They'll be watching for that. Celebrain, raise another banner! Ride downriver with a squadron of Guards. I will take the Queen the other way!"

The woman standing beside Birgitte's horse saluted. It was a death sentence! "Birgitte, no," Elayne said.

"Demandred has decided you'll draw out the Dragon Reborn for him," Birgitte said, turning her horse. "I'm not about to let that happen. Hya!" She pushed her horse into a gallop as lightning struck Elayne's guards, blowing bodies into the air.

Elayne ground her teeth. Her armies were in danger of being overwhelmed, surrounded—all while Demandred laid down blast after blast of balefire, lightning and weaves of Earth. That man was as dangerous as an army himself.

"I can't leave," Elayne said from behind Birgitte.

"Yes you can, and you are," she replied gruffly as their horse galloped on. "If Mat has fallen—Light send that isn't the case—then we'll need to set up a new command post. There's a reason Demandred struck at Dashar Knob and then directly at you. He's trying to destroy our command structure. Your duty is to assume command from someplace *safe* and *secret*. Once we're far enough away that Demandred's scouts can't sense you channeling, we'll make a gateway and you *will* be back in control. Right now though, Elayne, you need to shut your mouth and let me protect you."

She was right. Burn her, she was. Elayne hung on as Birgitte galloped across the battlefield, her horse churning clods of dirt behind them in a flight toward safety.

At least he's making it easy to find him, Galad thought as he rode, watching the lines of fire streak from the enemy position toward Elayne's army.

Galad's heels dug into the flanks of his stolen horse, tearing across the Heights toward its eastern edge. Over and over, he saw Gawyn's dying body in his arms.

"Face me, Lews Therin!" The thunder of Demandred's shout shook the ground from up ahead. He had taken Galad's brother. Now the monster hunted Galad's sister.

The right thing had always seemed clear to Galad before, but never had it felt as *right* as this. Those streaks of light were like indicators on a map, arrows pointing his way. The Light itself guided him. It had prepared him, placed him here at this moment.

He ripped through the back lines of the Sharan force to where Demandred stood, just above the riverbed looking down on Elayne's troops. Arrows sank into the earth around him, archers firing, heedless of the risk of hitting their own men. Sword out, Galad pulled his leg from the stirrup, preparing to leap free.

An arrow struck the horse. Galad threw himself from the animal. He hit hard, skidding to a stop, and sliced the hand from a crossbowman nearby. A growling male channeler came for him, and the foxhead medallion grew cold against Galad's chest.

Galad rammed his blade through the man's neck. The man raved, blood spurting from his neck with each beat of his heart. He didn't seem surprised as he died, just angry. His howls drew more attention.

"Demandred!" Galad yelled. "Demandred, you call for the Dragon Reborn! You demand to fight him! He is not here, but his brother is! Will you stand against me?"

Dozens of crossbows were raised. Behind Galad, his horse collapsed, expelling a bloody froth from its nostrils.

Rand al'Thor. His brother. The shock of Gawyn's death had numbed Galad to this revelation. He would have to deal with it eventually, if he survived. He still did not know if he would be proud or ashamed.

A figure in strange, coin-link armor stepped through the Sharan ranks here. Demandred was a proud man; one needed see only his face to know that. He looked like al'Thor, actually. They had a similar sense about them.

Demandred inspected Galad, who stood with bloody sword out. The dying channeler scraped the ground with clawed fingers before him.

"His brother?" Demandred said.

"Son of Tigraine," Galad said, "who became a Maiden of the Spear. Who gave birth to my brother on Dragonmount, the tomb of Lews Therin. I had two brothers. You killed the other on this battlefield."

"You have an interesting artifact, I see," Demandred said as the medallion grew cold again. "Surely you don't think that is going to keep you from meeting the same fate as your pathetic brother? The dead one, I mean."

"Do we fight, son of Shadows? Or do we talk?"

Demandred unsheathed his sword, herons on the blade and hilt. "May you give me a better match than your brother, little man. I grow displeased. Lews Therin can hate me or rail against me, but he should *not* ignore me."

Galad stepped forward into the ring of crossbowmen and channelers. If he won, he would still die. But Light, let him take one of the Forsaken with him. It would be a fitting end.

Demandred came at him, and the contest began.

Her back pressed against a stalagmite, seeing only by the light of *Callandor* reflected against the walls of the cavern, Nynaeve worked to save Alanna's life.

There were those who, in the White Tower, had mocked her reliance on ordinary healing techniques. What could two hands and thread do that the One Power could not?

If any of those women had been here instead of Nynaeve, the world would have ended.

The conditions were horrible. Little light, no tools besides the implements she kept in her pouch. Still, Nynaeve sewed, using the needle and thread she always carried. She had mixed a draught of herbs for Alanna and forced it through her lips. It wouldn't do much, but every little bit might help. It would keep Alanna's strength up, help her with the pain, keep her heart from giving out as Nynaeve worked.

The wound was messy, but she had sewn messy wounds before. Though she trembled inside, Nynaeve's hands were steady as she sewed up the wound and coaxed the woman back from the very precipice of death.

Rand and Moridin did not move. But she felt something thrumming from them. Rand was fighting. Fighting a fight she could not see.

"Matrim Cauthon, you bloody fool. You're still alive?"

Mat glanced over as Davram Bashere rode up beside him in the early evening darkness. Mat had moved with the Deathwatch Guard to the back of the Andoran lines fighting at the river.

Bashere was accompanied by his wife and a guard of Saldaeans. Judging by the blood on her clothing, she had seen her share of fighting.

"Yes, I'm alive," Mat said. "I'm usually pretty good at staying alive. I've only failed one time that I remember, and it hardly counts. What are you doing here? Aren't you . . . "

"They dug into my bloody mind," Bashere said, scowling. "That they did, man. Deira and I talked it over. I'm not going to lead, but why should that stop me from killing a few Trollocs?"

Mat nodded. At Tenobia's fall, this man had become king of Saldaea—but he had refused the crown, so far. The corruption in his mind had shaken him. All he had said was that Saldaea fights alongside Malkier, and told the troops to look toward Lan. The throne would be sorted out if they all survived the Last Battle.

"What happened to you?" Bashere asked. "I heard the command post fell."

Mat nodded. "The Seanchan have abandoned us."

"Blood and ashes!" Bashere cried. "As if this weren't bad enough. Bloody Seanchan dogs."

The Deathwatch Guards who stood around Mat made no response to that.

Elayne's forces held along the riverbank, just barely—but Trollocs were slowly working around them upriver. Elayne's lines held only because of tenacity and careful training. Each huge square of men held pikes outward, bristling like a hedgehog.

Those formations could be separated if Demandred drove wedges between them in the right way. Mat employed cavalry sweeps of his own, including Andoran cavalry and the Band— trying to keep the Trollocs from penetrating the pike squares or surrounding Elayne.

The rhythm of the battle pulsed beneath Mat's fingertips. He *felt* what Demandred was doing. To anyone else, the end of the battle probably seemed a simple matter now. Attack in force, break the pike formations, crack Mat's defenses. It was so much more subtle.

Lan's Borderlanders had finished crushing the Trollocs upriver, and needed orders. Good. Mat needed those men for the next step in his plan.

Three of the enormous pike formations were flagging, but if he could place a channeler or two in each center, he could shore them up. Light shelter whoever had distracted Demandred. The Forsaken's attacks had destroyed entire pike formations. Demandred didn't need to kill each man individually; he needed only to launch attacks of the One Power to shatter the square. That let the Trollocs overwhelm them.

"Bashere," Mat said, "please tell me that someone has heard from your daughter."

"Nobody has," Deira said. "I'm sorry."

Bloody ashes, Mat thought. *Poor Perrin.*

Poor him. How was he going to do this without the Horn? Light. He was not certain he could do it *with* the bloody Horn.

"Go," Mat called as they rode. "Ride to Lan; he's upriver. Tell him to engage those Trollocs trying to move around the Andorans' right flank! And tell him I'll have other orders for him coming soon."

"But I—"

"I don't *care* if you've bloody been touched by the Shadow!" Mat said. "Every man has had the Dark One's fingers on his heart, and that's the bloody truth. You can fight through it. Now ride to Lan and tell him what needs to be done!"

Bashere stiffened at first; then—strangely—he smiled a broad smile beneath drooping mustaches. Bloody Saldaeans. They *liked* being yelled at. Mat's words seemed to give him heart, and he galloped off, wife at his side. She threw Mat a fond look, which made him uncomfortable.

Now ... he needed an army. And a gateway. He needed a bloody gateway. *Fool*, he thought. He had sent the *damane* away. Could he not have at least kept one? Though they did make his skin crawl as if it were covered in spiders.

Mat halted Pips, the Deathwatch Guards stopping with him. A few of them lit torches. They had certainly gotten the drubbing they had wanted, joining Mat in fighting the Sharans. They seemed to itch for more, though.

There, Mat thought, heeling Pips toward a force of troops south of Elayne's pike formations. The Dragonsworn. Before the Seanchan left Dashar Knob, Mat had sent this army to reinforce Elayne's troops.

He still did not know what to make of them. He had not been at the Field when they had gathered, but he had heard reports. People from all ranks and stations, all nationalities, who had joined together to fight in the Last Battle, heedless of loyalties or national borders. Rand broke all vows and all other bonds.

Mat rode at a quick trot—the Deathwatch Guards jogging to keep up—around the back of the Andoran lines. Light, the lines were buckling. This was bad. Well, he'd made his bet. Now he could only ride the bloody battle and hope it did not buck too much.

As he galloped for the Dragonsworn, he heard something incongruous. Singing? Mat pulled to a halt. The Ogier had been caught up fighting the Trollocs, and had pushed across the dry riverbed to help fight at Elayne's left flank, across from the bogs, to keep Trollocs from coming around that way.

They stood their ground here, as immovable as oaks before a flood, hacking with axes as they sang. Trollocs lay in piles around them.

"Loial!" Mat yelled, standing up in his stirrups. "*Loial!*"

One of the Ogier stepped back from the fighting and turned. Mat was taken aback. His usually calm friend had ears laid low, teeth clenched in anger, and a blood-soaked axe in his fingers. Light, but that expression sent terror through Mat's body. He would rather stare down ten men who thought he had been cheating than fight a single angry Ogier!

Loial called something to the others, and then rejoined them in the fighting. They continued to lay into the Trollocs nearby, cutting them down. Trollocs and Ogier were near the same size, but the Ogier somehow seemed to tower over the Shadowspawn. They did not fight like soldiers, but like woodsmen felling trees. Chop one way, then the next, breaking Trollocs. But Mat knew that Ogier hated felling trees, while they seemed to relish felling Trollocs.

The Ogier broke the Trolloc fist they'd been fighting, making them flee. Elayne's soldiers moved in and blocked off the rest of the Trolloc army, and the several hundred Ogier pulled back to Mat. Among them, Mat noticed, were more than a few of the Seanchan Ogier—the Gardeners. He had not ordered that. The two groups fought together, but barely seemed to look at one another now.

Every one of the Ogier, male and female, had numerous cuts on their arms and legs. They did not wear armor, but many of the cuts seemed trivial, as if their skin had the strength of bark.

Loial walked up to Mat and the Deathwatch Guards, raising his axe to his shoulder. Loial's trousers were dark up to the thighs, as if he had been wading in wine. "Mat," Loial said, drawing a deep breath. "We have done as you asked, fighting here. No Trolloc got by us."

"You did well, Loial," Mat said. "Thank you."

He waited for a reply. Something long-winded and eager, no doubt. Loial stood breathing in and out with lungs that could hold enough air to fill a room. No words. The others with him, though many were senior to Loial, offered no words either. Some lifted torches. The glow of the sun had vanished beneath the horizon. Night was fully upon them.

Quiet Ogier. Now *that* was strange. Ogier at war, though ... it was not something Mat had ever seen. He did not have any memory of it in the memories that were not his.

"I need you," Mat said. "We have to turn this battle around or we're finished. Come on."

"The Hornsounder commands!" Loial bellowed. "Up axes!"

Mat winced. If he ever needed someone to yell a message from Caemlyn to Cairhien for him, he knew who to ask. Only they would probably hear it all the way up in the Blight, too.

He heeled Pips into motion, the Ogier falling in around him and the Deathwatch Guards. The Ogier had no trouble keeping up.

"Honored One," Karede said, "I and mine are ordered to—"

"To go die on the front lines. I'm bloody working on that, Karede. Keep your sword out of your own gut for the moment, kindly."

The man's expression darkened, but he held his tongue.

"She doesn't really want you dead, you realize," Mat said. He could not say more without revealing the plot to bring her back.

"If my death serves the Empress, may she live forever, then I give it willingly."

"You're bloody insane, Karede," Mat said. "Unfortunately, so am I. You're in good company. You there! Who leads this force?"

They had reached the back ranks, where the reserves of the Dragonsworn were located, the wounded and those who were resting from their time at the front ranks.

"My Lord?" one of the scouts said. "That would be Lady Tinna."

"Go fetch her," Mat said. Those dice kept rattling in his head. He also felt a pull from the north, a tugging, as if some threads around his chest were yanking on him.

Not now, Rand, he thought. *I'm bloody busy.*

No colors formed, only blackness. Dark as a Myrddraal's heart. The tugging grew stronger.

Mat dismissed the vision. *Not. Now.*

He had work to do here. He had a plan. Light, let it work.

Tinna turned out to be a pretty girl, younger than he had expected, tall and strong of limb. She wore her long brown hair in a tail, though curls of it seemed to want to break out here and there. She wore breeches, and had seen some fighting, judging by that sword on her hip and the dark Trolloc blood on her sleeves.

She rode up to him, looking him up and down with discerning eyes. "You've finally remembered us, have you, Lord Cauthon?" Yes, she definitely reminded him of Nynaeve.

Mat looked up at the Heights. The firefight between Aes Sedai and Sharans up there had turned messy.

You'd better win there, Egwene. I'm counting on you.

"Your army," Mat said, looking at Tinna. "I'm told some Aes Sedai joined you?"

"Some did," she said cautiously.

"You're one of them?"

"I am not. Not exactly."

"Not exactly? What do you mean by that? Look, woman, I need a gateway. If we don't have one, this battle could be lost. Please tell me we have some channelers here who can send me where I need to go."

Tinna drew her lips to a line. "I'm not trying to irritate you, Lord Cauthon. Old habits make for strong ropes, and I have learned not to speak of certain things. I was turned out of the White Tower myself, for . . . complicated reasons. I'm sorry, but I do not know the weave for Traveling. I do know for a fact that most who joined us are too weak for that weave. It requires a great deal of the One Power, beyond the capacity of many who—"

"I can make one."

A woman in a red dress stood up from the lines of wounded, where she had apparently been Healing. She was thin and bony and had a sour expression on her face, but Mat was so happy to see her, he could have kissed her. Like kissing broken glass, that would have been. He'd have done it anyway. "Teslyn!" he cried. "What are you doing here?"

"Fighting in the Last Battle, I believe," she said, dusting off her hands. "Aren't we all?"

"But the Dragonsworn?" Mat asked.

"I did not find the White Tower to be a comfortable place once I returned," she said. "It had changed. I availed myself of the opportunity here, as this need superseded any others. Now, you wish a gateway? How large?"

"Large enough to move as many of these troops as we can, the Dragonsworn, the Ogier, and this cavalry banner from the Band of the Red Hand." Mat said.

"I'll need a circle, Tinna," Teslyn said. "No complaining that you can't channel; I can sense it in you, and all former allegiances and promises are broken for us here. Gather the other women. Where are we going, Cauthon?"

Mat grinned. "To the top of those Heights."

"The Heights!" Karede said. "But you *abandoned* those at the beginning of the battle. You gave them up to the Shadowspawn!"

"Yes, I did."

And now . . . now he had a chance to finish this. Elayne's forces holding along the river, Egwene fighting in the west . . . Mat had to seize the northern part of the Heights. He knew that with the Seanchan gone and most of his own troops occupied around the lower part of the Heights, Demandred would send a strong force of Sharans and Trollocs across the top to the northeast, to swing down across the riverbed and behind Elayne's armies. The armies of Light would be surrounded and at Demandred's mercy. His only chance was to keep Demandred's troops from coming off the Heights, despite their superior numbers. Light. It was a long shot, but sometimes you had to take the only shot you had.

"You're spreading us dangerously thin," Karede said. "You risk everything by moving armies that are needed here up to the Heights."

"You *did* want to go to the front lines," Mat replied. "Loial, are you with us?"

"A strike at the enemy's core, Mat?" Loial asked, hefting his axe. "It will not be the worst place I've found myself, following one of you three. I do hope Rand is all right. You do think so, don't you?"

"If Rand were dead," Mat said, "we'd know it. He'll have to watch out for himself, without Matrim Cauthon saving him this time. Teslyn, let's have that gateway! Tinna, organize your forces. Have them ready to charge through the opening. We need to seize the northern slope of those Heights fast and then hold it *no matter* what the Shadow tosses at us!"

Egwene opened her eyes. Though she shouldn't have been in a room at all, she lay in one. And a fine one. The cool air smelled of salt, and she rested on a soft mattress.

I'm dreaming, she thought. Or perhaps she had died. Would that explain the pain? Such terrible pain. Nothingness would be better, far better, than this agony.

Gawyn was gone. A piece of herself, snipped away.

"I forget how young she is." Whispers drifted into the room. That voice was familiar. Silviana? "Care for her. I must return to the battle."

"How does it go?" Egwene knew that voice, too. Rosil, of the

Yellow. She had gone to Mayene, with the novices and Accepted, helping Heal.

"The battle? It goes poorly." Silviana was not one to put honey on her words. "Watch her, Rosil. She is strong; I do not doubt she will pull through this, but there is always a worry."

"I've helped women with lost Warders before, Silviana," Rosil said. "I assure you, I'm quite capable. She'll be useless for the next few days, but then she will begin to mend."

Silviana sniffed. "That boy . . . I should have known he would ruin her. The day I first saw how she looked at him, I should have taken him by his ears, hauled him to a distant farm, and set him to work for the next decade."

"You cannot so easily control a heart, Silviana."

"Warders are a weakness," Silviana said. "That is all they have ever been, and all they ever will be. That boy . . . that *fool* boy . . . "

"That fool boy," Egwene said, "saved my life from Seanchan assassins. I would not be here to mourn if he had not done so. I would suggest that you remember that, Silviana, when you speak of the dead."

The others were silent. Egwene tried to overcome the pain of loss. She was in Mayene, of course. Silviana would have taken her to the Yellows.

"I will remember it, Mother," Silviana said. She actually managed to sound contrite. "Rest well. I will—"

"Rest is for the dead, Silviana," Egwene said, sitting up.

Silviana and Rosil stood in the doorway of the beautiful room, which was draped with blue cloth below the ceiling of worked mother-of-pearl inlays. Both women folded their arms and gave her stern looks.

"You've been through something extremely hurtful, Mother," Rosil said. Near the doorway, Leilwin stood guard. "The loss of a Warder is enough to stop any woman. There is no shame in letting yourself deal with the grief."

"Egwene al'Vere can grieve," Egwene said, standing up. "Egwene al'Vere lost a man she loved, and she felt him die through a bond. The Amyrlin has sympathy for Egwene al'Vere, as she would have sympathy for any Aes Sedai dealing with such loss. And then, in the face of the Last Battle, the Amyrlin would expect that woman to pick herself up and return to the fight."

She walked across the room, each step firmer. She held out her hand to Silviana, nodding toward Vora's *sa'angreal*, which she held. "I will be needing that."

Silviana hesitated.

"Unless the two of you wish to discover just how capable I am at present," Egwene said softly, "I would not suggest disobedience."

Silviana looked to Rosil, who sighed and nodded reluctantly. Silviana handed over the rod.

"I do not condone this, Mother," Rosil said. "But if you are insistent ..."

"I am."

"... then I will give you this suggestion. Emotion will threaten to crush you. This is the danger. In the face of a lost Warder, summoning *saidar* will be difficult. If you do manage it, Aes Sedai serenity will likely be impossible. This can be dangerous. Very dangerous."

Egwene opened herself to *saidar*. As Rosil had suggested, it was difficult to embrace the Source. Too many emotions vied for her attention, overwhelming her, driving away her calm. She blushed as she failed a second time.

Silviana opened her mouth, undoubtedly to suggest that Egwene sit back down. At that moment, Egwene found *saidar*, the bud in her mind flowering, the One Power rushing into her. She gave Silviana a defiant look, then began weaving a gateway.

"You didn't hear the rest of my advice, Mother," Rosil said. "You will not be able to banish the emotions troubling you, not completely. Your only choice is a bad one, to overwhelm those emotions of grief and pain with *stronger* emotions."

"That should not be difficult at all," Egwene said. She drew a deep breath, pulling in more of the One Power. She allowed herself anger. Fury at the Shadowspawn who threatened the world, anger at them for taking Gawyn from her.

"I will need eyes to watch me," Egwene said, defying Silviana's previous words. Gawyn had *not* been a weakness to her. "I will need another Warder."

"But—" Rosil began.

Egwene stopped her with a look. Yes, most women waited. Yes, Egwene al'Vere was pained from her loss, and Gawyn could never be replaced. But she *believed* in Warders. The Amyrlin Seat needed someone to watch her back. Beyond that, every person with a Warder bond was a better fighter than those without. To go without a Warder was to deny the Light another soldier.

There was a person here who had saved her life. *No*, a piece of her said, her eyes falling on Leilwin. *Not a Seanchan.*

Another piece of her, the Amyrlin, laughed at that. *Stop being such a child.* She would have a Warder. "Leilwin Shipless," Egwene said loudly, "will you take this duty?"

The woman knelt, bowing her head. "I . . . yes."

Egwene formed the weave for the bond. Leilwin stood, looking less fatigued, taking a deep breath. Egwene opened a gateway to the other side of the chamber, then used her immediate knowledge of this room to open another one to where her people fought. Explosions, screams and the beating of weapons against shields poured through.

Egwene strode back onto the killing fields, bringing the fury of the Amyrlin with her.

Demandred was a blademaster. Galad had assumed this would be the case, but he preferred to test his assumptions.

The two danced back and forth inside the ring of watching Sharans. Galad wore lighter armor, mail under his tabard, and stepped more quickly. The interwoven coins Demandred wore were heavier than simple mail, but good against a sword.

"You are better than your brother was," Demandred said. "He died easily."

The man was trying to enrage Galad. He did not succeed. Cold, careful. Galad moved in. The Courtier Taps His Fan. Demandred responded with something very similar to The Falcon Stoops, slapping away Galad's attack. Demandred stepped back, walking around the perimeter of the ring, sword out to the side. At the beginning, he had spoken a great deal. Now he made only the occasional gibe.

They circled each other in the darkness, lit by torches held in Sharan hands. One rotation. Two.

"Come now," Demandred said. "I'm waiting."

Galad remained silent. Each moment he stalled was a moment

Demandred was not sending destruction upon Elayne or her armies. The Forsaken seemed to realize it, for he came in swiftly. Three strikes: down, side, backhand. Galad met each one, their arms a blur.

Motion to the side. It came from a rock that Demandred had thrown at Galad by channeling. Galad dodged it, barely, then raised his sword against the blows that came next. Furious strikes downward, The Boar Rushes Down the Mountain, crashing against Galad's blade. He held against that, but was not able to stop the following twist of the blade that cut his forearm.

Demandred stepped back, his sword dripping Galad's blood. They circled around again, watching one another. Galad felt warm blood inside his glove, from where it had seeped down his arm. A little blood loss could slow a man, weaken him.

Galad breathed in and out, abandoning thought, abandoning worry. When Demandred next struck, Galad anticipated it, stepping aside and striking down with two hands, biting deeply into the leather behind Demandred's knee guard. The sword glanced off the side of the armor, but cut true otherwise. As Galad whipped back around, Demandred was limping.

The Forsaken grimaced. "You've blooded me," he said. "It has been a very long time since someone did that."

The ground began to heave and break beneath Galad. Desperate, he leaped forward, getting close to Demandred—forcing him to stop channeling, lest he topple himself. The Forsaken grunted, swinging, but Galad was inside his enemy's guard.

Too close to do a full swing, Galad raised his sword and bashed it—pommel first—at Demandred's face. Demandred caught Galad's hand with his, but Galad grabbed Demandred by the helmet, holding tightly, trying to force the helmet down over the Forsaken's eyes. He grunted, both men locked, neither moving.

Then, with a sickening sound Galad heard quite distinctly, his muscle ripped in the arm where he'd been cut. His sword slipped from numb fingers, his arm spasming, and Demandred threw him backward and struck with a flash of the blade.

Galad fell to his knees. His right arm—severed at the elbow by Demandred's slice—flopped to the ground in front of him.

Demandred stepped back, panting. He had been worried. Good. Galad held to his bleeding stump, then spat at Demandred's feet.

Demandred snorted, then swung his blade once more. All went black.

Androl felt as if he'd forgotten what it was like to breathe fresh air. The land around him smoldered and quaked, smoke churning in the wind, bringing with it the stench of burning bodies.

He and the others had moved up across the top of the Heights to the western side, searching for Taim. Much of the Sharan army fought here, contending with the White Tower army.

Groups of channelers drew fire from one side or the other, so Androl crossed the horrid landscape alone. He stepped over broken patches of smoking earth, crouching low, trying to give off the air of a solitary wounded man trying to creep to safety. He still wore Nensen's face, but with his head down and his posture low, that mattered very little.

He sensed a spike of alarm from Pevara, who moved alone nearby.

What is it? he sent. *Are you all right?*

After a tense moment, her thoughts came. *I'm fine. A scare with some Sharans. I convinced them I was on their side before they attacked.*

It's a wonder anyone can tell friend from foe here, Androl sent back. He hoped Emarin and Jonneth were safe. The two had gone together, but if they—

Androl froze. Up ahead, through the shifting smoke, he saw a ring of Trollocs protecting something. They stood on an outcropping of rock that jutted out of the hillside like the seat of a chair.

Androl crept forward, hoping to steal a peek.

Androl! Pevara's voice in his mind made him jump nearly out of his skin.

What?

You were alarmed at something, she said. *I was reacting to you.*

He took a few calming breaths. *I've found something. Just a moment.*

He drew close enough, indeed, to sense channeling inside the ring. He didn't know if—

The Trollocs parted as someone inside barked a command. Mishraile peered out, then scowled. "It's only Nensen!"

Androl's heart thumped inside his chest.

A man wearing black turned from his contemplation of the battle. Taim. In his hands, he carried a thin disc of black and white. He rubbed his thumb across it as he overlooked the battlefield, sneering, as if disdainful of the lesser channelers struggling all about him.

"Well?" he barked at Androl, turning and dropping the disc into a pouch at his waist.

"I saw Androl," Androl said, thinking quickly. Light, the others expected him to approach. He did so, walking past the Trollocs, putting himself right in the belly of the beast. If he could draw close enough . . . "I followed him for a while." Nensen always spoke in a rough, gravelly voice, and Androl did his best to imitate it. Pevara could have worked the voice into the weave, but hadn't known it well enough.

"I don't *care* about that one! Fool. What is Demandred doing?"

"He saw me," Androl said. "He didn't like me being over there. He sent me back to you and said that if he saw any of us away from this position, he'd kill us."

Androl . . . Pevara sent, worried. He couldn't spare the concentration to reply. It took all he had to keep from shaking as he stepped up close to Taim.

Taim rubbed his forehead with two fingers, closing his eyes. "And I thought you could do this simple thing." Taim created a complex weave of Spirit and Fire. It struck like a viper at Androl.

Pain suddenly moved up Androl's body, starting in his feet, surging through his limbs. He screamed, collapsing to the ground.

"Do you like that?" Taim asked. "I learned it from Moridin. I do think he's trying to turn me against Demandred."

Androl screamed in his own voice. That horrified him, but the others did not seem to notice. When Taim finally released the weave, the pain faded. Androl found himself groveling on the dirty ground, his limbs still spasming from the memory of the pain.

"Get up," Taim growled.

Androl began to lurch to his feet.

I'm coming, Pevara sent.

Stay back, he replied. Light, he felt powerless. As he stood up, he stumbled into Taim, his legs refusing to work as they should.

"Fool," Taim said, shoving Androl back. Mishraile caught him. "Stand still." Taim began another weave. Androl tried to pay attention, but he was too nervous to catch the details of the weave. It hovered in front of him, then wrapped around him.

"What are you doing?" Androl asked. He didn't have to fake the tremor in his voice. That *pain*.

"You said you saw Androl?" Taim said. "I'm placing a Mask of Mirrors on you and inverting the weave, making you look like him. I want you to pretend to be the pageboy, find Logain, then *kill* him. Use a knife or a weave, I don't care which."

"You're . . . making me look like Androl," Androl said.

"Androl is one of Logain's pets," Taim said. "He shouldn't suspect you. This is an exceptionally *easy* thing I'm asking of you, Nensen. Do you think, for once, you could avoid making a complete mess of it?"

"Yes, M'Hael."

"Good. Because if you fail, I'll kill you." The weave fell into place and vanished.

Mishraile grunted, releasing Androl and stepping back. "I think Androl is uglier than that, M'Hael."

Taim snorted, then waved at Androl. "It's good enough. Get out of my sight. Return with Logain's head, or do not return at all."

Androl scrambled away, breathing heavily, feeling the others' eyes on his back. Once a good distance away, he ducked around some brush that was only mostly burned, and nearly tripped over Pevara, Emarin and Jonneth hiding there.

"Androl!" Emarin whispered "Your disguise! What *happened*? Was that Taim?"

Androl sat down in a heap, trying to still his heart. Then, he held up the pouch he had pulled off Taim's belt while stumbling to his feet. "It was him. You're not going to believe this, but . . ."

Arganda cupped the piece of paper, sitting in Mighty's saddle and pulling his list of ciphers out of his pocket. Those Trollocs kept launching arrows. So far, he'd avoided being hit. As had Queen

Alliandre, who still rode with him. At least she was willing to stay back a little way with his reserves, where she was more sheltered.

In addition to the Legion of the Dragon and the Borderlanders, his force, along with the Wolf Guard and the Whitecloaks, had moved downriver following the battle at the ruins. Arganda had more foot soldiers than the others, and had trailed behind them.

They'd found plenty of fighting here, with the Trollocs and Sharans in the dry riverbed trying to surround the armies of Andor. Arganda had been fighting here for a few hours now as the sun set, bringing on the shadows. He'd pulled back once he got the message, however.

"Bloody awful handwriting," Arganda grumbled, flipping through the little list of ciphers and turning it toward a torch. The orders were authentic. Either that, or someone had broken the cipher.

"Well?" Turne asked.

"Cauthon's alive," Arganda said with a grunt.

"Where is he?"

"Don't know," Arganda said, folding the paper and tucking away the ciphers. "The messenger said Cauthon opened a gateway in front of him, threw the letter in his face, and told him to find me."

Arganda turned to the south, peering through the darkness. In preparation for night, his men had brought oil through gateways and set piles of wood alight. By the firelight, he could see the Two Rivers men heading his way, sure as the orders had said.

"Ho, Tam al'Thor!" Arganda said, raising a hand. He hadn't seen his commander since parting after the battle at the ruins, hours ago now.

The Two Rivers men looked as worn down as Arganda felt. It had been a long, *long* day, and the fighting was by no means over. *I wish Gallenne were here*, Arganda thought, inspecting Trollocs at the river as al'Thor's men approached. *I could use someone to argue with.*

Just downriver, shouts and clangs sounded from where the Andorans' pike formations held off—barely—the Trolloc waves. By now, this battle was strung out along the Mora, almost up to Dashar Knob. His men had helped keep the Andorans from being flanked.

"What news, Arganda?" Tam asked as he came over.

"Cauthon lives," Arganda said. "And that's bloody amazing, considering that someone blew up his command post, set fire to his tent, killed a bunch of his *damane*, and chased off his wife. Cauthon crawled out of it somehow."

"Ha!" Abell Cauthon said. "That's my boy."

"He told me you were coming," Arganda said. "He said you'd have arrows. Do you?"

Tam nodded. "Our last orders sent us through the gateway to Mayene for Healing and resupply. I don't know how Mat knew arrows would be coming, but a shipment from the women in the Two Rivers came right as we were getting ready to return here. We have longbows for you to use, if you need them."

"I will. Cauthon wants all of our troops to move back upriver to the ruins, cut across the riverbed and march up the Heights from the northeastern side."

"Not sure what that's about, but I suppose he knows what he's doing . . ." Tam said.

Together, their forces moved upriver in the night, leaving behind the fighting Andorans, Cairhienin and Aiel. *Creator shelter you, friends*, Arganda thought.

They crossed the dry riverbed and began moving up the northeastern slopes. It was quiet on top, at this end of the Heights, but the glow from lines of torches was evident.

"That's going to be a tough nut to crack, if those are Sharans up there," Tam said softly, looking up the darkened slope.

"Cauthon's note said we'd have help," Arganda replied.

"What kind of help?"

"I don't know. He didn't—"

Thunder rumbled nearby, and Arganda winced. Most of the channelers were supposed to be fighting on the other side of the Heights, but that didn't mean he wouldn't see any here. He *hated* that feeling, the sensation that a channeler might be watching him, contemplating whether to kill him with fire, lightning or earth.

Channelers. The world would be just plain better without them. But that sound didn't turn out to be thunder. A group of galloping riders bearing torches appeared from the night, crossing the riverbed to join Arganda and his men. They flew the Golden Crane at the center of an array of Borderlander banners.

"Well I'll be a bloody Trolloc," Arganda called. "You Borderlanders decided to join us?"

Lan Mandragoran saluted by torchlight, silvery sword glistening. He looked up the slope. "So we're to fight here."

Arganda nodded.

"Good," Lan said softly from horseback. "I just received reports about a large Sharan army moving northeast across the top of the Heights. It's clear to me they want to swing down around behind our people fighting the Trollocs at the river; then we'd be surrounded and at their mercy. Looks like it's our job to keep that from happening."

He turned toward Tam. "Are you ready to soften them up for us, archer?"

"I think we can manage that," Tam replied.

Lan nodded, then raised his sword. A Malkieri man at his side raised the Golden Crane high. And then they charged right up that slope. Coming toward them was a huge enemy army spread out in wide ranks across the landscape, the sky lit up by the thousands of torches they carried.

Tam al'Thor shouted for his men to line up and fire. "Loose!" Tam yelled, sending flights of arrows at the Sharans.

Then arrows began to be returned in their direction, now that the distance between the two armies had narrowed. Arganda figured that the archers wouldn't be nearly as accurate in the darkness as they might have been by day—but that would be true for both sides.

The Two Rivers men released a wave of death, arrows as fast as diving falcons.

"Hold!" Tam yelled to his men. They stopped firing just in time for Lan's cavalry to hit the softened Sharan lines.

Where did *Tam get his battle experience?* Arganda thought, thinking of the times he'd seen Tam fight. Arganda had known seasoned generals with far less sense of a battlefield than this sheepherder.

The Borderlanders pulled back, letting Tam and his men loose more arrows. Tam signaled to Arganda.

"Let's go!" Arganda called to his foot soldiers. "All companies, forward!"

The one-two attack of archers and heavy cavalry was powerful, but it had limited advantage, once the enemy set their defenses. Soon the Sharans would get a solid shield-and-spear wall up to deflect the horsemen, or the archers would pick them off. That's where the infantry came in.

Arganda unhooked his mace—those Sharans wore chain mail and leather—and raised it high, leading his men across the Heights, meeting the Sharans halfway, as they'd advanced to engage. Tam's troops were Whitecloaks, Ghealdanin, Perrin's Wolf Guard and the Mayener Winged Guard, but they viewed themselves as one army. Not six months ago, Arganda would have sworn on his father's grave that men such as these would never fight together—let alone come to one another's aid, as the Wolf Guard did when the Whitecloak forces were being overrun.

Some Trollocs could be heard howling and began moving up alongside the Sharans. Light! Trollocs, too?

Arganda swung his mace until his arm burned, then switched hands and kept going, breaking bones, smashing hands and arms until Mighty's coat was flecked with blood.

Flashes of light suddenly launched from the opposite end of the Heights toward the Andorans defending below. Arganda barely noted it, consumed by the fighting as he was, but something inside of him whimpered. Demandred must have resumed his attack.

"I have defeated your brother, Lews Therin!" The voice boomed across the battlefield, loud as a crack of thunder. "He dies now, bleeding away his mortality!"

Arganda danced Mighty back, turning as a hulking Trolloc with an almost-human face shoved away the wounded Sharan beside it and bellowed. Blood streamed from a cut on its shoulder, but it didn't seem to notice. It twisted, heaving a short-chained flail with a head like a log covered in spikes.

The flail crashed to the ground right beside Mighty, spooking the horse. As Arganda fought for control, the immense Trolloc stepped forward and *punched* with its off hand, slamming a ham fist into the side of Mighty's head, knocking the horse to the ground.

"Have you any care for the flesh of this birth?" Demandred thundered in the distance. "Share you any love for the one who named you brother, this man in white?"

Mighty's head had cracked like an egg. The horse's legs

spasmed and jerked. Arganda hauled himself to his feet. He didn't remember leaping free as the horse fell, but his instincts had preserved him. Unfortunately, his roll had taken him away from his guards, who fought for their lives against a group of Sharans.

His men were advancing, and the Sharans were getting slowly pushed back. He didn't have time to look, though. That Trolloc was on him. Arganda hefted his mace and looked up at the towering beast before him, whipping its flail over its head as it stepped over the dying horse.

Never had Arganda felt so small.

"Coward!" Demandred roared. "You name yourself savior of this land? I claim that title! Face me! Do I need to kill this kin of yours to draw you out?"

Arganda took a deep breath, then leaped forward. He figured that was the last thing the Trolloc would anticipate. Indeed, the beast's swing went wide. Arganda scored a solid crack at its side, his mace hitting the Trolloc's pelvis, crushing bone.

Then the thing backhanded him. Arganda saw white, and the sounds of battle faded. Screaming, pounding of feet, yelling. Screams and yells. Yells and screams . . . Nothing.

Sometime later—he didn't know how long—he felt himself being lifted up. The Trolloc? He blinked, intent on at least spitting in the face of his killer, only to find himself being hauled into the saddle behind al'Lan Mandragoran.

"I'm alive?" Arganda said. A wave of pain across his left side informed him that yes, indeed, he was.

"You felled a big one, Ghealdanin," Lan said, spurring his horse to a gallop toward their rear lines. The other Borderlanders were riding with them, Arganda saw. "The Trolloc hit you in its death throes. I thought you were dead, but I could not come for you until we had pushed them back. We would have been hard pressed if that other army hadn't surprised the Sharans."

"Other army?" said Arganda, rubbing his arm.

"Cauthon had an army lying in wait on the northern side of the Heights. By the looks of it, Dragonsworn and a banner of cavalry, probably part of the Band. About the time you were tussling with that Trolloc, they fell on the Sharan's left flank, breaking them all apart. It's going to take them a while to regroup."

"Light," Arganda said, then groaned. He could tell his left arm was broken. Well, he lived. Good enough for now. He looked toward the front lines where his soldiers still held their ranks. Queen Alliandre rode in their midst, back and forth through the ranks, encouraging them. Light. He wished she'd been willing to serve at the hospital in Mayene.

There was peace here at the moment—the Sharans had been hit hard enough that they had pulled back, leaving a section of ground open between the opposing armies. They probably hadn't been expecting such a sudden and strong attack.

But wait. Shadows approached from Arganda's right, oversized figures walking from the darkness. More Trollocs? He set his jaw against the pain. He'd dropped his mace, but he still had his boot knife. He'd not go down without . . . Without . . .

Ogier, he realized, blinking. *Those aren't Trollocs. They're Ogier.* Trollocs wouldn't carry torches as these beings did.

"Glory to the Builders!" Lan called up to them. "So you were part of the army Cauthon sent to attack the Sharans' flank. Where is he? I would have words with him!"

One of the Ogier let out a rumbling laugh. "You are not the only one, Dai Shan! Cauthon moves about like a squirrel hunting nuts in the underbrush. One moment here, another moment gone. I am to tell you that we must hold back this Sharan advance, at all cost."

More light flashed from the distant side of the Heights. The Aes Sedai and Sharans fought there. Cauthon *was* trying to box the Shadow's forces in. Arganda shoved aside his pain, trying to think.

What of Demandred? Arganda could now see another swath of destruction launched from the Forsaken. It burned through defenders across the river. The pike formations had begun to shatter, each burst of light killing hundreds.

"Sharan channelers in the distance on one side," Arganda mumbled, "and one of the Forsaken on the other! Light! I didn't realize how many Trollocs there were. They're endless." He could see them now, confronting Elayne's troops; blasts of the One Power showed thousands of them in the distance below. "We're finished, aren't we?"

Lan's face reflected torchlight. Eyes like slate, a face of granite. He did not correct Arganda.

"What will we do?" Arganda said. "To win ... Light, to win we'd need to break these Sharans, rescue the pikemen—they will soon be surrounded by the Trollocs—and each man of ours would need to kill at least five of those beasts! That's not even counting Demandred."

No reply from Lan.

"We're doomed," Arganda said.

"If so," Lan said, "we stand atop the high ground, and we fight until we die, Ghealdanin. You surrender when you're dead. Many a man has been given less."

The threads of possibility *resisted* Rand as he wove them together into the world he imagined. He did not know what that meant. Perhaps what he demanded was highly unlikely. This thing he did, using threads to show what could be, was more than simple illusion. It involved looking to worlds that had been before, worlds that could be again. Mirrors of the reality he lived in.

He didn't create these worlds. He merely ... manifested them. He forced the threads to open the reality he demanded, and finally they obeyed. One last time, the darkness became light, and the nothing became *something*.

He stepped into a world that did not know the Dark One.

He chose Caemlyn as a point of entry. Perhaps because the Dark One had used the place in his last creation, and Rand wanted to prove to himself that the terrible vision was not inevitable. He needed to see the city again, but untainted.

He walked on the road before the palace, taking a deep breath. The butterchain trees were in bloom, the bright yellow blossoms spilling out of the gardens and hanging over the courtyard walls. Children played in them, throwing the petals into the air.

Not a cloud marred the brilliant sky. Rand looked up, raising his arms, and stepped out from beneath the blossoming branches into the deep warming sunlight. No guards stood at the way into the palace, only a kindly servant who answered questions for some visitors.

Rand strode forward, feet leaving tracks in golden petals as he approached the entrance. A child came toward him, and Rand stopped, smiling at her.

She stepped up, reaching to touch the sword at Rand's waist. The child seemed confused. "What is it?" she asked, looking up with wide eyes.

"A relic," Rand whispered.

Laughter from the other children turned the girl's head, and she left him, giggling as one of the children threw an armful of petals into the air.

Rand walked on.

IS THIS PERFECTION FOR YOU? The Dark One's voice felt distant. He could pierce this reality to speak to Rand, but he could not appear here as he had in the other visions. This place was his antithesis.

For this was the world that would exist if Rand killed him in the Last Battle.

"Come and see," Rand said to him, smiling.

No reply. If the Dark One allowed himself to be drawn too fully into this reality, he would cease to exist. In this place, he had died.

All things turned and came again. That was the meaning of the Wheel of Time. What was the point of winning a single battle against the Dark One, only to know that he would return? Rand could do more. He could do *this*.

"I would like to see the Queen," Rand asked of the servant at the Palace doors. "Is she in?"

"You should find her in the gardens, young man," the guide said. He looked at Rand's sword, but out of curiosity, not worry. In this world, men could not conceive that one would want to hurt another. It didn't happen.

"Thank you," Rand said, walking into the Palace. The hallways were familiar, yet different. Caemlyn had nearly been razed during the Last Battle, the Palace burned. The reconstruction resembled what had been there before, but not completely.

Rand strolled the hallways. Something worried him, a discomfort from the back of his mind. What was it . . .

Do not be caught here, he realized. *Do not be complacent*. This world was not real, not completely. Not yet.

Could this have been a plan of the Dark One? To trick Rand into creating paradise for himself, only to enter it and be trapped while the Last Battle raged? People were dying as they fought.

He had to remember that. He could not let this fancy consume him. That was difficult to remember as he entered the gallery— a long hallway, lined with what appeared to be windows. Only, those windows did not look out at Caemlyn. These new glass portals allowed one to see other places, like a gateway always in place.

Rand passed one that looked out into a submerged bay, colorful fish darting this way and that. Another gave a view of a peaceful meadow high in the Mountains of Mist. Red flowers pushed up through the green, like specks of paint scattered on the floor following a painter's daily work.

On the other wall, the windows looked at the great cities of the world. Rand passed Tear, where the Stone was now a museum to the days of the Third Age, with the Defenders as its curators. None of this generation had ever carried a weapon, and were baffled by the stories of their grandparents having fought. Another showed the Seven Towers of Malkier, built strong again—but as a monument, not a fortification. The Blight had vanished upon the Dark One's death, and the Shadowspawn had fallen dead immediately. As if the Dark One had been linked to them all, like a Fade leading a fist of Trollocs.

Doors did not bear locks. Coinage was a nearly forgotten eccentricity. Channelers helped create food for everyone. Rand passed a window to Tar Valon, where the Aes Sedai Healed any who came and created gateways to bring loved ones together. All had everything they needed.

He hesitated beside the next window. It looked out at Rhuidean. Had this city ever been in a desert? The Waste bloomed, from Shara to Cairhien. And here, through the window, Rand saw the Chora Fields—a forest of them, surrounding the fabled city. Though he could not hear their words, he saw the Aiel singing.

No more weapons. No more spears to dance. Once again, the Aiel were a people of peace.

He continued on. Bandar Eban, Ebou Dar, the Seanchan lands, Shara. Each nation was represented, though these days, people didn't pay much heed to borders. Another relic. Who cared who lived in what nation, and why would someone try to "own" land? There was enough for all. The blooming of the Waste had opened up room for new cities, new wonders. Many of the windows Rand passed looked at places he did not know, though he was pleased to see the Two Rivers looking so majestic, almost like Manetheren come again.

The last window gave him pause. It looked upon a valley in what had once been the Blasted Lands. A stone slab, where a body had been burned long ago, rested here alone. Overgrown with life: vines, grass, flowers. A furry spider the size of a child's hand scurried across the stones.

Rand's grave. The place where his body had been burned following the Last Battle. He lingered a long while at that window before finally forcing himself to move on, leaving the Gallery and making his way to the Palace gardens. Servants were helpful whenever he spoke to them. Nobody questioned why he wanted to see the Queen.

He assumed that when he found her, she would be surrounded by people. If anyone could see the Queen, wouldn't that demand all of her time? Yet when he approached her sitting in the Palace gardens beneath the boughs of the Palace's chora tree, she was alone.

This was a world without problems. A world where people worked out their own grievances easily. A world of giving, not dispute. What would someone need of the Queen?

Elayne was as beautiful as she'd been when they'd last parted. She was no longer pregnant, of course. A hundred years had passed since the Last Battle. She appeared to have not aged a day.

Rand approached her, glancing at the garden wall that he had once fallen over, tumbling down to meet her for the first time. These gardens were far different, but that wall remained. It had weathered the scouring of Caemlyn and the coming of a new Age.

Elayne looked at him from her bench. Her eyes widened immediately, and her hand went to her mouth. "Rand?"

He fixed his gaze on her, hand resting on the pommel of Laman's sword. A formal posture. Why had he taken it?

Elayne smiled. "Is this a prank? Daughter, where are you? Have you used the Mask of Mirrors to trick me again?"

"It is no trick, Elayne," Rand said, sinking down onto one knee before her so that their heads were level. He looked into her eyes.

Something was wrong.

"Oh! But how can it be?" she asked.

That wasn't Elayne ... was it? The tone seemed off, the mannerisms wrong. Could she have changed so much? It *had* been a hundred years.

"Elayne?" Rand asked. "What has happened to you?"

"Happened? Why, nothing! The day is grand, wonderful. Beautiful and peaceful. How I like to sit in my gardens and enjoy the sunlight."

Rand frowned. That simpering tone, that vapid reaction ... Elayne had never been like that.

"We shall have to prepare a feast!" Elayne exclaimed, clapping her hands. "I will invite Aviendha! It is her week off from singing, though she is probably doing nursery duty. She usually volunteers there."

"Nursery duty?"

"In Rhuidean," Elayne said. "Everyone so likes to play with the children, both here and there. There is grand competition to care for the children! But we understand the need to take turns."

Aviendha. Tending children and singing to chora trees. There was nothing wrong with that, really. Why shouldn't she enjoy such activities?

But it was wrong, too. He thought Aviendha would be a wonderful mother, but to imagine her seeking to spend all day playing with other people's children ...

Rand looked into Elayne's eyes, looked into them deeply. A shadow lurked back there, behind them. Oh, it was an innocent shadow, but a shadow nonetheless. It was like ... like that ...

Like that shadow behind the eyes of someone who had been Turned to the Dark One.

Rand jumped to his feet and stumbled backward. "What have you done here?" he shouted into the sky. "Shai'tan! Answer me!"

Elayne cocked her head. She wasn't afraid. Fear did not exist in this place. "Shai'tan? I swear I remember that name. It has been so long. I get forgetful sometimes."

"SHAI'TAN!" Rand bellowed.

I HAVE DONE NOTHING, ADVERSARY. The voice was distant. THIS IS YOUR CREATION.

"Nonsense!" Rand said. "You've changed her! You've changed them all!"

DID YOU THINK THAT REMOVING ME FROM THEIR
LIVES WOULD LEAVE THEM UNALTERED?

The words thundered through Rand. Aghast, he stepped away
as Elayne rose, obviously concerned for him. Yes, he saw it now,
the thing behind her eyes. She was not herself ... because Rand
had taken from her the ability to *be* herself.

I TURN MEN TO ME, Shai'tan said. IT IS TRUE. THEY
CANNOT CHOOSE GOOD ONCE I HAVE MADE THEM
MINE IN THAT WAY. HOW IS THIS ANY DIFFERENT,
ADVERSARY?

IF YOU DO THIS, WE ARE ONE.

"No!" Rand screamed, holding his head in his hand, falling to
his knees. "No! The world would be perfect without you!"

PERFECT. UNCHANGING. RUINED. DO THIS, IF YOU
WISH, ADVERSARY. IN KILLING ME, I WOULD WIN.

NO MATTER WHAT YOU DO, I WILL WIN.

Rand screamed, curling up as the Dark One's next attack
washed over him. The nightmare Rand had created exploded outward, ribbons of light spraying away like streaks of smoke.

The darkness around him shook and trembled.

YOU CANNOT SAVE THEM.

The Pattern—glowing, vibrant—wrapped around Rand again.
The real Pattern. The truth of what was happening. In creating his
vision of a world without the Dark One, he had created something
horrible. Something awful. Something worse than would have been
before.

The Dark One attacked again.

Mat pulled back from the fighting, resting his *ashandarei* on his
shoulder. Karede had demanded the chance to fight—the more
hopeless the situation, the better. Well, the man should be bloody
well pleased with this. He should be dancing and laughing! He
had his wish. Light, but he did.

Mat sat down on a dead Trolloc, the only seat available, and
drank deeply from his waterskin. He had the pulse of the battle,
its rhythm. The beat it played was forlorn. Demandred was clever.
He had not gone for Mat's bait at the ford, where he had positioned a smaller army. Demandred had sent Trollocs there, but

held back his Sharans. Had Demandred abandoned the Heights to attack Elayne's army, Mat would have swept his own armies across the top of the Heights from the west and the northeast to smash the Shadow from behind. Now Demandred was trying to get his troops behind Elayne's forces, and Mat had stopped him for the time being. But how long could he hold?

The Aes Sedai were not doing well. The Sharan channelers were winning that fight. *Luck*, Mat thought. *We'll need more than a little of you today. Don't abandon me now.*

That would be a fitting end for Matrim Cauthon. The Pattern did like to laugh at him. He suddenly saw its grand prank, offering him luck when it meant nothing, then seizing it all away when it really mattered.

Blood and bloody ashes, he thought, putting away the empty waterskin, seeing only by a torch that Karede carried. Mat could not feel his luck at the moment. That happened sometimes. He did not know if it was with him or not.

Well, if they could not have a lucky Matrim Cauthon, they would at least have a stubborn Matrim Cauthon. He did not intend to die this day. There was still dancing to be done; there were still songs to be sung and women to be kissed. One woman, at least.

He stood and rejoined the Deathwatch Guards, the Ogier, Tam's army, the Band, the Borderlanders—everyone he had put up here. The battle had resumed, and they fought hard, even pushing the Sharans back a couple of hundred paces. But Demandred had seen what he was doing, and had started sending Trollocs at the river up the slope to join the fray. It was the steep one—hardest to climb—but Demandred would know he had to pressure Mat.

Those Trollocs were a real danger. There were enough of them at the river to potentially surround Elayne *and* fight their way up to the Heights. If any one of Mat's armies broke, he was done for.

Well, Mat had thrown his dice and sent out his orders. There was nothing more to do but fight, bleed and hope.

A spray of light, like liquid fire, flared from the western side of the Heights. Burning drops of molten stone fell through the dark air. At first, Mat thought that Demandred had decided to attack from that direction, but the Forsaken was still intent on destroying the Andorans.

Another flash of light. That was where the Aes Sedai fought. Through the darkness and smoke, Mat was certain he saw Sharans fleeing across the Heights from west to east. Mat found himself smiling.

"Look," he said, slapping Karede on the shoulder and drawing the man's attention.

"What is it?"

"I don't know," Mat said. "But it's setting Sharans on fire, so I'm mostly certain that I like it. Keep fighting!" He led Karede and the others in another charge against Sharan soldiers.

Olver walked hunched under the bundle of arrows tied to his back. They had to have real weight; he'd insisted. What would happen if one of the Shadow's people inspected the goods, and found that his pack had light cloth stuffed in the middle?

Setalle and Faile didn't need to keep looking at him as if he'd break any moment. The bundle wasn't *that* heavy. Of course, that wouldn't stop him from squeezing some sympathy from Setalle once they were back. He needed to practice doing things like that, or he'd end up as hopeless as Mat.

Their line continued forward toward the supply dump here in the Blasted Lands, and as it did, he admitted to himself that he wouldn't have minded a pack that was a *little* lighter. Not because he was growing tired. How was he going to fight if he needed to? He'd have to drop the pack quickly, and this didn't seem the type of pack that let one do *anything* quickly.

Gray dust coated his feet. No shoes, and his clothing now wouldn't make good rags. Earlier, Faile and the Band had attacked one of the pitiful caravans trailing toward the Shadow's supply depot. It hadn't been much of a fight—only three Darkfriends and one oily merchant guarding a string of worn-out, half-fed captives.

Many of their supplies bore the mark of Kandor, a red horse. In fact, many of those captives had been Kandori. Faile had offered them freedom, sending them southward, but only half had gone. The rest had insisted on joining her and marching for the Last Battle, though Olver had seen beggars on the streets with more meat on them than those fellows. Still, they helped Faile's line look authentic.

That was important. Olver glanced up as they approached the supply dump, the path lined with torches in the cold night. Several of those red-veiled Aiel stood to the side, watching the line pass. Olver looked down again, lest they see his hatred. He'd known that Aiel couldn't be trusted.

A couple of guards—not Aiel, but more of those Darkfriends—called out for the line to stop. Aravine walked forward, wearing the clothing of the merchant they'd killed. Faile was obviously Saldaean, and it had been decided that she might be too distinctive to play the part of the merchant Darkfriend.

"Where are your guards?" the soldier asked. "This is Lifa's run, isn't it? What happened?"

"Those fools!" Aravine said, then spat to the side. Olver hid a smile. Her entire countenance changed. She knew how to play a part. "They're dead where I left them! I told them not to wander at night. I don't know what took the three, but we found them at the edge of camp, bloated, their skin black." She looked sick. "I think something laid eggs in their hollowed-out stomachs. We didn't want to find what hatched."

The soldier grunted. "You are?"

"Pansai," Aravine said. "Lifa's business partner."

"Since when has Lifa had a business partner?"

"Since I stabbed her and took over her run."

What information they had on Lifa had come from the rescued captives. It was thin. Olver felt himself sweating. The guard gave Aravine a long look, then began walking down the line of people. Faile's soldiers were mixed among the Kandori captives. They tried their best to hold the right posture.

"You, woman," the guard said, pointing at Faile. "A Saldaean, eh?" He laughed. "I thought a Saldaean woman would kill a man before letting him take her captive." He shoved Faile on the shoulder.

Olver held his breath. Oh, blood and bloody ashes! Lady Faile wasn't going to be able to take that. The guard was looking to see if the captives were really beaten down or not! Faile's posture, her manner, would give her away. She was noble, and—

Faile slumped down, becoming small, and whimpered a reply that Olver could not hear.

Olver found himself gaping, then forced his mouth shut and

looked down at the ground. How? How had a lady like Faile learned to act like a servant?

The guard grunted. "Go on," he said, waving to Aravine. "Wait there until we send for you."

The group shuffled to a patch of ground nearby where Aravine ordered everyone to sit down. She stood to the side, arms folded, tapping one toe as she waited. Thunder rumbled, and Olver felt an odd chill. He looked up, and into the eyeless face of a Myrddraal.

A shock ran through Olver, like he'd been dropped into an icy lake. He couldn't breathe. The Myrddraal seemed to glide as it moved, its cloak motionless and dead, as it rounded the group. After a horrible moment, it moved on, back toward the supply camp.

"Searching for channelers," Faile whispered to Mandevwin.

"Light help us," the man whispered back.

The wait was nearly insufferable. Eventually, a plump woman in white clothing strode up and wove a gateway. Aravine barked for them all to climb to their feet, then waved them through. Olver joined the line, walking near Faile, and they passed from the land of red soil and cold air to a place that smelled like it was on fire.

They entered a ramshackle camp filled with Trollocs. Several large cookpots boiled nearby. Just behind the camp, a slope led up sharply to some kind of large plateau. Streams of smoke rose from the top of it, and from there and somewhere to Olver's left could be heard the sounds of combat. Turning away from the slope, the boy saw the darkened outline of a tall, narrow mountain far in the distance, rising from the flat plain like a candle in the middle of a table.

He looked back up the slope behind the camp, and his heart leaped. A body was plummeting down from the top of the slope, still clutching in its hand a banner—a banner that bore a large red hand. The Band of the Red Hand! The man and banner fell among a group of Trollocs eating sizzling pieces of meat around a fire. Sparks flew in all directions, and the enraged beasts yanked the intruder out of the flames, but he was long past caring what they did to him.

"Faile!" he whispered.

"I see it." Her bundle concealed the sack with the Horn in it. She added, more to herself, "Light. How are we going to reach Mat?"

They moved off to the side as the rest of her group came through the gateway. They had swords, but carried them bundled up like arrows, in packs, atop the backs of a few of the men as if they were tied-up supplies for the battlefield.

"Blood and ashes," Mandevwin whispered, joining the two of them. Captives whimpered from a pen nearby. "Maybe they'll put us in there? We could sneak out in the night."

Faile shook her head. "They'll take our bundles. Leave us unarmed."

"Then what do we do?" Mandevwin asked, glancing to the side as a group of Trollocs passed, dragging corpses harvested from the front lines. "Start fighting? Hope Lord Mat sees us, and sends help?"

Olver didn't think much of that plan. He wanted to fight, but those Trollocs were *big*. One passed nearby, and its wolf-featured head swung his way. Eyes that could have belonged to a man looked him up and down, as if hungry. Olver stepped back, then reached toward his bundle, where he'd hidden his knife.

"We'll run," Faile whispered, once the Trolloc passed. "Scatter in a dozen different directions, and in doing so, try to disorient them. Maybe a few of us will escape." She frowned. "What is delaying Aravine?"

Almost as she said it, Aravine strode through the gateway. The woman in white who had channeled followed her out, and then Aravine pointed at Faile.

Faile jerked into the air. Olver gasped, and Mandevwin cursed, throwing down his bundle and digging for his sword while Arrela and Selande shouted. All three were hauled into the air by weaves moment later, and Aiel in red veils ran through the gateway, weapons out.

Pandemonium followed. A few of Faile's soldiers fell as they tried to fight back with their fists. Olver dove for the ground, hunting for his knife, but by the time he had his hand on its hilt, the skirmish was over. The others were all subdued or tied in air.

So fast! Olver thought with despair. Why hadn't anyone warned him that fighting happened so quickly?

They seemed to have forgotten him, but he didn't know what to do.

Aravine walked up to Faile, still hanging in the air. What was happening? Aravine ... *she* had betrayed them?

"I am sorry, my Lady," Aravine said to Faile. Olver could barely hear. Nobody paid any attention to him; the Aiel kept watch on the soldiers, shoving them into a group to be guarded. More than a few of their number lay bleeding on the ground.

Faile struggled in the air, her face growing red as she strained. Her mouth was obviously gagged. Faile would never remain quiet at a time like this.

Aravine untied the Horn's bag from Faile's back, then checked inside it. Her eyes widened. She pulled the sack tight at the top and held it close. "I had hoped," she whispered to Faile, "to leave my old life behind. To start fresh and new. I thought I could hide, or that I would be forgotten, that I could come back to the Light. But the Great Lord does not forget, and one cannot hide from him. They found me the very night we reached Andor. This is not what I intended, but it is what I must do."

Aravine turned away. "A horse!" she called. "I will deliver this package to Lord Demandred myself, as I have been commanded."

The woman in white walked up beside her, and the two started arguing in hushed tones. Olver glanced about. Nobody was looking at him.

His fingers started trembling. He'd known that Trollocs were big, and that they were ugly. But ... these things were *nightmares*. Nightmares all around. Oh, Light!

What would Mat do?

"*Dovie'andi se tovya sagain*," Olver whispered, unsheathing his knife. With a cry, he threw himself at the woman in white and rammed his knife into her lower back.

She screamed. Faile dropped free of her bonds of Air. And then, suddenly, the captive pens burst open and a group of yelling men scrambled to freedom.

"Raise it higher!" Doesine cried. "Flaming quickly!"

Leane obeyed, weaving Earth with the other sisters. The ground trembled in front of them, buckling and slumping like a bunched-up rug. They finished, then used the mound for cover as fire dropped from upslope.

Doesine led the motley bunch. A dozen or so Aes Sedai, a smattering of Warders and soldiers. The men clutched their weapons, but lately those had proven about as effective as loaves of bread. The Power crackled and sizzled in the air. The improvised bulwark thumped as Sharans pounded it with fire.

Leane peeked above the defences, clutching the One Power. She had recovered from her encounter with the Forsaken Demandred. It had been an unsettling experience—she had been totally in his power, and her life could have been snuffed out in an instant. She had also been unnerved by the intensity of his ravings; his hatred of the Dragon Reborn was unlike anything she had ever seen.

A group of Sharans moved down the slope, and together they sent weaves at the makeshift fortification. Leane sliced one weave from the air, working like a surgeon cutting away withered flesh. Leane was much weaker in the One Power now than she had once been.

She had to be more efficient with her channeling. It was remarkable what a woman could achieve with less.

The bulwark exploded.

Leane threw herself aside as clods of soil rained down. She rolled through curling smoke, coughing and clinging to *saidar*. It was those Sharan men! She couldn't see their weaves. She picked herself up, her dress tattered from the explosion, her arms scored by scratches. She caught a hint of blue peeking from a furrow nearby. Doesine. She scrambled over.

She found the woman's body there. Not her head, though.

Leane felt an immediate, almost overpowering, sense of loss and grief. Doesine and she had not been close, but they had been fighting together here. It was wearing on Leane—the loss, the destruction. How much could they take? How many more would she have to watch die?

She steeled herself with difficulty. Light, this was a disaster. They had anticipated enemy Dreadlords, but there were hundreds upon hundreds of those Sharans. An entire nation's worth of channelers, all trained in war. The battlefield was strewn with bright bits of color, fallen Aes Sedai. Their Warders charged up the hillside, screaming in rage at the loss of their Aes Sedai as they were cut down by blasts of the Power.

Leane stumbled toward where a group of Reds and Greens fought from a hollowed out piece of ground on the western slope. The terrain protected them for now, but how long could the women hold out?

Still, she felt proud. Outnumbered and overwhelmed, the Aes Sedai kept fighting. This was nothing like the night the Seanchan attacked, when a fractured Tower had broken from the inside out. These women held firm; each time a pocket of them was scattered, they grouped back together and continued fighting. Fire fell from above, but nearly as much flew back, and lightning struck on either side.

Leane carefully made her way over to the group, joining Raechin Connoral, who crouched next to a boulder while launching weaves of Fire at the advancing Sharans. Leane watched for return weaves, then deflected one with a quick weave of Water, making the ball of fire burn away in tiny sparks.

Raechin nodded to her. "And here I thought you'd stopped being useful for anything other than batting your eyes at men."

"The Domani art is about achieving what you want, Raechin," Leane said coolly, "with as little effort as possible."

Raechin snorted and launched a few fireballs toward the Sharans. "I should ask advice from you on that sometime," she said. "If there really *is* a way to make men do as you like, I should like very much to know it."

That idea was so absurd as to nearly make Leane laugh, despite the terrible circumstances. A Red? Putting on paints and powders and learning the Domani arts of manipulation? *Well, why not?* Leane thought, striking down another fireball. The world was changing, and the Ajahs—ever so subtly—changing with it.

The sisters' resistance was attracting the attention of more Sharan channelers. "We'll have to abandon this position soon," Raechin said.

Leane only nodded.

"Those Sharans . . ." the Red growled. "Look at that!"

Leane gasped. Many of the Sharan troops in this quarter had withdrawn earlier in the fight—something seemed to have drawn them away—but the channelers had replaced them with a large group of frightened-looking people and were herding them at the front of their line to absorb attacks. Many carried sticks or tools of some sort for fighting, but they bunched together, holding the weapons timidly.

"Blood and bloody ashes," Raechin said, causing Leane to raise an eyebrow at her. She continued weaving, trying to send lightning down behind the lines of the frightened people. It still hit many of them. Leane felt sick, but joined in the attacks.

As they worked, Manda Wan crawled up to them. Soot-stained and blackened, the Green looked horrible. *Probably much as I do*, Leane thought, glancing down at her own scratched and sooty arms.

"We're pulling back," Manda said. "Maybe we'll have to use gateways."

"And go where?" Leane said. "Abandon the battle?"

The three grew silent. No. There was no retreat from this fight. It was win here or nothing.

"We are too fragmented," Manda said. "We must at least fall back to regroup. We need to bring the women together, and this is the only thing I can think of. Unless you have a better idea."

Manda looked to Raechin. Leane was too weak in the power now for her opinion to hold much weight. She started cutting down weaves as the two continued to speak in hushed tones. The Aes Sedai nearby began pulling back out of the hollow and moving back down the slope. They'd regroup, make a gateway toward Dashar Knob and decide what to do next.

Wait. What was *that*? Leane sensed powerful channeling nearby. Had the Sharans created a circle? She squinted; they were well into night now, but enough of the landscape burned to give firelight. It also raised a lot of smoke. Leane wove Air to blow the smoke out of the way, but it lifted on its own, split as if by a powerful wind.

Egwene al'Vere strode past them up the slope, glowing with the power of a hundred bonfires. That was more than Leane had ever seen a woman hold. The Amyrlin walked forward with her hand thrust out, holding a white rod. Egwene's eyes seemed to shine.

With a burst of light and force, Egwene released a dozen separate flows of fire. A *dozen*. They battered the hillside above, throwing the bodies of Sharan channelers into the air.

"Manda," Leane said, "I think we have found you a better rallying point."

Talmanes lit a twig off the lantern, then used it to light his pipe. He took one puff before hacking and emptying the pipe's bowl on the rock floor. The tabac had gone bad somehow. Horribly bad. He coughed and ground the offending tabac into the floor with his heel.

"You all right, my Lord?" Melten asked, walking past, idly juggling a pair of hammers with his right hand as he walked.

"I'm still bloody alive," Talmanes said. "Which is far more than I likely have a right to expect."

Melten nodded without expression and continued on, joining one of the teams working on the dragons. The deep cavern around them echoed with the sounds of hammers on wood as the Band did its best to reconstruct the weapons. Talmanes tapped the lantern, judging the oil. It smelled awful when it burned, though he was growing used to that. They had enough for a few more hours yet.

That was good, since—so far as he knew—this cavern had no exits to the battleground above. It was accessible only by gateway. Some Asha'man had known of it. Strange fellow. What kind of man knew of caverns that could not be reached, except through the One Power?

Anyway, the Band was trapped down here, in a place of safety but isolation. Only rare bits of information came in Mat's messages.

Talmanes strained, thinking he could hear the distant sounds of channelers fighting above, but it was mere fancy. The land was silent, and these ancient stones had not seen the light since the Breaking, if then.

Talmanes shook his head, walking to one of the working teams. "How goes it?"

Dennel gestured toward a few sheets of paper Aludra had given him, instructions on how to repair this particular dragon. The woman herself gave precise directions to another of the work teams, her lightly accented voice echoing in the chamber.

"Most of the tubes are solid," Dennel said. "If you think about it, they were built to withstand a little fire and an explosion now and then . . . " He chuckled, then fell silent, looking at Talmanes.

"Do not let my expression dampen your good humor," Talmanes said, tucking his pipe away. "Nor let it bother you that we are fighting at the end of the world, that our armies are grossly outnumbered, and that if we lose, our very souls will be destroyed by the Dark Lord of all evil."

"Sorry, my Lord."

"That was a joke."

Dennel blinked. "That?"

"Yes."

"That was a joke."

"Yes."

"You have an interesting sense of humor, my Lord," Dennel said.

"So I have been told." Talmanes stooped down and inspected the dragon cart. The scorched wood was held together with screws and extra boards. "This does not seem very functional."

"It will work, my Lord. We won't be able to move it fast, though. I was saying, the tubes themselves fared well, but the carts . . . Well, we've done what we can with salvage and the supplies out of Baerlon, but we can only do so much with the time we have."

"Which is none," Talmanes said. "Lord Mat could call upon us at any moment."

"If they're still alive up there," Dennel said, looking upward.

A discomforting thought. The Band could end its days trapped down here. At least there wouldn't be many of those days. Either the world would end or the Band would run out of food. They wouldn't last a week. Buried here. In darkness.

Bloody ashes, Mat. You'd better not lose up there. You'd better not! The Band still had fight in them. They were not going to end this one starving underground.

Talmanes held up his lantern, turning to go, but noticed something. The soldiers working on the dragons cast a twisted shadow on the wall, like a man with a wide cloak and hat that obscured his face.

Dennel followed the glance. "Light. It looks like we're being watched over by old Jak himself, doesn't it?"

"That it does," Talmanes said. Then, in a louder voice, he shouted, "It's too quiet in here by far! Let's have some singing, men."

Some of the men paused. Aludra stood up, placing hands on her hips, and gave him a displeased glance.

So Talmanes started it himself.

> "We'll drink the wine till the cup is dry,
> And kiss the girls so they'll not cry,
> And toss the dice until we fly,
> To dance with Jak o' the Shadows!"

Silence.
Then they started it up:

> "We'll give a yell with a bloody curse,
> And hug the maids, it could be worse,
> As we ride away with the Dark One's purse,
> To dance with Jak o' the Shadows!"

Their loud voices beat against the stones as they worked, furiously preparing for the part they would play.

And they *would* play it. Talmanes would make certain they did. Even if they had to blast their way out of this tomb in a storm of dragonfire.

As Olver stabbed the woman in white, Faile's bonds vanished. She dropped to the ground, stumbling but remaining upright. Mandevwin dropped beside her with a curse.

Aravine. Light, *Aravine*. Docile, careful and capable. Aravine was a Darkfriend.

She had the Horn.

Aravine glanced at the fallen Aes Sedai that Olver had attacked, then panicked, grabbing the horse a servant had brought and jumping into the saddle.

Faile dashed for her as captives roared out of the nearby pens, throwing themselves at Trollocs and trying to wrestle weapons free. She had almost reached Aravine before the woman galloped away, carrying the Horn with her. She headed toward the gentler slopes that would allow her to ride to the top of the Heights.

"No!" Faile screamed. "Aravine! Don't do this!" Faile started to run after her, but saw that that was no use.

A horse. She needed a horse. Faile looked around, frantic, and found the few pack animals they had brought through the gateway. Faile scrambled to Bela's side, cutting free the saddle—and all of its burdens—with a few swipes of the knife. She leaped up onto the mare bareback and took the reins, then kicked her into motion.

The shaggy mare galloped after Aravine, and Faile leaned low on her back. "Run, Bela," Faile said. "If you've kept any strength back, now is the time to use it. Please. Run, girl. *Run.*"

Bela charged across the trampled ground, hoofbeats accompanying thunder from above. The Trolloc camp was a place of darkness, lit by cook fires and the occasional torch. Faile felt as if she were riding through a nightmare.

Ahead, a few Trollocs burst onto the path to head her off. Faile leaned lower, praying to the Light that they'd miss when they attacked. Bela slowed, and then two horsemen charged up alongside Faile, bearing lances. One pierced a Trolloc's neck, and though the other rider missed his mark, his horse shouldered another Trolloc aside, making way. Bela galloped between the disoriented Trollocs, catching up to two men riding ahead, one large of girth, the other lean. Harnan and Vanin.

"You two!" Faile yelled.

"Ho, my Lady!" Harnan said, laughing.

"How?" she yelled at them over the sound of the hooves.

"We let a caravan find us," Harnan yelled back, "and let them take us captive. They brought us through the gateway a few hours back, and we've been preparing the captives to break free. Your arrival gave us the opportunity we needed!"

"The Horn! You tried to steal the Horn!"

"No," Harnan yelled back, "we tried to steal some of Mat's tabac!"

"I thought you had buried it to leave it behind!" Vanin yelled from the other side. "I figured Mat wouldn't care. He owes me a few marks anyway! When I opened that sack and found the bloody Horn of Valere ... bloody ashes! I'll bet they heard my yell all the way in Tar Valon!"

Faile groaned, imagining the scene. The yell that Faile had heard was a yell of surprise, and *it* was what had drawn the bear-thing to attack.

Well, there was no going back to that moment. She clung to Bela with her knees, urging the horse forward. Ahead, Aravine galloped between Trollocs, heading toward where the steep slopes tapered off. Aravine yelled frantically for Trollocs to help her. The racing horses traveled faster than any Trollocs could, however.

Demandred. Aravine had said she would take the Horn to one of the Forsaken. Faile growled softly, leaning down further, and amazingly, Bela pulled ahead of Vanin and Harnan. She didn't ask where they'd found the horses. She directed her entire attention toward Aravine.

A cry went up through camp, and Vanin and Harnan split off, intercepting riders who came for Faile. She cut to the side, urging Bela to leap a pile of supplies and charging through the center of a group of people in strange clothing, eating beside a small fire. They yelled after her with thick accents.

Inch by inch, she gained on Aravine. Bela snorted and puffed, sweat darkening her coat. The Saldaean cavalry was among the best in the land, and Faile knew horses. She'd ridden all breeds. In those minutes on the battlefield, she would have put Bela up against the Tairen best. The shaggy mare, of no particular breed of note, moved like a champion runner.

Feeling the rhythm of the hoofbeats beneath her, Faile slipped a knife from her sleeve. She urged Bela to jump over a small dip in the land, and they hung in the air for a moment, Faile judging the wind, the fall, the moment. She reached her arm back, and flipped the knife through the air right before Bela's hooves touched the ground.

The knife flew true, burying itself in Aravine's back. The woman slipped from the saddle, crumpling to the ground, sack sliding from her grip.

Faile leaped off Bela, landing while still in motion and sliding to a stop beside the sack. She untied the strings that secured its opening, and saw the glittering Horn inside.

"I'm ... sorry ..." Aravine whispered, rolling over. Her legs did not move. "Don't tell Aldin what I did. He has ... such terrible taste ... in women ..."

Faile stood up, then looked down with pity. "Pray that the Creator shelters your soul, Aravine," Faile said, and climbed back onto Bela's back. "For if not, the Dark One will have you as his. I leave you to him." She nudged Bela back into motion.

There were more Trollocs ahead, and they fixed their attention on Faile. They shouted, and several Myrddraal slid forward, pointing toward Faile. They began to shift around her, blocking her path.

She set her jaw, grim, and heeled Bela back in the direction she had come, hoping to meet up with Harnan, Vanin or anyone else who would help.

The camp was abuzz with activity, and Faile picked up riders chasing after her, yelling, "She has the Horn of Valere!"

Somewhere high atop the hill, Mat Cauthon's forces fought the Shadow. So close!

An arrow hit the ground beside her, followed by others. Faile reached the captive pens, the broken fence lying in pieces and bodies littered about. Bela was huffing, perhaps at the end of her strength. Faile caught sight of another horse nearby, a roan gelding that was saddled, nudging at a fallen soldier at his feet.

Faile slowed. What to do? Switch horses, but then what? She glanced over her shoulder and then ducked down as another arrow passed overhead. She'd picked up some dozen Sharan soldiers on horseback, all chasing her, wearing cloth armor sewn with small rings. They were followed by hundreds of Trollocs.

Even with a fresh horse, she thought, *I can't outrun them.* She led Bela behind some supply wagons for cover and leaped off, intending to dash for the fresh mount.

"Lady Faile?" a small voice asked.

Faile glanced down. Olver huddled beneath the wagon, holding his knife.

The riders were almost upon her. Faile didn't have time to think. She whipped the Horn from its sack and pushed it into Olver's arms. "Keep this," she said. "Hide. Take it to Mat Cauthon later in the night."

"You're leaving me?" Olver asked. "Alone?"

"I must," she said, stuffing some bundles of arrows into her sack, her heart thundering in her chest. "Once those riders pass, find another place to hide! They will come back to search where I've been, after . . ."

After they catch me.

She would have to take her knife to herself, lest they torture out of her what she'd done with the Horn. She gripped Olver by the arm. "I'm sorry to place this upon you, little one. There is no one else. You did well earlier; you can do this. Take the Horn to Mat or all is lost."

She ran into the open, making the sack she carried obvious. Some of those strangely dressed foreigners saw her, pointing. She lifted the sack high and climbed into the saddle of the roan, then kicked it into a gallop.

The Trollocs and Darkfriends followed, leaving the young boy and his heavy burden to huddle beneath a wagon in the middle of the Trolloc camp.

Logain turned the thin disc over in his fingers. Black and white, split by a sinuous line. *Cuendillar*, supposedly. The flakes that rubbed off beneath his fingers seemed to make mockery of its eternal nature.

"Why didn't Taim break them?" Logain asked. "He could have. These are as brittle as old leather."

"I don't know," Androl said, glancing at the others of his team. "Maybe the time wasn't right yet."

"Break them at the right time, and it will help the Dragon," said the man who called himself Emarin. He sounded worried. "Break them at the wrong time . . . and what?"

"Nothing good, I suspect," Pevara said. A Red.

Would he ever have his vengeance against those who had gentled him? Once, that hatred—and it alone—had driven him to survive. He now found a new hunger inside of him. He had defeated Aes Sedai, he had beaten them down and claimed them as his own. Vengeance seemed . . . empty. His long-building thirst to kill M'Hael filled a little of that emptiness, but not enough. What more?

Once, he had named himself the Dragon Reborn. Once, he had prepared himself to dominate the world. To make it heel. He fingered the seal to the Dark One's prison while standing at the periphery of the battle. He was far to the southwest, below the bogs, where his Asha'man held a small base camp. Distant rumbles sounded from the Heights—explosions of weaves firing back and forth between Aes Sedai and Sharans.

A large number of his Asha'man had fought there, but the Sharan channelers outnumbered the Aes Sedai and Asha'man combined. Others prowled the battlefields, hunting down Dreadlords, killing them.

He had been losing men faster than the Shadow. There were too many enemies.

He held up the seal. There was a power to it. Power to protect the Black Tower, somehow? *If they do not fear us, fear me, what will happen to us once the Dragon is dead?*

Dissatisfaction radiated through the bond. He met Gabrelle's eyes. She had been inspecting the battle, but now her eyes were upon him. Questioning. Threatening?

Earlier, had he really been thinking that he'd tamed Aes Sedai? The idea should have made him laugh. No Aes Sedai could be tamed, not ever.

Logain pointedly placed the seal and its fellows in the pouch at his belt. He drew its strings closed, meeting Gabrelle's eyes. Her concern spiked. For a moment, he'd felt that concern of hers to be *for* him, not *because* of him.

Perhaps she was learning how to manipulate the bond, to send him feelings she thought would lull him. No, Aes Sedai could not be tamed. Bonding them hadn't contained them. It had made more complications.

He reached to his high collar, undoing the dragon pin he wore there, and offered it to Androl. "Androl Genhald, you have walked into the pit of death itself and returned. Twice now, I am in your debt. I name you full Asha'man. Wear the pin with pride." He had already given the man back his sword pin, restoring him to Dedicated.

Androl hesitated, then reached out and took the pin in reverent hands.

"And the seals?" Pevara asked, arms folded. "They belong to the White Tower; the Amyrlin is their Watcher."

"The Amyrlin," Logain said, "is as good as dead, from what I have heard. In her absence, I am a fitting steward." Logain seized the Source, subjecting it, dominating it. He opened a gateway back to the top of the Heights.

The war returned to him in full force, the confusion, the smoke and screams. He stepped through, the others following. The powerful channeling from Demandred shone like a beacon, the man's booming voice continuing to taunt the Dragon Reborn.

Rand al'Thor was not here. Well, the closest thing to him was Logain himself. Another substitute. "I'm going to fight him," he told the others. "Gabrelle, you will remain behind and wait for my return, as I may need Healing. The rest of you deal with Taim's men and those Sharan channelers. Let no man live who has gone to the Shadow, whether by choice or force. Bring justice to the one and mercy to the other."

They nodded. Gabrelle seemed impressed with him, perhaps for his decision to strike at the enemy's heart. She did not realize. Not even one of the Forsaken could be as powerful as Demandred seemed to be.

Demandred had a *sa'angreal*, and a powerful one. Similar in power to *Callandor*, maybe stronger. With that in Logain's hands, many things in this world would change. The world would know of him and the Black Tower, and they would tremble before him as they never had for the Amyrlin Seat.

Egwene led an assault the likes of which had not been seen in millennia. The Aes Sedai pulled themselves out of their defensive fortifications and joined with her, pushing up the western slope in a steady stride. Weaves flew in the air like an explosion of ribbons caught in the wind.

The sky broke with the light of a thousand bolts, the ground groaning and trembling with the hits. Demandred continued to fire upon the Andorans from the other side of the plateau, and each shot of balefire sent ripples through the air. The ground cracked with spiderwebs of black, but now tendrils of something sickly began to sprout from those cracks. It spread like a disease across the broken stones of the hillside.

The air felt alive with the Power, the energy so thick that Egwene almost thought the One Power had become visible to all.

Through this, she drew as much strength as she could hold through Vora's *sa'angreal*. She felt as she had when fighting the Seanchan, only somehow more in control. Then, her rage had been fringed by desperation and terror.

This time, it was a white-hot thing, like a metal heated beyond the point of being worked by a smith.

She, Egwene al'Vere, had been given stewardship of this land.

She, the Amyrlin Seat, would not be bullied by the Shadow any longer.

She would not retreat. She would not bow as her resources failed.

She would fight.

She channeled Air, building a swirling storm of dust, smoke and dead plants. She held it before herself, obscuring the view of those above as they tried to pinpoint her. Lightning crashed down around her, but she wove Earth, digging deeply in the rock and bringing up a spurt of iron that cooled in a spire next to her. The lightning struck at the spire, sparing her as she sent the windstorm howling up the incline.

A movement at her side. Egwene felt Leilwin nearing. That one . . . that one had proven faithful. Such a surprise. Having a new Warder did not take the edge off her despair at Gawyn's death, but it did help in other ways. That knot in the back of Egwene's mind had replaced itself with a new one, very different, yet shockingly loyal.

Egwene raised Vora's *sa'angreal* and continued her attacks, moving up the hillside, Leilwin at her side. Ahead, Sharans huddled down, weathering the winds. Egwene struck them with ribbons of fire. Channelers tried to attack her through the windstorm, but their weaves went astray, their eyes clogged with dust. Three regular soldiers attacked from the side, but Leilwin dispatched them efficiently.

Egwene brought the wind around and used it like hands, scooping the channelers up and flinging them into the air. The lightning bolts from above took the men in a fiery embrace, and smoking corpses plummeted to the hillside. Egwene pressed forward, her army of Aes Sedai advancing, flinging weaves like arrows of light.

Asha'man joined them. Those had fought alongside the White

Tower on and off, but now they seemed committed in force. Dozens of men gathered as she led the way. The air became thick with the One Power.

The winds stopped.

The dust storm suddenly fell, smothered like a candle beneath a blanket. No natural force had done that. Egwene mounted a rocky outcrop, looking up toward a man in black and red standing at the top, his hand out. She had finally drawn out the one who led this force. His Dreadlords fought alongside the Sharans, but she sought their leader. Taim. M'Hael.

"He's weaving lightning!" a man yelled behind her.

Egwene immediately brought up a spire of molten iron and cooled it to draw the lightning that fell a moment later. She glanced to the side. The one who had spoken was Jahar Narishma, Merise's Asha'man Warder.

Egwene smiled, looking toward Taim. "Keep the others off me," she commanded loudly. "All but you, Narishma and Merise. Narishma's warnings will prove useful."

She gathered her strength and began to release a storm at the traitor M'Hael.

Ila picked through the dead on the battlefield near the ruins. Though the fighting had moved downriver, she could hear distant shouts and explosions in the night.

She hunted for the wounded among the fallen, and ignored arrows and swords when she found them. Others would gather those, though she wished they would not. Swords and arrows had caused much of this death.

Raen, her husband, worked nearby, prodding at each body then listening for a heartbeat. His gloves were stained red, and blood smeared his colorful clothing, because he had been pressing his ear against the chests of corpses. Once they confirmed someone was dead, they left an X drawn on a cheek, often in the person's own blood. That would keep others from repeating the work.

Raen seemed to have aged a decade in the last year, and Ila felt as if she had, too. The Way of the Leaf was an easy master at times, providing a life of joy and peace. But a leaf fell in calm winds and in the tempest; dedication demanded that one accept the latter as well as the former. Being driven from country after country, suffering starvation as the land died, then finally coming to rest in the lands of the Seanchan . . . such had been their life.

None of it matched losing Aram. That had hurt far more deeply than had losing his mother to the Trollocs.

They passed Morgase, the former queen, who organized these workers and gave them orders. Ila kept moving. She cared little for queens. They had done nothing for her or hers.

Nearby, Raen stopped, raising his lantern to examine a full quiver of arrows that a soldier had been carrying as he died. Ila hissed, lifting her skirts up to step around corpses and reach her husband. "Raen!"

"Peace, Ila," he said. "I'm not going to pick it up. Yet, I wonder." He looked up, toward the distant flashes of light downriver and atop the Heights where the armies continued their terrible acts of murder. So many flashes in the night, like hundreds of lightning bolts. It was well past midnight now. They'd been on this field, looking for the living, for hours.

"You wonder?" Ila asked. "Raen . . ."

"What would we have them do, Ila? Trollocs will not follow the Way of the Leaf."

"There is plenty of room to run," Ila said. "Look at them. They came to meet the Trollocs when the Shadowspawn were barely out of the Blight. If that energy had been spent gathering the people and leading them away to the south . . ."

"The Trollocs would have followed," Raen said. "What then, Ila?"

"We have accepted many masters," Ila said. "The Shadow might treat us poorly, but would it really be worse than we have been treated at the hands of others?"

"Yes," Raen said softly. "Yes, Ila. It would be worse. Far, *far* worse."

Ila looked at him.

He shook his head, sighing. "I am not going to abandon the Way, Ila. It is my path, and it is right for me. Perhaps . . . perhaps I will not think quite so poorly of those who follow another path. If we live through these times, we will do so at the bequest of those who died on this battlefield, whether we wish to accept their sacrifice or not."

He trailed away. *It's just the darkness of the night*, she thought. *He will overcome it, once the sun shines again. That's the right of it. Isn't it?*

She looked up at the night sky. That sun ... would they be able to tell when it rose? The clouds, lit from the fires below, seemed to be growing thicker and thicker. She pulled her bright yellow shawl closer, feeling suddenly cold.

Perhaps I will not think quite so poorly of those who follow another path ...

She blinked a few tears from her eyes. "Light," she whispered, something twisting inside. "I shouldn't have turned my back on him. I should have tried to help him return to us, not cast him out. Light, oh Light. Shelter him ... "

Nearby, a group of mercenaries found the arrows and picked them up. "Hey, Hanlon!" one called. "Look at this!"

When the brutish men had originally started helping with the Tuatha'an work, she had been proud of them. Avoiding battle to help care for the wounded? The men had seen beyond their violent past.

Now, she blinked and saw something else about them. Cowards, who would rather pick through corpses and fish in their pockets than fight. Which was worse? The men who—misguided though they were—stood up to the Trollocs and tried to turn them back? Or these mercenaries who refused to fight because they found this path easier?

Ila shook her head. She had always felt as if she knew the answers in life. Today, most of those had slipped from her. Saving a person's life, though ... that she could cling to.

She headed back among the bodies, searching for the living among the dead.

Olver scuttled back under the wagon, clutching the Horn, as Lady Faile rode off. Dozens of riders followed her, and hundreds of Trollocs. It had grown so dark.

Alone. He'd been left alone again.

He squeezed his eyes shut, but that didn't do much. He could still hear men screaming and shouting in the distance. He could still smell blood, the captives who had been killed by the Trollocs as they tried to escape. Beyond the blood, he smelled smoke, thick and itchy. It seemed that the whole world was burning.

The ground trembled, as if something very heavy had hit it somewhere close by. Thunder rumbled in the sky, accompanied by sharp cracks as lightning struck time and time again at the Heights. Olver whimpered.

How brave he had thought himself. Now, here he was, finally at the battle. He could barely keep his hands from trembling. He wanted to hide, dig deep into the earth.

Faile had told him to find another place to hide because they might come back, looking for the Horn.

Dared he go out there? Dared he stay here? Olver cracked his eyes open, then nearly screamed. A pair of legs ending in hooves stood beside the wagon. A moment later, a snouted face leaned down and looked at him, beady eyes narrowing, nostrils sniffing.

Olver yelled, scrambling back, clutching the Horn. The Trolloc yelled something, heaving the wagon over and nearly smashing it down on Olver. The wagon's contents of arrows went scattering across the ground as Olver dashed away, looking for safety.

There was none. Dozens of the Trollocs turned toward him, and they called to one another in a language Olver did not recognize. He looked about, Horn in one hand, knife in the other, frantic. No safety.

A horse snorted nearby. It was Bela, chewing on some grain leaked from a supply cart. The horse raised her head, looking at Olver. She didn't have a saddle on, only a halter and bridle.

Blood and ashes, Olver thought, running for her, *I wish I had Wind.* This plump mare would end him in the cookpot for certain. Olver sheathed his knife and jumped up onto Bela's back, seizing the reins in one hand, clutching the Horn in the other.

The pig-snouted Trolloc from the wagon swung, nearly taking off Olver's arm. He cried out, kicking Bela into motion, and the mare galloped out from among the Trollocs. The beasts ran behind with howls and yells. Other calls sounded throughout the camp, which was nearly emptying out as they converged on the boy.

Olver rode as he'd been taught, down low, guiding with his

knees. And Bela ran. Light, but she *ran*. Mat had said that many horses were frightened of Trollocs, and would throw their rider if forced near them, but this animal did none of that. She thundered right past howling Trollocs, right through the center of the camp.

Olver looked over his shoulder. There were hundreds of them back there, chasing him. "Oh, Light!"

He'd seen Mat's banner atop those Heights, he was sure of it. But there were so many Trollocs in the way. Olver turned Bela to ride the way Aravine had gone. Perhaps he could round the Trolloc camp and get out that way, then come up the back of the Heights.

Take the Horn to Mat, or all is lost.

Olver rode for all he was worth, urging Bela on.

There is nobody else.

Ahead, a large force of Trollocs cut him off. Olver turned back the other way, but others approached from that direction, too. Olver cried out, turning Bela again, but a thick black Trolloc arrow hit her in the flank. She screamed and stumbled, then dropped.

Olver tumbled free. Hitting the ground knocked the air from his lungs and made him see a flash of light. He forced himself to crawl to his hands and knees.

The Horn must *reach Matrim Cauthon . . .*

Olver grabbed the Horn, and found that he was weeping. "I'm sorry," he said to Bela. "You were a good horse. You ran like Wind couldn't have. I'm sorry." She whinnied softly and drew a final breath, then died.

He left her and ran beneath the legs of the first Trolloc that arrived. Olver couldn't fight them. He knew he couldn't. He didn't unsheathe the knife. He just ran up the steep slope, trying to reach the top from where he had seen Mat's flag fall.

It might as well have been a continent away. A Trolloc grabbed at his clothing, pulling him down, but Olver ripped free, leaving cloth in its thick nails. He scrambled over broken ground, and with desperation, spotted a little cleft in a rocky outcrop at the base of the slope. The shallow crack looked up at the black sky.

He threw himself toward it, then wiggled in, clinging to the

Horn. He barely fit. Trollocs milled around above him, then began to reach in for him, tearing at his clothing.

Olver whimpered and closed his eyes.

Logain hurled himself through the gateway, weaves already forming before him as he struck at Demandred.

The man stood on the smoldering slope that looked over the dried river and toward the failing Andoran pike formations. The Aiel, Cairhienin and Legion of the Dragon fought there as well, and all were in danger of being surrounded.

The pikes were all but shattered, now. It would soon be a rout.

Logain launched twin columns of fire toward Demandred, but Sharans threw themselves in the way, interfering with his attack. Flesh burned away, bones charring to dust. Their deaths gave Demandred time to spin about and lash out with a weave of Water and Air. Logain's burst of fire hit that and turned to steam, then boiled away.

Logain had hoped that after so much channeling, Demandred would be weakened. Not so. A complex weave formed in front of the man, a weave such as Logain had never seen. It made a field that rippled in the air, and when Logain next attacked, his weave bounced free like a stick thrown against a brick wall.

Logain leaped to the side, rolling as lightning struck from the sky. Shards of rock pelted him as he wove Spirit, Fire and Earth, slicing at the strange wall. He ripped it down, then lobbed broken bits of stone from the ground to intercept fire from Demandred.

A *diversion*, Logain thought, realizing that Demandred had woven something else, more complex, behind the fire. A gateway opened and shot across the ground, opening to a maw of redness. Logain threw himself to the side as the Deathgate passed, but it left a trail of burning lava.

Demandred's next attack was a jet of air that hurled Logain backward, toward that lava. Logain desperately wove Water to cool the lava. He hit shoulder-first, passing a burst of steam that scalded his skin, but he had cooled the lava enough that it formed a crust atop the still-molten flow beneath. Holding his breath against the steam, he hurled himself to the side as another series of lightning bolts pulverized the ground where he had been.

Those bolts shattered the crust he'd made, reaching into the molten rock. Drops of lava splashed across Logain, searing his skin, burning pocks in his arm and face. He screamed and wove through his rage to send lightning down on his foe.

A slice of Spirit, Earth and Fire cut his weaves from the air. Demandred was just so *strong*. That *sa'angreal* was incredible.

The next flash of lightning blinded Logain, throwing him backward. He hit a patch of broken shale, the points of the rock biting into his skin.

"You are powerful," Demandred said. Logain could barely hear the words. His ears ... the thunder ... "But you are not Lews Therin."

Logain growled, weaving through his tears, hurling lightning at Demandred. He wove twice, and though Demandred cut one bolt from the air, the other struck true.

But ... what was that weave? It was another that Logain did not recognize. The lightning hit Demandred, but vanished, somehow sent down into the ground and dissipated. Such a simple weave of Air and Earth, but it rendered the lightning useless.

A shield rammed between Logain and the Source. Through his wounded eyes, he watched the weave for balefire begin in Demandred's hands. Snarling, Logain grabbed a piece of shale from the ground beside him, the size of his fist, and hurled it at Demandred.

Surprisingly, the stone hit, ripping skin, causing Demandred to stumble back. The Forsaken was powerful, but he could still make the mistakes of common men. Never focus all of your attention on the One Power, despite what Taim had always said. In that moment of distraction, the shield between Logain and the Source vanished.

Logain rolled to the side, beginning two weaves. One, a shield of his own that he did not intend to use. The other, a desperate, final gateway. The coward's choice.

Demandred growled, raising a hand to his face and lashing out with the Power. He chose to destroy the shield, immediately recognizing it as the greater risk. The gateway opened, and Logain rolled through, letting it snap closed. He collapsed on the other side, his flesh scalded, his arms flayed, his ears ringing, his sight almost gone.

He forced himself to sit up, back in the Asha'man camp below the bogs where Gabrelle and the others awaited his return. He howled in anger. Gabrelle's concern radiated through the bond. Real concern. He *hadn't* imagined it. Light.

"Quiet," she said, kneeling beside him. "You fool. What have you done to yourself?"

"I have failed," he said. Distantly, he felt the strikes of Demandred's power begin again as he continued bellowing for Lews Therin. "Heal me."

"You're not going to try that again, are you?" she said. "I don't want to Heal you only to let you—"

"I won't try again," Logain said, voice ragged. The pain was horrible, but it paled compared to the humiliation of defeat. "I won't, Gabrelle. Stop doubting my word. He's too strong."

"Some of these burns are bad, Logain. These holes in your skin, I don't know if I can Heal them completely. You will be scarred."

"That is fine," he growled. That would be where the lava had splashed on his arm and the side of his face.

Light, he thought. *How are we going to deal with that monster?*

Gabrelle put her hands on him and Healing weaves poured into his body.

The thunder of Egwene's battle with M'Hael rivaled that of the crashing clouds above. M'Hael. A new Forsaken, his name proclaimed by his Dreadlords across the battlefield.

Egwene wove without thought, hurling weave after weave toward the renegade Asha'man. She had not called upon the wind, but still it rushed and roared about her, whipping her hair and her dress, catching her stole and flipping it about. Narishma and Merise huddled with Leilwin on the ground beside her, Narishma's voice—barely audible above the battle—calling out weaves as M'Hael crafted them.

Following her advance, Egwene stood upon the top of the Heights, on even ground with M'Hael. She knew, somewhere deep, that her body would need rest soon.

For now, that was an unaffordable luxury. For now, only the fight mattered.

Fire flared toward her, and she slapped it aside with Air. The sparks caught in the wind, swirling about her in a spray of light as she wove Earth. She sent a ripple through the already-broken ground, trying to knock M'Hael down, but he split the wave with a weave of his own.

He's slowing, she thought.

Egwene stepped forward, swollen with power. She began two weaves, one above each hand, and spouted fire at him.

He responded with a bar of pure whiteness, wire-thin, which missed her by less than a handspan. The balefire left an after-image in Egwene's eyes, and the ground *groaned* beneath them as the air warped. Those spiderwebs sprang out across the ground, fractures into nothingness.

"Fool!" she yelled at him. "You will destroy the Pattern itself!" Already, their clash threatened that. This wind was not natural, this sizzling air. Those cracks in the ground spread from M'Hael, widening.

"He's weaving it again!" Narishma cried, voice caught in the tempest.

M'Hael released this second weave of balefire, fracturing the ground, but Egwene was ready. She sidestepped, her anger building. Balefire. She needed to counter it!

They don't care what they ruin. They are here to destroy. That is their master's call. Break. Burn down. Kill.

Gawyn . . .

She screamed in fury, weaving column after column of fire, one after another. Narishma shouted what M'Hael was doing, but Egwene couldn't hear for the rush of sound in her ears. She saw soon, anyway, that he had constructed a barrier of Air and Fire to deflect her attacks.

Egwene strode forward, sending repeated strikes at him. That gave him no time to recover, no time to attack. She stopped the rhythm only to form a shield that she held at the ready. A spray of fire off his barrier made him stumble back, his weave cracking, and he raised his hand, perhaps to attempt balefire again.

Egwene slammed the shield between him and the Source. It didn't quite cut him off, for he held it back by force of will. They were near enough now that she could see his incredulity, his anger. He fought back, but was weaker than she. Egwene pushed, bringing that shield closer and closer to the invisible thread that

connected him to the One Power. She forced it with all her
strength . . .

M'Hael, straining, released a small stream of balefire upward,
through the gap where the shield had not yet fallen into place.
The balefire destroyed the weave—as it did the air, and indeed,
the Pattern itself.

Egwene stumbled back as M'Hael directed the weave toward
her, but the white-hot bar was too small, too weak, to reach her.
It faded away before hitting. M'Hael snarled, then vanished,
warping the air in a form of Traveling Egwene did not know.

Egwene breathed deeply, holding her hand to her chest. Light!
She had almost been obliterated from the Pattern.

He disappeared without forming a gateway! The True Power, she
thought. The only explanation. She knew next to nothing about
it—it was the Dark One's very essence, the lure that had coaxed
channelers in the Age of Legends to drill the Bore in the first
place.

Balefire. Light. I was almost dead. Worse than dead.

She had no way to counter balefire.

It's only a weave . . . Only a weave. Perrin's words.

The moment was past now, and M'Hael had fled. She would
have to keep Narishma close to warn her if someone started channeling nearby.

*Unless M'Hael uses the True Power again. Would another man be able
to sense that being channeled?*

"Mother!"

Egwene turned as Merise gestured toward where most of the
Aes Sedai and Asha'man were still engaged in a resounding battle
with the Sharan forces. Many sisters in colorful dresses lay dead
across the hillside.

Gawyn's death haunted her thoughts like an assassin in black.
Egwene set her jaw and stoked her anger, drawing in the One
Power as she launched herself at the Sharans.

Hurin, his nostrils stuffed with cloth, fought on Polov Heights
with the other Borderlanders.

Even through the cloth, he smelled the war. So *much* violence,
the scents of blood, of rotting flesh all around him. They coated

the ground, his sword, his own *clothing*. He had already been ill, violently, several times during the battle.

Still he fought. He threw himself aside as a bear-snouted Trolloc crawled over the bodies and swung down at him. The beast's sword made the ground shake, and Hurin cried out.

The beast laughed an inhuman laugh, taking Hurin's cry to indicate fear. It lunged, so Hurin scuttled forward and under its reach, then opened up its stomach as he ran past. The creature stumbled to a stop, watching its own reeking innards pour out.

Have to buy time for Lord Rand, Hurin thought, backing away and waiting for the next Trolloc to come over the bodies. They were coming up the eastern side of the Heights, the river side. This steep slope was hard for them to climb, but Light, there were so *many* of them.

Keep fighting, keep fighting.

Lord Rand had come to *him*, making apologies. To him! Well, Hurin would do him proud. The Dragon Reborn did not need the forgiveness of a little thief-taker, but Hurin still felt as if the world had righted itself. Lord Rand was Lord Rand again. Lord Rand would preserve them, if they could give him enough time.

There was a lull in the action. He frowned. The beasts had seemed endless. Surely they hadn't all fallen. He stepped cautiously forward, looking over the corpses and down the slope.

No, no they weren't defeated. The sea of beasts seemed near-endless still. He could see them by the light of fires below. The Trollocs had paused their climb because they needed to move corpses out of their way on the slope, many of whom had been cut down by Tam's archers. Below them, at the riverbed, the greater army of Trollocs fought Elayne's army.

"We should have a few minutes," Lan Mandragoran said to the soldiers from where he sat on horseback. Queen Alliandre rode nearby as well, talking calmly with her men. Two monarchs within sight. Surely they knew how to exercise command. That made Hurin feel better.

"They're preparing for a final charge," Lan said, "a push to force us away from the slope so they can fight us up here on even ground. Rest while they clear bodies. Peace favor your swords, friends. The next assault will be the worst one." The next assault would be the *worst* one? Light!

Behind them on the middle of the plateau, the rest of Mat's army continued pressing the Sharan army, trying to push them back to the southwest. If he could do that, and force them down the slope into the Trollocs fighting Elayne's forces, it could create a right mess that Mat could take advantage of. But for the moment, the Sharans were not giving an inch of ground; in fact, they were pushing back Mat's army, which was beginning to founder.

Hurin lay back, listening to the moans all around, the distant shouts and ringing of weapons hitting metal, sniffing the stink of violence hanging around him in an ocean of stenches.

The worst still to come.

Light help them . . .

Berelain used a rag to wipe the blood from her hands as she strode into the feast hall of her palace. The tables had been chopped apart for firewood to stoke the enormous hearths at either end of the long room; in place of the furniture lay rows upon rows of wounded.

The doors from the kitchens burst open and a group of Tinkers entered, some carrying litters and others helping wounded men limp into the room. *Light!* Berelain thought. *More?* The palace was stuffed to bursting with the wounded.

"No, no!" she said, stalking forward. "Not in here. The back hallway. We're going to have to start putting them there. Rosil! We have new wounded."

The Tinkers turned toward the hallway, speaking in comforting tones to the wounded men. Only those who could be saved were brought back. She had been forced to instruct the leaders among the Tuatha'an women as to which types of wounds took too much effort to Heal. Better to save ten men with bad wounds than to expend the same energy trying to rescue one man who clung to life by a single blade of hope.

That moment of explanation had been one of the grimmest things she'd ever done.

The Tinkers continued moving in a line, and Berelain watched the wounded for glimpses of white clothing. There were Whitecloaks among them, but not the one she sought.

So many ... she thought again. The Tinkers had no help moving the wounded. Every able-bodied man in the palace, and most women, had gone to the battlefield to fight or help the Caemlyn refugees gather arrows.

Rosil bustled up, her clothing stained with blood that she ignored. She immediately took charge of the wounded, eyeing them for any who needed immediate attention. Unfortunately, the doors to the kitchen burst open at that moment, and a group of bloodied Andorans and Aiel stumbled through, sent by the Kinswomen from another area of the battlefield.

What followed was near madness as Berelain chivvied out everyone she had—grooms, the elderly, some children as young as five—to help settle the newcomers. Only the worst of the Aiel came through; they had a tendency to remain on the battlefield as long as they could hold a weapon. That meant many who came to her were beyond help. She had to settle them in space she couldn't afford and watch them heave bloody gasps as they died.

"This is foolish!" she said, standing up. Her hands were wet with blood again, and she hadn't a clean rag left. Light! "We need to send more help. You." She pointed to an Aiel who had been blinded. He sat with his back to the wall, a bandage around his eyes. "You, the blind Aiel."

"I am called Ronja."

"Well, Ronja. I have some *gai'shain* here helping me. By my count, there should be a lot more of them. Where are they?"

"They wait until the battle is through so that they may minister to the victors."

"We're going to fetch them," she said. "We need every person we can get to help fight."

"They may come to you here, Berelain Paendrag, and help with tending the sick," the man said. "But they will not fight. It is not their place."

"They will see reason," she said firmly. "It's the Last Battle!"

"You may be clan chief here," the Aiel said, smiling, "but you are not *Car'a'carn*. Even he could not command the *gai'shain* to disobey *ji'e'toh*."

"Then who could?"

That seemed to surprise the man. "No one. It is not possible."

"And the Wise Ones?"

"They would not," he said. "Never."

"We shall see," Berelain said.

The man smiled deeper. "I should think that no man or woman would wish to suffer your wrath, Berelain Paendrag. But if I had my eyes restored, I would put them out again before I watched *gai'shain* fight."

"They don't need to fight, then," Berelain said. "Perhaps they can help carry the wounded. Rosil, you have this group?"

The tired woman nodded. There wasn't an Aes Sedai in the palace who didn't look like she'd sooner fall over than take another step. Berelain kept her feet by using some herbs she did not think Rosil would approve.

Well, she could do no more here. She might as well check on the wounded in the storage rooms. They had—

"My Lady First?" a voice asked. It was Kitan, one of the palace maids who had remained behind to help with the wounded. The slight woman took her arm. "There is something you need to see."

Berelain sighed, but nodded. What disaster awaited her now? Another bubble of evil, locking away groups of wounded behind walls that hadn't been there before? Had they run out of bandages again? She doubted there was a sheet, drapery or piece of smallclothes in the city that hadn't already been made into a bandage.

The girl led her up the steps to Berelain's own quarters where a few of the casualties were being nursed. She stepped into one of the rooms, and was surprised to find a familiar face waiting for her. Annoura sat at a bedside, wearing red slashed with gray, her customary braids pulled back and tied in an unflattering way. Berelain almost didn't recognize her.

Annoura rose at Berelain's entrance, bowing, though she looked about ready to fall over with fatigue.

In the bed lay Galad Damodred.

Berelain gasped, rushing to his side. It *was* him, though he bore a vicious wound to his face. He still breathed, but he was unconscious. Berelain lifted his arm to take his hand in hers, but found that the arm ended in a stump. One of the surgeons had already cauterized it to keep him from bleeding to death.

"How?" Berelain asked, clutching his other hand, closing her eyes. His hand felt warm. When she had heard what Demandred bellowed, defeating the man in white . . .

"I felt that I owed it to you," Annoura said. "I located him on the battlefield after Demandred announced what he had done. I pulled him away while Demandred fought against one of the Black Tower's men." She sat back down on the stool beside the bed, then leaned forward, drooping. "I could not Heal him, Berelain. It was all I could do to make the gateway to bring him here. I'm sorry."

"It is all right," Berelain said. "Kitan, fetch one of the other sisters. Annoura, you will feel better once you have rested. Thank you."

Annoura nodded. She closed her eyes, and Berelain was shocked to see tears at the edges of her eyes.

"What is it?" Berelain asked. "Annoura, what is wrong?"

"It should not concern you, Berelain," she said, rising. "All are taught it, you see. Do not channel if you are too tired. There can be complications. I needed a gateway back to the palace, though. To bring him to safety, to restore . . ."

Annoura collapsed from her stool. Berelain dropped to her side, propping up her head. Only then did she realize that it wasn't the braids that had made Annoura look so different. The face was wrong, too. Changed. No longer ageless, but instead youthful.

"Oh, Light, Annoura," Berelain said. "You've burned yourself out, haven't you?"

The woman had lapsed into unconsciousness. Berelain's heart lurched. The woman and she had had differences recently, but Annoura had been her confidante—and friend—for years before that. The poor woman. The way Aes Sedai spoke, this was considered to be worse than death.

Berelain lifted the woman onto the room's couch and then covered her with a blanket. Berelain felt so powerless. *Maybe . . . maybe she can be Healed somehow . . .*

She went back to Galad's side to hold his hand for a time longer, righting the stool and sitting upon it. Just a little rest. She closed her eyes. He lived. It came at a terrible cost, but he lived.

She was shocked when he spoke. "How?"

She opened her eyes to find him looking at her.

"How am I here?" he asked softly.

"Annoura," she said. "She found you on the battlefield."

"My wounds?"

"Other Healers will come when they can be spared," she said. "Your hand . . ." She steeled herself. "Your hand is lost, but we can wash away that cut to your face."

"No," he whispered. "It is only . . . a little cut. Save the Healing for those who would die without it." He seemed so tired. Barely awake.

She bit her lip, but nodded. "Of course." She hesitated. "The battle fares poorly, doesn't it?"

"Yes."

"So now . . . we simply hope?"

He slipped his hand from hers and reached under his shirt. When an Aes Sedai arrived, they would have to undress him and care for his wounds. Only the stump had been tended to so far, as it was the worst.

Galad sighed, then trembled, his hand slipping away from his shirt. Had he been intending to remove it?

"Hope . . ." he whispered, then fell unconscious.

Rand wept.

He huddled in the darkness, the Pattern spinning before him, woven from the threads of the lives of men. So many of those threads ended.

So many.

He should have been able to protect them. Why couldn't he? Against his will, the names began to replay in his mind. The names of those who had died for him, starting with only women, but now expanded to each and every person he should have been able to save—but hadn't.

As humankind fought at Merrilor and Shayol Ghul, Rand was forced to watch the deaths. He could not turn away.

The Dark One chose then to attack him in force. The pressure came again, striving to crush Rand into nothing. He couldn't move. Every bit of his essence, his determination and his strength focused on keeping the Dark One from ripping him apart.

He could only watch as they died.

Rand watched Davram Bashere die in a charge, followed

quickly by his wife. Rand cried out at the fall of his friend. He wept for Davram Bashere.

Dear, faithful Hurin fell to a Trolloc attack as it struck for the top of the Heights where Mat made his stand. Rand wept for Hurin. The man with so much faith in him, the man who would have followed him anywhere.

Jori Congar lay buried beneath a Trolloc body, whimpering for help until he bled to death. Rand wept for Jori as his thread finally vanished.

Enaila, who had decided to forsake *Far Dareis Mai* and had laid a bridal wreath at the foot of the *siswai'aman* Leiran, speared through the gut by four Trollocs. Rand wept for her.

Karldin Manfor, who had followed him for so long and had been at Dumai's Wells, died when his strength for channeling gave out and he dropped to the ground in exhaustion. Sharans fell upon him and stabbed him with their black daggers. His Aes Sedai, Beldeine, stumbled and fell moments later. Rand wept for them both.

He wept for Gareth Bryne and Siuan. He wept for Gawyn.

So many. So *very many*.

YOU ARE LOSING.

Rand huddled down further. What could he do? His dream of stopping the Dark One . . . he would create a nightmare if he did that. His own intentions betrayed him.

GIVE IN, ADVERSARY. WHY KEEP FIGHTING? STOP FIGHTING AND REST.

He was tempted. Oh, how he was *tempted*. Light. What would Nynaeve think? He could see her, fighting to save Alanna. How ashamed would she and Moiraine be if they knew that in that moment, Rand wanted to just let go?

Pain washed across him, and he screamed again.

"Please, let it end!"

IT CAN.

Rand huddled down, writhing, trembling. But still, their screams assaulted him. Death upon death. He held on, barely.

"No," he whispered.

VERY WELL, the Dark One said. I HAVE ONE MORE THING TO SHOW YOU. ONE MORE PROMISE OF WHAT CAN BE . . .

The Dark One spun threads of possibility one last time.
All became darkness.

Taim lashed out with the One Power, thrashing Mishraile with weaves of Air. "Go back, then, you fool! Fight! We will *not* lose that position!"

The Dreadlord ducked back, gathering his two companions and slinking away to do as ordered. Taim smoldered, then shattered a nearby stone with a surge of power. That Aes Sedai ridgecat! How *dare* she best him?

"M'Hael," a calm voice said.

Taim ... M'Hael. He had to think of himself as M'Hael. He crossed the hillside toward the voice that had called to him. He had taken a gateway to safety, panicked, across the Heights, and he was now at the edge of the southeastern slope of the Heights. Demandred used this location to monitor the battle below and to send destruction down into the formations of Andorans, Cairhienin and Aiel.

Demandred's Trollocs controlled the entire corridor between the Heights and bogs, and were wearing down the defenders at the dry river. It was only a matter of time. Meanwhile, the Sharan army fought northeast of here on the Heights. It concerned him that Cauthon had arrived so quickly to stop the advance of the Sharans. No matter. That was a move of desperation for the man. He wouldn't be able to stand up against the Sharan army. But the most important thing right now was destroying those Aes Sedai on the other side of the Heights. That was key to winning this battle.

M'Hael passed between suspicious Sharans with their strange dress and tattoos. Demandred sat, cross-legged, at their center. His eyes closed, he breathed in and out slowly. That *sa'angreal* he used ... it took something out of him, something more than just the normal strength required for channeling.

Would that provide M'Hael with an opening? How it galled to continue to put himself beneath another. Yes, he had learned much from this man, but now Demandred was obviously unfit to lead. He coddled these Sharans, and he wasted energy on his vendetta with al'Thor. The weakness of another was M'Hael's potential opening.

"I hear that you are failing, M'Hael," Demandred said.

Before them, across the dry riverbed, the Andoran defenses were finally starting to buckle. Trollocs were always testing to find weak points in their lines, and they were breaking through pike formations in various areas all up and down the river. The Legion's heavy cavalry and the Cairhienin light were in constant motion now, making sweeps of desperation against Trollocs as they broke through the Andoran defenses. The Aiel were still holding them back down near the bogs, and the Legion's crossbowmen combined with Andoran pike were still keeping the Trollocs from sweeping around their right flank. But the pressure of the Trolloc onslaught was relentless, and Elayne's lines were gradually bowing out, moving deeper into Shienaran territory.

"M'Hael?" Demandred said, opening his eyes. Ancient eyes. M'Hael refused to feel intimidated, looking into them. He would *not* be intimidated! "Tell me how you failed."

"The Aes Sedai witch," M'Hael spat. "She has a *sa'angreal* of great power. I almost had her, but the True Power failed me."

"You are given only a trickle for a reason," Demandred said, closing his eyes again. "It is unpredictable for one unaccustomed to its ways."

M'Hael said nothing. He would practice with the True Power; he would learn its secrets. The other Forsaken were old and slow. New blood would soon rule.

With a relaxed sense of inevitability, Demandred stood. He gave off the impression of a massive boulder shifting its position. "You will return and kill her, M'Hael. I have slain her Warder. She should be easy meat."

"The *sa'angreal* . . ."

Demandred held out his scepter, with the golden goblet affixed atop it.

Was this a test? Such *power*. M'Hael had felt the strength radiating from Demandred as he used it.

"You say she has a *sa'angreal*," Demandred said. "With this, you will have one as well. I grant you Sakarnen to take from you any excuse for failure. Succeed or die in this, M'Hael. Prove yourself worthy to stand among the Chosen."

M'Hael licked his lips. "And if the Dragon Reborn finally comes to you?"

Demandred laughed. "You think I would use this to fight him? What would that prove? Our strengths must be matched if I am to show myself the better. By all accounts, he cannot use *Callandor* safely, and he foolishly destroyed the Choedan Kal. He *will* come, and when he does, I will face him unaided and prove myself the true master of this realm."

Darkness within . . . Taim thought. *He's gone completely mad, hasn't he?* Strange to look into those eyes, which seemed so lucid, and hear complete insanity from his lips. When Demandred had first come to M'Hael, offering him the chance to serve the Great Lord, the man had not been like this. Arrogant, yes. All of the Chosen were arrogant. Demandred's determination to kill al'Thor personally had burned like a fire within him.

But this . . . this was something different. Living in Shara had changed him. Weakened him, certainly. Now this. What man would willingly give such a powerful artifact to a rival?

Only a fool, M'Hael thought, reaching for the *sa'angreal*. *Killing you will be like putting down a horse with three broken legs, Demandred. Pity. I had hoped to vanquish you as a rival.*

Demandred turned away, and M'Hael pulled the One Power through Sakarnen, drinking gluttonously of its bounty. The sweetness of *saidin* saturated him, a raging torrent of succulent Power. He was *immense* while holding this! He could do anything. Level mountains, destroy armies, all on his own!

M'Hael itched to pull out flows, to weave them together and destroy this man.

"Take care," Demandred said. His voice sounded pathetic, weak. The squeaking of a mouse. "Do not channel through that toward me. I have bonded Sakarnen to me. If you try to use it against me, it will burn you from the Pattern."

Did Demandred lie? Could a *sa'angreal* be *attuned* to a specific person? He did not know. He considered, then lowered Sakarnen, bitter despite the power surging through him.

"I am not a fool, M'Hael," Demandred said dryly. "I will not hand you the noose in which to hang me. Go and do as you are told. You are my servant in this thing, the hand that holds my axe to chop down the tree. Destroy the Amyrlin; use balefire. We have been commanded, and in this, we will obey. The world must be unraveled before we reweave it to our vision."

M'Hael snarled at the man, but did as he was told, weaving a gateway. He *would* destroy that Aes Sedai witch. Then . . . then he would decide how to deal with Demandred.

Elayne watched in frustration as her pike formations were pushed back. That Birgitte had managed to convince her to remove herself from the immediate area of combat—a Trolloc breakthrough could come at any moment—did not sit well with her.

Elayne had retreated almost to the ruins, out of direct danger for the moment. A double ring of Guards surrounded her, most of them sitting and eating—gaining what little strength they could during the moments between fights.

Elayne did not fly her banner, but she sent messengers to let her commanders know that she still lived. Though she had tried to guide her troops against the Trollocs, her efforts had not been enough. Her forces were clearly weakening.

"We have to go back," she said to Birgitte. "They need to see me, Birgitte."

"I don't know if it will change anything," Birgitte said. "Those formations just can't hold in the face of both Trollocs and that bloody channeling. I . . . "

"What is it?" Elayne asked.

Birgitte turned away. "I swear I once remembered a situation like this."

Elayne set her jaw. She found Birgitte's loss of memory heart-wrenching, but it was only one woman's problem. Thousands of her people were dying.

Nearby, the refugees from Caemlyn still searched the area for arrows and wounded. Several groups approached Elayne's guards, speaking with them softly, asking after the battle or the Queen. Elayne felt a spike of pride at the refugees and their tenacity. The city had broken, but a city could be rebuilt. The people, the true heart of Caemlyn, would not fall so easily.

Another lance of light plunged into the battlefield, killing men, disrupting the pikemen. Beyond that, on the far side of the Heights, women channeled in a furious battle. She could see the lights flashing in the night, though that was all. Should Elayne join them? Her command here had not been good enough to save the soldiers, but it *had* provided guidance and leadership.

"I fear for our army, Elayne." Birgitte said. "I fear that the day is lost."

"The day cannot be lost," Elayne said, "because if it is, we all are lost. I refuse to accept defeat. You and I will return. Let Demandred try to strike us down. Perhaps seeing me will revitalize the soldiers, make them—"

A group of Caemlyn refugees nearby attacked her Guardsmen and Guardswomen.

Elayne cursed, turning Moonshadow and embracing the One Power. The group she had, at first, taken for refugees in dirty, soot-stained clothing wore mail beneath. They fought her Guards, killing with sword and axe. Not refugees at all, *mercenaries*.

"Betrayal!" Birgitte called, lifting her bow and shooting a mercenary through the throat. "To arms!"

"It's not a betrayal," Elayne said. She wove Fire and struck down a group of three. "Those aren't ours! Watch for thieves in the clothing of beggars!"

She turned as another group of "refugees" lunged at the weakened lines of Guards. They were all around! They had crept up while attention had been focused on the distant battlefield.

As a group of mercenaries broke through, she wove *saidar* to show them the folly of attacking an Aes Sedai. She released a powerful weave of Air.

As it hit one of the men charging her, the weave fell apart, unraveling. Elayne cursed, turning her horse to flee, but one of the attackers lunged forward and drove his sword into Moonshadow's neck. The horse reared, squealing in agony, and Elayne caught a brief glimpse of Guards fighting all around as she fell to the ground, panicked for the safety of her babes. Rough hands grabbed her by the shoulders and held her against the ground.

She saw something silver glisten in the night. A foxhead medallion. Another pair of hands pressed it to her skin just above her breasts. The metal was sharply cold.

"Hello, my Queen," Mellar said, squatting beside her. The former Guardsman—the one many people still assumed had fathered her children—leered down at her. "You've been very hard to track down."

Elayne spat at him, but he anticipated her, raising his hand to catch the spittle. He smiled, then stood up, leaving her held by two mercenaries. Though some of her Guards still fought, most had been pushed back or killed.

Mellar turned as two men dragged Birgitte over. She thrashed in their grip, and a third man came over to help hold her. Mellar took out his sword, regarded its blade for a moment, as if inspecting himself in its reflective gleam. Then he rammed it into Birgitte's stomach.

Birgitte gasped, falling to her knees. Mellar beheaded her with a vicious backhand blow.

Elayne found herself sitting very still, unable to think or react as Birgitte's corpse flopped forward, spilling lifeblood from the neck. The bond winked away, and with it came . . . pain. Terrible pain.

"I've been waiting to do that for a long time," Mellar said. "Blood and bloody ashes, but it felt good."

Birgitte . . . Her Warder was dead. Her Warder had been killed. That tough yet generous heart, that tremendous loyalty— destroyed. The loss made it . . . made it hard to think.

Mellar kicked at Birgitte's corpse as a man rode up with a body draped across the back of his saddle. The man wore an Andoran uniform, and the facedown corpse dangled golden hair. Whoever the poor woman was, she wore a dress exactly like Elayne's.

Oh no . . .

"Go," Mellar said. The man rode off, a few others forming around him, fake Guardsmen. They carried Elayne's banner, and one started shouting, "The Queen is dead! The Queen has fallen!"

Mellar turned to Elayne. "Your people still fight. Well, that ought to disrupt their ranks. As for you . . . well, apparently, the Great Lord has a use for those children of yours. I've been ordered to bring them to Shayol Ghul. It occurs to me that you needn't be with them at the time." He looked at one of his companions. "Can you make it work?"

The other man knelt beside Elayne, then pressed his hands against her belly. A jolt of sudden fright pushed through her numbness and her shock. Her babes!

"She's far enough along," the man said. "I can probably keep the children alive with a weave, if you cut them out. It will be difficult to do right. They are young yet. Six months along. But with the weaves I was shown by the Chosen . . . yes, I think I can keep them living for an hour. But you will have to take them to M'Hael to get them to Shayol Ghul. Traveling with a regular gateway won't work there any longer."

Mellar sheathed his sword and pulled a hunting knife from his belt. "Good enough for me. We'll send the children on, as the Great Lord asks. But you, my Queen . . . you are mine."

Elayne flailed, but the men's grip was tight. She clawed at *saidar* again and again, but the medallion worked like forkroot. She might as well have been trying to embrace *saidin* as reach *saidar*.

"No!" she screamed as Mellar knelt beside her. "NO!"

"Good," he said. "I was hoping you'd get around to screaming."

Nothing.

Rand turned. He *tried* to turn. He had no form or shape.

Nothing.

He tried to speak, but he had no mouth. Finally, he managed to *think* the words and make them manifest.

SHAI'TAN, Rand projected, WHAT IS THIS?

OUR COVENANT, the Dark One replied. OUR ACCOM-MODATION.

OUR ACCOMMODATION IS NOTHING? Rand demanded.

YES.

He understood. The Dark One was offering a deal. Rand could accept this . . . He could accept nothingness. The two of them dueled for the fate of the world. Rand pushed for peace, glory, love. The Dark One sought the opposite. Pain. Suffering.

This was, in a way, a balance between the two. The Dark One would agree not to reforge the Wheel to suit his grim desires. There would be no enslaving of mankind, no world without love. There would be no world at all.

IT IS WHAT YOU PROMISED ELAN, Rand said. YOU PROMISED HIM AN END TO EXISTENCE.

I OFFER IT TO YOU, TOO, the Dark One replied. AND TO ALL MEN. YOU WANTED PEACE. I GIVE IT TO YOU. THE PEACE OF THE VOID THAT YOU SO OFTEN SEEK. I GIVE YOU NOTHING AND EVERYTHING.

Rand did not reject the offer immediately. He grasped the offer and cradled it in his mind. No more pain. No more suffering. No more burdens.

An ending. Was that not what he had desired? A way to end the cycles finally?

NO, Rand said. AN END TO EXISTENCE IS NOT PEACE. I MADE THIS CHOICE BEFORE. WE WILL CONTINUE.

The Dark One's pressure began to surround him again, threatening to rip him apart.

I WILL NOT OFFER AGAIN, the Dark One said.

"I would not expect you to," Rand said as his body returned and the threads of possibility faded.

Then the true pain began.

Min waited with the gathered Seanchan forces, officers walking down the lines with lanterns to prepare the men. They had not returned to Ebou Dar, but instead had fled through gateways to a large open plain that she did not recognize. Trees with a strange bark and large, open fronds grew here. She could not tell if they were truly trees, or just very large ferns. It was particularly hard to tell because of the wilting; the trees had grown leaves, but now they drooped down at the sides as if they had not seen water in far too many weeks. Min tried to imagine what they would have looked like when healthy.

The air smelled different to her—of plants she did not recognize, and of seawater. The Seanchan forces waited in strict formations of troops, ready to march, each fourth man with a lantern, though only one in ten of those were currently lit. Moving an army could not be done fast, despite gateways, but Fortuona had access to hundreds of *damane*. The retreat had been carried out efficiently, and Min suspected that a return to the battlefield could be accomplished swiftly.

If Fortuona decided to return, that was. The Empress sat atop a pillar in the night, lifted up to it on her palanquin, lit by blue lanterns. It was not a throne, but a pure white pillar, about six feet high, erected on the top of a small hill. Min had a seat next to the pillar, and could hear reports as they arrived.

"This battle is not going well for the Prince of the Ravens,"

General Galgan said. He addressed his generals before Fortuona, speaking to them directly, so that they could respond to him without formally addressing the Empress. "His request for us to return came only just now. He has waited far too long to seek our aid."

"I hesitate to say this," Yulan said. "But, though the Empress's wisdom knows no bounds, I do not have confidence in the Prince. He might be the chosen consort of the Empress, and he was obviously a wise choice for that role. He has proven himself reckless in battle, however. Perhaps he is overly strained by what is happening."

"I'm sure he has a plan," Beslan said, earnest. "You have to trust Mat. He knows what he's doing."

"He impressed me earlier," Galgan said. "The omens seem to favor him."

"He is losing, Captain-General," Yulan said. "Losing badly. The omens for a man can change quickly, as can the fortune of a nation."

Min narrowed her eyes at the short Captain of the Air. He now wore the last two fingernails of each hand lacquered. He had been the one to lead the strike on Tar Valon, and the success of that attack had gained him great favor in Fortuona's eyes. Symbols and omens spun around his head, like those above Galgan's—and, indeed, Beslan's.

Light, Min thought. *Am I really starting to think of "omens" like Fortuona? I need to leave these people. They're mad.*

"I feel that the Prince views this battle too much as a game," Yulan said again. "Though his initial gambles were keen ones, he has over extended himself. How many a man has stood around the table of *dactolk* and looked like a genius because of his bets, when really just random chance made him seem capable? The Prince won at first, but now we see how dangerous it is to gamble as he has."

Yulan inclined his head toward the Empress. His assertions grew increasingly bold, as she gave him no reason to quiet himself. From the Empress, in this situation, that was an indication he should continue.

"I have heard . . . rumors about him," Galgan said.

"Mat's a gambler, yes," Beslan said. "But he's uncannily good at it. He wins, General. Please, you need to go back and help."

Yulan shook his head emphatically. "The Empress—may she live forever—pulled us away from the battlefield for good reason.

If the Prince could not protect his own command post, he is not in control of the battle."

Bolder and bolder. Galgan rubbed his chin, then looked at another person there. Min didn't know much of Tylee. She remained quiet at these meetings. With graying hair and broad shoulders, the dark-skinned woman had an indefinable strength to her. This was a general who had led her people directly, in battle, many times. Those scars proved it.

"These mainlanders fight better than I ever assumed they would," Tylee said. "I fought alongside some of Cauthon's soldiers. I think they will surprise you, General. I, too, humbly suggest that we return to help."

"But is it in the best interests of the Empire to do so?" Yulan asked. "Cauthon's forces will weaken the Shadow, as will the Shadow's march to Ebou Dar from Merrilor. We can crush the Trollocs with air attacks along the way. The long victory should be our goal. Perhaps we can send *damane* to fetch the Prince and bring him to safety. He has fought well, but he is obviously overmatched in this battle. We cannot save his armies, of course. They are doomed."

Min frowned, leaning forward. One of the images above Yulan's head ... it was so odd. A chain. Why would he have a chain above his head?

He's a captive, she thought suddenly. *Light. Someone is playing him like an instrument.*

Mat feared a spy. Min felt cold.

"The Empress, may she live forever, has made her decision," Galgan said. "We return. Unless her mind, in its wisdom, has been changed ... ?" He turned toward her, a questioning look on his face.

Our spy can channel, Min realized, inspecting Yulan. *That man is under Compulsion.*

A channeler. Black Ajah? Darkfriend *damane*? A male Dreadlord? It could be anyone. And the spy would be wearing a weave for disguise, too, in all likelihood.

So, then, how would Min ever spot this spy?

Viewings. Aes Sedai and other channelers always had viewings attached to them. Always. Could she find a clue in one of those? She knew, by instinct, that Yulan's chain meant he was a captive of another. He wasn't the true spy, then, but a puppet.

She started with the other nobility and generals. Of course, many of them had omens above their heads, and those types commonly did. How would she spot something out of the ordinary? Min scanned the watching crowd, and her breath caught as she noticed for the first time that one of the *so'jhin*, a youthful woman with freckles, carried an array of images above her head.

Min didn't recognize the woman. Had she been serving here the whole time? Min was certain she'd have noticed earlier if the woman had come close to her; people who were not channelers, Warders or *ta'veren* rarely had so many images attached to them. Oversight or happenstance, though, she hadn't thought to look specifically at the servants.

Now, the cover-up was obvious to her. Min looked away so as to not raise the servant's suspicions, and considered her next move. Her instincts whispered that she should just attack, take out a knife and throw it. If that servant were a Dreadlord—or, Light, one of the Forsaken—striking first might be the only way to defeat her.

There was also a chance, however, that the woman was innocent. Min debated, then stood up on her chair. Several of the Blood muttered at the breach of decorum, but Min ignored them. She stepped up onto the arm rest of her chair, balancing there to put herself even with Tuon. Min leaned in.

"Mat has asked for us to return," Min said softly. "How long will you debate doing what he asked?"

Tuon eyed her. "Until I am convinced this is best for my Empire."

"He is your husband."

"One man's life is not worth that of thousands," Tuon said, but she sounded genuinely troubled. "If the battle really does go as badly as Yulan's scouts say ... "

"You named me Truthspeaker," Min said. "What exactly does that mean?"

"It is your duty to censure me in public, if I do something wrong. However, you are untrained in the station. It would be best for you to hold yourself back until I can provide proper—"

Min turned to face the generals and the watching crowd, her heart beating frantically. "As Truthspeaker to the Empress Fortuona, I speak now the truth. She has abandoned the armies of humankind, and she withholds her strength in a time of need. Her pride will cause the destruction of all people, everywhere."

The Blood looked stunned.

"It is not so simple, young woman," General Galgan said. From the looks others gave him, it seemed he wasn't supposed to debate a Truthspeaker. He barreled forward anyway. "This is a complex situation."

"I would be more sympathetic," Min said, "if I didn't know there was a spy for the Shadow among us."

The freckled *so'jhin* looked up sharply.

I have you, Min thought, then pointed at General Yulan. "Abaldar Yulan, I denounce you! I have seen omens that prove to me you are not acting in the interests of the Empire!"

The real spy relaxed, and Min caught a hint of a smile on her lips. That was good enough. As Yulan protested loudly the accusation, Min dropped a knife into her hand and whipped it toward the woman.

It flipped end over end—but just before hitting the woman, it stopped and hung in the air.

Nearby *damane* and *sul'dam* gasped. The spy shot Min a hateful glare, then opened a gateway, throwing herself through. Weaves shot after her, but she was gone before most of the people at the meeting realized what was happening.

"I'm sorry, General Yulan," Min announced, "but you are suffering from Compulsion. Fortuona, it is obvious that the Shadow is doing whatever it can to keep us from this battle. With that in mind, will you *still* pursue this course of indecision?"

Min met Tuon's eyes.

"You play these games quite well," Tuon whispered, voice cold. "And to think that I worried for your safety by bringing you into my court. I should have worried for myself, it appears." Tuon sighed, ever so softly. "I suppose you give me the opportunity . . . perhaps the mandate . . . to follow what my heart would choose, whether or not it is wise." She stood. "General Galgan, gather your troops. We will return to the Field of Merrilor."

Egwene wove Earth and destroyed the boulders behind which the Sharans had hidden. The other Aes Sedai struck immediately, hurling weaves through the crackling air. The Sharans died in fire, lightning and explosions.

This side of the Heights was so piled with rubble and scarred with trenches it looked like the remains of a city following a terrible earthquake. It was still night, and they had been fighting ... Light, how long had it been since Gawyn died? Hours upon hours.

Egwene redoubled her efforts, refusing to let the thought of him pull her down. Over the hours, her Aes Sedai and the Sharans had fought back and forth across the western side of the Heights. Slowly, Egwene was pushing them eastward.

At times, Egwene's side had seemed to be winning, but lately, more and more Aes Sedai fell from the effects of fatigue or the One Power.

Another group of channelers approached through the smoke, drawing on the One Power. Egwene could sense them more than see them.

"Deflect their weaves!" Egwene yelled, standing at the forefront. "I will attack, you defend!"

Other women took up the call, yelling it along their battle line. No longer did they fight in pockets alone; women of all Ajahs lined up to either side of Egwene, concentration on their ageless faces. Warders stood in front of them; using their bodies to stop weaves was the only protection they could offer.

Egwene felt Leilwin approaching from behind. The new Warder took her duties seriously. A Seanchan, fighting as her Warder in the Last Battle. Why not? The world itself was unraveling. The cracks all around Egwene's feet proved that. Those had not faded, as earlier ones had—the darkness remained. Balefire had been used too much in this area.

Egwene launched a wave of fire like a moving wall. Corpses went up in flames as the wall passed, leaving behind smoking piles of bones. Her attack scored the ground, blackening it, and the Sharans banded together to fight back against the weave. She killed a few of them before they shattered the attack.

The other Aes Sedai deflected or destroyed their return weaves, and Egwene gathered her strength to try again. *So tired ...* a piece of her whispered. *Egwene, you're so tired. This is becoming dangerous.*

Leilwin stepped up, stumbling on broken rock but joining her at the front. "I bring word, Mother," she said in that Seanchan drawl. "The Asha'man have recovered the seals. Their leader carries them."

Egwene let out a relieved breath. She wove Fire and sent it forth in pillars this time, the flames illuminating the broken ground around them. Those cracks that M'Hael had caused worried her deeply. She began another weave, then stopped. Something was wrong.

She spun around as balefire—a column as wide as a man's arm—ripped through the Aes Sedai line, vaporizing half a dozen women. Explosions all around appeared as if from nowhere, and other women went from battle to death in a heartbeat.

The balefire burned away women who had stopped weaves from killing us ... but those women had been removed from the Pattern before they could weave those, and could no longer have stopped the Sharan attacks. Balefire burned a thread backward in the Pattern.

The chain of events was catastrophic. Sharan channelers who had been dead were now alive again, and they surged forward— men clawing across the broken ground like hounds, women walking in linked groups of four or five. Egwene sought out the source of the balefire. She had never seen such an immense bar of it, so powerful it must have burned threads a few hours back.

She found M'Hael standing atop the Heights, the air warped in a bubble around him. Black tendrils—like moss or lichen—crept out of gaps in the rock around him. A spreading sickness. Darkness, nothing. It would consume them all.

Another bar of balefire burned a hole through the ground and touched women, making their forms glow, then vanish. The air itself *broke*, like a bubble of force that exploded from M'Hael. The storm from before returned, stronger.

"I thought that I'd taught you to run," Egwene snarled, climbing to her feet and gathering her power. At her feet, the ground cracked and opened into nothing.

Light! She could feel the emptiness in that hole. She began a weave, but another strike of balefire coursed across the battlefield, killing women she loved. The trembling underfoot threw Egwene to the ground. Screams grew loud as Sharan attacks slaughtered Egwene's followers. Aes Sedai scattered, seeking safety.

The cracks on the ground spread, as if the top of the Heights here had been hit by a hammer.

Balefire. She needed her own. It was the only way to fight him! She rose to her knees and began crafting the forbidden weave, though her heart lurched as she did it.

NO. Using balefire would only push the world toward destruction.

Then what?

It's only a weave, Egwene. Perrin's words, when he had seen her in the World of Dreams and stopped balefire from hitting him. But it *wasn't* just another weave. There wasn't anything like it.

So exhausted. Now that she'd stopped for a moment, she could feel her numbing fatigue. In its depths, she felt the loss, the bitter loss, of Gawyn's death.

"Mother!" Leilwin said, pulling her shoulder. The woman had stayed with her. "Mother, we must go! The Aes Sedai have broken! The Sharans overrun us."

Ahead, M'Hael saw her. He smiled, striding forward, a scepter in one hand, the other pointed toward her, palm up. What would happen if he burned her away with balefire? The last two hours would vanish. Her rally of the Aes Sedai, the dozens upon dozens of Sharans she had killed . . .

Just a weave . . .

No other like it.

That isn't the way it works, she thought. *Two sides to every coin. Two halves to the Power. Hot and cold, light and dark, woman and man. If a weave exists, so must its opposite.*

M'Hael released balefire, and Egwene did . . . something. The weave she'd tried before on the cracks, but of a much greater power and scope: a majestic, marvelous weave, a combination of all Five Powers. It slid into place before her. She yelled, releasing it as if from her very soul, a column of pure white that struck M'Hael's weave at its center.

The two canceled one another, like scalding water and freezing water poured together. A powerful flash of light overwhelmed all else, blinding Egwene, but she could *feel* something from what she did. A shoring up of the Pattern. The cracks stopped spreading, and something welled up inside of them, a stabilizing force. A growth, like scab on a wound. Not a perfect fix, but at least a patch.

She yelled, forcing herself to her feet. She would not face him on her knees! She drew every scrap of the Power she could hold, throwing it at the Forsaken with the fury of the Amyrlin.

The two streams of power sprayed light against one another, the ground around M'Hael cracking as the ground near Egwene rebuilt itself. She still did not know what it was she wove. The opposite of balefire. A fire of her own, a weave of light and rebuilding.

The Flame of Tar Valon.

They matched one another, in stasis, for an eternal moment. In that moment, Egwene felt a peace come upon her. The pain of Gawyn's death faded. He would be reborn. The Pattern would continue. The very weave she wielded calmed her anger and replaced it with peace. She reached more deeply into *saidar*, that glowing comfort that had guided her so long.

And she drew on more of the Power.

Her stream of energy pushed its way through M'Hael's balefire like a sword thrust, spraying the Power aside and traveling right up the stream into M'Hael's outstretched hand. It pierced the hand and shot through his chest.

The balefire vanished. M'Hael gaped, stumbling, eyes wide, and then he crystallized from the inside out, as if freezing in ice. A multihued, beautiful crystal grew from him. Uncut and rough, as if from the core of the earth itself. Somehow Egwene knew that the Flame would have had much less effect on a person who had not given himself to the Shadow.

She clung to the Power she'd held. She had pulled in too much. She knew that if she released her grip, she would leave herself burned out, unable to channel another drop. The Power surged through her in this last moment.

Something trembled far to the north. Rand's fight continued. The gaps in the land expanded. M'Hael and Demandred's balefire had done its work. The world here was crumbling. Black lines radiated across the Heights, and her mind's eye saw them opening, the land shattering, and a void appearing here that sucked into it all life.

"Watch for the light," Egwene whispered.

"Mother?" Leilwin still knelt beside her. Around them, hundreds of Sharans picked themselves up off the ground.

"Watch for the light, Leilwin," Egwene said. "As the Amyrlin

Seat, I command you—find the seals of the Dark One's prison and *break* them. Do it the moment the light shines. Only then can it save us."

"But . . ."

Egwene wove a gateway and wrapped Leilwin in Air, shoving her through to safety. As she went, Egwene released the woman's bond, severing their brief tie.

"No!" Leilwin cried.

The gateway closed. Black cracks into nothingness expanded all around Egwene as she faced the hundreds of Sharans. Her Aes Sedai had fought with strength and valor, but those Sharan channelers still remained. They surrounded her, some timid, others smiling in triumph.

She closed her eyes and drew in the power. More than a woman should be able to, more than was right. Far beyond safety, far beyond wisdom. This *sa'angreal* had no buffer to prevent this.

Her body was spent. She offered it up and became a column of light, releasing the Flame of Tar Valon into the ground beneath her and high into the sky. The Power left her in a quiet, beautiful explosion, washing across the Sharans and sealing the cracks created by her fight with M'Hael.

Egwene's soul separated from her collapsing body and rested upon that wave, riding it into the Light.

Egwene died.

Rand screamed in denial, in rage, in sorrow.

"Not her! NOT HER!"

THE DEAD ARE MINE.

"Shai'tan!" Rand yelled. "Not her!"

I WILL KILL THEM ALL, ADVERSARY.

Rand bent over, squeezing his eyes shut. *I will protect you*, he thought. *Whatever else happens, I will see you safe, I swear it. I swear it . . .*

Oh, Light. Egwene's name joined the list of the dead. That list continued to grow, thundering in his mind. His failures. So many failures.

He should have been able to save them.

The Dark One's attacks persisted, trying to rip Rand apart and crush him all at once.

Oh, Light. Not Egwene.

Rand closed his eyes and collapsed, barely holding back the next attack.

Darkness enclosed him.

Leane raised her arm, shading her eyes against the magnificent burst of light. It washed the hillside of its darkness and—for a moment—left only brilliance. Sharans froze in place, casting shadows behind them as they crystallized.

The column of power rose high in the air, a beacon, then faded.

Leane dropped to her knees, one hand resting on the ground to steady herself. A blanket of crystals coated the ground, growing over broken rock, coating the scarred landscape. Where cracks had opened, they were now filled with crystal, looking like tiny rivers.

Leane climbed to her feet and crept forward, passing the Sharans frozen in crystal, dead in time.

At the very center of the explosion, Leane found a column of crystal as wide as an ancient leatherleaf tree, rising some fifty feet in the air. Frozen at its center was a fluted rod, Vora's *sa'angreal*. There was no sign of the Amyrlin herself, but Leane knew.

"The Amyrlin Seat has fallen," a nearby Aes Sedai cried amid the crystallized Sharans. "The Amyrlin Seat has fallen!"

Thunder rumbled. Berelain looked up from the side of the bed, then stood, Galad's hand slipping from hers as she walked to the window set in the stone wall.

The sea churned and broke against the rocks outside, roaring, as if in anger. Perhaps pain. White foam sprayed, violent, toward clouds where lightning cast a fractured light. While she watched, those clouds grew thicker in the night, if that was possible. Darker.

Dawn was still an hour off. The clouds were so black, though, she knew she would not see the sun when it rose. She went back to Galad's side, sat down and took his hand. When would an Aes Sedai come to Heal him? He was still unconscious, save for nightmare whispers. He twisted, and something sparkled at his neck.

Berelain reached under his shirt, taking out a medallion. It was in the shape of a fox's head. She rubbed her finger across it.

". . . back to Cauthon . . ." Galad whispered, eyes closed. ". . . Hope . . ."

Berelain thought for a moment, feeling that darkness outside as if it were the Dark One's own, smothering the land and crawling in through windows, under doors. She rose, left Galad and walked quickly away, carrying the medallion.

"The Amyrlin Seat is dead," Arganda reported.

Blood and bloody ashes, Mat thought. *Egwene. Not Egwene too?* It hit him like a punch to the face.

"What's more," Arganda continued, "the Aes Sedai report that they have lost over half their numbers. The ones remaining claim . . . and this is a quote . . . that they 'couldn't channel enough of the One Power to lift a feather.' They're out of the battle."

Mat grunted. "How many of the Sharan channelers did they take?" he asked, bracing himself.

"All of them."

Mat looked at Arganda and frowned. "What?"

"All of the channelers," Arganda said. "All the ones that were fighting the Aes Sedai."

"That's something," Mat said. But Egwene . . .

No. No thinking of that right now. She and her people had stopped the Sharan channelers.

The Sharans and Trollocs fell back from the front lines to regroup. Mat took the opportunity to do the same.

His forces—what remained of them—were strung out across the Heights. He had joined together everyone he had left. The Borderlanders, the Dragonsworn, Loial and the Ogier, Tam's troops, the Whitecloaks, soldiers of the Band of the Red Hand. They fought hard, but their foe greatly outnumbered them. It was bad enough when they just had the Sharans to contend with, but once the Trollocs had broken through on the eastern edge of the Heights, they were forced to defend themselves on two fronts. Over the past hour they had been pushed back more than a thousand paces, in a northerly direction, and their back ranks had almost reached the end of the plateau.

This would be the last push. The end of the battle. With the Sharan channelers gone, Mat would not be wiped out immediately, but Light ... there were still so many *bloody* Trollocs left. Mat had danced this dance well. He knew he had. But there was only so much a man could do. Even Tuon's return might not be enough, if it came.

Arganda handled reports from the other areas of the battle-field—the man was wounded badly enough he could not fight, and there was no one with enough of the Power left to spare for Healing. He did his job well. Good man. Mat could have used him in the Band.

The Trollocs gathered for their push, again moving bodies out of the way, forming into fists with Myrddraal leading them. That would give Mat five or ten minutes to get ready. Then it would come.

Lan walked over, expression grim. "What would you have my men do, Cauthon?"

"Get ready to fight those Trollocs," Mat said. "Has anyone checked with Mayene lately? Now would be a wonderful time to get back a few ranks of men who have been Healed."

"I will check on it for you," Lan said. "And then I will prepare my men."

Mat dug in his saddlebags as Lan withdrew. He pulled out Rand's banner, the one of the ancient Aes Sedai. He'd gathered it earlier, thinking perhaps it might have some use. "Somebody hoist this thing up. We're fighting in Rand's bloody name. Let's show the Shadow we're proud of it."

Dannil took the banner, finding a spear to use as a pole. Mat took a deep breath. The way the Borderlanders spoke, they thought this would end in a glorious, heroic, suicidal charge. That was how Thom's songs always ended ... the kinds of songs Mat had hoped to never find himself in. Faint hope that was, now.

Think, think. In the distance, the Trolloc horns started blowing. Tuon had delayed. Was she going to come? He hoped, secretly, she would not. With the battle going so poorly, even the Seanchan might not be enough.

He needed an opening. *Come on, luck!* Another gateway opened, and Arganda went to collect the messenger's report. Mat did not need to hear to realize the kind of news it was, as when Arganda returned, he was frowning.

"All right," Mat said, sighing. "Give me your news."

"The Queen of Andor is dead," Arganda said.

Bloody Ashes! Not Elayne! Mat felt a lurch inside. *Rand . . . I'm sorry.* "Who leads there? Bashere?"

"Dead," Arganda said. "And his wife. They fell during an attack against the Andoran pikemen. We've lost six Aiel clan chiefs as well. Nobody leads the Andorans or the Aiel at the riverbed. They're crumbling fast."

"This is the end!" Demandred's augmented voice washed across Mat from the other end of the plateau. "Lews Therin has abandoned you! Cry out to him as you die. Let him feel your pain."

They had arrived at the last few moves in their game, and Demandred had played well. Mat looked over his army of exhausted troops, many of them wounded. There was no denying it, they were in a desperate situation.

"Send for the Aes Sedai," Mat said. "I don't care if they say they can't lift a feather. Maybe when it comes down to their lives, they'll find a little strength for a fireball here and there. Besides, their Warders can still fight."

Arganda nodded. Nearby, a gateway opened, and two beleaguered-looking Asha'man stumbled out. Naeff and Neald bore scorch marks on their skins, and Naeff's Aes Sedai was not with them.

"Well?" Mat asked the three.

"It is done," Neald said with a growl.

"What of Tuon?"

"They found the spy, apparently," Naeff said. "The Empress is waiting to return on your mark."

Mat breathed in, tasting the battlefield air, feeling the rhythm of the fighting he had set up. He didn't know if he could win, even with Tuon. Not with Elayne's army in disarray, not with the Aes Sedai weakened to the point of being unable to channel. Not without Egwene, her Two Rivers stubbornness, her iron backbone. Not without a miracle.

"Send for her, Naeff," Mat said. He called for paper and a pen, and scribbled a note, which he handed off to the Asha'man. He shoved aside the selfish desire to let Tuon fly to safety. Bloody ashes, there was no safety, not anywhere. "Give this to the Empress, Naeff; tell her these instructions must be followed exactly."

Then Mat turned to Neald. "I want you to go to Talmanes," he said. "Have him move forward with the plan."

The two channelers left, off to deliver their messages.

"Will it be enough?" Arganda asked.

"No," Mat said.

"Then why?"

"Because I'll be a Darkfriend before I'll let this battle go without trying everything, Arganda."

"Lews Therin!" Demandred boomed. "Come face me! I know you watch this battle! Join it! Fight!"

"I sure am growing tired of that man," Mat said.

"Cauthon, look, those Trollocs have regrouped," Arganda said. "I think they are about to attack."

"Then this is it; let's form up," Mat said. "Where is Lan; has he come back yet? I'd hate to do this without him."

Mat turned, scanning the lines for him, as Arganda shouted orders. His attention was drawn back suddenly as Arganda grabbed his arm, pointing toward the Trollocs. Mat felt a chill as he saw in the light of bonfires a lone horseman on a black stallion charge into the right flank of the Trolloc horde, making for the eastern slope of the Heights. Toward Demandred.

Lan had gone to fight a war on his own.

The Trollocs ripped at Olver's arm in the night, reaching into the crack, trying to pry him free. Others dug at the sides, and soil streamed in onto him, sticking to the tears on his cheeks and the blood flowing from his scratches.

He couldn't stop shaking. He also couldn't make himself move. He trembled, terrified, as the beasts pried at him with filthy fingers, digging closer and closer.

Loial sat on a stump, resting before the battle picked up again.

A charge. Yes, that would be a good way for this to end. Loial felt sore all over. He had read a great deal about battle, and had been in fights before, so he had known what to expect. But knowing a thing and experiencing it were completely different; that was why he'd left the *stedding* in the first place.

After more than a day of nonstop fighting, his limbs burned with a deep, inner fatigue. When he raised his axe, the head felt so heavy he wondered why it didn't break the shaft.

War. He could have lived his life without experiencing this. It was so much more than the frantic battle at the Two Rivers had been. There, at least, they'd had time to remove the dead and care for their wounded. There, it had been a matter of standing firm and holding against waves of attacks.

Here, there was no time to wait, no time to think. Erith sat down on the ground beside his stump, and he put a hand on her shoulder. She closed her eyes and leaned against him. She was beautiful, with perfect ears and wonderful eyebrows. Loial did not look at the bloodstains on her clothing; he feared some of it was hers. He rubbed her shoulder with fingers so tired he could barely feel them.

Loial had taken some notes on the battlefield, for himself and for others, to keep track of how the battle had gone so far. Yes, a final attack. That would make for a good ending to the story, once he wrote it.

He pretended that he would still write the story. There was no harm to such a little lie.

One rider burst from the ranks of their soldiers, galloping toward the Trolloc right flank. Mat would not be happy about that. One man, alone, would die. Loial was surprised that he could feel sorrow for that man's life lost, after all of the death he had seen.

That man looks familiar, Loial thought. Yes, it was the horse. He'd seen that horse before, many times. *Lan*, he thought, numb. *Lan is the one riding out alone.*

Loial stood.

Erith looked up at him as he shouldered his axe.

"Wait," Loial said to her. "Fight alongside the others. I must go."

"Go?"

"I need to witness this," Loial said. The fall of the last king of the Malkieri. He would need to include it in his book.

*

"Prepare to charge!" Arganda yelled. "Men, form up! Archers at the front, cavalry next, foot soldiers prepare to come up behind!"

A charge, Tam thought. *Yes, that is our only hope.* They had to continue their push, but their line was so thin. He could see what Mat had been trying, but it wasn't going to work.

They needed to fight it through anyway.

"Well, *he* is dead," a mercenary said from near Tam, nodding toward Lan Mandragoran as he rode toward the Trolloc flank. "Bloody Borderlanders."

"Tam . . ." Abell said from beside him.

Above them, the sky grew darker. Was that possible, at night? Those terrible, boiling clouds seemed to come lower and lower. Tam almost lost Lan's figure atop the midnight stallion, despite the bonfires burning on the Heights. Their light seemed feeble.

He's riding for Demandred, Tam thought. *But there's a wall of Trollocs in the way.* Tam took out an arrow with a resin-soaked rag tied behind the head and nocked it into his bow. "Two Rivers men, prepare to fire!"

The mercenary nearby laughed. "That's a hundred paces at least! You'll fill him with arrows if anything."

Tam eyed the man, then took his arrow and thrust the end into a torch. The bundled rag behind the head came alight with fire. "First rank, on my signal!" Tam yelled, ignoring the other orders that came down the line. "Let's give Lord Mandragoran a little something to guide his way!"

Tam drew in a fluid motion, the burning rag warming his fingers, and loosed.

Lan charged toward the Trollocs. His lance, and its three replacements, had all shattered hours ago. At his neck, he wore the cold medallion that Berelain had sent through the gateway with a simple note.

I do not know how Galad ended up with this, but I believe he wished me to send it to Cauthon.

Lan did not consider what he was doing. The void did not allow such things. Some men would call it brash, foolhardy, suicidal. The world was rarely changed by men who were unwilling to try being at least one of the three. He sent what comfort he could to distant Nynaeve through the bond, then prepared to fight.

As Lan neared the Trollocs, the beasts set up a spear line to stop him. A horse would impale itself trying to push through that. Lan drew in breath, calm within the void, planning to slice the head off the first spear, then ram his way through the line.

It was an impossible maneuver. All the Trollocs would need to do was squeeze together and slow him. After that, they could overwhelm Mandarb and pull Lan from the saddle.

But someone had to destroy Demandred. With the medallion at his neck, Lan raised his sword.

A flaming arrow streaked down from the sky and hit the throat of the Trolloc right in front of Lan. Without hesitation, Lan used the fallen Trolloc as an opening in the line of spears. He crashed between the Shadowspawn, trampling the fallen one. He would need to—

Another arrow fell, dropping a Trolloc. Then another fell, and another, in quick succession. Mandarb crashed through the confused, burning and dying Trollocs as an entire *rain* of burning arrows dropped in front of him.

"Malkier!" Lan yelled, heeling Mandarb forward, trampling corpses but maintaining speed as the way opened. A hail of light dropped before him, each arrow precise, killing a Trolloc that tried to stand before him.

He thundered through the ranks, shoving aside dying Trollocs, flaming arrows guiding his way in the darkness like a roadway. The Trollocs stood thick on either side, but those in front of him dropped and dropped until there were no more.

Thank you, Tam.

Lan cantered his steed along the eastern slope of the Heights, alone now, past the soldiers, past the Shadowspawn. He was one with the breeze that streamed through his hair, one with the sinewy animal beneath him that carried him forward, one with the target that was his destination, his fate.

Demandred stood at the sound of the hoofbeats, his Sharan companions rising in front of him.

With a roar, Lan heeled Mandarb into the Sharans that blocked his path. The stallion leaped, front legs driving the guards before him into the ground. Mandarb wheeled around, his haunches knocking down more Sharans, his forelegs coming down on yet others.

Lan threw himself from the saddle—Mandarb had no protection against channeling, and so to fight from horseback would be to invite Demandred to kill his mount—and hit the ground at a run, sword out.

"Another one?" Demandred roared. "Lews Therin, you are beginning to—"

He cut off as Lan reached him and flung himself into Thistledown Floats on the Whirlwind, a tempestuous, offensive sword form. Demandred whipped his sword up, catching the blow on his weapon and skidding backward a step at the force of it. They exchanged three blows, quick as cracks of lightning, Lan still in motion until the last blow caught Demandred on the cheek. Lan felt a slight tug, and blood sprayed into the air.

Demandred felt at the wound in his cheek, and his eyes opened wider. "Who are *you*?" Demandred asked.

"I am the man who will kill you."

Min looked up from the back of her *torm* as it loped toward the gateway back to the battlefield at Merrilor. She hoped it would withstand the battle frenzy when they got there. Bonfires and torches shone in the distance, fireflies illuminating scenes of valor and determination. She watched the lights flicker, the last embers of a fire that would soon be extinguished.

Rand trembled, distant, far to the north.

The Pattern spun around Rand, forcing him to watch. He looked through eyes streaming with tears. He saw the people struggle. He saw them fall. He saw Elayne, captive and alone, a Dreadlord preparing to rip their children from her womb. He saw Rhuarc, his mind forfeit, now a pawn of one of the Forsaken.

He saw Mat, desperate, facing down horrible odds.

He saw Lan riding to his death.

Demandred's words dug at him. The Dark One's pressure continued to tear at him.

Rand had failed.

But in the back of his mind, a voice. Frail, almost forgotten. *Let go.*

Lan held nothing back.

He did not fight as he had trained Rand to fight. No careful testing, no judging the terrain, no careful evaluation. Demandred could channel, and despite the medallion, Lan couldn't give his enemy time to think, time to weave and hurl rocks at him or open the ground beneath him.

Lan burrowed deeply into the void, allowing instincts to guide him. He went beyond lack of emotions, burning away everything. He did not need to judge the terrain, for he felt the land as if it were part of him. He did not need to test Demandred's strength. One of the Forsaken, with many decades of experience, would be the most skilled swordsman Lan had ever faced.

Lan was vaguely aware of the Sharans spreading out to make a broad circle around the two combatants as they fought. Apparently Demandred was confident enough of his skills that he did not allow interference from others.

Lan spun into a sequence of attacks. Water Flows Downhill became Whirlwind on the Mountain which became Hawk Dives into the Brush. His forms were like streams blending into a larger and larger river. Demandred fought as well as Lan had feared. Though the man's forms were slightly different from those Lan knew, the years had not changed the nature of a swordfight.

"You are ... good ... " Demandred said with a grunt, falling back before Wind and Rain, a line of blood dripping from his chin. Lan's sword flashed in the air, reflecting the red light of a bonfire nearby.

Demandred came back with Striking the Spark, which Lan anticipated, countering. He took a scratch along the side, but ignored it. The exchange set Lan back a step, and gave Demandred the chance to pick up a rock with the One Power and hurl it at Lan.

Deep within the void, Lan felt the stone coming. It was an understanding of the fight—one that ran deeply into him, to the very core of his soul. The way Demandred stepped, the direction his eyes flickered, told Lan exactly what was coming.

As he flowed into his next sword form, Lan brought his weapon up across his chest and stepped backward. A stone the size of a man's head passed directly in front of him. Lan flowed forward, arm moving into his next form as another stone flew under his arm, tugging wind with it. Lan raised his sword and flowed around the path of a third stone, which missed him by a thumb's width, rippling his clothing.

Demandred blocked Lan's attack, but he breathed hoarsely. "Who *are* you?" Demandred whispered again. "No one of this Age has such skill. Asmodean? No, no. He couldn't have fought me like this. Lews Therin? It *is* you behind that face, isn't it?"

"I am just a man," Lan whispered. "That is all I have ever been."

Demandred growled, then launched an attack. Lan responded with Stones Falling Down the Mountain, but Demandred's fury forced him back a few steps.

Despite Lan's initial offensive, Demandred was the better swordsman. Lan knew this by the same sense that told him when to strike, when to parry, when to step and when to withdraw. Perhaps if they had come to the fight evenly, it would be different. They had not. Lan had been fighting for an entire day, and though he'd been Healed from his worst wounds, the smaller ones still ached. Beyond that, a Healing in and of itself was draining.

Demandred was still fresh. The Forsaken stopped talking and engrossed himself in the duel. He also stopped using the One Power, focused only on his swordplay. He did not grin as he took the advantage. He did not seem like a man who grinned very often.

Lan slipped away from Demandred, but the Forsaken pressed forward with Boar Rushes Down the Mountain, again pushing Lan back to the perimeter of the circle, battering at his defenses, cutting him on the arm, then the shoulder, then finally the thigh.

I've only time for one last lesson . . .

"I have you," Demandred finally growled, breathing heavily. "Whoever you are, *I have you*. You cannot win."

"You didn't listen to me," Lan whispered.

One last lesson. The hardest . . .

Demandred struck, and Lan saw his opening. Lan lunged forward, placing Demandred's sword point against his own side and ramming himself forward onto it.

"I did not come here to win," Lan whispered, smiling. "I came here to kill you. Death is lighter than a feather."

Demandred's eyes opened wide, and he tried to pull back. Too late. Lan's sword took him straight through the throat.

The world grew dark as Lan slipped backward off the sword. He felt Nynaeve's fear and pain as he did, and he sent his love to her.

CHAPTER
38

The Place That Was Not

Rand saw Lan fall, and it sent a spasm of anguish through him. The Dark One pressed in around Rand. Swallowing him, shredding him. Fighting that attack was too hard. Rand was spent.

Let go. His father's voice.

"I have to save them . . ." Rand whispered.

Let them sacrifice. You can't do this yourself.

"I have to . . . That's what it means . . ." The Dark One's destruction crawled on him like a thousand crows, picking at his flesh, pulling it from his bones. He could barely think through the pressure and the sense of loss. The death of Egwene and so many others.

Let go.

It is their choice to make.

He wanted so badly to protect them, the people who believed in him. Their deaths, and the danger they faced, were an enormous weight upon him. How could a man just . . . let go? Wasn't that letting go of responsibility?

Or was it giving the responsibility to them?

Rand squeezed his eyes shut, thinking of all those who had died for him. Of Egwene, whom he had sworn to himself to protect.

You fool. Her voice in his head. Fond, but sharp.

"Egwene?"

Am I not allowed to be a hero, too?

"It's not that . . ."

You march to your death. Yet you forbid anyone else from doing so?

"I . . ."

Let go, Rand. Let us die for what we believe, and do not try to steal that from us.

You have embraced your death. Embrace mine.

Tears leaked from the corners of his eyes. "I'm sorry," he whispered.

Why?

"I've failed."

No. Not yet you haven't.

The Dark One flayed him. He huddled before that vast nothingness, unable to move. He screamed in agony.

And then, he let go.

He let go of the guilt. He let go of the shame for having not saved Egwene and all the others. He let go of the need to protect her, to protect all of them.

He let them be heroes.

Names streamed from his head. Egwene, Hurin, Bashere, Isan of the Chareen Aiel, Somara and thousands more. One by one—first slowly, but with increasing speed—he counted backward through the list he had once maintained in his head. The list had once been only women, but had grown to include everyone he knew had died for him. He hadn't realized how large it had become, how much he had let himself carry.

The names *ripped* from him like physical things, like doves aflight, and each one carried away a burden. Weight vanished from his shoulders. His breathing grew steadier. It was as if Perrin had come with his hammer and shattered a thousand chains that had been dragging behind Rand.

Ilyena was last. *We are reborn,* Rand thought, *so we can do better the next time.*

So do better.

He opened his eyes and placed his hand before him, palm against blackness that felt solid. His self that had fuzzed, becoming indistinct as the Dark One ripped at it, pulled together. He placed his other arm down, then heaved himself to his knees.

And then, Rand al'Thor—the Dragon Reborn—stood up once again to face the Shadow.

"No, no," the beautiful Shendla whispered, looking down at Demandred's body. Her heart sank down inside of her and she tore at her hair with both hands, her body swaying. As she gazed on her beloved, Shendla slowly drew breath deep into her chest, and when it released, it was a fearful shriek: "Bao the Wyld is dead!"

The entire battlefield seemed to grow still.

Rand faced the Dark One in that place that was *not*, surrounded by all time and nothing at the same time. His body still stood in the cave of Shayol Ghul, locked into that moment of battle against Moridin, but his soul was here.

He existed in this place that was not, this place outside of the Pattern, this place where evil was born. He looked into it, and he knew it. The Dark One was not a being, but a force—an essence as wide as the universe itself, which Rand could now see in complete detail. Planets, stars in their multitudes, like the motes above a bonfire.

The Dark One still strove to destroy him. Rand felt strong despite the attacks. Relaxed, complete. With his burdens gone, he could fight again. He held himself together. It was difficult, but he was victorious.

Rand stepped forward.

The Darkness shuddered. It quivered, vibrated, as if disbelieving.

I DESTROY THEM.

The Dark One was not a being. It was the darkness between. Between lights, between moments, between eyeblinks.

ALL IS MINE THIS TIME. IT WAS EVER MEANT TO BE. IT WILL EVER BE.

Rand saluted those who died. The blood running across rocks. The weeping of those who witnessed others fall. The Shadow threw all of it at Rand, intent on Rand's destruction. But it did not destroy him.

"We will never give in," Rand whispered. "*I* will never give in."

The vast Shadow thundered and shook. It sent jolts through and across the world. The ground rent, the laws of nature fractured. Swords turned against their owners, food spoiled, rock turned to mud.

It came upon Rand again, the force of nothingness itself trying to pull him apart. The strength of the attack did not lessen. And yet, suddenly, it felt like an idle buzzing.

They would not give up. It wasn't just about Rand. All of them would keep fighting. The Dark One's attacks lost meaning. If they could not make him yield, if they could not make him relent, then what were they?

Within the tempest, Rand sought the void as Tam had taught him. All emotion, all worry, all pain. He took it and fed it into the flame of a single candle.

He felt peace. The peace of a single drop of water hitting a pond. The peace of moments, the peace between eyeblinks, the peace of the void.

"I will not give up," he repeated, and the words seemed a wonder to him.

I CONTROL THEM ALL. I BREAK THEM BEFORE ME. YOU HAVE LOST, CHILD OF HUMANKIND.

"If you think that," Rand whispered into the darkness, "then it is because you cannot see."

Loial was panting hard when he returned to the northern end of the Heights. He gave the news to Mat, about how Lan had fought so bravely before he went down, taking Demandred with him. Loial's report affected Mat deeply, as it did all members of his army, particularly the Borderlanders who had lost a king, a brother. There was a disturbance among the Sharans as well; somehow, news of Demandred's death was already percolating through their ranks.

Mat forced down his grief. That wasn't what Lan would have wanted. Instead, Mat raised his *ashandarei*. "*Tai'shar Malkier!*" he screamed with all the force he could. "Lan Mandragoran, you bloody wonderful man! You did it!"

His shouts rang in the silence as he charged toward the Shadow armies. Shouts rang behind him: *"Tai'shar Malkier!"* Shouts from all nationalities, all peoples, Borderlander and not. They surged across the Heights alongside Mat. Together, they attacked the stunned foe.

CHAPTER
39

Those Who Fight

YOU CANNOT FATHOM IT, CAN YOU? Rand demanded of the darkness. IT IS BEYOND YOU. YOU BREAK US, AND STILL WE FIGHT! WHY? HAVEN'T YOU KILLED US? HAVEN'T YOU RUINED US?

YOU, the Dark One replied. I HAVE YOU.

Rand stepped forward. In this place of nothing, the Pattern seemed to swirl around him like a tapestry. HERE IS YOUR FLAW, SHAI'TAN—LORD OF THE DARK, LORD OF ENVY! LORD OF NOTHING! HERE IS WHY YOU FAIL! IT WAS NOT ABOUT ME. *IT'S NEVER BEEN ABOUT ME!*

It was about a woman, torn and beaten down, cast from her throne and made a puppet—a woman who had crawled when she had to. That woman still fought.

It was about a man that love repeatedly forsook, a man who found relevance in a world that others would have let pass them by. A man who remembered stories, and who took fool boys under his wing when the smarter move would have been to keep on walking. That man still fought.

It was about a woman with a secret, a hope for the future. A woman who had hunted the truth before others could. A woman who had given her life, then had it returned. That woman still fought.

It was about a man whose family was taken from him, but who stood tall in his sorrow and protected those he could.

It was about a woman who refused to believe that she could not help, could not Heal those who had been harmed.

It was about a hero who insisted with every breath that he was anything but a hero.

It was about a woman who would not bend her back while she was beaten, and who shone with the Light for all who watched. Including Rand.

It was about them all.

He saw this, over and over, in the Pattern arrayed about him. Rand walked through eons and ages, his hand passing through ribbons of the Pattern's light.

HERE IS THE TRUTH, SHAI'TAN, Rand said, taking another step forward, arms out, woven Pattern spreading around them. YOU CANNOT WIN UNLESS WE GIVE UP. THAT'S IT, ISN'T IT? THIS FIGHT ISN'T ABOUT A VICTORY IN BATTLE. TAKING ME ... IT WAS NEVER ABOUT BEATING ME. IT WAS ABOUT BREAKING ME.

THAT'S WHAT YOU'VE TRIED TO DO WITH ALL OF US. IT'S WHY AT TIMES YOU TRIED TO HAVE US KILLED, WHILE OTHER TIMES YOU DIDN'T SEEM TO CARE. YOU WIN WHEN YOU BREAK US. BUT YOU HAVEN'T. YOU CAN'T.

The darkness trembled. The nothingness shook, as if the arches of the heavens themselves were cracking. The Dark One's shout was defiant.

Within the void, Rand continued forward, and the darkness trembled.

I CAN STILL KILL, the Dark One bellowed. I CAN STILL TAKE THEM ALL! I AM LORD OF THE GRAVE. THE BATTLE LORD, HE IS MINE. ALL ARE MINE EVENTUALLY!

Rand stepped forward, hand stretched out. In his palm sat the world, and upon that world a continent, and upon that continent a battlefield, and upon that battlefield two bodies on the ground.

*

Mat fought, Tam at his side with sword out. Karede and the Deathwatch Guard joined them, then Loial and the Ogier. The armies of a dozen nations and peoples fought, many joining him as he rushed across the plateau.

They were outnumbered three to one.

Mat fought, bellowing in the Old Tongue. "*For the Light! For honor! For glory! For life itself!*"

He slew one Trolloc, then another. Half a dozen in moments, but he felt he was fighting with the surf itself. Wherever he struck down blackness, more took its place. Trollocs moving in the shadows, lit only by the occasional lantern or burning arrow stuck in the ground.

The Trollocs didn't fight as one. *We can break them*, Mat thought. *We have to break them!* This was his chance. Push now, while the Sharans were dazed at Demandred's fall.

THE SON OF BATTLES. I WILL TAKE HIM. I WILL TAKE THEM ALL, ADVERSARY. AS I TOOK THE KING OF NOTHING.

Blood and Bloody ashes! What was that nothingness in his head? Mat beheaded a Trolloc, then wiped his brow, Karede and the Deathwatch Guards covering him for a moment.

Mat could *feel* the battlefield in the night. There were a lot of Trollocs and Sharans, so many of them.

"There are too many!" Arganda called from nearby. "Light, they'll overwhelm us! We need to fall back! Cauthon, can you hear me?"

I can do this, Mat thought. *I can win this battle.* An army could defeat superior numbers, but Mat needed momentum, an opening. A favorable toss of the dice.

Rand stood above the Pattern and looked down at the fallen men in a land where hope seemed to have died. "You have not been watching closely enough. About one thing, you are wrong. So very wrong . . ."

*

Cornered and alone, a boy huddled in a cleft in the rock. Horrors with knives and fangs—the Shadow itself made flesh—dug at his hiding place, reaching with nails like knives and ripping his skin.

Terrified, crying, bloodied, the boy raised a golden horn to his lips.

Mat squinted, the battle seeming to dim around him.

So very wrong, Shai'tan, Rand's voice whispered in Mat's mind.

Then the voice was no longer in Mat's mind. It could be heard distinctly by everyone on the battlefield.

That one you have tried to kill many times, Rand said, *that one who lost his kingdom, that one from whom you took everything . . .*

Lurching, bloodied from the sword strike to his side, the last king of the Malkieri stumbled to his feet. Lan thrust his hand into the air, holding by its hair the head of Demandred, general of the Shadow's armies.

That man, Rand shouted. *That man still fights!*

Mat felt the battlefield grow still. All were frozen in place.

At that moment, there rang out a soft but powerful sound, a clear note, golden; one long tone that encompassed everything. The sound of a horn, pure and beautiful.

Mat had heard that sound once before.

Mellar knelt beside Elayne, pressing the medallion against her head to stop her from channeling. "This could have gone in a very different way, my Queen," he said. "You should have been more accommodating."

Light. That leer was an awful thing. He had gagged her, of course, but she did not give him the satisfaction of crying.

She *would* find a way to escape this. She had to shake free of the medallion. Of course, if she did, there was still the channeler. But if she could evade the medallion, then strike quickly . . .

"Pity that your little Captain-General isn't alive to watch," Mellar said. "Fool that she was, I really do think she *believed* that she was Birgitte from the legends." Elayne heard a soft sound in the distance. The ground vibrated. An earthquake.

She tried to concentrate, but she could only think that Birgitte had been right all along. It was fully possible for the babes to be safe, as Min had foretold, while Elayne herself was left dead.

White mist climbed up from the ground around them, like the souls of the dead, curling.

Mellar stiffened, suddenly.

Elayne blinked, looking up at him. Something silvery jutted from the front of Mellar's chest. It looked like . . . an arrowhead.

Mellar turned, knife dropping from his fingers. Behind him, Birgitte Silverbow stood over her corpse, one foot to either side of the headless body. She raised a bow, bright as newly polished silver, and released another arrow, which seemed to trail light as it struck Mellar in the head and pitched him to the ground. Her next shot took Mellar's channeler, killing the Dreadlord with a silver arrow before the man could respond.

All around them, Mellar's men stood as if paralyzed, gaping at Birgitte. The clothing she now wore seemed to glow. A short white coat, a voluminous pair of pale yellow trousers and a dark cloak. Her long golden hair hung in an intricate braid, down to her waist.

"I am Birgitte Silverbow," Birgitte announced, as if to dispel doubt. "The Horn of Valere has sounded, calling all to the Last Battle. The heroes have returned!"

Lan Mandragoran held aloft the head of one of the Forsaken— their battle commander, supposedly invincible.

The Shadow's army could not ignore what had happened, none of them, wherever they were on the battlefield. The voice that had come out of nowhere had proclaimed it. That the attacker should stand while the Chosen lay dead . . . it stunned them. Frightened them.

And then the Horn sounded in the distance.

"Press forward!" Mat yelled. "Press forward!" His army threw themselves ferociously onto the Trollocs and Sharans.

"Cauthon, what was that sound?" Arganda demanded, stumbling up beside Pips. The man still had one arm in a sling and carried a bloodied mace in the other hand. Around Mat, the Deathwatch Guard fought and grunted, cutting down Trollocs.

Mat yelled, throwing himself into the fight. "That was the bloody Horn of Valere! We can still win this night!"

The Horn. How had the bloody Horn been sounded? Well, it looked like Mat wasn't tied to the thing any longer. His death at Rhuidean must have broken him from it.

Some other unlucky fool could bear that burden now. Mat howled a battlecry, shearing the arm off a Trolloc, then stabbing it through the chest. The Shadow's entire army became disoriented at the sound of the Horn. Those Trollocs nearest Lan scrambled back, clawing over one another in desperate urgency to escape him. That left the Trollocs fighting along the slope spread thin, without reserves. And nobody seemed to be in charge.

Myrddraal nearby raised swords against their own Trollocs, trying to get those that were fleeing to turn back and fight, but flaming arrows shot by the Two Rivers archers fell from the sky and riddled the Fades' bodies.

Tam al'Thor, Mat thought, *I'm going to bloody send you my best pair of boots. Light burn me, but I will.* "To me!" Mat shouted. "All riders that can hold a flaming weapon, to *me!*"

Mat kicked Pips into a gallop, shoving his way through Trollocs that were still fighting. Mat's attack opened the way for Furyk Karede and his few remaining men to punch the hole in the horde of Trollocs wider. Following that, the full force of the remaining Borderlanders poured through after Mat, toward Lan.

The Sharan army showed signs of weakening, but they continued their offensive, their discipline forcing them to do what their hearts were calling them to end. Lan's victory wouldn't win the battle outright—there were far too many enemies—but without Demandred, the Shadow had lost direction. Even the Fades were showing the lack of a leader. The Trollocs began to fall back and regroup.

Mat and the Borderlanders galloped southwest across the Heights and came to where Lan was standing. Mat jumped from his horse and grabbed Lan by the shoulder as the Malkieri king faltered. Lan looked at Mat with grim thanks, and then his eyes rolled back in his head and he started to fall, dropping Demandred's head to the ground.

A man in a black coat rode over. Mat hadn't realized that Narishma was still there, fighting alongside the Borderlanders.

The Kandori Asha'man threw himself off his horse and took Lan by the other arm, then concentrated.

The brief Healing was enough to bring Lan back to consciousness.

"Get him on a horse, Narishma," Mat said. "You can work on him more when we get back to our army. I don't want to be stuck behind enemy lines if those Trollocs below decide to come back up the Heights."

They rode back northeast, laying into the back of the Trollocs' right flank with swords and lances as they swept past, which unsettled the beasts even more. Once past, the Borderlanders swung their mounts around and charged directly into the Trolloc hordes again, who were looking around in all directions, not sure where the next attack would be coming from. Mat and Narishma continued to ride toward their own back lines, with Lan in tow. Narishma eased the Malkieri off his horse and had him lie on the ground to continue the Healing, while Mat paused to consider their situation.

Behind them, mist gathered. Mat was struck with a terrible thought. He had ignored a terrible possibility. The Horn of Valere still called, a distant—yet unmistakable—sound. *Oh, Light*, Mat thought. *Oh, bloody stumps on a battlefield. Who blew it? Which side?*

The fog formed, like worms crawling out of the ground after a rainstorm. It gathered into a billowing cloud, a thunderhead on the ground, and shapes on horses charged down it. Figures of legend. Buad of Albhain, as regal as any queen. Amaresu, holding aloft her glowing sword. Hend the Striker, dark-skinned, a hammer in one hand and a spike in the other.

A figure rode through the mists at the front of the heroes. Tall and imperious, with a nose like a beak, Artur Hawkwing carried Justice, his sword, on his shoulder as he rode. Though the rest of the hundred-odd heroes followed Hawkwing, one broke off in a streak of mist, galloping away. Mat didn't get a good look at the rider. Who had it been, and where was he going so quickly?

Mat pulled his hat on tighter, nudging Pips forward to meet the ancient king. *I suppose I'll know which side summoned him*, Mat thought, *if he tries to kill me.* Mat lifted the *ashandarei* across his saddle. Could he fight Artur Hawkwing? Light, could *anyone* beat one of the heroes of the Horn?

"Hello, Hawkwing," Mat called.

"Gambler," Hawkwing replied. "Do take better care of what has been alotted you. Almost, I worried we would not be summoned for this fight."

Mat let out a relaxing breath. "Bloody ashes, Hawkwing! You needn't have drawn it out like that, you bloody goat-kisser. So you fight for us?"

"Of course we fight for the Light," Hawkwing said. "We would never fight for the Shadow."

"But I was told—" Mat began.

"You were told wrong," Hawkwing said.

"Besides," Hend said, laughing. "If the other side had been able to summon us, you'd be dead by now!"

"I did die," Mat said, rubbing at the scar on his neck. "Apparently that tree claimed me."

"Not the tree, Gambler," Hawkwing said. "Another moment, one that you cannot remember. It is fitting, as Lews Therin did save your life both times."

"Remember him," Amaresu snapped. "I have seen you murmur that you fear his madness, but all the while you forget that every breath you breathe—every step you take—comes at his forbearance. Your life is a gift from the Dragon Reborn, Gambler. Twice over."

Blood and bloody ashes. Even *dead* women treated him the way Nynaeve did. Where did they learn it? Were there secret lessons?

Hawkwing nodded toward something nearby. Rand's banner; Dannil still held it aloft. "We arrive here to gather at the banner. We can fight for you because of it, Gambler, and because the Dragon leads you—though he does it from afar. It is enough."

"Well," Mat said, looking at the banner, "I guess since you're here, you can fight the battle now. I'll pull my men back."

Hawkwing laughed. "You think we hundred can fight this entire battle?"

"You're the bloody heroes of the Horn," Mat said. "That's what you *do*, isn't it?"

"We can be defeated," said pretty Blaes of Matuchin, dancing her horse to the side of Hawkwing's. Tuon couldn't be mad if he looked a little at a hero, right? People were supposed to stare at them. "If we are wounded in dire ways, we will have to withdraw and recover in the World of Dreams."

"The Shadow knows how to incapacitate us," Hend added. "Bind us hand and foot, and we can do nothing to aid the battle. It doesn't matter if one is immortal when one cannot move."

"We can fight well," Hawkwing said to Mat. "And we will lend you our strength. This is not our war alone. We are just one part of it."

"Bloody wonderful," Mat said. That Horn was still sounding. "Then tell me this. If I didn't blow that thing, and the Shadow didn't do it . . . who did?"

Thick Trolloc nails scored Olver's arm. He kept blowing the Horn through his tears, eyes squeezed shut, in the small cleft in the rocky outcrop.

I'm sorry, Mat, he thought as a dark-haired hand scrabbled for a hold on the Horn. Another grabbed him by the shoulder, nails digging deeply, making blood pulse down his arm.

The Horn was ripped from his hands.

I'm sorry!

The Trolloc yanked Olver upward.

Then dropped him.

Olver tumbled to the ground, dazed, and then jumped as the Horn fell into his lap. He grabbed it, shaking and blinking away his tears.

Shadows churned above. Grunting. What was happening? Cautiously, Olver raised his head, and found someone standing above, one foot planted on either side of him. The figure fought in a blur, facing down a dozen Trollocs at once, his staff whirling this way and that as he defended the boy.

Olver caught sight of the man's face, and his breath caught. "*Noal?*"

Noal clubbed a Trolloc arm, forcing the creature back, then glanced at Olver and smiled. Though Noal still appeared aged, the *weariness* was gone from his eyes, as if a great burden had been lifted from him. A white horse stood nearby, with a golden saddle and reins, the most magnificent animal that Olver had ever seen.

"Noal, they said you died!" Olver cried.

"I did," Noal said, then laughed. "The Pattern was not finished with me, son. Sound that Horn! Sound it proudly, Hornsounder!"

Olver did so, blowing the Horn as Noal fought the Trollocs back in a small circle around Olver. Noal. *Noal* was one of the heroes of the Horn! The hooves of galloping horses announced others, come to rescue Olver from the Shadowspawn.

Suddenly, Olver felt a deep warmth. He had lost so many people, but one of them . . . one . . . had come back for him.

CHAPTER
40

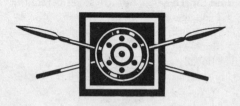

Wolfbrother

E layne's captors looked at Birgitte, stunned, and Elayne took the moment to jerk her body sideways. She rolled to her knees; her pregnancy made her awkward, but she was hardly incapable. The medallion that Mellar had been holding against her slipped to the ground, and she found the glow of *saidar* awaiting her grasp. She filled herself with the Power, and held her belly.

Her children stirred within. Elayne wove flows of Air, knocking her captors backward. Nearby, Elayne's Guards, having rallied, burst through Mellar's soldiers. A few stopped when they saw Birgitte.

"Keep fighting, you daughters and sons of goats!" Birgitte yelled, loosing arrows at the mercenaries. "I might be dead, but I'm still your bloody commander, and you *will* obey orders!"

That spurred them into motion. The rising mist curled upward, fogging the battlefield. It seemed to glow faintly in the darkness. In moments, Elayne's channeling, Birgitte's bow, and her Guards' work sent the remnants of Mellar's Darkfriend mercenaries running.

Birgitte dropped six of them with arrows as they fled.

"Birgitte," Elayne said through tears. "I'm sorry."

"Sorry?" Birgitte turned to her. "Sorry? Why do you mourn, Elayne? I have it all back! My memory has returned." She laughed. "It is wonderful! I don't know how you stood me these last few weeks. I moped worse than a child who'd just broken her favorite bow."

"I . . . Oh, Light." Elayne's insides told her she'd still lost her Warder, and the pain of the bond breaking was not a rational thing. It didn't matter that Birgitte stood before her. "Perhaps I should bond you again?"

"It would not work," Birgitte said, waving her hand with a dismissive gesture. "Are you hurt?"

"Nothing but my pride."

"Lucky for you, but luckier that the Horn was blown when it was."

Elayne nodded.

"I'm going to join the other heroes," Birgitte said. "You stay here and recover."

"Light burn *that*!" Elayne said, forcing herself to her feet. "I'm not bloody staying behind now. The babes are all right. I'm riding."

"Elayne—"

"My soldiers think I'm dead," Elayne said. "Our lines are breaking, our men dying. They have to see me to know that there is still hope. They won't know what this mist means. If they have ever needed their queen, this is the moment. Nothing short of the Dark One could stop me from returning now."

Birgitte frowned.

"You're not my Warder any longer," Elayne said. "But you're still my friend. Will you ride with me?"

"Stubborn fool."

"I'm not the one who just refused to stay dead. Together?"

"Together," Birgitte said, nodding.

Aviendha pulled up short, listening to new howls. Those didn't sound quite like wolves.

The tempest at Shayol Ghul continued. She didn't know which side was winning. Everywhere lay bodies, some ripped apart by wolves, others still smoldering from attacks of the One Power.

The storm winds whipped and raged, though no rain fell, and waves of dust and gravel washed across her.

She could feel channeling from the Pit of Doom, but it was like a quiet pulse, as opposed to the storm that had been the cleansing. Rand. Was he all right? What was happening?

The white clouds brought in by the Windfinders churned among the jet black storm clouds above, swirling together in a massive, writhing pattern above the mountain peak. From what she'd heard of the Windfinders—they had withdrawn up Shayol Ghul to a ledge far above the cave entrance, still working the Bowl of Winds—they were at a breaking point. More than two thirds of their numbers had collapsed from exhaustion. Soon, the storm would consume everything.

Aviendha prowled through the maelstrom, seeking the source of those howls. She didn't have any other channelers with whom to link, now that Rafela had left to join the Dragonsworn's last stand at the cavern. Out here, in the valley, different groups killed one another, shifting back and forth. Maidens, Wise Ones, *siswai'aman*, Trollocs, Fades. And wolves; hundreds of them had joined the battle so far. There were also some Domani, Tairens and Dragonsworn— though most of those fought near the path up to Rand.

Something hit the ground beside her, crooning, and she lashed out before thinking. The Draghkar burst into flames like a stick dried by a hundred days of sunlight. She took a deep breath, looking around her. *Howls.* Hundreds upon hundreds of them.

She broke into a run toward those howls, crossing the valley floor. As she did so, someone emerged from the dusty shadows, a wiry man with a gray beard and golden eyes. He was accompanied by a small pack of wolves. They glanced at her, then turned back in the direction they'd been going.

Aviendha stopped. Golden eyes.

"Ho, he who runs with wolves!" she called at the man. "Have you brought Perrin Aybara with you?"

The man froze. He acted like a wolf, careful yet dangerous. "I know of Perrin Aybara," he called back, "but he is not with me. He hunts in another place."

Aviendha walked closer to the man. He watched her, wary, and several of his wolves growled. It did not seem they trusted her or her kind much more than they trusted Trollocs.

"These new howls," she called over the wind, "they are from your . . . friends?"

"No," the man said, eyes growing distant. "No, not any longer. If you know of women who can channel, Aiel, you should bring them now." He moved off toward the sounds, his pack running with him.

Aviendha followed him, keeping her distance from those wolves, but trusting their senses above her own. They reached a small rise in the floor of the valley, one that she'd seen Ituralde use on occasion for overseeing the defense of the pass.

Pouring out of the pass were scores of dark shapes. Black wolves, the size of small horses. They loped across the rock, and though they were out of her sight, Aviendha knew they were leaving footprints melted into the stone.

Hundreds of wolves attacked the darker shapes, leaping on their backs, but were thrown free. They didn't seem to be doing much good.

The man with the wolves growled.

"Darkhounds?" Aviendha shouted.

"Yes," he called back, bellowing to be heard over the tempest. "This is the Wild Hunt, the worst of their kind. These cannot fall to mortal weapons. The bites of common wolves will not harm them, not permanently."

"Then why do they fight?"

The wolfbrother laughed. "Why do any of us fight? Because we must try to win somehow! Go! Bring Aes Sedai, some of those Asha'man if you can find them! These creatures will roll over your armies as easily as a wave over pebbles!"

The man took off down the slope, his wolves joining him. She understood why they fought. They might not be able to kill the Darkhounds, but they could slow the creatures. And that was their victory here—buying Rand enough time to do what he needed to.

She turned, alarmed, running to gather the others. The sensation of a powerful channeler wielding *saidar* nearby stopped her dead. She spun, looking toward the source of the sensation.

Graendal was *there*, up ahead—just barely visible. She calmly sent deadly weaves at a line of Defenders of the Stone. She had collected a small group of women—Aes Sedai, Wise Ones—and a few guards. The women knelt around her, and had to be feeding her their power, considering the strength of the weaves she unleashed.

Her guards were four Aiel men with black veils, not red. Under Compulsion for certain. Aviendha hesitated, wavering. What of the Darkhounds?

I have to take this chance, she thought. She wove, releasing a ray of blue light into the sky—the sign she, Amys and Cadsuane had agreed upon.

That, of course, alerted Graendal. The Forsaken spun on Aviendha and lashed out with Fire. Aviendha dodged, rolling. A shield came next, trying to cut Aviendha off from the Source. She desperately pulled in as much of the One Power as she could hold, drawing it through the turtle brooch. Cutting a woman off with a shield was like trying to snip a rope with shears—the thicker the rope, the more difficult it was to cut. In this case, Aviendha had taken in enough *saidar* to rebuff the shield.

She gritted her teeth, spinning weaves of her own. Light, she hadn't realized how tired she was. She almost slipped, the threads of the One Power threatening to drift from her control.

She drove them into place by force of will and released a weave of Air and Fire, although she knew that those captives included friends and allies.

They would rather die than be used by the Shaidw, she told herself as she dodged another attack. The ground exploded around her, and she dove to the ground.

No. Keep moving.

Aviendha leaped to her feet and ran. That saved her life as lightning began to rain down behind her, its might sprawling her to the ground again.

She came up bleeding from several cuts on her arm, and started making weaves. She had to drop them as a complex weave came near her. Compulsion. If that seized her, Aviendha would become another of the woman's thralls, forced to lend her strength to overthrowing the Light.

Aviendha wove Earth into the ground in front of herself, throwing up chips of rock, dust, smoke. Then she rolled away, seeking a hollow in the ground, peeking out carefully. She held her breath, and did not channel.

The whipping winds cleared the diversion she'd created. Graendal hesitated in the middle of the field. She could not sense Aviendha, who had earlier placed upon herself the weave that masked her ability. If she channeled, Graendal would know, but if she did not she would be safe.

Graendal's Aiel thralls stalked outward, their veils up, searching for Aviendha. Aviendha was tempted to channel right then and there, to end their lives. Any Aiel she knew would thank her for that.

She stayed her hand; she didn't want to give herself away. Graendal was too strong. She could not face the woman alone. But if she waited . . .

A weave of Air and Spirit attacked Graendal, trying to cut her off from the Source. The woman cursed, spinning. Cadsuane and Amys had arrived.

"Stand! Stand for Andor and the Queen!"

Elayne galloped through groups of pikemen, now in disarray, her hair streaming behind her, shouting with a Power-aided voice. She held aloft a sword, though the Light only knew what she would do with it if she had to swing it.

Men turned as she passed. Some were cut down by Trollocs as they did so. The beasts were pushing through the defenses, reveling in the broken lines and the slaughter.

My men are too far gone, Elayne thought. *Oh, Light. My poor soldiers.* The tale she saw was one of death and despair. The Andoran and Cairhienin pike formations had folded after taking horrible casualties; now men held in little bunches, many scattering, scrambling for their lives. "Stand!" Elayne cried. "Stand with your queen!"

More men stopped running, but they didn't go back to the fighting. What to do?

Fight.

Elayne attacked a Trolloc. She used the sword, despite just moments ago thinking that she'd be hopeless with it. She was. The boar-headed Trolloc actually looked surprised as she flailed at it.

Fortunately, Birgitte was there, and shot the beast in the

forearm as it swung for Elayne. That saved her life, but still didn't let her kill the blasted thing. Her mount—borrowed from one of her Guardsmen—danced around, keeping the Trolloc from cutting her down, as she tried to stab it. Her sword didn't move in the direction she willed. The One Power was far more refined a weapon. She would use that if she had to, but she would rather fight for the moment.

She didn't have to struggle long. Soldiers surrounded her, dispatching the beast and defending her from four others that had begun advancing on her. Elayne wiped her brow and pulled back.

"What was *that*?" Birgitte asked, riding up beside her, then loosing an arrow at a Trolloc before it could kill one of the soldiers. "Ratliff's nails, Elayne! I thought I'd seen the extent of your foolishness."

Elayne held up her sword. Nearby, men began to cry out. "The Queen lives!" they yelled. "For Light and Andor! Stand with the Queen!"

"How would you feel," Elayne said softly, "if you saw your queen trying to kill a Trolloc with a sword as you ran away?"

"I'd feel like I needed to bloody move to another country," Birgitte snapped, loosing another arrow, "one where the monarchs don't have pudding for brains."

Elayne sniffed. Birgitte could say what she wished, but the maneuver worked. Like a bit of yeast, the force of men she'd gathered grew, expanding to either side of her and building a battle line. She kept the sword raised high, shouting, and—after a moment of indecision—created a weave that made a majestic banner of Andor float in the air above her, the red lion to light the night.

That would draw direct fire from Demandred and his channelers, but the men needed the beacon. She would fight off attacks as they came.

They did not, as she rode down the battle lines, shouting words that gave hope to her men. "For Light and Andor! Your Queen lives! Stand and fight!"

Mat thundered forward across the top of the Heights with the remains of a once-great army, pushing southwest. The Trollocs were massed ahead on his left side, the Sharan army ahead on the right. Facing the enemy were the heroes, Borderlanders, Karede and his men, Ogier, Two Rivers archers, Whitecloaks, Ghealdanin and Mayeners, mercenaries, Tinna and her Dragonsworn refugees. And the Band of the Red Hand. His own men.

He remembered, within those memories that were not his, leading forces far grander. Armies that were not fragmented, half-trained, wounded and exhausted. But Light help him, he had never been so proud. Despite all that had happened, his men took up the shouts of attack and threw themselves into the battle with renewed vigor.

Demandred's death gave Mat a chance. He felt the armies surging, and through them flowed that instinctive rhythm of the battle. This was the moment he had been seeking. It was the card upon which to bet everything he had. Ten to one odds, still, but the Sharan army, the Trollocs and Fades had no head. No general to guide them. Different contingents took conflicting actions as various Fades or Dreadlords tried to give orders.

I'll have to watch those Sharans, Mat thought. *They'll have generals who can reinstitute command.*

For now, he needed to hit hard, hit powerfully. Push the Trollocs and Sharans off the Heights. Down below, the Trollocs filled the corridor between the bogs and the Heights, pressing hard the defenders at the riverbed. Elayne's death had been a lie. Her troops had been in disarray—they had lost more than a third of their soldiers—but just as they were about to be routed by the Trollocs, she rode into their midst and rallied them. Now they were miraculously holding their lines, despite being pushed back well into Shienaran territory. They could not resist much longer, though, with or without Elayne: more and more pikes on the front lines were being mobbed, soldiers were falling all across the field, and her cavalries and the Aiel were working furiously, with increasing difficulty, to contain the enemy. *Light, if I can push the Shadow off these bloody Heights into those beasts below, they'll fall all over each other!*

"Lord Cauthon!" Tinna shouted nearby. She leveled a bloody spear from horseback, pointing to the south.

Light shone distantly, toward the River Erinin. Mat wiped his brow. Was that . . .

Gateways in the sky. Dozens of them, and through them poured *to'raken* in flight, carrying lanterns. A fiery flight of arrows launched at the Trollocs in the corridor; the *to'raken*, carrying archers, flew in formation over the ford and the corridor beyond.

Over the battle, Mat heard sounds that must have made the enemy's blood run cold: hundreds, maybe thousands of animal horns blared out in the night their call to war; a thunderstorm of drums began to beat out a unified cadence that became louder and louder; and a rumble of footfalls made by an advancing army, man and animal alike, slowly approaching Polov Heights in the dark. No one could see them in the pre-dawn blackness, but everyone on the battlefield knew who they were.

Mat let out a whoop of joy. He could see the Seanchan movements playing out in his mind's eye now. Half their army would march directly north from the Erinin, joining with Elayne's harried army at the Mora to crush the Trollocs trying to force their way into Shienar. The other half would swing to the west around the bogs to the western side of the Heights, crushing the Trollocs in the corridor from behind.

Now the falling hail of arrows was accompanied by glowing lights popping into existence in the air—*damane*, making more light for their army to see by—a display that would have done the Illuminators proud! Indeed, the ground shook as the massive Seanchan army marched across the Field of Merrilor.

Thunder shattered the air off Mat's right flank on the Heights— a deeper thunder. Talmanes and Aludra had mended the dragons and were firing directly from the cavern through gateways into the Sharan army.

The pieces were almost all in place. There was one more bit of business that needed tending to before the final toss of the dice.

Mat's armies pressed forward.

Jur Grady fingered the letter from his wife, sent with Androl from the Black Tower. He couldn't read it in this darkness, but that didn't matter, so long as he could hold it. He'd memorized the words anyway.

He watched this canyon ten or so miles to the northeast along the River Mora, where Cauthon had positioned him. He was well out of sight of the battlefield at Merrilor.

He didn't fight. Light, it was hard, but he didn't fight. He watched, trying not to think of the poor people who had died trying to hold the river here. It was the perfect place for it—the Mora passed through a canyon here, where the Shadow could stop the river. And it had. Oh, the men Mat had sent had *tried* to fight the Dreadlords and the Sharans. What a fool's task that had been! Grady's anger smoldered at Cauthon. Everyone claimed that he was a good general. Then he went and did this.

Well, if he was a genius, why had he had sent five hundred simple folk from a mountain village in Murandy to hold this river? Yes, Cauthon had also sent about a hundred soldiers from the Band, but that wasn't nearly enough. They'd died after holding the river for a few hours. There were hundreds upon hundreds of Trollocs and several Dreadlords at the river canyon!

Well, those folk had been slaughtered, to a man. Light! There had been *children* in that group. The townsfolk and the few soldiers had fought well, defending the canyon for far longer than Grady would have thought possible, but then they'd fallen. And he'd been ordered not to help them.

Well, now Grady waited in the darkness atop the canyon walls, hiding among a cluster of rocks. Distant from him, perhaps a hundred paces, Trollocs moved by torchlight—the Dreadlords needed that to see. They, too, were atop the canyon walls, which gave them the height and position to look down on the river below—which had become a lake. The three Dreadlords had broken up large chunks of the canyon walls and created the barrier of rock that dammed the river.

That had dried out the Mora at Merrilor and let the Trollocs cross the river with ease. Grady could open that dam in a moment—a strike with the One Power would open it up and release the water from the canyon. So far, he hadn't dared. Cauthon had ordered him not to attack, but beyond that, he'd never be able to defeat three strong Dreadlords on his own. They'd kill him and dam the river again.

He caressed his wife's letter, then prepared himself. Cauthon had ordered him to make a gateway at dawn to that same village. Doing so would reveal Grady. He didn't know the purpose of the order.

The basin below was filled with water, covering the bodies of the fallen.

I guess now will do as well as any time, Grady thought, taking a deep breath. Dawn should be almost here, though the cloud cover kept the land dark.

He'd follow his orders. Light burn him, but he would. But if Cauthon survived the battle downriver, he and Grady would have words. Stern ones. A man like Cauthon, born of ordinary folk, should have known better than to throw away lives.

He took another deep breath, then began to weave a gateway. He opened it at that village the people had come from yesterday. He didn't know why he was to do this; the village had been depopulated to make up the group that had fought earlier. He doubted anybody remained. What had Mat called it? Hinderstap?

People roared through the gateway, yelling, holding aloft cleavers, pitchforks, rusty swords. With them came more soldiers of the Band, like the hundred who had fought here before. Except . . .

Except by the light of the Dreadlords' fires, the faces of those soldiers were the *same* as the ones who had fought here before . . . fought here and died.

Grady gaped as he stood up in the darkness, watching those people attack. They were *all* the same. The same matrons, the same farriers and blacksmiths, the very same people. He'd watched them die, and now they were back again.

The Trollocs probably couldn't tell one human from another, but the Dreadlords saw it—and understood that these were the same people. Those three Dreadlords seemed stunned. One of the Dreadlords yelled out about the Dark Lord abandoning them. He started flinging weaves at the people.

Those people just charged on, heedless of the danger as many of their number were blown apart. They fell on the Dreadlords, hacking at them with farming implements and kitchen knives. By the time the Trollocs attacked, the Dreadlords were down. Now he could . . .

Shaking off his stupor, Grady gathered his power and destroyed the dam blocking the canyon.

And in doing so, he released the river.

CHAPTER
41

A Smile

"Cauthon has the dragons back and fighting again," Jonneth said, trying to peer through the smoke. "Listen to them!" Pounding echoed across the top of the Heights. Pevara smiled. She, Androl, Jonneth, Emarin and Canler had joined Logain and the other Asha'man, along with some of the Aes Sedai who were bonded to them. They stood at the edge of the steep slopes opposite Dashar Knob, a half mile up from where Demandred's headless corpse lay.

Another round of dragonfire sounded across the Heights, though in the darkness, they couldn't see the smoke. "Those dragons won't last long, not if Taim's men have mixed in with the Sharans," Pevara said. "The dragoners can't defend themselves against channelers, and they're too easy to locate because of the noise."

"I doubt Cauthon has a choice but to use them," Androl said. "He can't hold anything back now."

"Asha'man!" Logain appeared through the smoke, striding among them, Gabrelle at his side. "It is time to move."

"We're going to go defend those dragons?" Androl asked. Around them, dozens of other exhausted Asha'man hauled themselves to their feet, turning to Logain.

"No," Logain said. "We're going to move west."

"To the west?" Pevara folded her arms. "That's *away* from the battle!"

"It is where your Amyrlin fought Taim," Logain said, turning away from her. "The ground there, as well as many of the Sharans, was entombed in crystal. I want every Asha'man, soldier and Dedicated to whom I have not given other specific orders to begin searching. There is—"

The ground shook, rumbling ominously, and Pevara stumbled. Androl caught her by the arm, though she sensed exhaustion through the bond to match her own. They didn't have much left in them.

As the trembling subsided, Logain continued. "Somewhere, inside that mass of crystals, is a golden scepter. Taim was said to have been holding it when Egwene al'Vere defeated him. We're going to find it. If any of you see it, do *not* touch it. Send for me."

Logain shouted the same orders to the next group of Asha'man. Androl watched him go, and Pevara sensed his frustration.

"If that scepter is an *angreal* or *sa'angreal*," Emarin said, "it could be of great use to us."

"Maybe," Pevara said. "I think those dragons need protecting more than we need that rod. I *swear* there's something about that horn sounding. We should be attacking now, not searching for battle spoils ..."

"The other Asha'man can do that," Androl said. "We don't have to."

"What?" Canler said, scowling. "You're going to disobey?"

"No," Androl said. "He said this is for men who didn't have any other orders. We do. Back at the start of the battle he told us to watch for Taim's lackeys and to do something about them."

"I'm not sure he remembers that order, Androl," Emarin said, rubbing his chin. "And I don't know that if he did remember, he'd want us to follow it now. He seems pretty intent on that scepter."

"He gave us the order nonetheless," Androl said.

"Androl," Canler said, sitting on his heels, "I feel so tired, I could hardly gather the strength to curse you if I wanted. None of these lads look any better, and you struggle to open a small gateway. How are we going to stand up to Mishraile and the others?"

Androl frowned, but had no argument in return. However, something occurred to Pevara. A way, perhaps, to accomplish something while exhausted . . .

Androl perked up, and his eyes widened, and then he grinned. "You're a genius, Pevara."

"Thank you," she said primly. "Canler, haul yourself to your feet. I'll bet you gentlemen anything that we'll find Taim's men trying to destroy those dragons. We're going to give them something of a surprise . . . "

What a mess this had become.

Moghedien kicked Demandred's corpse. It had been abandoned, the Sharans having gone to fight Cauthon's army and avenge their leader.

Demandred. The fool had let himself become distracted. If you focused too much on personal grudges, or if you let yourself be entangled with the worms you worked with . . . well, Demandred had earned his reward. Death, and likely eternal punishment at the Great Lord's hands.

Now that Demandred was indeed dead, she reached for the One Power—and found something else. A glowing river ten times as powerful, ten times as sweet. With so many of the Chosen having fallen, the Great Lord had opened himself to her. Survival was truly the best way to prove oneself to him.

This changed her plans dramatically. First, she burned Demandred's corpse to powder. Then she quickly wove the Mask of Mirrors—oh, how sweet the True Power was!—and replaced her form with an image of Demandred's. She always made certain she could imitate the other Chosen. Demandred would be difficult, as he had changed so much recently, but she had paid close attention. No one touching her would be fooled; she would be careful.

Disguise in place, she Traveled to the back lines of the Sharan army fighting Cauthon's troops. Here were the reserve units, waiting to move forward, as well as supply carts and some of the wounded.

The Sharans stopped sorting supplies to look at her. Gaping. They had been preparing to flee the battlefield itself. They were aware, as was everyone, that the huge Seanchan army had joined in the fight. She noticed that there were a handful of Ayyad in this group—only three, she could see. Two women with tattoos, and a grimy male channeler who squatted at their feet. Most of the others had been killed in the conflict with the Aes Sedai.

The Seanchan. Thinking of them and that imperious leader of theirs made Moghedien writhe. When the Great Lord discovered the mess she'd made . . .

No. He had given her the True Power. Moghedien had outlasted the others, and only that mattered, for now. He could not see everywhere, and probably did not yet know that she'd been uncovered. How had that girl seen through her disguise? It shouldn't have been possible.

Someone must have betrayed her. Still, she had been working closely with Demandred during this battle, and though she had never been as good a tactician as he—none of the Chosen had been, except maybe Sammael—she understood the battle well enough to take charge. She hated to do it, as it left her exposed in a way she disliked. But desperate times made for desperate actions.

And actually, as she considered, she thought that events were going fairly well for her. Demandred down, defeated by his own pride. M'Hael, that upstart, was also dead—and had conveniently removed the leader of the Aes Sedai from the battlefield. She still had the bulk of Demandred's Shadowspawn and some Dreadlords, some of the Black Ajah and a dozen of the Turned men M'Hael had brought.

"This is not him!" said an older man wearing the robes of a Sharan monk. He pointed at Moghedien. "This is not our Wyld! It is—"

Moghedien burned the man to nothingness.

As his bones fell in a heap, she remembered off-handedly from her eyes-and-ears that Demandred had shown that old man fondness. "Better you should die, old one," she said to the corpse, speaking as Demandred, "than live to denounce the one you should have loved. Does anyone else wish to deny me?"

The Sharans remained silent.

"Ayyad," Moghedien said to the three, "did you see me craft weaves?"

Both women and the grimy man shook their heads.

"I kill without weaves," Moghedien said, "only I, your Wyld, could have done this."

She had to remember not to smile, even in victory, as the people bowed their heads. Demandred was always solemn. As the people fell to their knees, Moghedien had to hold in her joy by force. Yes, Demandred had done good work here, and had handed her the army of an entire nation to play with. This would go quite well indeed!

"Dragonslayer," said a kneeling Ayyad woman. She was weeping! How weak these Sharans were. "We saw that you had fallen . . ."

"How could I fall? You have prophecies, do you not?"

The women looked at one another. "They say you will fight, Dragonslayer," the woman said. "But . . ."

"Gather five fists of the Trollocs from the back lines," Moghedien said, turning to the commander of the reserve unit, "and send them upriver to the ruins."

"The ruins?" the man asked. "Only the Caemlyn refugees are in that direction."

"Exactly, you fool. Refugees—children, the elderly, women who search for the dead. They can't fight back. Tell the Trollocs to start slaughtering. Our enemies are weak; an attack like this will force them to break off and protect the ones that true warriors would just let die."

The general nodded, and she saw approval in his face. He accepted her as Demandred. Good. He ran off to give the order.

"Now," Moghedien said as the dragons fired in the distance, "why haven't any of our Ayyad gone to remove those weapons from the battle?"

The Ayyad kneeling before Moghedien bowed her head. "We have fewer than a dozen Ayyad left, Wyld."

"Your excuses are weak," Moghedien said, listening as the explosions stopped. Perhaps some of M'Hael's remaining Dreadlords had just resolved the problem of the dragons.

She felt her skin itch as the Sharan commander strode toward a Myrddraal across the field. She *hated* being in the open like this. She was meant to remain in shadows, letting others lead battles. However, she would never have it said that when the situation demanded it, she was too frightened to go and—

A gateway split open behind her, and several of the Sharans yelled out. Moghedien spun, opening her eyes wide as she looked into what appeared to be a dark cavern. Dragons pointed out of it.

"Fire!" a voice yelled.

"Close the gateway!" Talmanes shouted, and the portal winked shut.

"This was one of Lord Mat's ideas, wasn't it?" Daerid yelled, standing beside Talmanes as the dragons were reloaded. They both had wax in their ears.

"What do you think?" Talmanes yelled back.

If the dragons were vulnerable when firing, what did you do? You fired them from a hidden location.

Talmanes smiled as Neald opened the next gateway in front of ten dragons. The fact that many of the dragon carts were too broken to roll well meant nothing when you could open a gateway in front of them, pointing them wherever you wanted.

This gateway opened up on several fists of Trollocs engaged in fierce combat against Whitecloaks. Some of the Shadowspawn turned horrified eyes toward the dragons.

"Fire!" Talmanes shouted, waving his hand down to give a visual cue, in case any of the men couldn't hear him.

Smoke filled the cavern, explosions echoing against Talmanes' earplugs, as the dragons recoiled, releasing a storm of death into the Trollocs. They broadsided the fists, sweeping them out of the way, leaving them broken and dying. The nearby Whitecloaks cheered and raised swords.

Neald shut the gateway, and the dragoners reloaded their weapons. Neald then made a gateway above them, facing downward, to vent the dragon smoke out of the cavern complex and away into empty air somewhere distant.

"Are you *smiling*?" Daerid asked.

"Yes," Talmanes said, satisfied.

"Blood and bloody ashes, Lord Talmanes . . . that expression is horrifying on you." Daerid hesitated. "You should probably do that more often."

Talmanes grinned as Neald opened the next gateway to a

point on Dashar Knob where Aludra stood with spyglass and scouts, deciding on the next place to target. She yelled through a position, Neald nodded, and they set up the next shot.

CHAPTER
42

Impossibilities

Aviendha felt as if the world itself were cracking, breaking apart, being *consumed*.

The lightning that fell on the valley of Shayol Ghul was no longer under control. Not by the Windfinders, not by anyone. It slew Shadowspawn and defender alike. Unpredictable. The air smelled of fire, burned flesh and something else—a distinctive, clean odor she had come to recognize as the scent of a lightning strike.

Aviendha moved like the twisting wind itself, trying to stay ahead of Graendal, who hurled bar after bar of white-hot balefire at her. With each shot, the ground *trembled*. Black lines spread all across the rocks.

The defenders of the valley had nearly fallen. Those people who had not retreated to the very back, near the path up the mountain, were being destroyed by Darkhounds. The ground shook, and Aviendha stumbled. Nearby, a group of Trollocs broke from the windy shadows, snarling. The creatures did not see her, but turned and attacked something else . . . Other Trollocs? They were fighting each other.

She wasn't surprised. It was not unusual for Trollocs to fight one another if not closely controlled by the Eyeless. But what was that odd mist?

Aviendha heaved herself to her feet and ran away from the Trollocs, moving up a nearby incline. Maybe from that vantage, she could pinpoint Graendal's location. At the top, she found that she was standing on an impossibility: an enormous chunk of rock that was floating precariously with very little underneath it. It had ripped from the ground and risen here.

All around the valley were similar impossibilities. A group of fleeing Domani horsemen galloped over a section of rock that rippled like water, and all four men and mounts sank into it, vanishing. That deep mist had started to enter the valley on one side. Men and Trollocs alike ran from it, screaming.

A liquid bar of balefire broke through the floating chunk of rock, passing just inches from her head. Aviendha gasped, falling flat against the ground. She heard a scrambling nearby, and she rolled over, preparing a weave.

Amys—her Wise One's clothing blackened and burned, the side of her face reddened—hurried up to Aviendha and huddled down beside her. "Have you seen Cadsuane or the others?"

"No."

Amys cursed softly. "We all need to attack the Shadowsouled at once. You go round the right; I will go left. When you sense me weaving, join in. Together, perhaps we can fell her."

Aviendha nodded. They rose and parted. Somewhere, fighting here, was Cadsuane's handpicked team. Talaan, a Windfinder who had somehow made her way to the Dragonsworn. Alivia, the former *damane*. They, with Amys and Aviendha, were some of the most powerful channelers the Light had.

The origin of the balefire was at least some indication of where Graendal was. Aviendha rounded the floating rock—the balefire had punctured it, rather than destroying it completely—growing disturbed as she saw other chunks of stone rising randomly across the valley. It was a bubble of evil, only on a much grander scale. As she crept, she heard a low *thrumming* sound coming from the mountain. The ground began to tremble, chips of stone bouncing about. Aviendha stayed low, only to see that the valley had begun to sprout—incredibly—new plants. The once-barren ground turned vibrantly green, the plants seeming to writhe as they grew tall.

Patches of those plants sprouted all across the valley, violent bursts of greenery. Above, the white and black clouds swirled together, white on black, black on white. Lighting crashed, then *froze* to the ground. The lightning, impossibly, seemed to have become a towering glass column, jagged, in the shape of the bolt that had struck, though it was no longer glowing.

Those clouds above formed a pattern that looked familiar. Black on white, white on black . . .

It's the symbol, she realized with a start. *The ancient symbol of the Aes Sedai.*

Under this sign . . . shall he conquer.

Aviendha held tightly to the One Power. That thrumming sound was him, somehow. The life growing was him. As the Dark One ripped the land apart, Rand stitched it back together.

She *had* to keep moving. She crouched as she ran, using the newly grown plants as cover. They had come right where she needed them to hide her approach. Happenstance? She chose to believe otherwise. She could feel him, in the back of her mind. He fought, a true warrior. His battle lent her strength, and she tried to return the same.

Determination. Honor. Glory. *Fight on, shade of my heart. Fight on.*

She came upon Graendal—still surrounded by minions under Compulsion—exchanging lethal flows of the One Power with Cadsuane and Alivia. Aviendha slowed, watching the three of them lob bursts of fire at one another, slicing at one another's weaves with Spirit, warping the air with heat and tossing weaves so quickly that it was difficult to make out what was happening.

She itched to help, but Amys was right. If she and Aviendha attacked together, particularly while Graendal was occupied, they had a better chance of killing the Forsaken. Assuming Cadsuane and Alivia could hold out, waiting was the better choice.

Could they hold out, though? Cadsuane was powerful, more powerful than Aviendha had thought. Those hair ornaments of hers included *angreal* and *ter'angreal* for certain, though Aviendha hadn't been able to handle them and tell for certain, using her Talent.

Graendal's women captives lay against the ground, obviously flagging. Two had collapsed; Sarene had fallen to her knees, and stared ahead with vacant eyes.

Cadsuane and Alivia didn't seem to mind if they hit the captives. That was the right choice. Still, could Aviendha somehow—

The tall brush beside her moved.

Aviendha spun without thought and wove Fire. She burned down a black-veiled attacker mere moments before his spear would have stabbed her in the neck. The weapon sliced the side of her shoulder as the man stumbled, then toppled forward, her strike having burned a hole in his chest as large as a fist.

Another channeler joined the melee, frantically sending out weaves. Amys had arrived. Fortunately, Graendal focused on her, rather than attacking Aviendha's just-revealed location.

That was good, for Aviendha was staring at the man she'd felled, a man Graendal had made to do her bidding through Compulsion. A man who looked familiar to Aviendha.

Horrified, trembling, she reached down and pulled aside the veil.

It was Rhuarc.

"I'm leaving," Mishraile said with a scowl, looking at the backs of the charging Sharan cavalry. They were standing on the western side of the Heights, far off the left flank of the Sharan army. "Nobody told us we'd be fighting the bloody heroes of the Horn."

"It is the Last Battle, child." Alviarin sounded snide. She had taken to calling all of them "child" lately. Mishraile was about ready to strangle her. Why had M'Hael allowed her to bond Nensen? Why would a *woman* be put in command of them?

They stood in a small group, Alviarin, Mishraile, Nensen, Kash, Rianna, Donalo, and Ayako—who had been Turned as he had. Mishraile didn't know a lot about battlefield fighting; when he killed people, he liked to wait for them to stumble someplace dark, where nobody was watching. All of this open air battle, all of this chaos, made him feel as if a knife tip were pressed against his back.

"There," Alviarin said to Nensen, pointing toward a flash of light as another explosion from those dragons sounded through gateways across the battlefield. "I think that came from the middle of the plateau. Make a gateway and go there."

"We're never going to—" Mishraile began.

"Go!" Alviarin said, face red with anger.

Nensen scrambled and did as she said. He liked following orders, feeling that someone was in charge.

I might have to kill her, Mishraile thought. *And Nensen as well.* Even without much experience of battle, Mishraile could see that this was not going to be an easy fight. The return of the Seanchan, the fall of Demandred and the Trollocs rampaging without any direction . . . Yes, the Shadow still had the numbers, but the fight wasn't nearly as one-sided as he'd have liked. One of the first rules he'd learned in life was to never fight a man when you had an equal chance of losing.

The six of them piled through the gateway, coming out in the middle of the plateau. The ground burnt by dragons and channelers emitted smoke to mix with the strange fog that had arisen; it was hard to tell what was going on where. Holes in the ground, splayed open by the dragons. Corpses . . . well, pieces of them . . . scattered about. An unusual scent in the air. It was after sunrise now, but barely any light came through the clouds.

Cries came from above, made by those strange flying creatures the Seanchan had brought. Mishraile shivered. Light. It was like standing in a house without a roof, knowing your enemy had archers positioned above you. He shot one of them down with a weave of Fire, satisfied with the way the wings crumpled and the beast spun about, swirling as it dropped.

Attacking like that exposed him, though. He really would have to kill the other Dreadlords, then escape. He was supposed to be on the *winning* side!

"To work," Alviarin said. "Do as I said. There are men making the gateways the devices fire through, so we will have to locate where the gateway was and have Donalo read the residue."

The men moved out, inspecting the ground, trying to find the place where the gateway had opened. People fought nearby, uncomfortably close—Sharans and men flying a banner with a wolf on it. If they came back this way . . .

Donalo fell in beside Mishraile as they searched, quickly, both holding to the Power. Donalo was a square-faced Tairen, with his graying beard in a point.

"When Demandred went down," Donalo whispered. "I figured this was a trap all along. We've been had."

Mishraile nodded. Perhaps Donalo would be an ally. They could escape together. Of course, then he'd have to kill Donalo. Mishraile wouldn't want any witnesses who could report back to the Great Lord what he had done.

He couldn't trust Donalo anyway. The man had joined them only because of that forced trick with the Myrddraal. If a man could change sides that quickly, what was to keep him from changing again? Besides, Mishraile didn't like the . . . feeling he got when looking at Donalo or the others who had been Turned. It was as if there was something unnatural deep within them, looking out at the world, seeking prey.

"We need to get out of here," Mishraile whispered. "Fighting here now is a fool's——" He cut off as they encountered someone moving through the smoke.

A tall man, with red-gold hair. A familiar man, scored with cuts, his clothing burned and blackened. Mishraile gaped and Donalo cursed as the Dragon Reborn himself saw them, started, then fled back across the plateau. By the time Mishraile thought to attack, al'Thor had crafted a gateway for himself and escaped through it.

The earth rumbled violently, and some chunks of earth actually broke apart, and a piece of the eastern slope went crashing down on to Trollocs below. This place was growing more and more unstable. Another reason to leave.

"That was the bloody Dragon Reborn!" Donalo said. "Alviarin! The bloody *Dragon Reborn* is on the battlefield!"

"What nonsense is this?" Alviarin asked, approaching with the others.

"Rand al'Thor was here," Mishraile said, still stunned. "Blood and bloody ashes, Donalo. You were right! That's the only way Demandred could have fallen."

"He did keep saying that the Dragon was on this battlefield somewhere," Kash noted.

Donalo stepped forward, cocking his head, as if studying something in the air. "I saw exactly where he made the gateway to escape. It was right here. Right here . . . Yes! I can feel the resonance. I know where he went."

"He defeated Demandred," Alviarin said, folding her arms skeptically. "Can we hope to fight him?"

"He looked exhausted," Mishraile said. "More than exhausted.

He panicked when he saw us. I think, if he did fight Demandred, it took a lot out of him."

Alviarin regarded the space in the air where al'Thor had vanished. Mishraile could practically see her thoughts. If they killed the Dragon Reborn, M'Hael might not be the only Dreadlord raised to the Chosen. The Great Lord would be grateful to the one who struck down al'Thor. Very grateful.

"I have it!" Donalo cried, opening a gateway.

"I need a circle to fight him," Alviarin said. Then hesitated. "But I will use Rianna and Nensen only. I don't want to risk us being too inflexible, all in the same circle."

Mishraile snorted, gathering his power and leaping through the opening. What she meant was that she didn't want one of the men leading the circle, potentially stealing the kill from her. Well, Mishraile would see about that.

He stepped from the battlefield to a clearing he did not recognize. The trees here didn't look as deeply under the Great Lord's touch as they did other places. Why was that? Well, the same dark sky thundered above, and the area was so dark that he had to weave a globe of light to make anything out.

Al'Thor rested on a stump nearby. He looked up, saw Mishraile, and cried out, scrambling away. Mishraile wove a fireball that sprouted in the air and flew after him, but al'Thor managed to cut it down with a weave of his own.

Ha! He is *weak!* Mishraile thought, dashing forward. The others followed him through the gateway, the women linked with Nensen, who trailed after Alviarin like a puppy. Donalo came through last, calling for them to wait for him.

A moment later they stopped running.

It hit Mishraile like a wave of cold water—like running face-first into a waterfall. The One Power vanished. It left him, just like that.

He stumbled, panicked, trying to figure out what had happened. He'd been shielded! No. He sensed no shield. He sensed . . . nothing.

The trees moved nearby, figures stepping from the shadows. Lumbering creatures with drooping eyebrows and thick fingers. They seemed as ancient as the trees themselves, with wrinkled skin and white hair.

He was in a *stedding*.

Mishraile tried to run, but firm arms grabbed him. Ogier ancients surrounded him and the others. Ahead, in the forest, al'Thor stepped forward—but it wasn't him. Not any longer. It had been a trick. Androl had been wearing the Dragon Reborn's face.

The others screamed and battered at the Ogier with their fists, but Mishraile fell to his knees, looking into that emptiness where the One Power had been.

Pevara moved next to Androl as the Ogier, those too ancient to join the battle, took the Dreadlords in strong hands and dragged them further into Stedding Sholoon. Lindsar—eldest among them, leaning on a cane as large as a man's thigh—approached Androl.

"We will care for the captives, Master Androl," Lindsar said.

"Execution?" Pevara asked.

"By the eldest trees, no!" The Ogier looked offended. "Not in this place, no, no killing here. We will hold them, and not let them escape."

"These are *very* dangerous people, good Ogier," Androl said. "Do not underestimate how devious they can be."

The Ogier chuckled, limping toward the *stedding*'s still beautiful trees. "Men assume that because we are calm, we cannot be devious ourselves," she said. "Let them see how crafty a mind can become with centuries worth of aging upon it. Do not worry, Master Androl. We will be careful. It will be well for these poor souls to live in the peace of the *stedding*. Perhaps a few decades of peace will change their outlook on the world."

She vanished into the trees.

Androl looked at Pevara, feeling her satisfaction pulse through the bond, though her face was calm. "You did well," he said. "The plan was excellent."

She nodded in satisfaction, and the two of them left the *stedding*—passing the invisible barrier back to the One Power. Though Androl was so tired he could barely think, he didn't have any trouble seizing *saidin*. He snatched it like a starving man taking a hunk of bread, though he'd only been without for a few minutes.

Almost, he felt sorry for what he had done to Donalo and the others. *Rest well here, my friend*, he thought, looking over his shoulder *Perhaps we can find a way to free you someday from the prison they put upon your mind.*

"Well?" Jonneth asked, running up.

"Done," Androl said.

Pevara nodded as they stepped out of the trees to overlook the Mora and the ruins outside the *stedding*. She stopped as they saw the area around the ruins before them, where the refugees from Caemlyn had been gathering the wounded and weapons.

It was now filled with Trollocs.

Slaughtering.

Aviendha knelt over Rhuarc's body.

Dead. She'd killed *Rhuarc*.

It was no longer him, she told herself. *Graendal killed him. Her weave might as well have burned him away. This is just a shell.*

It was just a . . .

It was just a . . .

It was just a . . .

Strength, Aviendha. Rand's determination filled her, radiating from the bond at the back of her mind. She looked up and felt all fatigue leave her, all distractions vanish.

Graendal was dueling with Amys, Talaan, Alivia and Cadsuane—and Graendal was winning. Weaves zipped back and forth, lighting the dusty air, but those coming from Cadsuane and the others were less and less vibrant. More defensive. As Aviendha watched, a storm of lightning fell around Amys, throwing her to the ground. Beside Graendal, Sashalle Anderly shook, then fell to the side; the glow of the One Power no longer surrounded her. Graendal had worn her out, pulling too much Power.

Aviendha stood up. Graendal was powerful and wily. She was *exceptionally* good at slicing weaves from the air as they were formed.

Aviendha held a hand out to her side, and wove Fire, Air, Spirit. A glowing, burning spear of light and fire appeared in her hand. She prepared five other weaves of Spirit, then dashed forward.

The thrumming of the trembling ground accompanied her

footsteps. Crystalline lightning fell from the heavens, then froze in place. Men and beasts howled as the Darkhounds reached the final lines of humans defending the pathway up to Rand.

Graendal saw Aviendha and began to weave balefire. Aviendha slashed the weave from the air with a flow of Spirit. Graendal cursed, weaving again. Aviendha struck, cutting the weave apart.

Cadsuane and Talaan sent bursts of fire. One of the captive Aiel threw himself in front of Graendal, dying with a long cry as the flames engulfed him.

Aviendha ran swiftly, the ground a blur beneath her, clutching a spear of light. She remembered her first race, one of the tests to join the Maidens. On that day, she had felt the wind behind her, urging her on.

This time, she felt no wind. Instead, she heard the cries of the warriors. The Aiel who fought seemed to drive her onward. The sound itself carried her toward Graendal.

The Forsaken made a weave before Aviendha could stop it, a powerful weave of Earth directed beneath Aviendha.

So she leaped.

The ground exploded, rocks flying upward as the blast threw her forward into the air. Stones flayed her legs, carrying ribbons of blood up through the air around her. Her feet were ripped apart, bones cracking, legs burning.

She gripped the spear of fire and light in two hands amid the storm of rock, skirt rippling as it shredded. Graendal looked up, eyes widening, lips parting. She was going to Travel with the True Power. Aviendha knew it. The woman had only avoided it so far because this method of Traveling seemed to require her to touch her companions to take them with her, and she didn't want to leave any.

Aviendha met the Shadowsouled's eyes during that brief moment when she hung in the air, and she saw true terror therein.

The air began to warp.

Aviendha's spear, point first, sank into Graendal's side.

In a moment, both of them vanished.

CHAPTER
43

A Field of Glass

Logain stood in the middle of a field of glass, hands clasped behind his back. The battle raged across the Heights. The Sharans appeared to be falling back from the onslaught of Cauthon's armies, and his scouts had just reported that the Shadow was being hit hard all across the Field of Merrilor.

"I guess they probably won't need you," Gabrelle said to him as his scouts retreated. "So you were right."

The bond sent dissatisfaction and even disappointment. "I need to look to the future of the Black Tower," Logain said.

"You aren't looking to its future," she said, soft, almost threatening. "You're looking to make certain you are a power in these lands, Logain. You cannot hide your emotions from me."

Logain shoved down his anger. He would not be subject to their power again. He would *not*. First the White Tower, then M'Hael and his men.

Days of torture. *Weeks.*

I will be stronger than any other, he thought. That was the only way out, wasn't it? *I will be feared.*

Light. He'd resisted their attempts to corrupt him, turn him to the Shadow ... but he couldn't help wondering if they had broken something else inside of him. Something profound. He leveled his gaze, looking across the field of crystal.

Another rumble came beneath, and some of the crystals shattered. This entire area was going to collapse soon. And with it, the scepter ...

Power.

"I'm warning you, mainlander," a calm voice said nearby. "I have a message to deliver. If I need see your arm broken to deliver it, I will see it done."

That's a Seanchan accent, Logain thought, turning with a frown. A Seanchan woman, accompanied by a large Illianer, was arguing with one of his guards. The woman knew how to make her voice carry without shouting. There was a self-possession to her that Logain found curious.

He walked over, and the Seanchan woman looked up at him. "You have the look of authority about you," she called to him. "You are the one called Logain?"

He nodded.

"The Amyrlin sends you her last words," the Seanchan woman called. "You must deliver the seals up to the White Tower to be broken. The sign is the coming of light! She says it will be known when it arrives."

Logain raised an eyebrow. He nodded to the woman, mostly to put her off, then walked back the other way.

"You don't intend to do it," Gabrelle said. "You fool. Those seals belong to—"

"To me," Logain said.

"Logain," Gabrelle said softly. "I know you have been hurt. But this is not a time for games."

"Why not? Has the White Tower's treatment of me been anything other than a great long game?"

"Logain." She touched him on the arm.

Light *burn* that bond! He wished he'd never forced her to it. Tied to her as he was, he could sense her sincerity. How much easier his life would be if he could continue to regard all Aes Sedai with suspicion.

Sincerity. Would that be his downfall?

"Lord Logain!" Desautel called from nearby. The Asha'man

Dedicated was as big as a blacksmith. "Lord Logain, I think I've found it!"

Logain broke eye contact with Gabrelle, looking toward Desautel. The Asha'man stood beside a large crystal. "It's here," Desautel said, wiping the crystal as Logain approached. "See?"

Logain knelt, weaving a globe of light. Yes ... there, within the crystal. It looked like a hand, made from a slightly different type of crystal, sparkling in his light. That hand held a golden scepter, the top vaguely cup-shaped.

Logain gathered the One Power, smiling broadly. He let *saidin* flow from him into the crystal, using a weave to shatter it as he would a stone.

The ground trembled. The crystal, whatever it was, resisted. The harder he pushed, the more violent the shaking became.

"Logain ... " Gabrelle said.

"Stand back," Logain said. "I think I'll need to try balefire."

Panic surged through the bond. Fortunately, Gabrelle did not try to tell him what was forbidden and what was not. Asha'man need not obey White Tower law.

"Logain!"

Another voice. Would they not leave him alone? He prepared his weave.

"Logain!" Androl was breathing deeply as he arrived. He fell to his knees, face scorched and burned. He looked worse than death itself. "Logain ... the refugees of Caemlyn ... The Shadow has sent Trollocs to kill them at the ruins. Light! They're being murdered."

Logain wove balefire, but held the weave in place, nearly complete as he looked at the crystal and its golden prize.

"Logain ... " Androl said, pained. "The others with me stayed to fight, but they are too tired. I can't find Cauthon, and the soldiers I went to are too busy fighting to help. I don't think any of the commanders know that the Trollocs are up there. Light."

Logain held his weave, feeling the One Power pulse within him. Power. Fear.

"Please," Androl whispered, so soft. "Children, Logain. They're slaughtering the children ... "

Logain closed his eyes.

*

Mat rode with the heroes of the Horn. Apparently, having once been the Hornsounder gave him a special place among them. They joined him, called to him, spoke to him as if they knew him. They looked so, well, heroic, tall in their saddles and surrounded by a mist that glowed against the breaking dawn's light.

Amid the fighting, he finally asked the question that had been haunting him for a long while now. "I'm not bloody . . . one of you, am I?" he asked Hend the Striker. "You know . . . since heroes are born sometimes, then die and . . . do whatever you do."

The big man laughed, riding a bay horse that could have almost gone shoulder-to-shoulder with a Seanchan boar-horse. "I knew that you would ask this thing, Gambler!"

"Well, then you should bloody well have an answer prepared." Mat felt his face flush as he anticipated the reply.

"No, you are not one of us," Hend said. "Be at ease. Though you have done more than enough to earn a place, you have not been chosen. I do not know why."

"Maybe because I don't like the idea of having to hop whenever anyone blows on that bloody instrument."

"Maybe!" Hend grinned and galloped toward a line of Sharan spears.

Mat no longer directed troop movements on the battlefield. The Light willing, he had set things up well enough that direct control would not be needed. He rode across the plateau, fighting, yelling, joining the heroes.

Elayne was back, and she had rallied her troops. Mat saw Elayne's banner glowing above them in the sky, crafted of the One Power, and caught a glimpse of someone who looked like her riding among the soldiers, hair glowing as if lit from behind her. She seemed a bloody hero of the Horn herself.

Mat let out a whoop of joy as he saw the Seanchan army marching north, about to merge with Elayne's army, and he continued riding along the eastern slope of the Heights. Soon after, he slowed, Pips just having trampled a Trolloc. That rushing sound . . . Mat looked down below as the river returned in a swift crash of muddy water. It broke the Trolloc army into two parts, washing away many of them, as it surged back into its bed.

Snow-haired Rogosh watched the water flow, then nodded to

Mat in respect. "Well done, Gambler," he said. The river's return had divided the Shadow's forces.

Mat rejoined the battle. He noticed as he galloped across the plateau that the Sharans—what remained of them—were fleeing through gateways. He let them go.

When the Trollocs atop the Heights saw the Sharans fleeing, their resistance cracked, and they panicked. Boxed in and being swept across the plateau by Mat's combined armies, they had no choice but to flee toward the long slope to the southwest.

It had become total mayhem off the Heights. The Seanchan army had joined with Elayne's, and both groups lit into the Trollocs with an intense fury. They formed a cordon around the beasts and advanced quickly, not allowing one to escape. The ground quickly turned to a deep, red mud as Trollocs fell by the thousands.

But the engagement on the Shienaran side of the Mora was nothing compared to the struggle taking place on the other side of the river. The corridor between the bogs and Polov Heights was choked with Trollocs trying to escape the Seanchan attacking them from the far side of the corridor on the west.

The vanguard sent in first against the Trollocs in the corridor was not composed of Seanchan soldiers, but squads of *lopar* and *morat'lopar*. On their hind legs, the *lopar* were no taller than Trollocs, but they outweighed them considerably. The *lopar* came at the Trollocs, raising up and slashing with their razor-sharp claws. Once a *lopar* softened up its prey, it grasped the Trolloc behind the neck with its paws and bit the beast's head off at the neck. This gave the *lopar* great pleasure.

The *lopar* were withdrawn as the corpses of Trollocs began to stack up at the far end of the corridor. Next into this pit of carnage came flocks of *corlm*, large, wingless, feathered creatures with long curved beaks designed to shred flesh. These carnivores easily ran over the stacks of corpses toward Trollocs still fighting, to separate the beasts' meat from bone. The Seanchan soldiers took little part in these proceedings, only setting their pikes to ensure that no Trollocs escaped through the corridor or off the western side of the Heights. The creatures assaulting them so unnerved the Trollocs that few had any notion of running toward the Seanchan troops.

On the slope, terror-stricken Trollocs, fleeing from Mat's army charging down after them, threw themselves onto the Trollocs that filled the corridor. The monsters tumbled on top of one another, and they fought among themselves, trying to be the ones to reach the top of the pile and continue breathing a while longer.

Talmanes and Aludra had set up their dragons across from the corridor and commenced firing dragons' eggs into the roiling masses of terrorized Trollocs.

It was all over quickly. The numbers of living Trollocs diminished from the many thousands to the hundreds. Those that remained, seeing death snatching at them from three sides, fled into the bogs, where many of them were sucked down into the shallow waters. Their deaths were less violent, but equally horrifying. The remainder received a more merciful end, shot with arrows, spears and crossbow bolts as they slogged through the mire toward the sweet scent of freedom.

Mat lowered his bloodied *ashandarei*. He checked the sky. The sun was hidden up there somewhere; he was not certain how long he had been riding with the heroes.

He would have to thank Tuon for returning. He did not go looking for her, though. He had a feeling that she would expect him to perform his princely duties, whatever they might be.

Only ... he did feel that strange tugging inside. Getting stronger and stronger.

Blood and bloody ashes, Rand, Mat thought. *I've done my part. You do yours.*

Amaresu's words returned to him. *Each breath you take is at his forbearance, Gambler ...*

Mat had been a good friend when Rand needed, had he not? Most of the time? Blood and ashes, you could not expect a fellow to not worry ... maybe stay a little distant ... when a madman was involved. Right?

"Hawkwing!" Mat called, riding up to the man. "The battle," Mat said, drawing a deep breath. "It's done, right?"

"You have sewn this one up tight, Gambler," Hawkwing said, sitting his mount regally. "Ah ... what I would give to go at you across the battlefield. What a grand fight it would be."

"Great. Wonderful. I didn't mean this battlefield. I mean the Last Battle. It's done, right?"

"You ask that under a sky of shadow, atop an earth that trembles in fear? What does your soul say, Gambler?"

Those dice still tumbled inside of Mat's head.

"My soul says I'm a fool," Mat growled. "That, and a *bloody* sparring dummy, set up and waiting to be attacked." He turned northward. "I need to go to Rand. Hawkwing, would you do me a favor?"

"Ask it, Hornblower."

"Do you know the Seanchan?"

"I am . . . familiar with them."

"I think their Empress would like very much to make your acquaintance," Mat said, galloping away. "If you could go to speak with her, I'd appreciate it. And if you do, kindly tell her I sent you."

YOU THINK I WILL RETREAT? the Dark One asked.

The thing that spoke those words was something that Rand could never truly comprehend. Even seeing the universe in its entirety did not allow him to understand Evil itself.

I NEVER EXPECT YOU TO RETREAT, Rand said. I BELIEVE YOU INCAPABLE OF IT. I WISH YOU COULD SEE, COULD KNOW, WHY IT IS YOU CONTINUE TO LOSE.

Beneath them, on the battlefield, the Trollocs had fallen, beaten by a young gambler from the Two Rivers. The Shadow shouldn't have lost. It made no *sense*. The Trollocs had the greater force.

However, Trollocs fought only because the Myrddraal forced them—on its own, a Trolloc would no more fight something stronger than a fox would attempt to kill a lion.

It was one of the most basic rules among predators. Eat that which was weaker than you. Flee from that stronger than you.

The Dark One seethed with a boiling anger that Rand felt in this place as a physical force.

YOU SHOULD NOT BE SURPRISED, Rand said. WHEN HAVE YOU EVER INSPIRED THE BEST IN MEN? YOU

CANNOT. IT IS OUTSIDE YOUR POWER, SHAI'TAN.
YOUR MINIONS WILL NEVER FIGHT ON WHEN HOPE
IS LOST. THEY WILL NEVER STAND BECAUSE DOING SO
IS RIGHT. IT IS NOT STRENGTH THAT BEATS YOU. IT IS
NOBILITY.

I WILL DESTROY! I WILL REND AND BURN! I WILL
BRING DARKNESS TO ALL, AND DEATH WILL BE THE
TRUMPET I SOUND BEFORE MY ARRIVAL! AND YOU,
ADVERSARY . . . OTHERS MAY ESCAPE, BUT YOU WILL
DIE. YOU MUST KNOW THIS.

OH, I DO, SHAI'TAN, Rand said softly. I EMBRACE IT,
FOR DEATH IS—AND ALWAYS HAS BEEN—LIGHTER
THAN A FEATHER. DEATH ARRIVES IN A HEARTBEAT,
NO MORE TANGIBLE THAN A FLICKER OF LIGHT. IT
HAS NO WEIGHT, NO SUBSTANCE . . .

Rand strode forward, speaking louder. DEATH CANNOT
KEEP ME AT BAY, AND IT CANNOT RULE ME. IT COMES
DOWN TO THIS, FATHER OF LIES. WHEN HAVE YOU
INSPIRED A PERSON TO GIVE THEIR LIFE FOR YOU?
NOT FOR THE PROMISES YOU GIVE, NOT FOR THE
RICHES THEY SEEK OR THE POSITIONS THEY WOULD
HOLD, BUT FOR YOU. HAS IT EVER HAPPENED?

The darkness grew still.

BRING MY DEATH, SHAI'TAN, Rand growled, throwing
himself into the blackness. FOR I BRING YOURS!

Aviendha dropped to a rocky ledge far above the floor of
Thakan'dar. She tried to stand, but her ruined feet and legs
couldn't support her weight. She collapsed on the ledge, the spear
of light vanishing from her fingers. Pain climbed up her legs as if
they'd been thrust into a fire.

Graendal stumbled back from her, gasping huge breaths, holding her side. Aviendha immediately wove an attack, flames of fire,
but Graendal cut them down with her own weaves.

"You!" Graendal spat. "You vermin, you detestable child!" The
woman was still strong, though wounded.

Aviendha needed help. Amys, Cadsuane, the others. Desperate,
clinging to the One Power despite her agony, she began weaving

a gateway back to where she had been. It was near enough that she did not need to know the area well.

Graendal let this weave pass. Blood gushed between the woman's fingers. While Aviendha worked, Graendal wove a thin trickle of Air and stanched the wound with it. Then she pointed bloody fingers at Aviendha. "Trying to escape?"

The woman began weaving a shield.

Frantic, her strength waning, Aviendha tied off her weave, leaving the gateway open and in place. *Please, Amys, see it!* she thought as she countered Graendal's shield.

She barely managed to block it; she was very weak. Graendal had been using borrowed power for their entire fight, while Aviendha had been using her own. Even with her *angreal*, in her state she was really no match for Graendal.

Graendal pulled herself upright, pain showing in her face. Aviendha spat at the woman's feet, then pulled herself away, leaving a trail of blood behind her.

Nobody came through the gateway. Had she made it to the wrong place?

She reached the rim of the ledge overlooking the battlefield of Thakan'dar below. If she went farther, she'd fall. *Better that than becoming another of her pets . . .*

Threads of Air wrapped around Aviendha's legs and jerked her back. She screamed through her clenched teeth, then twisted about; her feet seemed little more than stumps of raw flesh. The pain washed over her, and her vision darkened. She struggled to reach the One Power.

Graendal held her off, but the woman flagged and growled, then slumped down, gasping. The weave stanching her wound was still in place, but the woman's face grew pale. She seemed almost ready to faint.

The open gateway beside her invited Aviendha, a means of escape—but it might as well have been a mile away. Mind clouding, legs afire with pain, Aviendha slipped her knife from its sheath.

It fell from her trembling fingers. She was too weak to hold it.

CHAPTER
44

Two Craftsmen

Perrin awoke to something rustling. He cracked his eyes open, wary, and found himself in a dark room.

Berelain's palace, he remembered. The sound of the waves had grown softer outside, the calls of gulls silent. Thunder rumbled, distant.

What time was it? It smelled like morning, but it was dark outside still. He had trouble picking out the dark silhouette moving through the room toward him. He tensed until he picked out the scent.

"Chiad?" he asked, sitting up.

The Aiel did not jump, though he was certain from the way she stopped that he'd surprised her. "I should not be here," she whispered. "I push my honor to the very edge of what should be allowed."

"It's the Last Battle, Chiad," Perrin said. "You are allowed to push some boundaries . . . assuming we haven't won yet."

"The battle at Merrilor is won, but the greater battle—that at Thakan'dar—still rages."

"I need to return to work," Perrin said. He was in his small-clothes only. He didn't let that bother him. An Aiel like Chiad wouldn't blush. He pushed off his blanket.

Unfortunately, the bone-eating weariness inside him had subsided only a little. "Not going to tell me to stay in bed?" he asked, tiredly searching out his shirt and trousers. They were folded with his hammer at the foot of the bed. He had to lean against the mattress as he walked there. "You're not going to tell me I have no business fighting while tired? Every woman I know seems to think that is one of her primary jobs."

"I have found," Chiad said dryly, "that pointing out stupidity serves only to make men stupider. Besides, I'm *gai'shain*. It's not my place."

He looked at her, and though he couldn't see her blush in the darkness, he could smell her embarrassment. She wasn't acting much like *gai'shain*. "Rand should have just released you all from your vows."

"He does not have that power," she said hotly.

"What good is honor if the Dark One wins the Last Battle?" Perrin snapped, pulling up his trousers.

"It is everything," Chiad said softly. "It is worth death, it is worth risking the world itself. If we have no honor, better that we lose."

Well, he supposed there were things he'd say the same thing about. Not wearing silly white robes, of course—but he wouldn't do some of the things the Whitecloaks had done, even if the world was at stake. He didn't press her further.

"Why are you here?" he asked, putting on his shirt.

"Gaul," Chiad said. "Is he . . ."

"Oh, Light!" Perrin said. "I should have told you earlier. I've scrap iron for a brain lately, Chiad. He was fine when I left him. He's still in the dream, and time passes more slowly where he is. It has probably only been an hour or so in his time, but I need to return to him."

"In your condition?" she asked, ignoring the fact that she'd said she wouldn't chivvy him for that.

"No," Perrin said, sitting on the bed. "Last time, I nearly broke my neck. I need one of the Aes Sedai to cure me of my fatigue."

"This thing is dangerous," Chiad said.

"More dangerous than letting Rand die?" Perrin said. "More dangerous than leaving Gaul without an ally in the World of Dreams, protecting the *Car'a'carn* alone?"

"That one *is* likely to stab himself with his own spear if left to fight alone," Chiad said.

"I didn't mean—"

"Hush, Perrin Aybara. I will try." She left in a rustle of cloth.

Perrin lay back on the bed, rubbing his eyes with the heels of his palms. He'd been far more certain of himself when he'd fought Slayer this last time, yet still he'd failed. He gritted his teeth, hoping Chiad would return soon.

Something moved outside his room. He revived, hauling himself up to a sitting position again.

A large shape darkened the doorway, then removed the shield from a lamp. Master Luhhan was built like an anvil, with a compact--yet powerful—torso and arms that bulged. In Perrin's mind's eye, the man didn't have so much gray in his hair. Master Luhhan had grown older, but he was not frail. Perrin doubted he ever would be.

"Lord Goldeneyes?" he asked.

"Light, please," Perrin said. "Master Luhhan, you of all people should feel free to call me Perrin. If not 'that worthless apprentice of mine.'"

"Here, now," Master Luhhan said, walking into the room. "I don't believe I called you that except once."

"When I broke the new blade for Master al'Moor's scythe," Perrin said, smiling. "I was sure I could get it right."

Master Luhhan chuckled. He paused beside Perrin's hammer, which still lay on the table at the foot of the bed, and rested his fingers on it. "You have become a master of the craft." Master Luhhan seated himself on a stool beside the bed. "One craftsman to another, I'm impressed. I don't think I could have ever made something so fine as that hammer."

"You made the axe."

"I guess I did that," he said. "It was not a thing of beauty. It was a thing of killing."

"Killing sometimes needs to be done."

"Yes, but it's never beautiful. Never."

Perrin nodded. "Thank you. For finding me, bringing me here. For saving me."

"It was self-interest, son!" Master Luhhan said. "If we escape this, it will be because of you boys, mark my words on it as true."

He shook his head, as if he couldn't believe it. One man, at least, remembered the three of them as youths—youths who, in Mat's case at least, had been in trouble more often than not.

Actually, Perrin thought, *I'm pretty sure Mat's still in trouble more often than not.* At least, at the moment, he wasn't fighting but instead talking with some Seanchan, according to the spinning colors that resolved into an image.

"Chiad said that the fighting at Merrilor was finished?" Perrin asked.

"It is," Master Luhhan said. "I came through, carrying some of our wounded. I should be getting back to Tam and Abell soon, but I wanted to check on you."

Perrin nodded. That tugging inside of him . . . if anything, it was stronger now than it ever would be. Rand *needed* him. The war wasn't finished yet. Not by far.

"Master Luhhan," Perrin said with a sigh. "I've made a mistake."

"Mistake?"

"I ran myself ragged," Perrin said. "I pushed myself too hard." He made a fist, slamming it into the corner post of the bed. "I should know better, Master Luhhan. I always do this. I work myself so hard, I make myself useless the next day."

"Perrin, lad?" Master Luhhan said, leaning forward. "Today, I'm more worried that there's not going to *be* a next day."

Perrin looked up at him, frowning.

"If there was ever a time to push yourself, this is it," Master Luhhan said. "We've won one fight, but if the Dragon Reborn doesn't win his . . . Light, I don't think you've made a mistake at all. This is our last chance at the forge. This is the morning that the big piece is due. Today, you just keep working until it's done."

"But if I collapse . . ."

"Then you gave it your all."

"I could fail because I've run myself out of strength."

"Then at least you didn't fail because you held back. I know it sounds bad, and maybe I'm wrong. But . . . well, everything you're talking about is good advice for an average day. This isn't an average day. No, by the Light it's not."

Master Luhhan took Perrin by the arm. "You may see in yourself someone who lets himself go too far, but that's not the man I see. If anything, Perrin, I've seen in you someone who has learned to hold himself back. I've watched you hold a teacup with extreme delicacy, as if you feared breaking it with your strength. I've seen you clasp hands with a man, holding his hand in yours with such care, never squeezing too hard. I've watched you move with deliberate reserve, so that you don't shove anyone or knock anything over.

"Those were good lessons for you to learn, son. You needed control. But in you, I've seen a boy grow into a man who doesn't know how to let those barriers go. I see a man who's frightened of what happens when he gets a little out of control. I realize you do what you do because you're afraid of hurting people. But Perrin . . . it's time to stop holding back."

"I'm not holding back, Master Luhhan," Perrin protested. "Really, I promise."

"Is that the case? Well, maybe you're right." Master Luhhan suddenly smelled embarrassed. "Look at me. Here, acting like it's my business. I'm not your father, Perrin. I'm sorry."

"No," Perrin said as Master Luhhan stood to leave. "I no longer have a father."

Master Luhhan gave him a pained look. "What those Trollocs did . . . "

"My family wasn't killed by Trollocs," Perrin said softly. "It was Padan Fain."

"What? Are you certain?"

"One of the Whitecloaks told me," Perrin said. "He wasn't lying."

"Well, then," Luhhan said. "Fain . . . he's still out there, isn't he?"

"Yes," Perrin said. "He hates Rand. And there's another man. Lord Luc. You remember him? He's been ordered to kill Rand. I think . . . I think they're both going to try for him, before this is over."

"Then you'll have to make sure they don't succeed, won't you?"

Perrin smiled, then turned toward the footsteps outside. Chiad entered a moment later, and he could smell her annoyance that he'd sensed her coming. Bain followed, another figure in complete white. And after them . . .

Masuri. Not the Aes Sedai he would have chosen. Perrin felt his lips tighten.

"You do not like me," Masuri said. "I know this."

"I have never said that," Perrin replied. "You were a great help to me during our travels."

"And yet, you do not trust me, but that is beside the point. You wish to have your strength restored, and I am probably the only one willing to do it for you. The Wise Ones and the Yellows would paddle you like a babe for wanting to leave."

"I know," Perrin said, sitting down on the bed. He hesitated. "I need to know why you were meeting with Masema behind my back."

"I come here to fulfill a request," Masuri said, smelling amused, "and you tell me you won't let me do you that favor until I respond to interrogation?"

"Why'd you do it, Masuri?" Perrin said. "Out with it."

"I planned to use him," the slender Aes Sedai said.

"Use him."

"Having influence with one who called himself the Prophet of the Dragon could have been useful." She smelled embarrassed. "It was a different time, Lord Aybara. Before I knew you. Before any of us knew you."

Perrin grunted.

"I was foolish," Masuri said. "Is that what you wanted to hear? I was foolish, and I have since learned."

Perrin eyed her, then sighed, proffering his arm. It was still an Aes Sedai answer, but one of the straighter ones he had heard. "Do it," he said. "And thank you."

She took his arm. He felt his fatigue evaporate—felt it get shoved back, like an old quilt being stuffed into a small box. Perrin felt invigorated, strengthened. Powerful again. He practically leaped as he came to his feet.

Masuri sagged, sitting down on his bed. Perrin flexed his hand, looking down at his fist. He felt as if he could challenge anyone, even the Dark One himself. "That feels wonderful."

"I've been told I excel at this particular weave," Masuri said. "But be careful, it—"

"Yes," Perrin said. "I know. The body is still tired. I just can't feel it." And, as he considered, that last part wasn't exactly true. He *could* sense his fatigue, like a serpent deep within its hole, lurking and waiting. It would consume him again.

That meant he had to finish his job first. He inhaled deeply, then summoned his hammer to him. It didn't move.

Right, he thought. *This is the real world, not the wolf dream.* He walked over and slipped the hammer into its straps on his belt, the new ones that he had fashioned to hold the larger hammer. He turned toward Chiad, who stood by the doorway; he could smell Bain out there, too, where she'd retreated. "I will find him," Perrin said. "If he is wounded, I will bring him here."

"Do that," Chiad said, "but you will not find us here."

"You are going to Merrilor?" Perrin asked, surprised.

Chiad said, "Some of us are needed to bring the wounded in to be Healed. It is not a thing *gai'shain* have done in the past, but perhaps it is a thing we can do this time."

Perrin nodded, then closed his eyes. He imagined himself close to sleep, drifting. His time in the wolf dream had trained his mind well. He could fool himself, with concentration. That didn't change the world here, but it did change his perceptions.

Yes . . . drifting close to sleep . . . and there was the pathway. He took the branch toward the wolf dream in the flesh, and caught just a hint of a gasp from Masuri as he felt himself *shift* between worlds.

He opened his eyes and dropped into buffeting winds. He created a pocket of calm air, then hit the ground beneath with strengthened legs. Only a few teetering walls remained of Berelain's palace on this side. One of those broke apart, the stones shattering and pulled into the sky by the winds. The city beyond was mostly gone, heaps of rock here and there indicating where buildings had once stood. The sky groaned like bending metal.

Perrin summoned his hammer into his hand, then began the hunt one last time.

Thom Merrilin sat on a large, soot-blackened boulder, smoking his pipe, watching the world end.

He knew a thing or two about finding the best vantage to watch a performance. He judged this to be the finest seat in the world. His boulder was just next to the entrance into the Pit of Doom, close enough that if he leaned back and squinted, he could peer in and catch some of the lights and shadows playing inside. He glanced in. Nothing had changed.

Stay safe in there, Moiraine, he thought. *Please.*

He was also close enough to the edge of the path to overlook the valley below. He puffed on his pipe, knuckling his mustache.

Someone had to record this. He couldn't spend the entire time worrying about her. So, he searched his mind for the right words to describe what he was seeing. He set aside words like "epic" and "momentous." They were nearly worn out with overuse.

A wave of wind blew through the valley, ruffling the *cadin'sor* of Aiel fighting red-veiled enemies. Lightning surged, pounding at the Dragonsworn line holding the path up to the cave entrance. Those flashes sent men flying into the air. Then, that lightning started striking at the Trollocs instead. The clouds went back and forth like that, the Windfinders seizing control of the weather, the Shadow taking it back. Neither side yet had managed a clear advantage for long.

Hulking dark beasts ravaged the valley, killing with ease. The Darkhounds did not fall despite the work of dozens in concert. The right side of the valley was covered in a thick mist that, for some reason, the storm winds couldn't budge.

"Climactic"? Thom thought, chewing on the stem of his pipe. *No. Too expected.* If you used the words people expected, they grew bored. A great ballad needed to be unexpected.

Never be expected. When people start to expect you—when they started to anticipate your flourishes, to look for the ball you had hidden through sleight of hand, or to smile before you reached the twist line of your tale—it was time to pack up your cloak, bow once more for good measure, and stroll away. After all, that was what they'd least expect you to do when all was going well.

He leaned back again, peering into the tunnel. He couldn't see her, of course. She was too far in. But he could feel her, in his mind, because of the bond.

She stared at the end of the world, with grit and determination. Despite himself, he smiled.

Below, the battle churned like a meat grinder, ripping men and Trollocs into chunks of dead flesh. The Aiel fought at the periphery of the battlefield, engaging their Shadow-taken cousins. They seemed to be evenly matched, or they had been before those Darkhounds arrived.

They were relentless though, these Aiel. They didn't seem tired at all, though it had been ... Thom couldn't put his thumb on how much time had passed. He'd slept maybe five or six times since they'd come to Shayol Ghul, but he didn't know if that marked the days. He checked the sky. No sign of the sun, though the channeling of the Windfinders—and the Bowl of the Winds—had summoned a great line of white clouds to crash into the black ones. The clouds seemed to be having a battle of their own, a reverse image of the fighting below. Black against white.

"Perilous"? he thought. No, that wasn't the right word. He'd make a ballad of this for certain. Rand deserved it. Moiraine, too. This would be her victory as much as it was his. He needed *words*. The right words.

He searched for them while he heard the Aiel beating spears against shields as they ran to battle. While he heard the howling wind inside the tunnel, and while he could feel her standing at the end.

Below, the Domani crossbowmen cranked frantically. Once, thousands of them had been shooting. Now only a fraction remained.

Perhaps ... "terrifying."

That was a right word, but not the right word. It might not be unexpected, but it was very, very true. He felt it to his bone. His wife fighting for her life. The forces of Light pushed almost to the brink of death. Light, but he was frightened. For her. For them all.

But the word was pedestrian. He needed something better, something perfect.

Below, the Tairens thrust their polearms desperately at attacking Trollocs. The Dragonsworn fought with numerous types of weapons. One last steamwagon lay broken nearby, carrying arrows and bolts brought through the last gateway from Baerlon. They hadn't seen supplies in hours now. The distortion of time here, the tempest, was doing things to the One Power.

Thom took special note of the wagon—he would need to use it in a way that preserved its wonder, showing how its cold, iron sides had deflected arrows before its fall.

There was heroism in every line, in every pull of the bowstring and every hand that held a weapon. How to convey that? But how also to convey the fear, the destruction, the sheer strangeness of it all? The day before—in an odd sort of bloody truce—both sides had paused to clear away bodies.

He needed a word that gave the feel for the chaos, death, the cacophony, the sheer bravery.

Below, a tired group of Aes Sedai began moving up the pathway to where Thom waited. They passed archers keenly scanning the battlefield for Fades.

"Exquisite," Thom thought. *That is the word. Unexpected, but true. Majestically exquisite. No. Not "majestically." Let the word stand on its own. If it is the right word, it will work without help. If it's the wrong word, adding other words to it will just make it seem desperate.*

This was what the end *should* be like. The sky ripping apart as factions fought for control of the elements themselves, people from varied nations standing with their last strength. If the Light won, it would do so by the narrowest of margins.

That, of course, horrified him. A good emotion. It would have to go in the ballad. He drew on his pipe, and knew that he did so to keep himself from trembling. Nearby, an entire side of the valley wall exploded, showering rock down upon the people fighting below. He didn't know which of the channelers had done that. There were Forsaken on this battlefield. Thom tried to stay out of their way.

This is *what you get, old man*, he reminded himself, *for not knowing when to let go.* He was glad that he'd not been able to escape, that his attempts to leave Rand, Mat and the others behind had failed. Would he really have wanted to sit in some quiet inn somewhere while the Last Battle played out? While she went in there alone?

He shook his head. He was as much a fool as any man or woman. He just had enough experience to recognize it. It took a few seasons before a man could put that together.

The approaching group of Aes Sedai broke apart, some remaining below, one limping tiredly up toward the cavern. Cadsuane. There were fewer Aes Sedai here than there had been before; casualties were mounting. Of course, most who had come here had known that death waited for them. This battle was the most desperate, and fighters here were the least likely to survive. Of every ten who had come to Shayol Ghul to fight, only one still stood. Thom knew for a fact that old Rodel Ituralde had sent a farewell letter to his wife before accepting this command. Just as well that he had.

Cadsuane nodded toward Thom, then continued on toward the cavern where Rand was fighting for the fate of the world. As soon as her back was to Thom, he flipped a single knife—his other hand still holding the pipe in his mouth—through the air. It hit the Aes Sedai in the back, right in the middle, severing the spine.

She dropped like a sack of potatoes.

That's an overused term it is, Thom thought, puffing on his pipe. *A sack of potatoes? I'll need a different simile there. Besides, how often do sacks of potatoes drop? Not often.* She dropped like ... like what? Barley spilling from the ripped end of a sack, slumping to the ground in a heap. Yes, that worked better.

As the Aes Sedai hit the ground, her weave faded, revealing another face behind the "Cadsuane" mask she'd been using. He recognized this woman, vaguely. A Domani. What was her name? Jeaine Caide. That was it. She was a pretty one.

Thom shook his head. The walk had been all wrong. Didn't any of them realize that a person's walk was as distinctive as the nose on their face? Each woman who tried to slip past him assumed that changing her face and dress—maybe her voice—would be enough to fool him.

He climbed off his perch and grabbed the corpse under the arms, then stuffed it a hollow nearby—there were five bodies in there now, so it was getting crowded. He drew on his pipe and took his cloak off, placing it here so that it covered up the dead hand of the Black sister, which was peeking out.

He checked one more time down the tunnel—though he could not see Moiraine, it comforted him to look. Then he returned to his perch and took out a sheet of paper and his pen. And—to the thunder, the yells, the explosions, and the howl of the wind—he began to compose.

CHAPTER 45

Tendrils of Mist

Dice tumbling in his head, Mat found Grady with Olver and Noal on the Heights. He carried Rand's bloody banner wrapped up in a small bundle, under his arm. Bodies lay scattered around, fallen weapons and pieces of armor, and blood stained the rocks. But the fighting was done here, the place empty of foes.

Noal smiled at Mat from horseback; Olver rode in front of him, clutching the Horn. Olver looked exhausted from Grady's Healing—the Asha'man stood beside the horse—but also seemed proud as could be at the same time.

Noal. One of the heroes of the Horn. It bloody made sense. Jain Farstrider himself. Well, you wouldn't find Mat trading places with him. Noal might enjoy it, but Mat wouldn't dance at another man's command. Not for immortality itself, no he wouldn't.

"Grady!" Mat said. "You did a nice job upriver. That water came just when we needed it!"

Grady's face was ashen, as if he'd seen something he had not wanted to. He nodded. "What ... What were ... "

"I'll explain another time," Mat said. "Right now, I need a bloody gateway."

"Where to?" Grady asked.

Mat took a deep breath, pulling up. "Shayol Ghul." *And curse me for a fool.*

Grady shook his head. "It can't happen, Cauthon."

"You're too tired?"

"I *am* tired," Grady said. "It isn't that. Something's happening at Shayol Ghul. Gateways opened there are deflected. The pattern is . . . warped, if that makes any sense. The valley isn't one location any longer, but many, and a gateway can't pinpoint it."

"Grady," Mat said, "that made about as much sense to me as playing a harp with no fingers."

"Traveling to Shayol Ghul don't work, Cauthon," Grady said with annoyance. "Pick somewhere else."

"How close can you send me?"

Grady shrugged. "One of the scouting camps a day's hike out, probably."

A day's hike out. The tugging pulled at Mat.

"Mat?" Olver said. "I think I need to go with you, don't I? To the Blight? Won't the heroes be needed to fight there?"

That was a piece of it. The tugging was insufferable. *Bloody ashes, Rand. Leave me alone, you—*

Mat stopped himself, a thought occurring to him. Scout camps. "One of those Seanchan patrol camps, you mean?"

"Yes," Grady said. "They've been sending us status reports on the battle up there, now that the gateways are unreliable."

"Well, don't just sit there looking stupid," Mat said. "Get a gateway open! Come on, Olver. We have some more work to do."

"Ahhhh . . ." Shaisam rolled onto the battlefield at Thakan'dar. So perfect. So pleasurable. His enemies were killing one another. And he . . . he had grown vast.

His mind was in every tendril of mist that rolled down the side of the valley. The souls of Trollocs were . . . well, unsatisfying. Still, simple grain could be filling in plentitude. And Shaisam had consumed quite a number of them.

His drones stumbled down the hillside, cloaked in mists. Trollocs with their skin pocked, as if it had boiled. Dead white eyes. He hardly needed them any longer, as their souls had given him fuel to rebuild himself. His madness had retreated. Mostly. Well, not mostly. Enough.

He walked at the center of the bank of mist. He was not reborn yet, not completely. He would need to find a place to infest, a place where the barriers between worlds was thin. There, he could seep his *self* into the very stones and embed his awareness into that location. The process would take years, but once it happened, he would become more difficult to kill.

Right now, Shaisam was frail. This mortal form that walked at the center of his mind ... he was bound to it. Fain, it had been. Padan Fain.

Still, he was vast. Those souls had given rise to much mist, and it—in turn—found others to feed upon. Men fought Shadowspawn before him. All would give him strength.

His drones stumbled onto the battlefield, and immediately, both sides took to fighting them. Shaisam quivered in joy. They did not see. They did not understand. The drones weren't there to fight.

They were there to distract.

As the battle proceeded, he trailed his essence down in misty tendrils, then began stabbing it through the bodies of fighting men and Trollocs. He took Myrddraal. Converted them. Used them.

Soon, this entire army would be his.

He needed that strength in case his ancient enemy ... his dear friend decided to attack him.

Those two friends—those two enemies—were occupied with one another. Excellent. Shaisam continued his attack, striking down enemies on both sides and consuming them. Some tried to attack him by running into his mists, his embrace. Of course, that killed them. This was his *true* self. He had tried to create this mist before, as Fain, but he had not been mature enough.

They could not reach him. No living thing could withstand his mist. Once, it had been a mindless thing. It had not been him. But it had been trapped with him, inside of a seed carried away, and that death—that wonderful death—had been given fertile ground in the flesh of a man.

The three entwined within him. Mist. Man. Master. That wonderful dagger—his physical form carried it now—had grown something delightful and new and ancient all at once.

So, the mist was him, but the mist was also not him. Mindless, but it was his body, and it carried his mind. Wonderfully, with those clouds in the sky he did not have to worry about the sun burning him away.

So *nice* of his old enemy to welcome him so! His physical form laughed at the heart of the creeping mists, while his mind—the mists themselves—gloried in how perfect everything was.

This place would become his. But only after he had feasted upon Rand al'Thor, the strongest soul of them all.

What a wonderful celebration!

Gaul clung to the rocks outside the Pit of Doom. The winds ripped at him, driving sand and chips of rock against his body, slicing gashes in his skin. He laughed at the vortex of blackness above.

"Do your worst!" he shouted upward. "*I* have lived in the Three-fold Land. I had heard the Last Battle would be grand, not a stroll to my mother's roof picking simblossoms!"

The winds blew harder, as if in retribution, but Gaul flattened himself against the stone, giving the winds no purchase on him. He'd lost his *shoufa*—it had blown free—so he had tied part of his shirt over his lower face. He held one spear. The others were gone, broken or pulled away.

He crawled toward the opening to the cavern, which lay exposed, a thin veil of purple barring the way forward. A figure in dark leather appeared in front of the opening. Near this man, the winds stilled.

Eyes squinting against the storm, Gaul crawled silently up behind the man and thrust his spear forward.

Slayer spun with a curse, turning aside the spear with an arm suddenly as strong as steel. "Burn you!" he shouted at Gaul. "Stay still for once!"

Gaul jumped back, and Slayer came for him, but then the wolves arrived. Gaul withdrew and faded into the rocks. Slayer was very powerful here, but what he could not see, he could not kill.

The wolves harried Slayer until he vanished. There were hundreds of them here in this valley, roving through the winds. Slayer had killed dozens; Gaul whispered a farewell to another who had fallen in this attack. He could not speak to them as Perrin Aybara did, but they were spear brothers.

Gaul crawled slowly, carefully. His clothing and skin matched the color of the rocks—it felt right for them to be that way, so they were. The wolves and he could probably not defeat this Slayer; but they could try. Try hard.

How long had it been since Perrin Aybara had left? Two hours, perhaps?

If the Shadow has claimed you, my friend, he thought, *I pray you spat in Sightblinder's eye before you awoke.*

Slayer appeared on the rocks again, but Gaul did not crawl forward. The man had sent decoys before made only of rock. This figure did not move. Gaul looked about—carefully, slowly—as several wolves appeared near the decoy. They sniffed it.

It started killing them.

Gaul cursed, breaking out of his hiding place. This, apparently, was what Slayer had been wanting. Slayer launched a spear—one of Gaul's own. It hit Gaul in the side. Gaul grunted, falling to his knees.

Slayer laughed, then raised his hands. A jet of air blew out from him, flinging wolves away. Gaul could barely hear the whimpers over the rushing wind.

"Here," Slayer screamed into the tempest, "I am a *king*! Here, I am more than the Forsaken. This place is mine, and I will . . ."

Perhaps the pain of Gaul's wound was addling him; he thought that the winds were starting to die down.

"Here, I will . . ."

The winds stopped.

The entire valley grew silent. Slayer stiffened, then turned worried eyes toward the cavern beyond. Nothing there seemed to have changed.

"You are not a king," a soft voice said.

Gaul twisted about. A figure stood on a rocky protrusion behind him, wearing the greens and browns of a Two Rivers woodsman. His deep green cloak rippled faintly from the stilling winds. Perrin stood with his eyes closed, chin raised at a slight angle, as if toward the sun above—though, if there was one, it was blocked by clouds.

"This place belongs to the wolves," Perrin said. "Not to you, not to me, not to any man. You cannot be a king here, Slayer. You have no subjects, and you never will."

"Insolent pup," Slayer snarled. "How many times must I kill you?"

Perrin drew in a deep breath.

"I laughed when I found that Fain had killed your family," Slayer yelled. "I *laughed*. I was supposed to kill him, you know. The Shadow thinks him wild and rogue, but he's the first one who has managed to do something meaningful to bring you pain."

Perrin said nothing.

"Luc wanted to be part of something important," Slayer shouted. "In that, we're the same, though I sought the ability to channel. The Dark One cannot grant that, but he found something different for us, something better. Something that requires a soul to be melded with something else. Like what happened with you, Aybara. Like you."

"We are nothing alike, Slayer," Perrin said softly.

"But we are! That's why I laughed. And you know, there's a prophecy about Luc? That he'll be important to the Last Battle. That's why we're here. We'll kill you; then we'll kill al'Thor. Just like we killed that wolf of yours."

Standing on the rocky protrusion, Perrin opened his eyes. Gaul pulled back. Those golden eyes glowed like beacons.

The storm started again. And yet, that tempest seemed mild compared to the one Gaul saw in Perrin's eyes. Gaul felt a *pressure* from his friend. Like the pressure of the sun at noon after four days without having any water to drink.

Gaul stared up at Perrin for a few moments, then held a hand against his wound and ran.

The wind whipped at Mat as he clung to the saddle of a winged beast hundreds of feet in the air.

"Oh, blood and bloody ashes!" Mat yelled, one hand on his hat, the other clutching the saddle. He was tied in with some straps. Two little leather straps. Far too thin. Could they not have used more? Maybe ten or twenty? He would have been fine with a hundred!

Morat'to'raken were bloody insane. Every one of them! They did this every day! What was wrong with them?

Tied into the saddle in front of Mat, Olver laughed with glee.

Poor lad, Mat thought. *He's so frightened he's going mad. The lack of air up here is getting to him.*

"There it is, my Prince!" the *morat'to'raken*, Sulaan, called to him from her place at the front of the flying beast. She was a pretty thing. Completely insane, too. "We've reached the valley. Are you sure you want to set down in there?"

"No!" Mat shouted.

"Good answer!" The woman made her beast swoop.

"Blood and bloody—"

Olver laughed.

The *to'raken* brought them down over a long valley clogged with a frenzied battle. Mat tried to let his attention settle on the fighting, rather than on the fact that he was in the air flying on a lizard with two bloody lunatics.

Heaps of Trolloc bodies told that story as well as any map could have. The Trollocs had burst through defenses at the valley mouth behind Mat. He flew over that, toward the mountain of Shayol Ghul ahead, valley walls to his right and left.

It was mayhem below. Roving bands of Aiel and Trollocs moved through the valley, striking at each other here and there. Some soldiers, not Aiel, defended the way up to the Pit of Doom, but that was the only organized formation Mat could see.

Along the side of the valley a deep mist had begun to flood down onto its floor. At first, Mat was confused, thinking it had come from the heroes of the Horn. But no, the Horn was strapped to the saddle beside Mat's *ashandarei*. And this mist was too . . . silvery. If that was the right word. He thought he'd seen that mist before.

Then, Mat felt something. From that mist. A prickling cold sensation, followed by what he swore was whispering in his mind. He knew immediately what it was.

Oh, Light!

"Mat, look!" Olver called, pointing. "Wolves!"

A group of jet black animals, almost as large as horses, were assaulting the soldiers defending the path up to Shayol Ghul. The wolves were making quick work of the men. Light! As if things had not been difficult enough.

"Those aren't wolves," Mat said grimly. The Wild Hunt had come to Thakan'dar.

Maybe they and Mashadar would destroy one another? Was that too much to hope for? With the dice tumbling in his head, Mat was not going to bet on it. Rand's forces—what was left of the Aiel, Domani, Dragonsworn and Tairen soldiers who had come here—would be crushed by the Darkhounds. If they survived, Mashadar would take them. They could not fight either one.

That voice in there . . . It wasn't just Mashadar, the mindless mist. Fain was here somewhere, too. And the dagger.

Shayol Ghul loomed above. High in the air, clouds churned. Surprisingly, some white thunderheads had rolled in from the south, colliding with the black as they spun together. Actually, those two together looked an awful lot like the—

The *to'raken* turned and winged about, then swooped down lower, maybe only a hundred feet off the ground.

"Be careful!" Mat hollered, holding on to his hat. "Are you bloody trying to kill us!"

"Apologies, my Prince," the woman yelled back. "I just need to find a safe place to put you down."

"A *safe* place?" Mat said. "Good luck on that."

"It's going to be difficult. Dhana is strong, but I—"

A black-fletched arrow grazed the side of Sulaan's head, loosed from somewhere down below, along with a flight of a dozen others that zipped around Mat, one hitting the wing of the *to'raken*.

Mat cursed, dropping his hat and reaching for Sulaan as Olver cried out in shock. Sulaan went limp, dropping the reins. Below, a group of red-veiled Aiel prepared another volley.

Mat undid his straps. He leaped—well, more crawled—over Olver and the unconscious woman and grabbed the reins of the panicked *to'raken*. This could not be too much harder than riding a horse, could it? He pulled as he had seen Sulaan do, turning the *to'raken* as arrows cut the air behind them, several taking the beast in the wings.

They veered straight toward the rock wall, and Mat fou

himself on his feet, standing on the saddle and gripping the reins tightly as he tried to keep the wounded beast from bloody killing them all. That turn nearly tossed him free, but he held himself in place with feet wedged and holding the reins even tighter.

The rush of air as they turned caught up Olver's next words. The creature's badly wounded wings beat wildly and it screeched wretchedly. Mat was not certain *either* of them were in control as the beast twisted toward the ground.

They hit the floor of the valley in a heap. Bones cracked—Light, Mat hoped they belonged to the *to'raken*—and he found himself tumbling end over end across the broken ground.

He finally came to a rest, flopping over.

He breathed in and out, stunned by it all. "That," he finally groaned, "is the bloody worst idea I've ever had." He hesitated. "Maybe the second worst." He *had* decided to kidnap Tuon, after all.

He stumbled to his feet, and his legs still seemed to work. He did not limp too badly as he ran to the twitching *to'raken*. "Olver? Olver!"

He found the boy still tied in the saddle, blinking and shaking his head to clear it. "Mat," Olver said, "next time I think you should let me fly it. I don't think you did a very good job."

"If there is a next time," Mat said, "I'll eat a whole bag of Tar Valon gold." He yanked free the ties holding his *ashandarei* and Olver's Horn, then handed the instrument to the boy. He reached for the pack with Rand's banner, which he'd carried tied at his waist, but it was gone.

Panicked, Mat looked about. "The banner! I dropped the bloody banner!"

Olver smiled, looking up at the sign made by the swirling clouds. "It will be fine—we're beneath his banner already," he said, then lifted the Horn and blew a beautiful note.

CHAPTER
46

To Awaken

Rand broke free from the darkness and entered the Pattern fully again.

From his watching of the Pattern, he knew that although only minutes had passed here since he'd entered, in the valley outside this cavern, days had passed, and farther out into the world, it had been much longer.

Rand threw Moridin back from the position they'd held during those tense minutes with blades locked. Still full of the One Power, so sweet, Rand whipped the blade of *Callandor* at his old friend.

Moridin got his sword up in time to block, but only barely. He growled, pulling a knife from his belt and stepping back into a knife-and-sword stance.

"You don't matter any longer, Elan," Rand said, the torrent of *saidin* raging within him. "Let us finish this!"

"I don't?" Moridin laughed.

Then he spun and threw the knife at Alanna.

Nynaeve watched in horror as the knife spun through the air. The winds didn't touch it for some reason.

No! After she had coaxed the woman back to life. *I cannot lose her now!* Nynaeve tried to catch the knife or block it, but she moved just a hair too slowly.

The knife buried itself in Alanna's breast.

Nynaeve looked at it, horrified. This was not a wound that sewing and herbs could heal. That blade hit the heart.

"Rand! I need the One Power!" Nynaeve cried.

"It's . . . all right . . ." Alanna whispered.

Nynaeve looked at the woman's eyes. She was lucid. *The andilay,* Nynaeve realized, remembering the herb she'd used to give the woman strength. *It brought her out of her stupor. It awakened her.*

"I can . . ." Alanna said. "I can release him . . ."

The light faded from her eyes.

Nynaeve looked at Moridin and Rand. Rand glanced at the dead woman with pity and sorrow, but Nynaeve saw no rage in his eyes. Alanna had released the bond before Rand could feel the effects of her death.

Moridin turned back to Rand, another knife in his left hand. Rand raised *Callandor* to strike Moridin down.

Moridin dropped his sword, and stabbed his own right hand with the knife. Rand twitched suddenly, and *Callandor* dropped from his grip as if *his* hand somehow hurt from Moridin's attack.

The glow emanating from the blade winked out, and the crystalline blade rang as it hit the ground.

Perrin did not hold back in the fight with Slayer.

He did not try to distinguish between wolf and man. He finally let everything out, every bit of rage at Slayer, every bit of pain at the deaths of his family—pressures which had been growing inside him unnoticed for months.

He let it out. Light, he let it out. As he had on that terrible night when he'd killed those Whitecloaks. Ever since then, he'd clamped a firm grip on himself and his emotions. Just as Master Luhhan had said.

He could see it now, in a frozen moment. Gentle Perrin, always afraid of hurting someone. A blacksmith who had learned control. He had rarely let himself strike with all of his strength.

This day, he took the leash off the wolf. It had never belonged there anyway.

The storm *conformed* to his rage. Perrin didn't try to keep it back. Why would he? It matched his emotions perfectly. The fall of his hammer was like claps of thunder, the flashing of his eyes like lightning bolts. Wolves howled alongside the wind.

Slayer tried to fight back. He jumped, he *shifted*, he stabbed. Each time, Perrin was there. Jumping at him as a wolf, swinging at him as a man, buffeting him like the tempest itself. Slayer got a wild look in his eyes. He raised a shield, trying to put it between himself and Perrin.

Perrin attacked. Without thought, now, he became instinct only. Perrin roared, smashing his hammer into that shield time and time again. *Driving* Slayer before him. *Beating* the shield like a stubborn length of iron. *Pounding* away his anger, his fury.

His last blow threw Slayer back and flung the shield from the man's hands, sending it spinning a hundred feet in the air. Slayer hit the valley floor and rolled, gasping. He came to rest in the middle of the battlefield, shadowy figures rising all around him and dying as they fought in the real world. He looked at Perrin with panic, then vanished.

Perrin sent himself into the waking world to follow. He appeared amid the battle, Aiel against Trollocs in a furious fight. The winds were surprisingly strong on this side, and black clouds spun above Shayol Ghul, which rose like a crooked finger into the sky.

The nearby Aiel barely took time to notice him. The bodies of Trollocs and humans lay in heaps across the battlefield, and the place stank of death. The ground had once been dusty here, but now it churned with mud made from the blood of the fallen.

Slayer pushed through a group of Aiel nearby, growling, slashing with his long knife. He didn't look back—and it didn't seem that he knew Perrin had followed him into the real world.

A new wave of Shadowspawn pushed in off the slope, out of a silvery white mist. Their skin looked strange, pocked with holes, their eyes milky white. Perrin ignored these and barreled after Slayer.

Young Bull! Wolves. *The Shadowbrothers are here! We fight!*

Darkhounds. Wolves hated all Shadowspawn; an entire pack

would die pulling down a Myrddraal. But Darkhounds they feared.

Perrin looked around to spot the creatures. Ordinary men could not fight Darkhounds, whose mere saliva was death. Nearby, the human forces broke before a tide of black wolves the size of horses. The Wild Hunt.

Light! Those Darkhounds were enormous. Scores of the jet black, corrupted wolves ripped through the defensive lines, throwing Tairen and Domani soldiers about as if they were rag dolls. Wolves attacked the Darkhounds, but in vain. They screamed and howled and died.

Perrin raised his voice alongside their cries of death, a ragged yell of rage. For the moment, he could not help. His instincts and passions drove him. Slayer. He *had* to defeat Slayer. If Perrin did not stop Slayer, the man would shift to the World of Dreams and kill Rand.

Perrin turned and ran through the fighting armies, chasing after the distant figure ahead. Slayer had gained a lead by Perrin's distraction, but the man had slowed a little. He had not yet realized that Perrin could leave the World of Dreams.

Ahead, Slayer stopped and inspected the battlefield. He glanced back and saw Perrin—then his eyes widened. Perrin couldn't hear his words over the din, but could read Slayer's lips as he whispered, "No. No, it can't be."

Yes, Perrin thought. *I can follow you now, wherever you run. This is a hunt. You, finally, are the prey.*

Slayer vanished, and Perrin *shifted* into the wolf dream after him. The people fighting around him became patterns in the dust, exploding and reforming. Slayer yelled in fright at seeing him, then *shifted* back into the waking world.

Perrin did likewise. He could *smell* Slayer's trail. Slick with sweat, panicked. To the dream, then to the waking world again. In the dream, Perrin ran on four legs, as Young Bull. In the waking world, he was Perrin, hammer held aloft.

He *shifted* back and forth between the two as frequently as he blinked, chasing Slayer. When he hit a patch of fighting bodies, he would jump into the wolf dream and crash through the figures made of sand and blown dust, then *shift* back into the waking world to keep on the trail. The *shifting* started to happen so quickly, he flickered between the two with each heartbeat.

Thump. Perrin raised his hammer, leaping off a small ridge after the scrambling form ahead.

Thump. Young Bull howled, summoning the pack.

Thump. Perrin was close now. Only a few steps behind. Slayer's odor was pungent.

Thump. The spirits of wolves appeared around Young Bull, howling their thirst for the hunt. Never had a prey deserved it more. Never had a prey done more damage to the packs. Never had a man been more feared.

Thump. Slayer stumbled. He twisted as he fell, sending himself to the wolf dream by reflex.

Thump. Perrin swung *Mah'alleinir*, emblazoned with the leaping wolf. He who soars.

Thump. Young Bull leaped for the throat of the killer of his brothers. Slayer fled.

The hammer connected.

Something about this place, this moment, sent Perrin and Slayer into a spiraling series of flickers between worlds. Back and forth, back and forth, flashes of moments and thoughts. Flicker. Flicker. Flicker.

Men died around them. Some of dust, some of flesh. Their world, alongside shadows of other worlds. Men in strange clothing and armor, fighting beasts of all shapes and sizes. Moments where the Aiel became Seanchan, who became something between the two, with spears and light eyes but helmets shaped like monstrous insects.

In all of those moments, in all of those places, Perrin's hammer struck and Young Bull's fangs grabbed Slayer by the neck. He tasted the salty warmth of Slayer's blood in his mouth. He felt the hammer vibrate as it hit, and he heard bones crack. The worlds flashed like bolts of lightning.

Everything crashed, shook, then pulled together.

Perrin stood on the rocks in the valley of Thakan'dar, and Slayer's body crumpled in front of him, head crushed. Perrin panted, the thrill of the hunt clinging to him. It was over.

He turned, surprised to find that he was surrounded by Aiel. He frowned at them. "What are you doing?"

One of the Maidens laughed. "You looked like you were running to a great dance, Perrin Aybara. One learns to watch for warriors like you on the battlefield and follow. They often have the most fun."

He smiled grimly, surveying the battlefield. It was not going well for his side. The Darkhounds ripped apart the defenders in a ruthless frenzy. The way up to Rand was completely exposed.

"Who commands this battle?" Perrin asked.

"Nobody, now," the Maiden said. He did not know her name. "Rodel Ituralde did first. Then Darlin Sisnera led—but his command post fell to Draghkar. I have not seen any Aes Sedai or clan chiefs in hours."

Her voice was grim. Even the stalwart Aiel were flagging. A quick scan of the battlefield showed Perrin that the remaining Aiel fought wherever they were, often in small groups, doing as much harm as they could before being cut down. The wolves who had fought here in packs were broken, their sendings those of pain and fear. And Perrin didn't know what those Shadowspawn with the pocked faces meant.

The battle was finished, and the side of Light had lost.

The Darkhounds broke through the line of Dragonsworn nearby, the last group who held falling before them. A few tried to flee, but one of the Darkhounds leapt on them, pushing several to the ground and gnawing one. Frothing saliva sprayed across the others, and they dropped, twitching.

Perrin lowered his hammer, then knelt, pulling off Slayer's cloak and wrapping the cloth around his hands as he picked up his hammer again. "Don't let their spittle touch your skin. It is deadly."

The Aiel nodded, those with bare hands wrapping them. They smelled of determination, but also resignation. Aiel would run toward death if it was the only option, and would laugh while doing so. Wetlanders thought them mad, but Perrin could smell the truth on them. They were not mad. They did not fear death, but they did not welcome it.

"Touch me, all of you," Perrin said.

The Aiel did so. He *shifted* them to the wolf dream—taking so many was a strain, like bending a bar of steel—but he managed it. He immediately *shifted* them to the path up to the Pit of Doom. The spirits of wolves had gathered here, silent. Hundreds of them.

Perrin brought the Aiel back to the waking world, his *shift* placing him and his small force between Rand and the Darkhounds. The Wild Hunt looked up, corrupted eyes shining like silver as they fixed on Perrin.

"We will hold here," Perrin said to his Aiel, "and hope that some others aid us."

"We will stand," one of the Aiel said, a tall man wearing one of those headbands marked with Rand's symbol.

"And if we do not," another said, "and wake instead, then we will at least water the earth with our blood and let our bodies nourish the plants that will now grow here." Perrin had barely noticed the plants growing, incongruously, green and vibrant in the valley. Small, but strong. A manifestation of the fact that Rand still fought.

The Darkhounds slunk toward them, tails down, ears back, fangs exposed, gleaming like bloodstained metal. What was that he heard over the wind? Something very soft, very distant. It seemed so soft that he shouldn't have noticed it. But it pierced through the clamor of war. Faintly familiar . . .

"I know that sound," Perrin said.

"Sound?" the Aiel Maiden said. "What sound? The calls of the wolves?"

"No," Perrin said as the Darkhounds began to lope up the path. "The Horn of Valere."

The heroes would come. But upon which battlefield would they fight? Perrin could expect no relief here. Except . . .

Lead us, Young Bull.

Why must the heroes all be human?

A howl rose in the same pitch as that of the sounded Horn. He looked upon a field suddenly filled with a multitude of glowing wolves. They were great pale beasts, the size of Darkhounds. The spirits of those wolves who had died, then gathered here, waiting for the sign, waiting for the chance to fight.

The Horn had called them.

Perrin let loose a yell of his own, a howl of pleasure, then charged forward to meet the Darkhounds.

The Last Hunt had finally, truly arrived.

*

Mat left Olver with the heroes again. The boy looked like a prince, riding in front of Noal as they attacked the Trollocs and prevented anyone from climbing that path to kill Rand.

Mat borrowed a horse from one of the defenders who still had one, then galloped over to find Perrin. His friend would be among those wolves, of course. Mat did not know how those hundreds of big glowing wolves had entered the battlefield, but he was not going to complain. They met the Wild Hunt head-on, snarling and savaging the Darkhounds. Howls from both sides flooded Mat's ears.

He passed some Aiel fighting a Darkhound, but the people did not stand a chance. They tripped the beast, hacking at it, but it pulled back together as if it were made of darkness and not flesh—then ripped into them. Blood and bloody ashes! Those Aiel weapons did not even seem to scratch it. Mat continued galloping, avoiding the tendrils of silvery mist making their way across the whole valley.

Light! That mist was approaching the path up to Rand. It was picking up speed, rolling over Aiel, Trollocs and Darkhounds alike.

There, Mat thought, picking out a man fool enough to fight Darkhounds. Perrin slammed his hammer down on a Darkhound's head, cracking it and forcing it into the ground. When he raised his hammer, it trailed smoke behind it. The Darkhound, amazingly, remained dead.

Perrin turned, then stared. "Mat!" he called. "What are you doing here?"

"Coming to help!" Mat said. "Against my bloody better judgment!"

"You can't fight Darkhounds, Mat," Perrin said as Mat rode up beside him. "I can, and so can the Last Hunt." He cocked his head, then looked toward the sound of the Horn.

"No," Mat said, "I didn't sound it. That bloody burden has passed to someone who actually seems to enjoy it."

"It's not that, Mat." Perrin stepped up, reaching and taking him by the arm as he sat mounted. "My wife, Mat. Please. She had the Horn."

Mat looked down, feeling grim. "The lad said . . . Light, Perrin. Faile was at Merrilor, and led the Trollocs away from Olver so he could escape with the Horn."

"Then she could still be alive," Perrin said.

"Yes. Of course she could," Mat said. What else could he say? "Perrin, you need to know something else. Fain is here on this battlefield."

"Fain?" Perrin growled. "Where?"

"He's in that mist! Perrin, he's brought Mashadar, somehow. Don't let it touch you."

"I was in Shadar Logoth too, Mat," Perrin said. "I have a debt to settle with Fain."

"And I don't?" Mat said. "I—"

Perrin's eyes opened wide. He stared at Mat's chest.

There, a small white ribbon of silvery mist—Mashadar's mist—had speared Mat from behind through the chest. Mat looked at it, jerked once, then tumbled off his horse.

CHAPTER
47

Watching the Flow Writhe

Aviendha struggled on the slopes of the valley of Thakan'dar, trying to avoid the shield of Spirit Graendal was attempting to slip into place. A weave, like lace, defying her attempts to reach for the One Power. Her feet ruined, she could not stand. She lay, in pain, barely able to move.

She fought it off, but barely.

The Forsaken leaned against the rocks of the ledge, as she had been doing for a short time, muttering to herself. Her side bled bright red blood. Below them, in the valley, the battle raged. A silvery white mist was rolling across the dead and some of the living.

Aviendha tried to crawl toward her gateway. That lay open still, and through it she could see the valley floor. Something must have drawn Cadsuane and the others away—either that, or Aviendha had made the gateway to the wrong place.

The glow of *saidar* surrounded Graendal again. More weaves; Aviendha broke them, but they delayed her progress toward the gateway.

Graendal groaned, then pulled herself upright. She staggered in Aviendha's direction, though the woman looked dazed by her blood loss.

Aviendha could do little to defend herself, weak as she was from blood loss. She was helpless.

Except . . .

The weave for her gateway, the one she had tied off. It still hung there, holding the portal open. Ribbons of lace.

Carefully, hesitant but desperate, Aviendha reached out mentally and pulled one of the threads loose in the gateway. She could do it. The flow shivered and vanished.

It was something the Aiel did, but something Aes Sedai thought terribly dangerous. The results could be unpredictable. An explosion, a small shower of sparks . . . Aviendha could end up stilled. Or maybe nothing at all would happen. When Elayne had tried it, it had caused a devastating explosion.

That would be fine with her. If she brought down one of the Forsaken alongside her, that would be a wonderful death.

She had to try.

Graendal stopped near Aviendha and grumbled to herself, eyes closed. Then the woman opened her eyes and began crafting another weave. Compulsion.

Aviendha picked faster, pulling two, three, half a dozen threads free of the gateway. Almost, almost . . .

"What are you *doing*?" Graendal demanded.

Aviendha picked faster, and in her haste, picked at the wrong thread. She froze, watching the flow writhe, setting off the others near it.

Graendal hissed, and began to set the Compulsion on Aviendha.

The gateway exploded in a flash of light and heat.

Shaisam seized the battlefield, his mist shoving through those wolves and men who thought to bar his way to al'Thor.

Yes, *al'Thor*. The one he would kill, destroy, feast upon. Yes, al'Thor!

Something trembled at one edge of his senses. Shaisam hesitated, frowning to himself. What was wrong there? A piece of him . . . a piece of him had stopped sensing.

What was this? He ran his physical form across the ground through the mist. Blood trailed from his fingers, flayed by the dagger he carried, the wonderful seed, the last bit of his old self

He came upon a corpse, one that his mists had killed. Shaisam frowned, bending down. That body looked familiar . . .

The corpse's hand reached up and grabbed Shaisam by the throat. He gasped, thrashing, as the corpse opened its eye.

"There's an odd thing about diseases I once heard, Fain," Matrim Cauthon whispered. "Once you catch a disease and survive, you can't get it again."

Shaisam thrashed, panicked. No. No, this was not how a meeting with an old friend should go! He clawed at the hand holding him, then realized with horror that he'd dropped the dagger.

Cauthon pulled him down, slamming him to the ground. Shaisam called for his drones. Too late! Too slow!

"I've come to give you your gift back, Mordeth," Cauthon whispered. "I consider our debt paid in full."

Cauthon rammed the dagger right between the ribs, into Shaisam's heart. Tied to this pitiful mortal form, Mordeth screamed. Padan Fain howled, and felt his flesh melting from his bones. The mists trembled, began to swirl and shake.

Together they died.

Perrin *shifted* to the wolf dream and found Gaul by tracing the scent of blood. He had hated to leave Mat with Mashadar, but was confident—from a look Mat had given him after falling—that his friend could survive the mist, and knew what he was doing.

Gaul had hidden himself well, pushed up into a split in the rock just outside the Pit of Doom. Gaul still carried one spear and had darkened his clothing to match the rocks around him.

He was nodding off when Perrin found him. Gaul was not only wounded, but had been in the wolf dream far too long. If Perrin felt an aching exhaustion, it must be worse for Gaul.

"Come, Gaul," Perrin said, helping him out of the rocks.

Gaul looked dazed. "Nobody passed me by," he mumbled. "I watched, Perrin Aybara. The *Car'a'carn* is safe."

"You did well, my friend," Perrin replied. "Better than anyone could have expected. You have much honor."

Gaul smiled as he leaned on Perrin's shoulder. "I worried . . . when the wolves vanished, I worried."

"They fight on in the waking world." Perrin felt a need to return here. Finding Gaul had been part of that, but there was something else, a *drive* he couldn't explain.

"Hold on," Perrin said, grabbing Gaul about the waist. He *shifted* them to the Field of Merrilor, then *shifted* them out of the wolf dream and appeared in the center of the Two Rivers camp.

People immediately locked on Perrin, yells rising. "Light, Perrin!" a man said nearby. Grady rushed up, deep bags beneath his eyes. "I nearly burned you to char, Lord Goldeneyes. How did you appear like that?"

Perrin shook his head, setting Gaul down. Grady eyed the wound in the man's side, then called for one of the Aes Sedai to handle the Healing. They bustled around—some of the Two Rivers men calling out that Lord Goldeneyes had returned.

Faile. Faile had been here at Merrilor with the Horn.

I have to find her.

Rand was alone, unguarded in the wolf dream.

Burn it, that doesn't matter! Perrin thought. *If I lose Faile . . .*

If Rand died, he *would* lose Faile. And everything else. There were still Forsaken out there. Perrin wavered. He had to go look for her, didn't he? Wasn't that his duty, as her husband? Couldn't someone else look after Rand?

But . . . if not him, then who?

Though it ripped him apart, Perrin sought the wolf dream one last time.

Moridin scooped *Callandor* up off the floor. It burst alight with the One Power.

Rand stumbled away, holding his aching hand to his chest. Moridin laughed, raising the weapon high. "You are mine, Lews Therin. You are finally mine! I . . . " He trailed off, then looked up at the sword, perhaps in awe. "It can amplify the True Power. A True Power *sa'angreal*? How? Why?" He laughed louder.

A maelstrom churned about them.

"Channeling the True Power is death here, Elan!" Rand yelled. "It will burn you to a cinder!"

"It is oblivion!" Moridin yelled. "I will know that release, Lews Therin. I will take you with me."

The sword's glow turned a violent crimson. Rand could feel the power emanating from Moridin as he drew in the True Power.

This was the most dangerous part of the plan. Min had figured it out. *Callandor* had such flaws, such incredible flaws. Created so that a man using it needed women to control him, created so that if Rand used it, others could take control of him . . .

Why was Rand to need a weapon with such flaws? Why did the prophecies mention it so? A *sa'angreal* for the True Power. Why would he ever need such a thing?

The answer was so simple.

"Now!" Rand yelled.

Nynaeve and Moiraine channeled together, exploiting the flaw in *Callandor* as Moridin tried to bring it to bear against Rand. Wind whipped in the tunnel. The ground quivered, and Moridin yelled, eyes going wide.

They took control of him. *Callandor* was flawed. Any man using it could be forced to link with women, to be placed in their control. A trap . . . and one he used on Moridin.

"Link!" Rand commanded.

They fed it to him. Power.

Saidar from the women.

The True Power from Moridin.

Saidin from Rand.

Moridin's channeling the True Power here threatened to destroy them all, but they buffered it with *saidin* and *saidar*, then directed all three at the Dark One.

Rand punched through the blackness there and created a conduit of light *and* darkness, turning the Dark One's own essence upon him.

Rand felt the Dark One beyond, his immensity. Space, size, time . . . Rand understood how these things could be irrelevant now.

With a bellow—three Powers coursing through him, blood streaming down his side—the Dragon Reborn raised a hand of power and seized the Dark One through the Bore, like a man reaching through water to grab the prize at the river's bottom.

The Dark One tried to pull back, but Rand's claw was gloved by the True Power. The enemy could not taint *saidin* again. The Dark One tried to withdraw the True Power from Moridin, but the conduit flowed too freely, too powerfully to shut off now. Even for Shai'tan himself.

So it was that Rand used the Dark One's own essence, channeled in its full strength. He held the Dark One tightly, like a dove in the grip of a hawk.

And light exploded from him.

CHAPTER
48

A Brilliant Lance

Elayne trotted her horse among heaps of dead Trollocs. The day was won. She had everyone who could stand searching for the living among the dead.

So many dead. Hundreds of thousands of men and Trollocs, lying in piles all across Merrilor. The river's banks were slaughterhouses, the bogs mass graves, floating with corpses. Ahead of her, across the river, the Heights groaned and rumbled. She'd pulled her people away from there. She could barely sit on her horse.

The entire plateau collapsed upon itself, burying the dead. Elayne watched, feeling numb, feeling the ground shake. It—

Light.

She sat up straight, feeling the swelling of power in Rand. Her attention flew away from the Heights, instead focused on him. The feeling of supreme strength, the beauty of control and domination. A light shot into the sky far to the north, so bright that she gasped.

The end had come.

*

Thom stumbled back from the entrance to the Pit of Doom, shading his eyes with his arm as light—radiant as the sun itself—burst out of the cavern. Moiraine!

"Light," Thom whispered.

Light it was, breaking out of the top of the mountain of Shayol Ghul, a radiant beam that melted the mountain's tip and shot straight into the sky.

Min raised her hand to her breast, stepping away from the rows of wounded for whom she'd been changing linens.

Rand, she thought, feeling his agonized determination. Far to the north, a beam of light rose into the air, so bright that it lit the Field of Merrilor even such a great distance away. The helpers and the wounded alike blinked, stumbling to their feet, shading their faces.

That light, a brilliant lance in the heavens, burned away the clouds and opened up the sky.

Aviendha blinked at the light, and knew it was Rand.

It drew her back from the brink of darkness, flooding her with warmth. He was winning. He was *winning*. He was so strong. She saw the true warrior in him now.

Nearby, Graendal stumbled to her knees, eyes glazed over. The unraveling gateway had exploded, but not with as large a blast as last time. Weaves and the One Power had sprayed out, just as Graendal tried to spin Compulsion.

The Forsaken turned to Aviendha, and she adopted an adoring gaze. She bowed down, as if worshipping Aviendha.

The explosion, Aviendha realized, numb. It had done something to the Compulsion weave. Honestly, she had expected that blast to kill her. It had done something else instead.

"Please, glorious one," Graendal said. "Tell me what you wish of me. Let me serve you!"

Aviendha looked back to the light that was Rand and held her breath.

*

Logain stepped from the ruins, holding a toddler—maybe two years of age—in his arms. The child's weeping mother took her son from his hands. "Thank you. Bless you, Asha'man. *Light bless you.*"

Logain stumbled to a halt amid the people. The air stank of burned flesh and dead Trollocs. "The Heights are gone?" he asked.

"Gone," Androl said reluctantly from beside him. "The earthquakes took them."

Logain sighed. The prize . . . was it lost, then? Would he ever be able to dig it out?

I am a fool, he thought. He had abandoned that power for what? To save these refugees? People who would spurn him and hate him for what he was. People who . . .

. . . who looked at him with awe.

Logain frowned. These were common people, not like folk from the Black Tower who were accustomed to men who could channel. In that moment, he wouldn't have been able to tell the difference.

Logain watched with wonder as the people flocked around his Asha'man, weeping for their salvation. Elderly men took Asha'man by the hands, overcome, praising them.

Nearby a youth looked at Logain with admiration. A dozen youths. Light, a *hundred*. Not a hint of fear in their eyes.

"Thank you," the young mother said again. "Thank you."

"The Black Tower protects," Logain heard himself say. "Always."

"I will send him to you to be tested when he is of age," the woman promised, holding her son. "I would have him join you, if he has the talent."

The talent. Not the curse. The talent.

Light bathed them.

He stopped. That beam of light to the north . . . channeling like none he'd ever felt before, not even at the cleansing. Such *power*.

"It's happening," Gabrelle said, stepping up to him.

Logain reached to his belt, then took three items from his pouch. Discs, half white, half black. The nearby Asha'man turned toward him, pausing in Healing and comforting the people.

"Do it," Gabrelle said. "Do it, *Sealbreaker*."

Logain snapped the once unbreakable seals, one by one, and dropped the pieces to the ground.

CHAPTER
49

Light and Shadow

Everything was dead. In the wolf dream, Perrin stumbled across a rocky wasteland without plants or soil. The sky had gone black, the dark clouds themselves vanishing into that nothingness. As he climbed atop a ridge, an entire section of the ground behind him crumbled—his stone footing shaking violently—and was pulled into the air.

Beneath that was only emptiness.

In the wolf dream, all was being consumed. Perrin continued forward, toward Shayol Ghul. He could see it, like a beacon, glowing with light. Strangely, behind, he could make out Dragonmount, though it should have been far too distant to see. As the land between them crumbled, the world seemed to be shrinking.

The two peaks, pulling toward one another, all between shattered and broken. Perrin *shifted* to the front of the tunnel into the Pit of Doom, then stepped in, passing the violet barrier he'd erected earlier.

Lanfear lounged inside. Her hair was jet black, as it had been when he'd first met her, and her face was familiar. It looked as it once had.

"I find that dreamspike annoying," she said. "Did you have to place it here?"

"It keeps the other Forsaken away," Perrin said absently.

"I suppose it does that," she said, folding her arms.

"He is still ahead?" Perrin asked.

"It is the end," she said, nodding. "Something amazing just happened." She narrowed her eyes. "This might be the most important moment for humankind since we opened the Bore."

"Let's make sure nothing goes wrong, then," Perrin said, walking forward down the long maw of stone, Lanfear at his side.

At the end of the tunnel, they found an unexpected scene. Someone else was holding *Callandor*, the man that Rand had been fighting earlier. Maybe that was Demandred? Perrin did not know. He was certainly one of the Forsaken.

That man knelt on the floor, with Nynaeve's hand on his shoulder. She stood just behind Rand and to the left. Moiraine was on Rand's right, all three of them standing tall, with eyes forward, staring into the nothingness ahead.

The mountain rumbled.

"Perfect," Lanfear whispered. "I couldn't have dreamed that it could come out this well." She eyed the two women. "We will need to strike quickly. I will kill the taller woman, you the shorter one."

Perrin frowned. Something about that seemed very wrong. "Kill . . . ?"

"Of course," Lanfear said. "If we strike quickly, there will still be time to seize control of Moridin while he holds that blade. With that, I can force Lews Therin to bow." She narrowed her eyes. "He holds the Dark One between his fingers, needing only one squeeze to pinch the life—if it can be called that—away. Only one hand can save the Great Lord. In this moment, I earn my reward. In this moment, I become highest of the high."

"You . . . you want to save the Dark One?" Perrin said, raising a hand to his head. "You joined us. I remember . . ."

She glanced at him. "Such an inferior tool," she said, smelling dissatisfied. "I hate having to use it. This makes me no better than Graendal." She shivered. "If they had given me more time, I would have had you fairly." She patted Perrin fondly on the cheek. "You are troubled. The taller one is from your village, I remember. You grew up together, I presume? I won't make you kill her, my wolf. You can kill the short one. You hate her, don't you?"

"I . . . yes, I do. She stole me away from my family. It's because of her that they died, really. I would have been there, otherwise."

"That's right," Lanfear said. "We must be quick. Our moment of opportunity will not last long."

She turned toward the two women. Nynaeve and Moiraine. His *friends*. And then . . . and then *Rand*. She would kill him, Perrin knew. She would force him to bow, and then she would kill him. All along, her goal had been to put herself into a position where the Dark One himself would be helpless and she could step in to bring him salvation.

Perrin came up beside her.

"We strike together," Lanfear said softly. "The barriers between worlds have been broken here. They will be able to fight back unless we are quick. We must kill them at the same time."

This is wrong, Perrin thought. *This is very, very wrong.* He couldn't let it happen, and yet his hands rose.

IT IS WRONG. He didn't know why. His thoughts wouldn't allow him to think of why.

"Ready," Lanfear said, eyes on Nynaeve.

Perrin turned toward Lanfear.

"I will count to three," Lanfear said, not looking at him.

My duty, Perrin thought, *is to do the things Rand cannot.*

This was the wolf dream. In the wolf dream, what he felt became reality.

"One," Lanfear said.

He loved Faile.

"Two."

He loved Faile.

"Three."

He loved Faile. The Compulsion vanished like smoke in the wind, thrown off like clothing changed in the blink of an eye. Before Lanfear could strike, Perrin reached out and took her by the neck.

He twisted once. Her neck popped in his fingers.

Lanfear crumpled, and Perrin caught her body. She *was* beautiful. As she died, she changed back to the other form she had been wearing before, her new body.

Perrin felt a horrible stab of loss. He hadn't completely wiped what she'd done from his mind. He'd overcome it, perhaps overlaid

it with something new, something right. Only the wolf dream and
his ability to view himself as he *should* be had allowed him to
accomplish that.

Unfortunately, deep within, he still felt love for this woman.
That sickened him. The love was nowhere near as strong as his
love for Faile, but it was there. He found himself crying as he lowered her body, draped in sleek white and silver, to the stone floor.

"I'm sorry," he whispered. Killing a woman, particularly one
who wasn't threatening him personally . . . it was something he'd
never have thought himself capable of.

Someone had needed to do it. This was one test, at least, that
Rand would not need to face. It was one burden that Perrin could
carry for his friend.

He looked up toward Rand. "Go," Perrin whispered. "Do what
you must do. As always, I will watch your back."

The seals crumbled. The Dark One burst free.

Rand held the Dark One tightly.

Filled with the Power, standing in a column of light, Rand
pulled the Dark One into the Pattern. Only here was there time.
Only here could the Shadow itself be killed.

The force in his hand, which was at once vast and yet tiny,
trembled. Its screams were the sounds of planets grinding
together.

A pitiful object. Suddenly, Rand felt as if he were holding not
one of the primal forces of existence, but a squirming thing from
the mud of the sheep pens.

YOU REALLY ARE NOTHING, Rand said, knowing the
Dark One's secrets completely. YOU WOULD NEVER HAVE
GIVEN ME REST AS YOU PROMISED, FATHER OF LIES.
YOU WOULD HAVE ENSLAVED ME AS YOU WOULD
HAVE ENSLAVED THE OTHERS. YOU CANNOT GIVE
OBLIVION. REST IS NOT YOURS. ONLY TORMENT.

The Dark One trembled in his grip.

YOU HORRIBLE, PITIFUL MITE, Rand said.

Rand was dying. His lifeblood flowed from him, and beyond
that, the amount of the Powers he held would soon burn him
away.

He held the Dark One in his hand. He began to squeeze, then stopped.

He knew all secrets. He could see what the Dark One had done. And Light, Rand understood. Much of what the Dark One had shown him was lies.

But the vision Rand himself had created—the one without the Dark One—was truth. If he did as he wished, he would leave men no better than the Dark One himself.

What a fool I have been.

Rand yelled, thrusting the Dark One back through the pit from where it had come. Rand pushed his arms to the side, grabbing twin pillars of *saidar* and *saidin* with his mind, coated with the True Power drawn through Moridin, who knelt on the floor, eyes open, so much power coursing through him he couldn't even move.

Rand hurled the Powers forward with his mind and *braided* them together. *Saidin* and *saidar* at once, the True Power surrounding them and forming a shield on the Bore.

He wove something majestic, a pattern of interlaced *saidar* and *saidin* in their pure forms. Not Fire, not Spirit, not Water, not Earth, not Air. Purity. Light itself. This didn't repair, it didn't patch, it *forged anew*.

With this new form of the Power, Rand pulled together the rent that had been made here long ago by foolish men.

He understood, finally, that the Dark One was not the enemy.

It never had been.

Moiraine grabbed Nynaeve beside her, moving only by touch, for that light was blinding.

She pulled Nynaeve to her feet. Together, they ran. Away from the burning light behind. Up the corridor, scrambling. Moiraine burst into open air without realizing it, and almost ran off the edge of the path, which would have sent her stumbling down the steep slope. Someone caught her.

"I have you," Thom's voice said as she collapsed into his arms, completely drained. Nynaeve fell to the ground nearby, gasping.

Thom turned Moiraine away from the corridor, but she refused to look away. She opened her eyes, though she knew that the light was too intense, and she *saw* something. Rand and Moridin, standing in the light as it expanded outward to consume the entire mountain in its glow.

The blackness in front of Rand hung like a hole, sucking in everything. Slowly, bit by bit, that hole shrank away until it was just a pinprick.

It vanished.

EPILOGUE

To See the Answer

Rand slipped on his blood.

He couldn't see. He carried something. Something heavy. A body. He stumbled up the tunnel.

Closing, he thought. *It's closing.* The ceiling lowered like a shutting jaw, stone grinding against stone. With a gasp, Rand reached open air as the rocks slammed down behind him, locking together like clenched teeth.

Rand tripped. The body in his arms was so heavy. He slipped to the ground.

He could . . . see, just faintly. A figure kneeling down beside him. "Yes," a woman whispered. He did not recognize the voice. "Yes, that's good. That is what you need to do."

He blinked, his vision fuzzy. Was that Aiel clothing? An old woman, with gray hair? Her form retreated, and Rand reached toward her, not wanting to be alone. Wanting to explain himself. "I see the answer now," he whispered. "I asked the Aelfinn the wrong question. To choose is our fate. If you have no choice, then you aren't a man at all. You're a puppet . . ."

Shouting.

Rand felt heavy. He plunged into unconsciousness.

*

Mat stood up as the mist of Mashadar burned away from him and
vanished. The field was littered with the bodies of those eerie
pockmarked Trollocs. He looked upward through the vanishing
wisps and found the sun directly overhead.

"Well, you're a sight," he said to it. "You should come out
more often. You have a pretty face." He smiled, then looked down
at the dead man by his feet. Padan Fain looked like a bundle of
sticks and moss, the flesh slipping from his bones. The blackness
of the dagger had spread across his rotting skin. It stank.

Almost, Mat reached for that dagger. Then he spat. "For once,"
he said, "a gamble I don't want to touch." He turned his back on
it and walked off.

Three steps away, he found his hat. He grinned, snatched it up
and set it on his head, then began whistling as he rested the
ashandarei on his shoulder and strolled away. The dice had
stopped rolling in Mat's head.

Behind, the dagger, ruby and all, melted away into the mess
that had been Padan Fain.

Perrin walked wearily into the camp they had set up at the base
of Shayol Ghul after the fighting had ceased. He dropped his coat.
The air felt good on his bare chest. He tucked *Mah'alleinir* away
in its place at his belt. A good smith never neglected his tools, for
all that sometimes, carrying them felt as if they would bear him
down to the grave itself.

He thought that he could sleep a hundred days straight. But
not yet. Not yet.

Faile.

No. Deep down, he knew he had to face something horrible
about her. But not yet. For the moment, he shoved that worry—
that terror—away.

The last spirits of the wolves faded back into the wolf dream.

Farewell, Young Bull.

Find what you seek, Young Bull.

The hunt ends, but we will hunt again, Young Bull.

Perrin plodded among rows of wounded men and Aiel cele-
~·ing the defeat of the Shadowspawn. Some tents were filled
moans, others with yells of victory. People of all stripes ran

through the now-blooming valley of Thakan'dar, some hunting for the wounded, others crying in joy and whooping as they met with friends who had survived the last, dark moments.

Aiel called to Perrin, "Ho, blacksmith, join us!" But he did not enter their celebrations. He looked for the guards. Someone around here had to be levelheaded enough to worry about a rogue Myrddraal or Draghkar taking the opportunity to try for a little revenge. Sure enough, he found a ring of defenders at the center of camp guarding a large tent. What of Rand?

No colors swirled in his vision. No image of Rand. Perrin felt no more tugging, pulling him in any direction.

Those seemed like very bad signs.

He pushed through the guards, numb, and entered the tent. Where had they found a tent this large on this battlefield? Everything had been trampled, blown away or burned.

The inside smelled of herbs, and was partitioned with several hanging cloths.

"I've tried everything," a voice whispered. Damer Flinn's voice. "Nothing changes what is happening. He—"

Perrin pushed in on Nynaeve and Flinn standing beside a pallet behind one of the partitions. Rand, cleaned and dressed, lay there, eyes closed. Moiraine knelt beside him, her hand on his face, whispering so softly none but he could hear. "You did well, Rand. You did well."

"He lives?" Perrin asked, wiping the sweat from his face with his hand.

"Perrin!" Nynaeve said. "Oh, Light. You look horrible. Sit down, you lummox! You're going to fall over. I don't want *two* of you to tend."

Her eyes were red. "He's dying anyway, isn't he?" Perrin asked. "You got him out alive, but he's still going to die."

"Sit," Nynaeve commanded, pointing to a stool.

"Dogs obey that command, Nynaeve," Perrin said, "not wolves." He knelt down, resting a hand on Rand's shoulder.

I couldn't feel your tugging, or see the visions, Perrin thought. *You're no longer ta'veren. I suspect neither am I.* "Have you sent for the three?" Perrin asked. "Min, Elayne, Aviendha. They need to see him a last time."

"That's all you can say?" Nynaeve snapped.

He looked up at her. The way she folded her arms made her look as if she were holding herself together. Wrapping her arms about herself to stop from crying.

"Who else died?" Perrin asked, bracing himself. It was obvious from her expression. She had lost one already.

"Egwene."

Perrin closed his eyes, breathing out. Egwene. Light.

No masterwork comes without a price, he thought. *That doesn't mean it's not worth forging.* Still . . . Egwene?

"It's not your fault, Nynaeve," he said, opening his eyes.

"Of course it's not. I know it's not, you numb-brained fool." She turned away.

He stood up, embracing her and patting her back with his smith's hands. "I'm sorry."

"I left . . . to save you," Nynaeve whispered. "I only came along to protect you."

"You did, Nynaeve. You protected Rand so he could do what he had to do."

She shook, and he let her weep. Light. He shed a few tears himself. Nynaeve pulled away sharply after a moment, then barreled out of the tent.

"I tried," Flinn said desperately, looking at Rand. "Nynaeve did, too. Together, we tried, with Moiraine Sedai's *angreal*. Nothing worked. Nobody knows how to save him."

"You did what you could," Perrin said, peeking around the next partition. Another man lay on the pallet there. "What is he doing here?"

"We found them together," Flinn said. "Rand must have carried him out of the pit. We don't know why the Lord Dragon would save one of the Forsaken, but it doesn't matter. We can't Heal him either. They're dying. Both of them."

"Send for Min, Elayne and Aviendha," Perrin said again. He hesitated. "Did they all survive?"

"The Aiel girl took a beating," Flinn said. "She came stumbling into camp, half-carried by a horrid-looking Aes Sedai who
had made a gateway for her. She'll live, though I don't know how
she'll walk in years to come."

"Let them know. All of them."

Flinn nodded, and Perrin stepped out after Nynaeve. He found what he'd hoped to see, the reason why she'd left so quickly. Just outside the tent, Lan held her tightly. The man looked as bloodied and tired as Perrin felt. Their eyes met, and they nodded to one another.

"Several of the Windfinders have opened a gateway between here and Merrilor," Lan said to Perrin. "The Dark One is sealed away again. The Blasted Lands are blooming, and gateways can open here again."

"Thank you," Perrin said, passing him by. "Has anyone . . . heard anything about Faile?"

"No, blacksmith. The Hornsounder saw her last, but she left him and entered the battlefield to draw the Trollocs away from him. I'm sorry."

Perrin nodded. He'd already spoken with Mat, and Olver. It seemed to him that . . . that he'd been avoiding thinking about what must have happened.

Don't think about it, he told himself. *Don't you dare.* He steeled himself, then went to seek the gateway Lan had mentioned.

"Excuse me," Loial asked the Maidens sitting beside the tent. "Have you seen Matrim Cauthon?"

"*Oosquai?*" one of them asked, laughing, holding up the skin.

"No, no," Loial said. "I have to find Matrim Cauthon and get his account of the battle, you see. While it's fresh. I need everyone to tell me what they saw and heard, so that I can write it down. There will never be a better time."

And, he admitted to himself, he wanted to see Mat and Perrin. See that they were all right. So much had happened; he wanted to talk to his friends and make certain they were well. With what was happening to Rand . . .

The Aiel woman smiled at him drunkenly. Loial sighed, then continued through the camp. The day was coming to an end. The day of the Last Battle! It was the Fourth Age now, wasn't it? Could an age start in the middle of a day? That would be incon venient for the calendars, wouldn't it? But everyone agreed. Ra had sealed the Bore at noon.

Loial continued through the camp. They hadn't moved the base of Shayol Ghul. Nynaeve said she was too wor move Rand. Loial kept searching, peeking into tents. In the next, he found the grizzled general Ituralde, surrounded by four Aes Sedai.

"Look," Ituralde said. "I've served the kings of Arad Doman all of my life. I swore oaths."

"Alsalam is dead," Saerin Sedai said from beside the chair. "Someone has to take the throne."

"There is confusion in Saldaea," Elswell Sedai added. "The succession is messy, with the ties it has to Andor now. Arad Doman cannot afford to be leaderless. *You* must take the throne, Rodel Ituralde. You must do it quickly."

"The Merchant Council . . ."

"All dead or vanished," another Aes Sedai said.

"I swore oaths . . ."

"And what would your king have you do?" Yukiri Sedai asked. "Let the kingdom disintegrate? You must be strong, Lord Ituralde. This is not a time for Arad Doman to be without a leader."

Loial slipped away and shook his head, feeling sorry for the man. *Four* Aes Sedai. Ituralde would be crowned before the day was out.

Loial stopped by the main Healing tent again to check if anyone had seen Mat. He had been to this battlefield, and people said he was smiling and healthy, but . . . well, Loial wanted to see for himself. Wanted to talk to him.

Inside the tent, Loial had to slouch lest he brush his head on the ceiling. A large tent for humans was small by Ogier standards.

He peeked in on Rand. His friend looked worse than before. Lan stood by the wall. He wore a crown—it was just a simple silver band—where the *hadori* used to rest. That wasn't odd, but the matching one Nynaeve wore did give Loial a start.

"It's not fair," Nynaeve whispered. "Why should he die, when the other one gets better?"

Nynaeve seemed troubled. She still had red eyes, but before, ~~~he had chivvied anyone who mentioned them, so Loial said noth-~~~~. Humans often seemed to want him to say nothing, which ~~odd for people who lived lives so hastily.

~~ looked at Loial, and he bowed his head to her.

~~al," she said. "How goes your search?"

"Not well," he said with a grimace. "Perrin ignored me and Mat cannot be found."

"Your stories can wait a few days, Builder," Lan said.

Loial did not argue. Lan was a king now, after all. But . . . no, the stories could *not* wait. They had to be fresh so his history could be accurate.

"It's terrible," Flinn said, still looking at Rand. "But, Nynaeve Sedai . . . It's so strange. None of the three seem to care at all. Shouldn't they be more worried . . . ?"

Loial left them, though he did check in on Aviendha in a nearby tent. She sat while several women attended to her twisted, bleeding feet. She had lost several of her toes. She nodded her head to Loial; the Healings done so far had apparently taken away her pain, for though she seemed tired, she did not seem in agony.

"Mat?" he asked hopefully.

"I have not seen him, Loial, son of Arent son of Halan," Aviendha replied. "At least, not since you asked a short time ago."

Loial blushed, then left her. He passed Elayne and Min outside. He would get their stories—he had already asked a few questions—but the three *ta'veren* . . . they were most important! Why were humans always bustling around so quickly, never sitting still? Never any time to think. This was an important day.

It *was* odd, though. Min and Elayne. Shouldn't they be at Rand's side? Elayne seemed to be taking reports on casualties and refugee supplies, and Min sat looking up at Shayol Ghul, a far-off expression in her eyes. Neither went in to hold Rand's hand as he slipped toward death.

Well, Loial thought, *maybe Mat sneaked by me and went back to Merrilor.* Never staying put, these men. Always so hasty . . .

Matrim Cauthon sauntered into the Seanchan camp on the south side of Merrilor, away from the piles of the dead.

All around, Seanchan men and women gasped, hands to their mouths. He tipped his hat to them.

"The Prince of the Ravens!" Hushed tones moved throu~~gh the~~ camp ahead of him, passing from mouth to mouth like the ~~a~~ bottle of brandy on a cold night.

He walked right up to Tuon, who stood at a large map

the camp center talking to Selucia. Karede, Mat noticed, had survived. The man probably felt guilty about it.

Tuon looked at Mat and frowned. "Where have you been?"

Mat raised his arm, and Tuon frowned, looking upward at nothing. Mat spun and thrust his hand farther toward the sky.

Nightflowers began to explode high above the camp.

Mat grinned. Aludra had taken a little convincing, but only a little. She did so like to make things explode.

It was not truly dusk yet, but the show was still grand. Aludra now had half of the dragoners trained to build fireworks and handle her powders. She seemed far less secretive than she once had.

The sounds of the display washed over them.

"Fireworks?" Tuon said.

"The best bloody firework show in the history of my land *or* yours," Mat said.

Tuon frowned. The explosions reflected in her dark eyes. "I'm with child," she said. "The Doomseer has confirmed it."

Mat felt a jolt, as sure as if a firework had gone off inside of his stomach. An heir. A son, no doubt! What odds that it was a boy? Mat forced a grin. "Well, I guess I'm off the hook, now. You have an heir."

"I have an heir," Tuon said, "but I am the one off that hook. Now I can kill you, if I want."

Mat felt his grin widen. "Well, we'll have to see what we can work out. Tell me, do you ever play dice?"

Perrin sat down among the dead and finally started weeping.

Gai'shain in white and city women picked through the dead. There was no sign of Faile. None at all.

I can't keep going. How long had it been since he'd slept? That one night in Mayene. His body complained that it hadn't been nearly enough. He'd pushed himself long before that, spending the equivalent of weeks in the wolf dream.

Lord and Lady Bashere were dead. Faile would have been ..., if she'd lived. Perrin shook and trembled, and he could not ... himself move any more. There were hundreds of thousands ... on this battlefield. The other searchers ignored a body if it had no life, marking it and moving on. He had tried to spread the word for them to seek Faile, but the searchers had to look for the living.

Fireworks exploded in the darkening sky. Perrin buried his head in his hands, then felt himself slide sideways and collapse among the corpses.

Moghedien winced at the display in the sky. Each explosion made her see that deadly fire again, tearing through the Sharans. That flare of light, that moment of panic.

And then ... and then darkness. She'd awakened some time later, left for dead among the bodies of Sharans. When she'd come to, she had found these fools all across the battlefield, claiming to have won the day.

Claiming? she thought, wincing again as another round of fireworks sounded. *The Great Lord has fallen.* All was lost.

No. No. She continued forward, keeping her step firm, unsuspicious. She had strangled a worker, then taken her form, channeling only a tiny bit and inverting the weave. That should let her escape from this place. She wove around bodies, ignoring the stink to the air.

All was not lost. She still lived. And she was of the Chosen! That meant ... that meant that she was an empress among her lessers. Why, the Great Lord was imprisoned again, so he could not punish her. And certainly most, if not all, of the other Chosen were dead or imprisoned. If that were true, no one could rival her in knowledge.

This might actually work out. This might be a *victory*. She stopped beside an overturned supply cart, clutching her *cour'souvra*—it was still whole, thankfully. She smiled with a wide grin, then wove a small light to illuminate her way.

Yes ... Look at the open sky, not the thunderclouds. She could turn this to her advantage. Why ... in the matter of a few years, she could be ruling the world herself!

Something cold snapped around her neck.

Moghedien reached up with horror, then screamed. "No! ¹ *again*!" Her disguise melted away and the One Power left ¹

A smug-looking *sul'dam* stood behind. "They said we co⁻

take any who called themselves Aes Sedai. But you, you do not wear one of their rings, and you skulk like one who has done something wrong. I do not think you will be missed at all."

"Free me!" Moghedien said, scratching at the *a'dam*. "Free me, you—"

Pain sent her to the ground, writhing.

"I am called Shanan," the *sul'dam* said as another woman approached, a *damane* in tow. "But you may call me mistress. I think that we should return to Ebou Dar quickly."

Her companion nodded, and the *damane* made a gateway.

They had to drag Moghedien through.

Nynaeve emerged from the Healing tent at Shayol Ghul. The sun was almost below the horizon.

"He's dead," she whispered to the small crowd gathered outside.

Saying the words felt like dropping a brick onto her own feet. She did not cry. She had shed those tears already. That did not mean that she didn't hurt.

Lan came out of the tent behind her, putting an arm around her shoulders. She raised her hand to his. Nearby, Min and Elayne looked at one another.

Gregorin whispered to Darlin—he had been found, half dead, in the wreckage of his tent. Both of them frowned at the women. Nynaeve overheard part of what Gregorin said. ". . . expected the Aiel savage to be heartless, and maybe the Queen of Andor, but the other one? Not a tear."

"They're shocked," Darlin replied.

No, Nynaeve thought, studying Min and Elayne. *Those three know something I do not. I'll have to beat it out of them.*

"Excuse me," Nynaeve said, walking away from Lan.

He followed.

She raised an eyebrow at him.

"You shall not be rid of me in the next few weeks, Nynaeve," said, love pulsing through his bond. "Even if you want it."

"Stubborn ox," she grumbled. "As I recall, you are the one who ed on leaving me so that you could march alone toward your ed destiny."

"And you were right about that," Lan said. "As you so often are." He said it so calmly that it was hard to be mad at him.

Besides, it was the women she was mad at. She chose Aviendha first and stalked up to her, Lan by her side.

". . . with Rhuarc dead," Aviendha was saying to Sorilea and Bair, "I think that whatever I saw *must* be able to change. It has already."

"I saw your vision, Aviendha," Bair said. "Or something like it, through different eyes. I think it is a warning of something we must not let happen."

The other two nodded, then glanced at Nynaeve and grew as still-faced as Aes Sedai. Aviendha was just as bad as the others, completely calm as she sat in her chair, her feet wrapped in bandages. She might walk again someday, but she would never fight.

"Nynaeve al'Meara," Aviendha said.

"Did you hear me say that Rand is dead?" Nynaeve demanded. "He went silently."

"He that was wounded has woken from the dream," Aviendha said evenly. "It is as all must do. His death was accomplished in greatness, and he will be celebrated in greatness."

Nynaeve leaned down. "All right," she said menacingly, embracing the Source. "Out with it. I chose you because you can't run away from me."

Aviendha displayed a moment of what might have been fear. It was gone in a flash. "Let us prepare his pyre."

Perrin ran in the wolf dream. Alone.

Other wolves howled their sorrow for his grief. After he passed them, they would return to their celebrations, but that did not make their empathy any less real.

He did not howl. He did not cry out. He became Young Bull, and he ran.

He did not want to be here. He wanted slumber, true slumber. There, he could not feel the pain. Here he could.

I shouldn't have left her.

A thought of men. Why did it creep in!

But what could I do? I promised not to treat her like glass.

Run. Run fast. Run until exhaustion came!

I had to go to Rand. I had to. But in doing so, I failed her!

To the Two Rivers in a flash. Back out, along the river. The Waste, then back, a long run toward Falme.

How could I be expected to hold them both, then let one go?

To Tear. Then to the Two Rivers. A blur, growling, moving as quickly as he could. Here. Here he had wed her.

Here he howled.

Caemlyn, Cairhien, Dumai's Wells.

Here he saved one of them.

Cairhien, Ghealdan, Malden.

Here he had saved another.

Two forces in his life. Each had pulled at him. Young Bull finally collapsed near some hills somewhere in Andor. A familiar place.

The place where I met Elyas.

He became Perrin again. His thoughts were not wolf thoughts, his troubles not wolf troubles. He stared up at the sky that was now, after Rand's sacrifice, empty of clouds. He had wanted to be with his friend as he died.

This time, he would be with Faile where she had died.

He wanted to scream, but it would do no good. "I have to let go, don't I?" he whispered toward that sky. "Light. I don't want to. I learned. I *learned* from Malden. I didn't do it again! I did what I was supposed to, this time."

Somewhere nearby, a bird cried in the sky. Wolves howled. Hunting.

"I learned . . . "

A bird's cry.

It sounded like a falcon.

Perrin threw himself to his feet, spinning. *There.* He vanished in an instant, appearing on an open field he did not recognize. No, he *knew* this field. He knew it! This was Merrilor, only without the blood, without the grass churned to mud, without the land blasted and broken.

Here he found a tiny falcon—as small as his hand—crying softly, with a broken leg pinned beneath a rock. Its heartbeat was faint.

Perrin roared as he woke, clawing his way out of the wolf dream. He stood up on the field of bodies, shouting into the night. Searchers nearby scattered in fear.

Where? In the darkness, could he find the same place? He ran, stumbling over corpses, through pits made by channelers or dragons. He stopped, looking one way, then another. Where. *Where!*

Flowery soap. A hint of perfume in the air. Perrin dashed toward it, throwing his weight against the corpse of an enormous Trolloc, lying almost chest-high atop other bodies. Beneath it, he found the carcass of a horse. Unable to truly consider what he was doing, or of the strength it should have required, Perrin pulled the horse aside.

Beneath, Faile lay bloodied in a small hollow in the ground, breathing shallowly. Perrin cried out and dropped to his knees, cradling her in his arms, breathing in her scent.

It took him only two heartbeats to *shift* into the wolf dream, carry Faile to Nynaeve far to the north and *shift* out. Seconds later, he felt her being Healed in his arms, unwilling to let go of her even for that.

Faile, his falcon, trembled and stirred. Then she opened her eyes and smiled at him.

The other heroes were gone. Birgitte remained as evening approached. Nearby, soldiers prepared Rand al'Thor's pyre.

Birgitte could not stay much longer, but for now ... yes, she could stay. A short time. The Pattern would allow it.

"Elayne?" Birgitte said. "Do you know something? About the Dragon?"

Elayne shrugged in the waning light. The two stood at the back of the crowd gathering to watch the Dragon Reborn's pyre be lit.

"I know what you're planning," Birgitte said to Elayne. "With the Horn."

"And what am I planning?"

"To keep it," Birgitte said, "and the boy. To have it as an Andoran treasure, perhaps a nation's weapon."

"Perhaps."

Birgitte smiled. "It's a good thing I sent him away, then."

Elayne turned to her, ignoring those preparing Rand's pyre. "*What?*"

"I sent Olver away," Birgitte said. "With guards I trust. I

Olver to find someplace nobody would look, a place he could forget, and toss the Horn into it. Preferably the ocean."

Elayne exhaled softly, then turned back toward the pyre. "Insufferable woman." She hesitated. "Thank you for saving me from having to make that decision."

"I thought you'd feel that way." Actually, Birgitte had assumed it would take a long time before Elayne understood. But Elayne had grown in the last few weeks. "Anyway, I must be far from insufferable, since you've done an excellent job of suffering me these last months."

Elayne turned to her again. "That sounds like a farewell."

Birgitte smiled. She could feel it, sometimes, when it was coming. "It is."

Elayne looked sorrowful. "Must it be?"

"I'm being reborn, Elayne," Birgitte whispered. "Now. Somewhere, a woman is preparing to give birth, and I will go to that body. It's happening."

"I don't want to lose you."

Birgitte chuckled. "Well, perhaps we will meet again. For now, be happy for me, Elayne. This means the cycle continues. I get to be with him again. Gaidal . . . I'll be only a few years younger than he."

Elayne took her arm, eyes watering. "Love and peace, Birgitte. Thank you."

Birgitte smiled, then closed her eyes, and let herself drift away.

As evening settled onto the land, Tam looked up across what had once been the most feared place of all. Shayol Ghul. The last flickers of light showed plants growing here, flowers blooming, grass growing up around fallen weapons and over corpses.

Is this your gift to us, son? he wondered. *A final one?*

Tam lit his torch from the small, flickering flame that crackled in the pit nearby. He went forward, passing lines of those who stood in the night. They had not told many of Rand's funeral rites. All would have wanted to come. Perhaps all deserved to ome. The Aes Sedai were planning an elaborate memorial for wene; Tam preferred a quiet affair for his son.

and could finally rest.

He walked past people standing with heads bowed. None carried light save Tam. The others waited in the dark, a small crowd of perhaps two hundred encircling the bier. Tam's torch flickered orange off solemn faces.

In the evening, even with his light, it was hard to tell Aiel from Aes Sedai, Two Rivers man from Tairen king. All were shapes in the night, saluting the body of the Dragon Reborn.

Tam went up to the bier, beside Thom and Moiraine, who were holding hands, faces solemn. Moiraine reached over and gently squeezed Tam's arm. Tam looked at the corpse, gazing down into his son's face by the fire's light. He did not wipe the tears from his eyes.

You did well. My boy . . . you did so well.

He lit the pyre with a reverent hand.

Min stood at the front of the crowd. She watched Tam, with slumped shoulders, bow his head before the flames. Eventually the man walked back to join the Two Rivers folk. Abell Cauthon embraced him, whispering softly to his friend.

Heads in the night, shadows, turned toward Min, Aviendha and Elayne. They expected something from the three of them. A show of some sort.

Solemnly, Min stepped forward with the other two; Aviendha needed the help of two Maidens to walk, though she was able to stand by leaning on Elayne. The Maidens withdrew to leave the three of them alone before the pyre. Elayne and Min stood with her, watching the fire burn, consuming Rand's corpse.

"I've seen this," Min said. "I knew it would come the day I first met him. We three, together, here."

Elayne nodded. "So now what?"

"Now . . ." Aviendha said. "Now we make sure that everyone well and truly believes he is gone."

Min nodded, feeling the pulsing throb of the bond in the back of her mind. It grew stronger each moment.

Rand al'Thor—just Rand al'Thor—woke in a dark tent by himself. Someone had left a candle burning beside his pallet.

He breathed deeply, stretching. He felt as if he'd just slept long and deep. Shouldn't he be hurting? Stiff? Aching? He felt none of that.

He reached to his side and felt no wounds there. No wounds. For the first time in a long while, there was *no pain*. He almost didn't know what to make of it.

Then he looked down and saw that the hand prodding his side was his own left hand. He laughed, holding it up before him. *A mirror*, he thought. *I need a mirror.*

He found one beyond the next partition of the tent. Apparently, he'd been left completely alone. He held up the candle, looking into the small mirror. Moridin's face looked back at him.

Rand touched his face, feeling it. In his right eye hung a single *saa*, black, shaped like the dragon's fang. It didn't move.

Rand slipped back into the portion of the tent where he'd awakened. Laman's sword was there, sitting atop a neat pile of mixed clothing. Alivia apparently hadn't known what he would want to wear. She had been the one to leave these things, of course, along with a bag of coins from a variety of nations. She hadn't ever cared much for either clothing or coin, but she had known he'd need both.

She will help you die. Rand shook his head, dressing and gathering the coins and the sword, then slipping out of the tent. Someone had left a good horse, a dappled gelding, tied not far away. That would do him well. From Dragon Reborn to horsethief. He chuckled to himself. Bareback would have to do.

He hesitated. Nearby, in the darkness, people were singing. This was Shayol Ghul, but not as he remembered it. A blooming Shayol Ghul, full of life.

The song they sang was a Borderlander funeral song. Rand led the horse through the night to get a little closer. He peered between the tents to where three women stood around a funeral pyre.

Moridin, he thought. *He's being cremated with full honors as the Dragon Reborn.*

Rand backed away, then mounted the dapple. As he did so, he noticed one figure who was not standing by the fire. A solitary figure, who looked toward him when all other eyes were turned away.

Cadsuane. She looked him up and down, eyes reflecting

firelight from the glow of Rand's pyre. Rand nodded, waited for a moment, then turned the horse and heeled it away.

Cadsuane watched him go.

Curious, she thought. Those eyes had confirmed her suspicions. That would be information she could use. No need to keep watching this sham of a funeral, then.

She walked away through the camp, and there strolled directly into an ambush.

"Saerin," she said as the women fell in around her. "Yukiri, Lyrelle, Rubinde. What is this?"

"We would like direction," Rubinde said.

"Direction?" Cadsuane snorted. "Ask the new Amyrlin, once you find some poor woman to put into the position."

The other women continued to walk with her.

As it hit her, Cadsuane stopped in place.

"Oh, *blood and ashes*, no!" Cadsuane said, spinning on them. "No, no, *no*."

The women smiled in an almost predatory way.

"You always talked so wisely to the Dragon Reborn of responsibility," Yukiri said.

"You speak of how the women of this Age need better training," Saerin added.

"It is a new Age," Lyrelle said. "We have many challenges ahead of us . . . and we will need a strong Amyrlin to lead us."

Cadsuane closed her eyes, groaning.

Rand breathed a sigh of relief as he left Cadsuane behind. She did not raise an alarm, though she had continued to study him as he put distance between them. Glancing over his shoulder, he noticed her walking off with some other Aes Sedai.

She worried him; she probably suspected something he wished she did not. It was better than her raising an alarm, though.

He sighed, fishing in his pocket, where he found a pipe. *Than you, Alivia, for that*, he thought, packing it with tabac from a pou he found in the other pocket. By instinct, he reached for the Power to light it.

He found nothing. No *saidin* in the void, nothing. He paused, then smiled and felt an enormous relief. He could not channel. Just to be certain, he tentatively reached for the True Power. Nothing there either.

He regarded his pipe, riding up a little incline to the side of Thakan'dar, now covered in plants. No way to light the tabac. He inspected it for a moment in the darkness, then *thought* of the pipe being lit. And it was.

Rand smiled and turned south. He glanced over his shoulder. All three women at the pyre had turned from it to look directly at him. He could make them out, though not much else, by the light of the burning body.

I wonder which of them will follow me, he thought, then smiled deeper. *Rand al'Thor, you've built up quite a swelled head, haven't you? Assuming that one, or more, would follow.*

Maybe none of them would. Or maybe all of them would, in their own time. He found himself chuckling.

Which would he pick? Min . . . but no, to leave Aviendha? Elayne. No. He laughed. He couldn't pick. He had three women in love with him, and didn't know which he would like to have follow him. Any of them. All of them. *Light, man. You're hopeless. Hopelessly in love with all three, and there's no way out of it.*

He heeled the horse into a canter, heading farther south. He had a purse full of coin, a good horse and a strong sword. Laman's sword, which was a better sword than he'd have wanted. It might draw attention. It was a true heron-marked sword with a fine blade.

Did Alivia realize how much money she'd given him? She didn't know a thing about coins. She'd probably stolen the lot of it, so he wasn't just a horsethief. Well, he'd told her to get him some gold, and she'd done it. He could buy an entire farm in the Two Rivers with what he carried.

South. East or west would do, but he figured he wanted to go someplace away from it all for good. South first, then maybe out west, along the coast. Maybe he could find a ship? There was so much of the world he hadn't seen. He'd experienced a few battles, 'd gotten caught up in a huge Game of Houses. Many things he n't wanted anything to do with. He'd seen his father's farm. palaces. He'd seen a lot of palaces.

He just had not had the leisure to have a real look at much of the world. *That will be new*, he thought. Traveling without being chased, or having to rule here or there. Traveling where he could just sleep in a barn in exchange for splitting someone's firewood. He thought about that, and found himself laughing, riding on south and smoking his impossible pipe. As he did so, a wind rose up around him, around the man who had been called lord, Dragon Reborn, king, killer, lover and friend.

The wind rose high and free, to soar in an open sky with no clouds. It passed over a broken landscape scattered with corpses not yet buried. A landscape covered, at the same time, with celebrations. It tickled the branches of trees that had finally begun to put forth buds.

The wind blew southward, through knotted forests, over shimmering plains and toward lands unexplored. This wind, it was not the ending. There are no endings, and never will be endings, to the turning of the Wheel of Time.

But it was *an* ending.

And it came to pass in those days, as it had come before and would come again, that the Dark lay heavy on the land and weighed down the hearts of men, and the green things failed, and hope died. And men cried out to the Creator, saying, O Light of the Heavens, Light of the World, let the Promised One be born of the mountain, according to the prophecies, as he was in ages past and will be in ages to come. Let the Prince of the Morning sing to the land that green things will grow and the valleys give forth lambs. Let the arm of the Lord of the Dawn shelter us from the Dark, and the great sword of justice defend us. Let the Dragon ride again on the winds of time.

—from *Charal Drianaan te Calamon,*
The Cycle of the Dragon.
Author unknown, the Fourth Age.

He came like the wind, like the wind touched everything, and like the wind was gone.

—from *The Dragon Reborn.*
By Loial, son of Arent son of Halan,
the Fourth Age.

The End
of the Last Book of
The Wheel of Time

Robert Jordan was born in 1948 in Charleston, South Carolina, and died in 2007. He taught himself to read when he was four with the incidental aid of a twelve-year-old brother, and was tackling Mark Twain and Jules Verne by five. He is a graduate of The Citadel, the Military College of South Carolina, with a degree in physics, and served two tours in Vietnam with the US Army. Among his decorations are the Distinguished Flying Cross with bronze oak leaf cluster, the Bronze Star with "V" and bronze oak leaf cluster, and two Vietnamese Gallantry Crosses with Palm. He has written historical novels, and dance and theatre criticism, but it is the many volumes of his epic Wheel of Time series that have made him one of the bestselling and best loved fantasy writers of modern times.

Brandon Sanderson grew up in Lincoln, Nebraska. He teaches creative writing at Brigham Young University and lives in Provo, Utah, with his wife Emily, and their children.